The Oath of the Vayuputras

Amish is a 1974-born, IIM (Kolkata)-educated banker-turned-author. The success of his debut book, *The Immortals of Meluha* (Book 1 of the Shiva Trilogy), encouraged him to give up his career in financial services to focus on writing. Besides being an author, he is also an Indian-government diplomat, a host for TV documentaries, and a film producer.

Amish is passionate about history, mythology and philosophy, finding beauty and meaning in all world religions. His books have sold more than 6 million copies and have been translated into over 20 languages. His Shiva Trilogy is the fastest selling and his Ram Chandra Series the second fastest selling book series in Indian publishing history. You can connect with Amish here:

- www.facebook.com/authoramish
- www.instagram.com/authoramish
- www.twitter.com/authoramish

Other Titles by Amish

SHIVA TRILOGY

The fastest-selling book series in the history of Indian publishing

The Immortals of Meluha (Book 1 of the Trilogy)

The Secret of the Nagas (Book 2 of the Trilogy)

RAM CHANDRA SERIES

The second fastest-selling book series in the history of Indian publishing

Ram – Scion of Ikshvaku (Book 1 of the Series)

Sita – Warrior of Mithila (Book 2 of the Series)

Raavan – Enemy of Aryavarta (Book 3 of the Series)

War of Lanka (Book 4 in the Series)

INDIC CHRONICLES

Legend of Suheldev

NON-FICTION

Immortal India: Young Country, Timeless Civilisation

Dharma: Decoding the Epics for a Meaningful Life

www.authoramish.com

'{Amish's} writings have generated immense curiosity about India's rich past and culture.'

– Narendra Modi

(Honourable Prime Minister, India)

'{Amish's} writing introduces the youth to ancient value systems while pricking and satisfying their curiosity…'

– Sri Sri Ravi Shankar

(Spiritual Leader & Founder, Art of Living Foundation)

'{Amish's writing is} riveting, absorbing and informative.'

– Amitabh Bachchan

(Actor & Living Legend)

'{Amish's writing is} a fine blend of history and myth...gripping and unputdownable.'

– BBC

'Thoughtful and deep, Amish, more than any author, represents the New India.'

– Vir Sanghvi

(Senior Journalist & Columnist)

'Amish's mythical imagination mines the past and taps into the possibilities of the future. His book series, archetypal and stirring, unfolds the deepest recesses of the soul as well as our collective consciousness.'

– Deepak Chopra

(World-renowned spiritual guru and bestselling author)

'{Amish is} one of the most original thinkers of his generation.'

– Arnab Goswami

(Senior Journalist & MD, Republic TV)

'Amish has a fine eye for detail and a compelling narrative style.'

– Dr. Shashi Tharoor

(Member of Parliament & Author)

'{Amish has} a deeply thoughtful mind with an unusual, original, and fascinating view of the past.'

– Shekhar Gupta

(Senior Journalist & Columnist)

'To understand the New India, you need to read Amish.'

– Swapan Dasgupta

(Member of Parliament & Senior Journalist)

'Through all of Amish's books flows a current of liberal progressive ideology: about gender, about caste, about discrimination of any kind… He is the only Indian bestselling writer with true philosophical depth – his books are all backed by tremendous research and deep thought.'

– Sandipan Deb

(Senior Journalist & Editorial Director, Swarajya)

'Amish's influence goes beyond his books, his books go beyond literature, his literature is steeped in philosophy, which is anchored in bhakti, which powers his love for India.'

– Gautam Chikermane

(Senior Journalist & Author)

'Amish is a literary phenomenon.'

– Anil Dharker

(Senior Journalist & Author)

The Oath of the Vayuputras

Book 3
of the
Shiva Trilogy

Amish

HarperCollins *Publishers* India

www.authoramish.com

First published in 2013

This edition published in India by HarperCollins *Publishers* 2022
4th Floor, Tower A, Building No. 10, Phase II, DLF Cyber City,
Gurugram, Haryana – 122002
www.harpercollins.co.in

2 4 6 8 10 9 7 5 3 1

Copyright © Amish Tripathi 2013, 2022

P-ISBN: 978-93-5629-068-6
E-ISBN: 978-93-5629-078-5

This is a work of fiction and all characters and incidents described in this book are the product of the author's imagination. Any resemblance to actual persons, living or dead, is entirely coincidental.

Amish Tripathi asserts the moral right
to be identified as the author of this work.

All rights reserved. No part of this publication may be reproduced,
stored in a retrieval system, or transmitted, in any form or by any means, electronic,
mechanical, photocopying, recording or otherwise,
without the prior permission of the publishers.

Typeset in Garamond by Ram Das Lal

Printed and bound at
Thomson Press (India) Ltd

This book is produced from independently certified FSC® paper
to ensure responsible forest management.

To the late Dr Manoj Vyas, my father-in-law

Great men never die

They live on in the hearts of their followers

Har Har Mahadev

All of us are Mahadevs, All of us are Gods

For His most magnificent temple, finest mosque and greatest church exist within our souls

www.authoramish.com

Contents

Acknowledgements

The acknowledgments written below were composed when the book was published in 2013. I must also acknowledge those that are publishing this edition of **The Oath of the Vayuputras**. *The team at HarperCollins: Swati, Shabnam, Akriti, Gokul, Vikas, Rahul, and Udayan, led by the brilliant Ananth. Looking forward to this new journey with them.*

***

I hadn't imagined I would ever become an author. The life that I live now, a life spent in pursuits like writing, praying, reading, debating and travelling, actually feels surreal at times. There are many who have made this dream possible and I'd like to thank them.

Lord Shiva, my God, for bringing me back to a spiritual life. It is the biggest high possible.

Neel, my son, a rejuvenating elixir, who would regularly come and ask me while I was obsessively writing this book, *'Dad, aapka ho gaya kya?'*

Preeti, my wife; Bhavna, my sister; Himanshu, my brother-in-law; Anish and Ashish, my brothers; Donetta, my sister-in-law. They have worked so closely with me, that many times I feel that it isn't just my book, but a joint project, which just happens to have my name on it.

The rest of my family: Usha, Vinay, Meeta, Shernaz, Smita, Anuj and Ruta. For always being there for me.

Sharvani Pandit, my editor. She has battled severe health troubles, without asking for any sympathy. And despite the trying times she went through, she helped me fulfil my karma. I'm lucky to have her.

Rashmi Pusalkar, the designer of this book's cover. She's been a partner from the first book. In my humble opinion, she's one of the best book-cover designers in Indian publishing.

Gautam Padmanabhan, Satish Sundaram, Anushree Banerjee, Paul Vinay Kumar, Vipin Vijay, Renuka Chatterjee, Deepthi Talwar, Krishna Kumar Nair and the fantastic team at Westland, my publishers. They have shown commitment and understanding that very few publishers show towards their authors.

Anuj Bahri, my agent, a typically large-hearted, boisterous Punjabi. A man brought to me by fate, to help me achieve my dreams.

Sangram Surve, Shalini Iyer and the team at Think Why Not, the advertising and digital marketing agency for the book. I have worked with many advertising agencies in my career, including some of the biggest multinationals. Think Why Not ranks right up there, amongst the best.

Chandan Kowli, the photographer for the cover. He did a brilliant job as always. Also, Atul Pargaonkar, for fabricating the bow and arrow; Vinay Salunkhe, for the make-up; Ketan Karande, the model; Japheth Bautista, for the concept art for the background; the Little Red Zombies team and Shing Lei Chua for support on 3D elements and scene set-up; Sagar Pusalkar and team for the post processing work on the images; Julien Dubois for coordinating production. I hope you like the cover they have created. I loved it!

Omendu Prakash, Biju Gopal and Swapnil Patil for my photograph that has been printed in this book. Their composition was exceptional; the model, regrettably, left a lot to be desired!

Chandramauli Upadhyay, Shakuntala Upadhyay and Vedshree Upadhyay from Benaras; Santanu Ghoshroy and Shweta Basu Ghoshroy from Singapore. For their hospitality while I wrote this book.

Mohan Vijayan, a friend, whose advice on media matters is something I always treasure.

Rajesh Lalwani and the Blogworks team, a digital agency which works with my publisher, for their strong support in an area I don't understand too well.

Anuja Choudhary and the Wizspk team, the PR agency of my publisher, for the effective campaigns they've implemented.

Dr Ramiyar Karanjia, for his immense help in understanding the philosophies of Zoroastrianism.

Purnima, an old friend, for her impeccable legal advice. Caleb, for working with me on my film deals. Raajeev, for working with me on the music album created for the Shiva Trilogy.

And last, but certainly not the least, you the reader. Thank you from the depths of my being for the support you've given to the first two books of the Shiva Trilogy. I hope I can give you a sense of completion with this concluding book.

www.authoramish.com

The Shiva Trilogy

Shiva! The Mahadev. The God of Gods. Destroyer of Evil. Passionate lover. Fierce warrior. Consummate dancer. Charismatic leader. All-powerful, yet incorruptible. Quick of wit – and of temper.

No foreigner who came to India – be he conqueror, merchant, scholar, ruler, traveller – believed that such a great man could ever have existed in reality. They assumed he must have been a mythical God, a fantasy conjured within the realms of human imagination. And over time, sadly, this belief became our received wisdom.

But what if we are wrong? What if Lord Shiva was not simply a figment of a rich imagination but a person of flesh-and-blood like you and me? A man who rose to become God-like as a result of his karma. That is the premise of the Shiva Trilogy, which attempts to interpret the rich mythological heritage of ancient India, blending fiction with historical fact.

The Immortals of Meluha was the first book in a trilogy that chronicles the journey of this extraordinary hero. The story was continued in the second book, *The Secret of the Nagas*. And it will all end in the book that you are holding: *The Oath of the Vayuputras*.

This is a fictional series that is a tribute to my God; I found Him after spending many years in the wilderness of atheism.

www.authoramish.com

I hope you find your God as well. It doesn't matter in what form we find Him, so long as we do find Him eventually. Whether He comes to us as Shiva or Vishnu or Shakti Maa or Allah or Jesus Christ or Buddha or any other of His myriad forms, He wants to help us. Let us allow Him to do so.

Yadyatkarma karomi tattadakhilam shambho tavaaraadhanam
My Lord Shambo, My Lord Shiva, every act of mine is a prayer in your honour

List of Characters

Anandamayi: Ayodhyan princess, daughter of Emperor Dilipa, married to General Parvateshwar.
Athithigva: King of Kashi.
Ayurvati: The chief of medicine at Meluha.
Bappiraj: Prime minister of Branga.
Bhadra a.k.a. Veerbhadra: A childhood friend and a confidant of Shiva, married to Krittika.
Bhagirath: Prince of Ayodhya, son of Emperor Dilipa.
Bharat: An ancient emperor of the Chandravanshi dynasty married to a Suryavanshi princess.
Bhoomidevi: A revered non-Naga lady who established the present way of life of the Nagas a long time ago.
Bhrigu: A Saptrishi Uttradhikari (successor of the Saptarshis), rajguru of Meluha.
Brahaspati: Chief Meluhan scientist; belonged to the swantribe of Brahmins.
Brahmanayak: Father of Daksha, previous emperor of Meluha.
Chandraketu: King of Branga.
Chenardhwaj: Governor of Maika and Lothal; earlier the governor of Kashmir.
Daksha: Emperor of the Suryavanshi Empire of Meluha, married to Veerini and father of Sati and Kali.

Dilipa: Emperor of Swadweep, king of Ayodhya and chief of the Chandravanshis; father of Bhagirath and Anandamayi.
Divodas: The leader of the Brangas who live in Kashi.
Ganesh: Sati's first child, one of the Naga leaders.
Gopal: Chief of the Vasudevs.
Kali: Sati's twin sister and queen of the Nagas.
Kanakhala: The prime minister of Meluha, she is in charge of administrative, revenue and protocol matters.
Karkotak: Prime minister of the Nagas.
Kartik: Son of Shiva and Sati, named after Krittika, Sati's best friend and attendant.
Krittika: A close friend and attendant to Sati; wife of Veerbhadra.
Manobhu: Shiva's maternal uncle and teacher.
Manu: Founder of the Vedic way of life; he lived many millennia ago.
Mitra: Chief of the Vayuputras.
Mohini: An associate of Lord Rudra; respected by some as a Vishnu.
Nandi: A captain in the Meluhan army.
Parshuram: A dacoit in Branga; he was named after the sixth Vishnu.
Parvateshwar: Head of Meluhan armed forces, he was in charge of army, navy, special forces and police; married to Princess Anandamayi.
Ram: The seventh Vishnu, who lived centuries ago. He established the empire of Meluha.
Rudra: The earlier Mahadev, the Destroyer of Evil, who lived some millennia ago.
Sati: The royal princess of Meluha, daughter of King Daksha and Queen Veerini, married to Shiva, mother of Kartik and Ganesh.

Satyadhwaj: Grandfather of Parvateshwar.
Shiva: The chief of the Guna tribe; Neelkanth, the saviour of the land. Married to Sati, father of Kartik and Ganesh.
Siamantak: Prime minister of Swadweep.
Surapadman: Prince of Magadh.
Swuth: Chief of a tribe of Egyptian assassins.
Tara: A pupil of Bhrigu.
Vasudev pandits: Advisers to Shiva, tribe left behind by the previous Vishnu, Lord Ram.
Veerini: Queen of Meluha, wife of Emperor Daksha and mother of Sati and Kali.
Vidyunmali: Brigadier in the Meluhan army.
Vishwadyumna: A close associate of Ganesh.

Chapter 1

The Return of a Friend

Before the Beginning.

Blood dribbled into the water, creating unhurried ripples which expanded slowly to the edges of the cistern. Shiva bent over the container as he watched the rippling water distort his reflection. He dipped his hands in the water and splashed some on his face, washing off the blood and gore. Recently appointed Chief of the Gunas, he was in a mountain village far from the comforts of the Mansarovar Lake. It had taken his tribe three weeks to get there despite the punishing pace he had set. The cold was bone-chilling, but Shiva didn't even notice. Not because of the heat that emanated from the Pakrati huts that were being gutted by gigantic flames, but because of the fire that burnt within.

Shiva wiped his eyes and stared at his reflection in the water. Raw fury gripped him. Yakhya, the Pakrati chieftain, had escaped. Shiva controlled his breathing, still recovering from the exhaustion of combat.

He thought he saw his uncle, Manobhu's bloodied body in the water. Shiva reached out below the surface of the water with his hand. 'Uncle!'

The mirage vanished. Shiva squeezed his eyes shut.

The macabre moment when he had found his uncle's body replayed in his mind. Manobhu had gone to discuss a peace treaty with Yakhya, hoping the Pakratis and Gunas would end their incessant warmongering. When he hadn't returned at the appointed time,

Shiva had sent out a search party. Manobhu's mutilated body, along with those of his bodyguards, had been found next to a goat trail on the way to the Pakrati village.

A message had been written in blood; on a rock next to where Manobhu had breathed his last.

'Shiva. Forgive them. Forget them. Your only true enemy is Evil.'

All that his uncle wanted was peace and this is how they had repaid him.

'Where's Yakhya?' Bhadra's scream broke Shiva's chain of thoughts.

Shiva turned. The entire Pakrati village was up in flames. Some thirty dead bodies lay strewn across the clearing; brutally hacked by the enraged Gunas seeking vengeance for their former chief's death. Five Pakrati men knelt on the ground, tied together, a continuous rope binding their wrists and feet. Both ends of the rope had been hammered into the ground. The fierce Bhadra, bloodied sword in hand, led the twenty Guna guards. It was impossible for the Pakratis to escape.

At a distance, another contingent of Guna warriors guarded the shackled Pakrati women and children; unharmed thus far. The Gunas never killed or even hurt women and children. Never.

'Where is Yakhya?' repeated Bhadra, pointing his sword menacingly at a Pakrati.

'We don't know,' the Pakrati answered. 'I swear we don't know.'

Bhadra dug his sword point into the man's chest, drawing blood. 'Answer and you shall have mercy. All we want is Yakhya. He will pay for killing Manobhu.'

'We didn't kill Manobhu. I swear on all the mountain Gods, we didn't kill him.'

Bhadra kicked the Pakrati hard. 'Don't lie to me, you stinking arsehole of a yak!'

Shiva turned away as his eyes scanned the forests beyond the clearing. He closed his eyes. He could still hear his uncle Manobhu's words echo in his ears. 'Anger is your enemy. Control it! Control it!'

Shiva took deep breaths as he tried to slow down his furiously pounding heart.

'If you kill us, Yakhya will come back and kill all of you,' screamed a Pakrati at the end of the rope line. 'You will never know peace! We shall have the final vengeance!'

'Shut up, Kayna,' shouted another Pakrati, before turning to Bhadra. 'Release us. We had nothing to do with it.'

But the Pakrati seemed to have come unhinged. 'Shiva!' shouted Kayna.

Shiva turned.

'You should be ashamed to call Manobhu your uncle,' roared Kayna.

'Shut up, Kayna!' screamed all the other Pakratis.

But Kayna was beyond caring. His intense loathing for the Gunas had made him abandon his instinct for self-preservation. 'That coward!' he spat. 'Manobhu bleated like a goat as we shoved his intestines and his peace treaty down his throat!'

Shiva's eyes widened, as the rage bubbling under the surface broke through. Screaming at the top of his lungs, he drew his sword and charged. Without breaking a step, he swung viciously as he neared the Pakratis, beheading Kayna in one mighty blow. The severed head smashed into the Pakrati beside him, before ricocheting off to the distance.

'Shiva!' screamed Bhadra.

They needed the Pakratis alive if they were to find Yakhya. But Bhadra was too disciplined a tribesman to state the obvious. Besides, at that moment, Shiva didn't care. He swirled smoothly, swinging his sword again and again, decapitating the next Pakrati and the next. It was only a matter of moments before five beheaded Pakrati bodies lay in the mud, their hearts still pumping blood out of their gaping necks, making it pool around the bodies, almost as though they lay in a lake of blood.

Shiva breathed heavily, as he stared at the dead, his uncle's voice ringing loudly in his head.

'Anger is your enemy. Control it! Control it!'

— ⅄◯Ʊ⇑⊛ —

'I have been waiting for you, my friend,' said the teacher. He was smiling, his eyes moist. 'I'd told you, I would go anywhere for you. Even to *Patallok* if it would help you.'

How often had Shiva replayed these words uttered by the man who stood before him. But he had never fully understood the reference to *the land of the demons*. Now it all fell into place.

The beard had been shaved, replaced by a pencil-thin moustache. The broad shoulders and barrel chest were much better defined. The man must be getting regular exercise. The *janau, the holy thread of Brahmin identity,* was loosely slung over newly developed muscles. The head remained shaven, but the tuft of hair at the back appeared longer and neater. The deep-set eyes had the same serenity that had drawn Shiva to him earlier. It was his long-lost friend. His comrade in arms. His brother.

'Brahaspati!'

'It took you a very long time to find me.' Brahaspati stepped close and embraced Shiva. 'I have been waiting for you.'

Shiva hesitated for a moment before joyously embracing Brahaspati, allowing his emotions to take over. But no sooner had he regained his composure, than doubts started creeping into his mind.

Brahaspati created the illusion of his death. He allied with the Nagas. He destroyed his life's purpose, the great Mount Mandar. He was the Suryavanshi mole!

My brother lied to me!

Shiva stepped back silently. He felt Sati's hand on his shoulder, in silent commiseration.

Brahaspati turned to his students. 'Children, could you please excuse us?'

The students immediately rose and left. The only people left in the room were Shiva, Brahaspati, Sati, Ganesh and Kali.

Brahaspati stared at his friend, waiting for the questions. He could sense the hurt and anger in Shiva's eyes.

'Why?' he asked.

'I thought I would spare you the dreadful personal fate that is the inheritance of the Mahadevs. I tried to do your task. One cannot fight Evil and not have its claws leave terrible scars upon one's soul. I wanted to protect you.'

Shiva's eyes narrowed. 'Were you fighting Evil all by yourself? For more than five years?'

'Evil is never in a rush,' reasoned Brahaspati. 'It creeps up slowly. It doesn't hide, but confronts you in broad daylight. It gives decades of warnings, even centuries at times. Time is never the problem when you battle Evil. The problem is the will to fight it.'

'You say that you have been waiting for me. And yet you hid all traces of yourself. Why?'

'I always trusted you, Shiva,' said Brahaspati, 'but I could not trust all those who were around you. They would have prevented me from accomplishing my mission. I might even have been assassinated had they learnt about my plans. My mission, I admit, prevailed over my love for you. It was only when you parted ways with them, that I could meet you safely.'

'That's a lie. You wanted to meet me because you needed me for the success of your mission. Because you now know you cannot accomplish it by yourself.'

Brahaspati smiled wanly. 'It was never meant to be my mission, great Neelkanth. It was always yours.'

Shiva looked at Brahaspati, expressionless.

'You are partially right,' said Brahaspati. 'I wanted to meet you... No, I *needed* to meet you because I have failed. The coin of Good and Evil is flipping over and India needs the Neelkanth. It needs you, Shiva. Otherwise, Evil will destroy this beautiful land of ours.'

Shiva, while continuing to stare noncommittally at Brahaspati, asked, 'The coin is flipping over, you say?'

Brahaspati nodded.

Shiva remembered Lord Manu's words. *Good and Evil are two sides of the same coin.*

The Neelkanth's eyes widened. *The key question isn't 'What is Evil?' The key question is: 'When does Good become Evil? When does the coin flip?'*

Brahaspati continued to watch Shiva keenly. Lord Manu's rules were explicit; he could not suggest anything. The Mahadev had to discover and decide for himself.

Shiva took a deep breath and ran his hand over his blue throat. It still felt intolerably cold. It seemed as if the journey would have to end where it had begun.

What is the greatest Good; the Good that created this age? The answer was obvious. And therefore, the greatest Evil was exactly the same thing, once it began to disturb the balance.

Shiva looked at Brahaspati. 'Tell me why...'

Brahaspati remained silent, waiting... The question had to be more specific.

'Tell me why you think the Somras has tipped over from the greatest Good to the greatest Evil.'

— ⁂ —

Bits and pieces of the wreckage had been dutifully brought by the soldiers for examination by Parvateshwar and Bhagirath, who squatted at a distance.

Shiva had asked the Meluhan general and the Ayodhyan prince to investigate the wreckage. They had been tasked with determining the antecedents of the men who had attacked their convoy on the way to Panchavati. Parvateshwar and Bhagirath had stayed behind with a hundred soldiers while the rest of Shiva's convoy had carried on to Panchavati.

Parvateshwar glanced at Bhagirath and then turned back to the wooden planks. Slowly but surely, his worst fears were coming true.

He turned to look at the hundred Suryavanshi soldiers who stood at a respectable distance, as they had been instructed. He was relieved. It was best if they did not see what had been revealed. The rivets on the planks were clearly Meluhan.

'I hope Lord Ram has mercy on your soul, Emperor Daksha,' he shook his head and sighed.

Bhagirath turned towards Parvateshwar, frowning. 'What happened?'

Parvateshwar looked at Bhagirath, anger writ large on his face. 'Meluha has been let down. Its fair name has been tarnished forever; tarnished by the one sworn to protect it.'

Bhagirath kept quiet.

'These ships were sent by Emperor Daksha,' Parvateshwar said softly.

Bhagirath moved closer, his eyes showing disbelief. 'What? Why do you say that?'

'These rivets are clearly Meluhan. These ships were built in my land.'

Bhagirath narrowed his eyes. He had noticed something completely different and was stunned by the general's statement. 'Parvateshwar, look at the wood. Look at the casing around the edges.'

Parvateshwar frowned. He did not recognise the casing.

'It improves water-proofing in the joints,' said Bhagirath.

Parvateshwar looked at his brother-in-law, curious.

'This technology is from Ayodhya.'

'Lord Ram, be merciful!'

'Yes! It looks like Emperor Daksha and my weakling father have formed an alliance against the Neelkanth.'

— ⅄ⓞⅡ⇡⊗ —

Bhrigu, Daksha and Dilipa were in the Meluhan emperor's private chambers in Devagiri. Dilipa and Bhrigu had arrived the previous day.

'Do you think they have succeeded in their mission, My Lord?' asked Dilipa.

Daksha seemed remote and disinterested. He felt the intense pain of separation from his beloved daughter Sati. The terrible event at Kashi, more than a year ago, still haunted him. He'd lost his child and with it, all the love he ever felt in his heart.

A few months ago Bhrigu had hatched a plan to assassinate the Neelkanth, along with his entire convoy, en route to Panchavati. They had sent five ships up the Godavari River to first attack Shiva's convoy, and then move on to destroy Panchavati as well. There were to be no survivors who would bear witness to what actually took place. Attacking an unprepared enemy was not unethical. In one fell swoop, all those inimical to them would be destroyed. But it was possible only if Daksha and Dilipa joined hands, as they together had the means as well as the technology.

The people of India would be told that the ghastly Nagas had lured the simple and trusting Neelkanth to their city and assassinated him. Knowing the significance of simplicity in propaganda, Bhrigu had come up with a new title for Shiva: *Bholenath*, the *simple one*, the one who is easily misled. Laying the blame on the treachery of the Nagas and the simplicity of the Neelkanth would mean that Daksha and Dilipa would be spared the backlash. And the hatred for the Nagas would be strengthened manifold.

Bhrigu glanced at Daksha briefly and then turned his attention back to Dilipa. The *Saptrishi Uttradhikari* seemed to place his trust on Dilipa more than the Meluhan now. 'They should have succeeded. We'll soon receive reports from the commander.'

Dilipa's face twitched. He took a deep breath to calm his nerves. 'I hope it is never revealed that we did this. The wrath of my people would be terrible. Killing the Neelkanth with this subterfuge...'

Bhrigu interrupted Dilipa, his voice calm. 'He was not the Neelkanth. He was an imposter. The Vayuputra council did not create him. It did not even recognise him.'

Dilipa frowned. He had always heard rumours but had never really been sure as to whether the Vayuputras, the legendary tribe left behind by the previous Mahadev, Lord Rudra, actually existed.

'Then how did his throat turn blue?' asked Dilipa.

Bhrigu looked at Daksha and shook his head in exasperation. 'I don't know. It is a mystery. I knew the Vayuputra council had obviously not created a Neelkanth, for they are still debating whether Evil has risen. Therefore, I did not object to the Emperor of Meluha persisting with his search for the Neelkanth. I knew there was no possibility of a Neelkanth actually being discovered.'

Dilipa looked stunned.

'Imagine my surprise,' continued Bhrigu, 'when this endeavour actually led them to an apparent Neelkanth. But a blue throat did not mean that he was capable of being the saviour. He had not been trained. He had not been educated for his task. He had not been appointed for it by the Vayuputra council. But Emperor Daksha felt he could control this simple tribal from Tibet and achieve his ambitions for Meluha. I made a mistake in trusting His Highness.'

Dilipa looked at Daksha, who did not respond to the barb. The Swadweepan emperor turned back towards the great sage. 'In any case, Evil will be destroyed when the Nagas are destroyed.'

Bhrigu frowned. 'Who said the Nagas are evil?'

Dilipa looked at Bhrigu, nonplussed. 'Then, what are you saying, My Lord? That the Nagas can be our allies?'

Bhrigu smiled. 'The distance between Evil and Good is a vast expanse in which many can exist without being either, Your Highness.'

Dilipa nodded politely, not quite understanding Bhrigu's intellectual abstractions. Wisely though, he kept his counsel.

'But the Nagas are on the wrong side,' continued Bhrigu. 'Do you know why?'

Dilipa shook his head, thoroughly confused.

'Because they are against the great Good. They are against the finest invention of Lord Brahma; the one that is the source of our country's greatness. This invention must be protected at all costs.'

Dilipa nodded in affirmation. Once again, he didn't understand Bhrigu's words. But he knew better than to argue with the formidable maharishi. He needed the medicines that Bhrigu provided. They kept him healthy and alive.

'We will continue to fight for India,' said Bhrigu. 'I will not let anyone destroy the Good that is at the heart of our land's greatness.'

Chapter 2

What is Evil?

'That the Somras has been the greatest Good of our age is pretty obvious,' said Brahaspati. 'It has shaped our age. Hence, it is equally obvious that someday, it will become the greatest Evil. The key question is when would the transformation occur.'

Shiva, Sati, Kali and Ganesh were still in Brahaspati's classroom in Panchavati. Brahaspati had declared a holiday for the rest of the day so that their conversation could continue uninterrupted. The legendary 'five banyan trees', after which Panchavati had been named, were clearly visible from the classroom window.

'As far as I am concerned, the Somras was evil the moment it was invented!' spat out Kali.

Shiva frowned at Kali and turned to Brahaspati. 'Go on...'

'Any great invention has both positive and negative effects. As long as the positive outweighs the negative, one can safely continue to use it. The Somras created our way of life and has allowed us to live longer in healthy bodies. It has enabled great men to keep contributing towards the welfare of society, longer than was ever possible in the past. At first, the Somras was restricted to the Brahmins, who were expected to use the longer, healthier life – almost a second life – for the benefit of society at large.'

Shiva nodded. He had heard this story from Daksha many years ago.

'Later Lord Ram decreed that the benefits of the Somras should be available to all. Why should Brahmins have special privileges? Thereafter, the Somras was administered to the entire populace, resulting in huge progress in society as a whole.'

'I know all about this,' said Shiva. 'But when did the negative effects start becoming obvious?'

'The first sign was the Nagas,' said Brahaspati. 'There have always been Nagas in India. But they were usually Brahmins. For example, Ravan, Lord Ram's greatest foe, was a Naga and a Brahmin.'

'Ravan was a Brahmin?!' asked a shocked Sati.

'Yes, he was,' answered Kali, for every Naga knew his story. 'The son of the great sage Vishrava, he was a benevolent ruler, a brilliant scholar, a fierce warrior and a staunch devotee of Lord Rudra. He had some faults no doubt, but he wasn't Evil personified, as the people of the Sapt Sindhu would have us believe.'

'In that case, do you people think less of Lord Ram?' asked Sati.

'Of course not. Lord Ram was one of the greatest emperors ever. We worship him as the seventh Vishnu. His ideas, philosophies and laws are the foundation of the Naga way of life. His reign, *Ram Rajya*, will always be celebrated across India as the perfect way to run an empire. But you should know that it is believed by some that even Lord Ram did not see Ravan as pure evil. He respected his enemy. Sometimes there can be good people on both sides of a war.'

Shiva raised his hand to silence them, and turned

his attention back towards the Meluhan chief scientist. 'Brahaspati...'

'So the Nagas, though small in number initially, were usually Brahmins,' Brahaspati continued. 'But then, the Somras was used only by the Brahmins until then. Today, the connection seems obvious, but it didn't seem so at the time.'

'The Somras created the Nagas?' asked Shiva.

'Yes. This was discovered only a few centuries ago by the Nagas. I learnt it from them.'

'We didn't discover it,' said Kali. 'The Vayuputra council told us.'

'The Vayuputra council?' asked Shiva.

'Yes,' continued Kali. 'The previous Mahadev, Lord Rudra, left behind a tribe called the Vayuputras. They live beyond the western borders, in a land called *Pariha*, the *land of fairies*.'

'I know that,' said Shiva, recalling one of his conversations with a Vasudev Pandit. 'But I hadn't heard of the council.'

'Well, somebody needs to administer the tribe. And the Vayuputras are ruled by their council, which is headed by their chief, who is respected as a God. He is called Mithra. He is advised by the council of six wise people collectively called the Amartya Shpand. The council controls the twin mission of the Vayuputras. Firstly, to help the next Vishnu, whenever he appears. And secondly, have one of the Vayuputras trained and ready to become the next Mahadev, when the time comes.'

Shiva raised his eyebrows.

'You obviously broke that rule, Shiva,' said Kali. 'I'm sure the Vayuputra council must have been quite shocked when you appeared out of the blue. Because, quite clearly, they did not create you.'

'You mean this is a controlled process?'

'I don't know,' said Kali. 'But your friends will know a lot more.'

'The Vasudevs?'

'Yes.'

Shiva frowned, reached for Sati's hand, and then asked Kali, 'So how did you find out about the Somras creating the Nagas? Did the Vayuputras approach you or did you find them?'

'I did not find them. The Naga King Vasuki was approached by them a few centuries ago. They suddenly appeared out of nowhere, lugging huge hordes of gold, and offered to pay us an annual compensation. King Vasuki, very rightly, refused to accept the compensation without an explanation.'

'And?'

'And he was told that the Nagas were born with deformities as a result of the Somras. The Somras randomly has this impact on a few babies when in the womb, if the parents have been consuming it for a long period.'

'Not all babies?'

'No. A vast majority of babies are born without deformities. But a few unfortunate ones, like me, are born Naga.'

'Why?'

'I call it dumb luck,' said Kali. 'But King Vasuki believed that the deformities caused by the Somras were the Almighty's way of punishing those souls who had committed sins in their previous births. Therefore, he accepted the pathetic explanation of the Vayuputra council along with their compensation.'

'*Mausi* rejected the terms of the agreement with the Vayuputras the moment she ascended the throne,' said Ganesh, referring to his *aunt*, Kali.

'Why? I'm sure the gold could have been put to good use by your people,' exclaimed Shiva.

Kali laughed coldly. 'That gold was a mere palliative. Not for us, but for the Vayuputras. Its only purpose was to make them feel less guilty for the carnage being wrought upon us by the "great invention" that they protected.'

Shiva nodded, understanding her anger. He turned to Brahaspati. 'But how exactly is the Somras responsible for this?'

Brahaspati explained, 'We used to believe the Somras blessed one with a long life by removing poisonous oxidants from one's body. But that is not the only way it works.'

Shiva and Sati leaned closer.

'It also operates at a more fundamental level. Our body is made up of millions of tiny living units called cells. These are the building blocks of life.'

'Yes, I've heard of this from one of your scientists in Meluha,' said Shiva.

'Then you'd know that these cells are the tiniest living beings. They combine to form organs, limbs, and in fact, the entire body.'

'Right.'

'These cells have the ability to divide and grow. And each division is like a fresh birth; one old unhealthy cell magically transforms into two new healthy cells. As long as they keep dividing, they remain healthy. So your journey begins in your mother's womb as a single cell. That cell keeps dividing and growing till it eventually forms your entire body.'

'Yes,' said Sati, who had learnt all of this in the Meluha *gurukul*.

'Obviously,' said Brahaspati, 'this division and growth has to end sometime. Otherwise one's body would keep growing continuously with pretty disastrous consequences. So the Almighty put a limit on the number of times a cell can divide. After that, the cell simply stops dividing further and thus, in effect, becomes old and unhealthy.'

'And do these old cells make one's body age and thus eventually die?' asked Shiva.

'Yes, every cell reaches its limit on the number of divisions at some point or the other. As more and more cells in the body hit that limit, one grows old, and finally dies.'

'Does the Somras remove this limit on division?'

'Yes. Therefore, your cells keep dividing while remaining healthy. In most people, this continued division is regulated. But in a few, some cells lose control over their division process and keep growing at an exponential pace.'

'This is cancer, isn't it?' asked Sati.

'Yes,' said Brahaspati. 'This cancer can sometimes lead to a painful death. But there are times when these cells continue to grow and appear as deformities – like extra arms or a very long nose.'

'How polite and scientific!' said a livid Kali. 'But one cannot even begin to imagine the physical pain and torture that we undergo as children when these "outgrowths" occur.'

Sati stretched out and held her sister's hand.

'Nagas are born with small outgrowths, which don't seem like much initially, but are actually harbingers of years of torture,' continued Kali. 'It almost feels like a demon has taken over your body. And he's bursting out from within, slowly, over many years, causing soul-crushing pain that becomes your constant companion. Our bodies get twisted beyond recognition so that by adolescence, when further growth finally stops, we are stuck with what Brahaspati politely calls "deformities". I call it the wages of sins that we didn't even commit. We pay for the sins others commit by consuming the Somras.'

Shiva looked at the Naga queen with a sad smile. Kali's anger was justified.

'And the Nagas have suffered this for centuries?' asked Shiva.

'Yes,' said Brahaspati. 'As the number of people consuming the Somras grew, so did the number of Nagas. One will find that most of the Nagas are from Meluha. For that is where the Somras is used most extensively.'

'And what is the Vayuputra council's view on this?'

'I'm not sure. But from whatever little I know, the Vayuputra council apparently believes that the Somras continues to create good in most areas where it is used. The suffering of the Nagas is collateral damage and has to be tolerated for the larger good.'

'Bullshit!' snorted Kali.

Shiva could appreciate Kali's rage but he was also aware of the enormous benefits of Somras over several millennia. *On balance, was it still Good?*

He turned to Brahaspati. 'Are there any other reasons for believing that Somras is Evil?'

'Consider this: we Meluhans choose to believe that the Saraswati is dying because of some devious Chandravanshi conspiracy. This is not true. We are actually killing our mother river all by ourselves. We use massive amounts of Saraswati waters to manufacture the Somras. It helps stabilise the mixture during processing. It is also used to churn the crushed branches of the Sanjeevani tree. I have conducted many experiments to see if water from any other source can be used. But it just doesn't do the trick.'

'Does it really require that much water?'

'Yes, Shiva. When Somras was being made for just a few thousand, the amount of Saraswati water used didn't matter. But when we started mass producing Somras for eight million people, the dynamics changed. The waters started getting depleted slowly by the giant manufacturing facility at Mount Mandar. The Saraswati has already stopped reaching the Western Sea. It now ends its journey in an inland delta, south of Rajasthan. The desertification of the land to the south of this delta is already complete. It's a matter of time before the entire river is completely destroyed. Can you imagine the impact on Meluha? On India?'

'Saraswati is the mother of our entire *Sapt Sindhu* civilisation,' said Sati, speaking of *the land of the seven rivers.*

'Yes. Even our preeminent scripture, the Rig Veda, sings paeans to the Saraswati. It is not only the cradle, but also the lifeblood of our civilisation. What will happen to our future generations without this great river? The Vedic way of life itself is at risk. What we are doing is taking away the lifeblood of our future progeny so that our present generation can revel in the luxury of living for two hundred years or more. Would it be so terrible if we lived for only a hundred years instead?'

Shiva nodded. He could see the terrible side-effects and the ecological destruction caused by the Somras. But he still couldn't see it as Evil. An Evil which left only one option: a *Dharmayudh*, a *holy war,* to destroy it.

'What else?' asked Shiva.

'The destruction of the Saraswati seems a small price to pay when compared to another, even more insidious impact of the Somras.'

'Which is?'

'The plague of Branga.'

'The plague of Branga?' asked a surprised Shiva. 'What does that have to do with the Somras?'

Branga had been suffering continuous plagues for many years, which had killed innumerable people, especially children. The primary relief thus far had been the medicine procured from the Nagas. Or else exotic medicines extracted after killing the sacred peacock, leading to the Brangas being ostracised even in peace-loving cities like Kashi.

'Everything!' said Brahaspati. 'The Somras is not only difficult to manufacture, but it also generates large amounts of toxic waste. A problem we have never truly tackled. It cannot be disposed of on land, because it can poison entire districts through ground water contamination. It cannot be discharged into the sea. The Somras waste reacts with salt water to disintegrate in a dangerously rapid and explosive manner.'

A thought entered Shiva's mind. *Did Brahaspati accompany me to Karachapa the first time to pick up sea water? Was that used to destroy Mount Mandar?*

Brahaspati continued. 'What seemed to work was fresh river water. When used to wash the Somras waste, over a period of several years, fresh water appeared to reduce its toxic strength. This was proven with some experiments at Mount Mandar. It seemed to work especially well with cold water. Ice was even better. Obviously, we could not use the rivers of India to wash the Somras waste in large quantities. We could have ended up poisoning our own people. Therefore, many decades ago, a plan was hatched to use the high mountain rivers in Tibet. They flow through uninhabited lands and their waters are almost ice-cold. They would therefore work perfectly to clean out the Somras waste. There is a river high up in the Himalayas, called Tsangpo, where Meluha decided to set up a giant waste treatment facility.'

'Are you telling me that the Meluhans have come to my land before?'

'Yes. In secret.'

'But how can such large consignments be hidden?'

'You've seen the quantity of Somras powder required to feed an entire city for a year. Ten small pouches are all it takes. It is converted into the Somras drink at designated temples across Meluha when mixed with water and other ingredients.'

'So even the waste amount is not huge?'

'No, it isn't. It's a small quantity, making it easy to transport.

But even that small quantity packs in a huge amount of poison.'

'Hmmm... So this waste facility was set up in Tibet?'

'Yes, it was established in a completely desolate area along the Tsangpo. The river flowed east, so it would go to relatively unpopulated lands away from India. Therefore, our land would not suffer from the harmful effects of the Somras.'

Shiva frowned. 'But what about the lands farther ahead that the Tsangpo flowed into? The eastern lands that lie beyond Swadweep? What about the Tibetan land around Tsangpo itself? Wouldn't they have suffered due to the toxic waste?'

'They may have,' said Brahaspati. 'But that was considered acceptable collateral damage. The Meluhans kept track of the people living along the Tsangpo. There were no outbreaks of disease, no sudden deformities. The icy river waters seemed to be working at keeping the toxins inactive. The Vayuputra council was given these reports. Apparently, the council also sent scientists into the sparsely populated lands of Burma, which is to the east of Swadweep. It was believed the Tsangpo flowed into those lands and became the main Burmese river, the Irrawaddy. Once again, there was no evidence of a sudden rise in diseases. Hence it was concluded that we had found a way to rid ourselves of the Somras waste without harming anyone. When it was discovered that Tsangpo means "purifier" in the local Tibetan tongue, it was considered a sign, a divine message. A solution had been found. This came down to the scientists of Mount Mandar as received wisdom as well.'

'What does this have to do with the Brangas?'

'Well, you see, the upper regions of the Brahmaputra have never been mapped properly. It was simply assumed that the river comes from the east; because it flows west into Branga. The Nagas, with the help of Parshuram, finally mapped the upper course of the Brahmaputra. It falls at almost calamitous speeds from the giant heights of the Himalayas into the plains of Branga through gorges that are sheer walls almost two thousand metres high.'

'Two thousand metres!' gasped Shiva.

'You can well imagine that it is almost impossible to navigate a river course such as the Brahmaputra's. But Parshuram succeeded and led the Nagas along that path. Parshuram, of course, did not realise the significance of the discovery of the river's course. Queen Kali and Lord Ganesh did.'

'Did you go up the Brahmaputra as well?' asked Shiva. 'Where does the river come from? Is it connected to the Tsangpo in any way?'

Brahaspati smiled sadly. 'It *is* the Tsangpo.'

'What?'

'The Tsangpo flows east only for the duration of its course in Tibet. At the eastern extremities of the Himalayas, it takes a sharp turn, almost reversing its flow. It then starts moving south-west and crashes through massive gorges before emerging near Branga as the Brahmaputra.'

'By the Holy Lake,' said Shiva. 'The Brangas are being poisoned by the Somras waste.'

'Exactly. The cold waters of the Tsangpo dilute the poisonous impact to a degree. However, as the river enters India in the form of the Brahmaputra, the rising temperature reactivates the dormant toxin in the water. Though the Branga children also suffer from the same body-wracking pain as the Nagas, they are free from deformities. Sadly, Branga also has a high incidence of cancer. Being highly populous, the number of deaths is simply unacceptable.'

Shiva began to connect the dots. 'Divodas told me the Branga plague peaks during the summer every year. That is the time when ice melts faster in the Himalayas, making the poison flow out in larger quantities.'

'Yes,' said Brahaspati. 'That is exactly what happens.'

'Obviously, since both the Nagas and Brangas are being poisoned by the same malevolence, our medicines work on the Brangas as well,' Kali spoke up. 'So we send them our medicines to help ameliorate their suffering a little. Even though we told King Chandraketu how his kingdom was being poisoned, some Brangas prefer to believe that the plague strikes every year because of a curse that the Nagas have cast upon them. If only we were that powerful! But it appears that at least Chandraketu believes us. This is why he sends us men and gold regularly, to stealthily attack Somras manufacturing facilities, the root of all our problems.'

'Evil should never be fought with subterfuge, Kali,' said Shiva. 'It must be attacked openly.'

Kali was about to retort but Shiva had turned back to Brahaspati.

'Why didn't you say something? Raise the issue in Meluha or with the Vayuputras?'

'I did,' said Brahaspati. 'I took up the matter with Emperor Daksha. But he doesn't really understand scientific things or involve himself with technical details. He turned to the one intellectual he trusts, the venerable *royal priest*, *Raj guru* Bhrigu. Lord Bhrigu seemed genuinely interested and took me to the Vayuputra council so I could present my case before them, but they were not at all supportive. This was where the issue was effectively killed. Nobody was willing to believe me about the source of the Brahmaputra. They also laughed when they heard that I was ostensibly listening to the Nagas. According to them, the Nagas were now ruled by an extremist harridan whose frustration with her own karma made everyone else the object of her ire.'

'I'll take that as a compliment!' said Kali.

Shiva smiled at Kali before turning back to Brahaspati.

'But how did the Vayuputras rationalise what's happening in Branga?'

'According to them,' said Brahaspati, 'the Brangas were a rich but uncivilised lot, with strange eating habits and disgusting customs. So the plague could have been caused by their bad practices and karma rather than the Somras. Remember, there is little sympathy for the Brangas amongst the Vayuputras because it is well known that they drink the blood of peacocks, a bird that is held holy by any follower of Lord Rudra.'

'And you gave up?' retorted Shiva. 'Shouldn't you have pressed on? Emperor Daksha is weak and can be easily influenced. He could have brought about changes in Meluha. The Vayuputra council does not govern your country.'

'Well, there was a good reason for me to not persist with the argument.'

'What reason?'

'Tara, the woman I intended to marry, suddenly went missing,' continued Brahaspati. 'The last time I saw her, she was in Pariha. On returning to Meluha I received a letter from her telling me that she was disappointed with my tirades against the Somras. I asked Lord Bhrigu to check with his friends in Pariha. I was told that she had just disappeared.'

Shiva frowned.

'I know it sounds lame,' said Brahaspati. 'But somewhere deep within, I do believe Tara was taken hostage. It was a message for me. Keep quiet or else...'

'And you gave up?' Shiva repeated. 'Why would you do that if you believed you were right?'

'I didn't,' continued Brahaspati defensively. 'But by then I was losing credibility amongst the senior scientists of other realms. Had I made the issue any bigger within Meluha, I would have lost what little standing I have amongst the Suryavanshis as well. I would have lost my ability to do anything at all. Though I knew I had to do something, I also realised that the strategy of open lobbying and debate had become counter-productive. There were too many vested interests tied into the Somras. Only the Vayuputra council could have had the moral strength to stop it openly, through the institution of the Neelkanth. But they refused to believe that the Somras had turned evil.'

'What happened thereafter?' asked Shiva.

'I opted for silence,' said Brahaspati. 'At least on the surface. But I had to do something. Maharishi Bhrigu was convinced there was nothing to fear from the Somras waste. So the manufacturing of Somras continued at the same frantic pace. The Saraswati kept getting prodigiously consumed. Somras waste was being generated in huge quantities. Since the empire now believed that cold, fresh water had worked in disposing of the toxic waste, new plans were being drawn up to use other rivers. This time the idea was to use the upper reaches of either the Indus or the Ganga.'

'Lord Ram, be merciful,' whispered Shiva.

'Millions of lives would have been at risk. We were going to unleash toxic waste right through the heart of India. Almost as a message from the *Parmatma*, the *ultimate soul*, I was approached by Lord Ganesh around this time. He had formulated a plan, and I must admit his words made eminent sense. There could be only one possible solution. The destruction of Mount Mandar. Without Mount Mandar, there would be no Somras. And with the Somras gone, all these problems would disappear too.'

Shiva cast a quick look towards Sati.

'Whatever little doubts I may have had,' said Brahaspati, 'disappeared when I was confronted with a new scenario. When it happened, I knew in my heart that it was time for the destruction of Evil.'

'What new scenario?' asked Shiva.

'You appeared on the scene,' answered Brahaspati. 'Even without the Vayuputra council's permission, perhaps even without their knowledge... The Neelkanth appeared. It was the final sign for me: the time to destroy Evil was upon us.'

— ⅄⦾Ⴎ⇞⊗ —

Vishwadyumna quickly gave hand signals to his Branga soldiers. The hunting party went down on their knees.

Kartik, who was right behind Vishwadyumna, whistled softly as his eyes lit up. 'Magnificent!'

Vishwadyumna turned towards Kartik. While most of Shiva's convoy was settling itself into the visitor's camp outside Panchavati, a few hunting parties had been sent out to gather meat for the large entourage. Kartik, having proved himself as an accomplished hunter throughout the journey to Panchavati, was the natural leader of one of the groups. Vishwadyumna had accompanied the son of the Neelkanth. He intensely admired the fierce warrior skills of Kartik.

'It's a rhinoceros, My Lord,' said Vishwadyumna softly.

The rhinoceros was a massive animal, nearly four metres in length. It had bumpy brownish skin that hung over its body in multiple layers, suggestive of tough armour. Its most distinctive feature was its nasal horn, which stuck out like a fearsome offensive weapon, to a height of nearly fifty centimetres.

'I know,' whispered Kartik. 'They live around Kashi as well. They're nearly as big as a small elephant. These beasts have terrible eyesight, but they have a fantastic sense of smell and hearing.'

Vishwadyumna nodded at Kartik, impressed. 'What do you propose, My Lord?'

The rhinoceros was a tricky beast to hunt. They were quiet animals who kept to themselves, but if threatened, they could charge wildly. Few could survive a direct blow from their massive body and terrifying horn.

Kartik reached over his shoulder and drew out the two swords sheathed on his back. In his left hand was a short twin-blade, like the one his elder brother Ganesh favoured. In his right was a heavier one with a curved blade which was certainly not appropriate for thrusting. This weapon was perfect for swinging and slashing – a style of fighting Kartik excelled at.

Kartik spoke softly, 'Fire arrows at its back. Make as much noise as you can. I want you to drive it forward.'

Vishwadyumna's eyes filled with terror. 'That is not wise, My Lord.'

'This animal is huge. Too many soldiers charging in will cramp us. All it would need to do is swing its mighty horn and it would cause several casualties.'

'But we can fire arrows to kill it from a distance.'

Kartik raised his eyebrows. 'Vishwadyumna, you should know better. Do you really think our arrows can actually penetrate deep enough to cause serious damage? It's not the arrows but the noise that you will create, which will make it charge.'

Vishwadyumna continued to stare, still unsure.

'Also, it is standing upwind and your positioning behind it would be perfect. Along with the noise, the stench of your soldiers will also drive the animal forward. It's a good thing they haven't bathed in two days,' said Kartik, without any hint of a smile at the joke.

Like all warriors, Vishwadyumna admired humour in the face of danger. But he checked his smile, not sure if Kartik was joking. 'What will you do, My Lord?'

Kartik whispered, 'I'll kill the beast.'

Saying this, Kartik slowly edged forward. Right on to the path that the bull would charge on, when attacked by Vishwadyumna's soldiers. The soldiers meanwhile, moved upwind, behind the rhinoceros. Having reached his position, Kartik whistled softly.

'NOW!' shouted Vishwadyumna.

A volley of arrows attacked the animal as the soldiers began to scream loudly. The rhinoceros raised its head, ears twitching as the arrows bounced harmlessly off its skin. As the soldiers drew closer, some of the missiles managed to penetrate enough to agitate the beast. The animal snorted mightily and stomped the dirt, radiating strength and power as light gleamed off its tiny black eyes. It lowered its head and charged, its feet thundering against the ground.

Kartik was in position. The beast only had side vision and could not see straight ahead. Therefore, it was no surprise that it crashed into an overhanging branch in its path, which made it change its direction slightly. At which point, it saw Kartik standing to its right. The furious rhinoceros bellowed loudly, changed course back to the original path and charged straight towards the diminutive son of Shiva.

Kartik remained stationary and calm, with his eyes focused on the beast. His breathing was regular and deep. He knew that the rhinoceros couldn't see him since he stood straight ahead. The animal was running, guided by the memory of where it had seen Kartik last.

Vishwadyumna fired arrows into the animal rapidly, hoping to slow it down. But the thick hide of the beast ensured that the arrows did not make too much of a difference. It was running straight towards Kartik. Yet Kartik didn't move or flinch. Vishwadyumna could see the boy warrior holding his swords lightly. That was completely wrong for a stabbing action, where the blade needs to be firmly held. The weapon would fall out of his hands the moment he'd thrust forward.

Just when it appeared that he was about to be trampled underfoot, Kartik bent low and, with lightning speed, rolled towards the left. As the rhinoceros continued running, he slashed out, his left sword first, pressing the lever on the hilt as he swung. One of the twin-blades extended out of the other, slicing through the front thigh of the beast, cutting through muscles and veins. As blood spurted rapidly, the animal's injured leg collapsed from under it and it grunted, confused, trying to put weight on the appendage, now flopping uselessly against its belly. Admirably, it still continued its charge, its three good legs heaving against its bulk as it struggled to turn and face its attacker. Kartik ran forward, following the movement of the animal, now circling in from behind the beast. He hacked brutally with his right hand, which held the killer curved sword. The blade sliced through the thigh of the hind leg, cutting down to the bone with its deep curvature and broad metal. With both its right legs incapacitated, the rhinoceros collapsed to the ground, rolling sideways as it tried to stand with only two good legs, writhing in pain. Its blood mixed with the dusty earth to make a dark red-brown mud that smeared across its body as it flailed against the ground, panting in fear.

Kartik stood quietly at a short distance, watching the animal in its final throes.

Vishwadyumna watched from behind, his mouth agape. He had never seen an animal brought down with such skill and speed.

Kartik approached the rhinoceros calmly. Even though immobilised, the beast reared its head menacingly at him, grunting and whining in a high-pitched squeal. Kartik maintained a safe distance as the other soldiers rapidly ran up to him.

The son of the Neelkanth bowed low to the animal. 'Forgive me, magnificent beast. I am only doing my duty. I will finish this soon.'

Suddenly, Kartik moved forward and stabbed hard, right through the folds of the rhinoceros' skin, plunging deep into the beast's heart, feeling the shudder go through its body, until at last it was still.

— ⅄ⓄⅡ↑⊗ —

'My Lord, a bird courier has just arrived with a message for your eyes only,' said Kanakhala, the Meluhan prime minister. 'That's why I brought it personally.'

Daksha occupied his private chambers, a worried Veerini seated beside him. He took the letter from Kanakhala and dismissed her.

With a polite Namaste towards her Emperor and Empress, Kanakhala turned to leave. Glancing back, she glimpsed a rare intimate moment between them as they held each other's hands. The last few months had inured her to the strange goings-on in Meluha. Daksha's past betrayal of Sati during her first pregnancy had shocked her enormously. Kanakhala had lost all respect for her emperor. She continued with her job because she remained loyal to Meluha. She had even stopped questioning the strange orders from her lord; like the one he'd given the previous day about making arrangements for Bhrigu and Dilipa to travel to the ruins of Mount Mandar. She could understand Maharishi Bhrigu's interest in going there. But what earthly reason could there be for the Swadweepan emperor to go as well? Kanakhala saw Daksha letting go of Veerini's hand and breaking the seal of the letter as she shut the door quietly behind her.

Daksha began to cry. Veerini immediately reached over and snatched the letter from him.

As she read through it quickly, Veerini let out a deep sigh of relief as tears escaped from her eyes. 'She's safe. They're all safe...'

On the surface, the plan to assassinate the Neelkanth worked towards the unique interests of all the three main conspirators, Maharishi Bhrigu, Emperor Daksha and Emperor Dilipa. For Bhrigu, the greatest gain would be that the Somras would not be targeted by the Neelkanth. The faith of the people in the legend of the Neelkanth was strong. If the Neelkanth declared that the Somras was evil and decided to toe the Naga line, so would his followers. For Dilipa it meant the killing of two birds with a single stone. Not only would he continue to receive the elixir from Bhrigu, but he'd also do away with Bhagirath, his heir and greatest threat. Daksha would be rid of the troublesome Neelkanth and be able to blame all ills on the Nagas once again. The plan was perfect. Except that Daksha could not countenance the killing of his daughter. He was willing to put everything on the line to ensure that Sati was left unharmed. Bhrigu and Dilipa had hoped that with the rupture in relations between Daksha and his daughter, the Meluhan emperor would support this mission wholeheartedly. They were wrong. Daksha's love for Sati was deeper than his hatred for Shiva.

Upon Veerini's advice, Daksha had sent the Arishtanemi brigadier Mayashrenik, known for his blind loyalty to Meluha and deep devotion to the Neelkanth, on a secret mission. Mayashrenik was to accompany the five ships that had been sent to attack the Neelkanth's convoy. Veerini had covertly kept in touch with her daughter Kali through all these years of strife, and had made Daksha aware of the river warning and defence system of the Nagas. All that had to be done was to get the alarm triggered in time. Mayashrenik's mission was to ensure that the alarms went off. He was to escape and return to Meluha after that. The Arishtanemi brigadier and acting general of the Meluhan army had carried a homing pigeon with him to deliver the news of the subsequent battle to Daksha. The happy message for the Meluhan emperor was that the progeny Daksha cared for – Sati and Kartik – were alive and safe.

Veerini looked at her husband. 'If only you would listen to me a bit more.'

Daksha breathed deeply. 'If Lord Bhrigu ever finds out...'

'Would you rather your children were dead?'

Daksha sighed. He would do anything to ensure Sati's safety. He shook his head. 'No!'

'Then thank the *Parmatma* that our plan worked. And never breathe a word of this to anyone. Ever!'

Daksha nodded. He took the letter from Veerini and set it aflame, holding it by the edge for as long as possible, to ensure that every part of it had charred beyond recognition.

Chapter 3

The Kings Have Chosen

'Do you believe Brahaspati?' asked Shiva.

Night had fallen on the Panchavati guest colony just outside the main city. Injured and fatigued, Shiva's entourage had retired to their quarters for a well-deserved rest.

Sati and Shiva were in their chambers, having just returned from the city. They had not spoken to a soul about what they'd learnt at the Panchavati school. They had not even told the Suryavanshis that Brahaspati, their beloved chief scientist, was still alive. They were to meet him again the next day.

'Well, I don't think Brahaspati*ji* is lying,' said Sati. 'I do remember that more than two decades ago, Lord Bhrigu had spent many months in Devagiri, which was highly unusual for the *Raj guru*. He is a rare sight in Meluha, since he usually chooses to spend his time meditating in his Himalayan cave.'

'Aren't *Raj gurus* supposed to stay in the royal palace and guide the king?'

'Not someone like Lord Bhrigu. He helped my father get elected as emperor because he believed my father would be good for Meluha. Beyond that Lord Bhrigu has had no interest in the day-to-day governance of Meluha. He is a simple man, rarely seen in the so-called powerful circles.'

'So he spent a lot of time in Devagiri. That may have been unusual, but what about the other things that Brahaspati said?'

'Well, Lord Bhrigu, my father and Brahaspati*ji* were indeed away for many months. It had been announced as an important trade trip; but I can't imagine Lord Bhrigu or Brahaspati*ji* being interested in trade. Perhaps they were in Pariha at the time. And yes, the talented and lovely Tara*ji*, who worked at Mount Mandar and had been sent to Pariha for a project, did disappear suddenly. It was announced that she had taken *sanyas*. Renouncing public life is very common in Meluha. But what Brahaspati*ji* revealed today was something else altogether.'

'So you believe Brahaspati speaks the truth?'

'All I'm saying is that Brahaspati*ji* may believe this to be the truth. But is it actually so or is he mistaken? This decision of yours can change the course of history. What you do now will have repercussions for generations to come. It is a momentous occasion, a big battle. You have to be completely sure.'

'I must speak with the Vasudevs.'

'Yes, you must.'

'But that is not all you wanted to say to me, is it?'

'I think there is another aspect to be considered. What made Brahaspati*ji* disappear for over five years? What was he doing in Panchavati all this while? I feel this is an important question; perhaps linked to the back-up manufacturing facility for the Somras that father had told me about.'

'Yes, I didn't give it much importance then. But if the Somras is Evil, that facility is the key.'

'Actually, the Saraswati is the key. A manufacturing facility can always be rebuilt. But wherever it is built, it will always need the Saraswati waters. Kali told me at Icchawar that her people attacked Meluhan temples and Brahmins only if they were directly harming the Nagas. Maybe those temples were production centres that used the powder from Mount Mandar to manufacture the Somras drink for the locals. She also said that a final solution would emerge from the Saraswati. That the Nagas were working on it. I don't know what that cryptic statement meant. We need to find out.'

'You did not tell me about your conversation with Kali.'

'Shiva, this is the first honest conversation we are having about Kali and Ganesh since you met my son at Kashi.'

Shiva became quiet.

'I'm not blaming you,' continued Sati. 'I understood your anger. You thought that Ganesh had killed Brahaspati*ji*. Now that the truth has emerged, you are willing to listen.'

Shiva smiled and embraced Sati.

— ⁂ —

'Are you sure?' asked Shiva.

It was late the next morning, four hours into the second prahar. Shiva sat with Sati at his side in his private chambers. Parvateshwar and Bhagirath stood in front, holding a plank. The Meluhan general and the Ayodhyan prince had just returned after surveying the destroyed battleships.

'Yes, My Lord. The evidence is indisputable,' said Bhagirath.

'Show me.'

Bhagirath stepped forward. 'The rivets on these planks are clearly Meluhan. Lord Parvateshwar has identified them.'

Parvateshwar nodded in agreement.

'And the casing,' continued Bhagirath, 'that improves the water-proofing is clearly Ayodhyan.'

'Are you suggesting that Emperor Daksha and Emperor Dilipa have formed an alliance against us?' Shiva asked softly.

'They've used the best technologies available in both our

lands. These ships had navigated through a lot of sea water, judging by the molluscs on them. They needed the best to be able to make the journey quickly.'

Shiva breathed deeply, lost in thought.

'My Lord,' said Bhagirath. 'For all his faults, I cannot imagine my father would be capable of leading a conspiracy such as this. He simply does not have the capability. He is just a follower in this plot. You have to target him, of course. But don't make the mistake of thinking that he is the main conspirator. He is not.'

Sati leaned towards Shiva. 'Do you think my father can do this?'

Shiva shook his head. 'No. Emperor Daksha too is incapable of leading this conspiracy.'

Parvateshwar, still shame-faced at the dishonour brought upon his empire, said quietly, 'The Meluhan code enjoins upon us to follow the rules, My Lord. Our rules bid us to carry out our king's orders. In the hands of a lesser king, this can lead to a lot of wrong.'

'Emperor Daksha may have issued the orders, Parvateshwar,' said Shiva. 'But he didn't dream them up. There is a master who has brought the royalty of Meluha and Swadweep together. Someone who also managed to procure the feared *daivi astras*. Heaven alone knows if he has any more *divine weapons*. It was a brilliant plan. By Lord Ram's grace, we were saved by the skin of our teeth. It cannot be Emperor Daksha or Emperor Dilipa. This is someone of far greater importance, intelligence and resource. And, one who is clever enough to conceal his identity.'

— ⚘ —

'Return to Meluha?!' asked Veerbhadra.

Veerbhadra and Krittika were in Shiva's private chambers. Kali and Sati were also present.

'Yes, Bhadra,' said Shiva. 'It was the Meluhans and the Ayodhyans who attacked us together.'

'Are you sure Meluha is involved?' asked Veerbhadra.

'Parvateshwar has himself confirmed it.'

'And now you are worried about our people.'

'Yes,' said Shiva. 'I'm worried the Gunas will be arrested and held hostage as leverage over us. Before they do so, I want you to slip into Meluha quietly and take our people to Kashi. I will meet you there.'

'My scouts will guide Krittika and you through a secret route,' said Kali. 'Using our fastest horses and speediest boats, my people can get you close to Maika in two weeks. After that, you are on your own.'

'Meluha is a safe country to travel in,' said Krittika. 'We can hire fast horses up to the mouth of the Saraswati. After that we can travel on boats plying on the river. It's an easy route. With luck, we will reach Devagiri in another two weeks. The Gunas are in a small village not far from there.'

'Perfect,' said Shiva. 'Time is of the essence. Go now.'

'Yes Shiva,' said Veerbhadra as he turned to leave with his wife.

'And Bhadra...' said Shiva.

Veerbhadra and Krittika turned around.

'Don't try to be brave,' said Shiva. 'If the Gunas have been arrested already, leave Meluha quickly and wait for me at Kashi.'

Veerbhadra's mother was with the Gunas. Shiva knew Veerbhadra would not abandon her to her fate so easily.

'Shiva...' whispered Veerbhadra.

Shiva got up and held Veerbhadra's shoulder. 'Bhadra, promise me.'

Veerbhadra remained quiet.

'If you try to release them by yourself, you will be killed. You will be of no use to your mother if you are dead, Bhadra.'

Veerbhadra stayed silent.

'I promise you, nothing will happen to the Gunas. If you cannot get them out, I will. But do not do anything rash. Promise me.'

Veerbhadra placed his hand on Shiva's shoulder. 'There is something you aren't telling me. What have you discovered here? Why are you so afraid suddenly? Is there going to be a war? Is Meluha going to become our enemy?'

'I'm not sure, Bhadra. I haven't made up my mind as yet.'

'Then tell me what you do know.'

It was Shiva's turn to remain silent now.

'I'm going back to Meluha, Shiva. Had you asked me a month back, I would have said this would be the safest journey possible. A lot has changed since then. You have to tell me the truth. I deserve that.'

Shiva sat them down and revealed everything he had discovered during the course of the last few days.

— ⁂ —

'And you killed the rhino all by yourself?' asked an impressed Anandmayi, her face suffused with a broad smile.

'Yes, Your Highness,' said Kartik, stoic and expressionless as usual.

Anandmayi, Ayurvati and Kartik were settled comfortably on soft cushions in the dining room. Kshatriya in word and deed, Anandmayi and Kartik partook of the delicious rhinoceros meat. The Brahmin Ayurvati restricted herself to *roti*, *dal* and vegetables.

'Have you decided to stop smiling altogether?' asked

Anandmayi. 'Or is this just temporary?'

Kartik looked up at Anandmayi, a hint of a smile on his face. 'Smiling takes more effort than it's worth, Your Highness.'

Ayurvati shook her head. 'You are just a child, Kartik. Don't trouble yourself so much. You need to enjoy your childhood.'

Kartik turned to the Meluhan chief physician. 'My brother Ganesh is a great man, Ayurvati*ji*. He has so much to contribute to society, to the country. And yet, he was almost eaten alive by dumb beasts because he was trying to save me.'

Ayurvati reached across and patted Kartik.

'I will never be so helpless again,' swore Kartik. 'I will not be the cause of my family's misery.'

The door swung open. Parvateshwar and Bhagirath walked in.

Just by looking at them, Anandmayi could tell that they had discovered what she feared. 'Was it Meluha?'

Ayurvati winced. She could not imagine her great country's name being dragged into a vile conspiracy like the attack on the Neelkanth's convoy at the outskirts of Panchavati. And yet, after what she had discovered of Emperor Daksha's perfidy during Sati's pregnancy at Maika, she would not be surprised if Meluhan ships had carried out this dastardly act.

'It's worse,' sighed Bhagirath as he sat down.

Parvateshwar sat next to Anandmayi and held her hand. He looked at Ayurvati, his pained expression bearing witness to his stark misery. The general prized his country, his Meluha, as Lord Ram's ultimate legacy. It was the custodian of Ram Rajya. How could this great country's emperor have committed a dastardly act such as this?

'Even worse?' prompted Anandmayi.

'Yes. It seems Swadweep is in on the conspiracy as well.'

Anandmayi was stunned. 'What?!'

'It's either only Ayodhya or all of Swadweep. I cannot be sure if other kingdoms of Swadweep are following Ayodhya's lead. But Ayodhya is certainly involved.'

Anandmayi looked at Parvateshwar. He nodded, confirming Bhagirath's words.

'Lord Rudra, be merciful,' said Anandmayi. 'What is wrong with father?'

'I for one am not surprised,' said Bhagirath, barely able to conceal his contempt. 'He is weak and gets easily exploited. It doesn't take much for him to succumb.'

For once Anandmayi didn't rebuke her brother for denigrating their father. She looked at Parvateshwar. He seemed lost and unsure. Change was horrible for the Suryavanshis, for the people of the masculine, used as they were to unchanging rules and stark predictability. Anandmayi turned her husband's face towards herself and kissed him gently, reassuringly. She smiled warmly. He half-smiled back.

Kartik quietly put his plate down, washed his hands and walked out of the room.

— ⁂ —

It was early afternoon as Kartik and Ganesh's steps led them around the five banyan trees from whose existence Panchavati derived its name. Non-Nagas were not allowed inside the inner city. In truth, many of them, Brangas included, refused to enter due to a strong superstition about the misfortune that would befall those that did. But the Neelkanth's family did not believe in it. And anyway, nobody wanted to enforce an entry ban on them.

'Why have only Lord Ram's idols been depicted on these trees, *dada*?' Kartik asked his *elder brother*.

'You mean why have his wife, Lady Sita, and his brother,

Lord Lakshman, not been shown?'

'Not just them, even his great devotee, Lord Hanuman, is missing.'

Ganesh and Kartik were admiring the beautiful idols of Lord Ram sculpted into the main trunk of each of the five banyans. The five tree idols showed the ancient King, respected as the seventh Vishnu, in the five different roles of his life known to all: a son, a husband, a brother, a father and a Godly king. Each banyan trunk depicted him in a different form. In each form, in a manner that somehow appeared natural, the sculptors had made the idols look towards the temple of Lord Rudra and Lady Mohini at one corner of the square. Their idols, on the other hand, were placed in the front section of the temple as opposed to the back as in most temples, with the effect that the two deities appeared to be looking at all five tree idols as well. It seemed as if the architects intended to show the great Mahadev and the noble seventh Vishnu being respectful to each other.

'It's in keeping with Bhoomidevi's instructions,' answered Ganesh. 'I know his traditional depiction in the Sapt Sindhu is always along with his three favourite people in the world, Lady Sita, Lord Lakshman and Lord Hanuman. But it was an order of Bhoomidevi, our founding Goddess, that Lord Ram always be shown alone in Panchavati. Especially at the five banyans.'

'Why?'

'I don't know. Perhaps she wanted us to always remember that great leaders, like the Vishnus and the Mahadevs, may have millions following them. But at the end of the day, they carry the burden of their mission alone.'

'Like *baba*?' asked Kartik, referring to their *father*.

'Yes, like *baba*. He is the one who stands between Evil and India. If he fails, life in the subcontinent will be destroyed by Evil.'

'*Baba* will not fail.'

Ganesh smiled at Kartik's response.

'Do you know why?' asked Kartik.

Ganesh shook his head. 'No. Why?'

Kartik clasped Ganesh's right hand and held it to his chest, like the brother-warriors of yore. 'Because he is not alone.'

Ganesh smiled and embraced Kartik. They walked silently around the banyan trees, doing the holy *parikrama* of Lord Ram's idols.

'What is going on, *dada*?' asked Kartik, as they continued their circumambulation.

Ganesh frowned.

'Why have both the emperors allied against *baba*?'

Ganesh breathed deeply. He never lied to Kartik. He considered his brother an adult and treated him as such. 'Because *baba* threatens them, Kartik. They are the elite. They are addicted to the benefits they derive from Evil. *Baba's* mission is to fight for the oppressed; to be the voice of the voiceless. It is obvious that the elite will want to stop him.'

'What is the Evil that *baba* is fighting? How has it entrenched its claws so deeply?'

Ganesh took Kartik by the hand and made him sit at the foot of one of the banyans. 'This is for you alone, Kartik. You are not to tell anyone else. For it is *baba's* right to decide when and how others are to be informed.'

Kartik nodded in response.

Ganesh sat next to Kartik and explained to him about what Brahaspati and Shiva had discussed the previous day.

'What have you been doing these past five years, Brahaspati?'

asked Shiva.

Sati and Shiva had joined the chief scientist in the Naga queen's chambers. Brahaspati felt like he was being interrogated. But he could understand Shiva's need to get to the bottom of the issue.

'I was trying to find a permanent solution to the Somras problem,' answered Brahaspati.

'Permanent solution?'

'Destroying Mount Mandar is a temporary solution. We know it will get rebuilt. The Nagas tell me the reconstruction has been surprisingly slow. It shouldn't have taken five years. Not with Meluhan efficiency. But it's only a matter of time before it gets rebuilt.'

Shiva looked at Sati, but she didn't say anything.

'Once Mandar is back to full manufacturing capacity, the destruction of the Saraswati and the production of the toxic waste will begin in large measure once again. So we have to find a permanent solution. The best way to do that is to examine the Somras' ingredients. If we can somehow control that, we could possibly control the poisonous impact of the Somras waste. Many ingredients can be easily replaced. But two of them cannot. The first are the bark and branches of the Sanjeevani tree, and the second is the Saraswati water. We cannot control the availability of the Sanjeevani tree. Meluha has large plantations of it across its northern reaches. How many plantations can one destroy? Besides, trees can always be replanted. That brings us to the Saraswati. Can we somehow control its waters?'

Shiva remembered parts of a conversation with Daksha when he had first arrived in Devagiri. 'I was told by Emperor Daksha that the Chandravanshis did try to destroy the Saraswati more than a hundred years ago. By taking one of its main tributaries, the Yamuna, away from it and redirecting its flow towards the Ganga. It didn't really make much sense to me but the Meluhans seem to believe it.'

Brahaspati sniggered. 'The Chandravanshi ruling class cannot even build roads in their own empire. How can anyone think that they would have the ability to change the course of a river? What happened a hundred years ago was an earthquake that changed the course of the Yamuna. The Meluhans subsequently defeated the Chandravanshis and the resultant treaty mandated that the early course of the Yamuna would become no-man's land. And Meluhans do have the technology to change the course of rivers. They built giant embankments to block and change the course of the Yamuna to make it flow back into the Saraswati.'

'So what was your plan? Destroy the Yamuna embankments?'

'No. I had considered it, but that is impossible as well. They have many fail-safe options. It would take five brigades and months of open work to be able to destroy those embankments. We would obviously have had to work in secret with a small number of people.'

'So what was your plan?'

'An alternative. We cannot take the Saraswati away. But could we make the Saraswati much less potent in the production of the Somras? Is it possible to add something to the Yamuna waters, at its source, which would then flow into the Saraswati and control the amount of waste being produced? I thought that we had found one such ingredient.'

'What?'

'A bacterium which reacts with the Sanjeevani tree and makes it decay almost instantly.'

'I thought the Sanjeevani tree was already unstable and decayed rapidly. Ayurvati had told me the Naga medicine is created by mixing the crushed branches of another tree with the Sanjeevani bark to stabilise it. If the Sanjeevani is already unstable, why would it need bacteria to aid the decay? Wouldn't it just decay anyway?'

'The Sanjeevani bark becomes unstable once stripped off the branch. The entire branch, if used, is not. The bark is easier for small-scale manufacture, but for manufacturing the Somras in large quantities, we have to use crushed branches. This is what we did at Mount Mandar. But it is a method known only to my scientists.'

'So what you want to do is make the Sanjeevani branch also unstable.'

'Yes. And, I discovered that it was possible to do so with this bacterium. But it is only available in Mesopotamia.'

'Is this what you picked up from Karachapa when you accompanied me on my initial travels through Meluha? You had said you were expecting a shipment from Mesopotamia.'

'Yes,' said Brahaspati. 'And it would have worked perfectly. The Somras cannot be made without both the Sanjeevani tree and the Saraswati water. The presence of bacteria in the Saraswati water would render useless the Sanjeevani tree at the beginning of the process itself. And in any case, without the Saraswati water, the Somras cannot be made. Without the power of the Sanjeevani, the Somras would not be as potent. It will not triple or quadruple one's lifespan, but only increase it by twenty or thirty years. However, it would also mean that there would be practically no production of Somras waste. By sacrificing some of the powers of the Somras, we would take away all the poison of the Somras waste. Furthermore, these bacteria also mix with water and then multiply prodigiously. All we needed to do was release it in the Yamuna and the rest would follow.'

'Sounds perfect. Why didn't you?'

'There is no free lunch,' said Brahaspati. 'The bacteria came with its own problems. It is a mild toxin in itself. If we mix it in large quantities, as would be required in the Saraswati, we could create a new set of diseases for all living beings dependant not just on the Saraswati but also the Yamuna. We would have only replaced one problem with another.'

'So you were trying to see if the poisonous effect of the bacteria could be reduced or removed, without disturbing its ability to destroy the Sanjeevani tree?'

'Yes. Secrecy was required. If those who support the Somras knew about these bacteria, they would try to kill it at its source. Had they known I was working on an experiment such as this, they would have had me assassinated.'

'Aren't you afraid of being killed now?' asked Shiva. 'A lot of Meluhans will be angry with you when they discover you weren't the victim, but the perpetrator of the attack on Mount Mandar.'

Brahaspati breathed deeply. 'Earlier, it was important for me to remain alive since I alone could have done this research. But I have failed. And the solution to the Somras problem is not in my hands anymore. It's in your hands. It doesn't matter if I live any longer. Mount Mandar will be reconstructed. It's a matter of time. And Somras production will begin once again. You have to stop it, Shiva. For the sake of India, you have to stop the Somras.'

'The reconstruction is a charade, Brahaspati*ji*,' said Sati. 'It's to mislead enemies into thinking that it will take time to get Somras production back on track. To make them think that Meluha must be surviving on lower quantities of Somras.'

'What? Is there another facility?' asked Brahaspati, as he looked quickly at Kali. 'But that cannot be true.'

'It is,' answered Sati. 'I was told by father himself. Apparently, it was built years ago. As a back-up to Mount Mandar, just in case...'

'Where?' asked Kali.

'I don't know,' replied Sati.

'Damn!' exclaimed Kali, scowling darkly as she turned to Brahaspati. 'You had said that that was not possible. The churners needed materials from Egypt. They could not be built from Indian material. We have allies constantly watching those Egyptian mines. No material has gone to Meluha!'

Brahaspati's face turned white as the implications dawned on him. He held his head and muttered, 'Lord Ram, be merciful... How can they resort to this?'

'Resort to what?' asked Shiva.

'There's another way in which the Saraswati waters can be mixed with the crushed Sanjeevani branches. But it's considered wasteful and repugnant.'

'Why?'

'Firstly, it uses much larger quantities of the Saraswati water. Secondly, it needs animal or human skin cells.'

'Excuse me!' cried Shiva and Sati.

'It doesn't mean that one skins a live animal or human,' said Brahaspati, as though reassuring them. 'What is needed is old and dead skin cells that we shed every minute that we are alive. The cells help the Saraswati waters to grate the Sanjeevani branches at molecular levels. The waters mixed with dead skin cells are simply poured over crushed branches placed in a chamber. This process does not require any churning. But as you can imagine, it wastes a lot of water. Secondly, how would one find animals and humans who would come to a faraway facility and get into a pool of water above a chamber which contains crushed Sanjeevani branches? It is risky.'

'Why?'

'Dead skin cells of humans or animals are best shed while bathing. A human sheds between two to three kilograms every year. Bathing hastens the process.'

'But why is this risky?'

'Because Somras production is inherently unstable; the skin cell route even more so. One doesn't want large populations anywhere close to a Somras facility. If anything goes wrong, the resultant explosion can kill hundreds of thousands. Even in the usual, less risky churning process, we do not build Somras production centres close to cities. Can you imagine what would happen if the riskier skin cell process was being conducted close to a city with a large number of humans ritually bathing above a Somras production centre?'

Shiva's face suddenly turned white. 'Public baths in Meluhan cities...' he whispered.

'Exactly,' said Brahaspati. 'Build the facility within a city, below a public bath. One would have all the dead skin cells that one would need.'

'And if something goes wrong... If an explosion takes place...'

'Blame the *daivi astras* or the Nagas. Blame the Chandravanshis if you want,' fumed Brahaspati. 'Having created so many evil spectres, you can take your pick!'

— ⅄ⓄƱ⇞⊗ —

'Something is wrong,' said Bhrigu.

He was surveying the destroyed remains of Mount Mandar with Dilipa. The Somras manufacturing facility looked nowhere near completion though reconstruction was on.

Dilipa turned towards the sage. 'I agree, Maharishi*ji*. It has been more than five years since the Nagas destroyed Mandar. It's ridiculous that the facility has still not been reconstructed.'

Bhrigu turned to Dilipa and waved his hand dismissively. 'Mount Mandar is not important anymore. It's only a symbol. I'm talking about the attack on Panchavati.'

Dilipa stared wide-eyed at the sage. *Mount Mandar is not*

important? This means that the rumours are true. Another Somras manufacturing facility does exist.

'I had given a whole kit of homing pigeons to the attackers,' continued Bhrigu, not bothering with Dilipa's incredulous look. 'All of them had been trained to return to this site. The last pigeon came in two weeks back.'

Dilipa frowned. 'You can trust my man, My Lord. He will not fail.'

Bhrigu had appointed an officer from Dilipa's army to lead the attack on Shiva's convoy at Panchavati. He did not trust Daksha's ability to detach himself from his love for his daughter. 'Of that I am sure. He has proven himself trustworthy, strictly complying with my instructions to send back a message every week. The fact that the updates have suddenly stopped means that he has either been captured or killed.'

'I'm sure a message is on its way. We needn't worry.'

Bhrigu turned sharply towards Dilipa. 'Is this how you govern your empire, great King? Is it any wonder that your son's claim to the throne appears legitimate?'

Dilipa's silence was telling.

Bhrigu sighed. 'When you prepare for war, you should always hope for the best, but be ready for the worst. The last despatch clearly stated that they were but six days' sail from Panchavati. Having received no word, I am compelled to assume the worst. The attack must have failed. Also, I should assume Shiva knows the identity of the attackers.'

Dilipa didn't speak, but kept staring at Bhrigu. He thought Bhrigu was over-reacting.

'I'm not over-reacting, Your Highness,' said Bhrigu.

Dilipa was stunned. He hadn't uttered a word.

'Do not underestimate the issue,' said Bhrigu. 'This is not about you or me. This is about the future of India. This is about protecting the greatest Good. We cannot afford to fail! It is our duty to Lord Brahma; our duty to this great land of ours.'

Dilipa remained silent. Though one thought kept reverberating in his mind. *I am way out of my depth here. I have entangled myself with powers that are beyond mere emperors.*

Chapter 4

A Frog Homily

The aroma of freshly-cooked food emerged from Shiva's chambers as his family assembled for their evening meal. Sati's culinary skill and effort were evident in the feast she had lined up for what was practically their first meal together as a family. Shiva, Ganesh and Kartik waited for her to take a seat before they began the meal.

In keeping with custom, the family of the Mahadev took some water from their glasses and sprinkled it around their plates, symbolically thanking Goddess Annapurna for her blessings in the form of food and nourishment. After this, they offered the first morsel of food to the Gods. Breaking with age-old tradition though, Shiva always offered his first morsel to his wife. For him, she was divine. Sati reciprocated by offering her first morsel to Shiva.

And thus the meal began.

'Ganesh has got some mangoes for you today,' said Sati, looking indulgently at Kartik.

Kartik grinned. 'Yummy! Thanks *dada*!'

Ganesh smiled and patted Kartik on his back.

'You should smile a little more, Kartik,' said Shiva. 'Life is not so grim.'

Kartik smiled at his father. 'I'll try, *baba*.'

Looking at his other progeny, Shiva inhaled sharply. 'Ganesh?'

'Yes... *baba*,' said Ganesh, unsure of the response to his calling Shiva *father*.

'My son,' whispered Shiva. 'I misjudged you.'

Ganesh's eyes moistened.

'Forgive me,' said Shiva.

'No, *baba*,' exclaimed Ganesh, embarrassed. 'How can you ask me for forgiveness? You are my father.'

Brahaspati had told Shiva that he had made Ganesh take an oath of secrecy; nobody was to know that the former Meluhan chief scientist was alive. Brahaspati did not trust anyone and wanted his experiments on the Mesopotamian bacteria to remain secret. Ganesh had kept his word even at the cost of almost losing his beloved mother and of grievously damaging his relationship with Shiva.

'You're a man of your word,' said Shiva. 'You honoured your promise to Brahaspati, without sparing a thought for the price you would be paying.'

Ganesh remained quiet.

'I'm proud of you my son,' said Shiva.

Ganesh smiled.

Sati looked at Shiva, Kartik and then at Ganesh. Her world had come full circle. Life was as perfect as it could possibly be. She did not need anything else. She could live her life in Panchavati till the end of her days. But she knew that this was not to be. A war was coming; a battle that would require major sacrifices. She knew she had to savour these moments for as long as they lasted.

'What now, *baba*?' asked Kartik seriously.

'We're going to eat!' laughed Shiva. 'And then, hopefully, we will go to sleep.'

'No, no,' smiled Kartik. 'You know what I mean. Are we going to proclaim the Somras as the ultimate Evil? Are we going to declare war against all those who continue to use or protect the Somras?'

Shiva looked at Kartik thoughtfully. 'There has already been a lot of fighting, Kartik. We will not rush into anything.' Shiva turned to Ganesh. 'I'm sorry, my son, but I need to know more. I have to know more.'

'I understand, *baba*. There are only two groups of people who know all there is to know about this.'

'The Vasudevs and the Vayuputras?'

'Yes.'

'I'm not sure if the Vayuputra council will help me. But I know the Vasudevs will.'

'I'll take you to Ujjain, *baba*. You can speak to their chief directly.'

'Where is Ujjain?'

'It's up north, beyond the Narmada.'

Shiva considered it for a bit. 'That would be along the shorter route to Swadweep and Meluha, right?'

With the security of Panchavati uppermost in her mind, Kali had led Shiva and his entourage from Kashi to Panchavati via an elaborate route which took a year to traverse. The party had first headed east through Swadweep then south from Branga. They then moved west from Kalinga through the dangerous Dandak forests before they reached the headwaters of the Godavari where Panchavati lay. Shiva realised that there must be a shorter northern route to Meluha and Swadweep, which was impossible to traverse without a Naga guide, because of the impregnable forests that impeded the path.

'Yes, *baba*. Though *mausi* is very secretive about this route, I know that she would be happy to share it with the three of you.'

'I understand,' said Sati. 'The Nagas have many powerful enemies.'

'Yes, *maa*,' said Ganesh, before turning to Shiva. 'But that is not the only reason. Let's be honest. Though the war has not yet begun, we already know that the most powerful emperors in the land are against us. Which side everyone takes, including those waiting in the Panchavati guesthouse colony, will become clear over the next few months. Panchavati is a safe haven. It's not wise to give away its secrets just as yet.'

Shiva nodded. 'Let me figure out what I should do with my convoy. There aren't too many kings in the Sapt Sindhu I can readily trust at this point of time. Once I've made up my mind, we can make plans to leave for Ujjain.'

Kartik turned to Ganesh. '*Dada*, there's one thing I simply don't understand. The Vayuputras are the tribe left behind by Lord Rudra. They helped the great seventh Vishnu, Lord Ram, complete his mission. So how is it that these good people do not see the Evil that the Somras has become today?'

Ganesh smiled. 'I have a theory.'

Shiva and Sati looked up at Ganesh, while continuing to eat.

'You've seen a frog, right?' asked Ganesh.

'Yes,' said Kartik. 'Interesting creatures; especially their tongues!'

Ganesh smiled. 'Apparently, an unknown Brahmin scientist had conducted some experiments on frogs a long time ago. He dropped a frog in a pot of boiling water. The frog immediately jumped out. He then placed a frog in a pot full of cold water; the frog settled down comfortably. The Brahmin then began raising the temperature of the water gradually, over many hours. The frog kept adapting to the increasingly warm and then hot water till it finally died, without making any attempt to escape.'

Shiva, Sati and Kartik listened in rapt attention.

'Naga students learn this story as a life lesson,' said Ganesh.

'Often, our immediate reaction to a sudden crisis helps us save ourselves. Our response to gradual crises that creep up upon us, on the other hand, may be so adaptive as to ultimately lead to self-destruction.'

'Are you suggesting that the Vayuputras keep adapting to the incremental ill-effects of the Somras?' asked Kartik. 'That the bad news is not emerging rapidly enough?'

'Perhaps,' said Ganesh. 'For I refuse to believe that the Vayuputras, the people of Lord Rudra, would consciously choose to let Evil live. The only explanation is that they genuinely believe the Somras is not evil.'

'Interesting,' said Shiva.. 'And, perhaps you are right too.'

Sati chipped in with a smile, almost as if to lighten the atmosphere. 'But do you really believe the frog experiment?'

Ganesh smiled. 'It is such a popular story around here that I'd actually tried it, when I was a child.'

'Did you really boil a frog slowly to death? And it sat still all the while?'

Ganesh laughed. '*Maaaaa!* Frogs don't sit still no matter what you do! Boiling water, cold water or lukewarm water, a frog always leaps out!'

The family of the Mahadev laughed heartily.

— ⁂ —

Shiva and Sati were exiting the Panchavati Rajya Sabha, having just met with the Naga nobility. Many of the nobles were in agreement with Queen Kali, who wanted to attack Meluha right away and destroy the evil Somras. But some, like Vasuki and Astik, wanted to avoid war.

'Vasuki and Astik genuinely want peace. But for the wrong reasons,' said Shiva, shaking his head. 'They may be Naga nobility, but they believe that their own people deserve their cruel fate, because they are being punished for their past-life sins. This is nonsense!'

Sati, who believed in the concept of karma extending over many births, could not hold back her objection. 'Just because we don't understand something doesn't necessarily mean it is rubbish, Shiva.'

'Come on, Sati. There is only this life; this moment. That is the only thing we can be sure of. Everything else is only theory.'

'Then why were the Nagas born deformed? Why did I live as a Vikarma for so long? Surely it must be because in some sense we'd deserved it. We were paying for our past-life sins.'

'That's ridiculous! How can anyone be sure about past-life sins? The Vikarma system, like every system that governs human lives, was created by us. You fought the Vikarma system and freed yourself.'

'But I didn't free myself, Shiva. You did. It was your strength. And all the Vikarmas, including me, were set free because that was your karma.'

'So how does this work?' asked Shiva disbelievingly. 'That the compounded totality of sins committed by all the Vikarma over their individual previous lives was nullified at the stroke of a quill when I struck down this law? On that fateful day, in a flash, several lifetimes of sins sullying every Vikarma soul were washed away? A day of divine pardon, indeed!'

'Shiva, are you mocking me?'

'Would I ever do that, dear?' asked Shiva, but his smile gave him away. 'Don't you see how illogical this entire concept is? How can one believe that an innocent child is born with sin? It's clear as daylight: a new-born child has done no wrong. He has done no right either. He has just been born. He could not have done anything!'

'Perhaps not in this life, Shiva. But it's possible that the child committed a sin in a previous life. Perhaps the child's ancestors committed sins for which the child must be held accountable.'

Shiva was unconvinced. 'Don't you get it? It's a system designed to control people. It makes those who suffer or are oppressed, blame themselves for their misery. Because you believe you are paying for sins committed either in your own previous lives or those committed by your ancestors, or even community. Perhaps even the sins of the first man ever born! The system therefore propagates suffering as a form of atonement and at the same time does not allow one to question the wrongs done unto oneself.'

'Then why do some people suffer? Why do some get far *less* than what they deserve?'

'The same reason why there are others who get far *more* than what they deserve. It's completely random.'

Shiva gallantly reached out to help Sati mount her steed but she declined and gracefully slid onto the stallion. Her husband smiled. There was nothing he loved more than her intense sense of self-sufficiency and pride. Shiva leapt onto his own horse and with a quick spur matched Sati's pace.

'Really, Shiva,' said Sati, looking towards him. 'Do you believe that the *Parmatma* plays dice with the universe? That we are all handed our fate randomly?'

The Nagas on the road recognised Shiva and bowed low in respect. They didn't believe in the legend of the Neelkanth, but clearly, their queen respected the Mahadev. And that made most Nagas believe in Shiva as well. He politely acknowledged every person even as he replied to Sati without turning. 'I think the *Parmatma* does not interfere in our lives. He sets the rules by which the universe exists. Then, He does something very difficult.'

'What?'

'He leaves us alone. He lets things play out naturally. He lets His creations make decisions about their own lives. It's not easy being a witness when one has the power to rule. It takes a Supreme God to be able to do that. He knows this is our world, our *karmabhoomi*,' said Shiva, waving his hand all around as though pointing out the *land of their karma*.

'Don't you think this is difficult to accept? If people believe that their fate is completely random, it would leave them without any sense of understanding, purpose or motivation. Or why they are where they are.'

'On the contrary, this is an empowering thought. When you know that your fate is completely random, you have the freedom to commit yourself to any theory that will empower you. If you have been blessed with good fate, you can choose to believe it is God's kindness and ingrain humility within. But if you have been cursed with bad fate, you need to know that no Great Power is seeking to punish you. Your situation is, in fact, a result of completely random circumstances, an indiscriminate turn of the universe. Therefore, if you decide to challenge your destiny, your opponent would not be some judgemental Lord Almighty who is seeking to punish you; your opponent would only be the limitations of your own mind. This will empower you to fight your fate.'

Sati shook her head. 'Sometimes you are too revolutionary.'

Shiva's eyes crinkled. 'Maybe that is itself a result of my past-life sins!'

Laughing together, they cantered out of the city gates.

Seeing the Panchavati guest colony in the distance, Shiva whispered gravely, 'But one man will have to account to his friends for his karma in this life.'

'Brahaspati*ji*?'

Shiva nodded.

'What do you have in mind?'

'I had asked Brahaspati if he'd like to meet Parvateshwar and Ayurvati, to explain to them as to how he is still alive.'

'And?'

'He readily agreed.'

'I would have expected nothing less from him.'

— ⅄ⵀꀤꌦ⊛ —

'Are you all right?' asked Anandmayi.

Parvateshwar and Anandmayi were in their private room in the Panchavati guesthouse colony.

'I'm thoroughly confused,' said Parvateshwar. 'The ruler of Meluha should represent the best there is in our way of life – truth, duty and honour. What does it say about us if our emperor is such a habitual law-breaker? He broke the law when Sati's child was born.'

'I know what Emperor Daksha did was patently wrong. But one could argue that he is just a father trying to protect his child, albeit in his own stupid manner.'

'The fact that he did what was wrong is enough, Anandmayi. He broke the law. And now, he has broken one of Lord Rudra's laws by using the *daivi astras*. How can Meluha, the finest land in the world, have an emperor like him? Isn't something wrong somewhere?'

Anandmayi held her husband's hand. 'Your emperor was never any good. I could have told you that many years ago. But you don't need to blame all of Meluha for his misdeeds.'

'That's not the way it works. A leader is not just a person who gives orders. He is also the one who symbolises the society he leads. If the leader is corrupt, then the society must be corrupt too.'

'Who feeds this nonsense to you, my love? A leader is just a human being, like anyone else. He doesn't symbolise anything.'

Parvateshwar shook his head. 'There are some truths that cannot be challenged. A leader's karma impacts his entire land. He is supposed to be his people's icon. That is a universal truth.'

Anandmayi bent towards him with a soft twinkle in her eyes. 'Parvateshwar, there is your truth and there is my truth. As for the universal truth? It does not exist.'

Parvateshwar smiled as he brushed a stray strand of hair away from her face. 'You Chandravanshis are very good with words.'

'Words can only be as good or as bad as the thoughts they convey.'

Parvateshwar's smile spread wider. 'So what is your thought on what I should do? My emperor's actions have put me in a situation where my God, the Neelkanth, may declare war on my country. What do I do then? How do I know which side to pick?'

'You should stick to your God,' said Anandmayi, without any hint of hesitation in her voice. 'But this is a hypothetical question. So don't worry too much about it.'

— ⁂ —

'My Lord, you called,' said Ayurvati.

She had been as surprised as Parvateshwar when the both of them had been summoned to Shiva's chambers. Since their arrival in Panchavati, Shiva had spent most of his time with the Nagas. Ayurvati was convinced that the Nagas were somehow complicit in the attack on Shiva's convoy. She also believed the Neelkanth was perhaps investigating the roots of Naga treachery in Panchavati.

'Parvateshwar, Ayurvati, welcome,' said Shiva, 'I called you here because it is time now for you to know the secret of the Nagas.'

Parvateshwar looked up, surprised. 'But why only the two of us, My Lord?'

'Because the both of you are Meluhans. I have reason to suspect that the attack on us at the Godavari is linked to many things: the plague in Branga, the plight of the Nagas and the drying up of the Saraswati.'

Parvateshwar and Ayurvati were flummoxed.

'But I am certain about one thing,' said Shiva. 'The attack is connected to the destruction of Mount Mandar.'

'What?! How?'

'Only one man can explain it. One whom you believe is dead.'

Ayurvati and Parvateshwar spun around as they heard the door open.

Brahaspati walked in quietly.

'The Somras is Evil?' asked Anandmayi incredulously. 'Is that what the Lord Neelkanth thinks?'

Parvateshwar and Anandmayi were in their chambers at the Panchavati guest colony. Bhagirath had just joined them.

'I'm not sure about what he thinks,' said Parvateshwar. 'But Brahaspati seems to think so.'

'But Evil is supposed to be Evil for everybody,' said Bhagirath. 'Why should a Suryavanshi turncoat decide what Evil is? Why should we listen to him? Why should the Neelkanth listen to him?'

'Bhagirath, do you expect me to defend Brahaspati, the man who destroyed the soul of our empire?' asked Parvateshwar.

'Just a minute,' said Anandmayi, raising her hand. 'Think this through... If the plague in Branga is linked to the Somras, if the slow depletion of the river Saraswati is linked to the Somras, if the birth of the Nagas is linked to the Somras, then isn't it fair to think that maybe it is Evil?'

'So what is the Neelkanth planning to do? Does he want to ban the Somras?' asked Bhagirath.

'I don't know, Bhagirath!' snapped an irritated Parvateshwar, his world having turned upside down because of Daksha and now Brahaspati. 'You keep asking me questions, the answers to which I do not know!'

Anandmayi placed her hand on Parvateshwar's shoulders. 'Perhaps the Neelkanth is just as shocked as we are. He needs to think things over. He cannot afford to make hasty decisions.'

'Well, he has made one already,' said Parvateshwar.

Bhagirath and Anandmayi looked at Parvateshwar curiously.

'We are to leave for Swadweep once all have recovered from their injuries. The Lord has asked us to wait for him at Kashi till he decides his next move. He believes King Athithigva has not sold out to Ayodhya in the conspiracy to assassinate us on the Godavari.'

'But if we go to Kashi, my father will get to know that we are alive,' said Bhagirath. 'He will know his attack has failed.'

'We have to keep quiet about it. We have to pretend that nothing happened, that we were not attacked at all. That we made an uneventful journey to Panchavati and back.'

'Won't they wonder about their ships?'

'The Lord says that's all right. Many things can happen during long sea and river voyages. They may believe their ships met with an accident before they could attack us.'

Bhagirath raised his eyebrows. 'My father may be stupid enough to believe that story. But he is not the leader.

Whoever put together a conspiracy of this scale will certainly investigate what went wrong.'

'But investigations take time, allowing the Neelkanth to check whatever else it is that he needs to.'

'The Lord is not coming with us?' asked a surprised Anandmayi.

Parvateshwar shook his head. 'No. And the Lord has said we should let it be known that neither his family nor he is with us at Kashi. It should be publicised that he remains in Panchavati. The Lord believes that it will keep us safe as the attack was aimed at him.'

'That can mean only one thing,' said Bhagirath. 'He chooses to take Brahaspati at face value but wants to ascertain a few more things before he makes up his mind.'

Anandmayi looked at her husband with concern in her eyes. She knew that a war was approaching. Perhaps the biggest war that India had ever seen. And in all probability, Meluha and Shiva would be on opposite sides. Which side would her husband choose?

'Whatever happens,' said Anandmayi, holding Parvateshwar's face, 'we must have faith in the Neelkanth.'

Parvateshwar nodded silently.

— ⁂ —

Shiva, Parshuram and Nandi were sitting on the banks of the Godavari. Shiva took a deep drag from the chillum as he looked towards the river, lost in thought. He let out a sigh as he turned to his friends. 'Are you sure, Parshuram?'

'Yes, My Lord,' replied Parshuram. 'I can even take you to the uppermost point of the mighty Brahmaputra, where it is the Tsangpo. But I wouldn't recommend it, for fatalities can be high on that treacherous route.'

Shiva's silence provoked Parshuram to probe further, 'What is it about that river, My Lord?' He had been intrigued by the abnormal interest shown by the Nagas in the Brahmaputra's course as well. 'First the Nagas, now you; why is everyone so interested in it?'

'It may be the carrier of Evil, Parshuram.'

Nandi looked up in surprise. 'Doesn't the Tsangpo begin close to your own home in Tibet, My Lord?'

'Yes, Nandi,' said Shiva. 'It seems Evil has been closer than it initially appeared.'

Nandi remained quiet. He was one of the few who knew the ships that attacked Shiva's convoy were from Meluha. He knew what he had to do. If it came to a choice between Shiva and his country, he would choose Shiva. But it still hurt him immensely. He knew he might have to be a part of an army that would attack his beloved motherland, Meluha. He hated his fate for having put him in such a situation.

— ⁂ —

'I think I know how to find the mastermind, My Lord,' said Bhagirath.

He had sought an appointment with Shiva as soon as he had stepped out of Parvateshwar's chambers. He knew that his father had decided to oppose the Neelkanth. It made sense therefore for Bhagirath to immediately prove his loyalty to Shiva. He didn't expect Shiva to lose. Regardless of the opinion of the kings, the people would be with the Neelkanth.

'How?' asked Shiva.

'You'd agree that my father hardly has the wherewithal to draw up such an elaborate plan. I'd say his selfish needs have made him succumb to the evil designs of another.'

Shiva edged forward, intrigued. 'You think he has been bribed? Your father is in no need of money.'

'What can be a better bribe than life itself, My Lord? Had you seen my father a few years back, you would have thought he was but a small step away from the cremation pyre. A life of debauchery and drink had wreaked havoc within his body. But today, he looks younger than I have ever known.'

'The Somras?'

'I don't think so. I know he had tried the Somras in the past. It hadn't worked. Somebody is supplying him with superior medicines. Something that is otherwise unavailable to even a king.'

Shiva's eyes widened. *Who could be more powerful, more knowledgeable than a king?*

'Do you think a maharishi is helping him?'

Bhagirath shook his head. 'No, My Lord. I think a maharishi is *leading* him.'

'But who can that maharishi be?'

'I don't know. But when I go back to Ayodhya...'

'Ayodhya?'

'If we are to maintain that no ships attacked us on the Godavari, My Lord, then what reason can there be for my not going back to Ayodhya? It will arouse suspicion. More importantly, I can only uncover the true identity of the master when I'm in *Ayodhya*. Despite my father's best efforts, I still have eyes and ears in the *impregnable city*.'

Shiva considered this for a moment. He agreed with the train of thought. Moreover, now that Dilipa had chosen to align himself against Shiva, Bhagirath would be even more eager to prove his loyalty to him.

Shiva nodded. 'All right, go to Ayodhya.'

'But My Lord, when the time comes, I hope Ayodhya and Swadweep will be shown some kindness.'

'Kindness?'

'We have not used the Somras excessively, My Lord. Only a few Chandravanshi nobles use it, and that too, sparingly. It is the Meluhans who have abused its usage. That is what has made Evil rise. Therefore it is only fair that when the *Somras* is banned, this ban be imposed only on Meluha. Swadweep has not benefited from the *drink of the Gods*. I hope we will be allowed to use it.'

'You didn't *choose* to use less Somras, Bhagirath,' said Shiva. 'You just didn't have the opportunity to do so. If you had, the situation would have been very different. You know that just as much as I do.'

'But Meluha...'

'Yes, Meluha has used more. So naturally, they will suffer more. But let me make one thing clear. If I decide the Somras is Evil, then no one will use it. No one.'

Bhagirath kept silent.

'Is that clear?' asked Shiva.

'Of course, My Lord.'

Chapter 5

The Shorter Route

A caravan of five hundred people was moving up the northern path from Panchavati towards the Vasudev city of Ujjain. Shiva and his family were in the centre, surrounded by half a brigade of joint Naga and Branga soldiers in standard defensive formations. Kali did not want to reveal this route to anyone from Shiva's original convoy, so none of them were included. Nandi and Parshuram were the only exceptions. Brahaspati had been included for Shiva might need his advice in understanding what the Vasudevs had to say about the Somras.

Whereas Shiva persisted in his quest and questions with Brahaspati, the old brotherly love that they had shared was missing.

Parvateshwar, Ayurvati, Anandmayi and Bhagirath, along with the original convoy, had stayed back at Panchavati. They were to leave for Kashi in a few weeks, their eastern route going through the Dandak forest, onward through Branga. Vishwadyumna was to accompany them as a guide up to Branga.

'Ganesh, does Ujjain fall on the way from Panchavati to Meluha or do we take a detour?' asked Shiva, goading his horse forward over the path built through the forest. It was fenced by two protective hedges. The inner layer comprised the harmless Nagavalli creepers, while the outer one had poisonous vines to prevent wild animals from entering.

'Actually, *baba*, Ujjain is on the way to Swadweep. It's to the north-east. Meluha lies to the north-west.'

Sati tried to get her bearings of Meluha and Maika at the dried mouth of the Saraswati. The Meluhan city of births was not too far from the mouth of the Narmada. 'Does the Narmada serve as your waterway? One can sail west for Meluha and east for Ujjain and Swadweep.'

'Yes, *maa*,' answered Ganesh.

Shiva turned to his son. 'Have you ever been to Maika? How do abandoned Naga children get adopted?'

'Maika is the one place where there is no bias against the Nagas, *baba*. Perhaps the sight of helpless Naga babies, shrieking in pain as a cancerous growth bursts through their bodies, melts the hearts of the authorities. The Maika governor takes personal interest in attempting to save as many Naga babies as he can in the crucial first month after their birth. A Naga ship sails down the Narmada every month, docks at Maika late at night, and the babies born in that month are handed over to us by the Maika record-keeper. Some non-Naga parents choose to stay back and move to Panchavati for the sake of their children.'

'Don't the Maika authorities stop them?'

'Actually, the tenets of Meluhan law require parents to accompany their Naga children to Panchavati. In doing so, they are following their law. But others refuse to do so. They abandon their children and return to their comfortable life in Meluha. In such cases, only the child is handed over. The Maika governor pretends not to notice this breach of law.'

Sati shook her head. She had lived in Meluha for more than one hundred years, a few of which were in Maika as an infant.

She had never known any of this. It was almost like she was discovering her seemingly upright nation anew. Her father had not been the only one to break the law. It appeared as if many Meluhans valued the comforts of their land more than their duty towards their children or towards observing Lord Ram's laws.

Shiva looked ahead to see a large ship anchored in a massive lagoon. The waters were blocked on the far side by a dense grove. Having seen the grove of floating Sundari trees in Branga, Shiva assumed these trees must also have free-floating roots. The route ahead seemed obvious. 'I guess we have reached your secret lagoon. I assume the Narmada is beyond that grove.'

'There is a massive river beyond that grove, *baba*,' said Ganesh. 'But it is not the Narmada. It is the Tapi. We have to cross to the other side. After that it is a few more days' journey to the Narmada.'

Shiva smiled. 'The Lord Almighty has blessed this land with too many rivers. India can never run short of water!'

'Not if we abuse our rivers the way we are now abusing the Saraswati.'

Shiva nodded, silently agreeing with Ganesh.

— ⁂ —

Bhrigu tore open the letter. It was exactly what he had expected. The Vayuputras had excommunicated him.

Lord Bhrigu,

It has been brought to our attention that daivi astras *were loaded onto a fleet of ships in Karachapa. Investigations have led to the regrettable conclusion that you manufactured them, using materials that were given to you strictly for research. While we understand that you would never misuse the weapons expressly banned by our God, Lord*

Rudra, we cannot allow the unauthorised transport of these weapons to go unpunished. You are therefore prohibited from ever entering Pariha or interacting with a Vayuputra again. We do hope you will honour the greater promise that every friend of a Vayuputra makes to Lord Rudra: that of never using the daivi astras. *It is the expectation of the council that you will surrender the weapons at once to Vayuputra Security.*

What surprised Bhrigu was that the note had been signed by the Mithra, leader of the council. It was rare for the Mithra to sign orders personally. Usually, it was done by one of the Amartya Shpand, the six deputies on the council. The Vayuputras were clearly taking this very seriously.

But Bhrigu believed that he had not broken the law. He had already written to the Vayuputras that they were making the institution of the Neelkanth a mockery by not acting against this self-appointed imposter. But alas, the Vayuputras had done nothing. However, he could see how they would think he had misused their research material. Ironically, he had not. Even if he had got over his qualms about using that material, Bhrigu knew there was simply not enough to make the quantity of *daivi astras* that were needed. He had made his own stockpile of such weapons, using materials he himself had compiled over the years. Perhaps that was the reason why they did not have the destructive potency of the Vayuputra material. They had entire laboratories, whereas Bhrigu worked alone.

Bhrigu sighed. He had used all the weapons that he had manufactured. The only mystery was whether they had achieved their purpose; whether the Neelkanth had been assassinated. Talking to Daksha was an exercise in futility. He seemed to be in a state of shock since the rupture of his relations with his daughter. Bhrigu had sent off another ship, manned by men drawn from Dilipa's army, to the mouth of the Godavari to investigate the matter. But it would be months before he knew what had happened.

'Anything else, My Lord?' asked the attendant.

Bhrigu dismissed her with an absent-minded wave. Perhaps the job was done. Maybe the Neelkanth was no more. But it was also possible that Bhrigu's ships had failed. Even worse, the Neelkanth may have been persuaded by the Nagas and was plotting to turn the people against the Somras. Nothing was certain till he received news of the five ships he had sent earlier to attack Shiva's convoy. For now, much as he disliked living in Devagiri, he had no choice but to wait. He had to stay till he knew the Somras was safe. He believed India's future was at stake.

Bhrigu took a deep breath and went back into a meditative trance.

— ⁂ —

Shiva's convoy had covered ground quickly after crossing the Tapi and was waiting at the edge of another secret lagoon, while the Nagas prepared to set sail. Beyond the floating grove guarding this lagoon, flowed the mighty Narmada, mandated by Lord Manu as the southern border of the *Sapt Sindhu, the land of the seven rivers.*

'How much farther, *dada*?'

'Not too far, Kartik. Just a few more weeks,' answered Ganesh. 'We will sail east up the Narmada for a few days, then march on foot through the passes of the great Vindhya Mountains till we reach the Chambal River. We would then have to sail for only a few days down the Chambal to reach Ujjain.'

Sati watched the sailors pull the gangway plank towards the rudimentary dock, preparing the ship for loading. She wished that her sister Kali had accompanied them on this journey. But she also knew that being a queen, Kali had many responsibilities in Panchavati.

Her thoughts were interrupted by the ship's gangway plank landing on the dock with a loud thud.

Parvateshwar, Anandmayi, Bhagirath and Ayurvati were dining together in the late afternoon. They had just entered the first of five clearings on the *Dandakaranya* road from Panchavati. The road led to the hidden lagoon on the Madhumati in Branga. Accompanied by the convoy of sixteen hundred soldiers that had set out with Shiva more than a year ago, they were marching back to Kashi to await Shiva's return.

Bhagirath looked at the five paths in wonder. Only one of these was correct while the others were decoys that would lead trespassers to their doom. 'These Nagas are obsessive about security.'

Anandmayi looked up. 'Can we blame them? Do not forget that it was this attitude that saved our lives when those ships attacked us on the Godavari.'

'True,' said Bhagirath. 'The Nagas will no doubt prove to be good allies. Their loyalty to the Neelkanth isn't suspect, though the reasons might well be. When the moment of truth is upon us, all will have to answer a simple question: Will they fight the world for the Neelkanth? I know I will.'

Anandmayi's eyes flashed as she looked at Parvateshwar and then back at Bhagirath, chiding him. 'Get back to your food, little brother.'

Parvateshwar looked at Anandmayi with a tortured expression. 'I don't think the *Parmatma* will be so unkind to me. He could not have made me wait for more than a century to find my living God, only to force me to choose between my country and him. I'm sure the Almighty will find a way to ensure that Meluha and the Lord Neelkanth are not on opposite sides.'

Parvateshwar's sad smile told Anandmayi he himself did not believe that. She touched her husband's shoulder gently.

Bhagirath played with his *roti* absent-mindedly. He was beginning to believe they could not count on Parvateshwar. That would be a huge loss for the Neelkanth's army. Parvateshwar's strategic abilities had the capacity to turn the tide in any war.

Ayurvati looked at Parvateshwar with sympathy. She could identify with his inner conflict. In her case though, a decision had emerged that sat comfortably in her heart. Her emperor had committed heinous acts which dishonoured Meluha. This was no longer the country she had loved and admired all her life. She knew in her heart that Lord Ram would not have condoned the immorality that Meluha had descended into, under Daksha's watch. Her path was clear: in a fight between Meluha and Shiva, she would choose the Neelkanth. For he would set things right in Meluha as well.

— ⁂ —

The Naga ship was anchored close to the Chambal shore. Shiva, Sati, Ganesh and Kartik climbed down rope ladders to the large boat that had been tied to the ship's anchor line. Brahaspati, Nandi and Parshuram followed them, accompanied by ten Naga soldiers.

When everyone had disembarked, they began to row ashore. The Vasudevs being even more secretive than the Nagas, Shiva did not expect to find any sign of habitation close to the river.

Almost touching the river bank, a wall of dense foliage blocked the view beyond. Weeds had spread over the gentle Chambal waters, making rowing a back-breaking task. Ganesh navigated the boat towards a slender clearing between two immense palm trees. Shiva could sense something unnatural about the clearing, but couldn't put his finger on it. He turned towards Kartik, who was staring at the clearing as well.

'*Baba*, look at the trees behind the clearing,' said Kartik. 'You'll have to bend down to my level.'

As Shiva bent low the image became clear. The trees behind the clearing were organised unnaturally, given the dense, uncontrolled growth surrounding it. Placed equidistant, they seemed to grow in height as one looked farther away. This was because the ground itself sloped upwards in a gentle gradient. It was obviously not a natural hillock. A majority of the trees behind the clearing were the Gulmohur, their flaming orange flowers suggestive of fire. Shiva blinked at what appeared to be an optical illusion. He suddenly stood up, rocking the boat as Sati and Ganesh reached out to hold him steady. The Gulmohur trees had been placed in a specific pattern that was visible from a certain distance as one placed oneself directly in front of the small clearing between the twin palms. It was in the shape of a flame; a specific symbol that Shiva recognised.

'*Fravashi*,' whispered Shiva.

Surprised, Ganesh asked, 'How do you know that term, *baba*?'

Shiva looked at Ganesh and then back at the Gulmohur trees. The pattern had disappeared. Shiva sat down and turned towards Ganesh. 'How do *you* know that term?'

'It's a Vayuputra term. It represents the feminine spirit of Lord Rudra, which has the power to assist us in doing what is right. We are free to either accept it or reject it. But the spirit never refuses to help. Never.'

Shiva smiled as he began to understand his ancient memories.

'Who told you about *Fravashi*, *baba*?' asked Ganesh again.

'My uncle Manobhu,' said Shiva. 'It was among the many concepts and symbols that he made me learn. He said it would help me when the time came.'

'Who was he?'

'I thought I knew,' said Shiva. 'But I'm beginning to wonder if I knew him well enough.'

The conversation came to a halt as the boat hit the banks. Two Naga soldiers jumped out and pulled the boat farther up, onto dry land. Tugging hard on the line, they tied the craft to a conveniently placed tree stump. The landing party quickly disembarked. Kartik surveyed the palms that marked the clearing. He turned towards Ganesh, who was standing at the centre of the clearing.

'Can everyone stand behind me, please,' requested Ganesh. 'I do not want anybody between me and the palm trees.'

The others moved away as Ganesh closed his eyes to drown out the distractions surrounding him and find his concentration.

Ganesh breathed deeply and clapped hard repeatedly in an irregular beat. The claps were set in the Vasudev code and were being transmitted to the gatekeeper of Ujjain. *This is Ganesh, the Naga lord of the people, requesting permission to enter your great city with our entourage.*

Shiva heard the soft sounds of claps reverberating back. Ujjain's gatekeeper had answered. *Welcome, Lord Ganesh. This is an unexpected honour. Are you on your way to Swadweep?*

No. We have come to meet with Lord Gopal, the great chief Vasudev.

Was there something specific you needed to discuss, Lord Ganesh?

Clearly, the Vasudevs were still not comfortable with the Nagas, despite the fact that they had reached out to Ganesh for the Naga medicines to help with the birth of Kartik. The Ujjain gatekeeper was trying to parry off Ganesh's request while trying not to insult him.

Ganesh continued to clap rhythmically. *It is not I who seeks Lord Gopal, honoured gatekeeper. It is the Lord Neelkanth.*

Silence for a few moments. Then the sound of claps in quick succession. *Is the Lord Neelkanth at the palm clearing with you?*

He is standing with me. He can hear you.

Silence once again, before the gatekeeper responded. *Lord Ganesh, Lord Gopal himself is coming to the clearing. We will be honoured to host your convoy. It will take us a day to get there; please bear with us till then.*

Thank you.

Ganesh rubbed his palms together and looked at Shiva. 'It will take a day for them to get here, *baba*. We can wait in our ship till they arrive.'

'Have you ever been to Ujjain?' asked Shiva.

'No. I have met the Vasudevs just once at this very clearing.'

'All right, let's get back to our ship.'

— ⁂ —

'Are you telling me Lord Bhrigu visited Ayodhya eight times in the last year?' asked a surprised Surapadman.

The crown prince of Magadh maintained his own espionage network, independent of the notoriously inefficient Royal Magadh spy service. His man had just informed him of the goings-on in the Ayodhya royal household.

'Yes, Your Highness,' answered the spy. 'Furthermore, Emperor Dilipa himself has visited Meluha twice in the same period.'

'That, I am aware of,' said Surapadman. 'But the news you bring throws new light on it. Perhaps Dilipa was not going to meet that fool Daksha after all. Maybe he was going to meet Lord Bhrigu. But why would the great sage be interested in Dilipa?'

'That I do not know, Your Highness. But I'm sure you have heard of Emperor Dilipa's newly-acquired youthful appearance. Perhaps Lord Bhrigu has been giving him the Somras?'

Surapadman waved his hand dismissively. 'The Somras is easily available to Swadweepan royalty. Dilipa doesn't need to plead with a maharishi for it. I know Dilipa has been using the Somras for years. But when one has abused the body as much as he has, even the Somras would find it difficult to delay his ageing. I suspect Lord Bhrigu is giving him medicines that are even more potent than the Somras.'

'But why would Lord Bhrigu do that?'

'That's the mystery. Try to find out. Any news of the Neelkanth?'

'No, Your Highness. He remains in Naga territory.'

Surapadman rubbed his chin and looked out of the window of his palace chambers along the Ganga. His gaze seemed to stretch beyond the river into the jungle that extended to the south; the forests where his brother Ugrasen had been killed by the Nagas. He cursed Ugrasen silently. He knew the truth of his brother's murder. Addicted to bull-racing, Ugrasen had indulged in increasingly reckless bets. Desperate to get good child-riders for his bulls, he used to scour tribal forests, kidnapping children at will. On one such expedition he had been killed by a Naga, who was trying to protect a hapless mother and her young boy. What he could not understand though was why a Naga would risk his life to save a forest woman and her child.

But the death had narrowed Surapadman's choices. The Neelkanth would lead his followers against whoever he decided was Evil. A war was inevitable. There would be those who would oppose him. Surapadman did not care much about this war against Evil. All he wanted was to ensure that Magadh would fight on the side opposed to Ayodhya. He intended to use wartime chaos to establish Magadh as the overlord of Swadweep and himself as emperor. But Ugrasen's killing had deepened his father King Mahendra's distrust of the Nagas into unadulterated hatred. Surapadman knew Mahendra would force him to fight against whichever side the Nagas allied with. His only hope lay in the Nagas and the Emperor of Ayodhya choosing the same side.

— ⅄◎ꓴ↟⊛ —

Kanakhala waited patiently in the chambers of Maharishi Bhrigu at Daksha's palace. The maharishi was in deep meditation. Though his chamber was in a palace, it was as simple and severe as his real home in a Himalayan cave. Bhrigu sat on the only piece of furniture in the room, a stone bed. Kanakhala therefore had no choice but to stand. Icy water had been sprinkled on the floor and the walls. The resultant cold and clammy dampness made her shiver slightly. She looked at the bowl of fruit at the far corner of the room on a small stand. The maharishi seemed to have eaten just one fruit over the previous three days. Kanakhala made a mental note to order fresh fruit to be brought in. An idol of Lord Brahma had been installed in an indentation in the wall. Kanakhala stared fixedly at the idol as she repeated the soft chanting of Bhrigu.

Om Brahmaye Namah. Om Brahmaye Namah.

Bhrigu opened his eyes and gazed at Kanakhala contemplatively before speaking. 'Yes, my child?'

'My Lord, a sealed letter has been delivered for you by bird courier. It has been marked as strictly confidential. Therefore, I thought it fit to bring it to you personally.'

Bhrigu nodded politely and took the letter from Kanakhala without saying a word.

'As instructed, we have also kept the pigeon with us. It can return to where it came from. Of course, this would not be possible if the ship has moved. Please let me know if you'd like to send a message back with the pigeon.'

'Hmmm...'

'Will that be all, My Lord?' asked Kanakhala.

'Yes. Thank you.'

As Kanakhala shut the door behind her, Bhrigu broke the seal and opened the letter. Its contents were disappointing.

My Lord, we have found some wreckage of our ships at the mouth of the Godavari. They have obviously been blown up. It is difficult to judge whether they were destroyed as a result of sabotage or an accident owing to the goods they carried. It is also difficult to say if all the ships were destroyed or if there are any survivors. Await further instructions.

The words gave Bhrigu information without adding to his understanding of the situation. Not one of the five ships that he had sent to assassinate the Neelkanth and destroy Panchavati had returned or sent a message. The wreckage of at least some of the ships had been discovered, having drifted down the Godavari. Both the possible conclusions were disturbing: either the ships had been destroyed or some of them had been captured. Bhrigu could not afford to send another ship up the Godavari to try and dig deeper. He might end up gifting another well-built warship to the enemy just before the final war. Of course, there was also the possibility that the ships may have succeeded in their mission and had been destroyed subsequently. But Bhrigu simply could not be sure.

Bhrigu would have to wait. Maybe an angry Neelkanth would emerge from the jungles of Dandak. He could rally his followers and attack those allied against him. If that did not happen then the sage would assume that the Neelkanth threat had passed.

Bhrigu rang the bell, summoning the guard outside. He would send a message to the ship at the mouth of the Godavari with orders to return. He would also have to order Meluha and Ayodhya to prepare their armies for battle. Just in case.

Chapter 6

The City that Conquers Pride

It was a full moon night. Shiva stood at the anchored ship's balustrade as he looked into the dark expanse of forest on the Chambal's banks. Deep in the distance was what seemed to be a massive hill made of pure black stone. Shiva had been observing that hill all evening. It was too smooth to be natural. Even more unusually, it had an inverted bowl-like structure at the top that was distinctly a cupola. It was coloured a deeper hue of black as compared to the rest of the hill, which it was certainly not a part of.

'It's man-made, *baba*,' said Kartik.

Shiva, Ganesh and Brahaspati turned towards Kartik, who was crouching, looking at the bank of the river from a lower height. Shiva went down to the same level as Kartik. He observed the area behind the palm tree clearing; he could clearly see the pattern of the ancient Vayuputra image, *Fravashi*. As his eyes traced the path of the slope, he realised that had the incline continued, it would have ended at the very top of the black hill in the distance, at the cupola.

Brahaspati spoke up. 'The slope with the trees is probably the remnant of a very long ramp that was used to carry that stone cupola to the top of the hill.'

Shiva smiled at the precise engineering skills of the

Vasudevs. He had known his mysterious advisors for years. He looked forward to finally meeting their leader.

— ⋆ —

Daksha gazed at the full moon reflected in the shimmering Saraswati waters. He was standing by the large window of his private palace chamber. He had increasingly isolated himself in the last few months, avoiding meeting people as far as possible. He was especially terrified of meeting Maharishi Bhrigu, convinced as he was, that the maharishi would read his mind and realise that it was Daksha who had foiled the attack on Panchavati in an attempt to save his beloved daughter.

But this period of isolation had done wonders for Daksha and Veerini's relationship. They were conversing, even confiding in each other once again, almost like the first few years of their marriage. Before Daksha had developed ambitions to become the ruler of Meluha.

Veerini walked up to her husband and placed her hand on his shoulder. 'What are you thinking?'

Daksha pulled back from his wife. Veerini frowned. Then she noticed Daksha's hands. He was holding an amulet that showed his chosen-tribe, the self-declared ranking within the caste hierarchy that is adopted by young men and women. It was a subordinate rank, a lowly goat. Many Kshatriyas felt that the goat chosen-tribe was so low that it did not entitle its members to be considered complete Kshatriyas. In Daksha's case it was his father Brahmanayak who had selected his chosen-tribe, clearly reflecting his contempt for his son.

'What's the matter, Daksha?'

'Why does she think I'm a monster? I got rid of her son for her own good. And we didn't abandon Ganesh. He was well taken care of in Panchavati. And how can she imagine that I would even think of getting her husband killed? It wasn't me.'

Veerini stayed silent. Now was not the time to confront her husband with the truth. Had he wanted to, he could have saved Chandandhwaj, Sati's first husband. Daksha may not have got the killing done through commission, but he was complicit by omission. However, weak people never admit that they are responsible for their own state. They always blame either circumstances or others.

'I'm saying once again, Daksha, let's forget everything,' said Veerini. 'You have achieved all you wanted to. You are the Emperor of India. We cannot live in Panchavati anymore. We lost that opportunity long ago. Kali and Ganesh despise us. And I don't blame them for it. Let us take *sanyas,* retreat to the Himalayas and live out the rest of our lives in peace and meditation. We will die with the name of the Lord on our lips.'

'I will not run away!'

'Daksha...'

'Everything is clear to me now. I needed the Neelkanth to conquer Swadweep. He has now served his purpose. Sati will be back once he's gone and we will be happy again.'

A horrified Veerini stared at her husband. 'Daksha, what in Lord Ram's name are you thinking?'

'I can set everything right by...'

'Trust me, the best thing to do is to leave all this alone. You should never even have tried to become emperor. You can still be happy if...'

'Never tried to become emperor? What nonsense! I am the emperor. Not just of Meluha, but of India. You think some barbarian with a blue throat can defeat me? That a chillum-smoking, uncouth ingrate is going to take my family away from me?'

Veerini held her head in despair.

'I made him,' said Daksha. 'And I will finish him.'

— ᐁᗝᑌᐃ⊛ —

'My Lord,' exclaimed Parshuram. 'Look.'

Shiva turned to look towards the dense forests beyond the palm tree clearing.

In the distance, they saw a sudden flight of birds flying off into the sky, obviously disturbed by massive movement. The approaching mass was effortlessly pushing trees aside as it forged through the forest.

'They're here,' said Nandi.

Shiva turned around and spoke loudly. 'Ganesh, lower the boats.'

— ᐁᗝᑌᐃ⊛ —

Having left a majority of the soldiers onboard, Shiva and his entourage of two hundred were already at the clearing when enormous elephants burst through the jungle. They wore intricately carved, ceremonial forehead gear made of gold. The *human handlers of the elephants,* or *mahouts,* sat just behind the beasts' heads and were secured into their position with ropes. They were covered from head to toe in cane armour, which protected them from the whiplash of the branches that the elephants effortlessly pushed aside. With the aid of gentle prodding with their feet as well as the *hand-held hooks* called *ankush*, the *mahouts* expertly guided the elephants into the clearing. Firmly secured on the backs of the elephants were large, strong wooden *howdahs* fashioned to extend horizontally from the sides of the animals. Completely covered from all sides, they afforded protection to the people inside. Angled slats allowed access to air and a side door to the *howdahs* facilitated entry.

Shiva's eyes were fixed on the first elephant in the line. As it halted, the side door flung open and a rope ladder was flung down. A tall and lanky Pandit clad in a saffron *dhoti* and *angvastram*, climbed down. As soon as the Pandit's feet touched the ground he turned towards Shiva, his hands folded in a respectful Namaste. He had a flowing white beard and a long silvery mane. His wizened face, calm eyes and gentle smile showed a deep understanding of true wisdom. The wisdom of *sat-chit-anand*, of *truth-consciousness-bliss*; the unrelenting bliss of having one's consciousness and mind drowned in truth.

'Namaste, Pandit*ji*,' said Shiva. 'It's an honour to finally meet the Chief Vasudev.'

'Namaste, great Mahadev,' said Gopal politely. 'Believe me, the honour is all mine. I have lived for this moment.'

Shiva stepped forward and embraced Gopal. The surprised Chief Vasudev responded tentatively at first, and then returned the embrace as the open-heartedness of the Neelkanth made him smile.

Shiva stepped back and looked at the large number of men and elephants waiting patiently. 'It's a little crowded, isn't it?'

Gopal smiled. 'This is a small clearing, great Mahadev. We don't really meet too many people.'

'Well, let's climb aboard your elephants and leave for Ujjain.'

'Certainly,' said Gopal as he gestured towards his men.

— —

The *howdahs* were surprisingly spacious and could seat up to eight people in relative comfort. The carriage with Gopal and Shiva also carried Sati, Ganesh, Kartik, Brahaspati, Nandi and Parshuram.

'I hope your journey was comfortable,' said Gopal.

'Yes, it certainly was,' said Shiva, before pointing towards Ganesh. 'My son guided us well.'

'The Lord of the People has the reputation of a wise man,' agreed Gopal. 'And stories of the warrior spirit of your other son Kartik have already reached our ears.'

Kartik acknowledged the compliment with a slight nod and folded his hands into a respectful Namaste.

'Pandit*ji*, is it because of the distance that it takes us a day to reach Ujjain, or is it the density of the forest?' asked Shiva.

'A bit of both, great Neelkanth. We have not built any roads from the clearing on the Chambal into the city of Ujjain. We do not really meet a lot of people. But when we do need to travel, we have well-trained elephants that make it possible for us.'

— ⅄ⓄⅤ♆⊛ —

The people sitting in the *howdahs* had got used to the sounds of foliage crashing and scraping against the outside of the closed carriage. It had been a long and steady ride, due to which their attention was immediately drawn when the sounds stopped.

Gopal spoke up before any of them could make enquiries. 'We're here.'

As he said this, Gopal pressed a lever to his left. Hydraulic action made three sides of the *howdah*, the left, right and rear, slowly collapse outwards. Support pillars on the sides remained strong and held the *howdah* roof up. Horizontal metal railings ensured no passenger fell out. But none were paying attention to the engineering behind the *howdah*. They were all transfixed by *Ujjain*, the *city that conquers pride*.

The entirely circular city had been laid out within a giant, perfect-square clearing in the dense forest. A sturdy ring of stones, almost ten feet in depth and thirty feet in height, ran around the city; a strong and effective fort wall. The Shipra River, a tributary of the Chambal, which flowed along Ujjain, had been channelled into a moat around the walls. The moat followed the dimensions of the forest clearing. Therefore, the circular city was enclosed within a square moat. The moat was infested with crocodiles. The elephants ambled slowly towards the moat, where much to everyone's surprise, there did not appear to be any bridge.

Shiva had seen many forts across India with retractable drawbridges across their moats. These moats provided effective defence against the siege engines that an enemy used to attack a city's fort walls. He expected the elephants to stop and wait till the drawbridge was lowered. But neither did the elephants stop nor was there any sign of a drawbridge being lowered. Instead, there were twenty armed men who stood on the raised embankments which ran around the moat. As the elephants neared, two men stepped back and pushed hard on what appeared like cobbled ground. A button, the size of a stone block, depressed into the embankment with a soft hiss. This in turn triggered a part of the ground, just before the embankment, to slide sideways, revealing broad, gentle steps descending deep into the earth. The steps led to a well-lit tunnel which the elephants entered. The Vasudev guards went down on their knees in obeisance to the Neelkanth.

Kartik looked at Ganesh, smiling. 'What a brilliant idea, *dada*!'

'Yes. Instead of building a bridge over the moat they have built a tunnel underneath it. And the door to the tunnel merges completely into the cobbled ground, thus being effectively camouflaged.'

'The entire ground around the moat is cobbled. This will

prevent animal tracks from appearing around the tunnel entries.'

'Unless an enemy knows exactly where the entrance is, he can never find a way to cross the moat and enter the city.'

Nandi looked at Gopal. 'Your tribe is brilliant, Pandit*ji*.'

Gopal smiled politely.

As the elephants moved towards the city gates, the passengers noticed large geometric patterns along the walls. They were a series of concentric circles boxed within a single perfect square that skirted the outermost circle. It seemed to symbolise the aerial layout of Ujjain. The circular fort wall of the city was not an accident but the culmination of what the Vasudevs believed was the perfect geometric design.

'We have built the entire city in the form of a *mandal*,' said Gopal.

'What is the *mandal*, Pandit*ji*?' asked Shiva.

'It's a symbolic representation of an approach to spirituality.'

'How so?'

'The square boundary of the moat symbolises *Prithvi*, the land we live on. It is represented by a square that is bound on four sides, just like our land which is also bound by the four directions. The space within the square represents *Prakriti* or *nature*, as the land that we live on is uncultured and a wild jungle. Within it, the path of consciousness is the path of the *Parmatma,* which is represented by the circle.'

'Why a circle?'

'The *Parmatma* is the supreme soul. It is infinite. And if you want to represent infinity through a geometric pattern, you cannot do better than with a circle. It has no beginning. It has no end. You cannot add another side to it. You cannot remove a side from it. It is perfect. It is infinity.'

Shiva smiled.

A bird's eye view of Ujjain would show that within the

circular fort wall, there were five tree-lined ring roads that had been laid out in concentric circles. The outermost road skirted the fort walls. The remaining four were arranged in concentric circles of decreasing diameter. The smallest ring road circled the massive Vishnu temple at the centre of the city. Twenty paved radial roads extended in straight lines from the outermost ring road to the innermost.

These roads effectively divided Ujjain into five zones. The outermost zone, between the fourth and the fifth ring road, had massive wooden stables for various domesticated animals such as cows and horses. The pride of place was occupied by the thousands of well-trained elephants. The next zone, between the third and the fourth ring road, was for the residences of the novices and trainees. It also housed their schools, markets and entertainment districts. The zone between the second and the third ring road housed the Kshatriyas, Vaishyas and Shudras amongst the Vasudevs. The one between the first and the second ring road housed the Brahmins, the community which administered the tribe of Vasudevs. And within the first ring road, in the heart of the city, was the holiest place in Ujjain, their central temple.

The temple was made of black bricks and was what had appeared as a 'hill' to Shiva from the Chambal. Entirely man-made, this temple was in the shape of a perfect, inverted cone, with its base in a circle, supported by a thousand pillars running along its circumference. The conical temple was completely hollow inside and rose in ever smaller circles to reach its peak at a height of a gigantic two hundred metres. A central pillar, made of hard granite, had been erected within the temple, to support the massive weight of the ceiling. A giant cupola, made of black limestone, had been placed at the apex of the temple. Weighing almost forty tonnes, the cupola had been rolled onto the top of the temple by using elephants to pull the stone over a twenty-kilometre long gradual incline. It was the remnants of this incline that Shiva had seen at the Chambal.

Of course, Shiva and his entourage were yet to see this grandeur. As the elephants emerged from the tunnel onto the outer ring road along the inner fort wall, all eyes fell upon the vision that was impossible to miss from any part of Ujjain: the Vishnu temple at the centre. The entire entourage stared in wonder at the awe-inspiring sight. Only Brahaspati voiced what everyone felt within.

'Wow!'

Chapter 7

An Eternal Partnership

Shiva's entourage had been housed in Ujjain's Brahmin zone, abutting the central Vishnu temple. After a comfortable night's rest, Shiva had just finished breakfast with his family when a Vasudev pandit came over and then escorted him to the Vishnu temple. Shiva had a meeting with Gopal in the morning.

The simple grandeur of the massive Vishnu temple became even more apparent as Shiva approached it. It was built on a circular platform, of polished granite stones that were fixed together using metal. Contiguous holes and channels were drilled into stones and then molten metal poured into them; as the metal solidified, it bound the stones together in an unbreakable grip. Although expensive, this technique ensured strength as compared to the stones being bound together by mortar. There were no carvings on the platform at all, in keeping with its simplicity. In fact, statues and carvings would have been an unnecessary distraction given the marvel of engineering that the structure itself was. Steps had been chiselled all along the sides of the circular platform so that visitors could approach the great seventh Vishnu, Lord Ram, from all directions.

A thousand cylindrical pillars made of granite stood atop the platform, their bases buried deep. Lathe machines powered by elephants had achieved perfect evenness and uniform solidity in the pillars, which allowed them to efficiently bear the weight of the conical spire on top. The massive black-stone spire looked as smooth from up close as from a distance. Each stone block was of the same dimension, fitted in perfectly and polished smooth. A giant cupola made of black limestone had been placed on top of the spire. The Vasudev pandit remained silent as he watched Shiva climb the steps of the temple in wonder.

As he entered the main temple, he noticed that the spire was completely hollow from the inside, giving a magnificent view of the giant conical ceiling that enveloped a cavernous hall. This temple, unlike the others that Shiva had seen in India, did not have a separate sanctum sanctorum. The inside of the temple was an open, communal place of worship. The ceiling was ablaze with paintings in bright colours depicting the life of Lord Ram: his birth, his education, his exile and eventual triumphant return. Large frescoes on a prominent wall were devoted to the Lord's life after ascending the throne of Ayodhya; his real enemies, the wars he waged against them, his intense relationship with his inspirational wife, Lady Sita, and his founding of Meluha.

A giant pillar made of white granite stood in the centre of the hall. It was almost two hundred metres high, extending all the way to the top of the conical spire. Shiva was aware that granite was amongst the hardest stones known to man and extremely difficult to carve; hence he was surprised to see the detailed carvings on the pillar. They were giant images of Lord Ram and Lady Sita. Dressed simply, with no royal ornaments or crowns, they wore plain hand-spun cotton, the clothes of the poorest of the poor. These were the garments worn by the divine couple during their fourteen-year exile, most of it in dense jungles. Even more intriguing was the absence of Lord Lakshman and Lord Hanuman, who were normally included in all depictions of the seventh Vishnu. Lady Sita held his right hand from below, as if in support.

'Why has the worst phase of their life been chosen for depiction?' asked Shiva. 'This was when they had been banished from Ayodhya, when Lady Sita was later kidnapped by the demonic King Ravan and Lord Ram fought a fierce battle to rescue her.'

The Vasudev pandit smiled. 'Lord Ram had said that even if his entire life was forgotten, this phase, the one that he had spent in exile along with his wife, his brother and his follower Hanuman, should be remembered by all. For he believed that this was the period that had made him who he was.'

Gopal stood close to the base of the central pillar. Next to him were two ceremonial chairs, one at the feet of the statue of Lady Sita and the other at the feet of Lord Ram. A small ritual fire burned between the two chairs. The presence of the purifying Lord Agni, the God of Fire, signified that no lies could pass between those who sat on either side. Many Vasudev pandits stood patiently behind Gopal.

Gopal bowed to Shiva and joined his hands in a respectful Namaste. 'A Vasudev exists to serve but two purposes. The next Vishnu must arise from amongst us and we must serve the Mahadev, whenever he should choose to come.'

Shiva bowed low to Gopal in reciprocation.

'Every single one of us present here is honoured,' continued Gopal, 'that one of our missions will be fulfilled within our lifetime. We are yours to command, Lord Neelkanth.'

'You are not my follower, Lord Gopal,' said Shiva. 'You are my friend. I have come here to seek your advice, for I'm unable to come to a decision.'

Gopal smiled and gestured towards the chairs.

Shiva and Gopal took their seats as the other Vasudev pandits sat around them on the floor, in neat rows.

— ⅄⦶Ʊ⍋⊛ —

Ganesh, Kartik and Brahaspati had set off on a short tour of Ujjain, accompanied by a Vasudev Kshatriya. Ganesh was deeply interested in the animal enclosures in the outermost zone. Specifically, the elephant stables.

Pulling his horse close to Ganesh's mount, the Vasudev Kshatriya asked, 'Why are you so interested in the elephants, My Lord?'

'They are important for the impending war. They will play a big role if they are as well trained as I hope.'

The Vasudev smiled and prodded his horse forward, leading the way to the enclosures. He was happy to see the son of the Neelkanth interested in their war elephants. The Kshatriyas amongst the Vasudevs had revived the art of training them, much against the advice of the ruling Vasudev pandits. These magnificent beasts had once formed the dominant corps in Indian armies. However, counter tactics had been developed in recent times that offset their fearsome power; foremost among them was the use of specific drums, which disturbed the elephants and made them run amok, resulting in casualties within their own ranks. Most armies had stopped using them. But it was undeniable that well-trained elephants could be devastating on a battlefield. Ganesh had heard about the skilfully trained elephants in the Vasudev army. But their famous reticence made it difficult to believe whether this was true or in fact just rumours. Kartik leaned close to his brother. 'But *dada*, we've seen their elephants already when we rode them here from the Chambal. They are exceptionally well-trained and disciplined.'

'Yes they are, Kartik,' answered Ganesh. 'But those were female elephants that are not used in war. They are used for domestic work, like ferrying people or material. It is the male elephants that are required in times of war.'

'Is that because they're more aggressive?'

'Notwithstanding their otherwise calm temperament, elephants can be provoked, even trained, to be more aggressive. It is difficult to train a female elephant to be more aggressive though, for she will kill only with good reason, for example when her offspring is threatened. A male elephant, however, can be trained to be belligerent far more easily.'

'Why is that so?' asked Kartik. 'Are they less intelligent in comparison?'

'Well, I have heard that on average, the female of the species is smarter. But it's a little more complicated. Elephant herds are matriarchal and it's usually the oldest female who makes all the decisions in the wild: when they will move, where they will feed, who remains in the herd and who gets kicked out.'

'Kicked out?'

'Yes, male elephants are made to leave the herd when they reach adolescence. They either learn to fend for themselves or join nomadic male elephant herds.'

'That's unfair.'

'Nature is not concerned with fairness, Kartik. It's only interested in efficiency. The male elephant is not of much use to the herd. The females are quite capable of defending themselves and taking care of each other's calves. The male is only required when a female wants to have a child.'

'So how do they...'

'During the mating season, the female herd accepts a few nomadic male elephants for some time so that the females can get impregnated. Then the males are abandoned once again.'

Kartik shook his head. 'That's so cold.'

'Well, that is the way it is. The female wild elephants have well-defined social behaviour and group dynamics, enforced by the matriarch. The male elephant, on the other hand, is a nomad with no ties to anyone of his kind. Since he is usually a loner, he would have to be much more aggressive to survive. Therefore he is more difficult to break and one needs to catch him young. But once he is broken in, he is much easier to handle and remains loyal to the *mahout*, his rider. More importantly, unlike a female elephant, he will kill without sufficient reason, just because his *mahout* orders him to do so.'

'My Lords,' said the Vasudev Kshatriya, interrupting the conversation as he pointed forward, 'the elephant stables.'

— ⁂ —

'I guess you already know what I suspect is Evil,' said Shiva, looking at Gopal sitting across the small ritual fire.

'I wouldn't be much of a mind-reader if I didn't,' smiled Gopal. 'But I suppose you are more interested in knowing if I agree.'

'Yes. And if you do, what are your reasons?'

'Well, first things first. Of course we agree with you. Every single Vasudev agrees with you.'

'Why?'

'We are faithful followers of the institution of the Mahadev. We *have* to agree with you, once you have the right answer.'

Shiva caught on to something. 'Once I have the right answer?'

'Yes. Despite so many challenges, you have arrived at the right answer to the question posed to every Mahadev: What is Evil?'

'Does that mean you were already aware of the right answer?'

'Of course. What I did not know were the answers to the questions posed to me. The questions for the institution of the Vishnu are very different. The Mahadev's key question is: What is Evil? For the Vishnu, there are two key questions: What is the next great Good? And *when* does Good become Evil?'

'*When?*'

'Yes. While a Mahadev is an outsider, a Vishnu has to be an insider. His job is to use a great Good to create a new way of life and then lead men to that path. The great Good could be anything: a new technology like the *daivi astras* or a creation like the Somras; it could even be a philosophy. Most leaders just follow what has been ordained by a previous Vishnu. But once in a while a Vishnu emerges who uses a great Good to create a new way of life. Lord Ram used more than one, such as the idea that we can choose our own community rather than being stuck with the community that we are born into. He also allowed for the widespread use of the Somras so that not just the elite but everyone could benefit from its powers. But remember, great Good will, more often than not, lead to great Evil.'

'I understood that from the teachings of Lord Manu. I'd like to hear your reasons for why this is so.'

'We have a philosophical book in our community that answers this question beautifully. It contains the teachings of great philosophers who we have revered over the centuries, like Lord Hari and Lord Mohan. It also contains the teachings of the chiefs of the Vasudev tribe, beginning with our founder, Lord Vasudev. The book is called the "Song of our Lord".'

'*Song of our Lord?*'

'Yes. It is called the *Bhagavad Gita* in old Sanskrit. The Gita has a beautiful line that encapsulates what I want to convey:

Ati sarvatra varjayet. Excess should be avoided; excess of anything is bad. Some of us are attracted to Good. But the universe tries to maintain balance. So what is good for some may end up being bad for others. Agriculture is good for us humans as it gives us an assured supply of food, but it is bad for the animals that lose their forest and grazing land. Oxygen is good for us as it keeps us alive, but for anaerobic creatures that lived billions of years ago, it was toxic and it destroyed them. Therefore, if the universe is trying to maintain balance, we must aid this by ensuring that Good is not enjoyed excessively. Or else the universe will re-balance itself by creating Evil to counteract Good. That is the purpose of Evil: it balances the Good.'

'Why can't there be a Good that does not create Evil? Why can't we establish a way of life that does not imbalance the universe?'

'That is impossible. Our being alive itself creates imbalances. In order to live, we breathe. When we breathe, we take in oxygen and exhale carbon dioxide. Aren't we creating an imbalance by doing so? Isn't carbon dioxide evil for some? The only way we can stop creating evil is if we stop doing good as well; if we stop living completely. But if we have been born, then it is our duty to live. Let us look at it from the perspective of the universe. The only time the universe was in perfect balance was at the moment of its creation. And the moment before that was when it had just been destroyed; for that was when it was in perfect imbalance. Creation and destruction are the two ends of the same moment. And everything between creation and the next destruction is the journey of life. The universe's dharma is to be created, live out its life till its inevitable destruction and then be created once again. We are a downscaled version of the universe.'

'These are just theories, Pandit*ji*.'

'Yes they are. But they explain a lot of things that otherwise seem abstruse.'

'Even if I were to agree with you, how would it work at our level? We are minuscule compared to the universe.'

'Yes, that is true, but the universe lives within us in a minute model of itself. Good and Evil are a way of life for every living entity, including us. Our creation and destruction is through Good and Evil; through balance and imbalance. This is true for animals, plants, planets, stars, everything. What makes us humans special is that we can choose how to control Good and Evil. Most creatures are not given that opportunity. There were giant creatures that lived on Earth many millions of years ago. Climate change made them extinct. We have good reason to believe that they were not responsible for this but were victims of the "Evil" which suddenly reared its head. Humans, however, have been blessed with intelligence, the greatest gift of the Almighty. This allows us to make choices. We have the power to consciously choose Good and improve our lives. We also have the ability to stop Evil before it destroys us completely. Our relationship with nature is different from that of other living creatures. Others have nature's will forced upon them. We have the privilege, at times, of forcing our will upon nature. We can do this by creating and using Good, like we created agriculture. What is forgotten, however, is that many times the Good we create leads to the Evil that will destroy us.'

'Is that where the Mahadev comes in?'

'Yes. Good emerges from creative thinkers and scientists like Lord Brahma. But it needs a Vishnu to harness that Good and lead humanity on the path of progress. Paradoxically, imbalance in society is embedded in this very progress. At other times, a Vishnu arises and intervenes to move society away from the Evil which Good may be leading it to; he creates an alternative Good. By diluting the potency and hence the toxic effects of the Somras waste, Brahaspati was attempting just such an intervention. Had he succeeded, we Vasudevs would inevitably have helped him fulfil that mission. A new way of life based on a benign Somras would have been established. Alas, Brahaspati did not succeed and that path is closed. There exists only the path of the Mahadev now; to confront and then lead people away from the Good that has now become Evil.'

'So a Vishnu can make people move away from a Good that has turned Evil, by offering an alternate Good. But a Mahadev has to ask people to give up a Good without offering anything in return.'

'Yes. And that is not an easy thing to do. The Somras is still Good for a lot of people. It increases their lifespan dramatically and enables them to lead youthful, disease-free and productive lives. But it is evil for society as a whole. We are asking people to sacrifice their selfish interests for the sake of a greater good, while giving them nothing in return. This requires an outsider, a leader, who people will follow blindly. This requires a God who excites fervent devotion. This requires the Mahadev.'

'So you always knew the Somras was Evil?'

'We always knew it would eventually become Evil. What we didn't know is *when*. Remember, Good needs to run its course. If we remove a Good too early from society, we are obstructing the march of civilisation. However, if we remove it too late, we risk the complete destruction of society. So in the battle against Evil, the institution of the Vishnu has to wait for the institution of the Mahadev to decide if the time has come. In our case, a Mahadev emerged and his quest led him to the conclusion that the Somras is Evil. Therefore, we knew that it was time for Evil to be removed. The Somras had to be taken out of the equation.'

— ⁂ —

Ganesh, Kartik and Brahaspati stood at the entrance to the elephant stables. There were ten circular enclosures, built of massive stone-blocks. Each enclosure could house between eight hundred to one thousand animals. Five of the enclosures were for the female elephants and their calves. The remaining five were reserved for the male elephants that were regularly trained for war.

The female elephant enclosures had massive pools of water at their centre, allowing the beasts to submerge, have a mud bath, and spray themselves with water. The area around the pools was also a social meeting point for the animals. Piles of nutritious leaves around the central pool catered to the voluminous appetites of the animals. The female elephants were also taken to the jungle in small herds to feast on fresh vegetation. These outings also allowed the beasts to rub their skin against trees, which would scale off their dead skin. The resting areas in the female enclosure did not have partitions and they were allowed to mix freely. They usually grouped into herds, led by their specific matriarchs.

The enclosures for the male elephants though, were completely different. To begin with, the shelters were partitioned into separate sections for each elephant. The animal's individual *mahout* lived just above the elephant's enclosure, spending practically all his time with the beast under his control. This developed an attachment on the part of the elephant, for his *mahout*. The beasts were not expected to do any work. They did not rub their skin against rocks and trees to scrub the dead skin off; instead, the *mahouts* bathed them daily. They did not walk to a central area for their meals; instead, freshly-cut plants were supplied to them outside their own specific shelter. The male-elephants had only one task – train for war.

The central area of the male elephant enclosures had been

suitably prepared for that purpose. There was a pool of water in the central enclosure, just like in the female enclosure. But the pool was much deeper. Here the elephants were taught to put their inborn swimming skills to better use; they were taught to ram and sink boats. Around the pool were massive training grounds where the elephants were trained for specific tasks like mowing down opposing army lines. They were also toughened to survive the heat of battle. The Vasudevs were aware of the recent wide-spread use of drums with low frequency sounds to trouble elephants and drive them crazy. To combat this, the Vasudevs had developed an innovative ear plug for them. Furthermore, the elephants were also subjected to a daily bout of low frequency war drums, to help them get used to the sounds.

Ganesh, Kartik and Brahaspati were led into one of the male elephant enclosures. The Vasudev led them directly to one of the animals that he was personally proud of. As he reached the enclosure he called out to the *mahout*, instructing him to bring the elephant out of his shelter. The *mahout* immediately did so, sitting proudly on top of the beast, just behind its head. To Ganesh's surprise, the elephant's eyes had been covered by its head gear. The Vasudev Kshatriya clarified that the covers could be removed easily by the *mahout* from his position. It was used when they wanted the elephant to act solely on the *mahout's* instruction and not based on what it saw. A metallic cylindrical ball was tied to its trunk with a bronze chain. The Vasudev then proceeded to set up a round wooden board as a target. It was roughly three times the size of a human head.

'You may want to step back,' said the Vasudev to the assemblage.

As the visitors stepped back, the Vasudev looked towards the *mahout* and nodded. The man gently pressed his feet into the back of the elephant's ears, in a series of instructions.

The elephant stepped languidly up to the wooden target and shook his head, acknowledging the orders. Then all of a sudden, with the speed of lightning, it swung its mighty trunk, hitting the wooden board smack in the centre with the metallic ball, smashing the target to smithereens.

Kartik whistled softly in appreciation.

Ganesh looked towards the Vasudev. 'Can we make the target a little more interesting?'

The Vasudev was so confident of his elephant that he immediately agreed. Another wooden target was brought in, but placed on a board with wheels at the bottom, as Ganesh had instructed. He painted a smaller circle on the wooden board as a target; it was the size of a human head. In addition, Ganesh asked for the metallic ball tied to the elephant's trunk to be painted a bright red; thus they'd know exactly where the ball would hit the target. The *mahout* was tasked with ensuring that the elephant struck the smaller circle with his metallic ball, even as two other soldiers moved the board around with long ropes. The target simulated a man trying to avoid the elephant's blow. If the elephant could be used to kill a specific man rather than for mass butchery, then one could target the leader of an opposing army, rendering it headless.

Everyone stepped back. The *mahout* kept his eyes pinned to the board as he issued instructions through his feet, making the elephant move slowly towards the target. The soldiers with the ropes were alternately pulling and releasing their lines, keeping the target in constant motion. Suddenly, the *mahout* dug in deep with his right foot and the elephant swung his mighty trunk. The metallic ball hit the centre of the wooden board. It was a killer blow.

Ganesh smiled and swore in the name of the legendary *Lord of the Animals*. 'By the great *Pashupatinath* himself, what an elephant!'

Chapter 8

Who is Shiva?

'What if I had arrived at a different answer?' asked Shiva.

'Then we would have known that it is not yet time for Evil to have risen,' answered Gopal. 'That the Somras is still a force for Good.'

'Isn't that rather simplistic? Did you really believe that a random, untested foreigner would arrive at the right answer to the most important question of this age? Is this the way the system works?'

Gopal smiled. 'In truth, no. The system is very different. If I'm not mistaken, one of the Vasudev pandits has told you about the Vayuputras. Just like we are the tribe left behind by the previous Vishnu, the Vayuputras are the tribe left behind by the previous Mahadev, Lord Rudra. The institutions of the Vishnu and the Mahadev work in partnership with each other. The Vasudevs interact closely with the Vayuputras. We defer to them for the question that has been reserved by Lord Manu for them: What is Evil? And they defer to us for the question that has been reserved for us: What is the next great Good? The Vayuputras control the institution of the Neelkanth. They train possible candidates for the role of the Neelkanth and if they believe that Evil has risen, they allow the identification of a Neelkanth.'

'Kali did tell me about this. But how do the Vayuputras engineer a man's throat turning blue at a time of their choosing?'

'I have heard that they administer some medicine to the candidate as he enters adolescence. The effect of this medicine remains dormant in his throat for years till it manifests itself on his drinking the Somras at a specific age. I believe the Somras reacts with the traces of the medicine already present in the man's throat to make his neck appear blue. All of these activities have to be done at specific time periods in the man's life if this is to happen the way it has been conceptualised. For example, if a man drinks the Somras more than fifteen years after adolescence, his throat will not turn blue even if he had taken the Vayuputra medicine as a child.'

Shiva's eyes opened wide. 'This is seriously complicated!'

'It's a means by which the system could be controlled. As you can imagine, it is only the Vayuputras who could control the process such that a man's throat would turn blue at the appointed hour. People's blind faith in the legend would ensure that they would follow the Neelkanth and Evil would be taken out of the equation. I must mention that for some time now we had begun to believe that the Somras was turning evil. But we do not control the institution of the Neelkanth. The Vayuputras do. And they believed that the Somras was still Good. Therefore, they refused to release their Neelkanth nominee. Even though we were convinced that it was time for the Neelkanth to appear, it did not happen.'

'Did you present your case to the Vayuputras?'

'We did. But they did not agree. The only alternative available to us was to try and find a solution by the Vishnu method, of creating another Good. That is what we were deeply engaged with when an event occurred that stunned everyone, including the Vayuputras.'

Shiva pointed at himself. 'I suddenly emerged out of nowhere.'

'Yes. Nobody really understood what had happened. We knew you were not a Vayuputra-authorised candidate. Many Vayuputras in fact believed that you were a fraud who would be exposed soon enough. Some even wanted you assassinated in the interests of the institution of the Neelkanth. But the leader of the Vayuputras, the Mithra, prevailed upon them and decreed that you be allowed to live out your karma.'

'Why would the Mithra do that?'

'I don't know. That is a mystery. There was a lot of debate amongst us as well. Some of us believed that your emergence proved us right and we should use you to take the Somras out of the equation. There were others who thought that you were an unknown entity who could use the Neelkanth legend to create chaos; therefore we should have nothing to do with you. But there were also those amongst us who believed it is not our job to determine the fate of Evil. That is the sole preserve of the Neelkanth. Still others debated against us that you were after all, with due apologies, a mere barbarian, and chances were you'd arrive at an incorrect conclusion as to what constituted Evil. But the view that finally prevailed was that if the *Parmatma* has chosen to make you the Neelkanth, he will also lead you to the right answer. And we should, with all humility, accept that.'

'And I arrived at the Somras.'

'Doesn't it make the decision obvious then? You were not marked for this task. Yet somehow, you were given the Vayuputra medicine at the right age. Furthermore, you also arrived in Meluha at the appropriate time and were administered the Somras that made your throat turn blue. You were not trained for the role of a Neelkanth. Nobody gave you the answer to the key question. We consciously refused to say anything that would create a bias in your mind. We were very careful in our communications with you regarding your task. And yet, you arrived at the right answer. Isn't this ample proof that you have been chosen by the *Parmatma,* and that you are, truly, the Mahadev? Doesn't it make my decision easy then; that in following you, we are following the *Parmatma* Himself?'

Shiva leaned back on his chair, rubbing his forehead. His brow felt uncomfortable.

— ⁂ —

On returning from their short tour of Ujjain, Brahaspati, Ganesh and Kartik joined Sati, Nandi and Parshuram at the guesthouse.

'How is the city, Brahaspati*ji*?' asked Sati.

'Beautiful and well-organised,' answered Brahaspati. 'This city is a better rendition of Lord Ram's principles than even Meluha and Panchavati.'

Sati turned to Ganesh and Kartik. 'My sons, did you like the city?'

Ganesh's tactical mind reflected in his opinion. 'Though Ujjain is nice, what fascinated me were the elephant stables. We watched the *mahouts* tend to these beasts of war, each one of the five thousand of them equivalent to a thousand foot soldiers. I dare say our strength has increased manifold, given that the Vasudevs follow the Neelkanth. With these elephants on our side, we are not as precariously placed as we were earlier.'

'Precariously placed?' asked Parshuram. 'Lord Ganesh, forgive me for disagreeing with you. But how can you say that? We have the Neelkanth with us. That means a vast majority of Indians will be with us. I would say that the odds overwhelmingly favour us.'

'Parshuram, I have always admired your bravery and your utter devotion to the Neelkanth. But hope alone does not win battles. Only an honest evaluation of one's weaknesses, followed by their mitigation, can win the day.'

'What weaknesses can we have? We are led by the Neelkanth. The people will follow him.'

'The people will follow the Neelkanth, but their kings won't. And remember, the people do not control the army, kings do. Emperor Daksha is already against us. So is Emperor Dilipa. Together they have the technological wizardry of Meluha and the sheer numbers of Swadweep. That makes a very strong army.'

'But *dada*,' argued Kartik, 'even the most capable army is of little use if it is led by incapable leaders. Do you see any good generals on their side? I see none.'

Ganesh shook his head and looked at Brahaspati and Nandi before turning back to Kartik. 'They have the best. They have Lord Parvateshwar.'

Sati burst in angrily. 'Ganesh, I have warned you to desist from insulting *Pitratulya*.'

'I know he is *like a father* to you, *maa*,' said Ganesh politely. 'But the truth is Lord Parvateshwar will fight for Meluha.'

'No, he will not. Your father trusts him completely. How can you believe he will escape and join those who tried to kill the Neelkanth?'

'*Maa*, Parvateshwar*ji* has too much honour to escape. He will leave openly, once he has revealed his intentions to *baba*. And trust me, *baba* will let him go. He will not even try to stop him. For they are both honourable men who'd rather bring harm upon themselves than forsake their honour.'

'Indeed, he's an honourable man, Ganesh. Will that sense of duty not bind him to the path of the Neelkanth?'

'No. Parvateshwar*ji* is with *baba* because he is inspired

by him, not because he is honour-bound to follow him. He is supremely committed to one value alone, as in fact all Meluhans are: the protection of Meluha. You can ask any of the Meluhans here.'

Nandi's eyes flashed with anger as the normally affable man stared at Shiva's son, his eyes unblinking. 'Lord Ganesh, I have already made my choice. I live for the Neelkanth. And I will die for the Neelkanth. If that means I have to oppose my country, so be it. I will face my karma for having betrayed my country. But I will not have you questioning my loyalty again.'

Ganesh immediately reached out to Nandi. 'I was not questioning your loyalty, brave Nandi. I was wondering how you think General Parvateshwar will react.'

'I don't know what the General thinks. I only know what I think,' Nandi bristled.

'Well, I know how Parvateshwar thinks,' said Brahaspati. 'I realise this will hurt you Sati, but Ganesh is right. Parvateshwar will not abandon Meluha. In fact, he will battle those who seek to hurt Meluha. And if Shiva, as I hope, decides that the Somras is Evil, then Meluha will be our primary enemy. The battle lines are drawn, my child.'

Wordlessly, Sati looked out of the window at the Vishnu temple and sighed.

Shiva rubbed his throbbing brow as he pondered over the mysteries of his childhood.

Gopal bent forward. 'What is it, great Neelkanth?'

'It is not the hand of fate, Pandit*ji*,' said Shiva. 'Neither is it the grand plan of the *Parmatma* that I emerged as the Neelkanth. I suspect it was my uncle's doing. Though how he did all this is a mystery to me.'

'What do you mean?'

'I remember being administered some medicine in my childhood by my uncle. I used to suffer severe burning between my brows from when I was very young. My uncle's medicine helped me calm the burning sensation. The throbbing persists to this day but it is not as bad as it used to be. I still recall his words as he readied the medicine: "We will always remain faithful to your command, Lord Rudra, this is the blood oath of a Vayuputra". Then he'd pricked his index finger and let the blood drop into the potion. It was this mix that he gave to me, and bade me rub it into the back of my throat.'

Gopal's eyes had been pinned on Shiva, fascinated. He briefly looked at the Vasudev pandit from the Ayodhya temple, who was sitting in the first row.

The Ayodhya Vasudev spoke up. 'Great Neelkanth, what was the name of your uncle?'

'Manobhu,' said Shiva.

The stunned Ayodhya Vasudev turned to Gopal. 'In the great name of Lord Ram!'

'What is it?' asked a surprised Shiva.

'Lord Manobhu was your uncle?' asked Gopal.

'*Lord* Manobhu?'

'He was a Vayuputra Lord, one of the Amartya Shpand, a member of the council of six wise men and women who rule the Vayuputras under the leadership of the Mithra.'

'He was a Vayuputra Lord?!!'

'Yes, he was. Many years ago, when we were still trying to convince the Vayuputras about the Somras having turned evil, he was the only one amongst the Amartya Shpand who had agreed with us. Unfortunately, he got no support from the others in the council. The Mithra had also overruled Lord Manobhu.'

'What happened thereafter?'

'I remember that conversation as if it happened yesterday,' said Gopal. 'Lord Manobhu and I had spoken for hours about the Somras. It was obvious that we would not be able to convince the council. He had promised that he would ensure a Neelkanth arose. When I asked him how he would do it, he had said that Lord Rudra would help him. He made me promise that when the Neelkanth did rise, the Vasudevs and I would support him wholeheartedly. I had assured him that this was our duty in any case.'

'And then what happened?'

'Lord Manobhu disappeared. Nobody knew what happened to him. Some believed that he had gone back to his homeland of Tibet since he had been isolated in the Vayuputra council. Some thought he had been killed. I tended to believe the latter for only death could have stopped a man like him from fulfilling his promise. But he did not fail. He created you. Where is he now? How did he contrive to get you invited to Meluha and receive the Somras?'

'He didn't. He died many years ago, at a peace conference, in a cowardly ambush mounted on him by the Pakratis, our local enemies in Tibet.'

'Then how were you invited into Meluha within that specific period? As I've told you, your throat could turn blue only if you drank the Somras within fifteen years of entering adolescence.'

'I don't know,' answered Shiva. 'Nandi just happened to come to Mansarovar at that time, asking for immigrants.'

Gopal looked up at the central pillar of the temple, towards the idols of Lord Ram and Lady Sita. 'It is obvious then. It was the will of the Almighty that events unfolded the way they did.'

Shiva looked at Gopal, his eyes revealing his scepticism that his life was somehow all part of a divine plan.

Gopal tactfully changed the topic. 'My friend, you said that your brow has throbbed from a very young age. Did it happen after a specific incident? Did your uncle give you something which started the burning sensation?'

Shiva frowned. 'No, I've had it for as long as I can remember. I think from when I was born. Whenever I'd get upset, my brow would start throbbing.'

'Would this happen when your heart rate went up dramatically?'

Shiva thought about it for a second. 'Yes. Whenever I am angry or upset, my heart does beat dramatically. Or when I think of Sati, but that is a happy heartbeat.'

Gopal smiled. 'Which means your third eye has been active from the time of your birth, and that is very rare. It convinces me that you are the one chosen by the *Parmatma*.'

'Third eye?'

'It is the region between one's brows. It is believed that there are seven chakras or vortices within the human body which allow the reception and transmission of energy. The sixth chakra is called the *ajna chakra*, the vortex of the third eye. These chakras are activated by yogis after years of practice. Of course, they can also be activated by medicines. The Vayuputras use medicines to activate the third eye of those amongst their young who are potential candidates. But in all my one hundred and forty years, I have yet to hear of a child born with his third eye active.'

'So what is so special about that? It just causes me trouble. It burns dreadfully.'

Gopal smiled. 'That is just a small side-effect. I believe that your active third eye could be one of the reasons why your uncle thought you may have been the chosen one. For it set your body up to easily accept the Vayuputra medicine.'

'How so?'

'The Parihan system of medicine believes that the pineal gland, which exists deep within our brain, is the third eye. It is a peculiar gland. The cortical brain is divided into two equal hemispheres within which most components exist in pairs. The singular pineal gland, however, is present between the two hemispheres. It is a little like an eye and is impacted by light; darkness activates it and light inhibits it. A hyperactive pineal gland is regenerative. This is probably what made your body such that the Somras did not only lengthen your life but also repaired your injuries. Furthermore, the pineal gland is not covered by the blood barrier system.'

'Blood barrier system?'

'Yes. One's blood flows freely throughout the body. But there is a barrier when it approaches the brain. Perhaps this is so as to prevent germs and infections from affecting the brain, the seat of one's soul. However, the pineal gland, despite being lodged between the two hemispheres, is not covered by the blood barrier system. It is obvious why your third eye throbs when you are upset; this is the result of blood gushing through your hyperactive pineal gland.'

Shiva nodded slowly. 'Does this happen to others?'

'Yes, it does. But only amongst those who practice decades of yoga to train their third eye. Or it is active amongst those who are given medicines to stimulate it. What is unnatural about your case is that you were born with an active third eye. This is unheard of.'

Shiva shifted uneasily in his chair. 'So a congenital event just set me up for this role? My uncle could have got it all wrong. I could still be an erroneous choice and maybe I will not achieve the purpose set out for me.'

'But I am sure your uncle did not give you the medicine merely because of your active third eye. He would have judged your character and found you worthy. He must have trained you for this.'

'I was trained by him, no doubt. He taught me ethics, warfare, psychology, arts. But he did not say anything to me about my purported task. '

'You must concede he did an excellent job, though. For you have done well as the Neelkanth.'

'Just luck,' said Shiva wryly.

'Great Neelkanth, a non-believer will credit luck for one's achievements. But a believer in the *Parmatma*, like me, will know that the Neelkanth has achieved all that he has because the *Parmatma* willed it. And that means that the Neelkanth will complete his journey and eventually succeed in taking Evil out of the equation.'

Shiva smiled. 'Sometimes, faith can lean towards over-simplicity.'

Gopal smiled in return. 'Maybe simplicity is what this world needs right now.'

Shiva laughed softly and looked at the audience of Vasudev pandits, listening to the two of them with rapt attention. 'Well, many of my doubts have been cleared. The Somras is the greatest Good and will therefore, one day, certainly emerge as the greatest Evil. But how do we know that the moment has arrived? How can we be sure?'

One of the Vasudev pandits answered. 'We can never be completely sure, great Neelkanth. But if you allow me to express an opinion, we have had a Good which has had a glorious journey for thousands of years and humanity has grown tremendously with its munificence. However, we also know that it is close to becoming Evil now. It is possible that the Somras is taken out of the equation a trifle early, and the world will lose out on a few hundred years of additional good that it could do. But that pales in comparison to the enormous contribution it has already made for thousands of years. On the other hand, there is the risk that the Somras is getting closer to Evil and is likely to lead to chaos and destruction. It is already causing it in substantial measure; I'm not merely referring to the plague of Branga or the deformities of the Nagas. It is believed that the Somras is also responsible for the drastic fall in the birth rate of the Meluhans.'

'Really?'

'Yes,' answered Gopal. 'Perhaps in refusing to embrace death, they pay the price of not seeing their own genes propagate.'

Shiva acknowledged that he'd understood with a gentle nod. The massive images of Lord Ram and Lady Sita that formed the carved central pillar seemed to smile at him. Accepting their blessings, his eyes were drawn farther, towards a grand painting depicting Lord Ram at the feet of Lord Rudra in the backdrop of holy Rameshwaram. Shiva smiled at the giant circle of life. He joined his hands together in a respectful Namaste, closed his eyes and prayed. *Jai Maa Sita. Jai Shri Ram.*

Shiva was resolute as he opened his eyes and beheld Gopal. 'I have made my decision. We will strive to avoid war and needless bloodshed. But should our efforts prove futile, we shall fight to the last man. We will end the reign of the Somras.'

Chapter 9

The Love-struck Barbarian

'Your uncle was a Vayuputra Lord?' asked an amazed Sati.

Sati and Shiva were in their private chambers. Shiva had just related his entire conversation with the Vasudevs and the decision that he had arrived at.

'Not just an ordinary Lord!' smiled Shiva. 'An Amartya Shpand.'

Sati raised her arms and rested them on Shiva's muscular shoulders, her eyes teasing. 'I always knew there was something special about you; that you couldn't have been just another rough tribal. And now I have proof. You have pedigree!'

Shiva laughed loudly, holding Sati close. 'Rubbish! You thought I was an uncouth barbarian when you first laid your eyes on me!'

Sati edged up on her toes and kissed Shiva warmly on his lips. 'Oh, you are still an uncouth barbarian...'

Shiva raised his eyebrows.

'But you are *my* uncouth barbarian...'

Shiva's face lit up with the crooked smile he reserved for Sati; the smile that made her weak in the knees. He held her tight and lifted her up, close to his lips. Her feet dangling in the air, they kissed languidly; warm and deep.

'You are my life,' whispered Shiva.

'You are the sum of all my lives,' said Sati.

Shiva continued to hold her up in the air, embracing her tight, resting his head on her shoulders. Sati had her arms around her husband, her fingers running circles in his hair.

'So, are you going to let me down sometime?' asked Sati.

Shiva just shook his head in answer. He was in no hurry.

Sati smiled and rested her head on his shoulders, content to let her feet dangle in mid-air, playing with Shiva's hair.

— ⁂ —

'Here you go,' said Sati.

Shiva took the glass of milk from her. He liked his milk raw: no boiling, no jaggery, no cardamom, nothing but plain milk. Shiva drained the glass in large gulps, handed it to Sati and sank back on his chair with his feet up on the table. Sati put the glass down and sat next to him. Shiva looked across the balcony, towards the Vishnu temple. He took a deep breath and turned to Sati. 'You're right. Much as I respect Ganesh's tactical thinking, this time he is wrong. Parvateshwar will not leave me.'

Sati nodded emphatically in agreement. 'Without an inspirational leader like him, the armies of Meluha and Swadweep, though strong, will lack motivation as well as sound battle tactics.'

'That is true. But let us hope that the people themselves will rise up in rebellion and there will be no need for war.'

'How can we ensure that, though? If you send the proclamation banning the Somras to the kings, they will make sure that the general public will not know.'

'That's exactly what the Vasudevs and I discussed. My proclamation should not only reach the royalty but every citizen of India directly. The best way to ensure this is to display the proclamation in all the temples. All Indians visit temples regularly, and when they do, they will read my order.'

'And I'm sure the people will be with you. Let's hope that the kings listen to the will of their people.'

'Yes, I cannot think of another way to avoid war. I expect unflinching support from only the royalty of Kashi, Panchavati and Branga. Every other king will make his choice based on selfish interests alone.'

Sati held Shiva's hand and smiled. 'But we have the King of Kings, the *Parmatma* himself with us. We will not lose.'

'We cannot afford to lose,' said Shiva. 'The fate of the nation is at stake.'

— ⁂ —

'Are you sure you can do this, Kartik?' asked Ganesh.

Kartik looked up at his brother with eyes like still waters. 'Of course, I can. I'm your brother.'

Ganesh smiled and stepped away from the elephant mounting platform. Kartik and another diminutive Vasudev soldier were sitting on a *howdah* atop one of the largest bull elephants in the Ujjain stables. The *howdah* had been altered from its standard structure; the roof had been removed and the side walls cut by half. This reduced the protection to the riders, but dramatically improved their ability to fire weapons. Kartik had come up with an innovative idea that used the elephant as more than just a battering ram for enemy lines; instead, it could be used as a high platform from which to fire weapons in all directions.

This strategy envisioned a deliberate and co-ordinated movement of war elephants as opposed to a wild charge.

The issue of the choice of weapons, however, remained. Arrows discharged from elephant-back could never be so numerous as to cause serious damage. The Vasudev military engineers were ready with a solution – an innovative flame-thrower which used a refined version of the liquid black fuel imported from Mesopotamia. This devastating weapon spewed a continuous stream of fire, burning all that stood in its path. The fuel tanks occupied a substantial part of the *howdah,* leaving just enough room for two such weapons and infantrymen. The flame-throwers were not just heavy but released intense heat while operational. Therefore, they required strong operators. But constraints of space in the *howdah* also meant that the operators be, perforce, of short stature. Kartik, along with such a soldier, had volunteered to man this potential inferno.

Ganesh stood at a distance along with Parshuram, Nandi and Brahaspati. He shouted out to his brother. 'Are you ready, Kartik?'

Kartik shouted back, 'I was born ready, *dada*.'

Ganesh smiled as he turned towards the Vasudev commander. 'Let's begin, brave Vasudev.'

The commander nodded and waved a red flag.

Kartik and the Vasudev soldier immediately struck a flame and lit the weapons. Two devilishly long streams of fire burst out and reached almost thirty metres, on both sides of the elephant. A protective covering around the elephant's sides ensured it did not feel the heat. Kartik and the Vasudev had been tasked with reducing some thirty mud statues to ashes. The 'enemy' mud soldiers had been spread out, to test the range and accuracy of the weapon. Though heavy, the fire-weapons were surprisingly manoeuvrable. The *mahout* concentrated on following Kartik's orders and the mud-soldiers were reduced to ashes in no time.

Parshuram turned towards Ganesh. 'These can be devastating in war, Lord Ganesh. What do you think?'

Ganesh smiled as he borrowed a phrase from his father. 'Hell yes!'

— ⅄ⓄU♆⊛ —

'We have transcribed your proclamation, Lord Neelkanth,' said Gopal.

Gopal and Shiva were in the Vishnu temple, near the central pillar. Shiva read the papyrus scroll.

To all of you who consider yourselves the children of Manu and followers of the Sanatan Dharma, this is a message from me, Shiva, your Neelkanth.

I have travelled across our great land, through all the kingdoms we are divided into, met with all the tribes that populate our fair realm. I have done this in search of the ultimate Evil, for that is my task. Father Manu had told us Evil is not a distant demon. It works its destruction close to us, with us, within us. He was right. He told us Evil does not come from down below and devour us. Instead, we help Evil destroy our lives. He was right. He told us Good and Evil are two sides of the same coin. That one day, the greatest Good will transform into the greatest Evil. He was right. Our greed in extracting more and more from Good turns it into Evil. This is the universe's way of restoring balance. It is the Parmatma's *way to control our excesses.*

I have come to the conclusion that the Somras is now the greatest Evil of our age. All the Good that could be wrung out of the Somras has been wrung. It is time now to stop its use, before the power of its Evil destroys us all. It has already caused tremendous damage, from the killing of the Saraswati River to birth deformities to the diseases that plague some of our kingdoms. For the sake of our descendants, for the sake of our world, we cannot use the Somras anymore.

Therefore, by my order, the use of the Somras is banned forthwith.

To all those who believe in the legend of the Neelkanth: Follow me. Stop the Somras.

To all those who refuse to stop using the Somras: Know this. You will become my enemy. And I will not stop till the use of the Somras is stopped. This is the word of your Neelkanth.

Shiva looked up and nodded.

'This will be distributed to all the pandits in all the Vasudev temples across the Sapt Sindhu,' said Gopal. 'Our Vasudev Kshatriyas will also travel to other temples across the land. They will carry your proclamation carved on stone tablets and fix them on the walls of temples. All of them will be put up on the same night, one year from now. The kings will have no way to control it since it will be released simultaneously all over. Your word will reach the people.'

This is exactly what Shiva wanted. 'Perfect, Pandit*ji*. This will give us one year to prepare for war. I would like to be in Kashi when this proclamation is released.'

'Yes, my friend. Until then, we need to prepare for war.'

'I also need to use this one year to uncover the identity of my true enemy.'

Gopal frowned. 'What do you mean, great Neelkanth?'

'I don't believe that either Emperor Daksha or Emperor Dilipa is capable of mounting a conspiracy of this scale. They are obviously being led by someone. That person is my real enemy. I need to find him.'

'I thought you know who your real enemy is.'

'Do you know his identity?'

'Yes, I do. And you are right. He is truly dangerous.'

'Is he so capable, Pandit*ji*?'

'A lot of people are capable, Neelkanth. What makes a capable person truly dangerous is his conviction. If we believe that we're fighting on the side of Evil, there is moral weakness in our mind. Somewhere deep within, the heart knows that we're wrong. But what happens if we actually believe in the righteousness of our cause? What if your enemy genuinely believes that he is the one fighting for Good and that you, the Neelkanth, are fighting for Evil?'

Shiva raised his eyebrows. 'Such a person will never stop fighting. Just like I won't.'

'Exactly.'

'Who is this man?'

'He is a maharishi, in fact most people in India revere him as a *Saptrishi Uttradhikari*,' said Gopal, using the Indian term for the *successors of the seven great sages of yore*. 'His scientific knowledge and devotion to the *Parmatma* are second to none in the modern age. His immense spiritual power makes emperors quake in his presence. He leads a selfless, frugal life in Himalayan caves. He comes down to the plains only when he feels that India's interests are threatened. And he has spent the whole of last year in either Meluha or Ayodhya.'

'Does he genuinely believe that the Somras is Good?'

'Yes. And he believes that you are a fraud. He knows that the Vayuputras did not select you. In fact, we believe that the Vayuputras are on his side. For who else could have given him the *daivi astras* that were used in the attack at Panchavati?'

'Is there a possibility that he could have made the *daivi astras* himself? That is what I assumed must have happened.'

'Trust me, that is not possible. Only the Vayuputras have the know-how to make the *daivi astras*. Nobody else does; not even us.'

Shiva stared at Gopal, stunned. 'I didn't expect the Vayuputras to support me; I am not one of them. But I thought that they would at least be neutral.'

'No, my friend. We must assume that the Vayuputras are on the side of your enemy. They may even be in agreement with him about the Somras still being Good.'

Shiva breathed deeply. This man sounded formidable. 'Who is he? '

'Maharishi Bhrigu.'

— 人⨀ᑌ介⊛ —

Bhrigu's eyes scanned the distance, observing the Meluhan soldiers practising their art. Daksha stood next to him with his eyes pinned to the ground. Mayashrenik, the stand-in general of the Meluhan army in the absence of Parvateshwar, was a few metres ahead.

Bhrigu said softly, without turning towards Daksha, 'Your soldiers are exceptional, Your Highness.'

Daksha did not answer as he continued to study the ground.

Bhrigu shook his head. 'Your Highness, I said that your soldiers are well trained.'

Daksha turned his attention towards Bhrigu. 'Of course, My Lord. I'd already mentioned this to you. There is no need to worry. To begin with, a war is unlikely. But even the possibility of war leaves little to fear for I have the combined Ayodhyan and Meluhan armies at my command which...'

'We have much to fear,' said Bhrigu, interrupting Daksha. 'Your soldiers are well trained. But they are not well led.'

'But Mayashrenik...'

'Mayashrenik is not a leader. He is a great second-in-command. He will follow orders unquestioningly and implement them effectively. But he cannot lead.'

'But...'

'We need someone who can think; someone who can strategise; someone who is willing to suffer for the sake of the greater good. We need a leader.'

'But I am their leader.'

Bhrigu looked contemptuously at Daksha. 'You are not a

leader, Your Highness. Parvateshwar is a leader. But you sent him off with that fraud Neelkanth. I don't know if he is alive, or even worse, if he has switched loyalties to that barbarian from Tibet.'

Daksha took offence at Bhrigu's criticism. 'Parvateshwar is not the only great warrior in Meluha, My Lord. We can use Vidyunmali. He's a capable strategist and would make a great general.'

'I don't trust Vidyunmali. And I'd like to suggest that Your Highness is hardly the best judge of people.'

Daksha promptly went back to studying the ground that had held his fascination a few moments back.

Bhrigu took a deep breath. This discussion was pointless. 'Your Highness, I'm going to Ayodhya. Please make the arrangements.'

'Yes, Maharishi*ji*,' said Daksha.

— ⁂ —

Bhagirath and Anandmayi were in the last clearing of the forests of Dandak. It would take a few more months to reach Branga and from there on, Kashi. But the remaining journey was the last thing on Bhagirath's mind.

'What have they been talking about for so long?' asked Bhagirath.

Anandmayi turned in the direction of Bhagirath's gaze. Ayurvati and Parvateshwar were gesticulating wildly. But the tone of their voices, true to Meluhan character, remained soft and polite. They seemed to be in the middle of an intense debate.

Anandmayi shook her head. 'I don't have supernatural abilities. I can't hear what they're saying.'

'But I can take a good guess,' said Bhagirath. 'I hope that Ayurvati succeeds.'

Anandmayi turned towards Bhagirath, frowning.

'Ayurvati has already made her decision. She is with us. She is with the Mahadev. And now, I think, she is trying to convince Parvateshwar.'

Anandmayi knew that her brother was probably right, but love was forcing her to hope. 'Bhagirath, Parvateshwar has not made his decision as yet. He is devoted to the Mahadev. Don't assume...'

'Trust me, if it comes down to a war and he has to choose between Lord Shiva and his precious Meluha, your husband will choose Meluha.'

'Bhagirath, shut up!'

Bhagirath turned towards Anandmayi, irritated. 'I am only speaking the truth.'

'That is a matter of opinion.'

'I am the crown prince of Ayodhya. Many will say my opinion is the truth.'

Anandmayi tapped her brother on his head. 'And I, as the crown prince's elder sister, have the right to shut him up any time I choose!'

— ⁂ —

'Parvateshwar, you have not thought this through,' said Ayurvati.

Parvateshwar smiled sadly. 'I have not been thinking of much else in the last few months. I know the path that I must take.'

'But will you be able to act against the living God you worship?'

'Since there is no other choice, I must.'

'But Lord Ram had said that we must protect our faith. The Mahadevs and the Vishnus are our living Gods. How do we protect our religion if we do not fight alongside our living Gods?'

'You are confusing faith and religion. They are two completely different things.'

'No, they are not.'

'Yes, they are. The Sanatan Dharma is my religion. But it is not my faith. My faith is my country. My faith is Meluha. Only Meluha.'

Ayurvati sighed and looked up at the sky. She shook her head and turned back towards Parvateshwar. 'I know how devoted you are to the Neelkanth. Can you go to war against the Lord; do you have it in your heart to even harm him?'

Parvateshwar breathed deeply, his eyes moist. 'I will fight all who seek to harm Meluha. If Meluha must be conquered, it will be over my dead body.'

'Parvateshwar, do you really think that the Somras is not Evil? That it should not be banned?'

'No. I know it should be banned. I have already stopped using the Somras. I stopped using it the day Brahaspati told us about all the evil that it has been responsible for.'

'Then why are you willing to fight to defend this *halahal*?' asked Ayurvati, using an old Sanskrit term for *the most potent poison in the universe*.

'But I am not defending the Somras,' said Parvateshwar. 'I'm defending Meluha.'

'But the both of them are on the same side,' said Ayurvati.

'That is my misfortune. But defending Meluha is my life's purpose; this is what I was born to do.'

'Parvateshwar, Meluha is not what it used to be. You're well aware of the fact that Emperor Daksha is no Lord Ram. You are fighting for an ideal that does not exist anymore. You are fighting for a country whose greatness lives on only in memory. You are fighting for a faith that has been corrupted beyond repair.'

'That may be so, Ayurvati. But this is my purpose; to fight and die for Meluha.'

Ayurvati shook her head in irritation, but her voice was unfailingly polite. 'Parvateshwar, you are making a mistake. You are pitting yourself against your living God. You are defending the Somras, which even you believe has turned evil. And you are doing all this to serve some "purpose". Does the purpose of defending Meluha justify all the mistakes that you know you are making?'

Parvateshwar spoke softly, '*Shreyaan sva dharmo vigunaha para dharmaat svanushthitat.*'

Ayurvati smiled ruefully as she recalled the old Sanskrit *shloka*, a *couplet* attributed to Lord Hari, after whom the city of Hariyupa had been named. It meant that it was better to commit mistakes on the path that one's soul is meant to walk on, than to live a perfect life on a path that is not meant for one's soul. Discharge one's own *swadharma, personal law*, even if tinged with faults, rather than attempt to live a life meant for another.

Ayurvati shook her head. 'How can you be sure that this is your duty? Should you just be true to the role the world has foisted upon you? Aren't you blindly obeying what society is forcing you to do?'

'Lord Hari also said that those who allow others to dictate their own duties are not living their own life. They are, in fact, living someone else's life.'

'But that is exactly what you are doing. You are allowing others to dictate your duties. You are allowing Meluha to dictate the purpose of your soul.'

'No, I am not.'

'Yes, you are. Your heart is with Lord Shiva. Can you deny that?'

'No, I can't. My heart is with the Neelkanth.'

'Then how do you know that protecting Meluha is your duty?'

'Because I know,' said Parvateshwar firmly. 'I just know that this is my duty. Isn't that what Lord Hari had said? Nobody in the world, not even God, can tell us what our duty is. Only our soul can. All we have to do is surrender to the language of silence and listen to the whisper of our soul. My soul's whisper is very clear. Meluha is my faith; protecting my motherland is my duty.'

Ayurvati ran her hand over her bald pate, touching her *choti*, the knot of hair signifying Brahmin antecedents. She turned to look at Anandmayi and Bhagirath in the distance. She knew that there was nothing more to be said.

'You will be on the losing side, Parvateshwar,' said Ayurvati.

'I know.'

'And you will be killed.'

'I know. But if that is my purpose, then so be it.'

Ayurvati shook her head and touched Parvateshwar's shoulder compassionately.

Parvateshwar smiled wanly. 'It will be a glorious death. I shall die at the hands of the Neelkanth.'

Chapter 10

His Name Alone Strikes Fear

Reclining in an easy chair, his legs outstretched on a low table, Shiva, along with Sati, contemplated the Ujjain temple from their chamber balcony. Ganesh leaned against the doorway, while Kartik had balanced himself on the railing. Shiva had just related to his family his entire conversation with the Vasudevs, including the identity of their real enemy.

The Neelkanth looked up at the evening sky before turning towards Sati. 'Say something.'

'What can I say?' asked Sati. 'Lord Bhrigu... Lord Ram, be merciful...'

'He can't be all that powerful.'

Sati looked up at Shiva. 'He is one of the *Saptrishi Uttradhikaris*. His spiritual and scientific powers are legendary. But it is not the fear of his powers which has shaken me. It is the fact that a man of his strength of character has chosen to oppose us.'

'Why would you say that?'

'He is singularly unselfish and a man of unimpeachable moral integrity.'

'And yet, he sent five ships to eliminate us.'

'Yes. He must truly believe that the Somras is Good, and we are Evil to try to stop its usage. If he is convinced of it, could it be possible that we are wrong?'

Kartik was about to interject when Shiva raised his hand.

'No,' said Shiva. 'I am sure. The Somras is Evil and it has to be stopped There is no turning back.'

'But Lord Bhrigu...' said Sati.

'Sati, why would a man of such immense moral character use the *daivi astras*, which we all know have been banned by Lord Rudra himself?'

Sati looked at Shiva silently.

'Lord Bhrigu's attachment to the Somras has made him do this,' said Shiva. 'He thinks he is doing it for the greater good. But, in truth, he has become attached to the Somras. It is attachment that makes people forget not only their moral duties but even who they really are.'

Kartik finally spoke up. '*Baba* is right. And if this is what the Somras can do to a man of Lord Bhrigu's stature, then it surely must be Evil.'

Shiva nodded before turning back to Sati. 'What we are doing is right. The Somras must be stopped.'

Sati didn't say anything.

'We need to concentrate our minds on the impending war,' said Shiva. 'They admittedly have a leader of the calibre of Lord Bhrigu, along with the armies of Meluha and Ayodhya. The odds are stacked against us. How do we remedy this?'

'Divide their capabilities,' said Kartik.

'Go on.'

Kartik went into his bedchamber and returned with a map. '*Baba*, would you please...'

As Shiva lifted his feet off the table, Kartik laid out the map and looked at Ganesh before speaking. '*Dada* and I agreed that their strength lies in the technological wizardry of Meluha coupled with the sheer numbers of Ayodhya. If we can divide that, it would even out the odds.'

'By ensuring that Meluha and Ayodhya joined hands and

conspired to assassinate us at Panchavati, Lord Bhrigu has played his cards well. When they realise that I'm alive, they will be compelled to treat me as a common foe and hence ally with each other. After all, an enemy's enemy is a friend.'

Kartik smiled. 'I wasn't talking about breaking their alliance, *baba,* but dividing their capabilities.'

Sati, who had been studying the map all this while, was struck by the obvious. 'Magadh!'

'Exactly,' said Kartik as he tapped on the location of Magadh. 'The roads in Swadweep are either pathetic or non-existent. That is why the armies, especially the big ones, use rivers to mobilise. The Ayodhyan army will not come to Meluha's aid by cutting through dense forests. They will sail down the Sarayu in ships, then up the Ganga to the newly built pathway to Devagiri that Meluha has constructed.'

Shiva nodded. 'The Ayodhyan ships would have to pass Magadh, at the confluence of the Sarayu and Ganga rivers. If Magadh blockades that river, the ships will not be able to pass through. We can hold back their massive army with only a small naval force from Magadh.'

'Right,' said Kartik.

A smiling Shiva patted Kartik on his shoulder, 'I'm impressed, my boy.'

Kartik smiled at his father.

Sati looked at Shiva. 'We must first rally Prince Surapadman to our side. Bhagirath had told me it's the Magadhan prince who makes all the decisions and not his father King Mahendra.'

Shiva concurred before turning towards Ganesh.

Ganesh remained silent. He seemed a little unsettled by this new development.

'That is a good idea,' said Gopal.

Shiva, Sati, Ganesh and Kartik were with Gopal at the Vishnu temple.

'It should be relatively easy to bring Magadh to our side,' continued Gopal. 'King Mahendra is old and indecisive but his son, Surapadman, is a fearsome warrior and a brilliant tactician. And most importantly, he is a calculating and ambitious man.'

'His ambition should make him smell the opportunities in the coming war,' said Shiva. 'He can use it to bolster his position and declare independence from Ayodhya.'

'Exactly,' said Sati. 'Whatever may be the reason behind his choosing to back us, an alliance with him will help us win the war.'

Gopal suddenly noticed a pensive Ganesh. 'Lord Ganesh?'

Ganesh reacted with a start.

'Does something about this plan trouble you?' asked Gopal.

Ganesh shook his head. 'Nothing that needs to be mentioned at this point of time, Pandit*ji*.'

Ganesh was worried that he had inadvertently ruined any likelihood of an alliance with Magadh, for he had killed the elder Magadhan prince, Ugrasen. He had done so while trying to save an innocent mother and her son from Ugrasen. He hoped Surapadman was not aware of his identity.

'*Dada* and I have discussed this,' said Kartik. 'And we believe we should not assume Magadh will come to our side. We should also be prepared to conquer Magadh, if need be.'

'Well, hopefully that situation will not arise,' said Shiva, turning towards Ganesh. 'But yes, we should make contingent plans to fight Magadh. It could be one of our opening gambits in the war.'

'Then I shall start making plans for our departure to Magadh,' said Gopal.

'Are you going to come with us, Pandit*ji*?' asked a surprised Shiva. 'That would reveal your allegiance openly.'

'There was a time to remain hidden, my friend,' said Gopal. 'But now we need to come out in the open, for the battle with Evil is upon us. We have to pick our side openly. There are no bystanders in a holy war.'

— ⅄ ◎ ꓵ ⍋ ⊛ —

Parvateshwar and Anandmayi rode their favourite steeds, whispering to each other. He had leaned a bit to his right, holding Anandmayi's hand. He had just told her that if it came to a war, he would have no choice but to fight on the side of Meluha. Anandmayi, in turn, had told Parvateshwar that she would have no choice but to oppose Meluha.

'Aren't you even going to ask me why?' asked Anandmayi.

Parvateshwar shook his head. 'I don't need to. I know how you think.'

Anandmayi looked at her husband, her eyes moist.

'And I guess you know how I think,' said Parvateshwar. 'For you didn't ask me either.'

Anandmayi smiled sadly at Parvateshwar, squeezing his hand.

'What do we do now?' asked Parvateshwar.

Anandmayi took a deep breath. 'Keep riding together.'

Parvateshwar stared at his wife.

'Till our paths allow us...'

— ⅄ ◎ ꓵ ⍋ ⊛ —

Shiva leaned against the balustrade of the ship as it sailed gently down the Chambal. Beyond the banks, he could see dense forests. There was no sign of human habitation for miles in any direction. He looked back at the five ships following them, a small part of the fifty-ship Vasudev fleet. It had taken the Vasudevs a mere two months to mobilise for departure.

'What are you thinking, my friend?' asked Gopal.

Shiva turned to the chief Vasudev. 'I was thinking that the primary source of Evil is human greed. It's our greed to extract more and more from Good that turns it into Evil. Wouldn't it be better if this was controlled at the source itself? Can we really expect humans to not be greedy? How many of us would be willing to control our desire to live for two hundred years? The dominance of the Somras over many thousands of years has admittedly done both Good and Evil, but it will soon perish for all practical purposes. Isn't it fair to say then that it has served no purpose in the larger scheme of things? Perhaps it would have been better had the Somras not been invented. Why embark on a journey when you know that the destination takes you back to exactly where you began?'

'Are there any journeys which do not take you back to where you began?'

Shiva frowned. 'Of course there are.'

Gopal shook his head. 'If you aren't back to where you began, all it means is that the journey isn't over. Maybe it will take one lifetime. Maybe many. But you will end your journey exactly where you began. That is the nature of life. Even the universe will end its journey exactly where it began – in an infinitesimal black hole of absolute death. And on the other side of that death, life will begin once again in a massive big bang. And so it will continue in a never-ending cycle.'

'So what's the point of it all?'

'But that is the biggest folly, great Neelkanth; to think that we are on this path in order to get somewhere.'

'Aren't we?'

'No. The purpose is not the destination but the journey itself. Only those who understand this simple truth can experience true happiness.'

'So are you saying that the destination, even purpose, does not matter? That the Somras had to just experience all this; to create so much Good for millennia and then to descend into creating Evil in equal measure. And then to have a Neelkanth rise who would end its journey. If one believes this, then in the larger scheme of things, the Somras has achieved nothing.'

'Let me try to put it another way. I'm sure you're aware of how it rains in India, right?'

'Of course I am. One of your scientists had explained it to me. I believe the sun heats the waters of the sea, making it rise in the form of gas. Large masses of this water vapour coalesce into clouds, which are then blown over land by monsoon winds. These clouds rise when they hit the mountains, thus precipitating as rain.'

'Perfect. But you have only covered half the journey. What happens after the water has rained upon us?'

Shiva's knowing smile suggested that he was beginning to follow.

Gopal continued. 'The water finds its way into streams and then rivers. And finally, the river flows back into the sea. Some of the water that comes as rain is used by humans, animals, plants – anything that needs to stay alive. But ultimately, even the water used by us escapes into the rivers and then back into the sea. The journey always ends exactly where it began. Now, can we say that the journey of the water serves no purpose? What would happen to us if the sea felt that there is no point to this journey since it ends exactly where it begins?'

'We would all die.'

'Exactly. Now, one may be tempted to think that this

journey of water results in only Good, right? Whereas the Somras has caused both Good and Evil.'

'But of course,' Shiva smiled wryly, 'you would disabuse me of any such notion!'

Gopal's smile was equally dry. 'What about the floods caused by rains? What about the spread of disease that comes with the rains? If we were to ask those who have suffered from floods and disease, they may hold that rain is evil.'

'Excessive rains are evil,' corrected Shiva.

Gopal smiled and conceded. 'True. So the journey of water from the sea back into the sea serves a purpose as it makes the journey of life possible on land. Similarly, the journey of the Somras served a purpose for many, including you. For your purpose is to end the journey of the Somras. What would you do if the Somras hadn't existed?'

'I can think of so many things! Lazing around with Sati for example. Or whiling away my time immersed in dance and music. That would be a good life...'

Gopal laughed softly. 'But seriously, hasn't the Somras given purpose to your life?'

Shiva smiled. 'Yes it has.'

'And your journey has given purpose to my life. For what is the point of being a chief Vasudev if I can't help the next Mahadev?'

Shiva smiled and patted Gopal on his back.

'Rather than the destination it is the journey that lends meaning to our lives, great Neelkanth. Being faithful to our path will lead to consequences, both good as well as evil. For that is the way of the universe.'

'For instance, my journey may have a positive effect on the future of India. But it will certainly be negative for those who are addicted to the Somras. Perhaps that is my purpose.'

'Exactly. Lord Vasudev had held we should be under no

illusion that we are in control of our own breathing. We should realise the simple truth that we are "being breathed"; we are being kept alive because our journey serves a purpose. When our purpose is served, our breathing will stop and the universe will change our form to something else, so that we may serve another purpose.'

Shiva smiled.

Chapter 11

The Branga Alliance

Parvateshwar's entourage had sailed up the Madhumati to the point where it broke off from the mighty Branga River. There they had dropped anchor as they waited for Bhagirath's return. Bhagirath's ship had turned east and sailed down the main distributary of the Branga, the massive Padma. A week later his ship docked at the port of Brangaridai, the capital city of the Branga kingdom.

King Chandraketu had been informed of Bhagirath's arrival. The King of Branga had ensured that the Prince of Ayodhya was escorted with due honour to his palace. As Bhagirath was led into the private palace rather than the formal court, he acknowledged that Chandraketu was not treating him as the crown prince of Swadweep, but as a friend.

Bhagirath found Chandraketu waiting at the palace door along with his wife and daughter. The King of Branga folded his hands in a formal Namaste. 'How are you doing, brave Prince of Ayodhya?'

Bhagirath smiled and bowed his head as he returned the Namaste. 'I'm doing well, Your Highness.'

Chandraketu looked at his consort with a fond smile. 'Prince Bhagirath, this is my wife Queen Sneha.'

Bhagirath bowed towards Sneha. 'Greetings, Your Highness.'

A chivalrous Bhagirath then went down on one knee to face the six-year-old girl who looked at him with twinkling eyes. 'And who might this lovely lady be?'

Chandraketu smiled. 'That is my daughter, Princess Navya.'

'Namaste, young lady,' said Bhagirath.

Navya slid behind her mother, hiding her face.

Bhagirath smiled broadly. 'I am a friend of your father, my child. You don't have to be afraid of me.'

'You smell funny...' whispered Navya, sticking her face out.

A startled Bhagirath burst into laughter.

Chandraketu folded his hands together. 'My apologies, Prince Bhagirath. She can be a little direct sometimes.'

Bhagirath controlled his mirth. 'No. No. She's speaking the truth.' He turned to Navya. 'But young lady, I was always taught to be polite to strangers. Don't you think that's important as well?'

'Politeness does not mean lying,' said Navya. 'Lord Ram had said we should always speak the truth. Always.'

Bhagirath raised his eyebrows in surprise before turning to Chandraketu. 'Wow. Quoting Lord Ram at this age? She's smart.'

'Well, she is very intelligent,' said an obviously proud Chandraketu.

Bhagirath turned fondly towards Navya. 'Of course you're right, my child. I carry the odour of a long and rigorous voyage. I will make sure I bathe before I meet you next. You will not find my smell offensive the next time, I wager.'

Chandraketu laughed. 'Be warned, great Prince, little Navya has never lost a bet.'

Navya smiled at her mother. 'He does not seem all that bad, *maa*. I guess not all Ayodhyan royals are bad...'

Bhagirath laughed once again. 'King Chandraketu, I think we should retire to your chambers before any more assaults are made upon my dignity.'

A smiling Chandraketu nodded to his wife and then turned to Bhagirath. 'Come with me, Prince Bhagirath.'

— ⚹ —

'*Baba*...' whispered Ganesh.

Ganesh had just entered Shiva's chambers in the central ship of the joint Vasudev-Naga convoy.

Shiva looked up as he put the palm-leaf book aside. 'What is it, my son?'

A nervous Ganesh whispered, 'I need to speak with you.'

Shiva pointed to the chair next to him as he lifted his feet off the table.

Ganesh took a deep breath. '*Baba*, there may be some complications with Magadh.'

Shiva smiled. 'I was wondering when you were going to bring that up.'

Ganesh frowned. 'You knew?'

'I know Ugrasen was killed by a Naga. I understand that complicates things.'

Ganesh kept silent.

'Well? Do you know who killed him? If it was a criminal act then we should support Surapadman. Not only would justice be served but it would also help pull Magadh to our side.'

Ganesh didn't say anything.

Shiva frowned. 'Ganesh?'

'It was me,' confessed Ganesh.

Shiva's eyes widened. 'Well... this certainly complicates things...'

Ganesh stayed mute.

'Did you have a good reason?'

'Yes I did, *baba*.'

'What was it?'

'The Chandravanshi nobility has always patronised the tradition of bull racing. In the quest for the lightest riders, the sport has degenerated to the extent that innocent young boys are being kidnapped and forced to ride the charging bulls. This cruel sport has left innumerable children maimed and some have even died painful deaths.'

Shiva looked at Ganesh in horror. 'What kind of barbaric men would do that to children?'

'Men like Ugrasen. I found him trying to kidnap a young boy. The boy's mother was refusing to let him go, so Ugrasen and his men were on the verge of killing her. I had no choice...'

Shiva recalled something that Kali had mentioned. 'Is that the time when you were seriously injured?'

'Yes, *baba*.'

Shiva breathed deeply. Ganesh had once again shown tremendous character, fighting injustice even at risk to his own life. Shiva was proud of his son. 'You did the right thing.'

'I'm sorry if I have complicated the issue.'

Shiva smiled and shook his head.

'What happened, *baba*?'

'The ways of the world are really strange,' said Shiva. 'You protected an innocent child and his mother from an immoral prince. The Magadhans though, did not hesitate to spread a lie that Ugrasen died defending Magadh from a Naga terrorist attack. And people chose to believe that lie.'

Ganesh shrugged his shoulders. 'The Nagas have always been treated this way. The lies never stop.'

Shiva looked up at the ceiling of his cabin.

'What do we do now?' asked Ganesh.

'Nothing different. We'll stick to the plan. Let us hope

that Surapadman is ambitious enough to realise where the interests of Magadh lie.'

Ganesh nodded.

'And you stay in Kashi,' continued Shiva. 'Don't come with us to Magadh.'

'Yes, *baba*.'

— ⅄ⓄǗ⇞⊗ —

Fists clenched, Chandraketu tried hard to suppress the anger welling up within him. Bhagirath had just told him about the Somras waste being responsible for the plague that had been devastating Branga for generations.

'By all the fury of Lord Rudra,' growled Chandraketu, 'my people have been dying for decades, our children have suffered from horrific diseases and our aged have endured agonising pain, all so that privileged Meluhans can live for two hundred years!'

Bhagirath stayed silent, allowing Chandraketu to vent his righteous anger.

'What does the Lord Neelkanth have to say? When do we attack?'

'I will send word to you, Your Highness,' said Bhagirath. 'But it will be soon, perhaps in a few months. You must mobilise your army and be ready.'

'We will not only mobilise our army, but every single Branga who can fight. This is not just a war for us. This is vengeance.'

'My sailors are unloading some gifts from the Nagas and from Parshuram at the Brangaridai docks. As promised by the Neelkanth, all the materials required to make the Naga medicine are being delivered to you. A Naga scientist is also going to stay here and teach you how to make the medicine yourselves. These materials, combined with the herbs you already have in your kingdom, should keep you supplied with the Naga medicine for three years.'

Chandraketu smiled slightly. 'The Lord Neelkanth has honoured his word. He is a worthy successor to Lord Rudra.'

'That he is.'

'But I don't think we will need this much medicine. The combined might of Ayodhya and Branga will ensure the defeat of Meluha well within three years. We will stop the manufacturing of the Somras and destroy their waste facility in the Himalayas. Once the waste stops poisoning the Brahmaputra, there will be no plague and no further need for any medicine.'

Bhagirath narrowed his eyes, hesitating.

'What is it, Prince Bhagirath?'

'Your Highness, Ayodhya is probably not going to be with us in this war.'

'What? Are you saying Ayodhya may side with Meluha?'

'Yes. In fact, they have already thrown in their lot with Meluha.'

'Then why...'

Bhagirath completed the question. 'Why do I act against my own father and kingdom?'

'Yes. Why do you?'

'I am a follower of my Lord, the great Neelkanth. His path is true. And I will walk on it, even if it entails fighting my own kinsmen.'

Chandraketu rose and bowed to Bhagirath. 'It requires a special form of greatness to fight one's own for the ideal of justice. As far as I am concerned, you are fighting for justice for the Brangas. I shall remember this gesture, Prince Bhagirath.'

Bhagirath smiled, happy with the way the conversation had

progressed. He had accomplished the task that Shiva had given him, but in such a manner as to win the personal allegiance of the fabulously wealthy King of Branga. This alliance would prove useful when he made his move for the throne of Ayodhya. Having heard of Chandraketu's sentimental nature, Bhagirath thought it wise to seal the alliance in blood.

He pulled out his knife, slit his palm and held it up to the king. 'May my blood flow in your veins, my brother.'

A moist-eyed Chandraketu immediately pulled out his own knife, slit his palm and held it against Bhagirath's bloodied hand. 'And may my blood flow in yours.'

— ⅄ⓄƱ♆⊛ —

Sitting aft on the deck of the lead ship of the Vasudev-Naga fleet, Brahaspati, Nandi and Parshuram could make out the outlines of Ganesh and Kartik practising their swordsmanship in the vessel behind them. Farther back, Shiva sat with Sati on a higher deck.

Brahaspati's emotions were tinged with bitter regret. 'My mission has gained a leader but I have lost a friend.'

Nandi turned towards Brahaspati. 'Of course not, Brahaspati*ji*, the Lord Neelkanth continues to love you.'

Brahaspati raised his eyebrows and smiled. 'Nandi, lying does not behove you.'

Nandi laughed softly. 'If it makes you feel better, I can tell you that Lord Shiva missed you dearly when he believed that you were dead. You were always on his mind.'

'I wouldn't have expected any less,' said Brahaspati. 'But I don't think he understands why I did what I did.'

'To be honest,' said Nandi, 'neither do I. It was important to fake your death, I concede. But you probably should have revealed the truth to Lord Shiva.'

'I couldn't have,' said Brahaspati. 'Shiva is the son-in-law of Emperor Daksha, my prime enemy. Had Daksha known that I was alive, he would have sent assassins after me. I wouldn't have lived long enough to conduct the experiments I needed to. And I had no way of knowing whether Shiva would have enough faith in me to not reveal anything to Daksha.'

Parshuram tried to console Brahaspati. 'He has forgiven you. Trust me, he has.'

'He may have forgiven me, but I don't think he has understood me as yet,' said Brahaspati. 'I hope there comes a time when I will get my friend back.'

'It will happen,' said Parshuram. 'Once the Somras is destroyed, we will all go with the Lord to Mount Kailash and live happily ever after.'

Nandi smiled. 'Mount Kailash is far less hospitable than you imagine, Parshuram. I should know for I have been there. It is no luxurious paradise.'

'Any place would be paradise so long as we sit at the feet of Lord Shiva.'

— ⅄⊕⊍⍋⊛ —

'Have you worn *kajal* in your eyes?' asked a surprised Shiva.

Reclining in an easy chair on the raised private deck, Shiva had been gazing fondly at his children as they sparred with each other, swords at the ready. Sati seated herself and leaned close against him, briefly lost in the moment.

Shiva had rarely seen Sati use make-up. He believed her beauty was so ethereal that it did not need any embellishment.

Sati looked up at Shiva with a shy smile. Her pronounced Suryavanshi personality had been subtly influenced by Chandravanshi women, particularly Anandmayi. She was discovering the pleasures of beauty, especially when experienced through the appreciative eyes of the man she loved. 'Yes. I thought you hadn't noticed.'

The kohl accentuated Sati's large almond-shaped eyes and her bashful smile made her dimples spring to life.

Shiva was mesmerised, as always. 'Wow... It looks nice...'

Sati laughed softly as she edged up to Shiva's face, and kissed him lightly.

Ganesh and Kartik were engaged in a furious duel on the fore deck. As had become a tradition with them, they fought with real weapons instead of wooden swords. They believed that the risk of serious injury would focus their minds and improve their practice. They would halt just before a killer strike and demonstrate to the other that an opening had been found.

Converting his smaller size to his advantage, Kartik pressed close to Ganesh, cramping him and making it difficult for his taller opponent to strike freely. Ganesh stepped back and swung his shield down in a seemingly defensive motion, but halted the movement inches from Kartik's shoulder.

'Kartik, my shield has a knife,' said Ganesh, as he pressed a lever to release it. 'This is a strike on my account. I've said this to you before: fighting with two swords is too aggressive. You should use a shield. You ended up leaving an opening for me.'

Kartik smiled. 'No, *dada*. The strike is mine. Look down.'

Ganesh's eyes fell on his chest as he felt a light touch of metal. Kartik was holding his left sword the other way round, with a small blade sticking out of the hilt end. He had managed to turn the sword around, release the knife and bring it in close, all the while giving the feint of an open right flank to Ganesh. Shiva's elder son had assumed that Kartik had pulled his left sword out of combat.

Ganesh stood with his eyes wide open, seriously impressed

with his brother. 'How in Lady Bhoomidevi's name did you manage that?'

Shiva, who had seen the entire manoeuvre from his upper deck, was equally impressed with Kartik. He pulled back from Sati and shouted out, 'Bravo Kartik!'

Sensing angry eyes boring into him, Shiva immediately turned towards Sati. She was glaring at her husband, holding her breath irritably, her lips still puckered.

'I'm so sorry. I'm so sorry,' said Shiva, trying to draw close and kiss Sati again.

Sati pushed Shiva's face away with mock irritation. 'The moment's passed...'

'I'm so sorry. It's just that what Kartik did was...'

'Of course,' whispered Sati, shaking her head and smiling.

'It'll not happen again...'

'It better not...'

'I'm sorry...'

Sati shook her head and rested it on Shiva's chest. Shiva pulled her close. 'I love the *kajal*. I didn't think it was possible for you to look even more beautiful.'

Sati looked up at Shiva and rolled her eyes. She slapped him lightly on his chest. 'Too little, too late.'

Chapter 12

Troubled Waters

'How was it?' asked Anandmayi.

Bhagirath had sailed up the Padma and reached Parvateshwar's vessel which was anchored at the point where the river broke away from the Branga River. The captain was preparing to raise anchor and start sailing onward. Parvateshwar, Anandmayi and Ayurvati had been waiting for Bhagirath at the aft deck, eager for the news from Branga.

Bhagirath looked briefly at Parvateshwar and Ayurvati, before turning to Anandmayi. 'What do you think?'

'Did you tell him everything?' asked Ayurvati.

'That is exactly what the Lord Neelkanth had asked me to do,' answered Bhagirath.

Parvateshwar took a deep breath and walked away.

Anandmayi looked at her husband before turning back. 'So what did Branga say, Bhagirath?'

'King Chandraketu is livid that his people have been suffering from a murderous plague so that the Meluhans can live extra-long lives.'

'But I hope you told him that most Meluhans did not know this,' said Ayurvati. 'Had we known that the Somras was causing this evil in Branga, we would not have used it.'

Bhagirath looked disbelievingly at Ayurvati and sarcastically remarked, 'I did tell him that most Meluhans did not know about the devastation their addiction had caused. Strangely, it did not seem to lessen King Chandraketu's anger.'

Ayurvati remained silent.

Anandmayi spoke irritably, 'Can you stop being judgemental for a moment and just tell me what is going to happen in Branga now?'

'For now King Chandraketu is going to concentrate on manufacturing the medicines that his people need,' said Bhagirath. 'But at the same time, he has already started mobilising for war. He will be ready and waiting in three months for the Lord Neelkanth's orders.'

Ayurvati's eyes welled up with tears as she wistfully looked at Parvateshwar in the distance. She felt the anguish in his noble heart. For hers was just as heavy.

— ⅄ⵔⵡⵜ⊛ —

'My Lord,' said Siamantak, the Ayodhyan prime minister, as he entered Emperor Dilipa's chambers, 'I've just received word that Maharishi Bhrigu is on his way.'

'Lord Bhrigu?' asked a surprised Dilipa. 'Here?'

'The advance boat has just come in, Your Highness,' said Siamantak. 'Lord Bhrigu should be here by tomorrow.'

'Why wasn't I informed earlier?'

'I did not know either, Your Highness.'

'Meluha should not have done this. They should have informed us in advance before sending Lord Bhrigu here.'

'What can I say about Meluha, My Lord? Typically disdainful.'

A nervous Dilipa ran his hands across his face. 'Is there any news from the shipyard? Are our ships close to completion?'

Siamantak swallowed anxiously. 'No, Your Highness. You'd asked me to pay attention to the pavement dweller issue and...'

'I KNOW WHAT I'D ASKED YOU TO DO! JUST ANSWER MY QUESTION WITH A SIMPLE YES OR NO!'

'I'm sorry, Your Highness. No, the ships are nowhere near completion.'

'By when will the job be done?'

'If we stop doing everything else then I guess we should be ready in another six to nine months.'

Dilipa seemed to breathe easier. 'That's not so bad. Nothing's going to happen in the next nine months.'

'Yes, Your Highness.'

— ⁂ —

Emperor Dilipa was with Maharishi Bhrigu at the Ayodhya shipyard. The Meluhan brigadier, Prasanjit, stood at a distance.

Declining the hospitality which awaited him on landing, Bhrigu had headed directly for the shipyard. A flustered Dilipa had perforce followed him, courtiers and all. He gestured for Siamantak and all his courtiers to maintain a distance. He knew that Bhrigu was angry and expected an earful.

'Your Highness,' said Bhrigu slowly, keeping his temper on a tight leash, 'you had promised me that your ships would be ready.'

'I know, My Lord,' said Dilipa softly. 'But honestly, a few months' delay is not going to hurt us. It has been many months since our attack on Panchavati. There has been absolutely no news of the Neelkanth. I'm sure we have succeeded. We don't really need to be nervous. I honestly think that the likelihood of a war is substantially reduced.'

Bhrigu turned to Dilipa. 'Your Highness, may I request that you leave the thinking to me?'

Dilipa immediately fell silent.

'Was it not your suggestion to commandeer your trade ships and refit them for war?'

'Yes it was, My Lord,' said Dilipa.

'I had suggested that we are not likely to fight naval battles on the Ganga. I had told you that we will only need transport ships, for which your trade ships were good enough.'

'Yes, you had, My Lord.'

'Yet you had insisted that in the likelihood of there being river battles, it would be a good idea to have battleships.'

'Yes, My Lord.'

'And I agreed on one condition alone – that the battleships would be ready in six months. Correct?'

'Yes, My Lord.'

'It has been seven months now. You have stripped down the trade ships but have still not refitted them. So now, seven months later, not only do we not have any battleships, but we also don't have any trade-transport ships.'

'I know it looks very bad, My Lord,' said Dilipa, wiping his brow with his fingers. 'But the pavement-dwellers here had gone on a hunger strike.'

A confused Bhrigu raised his hands in exasperation. 'What does that have to do with the ships?'

'My Lord,' explained Dilipa patiently, 'in my benevolence, I had decreed that no Ayodhyan shall be roofless. Of course, this onerous task was assigned to the Royal Committee of Internal Affairs, which looks after both housing as well as the royal shipyard. The committee has been seriously debating the execution of this grand scheme over the last three years. Following our last conversation though, I thought it fit to direct the committee to focus on building ships. The resultant neglect of the free housing scheme angered the pavement-dwellers to the point of mass agitation. Public order being paramount, I redirected the committee to concentrate on the housing scheme. I am glad to say that the seventh version of the housing report, which judiciously takes into account the views of all the citizens, should be ready soon. Once accepted, obviously the committee can then give its undiluted attention to the matter of building ships.'

Bhrigu was staring wide-eyed at Dilipa, stunned.

'So you see, My Lord,' said Dilipa, 'I know this is not looking good, but things will be set right very soon. In fact, I expect the committee to start debating the shipyard issue within the next seven days.'

Bhrigu spoke softly, but his rage was at boiling point, 'Your Highness, the future of India is at stake and your committee is *debating*?!'

'But My Lord, debates are important. They help incorporate all points of view. Or else we may make decisions that are not...'

'In the name of Lord Ram, you are the king! Fate has placed you here so you can make decisions for your people!'

Dilipa fell silent.

Bhrigu maintained silence for a few seconds, trying to control his anger, then spoke in a low voice. 'Your Highness, what you do within your own kingdom is your problem. But I want the refitting of these ships to begin today. Understand?'

'Yes, Maharishi*ji*.'

'How soon can the ships be ready?'

'In six months, if my people work every day.'

'Make those imbeciles work day and night and have them ready in three. Am I clear?

'Yes, My Lord.'

'Also, please have your cartographers map the jungle route from Ayodhya to the upper Ganga.'

'Umm, but why should...'

Bhrigu sighed in exasperation. 'Your Highness, I expect Meluha to be the real battleground. Your Ayodhya is not likely to be at risk. These ships were needed to get your army to Meluha quickly, if necessary. Since they are not going to be ready now, we need an alternative plan if war is declared within the next few months. I would need your army to cut through the jungles in a north-westerly direction and reach the upper Ganga, close to Dharmakhet. Farther on, you can use the new road built by the Meluhans to reach Devagiri. Obviously, since you will be cutting through jungles, this route will be slow and could take many months, but it's better than reinforcements not getting to Meluha at all. And to ensure that your army does not get lost in the jungles, it would be good to have clear maps. I'm sure your commanders would want to reach Meluha in time to help your allies.'

Dilipa nodded.

'Also, I will be surprised if Ayodhya is attacked directly.'

'Of course. Why should anyone attack Ayodhya directly?' asked Dilipa. 'We have not harmed anyone.'

In truth, Bhrigu was not sure that Ayodhya would not be attacked. But he did not care. His only concern was the Somras. Meluha had to be protected in order to protect the Somras. Had it been possible to convince Dilipa to order the Ayodhyan army to leave for Devagiri right away, Bhrigu would not have hesitated to do so.

'I will order the cartographers to map the route through the jungles, My Lord,' said Dilipa.

'Thank you, Your Highness,' smiled Bhrigu. 'By the way, I notice that even your wrinkles are disappearing. Has the blood in your cough reduced?'

'Disappeared, My Lord. Your medicines are miraculous.'

'A medicine is only as good as the patient's responsiveness. All the credit is due only to you, Your Highness.'

'You are being too kind. What you have done to my body is magical. But My Lord, my knee continues to trouble me. It still hurts when I...'

'We'll take care of that as well. Don't worry.'

'Thank you.'

Bhrigu gestured behind him. 'Also, I have brought the Meluhan brigadier Prasanjit here. He will train your army on modern warfare.'

'Ummm, but...'

'Please ensure that your soldiers listen to him, Your Highness.'

'Yes, My Lord.'

— ⅄ⓄⅡ⇑⊛ —

The two ships carrying Parvateshwar and his team had just docked at the river port of Vaishali, the immediate neighbour of Branga. Shiva had asked Parvateshwar to speak to the King of Vaishali, Maatali, and get his support for the Neelkanth. However, keeping in mind his decision to oppose the Mahadev and protect Meluha, Parvateshwar was of the opinion that it would be unethical of him to approach the king. Therefore, he had requested Anandmayi to carry out the mission.

Bhagirath, Anandmayi and Ayurvati were standing aft while they waited for the gangplank to be lowered on to the Vaishali port. Parvateshwar, having opted to stay back, had decided to practise his sword skills with Uttanka on the lead ship. The waiting party gazed at the exquisite Vishnu temple dedicated to Lord Matsya, built very close to the river harbour. They bowed low towards the first Lord Vishnu.

'You will have to excuse me,' said Bhagirath, turning towards Anandmayi.

'Are you planning on leaving for Ayodhya right away?' asked Anandmayi.

'Yes. Why delay it? I intend to take the second ship and sail up the Sarayu to Ayodhya. The Vaishali King's allegiance is a given. He is blindly loyal to the Neelkanth. Your meeting him is a mere formality. I may as well concentrate on the other task that the Lord Neelkanth has given me.'

'All right,' said Anandmayi.

'Go with Lord Ram's blessings, Bhagirath,' said Ayurvati.

'You too,' said Bhagirath.

While the lead ships of Shiva's convoy berthed at the main Assi Ghat of Kashi, the others docked at the Brahma Ghat nearby. Along with a large retinue, King Athithigva waited in attendance for the ceremonial reception. On cue, drummers beat a steady rhythm and conches blared as Shiva stepped onto the gangplank. Ceremonial *aartis* and a cheering populace added to the festive air. Their living God had returned.

King Athithigva bowed low and touched Shiva's feet as soon as he stepped onto the Assi Ghat.

'*Ayushman bhav*, Your Highness,' said Shiva, blessing King Athithigva with *a long life*.

Athithigva smiled, his hands folded in a respectful Namaste. 'A long life is not of much use if we are not graced with your presence here in Kashi, My Lord.'

Shiva, always uncomfortable with such deference, quickly changed the subject. 'How have things been, Your Highness?'

'Very well. Trade has been good. But rumours have been going around that the Neelkanth is to make a big announcement soon. Is that so, My Lord?'

'Let us wait till we get to your palace, Your Highness.'

'Of course,' said Athithigva. 'I should also tell you that I have received word through a fast sailboat that Queen Kali is on her way to Kashi. She is just a few days' journey behind you. She should be here soon.'

With raised eyebrows, Shiva instinctively looked upriver from where Kali's ship would inevitably sail. 'Well, it will be good to have her here as well. We have a lot to plan for.'

Chapter 13

Escape of the Gunas

A delighted Shiva embraced Veerbhadra as Sati hugged Krittika. The duo had just entered Shiva's private chamber in the Kashi palace.

Veerbhadra and Krittika had had an uneventful journey through Meluha. Their reception at the village where the Gunas had been housed had taken them by surprise. There were no soldiers, no alarm, nothing out of the ordinary. Clearly, the Gunas were not being targeted as leverage against the Neelkanth. The system-driven Meluhans had achieved what their system had conceived – everybody being treated in accordance with the law with no special provisions for any particular people.

'Didn't you face any trouble?' asked Shiva.

'None,' said Veerbhadra. 'The tribe lived just like everyone else, in comfortable egalitarianism. We quickly bundled them into a caravan and quietly escaped. We arrived in Kashi a few months later.'

'That means they're not aware as yet of my escape at the Godavari,' said Shiva. 'Or else they would have arrested the Gunas.'

'That is the logical conclusion.'

'But it also means that if any Meluhan happens to check

the Guna village and finds them missing, they will assume that I'm alive and am planning a confrontation.'

'That is also a logical conclusion. But there's nothing we can do about that, can we?'

'No, there isn't,' agreed Shiva.

— ⅄ⵀ⅂ —

'*Didi*!' smiled Kali as she embraced her sister.

'How are you doing, Kali?' asked Sati.

'I'm tired. My ship had to race down the Chambal and Ganga to catch up with you!'

'Nice to meet you after so many months, Kali,' said Shiva.

'Likewise,' said Kali. 'How was Ujjain?'

'A city that is worthy of Lord Ram,' said Shiva.

'Is it true that some of the Vasudevs have accompanied you here?'

'Yes, including the chief Vasudev himself, Lord Gopal.'

Kali whistled softly. 'I was not even aware of the chief Vasudev's name till just the other day and now it looks like I will be meeting him soon. The scenario must be really grim for him to emerge from his seclusion like this.'

'Change doesn't happen easily,' said Shiva. 'I don't expect the supporters of the Somras to fade into the sunset. The Vasudevs in fact believe the war has already begun, regardless of whether it has been declared or not. That it's just a matter of time before actual hostilities break out. I agree.'

'Is that why my ship was dragged into the Assi River?' asked Kali. 'I was worried that it might not make it into the harbour. This river is so small that it should actually be called a culvert!'

'That is for the ship's protection, Kali,' said Shiva. 'It was Lord Athithigva's idea. The Kashi harbour, just like the city, is not protected by any walls. Our enemies may hesitate to attack the city itself due to their faith in Lord Rudra's protective spirit over Kashi. But any ships anchored on the Ganga would be fair game.'

'Hence the decision to move the ships into the Assi, which as you know, flows into the Ganga,' said Sati. 'The channel at the mouth of the river is narrow, thus not more than one enemy ship can come through at a time. Our ships therefore can be easily defended. Also, the Assi flows through the city of Kashi. Most Chandravanshis would not want to venture within, believing that the spirit of Lord Rudra would curse them for harming Kashi, even by mistake.'

Kali raised her eyebrows. 'Using an enemy's own superstition against him? I like it!'

'Sometimes good tactics can work better than a sword edge,' said Shiva, grinning.

'Aah,' said Kali, smiling. 'You're only saying that because you haven't encountered my sword!'

Shiva and Sati laughed convivially.

— ⁂ —

Shiva and his core group were in the main hall of the grand Kashi Vishwanath temple. Athithigva had stepped into the inner sanctum, along with the main pandit of the temple, to offer *prasad* to the idols of Lord Rudra and Lady Mohini. He returned thereafter with the *ritual offerings made to the Gods.*

'May Lord Rudra and Lady Mohini bless our enterprise,' said Athithigva, offering the *prasad* to Shiva.

Shiva took the *prasad* with both hands, swallowed it whole and ran his right hand over his head, thus offering his thanks to the Lord and Lady for their blessings. Meanwhile, the temple pandit distributed the *prasad* to everybody else. The ceremonies over, Athithigva sat down with the group to discuss the strategy for the war ahead. The pandit was led out of the temple by Kashi policemen and the entrance sealed. No one was to be allowed into the premises for the duration of the meeting.

'My Lord, my people are forbidden any acts of violence except if it is in self-defence,' said Athithigva. 'So we cannot join the campaign actively with you. But all the resources of my kingdom are at your command.'

Shiva smiled. The peace-loving Kashi people would, in any case, not really make good soldiers. He had no intention of leading them into battles. 'I know, King Athithigva. I would not ask anything of your people that they would be honour-bound to refuse. But you must be able to defend Kashi if attacked, for we intend to house many of our war resources here.'

'We will defend it to our last breath, My Lord,' said Athithigva.

Shiva nodded. He did not really expect the Chandravanshis to attack Kashi. He turned towards Gopal. 'Pandit*ji*, there are many things that we need to discuss. To begin with, how do we keep the Chandravanshis out of the war theatre in Meluha? Secondly, what strategy should we adopt with Meluha?'

'I think what Lord Ganesh and Kartik suggested is an excellent idea,' said Gopal. 'Let us hope we can rope in Magadh to our side.'

'Easier said than done,' said Kali. 'Surapadman would be compelled by his father to seek vengeance for his stupid brother Ugrasen. And I don't propose handing over Ganesh for what was, in fact, a just execution.'

'So what are you suggesting, Kali?' asked Sati.

'Well, I'm suggesting that we either fight Magadh right

away or we tell them that we will investigate and hand over the Naga culprit as soon as we lay our hands on him.'

Sati instinctively held Ganesh's hand protectively.

Kali laughed softly. '*Didi*, all I'm suggesting is that we make Surapadman *think* that we are going to hand him over. That way, we can buy some time and attack Ayodhya.'

'Are you saying that we lie to the Magadhans, Your Highness?' asked Gopal.

Kali frowned at Gopal. 'All I'm saying is we be economical with the truth, great Vasudev. The future of India is at stake. There are many who are counting on us. If we have to taint our souls with a sin for the sake of greater good, then so be it.'

'I will not lie,' said Shiva. 'This is a war against Evil. We are on the side of Good. Our fight must reflect that.'

'*Baba*,' said Ganesh. 'You know I would agree with you under normal circumstances. But do you think the other side has maintained the standards you are espousing? Wasn't the attack on us at Panchavati an act of pure deception and subterfuge?'

'I don't believe it is wrong to attack an unprepared enemy. Yes, their using *daivi astras* can be considered questionable. Even so, two wrongs don't make a right. I will not lie to win this war. We will win it the right way.'

Kartik remained silent. Whereas he agreed with the pragmatism of Ganesh's words, he was inspired by the moral clarity in Shiva's.

Gopal smiled at Shiva. '*Satyam vada. Asatyam mavada.*'

'What?' asked Shiva.

Kali spoke up. 'It's old Sanskrit. "Speak the truth, never speak the untruth".'

Sati smiled. 'I agree.'

'Well, I know some old Sanskrit too,' said Kali. '*Satyam bruyat priyam bruyat, na bruyat satyam apriyam.*'

Shiva raised his hands in dismay, 'Can we cut out the old Sanskrit one-upmanship? I don't follow what you people are saying.'

Gopal translated for Shiva. 'What Queen Kali said means "Speak the truth in a pleasing manner, but never speak that truth which is unpleasant to others".'

'It's not my line,' said Kali, turning to Shiva. 'It can be attributed to a sage of yore, I'm sure. But I think it makes sense. We don't have to reveal to Surapadman that we know who his brother's killer is. All we need to motivate him to do, is to wait till after we have attacked Ayodhya before choosing his friends and his enemies. His ambition will guide him in the direction that we desire.'

'The walls of Ayodhya are impregnable,' warned Gopal, drawing attention to another factor. 'We might be able to bog them down, but we won't be able to destroy the city.'

'I know,' said Ganesh. 'But our aim is not to destroy Ayodhya. It is to ensure that their navy is unable to sail their forces over to Meluha. Our main battle will be in Meluha.'

'But what if Surapadman attacks from the rear after we have laid siege on Ayodhya?' asked Gopal. 'Caught between Ayodhya in front of us and Surapadman behind us, we could get destroyed.'

'Actually, no,' said Ganesh. 'Surapadman attacking us from behind would make things easier for us. It's when he moves out of Magadh that we'll make our move.'

Shiva, Kartik and Sati smiled; they understood the plan.

'Brilliant,' exclaimed Parshuram.

The rest turned to Parshuram for a whispered explanation on the side.

'You don't have to lie,' continued Kali to Shiva. 'Refrain from telling Surapadman the entire truth, except for those portions which will make him pause. Let his ambition play out the rest. We require him to allow our ships to pass through the confluence of the Sarayu and Ganga, towards Ayodhya. Once that is done we will achieve our objective one way or the other; either by holding Ayodhya back or by destroying the Magadhan army.'

Shiva's brief nod acknowledged his assent. 'But what about Meluha? Should we launch a frontal attack with all our might? Or, should we adopt diversionary tactics to distract their armies while a small group searches for the secret Somras facility and destroys it?'

'Our Branga and Vaishali forces will battle in Magadh and Ayodhya, leaving the Vasudevs and the Naga armies for the Meluhan campaign,' said Sati. 'So we will have much smaller forces in Meluha. Of course, they will be exceptionally well-trained and will have superb technological skills, like the fire-spewing elephant corps that the Vasudevs have developed recently. But we have to respect the Meluhan forces; they're equally well-trained and technologically adept.'

'So are you suggesting that we avoid a direct attack?' asked Shiva.

'Yes,' said Sati. 'Our main aim has to be to destroy the Somras manufacturing facility. It will take them years to rebuild it. That much time is more than enough for your word to prevail amongst the people. The average Meluhan is devoted to the legend of the Neelkanth. The Somras will die a natural death. But if we attack directly, the war with Meluha will drag on for a long time. The more it drags on, the more innocent people will die. Also, the Meluhans will begin to look upon the war as an attack on their beloved country, and not the Somras. I'm sure there will be large numbers of Meluhans who would be willing to turn against the Somras, but if we challenge their patriotism, then we have no chance of winning.'

Kali was smiling.

'What?' asked Sati.

'I noticed that you said "they" instead of "we" when you referred to the Meluhans,' said Kali.

Sati seemed perplexed. She still believed Meluha was her own land. 'Umm, that's unimportant... It's still my country...'

'Sure it is,' smiled Kali.

Gopal cut in. 'Just for the sake of argument, let us imagine what would happen if there is a direct all-out war.'

'That is something we will have to avoid,' said Shiva. 'I see sense in what Sati is saying.'

'Nevertheless, let us consider what Lord Bhrigu and Daksha might think,' said Gopal. 'I agree, it is in our interest to not have a direct war. But it is in their interest to have one, and a destructive one at that. They will want tensions to escalate so that they can confuse the people. They will then say that the Neelkanth has betrayed Meluha. Like Lady Sati just pointed out, the patriotism of the Meluhans could drown out their faith in the Neelkanth.'

'I agree that Lord Bhrigu may want to escalate the situation,' said Shiva. 'What I do not understand is how he will manage it once it has. I have seen the Meluhan army from up close. It's a centralised, well-drilled unit. But the problem with such armies is their utter dependence on a good commander. Their general, Parvateshwar, is with us. Trust me, they do not have another man like him. If Lord Bhrigu is as intelligent as you say he is, he would know that too.'

Ganesh and Kartik sighed at the same time.

Shiva glared at his sons.

'*Baba...*' said Kartik.

'Dammit!' screamed Shiva. 'You will not doubt his loyalty! Am I clear?'

Ganesh and Kartik bowed their heads, their mouths pursed mutinously.

'Am I clear?' asked Shiva once again.

Kali frowned at Shiva before looking at Ganesh and Kartik, but remained silent.

Shiva turned back to Gopal. 'We have to avoid provocation. Our military formations have to be solidly defensive, so as to deter them from staging an open confrontation. The main task for our army is to keep them distracted, so that a smaller unit can search the towns on the Saraswati for signs of the Somras manufacturing facility. Once we succeed in destroying that facility, we will win the war.'

'Nandi,' said Sati, turning to the Meluhan major.

Nandi immediately laid out a map of Meluha. Everyone peered at it.

'Look,' said Sati. 'The Saraswati ends in an inland delta. The Meluhans will not be able to get their massive fleet from Karachapa into the Saraswati. Their defence doctrine covers just two possible threats – a naval attack via the Indus or a land-based army attack from the east. That is why they don't have a massive fleet on the Saraswati.'

Shiva grasped what Sati was alluding to. 'They're unprepared for a naval attack on the Saraswati...'

'You have to understand that this is with good reason. They assumed that no enemy ships could enter the Saraswati. No enemy-controlled rivers flow into it and the Saraswati does not open to the sea.'

'But isn't that just the problem?' asked a confused Athithigva. 'How will we get ships into the Saraswati?'

'We won't,' said Shiva. 'We will capture the Meluhan ships stationed in the Saraswati instead.'

Kali nodded. 'That is the last thing they would expect, which is the reason why it will work.'

'Yes,' said Sati. 'All we have to do is capture Mrittikavati, which is where most of the Saraswati command of the

Meluhan navy is stationed. Once we're in possession of those ships, we will control the Saraswati. We can quickly sail up, unchallenged, even as we continue our search for the Somras manufacturing facility.'

'That's correct,' said Brahaspati. 'The manufacturing facility can only be on the banks of the Saraswati. It cannot possibly be anywhere else.'

'This sounds like a good plan,' said Gopal. 'But how do we capture their ships? Where do we enter their territory from? Mrittikavati is not a border town. We will have to march in with an army. And we will obviously face resistance from the border town that falls on the way – Lothal.'

'Lothal?' asked Kartik.

'Lothal is the port of Maika,' said Gopal. 'They are practically twin cities. Maika is where all the Meluhan children are born and raised, while Lothal is the local army base.'

'Don't worry about Maika or Lothal,' said Kali. 'They will be on our side.'

Gopal, Shiva and Sati seemed genuinely surprised.

'If there are any Meluhans who will have sympathy for us, it will be the people of Maika,' continued Kali. 'They have seen the Naga children suffer. They have tried to help us on many occasions, even breaking their own laws in the process. The present Governor of Maika, Chenardhwaj, is also the administrator of Lothal. He was transferred from Kashmir a few years back. He is loyal to the institution of the Neelkanth. Furthermore, I have saved his life once. Trust me, both Maika and Lothal will be with us when hostilities break out.'

'I remember Chenardhwaj,' said Shiva. 'All right then, we will utilise the support of Lothal to conquer Mrittikavati. Then we'll use their ships to search the towns on the Saraswati. But remember, we must try and avoid a direct clash.'

Chapter 14

The Reader of Minds

'Do you believe we can convince him?' asked Shiva.

The Vasudev chief, Gopal, had just walked into Shiva's chamber. Sati and the Neelkanth were preparing to leave for Magadh with him. Ganesh and Kartik had come to say goodbye to their parents.

'I would have been worried had we been meeting Lord Bhrigu,' said Gopal. 'But it's only Surapadman.'

'What is so special about Lord Bhrigu?' asked Shiva. 'He is only human. Why are all of you so wary of him?'

'He is a maharishi, Shiva,' said Sati. 'In fact, like Gopal*ji* had mentioned, Lord Bhrigu is believed by many to be beyond a maharishi; he's a *Saptrishi Uttradhikari*.'

'You should respect a man, not his position,' said Shiva, before turning to Gopal. 'Once again I ask, my friend, why are you so nervous about him?'

'Well, for starters, he can read minds,' said Gopal.

'So?' asked Shiva. 'You and I can do that too. Every Vasudev pandit can, in fact.'

'True, but we can only do so while we're in one of our temples. Lord Bhrigu can read the mind of anyone around him, regardless of where he is.'

Ganesh looked genuinely surprised. 'How?'

'Well,' said Gopal, 'our brains transmit radio waves when we think. These thoughts can be detected by a trained person, provided he is within the range of a powerful transmitter. But it is believed that maharishis can go a step further. They do not need to wait till our thoughts are converted into radio waves, to be able to detect them. They can read our thoughts even as we formulate them.'

'But how?'

'Thoughts are nothing but electrical impulses in our brain,' said Gopal. 'These impulses make the pupils of our eyes move minutely. A trained person, like a maharishi, can decipher this movement in our pupils and read our thoughts.'

'Lord Ram, be merciful,' whispered a stunned Kartik.

'I still do not understand how this is possible,' remarked a sceptical Shiva. 'Are you saying all our thoughts are exposed by the movement of our pupils? What language would that communication be in? This makes no sense.'

'My friend,' said Gopal, 'you are confusing the language of communication with the internal language of the brain. Sanskrit, for example, is a language of communication. You use it to communicate with others. You also use it to communicate with your own brain, so that your conscious mind can understand your inner thoughts. But the brain itself uses only one language for its own working. This is a universal language across all brains of all known species. And the alphabet of this language has two letters, or signals.'

'Two signals?' asked Sati

'Yes,' said Gopal, 'only two – electricity on and electricity off. Our brain has millions of thoughts and instructions running simultaneously within. But at any one point of time, only one of these thoughts can capture our conscious attention. This particular thought gets reflected in our eyes through the language of the brain. A maharishi can read this conscious thought. So one has to be very careful about what one consciously thinks in the presence of a maharishi.'

'So the eye is indeed the window to one's soul,' said Ganesh.

Gopal smiled. 'It appears that it is.'

Shiva grinned, his brows raised. 'Well, I'll make sure that I keep mine shut when I meet Lord Bhrigu.'

Gopal and Sati laughed softly.

'Nevertheless, we will win,' said Gopal.

'Yes,' said Ganesh. 'We're on the side of Good.'

'That is true, without doubt. But that is not the reason, Lord Ganesh. We will win because of your father,' said Gopal.

'No,' said Shiva. 'It cannot be only me. We will win because we're all in this together.'

'It is you who brings us together, great Neelkanth,' said Gopal. 'Lord Bhrigu may be as intelligent as you are, maybe more. But he is not a leader like you. He uses, rather misuses his brilliance to cow down his followers. They don't idolise him; they are scared of him. You, on the other hand, are able to draw out the best in your followers, my friend. Don't think I did not understand what you did a few days back. You had decided upon your course of action already. But that did not stop you from having a discussion, allowing us to be a part of the decision. Somehow, you guided us all into saying what you wanted to hear. And yet, you made each one of us feel as if it was our own decision. That is leadership. Lord Bhrigu may have a bigger army than ours, but he fights alone. In our case, our entire army will fight as one. That, great Neelkanth, is a supreme tribute to your leadership.'

Shiva, embarrassed as always when complimented, quickly changed the topic. 'You are being too kind, Gopal*ji*. In any case, I think we should leave. Magadh awaits us.'

— ⁂ —

'Bhagirath is here?'

Siamantak nodded at his stunned emperor. 'Yes, My Lord.'

'But how did he...'

'Prime Minister Siamantak,' said Bhrigu, interrupting Dilipa. 'I would be delighted to meet him. Have Princess Anandmayi and her husband accompanied him?'

'No, My Lord,' said Siamantak. 'He has come alone.'

'That is most unfortunate,' said Bhrigu. 'Please show him in with complete honour into our presence.'

'As you wish, My Lord,' said Siamantak, as he bowed to Bhrigu and Dilipa before leaving the room.

As soon as he had left, Bhrigu turned towards Dilipa. 'Your Highness, you must learn to control yourself. Siamantak is unaware of the attack at the Godavari.'

'I'm sorry, My Lord,' said Dilipa. 'It's just that I'm shocked.'

'I'm not.'

Dilipa frowned. 'Why, My Lord! Did you expect this?'

'I can't say that I expected this specifically. But I had strong suspicions that our attack had failed. The only question was how they would be confirmed.'

'I don't understand, My Lord. Our ships could have got destroyed in so many ways.'

'It wasn't only the destruction of our ships. There is something else. I had asked Kanakhala to try and locate the Gunas.'

'Who are the Gunas?'

'They are the tribe of that fraud Neelkanth. The Gunas were immigrants in Meluha. There are standard policies in Meluha for immigrants, one of them being that their records are kept strictly secret. This system ensures that they are not targeted or oppressed, and are in fact, treated well. But the upshot was that the royal record-keeper was refusing to tell his own Prime Minister where the Gunas were settled.'

'How can the record-keeper do that? The Prime Minister's word would be the order of the Emperor. And his word is law!'

'Well,' smiled Bhrigu. 'Meluha is not like your empire, Lord Dilipa. They have this irritating habit of sticking to rules.'

Bhrigu's sarcasm was lost on Dilipa.

'So what happened, My Lord? Did you find the Gunas?'

'At first, Kanakhala seemed quite sure that the Gunas were in Devagiri itself. When that initial search yielded nothing, she had no choice but to approach Emperor Daksha. He passed an order through the Rajya Sabha that would force the Meluhan record-keeper to reveal the location of the Gunas. By the time we reached their village, they were gone.'

'Gone where?'

'I don't know. I was told this happens quite often. Many immigrants are not able to adapt to the civilised but regimented life in Meluha and choose to return to their homelands. So I was asked to believe that the Gunas must have gone back to the Himalayas.'

'And did you believe that?'

'Of course I didn't. I suspected the fraud Neelkanth must have spirited his tribe away before declaring war. But what could I do? I didn't know where the Gunas were.'

'But why is Bhagirath here? Why would the Neelkanth reveal his hand?'

'*Fraud* Neelkanth, Your Highness,' said Bhrigu, correcting Dilipa.

'I'm sorry, My Lord,' said Dilipa.

Bhrigu looked up at the ceiling. 'Yes, why has Shiva sent him here?'

'My God!' whispered Dilipa. 'Could he have been sent here to assassinate me?'

Bhrigu shook his head. 'That is unlikely. I don't think killing you, Your Highness, would serve any larger purpose.'

Dilipa opened his mouth to say something but decided instead to remain silent.

'Yes,' continued Bhrigu, narrowing his eyes, 'we do need to know why Prince Bhagirath is here. I look forward to meeting him.'

— ⚹ —

'Father,' said Bhagirath as he walked confidently into Dilipa's chamber.

Dilipa smiled as best he could. He didn't really like his son. 'How are you, Bhagirath?'

'I'm all right, father.'

'How was your trip to Panchavati?'

Bhagirath glanced at Bhrigu, wondering who the old Brahmin was, before turning back to his father. 'It was an uneventful trip, father. Perhaps the Nagas are not as bad as we think. Some of us have returned early. The Lord Neelkanth will join us later.'

Dilipa frowned, as if surprised, and turned towards Bhrigu.

Bhagirath arched his eyebrow before turning towards Bhrigu as well with a Namaste and quick bow of his head. 'Please accept my apologies for my bad manners, Brahmin. I was overwhelmed with emotions on seeing my father.'

Bhrigu looked deep into Bhagirath's eyes.

Bhagirath is consumed with curiosity about who I am. I better put this to rest so that his conscious mind can move on to more useful thoughts.

'Perhaps it is I who should apologise,' said Bhrigu. 'I have not introduced myself. I'm a simple sage who lives in the Himalayas and goes by the name of Bhrigu.'

Bhagirath straightened up in surprise. Of course he knew who Bhrigu was, although he hadn't met him. Bhagirath stepped forward and bent low, touching the sage's feet.

'Maharishi Bhrigu, it is my life's honour to meet you. I'm fortunate to have the opportunity to seek your blessings.'

'*Ayushman bhav*,' said Bhrigu, blessing Bhagirath with *a long life*.

Bhrigu then placed his hands on Bhagirath's shoulders and pulled him up, while once again looking directly into his eyes.

Bhagirath has realised that his imbecile father is not the true leader. I am. And he's scared. Good. Now all I have to do is make him think some more.

'I trust the Neelkanth is well?' asked Bhrigu. 'I have still not had the pleasure of meeting the man who commoners believe is the saviour of our times.'

'He is well, My Lord,' said Bhagirath. 'And is worthy of the title he carries. In fact, there are those of us who believe that he even deserves the title of the Mahadev.'

So, Bhagirath volunteered to uncover the identity of the true leader. Interesting. That Tibetan barbarian understands that this fool Dilipa could not have been the one. He has more intelligence than I thought.

'Allow posterity to prevail upon the present in deciding the honour and title bestowed upon man, my dear Prince of Ayodhya,' said Bhrigu. 'Duty must be performed for its own sake, not for the power and pelf it might bring. I am sure that even your Neelkanth is familiar with Lord Vasudev's nugget of wisdom which encapsulates this thought: *Karmanye vaadhikaa raste maa phaleshu kadachana*.'

'Oh, the Neelkanth is the embodiment of that thought, Maharishi*ji*,' said Bhagirath. 'He never calls himself the Mahadev. It is we who address him as such.'

Bhrigu smiled. 'Your Neelkanth must be truly great to inspire such loyalty, brave Prince. By the way, how was Panchavati? I have never had the pleasure of visiting that land.'

'It is a beautiful city, Maharishi*ji*.'

They were attacked at the outskirts of Panchavati... So our ships did make it through. And their devil boats got us. Well, at least our information about the location of Panchavati is correct.

'With Lord Ram's blessings,' said Bhrigu, 'I will visit Panchavati someday.'

'I'm sure that the Queen of the Nagas would be honoured, My Lord,' said Bhagirath.

Bhrigu smiled. *Kali would kill me if she had half a chance. Her temper is even more volatile than Lord Rudra's legendary anger.*

'But Prince Bhagirath,' said Bhrigu, 'I must complain about an iniquity that you have committed.'

An astonished Bhagirath folded his hands together in an apologetic Namaste. 'I apologise profusely if I have offended you in any way, My Lord. Please tell me how I can set it right.'

'It's very simple,' said Bhrigu. 'I was really looking forward to meeting the Emperor's daughter and her new husband. But you have not brought Princess Anandmayi along with you.'

'Apologies for my oversight, My Lord,' said Bhagirath. 'I overlooked this only because I rushed here to pay obeisance to my respected father, whom I have not met for a long time. And Princess Anandmayi has dutifully accompanied her husband General Parvateshwar to Kashi.'

Bhrigu suddenly held his breath as he read Bhagirath's thoughts. *Parvateshwar wants to defect? He wants to return to Meluha?*

'I guess I will only have the pleasure of meeting Princess Anandmayi and General Parvateshwar when the Almighty wills it,' said Bhrigu.

The smile on Bhrigu's face left Bhagirath with a sense of unease.

'Hopefully that will be soon enough, My Lord,' said Bhagirath. 'If I may now be excused, I'd like to meet up with some people and then head to Kashi for some unfinished tasks.'

Dilipa was about to say something when Bhrigu raised his hand and placed it on Bhagirath's head. 'Of course, brave Prince. Go with Lord Ram.'

'Why did you let him go, My Lord?' said Dilipa, as soon as Bhagirath had left. 'We could have arrested him. The interrogation would have surely revealed what happened in Panchavati.'

'I'm already aware of what happened,' said Bhrigu. 'Our ships did reach Panchavati and even managed to kill a large number from amongst their convoy. But they did not kill the main leaders. Shiva is still alive. And our ships were destroyed in the battle.'

'Even so, we should not allow Bhagirath to leave. Why are we letting one of their main leaders go back unharmed?'

'I have blessed him with a long life, Your Highness. I'm sure you don't want me to be proven a liar.'

'Of course not, My Lord.'

Bhrigu looked at Dilipa and smiled. 'I know what you are thinking, Your Highness. Trust me, in chess as in war, one sometimes sacrifices a minor piece for the strategic advantage of capturing a more important piece several moves later.'

Dilipa frowned.

'Let me make myself very clear, Your Highness,' said Bhrigu. 'Prince Bhagirath must not be harmed in Ayodhya. I imagine he will leave your city within a day. He should leave safe and sound. I want them to think that we are none the wiser from Bhagirath's brief visit.'

'Yes, My Lord.'

'Provision and ready a fast sailboat. I must leave for Kashi immediately.'

'Yes, My Lord.'

'Please have the manifest of my ship state that I am going to Prayag. Bhagirath still has friends in Ayodhya. I don't want him to know that I'm leaving for Kashi. Is that clear?'

'Of course, My Lord. I will have Siamantak take care of this immediately.'

Chapter 15

The Magadhan Issue

Shiva, Sati and Gopal had just been led into the guest chambers of Surapadman's royal palace by Andhak, the Magadhan minister for ports.

Gopal waited for him to leave and then remarked, 'It's interesting that we are being housed in Surapadman's private residence and not King Mahendra's palace.'

'Surapadman wants to serve as the exclusive channel of information between us and his father,' said Sati. 'Being the sole intermediary also allows him the discretion of passing on things selectively. It actually makes me more hopeful of success.'

'I am far less hopeful,' countered Shiva. 'No doubt it is actually Surapadman's writ that runs large in Magadh. Besides being the prince, he is also the keeper of the king's seal. But even he would be wary of his father's reaction following the killing of Prince Ugrasen. Perhaps that is why he wants to talk to us in private here.'

'Perhaps,' said Gopal. 'Maybe that's the reason why we were received in Magadh by Andhak and not King Mahendra's prime minister.'

'Yes,' said Shiva. 'I believe Andhak is loyal to Surapadman.'

'Let's hope for the best,' said Sati.

— ⁂ —

As Shiva, Sati and Gopal entered the prince's court, Surapadman rose from his ceremonial chair. He walked up to the Neelkanth and then went down on his knees. Surapadman placed his head on Shiva's feet. 'Bless me, great Neelkanth.'

'*Sukhinah bhav*,' said Shiva, placing his hand on Surapadman's head, *blessing him with happiness.*

Surapadman looked up at Shiva. 'I hope by the time this conversation ends, My Lord, you will find it in your heart to bless me with victory along with happiness.'

Shiva smiled and placed his hands on Surapadman's shoulders as he rose. 'Please allow me to introduce my companions, Prince Surapadman. This is my wife, Sati.'

Surapadman bowed low towards Sati. She politely returned Surapadman's greeting.

'And this is my close friend and the chief of the Vasudevs, Gopal,' said Shiva.

Surapadman's hands came together in a respectful Namaste as his eyes widened with surprise. 'Lord Ram, be merciful!'

'Pray to him,' said Gopal, 'and he will be.'

Surapadman smiled. 'My apologies, Gopal*ji*. My informants have always assured me that the legendary Vasudevs are for real. But I believed they would not interfere with worldly affairs unless an existential crisis was upon us.'

'Such a time is upon us, Surapadman,' said Gopal. 'And all the true followers of Lord Ram must align themselves with the Neelkanth.'

Surapadman remained silent.

'Let us make ourselves comfortable, brave Prince of Magadh,' said Shiva.

Surapadman led them to the centre of the court where ceremonial chairs had been placed in a circle. Gopal noticed there was no official from the royal Magadhan court except for Andhak. Rumours suggesting that Andhak would soon be taking over the command of the Magadhan army were perhaps true. It could also be deduced that the rest of the Magadhan court was not really aligned with the Neelkanth. Considering Magadh's traditional rivalry with Ayodhya, one would have imagined that they would choose to align with the Neelkanth. But Ugrasen's murder seemed to have effectively queered the pitch.

'What can I do for you, My Lord?' asked Surapadman.

'I will come straight to the point, Prince Surapadman,' said Shiva. 'Your elite intelligence officials would have already briefed you that a war is likely.'

Surapadman nodded silently.

'Perhaps you would also be aware that Ayodhya has not chosen wisely,' said Gopal.

'Yes, I'm aware of that,' said Surapadman, allowing himself a hint of a smile. 'But given Ayodhya's penchant for indecision and confusion, few can be sure about which side they will eventually find themselves on!'

Sati smiled. 'And what do you intend to do, brave Prince?'

'My Lady,' said Surapadman, 'I am a believer in the legend of the Neelkanth. And the Lord has shown that he is a worthy inheritor of the title of the Mahadev.'

Shiva shifted in his seat awkwardly, still not comfortable with being compared to the great Lord Rudra.

'Furthermore, Ayodhya is a terrible overlord,' continued Surapadman. 'It needs to be challenged in the interests of Swadweep. And only Magadh has the ability to do that.'

'I can see that only mighty Magadh has the strength to confront Ayodhya,' said Sati.

'There you have it,' said Surapadman, 'I have given you two good reasons why I should choose to stand with the army of the Neelkanth.'

Shiva, Gopal and Sati remained silent, waiting for the inevitable 'but'.

'And yet,' said Surapadman, 'circumstances have made my situation a little more complex.'

Turning towards Shiva, Surapadman continued, 'My Lord, you must already be aware of my dilemma. My brother, Ugrasen, was killed in a Naga terrorist attack and my father is hell-bent on seeking vengeance.'

Keeping the sensitivity of the issue in mind, Shiva spoke softly, 'Surapadman, I think the incident...'

'My Lord,' said Surapadman, 'please forgive me for interrupting you, but I know the truth.'

'I'm not sure you do, Prince Surapadman. Or else your reaction would have been different.'

Surapadman smiled, looked briefly at Andhak and continued. 'My Lord, Andhak and I have investigated the case personally. We've visited the spot where my brother and his men were killed. We're aware of the incident.'

Sati couldn't help inquiring, 'Then why...'

'What can I do, My Lady?' asked Surapadman. 'My father is a grieving old man who has convinced himself that his favourite son was a noble and valiant Kshatriya, who died while defending his kingdom from a cowardly Naga attack. How can I tell him the truth? How do I tell him that Ugrasen was in fact a compulsive gambler who was trying to kidnap a hapless boy-rider so that he could win some money? Should I tell my father that my great brother tried to murder a mother who was protecting her own child? That the apparently wicked Nagas were actually heroes who saved a subject of his own kingdom from his son's villainy? Do you think he will even listen to me?'

'There is nobility in truth,' said Sati, 'even if it hurts.'

Surapadman laughed softly. 'This is not Meluha, My

Lady. Meluhans' devotion to "the truth" is seen by many here as nothing but rigidity of thought. Chandravanshis prefer to choose from several alternative truths which may simultaneously co-exist.'

Sati remained silent.

Surapadman turned to Shiva. 'My Lord, my father thinks that I am an ambitious warmonger who's impatient to ascend the throne. He preferred my elder brother, who was more attuned to my father's views. I think he suspects that I engineered the death of Ugrasen, in pursuit of my goals.'

'I'm sure that's not true,' said Shiva. 'You are his capable son.'

'It takes a very self-assured man to appreciate the talents of another, My Lord,' said Surapadman. 'Even when it comes to one's own progeny. Ironically, the Nagas have in fact helped me, for my path to the throne is clear. All I have to do is wait for my father to pass on. And desist from doing anything that will make him disinherit me and offer the throne to some relative. Given this, if I were to tell my father that his favourite son's murder by the "evil" Nagas was absolutely justified, I would probably go down in history as the stupidest royal ever.'

Gopal smiled slightly. 'It appears that we are at an impasse, Prince Surapadman. What do we do?'

Surapadman narrowed his eyes. 'Just give me a Naga.'

'I can't,' said Shiva.

'I'm not asking for the one who actually killed Ugrasen, My Lord,' said Surapadman. 'I guess he is someone important. All I'm asking for is a random Naga. I will present him to my father as Ugrasen's killer and we'll have him executed forthwith. My father will then happily retire and go into *sanyas* to pray for my brother's soul. And I, along with all the resources of Magadh, will stand beside you. I know the Brangas are with you. Victory is assured if Magadh and

Branga are on the same side. You will win the war, My Lord, and Evil will be destroyed. All you need to do is sacrifice an insignificant Naga, who is suffering for the sins of his past lives in any case. We will actually be giving him an opportunity to earn good karma. What do you say?'

Shiva did not hesitate even for a second. 'I cannot do that.'

'My Lord...'

'I will not do that.'

'But...'

'No.'

Surapadman leaned back in his chair. 'We indeed seem to be at an impasse, great Vasudev. My father will not allow me to fight in an army that includes the Nagas unless we can assuage his thirst for vengeance.'

Shiva spoke up before Gopal could respond. 'What if you do not pick any side at all?'

Surapadman frowned, intrigued.

'Convince your father to remain neutral,' continued Shiva. 'Allow my ships to proceed to battle with Ayodhya. If we are able to beat them, then your primary enemies are weakened. If they beat us, our army, including the Nagas, would be in retreat. Your imagination can fill in the rest. You win both ways.'

Surapadman smiled. 'That does have an attractive ring to it.'

— ⁂ —

Parvateshwar and Anandmayi were housed in a separate wing of the massive Kashi palace, having arrived in the city recently. Anandmayi and Ayurvati had gone to meet Veerbhadra and the Gunas.

The Meluhan general was sitting in his chamber balcony, looking out towards the Ganga flowing in the distance.

'My Lord,' called out the doorman.

Parvateshwar turned. 'Yes?'

'A messenger has just delivered a note for you.'

'Hand it to me.'

'Yes, My Lord.'

As the doorman came in, Parvateshwar asked, 'Who brought the message?'

'The main palace door-keeper, My Lord.'

Parvateshwar raised his brows. 'An outsider would not be allowed in, would he? What I wanted to know was who gave the message to the palace door-keeper?'

The doorman looked lost. 'How would I know, My Lord?'

Parvateshwar sighed. These Swadweepans had no sense of systems and procedures. It's a wonder that an enemy didn't just stroll into their key installations. He took the neatly sealed papyrus scroll from the doorman and dismissed him. Parvateshwar couldn't recognise the symbol on the seal. It appeared to be a star, the kind used in ancient astrological charts. He shrugged and broke it open. The script surprised him; it was one of the standard Meluhan military codes. This one was used exclusively by senior Suryavanshi military officers. It was meant for top secret messages during times of war. For all others, the words in the scroll would have been absolute gibberish.

Lord Parvateshwar, it's time to prove your loyalty to Meluha. Meet me in the garden behind the Sankat Mochan temple at the end of the third prahar. Come alone.

Parvateshwar caught his breath. He instinctively looked towards the door. He was alone. He tucked the scroll into the pouch tied to his waistband.

He knew what he had to do.

The sound of bells, drums and prayer chants rent the morning air, day after day, at the Sankat Mochan temple. Having thus awoken Lord Hanuman, the devotees then sing *bhajans,* as Lord Hanuman would do, to gently wake his master, Lord Ram. At the end of this elaborate *puja*, the great seventh Vishnu proceeds to grant *darshan*, the divine pleasure of *beholding him.* The silence at dusk, however, belied the exuberance of the dawn. This was the time when Parvateshwar strode into the great temple.

Parvateshwar looked back to ensure that nobody was following him. Then he walked swiftly towards the garden behind the temple. It was quiet. Parvateshwar approached a tree at the far end of the garden and sat leaning against it.

'How are you, General?' asked a soft, polite voice.

Parvateshwar looked up. 'I'll do a lot better when I see you.'

'Are you alone?'

'I wouldn't have come had I not been alone.'

There was silence for some time.

Parvateshwar got up to leave. 'If you are a true Meluhan, you would know that Meluhans don't lie.'

'Wait, General,' said Bhrigu, as he emerged from the shadows.

Parvateshwar was stunned. He recognised the *Saptrishi Uttradhikari.* He knew that despite wielding tremendous influence, Bhrigu had never interfered in the workings of Meluha. He found it hard to believe that Bhrigu could involve himself in mundane matters of the material world.

'I am taking a huge risk in meeting you face-to-face,' smiled Bhrigu. 'I had to be sure that you were alone.'

'What are you doing here, *Maharishiji*?' asked Parvateshwar, bowing to the *great sage.*

'I'm doing my duty. As you are doing yours.'

'But you have never interfered in earthly matters.'

'I have,' said Bhrigu. 'But only on rare occasion. And this is one such.'

Parvateshwar remained silent. *So Bhrigu is the true leader. He was the one who had sent the joint Meluha-Ayodhya fleet to attack Lord Shiva's convoy by stealth outside Panchavati.* Parvateshwar's respect for Bhrigu went down a notch. The great sage was human after all.

'You already know what you have to do,' said Bhrigu. 'I know that you will not support the fraud Neelkanth in attacking your beloved motherland.'

Parvateshwar bristled with anger. 'Lord Shiva is not a fraud! He's the finest man to have walked the earth since Lord Ram!'

Bhrigu stepped back, astonished. 'Perhaps I was wrong. Perhaps you do not love Meluha as much as I thought you did.'

'Lord Bhrigu, I would die for Meluha,' said Parvateshwar. 'For it is my duty to do so. But please don't make the mistake of thinking that I despise the Lord Neelkanth. He is my living God.'

Bhrigu frowned, even more surprised. He looked into Parvateshwar's eyes. The normally restrained sage's mouth fell open ever so slightly. He realised that he was looking at a rare man who spoke exactly what he thought. Bhrigu's tenor changed and became respectful. 'My apologies, great General. I can see that your reputation does you justice. I misunderstood you. Sometimes the hypocritical nature of the world makes us immune to a rare sincere man.'

Parvateshwar remained silent.

'Will you fight for Meluha?' asked Bhrigu.

'To my last breath,' whispered Parvateshwar. 'But I will fight according to Lord Ram's laws.'

'Of course.'

'We will not break the rules of war.'

Bhrigu nodded silently.

'I suggest, Maharishi*ji*,' said Parvateshwar, 'that you return to Meluha. I will follow in a few weeks.'

'It would not be wise to remain here, General,' said Bhrigu. 'If anything were to happen to you, the consequences for Meluha would be disastrous. Your army needs a good leader.'

'I cannot leave without taking my Lord's permission.'

Bhrigu thought he hadn't heard right. 'Excuse me? Did you say that you wanted to take permission from the Neelkanth before leaving?'

He was careful not to say 'fraud Neelkanth'.

'Yes,' answered Parvateshwar.

'But why would he allow you to leave?'

'I don't know if he will. But I know I cannot leave without his permission.'

Bhrigu spoke carefully. 'Uhhh, Lord Parvateshwar, I don't think that you realise the gravity of the situation. If you tell the Neelkanth that you are going to lead his enemies, he will kill you.'

'No, he won't. But, if he chooses to do so, then that will be my fate.'

'My apologies for sounding rude, but this is foolhardy.'

'No, it's not. This is what a devotee does if he chooses to leave his Lord.'

'But...'

'Lord Bhrigu, this sounds peculiar to you because you haven't met Lord Shiva. His companions don't follow him out of fear. They do so because he is the most inspiring presence in their lives. My fate has put me in a position where I am being forced to oppose him. It's breaking my heart. I need his blessings and his permission to give me the strength to do what I have to do.'

Bhrigu's slow nod revealed a glimpse of grudging respect. 'The Neelkanth must be a special man to inspire such loyalty.'

'He is not just a special man, Maharishi*ji*. He is a living God.'

Chapter 16

Secrets Revealed

'I think we've achieved what we came here for,' said Sati.

Gopal, Sati and Shiva had retired to their chambers in Surapadman's palace. As a mark of goodwill, Surapadman had persuaded them to stay on for a few days and allow him to ready a few weapons for Shiva's army.

'Yes, I agree,' said Gopal. 'Surapadman's offer of weapons, though token in nature, is symbolic of his having allied with us.'

'Not one other person from the Magadhan court has visited us though,' said Shiva. 'I hope that King Mahendra doesn't prevail upon Surapadman to do something unwise.'

'Do you think he may prevent our ships from passing through to Ayodhya?' asked Gopal.

'I can't be sure,' said Shiva. 'It's most likely he will cooperate, but it depends on how his father reacts.'

'Let's hope for the best,' said Sati.

'What about my proclamation, Pandit*ji*?'

'It will be ready and distributed in a few weeks from now,' said Gopal. 'Vasudev pandits from across the country will give us constant updates as to the reaction of the people as well as the nobility.'

'But what if the Vasudev pandits are discovered?'

'No, they won't. The royals may know that the Vasudev tribe has allied with the Neelkanth, but they will never know the identity of the Vasudevs within their kingdoms.'

Shiva let out a long-drawn breath. 'And so it shall begin.'

Bhagirath arrived in Kashi late in the evening and proceeded directly to the palace. On reaching there, he was informed that Shiva had gone to Magadh to explore an alliance with Surapadman. Bhagirath, therefore, met Ganesh and Kartik to share his news with them.

'The Ayodhyans seem to have a back-up plan,' said Bhagirath. 'They expect Magadh to block their ships from carrying their soldiers onwards up the Ganga and towards Meluha. Hence, they intend to cut through the forests and have their army move north-west, right up to Dharmakhet. From there, they can cross the Ganga and then use the newly-built road to march to Meluha.'

'That's logical,' said Ganesh. 'But it will be slow. It will be many months before they can cut through the dense forests and reach Meluha. The war may actually be over by that time.'

Bhagirath agreed. 'True.'

Ganesh leaned forward. 'But I can see that there is more.'

Bhagirath could hardly contain himself. 'I know the identity of the one who leads our enemies.'

'Maharishi Bhrigu?' suggested Kartik.

Bhagirath was amazed. 'How did you know?'

'*Baba's* friends, the Vasudevs, told us,' answered Ganesh.

Bhagirath had heard stories about the legendary Vasudevs. 'Do the Vasudevs really exist?'

'Yes they do, brave Prince,' said Kartik.

Bhagirath smiled. 'With friends like them, Lord Shiva doesn't need followers like me!'

Ganesh laughed. 'He could not have known when he agreed to your suggestion, that the Vasudevs would reveal the identity of the main conspirator.'

'Of course,' said Bhagirath. 'But at least we now know about their back-up plan of marching through the impenetrable forests to the north-west of Ayodhya.'

'Yes, that is useful information, Bhagirath,' said Ganesh.

Kartik suddenly sat up. 'Prince Bhagirath, did you meet Maharishi Bhrigu personally?'

'Yes.'

Kartik looked at Ganesh with concern.

'What's the matter?' asked Bhagirath.

'Did he look into your eyes while speaking with you, Bhagirath?' asked Ganesh.

'Where else would he be looking if he was talking to me?'

Kartik looked up at the ceiling. 'Lord Ram, be merciful.'

'What happened?' asked a confused Bhagirath.

'We've been told that Lord Bhrigu can read your mind by looking into your eyes,' said Kartik.

'What? That's impossible!'

'He's a *Saptrishi Uttradhikari*, Bhagirath,' said Ganesh. 'Very few things are impossible for him. If he was distinctly looking into your eyes, chances are he has read your conscious thoughts. So he may have some very sensitive information about our plans.'

'Good Lord!' whispered Bhagirath.

'I want you to carefully recall what you were thinking about while speaking with Lord Bhrigu,' said Ganesh.

'I spoke about...'

Kartik interrupted Bhagirath. 'It doesn't matter what you spoke. What matters is what you thought.'

Bhagirath closed his eyes and tried to remember. 'I thought that my imbecile father could not have been the true leader of the conspiracy.'

'That's no secret,' said Ganesh. 'What else did you think about?'

'I remember a feeling of dread when I realised that Lord Bhrigu is the true leader.'

'I would have ideally not let him know your fears,' said Kartik. 'But this too cannot harm us.'

'I recall thinking that Lord Shiva had sent me to Ayodhya to discover the identity of the true leader.'

'Again,' said Ganesh, 'this is not very harmful information for an enemy to have.'

Bhagirath continued. 'I thought about being attacked by the joint Meluha-Ayodhya ships at Panchavati and how we repelled the attack.'

Ganesh cursed under his breath.

Bhagirath looked at Ganesh apologetically. 'So Maharishi Bhrigu knows about the Panchavati defences... I'm so sorry, Ganesh.'

Kartik patted Bhagirath reassuringly on his arm. 'You did not intend this to happen, Prince Bhagirath. Was there anything else?'

'Oh, Lord Rudra!' whispered Bhagirath.

Ganesh's eyes narrowed. 'What?'

'I thought about Parvateshwar wanting to defect to Meluha,' said Bhagirath.

Ganesh stopped breathing while Kartik held his head. 'What now, *dada*?'

'Get *mausi* here, Kartik,' said Ganesh, asking his brother to fetch the Queen of the Nagas, Kali. 'We know what we have to do, but *baba's* wrath will be terrible. *Mausi* can stand up to him. We need to know if she agrees with us.'

Kartik immediately left the room.

A shocked Bhagirath stared at Ganesh. 'I hope you are not thinking what I fear.'

'Do we have a choice, Bhagirath? Maharishi Bhrigu will try and contact Parvateshwar at the first opportunity and whisk him away.'

'Ganesh, Parvateshwar is my sister's husband. We cannot kill him!'

Ganesh raised his hands in exasperation. 'Kill him? What are you talking about, Bhagirath?'

Bhagirath remained silent.

'I only want to arrest General Parvateshwar so that he cannot escape.'

Bhagirath was about to say something when Ganesh interrupted him.

'We have no choice. If Parvateshwar goes over to their side, it would be disastrous for us. He is a brilliant strategist.'

Bhagirath sighed. 'I am not contradicting you. What needs to be done has got to be done. But we cannot kill him. I will not be responsible for making my sister a widow.'

'I wouldn't dream of killing a man like Parvateshwar. But we've got to arrest him. For all we know, Maharishi Bhrigu may already be attempting to make contact with him.'

— ⅄Ⓘ⋃↟⊛ —

A moonless night hung over an eerily quiet *Assi Ghat* in Kashi. The normally busy *Port of Eighty* did receive a small number of ships at night, but the darkness had kept away even the few brave captains who attempted night dockings.

A silent and pensive Parvateshwar was walking back from the ghat. He had just dropped a shrouded Bhrigu to a waiting rowboat which would take him to a ship anchored in the middle of the river. Bhrigu intended to stop at Prayag for a short while and then proceed to Meluha.

'General Parvateshwar!'

Parvateshwar looked up to see Kali. The flickering light from the torches revealed that she was accompanied by Ganesh, Kartik and about fifty soldiers. Parvateshwar smiled.

'You've brought fifty soldiers to down one man?' asked Parvateshwar, his hand resting on his sword hilt. 'You think too highly of me, Queen Kali.'

'Were you planning to escape, General?' asked Kali.

The soldiers rapidly surrounded Parvateshwar, making escape impossible.

Parvateshwar was about to answer when he saw a familiar figure next to Kartik.

'Bhagirath?'

'Yes,' answered Bhagirath. 'This is a sad day for me.'

'I'm sure it is,' said Parvateshwar sarcastically, before turning to Kali. 'So what do you plan on doing, Queen Kali? Kill me straight away or wait till the Lord Neelkanth returns?'

'So you admit that you are a traitor,' said Kali.

'I admit to nothing since you haven't asked anything.'

'I did ask you if you were attempting an escape.'

'If that were the case, I wouldn't be walking *away* from the Assi Ghat, Your Highness.'

'Have you met Maharishi Bhrigu?' asked Ganesh.

Parvateshwar never lied. 'Yes.'

Kali sucked in a sharp breath, reaching for her sword.

'*Mausi*,' said Ganesh, pleading with the Naga queen to keep her temper in check. 'Where is the Maharishi, General?'

'He's back on a boat,' said Parvateshwar, 'probably on his way to Meluha.'

'You know what comes next, don't you?' asked Kali.

'Do I get a soldier's death?' asked Parvateshwar. 'Will you

all attack me one by one so I have the pleasure of killing a few of you? Or will you just pounce on me like a pack of cowardly hyenas?'

'Nobody is getting killed, General,' said Ganesh. 'We Nagas have a justice system. Your treachery will be proven in court and then you will be punished.'

'No Naga is going to judge me,' said Parvateshwar. 'I recognise only two courts: the one sanctioned by the laws of Meluha and the other of the Lord Neelkanth.'

'Then you shall receive justice from the Neelkanth when he returns,' said Kali, before turning towards the soldiers. 'Arrest the General.'

Parvateshwar didn't argue. He stretched out his hands as he looked at the crestfallen face of the man handcuffing him. It was Nandi.

— ⅄⦶Ʊ⍋⊛ —

Shiva, Sati and Gopal were dining in the Neelkanth's chamber at Magadh.

'The captain of the ship met me in the evening,' said Sati. 'All the weapons have been loaded. We can sail for Kashi tomorrow morning.'

'Good,' said Shiva. 'We can begin our campaign within a few weeks.'

Gopal had anticipated this. 'I have already sent a message to the pandit of the Narsimha temple in Magadh. He will relay it to King Chandraketu, who will then set sail with an armada and await further instructions at the port of Vaishali.'

'Bhagirath, Ganesh and Kartik will travel with them to Ayodhya,' said Shiva. 'Ganesh will lead the Eastern Command.'

'A wise choice,' said Gopal.

'The Western Army, comprising the Vasudevs, the Nagas

and those Brangas who have been assigned to the Nagas, will attack Meluha under my command. We will set sail along with Kali and Parvateshwar within a week of reaching Kashi.'

'I have already sent a message to Ujjain,' said Gopal. 'The army has marched out with dismantled sections of our ships which will be reassembled on the Narmada. We will sail together to the Western Sea and farther up the coast, to Lothal.'

'What about your war elephants, Pandit*ji*?' asked Sati. 'How will they reach Meluha?'

'Our elephant corps will set out from Ujjain through the jungles, and meet us at Lothal,' answered Gopal.

'Gopal*ji*, can the Narsimha temple pandit send out a message to Suparna in Panchavati as well?' asked Shiva. 'Kali has appointed her the commander of the Naga army in her absence. They should join us at the Narmada.'

'I shall do that, Neelkanth,' said Gopal.

Chapter 17

Honour Imprisoned

An underground chamber beneath the royal palace had been converted into a temporary prison for General Parvateshwar. Though the public prisons of peaceful Kashi were humane, it would have been a slight to a man of Parvateshwar's stature to be imprisoned along with common criminals. The spacious chamber, though luxuriously appointed, was windowless. Not taking any chances, Parvateshwar's hands and legs had been securely shackled. While a platoon of crack Naga troops guarded the sole exit, two senior officers watched over Parvateshwar at all times. Nandi and Parshuram kept first watch.

'My apologies, General,' said Parshuram.

Parvateshwar smiled. 'You don't need to apologise, Parshuram. You are following orders. That is your duty.'

Nandi sat opposite Parvateshwar, but kept his face averted.

'Are you angry with me, Major Nandi?' asked Parvateshwar.

'What right do I have to be angry with you, General?'

'If there's something about me that's troubling you, then you have every right to be angry. Lord Ram had asked us to "always be true to ourselves".'

Nandi remained silent.

Parvateshwar smiled ruefully and then looked away.

Nandi gathered the courage to speak. 'Are you being true to yourself, General?'

'Yes, I am.'

'Forgive me, but you are not. You're betraying your living God.'

With visible effort, Parvateshwar kept his temper in check. 'It is only the very unfortunate who must choose between their God and their *swadharma*.'

'Are you saying that your *personal dharma* is leading you away from Good?'

'I'm saying no such thing, Major Nandi. But my duty towards Meluha is most important to me.'

'Rebelling against your God is treason.'

'Some may hold that rebelling against your country is a greater treason.'

'I disagree. Of course, Meluha is important to me, I would readily die for it. But I wouldn't fight my living God for the sake of Meluha. That would be completely wrong.'

'I'm not saying that you're wrong, Major Nandi.'

'Then you admit to being wrong yourself.'

'I didn't say that either.'

'How can that be, General?' asked Nandi. 'We're talking about polar opposites. One of us has got to be wrong.'

Parvateshwar smiled. 'It is such a staunch Suryavanshi belief: the opposite of truth has to be untruth.'

Nandi remained silent.

'But Anandmayi has taught me something profound,' said Parvateshwar. 'There is your truth and there is my truth. As for the universal truth, it does not exist.'

'The universal truth does exist, though it has always been an enigma to human beings,' smiled Parshuram. 'And it will continue to remain an enigma for as long as we are bound to this mortal body.'

— ⅄ ◎ ℧ ♆ ⊛ —

Anandmayi stormed into Bhagirath's chambers in the Kashi palace, brushing the guard aside.

'What the hell have you done?' she shouted.

Bhagirath immediately rose and walked towards his sister. 'Anandmayi, we had no choice...'

'Dammit! He is my husband! How dare you?'

'Anandmayi, it is very likely he will share our plans with...'

'Don't you know Parvateshwar? Do you think he will ever do anything unethical? He used to walk away whenever you spoke about the Lord Neelkanth's directives. He's not aware of any of your "confidential" military plans!'

'You're right. I'm sorry.'

'Then why is he under arrest?'

'Anandmayi, it wasn't my decision...'

'That's rubbish! Why is he under arrest?'

'He might escape if...'

'Do you think he couldn't have escaped had he wanted to? He is waiting to meet the Lord Neelkanth. Only then will he leave for Meluha.'

'That's what he said but...'

'But? What the hell do you mean "but"? Do you think Parvateshwar can lie? Do you think he is even capable of lying?'

'No.'

'If he has said that he will not leave till Lord Shiva returns, then believe me he's not going anywhere!'

Bhagirath remained silent.

Anandmayi stepped up to her brother. 'Are you planning to assassinate him?'

'No, Anandmayi!' cried a shocked Bhagirath. 'How can you even think I would do such a thing?'

'Don't pull this injured act on me, Bhagirath. If anything were to happen to my husband, even an accident, you know that the Lord Neelkanth's anger will be terrible. You and your allies may discount me, but you are scared of him. Remember his rage before you do something stupid.'

'Anandmayi, we are not...'

'The Lord Neelkanth will be back in a week. Until then, I'm going to keep a constant vigil outside the chamber where you have imprisoned him. If anyone wants to harm him, he will have to contend with me first.'

'Anandmayi, nobody is going to...'

She turned and strode away stiffly, causing Bhagirath to trail off mid-sentence. She pushed aside the diminutive Kashi soldier standing in her path and slammed the door behind her even as the soldier fell.

— ⁂ —

Ayurvati placed a hand on Anandmayi's shoulders. The Ayodhyan princess was sitting outside the chamber where Parvateshwar had been imprisoned. She had refused to move for the last few days.

'Why don't you go to your room and sleep,' said Ayurvati. 'I'll sit here.'

A determined Anandmayi shook her head. Wild horses couldn't drag her away.

'Anandmayi...'

'They aren't even letting me meet him, Ayurvati,' sobbed Anandmayi.

Ayurvati sat down next to Anandmayi. 'I know...'

Anandmayi turned towards the Naga soldiers standing guard at the door. 'MY HUSBAND IS NO CRIMINAL!'

Ayurvati took Anandmayi's hand in hers. 'Calm down... These soldiers are only following orders...'

'He's no criminal... He's a good man...'

'I know...'

Anandmayi rested her head on Ayurvati's shoulders and began to cry.

'Calm down,' said Ayurvati soothingly.

Anandmayi raised her head and looked at Ayurvati. 'I don't care if the entire world turns against him. I don't even care if the Neelkanth turns against him. I will stand by my husband. He is a good man... a good man!'

'Have faith in the Neelkanth. Have faith in his justice. Speak to him the moment he arrives in Kashi.'

— ⚹ —

The sun was directly overhead as Shiva's ship prepared to dock at Assi Ghat. Shiva, Sati and Gopal were at the balustrade.

'I do not understand why King Athithigva has to organise a grand reception every time I come here,' said Shiva as he looked at the giant canopy and vast throngs of people waiting.

Gopal smiled. 'I don't think Lord Athithigva orders his people to assemble, my friend. The people gather of their own accord to welcome their Neelkanth.'

'Yes, but it is so unnecessary,' said Shiva. 'They shouldn't be taking a break from their work to welcome me. If they really do want to honour me, they should work even harder at their jobs.'

Gopal laughed. 'People have a tendency to do what they want to do rather than what they should be doing.'

The ship was now close enough for them to see the expressions of the people on the dock, even the nobility standing farther away on higher ground.

'Something is not right,' said Sati.

'Why is everyone looking troubled?' asked Gopal.

Shiva studied the crowds carefully. 'You're right. Something's wrong.'

'King Athithigva seems disturbed,' said Sati.

'Kali, Ganesh, Kartik and Bhagirath are in a heated discussion,' said Shiva. 'What's troubling them so much?'

Sati tapped Shiva lightly. 'Look at Anandmayi.'

'Where?' asked Shiva, not finding her in the area cordoned off for the nobility.

'She's in the crowd,' said Sati, gesturing with her eyes. 'Right where the ship's gangplank will land.'

'Perhaps she wants to talk to you the moment you step off, my friend,' said Gopal.

'She looks deeply agitated, Shiva,' said Sati.

Shiva scanned the entire port area. And he softly asked, 'Where's Parvateshwar?'

— ⁂ —

The guards stepped aside as the Neelkanth stormed into the temporary prison. Sati, Gopal, Anandmayi and Kali could hardly keep pace.

He encountered Veerbhadra, Parshuram and Nandi in deep conversation with a fettered Parvateshwar.

'What the hell is the meaning of this?' shouted a livid Shiva.

'My Lord,' said Parvateshwar as he rose, the chains clinking.

Nandi, Veerbhadra and Parshuram rose too.

'Remove his chains!'

'Shiva,' said Kali softly, 'I don't think that is wise...'

'Remove his chains now!'

Nandi and Parshuram immediately set to work. The chains were removed with great haste. Parvateshwar rubbed his wrists, helping the blood flow freely.

'Leave me alone with Parvateshwar.'

'Shiva...' said Veerbhadra.

'Have I not made myself clear, Bhadra? Everybody leave right now!'

Kali shook her head disapprovingly, but obeyed. The others stepped out without any sign of protest.

Shiva turned to Parvateshwar, his eyes blazing with fury.

Parvateshwar was the first to speak. 'My Lord...'

Shiva raised his hand, signalling for him to keep quiet. Parvateshwar obeyed immediately. Shiva looked away as he walked back and forth, breathing deeply to calm his mind. He remembered his uncle Manobhu's words.

Anger is your enemy. Control it. Control it.

Much as he tried, Shiva could feel the fury welling up within him like a coiled snake waiting to strike. But his mind also told him that the issue at hand was far too important to allow anger to cloud his judgement.

Once he had breathed some calm into his mind and heart, Shiva turned to Parvateshwar. 'Tell me this is not true. Just say it and I will believe you, regardless of what anyone else says.'

'My Lord, this is the most difficult decision I have ever had to make in my life.'

'Do you intend to fight me, Parvateshwar?'

'No, My Lord. But I'm duty-bound to protect Meluha. I hope some miracle ensures that you and Meluha are not on opposite sides.'

'Miracle? Miracle? Are you a child, Parvateshwar? Do you think it is possible for me to compromise with Meluha where the Somras is concerned?'

'No, My Lord.'

'Do you think that the Somras is not evil?'

'No, My Lord. The Somras is evil. I have stopped using it from the moment you said that it was evil.'

'Then why would you fight to protect the Somras?'

'I will only fight to protect Meluha.'

'But they are on the same side!'

'That is my misfortune, My Lord.'

'You stubborn...'

Shiva checked himself in time. Parvateshwar remained silent. He knew the Neelkanth's anger was justified.

'Is Bhrigu forcing you to do this? Has he captured somebody who is important to you? We can take care of that. No one important to you will get hurt as long as I am alive.'

'Maharishi Bhrigu is not forcing me in any way, My Lord.'

'Then who in Lord Rudra's name is making you do this?'

'My soul. I have no choice. This is what I must do.'

'That does not make any sense, Parvateshwar. Do you actually believe that your soul is forcing you to fight for Evil?'

'My soul is only making me fight for my motherland, My Lord. This is a call that I cannot refuse. It is my purpose.'

'Your soul is taking you down a dangerous path, Parvateshwar.'

'Then so be it. No danger should distract one from walking one's path.'

'What nonsense is this? Do you think Bhrigu cares about you? All he cares for is the Somras. Trust me, once your purpose is served, you will be killed.'

'All of us will die when we have served our purpose. That is the way of the universe.'

Shiva covered his face with his hands in sheer frustration.

'I know you are angry, My Lord,' said Parvateshwar. 'But your purpose is to fight Evil. And you must do all that you can to accomplish it.'

Shiva continued to stare at Parvateshwar silently.

'All I am asking is for you to understand that just like you have to serve your purpose, I must serve mine. Your soul will not allow you to rest till you have destroyed Evil. My soul will not allow me to rest till I have done all that I can to protect Meluha.'

Shiva ran his hands over his face, trying desperately to maintain his calm. 'Do you think I am wrong, Parvateshwar?'

'Please, My Lord. How can I ever think that? You would never do anything that is wrong.'

'Then can you please explain the strange workings of your mind? You will not walk with me, although you admit that my path is right. Instead, you insist on walking on a path which leads to your death. In the name of Lord Rudra, why?'

'*Svadharma nidhanam shreyaha para dharmo bhayaavahah*,' said Parvateshwar. 'Death in the course of performing one's own duty is better than engaging in another's path, for that is truly dangerous.'

Shiva stared hard at Parvateshwar for what seemed like an eternity, then turned around and bellowed.

'Nandi! Bhadra! Parshuram!'

They rushed in.

'General Parvateshwar will continue to remain our prisoner,' said Shiva.

'As you command, My Lord,' said Nandi, saluting Shiva.

'And Nandi, the General will not be chained.'

Chapter 18

Honour or Victory?

'I say that we have no choice,' said Kali. 'I agree we cannot kill him, but he must remain our prisoner here till the end of the war.'

Shiva and his family, along with Gopal, were assembled in the Neelkanth's private chambers at the Kashi palace.

Ganesh glanced at a seething Sati and decided to hold his counsel.

Kartik, however, had no such compunctions. 'I agree with *mausi.*'

Shiva looked at Kartik.

'I know that it is a difficult decision,' continued Kartik. 'Parvateshwar*ji* has behaved with absolute honour. He was not privy to any of our strategy discussions. He could have escaped on multiple occasions, but did not. He waited till you returned so he could take your permission to leave. But you're the Neelkanth, *baba.* You have the responsibility for India on your shoulders. Sometimes, for the sake of the larger good, one has to do things that may not appear right at the time. Perhaps, a laudable end can justify some questionable means.'

Sati glared at her younger son. 'Kartik, how can you think that a great end justifies questionable means?'

'*Maa*, can we accept a world where the Somras continues to thrive?'

'Of course we can't,' said Sati. 'But do you think that this struggle is only about the Somras?'

Ganesh finally spoke up. 'Of course it is, *maa*.'

'No, it is not,' said Sati. 'It is also about the legacy that we will leave behind, of how Shiva will be remembered. People from across the world will analyse every aspect of his life and draw lessons. They will aspire to be like him. Didn't we all criticise Lord Bhrigu for using the *daivi astras* in the attack on Panchavati? The Maharishi must have justified what he did with arguments similar to what you're advocating. If we behave in the same way then what will differentiate us from him?'

'People only remember victors, *didi*,' said Kali. 'For history is written by victors. They can write it however they want. The losers are always remembered the way the victors portray them. What is important right now is for us to ensure our victory.'

'Please allow me to disagree, Your Highness,' said Gopal. 'It is not true that only victors determine history.'

'Of course, it is,' said Kali. 'There is a Deva version of events and an Asura version of events. Which version do we remember?'

'If you talk about the present-day India, then yes, the Deva version is remembered,' said Gopal. 'But even today, the Asura version is well known outside of India.'

'But we live here,' said Kali. 'Why should we bother about the beliefs that prevail elsewhere?'

'Perhaps I have been unable to make myself clear, Your Highness,' said Gopal. 'It's not just about the place, but also about the time. Will the Deva version of history always be remembered the way it is? Or is it possible that different versions will emerge? Remember, if there's a victor's version of events, then there's a victim's narrative that survives equally. For as long as the victors remain in command, their version holds ground. But if history has taught us one thing, it is that communities rise and fall in eminence just as surely as the tides ebb and flow. There comes a time when victors do not remain as powerful, when the victims of old become the elite of the day. Then, one will find that narratives change just as dramatically. This new version becomes the popular version in time.'

'I disagree,' dismissed Kali. 'Unless the victims escape to another land, like the Asuras, they will always remain powerless, their experiences dismissed as myths.'

'Not quite,' said Gopal. 'Let me talk about something that is close to your heart. In the times that we live, the Nagas are feared and cursed as demons. Many millennia ago, they were respected. After winning this war they will become respectable and powerful once again as loyal allies of the Neelkanth. Your version of history will then begin to gain currency once again, won't it?'

An unconvinced Kali chose to remain silent.

'An interesting factor is the conduct of the erstwhile victims in the new era,' said Gopal. 'Armed with fresh empowerment, will they seek vengeance on the surviving old elite?'

'Obviously the victims will nurse hatred in their hearts. Would you expect them to be filled with the milk of human kindness?' asked Kali, sarcastically.

'You hate the Meluhans, don't you?'

'Yes, I do.'

'But how do you feel about the founding father of Meluha, Lord Ram?'

Kali was quiet. She held Lord Ram in deep reverence.

'Why do you revere Lord Ram, but reject the people he left behind?' asked Gopal.

Sati spoke up on her sister's behalf. 'That is because Lord Ram treated even his enemies honourably, quite unlike the present-day Meluhans.'

Shiva observed Sati with quiet satisfaction.

'A man becomes God when his vision moves beyond the bounds of victors and losers,' said Sati. 'Shiva's message has to live on forever. And that can only happen if both the victors and the losers find validation in him. That he must win is a given. But equally critical is his winning the right way.'

Gopal was quick to support Sati. 'Honour must beget honour. That is the only way.'

Shiva walked to the balcony and gazed at the massive Kashi Vishwanath temple on the Sacred Avenue, and beyond it at the holy Ganga.

Everyone was poised for his decision.

He turned and whispered, 'I need some time to think. We will meet again tomorrow.'

— ⅄ⓄƱ♆⊛ —

Sati looked down. The clear waters of the lake lay below her. The fish swam rapidly, keeping pace with her as she flew over the water, towards the banks in the distance.

She looked up towards a massive black mountain, different in hue from all the surrounding mountains, topped by a white cap of snow. As she drew close, her vision fell upon a yogi on the banks of the lake. He wore a tiger-skin skirt. His long, matted hair had been tied up in a bun. His muscular body was covered by numerous battle scars. A small halo, almost like the sun, shone behind his head. A crescent moon was lodged in his hair while a snake slithered around his neck. A massive trident stood sentinel beside him, half-buried in the ground. The face of the yogi was blurred, though. And then the mists cleared.

'Shiva!' said Sati.

Shiva smiled at her.

'Is this your home? Kailash?'

Shiva nodded, never once taking his eyes off her.

'We shall come here one day, my love. When it's all over, we shall live together in your beautiful land.'

Shiva's smile broadened.

'Where are Ganesh and Kartik?'

Shiva didn't answer.

'Shiva, where are our sons?'

Suddenly, Shiva started ageing. His handsome face was rapidly overrun by wrinkles. His matted hair turned white almost instantaneously. His massive shoulders began to droop, his taut muscles dissolving before Sati's very eyes.

Sati smiled. 'Will we grow old together?'

Shiva's eyes flew wide open. Like he was looking at something that did not make sense.

Sati looked down at her reflection in the waters. She frowned in surprise. She hadn't aged a day. She still looked as young as always. She turned back towards her husband. 'But I've stopped using the Somras. What does this mean?'

Shiva was horror-struck. Tears were flowing fiercely down his wrinkled cheeks as his face was twisted in agony. He reached out with his hand, screaming loudly. 'SATI!'

Sati looked down. Her body was on fire.

'SATI!' he screamed once again, getting up and running towards the lake. 'DON'T LEAVE ME!'

Still facing Shiva, Sati began to fly backwards, faster and faster, the wind fanning the flames on her body. But even through the blaze she could see her husband running desperately towards her.

'SATI!'

Sati woke up with a start. The beautifully carved Kashi palace ceiling looked ethereal in the flickering torch-light.

The only sound was that of the water trickling down the porous walls, cooling the hot dry breeze as it flowed in. Sati instinctively reached out to her left. Shiva wasn't there.

Alarmed, she was up in a flash. 'Shiva?'

She heard him call out from the balcony. 'I'm here, Sati.'

Walking across, she could make out Shiva's silhouette in the darkness as he leaned back in an easy chair, focussed on the Vishwanath temple in the distance. Nestling comfortably against him on the armrest, she reached out her hand and ran it lovingly through her husband's locks.

It wasn't a full moon night, but there was enough light for Shiva to clearly see his wife's expression.

'What's the matter?' asked Shiva.

Sati shook her head. 'Nothing.'

'Something's wrong. You look disturbed.'

'I had a strange dream.'

'Hmmm?'

'I dreamt that we were separated.'

Shiva smiled and pulled Sati close to him, embracing her. 'You can dream all you want, but you're never getting away from me.'

Sati laughed. 'I don't intend to.'

Shiva held his wife close, turning his gaze back to the Vishwanath temple.

'What are you thinking?' asked Sati.

'I'm just thinking that marrying you was the best thing I ever did.'

Sati smiled. 'I'm not going to disagree with that. But what specifically brought that up at this time?'

Shiva ran his hand along Sati's face. 'Because I know that for as long as you're with me, you will always keep me centred on the right path.'

'So, you've decided to do the right thing with...'

'Yes, I have.'

Sati nodded in satisfaction. 'We will win, Shiva.'

'Yes, we will. But it has to be the right way.'

'Absolutely,' said Sati, and quoted Lord Ram. 'There is no wrong way to do the right thing.'

A select assembly awaited the arrival of Parvateshwar, who was to be produced in the court of Kashi during the second prahar. The Kashi nobility was represented by Athithigva alone. Shiva sat impassively, his closest advisors around him in a semi-circle: Gopal, Sati, Kali, Ganesh and Kartik. Bhagirath and Ayurvati stood at a distance. Anandmayi was missing.

Shiva nodded towards Athithigva.

Athithigva called out loudly. 'Bring the General in.'

Parshuram, Veerbhadra and Nandi escorted Parvateshwar into the hall. The Meluhan general was unchained, keeping in mind Shiva's explicit orders. He glanced briefly at Sati before turning to look at Shiva. The Neelkanth's rigid face was inscrutable. Parvateshwar expected to be put to death. He knew Shiva would not have wanted to do it, but the others would have convinced him of the necessity of getting rid of the general.

Parvateshwar also knew that regardless of what happened to him, he would treat the Neelkanth with the honour that the Lord deserved. The general clicked his heels together and brought his balled right fist up to his chest. And then, completing the Meluhan military salute, he bowed low towards the Neelkanth. He did not bother with anyone else.

'Parvateshwar,' said Shiva.

Parvateshwar immediately looked up.

'I do not want to drag this on for too long,' said Shiva. 'Your rebellion has shocked me. But it has also reinforced my conviction that we are fighting Evil and it'll not make things easy for us. It can lead even the best amongst us astray, if not through inducements then through dubious calls of honour.'

Parvateshwar continued to stare at Shiva, waiting for the sentence.

'But when one fights against Evil, one has to fight with Good,' said Shiva. 'Not just on the side of Good, but with Good in one's heart. Therefore, I have decided to allow you to leave.'

Parvateshwar couldn't believe his ears.

'Go now,' said Shiva.

Parvateshwar was only half listening. This magnificent gesture from the Neelkanth had brought tears to his eyes.

'But let me assure you,' continued Shiva coldly, 'the next time we meet, it will be on a battlefield. And that will be the day I will kill you.'

Parvateshwar bowed his head once again, his eyes clouded with tears. 'That will also be the day of my liberation, My Lord.'

Shiva stayed stoic.

Parvateshwar looked up at Shiva. 'But for as long as I live, My Lord, I shall fight to protect Meluha.'

'Go!' said Shiva.

Parvateshwar smiled at Sati. She brought her hands together in a polite but expressionless Namaste. Parvateshwar mouthed the word '*Vijayibhav*' silently, blessing his God-daughter with *victory*.

As he turned around to leave, he saw Ayurvati and Bhagirath standing by the door. He walked up to them.

'My apologies, Parvateshwar,' said Bhagirath.

'I understand,' replied Parvateshwar, impassively.

Parvateshwar looked at Ayurvati.

Ayurvati just shook her head. 'Do you realise that you are leaving one of the most magnificent men ever born?'

'I do,' said Parvateshwar. 'But I will have the good fortune of dying at his hands.'

Ayurvati breathed deeply and patted Parvateshwar on his shoulder. 'I will miss you, my friend.'

'I will miss you too.'

Parvateshwar scanned the room quickly. 'Where's Anandmayi?'

'She's waiting for you at the port,' said Bhagirath, 'beside the ship that will take you away.'

Parvateshwar nodded. He looked back one last time at Shiva and then walked out.

— ⁂ —

The harbour master came up to him just as Parvateshwar reached the Assi Ghat. 'General, your ship is berthed in that direction.'

He began walking in the direction indicated. Parvateshwar saw Anandmayi by the gangplank of a small vessel, obviously a merchant ship.

'Did you know that I would be allowed to leave honourably?' asked a smiling Parvateshwar as soon he reached her.

'When they told me this morning to arrange a ship to sail up the Ganga,' said Anandmayi, 'I could surmise it was not to carry your corpse all the way to Meluha and display it to the Suryavanshis.'

Parvateshwar laughed.

'Also, I never lost faith in the Neelkanth,' said Anandmayi.

'Yes,' said Parvateshwar. 'He's the finest man born since Lord Ram.'

Anandmayi looked at the ship. 'It's not much, I admit. It will not be comfortable, but it's quick.'

Parvateshwar suddenly stepped forward and embraced Anandmayi. It took a surprised Anandmayi a moment to respond. Parvateshwar was not a man given to public displays of affection. She knew that it was deeply uncomfortable for him so she never tried to embrace him in public.

Anandmayi smiled warmly and caressed his back. 'It's all over now.'

Parvateshwar pulled back a little, but kept his arms around his wife. 'I will miss you.'

'Miss me?' asked Anandmayi.

'You have been the best thing that ever happened to me,' said an emotional Parvateshwar, tears in his eyes.

Anandmayi raised her eyebrows and laughed. 'And I will continue to happen to you. Let's go.'

'Let's go?'

'Yes.'

'Where?'

'Meluha.'

'You're coming to Meluha?'

'Yes.'

Parvateshwar stepped back. 'Anandmayi, the path ahead is dangerous. I honestly don't think that Meluha can win.'

'So?'

'I cannot permit you to put your life in danger.'

'Did I seek your permission?'

'Anandmayi, you cannot...'

Parvateshwar stopped speaking as Anandmayi held his hand, turned around and started walking up the gangplank. Parvateshwar followed quietly with a smile on his face and tears in his eyes.

Chapter 19

Proclamation of the Blue Lord

'I have a brilliant plan,' said Daksha.

Daksha and Veerini were dining at the royal palace in Devagiri. A wary Veerini put the morsel of roti and vegetables back on her plate. She stole a quick glance towards the attendants standing guard at the door.

'What plan?' asked Veerini.

'Believe me,' said an excited Daksha. 'If we can implement it, the war will be over even before it has begun.'

'But, Lord Bhrigu...'

'Even Lord Bhrigu would be impressed. We will be rid of the Neelkanth problem once and for all.'

'Wasn't it the Neelkanth *opportunity* some years ago?' asked a sarcastic Veerini.

'Don't you understand what is happening?' asked an irritated Daksha. 'Do I have to explain everything to you? War is about to break out. Our soldiers are training continuously.'

'Yes, I'm aware of that. But I think we should keep out of this and leave the matter entirely to Lord Bhrigu.'

'Why? Lord Bhrigu is not the Emperor of India. I am.'

'Have you told Lord Bhrigu that?'

'Don't irritate me, Veerini. If you're not interested in what I have to say, just say so.'

'I'm sorry. But I think it's better to leave all the decision-making to Lord Bhrigu. All we should be concerned about is our family.'

'There you go again!' said Daksha, raising his voice. 'Family! Family! Family! Don't you care about how the world will see me? How history will judge me?'

'Even the greatest of men cannot dictate how posterity will judge them.'

Daksha pushed his plate away, shouting, 'You are the source of all my problems! It is because of you that I haven't been able to achieve all that I could have!'

Veerini looked at the attendants and turned back towards her husband. 'Keep your voice down, Daksha. Don't make a mockery of our marriage.'

'Ha! This marriage has been a mockery from the very beginning! Had I a more supportive wife, I would have conquered the world by now!'

Daksha got up angrily and stormed out.

— ⁂ —

'This is a huge mistake,' said Kali. 'In his obsession for the right way, your father may end up losing the war.'

Ganesh and Kartik were in her chamber in the Kashi palace.

'I disagree, *mausi*,' said Kartik. 'I think *baba* did the right thing. We have to win, but we must do it the right way.'

'I thought you were in agreement with us,' said a frowning Kali.

'I was. But *maa's* words convinced me otherwise.'

'In any case, *mausi*,' said Ganesh. 'It has happened. Let us not fret over it. We should focus on the war instead.'

'Do we have a choice?' asked Kali.

'*Baba* told me that I will lead the war effort in Ayodhya,' said Ganesh. 'Kartik, you will be with me.'

'We'll destroy them, *dada*,' said Kartik, raising his clenched right fist.

'That we will,' said Ganesh. '*Mausi*, are you sure about Lothal and Maika?'

'I've already asked Suparna to send ambassadors to Governor Chenardhwaj,' said Kali. 'Trust me, he is a friend.'

— ⅄ⵀⴲ ⏃ ⊗ —

Kartik bent and touched his mother's feet.

'*Vijayibhav*, my child,' said Sati, as she applied the red *tilak* on Kartik's forehead for good luck and victory.

Sati, Ganesh and Kartik were in the Neelkanth's chamber. Ganesh, whose forehead already wore the *tilak*, looked at his brother with pride. Kartik was still a child, but was already universally respected as a fearsome warrior. The two sons of Shiva were to set sail down the Ganga and meet their allies in Vaishali. From there, they were to turn back, sail up the Sarayu and attack Ayodhya. Ganesh turned towards his father and touched his feet.

Shiva smiled as he pulled Ganesh up into an embrace. 'My blessings are not as potent as those that emerge from your mother's heart. But I know that you will make me proud.'

'I'll try my best, *baba*,' smiled Ganesh.

Kartik turned and touched Shiva's feet.

Shiva embraced his younger son. 'Give them hell, Kartik!'

Kartik grinned. 'I will, *baba*!'

'You should smile more often, Kartik,' said Sati. 'You look more handsome when you do.'

Kartik smiled broadly. 'The next time we meet, I will certainly be grinning from ear to ear. For our army would have defeated Ayodhya by then!'

Shiva patted Kartik on his back before turning to Ganesh. 'If Ayodhya is willing to break ranks with Meluha after my proclamation is made public, then I would rather we don't attack them.'

'I understand, *baba*,' said Ganesh. 'This is why I'm taking Bhagirath along with me. His father may hate the Ayodhyan prince, but Bhagirath still has access to many members of the nobility. I'm hoping he'll be able to convince them.'

'When will the proclamation come out, *baba*?' asked Kartik.

'Next week,' answered Shiva. 'Stay in touch with the Vaishali Vasudev pandit for the reactions from across different kingdoms in Swadweep. You will know then what to expect in Ayodhya also.'

'Yes, *baba*,' said Kartik.

Shiva turned to Ganesh. 'I've been told that you have recruited Divodas and the Branga soldiers into the army.'

'Yes,' said Ganesh. 'We'll leave on board five ships and meet the combined Branga-Vaishali army at Vaishali. I'm told they have two hundred ships. Fifty of them have been deputed to the Western Army under your command and are on their way to Kashi. The remaining hundred and fifty ships will be with me. We will attack Ayodhya with a hundred and fifty thousand men.'

'That won't be enough to conquer them,' said Sati. 'But we should be able to tie them down.'

'Yes,' answered Ganesh.

'We'll hold them back, *baba*,' said Kartik. 'I promise you.'

Shiva smiled.

— ⸻ —

'How is she now?' asked Kali.

Kali was at the river gate of the eastern palace of the

Kashi king Athithigva. The palace had been built on the eastern banks of the Ganga, which was considered inauspicious for any permanent construction. The kings of Kashi had bought this land to ensure that no Kashi citizen lived on that side. It was in this palace that Athithigva had housed his Naga sister, Maya. Ganesh and Kali's open presence had given Athithigva the courage to let his sister come out of hiding.

'Your medicines have helped, Your Highness,' said Athithigva. 'At least she's not in terrible pain anymore. The *Parmatma* has sent you as an angel to help my sister.'

Kali smiled sadly. She knew it was a matter of time before Maya, a singular name for conjoined twins who were fused into one body from the chest down, would die. It was a miracle that Maya had lived for so long. On discovering her presence, Kali had immediately supplied Naga medicines to lessen her suffering. Since she was to leave with the Western Army the next day, she had come over to leave the rest of her medicines with Maya.

'I'm no angel,' said Kali. 'If the *Parmatma* had any sense of justice, he wouldn't make an innocent person like Maya suffer so much. I'm doing all I can to set right his injustices.'

Athithigva shrugged in resignation but was too pious to curse God.

Kali's gaze turned towards the Ganga where the fifty ships of the Branga armada had dropped anchor just the previous day. The mighty fleet covered the width of the river, stretching to the opposite bank. A nervous excitement was palpable throughout Kashi. The smell of war was in the air.

The flotilla's initial progress would be slow for they would first sail west against the current and then southwards up the Chambal. After disembarking, the soldiers would then march towards the Narmada. The second voyage would take them along the course of the Narmada out to the Western Sea and then north towards Meluha.

'Let's go in,' said Kali. 'I'd like to see Maya before I leave.'

— ⚹ —

'Your Highness!' said Kanakhala, running into Daksha's private office.

Daksha looked up at his prime minister as he slipped the papyrus he was reading back into the drawer of his desk. 'Where's the fire, Kanakhala?'

'Your Highness,' said a frantic Kanakhala, obviously carrying something within the folds of her *angvastram*, 'you need to see this.'

Kanakhala placed a thin stone tablet on her emperor's desk.

'What's this?' asked Daksha.

'You need to read it, Your Highness.'

Daksha bent over to read.

To all of you who consider yourselves the children of Manu and followers of the Sanatan Dharma, this is a message from me, Shiva, your Neelkanth.

I have travelled across our great land, through all the kingdoms we are divided into, met with all the tribes that populate our fair realm. I have done this in search of the ultimate Evil, for that is my task. Father Manu had told us Evil is not a distant demon. It works its destruction close to us, with us, within us. He was right. He told us Evil does not come from down below and devour us. Instead, we help Evil destroy our lives. He was right. He told us Good and Evil are two sides of the same coin. That one day, the greatest Good will transform into the greatest Evil. He was right. Our greed in extracting more and more from Good turns it into Evil. This is the universe's way of restoring balance. It is the Parmatma's *way to control our excesses.*

I have come to the conclusion that the Somras is now the greatest

Evil of our age. All the Good that could be wrung out of the Somras has been wrung. It is time now to stop its use, before the power of its Evil destroys us all. It has already caused tremendous damage, from the killing of the Saraswati River to birth deformities to the diseases that plague some of our kingdoms. For the sake of our descendants, for the sake of our world, we cannot use the Somras anymore.

Therefore, by my order, the use of the Somras is banned forthwith.

To all those who believe in the legend of the Neelkanth: Follow me. Stop the Somras.

To all those who refuse to stop using the Somras: Know this. You will become my enemy. And I will not stop till the use of the Somras is stopped. This is the word of your Neelkanth.

Daksha looked completely stunned. 'What the hell?!'

'I do not understand what this means, Your Highness,' said Kanakhala. 'Do we stop using the Somras?'

'Where did you find this?'

'I didn't, Your Highness,' said Kanakhala. 'It was hung on the outer wall of the temple of Lord Indra near the public bath. Half the citizens have seen this already and they would be talking to the other half by now.'

'Where is Maharishi Bhrigu?'

'My Lord, what about the Somras? Should I...'

'Where is Maharishi Bhrigu?'

'But if the Neelkanth has issued this order, we have no choice...'

'Dammit, Kanakhala!' screamed Daksha. 'Where is Maharishi Bhrigu?'

Kanakhala was silent for an instant. She did not like the way her Emperor had spoken to her. 'Maharishi Bhrigu had left Prayag a little more than a month back. That was the last I heard of him, Your Highness. It will take him at least two more months to reach Devagiri.'

'Then we will wait for him before deciding on a course of action,' said Daksha.

'But how can we oppose a proclamation from the Neelkanth, Your Highness?'

'Who is the Emperor, Kanakhala?'

'You are, Your Highness.'

'And have I taken a decision?'

'Yes, Your Highness.'

'Then that is the decision of Meluha.'

'But the people have already read this...'

'I want you to put up a notice stating that this proclamation is fraudulent. It cannot have been made by the true Neelkanth, for he would never go against the greatest invention of Lord Brahma, the Somras.'

'But is that true, Your Highness?'

Daksha's eyes narrowed, his temper barely in check. 'Kanakhala, just do what I tell you to do. Or I will appoint someone else as prime minister.'

Kanakhala brought her hands together in a formal but icy Namaste, and turned to leave. She couldn't resist a final parting shot, though. 'What if there are other notices like this?'

Daksha looked up. 'Send bird couriers across the empire. If they see such a notice anywhere, it must be pulled down and replaced with what I have asked you to put up instead. This notice is bogus, do you understand?'

'Yes, Your Highness,' said Kanakhala.

As she closed the door behind her, Daksha angrily flung the tablet on the floor. 'Mine is the only practical way to stop this. Maharishi Bhrigu *has* to listen to me.'

Chapter 20

The Fire Song

Gopal was shown into Shiva's private chamber the moment he arrived. He joined Shiva and Sati in the balcony and seated himself in an empty chair beside them.

'What news do you have, Pandit*ji*?' asked Shiva.

It had been a week since Shiva's proclamation banning the Somras had been released simultaneously across Meluha and Swadweep. He was hoping that the people would follow his edict.

'My pandits across the country have sent in their reports.'

'And?'

'The reactions in Meluha are very different from those in Swadweep.'

'I expected that.'

'It appears that the Swadweepan public has embraced the proclamation. It feeds into their bias against Meluha. It is seen as yet another instance of the Meluhans unfairly conspiring to stay ahead of the rest. And remember, none of them use the Somras anyway. So it's no real sacrifice for them.'

'But how have the kings reacted?' asked Sati. 'They are the ones in control of the armies.'

'It's too early to say, Sati*ji*,' said Gopal. 'But I do know that all the kings across Swadweep are in intense consultations with their advisors even as we speak.'

'But,' said Shiva, 'the Meluhans have rejected my proclamation, haven't they?'

Gopal took a deep breath. 'It's not so simple. My pandits tell me that the Meluhan public seemed genuinely disturbed by your proclamation initially. There were serious discussions in city squares and a lot of them believed that they needed to follow their Neelkanth's words.'

'Then what happened?'

'The Meluhan state is supremely efficient, my friend. The notices were taken down within the first three days, at least in all the major cities. They were replaced by a Meluhan royal order stating that they had been put up by a fraud Neelkanth.'

'And the people believed it?'

'The Meluhans have learnt to trust their government completely over many generations, Shiva,' said Sati. 'They will always believe everything that their government tells them.'

'Also,' said Gopal, 'you have been missing from Meluha for many years, my friend. There are some who are genuinely beginning to wonder if the Neelkanth has forgotten Meluha.'

Shiva shook his head. 'It looks like a war is inevitable.'

'Daksha, and more importantly Lord Bhrigu, will ensure that,' said Gopal. 'But at least our message has reached most Meluhans. Hopefully some of them will start asking questions.'

Shiva looked at the ships of the Brangas, Vasudevs and the Nagas anchored on the Ganga. 'We set sail in two days.'

— ⁂ —

'No, no!' Shiva shook his head in dismay. 'You've got it all wrong!'

Light and shadows from the bonfire danced on the faces of Brahaspati, Veerbhadra, Nandi and Parshuram as they looked at Shiva, suitably chastened. It was a moonless night and a cold wind swept in from the river. The Ganga's waters shimmered in the reflected light of the torches from the Branga fleet.

In keeping with ancient tradition, the Gunas sang paeans to the five holy elements ahead of major war campaigns, to invoke their protection and as a mark of manhood in the face of danger. The friends of the great Guna, Shiva, had gathered to honour this custom. For they would set sail at the crack of dawn tomorrow.

Shiva passed his chillum to Parshuram and decided to teach his friends the fine art of singing.

'The real trick is in here,' said Shiva, pointing towards his diaphragm.

'I thought it was in here,' said Veerbhadra playfully, pointing to his throat.

Shiva shook his head. '*Bhadra!* The vocal chords are basically a wind instrument. Your skill depends on the control over your breath, which means, essentially, the lungs. And lungs can be regulated through the diaphragm. Try to sing from here and you will find that you can project and modulate your voice with much greater ease.'

Nandi sang a note and then asked, 'Am I doing it right, My Lord?'

'Yes,' said Shiva, looking at Nandi's immense stomach. 'If you can feel the pressure of your diaphragm on your stomach, then you're doing it right. The other thing is to know when to take a breath. If you time it right, you will not have to struggle towards the end of the line. And if you don't struggle, then you will be able to finish your tune without having to rush through the last few notes at the end.'

Brahaspati, Parshuram and Nandi listened with rapt attention.

Veerbhadra however, was sarcastically nodding, his eyes mirthful. He didn't much care for tuneful singing. 'Shiva, you're taking it too seriously! It's the thought that counts. So long as I sing it with my heart, I don't think anybody should object even if I murder the song!'

Parshuram waved his hand at Veerbhadra before turning to Shiva. 'My Lord, why don't you sing and show us how it's done?'

As everyone pinned their eyes upon him, Shiva looked up at the sky, rubbed his cold neck and cleared his throat.

'Enough of the theatrics,' said Veerbhadra. 'Start singing now.'

Shiva slapped Veerbhadra playfully on his arm.

'All right now,' said Shiva with a genial grin. 'Silence!'

Veerbhadra light-heartedly put his finger on his lips as Brahaspati glared at him. Veerbhadra reached out, took the chillum from Parshuram, and inhaled deeply.

Shiva closed his eyes and went within himself. A sonorous hum emerged from within his very being, as he hit the perfect note right away. A lilting melody of words followed and the enraptured audience understood their significance. It was the prayer of a warrior to *agni* or *fire*, imploring it for a blessing. The warrior would repay this honour by feeding his enemies in combat to the hungry flames of a cremation pyre. The listeners intrinsically understood that Shiva's *prakriti* was closest to fire rather than the other four elements, each of which had Guna war songs dedicated to them.

It was a short song but the audience was spellbound. Shiva ended his performance to a robust round of applause.

'You still have it in you,' smiled Veerbhadra. 'That cold throat hasn't thrown your voice off.'

Shiva smiled and took the chillum from Veerbhadra. He

was about to take a drag when he heard someone cough softly near the entrance of the terrace. All the friends turned to find Sati standing there.

Shiva put the chillum down as he smiled. 'Did we wake you?'

Sati laughed as she walked up to Shiva. 'You were loud enough to awaken the entire city! But the song was so beautiful that I didn't mind being woken up.'

Sati took a seat next to Shiva as everyone laughed.

Shiva smiled. 'It's a song from back home. It steels a warrior's heart for battle.'

'I think the singing was more beautiful than the song,' said Sati.

'Yeah, right!' said Shiva.

'Why don't you try to sing it, My Lady?' asked Nandi.

'No, no,' said Sati. 'Of course not.'

'Why not?' asked Veerbhadra.

'I would love to hear you sing, my child,' said Brahaspati.

'Come on,' pleaded Shiva.

'All right,' said a smiling Sati. 'I'll try.'

Shiva picked up the chillum and offered it to Sati. She shook her head.

Sati had been playing close attention to Shiva's singing. The song, its melody and lyrics, had already been committed to memory. Sati closed her eyes, drew in a deep breath and entrusted herself to the music. The song began on a very low octave. She reproduced his earlier performance precisely, allowing the words to flow out in a flood when needed and letting them hang delicately when required. She quickened her breathing as she approached the end and took the notes higher and higher into a crescendo where the song finished in a flourish. Even the bonfire seemed to respond to the call of the elemental fire song from Sati.

'Wow!' exclaimed Shiva, embracing her as she finished. 'I didn't know you could sing so beautifully.'

Sati blushed. 'Was it really that good?'

'My Lady!' said a stunned Veerbhadra. 'It was fantastic. I always thought that Shiva was the best singer in the universe. But you are even better than him.'

'Of course not,' said Sati.

'Of course, yes,' said Shiva. 'It almost seemed like you had pulled all the surrounding fire into yourself.'

'And I shall keep it within me,' said Sati. 'We're going to be fighting the war of our lives. We need all the fire that we can get!'

— ⁂ —

Ganesh and Kartik had been housed in the private chambers of King Maatali of Vaishali. They were accompanied by the Ayodhyan prince Bhagirath and the Branga king Chandraketu. Their information was that Magadh was not preparing a blockade to stop their ships from sailing to Ayodhya. But the Magadhan army had been put on alert and training sessions had been doubled. Either this was a precautionary step taken by Surapadman or the Magadhans planned on attacking them once they had exhausted themselves against the Ayodhyans.

'We cannot afford to lose either men or ships as we pass Magadh,' said Ganesh. 'We've got to be prepared for the worst.'

'The way I see it,' said Bhagirath, pointing to the river map on the table, 'their primary catapults will be in the main fort on the west bank of the Sarayu. They have a small battlement on the east side as well, from where they can load catapults and throw fire barrels at us, but considering the size of this battlement, I don't think that the range will be long. So my suggestion is that we sail our ships closer to the eastern bank of the Sarayu.'

'But not too close though!' said Chandraketu.

'Of course,' said Bhagirath. 'We don't want to be the casualties of the smaller catapults from the east either.'

'Also, we can make sure that we don't just depend on our sails but also have our oarsmen in position to row the ships rapidly,' said the Vaishali king, Maatali.

'But no matter which side of the river we sail and how quickly we row, we will still lose people if they decide to attack,' said Ganesh. 'Remember, we are on ships, so we cannot get our men to disembark fast enough to retaliate.'

'Why don't we increase their risks?' asked Kartik.

'How?' asked Ganesh.

'Have half the soldiers from every ship go ashore before Magadh. We could get them to march on the eastern banks alongside our ships. The reduced load will make our ships move faster. Also, the Magadhan battlement on the eastern bank would know there is a massive contingent of enemy soldiers marching just outside their walls. They would have to think twice before doing anything stupid.'

'I like the idea,' said Bhagirath.

'I've thought of something even simpler,' said Chandraketu.

Ganesh looked at the Branga king.

'The Magadh royalty is amongst the poorest in Swadweep,' said Chandraketu. 'It's a powerful kingdom but King Mahendra has lost a considerable part of his fortune owing to both his son Ugrasen's as well as his own gambling addiction.'

'Do you want to bribe them?' asked Bhagirath.

'Why not?'

'For one, we would need massive amounts of money. A few thousand gold coins will not suffice. We won't be negotiating with some army officers but the royalty itself.'

'Will one million gold coins be enough?'

Bhagirath was stunned. 'One million?'

'Yes.'

'Just to make it through unharmed?'

'Yes.'

'Lord Rudra, be praised. That will be nearly six months of tax collections for the Magadhan royalty.'

'Exactly. I'll dispatch Divodas to Magadh with half the amount in the first ship. The other half can be handed over once our last ship has passed by safely.'

'But they could use this wealth to buy weapons,' said Kartik.

'They will not be able to do that quickly enough,' said Chandraketu. 'And what they do with the money after the war is over is not my concern.'

'Can you really afford to give away so much gold, Your Highness?' asked Ganesh.

Chandraketu smiled. 'We have more than enough, Lord Ganesh. But it means nothing to us. I would give away all the gold that we have to stop the Somras.'

'All right,' said Ganesh. 'I see no reason why it won't work.'

Chapter 21

Siege of Ayodhya

The cool northerly wind was a welcome relief for Shiva as he sat on the deck of the lead ship with Gopal, Sati and Kali clustered around him. As the fifty-six vessel armada made steady progress upriver, he knew that in just a few weeks they would reach close to the headwaters of the Chambal from where the soldiers would disembark and march to the Narmada.

'Pandit*ji*, do your ships that wait for us at the Narmada have the additional capacity to carry the fifty-five thousand soldiers who accompany us?' asked Kali.

'Yes, Your Highness,' said Gopal. 'Our ships have been specially designed to handle this additional load since we knew that we would not be able to use the ships we're currently on.'

'Judging by the maps we've seen,' said Sati, 'we should reach Lothal in three months, right Pandit*ji*?'

'Yes, Sati*ji*,' said Gopal. 'If the winds favour us, we may even make it earlier.'

'Have you received word from the Lothal governor, Kali?' asked Shiva.

'My ambassador will be waiting with the information at the Narmada,' answered Kali. 'Trust me, we will gain easy entry into Lothal. But don't expect a huge addition of troops into our army. Lothal doesn't have more than two or three thousand soldiers.'

'We don't really need their soldiers,' said Shiva. 'We have enough troops of our own. Along with the Vasudev army that waits for us at the Narmada, your own Naga army and this Branga force, we have more than a hundred thousand men. That's equal to the strength of the Meluhan army.'

'We can easily defeat them,' said Kali.

'I do not intend to attack,' said Shiva.

'I think you should.'

'All we need to do is destroy the Somras manufacturing facility, Kali.'

'But you have the Nagas with you. You shouldn't be afraid of a direct confrontation.'

'I'm not afraid. I just don't see the sense in it. It will distract us from our main purpose – the destruction of the Somras. We do not want to destroy Meluha. Don't forget that.'

'I'll count on you to remind me of that every time I forget,' said Kali.

Shiva smiled and shook his head.

— ⁂ —

The voyage up the Sarayu had been surprisingly uneventful. The Magadhans did not attack Ganesh's ships. The massive convoy was so long that the guards on the Magadhan towers spent an entire day watching ships go by.

A little over a week later, Ganesh ordered his ships to drop anchor. Kartik, Bhagirath, Chandraketu and Ganesh got into a small boat and rowed ashore. The forest had been cleared up to a fair distance. Divodas, the leader of the Branga immigrants in Kashi, waited there along with twenty men.

Ganesh jumped off as soon as the boat beached, and

waded through the shallow water to the river bank. The others followed. He touched his head to the ground as he reached the shore. He looked deep into the forest, remembering a time long ago when he had hidden behind the trees and observed his mother. 'Kartik, this is the Bal-Atibal Kund. This is where *Saptrishi* Vishwamitra taught Lord Ram his legendary skills.'

Kartik's eyes were wide open in awe. He bent down and touched the ground with his hand and whispered, 'Jai Shri Ram.'

The others around him repeated it. 'Jai Shri Ram.'

'Kartik,' said Ganesh, 'this ground was blessed by *Saptrishi* Vishwamitra and Lord Ram. But its greatness has been forgotten by many. We may have to redeem the honour of this land with blood.'

Kartik took a moment to understand. 'Do you think Surapadman might chase us?'

Ganesh smiled. 'He *will* chase us. Trust me. I see the siege of Ayodhya as a bait to draw Surapadman out of Magadh. Once he is out, we will destroy his army and capture his city. We'll be able to stop Ayodhyan ships easily with Magadh blockading the Ganga. And the battle to decide the fate of Magadh should be fought here. For this is where I would like *you* to attack him.'

'I would have thought that Surapadman would prevail on his father.'

'He is a clever man, Kartik. From what I have understood, his instinct was to support us but in the face of so much opposition, he will do what is now in his best interest. And he does have much to gain. He will win the favour of his father and his countrymen by taking revenge for his brother's death. He will come as the saviour for Ayodhya, albeit a little late so that Ayodhya is weakened. And who knows, he may even capture the sons of the Neelkanth...

Wouldn't that make him a strong ally of Bhrigu?' asked Ganesh with an ironic smile. 'Yes, brother, he will attack and he will learn that clever men should always listen to their instincts.'

Kartik took a deep breath and looked up at the sky before turning back to Ganesh with resolve writ large in his eyes. 'We will turn the river red with blood, *dada*.'

Bhagirath looked at Kartik with a familiar sensation of fascination and fear.

'Why this ground, Lord Ganesh?' asked Chandraketu.

'Your Highness,' answered Ganesh, 'as you can see, this stretch is long and narrow. That will lure Surapadman into anchoring his ships along the banks, thus stretching his army thin. The forest is not too far from the shore. Which means our main army can remain hidden behind the trees. We will leave only a small contingent on the beach.'

Bhagirath smiled. 'That will be a very juicy bait. Surapadman will probably imagine that this is a small brigade that has deserted the siege of Ayodhya. He'll want to kill them to give his soldiers a taste of victory.'

'Right,' said Ganesh. 'But the main battle will not be on land. We just have to pin him down here, which will, in all honesty, take a lot of courage, since he will have a large force. That is why I want Kartik here. But Surapadman will be defeated in the river itself.'

'How?' asked Chandraketu.

'I'll move back from Ayodhya and ram his ships from the front,' said Ganesh. 'I've also asked King Maatali to wait in the Sharda River along with thirty ships. The Sharda meets the Sarayu downriver. The Vaishali fleet will sail up the Sarayu once Surapadman's ships have passed, placing them behind the Magadhans. My contingent will attack from in front while the Vaishali forces will hit them from behind. Kartik has to hold Surapadman in position for long enough to make his fleet of ships immobile.'

'He will be sandwiched between King Maatali's ships and yours,' said Chandraketu. 'He won't stand a chance.'

'Exactly.'

'Sounds like a good plan,' said Bhagirath.

'The success of the battle hinges on two points,' said Ganesh. 'Firstly, Kartik has to entice Surapadman to anchor his ships and attack our soldiers on shore. In the absence of that he will keep moving, and his larger boats will ram through my smaller ships and possibly turn the tide in his favour. Our ships are light, manoeuvrable and built for speed. The Magadhan ships are bigger and have been built for strength. If Kartik fails to lure Surapadman ashore, my side of our fleet may face heavy casualties. I must be in command to take care of that possibility.'

'And the second point?' asked Bhagirath.

'King Maatali must be positioned to block Surapadman's escape back to Magadh. That will close the pincer trap.'

Chandraketu doubted neither Kartik's courage nor his strategic mind. His words to the young warrior bespoke respect. 'You're on your own, Kartik. It's all up to you now.'

Kartik narrowed his eyes, his hand on his sword hilt. 'I'll draw him in, King Chandraketu. And once I do, I assure you I'll obliterate his entire army myself. Our ships won't even be required to join the battle.'

Ganesh smiled at his brother.

— ⅄ⓂƱ⇞⊗ —

Ganesh reached for another document from the stack on the desk and began to read, then paused to rub his tired eyes. He was seated in his private cabin, surrounded by messages from his informants about the progress of the assault. There were dozens of missives telling him every aspect from the mood of the Ayodhyan populace to the progress of the armourers in meeting the archers' demand for arrows. He had hardly slept in the weeks since the battle had begun and his body ached for rest, but these reports could not wait. It appeared that Ayodhya stood poised on the brink of surrender, and any misstep now could spell disaster. Kartik and Chandraketu sat patiently by his side, assisting Ganesh with the endless stream of messages. The three sat together in silence as they awaited Bhagirath's return, to hear news of his mission.

The siege of Ayodhya had begun over a month ago. Ganesh's navy had assaulted the city in the classical manner of the ancient war manuals. A large part of the fleet had been anchored along the west banks of the Sarayu in a double line, out of the range of the catapults on the fort walls of the eastern banks. The lined ships had extended up to the north of Ayodhya, just shy of the sheer cliff upriver where the Sarayu descended in a waterfall. Small lifeboats had been tied to the right of the ships in Ganesh's convoy, with guards present round the clock. This was to prevent devil boats from attempting to set fire to the vessels from the Ayodhya end. A section of the army had camped to the left of the ships, on the shore itself, to thwart guerrilla attacks from the Ayodhyans.

Farther to the south, Ganesh had anchored his ships and tied them together, across the river in rows of ten. Another line-up was just behind the first level of the blockade ships. Behind these, five fast-moving cutters would patrol the river farther downstream to attack any Ayodhyans who attempted to escape. Thus, any Ayodhyan ship attempting to run the river blockade had to battle through a thick line of twenty enemy ships and five quick cutters.

The forest around Ayodhya had been cleared by the defending army to give it a clear line of sight in case of an attack. Prasanjit, the Meluhan brigadier who had been left behind by Bhrigu, had tried hard to convince the Ayodhyans to extend the clearing area farther, but he had been unsuccessful. Ganesh had got his troops to cut a second line of trees beyond the clearing, as a precautionary fire line. Once the outer fire line had been established, Ganesh had ordered that the trees within the two clearings be set aflame. The intense heat generated would have resulted in the collapse of any tunnels around Ayodhya that could have served as passages for food to be smuggled into the city. The fire had burned for four continuous days and had had a demoralising effect on the citizens of 'the impenetrable city', establishing the steely resolve of their blockaders.

A cataract on a sheer cliff to the north of Ayodhya served as a natural barrier, which prevented ships from navigating farther north on the Sarayu. The Ayodhyans had built a channel into their walled shipyard just short of the cataract. The singular narrow channel of entry had been designed to be easily defendable. While this channel, passing through a gated wall, protected the Ayodhyan shipyard, it also allowed the enemy to block the exit route of their ships. Ganesh had used the leftover logs from the forest clearing to block this channel, effectively extending the siege of the city to the shipyard as well. All he had wanted was to box them in, and blocking the channel had ensured that he did not have to divert too many ships to blockade the shipyard.

Ganesh had known that the Meluhans had set up a bird courier system for the Ayodhyans. He had hit upon a very simple strategy to destroy this. He had placed six hundred archers on various treetops outside Ayodhya and along the Sarayu. These archers worked in eight-hour shifts, changing three times a day, maintaining a continuous twenty-four hour vigil. The orders had been very simple: shoot any and every bird that they saw in the sky. Most of these dead birds were retrieved by trackers. In doing so, not only did they retrieve messages exchanged between Meluha and Ayodhya, but the dead pigeons and other game birds were also a source of fresh meat for the soldiers.

Ayodhya drew fresh drinking water from the Sarayu through channels that extended from the river to within the city walls. The channels were fed by ingeniously designed giant water wheels constructed along the Sarayu. These wheels used the flow of the river to rotate. A series of buckets tied around the diameter would fill up with water and disgorge into the channels as they reached the top. Tall walls had been built around the wheels to protect them from any attack. However, there was a breach in the wall just below the water surface, from where the buckets filled up with water. This opening was fortified with bronze bars that were wide enough to allow water to run through, but not so wide as to allow a man to swim in between. But that hadn't stopped Ganesh.

Ganesh had deployed soldiers to swim across the Sarayu at night pulling small, floating wooden barrels. Within these barrels were smaller iron cans filled with oil. Water in the space between the wooden barrel and the iron can, and a slow fuse made of hemp, completed the device. Once lit, the fuse would ignite the oil, bringing the water to a boil. The consequent pressure of escaping steam would cause an explosion with the iron and wood themselves serving as shrapnel. The task of the skilled swimmers had been to strategically place the devices within the buckets of the water wheels, thus destroying them. The existing wells of Ayodhya could never quench the thirst of its innumerable residents.

Ganesh had allowed a small number of non-combatant

women and priests to come out of the city every day, to draw small amounts of water for personal use. He had also ordered that this number be progressively reduced every day until the Ayodhyans surrendered. It was a slow squeeze designed to ultimately make the people rise against their leaders. Ganesh's soldiers had added to the psychological warfare by berating the emerging Ayodhyans for going against the wishes of their Neelkanth and siding with Meluha. They had been informed that the only reason why Ganesh had refrained from shooting missiles into Ayodhya was so as not to harm innocent citizens who had had nothing to do with the decision of their emperor, Dilipa.

The daily two-way traffic of some Ayodhyans had also served another important purpose. It had enabled the hidden Vasudev pandit of the Ramjanmabhoomi temple to send an emissary to Ganesh with information collected from all the Vasudev pandits from across the temples of India.

After a couple of weeks, Ganesh had offered to send Bhagirath to meet with the nobles of his father's kingdom to reach a mutually acceptable compromise. The opportunity had been instantly grabbed by the Ayodhyans.

Ganesh stretched his tired muscles and glanced at Kartik and Chandraketu seated beside him in the cabin. They also had hardly slept but masked their exhaustion and continued to peruse the documents. Ganesh smiled to himself. When this is done, he thought, we're all going to lock ourselves in our cabins and sleep for a week!

There was the sound of footsteps and a brief knock at the cabin door before it was pushed open. Bhagirath bowed slightly to Ganesh, his hair slightly ruffled from the wind, before entering to take a seat with the three men.

'What news, Bhagirath?' asked Ganesh, pushing the pile of messages to one side.

'I'm afraid it's not good.'

'Really?' asked Chandraketu. 'I thought the Ayodhyan army must be deeply divided. I cannot think of another reason why we were able to lay siege on the city so easily. No skirmishes, no guerrilla attacks, nothing. It could only mean that the army doesn't intend to fight.'

Bhagirath shook his head. 'You don't know Ayodhya, King Chandraketu. It was not the cowardice of their army but the indecisiveness of their nobility which worked in our favour. They have not been able to agree on the best way to attack us. Furthermore, Maharishi Bhrigu had brought in a Meluhan brigadier, Prasanjit, to oversee the Ayodhyan war preparations. All it achieved was further divisions within the city. By the time they agreed upon a strategy, we were already in control of the river. There was not much that they could do after that.'

'So?' asked Ganesh. 'Haven't their troubles opened the eyes of some at least?'

'No,' said Bhagirath. 'There is tremendous confusion within the city. Many Ayodhyans are fanatical devotees of Lord Shiva and are certain that the Neelkanth will not harm them. They refuse to believe that he has ordered this attack. This blind devotion seems to be working against us.'

'So who do they think has ordered this attack?' asked Chandraketu.

'Seeing the number of Brangas in the army, they think that it is you,' said Bhagirath.

Chandraketu raised his hands. 'Why would I attack Ayodhya?'

'They believe that Branga wants to be the overlord of Swadweep,' said Bhagirath. 'In the absence of Lord Shiva, there is nothing we can do to convince them otherwise. There are a few who do believe in the proclamation that was put up, but they are in a minority. They are outshouted by a very simple logic: "We have never used the Somras, so why would the Neelkanth attack us? He should attack Meluha." Of course, a few members of the nobility do use the Somras, but the people do not know that.'

'It is the opinion of the nobility that is more important right now,' said Kartik. 'The people do not control the army. So what do the nobles think?'

'The nobility is sharply divided. Some of them actually want us to succeed, which would give them a plausible reason to refuse to help Meluha. Others believe surrendering will mean terrible loss of face. These people want the army to gallantly strike out and sail to Meluha if only to prove to the rest of Swadweep that Ayodhya has the strength to do what it chooses to do.'

'How do we assist those who do not want to come to the aid of Meluha?' asked Ganesh.

'It's difficult,' said Bhagirath. 'My father made a brilliant move last week. He promised all of them a lifetime supply of the Somras.'

'What?'

'Yes. He told them that Lord Bhrigu has promised to supply the Somras powder to Ayodhya in massive quantities.'

'But how can Maharishi Bhrigu promise that?' asked Kartik. 'Where will it come from? Is the manufacturing facility capable of producing so much more?'

'It clearly must be,' said Bhagirath. 'In any case, this offer is open only to the nobility. So the numbers will be small.'

'Damn!' said Ganesh.

'My thoughts precisely,' said Bhagirath. 'This will allow them to remain alive for a hundred more years. No amount of gold can compete with that.'

'What do we do now?' asked Chandraketu.

'Prepare for war,' said Ganesh. 'They will make earnest attempts to break the siege.'

Chapter 22

Magadh Mobilises

Shiva, along with Sati, Gopal and Kali, watched the massive army board the Vasudev and Naga ships on the banks of the Narmada. The Vasudevs had tied some logs together to create floating platforms for the army to reach the anchored ships. A viewing platform had been built on a banyan tree near the banks. The leaves had been shorn off, to afford a panoramic view of the boarding operations. The line of ships stretched as far as the eye could see. Over one hundred thousand soldiers, comprising the Brangas, Vasudevs and Nagas, were boarding the vessels in an orderly manner. The voyage would be uncomfortable with two thousand men on every ship, but fortunately, the journey to Lothal would be short.

'We should be ready to sail out by tomorrow, Shiva,' said Kali.

'Has Suparna boarded?' asked Shiva.

Suparna, a fearsome warrior, was the leader of the Garuda Nagas.

'Not yet,' said Kali.

'May I meet her? I'd like to exchange some thoughts on the Nagas under her command.'

Kali raised her eyebrows. She had expected to lead the Nagas into the war.

'I'd like you to be with me, Kali,' said Shiva, mollifying her. 'I trust you. I'm going to be leading the search party into Meluhan cities to try and locate the Somras manufacturing facility. We'll have to work quietly and anonymously, while our army outside the city keeps the Meluhans busy.'

'You are very tactful, Shiva.'

Shiva frowned.

'You know how to get your way without making one feel that one has been cut down to size,' said Kali.

Shiva smiled, once again silent.

'But I understand that the search for the Somras facility is crucial,' said Kali. 'So it will be my honour to accompany you.'

'Excellent,' said Shiva, turning to Gopal. 'Any news from the Vasudevs, Pandit*ji*?'

'The siege of Ayodhya has been surprisingly easy,' said Gopal. 'The Ayodhyans have not fought back. Ganesh has a stranglehold over the city.'

'But has King Dilipa changed his stance?'

'Not yet. And Ganesh is, very wisely, not resorting to violence since that may rally the citizens around their king. We will have to be patient.'

'As long as the Ayodhyan army doesn't come to Meluha's aid, I'm happy. What about Magadh?'

'His ships are ready,' said Gopal. 'But Surapadman's army has not been mobilised as yet.'

Shiva raised his brows, clearly surprised. 'I didn't think Surapadman would let go of an opportunity like this. I would also imagine that his father, King Mahendra, would pressure him to attack us.'

'Let us see,' said Sati. 'Maybe Surapadman wants Ayodhya and our army to battle first. He would then be attacking a weakened enemy.'

Shiva nodded. 'Perhaps.'

— ⅄ⵀUⴷ⊛ —

'Look, Bhagirath,' said Ganesh.

The prince had just entered Ganesh's cabin. One of the soldiers had left a note from Meluha that was recovered from an injured bird. It was coded. But Bhagirath knew the encryption codes of Meluha-Ayodhya communication and had already trained Ganesh's soldiers on how to decrypt the messages.

Bhagirath read aloud. 'Prime Minister Siamantak, has Lord Bhrigu returned to Ayodhya? It has been months since he left Prayag but has still not reached Meluha. Should you have the knowledge, we would like to be informed about the location of Lord Shiva and General Parvateshwar.'

Ganesh didn't say anything, waiting for Bhagirath's reaction.

'It's been signed by Prime Minister Kanakhala,' said Bhagirath. 'Interesting.'

'Interesting indeed,' said Ganesh. 'Where is Lord Bhrigu? And why is the Meluhan Prime Minister enquiring about General Parvateshwar? Has he not reached as yet? Do they not know he has defected to their side?'

'Where do you think they are?' asked Bhagirath.

'They're certainly not in Meluha,' said Ganesh. 'That makes things easier for my father.'

'Do you think Lord Shiva has reached Meluha by now?'

'I think he's still a few weeks away.'

'And the Ayodhya army has not been able to leave,' said Bhagirath. 'The news just keeps getting better.'

Kartik suddenly rushed in. '*Dada!*'

'What's the matter, Kartik?'

'Magadh is mobilising.'

'Who told you? The Vasudev pandit?' asked Bhagirath.

'Yes,' said Kartik, turning back to Ganesh. 'I believe armaments are being loaded on to the ships. Soldiers have been asked to be on stand-by.'

Ganesh smiled. 'How many soldiers?'

'Seventy-five thousand.'

'Seventy-five thousand?' asked a surprised Bhagirath. 'Is Surapadman committing everything? Magadh will be left defenceless.'

'When are they expected to set sail?' asked Ganesh.

'Probably in two weeks' time,' said Kartik. 'At least that's what the Vasudev pandit surmised.'

'You should leave in the next few days,' said Ganesh. 'Take one hundred thousand men.'

'Why so many, *dada*?' asked Kartik. 'Don't you need some men here, with you?'

'I just need enough to be able to sail ships and shoot fire-arrows,' said Ganesh. 'If you do not succeed in holding Surapadman off at the Bal-Atibal Kund, he will just ram into us with his larger ships and drown us all. Our soldiers will be put to better use at your end, not mine.'

'I'll prepare to leave right away,' said Kartik.

— ⸻ —

A hundred thousand well-motivated soldiers reached the forests near the Bal-Atibal Kund in the early afternoon. The Ayodhyan prince had accompanied the army as the chief advisor to Kartik. King Chandraketu had stayed back with Ganesh to ensure that the Branga soldiers in Kartik's army would not be confused about the chain of command.

Immediately upon arrival, Kartik ordered the construction of water-proofed coracles which would serve as devil boats to set the Magadh fleet on fire. A thousand soldiers constructed them and then hid them on the eastern banks on the opposite side of the kund. They would destroy the enemy ships from the other side, even as the battle ensued in the area around the kund.

Hidden platforms had been constructed atop the trees to facilitate the relay of information back and forth between the two sides. A simple communication tool had been manufactured for these soldiers: small metallic pipes fitted on top of earthen pots containing anthracite, which burns with a short, but more importantly smokeless flame. The caps on these metallic pipes could be easily lifted open and then shut, allowing light out in a controlled manner. The apertures were small enough to give the impression of a collection of fire flies. For Kartik's soldiers though, the light signals would carry coded messages from both sides of the river.

Kartik wanted the area around the Bal-Atibal Kund to be left undisturbed. The army was to stay strictly within the forested area.

'I don't understand, Kartik. We do want our men on the beach if they're to serve as bait, don't we? At least, that is what Ganesh had in mind.'

'I would hesitate to underestimate Surapadman, Prince Bhagirath. And I daresay, he will not underestimate us either. If he sees a small number of our soldiers casually stationed in an area visible from the river, he may smell a trap. After all, if we were deserting our army, we wouldn't be stupid enough to camp where we could be seen, would we?'

'Fair enough. So what do you suggest?'

'We are on the west bank. Magadh is farther to our south, also on the west bank of the Sarayu. If we were to march along the river, where the forest is not too dense, Magadh would not be more than two or three weeks from here.'

Bhagirath smiled. 'You want Surapadman to guess our

actual strategy, that the Ayodhya siege was a feint to try to draw him out. He will realise that by conquering Magadh, we will have much more effective control over Ayodhyan ships sailing by, as compared to besieging Ayodhya itself.'

'Exactly. And if he is smart enough to suspect that, as I'm sure he is, he will have scouts looking out towards the forests running along the river. And when he gets reports of our massive army, he will draw the obvious conclusion: that we have marched out to conquer Magadh, while he is wasting his time sailing to Ayodhya.'

'Leave your home defenceless to conquer another land and you may find your own home getting conquered instead.'

'You got it,' said Kartik. 'Also, it will have credibility in Surapadman's eyes, for that's what he would expect a smart enemy to do. I do not see him underestimating us.'

'But what would stop him from just turning around and sailing back to Magadh?'

'Turning a large fleet of ships around in a river is easier said than done, especially if one is short of time. But even if Surapadman manages to do so, and speeds down the river to reach Magadh before us, he would know that our army could simply stop marching and not appear at the gates of his city. His own Magadhans may then believe that Surapadman ran away from the battle at Ayodhya using the false pretext of Magadh itself being in danger. A crown prince cannot afford to be perceived as a coward. So he would have no choice but to attack us here itself. What do you think?'

'I like the plan,' said Bhagirath. 'It should work with a good general like Surapadman, for he will have scouts riding along the river banks to keep him informed of what's going on. We have to be sure to attack those scouts but allow some of them to escape with information about the size of our army. Also, our camp in the forest stretches up to two kilometres.

When their ships pass our position, we should have soldiers disturb the birds on top of the trees at the beginning of our camp. Also, we could have some fires left "carelessly" aflame towards the end of our camp. Judging the vast distance between these two signals, Surapadman would assume that there is a massive enemy army marching south along the river bank. He would be forced to attack.'

'Right.'

'Let's have some devil boats on the western bank as well.'

'But the battle will be fought here on the west bank,' said Kartik, frowning. 'Their men would engage in battle here and our fire coracles would be clearly visible. Devil boats can set fire to ships only when they have an element of surprise. If they are visible then they can be easily sunk. That's why I have set up the devil boats on the eastern banks.'

'The fighting would happen on our side,' said Bhagirath. 'But Surapadman would be forced to land his men on the sands of the Bal-Atibal Kund, and nowhere else on the western side. It's almost impossible to land men in large numbers in the dense forest which runs along the river farther north. So if we keep our coracles up north, they would remain hidden from enemy eyes. As soon as his ships anchor to investigate our position, we'll attack them at the north end of his convoy.'

'Good point. I'll issue those orders.'

— ⅄ⵄⵙ —

Kartik's army was ready and poised for action as they heard the sounds of a massive navy rowing up the Sarayu. Judging by the dull drum-beats of the timekeepers and the faint sound of the oars negotiating the waters, it was fair to assume that the Magadhan ships would reach the Bal-Atibal Kund within the next hour or two.

Soldiers were immediately ordered to take battle positions. Weapons were checked, defences were tested.

Kartik walked up to the edge of the forest and surveyed the sands of the Bal-Atibal Kund as well as the river beyond. A crescent moon had failed to lift the darkness of the late hour of the night, which suited his strategy. A light seasonal fog had begun to spread along the river. Perfect! With a practiced eye he checked whether the communication pots were still visible in the fog and was pleased with what he saw.

Kartik turned to Bhagirath, and then looked farther ahead towards Divodas and the other commanders of the Branga army.

'My friends,' said Kartik. 'Unlike my father, I'm not good with words. So I will keep this short. The Magadhans will be fighting only for conquest and glory. Those are weak motivations. You are fighting for vengeance and retribution. For your families and for the soul of your nation. You are fighting to stop the Somras that has killed your children and crippled your people. You are fighting to stop the scourge of this Evil. You have to fight to the end; until they are finished. I don't want prisoners. I want them dead. If anyone takes the side of Evil, they forfeit the right to live. Remember! Remember the pain of your children!'

The Branga commanders roared together. 'Death to the Magadhans!'

'This land that we stand upon,' continued Kartik, 'has been blessed by the feet of Lord Ram. We shall honour him today with blood. Jai Shri Ram!'

'Jai Shri Ram!'

'To your positions!' ordered Kartik.

The Branga commanders hurried away. As soon as the men were out of earshot, Bhagirath spoke, 'Kartik, why do you want them all dead?'

'Prince Bhagirath, if there are too many Magadhan prisoners, we will have to leave behind a large force to keep watch over them. Our eventual purpose is to get as many soldiers as possible to Meluha. If the Magadhan army is decimated, we will not need to keep too many of our own soldiers in Magadh. Just a few thousand of them would be enough to control the city. Also, the killing of all the Magadhans would send a message to Ayodhya. It might make them reconsider their alliance with Meluha.'

Bhagirath was forced to accept Kartik's brutal but effective line of thought.

Chapter 23

Battle of Bal-Atibal Kund

The lead ship of the Magadhan navy passed the Bal-Atibal Kund. Kartik's army had heard the low monotonous sounds of rowing and the drumbeats of the timekeepers long before they had sighted the Magadhan ships.

Kartik motioned for a signal to be relayed by hand over a line of men who had been positioned for this purpose, till the message reached the southern end of the camp, more than a kilometre away. A group of soldiers pulled a rope quietly, releasing a net that had been tightly cast over a flock of birds. The birds took off suddenly, startled by their unexpected freedom. Kartik detected some movement in the Magadhan ships. They had clearly heard the birds.

Kartik strained his eyes. The Magadhan soldiers had their eyes pinned towards the top of the main masts.

'Shit!' whispered Bhagirath, as he realised the implications.

A small wry smile of appreciation for a worthy enemy flickered on Kartik's face. He turned to Divodas who stood right behind him. 'Divodas, send messages to our tree-top soldiers that the Magadhans have lookouts stationed on their crow's nests. Our soldiers should remain low to avoid detection.'

A crow's nest is built on top of the main masthead of the ship, where sailors would be stationed as lookouts to survey far and wide so as to report to the captain below on deck. This was a common practice on sea-faring ships, but was rarely used in river ships. Surapadman was obviously a cautious man for he had built crow's nests on his ships. Divodas left quietly to carry out Kartik's orders.

'The ships are pulling back their oars,' said Bhagirath, pointing forward.

As they were sailing against the natural flow of the river current, the Magadhan ships slowed down quickly. The sails were re-adjusted to bring the ships to a halt. Their earlier speed was such though, that at least ten ships passed the area where Kartik stood before Surapadman's fleet came to a standstill. The soldiers on the ships stared hard into the dense forests on the western banks.

'Now we wait,' said Kartik.

Bhagirath leaned over to Kartik. 'Their scout is a short distance behind us, close to the water's edge.'

Kartik stretched his arms in an exaggerated manner and then spoke to Divodas, loud enough for the Magadhan scout to hear. 'Check if their ships have started moving up ahead.'

Divodas moved towards the river, making the scout fall back silently. He returned almost instantaneously. 'Lord Kartik, their scout is swimming back to the ship.'

Kartik immediately rose and crept to the edge of the forest. He could see the Magadhan scout swimming noiselessly away.

'I expect the attack soon,' said Bhagirath. 'We should fall back to our positions.'

'Let's wait a few moments,' said Kartik. 'I want to see which ship he boards. It'll tell us where Surapadman is.'

'It's been almost half an hour,' said Bhagirath. 'What is he waiting for?'

Kartik and his army remained behind the forest line. They wanted to give Surapadman the impression that the Brangas did not wish to engage in a battle. They hoped he would be lulled into believing that he could launch a surprise attack.

Kartik suddenly exclaimed, 'Son of a bitch!'

'Lord Kartik?' asked Divodas.

'Send a message to our lookouts,' said Kartik. 'Tell them to communicate with those on the other side. I want to know what is happening there.'

Bhagirath slapped his forehead. 'Oh my God! We'd asked our lookouts to stay low!'

Divodas rushed off and messages were soon relayed across the Sarayu using light signals. He was back in no time with worrying news. 'They're mobilising on the other side, hidden by their massive vessels. Row boats are being lowered quietly into the river and soldiers are boarding it even as we speak. It looks like they're preparing to row downriver.'

'That cunning son of a flea-bitten dog!' said Bhagirath. 'He intends to row downriver, hidden by his own ships, and attack us from the south.'

'What do we do, Lord Kartik?' asked Divodas.

'Ask our lookouts if the Magadhans are disembarking from their tenth ship. That is where Surapadman is.' Turning to Bhagirath, Kartik continued. 'Prince Bhagirath, I suspect he will launch a two-pronged attack. There will be one at Bal-Atibal Kund. Surapadman would want to keep us busy here. In the meantime, another contingent of Magadhans would row down south, flank our southern side and aim to enter our camp from behind. We would be sandwiched between two sections of his army.'

'Which means we need to break up,' said Bhagirath. 'One

of us will stay here at the Bal-Atibal Kund, and the other will ride out to meet their southern force.'

'Exactly,' said Kartik.

Meanwhile, Divodas returned. 'Lord Kartik, they are disembarking from Surapadman's ship.'

'Prince Bhagirath,' said Kartik, 'You will lead our main force here. We have to ensure the Magadhans don't get past Bal-Atibal. I want this to be a death trap for them.'

'It'll be so, Kartik, I assure you. But do not leave too many from our forces with me. You will need a large number of soldiers to battle Surapadman in the south.'

'No I won't,' said Kartik. 'He's rowing downriver. He will not have any horses. I will.'

Bhagirath understood immediately. A single mounted cavalry warrior was equal to ten foot soldiers. He had the advantage of height as well as his horse's fearsome kicks. 'All right.'

Kartik snapped orders to Divodas even as he rose. 'Ride down south. Inform our forces to expect a Magadhan charge soon. You will be leading them. I'm going to ride out with two thousand cavalrymen in a giant arc from the west. I intend to attack Surapadman's forces from behind. Between my horses and your troops, we will crush them.'

Divodas smiled. 'That we will!'

'You bet!' said Kartik. 'Har Har Mahadev!'

'Har Har Mahadev!' said Divodas.

Divodas ran to his horse, swung onto the saddle and rode away.

Kartik appeared to be running over the instructions in his mind, not wanting to miss out a single detail.

'I have fought many battles, Kartik,' said Bhagirath with an amused look. 'Go fight yours. Let me take care of mine.'

Kartik smiled. 'We'll gift my father a famous victory.'

'That we shall,' said Bhagirath.

Kartik walked up to his horse, stretched up to put his left foot into the stirrup, for he was still quite short, and swung his right leg over to the other side, mounting his horse. Bhagirath, who had followed Kartik, saw the same steely look in the boy's eyes that he had seen many times during the animal hunts. A familiar sense of fear and fascination entered Bhagirath's heart. He smiled nervously and whispered, 'God have mercy on Surapadman...'

Kartik heard the remark and chuckled softly. 'He will have to be the one, for I won't.'

The son of the Neelkanth turned his horse and galloped away into the dark.

— ⅄ᴏᴜ⁂ —

The slender moon was now cloaked in clouds, its faint light hidden in the mist. Bhagirath could barely make out the lines of men in the wood beside him. He sensed them now by the sound of their breath rasping in the darkness. The metallic smell of sweat hung heavy in the air. Bhagirath could feel the perspiration beading on his upper lip, trickling into the corner of his mouth. Whispers came floating back to his ears from up and down the line – 'Har Har Mahadev... Har Har Mahadev...' – like a prayer as the men braced to face Surapadman's army.

Suddenly the moon burst through the clouds and Bhagirath could see men running up and down the length of the enemy ships carrying fire torches. They were lighting the arrows for the archers.

'Shields up!' screamed Bhagirath.

Bhagirath's soldiers, primarily Brangas, immediately prepared for the volley of arrows that would soon descend upon them. The sky lit up as the archers shot their fire arrows.

They flew out in a great arc before descending into the jungle. Bhagirath had kept his men strictly within the forest line, so the trees worked as their first line of defence. The few that got through were easily blocked by the raised shields.

The Magadhans had hoped that their fire arrows would set the forest aflame, causing chaos and confusion amongst the Brangas. But mist and the cold of the night had ensured dew formation on the leaves. The trees simply did not catch fire.

As the arrows stopped, Bhagirath roared loudly. 'Har Har Mahadev!'

His soldiers followed him as their cry rent the air, 'Har Har Mahadev!'

The Magadhans quickly lit another line of arrows and shot. Once again, the trees and the Branga shields ensured that Bhagirath's soldiers suffered no casualties.

The Brangas put their shields aside and let out their war cry, taunting their enemies. 'Har Har Mahadev!'

Bhagirath could see the rowboats being lowered from the ships. The attack was about to begin. The fire arrows were just a cover. As he watched the arrows being loaded again, he turned to his men. 'Shields!'

The Brangas effortlessly defended themselves against another volley of fire arrows.

'Send a message to our men on the other side to launch their fire coracles! Now!'

As his aide rushed away, Bhagirath saw his enemies rowing out towards the kund. And yet another shower of arrows was fired.

'Don't move!' shouted Bhagirath, keeping his men in check. 'Let them land first.'

In order to inflict maximum casualties Bhagirath would allow a large contingent of enemy soldiers to land ashore before launching a three-pronged attack from the adjoining forest. An impregnable phalanx of his infantry, standing shoulder to shoulder, shields in front, would advance and push at the frontline Magadhan soldiers with unstoppable force. The enemy soldiers bringing up the rear would inevitably be forced into the water. Weighed down by their weapons and armour, they would drown. The frontline, hopelessly outnumbered, would then be decimated.

'Shields!' ordered Bhagirath once again as he saw the arrows being lit.

His gut feel was that this would be the last volley. Enemy soldiers were jumping off their boats onto the sands of Bal-Atibal. Brutal hand-to-hand combat was moments away. Bhagirath could feel the adrenaline rushing through his veins. He could almost smell the blood that was about to be shed.

'Charge!' bellowed Bhagirath.

Kartik rode furiously with his two-thousand strong cavalry. Even through the dense foliage, he could see fire arrows being shot from Magadhan ships. They had commenced battle, which meant that the southern contingent of the Magadhan army was in position.

'Faster!' roared Kartik to his horsemen.

They could see that the ships at the centre of the fleet had already caught fire. The devil boats had struck. Bhagirath was obviously hurting the Magadhan navy. What was surprising though, was that the southern end was also aflame. The Vaishali forces must have arrived and were attacking the Magadhan navy from behind.

Kartik was distracted by the din up ahead; it was the sound of a fierce battle between the southern contingent of the Magadhans and Divodas' Brangas.

'Ride harder!'

Surapadman's men had probably shot fire arrows here as well, for parts of the camp were on fire. But this served as a beacon for Kartik's horsemen. They kicked their horses hard, spurring them on. The Brangas at the southern end were hard at work, holding almost twenty thousand soldiers at bay. The Magadhans, who had expected to decimate an unprepared enemy, were shocked by the fierce resistance they were facing. Things would get a lot worse though, for the Magadhans did not expect danger from the back as well.

'Har Har Mahadev!' yelled Kartik as he drew his long sword.

'Har Har Mahadev!' roared the Branga horsemen as they charged.

The last rows of the Magadhan foot soldiers, completely unprepared for a cavalry charge from the rear, were ruthlessly butchered within minutes. Kartik and his cavalry cut a wide swathe through the Magadhan units, their horses trampling hapless soldiers, their swords slicing all those who stood in their path.

Initially, the rear attack of the Branga cavalry went unnoticed due to the massive size of the rival armies and the brutal din and clamour of a battle well joined. Quickly overcoming their surprise, many brave Magadhan soldiers leapt at the horsemen, stabbing at the beasts and even fearlessly holding on to the stirrups, hoping to bring them down. Sensing that he led the cavalry charge, a clutch of infantrymen tripped Kartik's steed bringing them both down in a crash. They would soon wish that they hadn't.

With cat-like reflexes, Kartik sprang to his feet, viciously drawing his second sword as well, and cutting at the first of the soldiers pressing on to him. The Magadhan crumpled in midstep and fell silently to the ground, his windpipe severed, a gush of air bursting from his slit throat, splattering blood on those around him. A second soldier charged, and was cut down before he'd taken two steps, a single stroke of Kartik's blade slicing through his torso, almost to his spine.

The remaining soldiers paused, cautious now of this boy who could kill with such ease. They spread out in a circle around him, swords at the ready. Kartik knew they would charge together from all sides, and waited for them to make their move.

The charge came, two from the front, one from the back and a fourth from the left. Kartik crouched, and with near-inhuman speed sidestepped to the left and swung fiercely. Generating fearful blade speed through his swinging strikes, he brutally sliced limb, sinew, head and trunk all around him. Blood and entrails were splattered all over.

He paused, panting, the swords in his hands dripping red with blood. He looked around him, selected an opponent and charged again. As the *Bhagavad Gita* would say, Kartik had become Death, the destroyer of worlds.

The fighting raged for half an hour as the tide of the battle tipped more and more against the Magadhans. But they fought on as no quarter was given either by Kartik or his army.

Slowly the screams of the dying lessened, and then were silenced as Surapadman's army perished. Soldiers stopped their slaughter and stood quietly on the battlefield, leaning exhausted on their swords and panting. But Kartik did not slacken, pressing attack after attack on all those that remained standing.

Divodas tried to run as he approached Kartik, but his legs were weak and trembling, and he could scarcely manage more than a stumbling trot. He was covered in blood from a dozen small cuts, and a deep gash on his shoulder left his right arm dangling limply to his side. 'My Lord,' he called out, breathless and hoarse, 'My Lord!'

Kartik swung viciously, the speed of his movement building formidable power in his curved blade. Divodas took the blow on his shield as his hand reverberated with the shock of blocking the brutal blow, numbing his left arm to the shoulder.

'My Lord!' he pleaded in desperation. 'It is I, Divodas!'

Kartik suddenly stopped, his long sword held high in his right hand, his curved blade held low to his left, his breathing sharp and heavy, his eyes bulging with bloodlust.

'My Lord!' shrieked Divodas, his fear palpable. 'You have killed them all! Please stop!'

As Kartik's breathing slowed, he allowed his gaze to take in the scene of destruction all around him. Hacked bodies littered the battlefield. A once proud Magadhan army completely decimated. Divodas' frontal attack combined with the rear cavalry charge had achieved Kartik's plan.

Kartik could still feel the adrenalin coursing furiously through his veins.

Divodas, still afraid of Kartik, whispered. 'You have won, My Lord.'

Kartik raised his long sword high and shouted, 'Har Har Mahadev!'

The Brangas roared after him, 'Har Har Mahadev!'

Kartik bent down and flipped a Magadhan's decapitated head with his sword, then turned to Divodas. 'Find Surapadman. If there's life left in him, I want him brought to me alive.'

'Yes, My Lord,' said Divodas and rushed to obey.

Kartik wiped both his swords on the clothing of a fallen Magadhan soldier and carefully caged the blades in the scabbards tied across his back. The Branga soldiers maintained a respectful distance from him, terrified of the brutal violence they had just witnessed. He walked slowly towards the river, bent down, scooped some water in his palms and splashed it on his face. The river had turned red due to the massive bloodletting that had just occurred. He was covered with blood and gore. But his eyes were clean. Still. The bloodlust had left him.

Later in the day, when the dead were counted, it would emerge that seventy thousand of the Magadhan army from amongst seventy-five thousand had been slaughtered, burned or drowned. Kartik, on the other hand, had lost only five thousand of his one hundred thousand men. This was not a battle. It had been a massacre.

Kartik looked up at the sky. The first rays of the sun were breaking on the horizon, heralding a new day. And on this day, a legend had been born. The legend of Kartik, the Lord of War!

Chapter 24

The Age of Violence

The golden orb of a rising sun peeked from the mainland to the right as a strong southerly wind filled their sails, racing them towards the port of Lothal. Shiva, with Sati at his side, stood poised on the foredeck, eyes transfixed northwards, wishing their ship all speed.

'I wonder how the war has progressed in Swadweep,' said Sati.

Shiva turned to her with a smile. 'We do not know if there has been a war at all, Sati. Maybe Ganesh's tactics have worked.'

'I hope so.'

Shiva held Sati's hand. 'Our sons are warriors. They are doing what they are supposed to. You don't need to worry about them.'

'I'm not worried about Ganesh. I know that if he can avoid bloodshed, he will. Not that he's a coward, but he understands the futility of war. But Kartik... He loves the art of war. I fear he will go out of his way to court danger.'

'You're probably right,' said Shiva. 'But you cannot change his essential character. And in any case, isn't that what being a warrior is all about?'

'But every other warrior goes into battle reluctantly. He

fights because he has to. Kartik is not like that. He's enthused by warfare. It seems that his *swadharma* is war. That worries me,' said Sati, expressing her anxieties about what she felt was Kartik's *personal dharma*.

Shiva drew Sati into his arms and kissed her on her lips, reassuringly. 'Everything will be all right.'

Sati smiled and rested her head on Shiva's chest. 'I must admit that helped a bit...'

Shiva laughed softly. 'Let me help you some more then.'

Shiva raised Sati's face and kissed her again.

'Ahem!'

Shiva and Sati turned around to find Veerbhadra and Krittika approaching them.

'This is an open deck,' said a smiling Veerbhadra, teasing his friend. 'Find a room!'

Krittika hit Veerbhadra lightly on his stomach, embarrassed. 'Shut up!'

Shiva smiled. 'How're you, Krittika?'

'Very well, My Lord.'

'Krittika,' said Shiva. 'How many times do I have to tell you? You are my friend's wife. Call me Shiva.'

Krittika smiled. 'I'm sorry.'

Shiva rested his hand on Veerbhadra's shoulder. 'What did the captain say, Bhadra? How far are we?'

'At the rate we're sailing, just a few more days. The winds have been kind.'

'Hmmm... have you ever been to Lothal or Maika, Krittika?'

Krittika shook her head. 'It's difficult for me to get pregnant, Shiva. And that is the only way that an outsider can enter Maika.'

Shiva winced. He had touched a raw nerve. Veerbhadra did not care that Krittika couldn't conceive, but it still distressed her.

'I'm sorry,' said Shiva.

'No, no,' smiled Krittika. 'Veerbhadra has convinced me that we are good enough for each other. We don't need a child to complete us.'

Shiva patted Veerbhadra's back. 'Sometimes we barbarians can surprise even ourselves with our good sense.'

Krittika laughed softly. 'But I have visited the older Lothal.'

'Older Lothal?'

'Didn't I tell you?' asked Sati. 'The seaport of Lothal is actually a new city. The older Lothal was a river port on the Saraswati. But when the Saraswati stopped reaching the sea, there was no water around the old city, ending its vibrancy. The locals decided to recreate their hometown next to the sea. The new Lothal is exactly like the old city, except that it's a sea port.'

'Interesting,' said Shiva. 'So what happened to old Lothal?'

'It's practically abandoned, but a few people continue to live there.'

'So why didn't they give the new city a different name? Why call it Lothal?'

'The old citizens were very attached to their city. It was one of the greatest cities of the empire. They didn't want the name to disappear in the sands of time. They also assumed most people would forget old Lothal.'

Shiva looked towards the sea. 'New Lothal, here we come!'

— ⋯ —

The sun had risen high over Bal-Atibal Kund. It was the third hour of the second prahar. The bodies of the fallen Maghadans and Brangas were being removed to a cleared area in the forest where, to the drone of ritual chanting, their mortal remains were being cremated. Considering the massive number of Magadhan dead, this was back-breaking work. But Kartik had been insistent. Valour begot respect, whether in life or in the aftermath of death.

'Has Surapadman not been found yet?' asked Bhagirath, his eyes scanning the sands of the kund. Yesterday they were pristine white. Today they were a pale shade of pink, discoloured by massive quantities of blood.

'Not as yet,' said Kartik. 'Initially I thought he was fighting on the southern front. We were unable to find him there so I assumed he would be here.'

Maatali, the Vaishali king, had proved his naval acumen by destroying the rearguard of the Magadhan fleet. Having heard of Kartik's valour and ferocity, he now viewed him with newfound respect. Gone were the last traces of indulgence for the son of the Neelkanth.

'How far is my brother's fleet, King Maatali?' asked Kartik.

'I've sent some of my rowboats upriver. It is clogged with the debris of the Magadhan ships. Our boats are trying to clear up the mess, but it will take time. And Lord Ganesh is moving carefully so the ships don't sustain any damage. So he will take some time to get here.'

Kartik nodded.

'But he has been informed about your great victory, Lord Kartik,' said Maatali. 'He is very proud of you.'

Kartik frowned. 'It's not *my* victory, Your Highness. It's *our* victory. And it would not have been possible without my elder brother, who destroyed the northern end of the Magadhan navy.'

'That he did,' said Maatali.

'My Lord!' hailed Divodas, crossing over from the dense forest to the sands of the Bal-Atibal Kund. Still weak from injuries and bandaged across his shoulder, he was being assisted by five men as they together dragged something with ropes.

It took Kartik a moment to recognise what they were dragging. 'Divodas! Treat him with respect!'

Divodas stopped at once. Kartik ran towards them, followed by Bhagirath and Maatali. The corpse they had been dragging was that of a tall, well-built, swarthy man. His clothes and armour were soaked dark with blood, and his body was covered with wounds, some dried and black, others still fresh, red and wet. His skull had been split open near his temple, showing how he had died. His injuries were too numerous to be counted, clearly indicating the valour of this combatant. All the wounds were in the front, not one on the back. It had been an honourable death.

'Surapadman...' whispered Bhagirath.

'He was on the southern front, My Lord,' said Divodas.

Kartik pulled out his knife, bent down to cut the ropes tied around Surapadman's shoulders, and then gently lowered the fallen prince back onto the ground. He noticed Surapadman's right hand, still tightly gripping his sword. He touched the sword, its blade caked with dried blood. Divodas tried to pry open Surapadman's fingers.

'Stop,' commanded Kartik. 'Surapadman will carry his sword into the other world.'

Divodas immediately withdrew his hand and fell back.

Surapadman's mouth was half open. The ancient Vedic hymns on death claim that the soul leaves the body along with the last breath. Therefore, the mouth is open at the point of death. But there is a superstition that the mouth should be closed quickly after death, lest an evil spirit enters the soulless body.

Kartik closed Surapadman's mouth gently.

'Find the chief Brahmin,' said Kartik. 'Prepare Surapadman's body. He shall be cremated like the prince that he was.'

Divodas nodded.

Kartik turned to Bhagirath. 'We shall wait till my brother returns. Surapadman will then be cremated with full state honours.'

— ⴷⵀⵡⵠⴲ —

Ganesh stood at the ramparts of the Magadhan fort, watching the great Sarayu merge into the mighty Ganga. The setting sun had tinged the waters a brilliant orange. King Mahendra and the citizens of Magadh, stunned by the complete annihilation of their army and the death of their Prince Surapadman, had surrendered meekly when Ganesh's forces had entered the city. He did not expect any rebellion, since there were practically no soldiers left in Magadh. Ganesh planned to leave a small force of ten thousand soldiers to man the fort and blockade any Ayodhya ships. He would sail out with his other soldiers to meet with his father's army in Meluha. They were to leave the next day.

The war in Swadweep had worked perfectly for Ganesh. He was now able to block the movements of the Ayodhyan army with far less soldiers than would have been required if he was besieging Ayodhya itself.

'What are you thinking, *dada*?' asked Kartik.

Ganesh smiled at his brother as he pointed at the *confluence*. 'Look at the *sangam*, where the Sarayu meets the Ganga.'

Even before he turned his gaze, Kartik could hear the swirling waters of the *sangam*. What he saw was a young, impetuous Sarayu crashing into the mature, tranquil Ganga, jostling for space within her banks. Though she sometimes relented, the Ganga would often push aside the waters of the Sarayu with surprising ease, creating eddies and currents in its wake. This jostling continued till Ganga, the eternal mother, eventually drew the ebullient tributary into her bosom till they could be distinguished no more in the calm flow.

'There is always unity at the end,' said Ganesh, 'and it brings a new tranquillity. But the meeting of two worlds causes a lot of temporary chaos.'

Kartik smiled, bemused.

'This could not have been avoided,' said Ganesh. 'But the stricken visage of King Mahendra was heartbreaking. Every single house in Magadh has lost a son or a daughter in the Battle of Bal-Atibal.'

'But King Mahendra was the one who had forced Prince Surapadman to attack. He can only blame himself,' said Kartik. 'I've heard reports that Prince Surapadman had really wanted to remain neutral.'

'That may be true, Kartik. But that still doesn't take away from the fact that we have killed half the adult population of Magadh.'

'We had no choice, *dada*,' said Kartik.

'I know that,' said Ganesh, turning back to look at the sangam of the Ganga and the Sarayu. 'The rivers fight with each other with the only currency that they know: water. We humans fight with the only currency that we know in this age: violence.'

'But how else does one establish one's standpoint, *dada*?' asked Kartik. 'There are times when reason does not work, and peaceful efforts prove inadequate. Violence is ultimately the last resort. This is the way it has always been. The world will, perhaps, never be any different.'

Ganesh shook his head. 'It will be, one day. We live in the age of the Kshatriya. That's why we think that the only currency to bring about change is violence.'

'Age of the Kshatriya? I've never heard of that.'

'You would have heard of the four *yugs, cyclical eras* that time traverses repeatedly through a never-ending loop: the *Sat yug, Treta yug, Dwapar yug* and *Kali yug*.'

'Yes.'

'Within each of these yugs there are smaller cycles dominated by different caste-professions. There is the age of the Brahmin, of the Kshatriya, of the Vaishya and of the Shudra.'

'Age of the Brahmin, *dada*? I haven't heard of that either.'

'Sure you have. All of us have been told stories of the Prajapati; of a time of magic.'

Kartik smiled. 'Of course! Knowledge seems like magic to the ignorant.'

'Yes. The main currency of the age of the Brahmin was knowledge. And in our age, it is violence. Some philosophers believe that after our epoch will be the age of the Vaishya.'

'And the people in that age will not use violence to establish their writ?'

'Violence will never die, Kartik. Neither will knowledge. But they will not be the determining factors, since it will be an age dominated by the way of the Vaishya, which is profit. They will use money.'

'I can't imagine a world like that, *dada*.'

'It will come. I pray that it doesn't take too long. Not that I'm afraid of violence, but it leaves too many grieving hearts in its wake.'

'*Dada*, even if I do believe that such a time will come, are you saying that money will cause less devastation than violence? Will there not be winners and losers even then? Will sadness disappear?'

Ganesh raised his eyebrows, surprised. He smiled and patted his brother on his back. 'You are right. There will always be winners and losers. For that is the way of the world.'

Kartik put his arm around his brother's waist as Ganesh

put his around Kartik's shoulders. 'But that still doesn't take away from the grief of knowing that we have caused suffering to others.'

— ⅄⦶Ʊ⍋⊛ —

'This may sound strange to you,' said Shiva, reclining in the comfort of the Lothal governor's residence. 'But I feel as if I've come home. Meluha is where my journey began.'

Just as Kali had expected, the Lothal governor, Chenardhwaj, had broken ranks with the Meluhan nobility and opened the doors of his city for Shiva's army, pledging loyalty to the Neelkanth.

'And this is where it'll end,' said Sati. 'Then we can all go and live in Kailash.'

Shiva smiled. 'Kailash is not as idyllic as you imagine. It's a difficult, barren land.'

'But you will be there. That'll make it heaven for me.'

Shiva laughed, bent forward and kissed his wife lovingly, holding her close.

'But first, we need to deal with those who defend the evil Somras,' said Sati.

'That has already begun with the defeat of the Magadhans.'

'Hmmm... that's true, we can easily blockade the Ayodhyan navy, now that Magadh is firmly in our control. When will Ganesh and Kartik leave for Meluha?'

'They have left already.'

'And when do we leave for Mrittikavati?'

'In a few days.'

Sati had learnt to recognise the resolute expression Shiva now wore and couldn't help feeling a twinge of anxiety for her homeland. 'For their own sake, I hope they surrender.'

'I hope so too.'

Chapter 25

God or Country?

'By the great Lord Brahma!' growled Bhrigu.

Bhrigu had finally reached Devagiri. He had been delayed on the recently-built road between Dharmakhet in Swadweep and Meluha, by the floodwaters of an overflowing Yamuna, which had submerged the pathway. While he was stuck in this no-man's land between the Chandravanshi and Suryavanshi empires, Bhrigu availed of the facilities of the traveller's guesthouse, built by the Meluhans alongside the road. Not that its comforts calmed him though, for he needed to be in Devagiri. What did alleviate his stress was the arrival of Parvateshwar, along with Anandmayi. They travelled together from there onwards, and Bhrigu used this opportunity to discuss battle strategy with him. The flooding of the Yamuna had transformed what should have been a quick journey of a few weeks, into many months.

Bhrigu, Daksha, Parvateshwar and Kanakhala conferred in the private royal office of Devagiri, examining the ramifications of the Neelkanth's proclamation.

'May I see the notice, Maharishi*ji*?' asked Parvateshwar.

Bhrigu handed over the stone tablet and then turned to Daksha and Kanakhala. 'When were they put up?'

'A few months ago, My Lord,' said Daksha.

'At all major temples in practically every city within the Empire,' added Kanakhala.

'And was this a simultaneous event, orchestrated on the same day?' asked Parvateshwar, obviously impressed by the logistical feat.

'Yes,' said Kanakhala. 'Only the Neelkanth could have organised this. But why would he do it? He loves Meluha and we worship him. We therefore assumed that it had to be someone else who was trying to slander the reputation of our Lord. Sadly, we still haven't made any headway in our investigation and do not know who the real perpetrators are.'

'Do you have traitors in your administration, Your Highness?' asked Bhrigu.

Daksha bristled, but did not dare make his anger apparent. 'Certainly not, My Lord. You can trust the Meluhans like you trust me.'

Bhrigu's ironic smile did not leave much to the imagination. 'What do you make of it, Lord Parvateshwar?'

'I would have expected nothing less from the Neelkanth,' said Parvateshwar.

Kanakhala was stunned by this revelation, but prudently chose silence.

'But I must tell you that we responded well, My Lord,' said Daksha to Bhrigu. 'They were removed within a few days and were replaced with official notices stating that the earlier ones had been put up by a fraud and should not be believed.'

Kanakhala reeled from shock. She had inadvertently sinned when she put up the new notices that Daksha had asked her to, and become party to a lie. She considered resigning from her position. However, it was obvious that a war was imminent. And her war-time duties were clear: complete and unquestioning loyalty to the king and country. She had never faced a situation where her duties stood in direct conflict with her dharma. The confusion was bewildering.

'So you see, My Lord, this particular problem has been handled,' said Daksha. 'We need to now focus on how to repel Shiva's forces.'

Bhrigu gestured towards Daksha. 'Not now, Your Highness. Let me first confer with General Parvateshwar in private.'

Kanakhala was still lost in the turmoil within her conscience, and did not notice the exchange.

— ⁂ —

'The proclamation was made by the Lord Neelkanth. How can we go against his word? This is wrong. If the Lord says that the Somras is not to be used, then I don't see how we can go against this diktat.'

Parvateshwar had accompanied Kanakhala to her office after the meeting. He could tell that she was very disturbed by the events of the morning.

'I've already stopped using the Somras, Kanakhala.'

'As will I, from this instant. But that is not what troubles me. The Neelkanth wants the whole of Meluha to stop using the Somras. And the consequences of ignoring his decision are very clear from his message: if we don't, then we become his enemies.'

'I'm aware of that. For all practical purposes, war has already been declared. His army is mobilising even as we speak.'

'Meluha must stop using the Somras.'

'Does the law allow either you or me to pass an order banning the Somras?'

'No, only the Emperor can do that.'

'And he hasn't, has he? Also, the Emperor's orders are unquestionable in times of war.'

'Can't we avoid a war in some way? Why don't you speak to Maharishi Bhrigu? He respects you.'

'The Maharishi is not convinced that the Somras has turned evil.'

'Then we should approach the people directly.'

'Kanakhala, you know better than that. It would mean breaking your oath as prime minister, since you would be directly going against the order of your Emperor.'

'But why should I follow his orders? He made me lie to our own people!'

'I assure you that nothing like that will happen again for as long as I'm alive and in Meluha.'

Kanakhala looked away as she struggled to get a grip over her raging emotions.

'Kanakhala, let's say we do approach the Meluhans directly,' said Parvateshwar. 'We will have to convince our countrymen to voluntarily choose to end their life much before it normally would have. And we will have nothing to give them in return. Convincing people to do this is not an easy task, even with those as duty-bound and honourable as the Meluhans. It will take time. The Neelkanth, however, is not patient when it comes to the Somras. He wants its use to end right now. The only way he can do that is to attack the epicentre.'

'Which is Meluha...'

'Exactly. Right now our task is to protect our country. You know Lord Ram's laws state very clearly that our primary duty is towards our country. He had said that even if it comes to choosing between Lord Ram and Meluha, we should choose Meluha.'

'Who would have imagined that it would *actually* come down to such a choice, Parvateshwar? That we would need to choose between our God and our country?'

Parvateshwar smiled sadly. 'My duty to my country is above all others, Kanakhala.'

Kanakhala ran her hand over her bald pate and touched the knotted tuft of hair at the back of her head, trying to draw strength from it. 'What kind of challenge is fate throwing at us?'

'It's a stupid idea, Your Highness,' said Bhrigu. 'Your problem is that you do not look beyond the next three months when you dream up your strategies.'

Daksha had been sitting expectantly at the maharishi's feet, eagerly awaiting his response. For he had just unfolded to Bhrigu his 'brilliant' scheme to avoid the war altogether.

An unmoved Bhrigu then leaned towards him from his stone bed. 'We're not fighting with the Neelkanth, but the devotion that he inspires in your people. Making him a martyr will turn your people against you, and inevitably, the Somras.'

Daksha expressed acknowledgement. 'You're right, My Lord. Had we succeeded in killing him in Panchavati, the people would have blamed the Nagas. That failure was most unfortunate.'

'Also, Your Highness, while it is not unethical to attack an unprepared enemy, there are some codes that just cannot be broken, even in times of war, like killing a peace ambassador or even a messenger.'

'Of course, My Lord,' said a distracted Daksha. His mind, in fact, was already working on refining his plan.

'Are you listening, Your Highness?' asked an irritated Bhrigu.

A chastened Daksha looked up immediately. 'Of course I am, My Lord.'

Bhrigu sighed and waved his hand, dismissing him from his chamber.

— —

Parvateshwar strode into his house and nodded towards the attendant even as he ran up the steps that skirted the central courtyard. As he approached the first floor, he seemed to remember something and stepped back towards the landing overlooking the central courtyard.

'Rati!'

'Yes, My Lord?' answered the attendant.

'Isn't it the day of the week when Lady Anandmayi bathes in milk and rose petals?' asked Parvateshwar.

'Yes, My Lord. Warm water on all days of the week except the day of the Sun, when she bathes in milk and rose petals.'

Parvateshwar smiled. 'So, is it ready?'

Rati smiled indulgently. She had served Parvateshwar her entire life, but had never seen her master smile as much as he had in the last few days, since he had returned with the new mistress. 'It'll be ready any moment now, My Lord.'

'Be sure to inform the lady as soon as it's ready.'

'Yes, My Lord.'

Parvateshwar turned and ran up the remaining two flights of stairs, before reaching his private chamber on top. He found Anandmayi relaxing in the balcony on a comfortable chair, as she observed the goings-on in the street below. A cloth canopy screened out the evening sun. She turned around as she heard Parvateshwar rush in.

'What's the hurry?' asked a smiling Anandmayi.

Parvateshwar stopped, smiling broadly. 'I just wanted to know how you're doing.'

Anandmayi smiled and beckoned Parvateshwar. The

Meluhan general walked over and sat down beside her on the armrest. Anandmayi rested her head on his arm as she continued to study the street below. The markets were still open, but unlike the loud and garrulous Chandravanshis, the citizens of Devagiri were achingly polite. The road, the houses, the people, everything reflected the prized Suryavanshi values of sobriety, dignity and uniformity.

'What do you think of our capital?' asked Parvateshwar. 'Isn't it astonishingly well-planned and orderly?'

Anandmayi looked at Parvateshwar with an indulgent smile playing on her lips. 'It's heartbreakingly lacklustre and colourless.'

Parvateshwar laughed. 'You're more than enough to add colour to this city!'

Anandmayi placed her hand on Parvateshwar's as she remarked, 'So, this is the land where I will die...'

Parvateshwar turned his hand around and held hers, in reply.

'Any news?' asked Anandmayi. 'Has the Lord entered the territory of Meluha?'

'No reports as yet,' said Parvateshwar. 'But what is truly worrying is the absence of bird couriers from Ayodhya.'

Anandmayi's visage transformed as she straightened up with concern. 'Has Ayodhya been conquered?'

'I don't know, darling. But I don't think the Lord has enough men to conquer Ayodhya. The city has seven concentric walls, albeit badly designed. That is formidable defence, even if the soldiers are ill-trained.'

Anandmayi narrowed her eyes in irritation. 'They are poorly led, Parvateshwar, but the soldiers are brave men. My country's generals may be idiots, but the commoners will fight hard for their homeland.'

'This reinforces my argument that the Lord Neelkanth

couldn't have conquered Ayodhya with just the one hundred and fifty thousand soldiers of Branga and Vaishali.'

'So what do you think has happened?'

'Clearly, Meluhan interests are not being served in Ayodhya. One possibility is that your father, King Dilipa, has aligned with the Neelkanth.'

'Impossible. My father is too much in love with himself. He's getting medicines from Lord Bhrigu which is keeping him alive. He will not risk that for anything.'

'The people of Ayodhya may have rebelled against their King and thrown in their lot with the Neelkanth.'

'Hmmm... That's possible. My people are certainly more devoted to the Neelkanth than to my father.'

'And if the Neelkanth has Ayodhya under control, he will quickly turn his attention to his main objective: Meluha.'

'He aims to destroy the Somras, Parva. He will not indulge in wanton destruction. Why would he do that? It would turn your people against him. He will only go for the Somras.'

Parvateshwar's eyes flashed open. 'Of course! He will target the secret Somras manufacturing facility and its scientists. That would end the supply of the Somras. People will have no choice but to learn to live without it.'

'There you are. That's his target. Where *is* this secret Somras manufacturing facility?'

'I don't know. But I will find out.'

'Yes, you should.'

'In any case,' said Parvateshwar. 'I've told Kanakhala not to send any more messages to Ayodhya. We could just be passing on information to the enemy.'

'If Ayodhya is already in their control, and they leave now, they could be in Meluha quite soon.'

'Yes, it could be as early as six months. Also, along with Ayodhya, the Lord would have a massive army.'

'Redouble your preparations.'

'Hmmm... I'll also order Vidyunmali to leave for Lothal with twenty thousand soldiers.'

'Lothal? Just because they didn't send you their monthly report? Isn't that a bit of an over-reaction?'

'I don't have a good feeling about them,' said Parvateshwar, slowly shaking his head. 'They didn't respond to my bird courier.'

'Can you afford to send twenty thousand soldiers away based on a mere hunch?'

'Lothal is not too far away. Also, it's a border town. It is the closest Meluhan city from Panchavati. It may not be such a bad idea to reinforce it.'

Chapter 26

Battle of Mrittikavati

The exhausted scout stumbled into the military tent, barely able to conceal his anxiety. Shiva jerked his head up from the map he'd been poring over, as the soldier managed a hasty salute. 'What?'

Shot like an arrow, Shiva's voice made Kali, Sati, Gopal and Chenardhwaj look up too, worry creasing their faces. Shiva's army had marched in quickly from Lothal and was just a day away from Mrittikavati.

'My Lord, I have bad news.'

'Give me the facts. Don't jump to conclusions.'

'Mrittikavati is much better defended now than it had been earlier. Brigadier Vidyunmali sailed into the city a few days back. Apparently, he was on his way to Lothal to strengthen Meluha's defences at the border. Clearly, Emperor Daksha has no idea as yet that Lothal has pledged loyalty to you, My Lord.'

'How many men does Vidyunmali have?' asked Chenardhwaj.

'Around twenty thousand, My Lord. Added to which are the five thousand soldiers already stationed at Mrittikavati.'

'We're still at a substantial advantage in terms of numbers, My Lord,' said Chenardhwaj. 'But Mrittikavati's defences can make even twenty-five thousand men seem like a lot.'

Shiva shook his head. 'I don't think that should be a problem. It doesn't matter how many soldiers they have. We just want to commandeer their ships, not conquer their city. If Vidyunmali has sailed with twenty thousand soldiers, his transport ships would also be in the Mrittikavati port, right? So there are even more ships for us to capture.'

Kali smiled. 'That's true!'

'Prepare to march to Mrittikavati,' said Shiva. 'We attack in two days.'

— ⁂ —

Shiva could see the panic-stricken people rush back into the city as the warning conches were blown repeatedly from the ramparts of Mrittikavati. The unexpected appearance of a massive enemy force had shocked the Meluhans.

Atop his horse at a vantage point on the hill, Shiva could clearly see the city of Mrittikavati and its port. Like most Meluhan cities, it had also been built on a massive platform a kilometre away from the Saraswati, as a protection against floods. But it was the port, obviously built on the banks of the great river, which fascinated Shiva.

The circular harbour was massive, with the waters of the Saraswati going into it through a narrow opening. A semi-circular dock was separated by a pool of water from the outer ring of the port. A dome-covered inner dock protected the various repair yards. Ships were anchored along the outer side of the inner dock and the inner side of the outer pier. This ingenious design could hold nearly fifty ships in a relatively small space. The expanse of water between the two parallel circles of ships allowed for free movement of the vessels. The ships could move fairly quickly within the harbour in a single file. Being relatively small, the harbour gate afforded the entry or exit of only one ship at a time. But considering that ships could tail each other in the circular channel within the port, the narrow gate did not affect the speed at which the ships could enter or leave the port. However, it did allow for effective defence against enemy ships. The gate was shut and Shiva could see the numerous points across the harbour walls from where a defence could be mounted.

Shiva smiled. *Typically foolproof Meluhan planning.*

Kali leaned across to Shiva. 'The fortified pathway between the city and the port may be a weakness.'

'Yes,' said Sati. 'Let's attack from there. If we succeed in making them feel vulnerable, they will be forced to shut the gates of the city that lead to this pathway, and pull their soldiers within. The city and the port are not next to each other, which means they will have to sacrifice one or the other if the pathway walls are breached. I would imagine they would compromise and give up the port.'

Shiva looked at Sati. 'Vidyunmali is aggressive. He doesn't like to make compromises. Once he realises that we are after their ships and not the city itself, he may take a gamble. He may choose to step out of the city and mount a rearguard assault on our attacking forces. That may appear like a sensible choice to him. He may think that he can rout us on the pathway, thus saving both the port and the city. I hope he makes that mistake.'

— —

Shiva rode up and down the line of his all-inclusive army, consisting of Brangas, Vasudevs, Nagas and some Suryavanshis from Lothal. Sati and Kali were on horseback, leading their sections of the army. The soldiers were ready but knew that the Meluhans were well fortified.

'Soldiers!' roared Shiva. 'Mahadevs! Hear me!'

Silence descended on the men.

'We're told a great man walked this earth a thousand years ago. Lord Ram, *Maryada Purushottam*, the most celebrated amongst the kings. But we know the truth! He was more than a man! He was a God!'

The soldiers listened in pin-drop silence.

'These people,' said Shiva, pointing to the Meluhans stationed on the fort walls of Mrittikavati, 'only remember his name. They don't remember his words. But I remember the words of Lord Ram. I remember he had said: "If you have to choose between my people and dharma, choose dharma! If you have to choose between my family and dharma, choose dharma! Even if you have to choose between me and dharma, always choose dharma!"'

'Dharma!' bellowed the army in one voice.

'The Meluhans have chosen Evil,' bellowed Shiva. 'We choose dharma!'

'Dharma!'

'They have chosen death! We choose victory!'

'Victory!'

'They have chosen the Somras!' roared Shiva. 'We choose Lord Ram!'

'Jai Shri Ram!' shouted Sati.

'Jai Shri Ram!' Kali joined the war cry.

'Jai Shri Ram!' shouted all the soldiers.

'Jai Shri Ram!'

'Jai Shri Ram!'

The familiar cry from the Neelkanth's army reverberated within the walls of Mrittikavati; it was a cry that usually charged the Meluhans. But this time it infused fear.

Shiva turned to Kali, surrounded by the roars of his warriors, and nodded at her. A small cold smile curved Kali's lips and she nodded in return, her eyes glittering, and swung her sword so it flashed in the sun. Then she raised a single hand to the soldiers behind her, and a wave of silence rolled out across the army until all that could be heard was the wind snapping at the banners flying above their heads. She signalled again and the men tensed and readied their weapons. Then she raised one sword, pointed towards the sky, and with a blood-curdling scream, brought her blade forward to unleash a roaring tide of men at the walls.

— ⁂ —

Shiva keenly observed the battle raging in a narrow section of the fortified pathway. Kali was engaged in making repeated assaults with the Vasudev elephants and makeshift catapults, concentrating all resources on breaching one small section. A small number of exceptionally brave Naga soldiers fought against daunting odds as the Meluhans shot arrows and poured boiling oil from the battlements that lined the pathway. Famed for their superhuman courage, the Nagas were ideal for this battle of attrition. Small breaches began opening up on the pathway walls; Shiva's soldiers would soon be able to block the city's access to its port. This triggered the reaction that Shiva expected from Vidyunmali. The main gates of Mrittikavati were thrown open and the Meluhans marched out, arranged in a formation that they had learnt from Shiva himself.

The Meluhan soldiers had formed themselves into squares of twenty by twenty men. Each soldier covered the left half of his body with his shield and the right half of the soldier to the left of him. The soldier behind used his shield as a lid to cover himself and the soldier in front. Each warrior used the space between his own shield and the one next to him to hold out his long spear. This formation provided the defence of a tortoise but could also be used as a devastatingly offensive battering ram with long spears bearing in on the enemy.

However, the tortoise had one weakness that was known to the creator of the formation himself: Shiva. This chink in the armour was at its rear; if attacked from behind, there was little that the soldiers could do. They were weighed down with heavy spears which pointed ahead. It was difficult to turn around quickly. Furthermore, there was no shield protection at the back of the formation. So if an enemy were to get behind, he could attack the soldiers and rout them completely.

Shiva turned towards Sati with a smile. 'Vidyunmali is so predictable.'

Sati nodded. 'To formation?'

'To formation,' agreed Shiva.

Sati immediately turned her horse and rode out to the right, quickly extending the line of the army under her command towards the pathway wall. She steadily put herself between the Meluhan tortoises emerging from the city gates, and Kali's brave Nagas who were attacking the fortified pathway behind her. Her task was to first fight hard and then begin retreating slowly, giving the Meluhans a false sense of imminent victory, keeping them marching forward. It would be a tough battle which would lead to heavy casualties, as she would be right in front of the unstoppable tortoise formations. As the Meluhans moved ahead, space would open up behind them, allowing Shiva to ride out with his cavalry and attack them from the rear.

Shiva, meanwhile, rode towards the elephant corps and the cavalry on the left.

'Steady!' Shiva ordered the Vasudev brigadier in command of the elephant corps.

Shiva had to move quickly. But he also had to move at the right time. If he charged too early, Vidyunmali would smell the trap.

As Veerbhadra saw the Meluhan tortoise charge into Sati's army, he turned to Shiva, worried. 'The task is too difficult for Sati. We should…'

'Stay focused, Bhadra,' said Shiva. 'She knows what she is doing.'

The tortoise formations were bearing down hard on Sati and her soldiers. In the best traditions of Suryavanshi warfare, Sati led from the front. She could see the wall of shields moving steadily towards her at a slow, jostling run, a forest of spears bristling out of every crevice. The sun bounced off the polished metal with every thudding step they took. She breathed out slowly and urged her horse forward into a smooth canter, then a gallop as she held herself just out of the saddle, poised and still, waiting for her moment.

Closer and closer she came to the formation, eyes searching for a gap. For a moment a shield shifted slightly out of alignment as they ran, exposing the neck of a soldier. Without shifting in her seat, Sati drew a knife from her sheath and flung it with deadly accuracy, striking home and felling the soldier in midstep.

The tortoise was almost upon her. She pulled hard on the reins, her horse rearing up as she tried to turn backwards. She felt a sharp pain in her shoulder and heard her horse neigh desperately as it faltered beneath her. Gasping in pain from the spear thrust, she tried to kick free from her dying mount as it came to its knees. She looked up to see which soldier had stabbed her, but could not make out which pair of eyes, peering over their shields, held the spear that was buried in her shoulder. The spear was thrust deeper, and she cried out, half in pain and half in anger, her eyes watering. She swung her sword violently, hacking the spear in two, as she rolled off the horse and onto her feet.

A few arrows sped past Sati's shoulders, striking more soldiers in the tortoise through the gap she had just created. For a moment, the Meluhan charge slowed and faltered, the shield line crumbling in slightly as replacement soldiers struggled to come forward and seal the breach. Admirably though, the Meluhans were back in formation quickly and resumed their charge. Sati stepped back a pace and in the same movement, almost like they were in lock-step, her army stepped back as well, imperceptibly, as they fought on bravely. They kept withdrawing gradually, as though being mowed down by the unstoppable tortoise corps. Just a few more minutes of steady retreat by Sati's men and the Meluhans would have marched forward far enough for Shiva to ride out behind them and destroy their formations.

Shiva observed the battle raging in the distance. His eyes fell on the Meluhan chariots on the side of the tortoise formations, providing protection to their flanks. Each chariot had a charioteer to steer the horses and a warrior to engage in combat. The two-man team allowed for frightening speed and brutal force. These chariots could stall the impending charge of Shiva's cavalry.

'I want your elephants to take out those chariots. Now,' he ordered the Vasudev brigadier.

The Vasudev brigadier turned to his *mahouts*, quickly relaying the orders.

The elephants raced out at a fearsome pace, making the ground rumble with their charge. The Meluhan warriors on the chariots confidently observed the elephants approach. They immediately relieved their charioteers of the reins of their horses, who in turn pulled out drums stored for just such an occasion. The Meluhans still remembered the battles against Chandravanshi elephants. Loud noises from drums always disturbed the giant animals, making them run amuck, often crushing their own army. But these beasts had been trained by the Vasudevs to tolerate sudden loud sounds. Much to the shock of the Meluhan charioteers, the elephants continued their charge.

Seeing their tactic fail, they immediately abandoned the drums and took up the reins of their horses. The warriors pulled out their spears and readied themselves for battle. The Meluhan chariots moved quickly as the Vasudev elephants drew near, weaving around the pachyderms as they charged, throwing their spears at the giant beasts, hoping to injure or at least slow them down. But the elephants were prepared. There were massive metallic balls tied to their trunks. The elephants swung their trunks expertly, smashing the metallic balls into the bodies of the horses and the charioteers. Some of the Meluhans were fortunate enough to die instantly, but others had the balls smash through their bones, leaving them alive to suffer in agony. And as if this wasn't bad enough, a second surprise was in store for the Meluhan charioteers. All of a sudden, fire spewed out of the elephant *howdahs*!

The Vasudevs had fitted their elephants with machines designed by their engineers. Two Vasudev soldiers kept pushing the levers, shooting out an almost continuous stream of flames which burned all in its path. The few unfortunate Meluhan chariots that did not get burned were stamped out of existence under massive elephant feet. The chariot corps of the Meluhans was no match for the Vasudev elephants.

Shiva drew his sword and held it high. He turned to his cavalry, and shouted over the din, 'Ride hard into the rear of those formations! Charge into them! Destroy them!'

Even as Shiva's cavalry thundered out, Sati was playing her part perfectly. Her soldiers had been progressively stepping back, drawing the Meluhans farther and farther away into the open, exposing a massive breach between the rear of their tortoise formations and the fort walls. To maintain the credibility of the tactic and keep the Meluhans engaged in battle, Sati's soldiers were not running away in haste but continuing to fight, taking many casualties in the process. Sati herself had also been seriously injured, having been struck on both the shoulder and thigh. But she battled on. She knew she couldn't afford to fail. Her forces' success in their task was crucial to their overall victory.

Shiva's cavalry rode hard, in a great arc around the main battlefront. He could see the Vasudev elephants and the Meluhan chariots clashing on his right. Practically decimated, the chariots could not ride out to meet the new threat from the cavalry. Shiva rode fast, unchallenged, till he reached the unprotected rear of the Meluhan tortoise formations.

'Jai Shri Ram!' thundered Shiva.

'Har Har Mahadev!' bellowed his cavalry, kicking their horses hard.

Shiva's three thousand strong cavalry charged into the Meluhans. Locked into their formation as they faced the opposite side, weighed down by immensely heavy spears, they were unable to turn around. Shiva's mounted soldiers cut through the Meluhan tortoise corps, hacking away with their long swords. Within moments of this brutal attack, the Meluhan formations started breaking. Some soldiers surrendered while others simply ran away. By the time Vidyunmali, who was fighting at the head of his army, received the news of the decimation of his troops towards his rear, it was already too late. The Meluhans had been outflanked and defeated.

Chapter 27

The Neelkanth Speaks

The survivors had been disarmed and chained together in groups. The chains had been fixed into stakes buried deep in the ground. They were surrounded by four divisions of Shiva's finest. It was well nigh impossible for them to escape. Ayurvati had commandeered the outer port area and created a temporary hospital. The injured, of both the Meluhan as well as Shiva's armies, were being treated.

Shiva squatted next to a low bed where Sati had just received a quick surgery. The wound on her shoulder would heal quickly but the thigh injury would take some time. Kali and Gopal stood at a distance.

'I'm all right,' said Sati, pushing Shiva away. 'Go to Mrittikavati. You need to take control of the city quickly. They need to see you. You need to calm them down. We don't want skirmishes breaking out between the citizens of Mrittikavati and our army.'

'I know. I know. I'm going,' said Shiva. 'I just needed to check on you.'

Sati smiled and pushed him once again. 'I'm fine! I will not die so easily. Now go!'

'*Didi* is right,' said Kali. 'We need to do a flag march within the precincts of the city and cow them down.'

A surprised Shiva turned around. 'We are not taking our army into the city.'

Kali flailed her hands in exasperation. 'Then why did we conquer the city?'

'We haven't conquered the city. We've only defeated their army. We need to get the citizens of Mrittikavati on our side.'

'On our side? Why?'

'Because we will then be free to sail out of here with our entire army. We have ten thousand prisoners of the Meluhan army. Do you want to commit our soldiers to guarding prisoners of war? If Mrittikavati comes to our side, we can keep the Meluhan army imprisoned in the city itself.'

'They're not going to do that, Shiva. In fact, if they see any weakness in us, they will sense an opportunity to rebel.'

'It's not weakness, Kali, but compassion. People usually know the difference.'

'You've got to be joking! How in God's name are you going to show compassion after massacring their army?'

'I will do it by not marching into the city with my army. I will go there only with Bhadra, Nandi and Parshuram. And I will speak to the citizens.'

'How will that help?'

'It will.'

'You have just destroyed their army, Shiva! I don't think they would be interested in listening to anything you have to say.'

'They will be. I am their Neelkanth.'

Kali could barely contain her irritation. 'At least let me accompany you along with some Naga soldiers. You may need some protection.'

'No.'

'Shiva...'

'Do you trust me?'

'What does that have to...'

'Kali, do you trust me?'

'Of course I do.'

'Then let me handle this,' concluded Shiva, before turning to Sati. 'I'll be back soon, darling.'

Sati smiled and touched Shiva's hand.

'Go with Lord Ram, my friend,' said Gopal, as Shiva rose and turned to leave.

Shiva smiled. 'He's always with me.'

— ⁂ —

A collective buzz of a thousand voices hovered over the central square as the citizens of Mrittikavati came in droves for a glimpse of their Neelkanth. News of his presence in the city had spread like wildfire.

Was it the Neelkanth who attacked us?

Why would he attack us?

We are his people! He is our God!

Was it really him who banned the Somras and not a fraud Neelkanth? Did our Emperor lie to us? No, that cannot be...

Shiva stood tall on the stone podium, surveying the milling, excitable crowd. He allowed them to have a clear view of his uncovered *blue throat*, the *neel kanth*. Unarmed as ordered, Nandi, Veerbhadra and Parshuram stood apprehensively behind him.

'Citizens of Mrittikavati,' thundered Shiva. 'I am your Neelkanth.'

Whispers hummed through the square.

'Silence!' said Nandi, raising his hand, quietening the audience immediately.

'I come from a faraway land deep in the Himalayas. My life was changed by what I had believed was an elixir. But I was wrong. This mark I bear on my throat is not a blessing from the Gods but a curse of Evil, a mark of poison. I carry this mark,' said Shiva, pointing to his blue throat. 'But my fellow Meluhans, you bear this scourge as well! And you don't even know it!'

The audience listened, spellbound.

'The Somras gives you a long life and you are grateful for that. But these years that it gifts to you are not for free! It takes away a lot more from you! And its hunger for your soul has no limit!'

A sinister breeze rustled the leaves of the trees that lined the square.

'For these few additional transient years you pay a price that is eternal! It is no coincidence that so many women in Meluha cannot bear children. That is the curse of the Somras!'

Shiva's words found ready resonance in Meluhan hearts, many of which had been broken by the long lonely wait for children from the Maika adoption system. They knew the misery of growing old without a child.

'It is no coincidence that the mother of your country, the mother of Indian civilisation itself, the revered Saraswati is slowly drying to extinction. The thirsty Somras continues to consume her waters. Her death will also be due to the evil of the Somras!'

The Saraswati River was not just a body of water to most Indians; in fact, no river was. And the Saraswati was the holiest among them all. It was their spiritual mother.

'Thousands of children are born in Maika with painful cancers that eat up their bodies. Millions of Swadweepans are dying of a plague brought on by the waste of the Somras. Those people curse the ones who use the Somras. They are cursing you. And your souls will bear this burden for many births. That is the evil of the Somras!'

Veerbhadra looked at Shiva's back and then at the audience.

Shiva felt his blue throat and smiled sadly. 'It may appear that the Somras has my throat. But in actual fact, it has all of Meluha by the throat! And it is squeezing the life out of you slowly, so slowly, that you don't even realise it. And by the time you do, it will be too late. All of Meluha, all of India, will be destroyed!'

The citizens of Mrittikavati continued to be engrossed in his speech.

'I did try to stop this peacefully. I sent out a notice to every city, in every kingdom, all across this fair land of our India. But in Meluha, my message was replaced by another put up by your Emperor, stating that it wasn't I who banned the Somras, but some fraud Neelkanth.'

Nandi could sense the tide turning.

'Your Emperor lied to you!'

There was pin-drop silence.

'Emperor Daksha occupies the position that was Lord Ram's more than a thousand years ago. He represents the legacy of the great seventh Vishnu. He is supposed to be your Protector. And he lied to you.'

Parshuram looked at Shiva with reverence. He had swayed the Meluhans firmly to his side.

'As if that wasn't enough, he sent his army to drive a wedge between you and me. But I know that nothing can tear us apart; I know that you will listen to me. For I am fighting for Meluha. I am fighting for the future of your children!'

A collective wave of understanding swept through the crowd; the Neelkanth was fighting *for* them, not *against* them.

'You have heard myths about the tribe of Vasudev, left behind by our great lord, Shri Ram. Well, the legendary tribe does exist, the ones who carry the legacy of Lord Ram. And they are with me, sharing my mission. They also want to save India from the Somras.'

Almost every Meluhan was familiar with the fable of the Vasudevs, the tribe of Lord Ram himself. Now knowing that they not only existed in flesh and blood, but were with the Neelkanth as well, drove the issue beyond debate in their minds.

'I am going to save Meluha! I'm going to stop the Somras!' roared Shiva. 'Who is with me?'

'I am!' screamed Nandi.

'I am!' shouted every citizen of Mrittikavati.

'I love Meluha more than the Somras,' said Shiva, 'so I put up a proclamation banning the Somras. Your Emperor loves the Somras more than Meluha, so he decided to oppose me. Whose side are you on? Meluha or the Somras?'

'Meluha!'

'Then what do we do with the army that fights for your Emperor; that fights for the Somras?'

'Kill them!'

'Kill them?'

'Yes!'

'No!' shouted Shiva.

The people fell silent, dumbfounded.

'Your army was only following orders. They have surrendered. It would be against the principles of Lord Ram to kill prisoners of war. So once again, what should we do with them?'

The audience remained quiet.

'I want the soldiers to be imprisoned in Mrittikavati,' said Shiva. 'I want you to ensure that they do not escape. If they do, they will follow your Emperor's orders and fight me again. Will you keep them captive in your city?'

'Yes!'

'Will you ensure that not one of them escapes?'

'Yes!'

Shiva allowed a smile to escape. 'I see Gods standing before me. Gods who are willing to fight Evil! Gods who are willing to give up their attachment to Evil!'

The citizens of Mrittikavati absorbed the praise from their Neelkanth.

Shiva raised his balled fist high in the air. 'Har Har Mahadev!'

'Har Har Mahadev!' roared the people.

Nandi, Veerbhadra and Parshuram raised their hands and repeated the stirring cry of those loyal to the Neelkanth. 'Har Har Mahadev!'

'Har Har Mahadev!'

— ⁂ —

The governor's palace in Mrittikavati had been modified to serve as a prison for the surviving soldiers of the Meluhan army. Shiva's troops escorted the prisoners into the make-shift prison in small batches. Shiva, Kali, Sati, Gopal and Chenardhwaj were standing at a small distance from the entrance when Vidyunmali was led in. He tried to break free and lunge at Shiva. A soldier kicked Vidyunmali hard and tried to push him back in line.

'It's all right,' said Shiva. 'Let him approach.'

Vidyunmali was allowed to walk past the bamboo shields held by the soldiers, and move towards Shiva.

'You were doing your duty, Vidyunmali,' said Shiva. 'You were only following orders. I have nothing against you. But you will have to stay imprisoned till the Somras has been removed. Then you will be free to do whatever it is that you want to do.'

Vidyunmali stared at Shiva with barely concealed disgust. 'You were a barbarian when we found you and you are still a barbarian. We Meluhans don't take orders from barbarians!'

Chenardhwaj drew his sword. 'Speak with respect to the Neelkanth.'

Vidyunmali spat at the governor of Lothal-Maika. 'I don't speak to traitors!'

Kali drew her knife out, moving towards Vidyunmali. 'Perhaps you shouldn't speak at all...'

'Kali...' whispered Shiva, before turning towards Vidyunmali. 'I have no enmity with your country. I tried to achieve my purpose with peace. I had sent out a clear proclamation asking all of you to stop using the Somras, but...'

'We are a sovereign country! We will decide what we can and cannot use.'

'Not when it comes to Evil. When it comes to the Somras, you will do what is in the interest of the people and the future of Meluha.'

'Who are you to tell us what is in our interest?'

Shiva had had enough. He waved his hand dismissively. 'Take him away.'

Nandi and Veerbhadra immediately dragged a kicking Vidyunmali towards the make-shift prison.

'You will lose, you fraud,' screamed Vidyunmali. 'Meluha will not fall!'

— ⋏◎⊍⍋⊛ —

'Shiva, I'd like you to meet someone,' said Brahaspati.

Brahaspati had just walked into Shiva's private chamber in the Mrittikavati official guesthouse, accompanied by a Brahmin. Sati, Gopal and Kali were with the Neelkanth.

'Do you remember Panini?' asked Brahaspati. 'He was my assistant at Mount Mandar.'

'Of course I do,' said Shiva, before turning to Panini. 'How are you, Panini?'

'I am well, great Neelkanth.'

'Shiva,' said Brahaspati, 'I found Panini in Mrittikavati, leading a scientific project being conducted at the Saraswati delta. He has asked me if he can join us in our battle against the Somras.'

Shiva frowned, wondering why Brahaspati was disturbing him with such an inconsequential request at this time. 'Brahaspati, he was your assistant. I completely trust your judgement. You don't have to check with me about...'

'He has some news that may be useful,' interrupted Brahaspati.

'What is it, Panini?' asked Shiva politely.

'My Lord,' said Panini. 'I was recruited by Maharishi Bhrigu for some secret work at Mount Mandar.'

Shiva's interest was immediately piqued. 'I thought the Somras factory at Mount Mandar has not been rebuilt as yet.'

'My mission had nothing to do with the Somras, My Lord. I was asked to lead a small team of Meluhan scientists personally chosen by the Maharishi to make *daivi astras* from materials that he had provided.'

'What? Was it you who made the *daivi astras*?'

'Yes.'

'Did the Vayuputras come and help you?'

'We were trained by Maharishi Bhrigu himself on how to make them from the core material that he provided us. I do know a bit about the technology of *daivi astras*, but not enough to make any usable weapons. Perhaps I was selected because even my little knowledge is more than most.'

'But weren't any Vayuputras present, in order to assist you?' asked Shiva once again. 'Did you see them with Maharishi Bhrigu perhaps?'

'I don't think the core material that the Maharishi gave us was from the Vayuputras.'

A surprised Shiva looked at Gopal, before turning back to Panini. 'What makes you say that?'

'The little that I know of the *daivi astra* technology is based on Vayuputra knowledge. Maharishi Bhrigu's processes and the materials were completely different.'

'Did he have his own core material to make the *daivi astras*?'

'It appeared so.'

Shiva turned towards Gopal once again; the implications were obvious and portentous. To begin with, the Vayuputras were not on Bhrigu's side after all. But more importantly, Bhrigu was an even more formidable opponent if he could make the core material for the *daivi astras* all by himself.

'And I also think,' said Panini, 'that Maharishi Bhrigu may have used the last of the *daivi astra* core material that he had when he asked me to prepare the weapons.'

'Why do you think so?'

'Well, he was always exhorting me to be careful with the core material and not waste even small portions of it. I remember once when we had accidentally spoilt a minuscule amount of it. He was livid and had angrily rebuked us that this was all the *daivi astra* core material that he possessed; that we should be more careful.'

Shiva took a deep breath before turning to Gopal. 'He has no more *daivi astras*.'

'It appears so,' answered Gopal.

'And the Vayuputras are not with him.'

'That would be a fair assumption to make.'

'Shiva,' said Brahaspati, 'there's more.'

Shiva raised a brow and turned towards Panini.

'My Lord,' said Panini, 'I also believe that the secret Somras factory is in Devagiri.'

'How can you be sure?' asked Shiva.

'I'm sure you're aware that the Somras needs the Sanjeevani

tree in large quantities. I was brought to Devagiri on a regular basis but only in the night, to check the quality of the Sanjeevani logs coming into the city.'

'I don't understand. Isn't it a part of your normal duties to check the consignment before it is sent off to the Somras factory?'

'That's true. But I had a friend in the customs department with whom I checked whether the Sanjeevani logs ever left the city. He was unaware of any such movement. If such huge quantities of the Sanjeevani logs are being brought into Devagiri and not being taken out, then the most logical assumption is that this is the city where the Somras is being manufactured.'

Shiva's expression reflected his gratitude towards the Brahmin. 'Panini, thank you. You have no idea how useful your information is.'

'Magadh has fallen?' asked Parvateshwar.

Parvateshwar was in the office of the Meluhan Prime Minister Kanakhala. She had finally received a bird courier from Ayodhya after many months.

'There's more,' said Kanakhala. 'The entire army of Magadh has been routed. Prince Surapadman is dead. King Mahendra has gone into deep mourning. The Brangas are now in control of Magadh.'

Parvateshwar pressed the bridge of his nose as he absorbed the implications. 'If they control Magadh, they control the chokepoint on the Ganga. They would only have to keep a few thousand soldiers within the fort of Magadh to be able to attack any Ayodhyan ship that attempts to sail past.'

'*Exactly!* That means Ayodhya cannot come to our aid

quickly enough. They will have to march through forests to their west and then move towards us.'

'If Magadh has been conquered, it means the Lord Neelkanth can leave a small force in that city, sail up the Ganga with the rest of his forces and march into Meluha from Swadweep. We can expect an attack within as little as the next three or four months. We should ask our Ayodhyan allies to leave for Meluha at once. I will speak to Lord Bhrigu.'

'There's more,' said a worried Kanakhala. 'The courier also said that the army that besieged Ayodhya and attacked Magadh was led by Ganesh, Kartik, Bhagirath and Chandraketu.'

'Then where is the Lord Neelkanth?'

'Exactly!' said Kanakhala. 'Where is the Lord Neelkanth?'

Just then an aide rushed into Kanakhala's office. 'My Lord, My Lady, please come at once to His Highness' office. Lord Bhrigu has asked that the both of you come immediately.'

As Kanakhala and Parvateshwar rushed out of the office, another aide approached them with a message for the Meluhan general. From the stamp, it was clear that the message was from Vidyunmali. Parvateshwar broke the seal, intending to read the letter on the way to the emperor's office.

Chapter 28

Meluha Stunned

'What is it, Parvateshwar?' asked Kanakhala.

She had seen the Meluhan general's face turn white as he read Vidyunmali's message. Before Parvateshwar could answer, they found themselves at the door of Daksha's office.

No sooner had Parvateshwar and Kanakhala entered the emperor's chamber, than Daksha unleashed his fury. 'Parvateshwar! Are you in control of the army or not? What in Lord Ram's name have you been up to?'

Parvateshwar knew what the emperor was talking about. He also knew that speaking with the emperor on this topic was a waste of time. He wisely kept silent, saluting the emperor with a short bow of his head and his hands folded in a Namaste.

'Bad news, General,' spoke Bhrigu. 'Mrittikavati has been attacked and conquered by Shiva.'

'What?' asked a stunned Kanakhala. 'How did they even reach Mrittikavati? How could they get through the defences of Lothal?'

Lothal was an exceptionally well-designed sea fortress. Its defences were so solid that an attacker would have to fight overwhelming odds to have any hope of conquering it. It was also known that Lothal was the gateway to south-eastern Meluha, and an attacking army would have to cross this city to be able to march up to Mrittikavati.

Bhrigu raised five sheets of papyrus. 'This is from the governor of Mrittikavati. Apparently Chenardhwaj has pledged loyalty to Shiva. The traitor!'

'That swine!' growled Daksha. 'I knew I should never have trusted him!'

'Then why did you appoint him governor of Lothal, Your Highness?' asked Bhrigu.

Daksha lapsed into a sulk.

Bhrigu turned to Parvateshwar. 'Your suspicions about Lothal were correct, Lord Parvateshwar. I should apologise for not having listened to you earlier. Had we perhaps sent Vidyunmali to Lothal promptly with a strong force we would still be in control of that city.'

'We cannot undo what has happened, My Lord,' said Parvateshwar. 'Let's concentrate on what we can do now. I've received a message from Vidyunmali.'

Bhrigu looked at the letter in Parvateshwar's hand. 'What does the Brigadier say?'

'It sounds like an intelligence failure to me,' said Parvateshwar. 'He says Lord Shiva took them by surprise as he appeared at the gates of Mrittikavati with one hundred thousand soldiers. Vidyunmali put up a brave defence with a mere twenty-five thousand, but was routed.'

Kanakhala understood the strategic significance of Mrittikavati. 'Mrittikavati houses the headquarters of the Saraswati fleet. And Vidyunmali had taken what was left of our warships as well. If the Lord controls Mrittikavati, he now controls the Saraswati River.'

'Shiva is not a Lord!' screamed Daksha. 'How dare you? Who are you loyal to, Kanakhala?'

'Your Highness,' said Bhrigu, his calm tone belying the menace beneath.

Daksha recoiled in fear.

'Your Highness, perhaps it would be better if you retired to your personal chambers.'

'But...'

'Your Highness,' said Bhrigu. 'That was not a request.'

Daksha closed his eyes, shocked at the immense disrespect being shown to him. He got up and left his office, muttering under his breath about the respect due to the Emperor of India.

Bhrigu turned to Parvateshwar, unperturbed, as if nothing had happened. 'General, what else does Vidyunmali say?'

'The entire Saraswati fleet is under the Lord Neelkanth now. But it gets worse.'

'Worse?'

'The people of Mrittikavati have now pledged loyalty to him. The survivors of Vidyunmali's army have been held prisoner in Mrittikavati. Fortunately for us, Vidyunmali managed to escape with five hundred soldiers and send this message.'

'So the Neelkanth has stationed himself in Mrittikavati for now?' asked Bhrigu, careful not to use the term 'fraud Neelkanth' in Parvateshwar's presence. 'Because he will have to commit his own soldiers to guard ours, right?'

'No,' said Parvateshwar, shaking his head. 'Our army is being held prisoner by the citizens of Mrittikavati.'

'The citizens?!'

'Yes. So the Lord Neelkanth does not have to commit any of his own soldiers for the task. He has managed to take twenty-five thousand of our soldiers out of the equation but he still has practically his whole army with him. He has commandeered our entire Saraswati fleet. I'm sure he is making plans to sail up north even as we speak. Vidyunmali also writes about a fearsome corps of exceptionally well-trained elephants in the Lord's army, which are almost impossible to defeat.'

'Lord Ram, be merciful!' said a stunned Kanakhala.

'This is worse than we'd ever imagined,' said Bhrigu.

'But I don't understand one thing,' said Kanakhala. 'How does the Lord have an army of one hundred thousand in Meluha, when a hundred and fifty thousand of his soldiers were in Ayodhya a few weeks back?'

'Ayodhya?' asked a surprised Bhrigu.

'Yes,' said Kanakhala and proceeded to tell him about the message she had just received from Ayodhya about the siege and the destruction of the Magadhan forces.

'By the great Lord Brahma!' said Bhrigu. 'This means the Ayodhya army cannot sail past Magadh. They will have to march through the forest, which means it will take them forever to come to our aid.'

'But I still don't understand how the Lord Neelkanth has so many soldiers in Meluha,' persisted Kanakhala. 'The Branga and Naga armies together don't add up to this number.'

The truth finally dawned on Bhrigu. 'The Vasudevs have joined forces with Shiva. They are the only ones outside of the Suryavanshis and the Chandravanshis who can bring in so many soldiers. This also explains the presence of the exceptionally well-trained elephants Shiva used in the Battle of Mrittikavati. I have heard stories about the prowess of the Vasudev elephants.'

Bhrigu was not aware that the strongest strategic benefit of the Vasudevs was not their elephant corps, but their secretive Vasudev pandits hidden in temples across the Sapt Sindhu. These pandits were the eyes and ears of the Neelkanth, providing him with the most crucial advantage in war: timely and accurate information.

'Lord Shiva will be here soon with a large army,' said Parvateshwar. 'And the three hundred thousand soldiers of Ayodhya will not reach us in time. He has played his cards really well.'

'I do not have a military mind, General,' said Bhrigu. 'But even I can see that we are in deep trouble. What do you advise?'

Parvateshwar brought his hands together and rubbed his chin with his index fingers. He looked up at Bhrigu after some time. 'If Ganesh decides to enter Meluha from the north, we are finished. There is no way we can defend ourselves against a two-pronged attack. Our engineers have been working hard at repairing the road that was ruined by the Yamuna floods. I'll immediately send them instructions to leave the road as it is. If Ganesh chooses to cross from there, then we must make the journey difficult for him. Marching a hundred and fifty thousand strong army on a washed-out road is not going to be easy.'

'Good idea.'

'The Lord Neelkanth could be in Devagiri in a matter of weeks.'

'It's a good thing you have engaged the army in training exercises and simulations,' said Bhrigu.

'The Lord will not win here,' said Parvateshwar. 'That is my word to you, Maharishi*ji*.'

'I believe you, General. But what do we do about the Vasudev elephants? We cannot win against Shiva's army unless we stop his elephants.'

— ⅄◎Ʊ⇑⊛ —

'What do you think, Shiva?' asked Gopal.

Gopal, Sati and Kali were with Shiva in his chamber at

Mrittikavati, conferring. They were re-evaluating their strategy in the light of the news received from Panini.

Kali was clear in her mind. 'Shiva, I propose that you leave Mrittikavati and sail out to Pariha. If you can convince the Vayuputras to give you a lethal *daivi astra*, say the *Brahmastra*, this war will be as good as over.'

'We cannot actually use these *daivi astras*, Your Highness,' said Gopal. 'It will be against the laws of humanity. We can only use such weapons as deterrents to make the other side see sense.'

'Yes, yes,' said Kali dismissively, 'I agree.'

'How long will the journey to Pariha take, Pandit*ji*?' asked Shiva.

'Six months at the minimum,' said Gopal. 'It could take even nine to twelve months if the winds don't favour us.'

'Then the decision is clear,' said Shiva. 'I don't think going to Pariha at this stage makes sense.'

'Why?' asked Kali.

'We have momentum and time on our side, Kali,' said Shiva. 'Ayodhya's army cannot come into Meluha for another six to eight months at least. Ganesh and Kartik can reach the northern frontiers of Meluha within a few weeks. We will have a six-month window with two hundred and fifty thousand soldiers on our side against just seventy-five thousand on the side of Meluha. I like those odds. I say we finish the war here and now. In the time that it will take me to go to Pariha and return, the situation may have become very different. Also, don't forget, all we know is that the Vayuputras are not with Maharishi Bhrigu. That does not necessarily mean that they will choose to be with us. They may well decide to remain neutral.'

'That makes sense,' agreed Sati. 'If we conquer Devagiri and destroy the Somras factory, the war will be over regardless of what the Vayuputras choose to believe.'

'So what do you suggest, Shiva?' asked Gopal.

'We should divide our navy into two parts,' said Shiva. 'I'll move up the Saraswati and then north, up the Yamuna with a small sailing force of twenty-five ships. I'll meet Ganesh and Kartik as they march down the Yamuna road and we'll board their soldiers onto my ships. By sailing, we can get to Devagiri quicker, instead of waiting for them to march to the Meluhan capital. In the meantime, Sati will lead the other contingent of the navy, carrying our entire army from Mrittikavati up the Saraswati to Devagiri. Sati should leave three weeks after me so that we reach Devagiri around the same time. With two hundred and fifty thousand soldiers besieging Devagiri, they may actually see some sense.'

'Sounds good in theory,' said Kali. 'But coordination may prove to be a problem in practice. There could be delays. If one of our armies reaches Devagiri a few weeks earlier, it may leave them weakened against the Meluhans.'

'But Shiva is not suggesting that we mount an attack and conquer Devagiri as soon as either one of us reaches,' said Sati. 'We would just fortify ourselves and wait for the other. Once we have joined forces, only then should we attack.'

'True, but what if the Meluhans decide to attack?' asked Kali. 'Remember, anchored ships are sitting ducks for devil boats.'

'I don't see them stepping out of the safety of their fort,' said Shiva. 'The army that I will lead will have a hundred and fifty thousand soldiers who have just destroyed the mighty Magadhans; the Meluhans will not attack us with only seventy-five thousand soldiers. Sati's army will have a hundred thousand, and don't forget, she will also have the Vasudev elephants. So you see, even our separate armies are capable of taking on the Meluhans on an open field. General Parvateshwar has a calm head on his strong shoulders. He will know that it's better for them to remain in the safety of their fort, rather than marching out and attacking us.'

'But I get your point, Kali,' said Sati. 'If I reach early, I will encamp some ten kilometres south of Devagiri. There is a large hill on the banks of the Saraswati which can serve as a superb defensive position since it will give us the advantage of height. I will set up a *Chakravyuh* formation with our Vasudev elephants as the first line of defence. It will be almost impossible to break through.'

'I know that hill,' said Shiva to Sati. 'That is exactly where I will camp as well if I happen to reach before you do.'

'Perfect.'

— ⁂ —

'There is no respite from the speed, is there, My Lord?'

Shiva and Parshuram stood on the deck of his lead ship, battling to keep their eyes open against the onslaught of the wind upon a speedily moving object.

The fleet was racing up the Saraswati, skeletally staffed as it was, with just two thousand soldiers, not giving any opportunity for the Meluhans to launch small strikes. While none of the cities on the Saraswati were prepared for naval warfare – since the Meluhans never expected such an attack – Shiva had decided to not tempt fate. The Meluhans were not wanting in honour and courage. As an additional precaution, he had also inducted many of the courageous Naga soldiers into his navy. Kali, the Queen of the Nagas, was travelling in the rearguard ship of the convoy.

Shiva smiled. 'No Parshuram, there will be no respite. Speed is of the essence.'

In keeping with Shiva's orders, there had been no breaks in the rowing. Four teams had been set up on gruelling six-hour shifts. The timekeepers, beating on the drums to set the rhythm for the rowers, maintained it at battle-ramming speed. Shiva did not want to trust the unpredictable winds with determining how fast they moved. In the interest of fairness, Shiva had also added his own name to the roster for rowing duties. His six hours of rowing for the day were to come up soon.

'It's a beautiful river, My Lord,' said Parshuram. 'It's sad that we may have to kill it.'

'What do you mean?'

'My Lord, I have been researching the Somras. Lord Gopal has explained many things to me. And an idea has struck me...'

'What?'

'The Somras cannot be made without this,' said Parshuram, pointing to the Saraswati.

'Brahaspati tried that, Parshuram... He tried to find some way to make the Saraswati waters unusable. But that didn't work, remember?'

'That's not what I meant, My Lord. What if the Saraswati didn't exist? Neither would the Somras, would it?'

Shiva observed Parshuram closely with inscrutable eyes.

'My Lord, there was a time when the Saraswati, as we know it today, had ceased to exist. The Yamuna had started flowing east towards the Ganga. Saraswati cannot exist without the meeting of the Yamuna and the Sutlej.'

'We cannot kill the Saraswati,' said Shiva, almost to himself.

'My Lord, for all you know, maybe that's what Nature was trying to do more than a hundred years ago, when an earthquake caused the Yamuna to change its course and flow into the Ganga. If Lord Brahmanayak, the father of the present emperor, had not changed the Yamuna's course to flow back into the Sutlej and restore the Saraswati, history would have been very different. Maybe Nature was trying to stop the Somras.'

Shiva listened silently.

'We don't have to think the Saraswati would be dead. Its soul would still be flowing in the form of the Yamuna and the Sutlej. Only its body would disappear.'

Shiva stared at the Saraswati waters, perceiving her depths. Parshuram had a point but Shiva didn't want to admit it. Not even to himself. Not yet, anyway.

Chapter 29

Every Army Has a Traitor

'Any news, Ganesh?' asked Bhagirath.

Bhagirath and Chandraketu had just joined Ganesh and Kartik on the lead ship. The massive navy was sailing up the Ganga en route to Meluha from the north. Farther ahead, they were to take the Ganga-Yamuna road. They had slowed down only for a few hours to allow a boat to rendezvous with them. The boatman carried a message from a Vasudev pandit.

'I've just received word that my father's army has conquered Mrittikavati,' said Ganesh.

Chandraketu was thrilled. 'That is great news!'

'It is indeed,' answered Ganesh. 'And it gets even better; the citizens of Mrittikavati have been won over to my father's side. They have imprisoned what was left of the Meluhan army in the city.'

'And, have they discovered the location of the Somras factory?' asked Bhagirath.

'Yes,' said Kartik. 'It's Devagiri.'

'Devagiri? What are you saying? That is so stupid. It's their capital. One would think that the factory would be built in a secure, secret location.'

'But they could have built this factory only within cities

with large populations, right? And if so, which city would be better than Devagiri? They must have assumed that they could certainly keep their capital safe.'

'So what are our orders now?' asked Chandraketu.

'The Meluhans have only seventy-five thousand soldiers in Devagiri,' said Ganesh. 'So we're going to launch a coordinated attack.'

'What are the details of the plan?'

'We're to sail up the Ganga and reach the Ganga-Yamuna road. We will then march to Meluha. My father is going to sail up the Yamuna in a fleet to meet us as we march. Together, we will then sail down to Devagiri. My mother, in the meantime, will arrive with the hundred thousand soldiers under her command.'

'So we will have two hundred and fifty thousand soldiers, all fired up with the fervour of recent victories, against seventy-five thousand Meluhans holed up on their platforms,' said Bhagirath. 'I like the odds.'

'That's exactly what *baba* must have said!' grinned Kartik.

— ⁂ —

'You are going to give me the answer I want,' growled Vidyunmali, 'whether you like it or not.'

A Vasudev major, captured from Shiva's army, had been tied up on a moveable wooden rack with thick leather ropes. The stale air in the dark dungeon was putrid. The captured Vasudev was already drenched in his own sweat, but unafraid.

The Meluhan soldiers standing at a distance looked at Vidyunmali warily. What their brigadier was asking them to do was against the laws of Lord Ram. But they were too well-trained. Meluhan military training demanded unquestioning obedience to one's commanding officer. This training had forced the soldiers to suppress their misgivings and carry out Vidyunmali's orders until now. But their moral code was about to be challenged even more strongly.

Vidyunmali heard the Vasudev whispering something again and again. He bent close. 'Do you have something to say?'

The Vasudev soldier kept mumbling softly, drawing strength from his words. '*Jai Guru Vishwamitra. Jai Guru Vashishtha. Jai Guru Vishwamitra. Jai Guru Vashishtha...*'

Vidyunmali sniggered. 'They aren't here to help you, my friend.'

He turned and beckoned a startled Meluhan soldier. The brigadier pointed at a metallic hammer and large nail.

'My Lord?' whispered the nervous soldier, knowing full well that to attack an unarmed and bound man was against Lord Ram's principles. 'I'm not sure if we should...'

'It's not your job to be sure,' growled Vidyunmali. 'That's my job. Your job is to do what I order you to do.'

'Yes, My Lord,' said the Meluhan, saluting slowly. He picked up the hammer and nail. He walked slowly to the Vasudev and placed the nail on the captive's arm, a few inches above the wrist. He held the hammer back and flexed his shoulders, ready to strike.

Vidyunmali turned to the Vasudev. 'You'd better start talking...'

'*Jai Guru Vishwamitra. Jai Guru Vashishtha...*'

Vidyunmali nodded to the soldier.

'*Jai Guru Vishwamitra. Jai Guru...* AAAAHHHHHHHHH!'

The ear-splitting scream from the Vasudev resounded loudly in the confines of the dungeon. But this deep, abandoned underground hell-hole, somewhere between Mrittikavati and Devagiri, had not been used in centuries. There was nobody around to hear his screams except for the nervous Meluhan soldiers at the back of the room, who kept praying to Lord Ram, begging for his forgiveness.

The soldier kept robotically hammering away, pushing the nail deep into the Vasudev's right arm. The Vasudev kept screaming up to a point where his brain simply blocked the pain. He couldn't feel his arm anymore. His heart was pumping madly, as blood came out in spurts through the gaping injury.

Vidyunmali approached his ear as the Vasudev breathed heavily, trying to focus on his tribe, on his Gods, on his vows, on anything except his right arm.

'Do you need some more persuasion?' asked Vidyunmali.

The Vasudev looked away, focusing his mind on his chant.

Vidyunmali yanked the nail out, took a wet cloth and wiped the Vasudev's arm. Then he picked up a small bottle and poured its contents into the wound. It burned deeply, but the Vasudev's blood clotted almost immediately.

'I don't want you to die,' whispered Vidyunmali. 'At least not yet...'

Vidyunmali turned towards his soldier and nodded.

'My Lord,' whispered the soldier, with tears in his eyes. He had lost count of the number of sins that he was taking upon his soul. 'Please...'

Vidyunmali glared.

The soldier immediately turned and picked up another bottle. He walked up to the Vasudev and poured some of the viscous liquid into the wound he had inflicted.

Vidyunmali stepped back and returned with a long flint, its edge burning slowly. 'I hope you see the light after this.'

The Vasudev's eyes opened wide in terror. But he refused to talk; he knew he couldn't reveal the secret. It would be devastating for his tribe.

'Jai... Gu... ru... Vishwa...'

'Fire will purify you,' whispered Vidyunmali softly. 'And you will speak.'

'*...Mitra... Jai... Gu... ru... Vash...*'

The dungeon resonated once again with the desperate screams of the Vasudev, as the smell of burning flesh defiled the room.

— ⅄ⵀ ⵀ ⵀ —

'Are you sure?' asked Parvateshwar.

'As sure as I can ever be,' said a smiling Vidyunmali.

Parvateshwar took a deep breath.

He knew that it was Shiva who led the massive fleet of ships that had just sped past Devagiri two weeks back. Parvateshwar suspected that Shiva was sailing north to pick up Ganesh's army and bring them back to Devagiri. He had also received reports about the delays faced by Ganesh's army as they marched through the washed-out Ganga-Yamuna Road. It would probably take a month for Shiva to return to Devagiri, along with the hundred and fifty thousand soldiers in Ganesh's army.

He also knew that another contingent of the Neelkanth's army, being led by Sati, had just sailed out of Mrittikavati. They would reach Devagiri in a week or two. Knowing full well that Ganesh would be delayed, Parvateshwar expected Sati's army to reach Devagiri first. He also knew that this was a force of a hundred thousand soldiers against his own seventy-five thousand. Once Shiva and Ganesh's army sailed in, the strength of the enemy would rise to two hundred and fifty thousand. Parvateshwar knew that his best chance was to attack Sati's army before Shiva and Ganesh arrived.

The only problem was that he had no answer for the unstoppable Vasudev elephant corps under Sati's command. Until now.

'Chilli and dung?' asked Parvateshwar. 'It just seems so simple.'

'Apparently, the elephants don't like the smell of chilli, My Lord. It makes them run amuck. We should keep dung bricks mixed with chilli ready, burn them and catapult them towards the elephants. The acrid smoke will drive them crazy; and, hopefully, into their own army.'

'There are no elephants to test this on, Vidyunmali. The only way to test this would be in battle. What if this doesn't work?'

'My apologies, General, but do we have any other options?'

'No.'

'Then what's the harm in trying?'

Parvateshwar nodded and turned to stare at his soldiers practising in the distance. 'How did you get this information?'

Vidyunmali was quiet.

Parvateshwar returned his gaze to Vidyunmali, his eyes boring into him. 'Brigadier, I asked you a question.'

'There are traitors in every army, My Lord.'

Parvateshwar was stunned. The famous Vasudev discipline was legendary. 'You found a Vasudev traitor?!'

'Like I said, there are traitors in every army. How do you think I escaped?'

Parvateshwar turned and looked once again at his soldiers. No harm in trying this tactic. It just might work.

— ⁂ —

Devagiri, the abode of the Gods, had become the city of the thoroughly bewildered. Its two hundred thousand citizens could not recall a time in living memory when an enemy army had gathered the gumption to march up to their city. And yet, here they were, witness to unbelievable occurrences.

Just a few weeks earlier, they had seen a large fleet of warships race past their city, rowing furiously up the Saraswati. It was clear that these ships were a part of the Mrittikavati-based Meluhan fleet and that it was now in control of the enemy. Why those enemy ships simply sailed by without attacking Devagiri was a mystery.

News had also filtered in about a massive army garrisoning itself next to the Saraswati, about ten kilometres south of the city. The normally secure Devagiri citizens now confined themselves within the walls of the city, not venturing out unless absolutely necessary. Merchants had also halted all their trading activities and their merchant ships remained anchored at the port.

Rumours ran rife in the city. Some whispered that the enemy army stationed south of Devagiri was led by the Neelkanth himself. Others swore they saw the Neelkanth on the warships that had sailed past. However, they couldn't hazard a guess as to where Lord Shiva was headed in such a hurry. Facts had also found their way in, from other cities: that except for Mrittikavati, this mammoth army had not engaged in battle with any other Meluhan city while sailing up the Saraswati. They had not looted any city or plundered any village, nor had they committed any acts of wanton destruction, but had marched through Meluha with almost hermit-like restraint.

Some were beginning to believe that perhaps the purported gossip they had heard was in fact true; the Neelkanth was not against Meluha, but only the Somras. That the proclamation they had read many months ago was actually from their Lord and not a lie as their emperor had stated. That may be the Neelkanth's army waited at the banks of the Saraswati without attacking, because the Lord himself was negotiating possible terms of surrender with the emperor.

But there were also others, still loyal to Meluha, who refused to believe that their government could have lied. They had good reason to believe that the armies of Shiva comprised the Chandravanshis and the Nagas. That the Naga queen herself was a senior commander in the Neelkanth's army and the Neelkanth had been misled by the evil combination of the Chandravanshis and Nagas. They were willing to lay down their lives for Meluha. What they didn't understand was why their army was not engaging in battle as yet.

'Are you sure, General?' asked Bhrigu.

Parvateshwar was in Bhrigu's chamber in the Devagiri royal palace.

'Yes. It is a gamble, but we have to take it. If we wait too long, the Lord will lead Ganesh's army from the Yamuna to Devagiri. Combined with Sati's army, they will then have a vast numerical advantage and it will be impossible for us to win. Right now, our opponents are only Sati's soldiers who have garrisoned themselves close to the river. They are obviously not looking for a fight. I plan to draw them out and then try to cause some chaos amongst their elephants. If it works, their elephants may just charge back into their own army. They would have no room to retreat, with the river right behind them. If everything goes according to plan, we may just win the day.'

'Isn't Sati your God-daughter?' asked Bhrigu, looking deeply into Parvateshwar's eyes.

Parvateshwar held his breath. 'At this point of time, she is only an enemy of Meluha to me.'

Bhrigu continued to peer into his eyes, increasingly satisfied with what he read. 'If you are convinced, General, then so am I. In the name of Lord Ram, attack.'

— ⋏◎ᑌ♆⊛ —

Sati couldn't remain holed up on her anchored ships. Ships are unassailable from land when sailing fast, but sitting ducks when they are anchored, susceptible to bombardment and devil boat assaults. So she had decided to garrison herself on land, which would offer protection to her ships as well, by deterring the Meluhans from coming too close to the river banks.

She had chosen a good location to dig in her army. It was on a large, gently-rolling hill right next to the Saraswati. The trees between the hill and the city of Devagiri had been cut down. Therefore, from the vantage point of the hill, Sati had a clear line of sight of enemy movements at the Devagiri city gates ten kilometres away. The height of the hill also gave her another advantage: charging downhill was far easier than advancing uphill, which her enemies would have to do. The elevation also increased the range of her archers significantly.

Having occupied the high ground, Sati then opted to assume the most effective of defensive military formations: the *Chakravyuh*. The core of the *Chakravyuh* comprised columns of infantrymen in the tortoise position. The tortoises themselves were protected to the rear by the river and the Saraswati fleet at anchor, in the middle of the river. They would provide protection against any Meluhan forces that might attack from the river end. Rowboats had been beached and tied in the river shallows, as a contingency for retreating, if necessary. Rows of cavalry, three layers deep, reinforced the core towards the front. Two rows of war elephants formed an impregnable semi-circular outer shell, protecting the formations within. The giant *Chakravyuh,* comprising fifty thousand soldiers, left adequate space between the lines for inner manoeuvrability and for fortification of the outer shell by the cavalry in case of a breach.

All the animals had been outfitted with thin metallic armour and the soldiers had broad bronze shields to protect against any long-range arrows.

It was a near-perfect defensive formation, designed to avoid battle and allow a quick retreat if needed.

Sati intended to remain in this formation till she heard from Shiva.

Chapter 30

Battle of Devagiri

Sati sat on a tall wooden platform that had been constructed for her, behind the cavalry line. It gave her a panoramic view of the entire field and the city of Devagiri in the distance. She watched the city where she had spent most of her life, which she had once called home. A nostalgic corner of her heart longed to be able to revel in its quiet, sober efficiency and understated culture. To worship at the temple of Lord Agni, the purifying Fire God, a ritual she had adhered to as a Vikarma, an ostracised carrier of bad fate. Despite being so close, she couldn't even enter it now to meet her mother. She shook her head. This was no time for sentimentality. She had to focus.

Sati checked her horse, which had been tethered to the platform base. Nandi and Veerbhadra waited next to the platform, mounted on their stallions. They had been designated her personal bodyguards.

Sati knew this would be a difficult period – the time till Shiva returned with Ganesh's army. She had to keep her soldiers in war readiness, and yet, avoid war. As any general knows, this can sometimes breed restless irritability amongst the troops.

Her attention was pulled away as she detected some

movement in the far distance. She couldn't believe what she saw. The main gate of the *Tamra* or *bronze* platform of Devagiri was being opened.

What are they doing? Why would the Meluhans step out into the open? They are outnumbered!

'Steady!' ordered Sati. 'Everyone remain in their positions! We will not be provoked into launching an attack!'

Messengers below immediately relayed the orders to all the brigade commanders. It was important for Sati's soldiers to remain in line. As long as they did, it was almost impossible to beat them. It was especially crucial that the elephant line, at the periphery of Sati's formation, held position. They were the bulwark of her defence.

Sati continued to watch the small contingent of Meluhan soldiers marching out of Devagiri, perhaps no more than a brigade. As soon as they were out, the city gates were shut behind them.

Is it a suicide squad? For what purpose...

The Meluhan soldiers kept marching slowly towards Sati's position. She watched their progress, intrigued. Perched at a height, she soon observed that the soldiers were being followed by carts that were being pulled laboriously by oxen.

What do these thousand foot-soldiers hope to achieve? And what is in those carts?

As the Meluhans drew close to the hill, she saw that many of the soldiers carried long weapons in their left hands.

Archers.

She instantly knew what was about to happen, as she saw them stop. They even had a strong wind supporting them. The Meluhans had clearly planned this for when the winds would work in their favour. She knew the elements well in these parts and realised immediately that her archers would not have the pleasure of giving as much as receiving.

'Shields!' shouted Sati. 'Incoming arrows!'

But the archers were too far. They had clearly overestimated the wind. The arrows barely reached Sati's forces. The strong wind, though advantageous for the Meluhans, was not working to Sati's benefit. She couldn't reply to the Meluhan volley of arrows in kind with her own archers. She saw the Meluhans inch closer, lugging ox-drawn carts behind the archers. In all her years, Sati had never seen ox-drawn carts being used in warfare.

Sati frowned. *What in Lord Ram's name can oxen do against elephants? What is* Pitratulya *doing?*

Sati was clear that she did not want to test General Parvateshwar's strategy today. It was admittedly tempting because this small contingent would be wiped out in minutes if she sent her elephants. However, she smelt a trap and did not want to leave the high ground. She knew what had to be done: hold position till Shiva returned. She did not want to fight. Not today.

Having moved even closer, the Meluhan archers loaded their arrows again.

'Shields!' ordered Sati.

This time the arrows hit the shields at the right end of Sati's formation. Having tested the range, the Meluhan archers moved once again.

The Meluhans probably have some secret weapon that they are not absolutely sure about. The ox-drawn carts may have some role to play in it. They want to provoke some of my men into charging at them so that they can test their weapon.

The upshot was obvious. If her army refused to get provoked, no battle would take place. All the animals in her army were well-armoured. The soldiers had massive shields, prepared in defence for the very arrow attack that the Meluhans were attempting right now. Despite two showers of arrows, her army had not suffered a single casualty. There was nothing to gain by breaking formation. And, nothing to lose by staying in formation.

Sati also figured that since the enemy had already come close, ordering her own archers to shoot arrows now may prove counter-productive. The ox-drawn carts were not manned. A volley of arrows may well drive the animals crazy, making them charge in any direction, perhaps even at her own army, along with whatever evil they carried in the carts. She had a better idea. She instructed her messengers to tell a cavalry squad to ride out from behind the hill she was positioned on, thus hiding their movement, and go around to an adjoining hill towards the west. She wanted them to launch a flanking attack from behind the crest of that hill, surprise and decimate the Meluhan archers as well as drive the oxen away. All she had to do was wait for the Meluhans to move a little closer to her position. Then, she could have them blind-sided with her cavalry charge.

Sati shouted out her orders once again. 'Be calm! Hold the line! They cannot hurt us if we remain in formation.'

The Meluhan archers, having moved closer, arched their bows and fired once again.

'Shields!'

Sati's army was ready. Though the arrows reached right up to the centre of her army, not one soldier was injured. The Meluhans held their bows to their sides and prepared to draw nearer once again, this time a little tentatively.

They're nervous now. They know their plan is not working.

'What the hell!' growled an angry Vasudev elephant-rider as he turned to his partner. 'They are a puny brigade with oxen, against our entire army. Why doesn't General Sati allow us to attack?'

'Because she is not a Vasudev,' spat out the partner. 'She doesn't know how to fight.'

'My Lords,' said the *mahout* to the riders, 'our orders are to follow the General's orders.'

The Vasudev turned in irritation to the *mahout*. 'Did I ask you for your opinion? Your order is to only follow my orders!'

The *mahout* immediately fell silent as the distant shout of the brigadier's herald came through. 'Shields!'

Another volley of arrows. Again, no casualties.

'Enough of this nonsense!' barked one of the elephant-riders. 'We're Kshatriyas! We're not supposed to cower like cowardly Brahmins! We're supposed to fight!'

Sati saw a few elephants on the far right of her formation, the ones that were the closest to the Meluhan brigade, begin to rumble out.

'Hold the line!' shouted Sati. 'Nobody will break formation!'

The messengers carried forward the orders to the other end of the field immediately. The elephants were pulled back into formation by their *mahouts*.

'Nandi,' said Sati, looking down. 'Ride out to that end and tell those idiots to remain in formation!'

'Yes, My Lady,' said Nandi, saluting.

'Wait!' said Sati, as she saw the Meluhan archers loading another set of arrows. 'Wait out this volley and then go.'

The order of 'shields!' was relayed again and the arrows clanged harmlessly against the raised barriers. None of Sati's soldiers were injured.

As Sati put her shield down and looked up, she was horrified. Twenty elephants on the right had charged out recklessly.

'The fools!' yelled Sati, as she jumped onto her horse from the platform.

She galloped forward to cover the breach opened up by the recklessly charging elephants, closely followed by Veerbhadra and Nandi. While passing by the cavalry line, she ordered the reserve cavalry to follow her. Within a few minutes, Sati had stationed herself in the position left open by the Vasudev elephants that had charged out of formation.

'Stay here!' Sati ordered the soldiers behind her as she raised her hand.

She could see her elephants sprinting forward in the distance, goaded on by their *mahouts*, bellowing loudly. The Meluhan archers stood their ground bravely and shot another round.

The order resonated through Sati's army. 'Shields!'

The Vasudev elephant-riders screamed loudly as they crashed into the archers. 'Jai Shri Ram!'

The elephants swung their powerful trunks, tied to which were strong metallic balls. Meluhan soldiers were flung far and wide with the powerful swings. The few who remained were crushed under giant feet. Within just a few moments of this butchery, the archers began retreating.

Though it appeared as if the twenty Vasudev elephants were smashing the Meluhan archers to bits, Sati shuddered with foreboding as she felt a chill run down her spine. She screamed loudly, even though she knew that the elephant-riders couldn't hear her.

'Come back, you fools!'

The Vasudev elephant-riders though, were on a roll. Encouraged by the easy victory, they goaded their *mahouts* to keep the elephants moving forward.

'Charge!'

The elephant-riders primed their main weapon, pulling the levers on the flame throwers. Long, spear-like flames burst forth from the *howdahs*. The riders positioned the weapon, aiming for maximum effect as they crashed into the next line of Meluhans.

The elephants continued dashing forward, seeing the ox-drawn carts farther ahead. And then the tide turned. The retreating Meluhan archers spun around with arrows that had been set on fire, aiming straight for their own carts. The dry and volatile dung cakes on the carts had been mixed with chilli, and caught fire immediately. The startled oxen, sensing the blaze somewhere behind them, ran forward in panic, towards the advancing elephants.

It was the *mahouts* who had the first inkling that something was wrong. Attuned deeply to the beasts, they could sense their innate distress. Goaded on by the fiery elephant-riders behind them though, they continued to press their elephants ahead. Soon the contents on the carts were completely aflame, letting out a thick, acrid smoke. But the elephant-riders were too committed to the charge. They rode straight into the blinding smoke.

As soon as the smoke hit them, the elephants shrieked desperately. The *mahouts* recognised the smell.

Chilli!

'Retreat!' screamed a *mahout.*

'No!' shouted back a belligerent elephant-rider. 'We have them! Crush the oxen. Move forward!'

But the elephants were already in a state of frenzied panic. They turned from the source of their discomfort and ran. The hysterical oxen, with the fires burning hard on the carts, continued their frantic sprint forward as though to elude the blaze.

Sati could see the developing situation unfolding from the distance. Whatever the oxen were carrying was making the pachyderms hysterical. Within a matter of a few minutes the oxen would reach her remaining outer elephant line and spread the panic deep into her force. She saw a fire arrow being shot from the gates of Devagiri as they opened once again. The Meluhans could see their strategy was working and were committing themselves to a full attack. Her worst fears were confirmed as she saw the Meluhan cavalry thunder out of the Devagiri gates. The city was ten kilometres away, and she knew she had the luxury of some time before they reached her position. Her immediate concern was the oncoming oxen that could make all the Vasudev elephants charge madly back into her own force.

Turning back, she shouted out to her herald, 'Tell the lines at the back to retreat to the boats. NOW!'

She ordered the remaining elephant line to disband and escape southwards immediately. If the ox-driven carts reached the line of the lumbering animals and managed to spread panic among the hundreds of elephants under her command, her army would get destroyed completely by her own pachyderms.

She then ordered her cavalry forward.

'Charge at these beasts moving towards us! We have to deflect them on to a different path! We need time for our soldiers to retreat!'

Her cavalry drew their swords and roared: 'Har Har Mahadev!'

'Har Har Mahadev!' bellowed Sati, as she drew her sword and charged forward.

Sati's skilled cavalry kept up a steady volley of arrows as they drew near the elephants and oxen. While this did deflect many of the oxen away from Sati's army, the elephants continued their headlong charge. Many of the elephant *howdahs* had transformed into hell-holes, emitting fire continuously. The shocked elephant-riders, sitting atop the berserk animals, had fallen on some of their flame-throwers, breaking the levers.

Moments later, Sati's cavalry fearlessly charged headlong into her retreating elephants, riding expertly to avoid the wildly swinging trunks and metallic balls. They needed to bring their own elephants down. This required riding up close from behind and slashing the beasts' hamstrings, thus making their rear legs collapse. But this was easier said than done, with the malfunctioning flame-throwers spewing a continuous stream of fire. Sati bravely led her section of the cavalry in pursuit of the task at hand. Since there were only twenty elephants, they were brought down quickly. But not before many of the cavalrymen had lost their lives, some crushed, many burnt by the flame-throwers. Sati herself had had her face scorched on one side.

In the meantime, the rest of Sati's cavalry had managed to redirect all the charging oxen through the skilled use of spears and arrows. The bulls were still charging, panic-stricken with the burning carts tethered to them, but to the west and safely away from the rest of Sati's elephant corps. Sati looked back to the east, where many of her foot soldiers were already sailing out to the safety of the ships. Her cautious planning had ensured that a large number of rowboats had been kept ready for just such an eventuality.

But this would prove to be a minor victory, before absolute disaster. The Meluhan cavalry had been riding hard towards the battlefield, making good time. And, as the oxen stampeded away, the Meluhan riders charged into Sati's cavalry.

Swords clashed.

Sati's cavalry had numbered three thousand riders and was evenly matched with the Meluhans. But her riders had just emerged from a bruising encounter with the panic-stricken elephants and oxen. Their numbers had come down and their strength was already sapped. However, Sati knew that retreat was not an option. She had to battle on for a little longer so that all her foot soldiers could get away to the safety of the ships.

Then Sati heard the sounds of the elephants once again.

She killed the Meluhan in front of her and looked behind.

'Lord Ram, be merciful!'

Some of the elephant corps that she had ordered south were now thundering back. The elephants were trumpeting desperately, with fire spewing in all directions. The *mahouts* had already fallen off, leaving the animals totally out of control. Behind the elephants, were charging oxen with burning carts tethered to them.

The Meluhans had, in a brilliant strategic move ordered by Parvateshwar, kept another corps of ox-driven carts, laden with chilli-laced dung cakes, to the south of Sati's position. These carts had slipped out of Devagiri the previous evening, disguised as agricultural produce transport. Since Sati had not besieged the city, but only camped close to it, they only attacked armament transport and let non-lethal materials travel freely in and out of Devagiri. The reason was very obvious: a full siege would have committed too many soldiers and possibly even provoked a battle. Sati had wanted to avoid that. Little did Sati's Chandravanshi scouts realise that even dung and agricultural produce could be lethal for them.

As the elephants had charged towards these carts, they had also been set on fire. And, as expected, these retreating elephants turned around in alarm and charged back into the battlefield.

Sati was in a bind. The Meluhan cavalry was in front and a huge horde of charging, panic-stricken elephants spewing fire was behind her.

'Retreat!' yelled Sati.

Her cavalry disengaged and galloped towards the river. Fortunately for them, the Meluhan cavalry did not give chase. Alarmed by the sight of the terrified elephants speeding towards them, they turned around and rode towards the safety of their walls.

Many among Sati's horsemen were trampled or burned down by the rampaging elephants. Some of the riders managed to reach the river and rode into the waters without a second's hesitation. The horses swam desperately towards the ships, carrying their riders with them to safety. Many though, sank into the Saraswati under the weight of their light armour. Sati, Veerbhadra and Nandi were among the lucky few who managed to reach the vessels.

While most of the foot soldiers had been saved, the elephant and cavalry corps had been decimated. Memories of the elephants' killer blows in the battle of Mrittikavati were quickly forgotten as the magnitude of the disaster the animals had wreaked sank in.

Chenardhwaj, who was in charge of the ships, quickly ordered that they retreat, as soon as the last of the surviving soldiers was onboard. Without the protection of the land army, their stationary navy was a sitting duck for further attacks.

Chapter 31

Stalemate

'Absolute decimation,' crowed Vidyunmali. 'We should now chase those imbeciles and finish off what's left of the fraud's army. They should learn that nobody invades our fair motherland.'

Vidyunmali had joined Daksha, Bhrigu, Parvateshwar and Kanakhala in the Emperor's private office. Though brigadiers did not normally participate in strategy meetings, Daksha had insisted that he be allowed to attend, keeping in mind his sterling role in providing the information about the elephants.

Parvateshwar raised his hand to silence Vidyunmali. 'Let's not get ahead of ourselves, Vidyunmali. Remember, Sati's tactics under pressure were exceptional. She managed to save most of her army. So it's not as if we'll have a huge numerical advantage if we chase them.'

Vidyunmali fumed silently, keeping his eyes pinned on the floor. *Praise for a rival general? What is wrong with Lord Parvateshwar? She may have been a Meluhan princess once, but now she's a sworn enemy of our motherland.*

'And we should not forget,' said Kanakhala, 'that the Neelkanth is sailing down from the north with a large army. The safest place for our army right now is within these fort walls.'

Neelkanth? fumed Vidyunmali silently, unwilling to argue openly with senior officers of the empire. *He is not the Neelkanth. He is our enemy. And our army should be fighting, not keeping itself safe behind high walls!*

'Kanakhala is right,' said Daksha. 'We should keep our army here and attack that fraud Neelkanth the moment his ships dock. That coward left my daughter to fight alone while he went gallivanting up the Yamuna! He should pay for his cowardice!'

Vidyunmali couldn't believe what he was hearing. *Does anyone here put Meluha's interests above all else?*

'Let's worry about Meluha instead of Princess Sati and her husband's duties towards her,' said Bhrigu. 'Lord Parvateshwar is right. We have won a great victory. But we should measure our next steps carefully. What do you suggest, General?'

'My Lord, we have taken out their elephant corps and cavalry,' said Parvateshwar. 'Sati's army is in retreat. Hence, I do not expect the Neelkanth to stop and attack us here.'

'Of course he won't,' quipped Daksha. 'He's a coward.'

'Your Highness,' said Bhrigu, barely hiding his irritation. The maharishi turned to Parvateshwar. 'Why won't he stop here, General?'

'My scouts have sent back confirmation of our earlier estimates of Ganesh's army,' said Parvateshwar. 'They do have one hundred and fifty thousand soldiers. That is a big army, but it's not enough to defeat our forces if we remain within our fort walls, given that Sati's forces are no longer available to augment them. And from our defensive positions, we can slowly wear his army down. Therefore, the Neelkanth will not want to commit to a long siege here. He'll gain nothing and will unnecessarily lose men.'

'So what do you think he will do?'

'He will sail past Devagiri and join with Sati's army, perhaps in Mrittikavati or Lothal.'

'Then we should attack their ships,' interrupted Daksha.

'That will be difficult, Your Highness,' said Parvateshwar. 'Their ships are sailing downriver. We'll have to march on road since there are no warships on the Saraswati under our control. They will have the advantage of speed. We will not be able to catch up.'

'So where should we attack them?' asked Bhrigu.

'If we *have* to attack them, I would prefer to do so at Mrittikavati.'

'Why?'

'Lothal is not a good idea. I have designed the defences of Lothal myself, and sacrificing false modesty, I will say that those defences are solid. We would need a ten to one advantage in soldiers to conquer Lothal. We don't have that. We will be pitting eighty thousand of our men against more than two hundred thousand of the joint Sati-Ganesh army. Attacking Lothal will be a disaster for us; we will lose too many men. On the other hand, Mrittikavati's defences do not require that kind of numerical advantage. Also, we have twenty thousand of our own soldiers within Mrittikavati. I agree they may be imprisoned, but if they find out that their brother Meluhan soldiers are besieging the city, they may create a lot of trouble for the Lord from within. Having said that, I would expect the Lord to retreat to Lothal and not Mrittikavati, for this very reason.'

Bhrigu had an inkling that Parvateshwar preferred an altogether different strategy. 'I get the feeling that you would choose not to attack at all.'

'Not attack at all?' asked a surprised Daksha. 'Why not? Our army has tasted victory. Parvateshwar, you should...'

'Your Highness,' interrupted Bhrigu. 'Perhaps we should

leave it to an expert like Lord Parvateshwar to suggest what we should do. Go on, General.'

'The reason I suggest we avoid aggression right now is that the Lord Neelkanth would hope that we attack,' said Parvateshwar. 'One cannot attack a well-defended fort without the advantage of numbers. We don't have that. So by attacking them, we'll gain nothing and lose too many men. So I say that we stay within the safe walls of Devagiri. If we wait for six more months, Ayodhya's army will get here. Combined with their three hundred thousand soldiers, we will have a huge numerical advantage over the Lord's army.'

'So are you suggesting that we just sit around like cowards?' asked Daksha.

'It would not be cowardly to refrain from attacking when the situation is not in our favour,' said Bhrigu, before turning back to Parvateshwar. 'Go on, General.'

'Once Ayodhya's troops come in, we should march to Karachapa,' said Parvateshwar. 'We still have control over the Indus command of our navy. Along with Ayodhya's soldiers, we will have a four hundred thousand-strong army. Combine that with the vastly superior naval fleet that we have in the Indus, and we can mount a very solid attack on Lothal.'

'What you are saying appears to make sense,' said Bhrigu, before turning to Daksha. 'I suggest that we follow Lord Parvateshwar's strategy. Your Highness?'

Daksha immediately nodded his assent.

But Vidyunmali could guess that the Emperor's heart was not in this decision. He wondered if there was an opportunity for him to convince the emperor of a more aggressive course of action.

The stunned army of Ganesh was transfixed by the devastation on the hilly battlefield south of Devagiri, as they sailed down the Saraswati. Bloated carcasses of elephants and horses littered the hill, flies buzzing around them. Crows and vultures fought viciously over the beasts' entrails, even though there were enough corpses around for them all. The squawking and cawing of the feasting birds added pathos to the macabre scene.

Of particular interest to the soldiers though, was the fact that there were no human dead bodies on the battlefield. The Meluhans, true to their honourable traditions, had in all likelihood conducted funeral ceremonies for all their enemy warriors. Also, they noticed that there was no debris in the Saraswati. That meant Sati's ships had escaped the devastation, hopefully with most of her army intact.

Shiva stood on the deck of the lead ship, surveying the battlefield along with his sons and sister-in-law. He knew that he couldn't stop now and engage in a battle at Devagiri. He simply didn't have the strength of numbers anymore. He had to retreat farther south and find what was left of Sati's army. His scouts had already told him that the devastation looked worse than it actually must have been. Most of the infantrymen in Sati's army had survived and her ships were sailing south to safety. Shiva knew that with much of Sati's army intact, he still had a fighting chance in the war, but he would have to reformulate his strategy.

All that was for later, though. His mind was seized for the moment with one thought alone: was his Sati all right? Was she hurt? Was she alive?

'Neelkanth,' said Gopal, rushing up to Shiva. He had just received word from a Vasudev pandit envoy, who was hiding on the eastern bank of the Saraswati, waiting for Shiva's ships to arrive. 'Lady Sati was still alive when she was pulled aboard one of the retreating ships.'

'Still alive? What do you mean?'

'She was badly injured, Shiva. She personally led the cavalry against the rampaging elephants and Meluha's own horsemen. Nandi and Veerbhadra managed to pull her to safety. She was unconscious by the time she reached the ship. Unfortunately, the man I talked to didn't have any further information.'

Shiva made his decision immediately. He knew that his naval formation would only be able to sail as quickly as the slowest ship. He couldn't wait that long.

'Ganesh, I'm taking the fastest ship and sailing down south. I have to find your mother's ship. Kali, Kartik and you will remain with the fleet. Avoid all battles, sail as quickly as you can and meet me at Mrittikavati.'

Ganesh and Kartik stood mute, sick with worry about their mother.

'She's alive,' said Shiva, holding his sons' shoulders. 'I know she's alive. She cannot die without me.'

— ⁂ —

Shiva's ship had raced down the Saraswati and caught up with Sati's retreating fleet. He had clambered aboard his wife's ship to discover that his Sati was out of danger now, but still bed-ridden. However, this relief was accompanied by some terrible news received from a Vasudev pandit. Reports of the devastation of Sati's army in Devagiri had given the Meluhan prisoners of war in Mrittikavati the courage to challenge their citizen captors. They had broken out of their prison and taken control of the city. Three thousand citizens, loyal to the Neelkanth, had died in the process. Shiva had no choice but to avoid Mrittikavati for now, as it was no longer safe for his army. He decided to sail down another distributary of the Saraswati and then retreat to Lothal. Orders had been conveyed through a Vasudev pandit to Ganesh's army as well.

For the moment though, Shiva remained on Sati's ship as it sailed down the Saraswati. Having checked on the naval movements with the captain, Shiva descended to Sati's cabin.

Ayurvati sat by her bedside, applying soothing herbs on Sati's burnt face. Quickly and efficiently, she tied a bandage of neem leaves. 'This will ensure that your wound doesn't get infected.'

Sati nodded politely. 'Thank you, Ayurvati*ji*.'

'Also,' continued Ayurvati, thinking Sati may be concerned about the ugly mark which covered nearly a quarter of her face, 'don't worry about the scar. Whenever you are ready, I will perform a cosmetic surgery to smoothen out your skin.'

Sati nodded, her lips pursed tight.

Ayurvati looked at Shiva and then back at Sati. 'Take care, my child.'

'Thank you once again, Ayurvati*ji*,' said Sati, unable to smile due to the scar tissue forming on her face.

Ayurvati quickly walked out of the cabin. Shiva went down on his knees and held her hand.

'I'm sorry, Shiva. I failed you.'

'Please stop saying that again and again,' said Shiva. 'I've been told about the way our elephants reacted to the burning chilli; it's a miracle that you managed to save as many of our people as you did.'

'You are just being kind because I'm your wife. We have lost our elephant corps and most of our cavalry. This is a disaster.'

'Why are you so hard on yourself? What happened at Devagiri was not your fault. We'd lost our elephant corps the moment the Meluhans discovered that the smoke from burning chillies sends them into a state of panic.'

'But I should have withdrawn earlier.'

'You withdrew as soon as you saw the effect on the elephants. You had no choice but to go in with the cavalry, otherwise our soldiers would have got massacred. Practically our entire army is still intact. You did a great job to ensure that we didn't suffer even higher casualties.'

Sati looked away unhappily, still feeling terribly guilty.

Shiva touched her forehead gently. 'Sweetheart, listen to me...'

'Leave me alone for a while, Shiva.'

'Sati...'

'Shiva, please... please leave me alone.'

Shiva kissed Sati gently. 'It's not your fault. There are usually enough tragedies in life that we are genuinely responsible for. Feel guilty about them, for sure. But there is no point in burdening your heart with guilt over events that are not your fault.'

Sati turned to Shiva with a tortured expression. 'And what about you, Shiva? Do you really think a six-year-old child could have done anything to save that woman at Kailash?'

It was Shiva's turn to be silent.

'The honest answer is, no,' said Sati. 'And yet you carry that guilt, don't you? Why? Because you expected more from yourself.'

Shiva's eyes welled up with the agony of that childhood memory. There wasn't a day in his life when he didn't silently apologise to that woman he hadn't been able to save; the woman he hadn't even tried to save.

'I expected more from myself as well,' said Sati, her eyes moist.

They empathised with each other in a silent embrace.

— ⅄⦶Մ⍋⊗ —

Shiva and Sati's convoy of ships had just reached the last navigable point on this distributary of the Saraswati. From here on, the river was too shallow for the ships. Even farther, the Saraswati ran dry on land itself, unable to push through to the sea.

Shiva had avoided the distributary which led to Mrittikavati. He was on the southern-most part of the inland mouth of the Saraswati. From here on, his army would march to the frontier stronghold of Lothal. Leaving the empty ships behind was fraught with risk. It was only a matter of time before the Meluhans would get to know about it. Shiva would, in effect, be handing over twenty-five well-fitted military ships back to the Meluhans, which would allow them to move their army up and down the Saraswati with frightening speed. The decision was obvious. The ships had to be destroyed.

Once his entire army had disembarked and the caravan that would march on to Lothal had been readied, Shiva gave orders for the ships to be burned. Fortunately there had been a break in the rains which had arrived early this year, allowing the fire to consume the ships quickly.

Shiva stood observing the massive flames. He didn't hear Gopal and Chenardhwaj as they stepped up to him.

'Lord Agni consumes things rapidly,' said Gopal.

Shiva looked at Gopal before turning back to the burning ships. 'We have no choice, Pandit*ji*.'

'No, we don't.'

'What do you suggest we do, Pandit*ji*?' asked Shiva.

'The rainy season is here,' said Gopal. 'It will be difficult to mount a campaign to attack Devagiri any time soon. Even if we could, without the advantage of our cavalry it is unlikely that we will be able to conquer a well-designed citadel like Devagiri.'

'But it will be difficult for them to attack us in Lothal as well,' said Shiva. 'Lothal, in fact, is better designed for defence than even Devagiri.'

'True,' said Gopal. 'So it is a stalemate. Which suits the Meluhans just fine since all they will have to do is wait for the Ayodhyan forces to reach Meluha. They could be here in as little as six months.'

Silently, Shiva gazed at the burning ships, contemplating this unhappy turn of events.

Chenardhwaj spoke up. 'I have a suggestion, My Lord.'

Shiva turned to Chenardhwaj with a frown.

'We can draw up a crack force of Nagas and my troops,' said Chenardhwaj. 'The commandos will attack the Somras factory stealthily. It will be a suicide mission, but we will destroy it.'

'No,' said Shiva.

'Why, My Lord?'

'Because Parvateshwar will certainly be prepared for that. He's not an idiot. It will be a suicide mission all right, but not a successful one.'

'There is one other way,' whispered Gopal.

'The Vayuputras?' asked Shiva.

'Yes.'

Shiva looked back at the burning ships, his expression inscrutable. The Vayuputras appeared to be the only recourse now.

Chapter 32

The Last Resort

Shiva had pulled a light cloth over his head and wrapped it around his face, leaving his eyes open. His *angvastram* was draped across his muscular torso, affording protection from the fine drizzle. Sati lay in a covered cart as oxen pulled it gently. She was strong enough to walk now, but Ayurvati had insisted on exercising abundant caution during the march to Lothal. Shiva parted the curtains on the cart and looked at his sleeping wife. He smiled and drew the curtain shut again.

He kicked his horse into a canter.

'Pandit*ji*,' said Shiva, slowing his horse down as he approached Gopal. 'About the Vayuputras...'

'Yes?'

'What is that terrible weapon that they possess that Kali spoke of?'

'The *Brahmastra?*' asked Gopal, referring to the fearsome *weapon of Brahma*.

'Yes. How is it different from other *daivi astras?*' asked Shiva, for he didn't understand how a *Brahmastra* was so much more terrible than other *divine weapons*.

'Most *daivi astras* only kill men. But there are some, like the *Brahmastra*, that can destroy entire cities, if not kingdoms.'

'By the holy lake! How can one weapon do that?'

'The *Brahmastra* is the weapon of absolute destruction, my friend; a destroyer of cities and a mass-killer of men. When fired on some terrain, a giant mushroom cloud will rise, high enough to touch the heavens. Everyone and everything in the targeted place would be instantly vaporised. Beyond this inner circle of destruction will be those who are unfortunate enough to survive, for they will suffer for generations. The water in the land will be poisoned for decades. The land will be unusable for centuries; no crops will grow on it. This weapon doesn't just kill once; it kills again and again, for centuries after it has been used.'

'And people actually contemplate using a weapon such as this?' asked a horrified Shiva. 'Pandit*ji*, using such a dreadful weapon is against the laws of humanity.'

'Precisely, great Neelkanth. A weapon like this can never actually be used. The mere knowledge that one's enemy has this weapon, can strike terror in one's heart. No matter what the odds, one will surrender; one cannot win against the *Brahmastra*.'

'Do you think the Vayuputras will give this weapon to me? Or am I being too presumptuous? After all, I'm not one of them. They think I'm a fraud, don't they?'

'I can think of two reasons why they may help us. First, they have not tried to assassinate you, which they would have, had a majority of them believed that you were a fraud. Maybe a strong constituency amongst them still respects your uncle, Lord Manobhu.'

'And the second?'

'Lord Bhrigu used *daivi astras* in his attack on Panchavati. It was not the *Brahmastra*, but it was a *daivi astra* nevertheless. Even if it was fabricated from Lord Bhrigu's own material, he broke Lord Rudra's laws by actually using one. That, I suspect, would have turned the Vayuputras virulently against him. And an enemy's enemy...'

'...is a friend,' said Shiva, completing Gopal's statement. 'But I'm not sure these are reasons enough.'

'We don't have any other choice, my friend.'

'Perhaps... How do we get to the land of the Vayuputras?'

'Pariha is at a substantial distance towards our west. We can march overland, through the great mountains, to get there. But that is risky and time consuming. The other option is to take the sea route. But we will have to wait for the Northeasterly winds.'

'The Northeasterlies? But they begin only when the rains stop. We'll have to wait for one or two months.'

'Yes, we will have to.'

'I have an idea. I'm sure the Meluhans will set up spies and scouts in and around Lothal once they know that we have retreated into the city. So if we take the conventional route to Pariha, they will know that I have sailed west. Lord Bhrigu may guess that I've gone to the Vayuputras to seek help, which may encourage him to send assassins in pursuit. How about sailing south in a small convoy of military ships?'

Gopal immediately understood. 'We'll make them think that we're going to the Narmada, onwards perhaps to either Ujjain or Panchavati.'

'Exactly,' said Shiva. 'We could disembark from our military ships at a secret location and then set sail in a nondescript merchant ship to Pariha.'

'Brilliant. The Meluhans can keep searching for you along the Narmada while we are on our way to Pariha.'

'Right.'

'And if we use just one merchant ship instead of an entire convoy, we could keep the voyage secretive and be quick.'

'Right again.'

— ⅄ⓄՄ⍋⊗ —

Sati stood at a window in a lookout-shelter on the southern edge of Lothal fort, staring at the vast expanse of sea beyond its walls. The monsoon had arrived in earnest and heavy rain was pelting the city.

Shiva and his army were well fortified within the city walls. Ganesh was expected to arrive in Lothal within a week or two, along with his force.

Ayurvati rushed into the shelter with a loud whoop, propping her cane and cloth umbrella beside the entrance. 'Lord Indra and Lord Varun, be praised! They have decided to deliver the entire quota of this year's rain in a single day!'

Sati turned towards Ayurvati with a wan look.

Ayurvati sat next to her and squeezed the end of her drenched *angvastram*. 'I love the rain. It seems to wash away sorrows and bring new life with renewed hope, doesn't it?'

Sati nodded politely, not really interested. 'Yes, you are right, Ayurvati*ji*.'

Not one to give up, Ayurvati plodded on, determined to lighten Sati's mood. 'I'm quite free right now. There aren't too many injured and the monsoon diseases have, surprisingly, been very low this year.'

'That is good news, Ayurvati*ji*,' said Sati.

'Yes, it is. So, I was thinking that this would be a good time to do your surgery.'

Sati's face carried an ugly blemish on her left cheek, where scar tissue had formed over the remnants of the burns she had suffered during the Battle of Devagiri.

'There's nothing wrong with me,' said Sati politely.

'Of course there isn't. I was only referring to the scar on your face. It can be removed very easily through cosmetic surgery.'

'No. I don't want surgery.'

Ayurvati assumed that Sati was worried about the long

recovery time and the possible impact on her ability to participate in the next battle. 'But it is a very simple procedure, Sati. You will recover in a couple of weeks. We seem to be in for a good monsoon this year. This means there will be no warfare for a few months. You will not miss any battle.'

'Nothing would keep me away from the next battle.'

'Then why don't you want to do this surgery, my child? I'm sure it would make the Lord Neelkanth happy.'

A hint of a smile escaped her solemn demeanour. 'Shiva keeps telling me I'm as beautiful as ever, scar or no scar. I know I look horrendous. He's lying because he loves me. But I choose to believe it.'

'Why are you doing this?' asked an anguished Ayurvati. 'It won't hurt you at all; not that you are scared of pain...'

'No, Ayurvati*ji*.'

'But why? You have to give me a reason.'

'Because, I need this scar,' said Sati grimly.

Ayurvati paused for a moment. 'Why?'

'It constantly reminds me of my failure. I will not rest till I have set it right and recovered the ground that I lost for my army.'

'Sati! It wasn't your fault that...'

'Ayurvati*ji*,' said Sati, interrupting the former chief surgeon of Meluha. 'You of all people should not tell me a white lie. I was the Commanding Officer and my army was defeated. It was my fault.'

'Sati...'

'This scar stays with me. Every time I look at my reflection, it will remind me that I have work to do. Let me win a battle for my army, and then we can do the surgery.'

— ⁂ —

'*Dada*,' whispered Kartik, gently placing his hand on his angry brother's arm.

Ganesh's army had just arrived at Lothal. They too had avoided Mrittikavati as advised by a Vasudev pandit. Just like Shiva, Ganesh had ensured that all his ships were destroyed on the Saraswati before his army marched south to Lothal.

They were received at the gates of Lothal by Governor Chenardhwaj. Ganesh and Kartik had wanted to meet their parents immediately, but were informed by Chenardhwaj that Shiva wanted to meet them beforehand. Shiva wanted to prepare them for their first meeting with their mother after her defeat at the Battle of Devagiri.

Meanwhile, the allies of the Neelkanth – Bhagirath, the Prince of Ayodhya, Chandraketu, the King of Branga, and Maatali, the King of Vaishali – were led to their respective chambers in the Lothal governor's residence by protocol officers. The Chandravanshi royalty, used to the pomp and pageantry of their own land, were distinctly underwhelmed by the austere arrangements of the Meluhan accommodation. It was difficult to believe that the governor of one of the richest provinces of the richest Empire in the world lived in such simplicity. However, they accepted their housing with good grace, knowing it was the will of Shiva.

The army was accommodated in guesthouses and temporary shelters erected within the city. It was a tribute to the robust urban planning of Meluha that such a large number of new arrivals could be so quickly accommodated in reasonable comfort. All in all, a massive army, now totalling nearly two hundred and fifty thousand soldiers, had set up residence in Lothal.

Having been briefed by Shiva, Ganesh and Kartik rushed to meet their mother. They had been told about the nature of her injuries. Shiva did not want the brothers to inadvertently upset her further. While Kartik was, as instructed by Shiva, able to control his anger and shock, Ganesh's obsessive love for his mother did not allow him that ability.

Ganesh clenched his fists, staring at his mother's disfigured face. He gritted his teeth and breathed rapidly, his normally calm eyes blazing. His long nose was stretched out, trembling in anger. His big floppy ears were rigid.

Ganesh growled, 'I will kill every single one of those b...'

'Ganesh,' said Sati calmly, interrupting her son. 'The Meluhan soldiers were only doing their duty, as was I. They have done nothing wrong.'

Ganesh's silence was unable to camouflage his fury.

'Ganesh, these things happen in a war. You know that.'

'*Dada*, *maa* is right,' said Kartik.

Sati stepped close and embraced her elder son. She pulled his face down and kissed his forehead, smiling lovingly. 'Calm down, Ganesh.'

Kartik held his mother and brother as well. '*Dada,* battle scars are a mark of pride for a warrior.'

Ganesh held his mother tight, tears streaming down his face. 'You are not entering a battlefield again, *maa.* Not unless I am standing in front of you.'

Sati smiled feebly and patted Ganesh on his back.

— ⁂ —

Shiva walked into his suite of rooms in the governor's residence at Lothal. Sati had moved some of the furniture to create a training circle, and was practicing her sword movements. Shiva leaned against a wall and observed his wife quietly, so as not to disturb her. He admired every perfect warrior move, the sway of her hips as she transferred her weight; the quick thrusts and swings of her sword; the rapid movement of her shield, which she used almost like an independent weapon. Shiva breathed deeply at yet another reminder of why he loved her so much.

Sati swung around with her shield held high, as her eyes fell on Shiva.

'For how long have you been watching?' she asked, surprised.

'Long enough to know that I should never challenge you to a duel!'

Sati smiled slightly, not saying anything. She quickly sheathed her sword and put her shield down. Shiva stepped over and helped untie her scabbard.

'Thank you,' whispered Sati as she took the scabbard from Shiva, walked up to the mini-armoury and placed her shield and sheathed sword.

'We will not be able to go to Pariha together,' said Shiva.

'I know,' said Sati. 'I was told by Gopal*ji* that Parihans only allow Vayuputras and Vasudevs to enter their domain. I am neither.'

'Well, technically, nor am I.'

Sati pulled her *angvastram* over her head so as to cover her left cheek. She held the hem of the cloth between her teeth, covering her facial scar. 'But you are the Neelkanth. Rules can be broken for you.'

Shiva came forward, and pulled Sati close with one hand. With the other, he held the *angvastram* covering her face and tried to pull it back. Even though she knew he did not care, Sati liked to hide her scar from Shiva. It didn't matter to her if others saw it, but not Shiva.

'Shiva...' whispered Sati, holding her *angvastram* close.

Shiva tugged hard and pulled the *angvastram* free from her mouth. An upset Sati tried to yank it back but Shiva managed to overpower her, holding her close.

'I wish you could see through my eyes,' whispered Shiva, 'so you could see your own ethereal beauty.'

Sati rolled her eyes and turned away, still struggling within Shiva's grip. 'I'm ugly! I know it! Don't use your love to insult me.'

'Love?' asked Shiva, pretending mock surprise, wiggling his eyebrows. 'Who said anything about love? It's lust! Pure and simple!'

Sati stared at Shiva, her eyes wide. Then she burst out laughing.

Shiva pulled her close again, grinning. 'This is no laughing matter, my princess. I am your husband. I have rights, you know.'

Sati continued to laugh as she hit Shiva playfully on his chest.

Shiva kissed her tenderly. 'I love you.'

'You're mad!'

'That I am. But I still love you.'

Chapter 33

The Conspiracy Deepens

'Brilliant idea, Your Highness,' said Vidyunmali.

Daksha sat in his private office with his new confidant, Vidyunmali. The Meluhan brigadier's increasing frustration with Parvateshwar's cautious approach had forged a new alliance. According to Vidyunmali, this wait-and-watch strategy of General Parvateshwar was giving Shiva's army time to recover from its defeat at Devagiri. He had begun to spend more and more time with the emperor. Daksha had got him reassigned to head a brigade of a thousand soldiers that guarded the emperor, his family and his palace. This gave him a simple advantage: the brigade could carry out personal missions mandated by the emperor.

Sensing increasing comfort in the relationship, Daksha had finally confided in him about his idea to end the war. Much to Daksha's delight, Vidyunmali's reaction was very different from Bhrigu's.

'Exactly!' exclaimed a happy Daksha. 'I don't know why the others don't understand.'

'Your Highness, you are the emperor,' said Vidyunmali. 'It doesn't matter if others don't agree. If you have decided to go ahead, then that is the will of Meluha.'

'You really think we should go ahead...'

'It doesn't matter what I think, Your Highness. What do you think?'

'I think it is brilliant!'

'Then that is what Meluha thinks as well, My Lord.'

'I think we should implement it.'

'What are your orders for me, My Lord?'

'I haven't worked out the details, Brigadier,' said Daksha. 'You will need to think it through. My job is to look at the big picture.'

'Of course,' said Vidyunmali. 'My apologies, Your Highness. But I don't think we can execute our plan till the maharishi and the general leave Devagiri. They may try to stop us if they get the slightest whiff of our intentions.'

'They were planning to leave for Karachapa; or at least that was Parvateshwar's latest plan. I was not supportive of the idea earlier, but now I will encourage it and hasten their departure.'

'An inspired move, Your Highness. But we must also concentrate on getting the right assassins.'

'I agree. But where do we find them?'

'They must be foreigners, Your Highness. We do not want them recognised. They will be wearing cloaks and masks, of course. You want them to look like Nagas, right?'

'Yes, of course.'

'I know some people. They are the best in the business.'

'Where are they from?'

'Egypt.'

'By the great Lord Varun, that's too far! It will take too much time to get them here.'

'I will leave immediately, Your Highness. That is, if I have your permission.'

'Of course you have it. Accomplish this, Vidyunmali, and Meluha will sing your praises for centuries.'

— ⅄Ⓞ⋃⍋⊗ —

'Lord Gopal and I will leave within a week,' said Shiva.

Shiva and Gopal sat in the governor's office, surrounded by Sati, Kali, Ganesh, Kartik, Bhagirath, Chenardhwaj, Chandraketu and Maatali. The monsoons were drawing to an end, light smatterings of rain appearing occasionally, as if to bid farewell. Shiva and Gopal had decided to travel south, as planned, in their small convoy of military ships. They intended to rendezvous with a merchant ship at a secret location north of the Narmada delta. The Southwesterly winds would have receded by the time and the rains would have stopped. They would then board the merchant ship and use the Northeasterly winds to set sail towards the west, in the direction of Pariha. With luck, the deception would work and the Meluhans would be unaware of Shiva's actual destination.

'I want our destination to be kept secret,' continued Shiva. 'Victory is assured if our mission succeeds.'

'What are you planning to do, My Lord?' asked Bhagirath.

'Leave that to me, my friend,' said Shiva cryptically. 'In my absence, Sati will be in command.'

Everyone nodded in instant agreement. They were unaware though, that Sati had fought this decision. After Devagiri, she didn't think she deserved this command. But Shiva had insisted. He trusted her the most.

'Pray to Lord Ram and Lord Rudra that our mission is a success,' said Gopal.

— ⁂ —

Shiva stood on the shores of the Mansarovar lake, watching the slow descent of the sun in the evening sky. There was no breeze at all and it was eerily still. A sudden chill enveloped him, and he looked down, surprised to see that he was standing in knee-deep water. He turned around and began wading out of the lake. Thick fog had blanketed the banks of the Mansarovar. He couldn't see his village at all. As he stepped out of the lake, the mist magically cleared.

'Sati?' asked a surprised Shiva.

Sati sat calmly atop a thick pile of wood. Her metal armour had been secured around her torso, carved arm bands glistened in the dusky light, her sword lay by her side and the shield was fastened on her back. She was prepared for war. But why was she wearing a saffron angvastram, *the colour of the final journey?*

'Sati,' said Shiva, walking towards her.

Sati opened her eyes and smiled serenely. It appeared that she was speaking. But Shiva couldn't hear the words. The sound reached his ears with a delay of a few moments. 'I'll be waiting for you...'

'What? Where are you going?'

Suddenly, a hazy figure appeared bearing a burning torch. Without a moment's hesitation, he rammed it into the pile of wood that Sati sat upon. It caught fire instantly.

'SATI!' screamed a stunned Shiva as he raced towards her.

Sati continued to sit upon the burning pyre, at peace with herself. Her beatific smile presented an eerie contrast to the flames that leapt up around her.

'SATI!' shouted Shiva. 'JUMP OFF!'

But Sati was unmoved. Shiva was just a few metres away from her when a platoon of soldiers jumped in front of him. Shiva drew his sword in a flash, trying to push the soldiers aside. But they battled him relentlessly. The soldiers were huge and unnaturally hairy, like the monster from his dream. Shiva battled them tirelessly but could not push through. Meanwhile, the flames had almost covered his wife, such that he couldn't even see her clearly. And yet, she continued to sit on the pyre, without attempting to escape.

'SATI!'

Shiva woke up in a sweat as his hand stretched out desperately. It took a moment for his eyes to adjust to the darkness. He turned to his left instinctively. Sati was asleep, her burnt cheek clearly visible in the night light.

Shiva immediately bent over and embraced his wife.

'Shiva...' whispered a groggy Sati.

Shiva didn't say anything. He held her tight, as tears streamed down his face.

'Shiva?' asked Sati, fully awake now. 'What's the matter, darling?'

But Shiva couldn't say a word, choked with emotion.

Sati pulled her head back to get a better look in the dim light. She reached up and touched his cheeks. They were moist.

'Shiva? Sweetheart? What's wrong? Did you have a bad dream?'

'Sati, promise me that you will not go into battle till I return.'

'Shiva, you've made me the leader. If the army has to go into battle, I will have to lead them. You know that.'

Shiva kept quiet.

'What did you see?'

He just shook his head.

'It was just a dream, Shiva. It doesn't mean anything. You need to focus your attention on your journey. You're leaving tomorrow. You must succeed in your mission with the Vayuputras. That will bring an end to this war. Don't let anxieties about me distract you.'

Shiva remained impassive, refusing to let go.

'Shiva, you carry the future on your shoulders. I'm saying this once again. Don't let your love for me distract you. It was just a dream. That's all.'

'I can't live without you.'

'You won't have to. I'll be waiting for you when you return. I promise.'

Shiva pulled back a bit, looking deep into Sati's eyes. 'Stay away from fires.'

'Shiva, seriously, what...'

'Sati, promise me! You will stay away from fires.'

'Yes, Shiva. I promise.'

Chapter 34

With the Help of Umbergaon

Shiva was ready to leave. His bags had been sent to his ship. He had ordered all his aides out of his chamber. He'd wanted a few minutes alone with Sati.

'Bye,' whispered Shiva.

She smiled and embraced him. 'Nothing will happen to me, my good man! You will not get rid of me so easily.'

Shiva laughed softly, for Sati had used his own line on him. 'I know. It was just an overreaction to a stupid nightmare.'

Shiva pulled Sati's face up and kissed her affectionately. 'I love you.'

'I love you too.'

A couple of weeks later Shiva and Gopal stood on a beach in a hidden lagoon, a short distance to the north of the Narmada delta. The small convoy of military ships had sneaked into the lagoon the previous night. Shiva and Gopal had disembarked into rowboats, along with a skeletal crew, and stolen onto the beach. Early next morning, the merchant ship that would take them to Pariha arrived in the lagoon.

'Hmmm... good workmanship,' said an admiring Shiva.

It was, without doubt, a bulky ship, obviously designed to carry large cargo. However, any sailor could judge that with its double masts, high stern and low bow, this craft was also built for speed. In addition, the ship had been rigged with two banks of oars, to allow for 'human propulsion' if required.

'We won't really need the rowers,' said Gopal. 'Our vessel will have the Northeasterly winds in its sails.'

'Where is this beauty from?' asked Shiva.

'A small shipping village called Umbergaon.'

'Umbergaon? Where is it?'

'It's to the south of the Narmada River delta.'

'That's not a part of any empire, Swadweep or Meluha.'

'You guessed right, my friend. That makes it a perfect place to build ships that one doesn't want tracked. The local ruler, Jadav Rana, is a pragmatic man. The Nagas have helped him many times. He values their friendship. And, most importantly, his people are expert ship builders. This ship will get us to Pariha as fast as is humanly possible.'

'Interesting. We should be grateful for their invaluable help.'

'No,' said Gopal, smiling. 'It is Pariha that should be grateful to Umbergaon, for the Umbergaonis have ensured that the gift of the Neelkanth shall reach Pariha.'

'I'm no gift,' said a discomfited Shiva.

'Yes, you are. For you will help the Vayuputras achieve their purpose. You will help them fulfil their vow to Lord Rudra: to not let Evil win.'

Shiva remained silent, as always, embarrassed.

'And I'm sure,' continued a prescient Gopal, 'that one day, Pariha too shall send a gift in return to Umbergaon.'

— ⚹ —

'How're you feeling now, my friend?' asked Gopal, as soon as he entered Shiva's cabin.

The vessel bearing the two men had been sailing in the open seas for a little more than a week. They were far beyond the coastline and unlikely to run into any Meluhan military ships. They'd run into choppy waters though, in the last few days. The sailors, used to the ways of the sea, were not really troubled by it. Neither was Gopal, who had travelled on these great expanses of water many times. But Shiva had undertaken a sea voyage just once, from the Narmada delta to Lothal, where the ship had stayed close to the coast. It was, therefore, no surprise that the rough sea had given the Neelkanth a severe bout of seasickness.

Shiva looked up from his bed and cursed, his eyes half shut. 'I have no stomach left! It has all been churned out! A plague on these wretched waters!'

Gopal laughed softly, 'It's time for your medicines, Neelkanth.'

'What's the point, Pandit*ji*? Nothing stays inside!'

'For whatever little time the medicine remains, it will serve a purpose. Take it.'

Gopal gently poured a herbal infusion into a wooden spoon. Balancing it delicately, the Chief Vasudev offered it to Shiva, who swallowed it quickly and fell back on the bed.

'Holy Lake, help me,' whispered Shiva, 'let this medicine stay within me for a few minutes at least.'

But the prayer probably didn't reach Mansarovar Lake in time. Shiva lurched to his side and retched into the large pot that had been placed on the ground. A sailor standing by the bed rushed forward quickly and handed a wet towel to Shiva, who wiped his face slowly.

Shiva shook his head and looked up at the ceiling of his cabin in disgust. 'Crap!'

— ⅄ⵀ⊍⍋⊗ —

Bhrigu and Parvateshwar rode on horseback at the head of a massive army that had marched out of Devagiri. They were on their way to the Beas River, from which point, ships would sail them down to Karachapa.

'I was thinking that the powerful fleet in Karachapa is not the only advantage derived from our decision to shift our war command,' said Bhrigu.

Parvateshwar frowned. 'What other benefit does it serve, My Lord?'

'Well, there's also the fact that you will not have to suffer idiotic orders from your emperor. You will be free to conduct the war the way you deem fit.'

It was obvious that Bhrigu held Daksha in contempt, and did not think much of his harebrained schemes. But Parvateshwar was too disciplined a Meluhan to speak openly against his emperor. He was stoic in his silence.

Bhrigu smiled. 'You really are a rare man, General, a man of the old code. Lord Ram would have been proud of you.'

— ⸻ —

Aided by the Northeasterly winds pushing hard into its sails, the merchant ship was cutting through the waters with rapid speed. Having tossed and turned for a few days, Shiva had finally adapted to the sea. The Neelkanth was able, therefore, to enjoy the stiff morning breeze on the main deck at the bow, with Gopal for company.

'We are now crossing over from our Western Sea, through a very narrow strait,' said Gopal. 'It's just a little over fifty kilometres across.'

'What's on the other side?' asked Shiva.

'The Jam Zrayangh.'

'Sounds scary. What in Lord Ram's name does that mean?'

Gopal laughed. 'Something absolutely benign. Zrayangh simply means sea in the local language.'

'And what does Jam mean?'

'Jam means "to come to".'

'To come to?'

'Yes.'

'So this is the "sea that you come to"?'

'Yes, a simple name. This is the sea you must come to if you want to go to Elam or Mesopotamia or any of the lands farther west. But most importantly, this is the sea you must approach if you need to go to Pariha.'

'I've heard of Mesopotamia. It has strong trade relations with Meluha, right?'

'Yes. It's a very powerful and rich empire, established between two great rivers in the region, the Tigris and the Euphrates.'

'Is the empire bigger than Meluha and Swadweep?'

'No,' smiled Gopal. 'It's not even bigger than Meluha alone. But they believe human civilisation began in their region.'

'Really? I thought we Indians believed that human civilisation began here.'

'True.'

'So, who's right?'

Gopal shrugged. 'I don't know. This goes back many thousands of years. But frankly, does it matter who got civilised first so long as all of us eventually became civilised?'

Shiva smiled. 'True. And where is Elam?'

'Elam is a much smaller kingdom to the south-east of Mesopotamia.'

'South-east?' asked Shiva. 'So, Elam is closer to Pariha?'

'Yes. And Elam acts as a buffer state between Pariha and Mesopotamia, which is why the Parihans have occasionally helped the Elamites unofficially.'

'But I thought Pariha never got involved in local politics.'

'They try to avoid it. And most people in the region have not even heard of the Vayuputras. But they were concerned that an expanding Mesopotamia would encroach into their land.'

'Expanding Mesopotamia?'

'A gifted gardener had once conquered the whole of Mesopotamia.'

'A gardener? How did a gardener become a warrior? Did he train in secret?'

Gopal smiled. 'From what I've heard of the story, he wasn't trained.'

Shiva's eyes widened with amazement. 'He must have been very gifted.'

'Oh, he was talented. But not in gardening!'

Shiva laughed. 'What was his name?'

'Nobody knows his original name. But he called himself Sargon.'

'And he conquered the whole of Mesopotamia?'

'Yes, and surprisingly quickly at that. But it did not satiate his ambition. He went on to conquer neighbouring kingdoms as well, including Elam.'

'That would have brought him to the borders of Pariha.'

'Not exactly, my friend. But uncomfortably close.'

'Why didn't he move farther east?'

'I don't know. Neither he nor his successors did, though. But the Vayuputras were troubled enough to offer anonymous assistance to Elam. The Elamites were able to rebel because of this support, and the conquest of the Mesopotamians did not last for too long.'

'King Sargon seems like a very interesting man.'

'He was. He challenged the entire world, and even fate itself. He was so feisty that he dared to name his empire after the water-carrier who was his adopted father.'

'His father was a water-carrier?'

'Yes, named Akki. So they called themselves the Empire of the Akkadians.'

'And does this empire still exist?'

'No.'

'That's sad. I would have loved to meet these remarkable Akkadians.'

'The people of Elam would have thought very differently, Lord Neelkanth.'

— ★ —

'The soldiers are bored and restless,' said Ganesh. 'They have been mobilised, but there has been no action, no battle.'

Kartik and Ganesh had just entered Sati's chamber and were happy to find Kali with their mother.

'I was discussing just that, with *didi*,' said Kali. 'The men are spending their time gambling and drinking to keep themselves occupied. Training is suffering because they don't see the point of it when there is hardly any chance of combat in the near future.'

'This is the time when stupid incidents occur which can blow up into serious problems,' said Sati.

'Let's keep them busy,' suggested Kartik. 'Let's organise some animal hunts in the forests around the city. We know that the Meluhan army has still not moved out of Karachapa, so there is no risk in letting our soldiers out in large groups. Hunting will give them some sense of action.'

'Good idea,' agreed Kali. 'We can also use the excess meat to organise feasts for the citizens of Lothal. It will help assuage some of their irritation with having to host such a large army.'

'The excitement and the blood-rush will also prevent boredom from creeping into our troops,' said Ganesh.

'I agree,' said Sati. 'I'll issue the orders immediately.'

— ⅄ⓄႮ⇞⊗ —

It was nearly a month and a half since they had started their journey from the secret lagoon off the Narmada delta. Shiva's ship came to anchor off a desolate coast on the Jam Sea. There didn't seem to be any habitation of any kind at all; in fact it appeared as though this land had never been disturbed by humans. Shiva was not surprised. Just like the Vasudevs, the Vayuputras were secretive about their existence. He did not expect a welcoming port of landing. But he did expect some secret symbol, something like the emblematic Vasudev flame on the banks of the Chambal near Ujjain.

Then he thought he detected something. The coast was lined by a thick row of tall bushes, maybe three or four metres high. From the distance of the anchored ship, it seemed like these bushes had reddish-orange fruit hanging in abundance. The shrubs were covered with small dark-green leaves, except at the top, where it was bright red. These bright red leaves combined with the reddish-orange fruit to give the impression that the bush was on fire.

A burning bush...

Shiva immediately turned and began climbing the main mast, all the way up to the crow's nest. Once there, the symbol became obvious. The bushes, when combined with the white sand and brownish rocks, came together to form a symbol that Shiva recognised only too well: *Fravashi*, the holy flame, the feminine spirit.

Shiva came down to find Gopal standing below.

'Did you find something, my friend?' asked Gopal.

'I saw the holy flame; the pure being. I saw the *Fravashi*.'

Gopal was astonished at first, but not for long. 'Of course! Lord Manobhu... He would have told you about *Fravashi*.'

'Yes.'

'It's a symbol of the faith of Lord Rudra's people. The *Fravashi* represents pure spirits, the angels. They exist in large numbers, their scriptures say in the tens of thousands. They send forth human souls into this world and support them in the eternal battle between Good and Evil. They are also believed to have assisted God in creating the universe.'

Shiva nodded. 'The Vasudevs believe in the *Fravashi* as well, I assume.'

'We respect the *Fravashi*. But it is a Parihan symbol.'

'Then why do you have a *Fravashi* at the entrance to your land?'

Gopal frowned. 'A *Fravashi* symbol? Where?'

'At the clearing on the Chambal, from where we communicated with you through clapping signals.'

'Oh!' smiled Gopal, as understanding dawned upon him. 'My friend, we have a symbolic fire as well. But we don't call it *Fravashi*. We call it *Agni*, the God of Fire.'

'But the symbol is almost exactly like the *Fravashi*.'

'Yes, it is. I'm aware that the Parihans give enormous importance to fire rituals. So do we Indians. The first hymn of the first chapter in the Rig Veda is dedicated to the Fire God, Agni. The importance of the element of fire is, I believe, common across all religions of the world.'

'Fire is the beginning of human civilisation.'

'It is the beginning of all life, my friend. It is the source of all energy. For one way of looking at the stars is to see them as great balls of fire.'

Shiva smiled.

A sailor walked up to the two men. 'My Lords, the rowboat has been lowered. We are ready.'

— ⸻ —

The rowboat was a hundred metres from the coast when a tall man appeared from behind the bushes. He wore a long, brownish-black cloak and held what looked like a staff. Or, it could have been a spear. Shiva couldn't be sure. He reached for his sword.

Gopal reached out to stay Shiva's hand. 'It's all right, my friend.'

Shiva spoke without taking his eyes off the stranger. 'Are you sure?'

'Yes, he is a Parihan. He has come to guide us.'

Shiva relaxed his grip on the sword, but kept his hand close to the hilt.

He saw the stranger reach into the bushes and tug at what looked like ropes. Shiva immediately caught his breath and reached for his sword once again.

To his surprise though, four horses emerged from behind the thick row of bushes. Three of them were not carrying anything, clearly ready for their new mounts. The fourth was loaded with a massive sack. Perhaps, it was carrying provisions. Shiva moved his hand away from his sword and let it relax.

The stranger was a friend.

Chapter 35

Journey to Pariha

'I'm glad that the Vayuputras have sent someone to receive us,' said Gopal.

His sailors were offloading the provisions from the rowboat. Some of the luggage would be tied onto the three horses that would be mounted by Shiva, Gopal and the Parihan, while the rest would be loaded onto the severely-burdened fourth horse.

'How can the Vayuputras ignore the Chief Vasudev, My Lord?' asked the Parihan, bowing low towards Gopal. 'We received your message from the Vasudev pandit of Lothal well in time. You are our honoured guest. My name is Kurush. I will be your guide to our city, Pariha.'

Shiva observed Kurush intently. His long brownish-black cloak could not hide the fact that he carried a sword. Shiva wondered as to how the Parihan would draw his sword quickly in an emergency if it lay encumbered within the folds of his cloak.

The man was unnaturally fair-skinned, not seen often in the hot plains of India. While one may have expected this to make the Parihan look pale and unattractive, this was not so. The sharp long nose, combined with a full beard somehow enhanced the beauty of the man while giving him the look of a warrior nevertheless. The Parihan wore his hair long, something that was in common with the Indians. On his head was perched a square white hat, made of cotton. For Shiva, the most interesting aspect was his beard. It was just like that of Lord Rudra's image in the revered Vishwanath temple at Kashi; the distinctive beard of the previous Mahadev had many strands of hair curled into independent clumps.

'Thank you, Kurush,' said Gopal. 'Please allow me the pleasure of introducing the long-awaited Neelkanth himself, Lord Shiva.'

Kurush turned towards Shiva and nodded curtly. Clearly he was one amongst those Vayuputras who considered Shiva a usurper; a Neelkanth who had not been authorised by his tribe. Shiva did not say anything. He knew that the only opinion that mattered was that of their chief, Mithra.

Shiva mounted his horse, then turned and waved at the sailors as they rowed back to their ship. They intended to sail a little farther and anchor in a hidden cove. After a waiting period of two months, the captain would send out a rowboat once every two days to the spot where Gopal and Shiva had met Kurush, to check if they had returned.

Kurush had already begun riding in front, while also holding the reins of the horse bearing the provisions, when Gopal and Shiva kicked their horses into a trot. With the Parihan safely out of earshot, Shiva turned to Gopal. 'Why does the name Kurush sound familiar?'

'Kurush is sometimes also known as Kuru,' said Gopal. 'And Kuru, I'm sure you're aware, was a great Indian Emperor in ancient times.'

'So which name came first? Kuru or Kurush?'

'You mean who influenced whom?' asked Gopal. 'Did India influence Pariha or was it the other way around?'

'Yes, that's what I want to know.'

'I don't know. It was probably a bit of both. We learnt from their noble culture and they learnt from ours. Of course, we can go on about who learnt how much and from whom, but that is nothing but our ego, showing our desperation to prove that our culture is superior to others. That is a foolish quest. It is best to learn from everyone, regardless of the cultural source of that learning.'

— ⋆ —

The Parihan rode ahead in solitary splendour. They had been travelling for a week now, and Kurush had determinedly remained uncommunicative, giving monosyllabic answers to Shiva's companionable queries. The Neelkanth had finally stopped talking to him.

'Did the Lord grow up here?' Shiva asked Gopal.

'Yes, Lord Rudra was born around this area. He came to India when we needed him.'

'He was from the *land of fairies*. That would obviously make him our guardian spirit as well.'

'Actually, I believe he wasn't born in *Pariha*, but somewhere close to this region.'

'Where?'

'Anshan.'

'Doesn't *anshan* mean hunger in India?'

Gopal smiled. 'It means the same here as well.'

'They named their land "hunger"? Was it so bad?'

'Look around you. This is a harsh, mountainous desert. Life is perennially difficult here. Unless...'

'Unless what?'

'Unless great men are occasionally able to tame this land.'

'And Lord Rudra's tribe proved to be such men?'

'Yes, they set up the kingdom of Elam.'

'Elam? You mean the same one that the Akkadians conquered?'

'Yes.'

'That would explain the Vayuputra support, wouldn't it? The Elamites were the people of Lord Rudra.'

'No, that's not the reason why. The Vayuputras supported the Elamites because they genuinely felt the need for a buffer state between them and the Mesopotamians. In fact, Lord Rudra had made it very clear to his fellow Elamites: they could either join the Vayuputra tribe, giving up all links with any other identity that they had previously cherished, or they could choose to remain Elamites. Those who chose to follow Lord Rudra are the Vayuputras of today.'

'So Pariha is not where Anshan used to be.'

'No. Anshan is the capital of the Elamite kingdom. Pariha exists farther to the east.'

'It appears to me that the Vayuputras accepted other outsiders as well, and not just the Elamites. My uncle was a Tibetan.'

'Yes, Lord Manobhu was one. The Vayuputras accept members solely on merit, not by virtue of birth. There are many Elamites who try to become Vayuputras but do not succeed. The only people who were accepted in large numbers, because they were refugees, were a tribe from our country.'

'From India?'

'Yes, Lord Rudra felt personally guilty about what he had done to them. So he took them under his protection and gave them refuge in his land, amongst the Vayuputras.'

'Who were these people?'

'The Asuras.'

Before Shiva could react to this revelation, Kurush turned and addressed Gopal. 'My Lord, this is a good place to have some lunch. The path ahead goes through a narrow mountain pass. Shall we take a break here?'

— ⅄ⓞ⊍⍋⊛ —

Lunch was entirely unappetising and cold, with the harsh mountain winds adding to the discomfort. But the dry fruit that Kurush had brought along provided a boost of energy, much needed for the back-breaking ride that lay ahead.

Kurush quickly packed the remaining food, mounted his horse and kicked it into action after making sure that he had a good grip over the reins of the fourth horse. Gopal and Shiva settled into a canter behind him.

'The Asuras took refuge here?' asked Shiva, still in shock.

'Yes,' answered Gopal. 'Lord Rudra himself brought the few surviving Asura leaders to Pariha. Others, who were in hiding, were also led out of India by the Vayuputras. Some Asuras went farther west, even beyond Elam. I'm not really sure what happened to them. But many of them stayed on in Pariha.'

'And Lord Rudra accommodated these Asuras into the Vayuputra tribe, did he?'

'Not all of them. He found that a few of the Asuras were not detached enough to become members of the Vayuputra tribe. They were allowed to live in Pariha as refugees. But a vast majority of the remainder became Vayuputras.'

'A lot of them would have been the Asura royalty. Wouldn't they have wanted to attack India and take revenge on the Devas who had defeated them?'

'No. Once they entered the Vayuputra brotherhood, they ceased to be Asuras. They gave up their old identities and embraced the primary task Lord Rudra had set for the Vayuputras: to protect the holy land of India from Evil.'

Shiva inhaled deeply as he absorbed this news. The Asuras had been able to go beyond their hatred for their former enemies and work for the mission mandated by Lord Rudra.

'In a strange twist of fate, the Asuras, who to the Devas were demons, were in fact actively working behind the scenes to protect them from the effects of Evil,' said Gopal, as he guided his horse to the right and entered a narrow pass.

Shiva suddenly thought of something, and rode up to Gopal.

'But Pandit*ji*, I'm sure the Asuras would not have forgotten their old culture. They must surely have influenced the Parihan way of life. It's impossible to shed one's cultural memes even after having moved away to foreign lands generations ago. Unless, of course, one becomes as detached as the ascetics.'

'You're right,' said Gopal. 'The Asura culture did impact the Parihans. For instance, do you know the Parihan term for Gods?'

Shiva shrugged.

Gopal glanced at Shiva conspiratorially. 'Before you answer, know this, that in the old Parihan language, there was no place for the production and perception of the phonetic sound "s". It either became "sh" or "h". So, what do you think they called their Gods?'

Shiva frowned, making a wild guess. 'Ahuras?'

'Yes, Ahuras.'

'Good Lord! What were their demons called then?'

'Daevas.'

'By the great Lord Brahma!'

'It's the exact opposite of the Indian pantheon. We call our Gods Devas and demons Asuras.'

Shiva smiled slightly. 'They're different, but they're not evil.'

Chapter 36

The Land of Fairies

Shiva, Gopal and Kurush had been riding for a little over a month. Late winter made travelling through the harsh mountainous terrain a test of will. Shiva, who'd lived most of his life in the highlands of Tibet, managed the expedition quite well. But Gopal, who was used to the moist heat of the plains, was struggling due to the cold and rarefied atmosphere.

'We're here,' said Kurush out of the blue one day, as he raised his hand.

Shiva pulled his reins. They had been on a narrow pathway, no more than four or five metres wide. Shiva dismounted from his horse, tied the reins to a rocky outcrop and walked up to Gopal to assist him. He tied Gopal's horse, helped him sit with his back propped up against the mountain side, and offered his water to the Chief Vasudev. Gopal sipped the life-nurturing fluid slowly.

Having helped his friend, Shiva looked around. To the left was a sheer, rocky mountainside, almost as steep as a cliff, which extended upwards for several hundred metres. To the right was a steep drop, to a dry valley far below. As far as the eye could see, there was no sign of any life anywhere. No human habitation, no animal, not even the few valiant plants and trees that they had seen at lower heights.

Shiva looked at Gopal with raised eyebrows and whispered. 'We're here?'

Gopal gestured towards Kurush. The Parihan was carefully running his hands over the mountain wall, his eyes shut, trying to locate something. He suddenly stopped. He had found what he was seeking. Shiva had moved up in the meantime and saw the faint indentation of a symbol on the mountainside. A figurative flame he had come to recognise: *Fravashi.*

Kurush pressed the ring on his index finger into the centre of the symbol. A block of rock, the size of a human head, emerged from the right. Kurush quickly placed both his hands on the rock, stepped back to get some leverage, and pushed hard.

Shiva watched in wonder as the mountain seemed to come to life. A substantial section, nearly four metres across and three metres high, receded inward and then slid aside, revealing a pathway going deep into the mountain's womb.

Kurush turned towards Shiva and indicated that they were good to go. Shiva helped Gopal onto his horse and handed the reins to his friend. As he walked towards his horse, he noticed that while the rocky outcrop where he had tethered his animal looked natural, in fact, it was manmade. Shiva mounted his horse and quickly joined Gopal and Kurush, riding into the heart of the mountain.

— ⅄ⓄƱ⇞⊛ —

The rocky concealed entrance had closed behind them just as smoothly. It would have been pitch dark inside except for a flaming torch that was maintained by the Parihans on one of the walls, which threw its light ahead for a few metres. Beyond that, the light lost its struggle against the omnipresent darkness of the cavernous pathway. Kurush picked three unlit torches from a recess on the wall, lit them and handed one each to Gopal and Shiva. Thereupon he swiftly rode ahead, holding his torch aloft. Shiva and Gopal kicked their horses and made haste after him.

Soon the pathway split into a fork, but Kurush unhesitatingly led them up one, disregarding the other. Just like the Nagas in the Dandak forests, the Vayuputras too had ensured that in the unlikely scenario of any unauthorised person finding his way into the secret pathway, he would inevitably get lost within the mountain, unless led by a Vayuputra guide.

Shiva expected many more such misleading paths along the way. He was not disappointed.

— ⁂ —

A half hour later, after a long monotonous ride, the travellers emerged on the other side of the mountain, almost blinded by the sudden onslaught of bright sunlight. Even as his eyes adjusted, Shiva's jaw dropped with amazement as he took in what lay ahead.

The other side of the mountain was dramatically different from what they had seen up to now. A broad, winding road had been cut into the sides of the mountain. Called the Rudra Avenue by the local Parihans, a beautifully carved railing ran along its sides, affording protection for horses or carriages from slipping off the road to certain death in the sheer ravine below. The Rudra Avenue wound its way along the steep mountain in a gentle descent to the bottom. The valley itself, naturally dry as a bone, was surrounded on all sides by steep mountains. The splendour of nature notwithstanding, what Shiva was struck by was what the Parihans had done with it. Hidden away from prying eyes, surrounded by unconquerable mountains, in this secluded spot, they had truly created a *land of fairies, Pariha.*

The Rudra Avenue ended at the base of a terrace. This platform though, unlike the ones built by the Meluhans, had not been constructed as protection against flood. The problem with water in Pariha was not one of excess but that of scarcity. The platform had been built to create a smooth base atop the rough, undulating, mountainous valley, allowing for the construction of massive structures upon it. The city of Pariha had been built on it.

Kurush, Gopal and Shiva approached the platform at the lowest point of the valley. The platform was at its tallest here, nearly twenty metres high. A massive ceremonial gate had been erected at what was obviously the only entry point into the city. The road was surrounded by high walls on both sides, and narrowed down as it led to the well barricaded gate. Looking admiringly around, the warrior in Shiva understood that the approach to the city gates perforce funnelled an attacking force into a narrow neck, thus making defence easy for the Parihans.

The massive ornate city gates had been hewn out of the local brown stone that Shiva had frequently seen en route. The gate itself was flanked on either side by large pillars, on which crouched two imposing creatures, as if ready to pounce in defence of their city. This unfamiliar creature carried the head of a man on the body of a lion and sprouted the broad wings of an eagle. Parihan pride was unmistakable in the features of the face: a sharp forehead held high, a hooked nose, neatly beaded beard, a drooping moustache and lengthy locks emerging from under a square hat. The aggressive, warrior-like visage was tempered somewhat by calm, almost friendly eyes.

Shiva noted that Kurush's conversation with the gatekeeper was done. He walked back and spoke respectfully to Gopal.

'My Lord, the formalities have been completed. Please accept my apologies that it took us so long to get here. Shall we?'

'There's no need for an apology, Kurush,' said Gopal politely. 'Let's go.'

Shiva quietly followed Kurush and Gopal, keenly aware of the gatekeeper's quizzical, perhaps even judgemental eyes.

— ⅄ⓄՍⴷ⊛ —

They crossed a massive tiled courtyard, guiding their horses onto the cobbled pathway leading to the top of the platform. The gradient was gentle, making it easy to negotiate the single hair-pin bend they encountered. A few pedestrians sauntered along the accompanying steps, provided with long treads to facilitate the climb. All along the pathway, the rock face of the platform had been carved and painted. Against the relief of glazed tiles, sculpted Parihans gazed at passers-by with their distinguished features, long coats and square hats. As if from nowhere, water rippled down the centre of the rock face, leaving a lilting musical sound in its wake. Shiva made a mental note to ask Gopal the secret of this water source in the harsh desert.

Shiva's questions were quickly forgotten as he reached the top and exclaimed with wonder at the sheer beauty of all that he beheld.

'By the Holy Lake!'

He had just had his first vision of the exquisite, symmetrical gardens of Pariha. These artificial heavenly creations were so extraordinary that Parihans had named them *Paradaeza, the walled place of harmony*.

The Paradaeza extended along the central axis of the rectangular city, with buildings built around it. The park and the city extended all the way to the edge of a great mountain at the upper end of the valley, which had been named the Mountain of Mercy by the Asuras. A water channel emerged from the heart of the mountain, flowing through the garden in an unerringly straight line, filling up large square ponds intermittently. The ponds themselves had flamboyant fountains constructed in the centre, spewing water high into the air. The left and right halves of the gardens, divided by the water channel, were perfect mirror images of each other. The entire expanse was covered with a carpet of thick and carefully manicured grass, which provided the base around which flower beds and trees were arranged in perfect harmony. The flora had obviously been imported from around the world; roses, narcissus, tulips, lilacs, jasmine, orange and lemon trees dotted the landscape in poetic profusion.

Shiva was so lost in the beauty of the garden that he didn't hear his friend call.

'Lord Neelkanth?' repeated Gopal.

Shiva turned to the Chief Vasudev.

'We can always come back here, my friend. But for now, we need to retire to our guesthouse.'

Shiva and Gopal had been housed in the state guesthouse, reserved for elite visitors to Pariha. Here too, the duo encountered the Parihan obsession with beauty and elegance.

Dismounting from their horses, Shiva and Gopal strode into the building. The entrance led to a wide, comfortable veranda lined with neat rows of perfectly circular columns providing support to a great stone ceiling. The columns were coloured a vivid pink all the way to the top, at which point, near the ceiling, it contained discreet etchings of animal figurines. Shiva squinted to get a better look.

'Bulls,' remarked Shiva.

Bulls and cows were sacred amongst the Indians, central to the spiritual experience of life.

'Yes,' confirmed Gopal. 'Bulls are revered by the Parihans as well. They're symbolic of strength and virility.'

As they reached the other end of the veranda, they encountered three elegantly dressed Parihans. The one in front held out a tray with warm, moistened and scented towels. Gopal immediately picked one up and went on to wipe the accumulated dust and grime from his face and hands. Shiva followed his example.

A Parihan woman walked up to Gopal, bowed low and spoke softly. 'Welcome, honoured Chief Vasudev Gopal. We can scarce believe our good fortune in hosting the representative of the great Lord Ram.'

'Thank you, My Lady,' said Gopal. 'But you have me at a disadvantage. You know my name and I do not know yours.'

'My name is Bahmandokht.'

'The daughter of Bahman?' said Gopal, for he was familiar with their old language, Avesta.

Bahmandokht smiled. 'That is one of the meanings, yes. But I prefer the other one.'

'And, what is that?'

'A maiden with a good mind.'

'I'm sure you live by that name, My Lady.'

'I try my best, Lord Gopal.'

Gopal smiled and folded his hands into a Namaste.

Unlike most Parihans who had studiously ignored Shiva all this time, Bahmandokht addressed the Neelkanth with a polite bow. 'Welcome, Lord Shiva. I do hope we have given you no cause for complaint.'

'None at all,' said Shiva graciously.

'I know you are here on a mission,' said Bahmandokht.

'I do not make so bold as to speak for my entire tribe, but I personally hope that you succeed. India and Pariha are intertwined by ancient bonds. If something needs to be done that is in the interest of your country, I believe it is our duty to help. It is the dictate that Lord Rudra laid down for us.'

Shiva acknowledged the courtesy and held his hands together in a Namaste. 'That spirit is returned in full measure by my country, Lady Bahmandokht.'

Bahmandokht glanced at a woman standing at the back towards the end of the lobby. Shiva's eyes followed her and rested on a tall woman, dressed in traditional Parihan garb. Despite the attire, it was obvious that she wasn't native to Pariha. Bronze-complexioned with jet black hair, she had large attractive doe-eyes and a voluptuous body, unlike the slender locals. She was a gorgeous woman indeed.

'Lord Shiva,' said Bahmandokht, pulling the Neelkanth's attention back. 'My aide will show you to your chamber.'

'Thank you,' said Shiva.

As Gopal and Shiva were escorted away, the Neelkanth looked back. The mystery woman had disappeared.

Shiva and Gopal were led into a lavish suite of rooms with two separate bed chambers. The suite had been furnished with every luxury imaginable. Door-length windows at the far end opened on to a huge balcony with large recliners and a couple of cloth-covered pouffes that could double up as tables. The living room contained a mini fountain on the side, its cascading waters creating a soothing tinkle. Delicately woven wall-to-wall plush carpets covered every inch of the floor. Bolsters and cushions of various sizes were strewn on the carpets at several corners, making comfortable floor-seating areas. An ornately carved oak table was placed in one corner, accompanied with cushioned chairs on the side. Another corner was occupied by Parihan musical instruments, keeping in mind the role of leisure in hospitality. Lavish gold and silver plated accoutrements decorated the mantelpiece and shelves on the walls. This was ostentatious even by the standards of Swadweepan royalty.

The two bedrooms had comfortable soft beds with silk linen. Bowls of fruit had been thoughtfully placed on low tables next to the beds. Even clothes had been specially ordered and placed in cupboards for the two guests, including traditional Parihan cloaks.

Shiva looked at Gopal with a twinkle in his eye and chortled, 'I think these miserable quarters will have to suffice!'

Gopal joined in mirthfully.

Chapter 37

Unexpected Help

After a sumptuous dinner, Gopal and Shiva were back in their chambers, welcoming the opportunity for relaxation and inactivity. The fountain in the room having drawn his attention, Shiva quipped, 'Pandit*ji*, where do they get the water from?'

'For this fountain?' asked Gopal.

'For all the fountains, ponds and channels that we have seen. Quite frankly, building this city and these gardens would have required a prodigious amount of water. This is a desert land with almost no natural rivers. I was told that they don't even have regular rains. So where does this water come from?'

'They owe it to the brilliance of their engineers.'

'How so?'

'There are massive natural springs and aquifers to the north of Pariha.'

'That is water within the rocks and the ground, right?'

'Yes.'

'But springs can never be as bountiful.'

'True, but scarcity engenders ingenuity. When you don't have enough water, you learn to use it judiciously. All the fountain and canal water that you see in the city is recycled waste water.'

Shiva, who had dipped his hand into the fountain water, immediately recoiled.

Gopal laughed softly. 'Don't worry, my friend. That water has been treated and completely cleaned. It's even safe to drink.'

'I'll take your word for it.'

Gopal smiled as Shiva judiciously wiped his hands with a sanitised napkin.

'How far away are these springs and aquifers?'

'The ones that supply this city are a good fifty to hundred kilometres away,' answered Gopal.

Shiva whistled softly. 'That's a long distance. How do they get the water here in such large quantities? I haven't seen any canals.'

'Oh, they have canals. But you can't see them as they are underground.'

'They've built underground canals?' asked Shiva, stunned.

'They're not as broad as the canals we have back home. But they serve the purpose. They built canals that are the size of underground drains, which begin at the aquifers and springs.'

'But a hundred kilometres is a long way to transport water. How do they do that? Do they have underground pumps powered by animals?'

'No. They use one of the most powerful forces of nature to do the job.'

'What?'

'Gravity. They built underground channels with gentle gradients that slope over a hundred kilometres. The water naturally flows down due to the force of gravity.'

'Brilliant. But building something like this would require precision engineering skills of a high order.'

'You're right. The angle of the descent would have to be absolutely exact over very long distances. If the gradient is even slightly higher than required, the water would begin to erode the bottom of the channel, destroying it over time.'

'And if the slope is a little too gentle, the water would simply stop flowing.'

'Exactly,' said Gopal. 'You can imagine the flawless design and execution required, in implementing a project such as this.'

'But when did they...'

Shiva was interrupted by a soft knock on the door. He immediately lowered his voice to an urgent whisper. 'Pandit*ji*, were you expecting someone?'

Gopal shook his head. 'No. And, where is our guard? Isn't he supposed to announce visitors?'

Shiva pulled out his sword, indicating to Gopal that he should follow him, as he tiptoed to the door. The safest place for him was behind Shiva. The Vasudev chief was a Brahmin and not a warrior. Shiva waited near the door. The soft knock was heard again.

Shiva turned and whispered to Gopal. 'As soon as I pull the intruder in, shut the door and lock it.'

Shiva held his sword to the side, pulled the door open and in one smooth motion, yanked the intruder into the room, pushing the Parihan to the ground. Gopal, moving just as rapidly, shut the door and bolted it.

'I'm a friend!' spoke a feminine voice, her hands raised in surrender.

Shiva and Gopal stared at the woman on the ground, her face covered with a veil.

She slowly got up, keeping her eyes fixed on Shiva's sword. 'You don't need that. Parihans do not kill their guests. It is one of Lord Rudra's laws.'

Shiva refused to lower his blade. 'Reveal yourself,' he commanded.

The woman removed her veil. 'You've seen me earlier, great Neelkanth.'

Shiva recognised the intruder immediately. It was the dark-haired mystery woman he had seen in the lobby while he'd been talking to Bahmandokht.

Shiva smiled. 'I was wondering when I would see you next.'

'I've come to help,' said the woman, still unable to tear her eyes away from the sword. 'So I'll repeat that you really don't need that. We Parihans will never break Lord Rudra's laws.'

Shiva sheathed his sword. 'What makes you think we need your help?'

'For the same reason that you don't need your sword here: we Vayuputras never break Lord Rudra's laws. I am here to help you get what you came for...'

Shiva and Gopal joined the lady, having made her comfortable on the soft cushions.

'What is your name?' asked Shiva. 'Why do you want to help us?'

'My name is Scheherazade.'

Scheherazade was a name that harked back to ancient Parihan roots; *a person who gives freedom to cities.*

Shiva narrowed his eyes. 'That is a lie. You are not from this land. What is your real name?'

'I am a Parihan. This is my name.'

'How can we trust you if you don't even tell us your real name?'

'My name has nothing to do with your mission. What the Amartya Shpand, the Vayuputra Council, think of your mission is what truly matters.'

'And you can tell us what they think?' asked Gopal.

'That's why I am here. I can tell you what you need to do to fulfil your mission.'

— ⅄ ⊙ ᕫ ⍋ ⊗ —

The Mithra was a ceremonial title for the chief of the Vayuputra tribe. It literally translated as *'friend'*; for he was the deepest friend of the Vayuputra God, the Ahura Mazda.

Ahura Mazda was a formless God, much like the Hindu concept of *Parmatma.* And Mithra was his representative on earth. Lord Rudra had mandated that the ancient title of Mithra be used for the Chief Vayuputra. Once a man became the Mithra, all his earlier identities were erased, including his old name. He even dissociated himself completely from his former family. Everyone was to know him thereafter as Mithra.

Mithra was in the antechamber of his office, when he heard a soft noise from the veranda. The nascent moon cast a faint light, impairing vision, but Mithra knew who it was as he walked over.

He heard a soft, feminine voice call out in a whisper, 'Great Mithra, I have sent her to them.'

'Thank you, Bahmandokht. The Vayuputras will be indebted to you in perpetuity, for you have helped our tribe fulfil our mission and our vow to Lord Rudra.'

Bahmandokht bowed low. There had been a time when she had loved the man who'd become the Mithra. But once he had assumed his office as the chief, the only feelings she had allowed herself were those of devotion and respect.

She stepped away quietly.

The Mithra stared at Bahmandokht's retreating form and then returned to the antechamber. He sat on a simple chair, leaned back and closed his eyes. The ancient memory was still fresh in his mind, as if it had all happened yesterday – the conversation with his close friend and brother-in-law, Manobhu.

'Are you sure, Manobhu?' asked the Parihan, who would go on to become the Mithra.

The Tibetan feigned outrage as he looked at his friend and fellow Vayuputra.

'I mean no disrespect, Manobhu. But I hope you realise that what we're doing is illegal.'

Manobhu allowed himself a slight smile as he scratched his shaggy beard. His matted hair had been tied up in a bun with a string of beads, in the style favoured by his tribe, the fierce Gunas. His body was covered with deep scars acquired from a lifetime of battle. His tall, muscular physique was always in a state of alertness, ever ready for war. His demeanour, his clothes, his hair – all conveyed the impression of a ruthless warrior. But his eyes were different. They were a window to his calm mind, one that had found its purpose and was at peace. Manobhu's eyes had always intrigued the Parihan, compelling him to become a follower.

'If you are unsure, my friend,' said Manobhu, 'you don't have to do this.'

The Parihan looked away.

'Don't feel pressured to do this just because you're related to me,' continued Manobhu, whose brother had married the Parihan's sister.

The Parihan returned his gaze. 'How does the reason matter? What matters is the result. What matters is whether Lord Rudra's commandment is being followed.'

Manobhu continued to lock gaze with the Parihan, his eyes mirthful. 'You should know Lord Rudra's commandments better than I do. After all, he was a Parihan. Like you.'

The Parihan stole a look at the back of the room nervously, where a diabolical mixture was boiling inside a vessel, the fire below it steady and even.

Manobhu stepped forward and put his hand on the Parihan's shoulder. 'Trust me, the Somras is turning Evil. Lord Rudra would have wanted us to do this. If the council doesn't agree, then the hell with them. We will ensure that Lord Rudra's commandments are followed.'

The Parihan looked at Manobhu and sighed. 'Are you sure that your nephew has the potential to fulfil this mission? That he can one day be the successor to Lord Rudra?'

Manobhu smiled. 'He's your nephew too. His mother is your sister.'

'I know. But the boy doesn't live with me. He lives with you, in Tibet. I have never met him. I don't know if I ever will. And you refuse to even tell me his name. So I ask again: Are you sure he is the one?'

'Yes,' Manobhu was confident in his belief. 'He is the one. He will grow up to be the Neelkanth. He will be the one who will carry out Lord Rudra's commandment. He will take Evil out of the equation.'

'But he needs to be educated. He needs to be prepared.'

'I will prepare him.'

'But what is the point? The Vayuputra council controls the emergence of the Neelkanth. How will our nephew be discovered?'

'I'll arrange it at the right time,' said Manobhu.

The Parihan frowned. 'But how will you...'

'Leave that to me,' interrupted Manobhu. 'If he is not discovered, it will mean that the time for Evil has not yet come. On the other hand, if I'm able to ensure that he is discovered...'

'...then we will know that Evil has risen,' said the Parihan, completing Manobhu's sentence.

Manobhu shook his head, disagreeing partially with his brother-in-law. 'To be more precise, we would know that Good has turned into Evil.'

The conversation was interrupted by a soft hissing sound from the far corner of the room. The medicine was ready. The two friends walked over to the fire and peered into the vessel. A thick reddish-brown paste had formed; small bubbles were bursting through to the surface.

'It only needs to cool down now. The task is done,' said the Parihan.

Manobhu looked at his brother-in-law. 'No, my friend. The task has just begun.'

The Mithra breathed deeply as he came back to the present. He whispered, 'I never thought that our rebellion would succeed, Manobhu.'

He rose from his chair, walked over to the veranda and looked up at the sky. In the old days, his people believed that great men, once they had surrendered their mortal flesh, went up to live among the stars and keep watch over them all. Mithra focused his eyes on one particular star and smiled. 'Manobhu, it was a good idea to name our nephew Shiva. A good clue to help me guess that he is the one.'

— ⁂ —

'To begin with, let me tell you that most of the Vayuputras are against you,' said Scheherazade.

'That's not really much of a secret,' said Shiva wryly.

'Look, you can't blame the Vayuputras. Our laws state very clearly that only one of us, from amongst those who're authorised by the Vayuputra tribe, can become the Neelkanth. You have emerged out of nowhere. The laws don't allow us to recognise or help someone like you.'

'And yet, you are here,' said Shiva. 'I don't think you're working alone. You were standing right at the back, almost hidden, when I saw you in the lobby. I bet you are not a fully-accepted Parihan. I can't see someone like you having the courage to do this all by yourself. Some powerful Parihans are putting you up to it. Which makes me believe that some Vayuputras realise what I am saying is true, that Evil has risen.'

Scheherazade smiled softly. 'Yes. There are some very powerful Vayuputras who are on your side. But they cannot help you openly. Unlike most of the earlier Neelkanth pretenders, your blue throat is genuine. This leads to one inescapable conclusion; some Vayuputra has helped you many decades ago. Can you imagine the chaos this has caused? There were unprecedented accusations flying thick and fast after your emergence; people within Pariha were accusing each other of having broken Lord Rudra's laws and helping you clandestinely when you were young. It was tearing the Vayuputras apart till Lord Mithra put an end to it. He held that our tribe has not authorised you as the Neelkanth and perhaps it was the doing of someone from within your own country.'

'So, if any Vayuputra helps me, he will be seen as the traitor who started it all, many years ago.'

'Exactly,' answered Scheherazade.

'What is the way out?' asked Gopal.

'You, My Lord Chief Vasudev, must lead the mission,' said Scheherazade. 'Lord Shiva must stay in the background. Don't ask for assistance to be provided for the Neelkanth, but to *you* as a member of the Vasudev tribe, seeking justice. They cannot say no to a just demand from the representative of Lord Ram.'

'I am sorry? I didn't understand.'

'What does the Neelkanth need, Lord Gopal?' asked Scheherazade. 'He needs the *Brahmastra* to threaten Meluha...'

'How did you...'

'With due respect, don't ask superfluous questions, Lord Gopal. What Lord Shiva and you need is obvious. We have to devise the best way for you to get it. If you ask for the *Brahmastra* so that you can fight Evil, then you will open yourself to questions as to Lord Shiva's legitimacy in deciding what Evil is, for we all know that he has not been authorised or trained by the Vayuputras. Instead, seek redress for a crime committed on Indian soil by a person who the Vayuputras have supported in the past. And what crime was that? The unauthorised use of *daivi astras*.'

'Lord Bhrigu...' said Gopal, remembering the great maharishi's use of the *divine weapons* in Panchavati.

'Exactly. The laws of Lord Rudra make it clear that for

the first unauthorised use of *daivi astras*, the punishment is a fourteen-year exile into the forests. A second unauthorised use is punishable by death. Many in the council agree that Lord Bhrigu has got away lightly, despite having used *daivi astras*.'

'So the Vasudevs are to present themselves as the ones enforcing the justice of Lord Rudra?'

'Exactly. It is impossible for a Vayuputra to say no to this. You should state that the law on the *daivi astra* ban was broken and those who did this – Lord Bhrigu, the Emperor of Meluha and the King of Ayodhya – need to be punished. And, the Vasudevs have decided to mete out justice.'

'And we can tell the Vayuputras,' said Shiva, completing Scheherazade's thought, 'that they may well have more reserves of *daivi astras*. So we need the *Brahmastra* to encourage them to do the right thing.'

Scheherazade smiled. 'Use the laws to achieve your objective. Once you have the *Brahmastra*, use it to threaten the Meluhans. Evil must be stopped. But I've been asked to tell you that you shouldn't...'

'We will never use the *Brahmastra*,' said Gopal, interrupting Scheherazade.

'It's not just about the laws of Lord Rudra,' added Shiva. 'Using a weapon of such horrifying power goes against the laws of humanity.'

Scheherazade nodded. 'When you meet the council, insist on speaking with Lord Mithra in private. Tell them it is a matter of the *daivi astra* law being broken. Say that the Vasudevs cannot allow those who broke Lord Rudra's law to go unpunished. That will be enough. It will then be a private conversation between Lord Mithra and the two of you. You will get what you want.'

Shiva smiled as he understood who amongst the Vayuputras

was helping him. But he was still intrigued by Scheherazade, or whatever her real name was.

'Why are you helping us?' asked Shiva.

'Because I've been told to do so.'

'I don't believe that. Something else is driving you. Why are you helping us?'

Scheherazade smiled sadly and looked at the carpet. Then she turned towards the balcony, staring into the dark night beyond. She wiped a tear from the corner of her eye and turned back towards Shiva. 'Because there was a man whom I had loved once, who had told me that the Somras was turning evil. And I didn't believe him at the time.'

'Who is this man?' asked Gopal.

'It doesn't matter anymore,' said Scheherazade. 'He is dead. He was killed, perhaps by those who'd wanted to stop him. Ending the reign of the Somras is my way of apologising...'

Shiva leaned towards her, looked straight into Scheherazade's eyes and whispered, 'Tara?'

A stunned Scheherazade pulled back. Nobody had called her by that name in years. Shiva continued to observe her eyes.

'By the Holy Lake,' he whispered. 'It is you.'

Scheherazade did not say anything. Her relationship with Brahaspati had been kept a secret. Many amongst the Parihans believed that the Somras was still a force for Good, and that the former chief scientist of Meluha was deeply biased and misguided about it. Tara would have preferred not having to live in Pariha as Scheherazade. But her presence here had served a purpose for her guru, Lord Bhrigu. Believing Brahaspati was dead, she had found no reason to return to her homeland.

'But you are Lord Bhrigu's student,' said Shiva. 'Why are you going against him?'

'I'm not Tara.'

'I know you are,' said Shiva. 'Why are you going against your guru? Do you believe that it was Lord Bhrigu who got Brahaspati killed at Mount Mandar?'

Scheherazade stood up and turned to leave. Shiva rose quickly, stretched out and held her hand. 'Brahaspati is not dead.'

A dumbstruck Scheherazade stopped dead in her tracks.

'Brahaspati is alive,' said Shiva. 'He is with me.'

Tears poured from Scheherazade's eyes. She couldn't believe what she was hearing.

Shiva stepped forward and repeated gently. 'He is with me. Your Brahaspati is alive.'

Scheherazade kept crying, tears of confused happiness flowing down her cheeks.

Shiva gently held her hand in his own. 'Tara, you will come back with us when we're done here. I'll take you back. I'll take you back to your Brahaspati.'

Scheherazade collapsed into Shiva's arms, inconsolable in her tears. She would be Tara once again.

Chapter 38

The Friend of God

The strategy that Tara had suggested worked like a charm. The Amartya Shpand was genuinely taken by surprise when Gopal entered their audience chamber without Shiva. When he raised the issue of Maharishi Bhrigu's misuse of the *daivi astras*, they knew that they had been cornered. They had no choice but to grant Gopal an audience with the Mithra. That was the law.

The following day, Shiva and Gopal were led into the official audience hall and residence of the Mithra. It had been built at one end of the city, the last building abutting the Mountain of Mercy. Unlike the rest of Pariha, this structure was incredibly modest. It had a simple base made of stone, which covered the water channel that emerged from the mountain. On it were constructed austere pillars, which supported a wooden roof four metres high. On entry, one immediately stepped into a simple audience hall furnished with basic chairs and sombre carpets. The Mithra's personal quarters lay farther inside, separated by stone walls and a wooden door. Shiva could sense that this was almost a stone replica of a large ceremonial tent, the wooden tent-poles having been converted to stone pillars and the cloth canopy into a wooden roof. In a way, this was a link to the nomadic past of Lord Rudra's people, when everybody lived in simple, easily-built tents that could be dismantled and moved at short notice. Like a tribal leader of the old code, the Mithra lived in penurious simplicity while his people lived in luxury. The only indulgence that the Mithra had allowed himself was the beautiful garden that surrounded his abode. It was bountiful in its design, precise in its symmetry and extravagant in its colourful flora.

Shiva and Gopal were left alone in the audience hall, and the doors were shut. Within a few moments, the Mithra entered.

Shiva and Gopal immediately stood up. They greeted the Mithra with the ancient Parihan salute: the left hand was placed on the heart, fist open, as a mark of admiration. The right arm was held rigidly to the side of the body, bent upwards at the elbow. The open palm of the right hand faced outwards, as a form of greeting. The Mithra smiled genially and folded his hands together into the traditional Indian Namaste.

Shiva grinned, but remained silent, waiting for the Mithra to speak.

The Mithra was a tall, fair-skinned man, dressed in a simple brown cloak. A white hat covered his long brownish hair, with tiny beads wrapped around separated strands of his beard, much like all Parihans. Though the sack-like cloak made it difficult to judge, his body seemed strong and muscular. Of interest to Shiva were his delicate hands with long, slender fingers; like those of a surgeon rather than a warrior. But Shiva was most intrigued by the Mithra's nose: sharp and long. It reminded him of his beloved mother.

The Mithra walked up to Shiva and held the Neelkanth by his shoulders. 'What a delight it is to finally see you.'

Shiva noted that the Mithra didn't even cursorily glance at his blue neck, something most people could not resist. The Mithra's attention was focused on Shiva's eyes.

And then the Mithra said something even more intriguing. 'You have your father's eyes. And your mother's nose.'

He knew my father? And my mother?!

Before Shiva could react, the Mithra gently touched Shiva's back, as he smiled at Gopal. 'Come, let's sit.'

As soon as they had seated themselves, the Mithra turned towards the Neelkanth, 'I can see the questions that are running through your mind. How do I know your father and mother? Who am I? What was my name before I became the Mithra?'

Shiva smiled. 'This eye-reading business is very dangerous. It doesn't allow one to have any secrets.'

'Sometimes, it's important that there be no secrets,' said the Mithra, 'especially when such big decisions are being taken. How else can we be sure that we have taken the right step?'

'You don't have to answer if you don't wish to. The questions running in my mind are not important to our mission.'

'You're right. You have been trained well. These questions may trouble your mind, but they are not important. But then, can we really carry out our mission with troubled minds?'

'A troubled mind makes one lose sight of the mission,' admitted Shiva.

'And the world cannot afford to have you lose sight of your mission, great Neelkanth. You are too important for us. So let me answer your personal questions first.'

Shiva noticed that the Mithra had called him the Neelkanth, something which no Parihan had, until now.

'My name is not important,' said the Mithra. 'I don't hold that name anymore. My only identity is my title: the Mithra.'

Shiva nodded politely.

'Now, how do I know your mother? Simple. I grew up with her. She was my sister.'

Shiva's eyes opened wide in surprise. 'You are my uncle?'

Mithra nodded. 'I was your uncle before I became the Mithra.'

'Why have I not met you before?'

'It's complicated. But suffice it to say that your father's brother, Lord Manobhu, and I were good friends. I held him in deep regard. We'd decided to seal our friendship with a marriage between our two families. My sister went to live with Lord Manobhu's brother in Tibet, after their wedding. And you were born from that union.'

'But my uncle had rebellious ideas...' said Shiva, trying to guess why the Mithra had been forced to keep his distance from their family.

The Mithra shook his head. 'Manobhu didn't have rebellious ideas. He had inspiring ideas. But an inspiration before its time appears like a rebellion.'

'So you were not forced by the Vayuputras to stay away from my family?'

'Oh I was forced all right. But not by the Vayuputras.'

Shiva smiled. 'Uncle Manobhu could be stubborn at times.'

The Mithra smiled.

'When did you know that I was your long-lost relative?' asked Shiva. 'Did you have spies following me?'

'I recognised you the moment I heard your name.'

'Didn't you know my name?'

'No, Manobhu refused to tell me. Now I understand why. It was a clue he'd left for me. If you emerged at all, I would recognise you by your name.'

'How so?' asked Shiva, intrigued.

'Almost nobody, even from amongst the Vayuputras, knows that Lord Rudra's mother had had a special and personal name for him: Shiva.'

'What?!'

'Yes. Lord Rudra's name means "the one who roars". He

was named so because when he was born, he cried so loudly that he drove the midwife away!'

'I have heard that story,' said Shiva. 'But I have not heard the one about Lord Rudra's mother calling him Shiva...'

'It's a secret that only a few Vayuputras are aware of. Legend holds that Lord Rudra was actually stillborn.'

'What?' asked a genuinely surprised Gopal.

'Yes,' said the Mithra. 'The midwife and Lord Rudra's mother tried very hard to revive him. Finally, the midwife tried something very unorthodox. She tried to breastfeed the stillborn Lord Rudra. Much to his mother's surprise, the baby actually started breathing and, as history recalls, roared loudly.'

'By the Holy Lake,' whispered Shiva. 'What a fascinating story.'

'Yes, it is. The midwife walked away soon thereafter, and was never heard of again. Lord Rudra's mother, who was an immigrant and a believer in the Mother Goddess Shakti, was convinced that the midwife had been sent by the Goddess to save her son. She believed her son was born as *a body without life*, a *shava*, whom Goddess Shakti had infused with life; therefore, she felt the Goddess had converted a *Shava* to *Shiva*, or *the auspicious one*. So she started calling her son Shiva, in honour of the Mother Goddess and in acknowledgement of the state in which her son was born.'

An enthralled Shiva listened in rapt attention to the Mithra.

'So,' said the Mithra, 'the moment I heard your name, I knew that Manobhu had left a clue for me about you being the one he had trained.'

'So you knew that Lord Manobhu was planning this?'

The Mithra smiled. 'Your uncle and I made the medicine together.'

'You mean the medicine that is responsible for my throat turning blue?'

'Yes.'

'But didn't that have to be given to me at a specific time in my life?'

'I'm assuming that is what Manobhu did, for here you are.'

'But Lord Mithra, this is not the way the system was supposed to work, as an unfolding series of implausible coincidences. There are so many things that could have gone wrong. To begin with, I may not have been trained well. Or the medicine may not have been given to me at the right time. I may never have been invited to Meluha. And worst of all, I may not have stumbled upon the Somras as the true Evil.'

'You're right. This is not the way our *Vayuputra* system was designed to work. But Manobhu and I had faith that this is the way the *universe's* system is supposed to work. And it did, didn't it?'

'But is it right to leave such significant outcomes to a roll of the universe's dice?'

'You make it sound as if it was all left to dumb luck. We didn't leave it only to chance, Shiva. The Vayuputras were sure the Somras had not turned evil. Manobhu and I felt otherwise. Had Manobhu been alive, he would have guided you through this period, but in spite of his untimely death, Good prevailed. Manobhu always said let us allow the universe to make the decision, and it did. We decided to set in motion a chain of events, which would work out only if the universe willed it so. Frankly, I wasn't sure. But I didn't stop him. I just didn't think his plan would succeed. I did help him in making the medicine, though. And when I saw the plan coming to fruition, I knew that it was my duty to do whatever I could to help.'

'But what if I had failed? What if I hadn't identified the Somras as Evil? Then Evil would have won, right?'

'Sometimes, the universe decides that Evil is supposed to win. Perhaps a race or species becomes so harmful that it's better to allow Evil to triumph and destroy that species. It has happened before. But this is not one of those times.'

Shiva was clearly overwhelmed by the number of things that could have gone wrong.

'You are still troubled by something...' said the Mithra.

'I've talked to Pandit*ji* as well, about this,' said Shiva, pointing to Gopal. 'So much of what I have achieved in my mission can be attributed to pure luck; just a random turn of the universe.'

The Mithra bent forward towards Shiva and whispered, 'One makes one's own luck, but you have to give the universe the opportunity to help you.'

Shiva remained stoic, not quite convinced by the Mithra's words.

'You had every reason to turn away after arriving in Meluha for the first time. You were in a strange new land. Peculiar people, who were evidently so much more advanced than you, insisted on looking upon you as a God. You were tasked with a mission, the enormity of which would have intimidated practically anyone in the world. I'm sure that at the time, you didn't even think you could succeed. And yet, you didn't run away. You stood up and accepted a responsibility that was thrust upon you. That decision was the turning point in your journey against Evil, which had nothing to do with the twists and blessings of fate.'

Shiva looked at Gopal, whose demeanour suggested he was in full agreement with the Mithra.

'You are giving me too much credit, Lord Mithra,' said Shiva.

'I am not,' said the Mithra. 'You are on course to fulfil *my* mission, without having taken any help from me. But I will not allow you to do that. You must give me the privilege of offering some help. Otherwise, how will I face the Ahura Mazda and Lord Rudra when I meet with them?'

Shiva smiled.

The Mithra looked directly into Shiva's eyes. 'But there are some things I must be sure of. What do you plan to do with the *daivi astra*?'

'I plan to use it to threaten...' Shiva stopped speaking as the Mithra raised his hand.

'I've seen enough,' said the Mithra.

Shiva frowned.

'Thoughts move faster than the tongue, great Neelkanth. I know you will not use these terrible weapons of destruction. I can also see that the reason you will not do so is not just because of the Vayuputra ban but because you believe that these weapons are too horrifying to ever be used.'

'I do believe that.'

'But I cannot give you the *Brahmastra*.'

This was unexpected. Shiva had thought the discussion had been going his way.

'I cannot give you the *Brahmastra* because it is too uncontrollable. It destroys anything and everything. Most importantly, its effect spreads out in circles. The worst destruction is in the epicentre, where everything living is instantly incinerated into thin air. While there is less destruction in the outer circles, the damage is still significantly widespread in the vicinity. So even if those outside the primary impact zone are not immediately killed, they suffer from the immense radiation unleashed by the *astra*. With Lord Bhrigu on the other side, he is sure to bet that you are using the weapon only as a threat, because you would not want to hurt your own army, which would most certainly be in the zone of radiation exposure.'

'So what is the way forward?'

'The *Pashupatiastra*. It is a weapon designed by Lord Rudra. It has all the power of the *Brahmastra*, but with much greater control. Its destruction is concentrated in the inner circle. Life outside this zone is not impacted at all. In fact, with the *Pashupatiastra*, you can even focus the effect in only one direction, leaving everyone else in the other directions safe. If you threaten to use this weapon, Lord Bhrigu will know that you can destroy Devagiri without endangering your people or the adjoining areas. Then the threat will be credible.'

This made sense. Shiva agreed.

'But you cannot actually use the weapon, Neelkanth,' reiterated the Mithra. 'It will poison the area for centuries. The devastation is unimaginable.'

'I give you my word, Lord Mithra,' said Shiva. 'I will never use these weapons.'

The Mithra smiled. 'Then I have no problems in offering the *Pashupatiastra* to you. I will give the orders immediately.'

Shiva raised his chin as a faint smile played on his lips. 'I think you had already made your decision about this, even before you met me, uncle.'

The Mithra laughed softly. 'I am just Mithra. But you didn't expect it to be so easy, right?'

'No, I didn't.'

'I have heard stories about you, especially about the way you have fought your battles. You have behaved in an exemplary manner until now. Even when you could have gained by doing something wrong, you refrained from doing so. You didn't fall prey to the logic of doing a small wrong for the sake of the greater good; of the ends justifying the means. That takes moral courage. So yes, I had already made up my mind. But I wanted to see you in any case. You will be remembered as the greatest man of our age; generations will look up to you as their God. How could I not want to meet you?'

'I am no God, Lord Mithra,' said an embarrassed Shiva.

'Wasn't it you who had said *"Har Har Mahadev"*? That *all of us are Gods*?'

Shiva laughed. 'You've got me there.'

'We don't become Gods because we think we are Gods,' said the Mithra. 'That is only a sign of ego. We become Gods when we realise that a part of the universal divinity lives within us; when we understand our role in this great world and when we strive to fulfil that role. There is nobody striving harder than you, Lord Neelkanth. That makes you a God. And remember, Gods don't fail. You cannot fail. Remember what your duty is. You have to take Evil out of the equation. You shouldn't destroy all traces of the Somras, for it may become Good in times to come, when it might be required once again. You have to keep the knowledge of the Somras alive. You will also have to create a tribe which will manage the Somras till it is required once again. Once all this is done, your mission will be over.'

'I will not fail, Lord Mithra,' said Shiva. 'I promise.'

'I know you will succeed,' smiled the Mithra, before turning to Gopal. 'Great Chief Vasudev, once the Neelkanth creates his own tribe, the Vayuputras will not remain in charge of fighting Evil anymore. It will be the task of the Neelkanth's tribe. Our relationship with the Vasudevs will become like one between distant relatives rather than the one which has entailed a joint duty towards a common cause.'

'Your relationship with the Vasudevs and with my country will exist forever, Lord Mithra,' said Gopal. 'You have helped us in our hour of need. I'm sure that, in turn, we will help Pariha if it ever needs us.'

'Thank you,' said the Mithra.

Chapter 39

He is One of Us

The Mithra called the entire city to the town centre the following morning. Shiva and Gopal stood next to him as he addressed the crowd.

'My fellow Vayuputras, I'm sure your minds are teeming with many questions and doubts. But this is not the time for that; this is the time for action. We trusted a man who had worked closely with us; we trusted him with our knowledge. But he betrayed us. Lord Bhrigu broke the laws of Lord Rudra. Lord Gopal, the chief of the Vasudevs and the representative of Lord Ram, has come here demanding justice. But, in this moment, it is not just about retribution for what Lord Bhrigu has done. It's also about justice for India, justice to Lord Rudra's principles. There is a purpose that we all serve, Parihans; it is beyond laws; it is one that was defined by Lord Rudra himself.'

Pointing at Shiva, the Mithra continued. 'Behold this man. He may not be a Vayuputra. But he does bear the blue throat. He may not be a Parihan, but he fights like one, with honour and integrity. We may not have recognised him, but the Vasudevs consider him the Neelkanth. He may not have lived amongst us, but he respects and idolises Lord Rudra as much as we do. Above all, he is fighting for Lord Rudra's cause.'

The Vayuputras listened with rapt attention.

'Yes, he is not a Vayuputra, and yet he is one of us. I am supporting him in his battle against Evil. And so shall you.'

Many amongst the Vayuputras were swayed by the Mithra's words. Those who weren't, were nevertheless aware that it was within the Mithra's legal rights to choose whom to support within India. So, while their reasons to do so may have differed, all the Vayuputras fell in line with the Mithra's decision.

Shiva and Gopal received a large crate the following evening. An entire Parihan cavalry platoon had been arranged to transport this incredibly heavy trunk safely back to the sea. Never having seen the material of the *Pashupatiastra*, Shiva assumed from the size of the trunk that they were carrying a huge quantity; probably enough to threaten an entire city. He was therefore amazed by Gopal's clarification that they were carrying only a handful of the *Pashupatiastra* material.

'Are you serious?'

'Yes, Lord Neelkanth,' said Gopal. 'Just a handful is enough to destroy entire cities. The trunk has massive insulation, made of lead and wet clay, besides the leaves of imported bilva trees. Together, these will protect us from exposure to the *Pashupatiastra* radiation.'

'By the Holy Lake,' said Shiva. 'The more I learn about the *daivi astras,* the more I'm convinced that they are the weapons of the demons.'

'They are, my friend. That's why Lord Rudra called them evil and banned their use. That is also why we will not use the *Pashupatiastra*. We'll only threaten to use it. But to make it a credible threat to the Meluhans, we will actually have to set up the weapon outside Devagiri.'

'Do you know how to do that?'

'No, I don't. Most of the Vayuputras are not privy to that knowledge either; only a select few are authorised to be in the know. There is a combination of engineering construction, mantras and other preparations that we would have to follow in order to set up this weapon. We would have to do this properly so as to convey a credible threat to Lord Bhrigu, since he does know how the *Pashupatiastra* is prepared for use. Lord Mithra and his people will commence our training from tomorrow morning.'

— ⅄ⓄⅡ⇑⊗ —

Parvateshwar moved his attention away from those sitting with him and cast a look outside the window of the Karachapa governor's residence. They were on the *dwitiya* or second platform of the city, and from this height, Parvateshwar had a clear view of the Western Sea, which stretched far into the horizon.

'The sea is the only way we have,' said Parvateshwar.

Bhrigu and Dilipa turned towards Parvateshwar. Dilipa's Ayodhyan army had finally arrived in Meluha, many months after the Battle of Devagiri. They had sailed on to Karachapa to join Parvateshwar's Suryavanshi forces.

'But General, isn't that the entire idea behind coming to Karachapa?' asked Dilipa. 'To attack Lothal by sea? What's new about that idea?'

'I'm not talking about attacking the city, Your Highness.'

While there were now four hundred thousand troops based in Karachapa under the command of Parvateshwar, he knew that it was not really enough to defeat a well-entrenched force of two hundred and fifty thousand in the well-designed citadel of Lothal. And despite all attempts at provocation, Sati had resolutely refused to step out of Lothal, thus giving Parvateshwar no opportunity to bring his numerical superiority into play in an open battlefield. The war had, for all practical purposes, ground to a stalemate.

'Please explain, General,' said Bhrigu, hoping the Meluhan army chief had come up with some brilliant idea to end the stalemate. 'What is your plan?'

'I think we should send forth a fleet towards the Narmada River, making sure that these ships are visible.'

Dilipa frowned. 'Have your spies discovered the route that Lord Shiva took?'

The Meluhans were aware that Shiva and Gopal had sailed to the Narmada, but they had lost track of them thereafter. They assumed that the duo may have used the Narmada route to steal into Panchavati or Ujjain. To what purpose, was still a mystery to the Meluhans.

'No,' answered Parvateshwar.

'Then what's the point of making our ships sail out in that direction? The Neelkanth's scouts and spies will surely get to know that our ships are sailing to the Narmada. We'll lose the element of surprise.'

'That is precisely what I want,' said Parvateshwar. 'We don't want to hide.'

'By the great Lord Brahma!' exclaimed an impressed Bhrigu. 'General Parvateshwar, have you discovered the Narmada route to Panchavati?'

'No, My Lord.'

'Then I don't understand... Oh right...' Bhrigu stopped mid-sentence as he finally understood what Parvateshwar had in mind.

'I'm not aware of the Narmada route to Panchavati,' said Parvateshwar. 'But the Lord Neelkanth's army doesn't know that I don't know. They may assume that we have discovered this precious route and that the Lord's life is in danger. Furthermore, the Nagas are a substantial segment of the warriors in that army. Will they keep quiet in the face of an imminent danger to their capital Panchavati, the city established by their Goddess Bhoomidevi?'

'They will be forced to sail out of Lothal,' said Dilipa.

'Exactly,' said Parvateshwar. 'Since our contingent will be approximately fifty ships, they will have to match our numbers. We will make our ships wait in ambush in a lagoon far beyond the Narmada delta.'

'And once they've begun sailing up the Narmada, we'll charge in from behind and attack them,' said Dilipa.

'No,' said Parvateshwar.

'No?' asked a surprised Dilipa.

'No, Your Highness. I intend to send out a crack team of commandos in advance, to the Narmada. They will wait for the Naga ships to race upriver, till they have travelled a considerable distance away from the sea. Naval movements in a river are constricted, no matter how large the river. Their fleet will be sailing close to each other. Our commandos will have devil boats with firewood and flints ready for our enemies. Our task will be to take out the first as well as last line of ships simultaneously.'

'Brilliant. They will lose their fleet, their soldiers will be adrift. Then our own fleet can charge in from the hidden lagoon and cut their soldiers down.'

'No, Your Highness,' said Parvateshwar, thinking he wouldn't have needed to explain all this to someone with the strategic brilliance of Shiva. 'Our fleet is not going to engage in battle at all. It's only a decoy. Our main attack will be carried out by the commandos. If the first and last line of the enemy ships are set on fire, there's a pretty good chance that all the ships in between too will eventually catch fire.'

'But won't that take too long?' asked Bhrigu. 'Many of

their soldiers would be able to abandon ship and escape onto land.'

'True,' said Parvateshwar. 'But they will be stranded far from their base with no ships. I had learnt at Panchavati that there is no road between Maika-Lothal and the Narmada. It will take them at least six months to march back to Lothal through those dense impenetrable forests. I'm hoping that on seeing the size of our decoy fleet, Sati will commit at least one hundred thousand men to attack us. And with those hundred thousand enemy soldiers stuck in the jungles of the Narmada, our army would become vastly superior numerically; a ratio of almost four to one. We could then attack and probably take Lothal.'

Dilipa still hadn't understood the entire plan. 'But many of our own soldiers will also be in the decoy fleet, right? So we'll have to wait for them to come back to Karachapa and then...'

'I'm not planning on using our decoy fleet to engage in battle,' said Parvateshwar. 'So we're not going to load them up with soldiers. We'll only keep a skeletal staff, enough to set sail. We will not commit more than five thousand men. Imagine what we can achieve. Only five thousand of our men, including the commandos, will leave Karachapa but we would have removed nearly one hundred thousand of the enemy men, leaving them stranded in the jungles around the Narmada, at least six months away from Lothal. And not a single arrow would have been fired. We can then go ahead and easily march in to capture Lothal.'

'Brilliant!' said Bhrigu. 'We will move towards Lothal as soon as our ships leave for the Narmada.'

'No, My Lord,' said Parvateshwar. 'I'm sure Sati has scouts lurking in and around Karachapa. If they see four hundred thousand of our troops marching out of the city, they will know that our ships are thinly manned and will therefore understand our ruse. Our army will have to remain hidden within the walls of Karachapa to convince them that our attack on Panchavati is genuine.'

The customs officer at Karachapa frowned at the merchant ship manifest. 'Cotton from Egypt? Why would any Meluhan want cotton from Egypt? They are no match for our own cotton.'

The customs procedure in Meluha was based on a system of trust. Ship manifests would be accepted at face value and the relevant duty applied. It was also accepted that, on random occasions, a customs officer could cross-check the ship load if he so desired. This was possibly one of those random occasions.

The officer turned to his assistant. 'Go down to the ship hold and check.'

The ship captain looked nervously to his right, at the closed door of the deck cabin, and turned back to the customs officer. 'What is the need for that, Sir? Do you think that I would lie about this? You know that the amount of cotton I have declared matches the maximum carrying capacity of this ship. There is no way you can charge me a higher custom duty. Your search will serve no purpose.'

The Meluhan customs officer looked towards the cabin that the captain had surreptitiously glanced at. The door suddenly swung open and a tall, well-built man stepped out and stretched his arms as he lazily yawned. 'What's the delay, Captain?'

The customs officer held his breath as he recognised the man. He instantly executed a smart Meluhan military salute. 'Brigadier Vidyunmali, I didn't know you were on this ship.'

'Now you know,' said Vidyunmali, yawning once more.

'I'm sorry, My Lord,' said the customs officer, as he immediately handed the manifest back to the captain and ordered his assistant to issue the receipt for the duty payment.

The paperwork was done in no time.

The customs officer started to leave, but then turned back and hesitatingly asked Vidyunmali, 'My Lord, you are one of our greatest warriors. Why isn't our army deploying you at the battlefront?'

Vidyunmali shook his head with a wry grin. 'I'm not a warrior now, officer. I'm a bodyguard. And also, as it now appears, a transporter of royal fashions.'

The customs officer smiled politely, and then hurried off the ship.

— ⁂ —

'Why the delay?' asked the Egyptian.

Vidyunmali had just entered the hold below the lowermost deck, deep in the ship's belly. The only porthole, high in one corner, had been shut tight and it was unnaturally dark. As his eyes adjusted, he was able to see the countenance of about three hundred assassins sitting with cat-like stillness in a huddle.

'Nothing important, Lord Swuth,' said Vidyunmali to the Egyptian. 'A stupid customs officer got it in his head to check the ship's hold. It's been taken care of. We're sailing past Karachapa now. We will be in the heart of Meluha soon. There's no turning back.'

Swuth nodded silently.

'My Lord,' said the captain, as he entered quietly with a shielded torch.

Vidyunmali took the torch from the captain, who was

followed by two men carrying large jute bags. They left the bags next to Vidyunmali.

'Wait outside,' said Vidyunmali.

The captain and his men obeyed. Vidyunmali turned towards the Egyptian.

Swuth was the chief of the shadowy group of Egyptian assassins that Vidyunmali was escorting back to Devagiri. The sweaty heat of the closed ship hold had made Swuth and his assassins strip down to their loincloths. Vidyunmali could see the several battle scars that lined Swuth's body in the dim light of the flaming torch. But it was the numerous tattoos on him that drew his attention. The Meluhan brigadier was familiar with one of them: a black fireball on the bridge of his nose, with rays streaming out in all directions. It was usually the last thing that his hapless victims saw before being butchered. The fireball represented the God that Swuth and his assassins believed in: Aten, the Sun God.

'I thought that Ra was the Sun God for the Egyptians,' said Vidyunmali.

Swuth shook his head. 'Most people call him Ra. But they're wrong. Aten is the correct name. And this symbol,' said Swuth, pointing to the fireball on his nose, 'is his mark.'

'And the jackal tattoo on your arm?' asked Vidyunmali.

'It's not a jackal. It's an animal that looks like a jackal. We call it Sha. This is the mark of the God I am named after.'

Vidyunmali was about to move on to the other tattoos, but Swuth raised his hand.

'I have too many tattoos on my body and too little interest in small talk,' said Swuth. 'You're paying me good money, Brigadier. So I will do your job. You don't need to build a relationship with me to motivate me. Let's talk about what you really want.'

Vidyunmali smiled. It was always a pleasure to work with

professionals. They focused all their attention on the work at hand. The mission that Emperor Daksha had tasked him with was difficult. Any brute could kill, but to kill with so many conditions attached, required professionals. It needed artists who were dedicated to their dark art.

'My apologies,' said Vidyunmali. 'I'll get down to it right away.'

'That would be good,' said Swuth, sarcastically.

'We don't want anybody recognising you.'

Swuth narrowed his eyes, as though he'd just been insulted. 'Nobody ever sees us killing, Brigadier Vidyunmali. More often than not, even our victims don't see us while they're being killed.'

Vidyunmali shook his head. 'But I want you to be seen, only not recognised.'

Swuth frowned.

Vidyunmali walked over to one of the jute bags, opened it and pulled out a large black cloak and a mask. 'I need all of you to wear this. And I want you to be seen as you kill.'

Swuth picked up the cloak and recognised it instantly. It was the garment that the Nagas wore whenever they travelled abroad. He stared at the mask. He was aware that these were worn during Holi celebrations.

Swuth looked at Vidyunmali, his eyes two narrow slits. 'You want people to think the Nagas did it?'

Vidyunmali nodded.

'These cloaks will constrain our movements,' said Swuth. 'And the masks will restrict our vision. We're not trained with these accoutrements.'

'Are you telling me that the warriors of Aten can't do this?'

Swuth took a deep breath. 'Please leave.'

Vidyunmali stared at Swuth, stunned by his insolence.

'Leave,' clarified Swuth, 'so that we can wear these cloaks and practice.'

Vidyunmali smiled and rose.

'Brigadier,' said Swuth. 'Please leave the torch here.'

'Of course,' said Vidyunmali, fixing the torch on its clutch before walking out of the ship hold.

Chapter 40

Ambush on the Narmada

'They aren't coming here?' exclaimed a surprised Sati.

Together with Kali, Ganesh and Kartik, she had been enjoying a family moment accompanied by rounds of sweet saffron milk. They were soon joined by Bhagirath, Chandraketu, Maatali, Brahaspati and Chenardhwaj with some fresh news. The information received earlier from the Vasudevs had suggested that a fleet of nearly fifty ships had sailed out of Karachapa a few weeks back. They had expected them to head for Lothal. But the latest news was that the ships had turned south.

'It looks like they're heading towards the Narmada,' said the Vasudev pandit who had just walked in with the information.

'That can't be!' A panic-stricken Kali looked at Ganesh.

Kali had not agreed with Shiva's tactic of misleading the Meluhans by pretending to go to the Narmada and from there, sailing on to Pariha. She was afraid that this would give the Meluhans a clue as to the possible route to Panchavati. Shiva had dismissed her concerns, saying that Bhrigu knew that the river near Panchavati flowed from west to east, whereas the Narmada flowed east to west; clearly Panchavati was not on the Narmada itself. The Meluhans would know that, even if they sailed up the Narmada, they would have to pass the dense Dandak forests to be able to reach Panchavati. And doing so was fraught with danger without a Naga guide.

Therefore, the news of the Meluhan navy sailing towards the Narmada left Kali with only one logical conclusion: they had discovered the route to Panchavati.

'How would they know the Narmada path to Panchavati?' asked a bewildered Ganesh.

Kali turned on Sati. 'Your husband did not listen to me and stupidly insisted on sailing towards the Narmada.'

'Kali, the Meluhans are in the know of all our goings and comings on the Narmada,' said Sati calmly. 'It is no secret. But they would have no idea how to travel from the Narmada to Panchavati. Shiva has not given anything away.'

'Bullshit!' shouted Kali. 'And it's not just Shiva's fault, it's yours as well. I had told you to kill that traitor, *didi*. You and your misplaced sense of honour will lead to the destruction of my people!'

'*Mausi*,' said Ganesh to Kali, immediately springing to his mother's defence. 'I don't think we should blame *maa* for this. It is entirely possible that it's not General Parvateshwar but Lord Bhrigu who has discovered the Narmada route. After all, he did know the Godavari route, right?'

'Of course, Ganesh,' said Kali sarcastically. 'It's not General Parvateshwar. And it obviously cannot be your beloved mother's fault, either. Why would the most devoted son in the history of mankind think that his mother could make a mistake?'

'Kali...' whispered Sati.

Kali continued her rant. 'Have you forgotten that you are a Naga? That you are the Lord of the People, sworn to protect your tribe to the last drop of your blood?'

Bhagirath decided to step in before things got out of hand. 'Queen Kali, there is no point in going on about how the

Meluhans discovered the Narmada route. What we should be discussing is what are we going to do next? How do we save Panchavati?'

Kali turned to Bhagirath and snapped, 'We don't need to be maharishis to know what needs to be done. Fifty ships will set sail tomorrow with all the Naga warriors on it. The Meluhans will regret the day they decided to attack my people!'

— ⁂ —

Kali, Ganesh and Kartik had assembled at Lothal's circular port along with a hundred thousand men, comprising all the Nagas and many Branga warriors, clambering aboard their ships rapidly. They knew that time was at a premium.

Sati had come to the port to see her family off. She was going to stay in Lothal. She suspected the Meluhans might mount a siege on their city at the same time, to try and take advantage of her divided army.

'Kali...' approached Sati softly.

Kali gave her a withering look and then turned her back on her sister, screaming instructions to her soldiers. 'Board quickly! Hurry up!'

Ganesh and Kartik stepped forward, bent to touch her feet and take their mother's blessings.

'We'll be back soon, *maa*,' said Ganesh, smiling awkwardly.

Sati nodded. 'I'll be waiting.'

'Do you have any instructions for us, *maa*?' asked Kartik.

Sati looked at her sister, who still had her back turned stiffly towards her. 'Take care of your *mausi*.'

Kali heard what Sati said, but refused to respond.

Sati stepped up and touched Kali on her shoulder. 'I'm sorry about General Parvateshwar. I only did what I thought was right.'

Kali stiffened her shoulders. '*Didi,* one who clings to moral arrogance even at the cost of the lives of others, is not necessarily the most moral person.'

Sati remained quiet, staring sadly at Kali's back. She could see Kali's two extra arms on top of her shoulders quivering, a sure sign that the Naga queen was deeply agitated.

Kali turned and glared at her sister. 'My people will not suffer for your addiction to moral glory, *didi.*'

Saying this, Kali stormed off, verbally lashing out at her soldiers to board the ships quickly.

— ✻ —

Kanakhala couldn't believe what she was hearing. A real shot at peace!

'This is the best news I have heard in a long time, Your Highness,' said Kanakhala.

Daksha smiled genially. 'I hope you understand this has to be kept secret. There are many who do not want peace. They think that the only way to end this is an all-out war.'

Kanakhala looked at Vidyunmali, standing next to Daksha. She had always assumed he was a warmonger. She was surprised to see him agreeing with the Emperor.

Perhaps, thought Kanakhala, *the Emperor is referring to Lord Bhrigu as the one who doesn't want peace with the Neelkanth.*

'We've seen the loss of life and devastation caused by the minor battle that was staged outside Devagiri,' said Daksha. 'It was only Sati's wisdom that stopped it from descending into a massacre that would have hurt both Meluha and the Lord Neelkanth.'

Maybe it's his love for Sati that is forcing the Emperor's hand. He would never allow any harm to come to his daughter. Whatever the reason, I will support him in his peace initiative.

'What are you thinking, Kanakhala?'

'Nothing important, My Lord. I'm just happy that you are willing to discuss peace.'

'You have your work cut out,' said Daksha. 'An entire peace conference has to be organised at short notice. We will name it, in keeping with tradition, after our Prime Minister: the *yagna* of Kanakhala.'

An embarrassed Kanakhala smiled. 'You're most kind, My Lord. But the name doesn't matter. What matters is peace.'

'Yes, peace is paramount. That is why you must take my instruction of secrecy seriously. Under no circumstances should the news of the peace conference reach Karachapa.'

Karachapa was where Lord Bhrigu had stationed himself, along with King Dilipa of Ayodhya and General Parvateshwar.

'Yes, My Lord,' said Kanakhala.

A happy Kanakhala rushed to her office to get down to immediate work.

Daksha waited for the door of his private office to shut before turning to Vidyunmali. 'I hope Swuth and his people will not fail me.'

'They will not, My Lord,' said Vidyunmali. 'Have faith in me. This will be the end of that barbarian from Tibet. Everyone will blame the Nagas. They are perceived as bloodthirsty, irrational killers in any case. No reasonable citizen here has been able to swallow that fraud Neelkanth's championing of the Nagas; just like they didn't accept the freeing of the Vikarmas, regardless of the greatness of Drapaku. The people will readily believe that the Nagas killed him.'

'And my daughter will return to me,' said Daksha. 'She'll have no choice. We will be a family again.'

Delusions create the most compelling of beliefs.

— ⅄⓪Մ⍏⊛ —

Shiva, Gopal and Tara stood on the foredeck of their merchant ship. The Parihans had helped in loading their precious merchandise onto the vessel. With everyone having said their goodbyes, the Neelkanth had just ordered his ship to set sail on the Jam Sea.

'Scheherazade,' said Gopal, 'how long...'

'Tara, please,' she interrupted the Chief Vasudev.

'Sorry?'

'My name is Tara now, great Vasudev,' said Tara. 'Scheherazade was left behind in Pariha.'

Gopal smiled. 'Of course. My apologies. Tara it is.'

'What was your question?'

'I was wondering how long you'd lived in Pariha.'

'Too long,' said Tara. 'Initially, I had gone on an assignment that Lord Bhrigu had given me. I had thought that it would be a short stay. He had assigned me to work on the *daivi astras* with the Vayuputras and said I could return only when he gave his permission. But after I heard of Brahaspati's death, I saw no reason to return.'

'Well, Brahaspati is not too far off now,' said Gopal kindly. 'Just a couple of weeks more on the Jam Sea and then we will be sailing east on the Western Sea to Lothal and to Brahaspati.'

Tara smiled happily.

'Yes,' said Shiva, playfully cracking a joke on the meaning of Jam. 'But it's all very confusing. The sea that "you come to", will be the sea that "we go from" now! And then we have to travel east on the Western Sea! Only the Holy Lake knows where we'll finally land up!'

Tara raised her eyebrows.

'I know,' said Shiva. 'It's a terrible joke. I guess the law of averages catches up with everyone.'

Tara burst out laughing. 'It's not your joke that astonished me. Though I agree, it really was a terrible joke.'

'Thank you!' laughed Shiva softly. 'But what exactly were you surprised by?'

'I'm assuming you think "Jam" means "to come to".'

Shiva turned to Gopal with a raised eyebrow, for it was the Chief Vasudev who had told him the meaning.

'Doesn't "Jam" mean "to come to"?' asked Gopal.

'That is what everybody thinks,' said Tara. 'Except for the Parihans.'

'What do they believe?' asked Shiva.

'Jam is the Lord of Dharma. So, this sea is actually the Sea of the Lord of Dharma.'

Shiva smiled. 'But in India, the Lord of Dharma...'

'...is Yam,' said Tara, completing Shiva's statement. 'Also the Lord of Death.'

'Exactly.'

'Is there a relationship between the two names: Yam and Jam? Was there a great leader or God called Jam in Pariha?'

'I don't know about any relationship between the names. But in ancient times there was a shepherd called Jam who, blessed by the Ahura Mazda, went on to become a great king, one of the earliest in this area. He spread prosperity and happiness throughout the land. When a great catastrophe was to strike, that would have destroyed the entire world, he is believed to have built an underground city which saved many of his people. The citizens of his realm later began to call him Jamshed.'

'Why "shed"?'

'"Shed" means radiant. So Jamshed means the radiant Lord of Dharma.'

Chapter 41

An Invitation for Peace

Sati, Bhagirath, Chandraketu, Maatali and Brahaspati had collected in the Lothal governor Chenardhwaj's private office. They had just received a visitor from Devagiri with a message from Kanakhala. A message that had left them stunned.

'Peace conference?' asked Bhagirath. 'What deception are they planning?'

'Prince Bhagirath,' rebuked the Lothal governor, Chenardhwaj. 'This is Meluha. Laws are not broken here. And the laws of a peace conference are very clear; they were designed by Lord Ram himself. There is no question of there being any deception.'

'But what about the attack on Panchavati?' asked Maatali, the King of Vaishali. 'They have clearly found the Narmada route to the Naga capital and have sent their ships on an attack mission even as they try to sidetrack us.'

'How is that subterfuge, King Maatali?' asked Chenardhwaj. 'They are at war with us. They found a weak spot and decided to attack. That is how wars are conducted.'

'I don't have a problem with the Meluhans choosing to attack, Governor Chenardhwaj,' said Chandraketu, the King of Branga. 'What is worrying is that they chose to attack Panchavati and call a peace conference at the same time. That sounds fishy to me.'

'I agree,' said Bhagirath. 'Maybe it is a ruse to draw us out of the city with the call for a peace conference and then attack us. Without the protective defences of the Lothal fort, we may well be beaten by the Meluhans.'

'Prince Bhagirath,' said Brahaspati, 'we've also received word that the Meluhan army has still not marched out of Karachapa. If their plan was to trick us out of Lothal, why wouldn't they mobilise their army at the same time?'

Chandraketu nodded. 'That is confusing.'

'Maybe there are divisions within Meluha,' suggested Brahaspati. 'Maybe some people want peace while others want war?'

'We cannot trust this initiative blindly,' said Sati. 'But we cannot ignore it either. If there's a possibility that the Somras can be stopped without any more killing, it is worth grabbing, right?'

'But the message is for Lord Shiva,' said Bhagirath. 'Shouldn't we await his return?'

Sati shook her head. 'That may take months. We don't even know if he has succeeded in convincing the Vayuputras. What if he hasn't? We would then be in a very weak position to negotiate a ban on the Somras. It's a stalemate right now. Even the Meluhans know that. Who knows, we might be able to negotiate good terms at the conference.'

'We could,' said Chandraketu. 'Or we might just march straight into a trap and have our entire army destroyed.'

Sati knew that this was a difficult decision. It couldn't be made in a hurry.

'I need to think about this some more,' she said, ending the discussion.

Sati walked into the heavily guarded room. The visitor from Devagiri, who had carried Kanakhala's message, had been detained in a comfortable section of the Lothal governor's office. While the messenger had been treated well, the windows of his room had been boarded up and the doors kept locked at all times, as abundant caution. He had been blindfolded while being allowed into the city and was led straight to this room. His men had been made to wait outside the city. Sati did not want the peace envoy to take note of the defensive arrangements within the city.

'Your Highness,' said the Meluhan as he rose and saluted Sati. She was still the Princess of Meluha for him.

'Brigadier Mayashrenik,' said Sati with a formal Namaste. She had always thought well of the Arishtanemi brigadier.

Mayashrenik looked towards the door with a frown. 'Isn't the Neelkanth joining us?'

Bhrigu had decided against sharing intelligence with Daksha at Devagiri. It would only cause Daksha's unwelcome interference in war strategies to continue, which Parvateshwar, being a disciplined Meluhan, would find difficult to constantly withstand. Therefore Mayashrenik, like every Meluhan in Devagiri, did not know what Parvateshwar in Karachapa suspected: that Shiva may have sailed up the Narmada and then marched on to Panchavati.

Sati, obviously, didn't want to reveal to Mayashrenik that Shiva was not in Lothal. But she didn't want to lie either. 'No.'

'But...'

'When you speak with me,' said Sati, interrupting him, 'it's as good as speaking with him.'

Mayashrenik frowned. 'Is it that the Lord Neelkanth doesn't want to meet me? Doesn't he want peace? Does he think that destroying Meluha is the only way forward?'

'Shiva does not think that Meluha is evil. Only the Somras

is evil. And of course, he is very willing to sue for peace if Meluha meets just one simple demand: abandon the Somras. '

'Then he must come for the peace conference.'

'That's where the problem lies. How can we believe that Kanakhala's invitation is genuine?'

'Your Highness,' said a stunned Mayashrenik. 'Surely you don't think Meluha would lie about a peace conference. How can we? Lord Ram's laws forbid it.'

'Meluhans may always follow the law, Brigadier. My father doesn't.'

'Your Highness, the Emperor's efforts are genuine.'

'And why should I believe that?'

'I'm sure your spies have already told you that Maharishi Bhrigu is in Karachapa.'

'So?'

'Maharishi Bhrigu is the one who doesn't want any compromise, Your Highness. Your father wants peace. He has an opportunity for it while the Maharishi is away. You know that once your father signs a peace treaty, it will be very difficult for Maharishi Bhrigu to overrule it. Meluha recognises only the Emperor's orders. Even now, while Maharishi Bhrigu may give the orders, they are all issued in the name of the Emperor.'

'You want me to believe that my father has suddenly developed enough character to stand up for what he thinks is right?'

'You are being unfair...'

'Really? Don't you know that he killed my first husband? He has no respect for the law.'

'But he loves you.'

Sati rolled her eyes in disgust. 'Please, Mayashrenik. Do you really expect me to believe that he's pushing for peace because he loves me?'

'He saved your life, Your Highness.'

'What utter nonsense! Have you also fallen for that ridiculous explanation? Do you really believe that my father threw out my Naga child and kept him hidden from me for nearly ninety years so he could "save my life"? No, he didn't. He did it because he wanted to protect his own name; he didn't want people to know that Emperor Daksha has had a Naga grandchild. That is the reason why he broke the law.'

'I'm not talking about what happened ninety years ago, Your Highness. I'm talking about what happened just a few years ago.'

'What?'

'How do you think the alarm went off at Panchavati?'

Sati remained silent, stunned by the revelation.

'The timely triggering of that alarm saved your life.'

'How do you know about that?'

'Lord Bhrigu had sent the ships to destroy Panchavati. But your father sent me to sabotage that operation. I triggered the alarm that saved all of you. I did it on your father's orders. He harmed his empire and his interests in order to protect you.'

Sati stared at Mayashrenik, gobsmacked. 'I don't believe you.'

'It is the truth, Your Highness,' said Mayashrenik. 'You know I don't lie.'

Sati took a deep breath and looked away.

'Even if His Highness is thinking of peace only because of his love for you and not because of his duty towards Meluha, wouldn't our country benefit all the same? Do we really want this war to continue till Meluha is destroyed?'

Sati held her counsel, as she turned towards Mayashrenik.

'Please speak to the Neelkanth, My Lady. He listens to you. The peace offer is genuine.'

Sati didn't say anything.

'May I please have an audience with the Neelkanth, Your Highness?' asked Mayashrenik, still unsure of whether Sati had committed herself to peace.

'No, you may not,' said Sati. 'One of my guards will guide you to the city gates. Go back to Devagiri. I will give serious thought to what you have said.'

— ⁂ —

'We should consider attending the peace conference,' said Sati.

She was in conference with Bhagirath, Brahaspati, Chenardhwaj, Chandraketu and Maatali, at the governor's residence.

'That is not a wise idea, My Lady,' said Bhagirath. 'Only Lord Ram can know what traps they may have set for us.'

'On the contrary, I think it may be very wise. Is there a good possibility that the army in Karachapa doesn't know what my father is doing in Devagiri?'

'It's possible,' said Brahaspati. 'But do you actually think your father is driving the peace conference? Does he have the strength to push his way through?'

'Perhaps it's not him alone. Prime Minister Kanakhala is certainly involved, for one,' said Sati. 'The invitation is in her name.'

'Kanakhala has influence over the Emperor, no doubt,' agreed Chenardhwaj. 'And she is certainly not a warmonger. Her instincts are usually towards peace. Also, she is a devoted follower of the Neelkanth.'

'Does she have the capability to enforce the peace accord?' asked Bhagirath.

'Yes, she does,' said Sati. 'The Meluhan system works on

the principle of written orders. The supreme written order is the one that comes from the Emperor. Lord Bhrigu does not issue orders himself. He asks my father to ratify what he deems fit. If my father issues an order on peace before Lord Bhrigu gets to know of it, all Meluhans will be forced to honour it. So if Prime Minister Kanakhala can get my father to issue the order, she can enforce the peace accord.'

'If we can achieve the objective of removing the Somras without any further bloodshed, it will be a deed that Lord Rudra would be proud of,' said Maatali.

'But we should respond carefully,' persisted a cautious Bhagirath. 'If it is true that peace is being pursued only by Emperor Daksha and Prime Minister Kanakhala, we will put our army at risk if we march out. Karachapa is not very far.'

'Right,' said Sati, with healthy respect for the tactical brilliance of General Parvateshwar. 'If *Pitratulya* in Karachapa hears about our army moving out, he'll assume that we're attacking Devagiri. He'll race out of Karachapa to intercept us at the Saraswati River.'

'Damned if we respond and damned if we don't,' said Chandraketu.

'So what do we do?' asked Chenardhwaj.

'I'll go,' said Sati. 'The rest of you, including the army, should stay within the walls of Lothal.'

'My Lady,' said Maatali. 'That is most unwise. You will need the army's protection to prevent any possible harm to your person in Devagiri.'

'The Meluhans may fight with my army outside Devagiri,' said Sati. 'But they'll not fight me alone. It's my father's house.'

Bhagirath shook his head. 'My apologies, My Lady, but your father has not proved himself to be a paragon of virtue so far. I would be wary of your travelling to Devagiri without protection. We cannot discount the remote possibility that the peace conference is a ruse to draw our leaders to Devagiri and then assassinate them.'

Chenardhwaj was genuinely offended now. 'Prince Bhagirath, I say this for the last time, these things do not happen in Meluha. Arms cannot be used at a peace conference under any circumstances. Those are the rules of Lord Ram. No Meluhan will break the laws of the seventh Vishnu.'

Sati raised her hand, signalling a call for calm, and then turned towards Bhagirath. 'Prince, trust me. My father will never harm me. He loves me. In his own twisted way, he really does care for me. I'm going to Devagiri. This is our best shot at peace. It is my duty to not let it slip by.'

Bhagirath could not shake off his sense of foreboding. 'My Lady, I insist you allow me and an Ayodhyan brigade to travel with you.'

'Your men will be put to better use here, Prince Bhagirath,' said Sati. 'Also, you and your soldiers are Chandravanshis. Please don't misunderstand me, but I would much rather take some Suryavanshis along. After all, I'm going to the Suryavanshi capital. I'll go with Nandi and my personal bodyguards.'

'But, my child,' said Brahaspati, 'that is only one hundred soldiers. Are you sure?'

'It's a peace conference, Brahaspati*ji*,' said Sati. 'Not a battle.'

'But the invitation was for the Lord Neelkanth,' said Chandraketu.

'The Lord Neelkanth has appointed me as his representative, Your Highness,' said Sati. 'I can negotiate on his behalf. I have made up my mind. I am going to Devagiri.'

— ⚹ —

'I have a bad feeling about this, My Lady,' pleaded Veerbhadra. 'Please don't go.'

Also assembled in Sati's private chamber were Parshuram and Nandi, whose expressions were equally anguished.

'Veerbhadra, don't worry,' said Sati. 'I will return with a peace treaty that will end the war as well as the reign of the Somras.'

'But why aren't you allowing Veerbhadra and me to accompany you, My Lady?' asked Parshuram. 'Why is only Nandi being given the privilege of travelling with you?'

Sati smiled. 'I would have loved to have the both of you with me; it's just that I'm only taking Suryavanshis, that's all. They're familiar with the Meluhan customs and ways. This is going to be a sensitive conference, anyway. I wouldn't want anything going wrong inadvertently even before it begins.'

'But, My Lady,' continued Parshuram, 'we have sworn to protect you. How can we just let you go without us?'

'I will be with her, Parshuram,' said Nandi. 'Don't worry. I will not let anything happen to Lady Sati.'

'There is absolutely no reason why anything untoward should happen, Nandi. It's a peace conference. If we don't arrive at a peace settlement, the Meluhans will have to allow us to return unharmed. That is Lord Ram's law.'

Veerbhadra continued to brood silently, clearly unconvinced.

Sati reached out and patted Veerbhadra on his shoulder. 'We must make an attempt at peace, you know that. We can save the lives of so many. I have no choice. I must go.'

'You do have a choice,' argued Veerbhadra. 'Don't go yourself. I'm sure you can nominate someone to attend the conference on your behalf.'

Sati shook her head. 'No. I must go. I must... because it was my fault.'

'What?'

'It was my fault that so many of our soldiers died in Devagiri and our elephant corps was destroyed. I'm to blame for the loss of almost our entire cavalry. It is because of me that we do not have enough strength to beat them in an open battle now. Since it is my fault, it is now my responsibility to set it right.'

'The loss in Devagiri was not your fault, My Lady,' said Parshuram. 'Circumstances were aligned against us. In fact, you salvaged a lot from a terrible situation.'

Sati narrowed her eyes. 'If an army loses, it is always because of the general's poor planning. Circumstance is just an excuse for the weak to rationalise their failures. However, I have been given another chance to make up for my blunder. I cannot ignore it. I will not.'

'My Lady,' said Veerbhadra. 'Please listen to me...'

'Bhadra,' said Sati, using the name her husband did for his best friend. 'I am going. I will return unharmed. *And* with a peace treaty.'

Chapter 42

Kanakhala's Choice

The invitation for the peace conference had been accepted.

Kanakhala rushed to Daksha's private office the minute she received a bird courier from Lothal. The door attendant tried to stop her, saying the Emperor had asked him not to let anyone enter.

Kanakhala brushed him aside. 'That order would not have included me. He asked me to meet him as soon as I received this,' said Kanakhala, pointing to a folded letter.

The door attendant moved aside and Kanakhala heard whispers as soon as she opened the door. Vidyunmali and Daksha were speaking softly with each other. She gently shut the door behind her.

'Are you sure they are ready?' asked Daksha.

'Yes, My Lord. Swuth's men have been practising in Naga attire. That fraud Neelkanth won't know what hit him,' said Vidyunmali. 'The world will blame the terrorist Nagas for their beloved Neelkanth's assassination.'

Daksha suddenly stopped him as he noticed a shocked Kanakhala rooted at the entrance. Vidyunmali drew his sword.

Daksha raised his hand. 'Vidyunmali! Calm down. Prime Minister Kanakhala knows where her loyalties lie.'

'Your Highness...' whispered Kanakhala, her eyes wide with terror.

'Kanakhala,' said Daksha with eerie calm, walking up and placing his hands on her shoulders. 'Sometimes an Emperor has got to do what has to be done.'

'But we cannot break Lord Ram's laws,' said Kanakhala, her breathing quickening with nervousness.

'Lord Ram's laws on a peace conference apply to a king, not to his prime minister,' said Daksha.

'But...'

'No buts,' said Daksha. 'Remember your oath. This is war time. You have to do whatever your Emperor asks of you. If you reveal his secrets without his permission, the punishment is death.'

'But, Your Highness... This is wrong.'

'What will be wrong is for you, Kanakhala, to break your vow.'

'Your Highness,' said Vidyunmali. 'This is too risky. I think the Prime Minister should be...'

Daksha interrupted Vidyunmali. 'We're doing no such thing, Vidyunmali. If we don't have her here to organise the conference, Shiva's men will get suspicious the moment they arrive. It is, after all, the "Conference of Kanakhala".'

Kanakhala was speechless with horror.

'You have been loyal to me for decades, Kanakhala,' said Daksha. 'Remember your vows and you will live. You can continue to be prime minister. But if you break them, not only will you be given the death sentence, you will also be damned by the *Parmatma*.'

Kanakhala couldn't utter a word. She knew that the prime ministerial oath also said that if she betrayed her liege, no funeral ceremonies would be conducted for her. According to ancient superstitions, this was a fate worse than death.

Without funeral rituals, her soul would not be able to cross the mythical Vaitarni River to *Pitralok, the land of one's ancestors.* The onward journey of her soul, either towards liberation or to return to earth in another body, would be interrupted. She would exist in the land of the living as a *Pishach,* a *ghost.*

'Remember your vows and do your duty,' said Daksha. 'Focus on the conference.'

— ⁂ —

Kanakhala stood quietly on the terrace outside her home-office. She loved the sound of trickling water from the small fountain in the centre of the chamber. This sound was wafting gently towards her, all the way to the open balcony. It kept her mind focused and calm. She looked up; the sun was already on its way down.

She took a deep breath and looked towards the street. The soldiers weren't even trying to hide. Kanakhala did not feel any anger towards the men who kept watch outside her house. They were good soldiers. They were simply following orders given to them by their commander.

Kanakhala knew it was pointless to try and send a message to Lothal and warn the Neelkanth. She was sure Vidyunmali would have positioned expert archers along the route to bring down any bird courier. Furthermore, it was very possible that the Neelkanth's convoy had already left Lothal. Her only recourse was Parvateshwar. If Lord Bhrigu and he managed to reach Devagiri in time, this travesty that her Emperor and Brigadier Vidyunmali were planning could be stopped. But getting a message to Karachapa wouldn't be easy.

Kanakhala looked at the small message in her hand. She had personally addressed it to the Neelkanth. She rolled the message tightly and slipped it into a small canister attached to a pigeon's leg. She shut the canister, closed her eyes and whispered, 'Forgive me, noble bird. Your sacrifice will aid a greater cause. *Om Brahmaye Namah.*'

Then she threw the bird into the air.

She could immediately sense the soldiers below go into a tizzy. She saw an archer emerging from the rooftop of a building some distance away. He quickly loaded an arrow on to his bow and shot at the pigeon, hitting the bird unerringly. The stricken pigeon dropped like a stone, with the arrow pierced through its body. The soldiers quickly scattered to find the pigeon. The message would be taken to Vidyunmali instantly. It would appear genuine since it was in Kanakhala's handwriting and had been addressed to the Neelkanth.

Kanakhala looked towards the street once again. From the corner of her eye, she saw her servant slip quietly out of the side door, using the temporary distraction of the soldiers with the fallen bird. The servant would release a pigeon outside the city walls, a homing bird set for Karachapa. Kanakhala hoped Bhrigu and Parvateshwar would be able to arrive in Devagiri in time to stop this madness; to prevent this subversion of Lord Ram's laws. Subsequently, the servant had been instructed to ride hard southwards, towards Lothal, and attempt to stop the Neelkanth and his peace negotiators from walking into a trap. Kanakhala had done all that she possibly could.

The Prime Minister sighed. She had broken her vow of loyalty to the Emperor, but she sought solace from an ancient scriptural verse: *Dharma matih udgritah;* dharma is that which is well judged by your mind; think deeply about dharma and your mind will tell you what is right.

In this case, it appeared to Kanakhala that breaking her vows was the right thing to do. For that was the only way to stop an even bigger crime from being committed. But she was no fool. She knew her punishment. She would not give Daksha that pleasure, though.

Kanakhala smiled sadly and walked back into her office. She stopped at her writing desk and picked up a bowl, which contained a clear, greenish medicine that had been prepared recently. She swallowed it quickly. It would numb her pain and make her feel drowsy; exactly what she needed. She ambled up to the fountain. The small pool at the base of the fountain was perfect; deep enough to keep her hand submerged. Clotting would be arrested if the wound was continually washed by flowing water.

She picked up the sharp ceremonial knife that she carried on her person. For one brief moment, she wondered whether she would roam the earth forever as a ghost, if her funeral ceremony was not conducted in accordance with the prescribed rituals. Then she shook her head and dismissed her fears.

Dharmo rakshati rakshitaha; dharma protects those who protect it.

She shut her eyes, balled her left hand into a fist and submerged it in the water. She then took a deep breath and whispered softly, 'Jai Shri Ram.'

In a swift move, she slashed deep, slicing through the veins and arteries on her wrist. Blood burst out in a rapid flood. She rested her head on the side of the fountain and waited for death to take her away.

— —

'It doesn't change the plans at all, Your Highness,' said Vidyunmali.

A stunned Daksha was sitting in his private office, having just received word of Kanakhala's suicide.

'Your Highness,' said Vidyunmali, when he didn't get a response.

'Yes...' said Daksha, still reeling from shock, looking distracted.

'Listen to me,' said Vidyunmali. 'We will go ahead with the plans as before. Swuth's men are ready.'

'Yes...'

'Your Highness!' said Vidyunmali loudly.

Daksha's face suddenly showed some focus as he stared at Vidyunmali.

'Did you hear me, Your Highness?' asked Vidyunmali.

'Yes.'

'Everyone will be told that Kanakhala died in an accident. The peace conference will continue in her memory.'

'Yes.'

'Also, I have to go.'

'What?' Daksha seemed to panic.

'I told you, Your Highness,' said Vidyunmali patiently, as if he was talking to a child. 'One of Kanakhala's servants is missing. I fear he may have set out to warn the fraud Neelkanth. He has to be stopped. I'm going to ride out myself, towards the south, with a platoon.'

'But how will I manage all this?'

'You don't have to do anything. Everything is under control. My soldiers will find a way to bring Princess Sati into the palace. Nobody else from her party will be allowed to accompany her. The moment she is with you, signal my man who will wait at your window. He will shoot a fire arrow high in the air, which will signal to Swuth's assassins that the coast is clear. They will then quickly move in and kill the fraud Neelkanth. They will also leave a few of Shiva's people alive so that they can testify that they were attacked by Nagas.'

Daksha still looked nervous.

Vidyunmali stepped up and spoke gently. 'You don't have to worry. I have planned everything in detail. There will be no mistakes made. All you have to do is signal my man when Princess Sati enters your room. That's it.'

'That's it?'

'Yes, that's it. Now I really need to go, Your Highness. If Kanakhala's man manages to reach the fraud Neelkanth, it will be the end of our plans.'

'Of course. Go.'

— ⁂ —

'Those sons of bitches!' scowled Kali.

Jadav Rana, the ruler of Umbergaon had just rowed up to the Naga fleet in a fast cutter. His small kingdom lay to the south of the Narmada. The Nagas had helped him on many occasions. And, Jadav Rana was not an ungrateful man.

When the fishermen in his kingdom informed him of a large Meluhan fleet stationed in a hidden lagoon nearby, he had gone personally to investigate. Keeping himself concealed, Jadav had seen the massive fleet and immediately surmised that this had something to do with the war raging in the north between the Neelkanth's forces and the Meluhans. He had also received news that the Nagas themselves were racing down the western coast, towards the mouth of the Narmada. He'd immediately got into a fast cutter to intercept the Nagas before they entered the river that marked the southern boundary of the Sapt Sindhu. He was convinced the Meluhans intended to take the Nagas by surprise and attack them from the rear.

'Your Highness,' said Jadav Rana. 'I assumed the Meluhans would enter the Narmada after you and assault your rear guard. They could devastate your entire fleet before you even realised what had happened.'

'I wouldn't be surprised if they have a forward ambush planned for us as well,' said Kartik.

'We'll attack them in their hidden lagoon,' said Kali. 'We'll burn their ships down and hang their rotten carcasses on the coastal trees.'

Ganesh had remained silent till now. Something was amiss. 'Your Highness, how many Meluhans are there?'

'Fifty ships, Lord Ganesh,' said Jadav Rana. 'It's a reasonably large force. But you have more than enough ships to take them on.'

'I didn't ask you about the ships, Your Highness,' said Ganesh. 'I asked how many men...'

Jadav Rana frowned. 'I don't know, Lord Ganesh.' He then turned to his men. 'Do you people have any idea?'

'It's difficult to be sure, My Lord, since they have largely remained on ship,' said one of Jadav Rana's lieutenants. 'But judging by the amount of food they have been foraging, I don't think there would be more than five thousand. You have many more men, Lord Ganesh. You can win very easily.'

Ganesh held his head. 'Bhoomidevi, be merciful.'

A stunned Kali stared at Jadav Rana's lieutenant. 'Are you sure? Just five thousand?'

Jadav Rana was surprised. He didn't understand why the Nagas looked so upset. Logically, they should have been happy. They outnumbered the Meluhans dramatically.

'My men are well acquainted with these coasts, Your Highness,' said Jadav Rana. 'If they're saying that the Meluhans number only five thousand, I would go with that number.'

'We've been taken for a ride,' said Ganesh. 'There's no

attack planned on Panchavati. They were trying to divide our forces. And they succeeded.'

A worried Kartik looked at his elder brother. 'They're probably attacking Lothal even as we speak.'

'And we took a hundred thousand men away from *maa*,' said a distraught Ganesh.

Kali turned and yelled the order at her prime minister, Karkotak. 'Turn around, now! We're going back to Lothal! Double rowing till we get there! MOVE!'

Chapter 43

A Civil Revolt

Bhagirath and Brahaspati had come to the Lothal port, having been informed by an advance boat that Shiva's ship would be arriving soon. They could now see Shiva's merchant ship sailing in from the east, from the vantage position of the port walls. To the south, they could also see the naval contingent that had left under Kali's command, steaming forward. All the ships would probably dock at Lothal at the same time.

Brahaspati took a sharp intake of breath as he saw a woman on the foredeck of Shiva's ship.

Bhagirath couldn't help notice the dramatic transformation in Brahaspati. He turned towards Shiva's ship. They were still quite far, but he could make out the countenance of Shiva and Gopal. Standing next to them was a woman, an Indian-looking woman. But the Ayodhyan prince didn't have the foggiest clue about her identity.

'Who is she, Brahaspati*ji*?' asked Bhagirath.

Brahaspati was crying. 'Oh Lord Brahma! Oh Lord Brahma!'

'Who is she?'

Brahaspati seemed to be delirious now. Delirious but happy! He turned around, rushing down the steps towards the docks. He was rambling in pure delight. 'They let her go! Shiva freed her! Lord Ram be praised, he freed her!'

— ⚹ —

'Isn't that Shiva's ship?' said Kali, pointing ahead.

Kali, Ganesh and Kartik had rushed back to Lothal and were surprised to discover that there was no siege on the city at all. They saw the merchant ship just ahead, pulling into the circular port. Fifteen minutes later Kali's ship docked at a berth as well. Shiva's ship was anchored just ahead of theirs. As soon as they got off the gangway plank, they rushed towards Shiva. They could see that Bhagirath and Brahaspati had come to receive the Neelkanth and Gopal. A stunned Brahaspati had just embraced a woman. Both of them were crying profusely.

'Shiva!' shouted Kali from a distance, sprinting towards him.

Shiva turned and smiled at Kali. 'I saw the Naga ships behind us. Where had you gone?'

'We were led on a wild goose chase,' said Kali. 'We were led to believe that Panchavati was under attack.'

'The Meluhan ships were a decoy?' asked Bhagirath.

'Yes, Prince Bhagirath,' said Kartik. 'The ships had only five thousand men. They had no intention of attacking Panchavati.'

'That is good news,' said Bhagirath.

'Where's Sati?' asked Shiva, looking around.

'There's some good news regarding her as well,' said Bhagirath.

'Good news?' asked Ganesh.

'Yes, we may have found a solution to end the war,' said Bhagirath.

'We've come back with a solution as well,' said Gopal, pointing to the large trunk that was being lowered carefully onto the docks from their ship.

Shiva looked again at an obviously delighted Brahaspati who was refusing to let go of Tara. She was crying inconsolably, her head gently nestled against Brahaspati's chest. They appeared like teenagers in the first heady flush of love.

'Looks like there is good news all around,' said Shiva, smiling.

— ⅄◎Ʊ⍋⊗ —

'How in the Holy Lake's name can this be good news?'

Bhagirath maintained a nervous silence, fearful of Shiva's wrath.

'But, My Lord,' said Chandraketu, 'Lady Sati believed this was our best chance at peace. And it looks like Emperor Daksha himself wants it. If he signs a peace treaty, then the war is over. And we do not want to destroy Meluha, do we? All we want is the end of the Somras.'

'I don't trust that goat of a man,' said Kali. 'If he hurts my sister, I will burn his entire city to a cinder, with him in it.'

'He won't hurt her, Kali,' said Shiva, shaking his head. 'But I'm afraid that he may make her a prisoner and use that to negotiate with us.'

'But, My Lord,' said Chenardhwaj, 'that is impossible. The rules governing a peace conference are very clear. Both parties are free to return, unharmed, if a solution or compromise is not found.'

'What's to stop my grandfather from not following the laws?' asked Ganesh. 'It will not be the first time he's broken a law.'

'My Lord,' said a Vasudev pandit entering the chamber and addressing Gopal. 'I have urgent news.'

'I think we can talk later, Pandit*ji*,' said Gopal.

'No, My Lord,' insisted the pandit in charge of the Lothal temple. 'We must speak now.'

Gopal was surprised but he knew his Vasudev pandits did not panic unnecessarily. It had to be something important. He rose and walked up to the pandit.

'Lord Ganesh,' said Chenardhwaj, resuming his conversation with Ganesh. 'The peace conference rules were laid down by Lord Ram himself. They are amongst the fundamental rules that can never be amended. They have to be rigorously followed, on pain of a punishment worse than death. Even a man like Emperor Daksha will never break these rules.'

'I pray to the *Parmatma* that you are right, Chenardhwaj,' snarled Kali.

'I have no doubt, Your Highness,' said Chenardhwaj. 'The worst that can happen is that no deal will be struck. Then Lady Sati will return to us.'

'Lord Ram, be merciful,' exclaimed Gopal loudly.

Everyone turned sharply to look at the Chief Vasudev. Gopal was still standing close to the door, along with the Lothal Vasudev pandit.

'What happened, Pandit*ji*?' asked Shiva.

An ashen-faced Gopal turned to Shiva. 'Great Neelkanth, the news is disturbing.'

'What is it?'

'Parvateshwar's army finally mobilised and marched out of Karachapa three days back.'

A loud murmur erupted in the chamber. *They would have to prepare for battle...*

'Silence,' snapped Shiva, before turning to Gopal. 'And?'

'Surprisingly, they turned back within a few hours,' said Gopal.

'Turned back? Why?'

'I don't know,' said Gopal. 'My Vasudev pandit tells me the army has been sent back to the barracks. But Lord Parvateshwar and Lord Bhrigu have pressed on. They set sail up the Indus in a lone fast-ship, with just their personal bodyguards.'

'Where are they going?' asked an alarmed Shiva.

'I have been told that they're rushing towards Devagiri.'

Shiva felt a chill run up his spine.

'And a flurry of birds have been flying out of Karachapa,' said Gopal. 'All of them towards Devagiri. My pandit at Karachapa doesn't know the contents of those messages. But he says he has never seen so much communication between Karachapa and Devagiri.'

There was deathly silence in the chamber. All those present were aware of Parvateshwar's spotless reputation for honourable conduct. If he was rushing to Devagiri without a large army that would slow him down, it only meant that something terrible was going on in the Meluhan capital. And he was rushing to stop it.

Shiva was the first to recover. 'Get the army mobilised immediately. We're marching out.'

'Yes, My Lord,' said Bhagirath, rising quickly.

'And, Bhagirath, I want to leave within hours, not days,' said Shiva.

'Yes, My Lord,' said Bhagirath, hurrying out.

Chandraketu, Chenardhwaj, Maatali, Ganesh and Kartik hastily followed the Ayodhyan prince.

'*Maa* will be all right, *baba*,' said Kartik, allowing hope to triumph over confidence.

Shiva and his entourage had stopped for a quick meal, just a few hours outside of Lothal. The Neelkanth had marched out immediately with Kartik, Ganesh, Kali, Gopal, Veerbhadra, Parshuram, Ayurvati and an entire brigade. Their main army, led by Bhagirath, would move out the next morning. Shiva's entire being was wracked with worry. He couldn't wait till the entire army was mobilised. He had taken the *Pashupatiastra* with him, as insurance.

'Kartik is right, great Neelkanth,' said Gopal. 'It's possible that Emperor Daksha may break the rules of a peace conference, but he will not hurt Princess Sati. He may try to imprison her to improve his negotiating position. But we have the *Pashupatiastra*. That changes everything.'

Shiva nodded silently.

Kali listened intently to Gopal. But the words did not give her any solace. She did not trust her father. She was deeply troubled about the safety of her sister. She was consumed with guilt about the petulant way in which she had parted with Sati. The two extra arms on her shoulders were in a constant quiver.

Shiva held Kali's hand and smiled faintly. 'Relax, Kali. Nothing will happen to her. The *Parmatma* will not allow such an injustice.'

Kali was too pained to respond.

'Finish your food,' said Shiva. 'We have to leave in the next few minutes.'

As Kali began gulping down her food, Shiva turned towards Ganesh. The Neelkanth's elder son was staring into the forest, his eyes moist. Ganesh had not touched the food in front of him. Shiva could see he was praying under his breath, his hands clasped tightly, repeating a chant in rapid succession.

'Ganesh,' said Shiva. 'Eat.'

Ganesh was pulled back from his trance. 'I'm not hungry, *baba*.'

'Ganesh!' said Shiva firmly. 'We may have to engage in battle the moment we reach Devagiri. I will require all of you to be strong. And for that you need to eat. So if you love your mother and want to protect her, keep yourself strong. Eat.'

Ganesh nodded and looked at his banana-leaf plate. He had to eat.

Shiva turned towards Veerbhadra, who had already finished and was wiping his hands on a piece of cloth that Krittika had handed to him.

'Bhadra, order the heralds to make an announcement,' said Shiva. 'We'll leave in ten minutes.'

'Yes, Shiva,' said Veerbhadra and rose up immediately.

Shiva pushed his empty banana-leaf plate aside and walked away. He reached the wooden drum where the water was stored, scooped some water out with his hands and gargled.

A chill ran up his spine again. He looked up at the sky, towards the north, about to make a prayer to the Holy Lake. Then he shook his head. It wasn't required.

'He'll not hurt her. He cannot hurt her. If there's one person in this world that that fool loves, it is my Sati. He'll not hurt her.'

— ⁂ —

'You are behaving like traitors!' shouted Vraka.

Brigadier Vraka had been ordered by Parvateshwar to mobilise the army quickly and leave for Devagiri. Parvateshwar hadn't told them anything about why they were required in the Meluhan capital and the general himself had rushed out earlier with Maharishi Bhrigu. It had taken Vraka two days to get his soldiers boarded onto ships and begin their journey up the Indus. However, they had been waylaid at Mohan Jo Daro by a non-violent protest.

The governor of the city remained loyal to the emperor, but his people worshipped the Neelkanth. When they heard that their army was sailing up the Indus to battle with the Neelkanth, they decided to rebel. Almost the entire population of Mohan Jo Daro had marched out of the city, boarded their boats and anchored all across the river. The line of boats extended across the massive breadth of the Indus and covered nearly a kilometre in length. It was impossible for Vraka to ram his ships through such an effective blockade.

'We will be traitors to Emperor Daksha,' said the leader of the protestors, 'but we will not be traitors to the Neelkanth!'

Vraka drew his sword. 'I will kill you all if you don't move,' he warned.

'Go ahead. Kill us all. We will not raise our hands. We will not fight against our own army. But I swear by the great Lord Ram, we will not move!'

Vraka snorted in anger. By not fighting with him, the citizens were not giving him a legal reason to attack them. He had been stymied.

— ⚹ —

Slowly regaining consciousness, Vidyunmali saw that he was lying on a cart that was ambling along on the riverside road. He raised his head. The fresh stitches on his stomach hurt.

'Lie back down, My Lord,' said the soldier. 'You need to rest.'

'Is that traitor dead?' asked Vidyunmali.

'Yes,' said the soldier.

Vidyunmali and his platoon had raced down the riverside road leading from Devagiri to Lothal. They had managed to waylay Kanakhala's servant, who was rushing to Lothal to warn Shiva of the planned perfidy at Devagiri. The servant had been killed, but not before he had managed to stab Vidyunmali viciously in his stomach.

'How far are we from Devagiri?' asked Vidyunmali.

'At the pace we're going, another five days, My Lord.'

'That's too long...'

'You cannot ride a horse, My Lord. The stitches may burst open. You have to travel by bullock cart.'

Vidyunmali cursed under his breath.

Chapter 44

A Princess Returns

Sati and her entourage surveyed the scene from the docked ship in Devagiri. They had commandeered a fast merchant ship and sailed up the Saraswati speedily to reach in time for the peace conference.

Nandi stood beside Sati and gestured at the sky.

'Look,' he said, pointing to a small bird winging its way overhead. 'Another homing pigeon.'

It was not the first that they had spotted. Sati's warriors had seen more than a few pigeons flying in the direction of Devagiri.

'Lord Ganesh believes that eavesdropping can give us good intelligence on the enemy's plan,' said Nandi. 'Shall we shoot one of them and see what is being discussed?'

Sati shook her head. 'We will obey the laws Lord Ram set for us, Nandi, and negotiate in good faith. Lord Ram said that there is no such thing as a small wrong. Understanding your opponent's strategy prior to peace negotiations, through the use of subterfuge, will give us only a small advantage. But to behave without honour is against Lord Ram's way.'

Nandi bowed his head in Sati's direction. 'I'm Lord Ram's servant, Princess.'

Sati turned away, and Nandi glanced one last time at the tiny speck of a bird disappearing into Devagiri.

The docks of the port had been completely cleared out, with no sign of commerce or any other activity. From the vantage point of her ship deck, Sati could see the walls of Devagiri in the distance. She remembered that there were those who lovingly called the city Tripura, in honour of its three platforms named after Gold, Silver and Bronze. But the name had never really caught on. The citizens of Devagiri couldn't imagine tampering with the name that Lord Ram himself had given it.

With a loud thud, the gangway plank was lowered onto the dock.

Sati signalled to Nandi and whispered, 'Let's go.'

As she began leading her men out, a Meluhan protocol officer walked up to her, a broad smile plastered on his face. The Meluhan noticed Sati's disfigured left cheek, but wisely refrained from commenting on it. 'My Lady, it's an honour to meet you once again.'

'It's a pleasure to be back in my city, Major. And in better circumstances this time.'

The Meluhan acknowledged the reference with a solemn nod.

'I hope you will succeed in negotiating a lasting peace, My Lady,' said the Meluhan. 'You can't imagine how distressed we Meluhans are that our country is at war with our living God.'

'With Lord Ram's blessing, the war will end. And we shall have lasting peace.'

The Meluhan joined his hands together and looked up at the sky. 'With Lord Ram's blessing.'

Sati stepped out of the port area to find a large circular building that had been quickly constructed for the proceedings of the peace conference. One of the rules laid down for a peace conference was that it couldn't take place within the host city itself. The current venue was at a healthy distance from the city walls, almost adjacent to the port. The peace conference building had been constructed on a large rectangular base of standard Meluhan bricks, almost a metre high. Tall wooden columns had been hammered into holes on top of this base. The columns served as the skeleton for the structure. Smaller bamboo sticks had been tied together and stretched across these poles, creating an enclosed circular wooden building that was surprisingly strong despite no mortar having been used in its construction.

Sati looked up at the high ceiling as soon as she entered the structure and spoke loudly to check the acoustics. 'Good construction.'

The sound did not reverberate. Sati smiled. Meluhan engineers had not lost their talent.

A large idol of Lord Ram and Lady Sita had been placed near the entrance of this cavernous chamber. From the flowers and other oblations scattered around the idols, Sati knew that the chief priest of Devagiri had conducted the *Pran Prathishtha* ceremony; *the life force of the two deities had been infused into the idols.* A true Hindu would, therefore, believe that Lord Ram and Lady Sita themselves were residing in the idols and were supervising the proceedings. Nobody would dare to break the law in their presence. A separate enclosure had been walled off at one end; there was a large wooden door in the middle. The room within had been completely soundproofed so that even the most raucous sounds would not be able to travel beyond its walls. It had been set aside for private internal discussions for either party during the course of the conference.

Sati nodded. 'The arrangements are precisely in keeping with the ancient laws.'

'Thank you, My Lady,' said the Meluhan.

'Now the armoury,' said Sati.

'Of course, My Lady,' said the Meluhan. 'We can leave right away.'

As she stepped out of the conference hall, she saw her horse tethered outside. It had been unloaded from her ship and was saddled up and ready. The horses of her companions had been similarly saddled, girthed and groomed.

'My Lady,' said the Meluhan. 'You do know that according to the laws, the animals will also need to be locked up next to the armoury. All your horses will be taken away.'

'All except mine,' said Sati. Very few were more well-versed with the laws of Lord Ram than her. The leader of the visitors was allowed to keep his or her horse. 'My horse remains with me.'

'Of course, My Lady.'

'And the horses of my men will be returned as soon as the conference is over.'

'That is the law, My Lady.'

'And the animals within Devagiri would also be locked up.'

'Of course, My Lady,' said the Meluhan. 'That has already been done.'

'All right,' said Sati. 'Let's go.'

— ⁂ —

The temporary armoury had been built outside the city walls under the connecting bridge between the Svarna and Tamra platforms, once again, to exact specifications. A massive door with a double lock had been built at the entryway, making it almost impossible to break into. One of the keys was handed over to Sati, who personally checked that the door was locked. The Meluhan protocol officer used his key to double-lock the door, allowed Sati to check it again, and then fixed a seal on top of the lock. All the weapons in Devagiri had been effectively put out of reach.

Sati handed over her key to Nandi. 'Keep this carefully.'

Bowing and turning to leave, the officer hesitated, as if remembering something. 'My Lady, your weapons? Aren't they supposed to be locked in here as well?'

'No,' said Sati.

'Umm, My Lady, but the rules state that...'

'What the rules say, Major,' interrupted Sati, 'is that the armies have to be disarmed. But the personal bodyguards and the leaders at the peace conference are allowed to retain their weapons. I'm sure my father's bodyguards have not been disarmed, have they?'

'No, My Lady,' replied the Meluhan protocol officer, 'they still hold their weapons.'

'As will my bodyguards,' said Sati, pointing to Nandi and her other soldiers.

'But, My Lady...'

'Why don't you check with Prime Minister Kanakhala? I'm sure she will know the law...'

The Meluhan protocol officer didn't say anything further. He knew that Sati was legally correct. He also knew that Prime Minister Kanakhala could not be called upon for any clarifications. Meanwhile, Sati was looking at the giant animal enclosure a few hundred metres away. The horses of her men were being led in there for a temporary sequester.

'Also, My Lady,' said the protocol officer, 'Emperor Daksha has made a request for your presence at his palace for lunch.'

Sati turned towards Nandi. 'I'll ride ahead. You check the lock on the animal enclosures and then join me in...'

'My Lady,' said the officer, interrupting Sati. 'The instructions were very clear. He wanted you to come alone.'

Sati frowned. This was unorthodox. She was about to reject the suggestion when the officer spoke up again. 'My Lady, I don't think this has anything to do with the conference. You are His Highness' daughter. A father has the right to expect that he can have a meal with his daughter.'

Sati took a deep breath. She was in no mood to break bread with her father. But she would dearly like to meet her mother. In any case, the conference was scheduled for the following day. There was nothing much to do today. 'Nandi, once you have checked the enclosure, go back to the conference building and wait for me. I'll be back soon.'

'As you command, My Lady,' said Nandi. 'But may I have a word with you before you leave?'

'Of course,' said Sati.

'In private, My Lady,' said Nandi.

Sati frowned, but left the reins of her horse in the hands of a soldier standing discreetly at the back, and then walked aside.

When they were out of earshot, Nandi whispered, 'If I may be so bold as to make a suggestion, My Lady, please don't think you are going to meet your father. Think instead that you are going to meet the emperor with whom you will be negotiating. Please use this lunch as an opportunity to set the right atmosphere for the peace conference tomorrow.'

Sati smiled. 'You are right, Nandi.'

— ⁂ —

Sati tied her horse at the stables near the palace steps, refusing the proffered assistance of the attendant. Owing to the peace conference, there were no animals in Devagiri so Sati's was the only horse present. As she approached the main steps of her father's palace, the guards in attendance executed a smart military salute. Sati saluted back politely and continued walking.

She had grown up in this palace, sauntered around its attached gardens, run up and down the steps a million times, practised the fine art of swordsmanship on its grounds. Yet, the building felt alien to her now. Maybe it was because she had been away for so many years. Or more likely, it was because she didn't feel any kinship with her father anymore.

She knew her way around the palace and did not need the aid of the various soldiers who kept emerging to guide her onward. She was surprised though that she couldn't recognise any of them. Perhaps Vidyunmali had changed the troops after taking over her father's security. She waved the soldiers away repeatedly, walking unerringly towards her father's chamber.

'Her Highness, Princess Sati!' announced the chief doorman loudly as one of his lieutenants opened the door to the royal chamber.

Sati walked in to find Daksha, Veerini and a man she didn't recognise, who stood at the far end of the chamber. Judging by his arm band, he was a colonel in the Meluhan army.

As she turned towards her parents, the Meluhan colonel looked out of the window and imperceptibly nodded at someone standing outside.

'By the great Lord Ram, what happened to your face?' exclaimed Daksha.

Sati folded her hands together into a Namaste and bowed low, showing respect, as she must, to her father. 'It's nothing, father. Just a mark of war.'

'A warrior bears her scars with pride,' said the Meluhan colonel congenially, his hands held together in a respectful Namaste.

Sati looked at the Meluhan quizzically as she returned his Namaste. 'I'm afraid I don't know you, Colonel.'

'I've been newly assigned, My Lady,' said the Meluhan colonel. 'I have served as second-in-command to Brigadier Vidyunmali. My name is Kamalaksh.'

Sati had never really liked Vidyunmali. But that was no reason to dislike Kamalaksh. She nodded politely at the Meluhan colonel, before turning to her mother with a warm smile. 'How are you, *maa*?'

Sati had never addressed Veerini by the more affectionate '*maa*'. She'd always used the formal term 'mother'. But Veerini liked this change. She walked up and embraced her daughter. 'My child...'

Sati held her mother tight. Years spent with Shiva had broken the mould. She could now freely express her pent-up feelings.

'I've missed you, my child,' whispered Veerini.

'I've missed you too, *maa*,' said Sati, her eyes moist.

Veerini touched Sati's scar and bit her lip.

'It's all right,' said Sati, with a slight smile. 'It doesn't hurt.'

'Why don't you get Ayurvati to remove it?' asked Veerini.

'I will, *maa*,' said Sati. 'But the beauty of my face is not important. What is important is to find a way towards peace.'

'I hope Lord Ram helps your father and the Neelkanth to do so,' said Veerini.

Daksha smiled broadly. 'I have already found a way, Sati. And we'll all be together once again; a happy family, like before. By the way, I hope the Neelkanth didn't mind waiting in the camp outside. After all, it would not be considered a good omen for us to meet before the peace conference.'

Sati frowned at her father's strange suggestion that all of them would be living together 'as a family' once again. She was about to clarify that Shiva had not come with her to Devagiri, but Daksha turned to Kamalaksh.

'Order the attendants to bring in lunch. I'm famished. As I'm sure are the women in my family,' said Daksha.

'Of course, My Lord.'

Veerini was still holding Sati's hand. 'It is sad that Ayurvati wasn't here last week.'

'Why?' asked Sati.

'Had she been here, she would certainly have saved Kanakhala. Nobody has the medical skills that she possesses.'

From the corner of her eye, Sati could see Daksha's body stiffen. 'Veerini, you talk too much. We need to eat and...'

'One moment, father,' said Sati, turning back to her mother. 'What happened to Kanakhala?'

'Didn't you know?' asked a surprised Veerini. 'She died suddenly. I believe there was some kind of accident in her house.'

'Accident?' asked a suspicious Sati, whirling around to face Daksha. 'What happened to her, father?'

'It was an accident, Sati,' said Daksha. 'You don't need to make a mountain of every mole hill...'

On seeing Daksha's evasive reaction to Sati's question, Veerini got suspicious as well. 'What's going on, Daksha?'

'Will you two please give it a rest? We've come together for a meal after a very long time. So let us just enjoy this moment.'

'Everything will be fine soon, Princess,' said Kamalaksh, in a soft voice.

Sati did not turn her attention to Kamalaksh. But there was something creepy in his voice. Her instincts kicked in.

'Father, what are you hiding?'

'Oh, for Lord Ram's sake!' said Daksha. 'If you are so worried about your husband, I'll have some special food sent out for him as well!'

'I did not mention Shiva,' said Sati. 'You are avoiding my question. What happened to Kanakhala?'

Daksha cursed in frustration, slamming his fist on a desk. 'Will you trust your father for once? My blood runs in your veins. Would I ever do anything that is not in your interest? If I say Kanakhala died in an accident, then that is what happened.'

Sati stared into her father's eyes. 'You're lying.'

'Kanakhala got what she deserved, Princess,' said Kamalaksh, from directly behind her. 'As will everyone who dares to oppose the true Lord of Meluha. But you don't need to worry. You are safe because your father adores you.'

A stunned Sati glanced back briefly towards Kamalaksh and then turned to her father.

Daksha's eyes were moist as he spoke with a wry smile. 'If only you'd understand how much I love you, my child. Just trust me. I will make everything all right once again.'

Almost imperceptibly, Sati tensed her muscular frame and shot her right elbow back into Kamalaksh's solar plexus. The surprised colonel staggered back as he bent over with pain, thus bringing his head within her range. Losing no time, Sati sprung onto her left foot and swung her right leg in a great arc, a lethal strike that she had learnt from the Nagas. Her right heel crashed with brutal force into Kamalaksh's head, right between his ear and temple. It burst his ear drum and rendered him unconscious. The giant frame of the Colonel came crashing down onto the floor. Sati swung full circle in the same smooth motion and faced Daksha again. Quick as lightning, she drew her sword and pointed it at her father.

It all happened so quickly that Daksha had had no time to react.

'What have you done, father?' screamed Sati, her anger at boiling point.

'It's for your own good!' shrieked Daksha. 'Your husband will not trouble us anymore.'

Sati finally understood. 'Lord Ram, be merciful... Nandi and my soldiers...'

'My God!' cried Veerini, moving towards him. 'What have you done, Daksha?'

'Shut up, Veerini!' screamed Daksha, as he shoved her aside and rushed towards Sati.

Veerini was in shock. 'How could you break the laws of a peace conference? You have damned your soul forever!'

'You can't go out!' shouted Daksha, trying to get a hold of Sati.

Sati pushed Daksha hard, causing the emperor to fall on the floor. She turned and ran towards the door, her sword held tight in her hand, ready for battle.

'Stop her!' yelled Daksha. 'Guards! Stop her!'

The doorman opened the door, stunned to see the princess sprinting towards him. The guards at the door were immobilised by shock.

'Stop her!' bellowed Daksha.

Before the guards could react, Sati crashed into them, pushed them aside and burst through the door. She raced down the main corridor. She could still hear her father screaming repeatedly for his guards to stop her. She had to get to her horse. No one else was in possession of one in Devagiri at this time. Were she able to do so, she could easily speed past all the guards and ride out of the city.

'Stop the Princess!' screamed a guard from behind.

Sati saw a platoon of guards taking position up ahead. They held their spears out, blocking the way. She looked behind her without slowing down. Another platoon of soldiers was running towards her from the other end. She was trapped.

Lord Ram, give me strength!

Sati heard Daksha's distant voice. 'Don't hurt her!'

A window to the left was open, up ahead. She was on the third floor. It would be foolish to jump. But she knew this palace well; it had been home. She knew that there was a thin ledge above the window. A short jump from there would land her on the palace terrace. Thereafter, she could race away from a side entrance towards the palace gate before anyone would be able to reach her.

Sati sheathed her sword and raised her hands, as if in surrender. The soldiers thought they had her and moved forward, slowing their gait so as to calm the princess' nerves. Sati suddenly jumped to her side, and was out of the window in a flash. The soldiers gasped, thinking the princess had fallen to a certain death into the courtyard below. But Sati had stretched her hands out simultaneously and used the momentum to jump up, grab the edge of the protruding ledge, swing upwards, and then land safely on top of the ledge in a half-flip. She took a moment to balance herself. She then took a couple of quick steps and leapt onto the terrace.

'She's on the terrace!' screamed a soldier.

Sati knew the path the soldiers would take. She quickly ran the other way, towards the far end of the terrace, jumping onto another ledge. She crept along the ledge till she reached another terrace, leapt onto it and sprinted towards the staircase on the far side. She charged down the stairs, three steps at a time, till she reached the landing above the first floor, which led to a side entrance. While this entrance was usually not guarded, she didn't want to take a chance. She leapt out of the balcony into the small garden at the side. There was a tree right next to the wall. She clambered onto the tree, reached its highest branch and used the elevation to jump over the boundary wall. She landed right next to her horse. In one leap, she mounted her horse, freed its reins and kicked the animal into motion.

'There she is!' shouted a guard.

Twenty guards rushed towards Sati, but she pushed through, refusing to slow down. Her horse galloped out of the palace enclosure and within seconds she was out into the city. She could hear the distant shouts of the guards screaming and swearing behind her.

'Stop her!'

'Stop the Princess!'

Startled Meluhans scrambled out of the way to escape the flaying hooves of Sati's steed. She turned into a small lane to avoid a big crowd of citizens up ahead, and came out of a different access road which led straight to the city's main gates. She rode hard, pushing her horse to its limit and was through the iron gates in no time. As soon as she crossed to the other side, her horse reared ferociously onto its hind legs, disturbed by loud noises of battle in the distance.

From the vantage point of the Devagiri city platform, Sati had a clear view of the venue of the peace conference, right next to the Saraswati, nearly four kilometres away. Her people were under attack. A large number of cloaked and hooded men were battling Nandi and his vastly outnumbered soldiers, many of whom already lay on the ground.

'Hyaaah!' Sati kicked her horse hard, goading it into a swift gallop.

She raced down the central steps of the Svarna platform of Devagiri, straight towards the battling men, screaming the war cry of those loyal to the Neelkanth.

'Har Har Mahadev!'

Chapter 45

The Final Kill

As she sped towards the battleground, Sati could estimate that there were almost three hundred cloaked assassins. They wore masks, just like the Nagas. But their battle style was nothing like the warriors from Panchavati. They were obviously some other group, being made to look like the Nagas. Nearly half of Sati's one hundred bodyguards were already on the ground, either grievously injured or dead.

Since the assassins and her soldiers were completely locked in combat, there was no clear line of enemies whom she could ride her horse into and mow down. She knew she'd have to dismount and fight. As she neared the battle scene, she rode towards the area where Nandi was combating three assassins simultaneously.

She heard Nandi's loud scream as he brutally drove his sword into his enemy's heart. He turned to his left, easily lifted the diminutive assassin impaled on his sword, and flung the hapless soul's body onto an oncoming attacker. Another assassin had moved up to Nandi, ready to slash him from behind.

Sati pulled her feet out of the stirrups, jumped up and leveraged herself to crouch on top of her saddle, even as she drew her sword out. As she neared the assassin who was about to slash Nandi from the rear, she flung herself from her horse and swung her sword viciously at the same time, decapitating the assassin in one fell swoop. Sati landed on her side and smoothly rolled over to stand behind Nandi as the quivering body of the beheaded assassin collapsed to the ground, blood bursting through, his adrenalised heart pumping the life-giving fluid furiously out of his gaping neck.

'My Lady!' yelled Nandi over the din, slashing hard at another assassin in front. 'Run!'

Sati stood steadfast, defensively back-to-back with Nandi, covering all angles. 'Not without all of you!'

An assassin leapt at Sati from the side, as she pulled her shield forward. He reached into the folds of his robe and threw something at her eyes. Instinctively, she pulled her shield up. A black egg splattered against her shield, deflecting its contents – shards of metal – safely away from her eyes. Some of the shrapnel cut through her left arm.

Sati had heard of this combat manoeuvre; it was Egyptian. Eggs were drained of their contents through a small hole and then filled with bits and pieces of sharp metal. These were flung at the eyes of enemies, thus blinding them. Usually the next move was a low sword thrust. Though her vision was blocked by her shield, Sati moved instinctively and swerved to her side, to avoid the expected low blow. Then she pressed a lever on her shield, extending a short blade which she rammed into her opponent's neck, ferociously driving the blade through his windpipe. As the assassin began to choke on his own blood, Sati ran her sword through his heart.

Nandi, meanwhile, was effortlessly killing all those in front of him. He was a big man, and he towered over the diminutive Egyptians like a giant. Not one of the assassins could even come close as he hacked through anyone who dared to challenge him. They threw knives and the modified eggs at him. But nothing got through to any vital part of his body. With a knife buried in his shoulder and numerous metallic shrapnel pierced all over his body, a bloodied Nandi fought relentlessly against his enemies. But both Nandi and Sati could see that the odds were stacked heavily against them. Most of their soldiers were falling, overwhelmed by the surprise attack and the sheer numbers. Escape wasn't an option either, as they were now surrounded on all sides. Their only hope was that other Suryavanshis in Devagiri, who were not part of Daksha's conspiracy, would come to their aid.

An assassin swung at Sati from a high angle on the right. She swung back with vicious force, blocking his blow. The man turned and swerved from the left this time, hoping to push Sati on her back foot. Sati met his strike with equal ferocity. The assassin then attempted to drop low and stab Sati through her abdomen, but he was unaware of her special technique.

Most warriors can only swing their sword in the natural direction, away from their body. Very few can swing it towards their own body, because of a lack of strength and skill. Sati could. Hence, both the inner and the outer sides of her sword were sharpened, unlike the vast majority of swords which only have sharpened outer edges. Sati swung back, and with a near impossible stroke, masterfully pulled her sword arm towards herself with tremendous force. The surprised assassin had his throat cut cleanly before he could respond. The wound was deep, almost beheading the man. The Egyptian's head fell backwards, dangling tenuously from his body by a shred of tissue, his eyes still rolling in his head. Sati kicked his body away as it collapsed.

She saw movement on her left and realised her mistake too late. She tried to block the sword stroke from the second assassin but it glanced off her sword, and went up into her scarred left cheek, cutting through her eye and grating off her skull. Her left eye collapsed in its socket, and blood poured from the wound, obscuring the vision in her other eye. Blinded, she executed a desperate defensive block, hoping to ward off any blows while she tried to wipe the blood from her face. She heard a woman panting, almost sobbing and realised that it was she herself. She braced as the man moved forward for a second attack.

She detected a movement from the right, and through her pinkish blurred vision, she saw Nandi swing from his massive height, beheading the assassin in one fell swoop.

'My Lady!' screamed Nandi, pulling his shield forward to protect himself from another assassin's blow. 'Run!'

The world had slowed around her, and his voice came to her as if from a great distance. She could hear her own heart beating; hear her breath gasping as she gazed at the carnage. The bodies of her guards lay bloodied and broken at her feet. Some of the fallen still lived, reaching and clawing at the legs of the attackers in desperation, until they were kicked aside in annoyance, their lives finished with half-distracted sword-strokes of irritation.

My arrogance, a voice whispered in her head. *I have failed them. Again.*

Her brain had blocked out the throbbing in her mutilated eye. She spat out the blood streaking down her face and into her mouth. Using her good right eye, she swung back into battle. Stepping back to avoid a brutal stab from another assassin, she slashed her sword from the right and sliced through his hand. As the Egyptian howled in pain, Sati rammed her shield into his head, cracking open his skull. She stabbed the staggering assassin in his eye, pulled her sword back quickly and turned to face another.

The assassin flung a knife across the distance. It cut through Sati's upper left arm, getting stuck in her biceps, restricting the movement of her defensive limb. Sati snarled in fury and swung her sword viciously across the assassin's body, cutting through the cloak and slashing deep into his chest. As the man staggered back, Sati delivered the killer blow, a stab straight through his heart. But the flow of assassins was unrelenting. Another one ran in to battle Sati. Using sheer will to overpower her tiring body, Sati raised her blood-drenched sword once again.

Swuth was observing the battle from a short distance away. His orders had been to ensure the death of the one they called Neelkanth. Surely he was the tall one, the powerful warrior, cutting down all his opponents with such ease. Swuth moved into the fray, striding towards the embattled Nandi.

Nandi looked up and turned to face his new opponent, swinging his sword fiercely at Swuth's blade. The Egyptian stepped back, his hand stinging with the force of Nandi's blow. Swuth dropped his sword and drew out two curved blades, something he kept for special occasions. Nandi had never seen swords such as these. They were short, a little less than two-thirds the length of his own sword. They curved in sharply at their edges, almost like hooks. The hilts of the swords were also peculiar, since most of it was made of uncovered metal, instead of being enveloped in leather or wood. A sword fighter would have to be very skilled not to cut himself while holding such swords, for the handles were also unsheathed sharp metal.

Swuth was no amateur. He swung both swords in a circular motion skilfully and with frightening speed. Nandi, never having seen swords and a battle style such as this, was naturally cautious and kept his shield held high. He waited for the Egyptian to move in, while keeping a safe distance at the same time. Using the attention that Nandi had focused on Swuth, and Sati's distraction with battling the assassin on her side, an Egyptian moved in suddenly and slashed Nandi's back viciously with his sword. Nandi roared with fury as his body lurched forward in reaction to the excruciatingly painful wound.

Swuth used this moment to suddenly hook his left sword onto his right blade, thus extending its reach two-fold, and swung hard from a low angle, aiming a little below Nandi's defensive shield. The sharp edge on the metallic hilt sliced through Nandi's left arm, severing it cleanly, a few inches above his wrist. The Suryavanshi bellowed in pain as blood burst from his slashed limb, the shock of the massive blow causing his heart to pump furiously. Swuth stepped close to a paralysed Nandi and slashed at his right arm, hacking the sword-bearing limb just below the elbow. The mighty Suryavanshi, with blood bursting forth from both his severed limbs, collapsed on the ground. Swuth spat as he kicked both of Nandi's hacked hands away.

'Damn!' cursed Swuth as he wiped some of his spittle that had got stuck on the Naga mask that he wasn't used to wearing. But he was careful enough to curse in Sanskrit. He had strictly forbidden his people from speaking in their native Egyptian tongue. The charade of their being Nagas had to be strictly maintained.

'Nandi!' screamed Sati, as she swirled around and thrust her sword at Swuth.

Swuth moved aside, easily avoiding her attack. Another assassin swung his sword from behind Sati, cutting through her upper back and left shoulder.

'Wait!' said Swuth, as two of his men were about to plunge their swords into her heart.

The assassins immediately held Sati's arms, awaiting Swuth's instructions. The leader did not want to sully his tongue by speaking to a woman; a sex that he believed was far beneath men, only a little better than animals.

'Ask her who the blue-throated Lord is.'

One of his assistants looked at Sati and repeated Swuth's question.

A shocked Sati did not hear them. She continued to stare at Nandi, lying prone on the ground, losing blood at an alarming rate from his severed limbs. But the unconscious Suryavanshi was still breathing. She knew that since the wounds were only on the limbs, the blood loss would not be so severe as to cause immediate death. If she managed to keep him alive for some more time, expert medical help could still save him.

'Is this the blue-throated Lord?' asked Swuth, pointing at Nandi.

Swuth's assistant repeated his question to Sati. But Sati was looking towards the gates of Devagiri from the corner of her eye. She could see people at the top of the platform running towards her. They would probably reach in another ten to fifteen minutes. She had to keep Nandi alive for that much time.

Swuth shook his head when he did not get any response from Sati. 'A curse of Aten on these stupid baby-producing machines!'

Sati stared at Swuth, catching on to his mistake in swearing in his own God's name, sure at last of his identity. He was an Egyptian; an assassin of the cult of Aten. She had learnt about their culture in her youth. She knew immediately what she had to do.

Swuth pointed at Nandi and turned to his men. 'Behead this fat giant. He must be the blue-throated Lord. Leave the other injured alive. They will bear witness that they were attacked by the Nagas. And collect our dead. We'll leave immediately.'

'He's not the blue-throated one,' spat Sati. 'Can't you see his neck, you Egyptian idiot?'

The Egyptian holding Sati hit her hard across her face.

Swuth sniggered.

'Leave the giant alive,' said Swuth, before turning to one of his fighters. 'Qa'a, torture this hag before you kill her.'

'With pleasure, My Lord,' smiled Qa'a, who was not the best of assassins, but an expert in the fine art of torture.

Swuth turned to his other men. 'How many times do I have to repeat myself, you putrid remains of a camel's dung? Start gathering our dead. We leave in a few moments.'

As Swuth's assassins started implementing his order, Qa'a moved towards Sati, returning his blood-streaked sword to its scabbard. He then pulled out a knife. A smaller blade always made torture much easier.

Sati suddenly straightened up and shouted loudly, 'The duel of Aten!'

Qa'a stopped in his tracks, stunned. Swuth stared at Sati, surprised beyond measure. The duel of Aten was an ancient code of the Egyptian assassins, wherein anyone could challenge them to a duel. They were honour-bound to engage in the duel. It could only be a one-on-one fight; multiple assassins could not attack or they would suffer the wrath of their fiery Sun God – an everlasting curse from Aten.

Qa'a turned towards Swuth, unsure.

Swuth stared at Qa'a. 'You know the law.'

Qa'a nodded, throwing his knife away. He drew his sword, pulled his shield forward, and waited.

Sati wrenched herself free from the assassins who were holding her. She bent down and ripped out some cloth from a fallen assassin's cloak, tying the strip of cloth across her face, covering her mutilated eye in an effort to stem the blood from flowing across her face. She hoped this would give her unimpeded vision and not disturb the good eye. Then she slowly pulled out the knife buried in her upper arm and tied another strip of cloth around the injury, using her teeth to tighten the bind.

She then drew her sword and held her shield high. Ready. Waiting.

Qa'a suddenly threw his shield away. All the assassins standing around burst out laughing and began to clap. Clearly, Qa'a was taunting Sati, suggesting that he didn't even need his shield to combat a stupid woman. Much to Qa'a's surprise, Sati threw her shield away as well.

Qa'a bellowed loudly and charged, swinging his sword at a high angle. Sati smoothly leaned back and swerved to the left as she avoided the strike. Qa'a turned swiftly and swung his sword high again, catching Sati by surprise. The Egyptian's sword cut through Sati's left hand, slicing off four fingers. Much to his surprise, Sati didn't flinch from the injury but swung her sword from a height at Qa'a. Qa'a swerved and defended Sati's blow with an elevated strike.

Sati, meanwhile, had surmised that the swinging strike was Qa'a's standard attack. She played to that as she kept swinging at Qa'a from a high angle and the Egyptian kept striking back. Both of them kept changing the direction repeatedly to surprise the other, but the strikes were almost typical and therefore, no serious injury was caused. Suddenly, Sati dropped to one knee and swung hard. The strike hit home. Her blade hacked brutally through Qa'a's abdomen, cutting deep. He collapsed as his intestines spilled on to the ground.

Sati stood up, towering over a kneeling Qa'a, who had been paralysed by the intense pain. She held her sword high vertically, and thrust it through Qa'a's neck, straight down, deep into his body right up to his heart, killing him instantly.

Swuth stared at Sati, dumbfounded. It wasn't just her skill

with the sword that had surprised him; it was also her character. She hadn't beheaded Qa'a when she could easily have done so. She let him keep his head. She gave him an honourable death; a soldier's death. She had followed the rules of the duel of Aten, even though the rules were not her own.

Sati pulled aside and ran her bloodied sword into the soft muddy ground. She bent over and ripped another piece of cloth from the now dead Qa'a's cloak and tied it around her left palm, covering the area where her fingers had been amputated.

She stood tall, pulled up her sword from the ground and held it aloft, careful not to look at Nandi. *Just a few more minutes.*

'Who's next?'

Another assassin stepped forward, reached for his sword and then hesitated. He had seen Sati battle brilliantly with the long blade. He drew out a knife from his shoulder belt instead.

'I don't have a knife,' said Sati, putting her sword back in its scabbard, wanting to fight fair.

Swuth pulled out his knife and flung it high in Sati's direction. She reached out and caught the beautifully-balanced weapon easily. In the meantime, the assassin had removed his mask and pulled back his hood. He didn't want to suffer the disadvantage of a restricted vision against a skilled warrior.

Having lost four fingers of her left hand, Sati couldn't battle this assassin the way she had battled Tarak in Karachapa many years ago, where she had hidden the knife behind her back with the aim of confusing her opponent about the direction of attack. So she held the knife in front, in her right hand. But she kept the hilt forward with the blade pointing back, towards herself, much to the surprise of the gathered assassins.

The Egyptian adopted the traditional fighting stance, and

pointed the knife directly at Sati. He moved forward and slashed hard. Sati jumped back to avoid the blow, but the blade sliced her shoulder, drawing some blood. This emboldened the assassin to move in further, swinging the knife left and then right as he charged in. Sati kept stepping back, allowing the assassin to draw closer into the trap. The assassin suddenly changed tack and thrust forward with a jabbing motion. Sati swerved right to avoid the blow, raising her right hand. She now held the knife high above her left shoulder. But she hadn't moved back far enough. The assassin's knife sliced through the left side of her abdomen, lodging deep within her, right up to the hilt.

Without flinching at the horrifying pain, Sati brought her hand down hard from its height, stabbing the Egyptian straight through his neck. The blow had so much force that the knife cut all the way through, its point sticking out at the other end of the hapless Egyptian's throat. Blood burst forth from the assassin's mouth and neck. Sati stepped back as the Egyptian drowned in his own blood.

Swuth was staring at this strange woman, the sneer wiped off his face. She had killed two of his assassins one-on-one, in a free and fair fight. She was bleeding desperately, and yet she stood tall and proud.

Sati, meanwhile, was breathing slowly, trying to calm her rapidly beating heart. She had been cut up in too many places. A pulsating heart would work against her, pumping more blood out of her body. She also needed to conserve her energy for the duels that were to come. She looked at the knife buried deep in her abdomen. It hadn't penetrated any vital organ. The only danger was the continuous bleeding. She spread out her feet, took a deep breath, held the knife's handle and yanked it out. She didn't flinch or make any sound of pain while doing so.

'Who is this woman?' asked a stunned assassin standing next to Swuth.

Sati bent down, ripped a part of the bloodied cloak of the assassin she had just killed, and bandaged it tightly around her abdomen. It staunched the blood flow. While doing so, she'd seen from the corner of her eye that the Meluhans who were running towards her were probably a third of the way through. She knew she couldn't stop the duels now. She had seen the killers. They couldn't leave her alive. Her only chance was to continue duelling and hope that she would still be breathing when the Meluhans reached her.

Sati drew her sword. 'Who's next?'

Another assassin stepped forward.

'No!' said Swuth.

The assassin stepped back.

'She's mine,' said Swuth, drawing one of his curved swords.

Swuth didn't approach Sati with both his curved swords. That would have been unfair according to the rules of Aten, since Sati had only one sword hand. He held the sword forward in his right hand. As he neared Sati, he started swinging the sword around, building it into a stunning circle of death just ahead of him, moving inexorably towards her. Even as Swuth's sword whirred closer, Sati began to step back slowly. She suddenly thrust her sword forward quickly, deep into the ring of the circling blade of Swuth, inflicting a serious cut on the Egyptian's shoulder. She pulled her sword back just as rapidly, before Swuth's circling blade could come back to deflect her sword.

The wound must have hurt, but Swuth didn't flinch. He smiled. He'd never met anyone with the ability to penetrate his sword's circle of death.

This woman is talented.

Swuth stopped circling his sword and held it in a traditional sword-fighter stance. He stepped forward, swinging viciously from the right. Sati bent low to avoid the blow and thrust her blade at Swuth's arm, causing a superficial cut. But Swuth suddenly reversed the direction of his blade, slashing hard across Sati's shoulder.

Sati swerved back just in time, reducing the threat of what could have been a devastating blow. Swuth's sword grazed her right arm and shoulder. Sati growled in fury and stabbed with such rapid force that a surprised Swuth had to jump back.

Swuth stepped back even further. This woman was a very skilled warrior. His standard tactics would not work.. He decided to keep his distance, pointing his sword forward, thinking of what could be a good move against her. Sati remained stationary, conserving her strength. She couldn't afford to move too much for fear of increasing the blood loss from her numerous wounds. Also, she was playing for time. She didn't mind a few moments of reprieve.

An idea struck Swuth. Sati was primarily injured on her left side. This would impair her movements in that direction. He quickly took a giant step forward and swung viciously from his right. Sati twisted to the left and swung her blade up to block Swuth's strike. The Egyptian could see that the movement had made blood spurt out of her wounded abdomen. As Sati stabbed at Swuth again, she stepped a little to the left to improve her angle. But Swuth had anticipated her move. He stepped further to his right and kept on swinging again and again from that awkward angle.

The intense pain of continuously turning leftwards forced Sati to take a gamble. She pirouetted suddenly and swung her sword in a great arc from her right, hoping to decapitate him. But this was exactly what Swuth had expected. He ducked low and stepped forward rapidly, easily avoiding Sati's strike. At the same time, he brought his sword up in a low, brutal jab. His curved sword with its serrated edges went right through Sati's abdomen, ripping almost every single vital organ; her intestines, stomach, kidney and liver were slashed through viciously. A paralysed Sati, her face twisted in agony, lay impaled on Swuth's curved sword. Her own blade fell from her hand. The Egyptian bent back, used the leverage and rammed his sword in even further, till its point burst through to the other side, piercing her shattered back.

'Not bad,' said Swuth, twisting his blade as he pulled it out of Sati, ripping her organs to ribbons. 'Not bad for a woman.'

Sati collapsed to the ground, her body shivering as dark blood began to pool on the ground around her. She knew she was going to die. It was only a matter of time. The blood flow couldn't be staunched now. Her vital internal organs and the massive numbers of blood vessels in them had been mortally damaged. But she also knew something else very clearly. She wouldn't die lying on the ground, slowly bleeding to death.

She would die like a Meluhan. She would die with her head held high.

She lifted her quivering right hand and reached for her sword. Swuth stared at Sati in awe, transfixed as he watched her struggling to reach her blade. He knew that she must know she was going to die soon. And yet, her spirit hadn't been broken.

Could she be the final kill?

The cult of Aten had a belief that every assassin would one day meet a victim so magnificent, so worthy, that it would be impossible for the man to kill ever again. His duty would then be to give his victim an honourable death and give up his profession to spend the rest of his life worshipping that last victim.

As Sati's arm flopped to her side after another vain attempt to reach her sword, Swuth shook his head. *It can't be a woman. This cannot be the moment. The final kill cannot be a woman!*

Swuth turned around and screamed at his people. 'Move out, you filthy cockroaches! We're leaving!'

The man standing next to Swuth didn't obey his order. He continued to stare beyond Swuth, stupefied by the awe-inspiring sight.

Swuth whirled around, stunned. Sati was up on one knee. She was breathing rapidly, forcing some strength into her debilitated body. She had dug her sword into the ground and her right hand was on its hilt as she tried to use the leverage to push herself up. She failed, took quick breaths, fired more energy into her body, and tried once more. She failed again. Then she stopped suddenly. She felt eyes boring into her. She looked up and locked eyes with Swuth.

Swuth stared at Sati, dumbstruck. She was completely soaked in her own blood, there were cavernous wounds all over her body, and her hands were shivering with the tremendous pain she was in. Her soul must know that death was just minutes away. And yet, her eyes did not exhibit even the slightest hint of fear. She stared directly at Swuth with only one expression. An expression of pure, raw, unadulterated defiance.

Tears sprang into Swuth's eyes as his heart felt immeasurably heavy. His mind grasped his heart's message instantly. This indeed was his final kill. He would never, ever, kill again.

Swuth knew what he had to do. He drew both his curved swords, held them high by the hilt and thrust them in a downward motion. In a flash, the swords were buried in the ground. For the last time, he looked at both the half-buried, bloodied swords that had served him so well. He would never use them again. He went down on one knee, pulled his shoulders back to give himself leverage and then slammed the hilts with his palms in an outward motion, snapping both blades in two.

He then got up, pulled back his hood and removed his mask. Sati could see the tattoo of a black fireball with rays streaming out on the bridge of his nose. Swuth reached behind and pulled out a sword from a scabbard tied across his back. Unlike all his other weapons, this sword was marked. It was marked with the name of their God, Aten. Below that had been inscribed the name of the devotee, Swuth. The blade had never been used before. It had but one purpose alone: to taste the blood of the final victim. Thereafter, the sword would never be used again. It would be worshipped by Swuth and his descendants.

Swuth bowed low before Sati, pointed at the black tattoo on the bridge of his nose and repeated an ancient vow.

'The fire of Aten shall consume you. And the honour of putting out your fire shall purify me.'

Sati didn't move. She didn't flinch. She continued to stare silently at Swuth.

Swuth went down on one knee. He had to give Sati an honourable death; beheading her was out of the question. He pointed his sword at her heart, holding the hilt with his thumb facing up. He pressed his other hand into the back of the hilt to provide support.

Ready in every way, Swuth stared back at Sati, at a face that he knew would haunt him for the rest of his life, and whispered, 'Killing you shall be my life's honour, My Lady.'

'NOOOOOOOO!'

A loud scream came wafting in from the distance.

An arrow whizzed past and pierced Swuth's hand. As his sword dropped to the ground, a surprised Swuth turned to find another arrow flying straight into his shoulder.

'Run!' screamed the assassins.

One of them picked up Swuth and started dragging him along.

'Noooo!' roared Swuth, struggling against his people, who were bodily carrying him back. Not killing the final victim was one of the greatest sins for the followers of Aten. But his people wouldn't leave him behind.

Nearly a thousand Meluhans had reached Sati, a desperately distraught Daksha and Veerini in the lead.

'S-A-T-I-I-I-I,' screamed Daksha, his face twisted in agony.

'DON'T TOUCH ME!' bellowed Sati as she collapsed to the ground.

Daksha buckled, crying inconsolably, digging his nails into his face.

'Sati!' screamed Veerini as she lifted her daughter into her arms.

'*Maa*...' whispered Sati.

'Don't talk. Relax,' cried Veerini, before frantically looking back. 'Get the doctors! Now!'

'*Maa*...'

'Be quiet, my child.'

'*Maa*, my time has come...'

'No! No! We'll save you! We'll save you!'

'*Maa*, listen to me!' said Sati.

'My child...'

'My body will be handed over to Shiva.'

'Nothing will happen to you,' sobbed Veerini. The Queen of Meluha turned around once again. 'Will someone get the doctors?! Now!'

Sati held her mother's face with surprising strength. 'Promise me! Only to Shiva!'

'Sati...'

'Promise me!'

'Yes, my child, I promise.'

'And, both Ganesh and Kartik will light my pyre.'

'You're not going to die!'

'Both Ganesh and Kartik! Promise me!'

'Yes, yes. I promise.'

Sati slowed her breathing down. She had heard what she needed to. She blocked out the weeping she could hear all around her. She rested her head in her mother's lap and looked towards the peace conference building. The doors were open. Lord Ram and Lady Sita's idols were clearly visible. She could feel their kind and welcoming eyes upon her. She would be back with them soon.

A sudden wind picked up, swirling dust particles and leaves lying around her on the ground. Sati gazed at the swirl. The particles appeared to form a figure. She stared hard as Shiva's image seemed to emerge. She remembered the promise she had made to him; that she would see him when he returned.

I'm sorry. I'm so sorry.

The wind died down just as suddenly. Sati could feel her vision blurring. Blackness appeared to be taking over. Her vision seemed to recede into a slowly reducing circle, with darkness all around it. The wind burst into life once again. The dust particles and leaves rose in an encore and showed Sati the vision she wanted to die with: the love of her life, her Shiva.

I'll be waiting for you, my love.

Thinking of her Shiva, Sati let her last breath slip quietly out of her body.

Chapter 46

Lament of the Blue Lord

To reach the Meluhan capital as quickly as possible, Shiva had commandeered a merchant ship, which docked at Devagiri a little more than a week later.

'That must be the ship Sati commandeered,' said Shiva, pointing towards an anchored empty vessel.

'It means she's still in Devagiri,' said Ganesh. 'Bhoomidevi, be praised.'

Kali clenched her fist. 'If they've imprisoned her and hope to negotiate, I will personally destroy everything that moves in this city.'

'Let's not assume the worst, Kali,' said Shiva. 'We all know that whatever may be his faults, the Emperor will not harm Sati.'

'I agree,' said Kartik.

'And don't forget, Queen Kali,' said Gopal, 'We have the fearsome *Pashupatiastra*. Nobody can stand up to it. Nobody. The mere threat of this terrifying weapon would be enough to achieve our purpose.'

Their conversation came to a stop with the sound of the gangplank crashing on the deck.

'Where is everyone?' asked Shiva, frowning as he stepped onto the gangplank.

'How can the port be left abandoned?' asked a surprised Ayurvati, who had never seen something like this in all the years that she had lived in Meluha.

'Let's go,' said Shiva, unease trickling down his spine.

The entire brigade marched out in step with the Neelkanth. As Shiva's men stepped out of the port area their eyes fell on the large peace conference building. Inexplicably, a colony of tents had been set up outside the building.

'This area has been thoroughly cleaned recently,' said Gopal. 'Even the grass has been dug out.'

'Of course, it would be,' said Shiva, quietening his fears. 'They would need a pure area for the conference.'

A phalanx of Brahmins was conducting a *puja* next to the closed door of the peace conference hall.

'What are they praying for, Pandit*ji*?' asked Shiva.

'They're praying for peace,' said Gopal.

Shiva found nothing amiss in that.

'But... They're praying for peace for the souls,' said a surprised Gopal. 'The souls of the dead...'

Shiva instinctively reached to his side and pulled out his sword. His entire brigade did the same.

As they approached the colony, Parvateshwar and Anandmayi stepped out from one of the tents. Behind them was a short man in a simple white dhoti and *angvastram*, his head shaved clean except for a traditional tuft of hair at the crown signifying his Brahmin lineage, and sporting a long, flowing white beard.

'Lord Bhrigu,' whispered Gopal, immediately folding his hands together in a Namaste.

'Namaste, great Vasudev,' said Bhrigu politely, walking up to Gopal.

Shiva held his breath as he stared at his real adversary. A man he was meeting for the first time.

'Great Neelkanth,' said Bhrigu.

'Great Maharishi,' returned Shiva, his grip over his sword tightening.

Bhrigu opened his mouth to say something, hesitated and then looked at Parvateshwar, who had now walked up to stand next to him. Parvateshwar and Anandmayi bent low in respect to their living God. As Parvateshwar rose, Shiva got his first close look at his friend-turned-foe's face. He was stunned. The Meluhan general's eyes were red and swollen, like he hadn't slept in weeks.

'Isn't the Emperor allowing you into the city?' asked Shiva.

'We have chosen not to enter, My Lord,' said Parvateshwar.

'Why?'

'We don't recognise him as our Emperor anymore.'

'Is it because you don't agree with what the conference is trying to achieve? Is that why you are waiting here for us, with your Brahmins chanting death hymns?'

Parvateshwar could not speak.

'If you want a battle, Parvateshwar, you shall have it,' announced Shiva.

'The battle is over, My Lord.'

'The entire war is over, great Neelkanth,' added Bhrigu.

Shiva frowned, astonished. He turned towards Gopal.

'Has Princess Sati managed to convince the Emperor?' asked Gopal. 'We want nothing but the end of the Somras. So long as Meluha agrees to those terms, the Neelkanth is happy to declare peace.'

'My Lord,' said Parvateshwar as he touched Shiva's elbow, his eyes brimming with tears. 'Come with me.'

'Where?'

Parvateshwar glanced at Shiva briefly, and then looked at the ground again. 'Please come.'

Shiva sheathed his sword in its scabbard and followed

Parvateshwar as he walked towards the peace conference building. He in turn was followed by the others: Bhrigu, Kali, Ganesh, Kartik, Gopal, Veerbhadra, Krittika, Ayurvati, Brahaspati and Tara. Anandmayi remained outside her tent. She couldn't bear to see what was about to happen.

The Brahmins continued their drone of Sanskrit *shlokas* as Parvateshwar came up to the building's entrance. The general took a deep breath and pushed the large doors open. As Shiva walked in he was stunned by what he saw.

Twenty beds had been laid out in the massive hall. Each bed was occupied by an injured soldier, being tended to by a Brahmin doctor. On the first bed lay one of Shiva's most ardent devotees, the one who had found him in Tibet.

'Nandi!' screamed Shiva, racing to the bed in a few giant strides.

Shiva went down on his knees and touched Nandi's face. He was unconscious. Both his arms had been severed; the left one close to his wrist and the right close to the elbow. There were numerous tiny scars all over his body, perhaps the result of small projectiles. His face was pockmarked with wounds. The bed had been especially designed to keep a part of Nandi's back untouched. He'd probably suffered a serious injury on his back as well. Shiva could see that the wounds were healing, but it was equally obvious that the injuries were grave and his body would take a long time to recover.

'The wounds have been left open so they can be aired, great Neelkanth,' said the Brahmin doctor, avoiding his eyes. 'We will put in a fresh dressing soon. Major Nandi will heal completely. As will all the other soldiers here.'

Shiva continued to stare at Nandi, gently touching his face, anger rising within him. He got up suddenly, drew his sword out and pointed it straight at Parvateshwar.

'I should murder the Emperor for this!' growled Shiva.

Parvateshwar stood paralysed, staring at the ground.

'If the Emperor thinks he can force my hand by doing this and capturing Sati,' said Shiva, 'he is living in a fool's paradise.'

'Once *didi* knows we are here,' hissed Kali to Parvateshwar, 'she will escape. And believe me, our wrath will then be terrible. Tell that goat who rules your Empire to release my sister. NOW!'

But Parvateshwar remained still, silent. Then he started shaking imperceptibly.

'General?' said Gopal, trying to sound reasonable. 'There doesn't have to be any violence. Just let the Princess go.'

Bhrigu attempted to speak to Gopal, but was unable to find the strength to say what he had to.

'Lord Bhrigu,' said Gopal, keeping his voice low but stern. 'We have the *Pashupatiastra*. We will not hesitate to use it if our demands are not met. Release Princess Sati at once. Destroy the Somras factory in Devagiri. Do it now and we shall leave.'

Bhrigu seemed stunned by the news of the *Pashupatiastra*. He turned briefly towards Parvateshwar. But the general had failed to even register the risk from the terrible *daivi astra*. He was crying now, his whole body shaking with misery. He cried for the loss of the woman he had loved like the daughter he'd never had.

'Parvateshwar,' snarled Shiva, moving his sword even closer. 'Don't test my patience. Where is Sati?'

Parvateshwar finally looked at Shiva as tears streamed down his face.

Shiva stared at him, a horrific foreboding entering his heart. The space between his brows began to throb frantically.

'My Lord,' sobbed Parvateshwar. 'I'm so sorry...'

Shiva's sword slipped from his weakened grip as an excruciatingly painful thought entered his mind.

With terror-struck eyes, Shiva stepped towards the general. 'Parvateshwar, where is she?'

'My Lord... I did not reach in time...'

Shiva pulled Parvateshwar by his *angvastram* and grabbed his neck hard. 'PARVATESHWAR! WHERE IS SATI?'

But Parvateshwar could not speak. He continued to cry helplessly.

Shiva noticed that Bhrigu had glanced for one brief moment at a direction behind him. He let go of Parvateshwar and spun around instantly. He saw a large wooden door at the far end of the hall.

'S-A-T-I-I-I-I,' screamed Shiva as he ran towards the room.

The Brahmin doctors immediately stepped out of the raging Shiva's path.

'SATI!'

Shiva banged on the door. It was locked. He stepped back, gave himself room, and rammed his shoulder into the door. It yielded an inch before the strong lock snapped it back into place.

In that instant, through the crack, Shiva saw a tower made of massive blocks of ice, before the door slammed back. His brow was burning now, a pain impossible for most mortals to tolerate.

One of the Meluhans went running for the keys to the room.

'SATI!' cried Shiva and slammed into the door again, splinters sticking into his shoulder, drawing blood.

The door held strong.

Shiva stepped back and kicked hard. It finally fell open with a thundering crash.

The breath was sucked out of the Neelkanth.

At the centre of the room, within the tower of ice, lay the mutilated body of the finest person he had ever known. His Sati.

'SATIIIII!'

The Neelkanth stormed into the room. His brow felt like something had exploded within. Fire was consuming the area between his eyes.

He banged his fists repeatedly against the large ice block covering Sati's body, desperately trying to push it away. Blood burst forth from Shiva's shattered knuckles as he pounded against the immovable block. He kept hammering against the ice, breaking bits of it, trying to shove it away, trying to reach his Sati. His blood started seeping into the frozen water.

'SATIII!'

Some Meluhans came running in from the other side of the room, sinking hooks into the block of ice covering Sati. They pulled hard. The block gave way and started sliding back. Shiva continued to hit hard, desperately pushing against it.

The block was barely half-way out when Shiva leapt onto the tower. A small depression had been carved in the ice, like a tomb. Within that icy coffin lay Sati's body, her hands folded across her chest.

Shiva jumped into the tomb and pulled her body up, holding it tight in his arms. She was frozen stiff, her skin dulled to a greyish blue. There was a deep cut across her face, and her left eye had been gouged out. Her left hand had been partially sliced off. There were two gaping holes in her abdomen. Frozen blood, which had seeped out of her multiple injuries, lay congealed all across her mutilated body. Shiva pulled Sati close as he looked up, crying desperately, screaming incoherently, his heart inundated, his soul shattered.

'SATIIII!'

It was a wail that would haunt the world for millennia.

Chapter 47

A Mother's Message

The setting sun infused the sky with a profusion of colours, casting a dull glow on the peace conference building. Parvateshwar's camp had been cleared out. A raging Kartik had threatened to kill every single man present. Not wanting to further excite the justified fury of the Neelkanth's son, Bhrigu had ordered the retreat of Parvateshwar, Anandmayi and their men into Devagiri, a city they had refused to enter thus far.

Gopal was outside the peace conference building, in the temporary camp that had been set up for Shiva's brigade. The Vasudev chief was in discussion with the brigade commander on the best course of action. Everyone wanted vengeance, but attacking Devagiri with just one brigade was unwise. Though the main Meluhan army and its allies were waylaid in faraway Mohan Jo Daro by its citizens, Devagiri still had enough troops to defend itself. The defensive features of the capital, moreover, could not be scaled with an offensive force as small as the one under Shiva's command. Some of them suggested using the *Pashupatiastra.* Gopal immediately rejected it. There was no question of using the weapon. Both Shiva and he had given their word.

Ayurvati had busied herself in the outer room of the peace

conference building, supervising the recovery of Sati's injured bodyguards. As she attended to the medical infusions being administered to a patient, her eyes strayed towards the locked door of the inner room. Sati's dead body lay there, with her family mourning quietly behind closed doors. Ayurvati wiped a tear and got back to work. Keeping herself busy was the only way in which she could cope with her grief.

The inner room, where Sati's body had been kept temporarily, had been built by the Meluhans to fulfil the princess' last wish of preserving her body till Shiva arrived. Tiny holes had been drilled high in the inner chamber walls with many huge blacksmith's bellows fitted into them to push in air regularly. A massive wooden circular gear had been constructed outside the peace conference building with twenty bulls harnessed to it. The non-stop circular movement of the beasts made the gear move constantly. This in turn powered the steady squeezing and releasing of the blacksmith bellows, through a system of smaller gears and pulleys, thus pushing in air regularly into the inner room that stored Sati's body. A screen of jute, cotton and a special cooling material had been hung in front of the bellows. Through a system of pipes and capillaries, water dripped down the screen in a constant stream. The air pushed through the bellows would pass through this screen, and cool down rapidly before flowing into the room. The integrity of the ice tower had been maintained with this classic Meluhan technology, but now the ice within the heart of the tower had begun to gradually melt due to the heat emanating from Shiva's body and his rapid breathing. This had caused Sati's corpse to thaw slowly, making her frozen blood melt. A pale, colourless fluid oozed out, appearing almost to weep from her wounds ever so gently.

Shiva sat there, immobile, shivering due to the cold

and his grief, stunned into absolute silence, staring into nothingness, holding Sati's lifeless body in his arms. Despite sitting on ice, Shiva's brow throbbed desperately, as if a great fire raged within. An angry blackish-red blotch had formed between his brows. He had been sitting thus for many hours. He hadn't moved. He hadn't eaten. He had stopped crying. It was almost as if he had chosen to be as lifeless as the love of his life.

Kali sat near the door of the inner room, sobbing loudly, cursing herself for her behaviour during her last meeting with Sati. It was a guilt that she would carry for the rest of her life. Uncontrollable rage was rising within her slowly but steadily. At this point, though, it was still swamped by her grief.

Krittika sat next to the tower of ice, shaking uncontrollably. She had cried till she had no tears left. She kept touching the ice tower every few seconds. Veerbhadra, his eyes swollen red, sat quietly next to her. One arm was around his wife Krittika, drawing as well as giving comfort. But his other arm was stiff, its fist clenched tight. He wanted vengeance. He wanted to torture and annihilate every single person who'd done this to Sati; who had done this to his friend Shiva.

Brahaspati and Tara sat quietly at another end of the room. The former Meluhan chief scientist's face was soaked with tears. He respected Sati as an icon of the Meluhan way of life. He also knew that Shiva would never be the same again. Ever. Tara kept staring at Shiva as her heart went out to the unfortunate Neelkanth. He was a mere shadow of the confident and friendly man she had met at Pariha.

Kartik and Ganesh sat impassively next to each other on the icy floor, their backs resting against the wall. Their eyes were fixed on the tower, on their father's paralysed figure on top, holding their mother's mutilated body. The tears had almost blinded their eyes. The deluge of sorrow had stunned their hearts. They sat quietly, holding hands, desperately trying to make sense of what had happened.

Ganesh thought he saw some movement on top of the ice tower. He looked up to a bewildering sight. His mother seemed to have risen from her body and floated high up in the air. Ganesh moved his gaze back to his father to see another body of his mother, lying still in his father's arms. Ganesh looked up again at his mother's apparition, his mouth agape.

Sati flew in a great arc and landed softly in front of Ganesh. Her feet didn't touch the ground, remaining suspended in the air, just like those of mythical Goddesses. She wore a garland of fresh flowers, again like mythical Goddesses. But mythical Goddesses didn't bleed. Sati, on the other hand, was bleeding profusely. Ganesh could see her mutilated body as she stood in front of him, her left eye gouged out with a deep cut across her face, leaking blood slowly. The burn scar on her face was flaming red, as though still burning. Her left hand had been sliced through brutally, blood spurting out of the wound in sudden jerks, timed with her heartbeat. There were two massive wounds in her abdomen from which blood was streaming out with the ferocity of a young mountain river. There were several small serrations all across her body, each of them seeping out even more blood. Sati's right fist was clenched tight, her body shaking with fury. Her right eye was bloodshot, focused directly on Ganesh. Her blood-soaked hair was loose; fluttering, as if a great wind had been assaulting it.

It was a fearsome sight.

Maa...

Maa...

'Avenge me!' hissed Sati.

Maa...

'Avenge me!'

Ganesh pulled his hand away from Kartik's and clenched it tight. He gritted his teeth and whispered within the confines of his mind. *I will, maa!*

'Remember how I died!' snarled Sati.

I will! I will!

'Promise me! You will remember how I died!'

I promise, maa! I will always remember!

Sati suddenly vanished. Ganesh reached out with his hand, weeping desperately. 'Maa!'

At exactly the same time as Ganesh, Kartik too saw his mother's apparition.

Sati's spirit appeared to escape from her body and hovered for some time before landing in front of Kartik. Her feet were suspended a little above the ground, a garland of fresh flowers around her neck. But unlike the vision that Ganesh had seen, the apparition in front of Kartik was whole and complete.

There was no wound. She looked exactly the way Kartik remembered seeing her last. Tall of stature and bronze-skinned, she wore a beautiful smile which formed dimples on both her cheeks. Her bright blue eyes shone with gentle radiance, her black hair was tied demurely in a bun. Her erect posture and calm expression reminded Kartik of what she'd symbolised: an uncompromising Meluhan who always put the law and the welfare of others before herself.

Kartik burst out crying.

Maa...

'My son,' whispered Sati.

Maa, I will torture everyone! I will kill every single one of them! I will drink their blood! I will burn down this entire city! I will avenge you!

'No,' said Sati softly.

A dumbfounded Kartik fell silent.

'Don't you remember anything?'

I will remember you forever, maa. And I will make all of Devagiri pay for what they did to you.

Sati's face became stern.

'Don't you remember anything I've taught you?'

Kartik remained silent.

'Vengeance is a waste of time,' said Sati. 'I am not important. The only thing that matters is dharma. Do you want to prove your love for me? Do so by doing the right thing. Don't surrender to anger. Surrender only to dharma.'

Maa...

'Forget how I died,' said Sati. 'Remember how I lived.'

Maa...

'Promise me! You will remember how I lived.'

I promise, maa... I will always remember...

Chapter 48

The Great Debate

The ones amongst Shiva's brigade who were seeking vengeance got a boost the next morning. Against all expectations, Bhagirath sailed in at the head of the entire army of two hundred and fifty thousand troops. The Ayodhyan prince had been worried about what would happen to his Lord if the Meluhans tried some trickery at Devagiri. He had marched the troops all the way from Lothal to the Saraswati, through the broad Meluhan highways without a halt, breaking only for brief food breaks and minuscule rest sessions. At the Saraswati, he had commandeered as many merchant ships as possible and raced up the great river, to Devagiri.

'Oh Lord Ram!' whispered a stunned Bhagirath.

Gopal had just told Bhagirath about what had occurred at Devagiri and the brutal manner in which Sati had been killed.

'Where is the Princess' body?' asked Chenardhwaj, tears welling up in his eyes.

'In the peace conference building,' said Gopal. 'The Lord Neelkanth is with her. He hasn't moved from there in the last twenty-four hours. He hasn't eaten. He hasn't spoken. He's just sitting there, holding Princess Sati's body.'

Chandraketu looked up at the sky. He turned around and

wiped away a tear. Those pearls of emotion were signs of weakness in a Kshatriya.

'We'll kill every single one of those bastards!' growled Bhagirath, his knuckles whitening on his clenched fists. 'We'll obliterate this entire city. There will be no trace left of this place. They have hurt our living God.'

'Prince Bhagirath,' said Gopal, his palms open in supplication. 'We cannot punish the entire city. We must keep a clear head. We should only punish those who're responsible for this assassination. We should destroy the Somras factory. We must leave the rest unharmed. That is the right thing to do...'

'Forgive me, great Vasudev,' interrupted Chandraketu, 'but some crimes are so terrible that the entire community must be made to pay. They have killed Lady Sati; and, in such a brutal manner.'

'But not everyone came out to kill her. A vast majority was not even aware of what the Emperor was up to,' argued Gopal.

'They could have come out to stop the killing once it had begun, couldn't they?' asked Chandraketu. 'Standing by and watching a sin being committed is as bad as committing it oneself. Don't the Vasudevs say this?'

'This is an entirely different context, King Chandraketu,' said Gopal.

'I disagree, Pandit*ji*,' said Maatali, the King of Vaishali. 'Devagiri must pay.'

'I think Lord Gopal is right, King Maatali,' said Chenardhwaj, the Lothal governor. 'We cannot punish everyone in Devagiri for the sins of a few.'

'Why am I not surprised to hear this?' asked Maatali.

'What is that supposed to mean?' asked Chenardhwaj, stung to the quick.

'You are a Meluhan,' said Maatali. 'You will stand up for your people. We are Chandravanshis. We are the ones who are truly loyal to the Lord Neelkanth.'

Chenardhwaj stepped up close to Maatali threateningly. 'I rebelled against my own people, against my country's laws, against my vows of loyalty to Meluha because I am a follower of the Neelkanth. I am loyal to Lord Shiva. And, I don't need to prove anything to you.'

'Calm down everyone,' said Chandraketu, the Branga king. 'Let's not forget who the real enemy is.'

'The real enemy is Devagiri,' said Maatali. 'They did this to Lady Sati. They must be punished. It's as simple as that.'

'I agree,' said Bhagirath. 'We should use the *Pashupatiastra*.'

Gopal flared with anger. 'The *Pashupatiastra* is not some random arrow that can be fired without any thought, Prince Bhagirath. It will leave total death and devastation behind in this area for centuries to come.'

'Maybe that is what this place deserves,' said Chandraketu.

'These are *daivi astras*,' said an agitated Gopal. 'They cannot be used casually to settle disputes among men.'

'Lord Shiva is not just another man,' said Bhagirath. 'He is divine. We must use the weapon to...'

'We cannot use the *Pashupatiastra*. That is final,' said Gopal.

'I don't think so, Pandit*ji*,' said Chandraketu. 'Lady Sati was a great leader and warrior, with the highest moral standards. The Lord Neelkanth loved Lady Sati more than I've seen any man love his wife. I'm sure Lord Shiva wants vengeance. And frankly, so do we.'

'It's not vengeance that we need, King Chandraketu,' said Gopal. 'But justice. The people who did this to Lady Sati must face justice. But only those who were responsible for this perfidy. Nobody else should be punished. For that would be an even bigger injustice.'

'Yours is the voice of reason, Pandit*ji*,' said Maatali. 'But this is not the time for reason. This is the time for anger.'

'I don't think the Neelkanth will make a decision in anger,' said Gopal.

'Then, why don't we ask Lord Shiva?' asked Bhagirath. 'Let him decide.'

— ⅄ⓞ⊍⇞⊛ —

'Kill them all!' growled Kali. 'I want this entire city to burn with every one of its citizens in it.'

All the commanders of Shiva, including his family members, were seated in a secluded area on the peace conference platform, outside the main building. Brahaspati and Tara had also joined in, but remained mostly silent. The area had been cordoned off by soldiers to prevent anyone from listening in on the deliberations. Gopal had tried to get Shiva to attend, but the Neelkanth did not respond to any of his entreaties. He remained alone, within the freezing inner chamber, holding Sati.

'Queen Kali,' argued Gopal, 'my apologies for disagreeing with you, but we cannot do this. This is morally wrong.'

'Didn't the Meluhans give their word that this is a peace conference? Nobody is supposed to use arms at a peace conference, right? They did something that is very morally wrong. How come you didn't notice that, Pandit*ji*?'

'Two wrongs don't make a right.'

'I don't care,' said Kali, waving her hand dismissively. 'Devagiri will be destroyed. They will pay for what they did to my sister.'

'Queen Kali,' said Chenardhwaj carefully. 'I respect you immensely. You are a great woman. You have always fought for justice. But does punishing an entire city for the crimes of a few serve justice?'

Kali cast him a withering look. 'I saved your life, Chenardhwaj.'

'I know, Your Highness. How can I forget that? That is the reason...'

'You will do what I tell you to do,' interrupted Kali. 'My sister will be avenged.'

Chenardhwaj tried to argue. 'But...'

'MY SISTER WILL BE AVENGED!'

Chenardhwaj fell silent.

Bhagirath was carefully avoiding this discussion. While walking towards the peace conference building, he had learnt that his sister Anandmayi was in Devagiri. The city would be destroyed, but he had to save his sister first.

'I agree with Queen Kali,' said Chandraketu. 'Devagiri must be destroyed. We must use the *Pashupatiastra*.'

At the mention of the devastating *daivi astra*, Kartik spoke up for the first time. 'The *astra* cannot be used.'

Gopal looked at Kartik, grateful to have at least one member of the Neelkanth's family on his side.

'Justice will be done,' said Kartik. '*Maa's* blood will be avenged. But not with the *Pashupatiastra*. It cannot be done with that terrible weapon.'

'It must not,' agreed Gopal immediately. 'The Neelkanth has given his word to the Vayuputras that he will not use the *Pashupatiastra*.'

'If that is the case, then we cannot use it,' said Bhagirath.

Gopal breathed easy, glad to have pulled at least some of them back from the brink. 'The question remains, how do we give justice to Princess Sati?'

'By killing them all!' roared Kali.

'But is it fair to kill children who had nothing to do with this?' asked Bhagirath.

'You are assuming, Prince Bhagirath,' said Kali, 'that Meluhans care for their children.'

'Your Highness,' said Bhagirath. 'Please try to understand that children who had nothing to do with this crime should not be punished.'

'Fine!' said Kali. 'We will let their children out.'

'And non-combatants as well,' said Kartik.

'Particularly the women,' said Bhagirath. 'We must let them go. But once they are out, we should destroy the entire city.'

'Is there anyone else you would like to save?' asked Kali sarcastically. 'What about the dogs in Devagiri? Should we lead them out too? Maybe the cockroaches as well?'

Bhagirath did not respond. Anything he said would only inflame Kali further.

Kali cursed. 'All right! Children and non-combatants will be allowed out. Everyone else will remain prisoner in the city. And they will all be killed.'

'Agreed,' said Bhagirath. 'All I'm saying is that we should be fair.'

'That is not all there is to it, Prince Bhagirath,' erupted Kartik. 'The Somras is not to be destroyed. My father had been very clear about that. It is only supposed to be taken out of the equation. We do have to destroy the Somras factory. But we also have to ensure that the knowledge of the Somras is not lost. We have to save the scientists and take them to a secret location. They will be a part of the tribe that my father will leave behind. These people will keep the knowledge of the Somras alive. Today it is Evil, but there may come a time in the future when the Somras may be Good again.'

Gopal nodded. 'Kartik has spoken wisely.'

'This means that even if some of these scientists had something to do with my mother's death,' said Kartik, 'we have to set aside our pain and save them. We have to save them for the sake of India's future.'

Ganesh glared at Kartik with dagger eyes.

'Set aside our pain?'

Kartik became silent.

Ganesh was breathing heavily, barely able to keep a hold on his emotions. 'Don't you feel any anger about *maa's* death? Any rage? Any fury?'

'*Dada,* what I was trying to say...'

'You always received *maa's* love on a platter, from the day you were born. That's why you don't value it!'

'*Dada...*'

'Ask me about the value of a mother's love... Ask me how much you hanker for it when you don't have it!'

'*Dada,* I loved her too. You know I...'

'Did you see her body, Kartik?'

'*Dada...*'

'Did you? Have you looked at her body?'

'*Dada*, of course, I have...'

'There are fifty-one wounds on her! I counted them, Kartik! Fifty-one!'

'I know...'

Furious tears were pouring down Ganesh's face. 'Those bastards must have continued hacking at her even after she was dead!'

'*Dada*, listen...'

Ganesh's body was shaking with anger now. 'Didn't you feel any rage when you saw your mother's mutilated body?'

'Of course I did, *dada*, but...'

'But?! What but can there be? She was attacked by many of those Somras-worshipping demons simultaneously! It is our duty to avenge her! Our duty! It is the least we can do for the best mother in the world!'

'*Dada*, she was the best mother... But she taught us to always put the world before ourselves.'

Ganesh didn't say anything. His long floppy nose had

stiffened, like it did on the rare occasions when he was enraged.

Kartik spoke softly. '*Dada,* if we were any other family I would give in to my rage... But we are not.'

Ganesh looked away, too livid to even respond.

'We are the family of the Neelkanth,' said Kartik. 'We have a responsibility to the world.'

'Responsibility to the world?! My *parents* are my world!'

Kartik fell silent.

Ganesh pointed his finger threateningly towards Kartik. 'Not one of those Somras-worshipping bastards will get out of here alive.'

'*Dada...*'

'Every single one of them will be killed; even if I have to kill them myself.'

Kartik fell silent.

Gopal sighed as he looked at Kali, Ganesh and Kartik. There was too much anger. He couldn't figure out a way to save the Somras scientists from Ganesh and Kali's rage. But at least he had managed to take the conversation away from the dangerous talk of using the *Pashupatiastra*. And maybe there was still hope that, over the next few hours, he would convince the Neelkanth's family of the necessity of saving the Somras scientists.

— ⋏◎ᑌ⍋⊛ —

Shiva had been sitting quietly in the icy tomb, holding Sati's body. His eyes were sunken and expressionless, with no light of hope in them, with no reason to even exist. The blackish-red blotch on his brow was visibly throbbing; he was shivering due to the cold. A single droplet of fluid had escaped from Sati's good eye, now closed, and ran down her face like a tear. There was an unearthly silence in the room, except for the soft hissing of the cold air being pumped in at regular intervals. A sudden sharp noise startled Shiva, perhaps from the bulls harnessed to the Meluhan cooling system.

He looked around with cold, emotionless eyes. There was nobody in the chamber. He looked down at his dead wife. He pulled her body close and kissed her gently on her forehead. Then he carefully placed her back on the ice.

Caressing her face tenderly, Shiva whispered, 'Stay here, Sati. I'll be back soon.'

Shiva jumped off the ice tower and walked up to the door of the inner chamber. As soon as he opened it, Ayurvati stood up. Accompanied by her medical team, she had been tending to Nandi and the other soldiers for the last twenty-four hours.

'My Lord,' said Ayurvati, her eyes red and swollen from accumulated misery and lack of sleep.

Shiva ignored her and continued walking. Ayurvati looked at Shiva with foreboding and terror. She had never seen the Neelkanth's eyes look so hard and remote. He looked like he had gone beyond rage; beyond ruthlessness; beyond insanity.

Shiva opened the main door. He heard voices to his right. He turned to see his commanders in deep discussion. Tara was the first to notice him.

'Lord Neelkanth,' said Tara, immediately rising to her feet.

Shiva stared at her blankly for a few seconds, then took a deep breath and spoke evenly. 'Tara, the *Pashupatiastra* trunk is in my ship. Bring it here.'

A panic-stricken Gopal rushed towards Shiva. He knew that Shiva hadn't eaten in twenty-four hours. He hadn't slept. He had been sitting on top of an inhumanly cold tower. Grief had practically unhinged him. He knew the Neelkanth wasn't himself. 'My friend... Listen to me. Don't make a decision like this in haste.'

Shiva looked at Gopal, his face frozen.

'I know you are angry, Neelkanth. But don't do this. I know your good heart. You will repent it.'

Shiva turned around to walk back into the conference building. Gopal reached out and held Shiva's arm, trying to pull him back.

'Shiva,' pleaded Gopal, 'you've given your word to the Vayuputras. You've given your word to your uncle, Lord Mithra.'

Shiva gripped Gopal's hand tightly and removed it from his arm.

'Shiva, the power of this weapon is terrible and unpredictable,' pleaded Gopal, grasping at any argument to stop this tragedy. 'Even if the *Pashupatiastra's* destruction is restricted to the inner circle, any attempt to destroy all three platforms of Devagiri will widen this circle. It will not just destroy Devagiri, it will also destroy all of us. Do you really want to kill your entire army, your family and your friends?'

'Tell them to leave.'

Shiva's voice was soft, barely audible. His eyes remained remote and unfocused, staring into space. Gopal paused for a moment, watching Shiva with a glimmer of hope. 'Should I tell our people to leave? With the *Pashupatiastra*?'

Shiva did not move. There was no reaction on his face. 'No. Tell the people of this city to leave. All except those who have protected or made the Somras, and those directly responsible for Sati's death. For when I am done, there will be no more Daksha. There will be no more Somras. There will be no more Evil. It will be as if this place, this Evil, never existed. Nothing will live here, nothing will grow here, and no two stones will be left standing upon each other to show that there ever was a Devagiri. It all ends now.'

Gopal was grateful that at least the innocent people of

Devagiri would be saved. But what about Lord Rudra's law banning the use of *daivi astras*?

'Shiva, the *Pashupatiastra...*' whispered Gopal with hope.

Shiva stared at Gopal unemotionally and spoke in a voice that was eerily composed. 'I will burn down this entire world.'

Gopal stared at Shiva with foreboding. The Neelkanth turned around and walked back into the building, to his Sati.

Tara rose.

'Where are you going?' whispered Brahaspati.

'To get the *Pashupatiastra*,' answered Tara softly.

'You cannot! It will destroy us all!'

'No, it won't. These weapons can be triangulated in such a way that the devastation will remain confined within the city. We will not be affected if we remain more than five kilometres away.'

Tara began to walk away.

Brahaspati pulled her back and whispered urgently, 'What are you doing? You know this is wrong. I feel for Shiva, but the *Pashupatiastra...*'

Tara stared at Brahaspati without a hint of doubt in her eyes. 'Lord Ram's sacred laws have been shamelessly broken. The Neelkanth deserves his vengeance.'

'Of course, he does,' said Brahaspati, meeting her gaze without flinching. 'But not with the *Pashupatiastra*.'

'Don't you feel his pain? What kind of friend are you?'

'Tara, I had once considered doing something wrong. I had wanted to assassinate a man who was to duel Sati. Shiva stopped me. He stopped me from taking a sin upon my soul. If I have to be a true friend to him, I have to stop him from tarnishing his soul. I can't let him use the *Pashupatiastra*.'

'His soul is already dead, Brahaspati. It's lying on top of that ice tower,' said Tara.

'I know, but...'

Tara pulled her hand away from Brahaspati. 'You expect him to fight in accordance with the laws when his enemies have not. They have taken everything from him, his life, his soul, his entire reason for existence. He deserves his vengeance.'

Chapter 49

Debt to the Neelkanth

Shiva's army had been divided into three groups, led by Bhagirath, Chandraketu and Maatali. Each group was stationed outside the gates of the three platforms of Devagiri. Maatali's troops blocked the Svarna platform, Chandraketu's forces guarded the exit from the Rajat platform and Bhagirath's troops were at the steps of the Tamra platform. Shiva's instructions had been followed. Ignoring Kali's protests, Shiva's forces informed those within the city that they would be allowed to leave, all except those Kshatriyas who had fought to protect the Somras and those Brahmins who had worked to create the Somras. Daksha and his personal bodyguards, including Vidyunmali, had also been specifically excluded from the amnesty. An evacuation had begun. What amazed the Chandravanshis among Shiva's troops was the number of citizens who chose to stay on and die with Devagiri.

There were many who came in a disciplined line to the city gates, said a dignified goodbye to their families and walked silently back to their homes to await death. There was no acrimony; no fighting at the gates or attempts to save the city. Not even melodramatic farewells.

Gopal and Kartik had stationed themselves at the Tamra platform, along with Bhagirath's troops. The soldiers on this side were primarily Brangas. A tired Bhagirath, having just supervised the construction of the perimeter barricades, rejoined them.

The Ayodhyan prince nodded towards the odd movements of citizens at the gate, half of them leaving and the other half returning to the city. 'What's going on here?'

Kartik dropped his eyes and said nothing, while Gopal's eyes welled up.

'It is becoming a movement amongst the Meluhans,' said the chief of the Vasudevs. 'An act of honour. A cause that demands your life. Stay and die with your city. Have your soul purified by allowing yourself to be killed by the Neelkanth...' He stopped himself, obviously overcome with emotion.

Bhagirath raised his eyebrows. 'What do you mean?'

Gopal gestured towards the crowd, where yet another woman had said goodbye to a couple, before calmly turning back towards the city. 'See for yourself,' he said.

Bhagirath paused for a moment, brows knitted, to study Gopal's face before turning back to the woman.

'Excuse me, madam,' Bhagirath called out to her, and she stopped, turning to face him. 'Why are you returning to the city? Why are you not evacuating with the others?'

The folds of her *angvastram* wafted gently in the breeze around her. She had a kind face with dark, quiet eyes and a soft voice. She spoke calmly, as if she was discussing the weather. 'I am a Meluhan. To be Meluhan is not about the country you live in – it is about how you live, what you believe in. What is the purpose of a long life, if not to strive for something higher? Lord Ram's most sacred law has been broken. We have fallen. All that we are has already been destroyed. What can we now hope to strive for in this life, if this is our karma?'

Bhagirath couldn't believe his ears.

The Meluhan woman continued. 'I believe in the Neelkanth. I have waited for him for so many years, worshipped him. And this is what Meluha has done to him. To our Princess – the most exemplary Meluhan of us all, who lived every breath of her life strictly according to Lord Ram's code. This is what Meluha has done to our Laws that make us who we are.' She was quiet for a moment, her eyes searching his. 'I am guilty. I took the Somras. I followed the Emperor and, through my complacency and silence, was party to everything that conspired to bring this about. If this is Meluha's evil, then it is my evil too. My karma. I will pay my debt to the Neelkanth this day, and pray that it may allow me to be reborn with a little less sin upon my soul.'

Bhagirath was stunned. What logic was this? She inclined her head in a half nod towards him, and again began walking with perfect composure back into the city.

Gopal's voice came from behind him. 'I know. They all say the same thing. I am Meluhan. The Law has been broken. It is my karma.'

They stood in silence together and watched the woman go.

'Prince Bhagirath.' The two of them started slightly, pulled out of their silent contemplation.

'Yes, Kartik?' said Bhagirath, turning to face him.

'I want you to call General Parvateshwar.'

'I have already sent in a messenger to get Anandmayi,' said Bhagirath. 'But neither she nor her husband has come as yet. She will not leave without Parvateshwar. I'm still trying to convince the both of them.'

'Tell them,' said Gopal, 'Lord Kartik and I have invited them here. We need to talk about something that is important for India's future.'

Bhagirath frowned. He knew that what Gopal and Kartik were suggesting was the only way to get his sister and her husband out of Devagiri, tenuous though it may be.

'I will go into the city myself,' said Bhagirath.

'And, Prince Bhagirath...' Gopal hesitated.

'I understand, Pandit*ji*. I will not breathe a word of this to anyone.'

They stood in silence together, looking at a city that would no longer exist tomorrow.

'Excuse me,' said a voice. They turned around to see a small group of Meluhans.

'Yes?' asked Kartik.

'We left the city this morning but have changed our minds now. We would like to stay. May we go back in?'

Gopal stared at them in disbelief, and Bhagirath dropped his eyes, praying that he would be able to convince his sister to leave.

— ⁂ —

It was late into the third prahar and the sun was on its way down. This would be the last time that the sun would set on Devagiri. Veerini looked up at the sky as she walked out of the Devagiri royal palace.

'Your Highness,' saluted a guard smartly, falling into step behind her.

Veerini absently waved her hand and walked towards the gate.

'Your Highness? Are you leaving?' asked the shocked guard.

He seemed genuinely stunned that the Meluhan queen was abandoning them and taking up the Neelkanth's offer of amnesty.

Veerini didn't bother with a reply but continued walking down the road, towards the Svarna platform gate.

— ⁂ —

'Has this been ordered by the Neelkanth?' asked Anandmayi, before looking at her husband.

Parvateshwar and she were in a secluded section outside the Tamra platform, speaking with Gopal, Kartik and Bhagirath.

'It's what he would want,' said Gopal. 'He just doesn't know it at this point of time.'

Parvateshwar frowned. 'If the Neelkanth has said no, then it means no.'

'General, I appreciate your loyalty,' said Gopal. 'But there is also the larger picture. The Somras is evil now. But it's not supposed to be completely destroyed. You know as well as I do, it's only supposed to be taken out of the equation. We have to keep the knowledge of the Somras alive, for it may well be required again. It's the future of India that we are talking about.'

'Are you suggesting that the Lord Neelkanth doesn't care about India?' asked Parvateshwar.

'I'm saying no such thing, General,' said Gopal. 'But...'

Kartik suddenly stepped in. 'I appreciate your loyalty to my father. And, I'm sure you're aware of my love for him as well.'

Parvateshwar nodded, not saying anything.

'My father is distraught at this point in time,' said Kartik. 'You know of his devotion to my mother. The grief of her death has clouded his mind. He is furious, and rightly so. But you also know that his heart is pure. He would not want to do anything that is against his dharma. I only intend to keep the technology of the Somras alive till my father's rage subsides. If, after calm reflection, he still decides that everything associated with the Somras should be destroyed, I will personally see to it.'

Parvateshwar stared into space, his eyes brooding and dark.

'And in order to do that you must ensure the survival of the Brahmins, together with their Somras libraries,' he sighed.

'Many of those Somras-worshipping intellectuals would grab the opportunity to live. But there are some who have heard the call of honour. Kartik, you cannot coerce a man to forsake his honour. You cannot force him to live, particularly if it is to continue the Somras which his Neekanth has declared Evil, and which is causing the destruction of his homeland.'

Kartik held Parvateshwar's hand. 'General, my mother appeared in a dream to me. She told me to do the right thing. She told me to remember how she lived, and not how she died. Even you know she would have done exactly what I'm trying to do.'

Parvateshwar looked up at the sky and quickly wiped a tear. He was quiet for a long time. 'All right, Kartik,' he said at last. 'I will bring those people out. I will talk them out where I can, and force them out where I cannot. But remember, they are your responsibility. They cannot be allowed to propagate Evil any longer. Only the Lord Neelkanth can decide the fate of the Somras. Not you, not Lord Gopal, nor anyone else.'

— ⁂ —

Veerini rapidly walked down the Svarna platform steps as all the assembled people made way for their queen. Maatali's forces were in charge here, checking the papers and antecedents of everyone who sought to leave the city. The soldiers saluted Veerini. She acknowledged them distractedly but kept walking towards the massive wooden tower being constructed a good four kilometres from the city. That was the base from which the *Pashupatiastra* missile would be launched.

As she neared the tower, Veerini could see Shiva issuing instructions. She immediately recognised the woman who stood next to him: Brahaspati's love, Tara. Ganesh was working with Tara, his brilliant engineering skills coming in handy in building the solid tower. Kali sat a little distance away on a rock, seemingly lost in thought.

Kali was the first to see her. '*Maa!*'

Veerini walked up to Shiva as Kali and Ganesh stepped up.

Shiva looked at Veerini with glazed eyes, the now-constant throbbing pain in his brow making it difficult for him to focus. Veerini had always been struck by Shiva's eyes; the intelligence, focus and mirth that resided in them. She believed that it was his eyes rather than his blue throat that were the foundation of his charisma. But they now reflected nothing but pain and grief, giving a glimpse into a soul that had lost its reason to live.

Shiva had not for a moment suspected that Veerini was involved with Sati's assassination in any way. He bowed his head and brought his hands together in a respectful Namaste.

Veerini held Shiva's hand, her eyes drawn to the throbbing blackish-red blotch on his brow. 'My son, I can't even imagine the pain that you are going through.'

Shiva was quiet, looking lost and broken.

'I gave my word to Sati, a promise she extracted from me just before her death. I am here to fulfil it.'

Shiva's eyes suddenly found their focus. He looked up at Veerini.

'She insisted that she be cremated by both her sons.'

Ganesh, who was standing next to Veerini, sucked in his breath as tears slipped from his eyes. Tradition held that while the eldest child cremated the father, it was the youngest who conducted the funeral proceedings of the mother. Also, it was considered inauspicious for Nagas to be involved in any funeral ceremony. So Ganesh had not expected the honour of lighting his mother's pyre.

Kali turned and held Ganesh.

'But traditionally only the youngest child can perform the mother's last rites,' said Veerini to Shiva. 'If there is anyone who can challenge that tradition, it is you.'

'I don't give a damn about that tradition,' said Shiva. 'If Sati wanted it, then it will be done.'

'I'll tell Kartik as well,' said Veerini. 'I've been told he's at the Tamra platform.'

Shiva nodded silently before looking back towards the building where Sati's body lay entombed in ice.

Veerini stepped forward to embrace Shiva. He held his mother-in-law lightly.

'Try to find some peace, Shiva,' said Veerini. 'It's what Sati would have wanted.'

'Have *you* been able to find peace?'

Veerini smiled wanly.

'We will only find peace now when we meet Sati again,' said Shiva.

'She was a great woman. Any mother would be proud to have a daughter like her.'

Shiva kept quiet, wiping a tear from the corner of his eye.

Veerini held Shiva's hand. 'I have to tell you this. She could have been alive. When she found out about the conspiracy, she was in Devagiri, in our palace. She could have chosen to stay out of it. But she fought her way out of the city and rushed into the battle to save Nandi and her other bodyguards. And she did save many. She died a brave, honourable, warrior's death, fighting and challenging her opponents till her last breath. It was the kind of death she always wished for herself; that any warrior wishes for himself.'

Shiva's eyes welled up again. 'Sati set very high standards for herself.'

Veerini smiled sadly.

Shiva took a deep breath. He needed to focus on the *Pashupatiastra.* He folded his hands together into a polite Namaste. 'I should...'

'Of course,' said Veerini. 'I understand.'

Shiva bent and touched his mother-in-law's feet. She touched his head gently and blessed him. He turned and walked back to supervise the work on the weapon. This was the only thing that stopped his spirit from imploding.

Veerini turned and embraced her daughter Kali and grandson Ganesh.

'I have been unfair to the both of you,' said Veerini.

'No you haven't, *maa*,' said Kali. 'It was father who committed the sins. Not you.'

'But I failed in my duty as a mother. I should have abandoned my husband when he refused to accept you.'

Kali shook her head. 'You had your duty as a wife as well.'

'It is not a wife's duty to support her husband in his misdeeds. In fact, a good wife corrects her husband when he is wrong, even if she has to ram it down his throat.'

'I don't think he would have listened, *naani*,' said Ganesh to his *grandmother*, 'no matter how hard you tried. That man is...'

Veerini looked at her grandson as Ganesh checked himself from insulting his grandfather to her face. She noticed his eyes. They weren't calm and detached, like they had been the last time she had met him. They were full of rage; repressed fury over his mother's death.

'*Naani*, if you will excuse me. I need to work on the tower.'

'Of course, my child.'

Ganesh bent down, touched his grandmother's feet and walked back to Tara.

'*Maa*, wait for a bit and Ganesh will take you to our ship,' said Kali. 'You can stay there till this is over and then return with us to Panchavati. It would be so wonderful to have you in my home, even if it is a hundred years after it was meant to be. Having you with us will help us all cope with our grief and the vacuum left behind by Sati.'

Veerini smiled and embraced Kali. 'I'll have to wait for my next birth to live in your home, my child.'

Kali was taken aback. '*Maa!* You don't have to be punished for that old goat's crimes! You will not return to Devagiri!'

'Don't be ridiculous, Kali. I'm the Queen of Meluha. When Devagiri dies, so shall I.'

'Of course not!' cried Kali. 'There's no reason...'

'Would you leave Panchavati on the day of its destruction?'

Kali was stumped. But the Naga queen was not one who gave in easily. 'That's a hypothetical question, *maa*. What is important is that...'

'What is important, my child,' interrupted Veerini, 'is the identity of the man who helped your father execute the conspiracy. Many of the conspirators have escaped, as have the assassins. They will not die here tomorrow. You need to find them. You need to punish them.'

Chapter 50

Saving a Legacy

The sun had long set across the western horizon. Kartik, Gopal and Bhagirath were stationed at the far corner of the Tamra platform. Neither the other two Devagiri platforms nor Shiva's army encampment had a clear view of this area. It was the best place for Kartik to carry out his mission.

Twenty Branga soldiers from the command of Divodas, who had become fanatically loyal to Kartik after the Battle of Bal-Atibal Kund, were with him. These soldiers held on tightly to a rope, gently allowing it to roll away from them at a gradual pace. Divodas worked along with them. The rope was attached to a pulley that had been rigged on top of the Tamra platform wall. Circling the pulley, the rope went down to where it had been tied to a wooden cage, which could carry ten Brahmins at a time. Ten of them, together with their books and essential equipment, were descending towards Kartik's refuge. Secrecy was essential, for it was forbidden to remove any knowledge of the Somras from the city, the penalty being death.

As a failsafe, another rope had been tied to the wooden cage. This particular rope was also circled around a pulley that was rigged onto the fort wall. But the grasping end of this rope was in the hands of Suryavanshi soldiers at the top of the platform. They were being supervised by Parvateshwar. Both groups of soldiers worked in tandem to release their end of the ropes at the same pace, so that the cage could descend gently to the ground. The angle of the wall made it impossible for Parvateshwar to look over and judge the movement of the wooden cage as well as its distance from the ground. And if the Suryavanshis holding the rope on top did not synchronise their movement with Divodas' team below, it could lead to the cage becoming unbalanced, resulting in a possible accident.

To prevent this from happening, Bhagirath had been made to stand at a distance, far enough to be able to view both Divodas' team as well as the Suryavanshis above. The new moon helped aid Bhagirath's vision. His task was to keep whistling the way birds do, but in a steady rhythm, till the wooden cage touched the ground. He played the role of a time-keeper, setting the pace for the movements of the soldiers.

Kartik whirled around when Bhagirath's whistling stopped. Divodas and his team had not paused but continued releasing the rope at the same pace. The Suryavanshis on top of the fort walls however, used to following orders, had instantly come to a halt when Bhagirath stopped whistling. Immediately, the wooden cage became unbalanced and tilted heavily to one side.

'Stop!' hissed Kartik.

Divodas and his team stopped. The cage containing ten Brahmins of the Somras factory remained suspended dangerously in the air. To the admiration of Gopal, the Brahmins in the cage remained quiet despite the possibility of falling to their death. Any sharp noise would have alerted others to what was going on.

Kartik rushed towards Bhagirath, who seemed lost in his own world.

'Prince Bhagirath?'

Bhagirath immediately came out of his stupor and began to whistle. The Suryavanshis started releasing the rope at a steady pace and the wooden cage descended softly to the ground. The Brahmins caged within stepped out quickly in an orderly fashion.

As the two teams began pulling the empty cage back up, the whistling was no longer required. In the upward movement, what was necessary was speed, and not steadiness.

'Prince Bhagirath, please pay attention. The lives of many people are at stake.'

Kartik was aware of the reason behind Bhagirath's distress. Parvateshwar had refused to leave Devagiri. The Meluhan general had decided he would perish along with his beloved city. And to Bhagirath's utter dismay, Anandmayi had decided to stay with her husband.

Bhagirath had fought passionately with her over her decision. He had pleaded with her, had begged her to reconsider. 'Do you think Parvateshwar wants you to die? And what about me? Why are you trying to hurt me? Do you hate me so much? I am your brother. What have I done to deserve this?'

Anandmayi had only smiled, her eyes glistening with love and tears. 'Bhagirath, you love me and want me to live, with every fibre of your soul. So let me live. Let me live every last second of my life, in the way that I believe life should be lived. Let me go.'

Bhagirath shook his head as if to clear his mind. 'My apologies, Kartik.'

Kartik stepped forward and held Bhagirath's arm. 'Prince, your sister was right about you. You will make a far better king than your father.'

Bhagirath snorted. He already knew the Chandravanshi

army that had been ordered to march to Devagiri under the command of the Meluhan brigadier Vraka had rebelled against his father, Emperor Dilipa. The soldiers believed that the Ayodhyan emperor had led them into an ill-conceived battle where they were fighting on the side of their former enemies, the Meluhans, against their Neelkanth. Bhagirath knew that a section of the troops had already set out for Devagiri to convince him to ascend the throne. But he didn't care. He was tormented by the impending loss of his beloved sister.

'But do you know what the mark of a great king is?' asked Kartik.

Bhagirath looked at Kartik.

'It's the ability to remain focused, regardless of personal tragedy. You will have time to mourn your sister and brother-in-law, Prince Bhagirath. But not now. You are the only one here who can whistle like a night bird and make it sound natural. You cannot fail.'

'Yes, Lord Kartik,' said Bhagirath, addressing the young man as his Lord for the first time.

Kartik turned around. 'Come here.'

A Branga soldier marched up.

'Prince Bhagirath,' said Kartik, 'this man will remain here to support you in your task.'

Bhagirath didn't object. Kartik quickly walked back to Gopal.

Seeing the pensive look of the Vasudev chief, Kartik asked, 'What happened, Pandit*ji*?'

Gopal pointed to the Suryavanshi soldier. 'Lord Parvateshwar has sent a message. Maharishi Bhrigu has refused to leave the city.'

Kartik shook his head. 'Why are the Meluhans so bloody eager to die?'

'What do I do, Lord Kartik?' asked the Suryavanshi.

'Take me to Maharishi Bhrigu.'

— ⛤ —

A flickering sacrificial flame spread its light as best as it could in the night. Its reflection on the nearby Saraswati River aided its cause. Ganesh sat quietly on a *patla, a low stool,* with his legs crossed and his fleshy hands placed on his knees, his long fingers extended out delicately. He wore a white dhoti.

A barber was shearing Ganesh's hair, while Ganesh kept chanting a *mantra* softly and dropping some ghee into the sacrificial flame.

Having removed all of Ganesh's hair, the barber put his implement down and wiped his head with a cloth. Then he picked up a small bottle he had taken from Ayurvati, poured the disinfectant into his hands and spread it on Ganesh's head.

'It's done, My Lord.'

Ganesh didn't reply. He looked directly at the sacrificial flame and spoke softly. 'She was the purest among them all, Lord Agni. Remember that as you consume her. Take care of her and carry her straight to heaven, for that is where she came from. She was, is and forever will be a Goddess. She will be the Mother Goddess.'

— ⛤ —

It was late in the night when a tired Shiva trudged back to his Sati. The *Pashupatiastra* was ready. There were just a few more tests that needed to be conducted. Tara was at it. The peace conference area was within the external blast radius of the *Pashupatiastra*, so Sati's body would be moved from her icy tomb the next morning.

What nobody dared verbalise was that, without the Meluhan cooling mechanism, her body would start decomposing, and she would need to be cremated. That was something Shiva refused to contemplate.

Shiva opened the door of the inner chamber in the building, shivering at the sudden blast of cold air. He could see Ganesh, his son, standing next to the ice tower, holding his dead mother's hand. His head had been shaven clean. The Lord of the Nagas was on his toes, his mouth close to his mother's ear. Following an ancient tradition, he was whispering hymns from the Rig Veda into her ear.

Shiva walked up to Ganesh and touched his shoulder lightly. Ganesh immediately pulled up his white *angvastram* and wiped his eyes before turning to face his father.

Shiva embraced his son.

'I miss her, *baba*.' Ganesh held Shiva tightly.

'I miss her too...'

Ganesh began to cry. 'I abandoned her in her hour of need.'

'You weren't the only one, my son. I wasn't there either. But we will avenge her.'

Ganesh kept sobbing helplessly.

'I want to kill them all. I want to kill every single one of those bastards!'

'We will kill the Evil that took her life.' Shiva held his son quietly while he sobbed. He closed his eyes and pulled Ganesh in tighter, and whispered hoarsely, 'Whatever the cost.'

Veerbhadra and Krittika had come to the Rajat platform. Krittika had lived in Devagiri for a long time and knew most people, so she had been trying to speak to those who were choosing to stay back, trying to convince them to leave.

'Veerbhadra, I need to talk to you.'

Veerbhadra turned around to see Kali and Parshuram standing behind him.

'Yes, Your Highness,' said Veerbhadra.

'In private,' said Kali.

'Of course,' said Veerbhadra, touching Krittika lightly before walking away.

— ⁂ —

'Vidyunmali?' spat out Veerbhadra, his face hardening with fury.

'He's the main conspirator,' said Kali. 'He's hidden in the city, badly injured from some recent skirmish.'

Parshuram touched Veerbhadra's shoulder. 'We have to enter the city in a small group and locate him.'

Kali touched her knife, a serrated blade that delivered particularly painful wounds. 'We need to encourage him to talk. We need to know the identity of the assassins who escaped.'

'That son of a bitch deserves a slow, painful death,' growled Veerbhadra.

'That he does,' said Kali. 'But not before we've made him talk.'

Parshuram stretched his hand out, palm facing the ground. 'For the Lord Neelkanth.'

Veerbhadra placed his hand on Parshuram's. 'For Shiva.'

Kali placed her hand on top. 'For Sati.'

Chapter 51

Live On, Do Your Karma

'You want to enter Devagiri?' screeched Krittika. 'Are you mad?'

'I will be back soon, Krittika,' argued Veerbhadra. 'There is no lawlessness in the city. You've seen the way the Meluhans are behaving.'

'That may be so. But Vidyunmali's men will surely be prowling the streets. What do you think they're going to do? Welcome you with flowers?'

'They will not notice me, Krittika.'

'Nonsense! Most people in Devagiri recognise you as the Lord Neelkanth's friend.'

'They will recognise me only if they see me. It's late at night. I'm going to be hidden from view. Nobody will notice me.'

'Why can't you send someone else?'

'Because this is the least I can do for my friend. We need to find out who Princess Sati's actual killers are. Vidyunmali knows. He is the one who organised and implemented this peace farce.'

'But we are destroying the entire city. All the conspirators will be dead in any case!'

'Krittika, many of the killers got away,' said Veerbhadra.

'Except for Vidyunmali, nobody knows who they are. If we don't get to know their identities now, we will never know.'

Krittika looked away, having run out of arguments but still deeply troubled. 'I'm as angry as you are about Princess Sati's death. But the killing has to stop some time.'

'I have to go, Krittika.'

Veerbhadra tried to kiss her goodbye but she turned her face away. He could understand her anger. She had lost the woman she had idolised all her life. Her hometown, Devagiri, was about to be destroyed. She did not want to risk losing her husband as well. But Veerbhadra had to do this. Sati's killers had to be punished.

— ⁂ —

'Pandit*ji*,' said Kartik, his hands folded in a Namaste and his head bowed low.

Bhrigu opened his eyes. The maharishi had been meditating in the grand Indra temple next to the Public Bath.

'Lord Kartik,' said Bhrigu, surprised to see Kartik in Devagiri at this time of night.

'I'm too young for you to address me as Lord, great Maharishi,' said Kartik.

'Noble deeds make a man a Lord, not merely his age. I have heard about your efforts to ensure the Somras is not completely destroyed. History will thank you for it. Your glory will be recounted for ages.'

'I'm not working for my own glory, Pandit*ji*. My task is to be true to my father's mission. My task is to do what my mother would have wanted me to do.'

Bhrigu smiled. 'I don't think your mother would have wanted you to come here. I don't think she would have wanted you to save me.'

'I disagree,' said Kartik. 'You are a good man. You just picked the wrong side.'

'I didn't just pick this side, I *led* it into battle. And the dictates of dharma demand that I perish with it.'

'Why?'

'If the side I led committed such crimes, I must pay for it. If fate has determined that those that supported the Somras have sinned, then the Somras must be evil. I was wrong. And, my punishment is death.'

'Isn't that taking the easy way out?'

Bhrigu stared at Kartik, angered by the implied insult.

'So you think you have done something wrong, Pandit*ji*,' said Kartik. 'What is the way out? Escaping through death? Or, actually working to set things right by balancing your karma?'

'What can I do? I've conceded that the Somras is evil. There's nothing left for me to do now.'

'You have a *vast storehouse of knowledge* within you Pandit*ji*,' said Kartik. 'The Somras is not the only subject you excel at. Should the world be deprived of Lord Bhrigu's *Samhita*?'

'I don't think anyone is interested in my knowledge.'

'That is for posterity to determine. You should only do your duty.'

Bhrigu fell silent.

'Pandit*ji*, your karma is to spread your knowledge throughout the world,' said Kartik. 'Whether others choose to listen or not is their karma.'

Bhrigu shook his head as a wry smile softened his expression. 'You speak well, son of the Neelkanth. But I chose to support something that turned out to be evil. For this sin, I must die. There is no karma left for me in this life. I will have to wait to be born again.'

'One cannot allow a bad deed to arrest the wheel of karma. Don't banish yourself from this world as a punishment for your sin. Instead, stay here and do some good, so that you can cleanse your karma.'

Bhrigu stared at Kartik silently.

'One cannot undo what has happened. But the inexorable march of time offers the wise opportunities for redemption. I entreat you, do not escape. Stay in this world and do your karma.'

Bhrigu smiled. 'You are very intelligent for such a young boy.'

'I'm the son of Shiva and Sati,' smiled Kartik. 'I am the younger brother of Ganesh. When the gardeners are good, the flower will bloom.'

Bhrigu turned towards the idol of Lord Indra within the sanctum sanctorum. The great God, the killer of the primal demon Vritra, stood resplendent as he held his favourite weapon, *Vajra, the thunderbolt*. Bhrigu folded his hands into a Namaste and bowed, praying for the God's blessing.

The maharishi then turned back to Kartik and whispered, '*Samhita...*'

'The *Bhrigu Samhita*,' said Kartik. 'The world will benefit from your vast knowledge, Pandit*ji*. Come with me. Don't sit here and wait for death.'

— ⸙ —

The sun rose on the day that would be Devagiri's last. The *Pashupatiastra* was ready. After barring the gates, Shiva's soldiers had been asked to retreat beyond the safety line, out of the range of the expected radius of exposure. The relatives of those remaining within Devagiri too waited patiently, as they were herded back by Chandraketu's Brangas. They kept up a constant prayer for the souls of their loved ones who were left behind in the city.

Maharishi Bhrigu and another three hundred people, who knew the secrets of the Somras, had been successfully spirited out of Devagiri the previous night. They were now kept imprisoned in a temporary stockade ten kilometres north of Devagiri under the watchful eye of Divodas and his soldiers. Kartik intended to wait for his father's anger to subside before talking to him about Bhrigu and the others.

The peace conference building had been abandoned. Nandi and the other surviving bodyguards had been carefully evacuated onto Shiva's ship, where a medical team under the supervision of Ayurvati maintained a constant vigil.

Ayurvati was worried about the blackish-red mark on Shiva's brow. It had made its appearance many times before, especially when Shiva was angry. But very rarely had it stayed for so long. Shiva had brushed aside Ayurvati's concerns.

Shiva, Kali, Ganesh and Kartik carried Sati's body gently to a specially prepared cabin on the ship. Her corpse was laid with great care within another tomb of ice.

Shiva gently ran his hand across Sati's face and whispered, 'Devagiri will pay for its crimes, my love. You will be avenged.'

As Shiva stepped back, the soldiers placed another block of ice on top, enveloping Sati's body completely.

Shiva, Kali, Ganesh and Kartik took one last look at Sati before turning around and walking out of the ship. Gopal and the kings in Shiva's army waited at the port.

Shiva turned and nodded towards the ship captain. Soldiers marched into the rowing deck of the ship to row it back a fair distance down the Saraswati River, far away from the external blast radius of the *Pashupatiastra*.

'The weapon is armed, Lord Neelkanth,' said Tara.

Shiva cast an expressionless look at an unhappy Gopal and then turned back towards Tara. 'Let's go.'

— ⁂ —

It was the fourth hour of the second prahar, just a couple of hours before Devagiri was to be destroyed. Veerini knocked on Parvateshwar's door. There was no answer. Parvateshwar and Anandmayi were probably alone at home.

Veerini pushed open the door and stepped into the house. She walked past the lobby into the central courtyard.

'General!' called out Veerini.

No response.

'General!' said Veerini again, a little louder this time. 'It is I, the Queen of Meluha.'

'Your Highness!'

Veerini glanced up to see a surprised Parvateshwar looking down from the balcony on the top floor. His hair was dishevelled and an *angvastram* had been hastily thrown over his shoulders.

'My apologies if I have come at a bad time, General.'

'Not at all, Your Highness,' said Parvateshwar.

'It's just that we don't have much time left,' said Veerini. 'There is something I needed to tell you.'

'Please give me a moment, Your Highness. I'll be down shortly.'

'Of course,' said Veerini.

Veerini walked into the large waiting room next to the courtyard, settled on a comfortable chair and waited. A few minutes later Parvateshwar, clad in a spotless white dhoti and *angvastram*, his hair neatly in place, walked into the room. Behind him was his wife, Anandmayi, also clad in white, the colour of purity.

Veerini rose. 'Please accept my apologies for disturbing you.'

'Not at all, Your Highness,' said Parvateshwar. 'Please be seated.'

Veerini resumed her seat, as Parvateshwar and Anandmayi sat next to her.

'What did you want to talk about, Your Highness?' asked Parvateshwar.

Veerini seemed to hesitate. Then she looked at Anandmayi and Parvateshwar with a smile. 'I wanted to thank you.'

'Thank us?' asked a surprised Parvateshwar, casting a look at Anandmayi before turning back to Veerini. 'Thank us for what, Your Highness?'

'For keeping the legacy of Devagiri alive,' said Veerini.

Parvateshwar and Anandmayi remained silent, their expressions reflecting their confusion.

'Devagiri is not just a physical manifestation,' said Veerini, waving her hand around. 'Devagiri exists in its knowledge, its philosophies and its ideologies. You have managed to keep that alive by saving our intellectuals.'

An embarrassed Parvateshwar didn't know how to react. How could he openly acknowledge having broken the law to save the scientists who worked at the Somras factory? 'Your Highness, I didn't...'

Veerini raised her hand. 'Your conduct has been exemplary all your life, Lord Parvateshwar. Don't spoil it by lying on your last day.'

Parvateshwar smiled.

'The people you've saved are not merely the repositories of the knowledge of Somras, but also of the accumulated knowledge of our great land. They are the custodians of our philosophies, of our ideologies. They will keep our legacy alive. For that, Devagiri and Meluha will forever be grateful to you.'

'Thank you, Your Highness,' said Anandmayi, accepting the gratitude on behalf of her discomfited husband.

'It's bad enough that the both of you are dying for my

husband's sins,' said Veerini. 'It would have been really terrible had Maharishi Bhrigu and our intellectuals suffered for it as well.'

'I think what's really unfair is your suffering for your husband's sins, Your Highness,' said Anandmayi. 'Your husband may not have been a good emperor, but you have been an excellent queen.'

'No, that's not true. If it were, I would have stood up to my husband instead of standing by him.'

They sat quietly together for a moment, then Veerini straightened her shoulders and rose to leave. 'Time grows short,' she said, 'and there are preparations we still have to make for our final journey. Thank you, both of you, and let us say our farewells. For one last time.'

Chapter 52

The Banyan Tree

Daksha sat quietly in his chamber, staring out of the window, waiting for his death. He looked towards the door, wondering where Veerini had gone so early in the morning.

Has she abandoned me as well?

As death approached, he was honest enough at least with himself, to not blame her if she had.

Daksha took a deep breath, wiped a tear and turned his gaze back at the window, towards the banyan tree in the distance. It was a magnificent tree, centuries old, even older than Daksha. He had known this tree for as long as he could remember. He recalled its size when he was young and the fact that he always marvelled at how the tree never seemed to stop growing. Its branches spread themselves out over vast distances, and when they extended too far, they dropped thin reed-like roots into the ground. The drop-roots then matured, anchoring themselves deep, drawing nourishment and growing enough in bulk to eventually resemble another trunk, thus supporting the further extension of the branch that gave them birth. After a few decades, there were so many new trunks that it was impossible to tell which the original one was. It had been a single tree when Daksha was born. It still was, but now it was so massive, that it appeared like a jungle.

Daksha knew all Indians looked upon the grand banyan tree with utmost respect and devotion. It was considered holy in India; a tree that unselfishly gave its all to others, building an ecosystem that sustained many birds and animals. Innumerable plants and shrubs found succour and shade under its protective cover. It remained firm and solid, even in the face of the most severe storm. Indians believed that ancestral spirits, even the Gods, inhabited the banyan tree.

For most citizens of Devagiri, this massive tree represented the ideal of life. They worshipped it.

Daksha's perspective though, was very different.

At a very young age, he had noted that no offspring of a banyan was able to flourish, or even grow, around its parent. The roots of the tree were too strong; they twisted and pushed away any attempt by another banyan sapling to grow roots in the vicinity. For a young sapling to survive, it would have to move very far away from its parent.

I should have run away.

The banyan tree is pollinated by a particular species of wasp. But the tree extracts a terrible price from the tiny insect that aids its reproduction. It kills the wasp, kills it brutally, ripping the insect to shreds. Daksha's interpretation of this fact was very simple: the banyan hated its own progeny so much that it would murder the kindly wasp that tries to bring its offspring to life.

To a neglected child's imagination, the banyan tree's munificence was reserved for others. It did not care for its own. In fact, it went out of its way to harm its own.

So while everyone else looks upon the banyan tree with reverential eyes, Daksha viewed it with fear and hatred.

He was fearful because this was not the only banyan tree in his life. He had had another: his father.

He hated his father with venomous intensity; but at a

deeper level, perhaps loved and admired his abilities. Just like the desperate offspring of the banyan, he had always tried to prove that he could be as great as his father. He had carried this burden all his life. But there had been this one time when he had unshackled himself from his father's grip; when he had been free for a few magical moments. He remembered that day so clearly. It had been a long time ago; more than a hundred years.

Sati had just returned from the Maika gurukul, a headstrong, idealistic girl of sixteen. In keeping with her character, she had jumped in to save an immigrant woman from a vicious pack of wild dogs. Daksha remembered well that Parvateshwar and he had rushed in to her rescue. He also remembered that, despite not being an accomplished warrior, he had, with Parvateshwar's help, courageously fought back the dogs that were out to kill his daughter. He had been seriously injured in that terrible fight.

Fortunately, the medical teams had reached quickly. Parvateshwar and Sati's injuries were superficial and had been quickly dressed. Daksha knew that since he had been in the thick of the battle, his injuries were the most serious. The medical officers had decided to take him to the *ayuralay* so that senior doctors could examine him. However, due to massive blood loss, he had lost consciousness on the way.

When he had regained consciousness, he had found himself in the *ayuralay*. He remembered that he'd scolded Sati for risking her own life to save an insignificant immigrant woman. Later, when recuperating in his room, he had asked Veerini to bring Sati to him, in order to make peace with her now. But before Sati could be brought in, Daksha's father Brahmanayak had stormed into the chamber, accompanied by the doctor who had treated Daksha.

Brahmanayak, being one of the foremost warriors in

Meluha, had mocked Daksha about how he could have got himself so badly injured while fighting mere dogs. The doctor had pulled Brahmanayak out of the room using the excuse of a private conversation, wanting to save Daksha from any further mental anguish. As soon as Brahmanayak had left the room, Veerini had repeated the plea she had made many times earlier, that they should escape from Meluha and live in Panchavati with both their daughters, Kali and Sati.

'Daksha, trust me,' said Veerini. 'We'll be happy in Panchavati. If there was any other place where we could live with both Kali and Sati, I'd suggest it. But there isn't.'

Maybe Veerini's right. I can escape the old man. We can be happy. Also, Sati is the only pure one in my bloodline. Veerini's corrupt soul has led to Kali's birth. It's difficult to help them. But I have to protect Sati from the terrible fate of seeing her father being insulted every day. My elder daughter is the only one worthy of my love.

Daksha breathed deeply. 'But how...'

'You leave that to me. I'll make the arrangements. Just say yes. Your father is leaving tomorrow for Karachapa. You are not so badly injured that you can't travel. We'll be in Panchavati before he knows you're gone.'

Daksha stared at Veerini. 'But...'

'Trust me. Please trust me. It will be for our good. I know you love me. I know you love your daughters. Deep inside, I know you don't really care about anything else. Just trust me.'

Perhaps this is what we need.

Daksha nodded.

Veerini smiled, bent close and kissed her husband. 'I'll make all the arrangements.'

Veerini turned and walked out of the room.

In this moment of solitude, Daksha glanced at the ceiling, feeling light and relaxed; feeling free.

Everything happens for a reason, perhaps even this battle with the dogs. We can be happy in Panchavati. We will be away from my father. We will be free of that monster. To hell with Meluha. To hell with the throne. I don't want any of it. I just want to be happy. I just want to be with my Sati and be able to take care of her. I will also look after Veerini and Kali. Who do they have besides me?

He noticed Veerini's prayer beads on the chair. Next to the prayer beads was the tiger claw that Sati wore as a pendant. It must have fallen off during the battle with the dogs and Veerini must have recovered it to return it to their young daughter. Daksha stared at the blood stains on the tiger claw; his daughter's blood. His eyes became moist again.

I will be nothing like my father. I'll take care of Sati. I will love her like every father should love his child. I will not ridicule her in public. I will not deride her for the qualities she doesn't possess. Instead, I will cherish everything that she does have. She will be free to live her own dreams. I will not force my dreams upon her. I will love her for who she is; not for what I'd like her to be.

Daksha looked at his own injured body and shook his head.

All of this to save an immigrant woman! Sati can be so naive at times. But she is a child. I shouldn't have screamed at her. I should have explained things calmly to her. After all, who does she have to look up to besides me?

Just then the door opened and Sati walked in, looking grouchy; almost angry.

Daksha smiled.

She's only a child.

'Come here, my child,' said Daksha.

Sati stepped forward hesitantly.

'Come closer, Sati,' laughed Daksha. 'I'm your father. I'm not going to eat you up!'

Sati stepped closer. But her face still reflected the righteous anger she felt within.

Lord Ram, be merciful! This girl still thinks that she did the right thing in risking all our lives to save an unimportant immigrant woman.

Daksha reached out and held Sati's hand, speaking patiently. 'My child, listen to me. I care for you. I only had your best interests at heart. It was stupid of you to risk your life for that immigrant. But I admit I shouldn't have shouted at...'

Daksha fell silent as the door swung open suddenly and Brahmanayak strode in.

Sati suddenly withdrew her hand and turned around to look at Brahmanayak, her back towards her father.

'Aah!' said Brahmanayak as his face broke into a broad smile. He walked up to Sati and embraced her. 'At least one of my progeny has my blood coursing through her veins!'

Sati looked at Brahmanayak adoringly, pure hero-worship in her eyes. Daksha stared at him with impotent rage.

'I've heard about what you did,' said Brahmanayak to Sati. 'You risked your own life to protect a woman whom you didn't even know; a woman who was only a lowly immigrant.'

Sati smiled in embarrassment. 'It was nothing, Your Highness.'

Brahmanayak laughed softly and patted Sati's cheek. 'I am not "Your Highness" for you, Sati. I'm your grandfather.'

Sati nodded, smiling.

'I'm proud of you, my child,' said Brahmanayak. 'I am honoured to call you a Meluhan, honoured to call you my granddaughter.'

Sati's smile broadened as her heart felt light. She had done the right thing after all. She embraced her grandfather once again.

Brahmanayak bent down and kissed his adolescent granddaughter on her forehead. He then turned to Daksha, the smile immediately disappearing from his face. With barely concealed contempt, he told his son, 'I'm leaving for Karachapa tomorrow morning and will be gone for many weeks. Perhaps you will need that much time to recover from your so-called injuries. We'll talk about your future when I return.'

A seething Daksha refused to answer Brahmanayak, turning his face away.

Brahmanayak shook his head and rolled his eyes. He then patted Sati on her head. 'I'll see you when I return, my child.'

'Yes, grandfather.'

Brahmanayak opened the door and was gone.

Daksha glared at the closed door.

Thank God I'm going to be rid of you, you beast! Insulting me in front of my favourite daughter? How dare you! Take the throne away, take all the riches away, take the world away if you wish. But don't you dare take my good daughter away from me! She's mine!

He looked at Sati's back. She was still staring at the door, her body shaking.

Is she crying?

Daksha thought that perhaps Sati was angry with Brahmanayak for insulting her father. She was his daughter after all.

Daksha smiled. 'It's all right, my child. I'm not angry. Your grandfather doesn't matter anymore because...'

'Father,' interrupted Sati as she turned around, tears streaming down her cheeks. 'Why can't you be more like grandfather?'

Daksha stared at his daughter, dumbstruck.

'Why can't you be more like grandfather?' whispered Sati again.

Daksha was in shock.

Sati suddenly turned around and ran out of the room.

Daksha kept staring at the door as it slammed shut behind Sati. Fierce tears were pouring from his eyes.

More like grandfather?

More like that monster?

I am better than him!

The Gods know that! They know I will make a far better king! I will show you!

You will love me! I am your creator!

You will love me! Not him! Not that monster!

The sound of the door being opened broke his train of thought, bringing Daksha back to the present from that ancient memory.

He saw Veerini walk into the bed chamber. She glanced at Daksha for an instant, then shook her head, walked up to her private desk and rummaged through it to find what she was looking for: her prayer beads. She brought them up to touch her forehead reverentially, then both her eyes and then her lips. She held the beads tightly and turned to take one last look at her husband. The disgust she felt couldn't be expressed in words. She had no intention of desecrating her ears by listening to his voice. She hadn't spoken to him since Sati's death.

Daksha's eyes followed Veerini's passage. He couldn't muster the courage to speak, even if it was only to apologise for all that he'd done.

She walked into the private prayer room next to her bed chamber and shut the door. She bowed before the idol of Lord Ram, which was, as usual, surrounded by the idols of his favourite people, his wife, Lady Sita, his brother, Lord Lakshman and his loyal devotee, Lord Hanuman, the Vayuputra.

Veerini sat down cross-legged. She held the beads high, in front of her eyes and began chanting as she waited for her death. 'Shri Ram Jai Ram Jai Jai Ram; Shri Ram Jai Ram Jai Jai Ram...'

The faint echo of this chanting reached Daksha's ears. He

stared at the closed door of the attached chamber, his angry wife closeted within.

I should have listened to her. She was right all along.

'Shri Ram Jai Ram Jai Jai Ram; Shri Ram Jai Ram Jai Jai Ram....'

He continued to hear the soft chanting of his wife in the prayer room. Those divinely serene words should have brought him peace. But there was no chance of that. He would die a frustrated and angry man.

Daksha clenched his jaw and looked out of the window. He stared at the banyan tree in the distance, tears streaming down his face.

Damn you!

The banyan shook slightly and its leaves ruffled dramatically with the strong wind. It appeared as if the giant tree was laughing at him.

Damn you!

Chapter 53

The Destroyer of Evil

'The wind is too strong,' murmured a worried Tara, looking at the windsock that had been set up close to the *Pashupatiastra* missile tower.

Tara and Shiva were mounted on horses, stationed far from the *Pashupatiastra* launch tower. It was almost the end of the second prahar and the sun was just a few moments away from being directly overhead. Shiva's entire army and the refugees from Devagiri had been cordoned off seven kilometres from the launch tower, safely outside the *Pashupatiastra's* blast radius.

Shiva glanced at Tara and then up at the sky, trying to judge the wind from the movement of dust particles. 'Not a problem.'

Saying this, Shiva's attention returned to stringing his bow. Parshuram had been working on making this composite bow for months. Its basic structure was made of wood, reinforced with horn on the inside and sinew on the outside. It was also curved much sharper than normal, with its edges turning away from the archer. Due to the mix of different elements and the curve at the edges, the bow had exceptional draw strength for its small size. It was ideal for an archer to shoot arrows from, while riding a horse or a chariot. Parshuram had named the bow *Pinaka*, after the fabled great ancient longbow of Lord Rudra.

Though Parshuram didn't know this while designing the bow, the Pinaka would prove ideal for Shiva's purpose, as firing the *Pashupatiastra* was not easy.

The *Pashupatiastra* was a pure nuclear fusion weapon, unlike the *Brahmastra* and the *Vaishnavastra* which were nuclear fission weapons. In a pure nuclear fusion weapon, two *paramanoos*, the *smallest stable division of matter*, are fused together to release tremendous destructive energy. In a nuclear fission weapon, *anoos*, *atomic particles*, are broken down to release *paramanoos*, and this is also accompanied by a demonic release of devastating energy.

Nuclear fission weapons leave behind a trail of uncontrollable destruction, with radioactive waste spreading far and wide. A nuclear fusion weapon, on the other hand, is much more controlled, destroying only the targeted area with minimal radioactive spread.

So the *Pashupatiastra* would be the obvious weapon of choice for those who intended to destroy a specific target with the precision of a surgeon. The problem though, was its launch.

These *daivi astras* were usually mounted on launching towers, packed with a mixture of sulphur, charcoal, saltpetre and a few other materials which generated the explosive energy that propelled the *astra* towards the target. Once the *astra* was close to its target, another set of explosions would trigger the weapon.

The launch material within the tower had to be triggered from a safe distance or else the people firing the *astra* would be incinerated in the initial launch explosion. Keeping this in mind, archers were called upon to shoot flaming arrows from a distance to trigger the launch explosion. These archers usually used long bows with a range of more than eight hundred metres. To hit a target accurately from this distance required archers of great skill.

The *Brahmastra* and *Vaishnavastra* did not need a precise landing as their destruction spread far and wide. Since accuracy was not of the essence, the launch towers that cradled these weapons had huge firing targets.

The *Pashupatiastra* or *Weapon of the Lord of Animals* was a precise missile. It had to land at the exact spot. What complicated the issue even more at this particular time was that the attempt was to fire three missiles concurrently. The trajectory of the three missiles had been planned such that they would detonate over the Svarna, Rajat and Tamra platforms of Devagiri simultaneously, guaranteeing the complete and instantaneous destruction of the entire city. The risk with trying to destroy three platforms at the same time was that the inner circle of devastation would expand, since the weapons would have to be triggered from a greater height. Tara had planned the angles of descent of each missile such that, together, their simultaneous explosions would ensure the annihilation of Devagiri while their excess energies would be trapped within each other, thus preventing any fallout destruction outside the inner circle.

A precise descent needed a perfect take-off. Therefore, the *Pashupatiastra* missiles had been set at precise angles within the tower. The target area on the tower where the fiery arrow would be shot was small. Shiva had to fire an arrow to hit the target, placed more than eight hundred metres away. Moreover, he had to do this while seated on a horse, so that he could escape immediately after firing the arrow.

'Remember, great Neelkanth,' said Tara, 'the moment your arrow hits the target, you have to ride away. You will have less than five minutes before the *Pashupatiastra* explodes over Devagiri. You have to cover at least three kilometres within that time. Only then will you be out of the range of the minuscule number of neutrons from the *Pashupatiastra* which may escape that far.'

Shiva nodded distractedly, still testing his bow's draw strength.

'Neelkanth? It is crucial for you to ride as fast as you can. The blast can be fatal.'

Shiva didn't respond. He pulled out the arrows from the quiver. He smelt them and then rubbed the tip of one of the arrows against the rough leather of the pommel. The tip immediately caught fire. Perfect. Shiva threw the burning arrow away and returned the rest to the quiver.

'Did you hear me? You need to move away immediately.'

Shiva wiped his hand on his *dhoti* and turned to Tara. 'Ride beyond the safety line now.'

'Shiva! You shoot the arrow and move.'

Shiva looked at Tara, his gaze glassy. Tara could see the blackish-red blotch on his brow throbbing frantically.

'You will ride away immediately!' emphasised Tara. 'Promise me!'

Shiva nodded.

'Promise me!'

'I have already promised you. Now go.'

Tara stared at Shiva. 'Neelkanth...'

'Go, Tara. The sun is about to reach overhead. I need to fire the missiles.'

Tara pulled her horse's reins and spun it around.

'And Tara...'

Tara pulled up her horse and looked back over her shoulder.

'Thank you,' said Shiva.

Tara was still, watching the face of the Neelkanth with clouded eyes. 'Ride back quickly beyond the safety line. Remember, all those who love you are waiting for you.'

Shiva held his breath.

Yes, my love is waiting for me.

Tara kicked her horse into action and rode away.

Shiva pressed his forehead, right above the blackish-red mark. The pressure seemed to ease the horrendous burning sensation. The pain had been immense and continuous for the last few days, ever since he had seen Sati's body.

Shiva shook his head and focused his attention on the tower. He could see the target in the distance. It had been marked a bright red.

He took a deep breath and looked towards the ground.

Holy Lake, give me strength.

Shiva breathed once again and looked up.

Lord Ram, be merciful!

Arrayed in front of him was an army of clones, blocking his view of the *Pashupatiastra* launch tower; clones of the giant hairy monster who had tormented him in his nightmares since his childhood. Shiva looked carefully and noticed that none of the monsters had faces. There was a smooth, white slate where their faces should have been. All of them had their swords drawn, blood dripping from every single blade. He could clearly hear their ghastly roar. For a moment Shiva imagined he was a terrified little boy once again.

Shiva looked up at the sky and shook his head, as if to clear it.

Help me!

Shiva heard his uncle Manobhu's voice call out. 'Forgive them! Forget them! Your only true enemy is Evil!'

Shiva brought his eyes down and locked his gaze on the launch tower. The monsters had disappeared. He stared directly at the red spot, right at the centre of the tower.

Shiva pulled his horse's reins and turned it right, singing softly in its ear to calm it down. The horse stayed still, offering Shiva the stable base he needed to hit a target. He turned his head to his left, creating the natural angle for a right-handed archer to get a straight shot. He pulled his bow forward and tested the string once again. He liked the twang of the bowstring when it was pulled and released rapidly. It was as taut as it could be. He bent forward and pulled an arrow from the quiver. He held it to his side and looked up, judging the wind.

The art of shooting arrows from this huge distance was all about patience and judgement. It was about waiting for the right wind conditions; the ability to judge the parabolic movement of the arrow; determining the ideal angle of release; controlling the speed of the arrow at release; deciding the extent to which the string should be pulled. Shiva kept his eyes fixed on the windsock, keeping his breathing steady, trying to ignore the burning sensation between his eyes.

The wind is changing direction.

Pointing the bow towards the ground Shiva nocked an arrow, the shaft firmly gripped between his hooked index and middle finger.

The wind is holding.

He ignited the tip by rubbing it against the leather pommel. Taut muscles raised the bow and drew the string in one fluid motion, even as his warrior mind instinctively calculated the correct angle of flight. Master archer that he was, he kept his dominant eye focused on the target. His left hand held the bow rock-steady, ignoring the searing heat from the tip of the arrow.

The wind is perfect.

He released the arrow without hesitation.

He saw the arrow move in a parabola, as if in slow motion. His eyes followed its path till it hit the red target, depressing it with its force. The fire immediately spread to the waiting receptacle behind the target. The *Pashupatiastra's* initial launch had been triggered.

'Ride away!' screamed Tara from the distance.

'*Baba*, turn your horse around!' shouted Kartik.

But Shiva could not hear either of them. They were too far away.

Shiva kept staring at the rapidly spreading fire behind the target; the pain within his brow ratcheting up once again. He felt as if the insides of his forehead were on fire as well, just like the launch tower. He pulled the reins of his horse and turned it around.

He could see his troops far away. Beyond them, he could see his ship, anchored on the Saraswati. Sati's body was stored in there.

She's waiting for me.

Shiva kicked his horse. The animal didn't need much coaxing as it quickly broke into a gallop.

The fire within the launch tower finally triggered the initial explosion. The three *Pashupatiastras* shot out of their pods, the two that were directed at the Tamra and Swarna platforms taking off just a few milliseconds after the third. That was because the target of the third missile, the Rajat platform, was farther away.

Shiva kept kicking his horse as it galloped faster and faster. He was just a few seconds away from the safety line. The missiles flew in a great arc, leaving a trail of fire behind them. Seconds later, they began their simultaneous descent into the city, like giant harbingers of absolute destruction.

'S-H-I-V-A!'

Shiva could have sworn he heard the voice that he loved beyond all reason. But it couldn't have been for real. He kept riding on.

The *Pashupatiastra* missiles were descending rapidly.

'S-H-I-V-A! S-H-I-V-A!'

Shiva looked back.

A bloodied and mutilated Sati was running after him. Her left hand was spewing blood in bursts, in tune with each beat of her pounding heart. Two massive wounds on her abdomen gaped open as blood streamed out from them in a torrent. Her left eye was gouged out. Her burn scar seemed like it was on fire once again. She was struggling desperately, but she kept running towards Shiva.

'S-H-I-V-A! HELP ME! DON'T LEAVE ME!'

An army of soldiers chased Sati, holding bloodied swords aloft. Each warrior was the exact likeness of Daksha. The area between Shiva's brows began throbbing even more desperately. The fire within was struggling to burst through.

'SATI!' screamed Shiva, as he pulled the reins of his horse. He was not going to lose her again.

The horse balked at Shiva's anxious command and refused to slow down.

'SATI!'

Shiva desperately yanked at the reins. But the horse had a mind of its own. He was not going to either slow down or turn. The beast could sense the stench of death behind it.

Shiva pulled both his feet out of the stirrups and jumped to the ground, the speed of his fall making him lurch dangerously. He rolled quickly and was up on his feet in a flash.

'SATI!'

The horse kept galloping ahead towards the safety line as Shiva turned around, drew his sword and ran to protect the mirage of his wife.

'Baba!' shouted Ganesh. 'Come back!'

The blackish-red mark at the centre of Shiva's forehead burst open and blood spewed out. He ran desperately towards his wife, roaring at the army of Dakshas who chased her.

'LEAVE HER ALONE, YOU BASTARDS! FIGHT ME!'

The three *Pashupatiastra* missiles simultaneously exploded as planned, some fifty metres above the three platforms. A blinding burst of light erupted. Shiva's army and the Devagiri refugees shielded their eyes, only to be stunned by what they saw of their own bodies. Glowing and translucent, blood, muscle and even bone were visible. They even saw a demonic flash within their bodies, an echo of the devastating blasts over Devagiri. Sheer terror entered their hearts.

Almost immediately thereafter, three bursts of satanic fire descended from the heights where the three *Pashupatiastras* had exploded. They tore into *Devagiri* fiendishly, instantaneously incinerating all three platforms. The great *City of the Gods*, built and nurtured over centuries, was reduced to nothingness in a fraction of a second.

'Lord Ram, be merciful,' whispered Ayurvati in absolute horror as she saw the massive explosion from aboard the ship that was carrying Sati.

As the fire ripped through Devagiri, giant pillars of smoke shot up from the site of the explosions. As Tara had predicted, the energy blasts of the three missiles seemed to attract each other. All the three pillars of smoke crashed into each other with diabolical rage, as thunder and lightning cracked through the destructive field. The unified pillar of smoke now shot higher; higher than anything that any living creature watching the explosion had ever seen. The smoke column rose like a giant and steeply inclined pyramid and then it exploded into a massive cloud about one kilometre high in the air. And just as instantaneously, the pyramid of smoke collapsed into itself, closeted permanently within the ruins of Devagiri.

Shiva, unmindful of the terrible devastation taking place in front of him, kept running forward, his sword drawn, his brow spouting blood at an alarming rate.

As soon as the pyramid of smoke collapsed, another silent blast occurred. As this blast of neutrons raced out, the sound of the initial explosion reached Shiva's army cowering behind the safety line.

'*Baba!*' screamed Ganesh, as he jumped from the platform he was on and raced towards his horse.

The neutron blast was invisible. Shiva couldn't see it. But he could feel a demonic surge rolling towards him. He had to save his wife. He kept running forward, screaming desperately.

'SATI!'

His body was lifted high by the neutron blast wave. For a moment he felt weightless, and then the wave propelled him back brutally. His brow and throat were on fire, while blood spewed out from his mouth. He landed hard on the ground, flat on his back, his head jerking as he felt a sharp sensation on the crown of his head.

And yet, he felt no pain. He just kept screaming.

'SA...TI...!'

'SA...TI...!'

Suddenly, he saw Sati bending over him. There was no blood on her. No wounds. No scars. She looked just like she had on the day he'd met her, all those years ago at the Brahma temple. She bent forward and ran her hand along Shiva's face, her smiling visage suffused with love and joy; a smile that always set the world right for him.

She touched the crown of Shiva's head. The sharp sensation receded and was replaced by a calm that was difficult to describe. He felt like he had been set free. Strangely, his blue throat was not cold anymore. Equally strange was the realisation that his brow had stopped burning from within.

Shiva opened his mouth, but no sound emerged. So he thought of what he wanted to say.

Take me with you, Sati. There's nothing left for me to do. I'm done.

Sati bent forward and kissed Shiva lightly on his lips. She smiled and whispered, 'No, you are not done yet. Not yet.'

Shiva kept staring at his wife. *I can't live without you...*

'You must,' said Sati's shimmering image.

Shiva couldn't keep his eyes open anymore. Sati's beautiful and calm face began to blur. He collapsed into a peaceful dream-like state. As he was descending the depths of consciousness though, he thought he heard a voice, almost like a command.

'No more killing from now on. Spread life. Spread life.'

Chapter 54

By the Holy Lake

Thirty years later, Mansarovar Lake (at the foot of Mount Kailash, Tibet)

Shiva squatted on the rock that extended over the Mansarovar. Behind him was the Kailash Mountain, each of its four sides perfectly aligned with the four cardinal directions. It stood sentinel over the great Mahadev, the one who had saved India from Evil.

The long years and the tough Tibetan terrain had taken its toll on his body. His matted hair had greyed considerably, though it was still long and wiry enough to be tied in a traditional bun with beads. His body, honed with regular exercise and yoga, was still taut and muscular, but the skin had wrinkled and lost its tone. His *neel kanth,* the *blue throat* had not lost colour at all over the years. But it didn't feel cold anymore. Not since the day he had been hit by the neutron blast from the *Pashupatiastra* that had destroyed Devagiri. The area between his brows didn't burn or throb either; perhaps also due to the neutron blast. But it had taken on a darker hue, almost black, that contrasted sharply with his fair skin. It wasn't an indistinct, indeterminate mark either. It looked like the tattoo of an eye; an eye with the lids shut. Kali had named it Shiva's third eye, which stood vertical on his forehead, between his natural eyes.

Shiva looked across the lake at the setting sun. In the distance he spotted a pair of swans gliding over the shimmering waters. It appeared to Shiva as if the birds beheld the sight together; the setting sun cannot be enjoyed unless shared with the one you love.

He breathed deeply and picked up a pebble. When he was young, he could throw one such that it skipped off the surface of the lake. His record had been seventeen bounces. He flung the pebble, but he failed; it sank immediately into the lake with a plop.

I miss you.

Not a day passed in his life without his mind dwelling on his wife. He wiped a tear from his eye before turning back to look at the bonfires outside his village compound. A large crowd had gathered around the fires, eating, drinking and making merry.

Some members of his Guna tribe had followed him when he had returned to Kailash Mountain many years ago. In addition, nearly ten thousand people from across India had decided to leave their homes and migrate to the homeland of their Mahadev. Chief amongst them were Nandi, Brahaspati, Tara, Parshuram and Ayurvati. The deposed Ayodhyan ruler, Dilipa, who was still alive thanks to Ayurvati's medicines; former Maika-Lothal governor Chenardhwaj and former Naga Prime Minister Karkotak had also migrated to the shores of the Mansarovar. Shiva's followers had established new villages in close proximity to his. Seeing the massive contingent Shiva now commanded, even the Pakratis, the local Tibetans who had maintained a long-standing enmity with the Gunas, had made peace with the Neelkanth.

The fires reminded Shiva of one of the worst days of his life, the day he had destroyed Devagiri. Sati had been cremated on the same day, later on in the evening. But Shiva did not have memories of that event. He had been unconscious, having been battered by the neutron blast of the *Pashupatiastra.* He had been fighting for his life under Ayurvati's care. What he knew about Sati's cremation was from what Kali, Ganesh and Kartik had told him.

He had been told that a calm breeze had blown across the land, picking up the ashes from the ruins of Devagiri and scattering them around slowly. It was almost as if the ashes were trying to reach the waters of the Saraswati, to give some closure to the souls of the departed. Hazy specks had coloured the entire landscape around the Saraswati to a pale shade of grey.

The sandalwood pyre, lit by both Ganesh and Kartik, had taken some time to light, but once it did, it had raged like an inferno. It seemed as if even *Lord Agni*, the *God of Fire*, needed some coaxing to consume the body of the former Princess of Meluha. But once the task had begun, it must have been so painful for Lord Agni that he wanted to finish it as soon as possible.

Shiva had regained consciousness three days later, to find an anxiety-filled gathering of Kali, Ganesh and Kartik sitting next to him. After he had regained his strength, a tearful Ganesh had handed him an urn containing Sati's ashes.

A few drops of water splashed on Shiva, perhaps from a fish swimming vigorously below. They pulled him back from the thirty-year-old memory to the present.

Shiva tarried for some more time, allowing his gaze to dwell on the lake waters. As always, he could have sworn that he saw Sati's ashes swirling in it. Of course, it was a mirage. Her ashes had been immersed in the holy Saraswati, a day after Shiva had regained consciousness.

He remembered struggling weakly onto the boat thirty years ago, helped by Ganesh and Kartik. The Neelkanth had been rowed to the middle of the river, where Kali and he had jointly scattered some of Sati's ashes into the water. Shiva had refused to immerse all of it, regardless of what tradition held. He needed to keep some portion of Sati for himself.

Indians believe that the body is a temporary gift from Mother Earth. She lends it to a living being so that one's soul has an instrument with which to carry out its karma. Once the soul's karma is done, the body must be returned, in a pure form, so that the Mother may use it for another purpose. The ashes represent a human body that has been purified by the greatest purifier of them all: Lord Agni, the God of Fire. By immersing the ashes into holy waters, the body is offered back, with respect, to Mother Earth.

He recalled the Brahmins in an adjacent boat, chanting Sanskrit hymns throughout the ceremony. One specific chant from the *Isha Vasya Upanishad* had caught Shiva's attention and had been committed to memory.

Vayur anilam amritam; Athedam bhasmantam shariram

Let this temporary body be burned to ashes. But the breath of life belongs elsewhere. May it find its way back to the Immortal Breath.

'My Lord!' shouted Nandi loudly.

Shiva turned to see Nandi standing at a distance, two hooks where his arms used to be.

'My Lord, everyone is waiting,' said Nandi, keeping his voice loud enough to reach his ears.

Shiva held his hand up, signalling for Nandi to wait. He needed some more time with his memories. They had sent Nandi to call him as they knew that he had become Shiva's favourite; he had fought bravely alongside Sati thirty years ago, losing both his hands in his doomed attempt to save Shiva's wife.

Shiva glanced beyond Nandi and saw Maharishi Bhrigu, sitting away from the others, talking to Ganesh and Kartik. The sage seemed to be explaining something from a palm-leaf book. Both his sons listened attentively. Chandraketu, the King of Branga and Maatali, the King of Vaishali, were also listening intently to Maharishi Bhrigu.

He looked back towards the lake and took another deep breath.

Kartik saved my honour.

Kartik had chosen the moment wisely to tell Shiva how he had saved the Devagiri scientists who had the knowledge of the Somras. The Neelkanth had received the news with equanimity. Shiva was also happy that Bhrigu had been saved, as the great maharishi had had no role to play in Sati's death. Furthermore, the India of the future would be the proud inheritor of the legacy of his immense knowledge.

Shiva had decreed that the Somras scientists be given lands in central Tibet, far beyond the expanse of Indian empires; in fact, beyond the reach of any empire. The Somras scientists had established their home with the help of Suryavanshi and Chandravanshi troops. These survivors named their new dwelling place after their original city, *Devagiri*, the *Abode of the Gods*. This new city established in Tibet was given a name with the same meaning, albeit in the local Tibetan language: Lhasa. The knowledge of the Somras, the elixir of immortality, was to be the sacred secret of the citizens of Lhasa, till such a time as India needed that knowledge again.

Shiva had also decreed that his two sons would set up the tribe that would protect Lhasa. The tribe that Ganesh and Kartik established was drawn from an eclectic mix of Chandravanshis, Suryavanshis and Nagas. They had also inducted most of the Gunas, Shiva's tribesmen, and many other local Tibetan tribes. Veerbhadra, Shiva's friend and loyal follower, was appointed chief of this tribe. He was given the title of Lama, the Tibetan word for guru or master. The people of Lhasa and the followers of the Lama would protect India's ancient knowledge. Their sworn duty was to rise up and save India whenever it faced the onslaught of Evil again.

The Somras waste dump site that had been set up in Tibet, on the Tsangpo River, was dug out and its contents were removed. This waste was taken farther north, into an inhospitable, remote and mostly uninhabited part of the Tibetan plateau. It was buried there, deep into the ground, enclosed within sludgy cases made of wet clay and bilva leaves, which were further encased within boxes of thick lead. These boxes had been buried deep under vast quantities of earth, snow and permafrost. It was hoped that this poison would remain undisturbed forever. Fortunately, there would be no new toxic waste to be taken care of since the manufacturing of Somras had stopped with the destruction of Devagiri.

Shiva had also realised that, just removing the knowledge of the *Somras* was not enough to stop the *drink of the Gods*. If it had to be wiped out from India, its very foundation needed uprooting. In that sense, the idea that Parshuram had had was sound: without the Saraswati, the Somras couldn't be manufactured. Furthermore, the river's present course was picking up radioactive waste at Devagiri and poisoning the lands farther downstream. The Saraswati emerged from the confluence of the Sutlej and the Yamuna. If these two tributaries were separated, the Saraswati water itself would not be available for the manufacture of the Somras or for picking up radioactive waste.

Shiva had decided that, in the interest of India, the Sutlej and the Yamuna would part company forever. It was decreed that the Yamuna's course would be changed once again, back to the temporary course that it had taken more than a century before the destruction of Devagiri, when it had merged into the Ganga. But this was easier said than done. If the course of a river as mighty as the Yamuna was changed suddenly, the resultant flooding would cause havoc. The change had to be controlled.

Bhagirath, with the help of Meluhan engineers, had come up with a brilliant plan. The sides of the Yamuna were dug up and giant sluice gates were built along them. These gates, serving as locks, would be opened slowly to guide the Yamuna onto its new course in a deliberate and controlled manner, over many months. Bhagirath had named these sluice gates the 'Locks of Shiva'. The Yamuna was thus slowly diverted onto its new course, to unite with the Ganga at Prayag. The Locks of Shiva had thereby allowed the Ganga to take its new form, gradually, without the chaos of an uncontrolled flood.

The addition of the massive Yamuna, along with the already worthy presence of the enormous Brahmaputra, had enhanced the mighty Ganga into the biggest river system in India. It also came to be believed that the Yamuna carried the soul of the Saraswati into the Ganga, thus transforming it into the holiest river in India. In a sense, the devotion associated with the hallowed river Saraswati had been transferred onto the Ganga. Furthermore, the burst of fresh clean water from the Yamuna had cleansed the poisonous waters in Branga, freeing the great rivers in that land of the Somras poison. The Brangas living at Gangasagar, the place where the resurgent Ganga met the sea, began to believe in a legend over time: that the Ganga had purified their land. It was a myth that was not far from the truth.

Meluha, without the centralising presence of Devagiri, had devolved into its different provinces which became independent kingdoms. Without the incompetent rule of

Daksha and with the fresh breath of freedom, there had been a burst of creativity and an efflorescence of varied but equally beautiful cultures.

Shiva heard a loud laugh, which he knew could belong only to Bhagirath. He turned and looked at him, standing near a bonfire, talking animatedly to Gopal and Kali. Dilipa had been deposed by his army before the destruction of Devagiri. He was succeeded by Bhagirath, who had ruled Ayodhya wisely, heralding a new era of peace and prosperity. Judging by the expression on Dilipa's face as he stood close to Bhagirath, the former emperor seemed to have made peace with his fate.

Shiva turned his attention to the tall, lanky figure speaking with Bhagirath and Kali. The great Vasudev perhaps sensed that somebody was looking at him. He turned to look at Shiva, smiled, folded his hands into a Namaste and bowed low. Shiva returned Gopal's greeting with a formal Namaste. Gopal had made his peace with Shiva.

The outcome at Devagiri was certainly not what the Vasudev chief had desired. But what had given him peace was the realisation that Evil had been removed and the knowledge of the Somras saved. India had rejuvenated itself as the malevolent effects of Evil were removed. The Neelkanth had succeeded in his mission, and in that lay the success of the Vasudevs. Gopal had also established formal relations with Veerbhadra and the citizens of Lhasa, the new tribe of the Mahadev. The Vasudevs and the Lhasans would maintain their watch over India in tandem, ensuring that this divine land continued to prosper and grow with balance.

Seeing his friend Gopal also reminded Shiva of the Vayuputras. They had never forgiven Shiva for having used the *Pashupatiastra.* It had been a source of particular embarrassment for the Mithra since he had personally backed the announcement of Shiva as the Neelkanth, against some virulent opposition. The punishment for the unauthorised use of a *daivi astra* was a fourteen-year exile. As a form of atonement for breaking his word to them, and for having been the cause of the death of his mother-in-law Veerini and his friends Parvateshwar and Anandmayi, Shiva had punished himself with exile from India; not just for fourteen years, but for the entire duration of his remaining life.

'*Baba...*'

Shiva hadn't noticed Ganesh, Kartik and Kali sneak up on him.

'Yes, Ganesh?'

'*Baba*, it's the feast of the Night of the Mahadev,' said Ganesh. 'And the Mahadev needs to be a part of the celebration instead of brooding next to the lake.'

Shiva nodded slowly. His neck had begun to hurt a bit; the perils of old age.

'Help me up,' said Shiva, as he made an effort to rise.

Kartik and Ganesh immediately leaned forward, helping their father to his feet.

'Ganesh, you get fatter every time I see you.'

Ganesh laughed heartily. He had suffered intensely and taken a long time to recover from his mother's death, but had ultimately reconciled himself with that loss, choosing to learn from her life instead. He had taken it upon himself to spread the word of Shiva and Sati throughout India. That sense of purpose in his life had helped him return to his calm state of being; in fact, he was even jovial at times.

'Thanks to your wisdom, peace prevails all over India, *baba*,' said Ganesh. 'There are no more wars, no conflicts. So I do very little physical activity and eat a lot. Ultimately, the way I see it, it's your fault that I'm getting fatter.'

Kali and Kartik laughed loudly. Shiva nodded faintly, his eyes not losing their seriousness.

'You should smile sometimes, *baba*,' said Kartik. 'It will make us happy.'

Shiva stared at Kartik. It had been a long time since Sati's death, and even young Kartik was now beginning to acquire a smattering of white hair. Shiva knew that Kartik had travelled a very long distance to come to Kailash. After most of Shiva's tasks had been completed and he had decided to return to Kailash-Mansarovar, Kartik had migrated to the south of the Narmada, going deep into the ancient heartland of India; the land of Lord Manu.

History had recorded that Lord Manu was a prince of the Pandya dynasty. This dynasty had ruled the prehistoric land of Sangamtamil. That nation and its fine Sangam culture had been destroyed as sea levels had risen with the end of the last Ice Age. Kartik had discovered that many people continued to live in this ancient Indian fatherland, breaking Lord Manu's law that banned people from travelling south of the Narmada. Kartik had established a new Sangam culture on the banks of the southern-most major river of India, the Kaveri.

'I will smile when the three of you will reveal your secret,' said Shiva.

'What secret?' asked Kartik.

'You know what I'm talking about.'

Shiva did discover in due course that on the night before the destruction of Devagiri, Kali, Parshuram and Veerbhadra had kidnapped Vidyunmali. Under pain of vicious torture, Vidyunmali had revealed the names of Sati's assassins. He had then been tormented with a brutal and slow death.

A few years after the destruction of Devagiri, Kali, Ganesh, Kartik, Parshuram and Veerbhadra had slipped out of India. Nobody really knew where they had disappeared. They had consistently refused to tell Shiva, perhaps because he had prohibited any further reprisals for Sati's death. But Shiva had his suspicions...

Those suspicions were not unfounded, because around the same time, rumours had arisen in Egypt about the near complete destruction of the secretive tribe of Aten. It was said that the death of each of the tribe's leaders had been long, slow and painful, their blood-curdling screams echoing through the hearts of their followers. What Kali and the rest didn't know was that a few months earlier Swuth had exiled himself. He had gone south, to the source of the Nile River, and had spent the rest of his years bemoaning the fact that he had been unable to complete his holy duty of executing the final kill. But the magnificence of Sati had been branded upon his soul. He didn't know her name. So he worshipped her as a nameless Goddess till his last days. His descendants continued the tradition. The few remaining survivors of the tribe of Aten would have to wait for centuries before a revolutionary Pharaoh, the ruler of Egypt, reformed and revived the cult. That Pharaoh would be remembered as the great Akhenaten, the living spirit of Aten. But that is another story.

'*Baba*, we had gone to...'

Kali placed her hand on Kartik's lips. 'There's nothing to reveal, Shiva. Except that the food is extremely delicious. You need to eat. So follow me.'

Shiva shook his head. 'You still haven't lost your regal airs.'

Kali didn't have a kingdom anymore. Within a few years of her return from Egypt, she had renounced her throne and supported the election of Suparna as the new queen of the Nagas. Leaving her kingdom in capable hands, Kali, accompanied by Shiva, Ganesh and Kartik, had toured the land of India. The family of the Neelkanth had established fifty-one Shakti temples across the length and breadth of the country. Kali had also convinced Shiva to part with the portion of Sati's ashes that he had kept for himself. She had told him that Sati belonged to the whole of India and not just to Shiva. Therefore, small portions of Sati's ashes were consecrated at each of these fifty-one temples so that Indians would forever remember their great Goddess, Lady Sati.

Kali had finally settled down in north-eastern Branga, close to the Kamakhya temple, and devoted her life to prayer. Her spiritual presence had made the Kamakhya temple one of the foremost Shakti temples in India. Many Suryavanshis, Chandravanshis and Nagas who were inspired by the Naga queen, had followed her to her new abode. Over time, they set up their own individual kingdoms. The Suryavanshis had named their kingdom *Tripura*, the *Land of the Three Cities,* after the three platforms of their destroyed capital. The Chandravanshis, worshippers of the seventh Vishnu, Lord Ram, had called their land *Manipur*, the *Land of the Jewel*; for the seventh Vishnu was, no doubt, a crown jewel of India. Many of Kali's Naga followers established their own empire farther to the east. All of these different peoples followed the path of Kali; proud warriors forged from the womb of Mother India. Therefore, if treated with respect, these people would be your greatest strength. If you disrespected them, then no power on earth would be able to save you.

'I may not have a kingdom anymore, Shiva,' said Kali, her eyes dancing with mirth, 'but I will always be a queen!'

Ganesh and Kartik smiled broadly. Shiva just stared at Kali's face, a splitting image of Sati's; it reminded him of how happy his life had once been.

'Come, let's go eat,' said Shiva.

As the family of the Mahadev walked back towards the bonfires, Ganesh and Kartik started speaking to Shiva about the brilliant composition that Bhrigu had just shown them; it would be known over the millennia as the greatest classic on the ancient science of astrology, the *Bhrigu Samhita*.

Over the subsequent years, Shiva became increasingly ascetic. He began spending many days, even months, in isolation within the claustrophobic confines of mountain caves, performing severe penance. The only one allowed to meet him at such times was Nandi. Legends emerged that the only way to reach Shiva's ears was through Nandi.

Shiva also devoted long hours to the study of yoga. The knowledge that he developed helped create a powerful tool for finding physical, mental and spiritual peace through unity with the divine. Shiva also added many fresh thoughts and philosophies to the immense body of ancient Indian knowledge and wisdom. Many of his ideas were captured in the holy scriptures of the *Vedas, Upanishads* and the *Puranas*, benefiting humanity for millennia.

Notwithstanding the prodigious productivity of Shiva's mind, his heart never really found happiness ever again. Legend has it that despite repeated attempts by his family, nobody ever saw Shiva smile again after that terrible day in Devagiri. Nobody saw his ethereal dances or heard his soulful singing and music again. Shiva had given up everything that offered even a remote possibility of bringing him happiness. But legends also hold that Shiva did smile once, just once, only a moment before he was to leave his mortal body to merge once again with the God whom he had emerged from. He smiled, for he knew that the love of his life, his Sati, was just one last breath away.

Kartik's wisdom and courage ensured that the Sangam culture in South India continued to flourish and its power spread far and wide. While Kartik continued to be adored in northern India, especially in Kashi where he was born, his influence in southern India was beyond compare. He is remembered to this day as the Warrior God, the one who can solve any problem and defeat any enemy.

Meanwhile, the adoration for Kartik's elder brother, the wise and kind-hearted Ganesh, grew to astronomical heights in India. People revered him as a living God. A belief spread throughout the country that he should be the first God to be worshipped in all ceremonies, before all others. It was held that worshipping Ganesh would remove all obstacles from one's path. Thus, he came to be known as the God of Auspicious Beginnings. His profound intellect also led to him gradually becoming the God of Writers; thus his name acquired immense significance for authors, poets and other troubled souls.

The Somras had had an especially strong effect on Ganesh, so he lived for centuries, beyond all his contemporaries. And Ganesh did not mind this. He loved interacting with people from across India, helping them, guiding them. But there did come a time when, enfeebled by old age, Ganesh began to think that perhaps he had lived in this mortal body for too long.

For he would have to suffer the mortification of seeing the ancient Vedic Indians turn on each other in a catastrophic civil war. A minor dispute within a dysfunctional royal family escalated into a mighty conflict which sucked in all the great powers of the day. The calamitous blood-letting in that war destroyed not just all the powerful empires of the time but also the way of life of the ancient Vedic Indians. What was left behind was utter devastation. From these ruins, as is its wont, civilisation did rise again. But this new culture had lost too much. They knew only snippets of the greatness of their ancestors. The descendants were, in many ways, unworthy.

These descendants beheld Gods in what were great men

of the past, for they believed that such great men couldn't possibly have existed in reality. These descendants saw magic in what was brilliant science, for their limited intellect could not understand that great knowledge. These descendants retained only rituals of what were deep philosophies, for it took courage and confidence to ask questions. These descendants divined myths in what was really history, for true memories were forgotten in chaos as vast arrays of *daivi astras* used in the Great War ravaged the land. That war destroyed almost everything. It took centuries for India to regain its old cultural vigour and intellectual depth.

When the recreated history of that Great War was written, built through fragments of surviving information, the treatise was initially called *Jaya* or *victory*. But even the unsophisticated minds of the descendants soon realised that this name was inappropriate. That dreadful war did not bring victory to anyone. Every single person who fought that war, lost the war. In fact, the whole of India lost.

Today, we know the inherited tale of that war as one of the world's greatest epics: *The Mahabharat*. If the Lord Neelkanth allows it, the unadulterated story of that terrible war shall also be told one day.

Om Namah Shivāya
The universe bows to Lord Shiva. I bow to Lord Shiva.

Glossary

Agni: God of fire

Agniparikisha: A trial by fire

Angaharas: Movement of limbs or steps in a dance

Ankush: Hook-shaped prods used to control elephants

Annapurna: The Hindu Goddess of food, nourishment and plenty; also believed to be a form of Goddess Parvati

Anshan: Hunger. It also denotes voluntary fasting. In this book, Anshan is the capital of the kingdom of Elam

Apsara: Celestial maidens from the court of the Lord of the Heavens – Indra; akin to Zeus/Jupiter

Arya: Sir

Ashwamedh yagna: Literally, the Horse sacrifice. In ancient times, an ambitious ruler, who wished to expand his territories and display his military prowess, would release a sacrificial horse to roam freely through the length and breadth of any kingdom in India. If any king stopped/captured the horse, the ruler's army would declare war against the challenger, defeat the king and annexe that territory. If an opposing king did not stop the horse, the kingdom would become a vassal of the former

Asura: Demon

Ayuralay: Hospital
Ayurvedic: Derived from Ayurved, an ancient Indian form of medicine
Ayushman bhav: May you have a long life
Baba: Father
Bhang: Traditional intoxicant in India; milk mixed with marijuana
Bhiksha: Alms or donations
Bhojan graham: Dining room
Brahmacharya: The vow of celibacy
Brahmastra: Literally, the weapon of Brahma; spoken of in ancient Hindu scriptures. Many experts claim that the description of a Brahmastra and its effects are eerily similar to that of a nuclear weapon. I have assumed this to be true in the context of my book
Branga: The ancient name for modern West Bengal, Assam and Bangladesh. Term coined from the conjoint of the two rivers of this land: *Bra*hmaputra and Ga*nga*
Brangaridai: Literally, the heart of Branga. The capital of the kingdom of Branga
Chandravanshi: Descendants of the moon
Chaturanga: Ancient Indian game that evolved into the modern game of chess
Chillum: Clay pipe, usually used to smoke marijuana
Choti: Braid
Construction of Devagiri royal court platform: The description in the book of the court platform is a possible explanation for the mysterious multiple-column buildings made of baked brick discovered at Indus Valley sites, usually next to the public baths, which many historians suppose could have been granaries
Dada: Elder brother

Daivi Astra: Daivi = Divine; Astra = Weapon. A term used in ancient Hindu epics to describe weapons of mass destruction

Dandakaranya: Aranya = forest. Dandak is the ancient name for modern Maharashtra and parts of Andhra Pradesh, Karnataka, Chhattisgarh and Madhya Pradesh. So Dandakaranya means the forests of Dandak

Deva: God

Dharma: Dharma literally translates as religion. But in traditional Hindu belief, it means far more than that. The word encompasses holy, right knowledge, right living, tradition, natural order of the universe and duty. Essentially, dharma refers to everything that can be classified as 'good' in the universe. It is the Law of Life

Dharmayudh: The holy war

Dhobi: Washerman

Divyadrishti: Divine sight

Dumru: A small, hand-held, hour-glass shaped percussion instrument

Egyptian women: Historians believe that ancient Egyptians, just like ancient Indians, treated their women with respect. The anti-women attitude attributed to Swuth and the assassins of Aten is fictional. Having said that, like most societies, ancient Egyptians also had some patriarchal segments in their society, which did, regrettably, have an appalling attitude towards women

Fire song: This is a song sung by Guna warriors to agni (fire). They also had songs dedicated to the other elements viz: *bhūmi* (earth), *jal* (water), *pavan* (air or wind), *vyom* or *shunya* or *akash* (ether or void or sky)

Fravashi: Is the guardian spirit mentioned in the *Avesta*, the sacred writings of the Zoroastrian religion. Although, according to most researchers, there is no physical description of Fravashi, the language grammar of *Avesta* clearly shows it to be feminine. Considering the importance given to fire in ancient Hinduism and Zoroastrianism, I've assumed the Fravashi to be represented by fire. This is, of course, a fictional representation

Ganesh-Kartik relationship: In northern India, traditional myths hold Lord Kartik as older than Lord Ganesh; in large parts of southern India, Lord Ganesh is considered elder. In my story, Ganesh is older than Kartik. What is the truth? Only Lord Shiva knows

Guruji: Teacher; ji is a term of respect, added to a name or title

Gurukul: The family of the guru or the family of the teacher. In ancient times, also used to denote a school

Har Har Mahadev: This is the rallying cry of Lord Shiva's devotees. I believe it means 'All of us are Mahadevs'

Hariyupa: This city is currently known as Harappa. A note on the cities of Meluha (or as we call it in modern times, the Indus Valley Civilisation): historians and researchers have consistently marvelled at the fixation that the Indus Valley Civilisation seemed to have for water and hygiene. In fact historian M Jansen used the term 'wasserluxus' (obsession with water) to describe their magnificent obsession with the physical and symbolic aspects

of water, a term Gregory Possehl builds upon in his brilliant book, *The Indus Civilisation — A Contemporary Perspective.* In the book, *The Immortals of Meluha*, the obsession with water is shown to arise due to its cleansing of the toxic sweat and urine triggered by consuming the Somras. Historians have also marvelled at the level of sophisticated standardisation in the Indus Valley Civilisation. One of the examples of this was the bricks, which across the entire civilisation, had similar proportions and specifications

Holi: Festival of colours

Howdah: Carriage placed on top of elephants

Indra: The God of the sky; believed to be the King of the Gods

Jai Guru Vishwamitra: Glory to the teacher Vishwamitra

Jai Guru Vashishtha: Glory to the teacher Vashishtha. Only two Suryavanshis were privileged to have had both Guru Vashishtha and Guru Vishwamitra as their gurus (teachers) viz. Lord Ram and Lord Lakshman

Jai Shri Brahma: Glory to Lord Brahma

Jai Shri Ram: Glory to Lord Ram

Janau: A ceremonial thread tied from the shoulders, across the torso. It was one of the symbols of knowledge in ancient India. Later, it was corrupted to become a caste symbol to denote those born as Brahmins and not those who'd acquired knowledge through their effort and deeds

Ji: A suffix added to a name or title as a form of respect

Kajal: Kohl, or eye liner

Karma: Duty and deeds; also the sum of a person's actions in this and previous births,

considered to limit the options of future action and affect future fate

Karmasaathi: Fellow traveller in karma or duty

Kashi: The ancient name for modern Varanasi. Kashi means the city where the supreme light shines

Kathak: A form of traditional Indian dance

Kriyas: Actions

Kulhads: Mud cups

Maa: Mother

Mandal: Literally, Sanskrit word meaning circle. Mandals are created, as per ancient Hindu and Buddhist tradition, to make a sacred space and help focus the attention of the devotees

Mahadev: Maha = Great and Dev = God. Hence Mahadev means the greatest God or the God of Gods. I believe that there were many 'destroyers of evil' but a few of them were so great that they would be called 'Mahadev'. Amongst the Mahadevs were Lord Rudra and Lord Shiva

Mahasagar: Great Ocean; Hind Mahasagar is the Indian Ocean

Mahendra: Ancient Indian name meaning conqueror of the world

Mahout: Human handler of elephants

Manu's story: Those interested in finding out more about the historical validity of the South India origin theory of Manu should read Graham Hancock's pathbreaking book, *Underworld*

Mausi: Mother's sister, literally translating as *maa si* i.e. like a mother

Maya: Illusion

Mehragarh: Modern archaeologists believe that Mehragarh is the progenitor of the Indus

Valley civilisation. Mehragarh represents a sudden burst of civilised living, without any archaeological evidence of a gradual progression to that level. Hence, those who established Mehragarh were either immigrants or refugees

Meluha: The land of pure life. This is the land ruled by the Suryavanshi kings. It is the area that we in the modern world call the Indus Valley Civilisation

Meluhans: People of Meluha

Mudras: Gestures

Naga: Serpent people

Namaste: An ancient Indian greeting. Spoken along with the hand gesture of open palms of both the hands joined together. Conjoin of three words. 'Namah', 'Astu' and 'Te' – meaning 'I bow to the Godhood in you'. Namaste can be used as both 'hello' and 'goodbye'

Nirvana: Enlightenment; freedom from the cycle of rebirths

Oxygen/ anti-oxidants theory: Modern research backs this theory. Interested readers can read the article 'Radical Proposal' by Kathryn Brown in the *Scientific American*

Panchavati: The land of the five banyan trees

Pandit: Priest

Paradaeza: An ancient Persian word which means 'the walled place of harmony'; the root of the English word, Paradise

Pariha: The land of fairies. Refers to modern Persia/Iran. I believe Lord Rudra came from this land

Parmatma: The ultimate soul or the sum of all souls

Parsee immigration to India: Groups of Zoroastrian refugees immigrated to India perhaps between the 8th and 10th century AD to escape religious persecution. They landed in Gujarat, and the local ruler Jadav Rana gave them refuge

Pashupatiastra: Literally, the weapon of the Lord of the Animals. The descriptions of the effects of the Pashupatiastra in Hindu scriptures are quite similar to that of nuclear weapons. In modern nuclear technology, weapons have been built primarily on the concept of nuclear fission. While fusion-boosted fission weapons have been invented, pure fusion weapons have not been invented as yet. Scientists hold that a pure nuclear fusion weapon has far less radioactive fallout and can theoretically serve as a more targeted weapon. In this trilogy, I have assumed that the Pashupatiastra is one such weapon

Patallok: The underworld

Pawan Dev: God of the winds

Pitratulya: The term for a man who is 'like a father'

Prahar: Four slots of six hours each into which the day was divided by the ancient Hindus; the first prahar began at twelve midnight

Prithvi: Earth

Prakrati: Nature

Puja: Prayer

Puja thali: Prayer tray

Raj dharma: Literally, the royal duties of a king or ruler. In ancient India, this term embodied pious and just administration of the king's royal duties

Raj guru: Royal sage

Rajat: Silver

Rajya Sabha: The royal council

Rakshabandhan: Raksha = Protection; Bandhan = thread/tie. An ancient Indian festival in which a sister ties a sacred thread on her brother's wrist, seeking his protection

Ram Chandra: Ram = Face; Chandra = Moon. Hence Ram Chandra is 'the face of the moon'

Ram Rajya: The rule of Ram

Rangbhoomi: Literally, the ground of colour. Stadia in ancient times where sports, performances and public functions would be staged

Rangoli: Traditional colourful and geometric designs made with coloured powders or flowers as a sign of welcome

Rishi: Man of knowledge

Sankat Mochan: Literally, reliever from troubles. One of the names of Lord Hanuman

Sangam: A confluence of two rivers

Sanyasi: A person who renounces all his worldly possessions and desires to retreat to remote locations and devote his time to the pursuit of God and spirituality. In ancient India, it was common for people to take sanyas at an old age, once they had completed all their life's duties

Sapt Sindhu: Land of the seven rivers – Indus, Saraswati, Yamuna, Ganga, Sarayu, Brahmaputra and Narmada. This was the ancient name of North India

Saptrishi: One of the 'Group of seven Rishis'

Saptrishi Uttradhikari: Successors of the Saptrishis

Shakti Devi: Mother Goddess; also Goddess of power and energy

Shamiana: Canopy

Shloka: Couplet

Shudhikaran: The purification ceremony

Sindhu: The first river
Somras: Drink of the Gods
Sundarban: Sundar = beautiful; ban = forest. Hence, Sundarban means beautiful forest
Svarna: Gold
Swadweep: The Island of the individual. This is the land ruled by the Chandravanshi kings
Swadweepans: People of Swadweep
Swaha: Legend has it that Lord Agni's wife is named Swaha. Hence it pleases Lord Agni, the God of Fire, if a disciple takes his wife's name while worshipping the sacred fire. Another interpretation of Swaha is that it means offering of self
Tamra: Bronze
Thali: Plate
Varjish graha: The exercise hall
Varun: God of the water and the seas
Vijayibhav: May you be victorious
Vikarma: Carrier of bad fate
Vishnu: The protector of the world and propagator of good. I believe that it is an ancient Hindu title for the greatest of leaders who would be remembered as the mightiest of Gods
Vishwanath: Literally, the Lord of the World. Usually refers to Lord Shiva, also known as Lord Rudra in his angry avatar. I believe Lord Rudra was a different individual from Lord Shiva. In this trilogy, I have used the term Vishwanath to refer to Lord Rudra
Yagna: Sacrificial fire ceremony

Other Titles by Amish

The Shiva Trilogy

The fastest-selling book series in the history of Indian publishing

THE IMMORTALS OF MELUHA
(Book 1 of the Trilogy)

1900 BC. What modern Indians mistakenly call the Indus Valley Civilisation, the inhabitants of that period knew as the land of Meluha – a near perfect empire created many centuries earlier by Lord Ram. Now their primary river Saraswati is drying, and they face terrorist attacks from their enemies from the east. Will their prophesied hero, the Neelkanth, emerge to destroy evil?

THE SECRET OF THE NAGAS
(Book 2 of the Trilogy)

The sinister Naga warrior has killed his friend Brahaspati and now stalks his wife Sati. Shiva, who is the prophesied destroyer of evil, will not rest till he finds his demonic adversary. His thirst for revenge will lead him to the door of the Nagas, the serpent people. Fierce battles will be fought and unbelievable secrets revealed in the second part of the Shiva trilogy.

Indic Chronicles

LEGEND OF SUHELDEV

Repeated attacks by Mahmud of Ghazni have weakened India's northern regions. Then the Turks raid and destroy one of the holiest temples in the land: the magnificent Lord Shiva temple at Somnath. At this most desperate of times, a warrior rises to defend the nation. Read this epic adventure of courage and heroism that recounts the story of King Suheldev and the magnificent Battle of Bahraich.

www.authoramish.com

The Ram Chandra Series

The second fastest-selling book series in the history of Indian publishing

RAM – SCION OF IKSHVAKU
(Book 1 of the Series)

He loves his country and he stands alone for the law. His band of brothers, his wife, Sita, and the fight against the darkness of chaos. He is Prince Ram. Will he rise above the taint that others heap on him? Will his love for Sita sustain him through his struggle? Will he defeat the demon Raavan who destroyed his childhood? Will he fulfil the destiny of the Vishnu? Begin an epic journey with Amish's latest: the Ram Chandra Series.

SITA – WARRIOR OF MITHILA
(Book 2 of the Series)

An abandoned baby is found in a field. She is adopted by the ruler of Mithila, a powerless kingdom ignored by all. Nobody believes this child will amount to much. But they are wrong. For she is no ordinary girl. She is Sita. Through an innovative multi-linear narrative, Amish takes you deeper into the epic world of the Ram Chandra Series.

RAAVAN – ENEMY OF ARYAVARTA
(Book 3 of the Series)

Raavan is determined to be a giant among men, to conquer, plunder, and seize the greatness that he thinks is his right. He is a man of contrasts, of brutal violence and scholarly knowledge. A man who will love without reward and kill without remorse. In this, the third book in the Ram Chandra Series, Amish sheds light on Raavan, the king of Lanka. Is he the greatest villain in history or just a man in a dark place, all the time?

www.authoramish.com

Non-fiction

IMMORTAL INDIA

Explore India with the country's storyteller, Amish, who helps you understand it like never before, through a series of sharp articles, nuanced speeches and intelligent debates. In *Immortal India*, Amish lays out the vast landscape of an ancient culture with a fascinatingly modern outlook.

DHARMA – DECODING THE EPICS FOR A MEANINGFUL LIFE

In this genre-bending book, the first of a series, Amish and Bhavna dive into the priceless treasure trove of the ancient Indian epics, as well as the vast and complex universe of Amish's Meluha, to explore some of the key concepts of Indian philosophy. Within this book are answers to our many philosophical questions, offered through simple and wise interpretations of our favourite stories.

The Secret of the Nagas

Amish is a 1974-born, IIM (Kolkata)-educated banker-turned-author. The success of his debut book, *The Immortals of Meluha* (Book 1 of the Shiva Trilogy), encouraged him to give up his career in financial services to focus on writing. Besides being an author, he is also an Indian-government diplomat, a host for TV documentaries, and a film producer.

Amish is passionate about history, mythology and philosophy, finding beauty and meaning in all world religions. His books have sold more than 6 million copies and have been translated into over 20 languages. His Shiva Trilogy is the fastest selling and his Ram Chandra Series the second fastest selling book series in Indian publishing history. You can connect with Amish here:

- www.facebook.com/authoramish
- www.instagram.com/authoramish
- www.twitter.com/authoramish

Other Titles by Amish

SHIVA TRILOGY

The fastest-selling book series in the history of Indian publishing

The Immortals of Meluha (Book 1 of the Trilogy)

The Oath of the Vayuputras (Book 3 of the Trilogy)

RAM CHANDRA SERIES

The second fastest-selling book series in the history of Indian publishing

Ram – Scion of Ikshvaku (Book 1 of the Series)

Sita – Warrior of Mithila (Book 2 of the Series)

Raavan – Enemy of Aryavarta (Book 3 of the Series)

War of Lanka (Book 4 in the Series)

INDIC CHRONICLES

Legend of Suheldev

NON-FICTION

Immortal India: Young Country, Timeless Civilisation

Dharma: Decoding the Epics for a Meaningful Life

www.authoramish.com

'{Amish's} writings have generated immense curiosity about India's rich past and culture.'

– Narendra Modi
(Honourable Prime Minister, India)

'{Amish's} writing introduces the youth to ancient value systems while pricking and satisfying their curiosity…'

– Sri Sri Ravi Shankar
(Spiritual Leader & Founder, Art of Living Foundation)

'{Amish's writing is} riveting, absorbing and informative.'

– Amitabh Bachchan
(Actor & Living Legend)

'{Amish's writing is} a fine blend of history and myth...gripping and unputdownable.'

– BBC

'Thoughtful and deep, Amish, more than any author, represents the New India.'

– Vir Sanghvi
(Senior Journalist & Columnist)

'Amish's mythical imagination mines the past and taps into the possibilities of the future. His book series, archetypal and stirring, unfolds the deepest recesses of the soul as well as our collective consciousness.'

– Deepak Chopra
(World-renowned spiritual guru and bestselling author)

'{Amish is} one of the most original thinkers of his generation.'

– *Arnab Goswami*

(Senior Journalist & MD, Republic TV)

'Amish has a fine eye for detail and a compelling narrative style.'

– *Dr. Shashi Tharoor*

(Member of Parliament & Author)

'{Amish has} a deeply thoughtful mind with an unusual, original, and fascinating view of the past.'

– *Shekhar Gupta*

(Senior Journalist & Columnist)

'To understand the New India, you need to read Amish.'

– *Swapan Dasgupta*

(Member of Parliament & Senior Journalist)

'Through all of Amish's books flows a current of liberal progressive ideology: about gender, about caste, about discrimination of any kind… He is the only Indian bestselling writer with true philosophical depth – his books are all backed by tremendous research and deep thought.'

– *Sandipan Deb*

(Senior Journalist & Editorial Director, Swarajya)

'Amish's influence goes beyond his books, his books go beyond literature, his literature is steeped in philosophy, which is anchored in bhakti, which powers his love for India.'

– *Gautam Chikermane*

(Senior Journalist & Author)

'Amish is a literary phenomenon.'

– *Anil Dharker*

(Senior Journalist & Author)

www.authoramish.com

The Secret of the Nagas

Book 2
of the
Shiva Trilogy

Amish

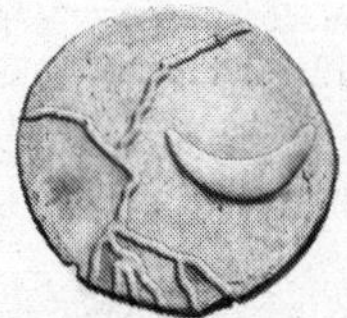

HarperCollins *Publishers* India

www.authoramish.com

First published in 2011

This edition published in India by HarperCollins *Publishers* 2022
4th Floor, Tower A, Building No. 10, Phase II, DLF Cyber City,
Gurugram, Haryana – 122002
www.harpercollins.co.in

2 4 6 8 10 9 7 5 3 1

Copyright © Amish Tripathi 2011, 2022

P-ISBN: 978-93-5629-060-0
E-ISBN: 978-93-5629-067-9

This is a work of fiction and all characters and incidents described in this book are the product of the author's imagination. Any resemblance to actual persons, living or dead, is entirely coincidental.

Amish Tripathi asserts the moral right
to be identified as the author of this work.

All rights reserved. No part of this publication may be reproduced, stored in a retrieval system, or transmitted, in any form or by any means, electronic, mechanical, photocopying, recording or otherwise, without the prior permission of the publishers.

Typeset by by Ram Das Lal

Printed and bound at
Thomson Press (India) Ltd

This book is produced from independently certified FSC® paper
to ensure responsible forest management.

To Preeti & Neel...

Unlucky are those who search the seven seas for paradise,

Fortunate are those who experience the only
heaven that truly exists,

The heaven that lives in the company of our loved ones

I am truly fortunate

www.authoramish.com

Satyam Shivam Sundaram

Shiva is truth. Shiva is beauty

Shiva is the masculine. Shiva is the feminine

Shiva is a Suryavanshi. Shiva is a Chandravanshi

www.authoramish.com

Contents

Acknowledgements

The acknowledgments written below were composed when the book was published in 2011. I must also acknowledge those that are publishing this edition of **The Secret of the Nagas**. *The team at HarperCollins: Swati, Shabnam, Akriti, Gokul, Vikas, Rahul, and Udayan, led by the brilliant Ananth. Looking forward to this new journey with them.*

***

The first book of the Shiva Trilogy, *The Immortals of Meluha*, was surprisingly well received. To be honest, I felt the pressure of trying to match up to the first book with *The Secret of the Nagas*. I don't know if I have succeeded. But I have had a great time bringing the second chapter in Shiva's grand adventure to you. I would like to take a minute to acknowledge those who made this journey possible for me.

Lord Shiva, my God, my Leader, my Saviour. I have been trying to decipher why He blessed an undeserving person like me with this beautiful story. I don't have an answer as yet.

My father-in-law and a devoted Shiva Bhakt, the late Dr Manoj Vyas, who passed away just a few months before the release of this book. A man I intensely admired, he continues to live in my heart.

Preeti, my wife. The bedrock of my life. My closest advisor. Not just the wind beneath my wings, but the wings themselves.

My family: Usha, Vinay, Bhavna, Himanshu, Meeta, Anish, Donetta, Ashish, Shernaz, Smita, Anuj, Ruta. For their untiring support and love. Bhavna needs an additional mention for helping me with the copy editing. As does Donetta for building and maintaining my first website.

Sharvani Pandit, my editor. Stubborn and fiercely committed to the Shiva Trilogy. It's an honour to work with her.

Rashmi Pusalkar, the designer of this book's cover. A fine artist, a magician. She is headstrong and always delivers.

Gautam Padmanabhan, Paul Vinay Kumar, Renuka Chatterjee, Satish Sundaram, Anushree Banerjee, Vipin Vijay, Manisha Sobhrajani and the fantastic team at Westland, my publishers. For their hard work, drive and supreme belief in the Shiva Trilogy.

Anuj Bahri, my agent. He has been a friend and has supported me when I needed it the most. And if I connect the dots of my serendipitous journey into writing, I must also thank Sandipan Deb, who introduced me to Anuj.

Chandan Kowli, the photographer for the cover. Talented and brilliant, he shot the required photograph perfectly. Chintan Sareen, for creating the snake in CG and Julien Dubois for assisting him. Prakesh Gor, for the make-up. Sagar Pusalkar, for the system work. They have truly created magic.

Sangram Surve, Shalini Iyer and the team at Think Why Not, the advertising and digital marketing agency for the book. It is a pleasure to work with these marketing geniuses.

Kawal Shoor and Yogesh Pradhan for their good advice during the formulation of the initial marketing plan. They helped me get my thoughts together on how the book should be marketed.

And last, but certainly not the least, you the reader. For accepting my first book with open arms. Your support has left me humbled. I hope I don't disappoint you with this second installment of the Shiva Trilogy. Everything that you may like in this book is the blessing of Lord Shiva. Everything that you don't like is due to my inability to do justice to that blessing.

The Shiva Trilogy

Shiva! The Mahadev. The God of Gods. Destroyer of Evil. Passionate lover. Fierce warrior. Consummate dancer. Charismatic leader. All-powerful, yet incorruptible. A quick wit, accompanied by an equally quick and fearsome temper.

Over the centuries, no foreigner who came to India – conqueror, merchant, scholar, ruler, traveller – believed that such a great man could possibly have existed in reality. They assumed that he must have been a mythical God, whose existence was possible only in the realms of human imagination. Unfortunately, this belief became our received wisdom.

But what if we are wrong? What if Lord Shiva was not a figment of a rich imagination, but a person of flesh and blood? Like you and me. A man who rose to become godlike because of his karma. That is the premise of the Shiva Trilogy, which interprets the rich mythological heritage of ancient India, blending fiction with historical fact.

This work is therefore a tribute to Lord Shiva and the lesson that his life is to us. A lesson lost in the depths of time and ignorance. A lesson, that all of us can rise to be better people. A lesson, that there exists a potential God in every single human being. All we have to do is listen to ourselves.

The Immortals of Meluha was the first book in the trilogy that chronicles the journey of this extraordinary hero. You are holding the second book, *The Secret of the Nagas*, in your hands. One more book is to follow: *The Oath of the Vayuputras*.

Note from the Author

The Secret of the Nagas is revealed from this page forth. This is the second book of the Shiva Trilogy and begins from the moment where its prequel, *The Immortals of Meluha*, ended. While I believe that you can enjoy this book by itself, perhaps, you may enjoy it more if you read *The Immortals of Meluha* first. In case you have already read *The Immortals of Meluha*, please ignore this message.

I hope you enjoy reading this book as much as I have loved writing it.

Also, there are many people from various different religions who write in to me, asking whether I believe that Lord Shiva is superior to other Gods. If I may, I would like to repeat my response here. There is a lovely Sanskrit line in the Rig Veda which captures the essence of my belief.

Ekam Sat Vipra Bahudha Vadanti.

Truth is one, though the sages know it as many.

www.authoramish.com

God is one, though different religions approach Him differently.
Call Him Shiva, Vishnu, Allah, Jesus or any other form of God that you believe in.
Our paths may be different. Our destination is the same.

www.authoramish.com

List of Characters

Anandamayi: Ayodhyan princess, daughter of Emperor Dilipa.

Athithigva: King of Kashi.

Ayurvati: The chief of medicine at Meluha.

Bappiraj: Prime minister of Branga.

Bhadra a.k.a. Veerahadra: A childhood friend and a confidant of Shiva; married to Krittika.

Bhagirath: Prince of Ayodhya, son of Emperor Dilipa.

Bharat: An ancient emperor of the Chandravanshi dynasty married to a Suryavanshi princess.

Bhoomidevi: A revered non-Naga lady who established the present way of life of the Nagas a long time ago.

Bhrigu: A Saptrishi Uttradhikari (successor of the Saptarshis), rajguru of Meluha.

Brahaspati: Chief Meluhan scientist; belonged to the swan-tribe of Brahmins.

Brahma: A great scientist from the very ancient past.

Brahmanayak: Father of Daksha, previous emperor of Meluha.

Chandraketu: King of Branga.

Chenardhwaj: Governor of Kashmir, based at Srinagar.

Daksha: Emperor of the Suryavanshi Empire of Meluha, married to Veerini and father of Sati.

Dilipa: Emperor of Swadweep, king of Ayodhya and chief of the Chandravanshis.

Divodas: The leader of the Brangas who live in Kashi.

Drapaku: A resident of Kotdwaar in Meluha

Kanakhala: The prime minister of Meluha, she is in charge of administrative, revenue and protocol matters.

Karkotak: Prime minister of the Nagas.

Kartik: Son of Shiva and Sati, named after Kritika, Sati's best friend and attendant.

Krittika: A close friend and attendant to Sati; wife of Veerbhadra.

Manu: Founder of the Vedic way of life; he lived many millennia ago.

Mohini: an associate of Lord Rudra; respected by some as a Vishnu.

Nandi: A captain in the Meluhan army.

Parshuram: A dacoit in Branga; he was named after the sixth Vishnu.

Parvateshwar: Head of Meluhan armed forces, in charge of army, navy, special forces and police.

Purvaka: Drapaku's blind father.

Ram: The seventh Vishnu, who lived many centuries ago. He established the empire of Meluha.

Rudra: The earlier Mahadev, the Destroyer of Evil, who lived some millennia ago.

Sati: Daughter of King Daksha and Queen Veerini, the royal princess of Meluha. Married to Shiva.

Satyadhwaj: Grandfather of Parvateshwar.

Shiva: The chief of the Guna tribe. Hails from Tibet. Later called Neelkanth, the saviour of the land.

Siamantak: Prime minister of Swadweep.
Surapadman: Prince of Magadh.
Tara: A pupil of Bhrigu.
The hooded Naga: The mysterious leader of the Nagas.
Vasudev pandits: Advisers to Shiva; tribe left behind by the previous Vishnu, Lord Ram.
Veerini: Queen of Meluha, wife of Emperor Daksha and mother of Sati.
Vishwadyumna: A close associate of the hooded Naga.

Before the Beginning

The boy was running as fast as his feet could carry him, the frost-bitten toe sending shards of icy pain up his leg. The woman's plea kept ringing in his ears: 'Help me. Please help me!'

He refused to slow down, sprinting towards his village. And then, he was yanked effortlessly by a large hairy arm. He was dangling in the air, desperately trying to get a foothold. The boy could hear the monster's sickening laugh as he toyed with him. Then, the other grotesque arm spun him around and held him tight.

The boy was shocked into stillness. The body was that of the hairy monster, but the face was of the beautiful woman he had just fled away from moments ago. The mouth opened, but the sound that emanated was not a mellifluous feminine one, but a blood-curdling roar.

'You enjoyed this, didn't you? You enjoyed my distress at being tortured, didn't you? You ignored my pleas, didn't you? Now this face will haunt you for the rest of your life!'

Then a grotesque arm holding a short sword came up from nowhere and decapitated the gorgeous head.

'Noooooooo!' screamed the little boy, snapping out of his dream.

He looked around his straw bed, disoriented. It was late evening. A little bit of sunshine had made its way into the otherwise dark hut. A small fire was dying out near the door. It suddenly burst into flames with a fresh breath of oxygen as a person rushed into the tiny room.

'Shiva? What happened? Are you alright, my son?'

The boy looked up, completely bewildered. He felt his mother's hand wrap itself around him and pull his tired head down to her bosom. He heard her soothing voice, sympathetic and understanding. 'It's all right, my child. I am here. I am here.'

The boy felt the fear release from his taut body as his eyes shed long held back tears.

'What is it, my son? The same nightmare?'

The boy shook his head. The tears turned into an angrier deluge.

'It's not your fault. What could you have done, son? He was three times larger than you. A grown man.'

The boy didn't say anything, but stiffened. The mother continued to gently run her hand over his face, wiping the tears away. 'You would have been killed.'

The boy suddenly jerked back.

'THEN I SHOULD HAVE BEEN KILLED! I DESERVED IT!'

The mother was shocked into silence. He was a good son. He had never raised his voice at her before. Never. She quickly set this thought aside as she reached out to soothe his face. 'Don't say that again, Shiva. What would happen to me if you died?'

Shiva curled his small fist, banging it against his forehead. He kept at it till his mother pulled his fist away. An angry, reddish-black mark had formed right between his eyebrows.

The mother held his arms down again, pulling him towards her. Then she said something her son was not prepared to hear. 'Listen, my child! You yourself had said that she didn't fight back. She could have reached for his knife and stabbed him, couldn't she?'

The son didn't say anything. He just nodded.

'Do you know why she didn't do that?'

The boy looked up at his mother, curious.

'Because she was practical. She knew she would probably be killed if she fought back.'

Shiva continued to stare blankly at his mother.

'The sin was being committed against her. And yet, she did what she could to stay alive — not fight back.'

His eyes didn't waiver for one instant from his mother's face.

'Why is it wrong for you to be as pragmatic and want to stay alive?'

The boy started sobbing again as some sense of comfort seeped silently into him.

Chapter 1

The Strange Demon

'Sati!' screamed Shiva, as he rapidly drew his sword and started sprinting towards his wife, pulling his shield forward as he ran.

She'll run into a trap!

'Stop!' yelled Shiva, picking up his pace as he saw her dash into a cluster of trees alongside the road leading to the Ramjanmabhoomi temple in Ayodhya.

Sati was totally focused on chasing the retreating hooded Naga, her sword drawn and held far from her body, like a seasoned warrior with her prey in sight.

It took a few moments for Shiva to catch up with Sati, to ascertain that she was safe. As they continued to give chase, Shiva's focus shifted to the Naga. He was shocked.

How did that dog move so far ahead?

The Naga, showing surprising agility, was effortlessly navigating between the trees and undulating ground of the hillside, picking up pace. Shiva remembered battling with the Naga at the Brahma temple at Meru, when he had met Sati for the first time.

His slow leg movements at the Brahma temple were just a battle strategy.

Shiva flipped his shield, clipping it on to his back, to get room to run faster. Sati was keeping pace to his left. She suddenly made a grunting sound and pointed to the right, to a fork in the path that was coming up. Shiva nodded. They would split up and try to cut off the Naga from opposite ends on the narrow ridge ahead.

Shiva dashed to his right with a renewed burst of speed, sword at the ready. Sati stayed her course behind the Naga, running equally hard. The ground beneath Shiva's feet on the new path had evened out and he managed to cover the distance rapidly. He noticed that the Naga had pulled his shield into his right hand. The wrong hand for defence. Shiva frowned.

Quickly coming up to the Naga's right, with Sati still some distance away, Shiva reached with his left hand, drew a knife and flung it at the Naga's neck. A stunned Shiva then saw a magnificent manoeuvre that he hadn't imagined possible.

Without turning to look at the knife or even breaking a step, the Naga pulled his shield forward in the path of the knife. With the knife safely bouncing off the shield, the Naga effortlessly let the shield clip on to his back, maintaining his pace.

Shiva gaped in awe, his speed slackening.

He blocked the knife without even looking at it! Who the hell is this man?

Sati meanwhile had maintained her pace, edging closer to the Naga as Shiva ran in from the other trail onto the path that the Naga was on.

Seeing Sati cross the narrow ridge, Shiva picked up speed, closing in on his wife. Because of the steep angle of the sloping ridge, he could see the Naga further ahead, reaching the wall at the bottom of the hill. The wall protected the Ramjanmabhoomi temple at the base from animal attacks and trespassers. The height of the wall gave Shiva hope. There was no way the Naga could jump over it. He would have to climb, giving Sati and him the crucial seconds needed to catch up and mount an attack.

The Naga came to the same realisation as well. As he neared the wall, he pirouetted on his heels, hands reaching to his sides, drawing out two swords. The sword in his right hand was a traditional long sword, glinting in the evening sun. The one in his left, a short sword with a strange double blade mounted on a central pivot at the hilt. Shiva pulled his shield forward as he neared the Naga. Sati attacked the Naga from his right.

The Naga swung the long sword hard, forcing Sati to step back. With Sati on the back foot, the Naga swerved with his left hand, making Shiva duck to avoid a strike. As the Naga's sword swept safely away, Shiva jumped high and struck down from his height, a blow almost impossible to defend if the opponent is not holding a shield. The Naga, however, effortlessly stepped back, avoiding the strike, while thrusting forward with his short sword, putting Shiva on the back foot. The Neelkanth had to quickly swing his shield up to deflect the blow.

Sati again moved forward, her sword forcing the Naga back. Reaching behind with her left hand, she pulled out a knife and threw it. The Naga bent his head at the exact moment, letting the knife sail harmlessly into the wall. Shiva and Sati were yet to get a single strike on the Naga, but he was progressively being forced to retreat. It was a matter of time before he would be pinned against the wall.

By the Holy Lake, I finally have him.

And then, the Naga swung ferociously with his left hand. The sword was too short to reach Shiva and it appeared to be a wasted manoeuvre. Shiva pushed forward, confident he would strike the Naga on his torso. But the Naga swung back, this time his thumb pressing a lever on the pivot of the short sword. One of the twin blades suddenly extended beyond the length of the other, doubling the reach of the sword. The blade cut Shiva on his shoulder. Its poisoned edge sent a jolt of electricity through his body, immobilising him.

'Shiva!' screamed Sati, as she swung down on the sword in the Naga's right hand, hoping to knock the blade out. Moments before the impact, the Naga dropped his long sword, causing Sati to lurch, her sword slipping out of her hand as she struggled to regain her balance.

'No!' screamed Shiva, helpless on his back, unable to move.

He had noticed what Sati had forgotten. The knife Sati had flung at the Naga, when he had been discovered hiding behind a tree at the Ramjanmabhoomi temple, was tied to his right hand. The Naga swiped with his right hand at the falling Sati's abdomen. Sati realised her mistake too late.

But the Naga pulled his hand back at the last moment. What would have been a lethal blow turned into a surface wound, running a trickle of blood. The Naga jabbed Sati hard with his left elbow, breaking her nose and knocking her down.

With both his enemies immobilised, the Naga quickly flicked his long sword up with his right foot. He swung both his weapons into their scabbards, eyes still on Shiva and Sati. The Naga then jumped high, holding the top of the wall behind him with his hands.

'Sati!' screamed Shiva, rushing towards his wife as the poison released its stranglehold.

Sati was clutching her abdomen. The Naga frowned, for the wound was just a surface nick. Then his eyes flashed wide.

She is carrying a baby.

The Naga crunched his immense stomach, pulling his legs up in one smooth motion, soaring over the wall.

'Press tight!' shouted Shiva, expecting a deep gash.

Shiva breathed easy when he realised that it was a minor wound, though the blood loss and the knock on Sati's nose was causing him worry.

Sati looked up, blood running down her nose and her eyes ablaze with fury. She picked up her sword and growled, 'Get him!'

Shiva turned around, picking up his sword and pushing it into his scabbard as he reached the wall. He clambered quickly over. Sati tried to follow. Shiva landed on the other side on a crowded street. He saw the Naga at a far distance, still running hard.

Shiva started sprinting after the Naga. But he knew the battle was already lost. He was too far behind. He now hated the Naga more than ever. The tormentor of his wife! The killer of his brother! And yet, deep inside, he marvelled at the sheer brilliance of the Naga's martial skills.

The Naga was running towards a horse tied outside a shop. In an inconceivable movement, he leapt up high, his right hand stretched out. As the Naga landed smoothly on top of the horse, the knife in his right hand slickly cut the reins, freeing the tethered horse. The rearing of the startled horse had caused the reins to fly back. The

Naga effortlessly caught them in his left hand. Instantly, he kicked the horse, whispering in the animal's ear. The horse sprang swiftly to the Naga's words, breaking into a gallop.

A man came hurtling out of the shop, screaming loudly, 'Stop! Thief! That's my horse!'

The Naga, hearing the commotion, reached into the folds of his robe and threw something back with tremendous force while continuing to gallop away. The force of the blow caused the horseman to stagger, falling flat on his back.

'By the Holy Lake!' shouted Shiva, sprinting towards what he thought was a grievously injured man.

As he reached the horseman, he was surprised to see him get up slowly, rubbing his chest in pain, cursing loudly, 'May the fleas of a thousand dogs infest that bastard's armpits!'

'Are you all right?' asked Shiva, as he examined the man's chest.

The horseman looked at Shiva, scared into silence at seeing his blood-streaked body.

Shiva bent down to pick up the object that the Naga had thrown at the horseman. It was a pouch, made of the most glorious silk he had ever seen. Shiva opened the pouch tentatively, expecting a trap, but it contained coins. He pulled one out, surprised to see that it was made of gold. There were at least fifty coins. He turned in the direction that the Naga had ridden.

What kind of a demon is he? He steals the horse and then leaves enough gold to buy five more!

'Gold!' whispered the horseman softly as he snatched the pouch from Shiva. 'It's mine!'

Shiva didn't look up, still holding one coin, examining its markings. 'I need one.'

The horseman spoke gingerly, for he did not want to battle a man as powerful-looking as Shiva, 'But...'

Shiva snorted in disgust. He pulled out two gold coins from his own pouch and gave it to the horseman, who, thanking his stars for a truly lucky day, quickly escaped.

Shiva turned back and saw Sati resting against the wall, holding her head up, pressing her nose hard. He walked up to her.

'Are you all right?'

Sati nodded in response, dried blood smeared on her face. 'Yes. Your shoulder? It looks bad.'

'It looks worse than it feels. I'm fine. Don't worry.'

Sati looked in the direction that the Naga had ridden off. 'What did he throw at the horseman?'

'A pouch full of this,' said Shiva as he showed the coin to Sati.

'He threw gold coins?!'

Shiva nodded.

Sati frowned and shook her head. She took a closer look at the coin. It had the face of a strange man with a crown on his head. Strange, because unlike a Naga, he had no deformity.

'He looks like a king of some kind,' said Sati, wiping some blood off her mouth.

'But look at these odd markings,' said Shiva as he flipped the coin.

It had a small symbol of a horizontal crescent moon. But the bizarre part was the network of lines running across the coin. Two crooked lines joined in the middle in the shape of an irregular cone and then they broke up into a spidery network.

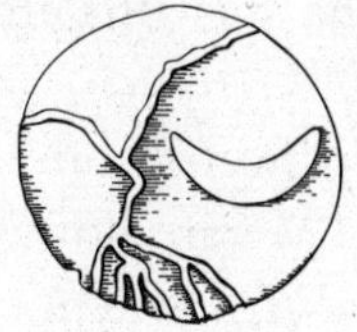

'I can understand the moon. But what do these lines symbolise?' asked Sati.

'I don't know,' admitted Shiva. But he did know one thing clearly. His gut instinct was unambiguous.

Find the Nagas. They are your path to discovering evil. Find the Nagas.

Sati could almost read her husband's mind. 'Let's get the distractions out of the way then?'

Shiva nodded at her. 'But first, let's get you to Ayurvati.'

'You need her more,' said Sati.

— ⁂ —

'You have nothing to do with our fight?' asked a startled Daksha. 'I don't understand, My Lord. You led us to our greatest victory. Now we have to finish the job. The evil Chandravanshi way of life has to end and these people have to be brought to our pure Suryavanshi ways.'

'But, Your Highness,' said Shiva with polite firmness, shifting his bandaged shoulder slightly to relieve the soreness. 'I don't think they are evil. I understand now that my mission is different.'

Dilipa, sitting to the left of Daksha, was thrilled. Shiva's words were a balm to his soul. Sati and Parvateshwar, to

Shiva's right, were quiet. Nandi and Veerbhadra stood further away, on guard but listening in avidly. The only one as angry as Daksha was Bhagirath, the crown prince of Ayodhya.

'We don't need a certificate from a foreign barbarian to tell us what is obvious! We are not evil!' said Bhagirath.

'Quiet,' hissed Dilipa. 'You will not insult the Neelkanth.'

Turning towards Shiva with folded hands, Dilipa continued, 'Forgive my impetuous son, My Lord. He speaks before he thinks. You said your mission is different. How can Ayodhya help?'

Shiva stared at a visibly chafing Bhagirath before turning towards Dilipa. 'How do I find the Nagas?'

Startled and scared, Dilipa touched his Rudra pendant for protection as Daksha looked up sharply.

'My Lord, they are pure evil,' said Daksha. 'Why do you want to find them?'

'You have answered your own question, Your Highness,' said Shiva. He turned towards Dilipa. 'I don't believe you are allied with the Nagas. But there are some in your empire who are. I want to know how to reach those people.'

'My Lord,' said Dilipa, swallowing hard. 'It is rumoured that the King of Branga consorts with the dark forces. He would be able to answer your questions. But the entry of any foreign person, including us, is banned in that strange but very rich kingdom. Sometimes, I actually think the Brangas pay tribute to my empire only to keep us from entering their land, not because they are scared of being defeated by us in battle.'

'You have another king in your empire? How is that possible?' asked a surprised Shiva.

'We aren't like the obsessive Suryavanshis. We don't insist

on everyone following one single law. Every kingdom has the right to its own king, its own rules and its own way of life. They pay Ayodhya a tribute because we defeated them in battle through the great *Ashwamedh yagna*.'

'*Horse sacrifice?*'

'Yes, My Lord,' continued Dilipa. 'The sacrificial horse travels freely through any kingdom in the land. If a king stops the horse, we battle, defeat and annexe that territory. If they don't stop the horse, then the kingdom becomes our colony and pays us tribute, but is still allowed to have its own laws. So we are more like a confederacy of aligned kings rather than a fanatical empire like Meluha.'

'Mind your words, you impudent fool,' ranted Daksha. 'Your confederacy seems a lot like extortion to me. They pay you tribute because if they don't, you will attack their lands and plunder them. Where is the Royal Dharma in that? In Meluha, being an emperor does not just give you the right to receive tribute, but it also confers the responsibility to work for the good of all the empire's subjects.'

'And who decides what is good for your subjects? You? By what right? People should be allowed to do whatever they wish.'

'Then there will be chaos,' shouted Daksha. 'Your stupidity is even more apparent than your immoral values!'

'Enough!' asserted Shiva, struggling to tame his irritation. 'Will both your Highnesses please desist?'

Daksha looked at Shiva in surprised anger. Seeing a much more confident Shiva, not just accepting, but living his role as the Neelkanth. Daksha's heart sank. He knew that fulfilling his father's dream of a member of their family being Emperor of all India, and bringing the Suryavanshi way of life to all its citizens, was becoming increasingly remote. He could defeat the Swadweepans in battle due to his army's superior tactics and technology, but he did not have enough soldiers to control the conquered land. For that, he needed the faith that the Swadweepans had in the Neelkanth. If the Neelkanth didn't go along with his way of thinking, his plans were bound to fail.

'Why do you say that the Brangas are allied with the Nagas?' asked Shiva.

'I can't say for sure, My Lord,' said Dilipa. 'But I am going on the rumours that one has heard from traders in Kashi. It is the only kingdom in Swadweep that the Brangas deign to trade with. Furthermore, there are many refugees from Branga settled in Kashi.'

'Refugees?' asked Shiva. 'What are they fleeing from? You said Branga was a rich land.'

'There are rumours of a great plague that has struck Branga repeatedly. But I'm not quite certain. Very few people can be certain about what goes on in Branga! But the King of Kashi would certainly have better answers. Should I summon him here, My Lord?'

'No,' said Shiva, unsure whether this was another wild goose chase or whether the Brangas actually had something to do with the Nagas.

Sati suddenly piped up as a thought struck her and turned towards Dilipa. Her voice was nasal due to the bandage on her nose. 'Forgive me, Your Highness. But where exactly is Branga?'

'It is far to the East, Princess Sati, where our revered river Ganga meets their holy river which comes in from the northeast, Brahmaputra.'

Shiva started as he realised something. He turned to Sati, smiling. Sati smiled back.

They aren't lines! They are rivers!

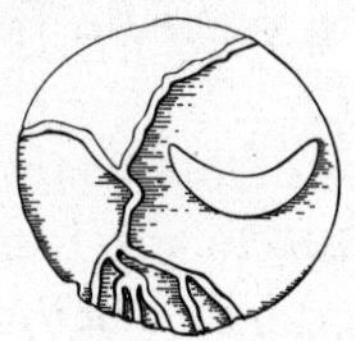

Shiva reached into his pouch and pulled out the coin he had recovered from the Naga and showed it to Dilipa. 'Is this a Branga coin, Your Highness?'

'Yes, My Lord!' answered a surprised Dilipa. 'That is King Chandraketu on one side and a river map of their land on the other. But these coins are rare. The Brangas never send tribute in coins, only in gold ingots.'

Dilipa was about to ask where Shiva got the coin from, but was cut off by the Neelkanth.

'How quickly can we leave for Kashi?'

'Mmmm, this is good,' smiled Shiva, handing the chillum to Veerbhadra.

'I know,' smiled Veerbhadra. 'The grass is much better here than in Meluha. The Chandravanshis certainly know how to savour the finer things in life.'

Shiva smiled. The marijuana was working its magic on him. The two friends were on a small hill outside Ayodhya, enjoying the evening breeze. The view was stunning.

The gentle slope of the grassy hill descended into a sparsely forested plain, which ended in a sheer cliff at a far distance. The tempestuous Sarayu, which had cut through the cliff over many millennia, flowed down south, rumbling passionately. The sun setting gently beyond the horizon completed the dramatic beauty of the tranquil moment.

'I guess the Emperor of Meluha is finally happy,' smiled Veerbhadra, handing the chillum back to Shiva.

Shiva winked at Veerbhadra before taking a deep drag. He knew Daksha was unhappy about his changed stance on the Chandravanshis. And as he himself did not want any distractions while searching for the Nagas, he had hit upon an ingenious compromise to give Daksha a sense of victory and yet keep Dilipa happy as well.

Shiva had decreed that Daksha would henceforth be known as Emperor of India. His name would not only be taken first during prayers at the royal court at Devagiri, but also at Ayodhya. Dilipa, in turn, would be known as Emperor of Swadweep within the Chandravanshi areas, and the 'brother of the Emperor' in Meluha. His name would be taken after Daksha's in court prayers in both Devagiri and Ayodhya. Dilipa's kingdom would pay a nominal tribute of a hundred thousand gold coins to Meluha, which Daksha had pronounced would be donated to the Ramjanmabhoomi temple in Ayodhya.

Thus Daksha had at least one of his dreams fulfilled: Being Emperor of India. Content, Daksha had returned to Devagiri in triumph. The ever pragmatic Dilipa was delighted that despite losing the war with the Suryavanshis, for all practical purposes, he retained his empire and his independence.

'We leave for Kashi in a week?' asked Veerbhadra.

'Hmmm.'

'Good. I'm getting bored here.'

Shiva smiled handing the chillum back to Veerbhadra. 'This Bhagirath seems like a very interesting fellow.'

'Yes, he does.' Veerbhadra took a puff.

'What have you heard about him?'

'You know,' said Veerbhadra, 'Bhagirath was the one who had thought of taking that contingent of hundred thousand soldiers around our position at Dharmakhet.'

'The attack from the rear? That was brilliant. May have worked too, but for the valour of Drapaku.'

'It would certainly have worked if Bhagirath's orders had been followed to the T.'

'Really?' asked Shiva, smoking.

'I have heard Bhagirath wanted to take his army in the quiet of the night through a longer route that was further away from the main battleground. If he had done that, we would not have discovered the troop movement. Our delayed response would have ensured that we would have lost the war.'

'So what went wrong?'

'Apparently, the War Council didn't want to meet at night, when Bhagirath called them.'

'Why in the name of the holy lake wouldn't they meet urgently?'

'They were sleeping!'

'You're joking!'

'No, I'm not,' said Veerbhadra, shaking his head. 'And what is worse, when they did meet in the morning, they ordered Bhagirath to stick close to the valley between Dharmakhet and our position, helping us discover their movement.'

'Why the hell did the War Council make such a stupid decision?' asked a flabbergasted Shiva.

'Apparently, Bhagirath is not trusted by his father. And therefore, not by most Swadweepan kings or generals either. They believed he would have taken the soldiers, escaped to Ayodhya and declared himself Emperor.'

'That's ridiculous. Why does Dilipa not trust his own son?'

'Because he believes Bhagirath thinks he is a fool and a terrible emperor.'

'I'm sure Bhagirath doesn't actually think that!'

'Well, from what I've heard,' smiled Veerbhadra as he junked out the ash from the chillum, 'Bhagirath actually *does* think so of his father. And he's not far from wrong, is he?'

Shiva smiled.

'And then, to make matters worse,' continued Veerbhadra, 'the entire fiasco was blamed on Bhagirath. It was said that because he took a hundred thousand soldiers away, they lost the war.'

Shiva shook his head, saddened to see an intelligent man being rubbished by the idiots surrounding him. 'I think he is a capable person, whose wings have been clipped.'

The tranquil moment was suddenly shattered by a loud scream. Shiva and Veerbhadra looked up to see a rider galloping away, while his companion, lagging far behind, was screeching loudly: 'Help! Somebody help, Prince Bhagirath!'

Bhagirath had lost control of his speeding horse and was hurtling towards the cliff. A near certain death. Shiva jumped onto his horse and charged towards him with Veerbhadra in tow. It was a long distance, but the gentle slope helped Shiva and Veerbhadra make up the expanse quickly. Shiva rode in an arc to intercept Bhagirath's horse.

A few minutes later, Shiva was galloping along Bhagirath's path. He was impressed that Bhagirath seemed calm and focussed, despite facing a life threatening situation.

Bhagirath was pulling hard on his reins, trying to slow his horse down. But his action agitated the horse even further. It picked up more speed.

'Let the reins go!' shouted Shiva, over the loud rumble of the threateningly close Sarayu river.

'What?!' screamed Bhagirath. All his training told him letting the reins go was the stupidest thing to do when a horse was out of control.

'Trust me! Let it go!'

Bhagirath would later explain it to himself as fate guiding him towards the Neelkanth. At this moment, his instinct told him to forget his training and trust this barbarian from Tibet. Bhagirath let go. Much to his surprise, the horse immediately slackened.

Shiva rode in close. So close that he could almost whisper into the animal's ear. Then he began to sing a strange tune. The horse gradually started calming down, reducing its speed to a canter. The cliff was coming close. Very close.

'Shiva!' warned Veerbhadra. 'The cliff is a few hundred metres away!'

Shiva noted the warning, matching the pace of his horse with Bhagirath's. The prince kept his control, staying on the horse, while Shiva kept singing. Slowly but surely, Shiva was gaining control. It was just a few metres before the cliff that Bhagirath's horse finally came to a halt.

Bhagirath and Shiva immediately dismounted as Veerbhadra rode in.

'Damn!' said Veerbhadra, peering towards the cliff. 'That was too close!'

Shiva looked at Veerbhadra, before turning towards Bhagirath. 'Are you all right?'

Bhagirath kept staring at Shiva, before lowering his eyes in shame. 'I'm sorry for putting you through so much trouble.'

'No trouble at all.'

Bhagirath turned to his horse, hitting its face hard for embarrassing him.

'It's not the horse's fault!' shouted Shiva.

Bhagirath turned back to Shiva, frowning. Shiva walked towards Bhagirath's horse, gently cradling its face, almost like it was a child being punished unfairly. Then he carefully pulled its reins out, signalled to Bhagirath to come closer and showed him the nail buried in the leather close to the horse's mouth.

Bhagirath was shocked. The inference was obvious.

Shiva pulled the nail out, handing it to Bhagirath. 'Somebody doesn't like you, my friend.'

Meanwhile, Bhagirath's companion had caught up with them. 'My Prince! Are you all right?'

Bhagirath looked towards his companion. 'Yes I am.'

Shiva turned towards the man. 'Tell Emperor Dilipa his son is an exceptional rider. Tell him that the Neelkanth has yet to see a man with greater control over an animal, even when the odds were stacked so desperately against him. Tell him the Neelkanth requests the honour of Prince Bhagirath accompanying him to Kashi.'

Shiva knew that for Dilipa, this would not be a request but an order. This was probably the only way of keeping Bhagirath safe from the unknown threat to his life. The companion immediately went down on his knee. 'As you command, My Lord.'

Bhagirath stood dumbfounded. He had come across people who plotted against him, people who took credit for his ideas, people who sabotaged him. But this... This was unique. He turned to his companion. 'Leave us.'

The man immediately rode away.

'I have experienced such kindness from only one person up until now,' said Bhagirath, his eyes moist. 'And that is my sister, Anandmayi. But blood justifies her actions. I don't know how to react to your generosity, My Lord.'

'By not calling me Lord,' smiled Shiva.

'That is one order I would request you to allow me to refuse,' said Bhagirath, his hands folded in a respectful namaste. 'I will follow any other order you give. Even if it is to take my own life.'

'Now don't get so dramatic! I am not about to ask you to commit suicide right after having worked strenuously to save your life.'

Bhagirath smiled softly. 'What was it you sang to my horse, My Lord?'

'Sit with me over a chillum sometime and I will teach you.'

'It will be my honour to sit at your feet and learn, My Lord.'

'Don't sit at my feet, my friend. Sit beside me. The sound carries a little better there!'

Bhagirath smiled as Shiva patted him on the shoulder.

Chapter 2

Sailing Down the Sarayu

'Tell Princess Anandmayi,' said Parvateshwar to the Captain of the Women's Guard at Anandmayi's palace entrance, 'that General Parvateshwar is waiting outside.'

'She had told me she was expecting you, General,' said the Captain bowing low. 'May I request you to wait a moment while I go and check on her?'

As the Captain walked into Anandmayi's chamber, Parvateshwar turned around. Shiva had made him in-charge of the expedition to Kashi. Shiva knew if he left the organisation to one of Ayodhya's administrators, they would probably be debating the mode of transport for the next three years. Parvateshwar, with his typical Suryavanshi efficiency, had seen to the arrangements within a week. The contingent was to travel east down the Sarayu on royal boats, to the city of Magadh, where the river merged into the mighty Ganga. From there, they would turn west to sail up the Ganga to *Kashi, the city where the supreme light shines.*

Parvateshwar had been inundated with inane requests from some of the Ayodhya nobility who were taking the opportunity to travel with the Neelkanth. He did plan to honour some strange appeals, like one from a superstitious nobleman who wanted his boat to leave exactly thirty two minutes after the beginning of the third prahar. Others he had flatly refused, such as a request from another nobleman for his boat to be staffed only by women. The General was quite sure that Anandmayi must also have some special arrangements she wanted made.

Like carrying a ship hold of milk for her beauty baths!

The Captain was back shortly. 'You may go in, General.'

Parvateshwar marched in smartly, bowed his head, saluted as he must to royalty and spoke out loud, 'What is it you want, Princess?'

'You needn't be so coy, General. You can look up.'

Parvateshwar looked up. Anandmayi was lying on her stomach next to a picture window overlooking the royal gardens. Kanini, her masseuse, was working her magic on the princess' exotic and supple body. Anandmayi only had one piece of cloth draped loosely from her lower back to her upper thighs. The rest of her, a feast for his eyes.

'Beautiful view, isn't it?' asked Anandmayi.

Parvateshwar blushed a deep red, his head bowed, eyes turned away. To Anandmayi, he appeared to be like the rare cobra male that bows his head to its mate at the beginning of their mating dance, as though accepting the superiority of its partner.

'I'm sorry, Princess. I'm so sorry. I didn't mean to insult you.'

'Why should you apologise for looking at the royal gardens, General? It is allowed.'

Parvateshwar, a lifelong celibate, was mollified. It did not appear as though Anandmayi had misunderstood his intentions. He whispered in a soft voice, eyes on the floor, 'What can I do for you, Princess?'

'It's quite simple really. A little further south down the Sarayu is the spot where Lord Ram had stopped with his Guru Vishwamitra and brother Lakshman on his way to slay the demon Tadaka. It is the spot where Maharishi Vishwamitra taught Lord Ram the arts of Bal and Atibal, the fabled route to eternal good health and freedom from hunger and thirst. I would like to halt there and offer a puja to the Lord.'

Parvateshwar, pleased at her devotion to Lord Ram, smiled. 'Of course, we can stop there Princess. I will make the arrangements. Would you need any special provisions?'

'None whatsoever. An honest heart is all that is needed for a prayer to reach the Lord.'

Parvateshwar looked up for a brief moment, impressed. Anandmayi's eyes, however, seemed to be mocking him. He growled softly. 'Anything else, Princess?'

Anandmayi grimaced. She was not getting the reaction that she had desired. 'Nothing else, General.'

Parvateshwar saluted smartly and left the room.

Anandmayi kept staring at Parvateshwar's retreating form. She sighed loudly and shook her head.

— ⁂ —

'Gather around please,' said the Pandit, 'we will commence the puja.'

Shiva's contingent was at Bal-Atibal kund, where Guru Vishwamitra had taught Lord Ram his legendary skills.

The Neelkanth was unhappy that many of Ayodhya's nobility had inveigled their way into the voyage to Kashi.

What should have been a super-fast five ship convoy had turned into a lethargic fifty ship caravan. The straightforward Parvateshwar had found it difficult to deny the convoluted logic of the Chandravanshi nobility. Therefore, Shiva was delighted that Bhagirath had found an ingenious method to cut down the numbers. Craftily, he had suggested to one noble that he should rush to Kashi and set up a welcoming committee for the Neelkanth, and thus gain favour with the powerful Lord. Seeing one noble hustle away, many others had followed, in a mad dash to be the first to herald the arrival of the Neelkanth at Kashi. Within hours, the convoy had been reduced to the size that Shiva desired.

The puja platform had been set up some fifty metres from the riverbank. It was believed that anyone who conducted this prayer with full devotion would never be inflicted with disease. Shiva, Sati, Parvateshwar, Ayurvati, Bhagirath and Anandmayi sat in the innermost circle next to the Pandit. Others like Nandi, Veerbhadra, Drapaku, Krittika and the men of the joint Suryavanshi-Chandravanshi brigade sat a little further back. The earnest Brahmin was reciting Sanskrit shlokas in the exact same intonations that had been taught to him by his Guru.

Sati was uneasy. She had an uncomfortable feeling that someone was watching her. For some strange reason, she felt intense hatred directed at her. Along with that she also felt boundless love and profound sadness. Confused, she opened her eyes. She turned her head to her left. Every single person had his eyes closed, in accordance with the guidelines of this particular puja. She then turned to the right and started as she saw Shiva gazing directly at her. His eyes open wide, reflecting an outpouring of love, Shiva's face sported a slight smile.

Sati frowned at her husband, gesturing with her eyes that he should concentrate on his prayers. Shiva, however, pursed his lips together and blew her a kiss. A startled Sati frowned even more. Her Suryavanshi sensibilities felt offended at such frivolous behaviour, which she considered a violation of the code. Shiva pouted like a spoilt child, closed his eyes and turned towards the fire. Sati turned too, eyes closed, allowing herself a slight smile at the fact that she had been blessed with an adoring husband.

But she still felt she was being watched. Stared at intently.

— ⁂ —

The last ship of the Neelkanth's convoy turned round the bend in the Sarayu. With his enemies out of sight, the Naga emerged from the trees. He walked briskly to the place where the Brahmin had just conducted the puja. He was followed by the Queen of the Nagas and a hundred armed men. They stopped at a polite distance from the Naga, leaving him alone.

Karkotak, Prime Minister to the Queen of the Nagas, looked up at the sky, judging the time. Then he looked disconcertedly at the Naga in the distance. He wondered why the Lord of the People, as the Naga was referred to in his lands, was so interested in this particular puja. The Lord had far greater powers and knowledge. Some even considered him better than the Naga Queen.

'Your Highness,' said Karkotak to the Queen, 'do you think it advisable to emphasise to the Lord of the People the importance of returning home?'

'When I want your advice, Karkotak,' said the Queen in

a curt whisper, 'I will ask for it.'

Karkotak immediately retreated, terrified as always of his Queen's temper.

The Queen turned back towards the Naga, her mind considering Karkotak's words. She had to admit that her Prime Minister was right. The Nagas had to return to their capital quickly. There was little time to waste. The *Rajya Sabha*, the Naga *Royal Council* was to be held soon. The issue of medical support to the Brangas would come up again. She knew that the severe cost of that support was turning many Nagas against the alliance with the Brangas, especially the peace-loving ones who wanted to live their ostracised lives quietly, calling it a product of their bad karma. And without the alliance, her vengeance was impossible. More importantly, she could not desert the Brangas in their hour of need when they had been unflinchingly loyal to her.

On the other hand, she could not abandon her nephew, the Lord of the People. He was troubled; the presence of that vile woman had disturbed his usual calm demeanour. He was taking unnecessary risks. Like the idiotic attack on Sati and Shiva at the Ramjanmabhoomi temple. If he didn't want to kill her, why the hell did he put his own person in such grave peril? What if he had been killed? Or worse, caught alive? He had justified it later as an attempt to draw Sati out of Ayodhya, as capturing her within the city was impossible. For what it was worth, he had succeeded in drawing her out on a voyage to Kashi. But she was accompanied by her husband and a whole brigade. It was impossible to kidnap her.

The Queen saw her nephew move slightly. She stepped forward a little distance, motioning for Karkotak and the men to remain behind.

The Naga had taken out a knife from a newly built hold on his belt. It was the knife Sati had flung at him at the Ramjanmabhoomi temple. He looked at it longingly, letting the blade run up his thumb. Its sharp edge cut his skin lightly. He shook his head angrily, dug the knife hard into the sand and turned around to walk towards the Queen.

He stopped abruptly. Oddly hesitant.

The Queen, clearly out of her nephew's earshot, willed her thoughts in a quiet whisper. 'Let it go, my child. It's not worth it. Let it go.'

The Naga stood rooted to his spot. Indecision weighed heavy on him. The men in the distance were shocked to see their Lord in such a weak state. To the Queen's dismay, the Naga turned around and walked back to the spot where he had buried the knife. He picked it up carefully, held it reverentially to his forehead and put it back into his side hold.

The Queen snorted in disgust and turned around, signalling Karkotak to come forward. She knew she had no choice. She would have to leave her nephew with bodyguards, while she herself would ride out towards Panchavati, her capital.

'Portage charges? What rubbish!' bellowed Siamantak, Ayodhya's Prime Minister. 'This ship belongs to the Emperor of Swadweep. It carries a very important individual, the most important in the land.'

Siamantak was in the pilot boat of Andhak, Port Minister of Magadh, who unlike typical Chandravanshis, was known to turn a blind eye to everything except the letter of the law. Siamantak turned to look nervously at the massive ship that carried the Neelkanth. Shiva was standing on the balustrade with Parvateshwar and Bhagirath. Siamantak was aware that Shiva wanted to stop at Magadh. He had expressed a desire to visit the Narsimha temple on the outskirts of the city. Siamantak did not want to disappoint the Neelkanth. However, if he paid portage charges for the ship, it would set a dangerous precedent. How could the Emperor's ship pay portage in his own empire? It would open a can of worms with all the river port kingdoms across the empire. The negotiations with Andhak were delicate.

'I don't care who the ship belongs to,' said Andhak. 'And I don't care if you have Lord Ram himself on that ship. The law is the law. Any ship that ports at Magadh has to pay portage. Why should Emperor Dilipa be worried about a small fee of one thousand gold coins?'

'It's not the money. It's the principle,' argued Siamantak.

'Precisely! It is the principle. So please pay up.'

Shiva was getting impatient. 'What the hell are they talking about for so long?'

'My Lord,' said Bhagirath. 'Andhak is the Port Minister. He must be insisting that the law of portage charges be followed. Siamantak cannot allow any ship owned by my father to pay portage. It is an insult to my father's fragile ego. Andhak is an idiot.'

'Why would you call a person who follows the law stupid?' frowned Parvateshwar. 'On the contrary, he should be respected.'

'Sometimes even circumstances should be looked at, General.'

'Prince Bhagirath, I can understand no circumstance

under which the letter of the law should be ignored.'

Shiva did not want to witness yet another argument between the Suryavanshi and Chandravanshi way of life. 'What kind of ruler is the King of Magadh?'

'King *Mahendra*?' asked Bhagirath.

'Doesn't that mean *the conqueror of the world?'*

'Yes, it does, My Lord. But he does not do justice to that name. Magadh was a great kingdom once. In fact, there was a time when it was the overlord kingdom of Swadweep and its kings were widely respected and honoured. But as it happens with many great kings, their unworthy descendants frittered away the wealth and power of their kingdoms. They have been trying hard to live up to Magadh's past glory, but have been spectacularly unsuccessful. We share a prickly relationship with them.'

'Really, why?'

'Well, Ayodhya was the kingdom that defeated them more than three hundred years ago to become the overlord of Swadweep. It was a glorious Ashwamedh Yagna, for this was a time when Ayodhya had still not fallen prey to the wooden kings who rule it today. As you can imagine, Magadh was not quite pleased about the loss of status and revenue from tributes.'

'Yes, but three hundred years is a long time to carry a grudge!'

Bhagirath smiled. 'Kshatriyas have long memories, My Lord. And they still suffer from their defeat to Ayodhya. Magadh could theoretically benefit from the fact that it is at the confluence of two rivers. It becomes the most convenient trading hub for merchants travelling on river ports on the Sarayu or the Ganga. This advantage was negated after they lost the Ashwamedh to us. A ceiling was imposed on their portage and trading hub charges. And then, our enmity received a fresh lease of life a hundred years back.'

'And how did that happen?'

'There is a kingdom to the west, up the Ganga, called Prayag. It had historically been in close alliance with Magadh. In fact the ruling families are very closely related.'

'And...'

'And when the Yamuna changed course from Meluha and started flowing into Swadweep, it met the Ganga at Prayag,' said Bhagirath.

'That would have made Prayag very important?' asked Shiva.

'Yes, My Lord. Just like Magadh, it became a crucial junction for river trade. And unlike Magadh, it was not bound by any treaty on its portage and trading charges. Any trader or kingdom wanting to settle or trade in the newly opened hinterlands of the Yamuna had to pay charges at Prayag. Its prosperity and power grew exponentially. There were even rumours that they were planning to support Magadh in an Ashwamedh Yagna to challenge Ayodhya's suzerainty. But when my great grandfather lost the battle to the Suryavanshis and a dam was built on the Yamuna to turn the flow towards Meluha, Prayag's importance fell again. They have blamed Ayodhya ever since. They actually believe we purposely lost the war to give them a devastating blow.'

'I see.'

'Yes,' said Bhagirath, shaking his head. 'But to be honest, we lost the war because my great grandfather employed terrible battle strategy.'

'So you people have hated each other forever?'

'Not forever, My Lord. There was a time when Ayodhya and Magadh were close allies.'

'So will you be welcome here?'

Bhagirath burst out laughing. 'Everyone knows I don't really represent Ayodhya. This is one place I will not be suspect. But King Mahendra is known to be highly suspicious. We should expect spies keeping a close tab on us all the time. He does that to every important visitor. Having said that, their spy network is not particularly efficient. I do not foresee any serious problems.'

'Will my blue neck open doors here?'

Bhagirath looked embarrassed. 'King Mahendra does not believe in anything my father believes in, My Lord. Since the Emperor of Ayodhya believes in the Neelkanth, the Magadh king will not.'

Their conversation was interrupted by Siamantak climbing up the ship ladder. He came up to the Neelkanth, saluted smartly and said, 'A deal has been struck, My Lord. We can disembark. But we will have to stay here for at least ten days.'

Shiva frowned.

'I have temporarily transferred the ownership of the ship to a palace guesthouse owner in Magadh, My Lord. We will stay in his guesthouse for ten days. He will pay the portage charges to Andhak from the guesthouse rent we pay. When we wish to leave, the ownership of the ship will be transferred back to King Dilipa. We have to stay for ten days so that the guesthouse owner can earn enough money for his own profit and for portage charges.'

Shiva gaped at Siamantak. He didn't know whether to laugh at this strangely convoluted compromise or be impressed at Siamantak's bureaucratic brilliance in achieving

Shiva's objective of visiting Magadh while upholding his Emperor's prestige. The portage charges would be paid, but technically not by Emperor Dilipa.

— ⅄OƱ↑⊗ —

The Naga and his soldiers had been silently tracking the fleet carrying Shiva, Sati and their entourage. The Naga Queen, Prime Minister Karkotak and her bodyguards had left for Panchavati, the Naga capital. The smaller platoon allowed the Naga to maintain a punishing pace, staying abreast with the fast moving ships of Shiva's convoy.

They had wisely remained away from the banks. Far enough to not be visible to the boat look-outs but close enough to follow their paths. They had moved further inland to avoid Magadh and intended to move closer to the river once they had bypassed the city.

'A short distance more, My Lord,' said Vishwadyumna. 'Then we can move back towards the river.'

The Naga nodded.

Suddenly, the still of the forest was shattered by a loud scream. 'NOOOOO!'

The Naga immediately went down on his knees, giving Vishwadyumna rapid orders with hand signals. The entire platoon went down quickly and quietly, waiting for the danger to pass.

But trouble had just begun.

A woman screamed again. 'No! Please! Leave him!'

Vishwadyumna silently gestured to his soldiers to stay down. As far as he was concerned, there was only one course of action to take. Retrace their steps, take a wide arc around this area and move back towards the river. He turned towards his Lord, about to offer this suggestion. The Naga, however, was transfixed, eyes glued to a heartbreaking sight.

At a distance, partially hidden by the trees and underbrush, lay a tribal woman, frantically clutching a boy, no older than six or seven years. Two armed men, possibly Magadhan soldiers, were trying to pull the child away. The woman, showing astounding strength for her frail frame, was holding on to the child desperately.

'Dammit!' screamed the leader of the Magadhans. 'Push that woman off, you louts!'

In the wild and unsettled lands between the Ganga and Narmada lived scattered tribes of forest people. In the eyes of the civilised city folk living along the great rivers, these tribals were backward creatures because they insisted on living in harmony with nature. While most kingdoms ignored these forest tribes, others confiscated their lands at will as populations grew and need for farmlands increased. And a few particularly cruel ones preyed on these helpless groups for slave labour.

The Magadhan leader kicked the woman hard. 'You can get another son! But I need this boy! He will drive my bulls to victory! My father will finally stop his endless preening about winning every race for the last three years!'

The Naga looked at the Magadhan with barely concealed hate. Bull-racing was a craze in the Chandravanshi areas, subject to massive bets, royal interest and intrigue. Riders were needed to scream and agitate the animals to keep them running on course. At the same time, if the riders were too heavy, they would slow down the animal. Therefore, boys between the ages of six and eight were considered perfect. They would shriek out of fear and their weight was inconsequential. The children would be tied to the beasts. If the bull went down, the boy rider would be seriously injured or killed. Therefore, tribal children were often kidnapped to slave away as riders. Nobody important missed them if they died.

The Magadhan leader nodded to one of his men who drew his sword. He then looked at the woman. 'I am trying to be reasonable. Let your son go. Or I will have to hurt you.'

'No!'

The Magadhan soldier slashed his sword, cutting across the mother's right arm. Blood spurted across the child's face, making him bawl inconsolably.

The Naga was staring at the woman, his mouth open in awe. Her bloodied right arm hanging limply by her side, the woman still clung to her son, wrapping her left arm tightly around him.

Vishwadyumna shook his head. He could tell it was a matter of time before the woman would be killed. He turned towards his soldiers, giving hand signals to crawl back. He turned back towards his Lord. But the Naga was not there. He had moved swiftly forward, towards the mother. Vishwadyumna panicked and ran after his Lord, keeping his head low.

'Kill her!' ordered the Magadhan leader.

The Magadhan soldier raised his sword, ready to strike. Suddenly, the Naga broke out from the cover of the trees, his hand holding a knife high. Before the soldier knew what had happened, the knife struck his hand and his sword dropped harmlessly to the ground.

As the Magadhan soldier shrieked in agony, the Naga drew out two more knives. But he had failed to notice the platoon of Magadhan soldiers at the back. One had his bow at the ready, with an arrow strung. The soldier released it at the Naga. The arrow rammed into his left shoulder, slipping between his shoulder cap and torso armour, bursting through to the bone. The force of the blow caused the Naga to fall to the ground, the pain immobilising him.

Seeing their Lord down, the Naga's platoon ran in with a resounding yell.

'My Lord!' cried Vishwadyumna, as he tried to support the Naga back to his feet.

'Who the hell are you?' screamed the cruel Magadhan leader, retreating towards the safety of his platoon, before turning back to the Naga's men.

'Get out of here if you want to stay alive!' shouted one of the Naga's soldiers, livid at the injury to his Lord.

'Bangas!' yelled the Magadhan, recognising the accent. 'What in the name of Lord Indra are you scum doing here?'

'It's Branga! Not Banga!'

'Do I look like I care? Get out of my land!'

The Branga did not respond as he saw his Naga Lord getting up slowly, helped by Vishwadyumna. The Naga signalled Vishwadyumna to step back and tried to pull the arrow out of his shoulder. But it was buried too deep. He broke its shaft and threw it away.

The Magadhan pointed at the Naga menacingly. 'I am Ugrasen, the Prince of Magadh. This is my land. These people are my property. Get out of the way.'

The Naga did not respond to the royal brat.

He turned around to see one of the most magnificent sights he had ever seen. The mother lay almost unconscious behind his soldiers. Her eyes closing due to the tremendous loss of blood. Her body shivering desperately. Too terrified to even whimper.

And yet, she stubbornly refused to give up her son. Her left hand still wrapped tight around him. Her body protectively positioned in front of her child.

What a mother!

The Naga turned around. His eyes blazing with rage. His body tense. His fists clenched tight. He whispered in a voice that was eerily calm, 'You want to hurt a mother because she is protecting her child?'

Sheer menace dripped from that soft voice. It even managed to get through to a person lost in royal ego. But Ugrasen could not back down in front of his fawning courtiers. Some crazy Branga with an unseasonal holi mask was not going to deprive him of his prize catch. 'This is my kingdom. I can hurt whoever I want. So if you want to save your sorry hide, get out of here. You don't know the power of...'

'YOU WANT TO HURT A MOTHER BECAUSE SHE IS PROTECTING HER CHILD?'

Ugrasen fell silent as terror finally broke through his thick head. He turned to see his followers. They too felt the dread that the Naga's voice emanated.

A shocked Vishwadyumna stared at his Lord. He had never heard his Lord raise his voice so loud. Never. The Naga's breathing was heavy, going intermittently through gritted teeth. His body stiff with fury.

And then Vishwadyumna heard the Naga's breathing return slowly to normal. He knew it instantly. His Lord had made a decision.

The Naga reached to his side and drew his long sword.

Holding it away from his body. Ready for the charge. And then he whispered his orders. 'No mercy.'

'NO MERCY!' screamed the loyal Branga soldiers. They charged after their Lord. They fell upon the hapless Magadhans. There was no mercy.

Chapter 3

The Pandit of Magadh

It was early morning when Shiva left the guesthouse for the Narsimha temple. He was accompanied by Bhagirath, Drapaku, Siamantak, Nandi and Veerbhadra.

Magadh was a far smaller town than Ayodhya. Not having suffered due to commercial or military success and the resultant mass immigration, it remained a pretty town with leafy avenues. While it did not have the awesome organisation of Devagiri or the soaring architecture of Ayodhya, it was not bogged down by the boring standardisation of the Meluhan capital or the grand chaos of the Swadweepan capital.

It did not take Shiva and his entourage more than just half–an–hour to get across to the far side of the city where the magnificent Narsimha temple stood. Shiva entered the compound of the grand shrine. His men waited outside as per his instructions, but only after scoping the temple for suspects.

The temple was surrounded by a massive square garden, a style from Lord Rudra's land, far beyond the western borders of India. The garden had an ingeniously designed gargantuan fountain at its heart and rows of intricate waterways, flowerbeds and grass spread out from the centre in simple, yet stunning symmetry. At the far end stood the Narsimha temple. Built of pure white marble, it had a giant staircase leading up to its main platform, a spire that shot up at least seventy metres and had ornately carved statues of Gods and Goddesses all across its face. Shiva was sure this awe-inspiring and obviously expensive temple had been built at a time when Magadh had the resources of the entire Swadweep confederacy at its command.

He took off his sandals at the staircase, climbed up the steps and entered the main temple. At the far end was the main sanctum of the temple, with the statue of its God, Lord Narsimha, on a majestic throne. Lord Narsimha had lived many thousands of years ago, before even Lord Rudra's time. Shiva mused that if the Lord's idol was life size, then he must have been a powerful figure. He looked unnaturally tall, at least eight feet, with a musculature that would terrify even the demons. His hands were unusually brawny with long nails, making Shiva think that just the Lord's bare hands must have been a fearsome weapon.

But it was the Lord's face that stunned Shiva. His mouth was surrounded by lips that were large beyond imagination. His moustache hair did not flow down like most men, but came out in rigid tracks, like a cat's whiskers. His nose was abnormally large, with sharp eyes on either side. His hair sprayed out a fair distance, like a mane. It almost looked as though Lord Narsimha was a man with the head of a lion.

Had he been alive today, Lord Narsimha would have been considered a Naga by the Chandravanshis and hence feared, not revered. Don't they have any consistency?

'Consistency is the virtue of mules!'

Shiva looked up, surprised how someone had heard his thoughts.

A Vasudev Pandit emerged from behind the pillars. He was the shortest Pandit that Shiva had met so far; just a little over five feet. But in all other aspects, his appearance was like every other Vasudev, his hair snowy white and his face wizened with age. He was clad in a saffron *dhoti* and *angvastram.*

'How did you...'

'That is not important,' interrupted the Pandit, raising his hands, not finding it important to explain how he discerned Shiva's thoughts.

That conversation... another time... great Neelkanth.

Shiva could have sworn he heard the Pandit's voice in his head. The words were broken, like the voice was coming from a great distance. Very soft and not quite clear. But it was the Pandit's voice. Shiva frowned, for the Pandit's lips had not moved.

Oh Lord Vasudev... this foreigner's...impressive.

Shiva heard the Pandit's voice again. The Pandit was smiling slightly. He could tell that the Neelkanth could hear his thoughts.

'You're not going to explain, are you?' asked Shiva with a smile.

No. You're certainly... not ready... yet.

The Pandit's appearance may have been like other Vasudevs, but his character was clearly different. This Vasudev was straightforward to the point of being rude. But Shiva knew the apparent rudeness was not intended. It was just a reflection of the mercurial nature of this particular Pandit's character.

Maybe the Pandit was a Chandravanshi in another life.

'I'm a Vasudev,' said the Pandit. 'There is no other identity I carry today. I'm not a son. Or husband. Or father. And, I'm not a Chandravanshi. I am only a Vasudev.'

A man has many identities, Panditji.

The Pandit narrowed his eyes.

'Were you born a Vasudev?'

'Nobody is born a Vasudev, Lord Neelkanth. You earn it. There is a competitive examination, for which Suryavanshis or Chandravanshis can appear. If you pass, you cease to be anything else. You give up all other identities. You become a Vasudev.'

'But you were a Chandravanshi before you earned your right to be a Vasudev,' smiled Shiva, as though merely stating a fact.

The Pandit smiled, acknowledging Shiva's statement.

Shiva had many questions he wanted answered. But there was a most obvious one for this particular Vasudev.

'A few months back, the Vasudev Pandit at the Ramjanmabhoomi temple had told me that my task is not to destroy evil, but to find out what evil is,' said Shiva.

The Vasudev Pandit nodded.

'I'm still digesting that idea. So my question is not on that,' continued Shiva. 'My query is about something else he said. He had told me that the Suryavanshis represent the masculine life force and the Chandravanshis represent the feminine. What does this mean? Because I don't think it has anything to do with men and women.'

'You can't get more obvious than that, my friend! You're right, it has nothing to do with men and women. It has to do with the way of life of the Suryavanshis and Chandravanshis.'

'Way of life?'

— ⅄ⵔ Ʊ ⴷ ⊛ —

'Prince Ugrasen has been killed?' asked Bhagirath.

'Yes, Your Highness,' said Siamantak softly. 'The news is from a source I trust implicitly.'

'Lord Ram help us! This is all we need. King Mahendra will think Ayodhya arranged the assassination. And you know how vengeful he can get.'

'I hope that he doesn't think that, Your Highness,' said Siamantak, 'It's the last thing we need.'

'Their spies have been following us,' said Nandi. 'I'm sure they have a report of our whereabouts and movements since we have entered the city. We cannot be blamed.'

'No, Nandi,' said Bhagirath. 'King Mahendra can also think that we hired assassins to do his son in. By the way, where are the spies?'

'Two of them,' said Drapaku, pointing with his eyes in the direction of the spies. 'They are quite amateurish. That tree doesn't really hide them!'

Bhagirath smiled slightly.

'It could be Surapadman,' said Siamantak. 'Everyone in Swadweep is aware that the younger Magadh Prince is ruthless. He could have arranged the killing to claim the throne.'

'No,' said Bhagirath, narrowing his eyes. 'Surapadman is by far the more capable son of King Mahendra. For all his faults, the king of Magadh does respect capability, unlike some other rulers I know. Surapadman practically has the throne. He doesn't need to kill his brother for it.'

'But how come there is no public mourning as yet?' asked Drapaku.

'They're keeping the news secret,' said Siamantak. 'I don't know why.'

'Maybe to arrange a credible story to give at least some respectability to Ugrasen's memory,' said Bhagirath. 'That idiot was quite capable of stumbling upon his own sword!'

Siamantak nodded before turning towards Drapaku. 'Why does the Lord want to spend so much time in the temple alone? It's quite unorthodox.'

'That's because the Lord himself is quite unorthodox. But why are we keeping his identity secret in Magadh?'

'Not everyone who believes in the legend is a follower of the Neelkanth, Drapaku,' said Bhagirath. 'The present king of Magadh does not follow the Neelkanth. And the people here are loyal followers of the King. The Lord's identity is best kept undisclosed here.'

— ⅄⦶Ʊ⍏⊛ —

'You know what makes humans special when compared to animals?' asked the Pandit.

'What?' asked Shiva.

'The fact that we work together. We collaborate to achieve combined goals. We pass on knowledge to each other, so every generation begins its journey from the shoulders of the previous generation and not from scratch.'

'I agree. But we are not the only ones who work in a pack. Other animals, like the elephants or lions, do it as well. But nobody does it on the scale that we do.'

'Yes, that's true. But it's not always about collaboration. It is sometimes about competition as well. It's not always about peace. Many times, it's also about war.'

Shiva smiled and nodded.

'So the key point is that we humans are nothing individually,' said the Pandit. 'Our power flows from all of us. From the way all of us live together.'

'Yes,' agreed Shiva.

'And if we have to live together, we must have a way of life, right?'

'Yes. Some method for all of us to collaborate or compete with each other.'

'Most people believe there are many hundred ways of life in the world,' said the Pandit. 'Every civilisation thinks that it is unique in some way.'

Shiva nodded in agreement.

'But if you actually distil the way people live, there are only two ways: The Masculine and the Feminine.'

'And what do these ways of life mean?'

'The masculine way of life is "life by laws". Laws that could be made by a great leader, perhaps a Vishnu like Lord Ram. Or laws that come down from a religious tradition. Or collective laws decreed by the people themselves. But the masculine way is very clear. Laws are unchangeable and they must be followed rigidly. There is no room for ambiguity. Life is predictable because the populace will always do what has been ordained. Meluha is a perfect example of such a way of life. It is obvious, therefore, why the people of this way of life live by the code of Truth, Duty and Honour. Since that's what they need to be successful in this system.'

'And the feminine?'

'The feminine way of life is "life by probabilities". There are no absolutes. No black or white. People don't act as per some preordained law, but based on probabilities of different outcomes perceived at that point of time. For example, they will follow a king who they think has a higher probability of remaining in power. The moment the probabilities change, their loyalties do as well. If there are laws in such a society, they are malleable. The same laws can be interpreted differently at different points of time. Change is the only constant. Feminine civilisations, like Swadweep, are comfortable with contradictions. And the code for success in such a system? Unmistakeably, Passion, Beauty and Freedom.'

'And no one way of life is better?'

'Obviously. Both types of civilisations must exist. Because they balance each other.'

'How?'

'You see, a masculine civilisation at its peak is honourable, consistent, reliable and spectacularly successful in an age suitable for its particular set of laws. There is order and society moves coherently in a preordained direction. Look at the Suryavanshis today. But when masculine civilisations decline, they cause horrible turmoil, becoming fanatical and rigid. They will attack those that are different, try to "convert" them to their "truth", which will lead to violence and chaos. This especially happens when an age changes. Change is difficult for the masculine. They will cling even more rigidly to their laws, even though those laws may be unsuitable for the new age. Masculine civilisations enforce order which is welcome when they are strong, but is suffocating when they decline. The Asuras, who were followers of the masculine way, had faced similar problems when their power started waning.'

'So when fanaticism causes rebellions born of frustration, the openness of the feminine brings a breath of fresh air.'

'Exactly. The feminine way incorporates all differences.

People of varying faiths and belief can coexist in peace. Nobody tries to enforce their own version of the truth. There is a celebration of diversity and freedom, which brings forth renewed creativity and vigour causing tremendous benefits to society. The Devas, who were followers of the feminine way, brought in all this when they defeated the Asuras. But as it happens with too much freedom, the feminine civilisations overreach into decadence, corruption and debauchery.'

'Then the people once again welcome the order of the masculine.'

'Yes. The feminine Deva way was in decline during Lord Ram's times. The country was corrupt, immoral and depraved. People clamoured for order and civility. Lord Ram ushered that in as he created a new masculine way of life. Very intelligently, to prevent unnecessary rebellions, he never decried the Deva way. He just called his rule a new way of life: the Suryavanshi path.'

'But can you really say the masculine and the feminine only exist at the level of civilisations?' asked Shiva. 'Doesn't it really exist within every man and woman? Doesn't everyone have a little bit of the Suryavanshi and a bit of the Chandravanshi within themselves? Their relative influence within the individual changing, depending upon the situations he faces?'

'Yes, you are right. But most people have a dominant trait. Either the masculine or the feminine.'

Shiva nodded.

'The reason why you need to know the two ways of life is because once you have discovered evil, you would have to tailor your message depending on which people you speak to. You will have to convince the Suryavanshis in one manner and the Chandravanshis in an altogether different manner in the battle against evil.'

'Why would I need to convince them? I don't think either the Suryavanshis or Chandravanshis lack in courage.'

'It has nothing to do with courage, my friend. Courage is only needed once the war begins. To begin with you need to persuade the people to embark upon the war against evil. You will need to influence them to give up their attachment to evil.'

'Attachment! To evil!' cried a flabbergasted Shiva. 'Why in the name of the holy lake would anyone be attached to evil?'

The Pandit smiled.

Shiva sighed. 'Now what? What's the explanation for stopping the conversation at this moment? I'm not ready? The time is not right?'

The Pandit laughed. 'I can't explain it to you right now, O Neelkanth. You would not understand. And when you discover evil, you would not need my explanation in order to understand. Jai Guru Vishwamitra. Jai Guru Vashishtha.'

Chapter 4

The City Where the Supreme Light Shines

'Prince Surapadman?' asked a surprised Bhagirath. 'Here!'

'Yes, Your Highness,' said Siamantak, worried.

Bhagirath turned towards Shiva. The Neelkanth nodded.

The prince of Ayodhya turned towards Siamantak. 'Let Prince Surapadman in.'

Moments later a dashing figure marched in. Tall, well-built and swarthy, Surapadman sported a handle bar moustache smoothly oiled and curled up at the edges. His well-maintained hair was long and neatly arranged under an extravagant yet tasteful crown. He wore an ochre *dhoti* with a white *angvastram*, sober for a Chandravanshi royal. There were numerous battle scars on his body, a sign of pride on any Kshatriya.

He walked straight up to Shiva, went down on his haunches and touched the Neelkanth's feet with his head. 'My Lord, it is an honour to finally have your presence in India.'

A surprised Shiva had the presence of mind not to step back. That could easily have been seen as an insult.

He blessed Surapadman with a long life. '*Ayushman Bhav*, Prince. How did you know who I am?'

'Divine light cannot be kept secret, My Lord,' said Surapadman, turning towards Bhagirath with a knowing smile. 'No matter how strong a veil one puts on it.'

Bhagirath smiled and nodded at Surapadman.

'I heard about your brother,' said Shiva. 'Please accept my condolences.'

Surapadman didn't say anything to acknowledge the commiseration. He bowed politely and changed the subject. 'I would like to apologise to you for not receiving you with the ceremonial honour due to the long-awaited Neelkanth. But my father can be a little stubborn.'

'That's all right. I've not given anybody any reason to honour me just as yet. Why don't we talk about what you actually came here for, Surapadman?'

'My Lord, I suppose nothing remains a secret from you. My brother was killed a few days back while in the forest with some friends and his bodyguards. There is a belief that Ayodhya may have carried out this dastardly act.'

'I can assure you we didn't...,' started Bhagirath. Surapadman stretched out his hand, requesting for silence.

'I know that, Prince Bhagirath,' said Surapadman. 'I have a different theory about his murder.'

Surapadman reached into the pouch tied to his waist band and fished out a Branga gold coin. It was exactly similar to the gold coin that Shiva had recovered from the Naga *Lord of the People*.

'My Lord,' said Surapadman. 'This is something I found near my brother's body. I believe that you had recovered a gold coin from a Naga while you were in Ayodhya. Is this similar to that coin?'

Bhagirath stared at Surapadman with shock. He was wondering how Surapadman knew about the Neelkanth's discovery. Rumours about Surapadman building his own spy network must be true. A network independent of the outrageously incompetent Magadh intelligence services.

Shiva took the coin from Surapadman, staring at it hard, his body taut with anger. 'I don't suppose that filthy rat has been caught?'

Surapadman was surprised at Shiva's intense reaction. 'No, My Lord, regrettably not. I fear he may have escaped into the rat hole he emerged from.'

Shiva handed the coin back to Surapadman. He was quiet.

Surapadman turned towards Bhagirath. 'This is all the confirmation I needed, Prince. I will report to the King that my brother, Prince Ugrasen, died while valiantly defending Magadh from a Naga terrorist attack. I will also report that Ayodhya had nothing to do with this. I am sure even you don't want a pointless war between the two pillars of the Chandravanshi confederacy. Especially not now, when we have suffered such a grievous loss to the Suryavanshis.'

The last comment was a jibe. Ayodhya had lost face amongst Chandravanshis due to its leadership in the disastrous war against the Meluhans at Dharmakhet.

'Your words assuage a deep concern of mine, Prince Surapadman,' said Bhagirath. 'I assure you of Ayodhya's friendly intentions towards Magadh. And please allow me to officially convey Ayodhya's condolences on your brother's untimely death.'

Surapadman nodded politely. He turned towards Shiva again with a low bow. 'My Lord, I can see that you too have a bone to pick with the Nagas. I request you to call me to your service when the war with this particular demon is to be fought.'

Shiva looked at Surapadman with a surprised frown. The prince had not given an impression till now that he loved his brother or even sought vengeance.

'My Lord, whatever he may have been like,' said Surapadman, 'he was my brother. I must avenge his blood.'

'That Naga killed my brother as well, Prince Surapadman,' said Shiva, referring to Brahaspati, the Chief Scientist of Meluha, who was like a brother to him. 'I will call you to battle when the time is right.'

— ⁂ —

Shiva's entourage left Magadh quietly. Unlike any other city that Shiva had been to, both in Meluha and Swadweep, there was no jamboree organised to see him off. His coming and going had been secret from most people in Magadh. Surapadman however had come to the Magadh port incognito to pay his respects to the Neelkanth before his departure.

The ships sailed in the standard Meluhan convoy formation with the main ship carrying the Neelkanth and his companions, surrounded on all four sides by a ship each. Regardless of which side an enemy cutter came from, they would have to fight through an entire battleship before reaching the Neelkanth's craft. A crucial role in this formation was played by the lead ship. It was the speed controller for the entire convoy. It had to sail slow enough to protect the Neelkanth's ship from the front, but be fast enough to afford enough space for Shiva's ship to slip through and escape if need be.

A Chandravanshi captain was in command of the lead ship and he was doing a spectacularly inept job. He was speeding at a maniacal pace, perhaps to show the prowess of his vessel. This kept opening up a breach between his lead boat and Shiva's vessel. Parvateshwar had to keep blowing the ship horn to alert the lead boat Captain and slow him down.

Tired of this inefficiency, Parvateshwar had decided to travel in the lead ship to teach a thing or two to the Chandravanshi captain about the basics of naval defence formations. Considering the task at hand, Parvateshwar was distressed that Anandmayi had, for some inexplicable reason, decided to also travel on the lead ship.

'So why are we so slow?' asked Anandmayi.

Parvateshwar turned from the balustrade at the fore of the ship. He had not seen her tip-toe to his side. She was standing with her back to the railing, her elbows resting on it lightly with one of her heels placed on the block at the bottom of the railing. Her posture had the effect of raising her already short *dhoti* a fair distance up her right leg and stretching her bosom out provocatively. Parvateshwar, uncomfortable for some reason he could not fathom, stepped back a bit.

'This is a naval defence formation, Princess,' laboured Parvateshwar, as if explaining complicated mathematics to a child unprepared to understand. 'It would take me a lifetime to explain it to you.'

'Are you asking me to spend a lifetime with you? You old devil, you.'

Parvateshwar turned red.

'Well,' continued Anandmayi, 'it will certainly not take me a lifetime to tell you something quite basic. Instead of trying to keep our lead boat agonisingly slow, simply tie a rope of approximately the right length from here to the main ship. Then have a soldier posted at the back who signals every time the rope touches the water, which would mean that the lead vessel is too slow and should speed up. And if the rope becomes taut, the soldier can relay a signal that the lead ship should slow down.'

Anandmayi slipped her hands into her hair to straighten them out. 'You'll make much better time and I will be able to get off these ridiculously small quarters into a more comfortable Kashi palace.'

Parvateshwar was struck by the ingenuity of her suggestion. 'That is brilliant! I will immediately have the captain execute these orders.'

Anandmayi reached out a delicate hand, catching hold of Parvateshwar and pulling him back. 'What's the hurry, Parva? A few minutes will make no difference. Talk to me for a while.'

Parvateshwar turned beet red at both the corruption of his name and Anandmayi's unyielding grip on his arm. He looked down at her hands.

Anandmayi frowned and pulled her hands back. 'They're not dirty, General.'

'That's not what I was implying, Princess.'

'Then what?' asked Anandmayi, her tone slightly harsher.

'I cannot touch a woman, Princess. Especially not you. I am sworn to lifelong celibacy.'

Anandmayi was aghast, staring as though Parvateshwar was an alien. 'Hold on! Are you saying you are a 180-year-old *virgin?!*'

Parvateshwar, chagrined at the completely inappropriate

conversation, turned around and stormed off. Anandmayi collapsed into a fit of giggles.

Vishwadyumna heard the soft footfalls. He immediately drew his sword, giving hand signals to his platoon to do likewise.

Their platoon had moved deeper into the forests south of Magadh after the skirmish with Prince Ugrasen and his platoon. The Naga had been injured seriously and was not in a position to travel far. They had travelled as fast as they could without risking the Naga's life, as the angry Magadhans scoured the land for the killers of their prince.

Vishwadyumna hoped the sounds he was hearing did not come from the Magadhans. His Lord was in no state to fight. Or flee.

'Put your sword down, you imbecile,' whispered a strong feminine voice. 'If I'd really wanted to kill you, I would have done it even before you drew your weapon.'

Vishwadyumna did not recognise the hoarse whisper. Perhaps, the tiredness of long travel or the cold of winter had roughened the voice. But he certainly recognised the tone. He immediately put his sword down and bowed his head.

The Queen of the Nagas emerged from the trees, leading her horse quietly. Behind her was her trusted Prime Minister, Karkotak, and fifty of her elite bodyguards.

'I asked you to do just one simple thing,' hissed the Queen. 'Can't you ensure the protection of your Lord? Is that so difficult to do?'

'My Lady,' whispered a nervous Vishwadyumna, 'the situation suddenly got out of...'

'Shut up!' glared the Queen, throwing the reins of her horse to one soldier, as she walked quickly towards the cloth tent at the centre of the clearing.

She entered the cramped tent and took off her mask. On a bed of hay lay her nephew, the Lord of the People. He was covered in bandages, his body limp and weak.

The Queen looked at her nephew with concerned eyes, her tone kind. 'Are we now in alliance with the tribals also?'

The Naga opened his eyes and smiled. He whispered weakly, 'No, Your Highness.'

'Then in the name of the Parmatma, why are you risking your own life to save one of the forest people? Why are you causing me so much grief? Don't I have enough on my plate already?'

'Forgive me, *Mausi*, but haven't I already taken care of your biggest source of tension?'

'Yes, you have. And that is the only reason why I have come all this way for you. You have earned the devotion of all the Nagas. But your karma is still not complete. There are many things you need to do. And stopping some royal brat from what you believe is wrong does not figure high on that list. This country is full of repulsive royals who abuse their people. Are we going to fight every single one?'

'It is not that simple, *Mausi*.'

'Yes, it is. The Magadh prince was doing something wrong. But it is not your duty to stop every person who does something wrong. You are not Lord Rudra.'

'He was trying to kidnap a boy for a bull race.'

The Queen sighed. 'It happens all over. It happens to

thousands of children. This bull fighting is an addictive disease. How many will you stop?'

'But he didn't just stop there,' whispered the Naga. 'He was about to kill the boy's mother, because she was trying to protect her child.'

The Queen stiffened. Quick anger rose within her.

'There aren't too many mothers like this,' whispered the Naga with rare emotion. 'They deserve protection.'

'Enough! How many times have I told you to forget this?'

The Queen rapidly put her mask back on her face and stormed out. Her men kept their heads bowed, terrified of her fearsome rage. 'Karkotak!'

'Yes, my lady.'

'We leave within the hour. We're going home. Make preparations.'

The Lord of the People was in no position to travel. Karkotak knew that. 'But, Your Highness...'

His words were cut short by a petrifying glare from the Queen.

— ⁂ —

It was just a little over three weeks when Shiva's convoy was closing in on *Kashi, the city where the supreme light shines.* The city had been settled along a voluptuous bend of the holy Ganga river as it took a leisurely northwards meander before flowing East again. If looked at from the sky, this meander gave the impression of a crescent moon, incidentally the royal insignia of the Chandravanshis. Therefore, in the eyes of the Swadweepans, Kashi was the most natural Chandravanshi city.

Kashi also had its own superstition. The city had been built only along the western banks of the river meander, leaving its eastern banks bare. It was believed that whoever built a house on the eastern side at Kashi would suffer a terrible fate. The royal family of Kashi had therefore bought all the land to the East, ensuring that nobody, even by mistake, would suffer the wrath of the Gods.

As Shiva's ship was moving towards the legendary *Assi Ghat* or *Port of Eighty,* one of the main docking points of this thriving city, the crowd on the steps started beating their drums for the ceremonial welcome aarti.

'It's a beautiful city,' whispered Sati, running her hand over her protruding belly.

Shiva looked at her and smiled, taking her hand, kissing it gently and holding it close to his chest. 'For some reason, it feels like home. This is where our child should be born.'

Sati smiled back. 'Yes. This shall be the place.'

Even from afar, Bhagirath could make out the countenance of many Ayodhya nobles jostling with the Kashi aristocracy, striving to raise their welcome lamps while berating their aides to hold their family pennants higher. They wanted the Mahadev to notice and favour them. But the Neelkanth noticed something more unusual.

'Bhagirath,' said Shiva, turning to his left, 'this city has no fortifications. Why in the name of the Holy Lake do they have no protection?'

'Oh! That's a long story, My Lord,' said Bhagirath.

'I have all the time in the world. Tell me the entire tale, for this is one of the strangest sights I have seen in India.'

'Well, My Lord, the story starts at Assi Ghat, where we are about to dock.'

'Hmm.'

'This dock did not get its peculiar name because it has eighty steps. Neither did it get its name from the small Assi rivulet that flows close by. It got its name due to an execution that took place here. In fact, eighty executions in just one day.'

'Lord Ram be merciful,' said a flabbergasted Sati. 'Who were these unfortunate people?'

'They were not unfortunate, My Lady,' said Bhagirath. 'They were the worst criminals in history. Eighty members of the Asura royalty were put to death by Lord Rudra for war crimes. Many believe that it was not the exhausting battles between the Devas and Asuras that put an end to the evil Asura menace, but this sublime act of justice that Lord Rudra performed. Without their key leaders, the Asura insurrection against the Devas fizzled out.'

'And then?' asked Shiva, remembering what the Vasudev Pandit at Ayodhya had told him.

Who said the Asuras were evil?

'And then, something strange happened. Soon thereafter, Lord Rudra, the greatest and most fearsome warrior in history, abandoned all violence. He banned the use of *Daivi Astras* that had caused enormous casualties in the Deva-Asura war. Anyone who disobeyed this order would feel the wrath of Lord Rudra who said he would even break his vow of non-violence and destroy seven generations of the man who used any divine weapons.'

'I know of Lord Rudra's order on the *Daivi Astras*,' said Sati, as the Meluhans were also aware of the Mahadev's ban on *divine weapons*. 'But I didn't know the story behind it. What made him give this order?'

'I don't know, My Lady,' said Bhagirath.

I know, mused Shiva. *This must have been the moment when*

Lord Rudra realised the Asuras were not evil, just different. He must have been racked by guilt.

'But the story did not end there. Lord Rudra also said Assi Ghat and Kashi had become holy. He didn't explain why, but the people of that time assumed that it must be because this was the place that ended the war. Lord Rudra said there would be no further killing at Assi Ghat. Ever. That the place should be respected. That the spirits at Assi Ghat and Kashi would forgive the sins of even the most sinful and guide them to salvation if their dead body was cremated there.'

'Interesting,' said Sati.

'The Kashi kings, who were great followers of Lord Rudra, not only banned any executions or killing at Assi Ghat, they also threw it open for cremations for people from any kingdom, without prejudice of caste, creed or sex. Any person can find salvation here. Over time, the belief in Kashi being the gateway to a soul's deliverance gained ground and vast numbers of people started coming here to spend their final days. It was impossible for the small Assi Ghat to cater to such large numbers of the dead. So cremations were stopped at Assi and the city converted another massive ghat, called Manikarnika, into a giant crematorium.'

'But what does that have to do with there being no fort walls?' asked Shiva.

'The point is that if the most influential people in Swadweep came here at the time of their death, with the belief that this would be a place where their sins would be forgiven and they could attain salvation, very few would want Kashi to be destroyed or even be involved in the regular wars that raged in the confederacy. In addition,

Kashi kings took Lord Rudra's orders of nonviolence to what they believed was its logical conclusion. The royal family publicly swore that neither they, nor their descendants, would ever indulge in warfare. In fact, they foreswore any killing, except in the case of self-defence. To prove their commitment to their words, they actually tore down their fort ramparts and built an open ring road around the city. They then erected great temples all along the road, giving it an aura of spirituality.'

'Kashi wasn't attacked and conquered?'

'On the contrary, My Lord,' continued Bhagirath, 'their intense commitment to Lord Rudra's teachings almost made Kashi sacred. Nobody could attack this city, for it would be seen as an insult to Lord Rudra. It became a land of supreme peace and hence prosperity. Suppressed people from across the confederacy found solace here. Traders found that this was the safest place to base their business. Peace and nonalignment to any other kingdom in Swadweep has actually made Kashi an oasis of stability.'

'Is that why you find so many Brangas here?'

'Yes, My Lord. Where else would they be safe? Everybody is out of harm's way in Kashi. But the Brangas have tested even the famed Kashi patience and hospitality.'

'Really?'

'Apparently, they are very difficult to get along with. Kashi is a cosmopolitan city and nobody is forced to change their way of life. But the Brangas wanted their own area because they have certain special customs. The Kashi royal family advises its citizens that the Brangas have suffered a lot in their homeland and that Kashi denizens should be compassionate. But most people find that difficult. In fact, a few years back, it was rumoured that the situation came to such a pass that the king of Kashi was about to order the eviction of the Brangas.'

'And then what happened?' asked Shiva.

'Gold managed to do what good intentions couldn't. Branga is by far the richest land today. The king of Branga had apparently sent gold equivalent to ten years of Kashi's tax collections. And the eviction order was buried.'

'Why would the Branga king spend his own money to help people who have abandoned his country?'

'I don't know, My Lord. I think we can put that down as another strange characteristic of the Brangas.'

The ship docked softly at Assi Ghat and Shiva looked towards the multitudes gathered there to welcome him. Parvateshwar was already organising the place so that Shiva could alight. He saw Drapaku at a distance giving orders to Nandi and Veerbhadra. Bhagirath had already bounded down the gangway in search of the Kashi head of police. Sati tapped Shiva lightly. He turned to look at her and she gestured delicately with her eyes. Shiva looked in the direction she had indicated. In the distance, away from the melee, letting his nobles and the Ayodhya aristocracy hog the frontlines of the Neelkanth's welcome, under an understated royal umbrella, stood a sombre old man. Shiva joined his hands in a polite namaste and bowed slightly to Athithigva, the king of Kashi. Athithigva in turn bowed low in respect to the Neelkanth. Sati could not be sure from the distance, but it appeared as though the king had tears in his eyes.

Chapter 5

A Small Wrong?

'Mmm,' mumbled Shiva as Sati softly kissed him awake. He cupped her face gently. 'Are my eyes deceiving me or are you getting more beautiful every day?'

Sati smiled, running her hand along her belly. 'Stop flattering me so early in the morning!'

Shiva edged up on his elbows, kissing her again. 'So there is a fixed schedule for compliments now?'

Sati laughed again, slowly getting off the bed. 'Why don't you go wash? I have requested for breakfast to be served in our room.'

'Ahh! You are finally learning my ways!' Shiva always hated eating at the organised and civilised dining room gatherings that Sati liked.

As Shiva walked into the comfortable washroom attached to their chamber at the Kashi palace, Sati looked out. The famous ring road, also called the Sacred Avenue, was clearly visible. It was an awe-inspiring sight. Unlike the congested city of Kashi itself, the avenue was very broad, allowing even six carts to pass simultaneously. There was a breathtaking profusion of trees around the road, with probably all the species of flora from the

Indian subcontinent represented. Beyond the trees lay the plethora of temples. The boulevard extended upto a roughly semi-circular distance of more than thirty kilometres and not one of the buildings built on its sides was anything but a place of worship. The Chandravanshis liked to say that almost every Indian God has a home on Kashi's Sacred Avenue. But of course, that belief was scarcely built on reality, considering that the Indians worshipped over thirty million Gods. But one could safely state that practically all the popular Gods had a temple dedicated to them on this holy pathway. And the most majestic temple of them all was dedicated, but of course, to the most admired of them all, the great Mahadev himself, Lord Rudra. It was this temple that Sati was staring at. It had been built close to the Brahma Ghat. Legend had it that the original plan for the temple, hatched by the Devas during the life of Lord Rudra himself, was to have it close to Assi Ghat, the scene of Lord Rudra's deliverance of justice. But the great Mahadev, the scourge of the Asuras, had ordered that no memorial to him must ever be built near Assi Ghat, with one of his most unfathomable lines — '*Not here. Anywhere else. But not here*'. No one had understood why. But at the same time, no one argued with the fearsome Lord Rudra.

'They call it the *Vishwanath* temple,' said Shiva, startling Sati with his sudden appearance. 'It means the *Lord of the World*.'

'He was a great man,' whispered Sati. 'A true God.'

'Yes,' agreed Shiva, *bowing to Lord Rudra*. '*Om Rudraiy namah*.'

'*Om Rudraiy namah*.'

'It was good of King Athithigva to leave us alone last night. We certainly needed the rest after the string of ceremonies at Assi Ghat.'

'Yes, he seems to be a good man. But I fear he will not be leaving you alone today. I could make out that he has a lot to talk to you about.'

Shiva laughed. 'But I do like his city. The more I see it, the more it feels like home.'

'Let's eat our breakfast,' said Sati. 'I think we have a long day ahead!'

— ⁂ —

'*Especially not you*?' asked Kanini. 'He actually said that?'

'Those very words,' said Anandmayi. 'He said he cannot touch any woman. Especially not me!'

Kanini expertly massaged the rejuvenating oil into Anandmayi's scalp. 'That does make sense, Princess. There are only two women who can make a man break the vow of lifelong celibacy. Either the *apsara* Menaka or you.'

'Two?' Anandmayi had her eyebrows raised at being considered akin to the *celestial nymph*.

'My apologies,' chuckled Kanini. 'What is Menaka compared to you!'

Anandmayi laughed.

'But this is a far tougher challenge than Menaka's, Princess,' continued Kanini. 'Sage Vishwamitra had taken the vow late in his life. He had already experienced the pleasures of love. Menaka just had to remind him, not create the need. The General on the other hand is a virgin!'

'I know. But when something is so beautiful, achieving it cannot be easy, can it?'

Kanini narrowed her eyes. 'Don't lose your heart before you have won his, Princess.'

Anandmayi frowned. 'Of course I haven't!'

Kanini stared hard at Anandmayi and smiled. The Princess was obviously in love. She hoped Parvateshwar had the good sense to realise his good fortune in time.

— ⁂ —

'You have a beautiful capital, Your Highness,' said Shiva.

The sun had already covered a third of its daily journey. Shiva was sitting in King Athithigva's private chambers with Sati. Drapaku, Nandi and Veerbhadra stood guard at the door supporting the baton-wielding Kashi royal guard. It was a mystery to Drapaku how only batons could be used to protect a royal family. What if there was a serious attack? Meanwhile, Parvateshwar had set off on a tour with the Kashi police chief. He wanted to ensure that the path from the palace to the Kashi Vishwanath temple was well-protected for the Neelkanth's planned visit in the afternoon. It was expected that practically the entire city would be lining the Sacred Avenue to catch a glimpse of the Neelkanth, for only the nobility had been allowed to meet him at his arrival at Assi Ghat.

'Actually, this is your city, My Lord,' said Athithigva with a low bow.

Shiva frowned.

'Lord Rudra had spent most of his time in Kashi, calling it his adopted home,' explained Athithigva. 'After his departure to his birth land to the West, the Kashi royal family conducted a puja at Assi Ghat, effectively making Lord Rudra and his successors our true kings for eternity.

My family, while being different from the royal family that conducted that puja, honours the promise to this day. We only function as the caretakers of the birthright of Lord Rudra's successors.'

Shiva was getting increasingly uncomfortable.

'Now that Lord Rudra's successor is here, it is time for him to ascend the throne of Kashi,' continued Athithigva. 'It will be my honour to serve you, My Lord.'

Shiva almost choked on a combination of surprise and exasperation.

These people are all mad! Well intentioned, but mad!

'I have no intentions of becoming a King, Your Highness,' smiled Shiva. 'I certainly don't think of myself as worthy of being called Lord Rudra's successor. You are a good king and I suggest you continue to serve your people.'

'But, My Lord...'

'I have a few requests though, Your Highness,' interrupted Shiva. He did not want to continue the discussion on his royal antecedents.

'Anything, My Lord.'

'Firstly, my wife and I would like our child to be born here. May we impose on your hospitality for this duration?'

'My Lord, my entire palace is yours. Lady Sati and you can stay here for all time to come.'

Shiva smiled slightly. 'No, I don't think we will stay that long. Also, I want to meet the leader of the Brangas in your city.'

'His name is Divodas, My Lord. I will certainly summon him to your presence. Speaking to anyone else from that unfortunate tribe is useless. Divodas is the only one sensible or capable enough to interact with others. I believe he is out on a trading trip and should be returning by tonight. I'll ensure that he is called here at the earliest.'

'Wonderful.'

'The crowd out there looks like it is slipping out of control, Drapaku,' pointed Parvateshwar.

Parvateshwar was with Bhagirath, Drapaku and Tratya, the Kashi police chief, upon a raised platform on the Sacred Avenue. It almost seemed like all of Kashi's 200,000 citizens had descended there to catch a glimpse of the Neelkanth. And the Kashi police appeared woefully ill-trained to manage the crowd. They were polite to a fault, which usually worked with the courteous Kashi citizens. But on an occasion like this, when every person was desperate to jump up front and touch the Lord, the firm hand of the Suryavanshis was called for.

'I'll take care of it, General,' said Drapaku as he bounded off the platform to issue instructions to Nandi waiting at the bottom.

'But he must not raise his hand,' said Tratya.

'He'll behave as required by the situation, Tratya,' said Parvateshwar, irritated.

Nandi, on hearing Drapaku's orders, was off with his platoon. Drapaku, using the hook on his amputated left hand, pulled himself back onto the platform with surprising agility.

'It's done, General,' said Drapaku. 'That crowd will be pushed back.'

Parvateshwar nodded and turned to look at Shiva and his party. Shiva, holding Sati's hand, walked slowly with a broad smile, acknowledging almost every single person who screamed out his name. Krittika, Sati's companion, paced slightly behind Sati while Athithigva, beaming with the commitment of a true devotee, marched silently, with his family and ministers in tow.

'Chief Tratya,' shouted a panicked Kashi policeman bounding up the platform.

Tratya looked down. 'Yes, Kaavas?'

'A riot is breaking out in the Branga quarter!'

'Tell me exactly what happened.'

'They have killed a peacock once again. But this time they were caught red-handed by some of their neighbours, who are swearing retribution for this sin.'

'I'm not surprised! I don't know why His Highness insists on keeping those uncivilised dolts in our city. It was only a matter of time before some citizens lost their patience and did something.'

'What happened?' asked Parvateshwar.

'It's the Brangas. They know that killing peacocks is banned in Kashi as they were Lord Rudra's favourite amongst the birds. There is a widespread belief that they sacrifice the bird in some bizarre ceremonies in their colony. Now they have been caught red-handed and are going to be taught a lesson.'

'Why don't you send some of your men there to break up the riot?'

Tratya looked at Parvateshwar strangely. 'You won't understand some things. We accept every community from India in Kashi. All of them live peacefully, making this great city their home. But the Brangas purposely want to infuriate every one of us. This riot is actually a bad path to a good end. Just let it happen.'

Parvateshwar was shocked at the words of the same police chief who had been propagating the virtues of non-violence just a while back. 'If they have committed a crime, they should be punished by your courts. Your citizens do not have the right to riot and hurt innocent people who may have had nothing to do with the killing of the bird.'

'It doesn't matter if some of them were innocent. It's a small price to pay if it rids the city of the Brangas and their evil ways. I cannot and will not do anything on this.'

'If you won't do anything, I will,' warned Parvateshwar.

Tratya looked at Parvateshwar in exasperation and turned back to look at the Neelkanth's entourage. Parvateshwar stared hard at Tratya. It took only a moment for him to make up his mind.

'Drapaku, you have the command,' said Parvateshwar. 'Make sure the crowd breaks as soon as the Lord is in the Vishwanath temple. Prince Bhagirath, will you accompany me? I would need some help as I don't know Chandravanshi customs.'

'It will be my honour, General,' said Bhagirath.

'This is not your job,' said Tratya, raising his voice for the first time in the day. 'You have no right to interfere in our internal affairs.'

'He has every right,' interjected Bhagirath, with the arrogance that only a royal can possess. 'Have you forgotten Lord Ram's words? Standing by and doing nothing while a sin is committed is as bad as committing the sin yourself. You should be thanking the General for doing your job.'

Parvateshwar and Bhagirath quickly stepped down from the platform along with Kaavas, ordered Veerbhadra to follow them with a hundred men and rushed towards the Branga quarters.

— ⅄◎℧⍋⊛ —

'This is tough and tricky,' said Bhagirath.

They were in front of the Branga quarters. The legendary hoards of gold brought in by the refugees from the East had transformed this particularly congested part of the city into spacious residences. Brangas lived in a lavishly designed and intricately carved multi-storey building, the tallest in all of Kashi, save for the Vishwanath temple and the royal palaces. The building was surrounded on all sides by a large garden, strangely enough both lusciously landscaped and conservatively symmetrical, much like the one at the Narsimha temple in Magadh. A board at its entrance proudly proclaimed the loyalty of its residents: 'May Lord Rudra bless the most divine land of Branga.'

The city's congestion and confusion began immediately at the border of the fenced garden. Narrow paths led out into what were suburbs dominated by immigrants from Ayodhya, Magadh, Prayag and other parts of the Chandravanshi confederacy. A little known fact was that even some Meluhans, tired of the regimented life in their homeland and fearful of giving up their birth children at Maika, had found refuge in Kashi. They tolerated the chaos of the Chandravanshi ways for the pleasure of watching their children grow.

'I'm sure it's not just anger at their customs,' said Veerbhadra, taking in the stark difference in the lifestyles of the common folk of Kashi and the Brangas, 'Resentment about their wealth must also drive the hatred towards the Brangas.'

Bhagirath nodded before turning towards Parvateshwar, who was evaluating the situation. 'What do you think, General?'

From a perspective of defence, the location was a disaster. The Brangas were stuck between a rock and a hard place. They were surrounded on all four sides by a hostile population living in densely-populated areas along congested streets leading to the Branga quarters. Escape was out of the question. They would be easily mobbed in the narrow lanes. The garden gave them some measure of protection. Any mob attacking the Brangas would be exposed in that area for at least a minute till they reached the building itself.

The Brangas, perhaps always fearful of their status in Kashi, had stocked the roof of their building with a huge horde of rocks. Thrown from that height, the rocks were like missiles, capable of causing serious injury, possibly even death if it hit the right spot.

The Kashi mob, meanwhile, was releasing dogs, which the Brangas considered unclean, into the closed compound. They knew the Brangas would respond with stones to chase the animals back. Parvateshwar realised that in this battle of attrition, it was a matter of time before the Branga rocks ran out and they were susceptible to a full frontal attack. Outnumbered at more than a hundred to one, despite the fact that their enemies were armed with such laughable weapons as kitchen knives and washing clubs, the Brangas had little chance of survival.

'It doesn't look good for the Brangas,' said Parvateshwar. 'Can we reason with the Kashi mob?'

'I already tried, General,' said Bhagirath. 'They will not listen. They believe the Brangas can buy out the courts with their gold.'

'It's probably true,' mumbled the Kashi Captain Kaavas, quietly revealing his own leanings.

Bhagirath turned towards Kaavas, who immediately recoiled with fear, for Bhagirath's reputation was legendary in Kashi.

'You don't agree with the mob, do you?' asked Bhagirath.

Kaavas' face glowered, 'I detest the Brangas. They are dirty scoundrels who break every law, even as they throw their gold around.' Having said his piece, Kaavas seemed to calm down. He looked down and whispered. 'But is this the way they should be treated? Would Lord Rudra have done this? No, Your Highness.'

'Then find us a solution.'

Pointing to the angry Kashi citizens surrounding them, Kaavas said, 'This horde will not back off till the Brangas are punished in some form, Prince Bhagirath. How can we ensure that, while keeping the Brangas alive and safe? I don't know.'

'What if the Suryavanshis attack them?' asked Parvateshwar, shocked at the effective but borderline ethical solution that had entered his mind.

Bhagirath smiled immediately, for he could suspect where Parvateshwar was going. 'We'll use the batons of the Kashi police, not our weapons. We'll only injure, not kill.'

'Exactly,' said Parvateshwar. 'The mob will get its justice and back off. The Brangas will be injured, but alive. I know this is not entirely right. But sometimes, the only way to prevent a grave wrong is to commit a small wrong.

I will have to take full responsibility for this and answer to the Parmatma.'

Bhagirath smiled softly. Some Chandravanshi ways were entering Parvateshwar's psyche. It had not escaped his notice that his elder sister had been lavishing attention on the Meluhan General.

Parvateshwar turned to Kaavas. 'I will need a hundred batons.'

Bhagirath shot off with Kaavas towards the Sacred Avenue. They were back in no time. Parvateshwar had meanwhile spoken to the leaders of the Kashi mob, promising them justice if they dropped their weapons. They waited patiently for the Suryavanshis to deliver.

Parvateshwar gathered the Suryavanshis in front of him. 'Meluhans, do not use your swords. Use the batons. Limit the blows to their limbs, avoid their heads. Keep your shield rigidly in the tortoise formation. Rocks from that height can kill.'

The Suryavanshis stared at their General.

'This is the only way the Brangas can be saved,' continued Parvateshwar.

The Meluhans moved quickly into battle formation, with Parvateshwar, Bhagirath and Veerbhadra in the lead. Kaavas, who was unfamiliar with such tactics, was placed in the middle, where it was safest. As the soldiers marched into the Branga garden, there was a hailstorm of stones. Their shields kept them safe as they strode slowly but surely towards the building entrance.

The entrance itself was, naturally, narrower than the garden path. The tortoise formation would have to be broken here. Parvateshwar ordered a double file charge into the building, shields held left-right to prevent attacks from the sides. He had assumed the rocks could not be used within the building. A grave miscalculation.

— ⩓⦾Ʊ⇞⊛ —

'What a statue,' whispered Sati, shuddering slightly at the awe-inspiring sight of Lord Rudra.

Shiva and Sati had just entered the massive Vishwanath temple.

The temple, built a little distance away from the Brahma Ghat, was an imposing structure. It wasn't just the gargantuan height of one hundred metres, but also the overwhelming simplicity of the edifice that inspired wonder. An open garden, built in the symmetrical style of Lord Rudra's native land, provided the entry from the Sacred Avenue to the temple. The red sandstone structure, almost the colour of blood, was startlingly sober. The giant platform, almost twenty metres in height, which soared from the farthest point of the garden, had absolutely no carvings or embellishments, unlike any other temple Shiva had seen so far. A hundred steps had been carved into the platform. Devotees, who reached atop the platform, would be stunned by the main temple spire, again of red sandstone, which soared an improbable eighty metres. Just like the platform, the main temple also had no carvings. There were a hundred square pillars to hold up the spire. Unlike other temples, the sanctum sanctorum was in the centre and not at the far end. Within the sanctum was the statue that drew devotees from across the land: The formidable Lord Rudra.

Legend had it that Lord Rudra mostly worked alone. He had no known friends whose stories could be immortalised in frescoes on the temple walls. There was no favourite devotee whose statue could be placed at his feet. The only partner Lord Rudra had, the only one he listened to, was Lady Mohini. Hence Krittika found it odd that her legendary beauty had not been rendered into an idol.

'How come Lady Mohini's statue is not here?' whispered Krittika to an aide of Athithigva.

'You know the stories of the Lord well,' replied the aide. 'Come.'

She led Krittika to the other side of the sanctum. To her surprise, Krittika discovered that the sanctum had another entrance from the back. Through that entrance a devotee would see an idol of Lady Mohini, rumoured to be the most gorgeous woman of all time, sitting on a throne. Her beautiful eyes were in an enchanting half stare. But Krittika noticed that in her hand, surreptitiously hidden at first view, was a knife. Mohini, ever capricious and deadly. Krittika smiled. It seemed fitting that the idols of Lady Mohini and Lord Rudra were back to back. They shared a complex relationship; partners but with vastly different outlooks.

Krittika bowed low to Lady Mohini. While some refused to honour her as *Vishnu*, Krittika was amongst the majority which believed that Lady Mohini deserved the title of *the Propagator of Good.*

On the other side of the sanctum, Shiva was staring at Lord Rudra's idol. The Lord was an imposing and impossibly muscled man. His hirsute chest sported a pendant. Upon closer examination, Shiva realised the pendant was a tiger claw. The Lord's shield had been laid at the side of his throne and while the sword too rested along the seat, the Lord's hand was close to the hilt. Clearly, the sculptor wanted to signify that while the most ferocious warrior in history had renounced violence, his weapons lay close at hand, ready to be used on anyone who dared to break his laws. The sculptor had faithfully recreated the proud battle scars that must have adorned Lord Rudra's body. One of the scars ran across his face from his right temple to his left cheek. The Lord also sported a long beard and moustache, many strands of which had been painstakingly curled with beads rolled into them.

'I have never seen anyone in India wear beads in their beard,' said Shiva to Athithigva.

'This is the way of the Lord's native people in Pariha, My Lord.'

'*Pariha*?'

'Yes, My Lord. The *land of fairies*. It lies beyond the western borders of India, beyond the Himalayas, our great mountains.'

Shiva turned back to the Lord's idol. The strongest feeling he had in the temple was fear. Was it wrong to feel like this about a God? Wasn't it always supposed to be love? Respect? Awe? Why fear?

Because sometimes, nothing clarifies and focuses the mind except fear. Lord Rudra needed to inspire fear to achieve his goals.

Shiva heard the voice in his head. It appeared to come from a distance, but it was unquestionably clear. He knew it was a Vasudev Pandit.

Where are you, Panditji?

Hidden from view, Lord Neelkanth. There are too many people around.

I need to talk to you.

All in good time, my friend. But if you can hear me, can't you hear the desperate call of your most principled follower?

Most principled follower?

The voice had gone silent. Shiva turned around, concerned.

Chapter 6

Even a Mountain Can Fall

'Take cover!' shouted Parvateshwar.

Bhagirath and he had entered the Branga building to be greeted by a volley of stones.

The building had a huge atrium at the entrance, with a sky light. It was a brilliant design that allowed natural sunlight and fresh air to come in unhindered. There was a cleverly constructed retractable ceiling to cover the atrium during the rains. At present, however, the atrium was like a valley of death for the Suryavanshis, surrounded as it was on all sides by balconies from where the Brangas rained stones upon them.

A sharp missile hit Parvateshwar on his left shoulder. He felt his collar bone snap. A furious Parvateshwar drew his baton high and bellowed, 'Har Har Mahadev!'

'Har Har Mahadev!' yelled the Suryavanshis.

They were Gods! Mere stones wouldn't stop them. The Suryavanshis charged up the stairs, clubbing all who came in their path, including women. But even in their fury, they were mindful of Parvateshwar's instructions: No strikes on the head. They injured the Brangas, but killed none.

The Brangas started falling back, faced with the relentless

and disciplined Suryavanshi attack. Soon the Suryavanshis were charging up the building to the top. Parvateshwar found it strange that there appeared to be no leader. The Brangas were just a random mob, which was fighting heroically, but in a disastrously incompetent manner. By the time the Suryavanshis reached the top, practically all the Brangas were on the floor, writhing in agony. Injured, but alive.

It was then that Parvateshwar heard the noise. Even in the commotion of the numerous Brangas howling in pain, the horrifying din could not be missed. It sounded like hundreds of babies were howling desperately, as if their lives depended on it.

Parvateshwar had heard rumours of ghastly ritual sacrifices that the Brangas committed. Fearing the worst, he ran towards the room where the sound emanated from. The General broke open the door with one kick. He was sickened by what he saw.

The limp body of the decapitated peacock was held at a corner of the room, its blood being drained into a vessel. Around it were many women, each holding a baby writhing in pain. Some babies had blood on their mouths. A horror-struck Parvateshwar dropped his club and reached for his sword. There was a sudden blur to his left. Before he could react, he felt a sharp pain on his head. The world went black.

Bhagirath screamed, drawing his sword, as did the Suryavanshis. He was about to run his sword through the man who had clubbed Parvateshwar when a woman screamed: 'PLEASE DON'T!'

Bhagirath stopped. The woman was very obviously pregnant.

The Branga man was about to raise his club again. The woman screamed once more. 'NO!'

To Bhagirath's surprise, the man obeyed.

The other Branga women at the back were carrying on with their sickening ritual.

'Stop!' screamed Bhagirath.

The pregnant Branga woman fell at Bhagirath's feet. 'No, brave Prince. Don't stop us. I beg you.'

'High priestess, what are you doing?' asked the Branga man. 'Don't humiliate yourself!'

Bhagirath looked at the scene once again, and this was when the real inference dawned on him. He was stunned. The only children crying were the ones who did not have blood on their mouths. Their limbs were twisted in painful agony, as if a hideous force was squeezing their tiny bodies. The moment some of the peacock blood was poured into a baby's mouth, the child quietened down.

Bhagirath whispered in shock. 'What the hell...'

'Please,' pleaded the Branga high priestess. 'We need it for our babies. They will die without it. I beg you. Let us save them.'

Bhagirath stood silent. Bewildered.

'Your Highness,' said Veerbhadra. 'The General.'

Bhagirath immediately bent down to check on Parvateshwar. His heart was beating, but the pulse was weak.

'Suryavanshis, we need to carry the General to an *ayuralay*. Quickly! We don't have much time!'

Bearing their leader along, the Suryavanshis rushed out. Parvateshwar had to be taken to a *hospital*.

— ⅄ⵀⵡ ⊕ —

Ayurvati came out of the operating room. Chandravanshi doctors simply did not have the knowledge to deal with Parvateshwar's injury. Ayurvati had been sent urgent summons.

Shiva and Sati immediately rose. Sati's heart sank on seeing the dejected look on Ayurvati's face.

'How soon will he be all right, Ayurvati?' asked Shiva.

Ayurvati took a deep breath. 'My Lord, the club hit the General at a most unfortunate spot, right on his temple. He is suffering severe internal haemorrhaging. The blood loss could be fatal.'

Shiva bit his lip.

'I...,' said Ayurvati.

'If anyone can save him, it is you Ayurvati,' said Shiva.

'There is nothing in the medical manuals for such a severe injury, My Lord. We could do brain surgery, but that cannot be performed while the patient is unconscious. In the surgery, we apply local pain relievers to allow the conscious patient to guide us with his actions. Taking this risk while Parvateshwar is unconscious could prove more dangerous than the injury itself.'

Sati's eyes were welling up.

'We cannot allow this to happen, Ayurvati,' said Shiva. 'We cannot!'

'I know, My Lord.'

'Then think of something. You are Ayurvati, the best doctor in the world!'

'I have only one solution in mind, My Lord,' said Ayurvati. 'But I don't even know if it would work.'

'The Somras?' asked Shiva.

'Do you agree?'

'Yes. Let's try it.'

Ayurvati rushed off to find her assistants.

Shiva turned towards Sati, worried. He knew how close Sati was to her *Pitratulya.* Her obvious misery would also impact their unborn child. 'He'll be all right. Trust me.'

— ⁂ —

'Where is the damn Somras?' asked an agitated Shiva.

'I'm sorry, My Lord,' said Athithigva. 'But we don't really have large quantities of the Somras. We don't keep any at the ayuralay.'

'It's coming, My Lord,' assured Ayurvati. 'I have sent Mastrak to my quarters for some.'

Shiva snorted in frustration and turned towards Parvateshwar's room. 'Hang on, my friend. We will save you. Hang on.'

Mastrak came in panting, holding a small wooden bottle. 'My lady!'

'You've prepared it correctly?'

'Yes, my lady.'

Ayurvati rushed into Parvateshwar's room.

— ⁂ —

Parvateshwar was lying on a bed in the far corner. Mastrak and Dhruvini, Ayurvati's assistants, sat at the bedside, rubbing the juice of neem leaves under his nails. There was a pumping apparatus attached to the General's nose in order to ease his breathing.

'The haemorrhaging has stopped, My Lord,' said Ayurvati. 'He is not getting worse.'

The vision of the apparatus attached to the General's

nose shook Shiva. To see a man such as Parvateshwar in this helpless state was too much for him. 'Then why is that apparatus required?'

'The bleeding has harmed the parts of his brain that control his breathing, My Lord,' said Ayurvati, in the calm manner she always willed herself into when faced with a medical crisis. 'Parvateshwar cannot breathe on his own. If we remove this apparatus, he will die.'

'Then why can't you repair his brain?'

'I told you, My Lord, a brain surgery cannot be done while the patient is unconscious. It is too risky. I may injure some other vital function with my instruments.'

'The Somras...'

'It has stopped the bleeding, My Lord. He is stable. But it doesn't appear to be healing his brain.'

'What do we do?'

Ayurvati remained silent. She didn't have an answer. At least an answer that was practical.

'There must be a way.'

'There is one remote possibility, My Lord,' said Ayurvati. 'The bark of the Sanjeevani tree. It is actually one of the ingredients in the Somras. A very diluted ingredient.'

'Then why don't we use that?'

'It is very unstable. The bark disintegrates very rapidly. It has to be taken from a live Sanjeevani tree and used within minutes.'

'Then find a...'

'It doesn't grow here, My Lord. It grows naturally in the foothills of the Himalayas. We have plantations in Meluha. But getting it could take months. By the time we return with the bark, it would have disintegrated.'

There has to be a way! Holy lake, please find me a way!

— ⸻ —

'Your Highness,' said Nandi, who had been promoted from the rank of Captain.

'Yes, Major Nandi,' said Bhagirath.

'Can you come with me please?'

'Where?'

'It's important, Your Highness.'

Bhagirath thought it was odd that Nandi wanted him to leave the ayuralay at a time when Parvateshwar was fighting for his life. But he knew that Nandi was the Neelkanth's close friend. More importantly, he also knew that Nandi was a level-headed man. If he was asking him to go somewhere, it would be important.

Bhagirath followed.

— ⸻ —

Bhagirath could not hide his surprise as Nandi took him to the Branga building.

'What is going on, Major?'

'You must meet him,' said Nandi.

'Who?'

'Me,' said a tall, dark man stepping out of the structure. His long hair was neatly oiled and tied in a knot. His eyes were doe-shaped, his cheekbones high. He had a clear complexion. His lanky frame was draped in a white starched *dhoti*, with a cream *angvastram* thrown over his shoulder. His face bore the look of a man who had seen too much sadness for one lifetime.

'Who are you?'

'I am Divodas. The chief of the Brangas here.'

Bhagirath gritted his teeth. 'The General saved all your sorry hides. And your men have brought him to the brink of death!'

'I know, Your Highness. My men thought the General would have stopped us from saving our children. It was a genuine mistake. Our most sincere apologies.'

'You think your apology is going to save his life?'

'It will not. I know that. He has saved my entire tribe from a certain death. He has saved my wife and unborn child. It is a debt that must be repaid.'

The mention of payment made Bhagirath even more livid. 'You think your filthy gold will get you out of this? Mark my words, if anything happens to the General, I will personally come here and kill every single one of you. Every single one!'

Divodas kept quiet. His face impassive.

'Your Highness,' said Nandi. 'Let us hear him out.'

Bhagirath grunted in an irritated manner.

'Gold means nothing, Your Highness,' said Divodas. 'We have tonnes of it back home. It still cannot buy us out of our suffering. Nothing is more important than life. Nothing. You realise the simplicity of that point only when you confront death every day.'

Bhagirath didn't say anything.

'General Parvateshwar is a brave and honourable man. For his sake, I will break the vow I took on the name of my ancestors. Even if it damns my soul forever.'

Bhagirath frowned.

'I am not supposed to share this medicine with anyone who is not Branga. But I will give it to you for the General.

Tell your doctor to apply it on his temple and nostrils. He will live.'

Bhagirath looked suspiciously at the small silk packet. 'What is this?'

'You don't need to know what it is, Your Highness. You just need to know one thing. It will save General Parvateshwar's life.'

— ⅄ⓄU⇞⊛ —

'What is this?'

Ayurvati was looking at the silk pouch Bhagirath had just handed over to her.

'That doesn't matter,' said Bhagirath. 'Just apply it on his temples and nostrils. It may save his life.'

Ayurvati frowned.

'Lady Ayurvati, what is the harm in trying?' asked Bhagirath.

Ayurvati opened the pouch to find a reddish-brown thick paste. She had never seen anything like it. She smelt the paste and immediately looked up at Bhagirath, stunned. 'Where did you get this?'

'That doesn't matter. Use it.'

Ayurvati kept staring at Bhagirath. She had a hundred questions running through her mind. But she had to do the most obvious thing first. She knew this paste would save Parvateshwar.

— ⅄ⓄU⇞⊛ —

Parvateshwar opened his eyes slowly, his breathing ragged.

'My friend,' whispered Shiva.

'My Lord,' whispered Parvateshwar, trying to get up.

'No! Don't!' said Shiva, gently making Parvateshwar lie back. 'You need to rest. You are strong-headed, but not that strong!'

Parvateshwar smiled wanly.

Shiva knew the question that would arise first in the General's mind. 'All the Brangas are safe. What you did was brilliant.'

'I don't know, My Lord. I will have to do penance. I have committed a sin.'

'What you did saved lives. There is no need for any penance.'

Parvateshwar sighed. His head still throbbed immensely. 'They had some ghastly ritual going on...'

'Don't think about it, my friend. Right now you need to relax. Ayurvati has ordered strictly that nobody is to disturb you. I will leave you alone. Try to catch some sleep.'

'Anandmayi!'

— ⁂ —

Bhagirath tried to stop his sister. Anandmayi was rushing into the ayuralay chamber where Parvateshwar lay. She had been out of the city the whole day attending a music lesson at a nearby ashram. She ran into her brother's arms.

'Is he all right?'

'Yes,' said Bhagirath.

Anandmayi glowered. 'Who is the bastard who did this? I hope you killed that dog!'

'We will let Parvateshwar decide what to do.'

'I heard he was hit on the temple. That there was blood

haemorrhaging.'

'Yes.'

'Lord Agni be merciful. That can be fatal.'

'Yes. But some medicines from the Brangas have saved him.'

'Brangas? First they nearly kill him and then give medicines to save him? Is there no limit to their madness?'

'The medicine was given by their leader, Divodas. He arrived in Kashi a few hours back and heard about this incident. He seems like a good man.'

Anandmayi was not interested in the Branga leader. 'Has Parvateshwar woken up?'

'Yes. The Lord Neelkanth just met him. He has gone back to sleep. He is out of danger. Don't worry.'

Anandmayi nodded, her eyes moist.

'And, by the way,' said Bhagirath. 'I've also recovered from my injuries.'

Anandmayi burst out laughing. 'I'm sorry, my brother! I should have asked.'

Bhagirath made a dramatic pose. 'Nobody can hurt your brother. He's the greatest Chandravanshi warrior ever!'

'Nobody hurt you because you must have been hiding behind Parvateshwar!'

Bhagirath burst out laughing and reached out playfully to chuff his sister. Anandmayi pulled her younger brother into her arms.

'Go,' said Bhagirath. 'Looking at him may make you feel better.'

Anandmayi nodded. As she entered Parvateshwar's room, Ayurvati emerged from another chamber. 'Your Highness.'

'Yes, Lady Ayurvati,' said Bhagirath with a namaste.

'The Lord Neelkanth and I would like to talk to you. Could you come with me?'

'Of course.'

— ⅄ⵀⵒ —

'Where did you get the medicine from, Bhagirath?' asked Shiva.

Bhagirath was surprised at Shiva's tone. The Lord had always appeared kind. He now seemed cold. Angry.

'What is the matter, My Lord?' asked Bhagirath, worried.

'Answer my question, Prince. Where did you get the medicine from?'

'From the Brangas.'

Shiva stared hard into Bhagirath's eyes. Bhagirath could gauge the Neelkanth was struggling to believe his words.

'I'm not lying, My Lord,' said Bhagirath. 'And why would I? This medicine has saved the General's life.'

Shiva continued to stare.

'My Lord, what is the problem?'

'The problem, Your Highness,' said Ayurvati, 'is that this medicine is not available in the Sapt Sindhu. I could tell that it was made from the bark of the Sanjeevani tree. But the problem with any Sanjeevani medicine is that it deteriorates rapidly. It cannot be used unless freshly taken from a live tree. This medicine was stabilised. It was a paste. We could use it.'

'My apologies Lady Ayurvati, but I still do not understand the problem.'

'There is only one element, the crushed wood of another specific tree, which is capable of mixing with the Sanjeevani and stabilising it. That tree does not grow in the Sapt Sindhu.'

Bhagirath frowned.

'That tree only grows south of the Narmada river. In Naga territory.'

The prince of Ayodhya froze. He knew what the Neelkanth would be thinking. 'My Lord, I have nothing to do with the Nagas. I got this medicine from the Branga leader Divodas. I swear on Ayodhya. I swear on my beloved sister. I have nothing to do with the Nagas.'

Shiva continued to stare at Bhagirath. 'I want to meet Divodas.'

'My Lord, I swear I have nothing to do with the Nagas.'

'Get me Divodas within the next hour, Prince Bhagirath.'

Bhagirath's heart was beating madly. 'My Lord, please believe me...'

'We will talk about this later, Prince Bhagirath,' said Shiva. 'Please get Divodas.'

'I believe King Athithigva has already arranged for Divodas to have an audience with you tomorrow morning, My Lord.'

Shiva stared at Bhagirath, eyes narrowing a bit.

'I will arrange for Divodas to come here right away, My Lord,' said Bhagirath, rushing from the room.

Anandmayi sat silently on a chair next to Parvateshwar's bed. The General was asleep, breathing slowly. The Princess ran her fingers slowly down Parvateshwar's powerful shoulder, arm and all the way to his fingers. The General's body seemed to shiver a bit.

Anandmayi laughed softly. 'For all your vows, you are a

man after all!'

As if driven by instinct, Parvateshwar withdrew his hand. He blabbered something in his sleep. The voice not clear enough to reach Anandmayi's ears. She leaned forward.

'I'll never break my vow... father. That is my... Dashrath promise. I will never break... my vow.'

A Dashrath promise, named after a vow that Lord Ram's father had once taken, was an open-ended word of honour that could never be broken. Anandmayi shook her head and sighed. Parvateshwar was repeating his vow of *brahmacharya*, or *eternal celibacy*, once again.

'I'll never break... my vow.'

Anandmayi smiled. 'We'll see.'

— ⁂ —

'My Lord,' said Divodas, immediately bending to touch the Neelkanth's feet.

'*Ayushman bhav*, Divodas,' said Shiva, blessing the man with *a long life*.

'Such an honour to meet you, My Lord. The dark days are over. You will solve all our problems. We can go home.'

'Go home? You still want to go back?'

'Branga is my soul, My Lord. I would never have left my homeland if it weren't for the plague.'

Shiva frowned, before coming to the point that concerned him. 'You are a good man, Divodas. You saved my friend's life. Even at your own cost.'

'It was a matter of honour, My Lord. I know all that happened. General Parvateshwar saved my tribe from certain death. We had to return the favour. And there was no cost to me.'

'That depends on you, my friend. Remember your code of honour when you answer this.'

Divodas frowned.

'How did you get the Naga medicine?' asked Shiva.

Divodas froze.

'Answer me, Divodas,' repeated Shiva gently.

'My Lord...'

'I know that medicine could only be made by the Nagas. The question, Divodas, is how you came by it.'

Divodas did not want to lie to the Neelkanth. Yet he was afraid of speaking the truth.

'Divodas, be truthful,' said Shiva. 'Nothing angers me more than lies. Speak the truth. I promise you that you will not be harmed. It is the Nagas I seek.'

'My Lord, I don't know if I can. My tribe needs the medicines every year. You saw the chaos that a few days of delay led to. They will die without it, My Lord.'

'Tell me where to find those scum and I give you my word, I will get you the medicines every year.'

'My Lord...'

'It is my word, Divodas. You will always have your medicine. Even if it's the only thing I do for the rest of my life. Nobody in your tribe will die for the lack of medicine.'

Divodas hesitated. Then his faith in the Neelkanth legend overcame his fear of the unknown. 'I have never met a Naga, My Lord. Many of us believe that they have put a curse on Branga. The plague peaks every year, without fail, during the summer. The only medicines that can save us are the ones the Nagas supply. King Chandraketu gives the Nagas untold amounts of gold and a large supply of men in return for the medicines.'

Shiva was stunned. 'You mean King Chandraketu is forced to deal with the Nagas? He is their hostage?'

'He is a virtuous king, My Lord. Even the few of us who have escaped and found refuge outside Branga are given gold by him to sustain ourselves. We go back to Branga every year to get the medicines.'

Shiva stayed silent.

Divodas had a smidgeon of moisture in his eyes. 'Our king is a great man, My Lord. He has made a deal with the devils and cursed his own soul, only to save the people of Branga.'

Shiva nodded slowly. 'Is the King the only one who deals with the Nagas?'

'From what I know, he and a few trusted advisors, My Lord. Nobody else.'

'Once my child is born, we will leave for Branga. I will need you to accompany me.'

'My Lord!' cried Divodas in shock. 'We cannot bring any non-Branga into our land. Our secrets must remain within our borders. My tribe's future is at stake. My land's future is at stake.'

'This is much bigger than you, your tribe or me. This is about India. We must find the Nagas.'

Divodas gazed at Shiva, torn and confused.

'I believe I can help, Divodas,' said Shiva. 'Is this a life worth leading? Desperately begging for the medicines every year? Not even knowing what ails your tribe? We have to solve this problem. I can do it. But not without your help.'

'My Lord...'

'Divodas, think. I have heard that peacock blood has

many other side-effects that are just as bad. What if you had not reached in time with the Naga medicines? What would have happened to your tribe? Your wife? Your unborn child? Don't you want this resolved once and for all?'

Divodas nodded slowly.

'Then take me to your kingdom. We will free your King and the land of Branga from the clutches of the Nagas.'

'Yes, My Lord.'

— ⁂ —

'I swear I have nothing to do with the Nagas, My Lord,' said Bhagirath, his head bowed.

Nandi, standing at the door of Shiva's chamber, was looking on sympathetically.

'I swear, My Lord, I would never go against you,' said Bhagirath. 'Never.'

'I know,' said Shiva. 'I think the presence of the medicine shook me. Nandi has already spoken to me. I know how you came by the medicine. My apologies that I doubted you.'

'My Lord,' cried Bhagirath. 'You don't need to apologise.'

'No Bhagirath. If I have made a mistake, I must apologise. I will not doubt you again.'

'My Lord...' said Bhagirath.

Shiva pulled Bhagirath close and embraced him.

— ⁂ —

'Thank you once again for gracing us with your presence, My Lord,' said Kanakhala, the Meluhan Prime Minister, bowing down to touch the *great sage, Maharishi* Bhrigu's feet. 'I will take your leave.'

'*Ayushman Bhav*, my child,' said Bhrigu with a slight smile.

Kanakhala was astonished at the sudden appearance of the reclusive Maharishi in Devagiri, the capital city of Meluha. But her Emperor, Daksha, did not seem the least bit surprised. Kanakhala knew how the strict *Saptrishi Uttradhikari*, *a successor to the seven great sages*, liked to live. She had organised his chamber to be exactly like the Himalayan cave that was Bhrigu's home. No furniture except for a stone bed, on which Bhrigu was sitting presently. Cold water had been sprinkled on the floor and the walls to simulate the uncomfortable chilly and damp atmosphere of the mountains. Light had been restricted through the presence of thick curtains on all the windows. A bowl of fruit had been placed in the room; the only food for the sage for days. And most importantly, an idol of Lord Brahma had been installed on an indentation in the wall, at the north end of the chamber.

Bhrigu waited for Kanakhala to leave before turning to Daksha, speaking in a calm, mellifluous voice. 'Are you sure about this, Your Highness?'

Daksha was sitting on the floor, at Bhrigu's feet. 'Yes, My Lord. It is for my grandchild. I have never been surer of anything in the world.'

Bhrigu smiled slightly, but his eyes were unhappy. 'Your Highness, I have seen many kings forget their dharma in their love for their child. I hope your obsession with your daughter doesn't make you forget your duty to your nation.'

'No, My Lord. Sati is the most important person in the world to me. But I will not forget my duties towards the cause.'

'Good. That is the reason I supported you in becoming Emperor.'

'I know, My Lord. Nothing is more important than the cause. Nothing is more important than India.'

'You don't think your son-in-law is intelligent enough to start asking questions when he sees it?'

'No, My Lord. He loves my daughter. He loves India. He will not do anything to hurt the cause.'

'The Vasudevs have begun to influence him, Your Highness.'

Daksha looked shocked, at a loss for words. Bhrigu realised the futility of carrying on this conversation. Daksha was too simple-minded to understand the implications. He would have to fight for the cause by himself.

'Please go ahead then, if that is what you believe,' said Bhrigu. 'But you are not to answer any questions on where it came from. To anyone. Is that clear?'

Daksha nodded. He was still shocked by the statement Bhrigu had made about Shiva and the Vasudevs.

'Not even to your daughter, Your Highness,' said Bhrigu.

'Yes, My Lord.'

Bhrigu nodded. He breathed deeply. This was troubling. He would have to fight hard to save the legacy. It was imperative. He believed the very future of India was at stake.

'There is nothing to fear in any case, My Lord,' said Daksha, feigning a brilliance he didn't quite feel. 'Whatever may have happened with Brahaspati, the secret is safe. It will remain alive for centuries. India will continue to prosper and rule the world.'

'Brahaspati was a fool!' said Bhrigu, his voice rising.

'Even worse, maybe he was a traitor to the cause.'

Daksha kept quiet. As always, he was afraid of Bhrigu's temper.

Bhrigu calmed down. 'I can't believe I even considered giving my disciple Tara to him in marriage. The poor girl's life would have been destroyed.'

'Where is Tara, Your Highness? I hope she is safe and happy.'

'She is safe. I have kept her in the land of Lord Rudra. Some of them remain true to me. As for happiness...,' Bhrigu shook his head wearily.

'She still loves him?'

'Stupidly so. Even though he is no more.'

'No point in talking about Brahaspati,' said Daksha. 'Thank you so much for your permission, My Lord. From the deepest corner of my heart, thank you.'

Bhrigu nodded, bending lower and whispering, 'Remain careful, Your Highness. The war is not over. Don't think that you are the only one who can use the Neelkanth.'

Chapter 7

Birth Pangs

Shiva stood at the edge of the Dasashwamedh Ghat in a royal enclosure. On his side stood Their Highnesses Dilipa and Athithigva, with other key members of the nobility behind them. The citizens of Kashi stood away from the enclosure. They were not over excited. They had got used to the constant attention that came the way of their city since the Neelkanth had made it his temporary home.

It was a busy day for Kashi's diplomatic staff. Dilipa had arrived just that morning. The standard protocols for the Emperor of Swadweep had been followed, right down to the single white flag at the royal enclosure with the Chandravanshi crescent moon darned on it. Now, they were waiting for Daksha, the Emperor of India.

The protocol had been tricky. But they had finally decided to have a red Suryavanshi flag placed at the highest point of the enclosure. After all, the Lord Neelkanth had declared Daksha the Emperor of all of India. Bowing to the sensitivities of Dilipa, Kashi protocol officers had also placed a Chandravanshi flag in the enclosure at a slightly lower height as compared to the Suryavanshi flag.

Shiva, of course, did not really care about the ceremonies. He was more interested in the workers busy at the temporary shipyard across the river, where the Brangas, led by Divodas himself, had been furiously working away for the last three months. Given the superstition about not living on the eastern side of the Ganga's meander, it was naturally the safest place for the Brangas to do their job. They had been constructing special ships that could sail through the great Gates of Branga, massive barriers across the main river access to their land. Shiva couldn't imagine how barricades could be built in a river as broad as the Ganga. But Divodas had said that these special ships would be required. Shiva remembered telling a sceptical Athithigva, who had opposed this move of the Brangas: 'Just because you can't imagine it, doesn't mean it doesn't exist.' But Athithigva had refused the usage of the royal palace and grounds on the eastern bank as a shipyard. So the Brangas worked on a dangerous, recently dried stretch of the riverbank.

Divodas had begun work the very next day after promising the Neelkanth that he would accompany him to Branga.

Divodas has been true to his word. He is a good man.

The sound of Daksha's ship finally docking at the ghat brought Shiva back from his thoughts. He saw the rope pulley lowering the walkway. Daksha, without caring for royal protocol, immediately bounded onto the walkway and almost ran to Shiva. He bowed low and spoke breathlessly. 'Is it a boy, My Lord?'

Shiva stood up to welcome the Emperor of India, did a formal namaste and spoke with a smile. 'We still don't know Your Highness. She is not due till tomorrow.'

'Oh wonderful. I have not been late then! I was very scared that I would miss this joyous day.'

Shiva laughed out loud. It was difficult to say who was more excited — the father or the grandfather!

— ⅄ⵀⵡⴷⵣ —

'Such a delight to meet you again, Purvaka*ji*,' said Shiva, rising from his chair and bending down to touch the blind man's feet. The suffix *ji* was a form of respect.

Purvaka, Drapaku's blind father, was the same Vikarma whose blessings Shiva had sought at Kotdwaar in Meluha a few years ago. Kotdwaar residents had been stunned by the Neelkanth's public rejection of the Vikarma law. Leave alone finding the touch of a Vikarma polluting, Shiva had actually sought to be blessed by one.

Purvaka had come along in Emperor Daksha's convoy to Kashi. He immediately stepped back, as though sensing what Shiva was about to do. 'No, My Lord. You are the Neelkanth. How can I allow you to touch my feet?'

'Why not, Purvakaji?' asked Shiva

'But My Lord, how can you touch my father's feet?' said Drapaku. 'You are the Mahadev.'

'Isn't it my choice as to whose feet I touch?' asked Shiva.

Turning back to Purvaka, Shiva continued, 'You are elder to me. You cannot deny me the right to seek your blessings. So please do so quickly. My back is hurting from bending for so long.'

Purvaka laughed, placing his hand on Shiva's head. 'Nobody can refuse you, great one. *Ayushman bhav*.'

Shiva rose, satisfied with the *blessing for a long life*. 'So you intend to spend your time with your son now?'

'Yes, My Lord.'

'But we would be going on a dangerous voyage. Are you sure?'

'I was a warrior too once, My Lord. I still have the strength. I can kill any Naga who stands in front of me!'

Shiva smiled, turning towards Drapaku, his eyebrows raised. Drapaku smiled back, signalling with his hand that he would protect his father.

'My boy, don't think I cannot sense what you are saying,' said Purvaka. 'I may be blind, but you learnt to wield the sword holding my hands. I will protect myself. And, you as well.'

Both Shiva and Drapaku burst out laughing. Shiva was delighted to see that the diffident Purvaka he had met at Kotdwaar, a man who had suppressed his natural valour in a defeatist manner against the assaults of fate, was rediscovering his old fire.

'Forget about your son,' said Shiva, 'I would be delighted to have you as *my* bodyguard!'

— ⁂ —

'I am scared, Shiva.'

Sati was sitting on her bed in their chamber. Shiva had just entered the room with a plateful of food. Much to the horror of the royal cook, the Neelkanth had insisted on cooking for his wife himself.

Pretending to be hurt, Shiva said, 'My cooking isn't that bad!'

Sati burst out laughing. 'That's not what I meant!'

Shiva came closer and smiled. Setting the plate aside on the table, he caressed her face. 'I know. I have insisted on

Ayurvati overseeing the delivery. She is the best doctor in the world. Nothing will go wrong.'

'But what if this child too is stillborn? What if my past life's sins affect our poor child?'

'There are no past life sins, Sati! There is only this life. That is the only reality. Everything else is a theory. Believe the theory that gives you peace and reject the one that causes you pain. Why believe in a theory if it causes you unhappiness? You have done all you can to take care of your child and yourself. Now have faith.'

Sati kept quiet, her eyes still mirroring the foreboding she felt inside.

Shiva ran his hand along Sati's face again. 'My darling, trust me. Your worrying is not going to help. Just think positive and happy thoughts. That is the best you can do for our child. And leave the rest to fate. In any case, fate has ensured that you will lose your bet tomorrow.'

'What bet?'

'You can't wriggle out of it now!' said Shiva.

'Seriously, what bet?'

'That we will have a daughter.'

'I had forgotten about that,' smiled Sati. 'But I have a strong feeling it will be a son.'

'Nah!' laughed Shiva.

Sati laughed along and rested her face against Shiva's hand.

Shiva broke a piece of the roti, wrapped some vegetables in it and held out the morsel for Sati. 'Is the salt all right?'

'Are there really past life sins?' asked Shiva.

The Neelkanth was in the Kashi Vishwanath temple. Seated in front of him was a Vasudev pandit. The setting sun shone through the spaces between the temple pillars. The red sandstone shone even brighter, creating an awe-inspiring atmosphere.

'What do you think?' asked the Vasudev.

'I don't believe anything till I've seen the proof. For anything without proof, I think we should believe the theory that gives us peace. It doesn't matter whether the theory is true or not.'

'That is a good strategy for a happy life, no doubt.'

Shiva waited for the pandit to say more. When he didn't, Shiva spoke again. 'You still haven't answered my question. Are there really past life sins that we suffer for in this life?'

'I didn't answer the question because I don't have the answer. But if people believe that sins of the past life can impact this life, won't they at least try to lead a better life this time around?'

Shiva smiled. *Are these people just talented wordsmiths or great philosophers?*

The Pandit smiled back. *Once again, I don't have the answer!*

Shiva burst out laughing. He had forgotten the Pandit could receive his thoughts and that he could, in turn, do the same with the Pandit's.

'How does this work? How is it that I can hear your thoughts?'

'It's a very simple science really. The science of radio waves.'

'This is not a theory?'

The Pandit smiled. 'This is certainly not a theory. This is a fact. Just like light, which helps you see, there are radio waves to help you hear. While all humans can easily use the properties of light to see, most don't know how to use radio waves to hear. We are dependent on sound waves to hear. Sound waves travel much slower through the air and for much shorter distances. Radio waves travel far and fast, just like light.'

Shiva remembered his uncle, who he always thought could hear his thoughts. In his youth, he had thought it was magic. Now he knew better, that there was a science behind it. 'That's interesting. Then why can't you create a machine to convert radio waves into sound waves?'

'Aah! That is a tough one. We haven't succeeded in that as yet. But we have succeeded in training our brains to pick up radio waves. It takes years of practice to do it. That's why we were shocked that you could do it without any training.'

'I got lucky, I guess.'

'There is no luck, great one. You were born special.'

Shiva frowned. 'I don't think so. In any case, how is it supposed to work? How do you pick up radio waves? Why can't I hear everyone's thoughts?'

'It takes effort to be able to even transmit your thoughts clearly as radio waves. Many people do it unconsciously, even without training. But picking up radio waves and hearing other people's thoughts? That is completely different. It is not easy. We have to stay within the range of powerful transmitters.'

'The temples?'

'You are exceptionally intelligent, O Neelkanth!' smiled the Pandit. 'Yes, the temples work as our transmitters. Therefore the temples we use have to have a height of at least fifty metres. This helps in catching radio waves from other Vasudevs and in turn transmitting my thoughts to them as well.'

You mean other Vasudevs are hearing us all the time, Panditji?

Yes. Whoever chooses to hear our conversation. And very few Vasudevs would choose not to hear the saviour of our times, great Neelkanth.

Shiva frowned. If what the Pandit was saying was true, then he could speak to any Vasudev Pandit at any of their temples across India right now. *Then tell me this O Vasudev of the Magadh temple, what did you mean by saying that people are attached to evil?*

Shiva heard a loud laugh. It appeared to be coming from a distance. The Vasudev Pandit of the Narsimha temple at Magadh. *You are too smart, Lord Neelkanth.*

Shiva smiled. *I would prefer answers to flattery, great Vasudev.*

Silence.

Then Shiva heard the voice from Magadh clearly. *I really liked your speech at the Dharmakhet war. Har Har Mahadev. All of us are Mahadevs. There is a God in every single one of us. What a beautiful thought.*

What does that have to do with my question? I asked why people should be attached to evil.

It does. It very profoundly does. There is a God in every single one of us. What is the obvious corollary?

That it is the responsibility of every single one of us to discover the God within.

No, my friend. That is the moral. I asked what the corollary was.

I don't understand, Panditji.

Everything needs balance, Neelkanth. The masculine needs the feminine. The energy requires the mass. So think! Har Har Mahadev. What is the corollary? What balances this statement?

Shiva frowned. A thought occurred to him. He didn't like it.

The Vasudev of Ayodhya urged Shiva. *Don't stop your*

thoughts, my friend. Free flow is the only way to discover the truth.

Shiva grimaced. *But this cannot be true.*

Truth doesn't have to be liked. It only has to be spoken. Speak it out. The truth may hurt you, but it will set you free.

But I can't believe this.

The truth doesn't ask for belief. It just exists. Let me hear what you think. There is a God in every single one of us. What is the obvious corollary?

There is evil in every single one of us.

Exactly. There is a God in every single one of us. And there is evil in every single one of us. The true battle between good and evil is fought within.

And the great evil connects itself to the evil within us. Is that why people get attached to it?

I believe that when you discover the great evil of our times, you will not need any explanation about how it attaches itself so deeply to us.

Shiva stared at the Pandit in front of him. The conversation had shaken him. His task was not just to discover evil. That would probably be easy. How would he get people to give up their attachment to evil?

'You don't have to find all the answers now, my friend,' said the Kashi Vasudev.

Shiva smiled weakly, uneasy. Then he heard the distant voice of someone he didn't recognise. A commanding voice, a voice that appeared to be used to being powerful. Strong, yet calm.

The medicine...

'Of course,' said the Kashi Pandit, as he got up quickly. He was back in no time, with a small silk pouch.

Shiva frowned.

'Apply this on your wife's belly, my friend,' said the

Kashi Pandit. 'Your child will be born healthy and strong.'

'What is this?'

'Its identity doesn't matter. What matters is that it will work.'

Shiva opened the pouch. There was a thick reddish-brown paste inside. *Thank you. If this ensures my child's safety, I will be forever grateful to you.*

The voice that Shiva had not recognised, the one that had ordered the Kashi Vasudev, spoke. *You don't need to be grateful, Lord Neelkanth. It is our duty, and honour, to be of any assistance to you. Jai Guru Vishwamitra. Jai Guru Vashishtha.*

— ⁂ —

Shiva was at the window. From the height of the palace walls, he could see the congested city and beyond that the wide Sacred Avenue. On its edge, close to the Brahma Ghat stood the mighty Vishwanath temple. Shiva was staring at it, his hands clasped together in prayer.

Lord Rudra, take care of my child. Please. Let nothing go wrong.

He turned around as he heard a soft cough.

The most important people in India were waiting with bated breath for news of Sati and Shiva's child. Daksha was fidgeting nervously, deeply afraid.

He is truly concerned about Sati. Whatever else he may or may not be, he is a devoted father.

An impassive Veerini was holding Daksha's hand. Emperor Dilipa sat quietly, watching his children, Bhagirath and Anandmayi, who were in an animated, but soft conversation.

Dilipa kept staring at Bhagirath...

Parvateshwar, who had recovered completely from his

injuries in the past three months, stood strong at a corner of the chamber. King Athithigva paced up and down the room, upset that his own doctors had not been given the honour to deliver the Neelkanth's first-born. But Shiva was not about to take chances. Only Ayurvati would do.

Shiva turned around. He saw Nandi standing near the wall and gestured with his eyes.

'Yes, My Lord?' asked Nandi, coming up to Shiva.

'I feel so helpless, Nandi. I'm nervous.'

'Give me a moment, My Lord.'

Nandi rushed out of the chamber. He was back with Veerbhadra.

Both friends went up to the window.

'This one is good!' said Veerbhadra.

'Really?' asked Shiva.

Veerbhadra lit the chillum and gave it to Shiva, who took a deep puff.

'Hmmm...,' whispered Shiva.

'Yes?'

'I'm still nervous!'

Veerbhadra started laughing. 'What do you hope it will be?'

'A girl.'

'A girl? Sure? A girl can't be a warrior.'

'What nonsense! Look at Sati.'

Veerbhadra nodded. 'Fair point. And the name?'

'Krittika.'

'Krittika! You don't have to do this for me my friend.'

'I'm not doing it for you, you fool!' said Shiva. 'If I wanted to do that, I would name my daughter Bhadra! I am doing it for Krittika and Sati. Krittika has been a rock of support in my wife's life. I want to celebrate that.'

Veerbhadra smiled. 'She is a good woman, isn't she?'

'That she is. You have done well.'

'Hey, she hasn't done so badly either. I'm not that terrible a husband!'

'Actually, she could have done better!'

Bhadra playfully slapped Shiva on his wrist, as both friends shared a quiet laugh. Shiva handed the chillum back to Veerbhadra.

Suddenly, the door to the inner chamber opened. Ayurvati rushed out to Shiva. 'It's a boy, My Lord! A strong, handsome, powerful boy!'

Shiva picked up Ayurvati in his arms and swung her around, laughing heartily. 'A boy will also do!'

Setting an embarrassed Ayurvati back on the ground, Shiva rushed into the inner chamber. Ayurvati stopped everyone else from entering. Sati was on the bed. Two nurses were hovering close by. Krittika was sitting on a chair next to Sati, holding her hand. The most beautiful baby that Shiva had ever seen was next to Sati. He had been wrapped tight in a small white cloth and was sleeping soundly.

Sati smiled softly. 'It's a boy. Looks like I won, darling!'

'That's true,' whispered Shiva, scared of touching his son. 'But I haven't lost anything!'

Sati laughed, but immediately quietened down. The stitches hurt. 'What do we call him? We certainly cannot call him Krittika.'

'Yes, that is out of the question,' smiled Sati's handmaiden. 'Krittika is a woman's name.'

'But I still want him named after you, Krittika,' said Shiva.

'I agree,' said Sati. 'But what can that name be?'

Shiva thought for a moment. 'I know! We'll call him Kartik.'

Chapter 8

The Mating Dance

Daksha rushed into the room as soon as he was allowed, followed closely by Veerini.

'Father,' whispered Sati. 'Your first grandchild...'

Daksha didn't answer. He gently picked up Kartik and much to Sati's irritation, unfastened the white cloth that had bound the baby tightly, letting it fall back to the bed. Daksha held up Kartik, turning him around, admiring every aspect of his grandson. Tears were flowing furiously down the eyes of the Emperor of India. 'He's beautiful. He's just so beautiful.'

Startled, Kartik woke up and immediately began crying. It was the loud, lusty cry of a strong baby! Sati reached out for her son. Daksha, however, handed the baby over to a beaming Veerini. To Sati's surprise, Kartik immediately calmed down in Veerini's arms. The Queen placed Kartik on the white cloth and swaddled him again. Then she placed him in Sati's arms, his tiny head resting on her shoulders. Kartik gurgled and went back to sleep.

Daksha's tears had seemed to develop a life of their own. He embraced Shiva tightly. 'I'm the happiest man in all of history, My Lord! The happiest ever!'

Shiva patted the Emperor lightly on his back, smiling slightly. 'I know, Your Highness.'

Daksha stepped back and wiped his eyes. 'Everything is all right. You, Lord Neelkanth, have purified all that went wrong with my family. Everything is all right once again.'

Veerini stared at Daksha, her eyes narrowed, her breathing ragged. She gritted her teeth, but kept her silence.

— ⁂ —

Bhagirath was walking back from the riverbank after checking on the progress of the ships being built by Divodas' men. As it was late, he had sent his bodyguards home. After all, this was Kashi, the city where everyone sought refuge. The city of peace.

The streets were deathly quiet. So silent that he clearly heard a soft crunch behind him.

The Prince of Ayodhya continued walking, appearing nonchalant. His hand on the hilt of his blade, ears focussed. The soft tread was gaining ground. A sword was drawn softly. Bhagirath spun around suddenly, drew his knife and flung it, piercing his assailant through his stomach. The blow was enough to paralyse his attacker. He would be in excruciating pain, but not dead.

Through the corner of his eye, Bhagirath saw another movement. He reached for his other knife. But the new threat crashed against a wall, a short sword buried in his chest. Dead.

Bhagirath turned to see Nandi to the left. 'Anyone else?' he whispered.

Nandi shook his head.

Bhagirath rushed to the first assailant. Shaking him from the shoulders, Bhagirath asked, 'Who sent you?'

The assassin remained mute.

Bhagirath twisted the knife in the man's stomach.

'Who?'

The man's mouth suddenly started frothing. The rat had eaten his poison. He died within seconds.

'Dammit!' said a frustrated Bhagirath.

Nandi looked at the Prince of Ayodhya, alert for any new threat, sword drawn.

Bhagirath shook his head and rose. 'Thank you, Nandi. Lucky that you were around.'

'It wasn't luck, Your Highness,' said Nandi softly. 'The Neelkanth has asked me to follow you for the duration of your father's visit. I honestly thought the Lord was over-reacting. No father would make an attempt on his child's life. I guess I was wrong.'

Bhagirath shook his head. 'It's not my father. At least not directly.'

'Not directly? What do you mean?'

'He doesn't have the guts. But he makes it well–known that I am not in his favour. That obviously encourages rival claimants to the throne, people who travel in his court. All they have to do is take me out of the equation. Make it appear as if I died in an accident.'

'This,' said Nandi, pointing to the dead assassins, 'wouldn't look like an accident.'

'I know. It just means that they're getting desperate.'

'Why?'

'My father's health is not good. I think they feel that they don't have time. If he dies while I am alive, I will be crowned king.'

Nandi shook his head.

Bhagirath patted Nandi. 'I'm in your debt, my friend. Forever grateful. As long as I live.'

Nandi smiled. 'And you will live a long life, Your Highness. Nothing will happen to you as long as I am around. I will stand between you and any man who dares to attack you. And there is a lot of me to cover you with!'

Bhagirath smiled at Nandi's attempt at humour on his elephantine girth.

— ⚹ —

'Did you get any names? Who sent them?'

'I don't know, My Lord,' said Bhagirath. 'They died before I could get any answers.'

Shiva sighed. 'The dead bodies?'

'Handed over to the Kashi police,' said Bhagirath. 'But I don't expect that they will be able to gather any leads.'

'Hmm,' said Shiva.

'For the second time, I owe you my life, My Lord.'

'You owe me nothing,' said Shiva, before turning towards Nandi. 'Thank you, my friend. It is you who deserves credit.'

Nandi bowed low. 'It's my honour to serve you, My Lord.'

Shiva turned back to Bhagirath. 'What are you going to tell Anandmayi?'

Bhagirath frowned. 'Nothing. I don't want her getting troubled unnecessarily. I am fine. There is no need for anyone to know.'

'Why?'

'Because I am sure that father will not even try to

investigate this attack. Other nobles will see this as a sign of his tacit acceptance of a more aggressive attack on me rather than difficult-to-organise "accidents". Letting this news become public will only encourage rival claimants further.'

'Are there so many nobles after you?'

'Half the court is related to my father, My Lord. All of them think that they have a right to the throne.'

Shiva breathed deeply. 'Never stay alone while your father's here. And you are coming with me on the voyage to Branga, far away from here.'

Bhagirath nodded.

Shiva patted Bhagirath on his shoulder. 'Make sure that you don't get yourself killed. You are important to me.'

Bhagirath smiled. 'I will try to remain alive for you, My Lord!'

Shiva laughed softly. So did Nandi.

'Your Highness, I don't think it is wise for you to give away so much Somras powder,' said Shiva.

Shiva and Daksha were in Shiva's quarters. It had been a week since Kartik's birth. Sati and Kartik were sleeping in the next room, with Krittika and a bevy of nurses in close attendance. Shiva was shocked at the large amount of Somras powder Daksha had got with him as a present for Kartik. Daksha wanted Kartik to start taking the Somras from birth, every day, so that he would grow to be a strong, powerful warrior. He had got enough powder to last until Kartik's eighteenth birthday!

'My Lord,' said Daksha, 'it's not fair for you to tell a

doting grandfather what he can or cannot give his first grandchild.'

'But My Lord, with the destruction of Mount Mandar, you must be running short on Somras supplies. I don't think it is right for so much to be given to my son, when your entire country could use the blessings of the Somras.'

'Let me worry about that, My Lord. Please don't say no.'

Shiva gave up. 'How are the plans to rebuild Mount Mandar coming along?'

'It's taking too long,' said Daksha, waving his hand dismissively. 'Let's forget about that. This is such a happy event. I have a grandchild. A whole, complete, handsome grandchild who will grow up to be the Emperor of India!'

— ⁂ —

The citizens of Kashi customarily celebrated the birth of a child with music and dance after exactly seven days of its birth. Shiva decided to honour the traditions of his hosts.

The Neelkanth was sitting on a throne in the dance theatre. Next to him, on the throne meant for the Queen of Kashi, sat Sati, cradling a sleeping Kartik in her arms. Daksha and Dilipa had the seat of honoured guests next to Shiva and Sati. The royal family of Kashi sat beyond them. It was unorthodox for the King of the kingdom to occupy such a low place in the seating protocol. But Athithigva did not mind.

Sati bent towards Shiva and whispered, 'You danced marvellously. As always!'

'You noticed?' teased Shiva.

Earlier in the evening, Shiva had insisted on opening the

celebrations with his own performance. The audience could not believe their good fortune at seeing the Neelkanth himself dance. And they applauded his fabulous dancing skills with a five-minute long standing ovation. The dance was one of his best ever. And the audience was moved to raptures. But Shiva had noticed, much to his chagrin, that Sati was distracted during his performance. She had been troubled since the time Shiva had told her of the Somras powder brought by Daksha.

'Of course, I did,' smiled Sati. 'I'm just troubled that father is giving away so much Somras. It's not right. It is for all of Meluha. Kartik should not get any special treatment just because he is a royal. This is against Lord Ram's principles.'

'Then, speak to your father.'

'I will. At the right time.'

'Good. For now, however, look at Anandmayi when she dances. She may not be as forgiving as me.'

Sati smiled and rested her head on Shiva's shoulders as she turned to look at the stage just in time to see Anandmayi walk onto it. She was wearing a shockingly tiny *dhoti* and a tight blouse, leaving very little to the imagination. Sati raised her eyebrow and looked at Shiva. Shiva was smiling.

'It's the right costume for this dance,' said Shiva.

Sati nodded and turned towards the stage again. Shiva sidled a glance at Parvateshwar and smiled. The General's face was an impenetrable mask. His Suryavanshi training had kicked in, but the man's clenched jaw and tick near his brow betrayed that he was far from unmoved.

Anandmayi bent low to touch the stage with her forehead, seeking blessings and inspiration for her performance. The Chandravanshis in the front row leaned forward to get a better view of the ample cleavage that was revealed. If it had been any other dancer, the audience would probably have been whistling by now. But this was the Princess of Swadweep. So, they just kept ogling silently at her.

Then another dancer walked onstage: Uttanka. The progeny of a famed Magadhan brigadier, Uttanka's military career was cut short by an injury which left him with a severe hump on his right shoulder. Like most people frustrated with their lot in life, he too had sought refuge in Kashi, where he discovered the beauty of dance. But the same injury which had stumped his military career held back his dancing career as well. His shoulder movements were restricted, keeping him from becoming a truly great performer. There were whispers that Anandmayi, a true Chandravanshi whose heart automatically reached out towards the weak, had felt pity for Uttanka and hence had agreed to partner him.

But there was also a feeling that this sympathy was misplaced. Uttanka would probably be humiliated on stage. They were expected to perform a complex dance which encaptured the enticement of the legendary sage Vishwamitra by the celestial nymph Menaka. Would Uttanka be equal to the task?

Anandmayi, unmindful of such speculation, bowed towards Uttanka. He bowed back. Then, they stepped close to each other. Far closer than the standard position for commencing this dance. Probably a necessary adjustment as Uttanka's arm could not extend very far. Shiva turned once again towards Parvateshwar. He had narrowed his eyes a bit and seemed to be holding his breath.

Is he jealous?

The Princess of Ayodhya had choreographed their dance

well, having changed the ancient rules of this particular act, in order to suit Uttanka's restricted arm movements. But the changes also ensured that the two of them danced very close to each other throughout the performance, creating an air of intense sensuality. The audience first watched in shock, their jaws open. How could a former soldier be allowed to hold Princess Anandmayi so close? But then they were pulled in by the sheer quality of the act. Nobody had seen the dance of Vishwamitra and Menaka in such a blatantly passionate form before.

As the piece ended, the audience stood up, applauding wildly and whistling. It had been a truly remarkable performance. Anandmayi bowed low and then pointed at Uttanka, graciously giving the credit to the physically-challenged former soldier. Uttanka beamed at the appreciation he received, finding meaning in his life, perhaps for the first time.

Parvateshwar was the only one present who wasn't clapping.

— ⅄◎Ʊ⇞⊛ —

Next day, Parvateshwar was sparring with Purvaka within the temporary military training grounds that had been constructed in the Kashi royal palace. The former brigadier was rediscovering his seemingly lost fearsome powers. Despite the lack of sight, Purvaka could sense Parvateshwar's actions with his keen hearing and was responding brilliantly, dodging when necessary, jabbing when possible.

Parvateshwar was delighted.

Calling a halt, Parvateshwar turned towards Drapaku

and nodded. He then turned towards Purvaka and executed the formal Meluhan salute, with a slight bow of his head. Purvaka too beat his chest with his fist and bent low, far lower than Parvateshwar had bowed. He respected Parvateshwar's legendary prowess.

'It will be my honour to include you in the Suryavanshi brigade travelling with the Neelkanth, Brigadier Purvaka,' said Parvateshwar.

Purvaka smiled. This was the first time he had been called Brigadier in decades. 'The honour is all mine, General. And thank you for not shafting me into the Chandravanshi brigade. I don't think I could tolerate their inefficiency!'

Bhagirath, standing at one end of the room, could not stop himself from laughing. 'We'll see who works harder for the Neelkanth, Purvaka! Don't forget, you are in Chandravanshi territory now. Battles are fought differently here.'

Purvaka did not respond. His training forbade him from talking back to a royal. He nodded.

Just then, Anandmayi entered the room. Bhagirath smiled and glanced at Parvateshwar, before looking back at her. She was in a bright, harlequin-green blouse and short *dhoti*, a colour so loud that only a woman of Anandmayi's beauty and chutzpah could have carried it off. He suspected that Anandmayi's need to gain Parvatshwar's attention was making her become more brazen by the day. He had never seen his sister quite this way and wasn't sure whether to have a chat with her or to draw Parvateshwar out and ask him about his intentions.

Waving to her brother, Anandmayi marched straight up to Parvateshwar, Uttanka at her heels. She came uncomfortably close to Parvateshwar, forcing him to step back. 'How is my favourite Meluhan General doing?' she asked, arching her brows after giving him the once over.

'We don't have different kingdoms within Meluha, Your Highness. We have only one army,' said Parvateshwar.

Anandmayi frowned.

'It means that there is no need to play favourites since there is only one Meluhan General.'

'I agree. There is only one Parvateshwar...'

Parvateshwar turned red. Drapaku grimaced with distaste.

'Is there anything I can do for you, Princess?' Parvateshwar wanted to quickly find a way to end this conversation.

'I thought you'd never ask,' smiled Anandmayi, pointing towards Uttanka. 'This young man here is a refugee from Magadh. His name is Uttanka. He always wanted to be a warrior. But a riding accident left him with an injured shoulder. The idiotic, apparently merit-obsessed, Prince Surapadman dismissed him. Like most unhappy souls, he found his way to Kashi. I'm sure you saw him dance yesterday. He dances brilliantly. I want you to include him in the Neelkanth's brigade.'

'As a dancer?' asked a flabbergasted Parvateshwar.

'Do you like being deliberately stupid or is this just an act?'

Parvateshwar frowned.

'Obviously not as a dancer,' shrugged an exasperated Anandmayi. 'As a soldier.'

Parvateshwar turned towards Uttanka. Feet spread. Arms close to his side weapons. Ready for battle. Uttanka had obviously been trained well. Then Parvateshwar's eyes settled on Uttanka's shoulders. The hump caused by the injury restricted his right arm's movements. 'You will not be able to battle a taller man.'

'I will die before retreating, My Lord,' said Uttanka.

'I have no use for soldiers who die,' said Parvateshwar. 'I need soldiers who will kill and live. Why don't you stick to dancing?'

'Are you saying that dancers cannot be warriors?' butted in Anandmayi.

Parvateshwar glared. The Neelkanth was a celebrated dancer and a fearsome warrior. He turned around, picked up two wooden swords and shields, throwing one pair to Uttanka. He held up his sword, adjusted his shield and gestured to the Magadhan to get into position.

'You're going to fight him?' asked a shocked Anandmayi. She knew Uttanka would be no match for Parvateshwar. 'What is wrong with you? Why can't he just come along...'

Anandmayi stopped as Bhagirath touched her arm. He pulled her back. Purvaka and Drapaku too stepped back.

'You still have a choice, soldier,' said Parvateshwar. 'Walk away.'

'I'd rather be carried out, My Lord,' said Uttanka.

Parvateshwar narrowed his eyes. He liked the man's spirit. But he had to test his ability now. For spirit without ability usually led to a gruesome death on the battlefield.

Parvateshwar moved slowly, waiting for Uttanka to charge. But the man kept still. Parvateshwar realised that the Magadhan was being defensive. Uttanka's shoulder injury prevented a high arm assault that would be required to attack a taller man like Parvateshwar.

The General charged. It was an unorthodox assault.

He struck only from above, keeping his shield upfront at medium height. Uttanka had to keep stepping back, holding his shield high with his left hand to defend against the powerful blows. If he could have raised his right arm high, he would have struck Parvateshwar's exposed head and shoulder. But he couldn't. So he kept jabbing back at chest height. Parvateshwar easily parried the blows with his shield. Slowly, but surely, Parvateshwar kept pushing Uttanka back towards the wall. It was a matter of time before he would have no place to retreat.

Anandmayi, while happy at what she thought was the Meluhan General's jealousy, was also worried about Uttanka. 'Why can't he show some compassion?'

Bhagirath turned to his sister. 'Parvateshwar is doing the right thing. An enemy will show no quarter in battle.'

Just then Uttanka's back hit the wall. His shield bobbed. Parvateshwar immediately swung from the right and hit Uttanka hard on his chest.

'That would be a death blow with a real sword,' whispered Parvateshwar.

Uttanka nodded. He did not try to rub his obviously hurting chest.

Parvateshwar walked calmly back to the centre of the room and called out loudly. 'Once more?'

Uttanka trudged back into position. Parvateshwar attacked once more. Again with the same result.

Seeing Uttanka in pain, Anandmayi hissed. She was about to step forward, but Bhagirath held her back. He too was worried. But he knew he couldn't step in. That would be an insult to the General and the foolishly brave soldier who was trying to combat him.

'Why did you bring that man here?' asked Bhagirath.

'Uttanka dances beautifully. I thought it would be fun to have him along on the voyage to Branga.'

Bhagirath turned towards his sister with narrowed eyes. 'That is not the whole truth. I know what you are doing. And it's not fair.'

'Everything's fair in love and war, Bhagirath. But I certainly don't want Uttanka getting hurt.'

'Then you shouldn't have brought him here!'

Parvateshwar was back in the centre. 'Again?'

Uttanka lumbered back. He was evidently in pain, his face revealing his increasing rage and frustration. Parvateshwar, on the other hand, was worried. He was afraid that he would end up breaking the soldier's ribs if they had one more joust. But he had to stop this foolhardiness. If this was a real battle, Uttanka would have already been killed twice over.

He charged at Uttanka again. To his surprise, Uttanka stepped to the side, letting Parvateshwar move forward with his momentum. Then Uttanka turned and charged as an aggressor. He swung to the left, letting his shield come down, leaving his flank open. Parvateshwar pushed his sword forward. Uttanka turned right to avoid the blow and in the same motion rolled his right arm in a swing, letting the momentum carry the sword higher than his injured shoulder would normally have allowed. He struck Parvateshwar on his neck. A kill strike, if it had been a real blade and not a practice weapon.

Parvateshwar stood stunned. How had Uttanka managed to do that?

Uttanka himself looked shocked. He had never managed to strike that high after his injury. Never.

Parvateshwar's face broke into a slight smile. Uttanka

had given up being defensive, turned into an aggressor, and won.

'Give up your attachment to your shield,' said Parvateshwar. 'When you attack hard, you do have the ability to kill.'

Uttanka, still panting hard, smiled slowly.

'Welcome to the Meluhan army, brave soldier.'

Uttanka immediately dropped his sword and fell at Parvateshwar's feet, his eyes moist.

Parvateshwar pulled Uttanka up. 'You are a Meluhan soldier now. And my soldiers don't cry. Conduct yourself in the manner befitting a Meluhan military man.'

Bhagirath sighed in relief and turned towards Anandmayi. 'You were lucky this time.'

Anandmayi nodded slowly. But her heart was already racing a few steps ahead. What really impressed Parvateshwar was military prowess. Anandmayi developed a new plan to ensnare her General.

— ⁂ —

'Shiva is right, father,' said Sati. 'You can't give away so much Somras. Meluha needs it.'

It had been ten days since Kartik's birth. Emperor Dilipa and his entourage had left for Ayodhya. Shiva had gone to the banks of the Ganga to supervise the ship building. Daksha and Veerini were sitting in Sati's private chambers as the proud mother gently rocked Kartik's crib.

Veerini looked at Daksha, but did not say anything.

'Let Meluha be my concern, my child,' said Daksha. 'You worry your pretty little head only with Kartik.'

Sati hated being spoken to in such a patronising manner.

'Father, of course I am thinking about Kartik. I am his mother. But I cannot forget our duties to Meluha.'

'My child,' smiled Daksha. 'Meluha is safe. Safer than it has ever been. I don't think you need to doubt my abilities to care for my people.'

'Father, I'm not doubting your abilities. Or your commitment. All I'm saying is that I feel it's wrong for Kartik to receive such a large share of Somras that rightly belongs to the people of Meluha. I am sure there is an immense shortage of the Somras after the destruction of Mount Mandar. Why give so much to my son? Just because he is the Emperor's grandson? This is against Lord Ram's rules.'

Daksha laughed out loud. 'My darling daughter, nowhere do Lord Ram's rules say that an emperor cannot give Somras powder to his grandchild.'

'Of course the exact words will not be there, father,' argued Sati, irritated. 'And it is not about the exact words. It is the principles that Lord Ram had set up. An emperor must always put his people above his family. We are not following that principle.'

'What do you mean we are not following that principle?' asked Daksha, sounding angry. 'Are you calling me a law-breaker?'

'Father, please keep your voice low. Kartik will wake up. And if you are favouring Kartik over the common Meluhans, then yes, you are breaking Lord Ram's laws.'

Veerini cringed. 'Please...'

Ignoring Veerini's plea, Daksha ranted. 'I am not breaking Lord Ram's laws!'

'Yes, you are,' said Sati. 'Are you saying you have enough Somras for the Suryavanshis? That Kartik is not benefiting at the cost of another less fortunate Meluhan? Unless you promise me that, this Somras powder will just lie waste. I will not let anyone give it to Kartik.'

'You will hurt your own son?' asked Daksha, turning briefly to glance at his sleeping grandson, before glaring at Sati.

'Kartik is my son. He will not like to benefit at the cost of others. Because I will teach him what *raj dharma* is.'

His own daughter accusing him of not following his *royal duties?* Daksha exploded. 'I HAVE TAKEN CARE OF MY RAJ DHARMA!'

Kartik woke with a start and Sati reached out for him instinctively. His mother's familiar fragrance calmed him instantly. Sati turned and glared at her father.

'I didn't want to tell you this,' said Daksha, 'but since you are bent on hurting Kartik's interests, listen. Another Somras manufacturing facility exists. Maharishi Bhrigu ordered me to build it secretly many years ago. It was a back-up for Mount Mandar. We kept it secret because there are traitors in our midst.'

Sati stared at her father in shock. Veerini was holding her head.

'So my beloved child,' said a sarcastic Daksha. 'I have followed my raj dharma. There is enough Somras for all of Meluha for centuries to come. Now give the drink of the Gods to Kartik every day till he turns eighteen. He will go down in history as the greatest man ever.'

Sati didn't say anything. She still appeared shocked by the news of the secret Somras manufacturing facility. There were hundreds of questions running through her head.

'Did you hear me?' asked Daksha. 'You will give the Somras to Kartik every day. Every day!'

Sati nodded.

— ⅄ⵀⵡ⇑ⴲ —

Shiva was standing on the dried river bed where the Brangas had made their temporary workshop. Five ships were being constructed. Shiva, who had seen some massive ships being built at Karachapa, the Meluhan sea port, was amazed at the radically different design of the Branga ships. So was Parvateshwar.

They walked together around the great wooden stands on which the ships rested. The size and structure of the ships was vastly superior to the standard Swadweepan vessels. They were almost the size of Meluhan crafts. But the difference was at the bottom of the hull. Below the waterline, the hull had been thinned out to a ridiculously narrow range and it went down flat for a good two or three metres.

'What is the point of this, Parvateshwar?' asked Shiva.

'I don't know, My Lord,' said Parvateshwar. 'It is the strangest design I have ever seen.'

'You think it helps the ship cut through the water faster?'

'I'm not sure. But shouldn't this extension make the ship less stable?'

'The coating on it should make it heavy,' said Shiva as he touched the metal plates that had been hammered into the wood. 'Is this that strange new metal your people have discovered recently?'

'Yes, My Lord. It does look like iron.'

'In that case its heaviness probably increases stability.'

'But the heaviness would also slow down the ship.'

'That's true.'

'I wonder what these strange grooves are for?' asked Parvateshwar, running his hand over a deep furrow which ran all along the metal plates on the hull extension.

'Or these hooks for that matter,' said Shiva as he looked up at the many large hooks on the hull, around two metres above the furrow.

Just then Divodas, accompanied by Ayurvati, joined them. Working in the sun for double shifts was tiring out the Brangas. Divodas had requested Shiva for Ayurvati's help. Ayurvati was only too delighted to have her team prepare some ayurvedic energy infusions for the Brangas.

'My Lord,' said Divodas, smiling. 'Lady Ayurvati is a genius. Drinking her medicines is like getting a shot of pure energy. My worker's efforts have doubled over the last few days.'

An embarrassed Ayurvati turned red. 'No, no, it's nothing.'

'What is it with you Suryavanshis?' asked Divodas. 'Why can't you take a compliment properly?'

Shiva and Ayurvati laughed out loud. Parvateshwar did not find it funny. 'Lord Ram said humility is the mark of a great person. If we forget our humility, we insult Lord Ram.'

'Parvateshwar, I don't think Divodas was suggesting anything that would hurt Lord Ram,' said Ayurvati. 'We all respect the Lord. I think Divodas was only suggesting we enjoy the better aspects of our life a little more uninhibitedly. Nothing wrong with that.'

'Well,' said Shiva, changing the topic, 'what I'm more interested in is this strange extension at the bottom of the ship. First of all, it must have been very difficult to design. You would have to get the weight and dimensions exactly right or else the ship would keel over. So I must compliment your engineers.'

'I have no problems with accepting compliments, My Lord,' smiled Divodas. 'My engineers are brilliant!'

Shiva grinned. 'That they are. But what is the purpose of this extension? What does it do?'

'It opens locks, My Lord.'

'What?'

'It is a key. You will see how it works when we reach the gates of Branga.'

Shiva frowned.

'Any ship without this can never enter Branga. It will be crushed.'

'The gates on the mighty Ganga?' asked Parvateshwar. 'I had thought that was a myth. I can't imagine how a gate could be built across a river of this size and flow.'

Divodas smiled. 'You need legendary engineers to build reality out of myth. And we have no shortage of such men in Branga!'

'So how does that gate work?' asked Shiva.

'It will be much better if you see it, My Lord,' said Divodas. 'Awesome structures like that cannot be described. They can only be seen.'

Just then, a woman holding a one-month old baby came up. It was the Branga high priestess. The same one who had stopped Bhagirath's attack at the Branga building.

Shiva looked at the child and smiled. 'What a lovely baby!'

'That's my daughter, My Lord,' said Divodas. 'And this is Yashini, my wife.'

Yashini bent down to touch Shiva's feet and then placed her daughter there. Shiva immediately bent down and picked up the child. 'What's her name?'

'Devayani, My Lord,' said Yashini.

Shiva smiled. 'She's been named after the daughter of Shukra, the teacher?'

Yashini nodded. 'Yes, My Lord.'

'It's a beautiful name. I'm sure she will teach the world great knowledge as she grows up,' said Shiva, as he handed the baby back to Yashini.

'Dreaming for our children's careers is too ambitious for us Brangas, My Lord,' said Yashini. 'All we can hope for is that they live to see their future.'

Shiva nodded in sympathy. 'I will not stop till I change this, Yashini.'

'Thank you, My Lord,' said Divodas. 'I know you will succeed. We do not care for our own lives. But we have to save our children. We will be forever grateful to you when you succeed.'

'But Divodas,' interrupted Ayurvati. 'Even the Lord is grateful to you.'

Both Shiva and Divodas turned towards Ayurvati. Surprised.

'Why?' asked Divodas.

'Your medicine saved Kartik's life,' explained Ayurvati.

'What are you talking about?'

'Well, many a times, within the womb, the umbilical cord gets wrapped around the baby's neck. In some of these cases, the baby cannot survive the journey of birthing. It suffocates and dies. I'm not sure since I wasn't there, but I think that is what may have happened with Princess Sati's first child as well. Kartik had the umbilical cord wrapped around his neck. But this time, I applied your medicine on Princess Sati's belly. It somehow permeated the womb and gave Kartik the strength to survive those few crucial moments till he slipped out. Your medicine saved his life.'

'What medicine?' asked Divodas.

'The Naga medicine,' said Ayurvati, frowning. 'I recognised the paste as soon as I smelt it. And only you could have given it, right?'

'But I didn't!'

'You didn't?' asked a shocked Ayurvati, turning to Shiva. 'Then... Where did you get the medicine from, My Lord?'

Shiva was stunned. Like someone had cruelly destroyed one of his most precious memories.

'My Lord? What is it?' asked Ayurvati.

Shiva, looking furious, abruptly turned around. 'Nandi! Bhadra! Come with me.'

'My Lord, where are you going?' asked Parvateshwar.

But Shiva was already walking away. Followed by Nandi, Veerbhadra and their platoon.

— ⁂ —

'PANDITJI!'

Shiva was in the Kashi Vishwanath temple. As ordered, Nandi and Veerbhadra waited outside, along with their platoon.

'PANDITJI!'

Where the hell is he?

And then Shiva realised he didn't need to shout. All he needed to do was transmit his thoughts. *Vasudevs! Are any of you listening?*

No answer. Shiva's anger rose another notch.

I know you can hear me! Will one of you have the guts to speak?

Still no answer.

Where did you get the Naga medicine from?

Absolute silence.

Explain yourself! What relationship do you and the Nagas have? How deep does this go?

No Vasudev responded.

By the holy lake, answer me! Or I add your name to the enemies of Good!

Shiva didn't hear a word. He turned towards the idol of Lord Rudra. For some strange reason, it didn't appear as fearsome as he remembered. It seemed peaceful. Serene. Almost like it was trying to tell Shiva something.

Shiva turned around and screamed one last time. 'VASUDEVS! ANSWER ME NOW OR I ASSUME THE WORST!'

Hearing no answer, Shiva stormed out of the temple.

Chapter 9

What is Your Karma?

'What happened, Shiva?'

The little boy turned around to find his uncle standing behind him. The boy quickly wiped his eyes, for tears were a sign of weakness in Guna men. The uncle smiled. He sat down next to Shiva and put his arm around his diminutive shoulder.

They rested in silence for a while, letting the waters of the Mansarovar lake lap their feet. It was cold. But they didn't mind.

'What ails you, my child?' asked the uncle.

Shiva looked up. He had always wondered how a fierce warrior like his uncle always sported such a calm, understanding smile.

'Mother told me that I shouldn't feel guilty about...'

The words stopped as tears choked Shiva. He could feel his brow throbbing once again.

'About that poor woman?' asked the uncle.

The boy nodded.

'And, what do you think?'

'I don't know what to think anymore.'

'Yes, you do. Listen to your heart. What do you think?'

Shiva's little hands kept fidgeting with his tiger skin skirt. 'Mother thinks I couldn't have helped her. That I am too small, too young, too powerless. I would have achieved nothing. Instead of helping her, I would probably have just got myself injured.'

'That's probably true. But does that matter?'

The little boy looked up, his eyes narrowed, tears welling up. 'No.'

The uncle smiled. 'Think about it. If you had tried to help her, there is a chance that she would still have suffered. But there is also a chance, however small, that she may have escaped. But if you didn't even try, there was no chance for her. Was there?'

Shiva nodded.

'What else did your mother tell you?'

'That the woman didn't even try to fight back.'

'Yes, that may be true.'

'And mother says that if the woman didn't try to fight, why would it be wrong for me to do the same?'

'That is an important point. The sin was being committed against her. And yet she was accepting it.'

They kept quiet for some time, staring at the setting sun.

'So, even if the woman didn't fight back,' said the uncle. 'What do you think you should have done?'

'I...'

'Yes?'

'I think it doesn't matter if the woman didn't fight to protect herself. No matter what, I should have fought for her.'

'Why?'

Shiva looked up. 'Do you also think I should have been pragmatic? That it wasn't wrong to run away?'

'What I think doesn't matter. I want to hear your interpretation. Why do you think it was wrong for you to run away?'

Shiva looked down, fidgeting with his skirt. His brow was throbbing madly. 'Because it feels wrong to me.'

The uncle smiled. 'That is the answer. It feels wrong, because what you did was against your karma. You don't have to live with the woman's karma. What she did was her choice. You have to live with your own karma.'

Shiva looked up.

'It is your karma to fight evil. It doesn't matter if the people that evil is being committed against don't fight back. It doesn't matter if the entire world chooses to look the other way. Always remember this. You don't live with the consequences of other people's karma. You live with the consequences of your own.'

Shiva nodded slightly.

'Does that hurt?' asked the uncle, pointing at the blackish-red blotch on Shiva's brow, right between his eyes.

Shiva pressed it hard. The pressure provided some relief. 'No. But it burns. It burns a lot.'

'Especially when you are upset?'

Shiva nodded.

The uncle reached into his coat and pulled out a small pouch. 'This is a very precious medicine. I have carried it for a long time. And I feel you are the correct person to receive it.'

Shiva took the pouch. Opening it, he found a reddish-brown thick paste inside. 'Will it make the burning go away?'

The uncle smiled. 'It'll set you on the path of your destiny.'

Shiva frowned. Confused.

Pointing towards the gargantuan Himalayas extending beyond the Mansarovar, the uncle continued. 'My child, your destiny is much larger than these massive mountains. But in order to realise it, you will have to cross these very same massive mountains.'

The uncle didn't feel the need to explain any more. He took some of the reddish-brown paste and applied it on Shiva's brow, in a neat vertical line, up from between his eyes to his hair line. Shiva felt immediate relief as his brow cooled down. Then the uncle applied some paste around Shiva's throat. He took the remaining portion of the medicine and placed it in Shiva's right palm. Then he cut his finger lightly and dropped a little bit of blood into the paste, whispering, 'We will never forget your command, Lord Rudra. This is the blood oath of a Vayuputra.'

Shiva looked at his uncle and then down at his palm, which cradled the strange reddish-brown paste mixed with his uncle's blood.

'Put it at the back of your mouth,' said the uncle. 'But don't swallow it. Massage it with your tongue till it gets absorbed.'

Shiva did that.

'Now you are ready. Let fate choose the time.'

Shiva didn't understand. But he felt the relief the medicine gave. 'Do you have any more of this medicine?'

'I have given you all that I have, my child.'

— ⁂ —

'The Vasudevs had the Naga medicine?' asked a shocked Sati.

She had intended to speak to Shiva about the disturbing conversation with her father in the morning. She was still stunned that a back-up manufacturing facility for the Somras existed and that no one knew about it. But that was immediately forgotten on seeing Shiva's enraged face.

'I have been misled. They are probably in alliance with the Nagas! Can't you trust anyone in this country?'

Something within Sati told her that the Vasudevs couldn't be evil. It didn't add up. 'Shiva, are you probably jumping to...'

'Jumping? Jumping to conclusions?' glared Shiva. 'You know what Ayurvati said. That medicine could only be made in Naga lands. We know how the Brangas got it. They are being blackmailed. What is the explanation for the Vasudevs? They needed the Nagas to build their temples?'

Sati kept quiet.

Shiva walked up to the window and stared hard at the Vishwanath temple. For some strange reason, he could hear his inner voice repeating the same thought. *Stay calm. Don't jump to conclusions.*

Shiva shook his head.

'I'm sure the Vasudevs would have assumed that you would figure out where the medicine came from,' said Sati. 'So there can be only two explanations as to why the Vasudevs gave it to you.'

Shiva turned around.

'Either they are stupid. Or they think the safe birth of your son is so important that they are willing to risk your anger.'

Shiva frowned.

'From what I have gathered from you, I don't think they are stupid,' said Sati. 'That leaves us with only one choice. They think that if anything happened to our son, you would be so devastated that it would harm their cause against evil.'

Shiva chose silence.

— ⁂ —

The Naga Lord of the People sat on his chair in his personal chambers, right next to the window. He could hear the songs of the choir that paraded the streets of Panchavati at this time of the evening, once a week. The Queen had wanted to ban the sad songs they sang. She despised them as defeatist. But the Naga *Rajya Sabha*, the elected *Royal Council*, had voted against her move, allowing the songs to continue.

The song triggered powerful emotions in the Naga, but he held them within.

You were my world, my God, my creator,

And yet, you abandoned me.

I didn't seek you, you called me,

And yet, you abandoned me.

I honoured you, lived by your rules, coloured myself in your colours,

And yet, you abandoned me.

You hurt me, you deserted me, you failed in your duties,

And yet, I am the monster.

Tell me Lord, what can I...

'Disgusting song,' said the Queen, interrupting the Naga's thoughts. 'Shows our weakness and our attachments!'

'*Mausi*,' said the Naga as he rose. 'I didn't hear you come in.'

'How could you? These nauseating songs drown out the world. Drown out any positive thought.'

'Vengeance is not a positive thought, Your Highness,' smiled the Naga. 'Also the choir does sing happy songs as well.'

The Queen waved her hand. 'I have something more important to discuss.'

'Yes, *Mausi*.'

The Queen took a deep breath. 'Did you meet the Vasudevs?'

The Naga narrowed his eyes. He was surprised that it had taken the Queen so long to find out. 'Yes.'

'Why?' asked the Queen, barely restraining her temper.

'Your Highness, I believe we can use their help.'

'They will never support us. They may not be our enemies. But they will never be our friends!'

'I disagree. I think we have a common enemy. They will come to our side.'

'Nonsense! The Vasudevs are fanatic purveyors of an ancient legend. Some foreigner with a blue throat is not going to save this country!'

'But another foreigner with a beaded beard saved this country once, didn't he?'

'Don't compare this tribal to the great Lord Rudra. This country is probably fated for destruction. All India has given us is pain and sorrow. Why should we care?'

'Because whatever it may be, it is our country too.'

The Queen grunted angrily. 'Tell me the real reason why you gave them our medicine. You know it is in short supply. We have to send the annual quota to the Brangas. I am not breaking my word. They are the only decent people in this wretched land. The only ones who don't want to kill us all.'

'The quota of the Brangas will not be affected, Your Highness. I have only given my personal share.'

'In the holy name of Bhoomidevi, why? Have you suddenly started believing in the Neelkanth too?'

'What I believe doesn't matter, Your Highness. What matters is that the people of India believe.'

The Queen stared hard at the Naga. 'That is not the real reason.'

'It is.'

'DON'T LIE TO ME!'

The Naga kept quiet.

'You did it for that vile woman,' stated the Queen.

The Naga was disturbed, but his voice remained calm. 'No. And at least you shouldn't speak of her that way, Your Highness.'

'Why not?'

'Because besides me, you are the only one who knows the truth.'

'Sometimes I wish I didn't!'

'It's too late for that now.'

The Queen sniggered. 'It's true that the Gods don't give all abilities to one person. You truly are your own worst enemy.'

— ⅄⦾Ʊ⍋⊛ —

Daksha was sitting on the ground. He had been shocked at the unscheduled appearance of Maharishi Bhrigu in Devagiri. The Emperor of Meluha had not sought an audience with the sage.

Bhrigu looked down hard at Daksha, deeply unhappy. 'You disobeyed a direct command, Your Highness.'

Daksha remained quiet, head bowed low. *How did the Maharishi get to know? Only Sati, Veerini and I had been in on the conversation. Is Veerini spying on me? Why is everyone against me? Why me?*

Bhrigu stared at Daksha, reading his thoughts. The sage always knew that Daksha was weak. But the Emperor had never dared disobey a direct order. Furthermore, Bhrigu didn't really give that many orders. He was concerned about only one thing. On all other matters, he let Daksha do whatever he liked.

'You have been made Emperor for a reason,' said Bhrigu. 'Please don't make me question my judgement.'

Daksha kept quiet, scared.

Bhrigu bent down and turned Daksha's face up. 'Did you also tell her the location, Your Highness?'

Daksha whispered softly. 'No, My Lord. I swear.'

'Don't lie to me!'

'I swear, My Lord.'

Bhrigu read Daksha's thoughts. He was satisfied.

'You are not to mention this to anyone. Is that clear?'

Daksha remained silent.

'Your Highness,' said Bhrigu, his voice louder. 'Is that clear?'

'Yes, My Lord,' said a scared Daksha, holding Bhrigu's feet.

— ⁂ —

Shiva stood at the Assi Ghat. The sails of the five gleaming Branga ships had been folded in all but one of the ships. On the ship anchored closest to port, the sails had been pulled up, creating a grand sight, much to the appreciative glances of the people present.

'They look good, Divodas,' said Shiva.

'Thank you, My Lord.'

'I can't believe that your tribe built all this in just nine months.'

'We Brangas can do anything, My Lord.'

Shiva smiled.

Athithigva, standing next to Shiva, spoke up. 'Divodas, are you sure the ships will sail? This ship here has all its sails open and the winds are strong. And yet, it doesn't seem to be shaking the ship at all.'

Clearly the king did not know much about sailing.

'That is a very good point, Your Highness,' said Divodas. 'But the ship is not moving because we don't want it sailing off without us. The sails have been aligned such that they are directly against the wind. Can you see the main sail fluttering dramatically?'

Athithigva nodded.

'That means that the sail is laughing at us since it's not catching any wind.'

Shiva smiled. 'Laughing?'

'That's the term we use when the sail has been set wrong and is fluttering, My Lord,' said Divodas.

'Well,' said Shiva. 'I'll be serious then. We leave in three days for Branga. Make all the preparations.'

Sati was staring at the Ganga from her chamber window. She could see a small entourage of boats carrying King Athithigva across the river to his palace on the eastern banks.

Why does he keep going there? Why does he only take his family?

'What are you thinking, Sati?'

Shiva was standing behind her. She embraced him. 'I'm going to miss you.'

He pulled her face up, kissed her and smiled. 'That's not what you were thinking.'

Sati patted him lightly on his chest. 'You can read my mind as well?'

'I wish I could.'

'I wasn't thinking anything serious. Just wondering why King Athithigva goes to the Eastern palace so often. Even more oddly, he only takes his family there.'

'Yes, even I've noticed that. I'm sure he has some good reason. There is the superstition of the eastern banks being inauspicious, right?'

Sati shrugged. 'Is it fixed? You're leaving in three days?'

'Yes.'

'How long do you think you'll be gone?'

'I don't know. Hopefully, not too long.'

'I wish I could come.'

'I know. But Kartik is simply not old enough for a voyage like this.'

Sati looked at Kartik sleeping on his bed. He had grown so fast that he didn't fit in his crib any more. 'He looks more and more like you.'

Shiva smiled. 'It's been just six months, but he looks like a two–year–old!'

Sati had to take Shiva's word for it. Being a Meluhan who did not live in Maika, she had never seen a child younger than sixteen years of age.

'Maybe it's the blessings of the Somras,' said Sati.

'Possible. Ayurvati was surprised that he didn't fall sick the first time he took the Somras.'

'That was surprising. But maybe that's simply because he is a special boy!'

'That he is. I've never seen a baby who could walk at six months.'

Sati smiled. 'He will make us proud.'

'I'm sure he will.'

Sati looked up and kissed Shiva again. 'Just find a path to the Nagas and come back to me soon.'

'I certainly will, my love.'

— ⁂ —

The ships had been provisioned. They did not intend to wait at any port along the way. Speed was of the essence.

Much to the mortification of Parvateshwar, a joint brigade of Suryavanshis and Chandravanshis had been created. It was difficult to carry more men in the five ships. But the saving grace was that the overall command remained with Drapaku.

Shiva looked at the ships from the steps of the Assi Ghat. Drapaku, as the commander, was on the lead craft, accompanied by his father Purvaka. The key companions of the Neelkanth were stationed on the main vessel, which would sail in the safest zone, surrounded by the other four boats. Parvateshwar, Bhagirath, Anandmayi, Ayurvati, Nandi and Veerbhadra, all stood at the balustrade of this ship. Shiva was surprised to find Uttanka too on the main ship.

Anandmayi must have insisted. If there is one woman who can entice Parvateshwar into breaking his vow of celibacy, it is her.

'My Lord,' said Athithigva, interrupting Shiva's thoughts.

The King of Kashi bent down to touch the Neelkanth's feet.

Shiva touched Athithigva's head gently. '*Ayushman Bhav.*'

With folded hands, Athithigva whispered, 'I beg you to return to Kashi quickly, My Lord. We are orphans without you.'

'You don't need me, Your Highness. You don't really need anyone else. Have faith in the one person that loves you the most: Yourself.'

Shiva turned towards a moist-eyed Sati, who was holding Kartik's hand as he stood by her side, wobbling slightly due to the strong winds.

Kartik pointed up at Shiva and said, 'Ba-ba.'

Shiva smiled and picked Kartik up. 'Ba-ba will be back soon, Kartik. Don't give your mother too much trouble.'

Kartik pulled Shiva's hair and repeated. 'Ba-ba.'

Shiva smiled even more broadly and kissed Kartik on his forehead. Then he held Kartik to his side and stepped forward to embrace Sati. Some Suryavanshi habits were too hard to break. Sati embraced Shiva lightly, for she was embarrassed of such public displays of affection. Shiva didn't let go. Sati's love for Shiva conquered her Suryavanshi reserve. She looked up and kissed Shiva. 'Come back soon.'

'I will.'

Chapter 10

The Gates of Branga

The waters were rising fast, flooding the small boat.

Shiva tried desperately to control the vessel, fighting the raging river with his oars, labouring to reach his friend.

Brahaspati was struggling. Suddenly his eyes opened wide in surprise. What seemed like a rope came out of nowhere and bound itself to his legs. He started getting pulled in rapidly.

'Shiva! Help! Please help me!'

Shiva was rowing hard. Desperately so. 'Hold on! I'm coming!'

Suddenly a massive three headed snake rose from the river. Shiva noticed the rope around Brahaspati slithering up and around him, crushing him ruthlessly. It was the serpent!

'Nooooo!'

Shiva woke up with a start. He looked around in a daze. His brow was throbbing hard, his throat intolerably cold. Everyone was asleep. He could feel the ground beneath him sway as the ship rocked gently, in tune with the Ganga waters. He walked up to the porthole of his cabin, letting the gentle breeze slow his heart rate down.

He curled his fist and rested it against the ship wall. 'I will get him, Brahaspati. That snake will pay.'

It had been two weeks since Shiva's entourage had left Kashi. Making good time since they were sailing downriver, they had just crossed the city of Magadh.

'We should be reaching Branga in another three weeks, My Lord,' said Parvateshwar.

Shiva, who was staring upriver, towards Kashi, turned around with a smile. 'Did you speak to Divodas?'

'Yes.'

'Where is he right now?'

'At the mast head, My Lord, trimming his sails to the prevailing wind. Obviously, he too wants to get to Branga quickly.'

Shiva looked at Parvateshwar. 'No, I don't think so. I think he yearns to play his role in my quest and then get back to his wife and daughter. He really misses them.'

'As you miss Sati and Kartik, My Lord.'

Shiva smiled and nodded, both of them leaning against the ship rail, looking at the tranquil Ganga. A school of dolphins emerged from the river and flew up into the air. Falling gracefully back into the waters, they jumped up once again, continuing this handsome dance, in graceful symphony. Shiva loved looking at the dolphins. They always seemed happy and carefree. 'Carefree fish in a capricious river! Poetic, isn't it?'

Parvateshwar smiled. 'Yes, My Lord.'

'Speaking of carefree and capricious, where is Anandmayi?'

'I think the Princess is with Uttanka, My Lord. She keeps going to the practice room with him. Perhaps they are perfecting some other dance moves.'

'Hmm.'

Parvateshwar kept looking at the river.

'She does dance well, doesn't she?' asked Shiva.

'Yes, My Lord.'

'Exceptionally well, actually.'

'That would be a fair comment to make, My Lord.'

'What do you think of Uttanka's dancing skills?'

Parvateshwar looked at Shiva and then towards the river once again. 'I think there is scope for improvement, My Lord. But I'm sure Princess Anandmayi will teach him well.'

Shiva smiled at Parvateshwar and shook his head. 'Yes, I'm sure she will.'

— ⅄◎Ʊ⇑⊗ —

'The Neelkanth and his entourage left for Branga a month back, Your Highness,' said the Naga Lord of the People to the Queen.

They were sitting in her private chambers.

'Good to see you focus once again. I'll send a warning message to King Chandraketu.'

The Naga nodded. He was about to say something more, but kept silent. Instead, he looked out of the window. From this position in Panchavati, he could see the calm Godavari river in the distance.

'And?' asked the Queen.

'I'd like your permission to go to Kashi.'

'Why? Do you want to open trade relations with them?' asked the Queen, highly tickled.

'She did not go with the Neelkanth.'

The Queen stiffened.

'Please, Your Highness. This is important to me.'

'What do you hope to achieve, my child?' asked the Queen. 'This is a foolhardy quest.'

'I want answers.'

'What difference will that make?'

'It will give me peace.'

The Queen sighed. 'This quest will be your downfall.'

'It will complete me, Your Highness.'

'You are forgetting that you have duties towards your own people.'

'I first have a duty unto myself, *Mausi*.'

The Queen shook her head. 'Wait till the Rajya Sabha is over. I need you here to ensure that the motion to support the Brangas is not defeated. After that you can go.'

The Naga bent low and touched the Queen's feet. 'Thank you, *Mausi*.'

'But you will not go alone. I don't trust you to take care of yourself. I will come with you.'

The Naga smiled softly. 'Thank you.'

Shiva's entourage was just a week's distance from the gates of Branga. The ships had maintained a punishing schedule. Parvateshwar and Divodas had taken a clipper to the lead boat in order to confer with Drapaku about the protocol on reaching the gates. Parvateshwar made it very clear that the Lord Neelkanth did not want any bloodshed. Divodas was to complete the negotiations necessary in order to enter the restricted Branga territory. He felt it would be impossible to enter without showing the Neelkanth, for the Brangas too believed in the legend. Parvateshwar advised him to try and enter without having to resort to that.

Divodas was left with Drapaku so they could plan the

flag display as well, while Parvateshwar returned to the central vessel. He wanted to take the Lord Mahadev's advice on how he would like the Branga border guards handled. Parvateshwar did not want to let his guard down and yet, given the delicacy of the mission, it was imperative that the Brangas did not view the five ship fleet as a threat.

His rowers tied the cutter to the main ship and he climbed up to the aft section. He was taken aback to see Anandmayi there. She had her back to him. Six knives in her hand. The standard target board at the wall had been removed and the expert board, much smaller in size, had been hung up there. Bhagirath and Uttanka were standing a short distance away.

Uttanka turned towards Anandmayi. 'Remember what I've taught you, Princess. No breaks. A continuous shower of knives.'

Anandmayi rolled her eyes. 'Yeeesss Guruji. I heard you the first time. I'm not deaf.'

'I'm sorry, Your Highness.'

'Now stand aside.'

Uttanka moved away.

Parvateshwar standing at the back was dumbfounded by what he saw. Anandmayi was standing correctly. Like a trained warrior. With her feet slightly spread in a stable posture. Her right hand relaxed to her side. The left hand holding the six knives from the hilt, positioned close to her right shoulder. Her breathing, light and calm. Perfect.

Then she raised her right hand. And in a dramatically rapid action, pulled the first knife from her left hand and threw. Almost simultaneously, she reached for the second knife and released it. And then the third, fourth, fifth and sixth.

Anandmayi's movements were so flawless that Parvateshwar did not even see the target. He stood there admiring her action. His mouth open in awe. Then he heard Uttanka and Bhagirath applauding. He turned towards the board. Every knife had hit dead centre. Perfect.

'By the great Lord Ram!' marvelled Parvateshwar.

Anandmayi turned with a broad smile. 'Parva! When did you get here?'

Parvateshwar, meanwhile, had found something else to admire. He was staring at Anandmayi's bare legs. Or so it seemed.

Anandmayi shifted her weight, relaxing her hips to the side saucily. 'See something you like, Parva?'

Parvateshwar whispered softly, pointing with a bit of wonder at the scabbard hanging by Anandmayi's waist. 'That is a long sword.'

Anandmayi's face fell. 'You really know how to sweep a woman back onto her feet, don't you?'

'Sorry?' asked Parvateshwar.

Anandmayi just shook her head.

'But that is a long sword,' said Parvateshwar. 'When did you learn to wield that?'

Wielding a sword that was significantly longer than a warrior's arm length was a rare skill. Difficult to master. But those who mastered it, dramatically improved their chances of a kill.

Bhagirath and Uttanka had now walked up close.

Bhagirath answered, 'Uttanka has been teaching her for the last month, General. She is a quick student.'

Parvateshwar turned back to Anandmayi, bowed his head slightly. 'It would be my honour to duel with you, Princess.'

Anandmayi raised her eyebrows. 'You want to duel with me? What the hell do you think you're trying to prove?'

'I'm not trying to prove anything, Your Highness,' said Parvateshwar, surprised at Anandmayi's belligerence. 'It would just be a pleasure to duel with you and test your skills.'

'*Test* my skills? You think that's why I'm learning the art of warfare? So that you can test me and prove yourself superior? I already know you're better. Don't exert yourself.'

Parvateshwar breathed deeply, trying to control his rising temper. 'My lady, that's not what I was trying to imply. I was just...'

Anandmayi interrupted him. 'For a sharp man, you can be remarkably stupid sometimes, General. I just don't know what I was thinking.'

Bhagirath tried to step in. 'Umm listen, I don't think there is a need to...'

But Anandmayi had already turned and stormed off.

— ⁂ —

The sun had just risen over the Ganga, tinting it a stunning orange. Sati was standing at her chamber window, looking down at the river. Kartik was playing in the back with Krittika. Sati turned to look at her friend and son. She smiled.

Krittika is almost like a second mother to Kartik. My son is so lucky.

Sati turned back towards the river. She noticed a movement. Peering harder, she saw what was going on and frowned. Emperor Athithigva was off again to his mystery palace. Apparently, for yet another puja for the future of Kashi. She found this odd.

The entire city of Kashi was celebrating *Rakshabandhan* that day. A day when each sister *tied a thread on her brother's wrist, seeking his protection in times of distress.* This festival was celebrated in Meluha as well. The only difference in Swadweep was that the sisters also demanded gifts from their brothers. And the brothers had no choice but to oblige.

Shouldn't he be spending his time in Kashi? In Meluha, women would come to tie a rakhi to the local governor. And, it was his duty to offer protection. This had been clearly established by Lord Ram. Why is King Athithigva not following this tradition and is instead going to his other palace? And why in Lord Ram's name is he carrying so many things? Are they part of some ritual to rid the eastern banks of bad fate? Or are they gifts?

'What are you thinking, Your Highness?'

Sati turned around to find Krittika staring at her. 'I must find an answer to the mystery of this Eastern palace.'

'But nobody is allowed in there. You know that. The king even made some strange excuses to not take the Neelkanth there.'

'I know. But something is not right. And why is the King taking so many gifts there today?'

'I don't know, Your Highness.'

Sati turned towards Krittika. 'I'm going there.'

Krittika stared at Sati in alarm. 'My Lady, you cannot. There are lookouts at the palace heights. It is surrounded by walls. They will see any boat approaching.'

'That's why I intend to swim across.'

Krittika was now in panic. The Ganga was too broad to swim across. 'My Lady...'

'I've been planning this for weeks, Krittika. I've practised many times. There's a sand bank in the middle of the river where I can rest, unseen.'

'But how will you enter the palace?'

'I can hazard a guess about the structural layout from the terrace of our chamber. The Eastern palace is guarded heavily only at the entrance. I have also noticed that guards are not allowed into the main palace. There is a water drain at the far end of the palace. I can swim in through it, without leaving anyone the wiser.'

'But...'

'I'm going. Take care of Kartik. If all goes well, I will be back by nightfall.'

— ⁂ —

The ships turned the last meander of the Ganga to emerge a short distance from the legendary gates of Branga.

'By the Holy Lake!' whispered Shiva in awe.

Even the Meluhans, used to their own renowned engineering skills and celebrated monuments, were dumbstruck.

The gates gleamed in the midday sun, having been built almost entirely of the newly discovered metal, iron. The barrier was spread across the river, and it extended additionally into fort walls along the banks which ran a further hundred kilometres inland. This was to prevent anyone from dismantling a smaller ship, carrying it across land and then reassembling it on the other side. There were no roads at the Branga border. The Ganga was the only way in. And anyone stupid enough to go deep into the jungle would probably be killed by wild animals and disease before meeting any Branga man.

The barrier's base was a cage built of iron, which allowed the waters of the mighty Ganga to flow through, but prevented any person or large fish from swimming through underwater. The barrier had, oddly enough, five open spaces in between, to allow five ships to sail through simultaneously. It seemed odd at first sight because it appeared that a fast cutter could just race through the gap before any Branga could attack it.

'That seems bizarre,' said Bhagirath. 'Why build a barrier and then leave openings through it?'

'Those aren't openings, Bhagirath,' said Shiva. 'They are traps.'

Shiva pointed at a Branga ship that had just entered the gates. At the beginning of the opening was a deep pool of water with a base made of water-proofed teak, into which the ship had sailed in. There was a cleverly designed pump system that allowed the waters of the Ganga to come into the pool. This raised the ship to the correct height. And then, they saw the fearsome magic of the gates of Branga. Two thick iron platforms rapidly extended from both sides of the pool onto the ship, fitting onto the groove on the extended iron base at the bottom of the hull. The platform had rollers on its edge which fit snugly within the channel of the iron base of the ship.

Shiva looked at Parvateshwar. 'So that's why Divodas built the base at the bottom of our hulls.'

Parvateshwar nodded in awe. 'The platforms extended with such rapid force. If we didn't have the iron base at the bottom, it would just crush the hull of our ship.'

Iron chains were being fitted onto the hooks on the hull

of the ship. The chains were then attached to a strange looking machine which appeared to be like a medley of pulleys.

'But what animal did they use to make the platform move so fast?' asked Bhagirath. 'This force is beyond any animal's capability. Even a herd of elephants!'

Shiva pointed to the Branga ship. The pulleys had started moving with rapid force, extending the chains, pulling the vessel forward. The rollers on the platform permitted the ship to move with minimum friction, allowing it to maintain its amazing speed.

'My God!' whispered Bhagirath again. 'Look at that! What animal can make the pulleys move so quickly?'

'It's a machine,' said Shiva. 'Divodas had told me about some accumulator machines, which store the energy of various animals over hours and then release them in seconds.'

Bhagirath frowned.

'Look,' said Shiva.

A massive cylinder of rock was coming down rapidly. Next to it was another similar cylinder, being slowly pushed up by pulleys, as twenty bulls, yoked to the machine, gradually went around it in circles.

'The bulls are charging the machine with hours of labour,' said Shiva. 'The massive rock is locked at a height. When the platform is to be extended or a ship pulled, they remove the lock on the rock. It comes crashing down, the momentum releasing a tremendous force that propels the platforms.'

'By the great Lord Indra,' said Bhagirath. 'A simple design. But so brilliant!'

Shiva nodded. He turned towards the Branga office at the entry gates.

Their ships had anchored close to the gates. Divodas had already stepped off to negotiate with the Branga Officer in-charge.

— ⅄ⵁႮ⇡⊛ —

'Why are you back so soon? You have enough medicines for a year.'

Divodas was shocked at the manner in which Major Uma was speaking. She was always strict, but never rude. He had been delighted that she had been posted at the gates. Though he hadn't met her in years, they had been friends a long time back. He had thought he could use his friendship with her to gain easy passage into Branga.

'What is the matter, Uma?' asked Divodas.

'It is Major Uma. I am on duty.'

'I'm sorry Major. I meant no disrespect.'

'I can't let you go back unless you give me a good reason.'

'Why would I need a reason to enter my own country?'

'This is not your country anymore. You chose to abandon it. Kashi is your land. Go back there.'

'Major Uma, you know I had no choice. You know the risks to the life of my child in Branga.'

'You think those who live in Branga don't? You think we don't love our children? Yet we choose to live in our own land. You suffer the consequences of your choice.'

Divodas realised this was getting nowhere. 'I have to meet the King on a matter of national importance.'

Uma narrowed her eyes. 'Really? I guess the King has some important business dealings with Kashi, right?'

Divodas breathed in deeply. 'Major Uma, it is very important that I meet the King. You must trust me.'

'Unless you are carrying the Queen of the Nagas herself on one of your ships, I can't see anything important enough to let you through!'

'I'm carrying someone far more important than the Queen of the Nagas.'

'Kashi has really improved your sense of humour, Divodas,' sneered Uma. 'I suggest you turn back and shine your supreme light somewhere else.'

The snide pun on Kashi's name convinced Divodas that he was facing a changed Uma. An angry and bitter Uma, incapable of listening to reason. He had no choice. He had to get the Neelkanth. He knew Uma used to believe in the legend.

'I'll come back with the person who is more important than the Queen of the Nagas herself,' said Divodas, turning to leave.

— ⁂ —

The small cutter had just docked at the Branga office. Divodas alighted first. Followed by Shiva, Parvateshwar, Bhagirath, Drapaku and Purvaka.

Uma, standing outside her office, sighed. 'You really don't give up, do you?'

'This is very important, Major Uma,' said Divodas.

Uma recognised Bhagirath. 'Is this the person? You think I should break the rules for the Prince of Ayodhya?'

'He is the Prince of Swadweep, Major Uma. Don't forget that. We send tribute to Ayodhya.'

'So you are more loyal to Ayodhya as well now? How many times will you abandon Branga?'

'Major, in the name of Ayodhya, I respectfully ask you

to let us pass,' said Bhagirath, trying hard not to lose his temper. He knew the Neelkanth did not want any bloodshed.

'Our terms of the Ashwamedh treaty were very clear, Prince. We send you a tribute annually. And Ayodhya never enters Branga. We have maintained our part of the agreement. The orders to me are to help you maintain your part of the bargain.'

Shiva stepped forward. 'If I may...'

Uma was at the end of her patience. She stepped forward and pushed Shiva. 'Get out of here.'

'UMA!' Divodas pulled out his sword.

Bhagirath, Parvateshwar, Drapaku and Purvaka too drew out their swords instantly.

'I will kill your entire family for this blasphemy,' swore Drapaku.

'Wait!' said Shiva, his arms spread wide, stopping his men.

Shiva turned towards Uma. She was staring at him, shocked. The *angvastram* that he had wrapped around his body for warmth had come undone, revealing his *neel kanth,* the prophesied blue throat. The Branga soldiers around Uma immediately went down on their knees, heads bowed in respect, tears flooding their eyes. Uma continued to stare, her mouth half open.

Shiva cleared his throat. 'I really need to pass through, Major Uma. May I request your cooperation?'

Uma's face turned mottled red. 'Where the hell have you been?'

Shiva frowned.

Uma bent forward, tears in her eyes, banging her small fists on Shiva's well-honed chest. 'Where the hell have you been? We have been waiting! We have been suffering! Where the hell have you been?'

Shiva tried to hold Uma, to comfort her. But she sank down holding Shiva's leg, wailing. 'Where the hell have you been?'

A concerned Divodas turned to another Branga friend also posted at the border. His friend whispered, 'Last month, Major Uma lost her only child to the plague. Her husband and she had conceived after years of trying. She was devastated.'

Divodas looked at Uma with empathy, understanding her angst. He couldn't even begin to imagine what would happen to him if he lost his baby.

Shiva, who had heard the entire conversation, squatted. He cradled Uma in the shelter of his arms, as though trying to give her his strength.

'Why didn't you come earlier?' Uma kept crying, inconsolable.

Chapter 11

The Mystery of the Eastern Palace

Sati was resting on the sandbank in the middle of the Ganga. She kept low to avoid being seen from the Eastern palace. Her brown clothes, an effective camouflage.

She kept her breathing steady, rejuvenating her tired muscles. Reaching back, she again checked the hold on her sword and shield. It was secure on her back. She didn't want it slipping out into the Ganga, leaving her defenceless when she entered the palace.

Reaching to her side, she pulled out a small pouch. She ate the fruit inside quickly. Once done, she tucked the empty pouch back. Then slipped quietly back into the Ganga.

A little while later Sati crept gradually onto the eastern banks. Far from the well guarded ghats of the palace, where the King's boats had been anchored, was a concealed drain. It was impossible to see from anywhere in Kashi or the Ganga. But the elevation of the palace that was Sati's quarters for the duration of her visit to the city, the only building of that height in Kashi, allowed her to chance upon it. She crept slowly into the foliage, suspecting the channel was behind it.

She quietly slipped into the drain, swimming with powerful strokes towards the palace. The drain was surprisingly clean. Not too many people in the palace perhaps. Closer to the palace wall, the drain disappeared underground. Sati dived underwater. Metal bars protected the drain opening near the palace premises. Sati pulled out a file from her pouch and started cutting away at the bar. She only went up for air when her lungs started burning for oxygen. She dived back and continued filing the rusty, old metal bars. With only five trips up for air, Sati was able to cut through two of the rods, space enough for her to slip through.

Sati emerged along the western wall of the palace to find herself in a breathtaking garden. The area was completely deserted. Perhaps nobody expected an intruder from this end. While the ground was covered with lush green grass, flowers and trees appeared to have been allowed to go wild, giving the garden the appearance of a barely restrained forest. Picturesque and natural.

Sati hurried through the garden, careful not to step on any dried twigs. She reached a side entrance and walked in.

The eeriness of the palace was starting to get her. There was no sound. No servants toiling away. No sounds of royalty making merry. No sounds of birds in the garden. Nothing. It was like she had stepped into a vacuum.

She hurried through the corridors. Not finding anyone to obstruct or challenge her, she went through the luxurious palace, which looked like it had never been lived in!

Suddenly she heard the soft sounds of laughter. She crept in that direction.

The corridor opened into the main courtyard. Sati hid behind a pillar. She could see King Athithigva sitting in the centre on a throne. Standing next to him were his wife and son. Three ancient-looking attendants, who Sati had never seen before, stood next to them, holding puja thalis with all the necessary accoutrements for a rakhi ceremony, including the sacred thread itself.

Why is he getting his rakhi tied here?

And then, a woman stepped forward.

Sati's breathing stopped in horror.

Naga!

— ⅄ⓄⓊⓅ⊛ —

The entire crew on all five ships was crowded on the port and starboard side, watching the operation with awe and wonder. Shiva's men were completely astounded by the Branga gates. They had seen the platform close in on their ship with frightening force. Then the hooks were secured to the chains. The Brangas, after the go-ahead from the respective ship captains, began towing the fleet.

Shiva was standing aft, looking at the office at the gate entrance.

Every Branga not working on the gate machinery was on his knees, paying obeisance to the Neelkanth. But Shiva was staring at a broken woman curled up against the wall in a foetal position. She was still crying.

Shiva had tears in his eyes. He knew Uma believed that fate had cheated her daughter. She believed that if the Neelkanth had arrived a month earlier, her child would still be alive. But the Neelkanth himself was not so sure.

What could I have done?

He continued to stare at Uma.

Holy Lake, give me strength. I will fight this plague.

The ground staff got the signal. They released the accumulator machines and the pulleys began turning, moving the ship rapidly forward.

Seeing the vision of Uma retreating swiftly, Shiva whispered, 'I'm sorry.'

— ⁂ —

Sati was stunned. A Naga woman with the King of Kashi!

The Naga woman was actually two women in one body. The body was one from the chest down. But there were two sets of shoulders, fused to each other at the chest, each with a single arm dangling in either direction. The Naga had two heads.

One body, two arms, four shoulders and two heads. Lord Ram, what evil is this?

Sati realised quickly that each head was fighting for control over their common body. One head seemed docile, wanting to come forward to tie the rakhi on the King's extended arm. The other head, playful and mischievous, intent on playing pranks on her brother, was pulling back.

'Maya!' said Athithigva. 'Stop playing pranks and tie the rakhi on my wrist.'

The mischievous head laughed and commanded the body to come forward, to fulfil her brother's wish. Athithigva proudly displayed his rakhi to his wife and son. Then he took some sweets from the plates held by the attendants and gave them to his sister. The attendant then came forward with a sword. Athithigva looked at the mischievous sister and gave the sword to her. 'Practice well. You are really improving!'

The attendant then gave a *Veena*, a stringed musical instrument to the King. Athithigva turned to the other sister and gave the instrument to her. 'I love to hear you play.'

The arms seemed to be in a quandary as to which gift to hold.

'Now don't you squabble over the gifts dear sisters. I mean for you to share them sensibly.'

Just then one of the attendants noticed Sati. She screamed out loud.

Sati immediately drew her sword. Maya did as well. But the heads hadn't come to a consensus. She seemed to be hesitating. Ultimately, the docile head won. She ran behind her brother. Athithigva's wife and son stood rooted to their spot.

Athithigva however was staring hard at Sati, eyes defiant, arm protectively drawn around his sister.

'Your Highness,' said Sati. 'What is the meaning of this?'

'I'm only getting a rakhi tied by my sister, My Lady,' said Athithigva.

'You are sheltering a Naga. You are hiding this from your people. This is wrong.'

'She is my sister, My Lady.'

'But she is a Naga!'

'I don't care. All I know is that she is my sister. I am sworn to protect her.'

'But she should be in the Naga territory.'

'Why should she be with those monsters?'

'Lord Rudra would not have allowed this.'

'Lord Rudra said judge a person by his karma, not his appearance.'

Sati kept quiet, troubled.

Maya suddenly stepped forward. The aggressive personality had come up front. The docile one seemed to be struggling to pull the body back.

'Let me go!' screamed the aggressive one.

The docile head capitulated. Maya moved forward and dropped her sword, not wanting to convey any threat.

'Why do you hate us?' said the Naga's aggressive head.

Sati stood dumbfounded. 'I don't hate you... I was just talking about the rules to be followed...'

'Really? So rules made thousands of years back, in a different land, by people who don't know us or our circumstances, will govern every aspect of our life?'

Sati kept silent.

'You think that is how Lord Ram would have liked it?'

'Lord Ram ordered his followers to obey the rules.'

'He also said rules are not an end in itself. They are made to create a just and stable society. But what if the rules themselves cause injustice? Then how do you follow Lord Ram? By following those rules or breaking them?'

Sati didn't have an answer.

'Brother has spoken a lot about the Lord Neelkanth and you,' said Maya. 'Aren't you supposed to be a Vikarma?'

Sati stiffened. 'I followed those rules as long as they were active.'

'And why was the Vikarma law changed?'

'Shiva didn't change it for me!'

'Believe what you want. But the change in the law helped you as well, right?'

Sati kept quiet, disturbed.

Maya continued. 'I have heard many tales about the Neelkanth. I'll tell you why he changed it. The Vikarma law may have made sense a thousand years back. But in this day and age, it was unfair. It was just a tool to oppress people one doesn't understand.'

Sati was about to say something, but kept quiet.

'And who is more misunderstood today than a person with a deformity? Call us Naga. Call us a monster. Throw us to the South of the Narmada, where our presence will not trouble your lily white lives.'

'So what you are saying is that all Nagas are paragons of virtue?'

'We don't know! And we don't care! Why should we answer for the Nagas? Just because we were born deformed? Will you answer for any Suryavanshi who breaks the law?'

Sati kept silent.

'Isn't it punishment enough that we live alone in this godforsaken palace, with only three servants for company? That the only excitement in our lives is the periodic visits of our brother? How much more do you want to punish us? And will you kindly explain what we are being punished for?'

The docile personality suddenly seemed to assert herself and Maya abruptly moved back, hiding behind Athithigva.

Athithigva bent low. 'Please, Lady Sati. I beg you. Please don't tell anyone.'

Sati remained quiet.

'She's my sister,' pleaded Athithigva. 'My father made me swear on his deathbed that I would protect her. I cannot break my pledge.'

Sati looked at Maya and then at Athithigva. For the first time in her life, she was confronted with the viewpoint of a Naga. And she could see the unfairness that they faced.

'I love her,' said Athithigva. 'Please.'

'I promise to keep quiet.'

'Will you swear in the name of Lord Ram, My Lady?'

Sati frowned. 'I am a Suryavanshi, Your Highness. We don't break our promises. And everything that we do is in the name of Lord Ram.'

As soon as the ships were through the gates, Drapaku ordered the sails up full mast. He directed the other ships to quickly fall into formation.

They had just gone a short distance when they beheld the mighty Brahmaputra flowing down to marshal with the Ganga, and together form probably one of the largest fresh water bodies in the world.

'By the great Lord *Varun*,' said Drapaku in awe, remembering the *God of water and seas*. 'That river is almost as big as an ocean!'

'Yes,' said Divodas proudly.

Turning to Purvaka, Drapaku said, 'I wish you could see this, father. I have never seen a river so massive!'

'I can see through your eyes, my son.'

'Brahmaputra is the largest river in India, Brigadier,' said Divodas. 'The only one with a masculine name.'

Drapaku thought about it for a moment. 'You are right. I never thought of that. Every other river in India has a feminine name. Even the great Ganga that we sail on.'

'Yes. We believe the Brahmaputra and Ganga are the father and mother of the Branga.'

Purvaka started. 'Of course! That must be the source of the names of your main river and your kingdom. The *Bra*hmaputra and Ga*nga* conjugate to create *Branga!*'

'Interesting point, father,' said Drapaku. He then turned to Divodas. 'Is that true?'

'Yes.'

The ships set sail, down the Branga river, to the capital city of the kingdom, *Brangaridai*, literally, *the heart of Branga.*

— ⁂ —

Parvateshwar was standing alone at the stern, watching the lead boat. The system that Anandmayi had suggested, of tying a line from the lead boat to the central boat, was being followed. The General still marvelled at the brilliant simplicity of this idea.

'General.'

Parvateshwar turned around to find Anandmayi standing behind him. Due to the cold, she had wrapped a long *angvastram* around her.

'Your Highness,' said Parvateshwar. 'I'm sorry, I didn't hear you come.'

'It's all right,' said Anandmayi with a slight smile. 'I have soft feet.'

Parvateshwar nodded, about to say something, but he hesitated.

'What is it, General?'

'Your Highness,' said Parvateshwar. 'I meant no insult when I asked you to duel with me. In Meluha, it is a form of fellowship.'

'Fellowship! You make our relationship sound so boring, General.'

Parvateshwar kept silent.

'Well, if you have called me a friend,' said Anandmayi, 'perhaps you can answer a question.'

'Of course.'

'Why did you take the vow of lifelong celibacy?'

'That is a long story, Your Highness.'

'I have all the time in the world to hear you.'

'More than two hundred and fifty years ago, noblemen in Meluha voted for a change in Lord Ram's laws.'

'What is wrong with that? I thought Lord Ram had said his laws can be changed for the purpose of justice.'

'Yes, he did. But this particular change did not serve justice. You know about our Maika system of child management, right?'

'Yes,' said Anandmayi. How a mother could be expected to surrender her child without any hope of seeing him ever again was something she did not understand. But she didn't want to get into an argument with Parvateshwar. 'So what change was made in it?'

'The Maika system was relaxed so that the children of nobility would not be surrendered into the common pool. They would continue to be tracked separately and returned to their birth parents when they turned sixteen.'

'What about the children of common people?'

'They were not a part of this relaxation.'

'That's not fair.'

'That's exactly what my grandfather, Lord Satyadhwaj, thought. Nothing wrong with the relaxation itself. But one of Lord Ram's unchangeable rules was that the law should apply equally to everyone. You cannot have separate sets of rules for the nobility and the masses. That is wrong.'

'I agree. But didn't your grandfather oppose this change?'

'He did. But he was the only one opposing it. So the change still went through.'

'That is sad.'

'To protest against this corruption of Lord Ram's way, my grandfather vowed that neither he nor any of his adopted Maika descendants would ever have birth children.'

Anandmayi wondered who gave Lord Satyadhwaj the right to make a decision for all his descendants in perpetuity! But she didn't say anything.

Parvateshwar, chest puffed up in pride, said, 'And I honour that vow to this day.'

Anandmayi sighed and turned towards the riverbank, watching the dense forest. Parvateshwar too turned to look at the Branga river, heavily laden with silt, flowing sluggishly on.

'It's strange how life works,' said Anandmayi, without turning towards Parvateshwar. 'A good man rebelled against an injustice in a foreign land more than two hundred and fifty years ago. Today, that very rebellion is causing me injustice...'

Parvateshwar turned to glance at Anandmayi. He stared hard at her beautiful face, a soft smile on his lips. Then he shook his head and turned back towards the river.

Chapter 12

The Heart of Branga

The Branga river carried too much water and silt to remain whole for long. It rapidly broke up into multiple distributaries, which spread their bounty across the land of Branga before disgorging themselves into the Eastern Sea, creating what was probably the largest river delta on earth. It was rumoured that the land was so fertile with the flood-delivered silt and so bountiful in water that the farmers did not have to labour for their crops. All they had to do was fling the seeds and the rich soil did the rest!

Brangaridai lay on the main distributary of the Branga river, the Padma.

Shiva's fleet closed in on Brangaridai a little over two weeks after crossing the gates of Branga. They had sailed through lands that were prosperous and wealthy. But there was an air of death, of pathos, which hung heavy.

The walls of Brangaridai spread over an area of a thousand hectares, almost the size of Devagiri. While the city of Devagiri had been built on three platforms, Brangaridai spread itself on naturally higher ground, around a kilometre inland from the Padma, as a safeguard against floods. Surrounded by high walls, the capital stayed true to the Chandravanshi disdain for any long term planning. The roads were laid out in a haphazard manner and not in the grid form of the Meluhan cities. But the streets were still broad and tree-lined. Vast quantities of Branga wealth ensured that their buildings were superbly built and maintained, while their temples were lofty and grand. A large number of public monuments had been constructed over the centuries: stadia for performances, halls for celebrations, exquisite gardens and public baths. Despite their superb condition, these public buildings were rarely used. The repeated bouts of the plague ensured that the Brangas saw death every day. There was very little zest left for life.

The river port off the city had multiple levels to allow for the vastly varying depth of the Padma at different times of the year. At this time of the year, the peak of winter, the Padma was at its medium flow. Shiva and his entourage disembarked on the fifth level of the port. Shiva saw Parvateshwar, Drapaku, Purvaka and Divodas waiting for him on the comfortable concourse at this port level.

'It's a massive port, Purvaka ji,' said Shiva.

'I can sense it, My Lord,' smiled Purvaka. 'I think these Brangas may probably have the capability to be as efficient as the Meluhans.'

'I don't think they care about efficiency, father,' said Drapaku. 'I sense that the bigger challenge for them is to simply stay alive.'

Just then a short, rotund Branga man, wearing an impossibly large array of gold jewellery, came rushing down the steps. He saw Parvateshwar and went down on his knees, bringing his head down to his feet. 'My Lord, you have come! You have come! We are saved!'

Parvateshwar bent down to pick up the man sternly. 'I am not the Neelkanth.'

The Branga man looked up, confused.

Parvateshwar pointed towards Shiva. 'Bow down to the true Lord.'

The man rushed towards Shiva's feet. 'My apologies, My Lord. Please don't punish Branga for my terrible mistake.'

'Get up, my friend,' smiled Shiva. 'How could you recognise me when you had never seen me before?'

The Branga stood up, tears flooding his eyes. 'Such humility, despite so much power. It could only be you, the great Mahadev.'

'Don't embarrass me. What is your name?'

'I am Bappiraj, Prime Minister of Branga, My Lord. We have set up the welcoming party for you at ground level, where King Chandraketu awaits.'

'Please take me to your king.'

— ⋆ —

Bappiraj proudly climbed the last step to the ground level, followed by Shiva. Bhagirath, Parvateshwar, Anandmayi, Ayurvati, Divodas, Drapaku, Purvaka, Nandi and Veerbhadra followed.

As soon as Shiva ascended, loud conch shells were blown by a posse of pandits. A large herd of elephants, decked in fine gold ornaments, standing a little further away, trumpeted loud enough to startle Purvaka. The splendidly-carved stone pavilion at the ground level had been sheathed in gold plates to honour the Mahadev. It seemed as though almost the entire population — 400,000 citizens — of Brangaridai had gathered to receive the

Neelkanth. At the head was the poignant figure of King Chandraketu.

He was a man of medium height, with a bronzed complexion, high cheekbones and doe-eyes. King Chandraketu's black hair was long like most Indians and had been neatly oiled and curled. He didn't have the muscular physique one expected of a Kshatriya. His lanky frame was clothed in a simple cream *dhoti* and *angvastram*. Despite ruling a kingdom with legendary hordes of gold and fabulous wealth, Chandraketu did not have a smidgeon of gold on his body. His eyes had the look of a defeated man, struggling against fate.

Chandraketu went down on his knees, his head touching the ground and his hands spread forward, as did every other Branga present.

'*Ayushman bhav*, Your Highness,' said Shiva, blessing King Chandraketu *with a long life*.

Chandraketu looked up, still on his knees, his hands folded in a namaste, copious tears rolling down his eyes. 'I know I will live long now, My Lord. And so will every Branga. For you have come!'

— ⁂ —

'We must stop this senseless war,' said Vasuki, looking around the Naga Rajya Sabha. Many heads nodded in agreement. He was the descendant of one of the celebrated kings of the Nagas in the past. His lineage earned him respect.

'But the war is over,' said the Queen. 'Mount Mandar has been destroyed. The secret is with us.'

'Then why are we sending the medicine to the Brangas?'

asked Nishad. 'We don't need them anymore. Helping them only gives reasons to our enemies to keep hostilities alive.'

'Is that how Nagas will work from now on?' asked the Queen. 'Abandoning a friend when not needed?'

Suparna, whose face seemed to resemble that of a bird, spoke up. 'I agree with the Queen. The Brangas were and are our allies. They are the only ones who supported us. We must help them.'

'But we are Nagas,' said Astik. 'We have been punished for the sins of our previous births. We must accept our fate and live out our lives in penance. And we should advise the Brangas to do the same.'

The Queen bit her lip. Karkotak looked at her intensely. He knew his Queen hated this defeatist attitude. But he also knew what Astik said was the majority opinion.

'I agree,' said Iravat, before looking at Suparna. 'And I wouldn't expect the people of Garuda to understand that. They are hungry for war all the time.'

That comment hurt. The people of Garuda, or Nagas with the face of birds, had been the enemies of the rest of the Nagas for long. They used to live in the fabled city of Nagapur, far to the east of Panchavati, but still within the Dandak forest. The great Lord of the People had brokered peace many years back and Suparna, their present leader, had joined the Rajya Sabha as a trusted aide of the Queen. Her people now lived in Panchavati.

The Queen spoke firmly. 'That is uncalled for, Lord Iravat. Please don't forget Lady Suparna has brought the people of Garuda into the joint Naga family. We are all siblings now. Anyone who insults Lady Suparna shall incur my wrath.'

Iravat immediately backtracked. The Queen's anger was legendary.

Karkotak looked around with concern. Iravat had withdrawn but the discussion was going nowhere. Would they be able to continue sending the medicines to the Brangas as the Queen had promised? He looked at the Lord of the People, who rose to speak.

'Lords and Ladies of the Sabha, please excuse me for the impertinence of speaking amongst you.'

Everybody turned to the Lord of the People. While he was the youngest member of the Rajya Sabha, he was also the most respected.

'We are looking at this the wrong way. This is not about the war or our allies. This is about being true to the principles of Bhoomidevi.'

Everybody frowned. Bhoomidevi, a mysterious non-Naga lady who had come from the North in the ancient past and established the present way of life of the Nagas, was respected and honoured as a Goddess. To question Bhoomidevi's principles was sacrilegious.

'One of her clear guidelines was that a Naga must repay in turn for everything that he receives. This is the only way to clear our karma of sins.'

Most Rajya Sabha members frowned. They didn't understand where the Lord of the People was going with this. The Queen, Karkotak and Suparna, however, smiled softly.

'I would encourage you to look inside your pouches and see how many gold coins in there have the stamp of King Chandraketu. At least three quarters of the gold in our kingdom has come from Branga. They have sent it as allied support. But let us recognise it for what it really is: Advance payment for the medicine.'

The Queen smiled at her nephew. It was his idea to tell King Chandraketu not to send plain gold ingots but coins bearing his stamp, to remind the Nagas of what they received from the Brangas.

'By my simple calculations, we have received enough gold to supply medicines for the next thirty years. If we are to honour Bhoomidevi's principles, I say we have no choice but to keep supplying the medicines to them.'

The Rajya Sabha had no choice. How could they question Bhoomidevi's guidelines?

The motion was passed.

— ⁂ —

'My Lord, how do we stop the plague?' asked Chandraketu.

Shiva, Chandraketu, Bhagirath, Parvateshwar, Divodas and Bappiraj were in the king's private chambers in the Brangaridai palace.

'The route will be through the Nagas, Your Highness,' said Shiva. 'I believe they are the cause of the troubles of India. And, your plague. I know that you know where they live. I need to find them.'

Chandraketu stiffened, his melancholic eyes shutting for a bit. He then turned to Bappiraj. 'Please excuse us for a little while, Prime Minister.'

Bappiraj tried to argue. 'But, Your Highness...'

The King narrowed his eyes and continued to stare at his Prime Minister. Bappiraj immediately left the chambers.

Chandraketu went to a side wall, took off a ring from his forefinger and pressed it into an indentation. A small box sprang out of the wall with a soft click. The king picked up a parchment from it and walked back towards Shiva.

'My Lord,' said Chandraketu. 'This is a letter I received from the Queen of the Nagas just a few days back.'

Shiva scowled softly.

'I beg you to hear it with an open mind, My Lord,' said Chandraketu, before lifting the parchment and reading aloud. '*My friend Chandraketu. My apologies for the delay in the delivery of this year's supply of the medicines. The troubles with my Rajya Sabha continue. But whatever the situation, the medicines will be delivered soon. That is my word. Also, I have been informed that a charlatan claiming to be the Neelkanth is coming to your kingdom. I believe he wants to find a way to our land. All that he has to offer you are promises. What you get from us is our medicine. What do you think will keep your people alive? Choose wisely.*'

Chandraketu looked up at Shiva. 'It has the seal of the Naga Queen.'

Shiva did not have an answer.

Divodas spoke up. 'But, Your Highness, I think that the Nagas have cast this spell on us. The plague is their creation. Fight it we must. But to battle it properly, we have to attack the source. Panchavati, the city of the Nagas.'

'Divodas, even if I agree with you, we cannot forget that what keeps us alive is their medicine. Until the plague is stopped we cannot survive without the Nagas.'

'But they are your enemies, Your Highness,' said Bhagirath. 'How can you not seek vengeance for the plague they have wrought upon you?'

'I'm fighting everyday to keep my people alive, Prince Bhagirath. Vengeance is a luxury I cannot afford.'

'It's not about vengeance. It is about justice,' said Parvateshwar.

'No General,' said Chandraketu. 'It is not about

vengeance or justice. It is only about one thing: Keeping my people alive. I am not a fool. I do know that if I give you the route to Panchavati, the Lord will attack it with a massive army. The Nagas will be destroyed. Along with them, their medicine too, thus demolishing the only means to Branga's survival. Unless you can guarantee me another supply source, I cannot tell you where Panchavati lies.'

Shiva stared hard at Chandraketu. Though he didn't like what he was hearing, he knew what the Branga King said was right. He had no choice.

Chandraketu folded his hands together, as though pleading, 'My Lord, you are my leader, my God, my saviour. I believe in your legend. I know you will set everything right. However, while my people may forget the details, I remember the tales of Lord Rudra. I remember that legends take time to fulfil their promise. And time is the only thing my people don't have.'

Shiva sighed. 'You are right, Your Highness. I cannot guarantee supply of the medicines right now. And until I can, I have no right to demand this sacrifice of you.'

Divodas started to say something, but Shiva silenced him with a wave.

'I will take your leave, Your Highness,' said Shiva. 'I need to think.'

Chandraketu fell at Shiva's feet. 'Please don't be angry with me, My Lord. I have no choice.'

Shiva pulled Chandraketu up to his feet. 'I know.'

As Shiva turned to leave, his eyes fell upon the Naga Queen's letter. He stiffened as he saw the seal at the bottom. It was an Aum symbol. But not the standard one. At the meeting point of the top and bottom curve of the Aum were two serpent heads. The third curve, surging out to the East, ended in a sharp serpent head, with its fork tongue struck out threateningly.

Shiva growled softly, 'Is this the Naga Queen's seal?'

'Yes, My Lord,' said Chandraketu.

'Can any Naga man use this seal?'

'No, My Lord. Only the Queen can use it.'

'Tell me the truth. Does any man use this seal?'

'No, My Lord. Nobody.'

'That is not true, Your Highness.'

'My Lord from what I know...' Suddenly Chandraketu stopped. 'Of course, the Lord of the People also uses this seal. He is the only one in the history of the Nagas, besides the ruler, who has been allowed to do so.'

Shiva snarled. 'The Lord of the People? What is his name?'

'I don't know, My Lord.'

Shiva narrowed his eyes.

'I swear on my people, My Lord,' said Chandraketu. 'I don't know. All I know is that his formal title is the Lord of the People.'

'My Lord,' said Bhagirath. 'We have to insist with King Chandraketu.'

Bhagirath, Parvateshwar and Divodas were sitting in Shiva's private chambers in the Brangaridai palace.

'I agree, My Lord,' said Divodas.

'No,' said Shiva. 'Chandraketu has a point. We have to guarantee the supply of the Naga medicine before we attack Panchavati.'

'But that is impossible, My Lord,' said Parvateshwar. 'Only the Nagas have the medicine. The only way we can get the medicine is if we control the Naga territories. And how can we attack and control the Naga territories if the Branga king does not tell us where Panchavati is?'

Shiva turned to Divodas. 'There must be another way to get the Naga medicine.'

'There is a very bizarre one, My Lord,' said Divodas.

'What?'

'But it's the worst possible way, My Lord.'

'Let me be the judge of that. What is the way?'

'There is a bandit in the forests beyond the Madhumati river.'

'Madhumati?'

'Also a distributary of the Branga, My Lord. To our West.'

'I see.'

'It is rumoured that this bandit knows how to make the Naga medicine. Apparently, he does it with the help of a secret plant he sources from beyond the Mahanadi river, which lies to the South–west.'

'So why doesn't this bandit sell it? After all a bandit should be interested in money.'

'He is a strange bandit, My Lord. It is rumoured that he was born a Brahmin, but has long given up the path of knowledge for violence. Most of us believe he has serious psychological problems. He refuses to make money. He has a pathological hatred for Kshatriyas and kills any warrior who ventures into his territory, even if the poor Kshatriya had just lost his way. And, he refuses to share the Naga medicine with anyone, even for untold amounts of gold, using it only for his gang of criminals.'

Shiva frowned. 'How bizarre.'

'He is a monster, My Lord. Even worse than the Nagas. It is rumoured that he even beheaded his own mother.'

'My God!'

'Yes, My Lord. How do you reason with a madman like that?'

'Is there any other way to get to the Naga medicine?'

'I don't think so.'

'Then our choice is made. We must capture that bandit.'

'What is the name of this bandit, Divodas?' asked Bhagirath.

'Parshuram.'

'Parshuram!' cried Parvateshwar in shock. 'That is the name of the sixth Lord Vishnu who lived thousands of years ago.'

'I know, General,' said Divodas. 'But trust me. This bandit does not have any of the qualities of the great sixth Lord Vishnu.'

Chapter 13

Man-eaters of Icchawar

'Maharishi Bhrigu! Here?' asked a surprised Dilipa.

All the nobles in India knew that Bhrigu was the *raj guru*, the *royal sage* of Meluha and strongly backed the Suryavanshi royalty. His sudden appearance in Ayodhya, therefore, had Dilipa bewildered. But it was also a rare honour, for Bhrigu had never ever visited Dilipa's capital before.

'Yes, My Lord,' said the Swadweepan Prime Minister, Siamantak.

Dilipa immediately rushed to the chambers Siamantak had housed the great sage in. Bhrigu's room, as expected, had been kept cold, severe and damp, just like his Himalayan abode.

Dilipa immediately fell at Bhrigu's feet. 'My Lord Bhrigu, in my city, my palace. What an honour!'

Bhrigu smiled, speaking softly, 'The honour is mine, great Emperor. You are the light of India.'

Dilipa raised his eyebrows, even more surprised. 'What can I do for you, Guruji?'

Bhrigu stared hard at Dilipa. 'I personally need nothing, Your Highness. Everything in the world is *maya*, an *illusion*.

The ultimate truth one has to realise is that we actually need nothing. Because to possess an illusion is as good as possessing nothing.'

Dilipa smiled, not quite understanding what Bhrigu said, but too terrified of disagreeing with the powerful Brahmin.

'How is your health now?' asked Bhrigu.

Dilipa wiped his lips with a damp cotton cloth, absorbing the medicine his royal doctor had applied on it. The Emperor of Swadweep had coughed some blood the previous morning. His doctors had told him that he had but a few months to live. 'Nothing is a secret from you, My Lord.'

Bhrigu nodded, not saying anything.

Dilipa smiled bravely. 'I have no regrets, My Lord. I have lived a full life. I am content.'

'True. How is your son, by the way?'

Dilipa narrowed his eyes. There was no point in lying. This was Maharishi Bhrigu, considered by many to be a *Saptrishi Uttradhikari*, a *successor to the seven sages*. 'Looks like he will not have to kill me. Fate will do his work for him. Anyway, who can fight destiny?'

Bhrigu bent forward. 'Fate controls only the weak, Your Highness. The strong mould the providence they want.'

Dilipa frowned. 'What are you saying, Guruji?'

'How long would you like to live?'

'Is it in my hands?'

'No. In mine.'

Dilipa laughed softly. 'The Somras will have no impact, My Lord. I have smuggled in large amounts from Meluha. I have found out the hard way that it cannot cure diseases.'

'The Somras was the greatest invention of the Saptrishis, Your Highness. But it wasn't the only one.'

'You mean to say that...'

'Yes.'

Dilipa edged back. Breathing quicker. 'And, in return?'

'Just remember your debt.'

'If you give me this blessing, Guruji, I will be forever indebted to you.'

'Not to me,' said Bhrigu. 'Remain indebted to India. And, I shall remind you when the time comes for you to serve your country.'

Dilipa nodded.

— ⁂ —

A few days later, a single ship bearing Shiva, Bhagirath, Parvateshwar, Anandmayi, Divodas, Drapaku, Purvaka, Nandi and Veerbhadra set off up the Padma. With them were around five hundred men, half the brigade that had set off from Kashi. Only the Suryavanshis. Shiva needed disciplined warriors to take on the fearsome bandit and his gang. He suspected that too large an army might hinder his attempt at drawing the brigand out. Four vessels and the five hundred Chandravanshis had been left behind to savour Brangaridai hospitality.

Of course, Ayurvati was also on the ship. Her medical skills were certainly needed, especially since Divodas had warned of a bloody confrontation.

After a few days of sailing, the ship reached the part of the Branga river where the Madhumati broke off. They swept down the Madhumati, the western-most edge of the Branga country and its most sparsely populated areas. The land became more wild, with dense forests on both banks.

'A perfect place for a bandit,' said Shiva.

'Yes, My Lord,' nodded Drapaku. 'This land is close enough to civilisation to mount raids. And yet, dense and impenetrable enough to hide quickly. I can imagine why the Brangas have had trouble arresting this man.'.

'We need him alive, Drapaku. We need the conduit to the Naga medicine.'

'I know, My Lord. General Parvateshwar has already issued those instructions to us.'

Shiva nodded. The dolphins were dancing upon the waters. Birds chirped in the dense sundari trees. A large tiger lounged lazily along one bank. It was a picturesque scene of natural bounty, every animal enjoying the gifts of the Brahmaputra and Ganga.

'It is a beautiful land, My Lord,' said Drapaku.

Shiva didn't answer. He continued to stare hard at the banks.

'My Lord,' said Drapaku. 'Did you see something?'

'We're being watched. I can feel it. We're being watched.'

— ⁂ —

Ever since her trespass into the Eastern palace, Sati's relationship with Athithigva had deepened considerably, almost to a filial level. Shared secrets have a way of creating bonds. Sati had remained true to her word, not whispering to a soul about Maya. Not even to Krittika.

Athithigva routinely sought Sati's advice on matters of state, however inconsequential. Sati's counsel was always wise, bringing some order and control to the Chandravanshi penchant for unbridled freedom and chaos.

The problem this time around, however, was a knotty one.

'How can just three lions cause so much chaos?' asked Sati.

Athithigva had just told her about the most recent plea for help from the villagers of Icchawar. They had been living under a mortal threat of man-eating lions for many months. Representations had been coming to Kashi for a long time. Kashi had in turn requested Ayodhya, as the overlord of Swadweep, to come to its aid. Chandravanshi bureaucrats had so far been arguing over the terms of the Ashwamedh treaty; the main stalemate being on how the vow of protection made by Ayodhya did not cover animal attacks. Kashi, of course, had no warrior of note to lead them against even a few lions.

'What do we do, My Lady?'

'But you had sent a platoon of Kashi police a month back, right?'

'Yes, My Lady,' said Athithigva. 'They tried their best, having devised a brilliant plan to trap the lions, using the villagers to create commotion with their drums in order to drive the lions to a well-covered ditch with giant spikes in it. But to their surprise, most of the lions seemed to have escaped and attacked a school where the village children had been huddled for safe-keeping.'

Sati suppressed a gasp of shock.

Athithigva, with tears in his eyes, whispered, 'Five children were killed.'

'Lord Ram be merciful,' whispered Sati.

'The beasts didn't even drag the children's bodies away. Maybe they wanted vengeance for the single lion killed when he fell into the trap.'

'They are not humans, Your Highness,' said Sati, irritated. 'They do not feel anger or the need for vengeance. Animals kill for only two reasons: hunger or self-defence.'

But why would they kill and then leave the bodies there?

'Is there more to this than meets the eye?' asked Sati.

'I don't know, My Lady. I'm not sure.'

'Where are your men?'

'They are still in Icchawar. But the villagers are preventing them from mounting any more traps. They are saying that their own lives are in greater danger when the lions are lured. They want my police to venture into the jungle and hunt the lions down.'

'Which they don't want to do?'

'It's not that they don't want to, My Lady. They don't know *how* to. They're citizens of Kashi. We don't hunt.'

Sati sighed.

'But they are willing to fight,' said Athithigva.

'I'll go,' said Sati.

'Of course not, My Lady,' said Athithigva. 'That's not what I wanted from you. I only wanted you to send word to Emperor Dilipa for help. He cannot refuse you.'

'That would take forever, Your Highness. I know how the Swadweepan bureaucracy works. And your people will keep dying. I'll go. Assign two platoons of the Kashi police to travel with me.'

Sixty soldiers, forty travelling with me and another twenty already in Icchawar. That should do.

Athithigva did not want Sati to venture into the forest. He had come to love her as his sister. 'My Lady, I can't bear to see anything...'

'Nothing will happen to me,' interrupted Sati. 'Now assign two Kashi platoons. Sixty men ought to be enough against two lions. I want the joint platoon led by that man who helped General Parvateshwar protect the Brangas. His name was Kaavas, right?'

Athithigva nodded. 'My Lady, please don't think I'm unsure about your abilities... But you are like a sister to me. I cannot allow you to put yourself in danger like this. I don't think you should go.'

'And I think I must go. Innocents are being killed. Lord Ram would not allow me to stay here. Either I can leave Kashi alone, or with forty soldiers. Which option would you prefer?'

The ship was sailing slowly along the Madhumati. There had been no attack from Parshuram. No devil boats to set Shiva's ship on fire. No arrows to injure the lookouts. Nothing.

Parvateshwar and Anandmayi were standing against the balustrade at the stern of the ship, staring at the reflection of the sun rising gently in the sluggish Madhumati.

'The Lord is right,' said Parvateshwar. 'They are watching us. I can feel it. It irritates me.'

'Really?' smiled Anandmayi. 'I have had people staring at me all my life. It's never irritated me!'

Parvateshwar turned to Anandmayi as if trying to explain his point. Then, as he understood the pun, he smiled.

'By Lord Indra!' exclaimed Anandmayi. 'I got you to smile! What an achievement!'

Parvateshwar smiled even more broadly. 'Yes, well, I was only talking about why the bandits were not attacking...'

'Now don't spoil the moment,' said Anandmayi. She slapped Parvateshwar's wrist with the back of her hand. 'You know you look very nice when you smile. You should do so more often.'

Parvateshwar blushed.

'And you look even better when you blush,' laughed Anandmayi.

Parvateshwar blushed even deeper. 'Your Highness...'

'Anandmayi.'

'Sorry?'

'Call me Anandmayi.'

'How can I?'

'Very simple. Just say Anandmayi.'

Parvateshwar kept quiet.

'Why can't you call me Anandmayi?'

'I can't, Your Highness. It is not correct.'

Anandmayi sighed. 'Tell me Parvateshwar. Who exactly defines what is correct?'

Parvateshwar frowned. 'Lord Ram's laws.'

'And, what was Lord Ram's fundamental law on punishment for a crime?'

'Not even one innocent man should be punished. Not even one criminal must get away.'

'Then you are breaking his laws.'

Parvateshwar frowned. 'How so?'

'By punishing an innocent person for a crime she didn't commit.'

Parvateshwar continued to frown.

'Many noblemen committed a crime by breaking Lord Ram's law two hundred and fifty years ago. They got away with the crime. Nobody punished them. And, look at me. I had nothing to do with that crime. I wasn't even born then. And yet, you are punishing me today for it.'

'I am not punishing you, Your Highness. How can I?'

'Yes, you are. You know you are. I know how you feel. I

am not blind. Don't pretend to be deliberately stupid. It's insulting.'

'Your Highness...'

'What would Lord Ram have told you to do?' interrupted Anandmayi.

Parvateshwar clenched his fist. He looked down, sighing deeply. 'Anandmayi. Please understand. Even if I want to, I can't...'

Just then Drapaku marched up. 'My Lord, the Lord Neelkanth requests your presence.'

Parvateshwar stood rooted to his spot. Still staring at Anandmayi.

'My Lord...,' repeated Drapaku.

Parvateshwar whispered. 'Forgive me, Your Highness. I will speak with you later.'

The Meluhan General turned and marched away, followed by Drapaku.

Anandmayi hissed at Drapaku's retreating form. 'Impeccable timing!'

— ⁂ —

'Do you have to go, My Lady?' asked Krittika, gently rocking a sleeping Kartik.

Sati looked at Krittika, bemused. 'There are innocents dying, Krittika. Do I have a choice?'

Krittika nodded before looking at Kartik.

'My son will understand,' said Sati. 'He would do the same. I am a Kshatriya. It is my dharma to protect the weak. Dharma comes before anything else.'

Krittika took a deep breath and whispered, 'I agree, My Lady.'

Sati gently ran her hand across Kartik's face. 'I need you to take good care of him. He is my life. I have never known the pleasures of motherhood. I never imagined there would be another person I would love as deeply as I love Shiva. But in such a short span of time, Kartik...'

Krittika looked at Sati with a smile, touching the Princess' hand. 'I will take care of him. He's my life as well.'

— ⁂ —

The Naga Lord of the People was kneeling in the cold waters of the Chambal river. He scooped some water in the palm of his hands and allowed it to pour slowly, mumbling quietly. He then brushed his hands across his face.

The Queen, kneeling next to him, raised an eyebrow. 'A prayer?'

'I don't know if prayers will help. I don't think anybody up there is really interested in me.'

The Queen smiled and looked back at the river.

'But there are times when you wouldn't mind the help of the Almighty,' whispered the Naga.

The Queen turned towards him and nodded. Getting up slowly, she put the mask back on her face. 'I've received a report that she has left Kashi and is riding towards Icchawar.'

The Naga breathed deeply. He rose slowly and put the mask back on his face.

'She rides with only forty soldiers.'

The Naga's breathing picked up pace. At a distance, Vishwadyumna was sitting quietly with a hundred Branga soldiers. This could be the moment. Capturing her in a teeming city of two hundred thousand was well nigh impossible. The remoteness of Icchawar improved the odds dramatically. And they finally had the advantage of numbers. The Naga slowly brought his breathing back to normal. Trying to keep his voice calm, he whispered, 'That is good news.'

The Queen smiled and patted the Naga gently on his shoulder. 'Don't be nervous, my child. You are not alone. I am with you. Every step of the way.'

The Naga nodded. His eyes narrowed.

— ⁂ —

It was just the beginning of the second prahar when Sati rode into Icchawar at the head of her platoon, with Kaavas by her side. She was shocked to see a massive pyre at the far end of the village. She rode hard, followed by her men.

A man rushed up, breathless and panic-stricken, waving. 'Please leave! Please leave!'

Sati ignored him and kept riding up to the giant pyre.

'You cannot ignore me! I am the Headman of Icchawar!'

Sati noticed the faces of the villagers. Every single one had terror writ large on his face.

'Things have only gotten worse since you people came!' shouted the Headman.

Sati noticed the Brahmin who had just finished the puja at the pyre, praying for the safety of the departed souls. He was the only one who seemed to be in control.

Sati rode up to him. 'Where are the Kashi soldiers?'

The Brahmin pointed at the giant pyre. 'In there.'

'All twenty of them?' asked a stunned Sati.

The Brahmin nodded. 'They were killed by the lions last

night. Just like our villagers here, your soldiers didn't know what they were doing.'

Sati looked around the pyre. It was an open area, a little outside the village, which opened straight into the forest. To the far left were some blankets and the remnants of a camp fire. There was blood all over that area.

'Did they sleep here?' asked Sati in horror.

The Brahmin nodded.

'This is a suicide zone with man-eating lions around! Why in Lord Ram's name did they sleep here at night?'

The Brahmin looked at the Headman.

'It was their decision!' said the Headman defensively.

'Don't lie,' said the Brahmin. 'It wasn't solely their decision.'

'Don't you dare call me a liar, Suryaksh!' said the Headman. 'I told them their presence in any house only attracts the lions and leads to deaths. The decision to not stay in any house was their own!'

'You actually think the lions are interested only in the soldiers?' asked Suryaksh. 'You are wrong.'

Sati had stopped listening. She was surveying the area where the Kashi soldiers had been killed. Despite the immense amounts of blood and gore, she could clearly make out the tracks of some lions and maybe lionesses. There were at least seven distinct marks. The information they had was clearly wrong. She turned around and growled. 'How many lions are here?'

'Two,' said the Headman. 'We've never seen more than two lions. The third lion was killed in a trap.'

Sati ignored him and looked at Suryaksh. The Brahmin responded, 'Judging from the tracks, at least five to seven.'

Sati nodded. Suryaksh was the only one who appeared

to know what he was talking about. Turning towards the village, Sati told Suryaksh, 'Come with me.'

Seven. That means five lionesses at least. A standard pride. But counting the one that died, there were three lions in this pride? That is strange. There is usually just one adult male in a pride. Something isn't right!

— ⁂ —

'He is smarter than we have been told,' said Shiva. 'Every ruse we have tried for weeks has failed.'

The sun was directly overhead. The ship was anchored close to a beach. Due to the heavy silt it carried, which settled and turned into natural dams, the Madhumati kept changing course all the time. The result was that there were many recently formed sandbanks along the current course of the river. These were areas clear of vegetation, which afforded enough open space for a fierce battle to be fought. Shiva had held the ship close to one such beach, firing arrows into the trees, hoping Parshuram would be goaded into coming out in the open. The plan had not succeeded so far.

'Yes, My Lord,' agreed Parvateshwar. 'He will not be provoked into attacking out of blind hatred.'

Shiva stared hard at the river bank.

'I think it is the ship,' said Parvateshwar.

'Yes, he cannot judge how many men we have.'

Parvateshwar agreed. 'My Lord, we have to take more risks to lure him out.'

'I have a plan,' Shiva whispered softly. 'Further ahead is another beach. I plan to go ashore with a hundred men. Once I've taken the soldiers deep inside the forest, the ship should turn back, giving Parshuram the impression that there is dissension in the ranks. That the vessel is deserting us and departing for Branga. I'll continue into the jungle and flush him out onto the beach. When I have him there, I'll send out a fire arrow as a signal.'

'Then Bhagirath can quickly get the ship over there, pull down the cutters and land on the beach with four hundred men, overwhelming them. Just two key things to remember, My Lord. They must be with their backs to the river. So that they can't escape when the cutters arrive. And of course, the ship must not depend only on the sails, but rowers as well. Speed will be of the essence.'

Shiva smiled. 'Exactly. Just one more thing. It will not be us on the beach. Only me. I need you on the ship.'

'My Lord!' cried Parvateshwar. 'I cannot let you take that risk.'

'Parvateshwar, I will lure the bastard out. But I need you watching my back. If the cutters don't come on time, we will be slaughtered. We will be trying to capture, not kill. He will show no such restraint.'

'But My Lord...' said Parvateshwar.

'I have decided, Parvateshwar. I need you on the ship. I can trust only you. Tomorrow is the day.'

'This is where we'll camp,' said Sati, pointing to the school building, the only unoccupied structure in Icchawar. It had no doors and could not be barricaded against the lions. But it had a terrace, with one defendable flight of stairs leading up.

It was halfway through the third prahar. Nightfall,

the favourite time for lions to attack, was just a few hours away. The villagers had all retired and barricaded themselves inside their homes. The massacre of the Kashi soldiers the night before had shaken all of them. Perhaps the Headman was right they thought. The presence of the Kashi soldiers was bad luck.

The Headman walked behind Sati, trailed by Suryaksh. 'You must leave. The presence of the foreigners is angering the spirits.'

Sati ignored him and turned to Kaavas. 'Station our men on the terrace. Pull the horses up as well.'

Kaavas nodded and rushed to carry out the orders.

The Headman continued, 'Look, they were only killing animals earlier. Now they're killing humans as well. All because of your soldiers. Just leave and the spirits will be calmed.'

Sati turned towards the Headman. 'They have tasted human blood. There is no escape. Either you abandon the village or we have to stay here and protect you till all the lions are killed. My advice is you gather all the villagers and we leave tomorrow morning.'

'We cannot abandon our motherland!'

'I will not allow you to condemn your people to death. I will leave tomorrow and I am taking your people as well. What you do for yourself is up to you.'

'My people are not going to desert Icchawar. Never!'

Suryaksh spoke up. 'If the villagers had listened to me, we would have left a long time back! And this suffering would never have happened.'

'If you were half the priest your father was,' snapped the Headman, 'you would have conjured up a puja to calm the spirits and drive the lions away.'

'Pujas will not drive them away, you fool! Can't you smell

it? The lions have marked this land. They think our village is their territory. There are only two options now. Fight or flee. We obviously don't want to fight. We have to flee.'

'Enough!' said Sati, irritated. 'No wonder the lions got the better of you. Go home. We'll meet tomorrow.'

Sati walked up the steps of the school. She was happy to note a large pile of kindling half-way up the steps. She jumped over it and continued climbing. As she entered the terrace, she saw a massive pile of firewood to the left.

She turned toward Kaavas. 'Enough to last the night?'

'Yes, My Lady.'

Sati scanned the forest and whispered, 'Light the fire on the staircase as soon as the sun goes down.'

She stared up ahead to see a goat tied at the spot where the lions had killed the Kashi soldiers. It was a clear shot from her elevated position. She anticipated that she would be able to fire arrows upon at least a few lions. Hoping the bait would work, Sati settled down on the terrace and waited.

Chapter 14

The Battle of Madhumati

Shiva, Parvateshwar, Bhagirath, Drapaku and Divodas were seated aft on the ship. The moon was absent, cloaking the entire area in darkness. The quietness of the jungle, except for the incessant beating of crickets, automatically made them speak softly.

'The problem is how do we make him believe that there is a rebellion and he has to fight only one hundred men, not the entire crew,' whispered Shiva.

'His spies would be watching us all the time,' murmured Divodas. 'It has to be a believable act. We can't let our guard down for even a minute.'

Shiva suddenly started. Motioning with his hands for everyone to keep talking, he slowly rose and crawled to the rail of the ship, picking his bow quietly, stealthily placing an arrow. And then, quick as lightening, he rose above the railing and shot the arrow. There was a loud scream of pain as one of the brigand's men, swimming towards the ship, was hit.

'COME OUT YOU COWARD!' yelled Shiva. 'FIGHT LIKE A MAN!'

There was commotion in the jungle as animals shrieked at

the sudden disturbance. Birds fluttered loudly. Hyenas howled, tigers roared, deer bleated. There was some splashing in the river. Someone possibly trying to rescue an injured comrade. Shiva thought he heard the sound of foliage breaking as someone or something broke through and retreated.

As his followers rushed up, Shiva whispered, 'It wasn't a kill wound. We need Parshuram alive. Remember. It makes our task tougher. But we need him alive.'

And then they heard a strong voice from the jungle. 'WHY DON'T YOU GET OUT OF THE SHIP, YOU SPINELESS WIMP? AND I'LL SHOW YOU HOW A MAN FIGHTS!'

Shiva smiled. 'This is going to be interesting.'

— ⁂ —

Sati woke up with a start. Not due to some sudden noise. But because the noise had stopped.

She looked towards the left. The flames were burning strong. Two men with swords drawn were at the top of the stairs, supervising the fire.

'More wood,' whispered Sati.

One of the soldiers immediately crept to the stack of firewood and dropped some more onto the raging fire in the middle of the staircase. Meanwhile, Sati tiptoed to the parapet. The goat had been bleating desperately all night. But no more.

She looked gingerly over the railing. The night had thrown a pitch-black shroud all around. But the flames of the school fire spread a bit of glow. The goat was still there. It wasn't standing anymore. Its hind legs had collapsed. And it was shivering desperately.

'Are they here, My Lady?' asked Kaavas, crawling quietly to Sati.

'Yes,' whispered Sati.

They heard a soft, deep roar. A sound which would terrorise any living creature in the jungle. Kaavas quickly woke the rest of the platoon, who drew their swords and crawled to the doorway at the end of the staircase, to defend the one passage from where the lions could charge up. Sati kept staring at the goat. Then she heard the sound of something being dragged softly.

She strained her eyes. One. Two. Three. Four. It wasn't their full pride. The fourth lion seemed to be dragging something.

'Oh Lord,' whispered Sati in horror.

The body being dragged was that of Suryaksh, the village Brahmin. His hand was moving a little. He was still alive. But barely so.

The largest lion, obviously the leader of the pack, came into full view. It was abnormally massive. The largest Sati had ever seen. And yet the mane was not dense. It was clearly an adolescent. Not more than a year old perhaps.

Then a troubling thought struck Sati. She stared at the lead animal's skin. It had the stripes of a tiger. It wasn't an adolescent at all! She gasped in shock. 'Liger!'

'What?' whispered Kaavas.

'A rare animal. The offspring of a lion and a tigress. It grows almost twice as big as its parents. And has many times their ferocity.'

The liger sauntered up to the goat. The goat's front legs too buckled, as it collapsed onto the ground in terror, waiting for its imminent death. But the liger didn't strike out. He just walked around the goat, whipping it with his tail. He was toying with the bait.

The lion dragging Suryaksh dropped the body and bent to bite into the Brahmin's leg. Suryaksh should have screamed in pain. But his neck was bleeding profusely. He simply didn't have the strength. The liger suddenly growled at the lion who was chewing Suryaksh's leg. The lion growled back, but retreated. The liger clearly didn't want Suryaksh eaten just as yet.

The liger is a recent leader. The other lion still seems to have the strength to at least protest.

Followed by the lionesses, the liger walked back to the goat, lifted his hind leg and urinated around the area, marking his territory again. Then he roared. Loud and strong.

The message was clear. This was his territory. Anyone in it was fair game.

Sati reached silently for her bow. The aggression of the pride would be cut if the liger was dead. She softly loaded an arrow and aimed. Unfortunately, just as she released the arrow, the liger stumbled on Suryaksh's body. The arrow flew past him and rammed deep into the eye of the lioness behind. She snarled in pain and ran into the forest. So did the others. But the liger turned around, baring his teeth ferociously at this intrusion, growling. He reached out with his paw and struck Suryaksh hard across the face. A fatal blow. Sati reloaded and fired again. This one hit the liger on his shoulder. The liger roared and retreated.

'The lioness will be dead soon,' said Sati.

'But the liger will come back,' said Kaavas. 'Angrier than ever. We better leave tomorrow with the villagers.'

Sati nodded.

— ⅄◎ᙀ⍋⊛ —

The sun had just broken through the night.

'You must leave. You have no choice,' said Sati. She couldn't believe she had to argue with the villagers about what was blatantly obvious.

It was the beginning of the second prahar. They were standing next to the pyre consuming Suryaksh's body. Sadly, there was nobody to say prayers for his brave soul.

'They will not come back,' said one villager. 'What the Headman says is right. The lions will not come back.'

'What nonsense!' argued Sati. 'The liger has marked his territory. You either kill him or leave this place. There is no third option. He cannot let you have a free run in this land. He will lose control over his pride.'

A village woman stepped up to argue. 'The spirits have been partially appeased by the blood of Suryaksh. At the most we will have to make one more sacrifice and they will leave.'

'One more sacrifice?' asked a flabbergasted Sati.

'Yes,' said the headman. 'The village cleaner is willing to sacrifice himself and his family for the good of the rest of the village.'

Sati turned to see a thin, wiry little man, who also had the onerous task of collecting firewood and cremating the dead over the last few days. Behind him stood his equally puny wife, with a look of utter determination on her face. Holding onto her *dhoti* were two little children, no older than two or three, wearing nothing but torn loincloths, unaware of the fate chosen for them by their parents.

Sati turned towards the Headman, fists clenched. 'You are sacrificing this poor man and his family because he is the most powerless! This is wrong!'

'No, My Lady,' said the cleaner. 'This is my choice. My fate. I have been born low in this birth because of my past life karma. My family and I will sacrifice ourselves willingly for the good of the village. The Almighty will see our good deed and bless us in our next birth.'

'I admire your bravery,' said Sati. 'But this will not stop the lions. They will not stop till all of you are either driven out or killed.'

'Our blood will satisfy them, My Lady. The headman has told me so. I am sure of this.'

Sati stared hard at the cleaner. Blind superstition can never be won over by logic. She looked down at his children. They were poking each other and laughing uproariously. They suddenly stopped and looked up at her. Surprised. Wondering why this foreign woman was staring at them.

I can't let this happen.

'I will stay here. I will stay till every lion has been killed. But you will not sacrifice yourself. Or your family. Is that clear?'

The cleaner stared at Sati, confused at what to him seemed a strange suggestion. Sati turned towards Kaavas. He immediately started leading the soldiers back to the school. Some of them were arguing, clearly unhappy at this turn of events.

— ⁂ —

The spies of Parshuram, high in the trees, were watching

attentively. Shiva and Bhagirath were on the deck. They appeared to be arguing. Three cutters, lowered from the ship onto the Madhumati, were bobbing gently.

Finally, Shiva made an angry gesture and started climbing down onto his cutter, which had Drapaku, Nandi, Veerbhadra and thirty soldiers. He looked at two more cutters behind them, full of soldiers. Shiva gave a signal and they started rowing towards the bank.

The ship on the other hand appeared to be preparing to pull anchor.

One spy looked at the other with a smile. 'A hundred soldiers. Let's go tell Lord Parshuram.'

— ⁂ —

The rich waters of the Madhumati and the fertile soil of Branga had conspired to grow a jungle of ferocious density. Shiva looked up at the sky. A little bit of sunshine pierced through the dense foliage. The direction of the rays told Shiva that the sun had already begun its downward journey.

His platoon had hacked through the almost impenetrable forest for a good eight hours, tracking the movements of the brigand. Shiva had broken for lunch two hours earlier. Though physically satiated, his soldiers were getting restless, waiting for action. Parshuram seemed to be avoiding battle even here.

Suddenly Shiva raised his hand. The platoon halted. Drapaku slipped up to Shiva and whispered, 'What is it, My Lord?'

Shiva pointed with his eyes and whispered, 'This territory has been marked.'

Drapaku stared, confused.

'See the cut on this bush,' said Shiva.

Drapaku stared harder. 'They have passed through here. This route has been hacked.'

'No,' said Shiva, looking ahead, 'This hasn't been hacked to walk through. It has been cut from the right side to make us think they have walked through here. There is a trap straight ahead.'

'Are you sure, My Lord?' asked Drapaku, noticing Shiva reach slowly for his bow.

Shiva suddenly turned around, pulling an arrow simultaneously and loading it onto his bow. He fired it immediately onto the top of one of the trees. There was a loud noise as an injured man came crashing down.

'This way!' said Shiva, running hard to the right.

The soldiers followed, desperately keeping pace with their charging Lord. They ran hard for what must have been a few minutes. Shiva suddenly emerged onto a beach. And stopped dead.

Standing in front, at a distance of around one hundred metres, was Parshuram with his gang. There were at least one hundred men, an equal match for the Suryavanshis. Shiva's soldiers kept running out of the jungle in a single file and started getting into formation quickly on the beach.

'I'll wait!' said Parshuram sarcastically, his gaze locked onto Shiva. 'Get your men into position.'

Shiva stared right back. Parshuram was a powerful man. Though a little shorter than Shiva, he was ridiculously muscled. His shoulders spread wide, his barrel chest heaving. In his left hand was a mighty bow, much too big for any man. But clearly, his powerful arms had enough strength to pull the string clean. On his back was a quiver full of arrows. But slung the other way was the weapon that had made him famous. The weapon he used to decapitate his hapless victims. His battleaxe. He wore a simple saffron *dhoti*, but no armour. In a sign of his Brahmin antecedents, Parshuram's head was shaved clean except for a neat tuft of hair tied at the back and a *janau* thread tied loosely down from his left shoulder across his torso to his right. His face bore a long, mighty beard.

Shiva looked to his side, waiting for all his soldiers to get into line. He sniffed.

What is that?

It seemed like the paraffin used by the Meluhans to light their prahar lamps. He looked down. The sand was clean. His men were safe. Shiva drew his sword and bellowed. 'Surrender now, Parshuram. And you shall get justice.'

Parshuram burst into laughter. 'Justice?! In this wretched land?'

Shiva turned his eyes to his sides. His men were in position. Ready. 'You can either bow your head towards justice. Or you can feel its flames bear down on you! What do you want?'

Parshuram sniggered and nodded at one of his men. The man raised an arrow, touched it to a flame, and shot the burning arrow high into the air, way beyond the range of the Suryavanshis.

What the hell?

Shiva lost sight of the arrow in the light of the sun for a moment. It landed quite some distance behind Shiva's men, and immediately set off the paraffin lying there. The flames spread quickly, making an impenetrable border. The Suryavanshis were trapped on the beach. No retreat was possible.

'You're wasting your arrows, you idiot!' shouted Shiva. 'Nobody is retreating from here!'

Parshuram smiled. 'I am going to enjoy killing you.'

To Shiva's surprise, Parshuram's archer turned around, lit another arrow and shot it towards the river.

Shit!

Parshuram's men had tied thin canoes, touching each other, across the bend of the river arching the beach. Full of large quantities of paraffin, these boats immediately burst into flames as the fiery arrow hit one of them. The massive blaze made it appear like the entire river was on fire. The inferno reached high, making it almost impossible for Parvateshwar's back-up cutters to row through.

Parshuram looked towards Shiva with a chilling sneer. 'Let's keep our merriment to ourselves, shall we?'

Shiva turned and nodded at Drapaku, who immediately passed an order. An arrow shot up high into the sky and burst into blue flames. Parvateshwar had been summoned. But Shiva didn't see how the Meluhan General would be able to get through the wall of fire on the Madhumati. Small cutters couldn't slip through. And the ship itself could not come so close to the banks as it would run aground.

Nobody's coming. We have to finish this ourselves.

'This is your last chance, barbarian!' screamed Shiva, pointing forward with his sword.

Parshuram dropped his bow. So did every archer at his command, drawing their *anga* weapons out. Parshuram pulled his battleaxe out. He clearly wanted brutal close combat. 'No, Brangan! It was your last chance. I'm going to make your end slow and painful.'

Shiva dropped his bow and drew his shield forward.

And spoke to his soldiers. 'On guard! Go for their sword arms. Injure, don't kill. We want them alive.'

The Suryavanshis pulled their shields forward and drew their swords. And waited.

Parshuram charged. Followed by his vicious horde.

The bandits ran into Shiva's men with surprising speed and agility, Parshuram racing in the lead. He had no shield to protect himself. His heavy battleaxe required both arms to wield. He was charging straight at Shiva. However, Drapaku swung to his left and charged. The bandit was momentarily surprised by Drapaku's charge. He swerved back to avoid the sword and with the same smooth motion, brought his battleaxe up in a brutal swing. Drapaku pushed out the shield fixed on the hook on his amputated left hand to defend himself. The formidable axe severed through a part of the hide-covered bronze shield. A stunned Drapaku swung his shield back, bringing his sword down, glancing a swerving Parshuram's left shoulder.

Meanwhile Shiva pirouetted smartly to avoid a vicious stab from one of the bandits, pushing the sword away with his shield. As the bandit lost balance, Shiva swung his sword down in a smooth arc, severing his enemy's sword arm from the elbow. The thug fell down. Incapacitated, but alive. Shiva immediately turned and pulled his sword up to deflect a strike from another man.

Nandi, pulling his sword out from the right shoulder of an enemy, pushed him down with his shield, hoping the brigand would remain down and surrender. To Nandi's surprise and admiration, the bandit dropped his shield, smoothly transferring his sword to his uninjured left hand, and jumped into the fray again. Nandi pulled his shield forward to prevent the sword strike and pushed his sword in once again into the injured right shoulder of the thug, shouting over the din, 'Surrender, you fool!'

Veerbhadra, however, was not having much luck keeping his enemies alive. He had already killed two and was trying desperately to avoid killing a very determined third. Ignoring his injured sword arm, the bandit had picked up his sword with his left hand. An exasperated Veerbhadra swung down hard with his shield on the brigand's head, hoping to knock the man out. The thug arched his shoulder, taking the blow on it while swinging his sword in a brutal cut at Veerbhadra. The sword slashed Veerbhadra across his torso. Enraged, he thrust his sword straight at the exposed flank of the bandit, driving the blade through his heart.

'Dammit!' screamed a frustrated Veerbhadra. 'Why didn't you just surrender?'

In another corner of the battlefield, Shiva swung his shield sideward at the outlaw he was combating. The brigand swung his head back, getting a slash across his face but preventing a knockout blow.

Shiva was now getting worried. Too many people were getting killed, mostly on Parshuram's side. He wanted them alive. Or the secret of the Naga medicine would be lost. Then he heard a loud sound. It was Parvateshwar's conch shell.

They're coming!

Brutally stabbing his enemy, Shiva also rammed his shield onto the bandit's head again, this time successfully knocking him cold. Then he looked up and smiled.

The massive Suryavanshi ship burst through the flaming canoes, running aground onto the beach, its hull cracking.

The flames on the Madhumati were high for a cutter, but not high enough for a large ship. Parshuram had banked on the idea that the Suryavanshis would not ground their ship as this would mean that they would have no way of returning to Branga. He had, however, miscalculated the determination of the Suryavanshi troops as well as the valour of their General, Parvateshwar.

The ship rammed through many of Parshuram's men, killing them instantly.

Parvateshwar, standing at the bow, jumped down as soon as the ship hit the sandbank. The rope tied around his waist broke his fall from the great height. As he swung close to the ground, Parvateshwar slashed his sword above him, cutting the rope neatly and landing free. Four hundred Suryavanshis followed their General into battle.

Drapaku had been momentarily distracted by the sight of the ship. As he swung his sword at Parshuram's axe, he failed to notice the bandit pull out a knife from behind. Parshuram brought up his left hand in a smooth action, thrusting the knife into Drapaku's neck. Pain immobilised the Suryavanshi Brigadier momentarily. Parshuram rammed the knife in brutally, right up to the hilt. Drapaku staggered back, bravely retaining his hold on his sword.

Meanwhile, the Suryavanshis, outnumbering Parshuram's men five times over, were rapidly taking control of the situation. Many brigands were surrendering, finally seeing the futility of their situation.

At the centre of the battle, Parshuram released the knife from a tottering Drapaku's neck. He gripped his battleaxe with both hands, pulled back and swung viciously. The axe rammed hard into Drapaku's torso, smashing through his hide and bronze armour. It struck deep, breaking through skin and flesh, right down to the bone. The mighty Suryavanshi Brigadier fell to the ground. Parshuram tried to pull the axe away, but it was stuck. He yanked hard. Ripping Drapaku's chest, the axe finally came out. Much to Parshuram's admiration, the Suryavanshi was still alive. The Brigadier tried to raise his drastically weakened sword arm, still attempting to fight.

Parshuram stepped forward and pinned Drapaku's arm down. He could feel the weakened motions of the Brigadier's limb. Attempts by a dying man to not give up the fight, the sword still held tight. Parshuram was awed. He had never needed more than one clear blow with his battleaxe to kill his opponents. His soldiers were rapidly losing the battle, but he didn't seem to notice. His eyes were transfixed upon the magnificent man dying at his feet.

Parshuram bowed his head slightly and whispered, 'It is an honour to slay you.'

The brigand raised his axe, ready for the decapitation strike. At the same instant, Anandmayi flung her knife from a distance. It pierced straight through Parshuram's left hand, causing the axe to fall safely away. Bhagirath, with the help of Divodas and two Suryavanshi soldiers, wrestled Parshuram to the ground without any further injury to the bandit.

Shiva and Parvateshwar ran to Drapaku. He was bleeding profusely, barely alive.

Shiva turned back and shouted, 'Get Ayurvati! Quickly!'

— ⁂ —

The sun still had a few hours of life left. Sati was on the school terrace, supervising the making of improvised bows and arrows. The Kashi soldiers were simply incapable of taking on the lions from close quarters. Neither were they skilled at shooting arrows. Sati was hoping that as long as they fired some in the general direction, the arrows might find their mark.

Sati double-checked the pile of wood near the staircase. The soldiers had replenished the stock and it appeared as though they would be able to last the night without running out.

She hoped to kill some members of the pride from the safety of the terrace. If fortune favoured her, she hoped to kill the liger and finish the key source of the menace. A few days of watch thereafter might solve the problem once and for all. After all, there were only seven animals. Not a very large pride.

She looked up at the sky, praying softly that nothing would go wrong.

Chapter 15

The Lord of the People

The sun was rapidly descending into the horizon, the twilit sky a vibrant ochre. The Suryavanshi camp was a hub of feverish activity.

Bhagirath was supervising the key task of the securing of the prisoners. Using bronze chains from the ship, Parshuram's men had been tied up, hand and foot, and forced to squat in a line in the centre of the sandbank. The chains had been hammered into stakes deep in the ground. As if that wasn't enough, another chain ran through their anklets, effectively binding them to each other. The Suryavanshi soldiers were stationed all around the prisoners. They would maintain a constant vigil. Escape was impossible for Parshuram and his men.

Divodas walked up to Bhagirath. 'Your Highness, I've inspected the ship.'

'And?'

'It will take at least six months to repair.'

Bhagirath cursed. 'How the hell do we get back?'

At the other end of the beach, ayuralay tents had been set up. Ayurvati and her medical unit were working desperately to save as many as they could, both the Suryavanshis and the bandits. They would succeed with most. But Ayurvati was presently in a tent where there was no hope.

Shiva was on his knees, holding Drapaku's hand. Ayurvati knew nothing could be done. The injuries were too deep. She stood at the back, with Nandi and Parvateshwar. Drapaku's father, Purvaka, was kneeling on the other side, looking lost once again.

Drapaku kept opening his mouth, trying to say something.

Shiva bent forward. 'What is it, my friend?'

Drapaku couldn't speak. Blood continued to ooze from his mouth. He turned towards his father and then back to Shiva. The movement caused his heart to spurt, spilling some more blood out of his gaping chest onto the sheet covering him.

Shiva, his eyes moist, whispered, 'I will take care of him, Drapaku. I will take care of him.'

A long breath escaped Drapaku. He had heard what he needed to. And he let himself die, at peace finally.

A gasp escaped Purvaka's lips. His head collapsed on his son's shoulders, his body shaking. Shiva reached out and touched Purvaka gently on his shoulders. Purvaka looked up, his forehead covered with his son's brave blood, tears flowing furiously. He looked at Shiva, devastated. The proud, confident Purvaka was gone. It was the same broken man that had met Shiva at Kotdwaar in Meluha. His only reason to stay alive had been brutally hacked away.

Shiva's heart sank. He couldn't bear to look at this Purvaka. And then, rage entered his heart. Pure, furious rage!

Shiva rose.

To Parvateshwar's surprise, Nandi lunged forward, grabbing Shiva. 'No, My Lord! This is wrong.'

Shiva angrily pushed Nandi aside and stormed out. He began running to where Parshuram had been tied up.

Nandi was running behind, still screaming. 'No, My Lord! He's a prisoner. This is wrong.'

Shiva was running even harder. As he came close to where Parshuram had been tied, he drew out his sword.

Bhagirath standing at the other end of the line screamed out. 'No, My Lord! We need him alive!'

But Shiva was frenzied, screaming, racing quickly towards Parshuram, his sword high, ready to behead the bandit.

Parshuram continued to stare blankly, not a hint of fear on his face. And then he shut his eyes and shouted the words he wanted to die with. 'Jai Guru Vishwamitra! Jai Guru Vashishtha!'

A stunned Shiva stopped in his tracks. Paralysed.

Not feeling the sword strike on his neck, Parshuram opened his eyes and stared at Shiva, confused.

The sword slipped from Shiva's hands. 'Vasudev?'

Parshuram looked as shocked as Shiva. He finally got a good look at Shiva's throat, deliberately covered by a cravat. Realisation dawned. 'Oh Lord! What have I done? Neelkanth! Lord Neelkanth!'

Parshuram brought his head down towards Shiva's feet, tears flooding his eyes. 'Forgive me, Lord. Forgive me. I didn't know it was you.'

Shiva just stood there. Paralysed.

A half-asleep Sati heard the throaty roars. She immediately became alert.

They're here.

She turned towards the doorway. The fire was burning strong. Two soldiers were sitting guard.

'Kaavas, they're here. Wake everyone up.'

Sati crept up to the terrace railing. She couldn't see any lion as yet. The moon had a bit of strength tonight. She wasn't dependant only on the fire.

Then she saw the liger emerge from the tree line. The arrow Sati had shot was still buried in his shoulder, its shaft broken. It made him drag his front foot marginally.

'There's another male lion,' whispered Kaavas, pointing.

Sati nodded. She drew her bow forward. But before she could shoot, the sight in front of her stunned her.

Numerous lionesses were pouring out from behind the liger. The pride was far larger than the seven animals she had assumed there would be. She continued to watch in horror as more and more animals emerged. One lioness after another, till there were nearly thirty of them on display.

Lord Ram be merciful!

After the attack the previous night, the liger had brought his whole army to combat the threat. And it was a massive pride.

This explains the three male lions. The liger has actually taken over and merged three prides into one.

Sati slunk back and turned around. She couldn't shoot so many lionesses. She looked around her. There was pure terror in the eyes of the Kashi soldiers.

She pointed to the doorway. 'Two more men there. And more wood into the fire.'

The Kashi soldiers rushed to obey. Sati's brain was whirring, but no idea struck her. That's when she heard it.

She immediately turned around and crept to the railing, hearing the sound clearer. Two children were crying. Howling desperately for their lives.

Sati opened her eyes wide in panic.

Please... No...

The village cleaner and his wife were walking determinedly towards the lions. They wore saffron, to signify their sacrifice, their final journey. The children, naked to the elements, were held one each by their parents. They were bawling frantically.

The liger turned towards the couple and growled.

Sati drew her sword. 'Noooo!'

'No, My lady!' screamed Kaavas.

But Sati had already jumped over onto the ground. She charged towards the lions, sword held high.

The lions turned towards her, surprised, forgetting about the cleaner and his family. Then the liger registered Sati. He roared loudly. And, his pride charged.

The Kashi soldiers jumped onto the ground after Sati, inspired by the sheer bravery displayed by their leader. But inspiration is no substitute for skill.

Sati swung as she neared a massive lioness, turning smoothly with the movement, slicing through the nose and eye of the beast. As the lioness retreated, howling, Sati turned in the same smooth motion to attack a lion in front of her. Another lioness charged her from the right. A brave Kashi soldier jumped in front. The lioness grabbed the unfortunate soldier from his throat, shaking him like a rag doll. The soldier, however, had managed to lodge his sword deep into the lioness' chest. As he died, so did the lioness. Kaavas was frantically battling a lioness that had sunk her teeth into his leg, gouging his flesh. He was swinging down with his sword, hitting her on her shoulder again and again with ineffective strikes.

The Kashi men were fighting desperately. Bravely. But it was clearly a matter of time before they would be overwhelmed. They didn't have the training or the skill to battle this well coordinated pride. Sati knew it was but a matter of time before they would succumb.

Lord Ram, let me die with honour!

Then, a resounding yell rose above the mayhem. A hundred soldiers broke through the tree-line, rushing into the melee. One of them was blowing a conch shell. The fierce call of a Naga attack!

A stunned Sati continued fighting the lioness in front of her, but her thoughts were distracted, wondering why these soldiers had come to the village, to their aid.

The tide of the battle turned immediately. The new soldiers, clearly more skilled than their Kashi counterparts, charged at the lions viciously.

Sati killed the lioness in front of her and turned to see numerous lion carcasses around her. She perceived a movement to her left. The liger had sprung high at her. From nowhere, a massive hooded figure emerged. He caught hold of the liger and flung the animal off. The liger's claws struck at the hooded figure, tearing deep through his shoulder. As the liger regained balance and swung to face this new threat, the hooded figure stood protectively in front of Sati, his sword drawn.

Sati looked at the back of her fearless protector.

Who is this man?

The hooded figure charged at the liger. Just then another lioness charged at Sati. She bent low and struck her sword up brutally through the lioness' chest, deep into the beast's heart. The lioness fell on Sati, dead. She tried to push the lioness off, her head turned to the right. She could see the hooded figure battling the gargantuan liger on his own. Then she screamed, 'Watch out!'

Another lioness charged from the right towards the hooded figure, grabbing his leg viciously. The hooded figure fell but not before stabbing deep through the eyes of the lioness mauling his leg. The liger jumped once again on the hooded figure.

'No!' screamed Sati, desperately trying to push the lioness off her.

Then she saw various soldiers rushing at the liger, swinging their swords at the same time. The liger, overwhelmed, turned and ran. Only three of the pride of thirty beasts were able to escape. The rest lay on the village grounds, dead. Along with them were the bodies of ten brave Kashi soldiers.

A soldier came to assist Sati, pushing the lioness' carcass off her. She immediately got up and ran towards the hooded figure, who was being helped to his feet.

Then she stopped. Stunned.

The hooded figure's mask had slipped off.

Naga!

The Naga's forehead was ridiculously broad, his eyes placed on the side, almost facing different directions. His nose was abnormally long, stretching out like the trunk of an elephant. Two buck teeth struck out of the mouth, one of them broken. The legacy of an old injury, perhaps. The ears were floppy and large, shaking of their own accord. It almost seemed like the head of an elephant had been placed on the body of this unfortunate soul.

The Naga was standing with his fists clenched tight,

fingers boring into his palms. He had dreamt of this moment for ages. Emotions were raging through his soul. Anger. Betrayal. Fear. Love.

'Ugly, aren't I?' whispered the Naga, his eyes wet, teeth gritted.

'What? No!' cried Sati, controlling her shock at seeing a Naga. How could she insult the man who had saved her life? 'I'm sorry. It's just that I...'

'Is that why you abandoned me?' whispered the Naga, ignoring what Sati had said. His body was shaking, his fists clenched tight.

'What?'

'Is that why you abandoned me?' Soft tears were rolling down the Naga's cheeks. 'Because you couldn't even bear to look at me?'

Sati stared at the Naga, confused. 'Who are you?'

'Stop playing innocent, you daddy's spoilt little girl!' shrieked a strong feminine voice from behind.

Sati turned and gasped.

Standing a little to her left was the Naga Queen. Her entire torso had an exoskeleton covering it, hard as bone. There were small balls of bone which ran from her shoulders down to her stomach, almost like a garland of skulls. On top of her shoulders were two small extra appendages, serving as a third and fourth arm. One was holding a knife, clearly itching to fling it at Sati. But it was the face that disturbed Sati the most. The colour was jet black, but the Naga Queen's face was almost an exact replica of Sati's.

'Who are you people?' asked a stunned Sati.

'Let me put this phony out of her misery, my child.' The Naga Queen's hand holding the knife was shaking.

'She will never acknowledge the truth. She is just like her treacherous father!'

'No, *Mausi*.'

Sati turned to the Naga again, before returning her gaze to the Naga Queen. 'Who are you?'

'Bullshit! You expect me to believe that you don't know?!'

Sati continued to stare at the Naga Queen, confused.

'*Mausi*...,' whispered the Naga. He was on his knees, crying desperately.

'My child!' cried the Naga Queen as she sprinted towards him. She tried to hand him her knife. 'Kill her! Kill her! That is the only way to find peace!'

The Naga was trembling, shaking his head, tears streaking down his face. Vishwadyumna and the Brangas were holding the Kashi soldiers at a distance.

Sati asked once again. 'Who are you people?'

'I've had enough of this!' screamed the Naga Queen, raising the knife.

'No *Mausi*,' whispered the Naga through his tears. 'She doesn't know. She doesn't know.'

Sati stared at the Naga Queen. 'I swear I don't know. Who are you?'

The Naga Queen shut her eyes, took a deep breath and spoke with all the sarcasm at her command. 'Then listen, oh exalted Princess. I am your twin sister, Kali. The one whom your two-faced father abandoned!'

Sati stared at Kali, mouth half-open, too shocked to react.

I have a sister?

'And this sad soul,' said Kali, pointing at the *Lord of the People*, 'is the son you abandoned, *Ganesh*.'

Sati gasped in shock.

My son is alive?

She stared at Ganesh.

My son!

Angry tears were flooding down Ganesh's face. His body was shaking with misery.

My son...

Sati's heart was crying in pain.

But... but father said my son was stillborn.

She continued to stare.

I was lied to.

Sati held her breath. She stared at her twin sister. An exact replica of her. A visible proof of the relationship. She turned to Ganesh.

'My son is alive?'

Ganesh looked up, tears still rolling down his eyes.

'My son is alive,' whispered Sati, tears spilling from her eyes.

Sati stumbled towards the kneeling Ganesh. She went down on her knees, holding his face. 'My son is alive...'

She cradled his head. 'I didn't know, my child. I swear. I didn't know.'

Ganesh didn't raise his arms.

'My child,' whispered Sati, pulling Ganesh's head down, kissing his forehead, holding him tight. 'I'll never let you go. Never.'

Ganesh's tears broke out in a stronger flood. He wrapped his arms around his mother and whispered that most magical of words. '*Maa...*'

Sati started crying again. 'My son. My son.'

Ganesh cried like the sheltered little child he had always

wanted to be. He was safe. Safe at last. Safe in his loving mother's arms.

— ⅄ⓄⓊ⍋⊗ —

Parshuram was biding time.

The water holds of the Branga ship had been destroyed when it grounded. The Suryavanshis had no choice but to drink the Madhumati water. Divodas had insisted the water be boiled first. But Parshuram knew that people drinking Madhumati water for the first time would be knocked out for a few hours if they didn't have the antidote beforehand.

He waited patiently for the water to take effect. He had a task to carry out.

As the camp slept, Parshuram set to work. He found the weak link in his chain and banged it lightly with a stone till it broke. His lieutenant next to him expected to be set free. But Parshuram hammered the chain back into the stake.

'Nobody escapes. Is that clear? Anyone who dares to will be hunted down by me.'

The lieutenant frowned, thoroughly confused, but did not dare question his fearsome chieftain. Parshuram turned towards the kitchen area of the beach. His battleaxe gleamed in the moonlight. He knew what he had to do.

It had to be done. He had no choice.

Chapter 16

Opposites Attract

The fire was raging.

Shiva had never seen flames so high near the Mansarovar Lake. The howling winds, the open space, the might of the Gunas, his tribe, simply didn't allow any fire to last too long.

He looked around. His village was deserted. Not a soul in sight. The flames were licking at the walls of his hamlet.

He turned towards the lake. 'Holy Lake, where are my people? Have the Pakratis taken them hostage?'

'S-H-I-V-A! HELP ME!'

Shiva turned around to find a bloodied Brahaspati racing out of the village gates, through the massive inferno. He was being followed by a giant hooded figure, his sword drawn, his gait menacing in its extreme control.

Shiva pulled Brahaspati behind him, drew his sword and waited for the hooded Naga to come closer. When within shouting distance, Shiva screamed, 'You will never get him. Not as long as I live!'

The Naga's mask seemed to develop a life of its own. It smirked. 'I've already got him.'

Shiva spun around. There were three massive snakes behind him. One was dragging Brahaspati's limp body away, punctured by numerous massive bites. The other two stood guard, spewing fire from their mouths, preventing Shiva from moving closer. Shiva watched in helpless rage as they dragged Brahaspati towards the Naga. A furious Shiva turned towards the Naga.

'Lord Rudra be merciful!' whispered Shiva.

A severely bleeding Drapaku was kneeling next to the Naga. Defeated, forlorn, waiting to be killed.

Next to Drapaku, down on her knees was a woman. Streaks of blood ran down her arms. Her billowing hair covered her downcast face. And then the wind cleared. She looked up.

It was her. The woman he couldn't save. The woman he hadn't saved. The woman he hadn't even attempted to save. 'HELP! PLEASE HELP ME!'

'Don't you dare!' screamed Shiva, pointing menacingly at the Naga.

The Naga calmly raised his sword and without a second's hesitation, beheaded the woman.

Shiva woke up in cold sweat, his brow burning again. He looked around the darkness of his small tent, hearing the soft sounds of the Madhumati lapping the shores. He looked at his hand, the serpent Aum bracelet was in it. He cursed out loud, threw the bracelet onto the ground and lay back on the bed. His head felt heavy. Very heavy.

— ⁂ —

The Madhumati flowed quietly that night. Parshuram looked up. The moonlight gave just enough visibility for him to do his task.

He checked the temperature on the flat griddle heating up on the small fire. Scalding. It had to be. The flesh would have to be seared shut quickly. Otherwise the bleeding would not stop. He went back to sharpening the axe.

He tested the sharpness of the blade once again. Razor sharp. It would afford a clean strike. He looked back. There was nobody there.

He threw away his cloak and took a deep breath.

'Lord Rudra, give me strength.'

He curled up his left hand. The sinning hand that had dared to murder the Neelkanth's favourite. He held the outcrop of a tree stump. Held it tight. Giving himself purchase to pull his shoulder back.

The trunk had been used earlier to behead many of his enemies. The blood of those unfortunate victims had left deep red marks on the wood. Now his blood would mix with theirs.

He reached out with his right hand and picked up the battleaxe, raising it high.

Parshuram looked up one last time and took a deep breath. 'Forgive me, My Lord.'

The battleaxe hummed through the air as it swung down sharply. It sliced through perfectly, cutting the hand clean.

— ⁂ —

'How in the name of the holy lake did he escape?' shouted Shiva. 'What were you doing?'

Parvateshwar and Bhagirath were looking down. The Lord had justifiable reasons to be angry. They were in his tent. It was the last hour of the first prahar. The sun had just risen. And with that had come to light Parshuram's disappearance.

Shiva was distracted by commotion outside. He rushed out to find Divodas and a few other soldiers pointing their sword at Parshuram. He was staggering towards Shiva, staring at him. Nobody else.

Shiva held his left hand out, telling his men to let Parshuram through. For some reason, he didn't feel the need to reach for his sword. Parshuram had his cloak wrapped tightly around himself. Bhagirath stepped up to check Parshuram for weapons. But Shiva called out loudly. 'It's alright, Bhagirath. Let him come.'

Parshuram stumbled towards Shiva, obviously weak, eyes drooping. There was a massive blood stain on his cloak. Shiva narrowed his eyes.

Parshuram collapsed on his knees in front of Shiva.

'Where had you gone?'

Parshuram looked up, his eyes melancholic. 'I... penance... My Lord...'

Shiva frowned.

The bandit dropped his cloak and with his right hand, placed his severed left one at Shiva's feet. 'This hand... sinned... My Lord. Forgive me...'

Shiva gasped in horror.

Parshuram collapsed. Unconscious.

— ⚹ —

Ayurvati had tended to Parshuram's wound. She had cauterised it once again in order to prevent any chance of infection. Juice of neem leaves had been rubbed into the open flesh. A dressing of neem leaves had been created and wound tight around the severed arm.

She looked up at Shiva. 'This fool is lucky the axe was sharp and clean. The blood loss and infection from a wound like this can be fatal.'

'I don't think the cleanliness or sharpness was an

accident,' whispered Bhagirath. 'He made it so. He knew what he was doing.'

Parvateshwar continued to stare at Parshuram, stunned.

Who is this strange man?

Shiva had not uttered a word so far. He just kept looking at Parshuram, his face devoid of any expression. His eyes narrowed hard.

'What do we do with him, My Lord?' asked Parvateshwar.

'We use him,' suggested Bhagirath. 'Our ship will take up to six months to repair. We can't stay here for that long. I say we carry Parshuram in one of our cutters to the closest Branga outpost and hand him over. We'll use the leverage of handing over the most wanted criminal in Branga to wrangle a ship from them. They'll force the medicine out of him and we get our path to the Nagas.'

Shiva didn't say anything. He continued to stare at Parshuram.

Parvateshwar didn't like Bhagirath's solution. But he also knew it was the most practical thing to do. He looked at Shiva. 'My Lord?'

'We're not handing him over to the Brangas,' said Shiva.

'My Lord?' cried Bhagirath, shocked.

Shiva looked at Bhagirath. 'We're not.'

'But My Lord, how do we get to the Nagas? We have sworn to get the medicines to the Brangas.'

'Parshuram will give us the medicines. I'll ask him when he is conscious.'

'But, My Lord,' continued Bhagirath. 'He's a criminal. He will not help unless he is coerced. I admit he has made a sacrifice. But we need a ship to get out of here.'

'I know.'

Bhagirath continued to stare at Shiva. Then he turned

towards Parvateshwar. The Meluhan General gestured to the Ayodhya Prince to be quiet.

But Bhagirath would have none of it. What the Neelkanth was suggesting was not practical. 'Please forgive me for saying it again, My Lord. But the only practical way to get a ship is by letting the Brangas get their hands on him. And that's not the only reason to do so. Parshuram is a criminal, a mass murderer. Why shouldn't we surrender him to suffer the righteous Branga justice?'

'Because I said so.'

Saying this, Shiva walked out. Bhagirath kept staring at Parvateshwar, not saying a word.

Parshuram's eyes opened slightly. He smiled faintly. And then went back to sleep.

— ⁂ —

As the second prahar came to a close, the sun shone brightly, right over head.

The Branga and Kashi soldiers had been hard at work, with Vishwadyumna having taken charge. Kaavas didn't seem to mind following orders from the capable Branga. The Branga travelling doctor had tended to all the wounded. They were all on the road to recovery. The dead had been cremated in the Icchawar village ground. While nobody expected the few remaining lionesses and the liger to return back to the village, for abundant precaution, the soldiers had dug ditches around the village. Temporary quarters had been erected for both Branga as well as Kashi soldiers in the school building. The villagers had been commandeered to arrange the food supplies.

The villagers, though rejoicing at the decimation of the

pride, stayed warily at a distance, carrying out the tasks assigned to them by Vishwadyumna. Their mortal fear of the Nagas, despite the fact that their lives had just been saved by them, kept them suppressed.

The cleaner's children, however, seemed to delight in playing with Kali. They pulled her hair, jumped on her and laughed uproariously every time she pretended to get angry.

'Children!' spoke their mother sternly. They turned and ran towards her, holding on to her *dhoti*. The cleaner's wife spoke to Kali. 'My apologies for this, Your Highness. They will not disturb you.'

In the presence of an adult Kali's demeanour became serious once again. She merely nodded wordlessly.

She turned to her right to find Ganesh sleeping with his head on Sati's lap, his face a picture of bliss. His wounds had been dressed. The doctor was especially worried about the mutilation caused by the lioness on Ganesh's leg. It had been cleaned and bandaged tight.

Sati looked up at Kali and smiled. She held her sister's hand.

Kali smiled softly. 'I've never seen him sleep so peacefully.'

Sati smiled and lovingly ran her hand along Ganesh's face. 'I must thank you for taking care of him for so long.'

'It was my duty.'

'Yes, but not everyone honours their duty. Thank you.'

'Actually, it was my pleasure as well!'

Sati smiled. 'I can't imagine how tough life must have been for you. I will make it up to you. I promise.'

Kali frowned slightly, but kept quiet.

Sati looked up once again as a thought struck her. 'You

had said something about father. Are you sure? He is weak. But he loves his family dearly. I can't imagine him consciously hurting any of us.'

Kali's face hardened. Suddenly, they were disturbed by a noise from Ganesh. Sati looked down at her son.

Ganesh was pouting. 'I'm hungry!'

Sati raised her eyebrows and burst out laughing. She kissed Ganesh gently on his forehead. 'Let me see what I can rustle up.'

As Sati walked away, Kali turned to Ganesh, about to scold him for his behaviour. But Ganesh himself was up in a flash. 'You will not tell her, *Mausi*.'

'What?' asked Kali.

'You will not tell her.'

'She's not stupid, you know. She will figure it out.'

'That she may. But she will not find out from you.'

'She deserves the truth. Why shouldn't she know?'

'Because some truths can only cause pain, *Mausi*. They're best left buried.'

'My Lord,' whispered Parshuram.

Shiva, Parvateshwar and Bhagirath were huddled together around him in the tiny tent. It was the last hour of the third prahar. The sun was sinking into the horizon, turning the sludgy Madhumati waters orange-brown. Divodas and his team had already started working on repairing the ship. It was a daunting task.

'What is it, Parshuram?' asked Shiva. 'Why did you want to meet me?'

Parshuram closed his eyes, gathering strength. 'I will

have one of my people give the secrets of the Naga medicine to the Brangas, My Lord. We will help them. We will take them to Mount Mahendra in Kaling from where we get the stabilising agent for the medicine.'

Shiva smiled. 'Thank you.'

'You don't need to thank me, My Lord. This is what you want. Doing your bidding is my honour.'

Shiva nodded.

'You also need a ship,' said Parshuram.

Bhagirath perked up.

'I have a large ship of my own,' said Parshuram, before turning to Parvateshwar. 'Give me some of your men, brave General. I will tell them where it is. They can sail it here and we can leave.'

A surprised Parvateshwar smiled, looking at Shiva.

Shiva nodded. The bandit looked tired. Shiva bent down, touching Parshuram on his shoulder. 'You need to rest. We can talk later.'

'One more thing, My Lord,' said Parshuram, insistent. 'The Brangas are only a conduit.'

Shiva frowned.

'Your ultimate goal is to find the Nagas.'

Shiva narrowed his eyes.

'I know where they live,' said Parshuram.

Shiva's eyes widened in surprise.

'I know my way through the Dandak forests, My Lord,' continued Parshuram. 'I know where the Naga city is. I will tell you how to get there.'

Shiva patted Parshuram's shoulder. 'Thank you.'

'But I have one condition, My Lord.'

Shiva frowned.

'Take me with you,' whispered Parshuram.

Shiva raised his eyebrows, surprised. 'But why...'

'Following you is my life's duty. Please let me give my wretched life at least a little bit of meaning.'

Shiva nodded. 'It will be my honour to travel with you, Parshuram.'

— ⅄⅏ℿ⅍⊛ —

It had been three days since the battle of Madhumati. Parvateshwar's men had located Parshuram's ship. It was even bigger than the one they had travelled in. Clearly a Branga ship, it even had hull extensions to allow passage through the gates of Branga. The ship must have been captured by Parshuram's men from one of the unfortunate Branga Kshatriya bands sent to arrest or kill him.

All the soldiers had boarded the ship. Parshuram's men were not prisoners anymore. They had been allotted comfortable quarters of the same order as the Suryavanshi soldiers who had beaten them.

Shiva had personally seen to the comfort of both Purvaka and Parshuram. Ayurvati had stationed her assistant Mastrak alongside Parshuram, who was still extremely weak from tremendous blood loss.

The ship was sailing comfortably up the Madhumati. When they would reach the Branga river, a fast cutter with one of Parshuram's men would be sent to guide King Chandraketu in finding the alternative source of the Naga medicine. The man would also inform the rest of Shiva's men at Brangaridai to leave immediately and rejoin the brigade at the point where the Madhumati broke away from the Branga.

The brigade would then sail back to Kashi. Shiva was

desperate to meet Sati and Kartik. He had been missing his family. After that he planned to raise an army and quickly turn South to find the Nagas.

Shiva was standing at the head of the ship, smoking some marijuana with Veerbhadra. Nandi stood next to them. They stared into the swirling waters of the Madhumati.

'This expedition went better than expected, My Lord,' said Nandi.

'That it did,' smiled Shiva, pointing at the chillum. 'Unfortunately, the celebration isn't quite up to the mark.'

Veerbhadra smiled. 'Let me get to Kashi. They really know how to roll good grass there.'

Shiva laughed aloud. So did Nandi. Shiva offered the chillum to Nandi but the Meluhan Major declined. Shiva shrugged and took another drag, before passing the chillum back to Veerbhadra.

Shiva was distracted as he saw Parvateshwar come up to them, hesitate and turn back.

'I wonder what he wants to talk about now,' asked Shiva, frowning.

'It's obvious, isn't it?' smiled Veerbhadra.

Nandi looked down and smiled, not saying a word.

'Why don't you two idiots excuse me for a minute?' smiled Shiva, as he walked away from his friends.

Parvateshwar was standing at a distance, deep in thought.

'General? A word, General.'

Parvateshwar immediately turned around and saluted. 'Your command, My Lord.'

'Not a command, Parvateshwar. Just a request.'

Parvateshwar frowned.

'In the name of the Holy Lake,' said Shiva. 'For once, listen to your heart.'

'My Lord?'

'You know what I am saying. She loves you. You love her. What else is there to think about?'

Parvateshwar turned beet red. 'Has it been that obvious?'

'Obvious to everyone, General!'

'But My Lord, this is wrong.'

'How? Why? You think Lord Ram purposely designed laws for you to be unhappy?'

'But my grandfather's vow...'

'You have honoured it for long enough. Trust me, even he would want you to stop now.'

Parvateshwar looked down, not saying anything.

'I remember hearing that one of Lord Ram's commandments was that laws are not important. What is important is justice. If the purpose of justice is served by breaking a law, then break it.'

'Lord Ram said that?' asked Parvateshwar, surprised.

'I'm sure he must have,' smiled Shiva. 'He never wanted his followers to be unhappy. You are not hurting anyone else by being with Anandmayi. You are not hurting the protest begun by your grandfather. You have served that purpose quite enough. Now let your heart serve another purpose.'

'Are you sure, My Lord?'

'I've never been surer of anything else in my life. In the name of Lord Ram, go to her!'

Shiva slapped Parvateshwar hard on his back.

Parvateshwar had been thinking about this for long. Shiva's words only helped him gather his dwindling courage. He saluted Shiva and turned. A man on a mission. Ready to take the plunge.

— ⁂ —

Anandmayi was leaning against the railing astern of the ship, enjoying the strong evening breeze.

'Your Highness?'

Anandmayi spun around, surprised to find Parvateshwar there, looking sheepish. The Princess of Ayodhya was about to open her mouth, when he corrected himself.

'I meant Anandmayi,' whispered Parvateshwar.

Anandmayi stood up in surprise.

'Yes, General? You wanted something?' asked Anandmayi, her heart racing.

'Ummm... Anandmayi... I was thinking...'

'Yes?'

'Well, it's like this... It's about what we were talking about...'

Anandmayi was aglow, smiling from deep within her heart. 'Yes, General?'

'Ummm... I never thought I would face this day. So... Ummm...'

Anandmayi nodded, keeping quiet, letting him take his time. She could figure out exactly what Parvateshwar wanted to say. But she also knew that it would be very difficult for the Meluhan General.

'My vows and Suryavanshi laws have been the bedrock of my life,' said Parvateshwar. 'Unquestionable and unchanging. My destiny, the destination of my life and my role in it, has so far been clearly defined. This predictability is comforting. Rather, *had been* comforting, for many decades.'

Anandmayi nodded, silent.

'But,' said Parvateshwar, 'the last few years have turned my world upside down. First came the Lord, a living man that I could look up to. A person beyond the laws. I thought this would be the biggest change my simple heart had been forced to handle.'

Anandmayi continued to nod. Trying her best not to frown or laugh, touched to see this proud man baring his heart in what she thought was one of the most wooden attempts at courtship in history. But she was wise enough to know that her Parva had to say his piece or he would never be comfortable with himself or in the life she hoped he was choosing to make with her.

'But then... most unexpectedly, I also found a woman that I could look up to, could admire and adore. I have reached a crossroads in my life, where my destination is a blur. I do not know where my life is going. The road ahead is unclear. But to my surprise, I find that I am happy with that. Happy, as long as you walk this road with me...'

Anandmayi remained silent. Smiling. Tears in her eyes. He had really pulled it together at the end.

'It'll be one hell of a great journey.'

Anandmayi lunged forward and kissed Parvateshwar hard. A deep, passionate kiss. Parvateshwar stood stunned, his hands to his side, taking in a pleasure he hadn't ever imagined. After what seemed like a lifetime, Anandmayi stepped back, her eyes a seductive half-stare. Parvateshwar staggered, his mouth half open. Not even sure how to react.

'Lord Ram be merciful,' the General whispered.

Anandmayi stepped closer to Parvateshwar, running her hand across his face. 'You have no idea what you have been missing.'

Parvateshwar just continued to stare at her, dumbfounded.

Anandmayi held Parvateshwar's hand and pulled him away. 'Come with me.'

— ⅄ⓄᎱ⍋⊗ —

It had been a week since the battle with the liger. The few surviving lionesses and the liger had not come back. They were still licking their wounds. The villagers of Icchawar were using the moments of peace to start tilling their lands, preparing for the seasonal crops. It was a time of unexpected joy and relief.

The Chandravanshi soldiers were recovering. Ganesh's wounds were too deep. He still limped from the severe mauling his leg had taken. But he knew it was only a matter of time before he would be alright. He had to start preparing for the inevitable.

'*Maa*,' whispered Ganesh.

Sati looked at Ganesh, covering the dish she was cooking with a plate. She had spent the previous week listening to Kali share stories of Ganesh's childhood, sharing in his joys and sorrows, understanding her child's personality and character, right down to his favourite dishes. And she was satiating his stomach and soul with what she had learnt. 'What is it, my son?'

Kali had just stepped up close as requested by Ganesh.

'I think we have to start preparing to leave. I should be strong enough to travel in another week.'

'I know. The food I've been giving you has some rejuvenating herbs. They're giving you strength.'

Ganesh knelt and held his mother's hand. 'I know.'

Sati patted her son's face lightly.

Ganesh took a deep breath. 'I know you cannot come

to Panchavati. It will pollute you. I will come to visit you regularly in Kashi. I will come in secret.'

'What are you talking about?'

'I have also sworn the Kashi soldiers to an oath of silence, on pain of a gruesome death,' grinned Ganesh. 'They're terrified of us Nagas. They will not dare break this oath! The secret of my relationship with you will not be revealed.'

'Ganesh, what in Lord Ram's name are you talking about?'

'I will not embarrass you. Your acceptance of me is enough for my soul.'

'How can you embarrass me? You are my pride and joy.'

'*Maa*...' smiled Ganesh.

Sati held her son's face. 'You're not going anywhere.'

Ganesh frowned.

'You are staying with me.'

'*Maa*!' said Ganesh, horrified.

'What?'

'How can I? What will your society say?'

'I don't care.'

'But your husband...'

'He is your father,' said Sati firmly. 'Speak of him with respect.'

'I meant no disrespect, *Maa*. But he will not accept me. You know that. I am a Naga.'

'You are my son. You are his son. He will accept you. You don't know the size of your father's heart. The entire world can live in it.'

'But Sati...,' said Kali, trying to intervene.

'No arguments, Kali,' said Sati. 'Both of you are coming to Kashi. We travel when you are strong enough to do so.'

Kali stared at Sati, at a loss for words.

'You are my sister. I don't care what society says. If they accept me, they will accept you. If they reject you, I leave this society too.'

Kali smiled slightly, teary eyed. 'I was very wrong about you, *didi*.'

It was the first time Kali had called Sati her *elder sister*. Sati smiled and embraced Kali.

Chapter 17

The Curse of Honour

It had been ten days since the battle of the Madhumati. The ship carrying the now reconciled enemies — the Suryavanshis and Parshuram's men — was anchored where the Madhumati broke off from the Branga. They were waiting for their comrades to sail upriver from Brangaridai and join them.

A Branga Pandit had been called aboard to preside over Parvateshwar and Anandmayi's wedding. Bhagirath desired to conduct the ceremony at Ayodhya with regal pomp and grandeur befitting a princess. But Anandmayi would have none of it. She did not want to take any chances. Parvateshwar had taken his own sweet time to say yes and she wanted to have their relationship iron-tight 'as soon as humanly possible.' As Shiva had blessed the couple, all arguments about the hastiness of the ceremony had come to an end.

Shiva was standing at the ship railing, smoking with Veerbhadra.

'My Lord!'

Shiva turned around.

'By the Holy Lake! What are you doing, Parshuram?' asked a horrified Shiva. 'You should be resting.'

'I'm bored, My Lord.'

'But you were up for a long time yesterday for the wedding. Two days of continuous activity will be a bit too much. What does Ayurvati have to say?'

'I will go back in a little while, My Lord,' said Parshuram. 'Let me stand next to you for some time. It soothes me.'

Shiva raised an eyebrow. 'I'm not special. It's all in your mind.'

'I disagree, My Lord. But even if what you're saying is true, I'm sure you will find it in your heart to let me indulge my mind if it doesn't hurt anyone.'

Shiva burst out laughing. 'You're quite good with words for a...'

Shiva suddenly stopped.

'For a bandit,' grinned Parshuram.

'I meant no insult. I apologise.'

'Why apologise, My Lord? It is the truth. I was a bandit.'

Veerbhadra had become increasingly fascinated with this strange bandit. Intelligent, disturbed and ferociously devoted to Shiva. He spoke up, changing the topic, 'You were delighted about General Parvateshwar and Princess Anandmayi's wedding. I found that interesting.'

'Well, they are completely different,' said Parshuram. 'In terms of personality, thought, belief and region. Actually, pretty much everything. They are polar opposites. Extremes of the Chandravanshi and Suryavanshi thought processes. Traditionally, they should be enemies. Yet they found love in each other. I like stories like that. Reminds me of my parents.'

Shiva frowned. He remembered the terrible rumour he had heard about Parshuram beheading his own mother. 'Your parents?'

'Yes, My Lord. My father, Jamadagni, was a Brahmin, a scholarly man. My mother, Renuka, was from a Kshatriya clan. Rulers who were vassals of the Brangas.'

'So how did they get married?' smiled Shiva.

'Due to my mother,' smiled Parshuram. 'She was a very strong woman. My parents were in love. But it was her strength of character and determination that propelled their love to its logical conclusion.'

Shiva smiled.

'She worked at his *gurukul*. That in itself was against the norm in her clan.'

'How is working in *a school* a rebellion?'

'Because in her clan it was prohibited for women to go out and work.'

'They couldn't work? Why? I know that some clans have rules that do not allow women on the battlefield. Even the Gunas had that rule. But why against work in general?'

'Because my mother's clan was amongst the stupidest on the planet,' said Parshuram. 'My mother's people believed a woman should remain at home. That she shouldn't meet "strange" men.'

'What rubbish!' said Shiva.

'Absolutely. In any case, like I said, my mother was wilful. And, also her father's darling. So she convinced him to allow her to work at my father's gurukul.'

Shiva smiled.

'Of course, my mother had her own agenda,' said Parshuram, 'She was desperately in love. She needed time to convince my father to give up his vows and marry her.'

'Give up vows?'

'My father was a Vasudev Brahmin. And a Vasudev

Brahmin cannot marry. Other castes within the Vasudevs can, but not Brahmins.'

'There are non-Brahmins amongst the Vasudevs?'

'Of course. But Brahmins steer the community. To ensure that they remain true to the cause of the Vasudevs, they have to give up all earthly attachments like wealth, love and family. Therefore, one of their vows is that of lifelong celibacy.'

Shiva frowned. *What is this obsession among the Indians about giving up earthly attachments? How, in the Holy Lake's name, can that guarantee that you will evolve into a better human being?*

'So,' continued Parshuram, his eyes crinkling, 'my mother finally convinced my father to break the rules. He was in love with her, but she gave him the courage to give up his Vasudev vows so he could spend his life with her. Even more, she also convinced her own father to bless their relationship. Like I said, when she wanted something, she made it happen. My parents got married and had five sons. I was the youngest.'

Shiva looked at Parshuram. 'You are really proud of your mother, aren't you?'

'Oh yes. She was quite a woman!'

'Then why did you...'

Shiva stopped talking. *I shouldn't have said that.*

Parshuram became serious. 'Why did I... behead her?'

'You don't have to speak about it. I cannot even imagine the pain.'

Parshuram took a deep breath, sliding down to sit on the deck. Shiva sat on his haunches, touching Parshuram on his shoulder. Veerbhadra stood, staring directly into Parshuram's pain-ridden eyes.

'You don't need to say anything, Parshuram,' said Shiva.

Parshuram closed his eyes, right hand over his heart. He chanted repeatedly, *bowing to Lord Rudra* in his prayer. '*Om Rudraiy namah. Om Rudraiy namah.*'

Shiva watched the Brahmin warrior quietly.

'I have never spoken about it with anyone, My Lord,' said Parshuram. 'It was the trigger that set my life on the path it has taken.'

Shiva reached out and touched Parshuram's shoulder again.

'But I must tell you. If there is one person who can heal me, it is you. I had just completed my studies. And like my father, I too wanted to be a Vasudev. He didn't want me to. He didn't want any of his sons to become Vasudevs. He had been expelled from their tribe when he had chosen to marry my mother. He didn't want any of us to suffer his fate in the future.'

Veerbhadra sat down as well, all ears for Parshuram's story.

'But I had my mother's doggedness in me. Unlike my brothers, I was determined. I thought I would enter the tribe of Vasudevs as a Kshatriya, as this way, I wouldn't be bound by their detachment vows. I trained as a warrior. My father sent a letter to Ujjain, the Vasudev capital, to a few elders who still sympathised with him and requested them to consider my application. When the day finally arrived, I departed to the closest Vasudev temple for my examination.'

What did this have to do with his mother?

'What I didn't know when I left was that my grandfather had died. He was the only one holding back my mother's barbarian horde of a family. The moment his influence was gone, they decided to do what they had always wanted to do. Honour kill.'

'Honour kill?'

Parshuram looked at Shiva. 'When the people in the clan believe a woman in their community has insulted the honour of her family, the clan has the right to kill that woman and everyone else with her to avenge their loss of face.'

Shiva just stared, stunned.

What honour can there be in this barbarism?

'The men of my mother's family, her own brothers and uncles, attacked my father's gurukul.'

Parshuram stopped talking. A long-held back tear escaped from his eyes.

'They...' Parshuram held his breath and then found the strength to continue. 'They killed my brothers, all my father's students. They tied my mother to a tree and forced her to watch as they tortured my father for an entire day, doing unspeakable horrors. Then, they beheaded him.'

Veerbhadra squirmed, unable to comprehend such insanity, such evil.

'But they didn't kill my mother. They told her that they wanted her to live, to relive that day again and again. That she had to serve as an example to the other women so that they would never dare bring dishonour to their families. I returned to find my father's gurukul destroyed. My mother was sitting outside our house, holding my father's severed head in her lap. She looked like her soul had been burnt alive. Her eyes wide, blank. A shadow of the woman she had been, broken and brutalised.'

Parshuram stopped talking and turned to look at the river. This was the first time he was talking about his mother since that terrible day. 'She looked at me as though I was a stranger. And then she said words that would haunt me forever. She said: "Your father died because of me. It is my sin. I want to die like him."'

Shiva's mouth fell open in shock, his heart going out to the unfortunate Brahmin.

'At first I didn't understand. And then she commanded: "Behead me!" I didn't know what to do. I hesitated. Then she said once again: "I am your mother. I am ordering you. Behead me."'

Shiva pressed Parshuram's shoulder.

'I had no choice. My mother was catatonic. Without my father's love, she was nothing but an empty shell. As I picked up my axe to carry out her order, she looked straight into my eyes: "Avenge your father. He was the finest man that God ever created. Avenge him. Kill every single one of them! Every single one!"'

Parshuram fell silent. Shiva and Veerbhadra were too stunned to react. The only sounds were those of the somnolent waves of the Madhumati breaking gently against the ship.

'I did as she said. I beheaded her,' said Parshuram, taking a deep breath and wiping his tears. Then his eyes lit in remembered anger as he spoke through gritted teeth. 'And then I hunted down every single one of those bastards. I beheaded every single one of them. Every single one. The Vasudevs expelled me. I had killed people without the permission of their tribe, they said. Without a fair trial, they said. I had committed a wrong, they said. Did I, My Lord?'

Shiva looked straight into Parshuram's eyes, his heart heavy. He could feel the Brahmin's intense pain. He knew that Lord Ram would have probably acted as the Vasudevs had. The great Suryavanshi would have wanted the criminals to be punished but only after a fair trial. However, he also knew that if anyone had dared to do this to his own family, he would have burnt down their entire world. 'No. You didn't do anything wrong. What you did was in accordance with justice.'

Parshuram sighed as a dam burst.

What I did was just.

Shiva held Parshuram's shoulder. Parshuram covered his eyes with his hand, sniffing. At long last he shook his head slightly and looked up. 'The Branga king sent bands of Kshatriyas to arrest me. To apparently bring me to justice for annihilating his most important vassals. Twenty–one times they sent brigades to catch me. And twenty–one times I beat them. Finally they stopped.'

'But how did you fight the Brangas alone?' asked Veerbhadra.

'I wasn't alone. Some angels knew of the injustice I had suffered. They brought me to this haven, introduced me to the few unfortunate, ostracised brigands who lived here. I could build my own army. They gave me medicines so that I could survive despite the unclean waters here and food till I had established my people in the forests. They gave me weapons to fight the Brangas. And all this without any expectations from me. The battles with Brangaridai were also brought to an end because they finally threatened the Branga king. And King Chandraketu could not refuse them. They are the best people amongst us all. Angels who fight for the oppressed.'

Shiva frowned. 'Who?'

'The Nagas,' replied Parshuram.

'What?!'

'Yes, My Lord. That is why you are looking for them,

right? If you want to find Evil, you must make the Good your ally, right?'

'What are you talking about?'

'They never kill innocents. They fight for justice, despite the injustices they endure. They help the oppressed whenever and wherever they can. They truly are the best amongst us all.'

Shiva stared hard at Parshuram, not saying a word. Completely staggered.

'You are looking for their secret, aren't you?' asked Parshuram.

'What secret?'

'I don't know. But I have heard that the secret of the Nagas has a deep connection to Evil. Isn't that why you are searching for them?'

Shiva didn't answer. He was looking into the horizon, deep in thought.

— ★ —

It had been two weeks since the battle with the liger's pride. All the injured soldiers were well on the path to recovery. But Ganesh's wounded leg had still not completely healed.

Sati had been supervising the building of some defences at the Icchawar village perimeter as a precaution against future animal attacks. She returned to the camp to see Kali changing the dressing on Ganesh's wound.

Both Kali and Ganesh, perhaps encouraged by Sati's complete acceptance of their appearance, had not worn their masks for the last two weeks. The Chandravanshi soldiers, however, still averted their eyes in dread when they saw them.

Kali had just finished applying the neem bandage. She patted Ganesh on his head and rose to walk towards the fire at one corner of the clearing. Sati saw the gesture and smiled. She turned to instruct Kaavas to carry on with his work and walked up to Kali.

'How is his wound?'

'It'll take another week, *didi.* The healing process has slowed down since last week.'

Sati grimaced, unhappy. 'The poor child lost a lot of blood and flesh.'

'Don't worry,' said Kali. 'He is very strong. He will recover.'

Sati smiled. Kali threw the bandage into the fire. The paste on the bandage, having drawn out much of the infection, burned a deep blue.

Sati looked up at Kali, took a deep breath and asked what had been troubling her since they had met. 'Why?'

Kali frowned.

'You are good people. I've seen the way you treat Ganesh and your men. You are tough, but fair. Then why did you do all those terrible things?'

Kali held her breath. She looked up at the sky and shook her head. 'Think again, *didi.* We have not done anything wrong.'

'Kali, you and Ganesh may not have personally done anything wrong. But your people committed grave crimes. They killed innocents.'

'My people work according to my orders, *didi.* If you want to blame them, then you cannot absolve me. Think once again. No innocents were killed in our attacks.'

'I'm sorry Kali, but that is not true. You attacked non-combatants. I have been thinking for some time. I agree that the Nagas are treated unfairly. The way Meluha treats Naga babies is unjust. But that doesn't mean every Meluhan, even if he personally hasn't done anything to hurt you, is your enemy.'

'*Didi*, you think we would attack people just because they were a part of a system which humiliated and wounded us? That is wrong. We never attacked anyone who hasn't directly harmed us.'

'You did. Your people attacked temples. They attacked innocents. They killed vulnerable Brahmins.'

'No. In every attack, we would let all the people except the temple Brahmins leave. Everyone. No innocents were killed. Ever.'

'But you did kill temple Brahmins. They're not warriors. They're innocent.'

'I disagree.'

'Why?'

'Because they directly hurt our people.'

'What? How? What wrong did the temple Brahmins do to you?'

'I'll tell you.'

— ⁂ —

Shiva's caravan of ships was anchored at Vaishali, a pretty city on the Ganga river and an immediate neighbour of Branga. It had been three weeks since Shiva had allied with Parshuram. Vaishali had a massive Vishnu temple dedicated to the legendary fish God, Lord Matsya. Shiva was deeply disturbed by what Parshuram had said about the Nagas. He wanted to speak with a Vasudev, one who was other than the ostracised Vasudev Brahmin-Kshatriya on board. Time and space had dimmed his anger towards the tribe.

The temple was very close to the city's harbour. A massive crowd, including the King, had been waiting to receive him, but Shiva had requested that he be allowed to meet them later. He headed straight for the Matsya temple. It was a little taller than seventy metres, comfortably above the minimum height needed for the Vasudevs to transmit radio waves.

The temple was on the banks of the Ganga. Usually temples would have had most of the space outside dedicated to landscaped gardens or grand enclosures. This temple was different. The land outside was dominated by intricate water bodies. Water from the Ganga had been routed into a system of elaborate canals around the main temple. And these canals made some of the most ethereal designs that Shiva had ever seen. It formed a map of ancient India at a time when sea-levels were a lot lower. It told the story of Lord Manu and how he had led his band of followers out of his devastated homeland, the Sangamtamil. Despite his urgency to meet the Vasudevs, Shiva held back, enthralled by the breathtaking designs. At long last, he tore his eyes away and walked up the steps to the main temple. Crowds hung outside, waiting quietly in accordance with their Neelkanth's request.

Shiva looked at the sanctum sanctorum at the far corner of the temple. It was far bigger than in any other temple he had seen so far. Probably to accommodate the enormous statue of its reigning God. On a raised platform lay Lord Matsya, a giant fish, who had helped bring Manu and his band of refugees from Sangamtamil to safety. Manu, the founder of the Vedic civilisation, had made it clear in his guidelines to his descendants that Lord Matsya must always be respected and worshipped as the first Lord Vishnu. If any of them were alive, it was due to the benefaction of the great Lord Matsya.

Lord Matsya looks so much like the dolphins I've seen in the rivers here. Only He is much larger.

Shiva bowed down and paid his respects to the Lord. He said a quick prayer and then sat down against one of the pillars. And then he thought out loud.

Vasudevs? Are you here?

Nobody responded. No one from the temple came to see him.

Is there no Vasudev here?

Absolute silence.

Is this not a Vasudev temple? Have I come to the wrong place?

Shiva heard nothing except the gentle tinkle of the fountains in the temple compound.

Damn!

Shiva realised that maybe he had made a mistake. This temple probably wasn't a Vasudev outpost. His thoughts went back to the advice Sati had given to him.

Maybe what Sati said is right. Maybe the Vasudevs were trying to help me. They did help! I would have been devastated if anything had happened to Kartik.

A calm clear voice rang out loud in his head. *Your wife is wise, great Mahadev. It is rare to find such beauty and wisdom in one person.*

Shiva looked up and around quickly. There was nobody. The voice was from one of the other Vasudev temples. He recognised it. It was the one that had commanded the Kashi Vasudev to give him the Naga medicine. *Are you the leader, Panditji?*

No, my friend. You are. I am but your follower. And I bring the Vasudevs with me.

Where are you? Ujjain?

There was silence.

What is your name, Panditji?

I am Gopal. I am the Chief Guide of the Vasudevs. I bear the key task that Lord Ram had set us: Assisting you in your karma.

I need your advice, Panditji.

As you wish, great Neelkanth. What do you want to talk about?

— ⸙ —

Sati, Kali, Ganesh and the Branga-Kashi soldiers were marching towards Kashi. Loud conversation amongst them disturbed the silence of the forest.

Vishwadyumna turned to Ganesh. 'My Lord, don't you find the forest oddly silent?'

Ganesh raised his eyebrows, for the soldiers were creating quite a racket. 'You think our men should be talking even louder?!'

'No, My Lord. We are loud enough! It is the rest of the forest that I'm talking about. It is too quiet.'

Ganesh tilted his head. Vishwadyumna was right. Not a single animal or bird sound. He looked around. His instincts told him that something was wrong. He stared hard into the woods. Then, shaking his head, he looked ahead and goaded his horse into moving faster.

A short distance away, an injured animal, massive in his proportions, with his wounds partially healed, crept slowly forward. The shaft of a broken arrow, buried deep in his shoulder, caused the liger to limp a little. Two lionesses followed him silently.

Chapter 18

The Function of Evil

This country is very confusing.

Gopal thought softly: *Why would you say that, my friend?*

The Nagas are obviously the people who are evil, right? Almost everyone seems to agree. And yet, the Nagas helped a man in need, in the interests of justice. That's not how evil is supposed to be.

A good point, great Neelkanth.

Considering the mistake I've already made, I'm not about to attack anyone till I'm sure.

A wise decision.

So do you also think the Nagas may not be evil?

How can I answer that, my friend? I do not have the wisdom to find that answer. I am not the Neelkanth.

Shiva smiled. *But you do have an opinion, don't you?*

Shiva waited for Gopal to speak. When the Vasudev Pandit didn't, Shiva smiled even more broadly, giving up this discussion. Suddenly a disturbing thought struck him. *Please don't tell me the Nagas also believe in the legend of the Neelkanth.*

Gopal remained silent for a moment.

Shiva repeated, frowning. *Panditji? Please answer me. Do the Nagas also believe in the Neelkanth legend?*

As far as I know, great Mahadev, most of them do not believe in the Neelkanth. But do you think that would make them evil?

Shiva shook his head. *No, of course not.*

Silence for some time.

Shiva breathed deeply. *So what is the blessed answer? I have travelled through all of India. Met practically all the tribes except the Nagas. And if none are evil, maybe Evil hasn't arisen. Maybe I'm not required.*

Are you sure it is only people who can be Evil, my friend? There may be attachment to Evil within some. There may be a small part of Evil within them. But could the great Evil, the one that awaits the Neelkanth, exist beyond mere humans?

Shiva frowned. *I don't understand.*

Can Evil be too big to be concentrated within just a few men?

Shiva remained silent.

Lord Manu had said it's not people who are evil. True Evil exists beyond them. It attracts people. It causes confusion amongst its enemies. But Evil in itself is too big to be confined to just a few.

Shiva frowned. *You make it sound like Evil is a power as strong as Good. That it doesn't work by itself, but uses people as its medium. These people, maybe even good people, find purpose in serving Evil. How can it be destroyed if it serves a purpose?*

That is an interesting thought, O Neelkanth, that Evil serves a purpose.

What purpose? The purpose of destruction? Why would the universe plan that?

Let's look at it another way. Do you believe there is nothing random in the universe? That everything exists for a reason. That everything serves a purpose.

Yes. If anything appears random, it only means that we haven't discovered its purpose just as yet.

So why does Evil exist? Why can't it be destroyed once and for all? Even when it is apparently destroyed, it rises once again. Maybe after much time has elapsed, perhaps in another form, but Evil does rise and will keep rising again and again. Why?

Shiva narrowed his eyes, absorbing Gopal's words. *Because even Evil serves a purpose...*

That is what Lord Manu believed. And the institution of the Mahadev acts as the balance, the control for that purpose. To take Evil out of the equation at the correct time.

Take it out of the equation? asked a surprised Shiva.

Yes. That is what Lord Manu said. It was just a line in his commandments. He said that the destroyers of Evil would understand what he means. My understanding of it is that Evil cannot and should not be destroyed completely. That it needs to be taken out of the equation at the right time, the time when it rises to cause total annihilation. Do you think he said that because the same Evil may serve the purpose of Good in another time?

I came here for answers, my friend. You are only throwing more questions at me.

Gopal laughed softly. *I'm sorry my friend. Our job is to give you the clues that we know. We are not supposed to interfere in your judgement. For that could lead to the triumph of Evil.*

I have heard that Lord Manu said Good and Evil are two sides of the same coin?

Yes, he did say so. They are two sides of the same coin. He didn't explain any further.

Strange. That doesn't make sense.

Gopal smiled. *It does sound strange. But I know you will make sense of it when the time is right.*

Shiva was silent for some time. He looked out across the temple pillars. In the distance, he could see the people of Vaishali outside the gates, waiting patiently for their Neelkanth. Shiva stared hard, then turned back towards the idol of Lord Matsya. *Gopal, my friend, what is the Evil that Lord Rudra took out of the equation. I know the Asuras were not evil. So what Evil did he destroy?*

You know the answer.

No, I don't.

Yes, you do. Think about it, Lord Neelkanth. What is the enduring legacy of Lord Rudra?

Shiva smiled. The answer was obvious. *Thank you, Panditji. I think we've spoken enough for today.*

May I offer my opinion on your first question?

Shiva was surprised. *About the Nagas?*

Yes.

Of course! Please.

It is obvious that you feel drawn to the Nagas. That you feel that your path to Evil lies through them.

Yes.

That can be due to two reasons. Either Evil exists at the end of that path.

Or?

Or Evil has caused its greatest destruction on that path.

Shiva took a deep breath. *You mean the Nagas may be the ones who suffered the most at the hands of Evil?*

Maybe.

Shiva leaned back against the pillar. He closed his eyes. *Maybe the Nagas deserve a hearing. Maybe everyone else has been unfair to them. Maybe they deserve the benefit of the doubt. But one of them has to answer to me. One of them awaits justice for Brahaspati's assassination.*

Gopal knew who Shiva was thinking about. He kept quiet.

— ⁂ —

Sati stood in front of Athithigva in his private chambers. Standing next to her were Kali and Ganesh. The stunned King of Kashi did not know how to react.

Sati had returned from Icchawar that morning with twenty-seven lion skins, proof of the destruction of the man-eating pride. Special prayers had been intoned at the Vishwanath temple for the brave Kashi soldiers who had died there. Kaavas had been promoted to the rank of Major. The courage of the Branga platoon had also been acknowledged. The Brangas of Kashi would be exempt from taxes for the next three months. But this specific problem was particularly knotty for Athithigva. He did not know how to react to the presence of the two Nagas beside Sati. He dare not expel the relatives of the wife of the Neelkanth from his city. At the same time, he couldn't allow them to live openly in Kashi. His people would consider it a crime against the laws of Karma. Superstitions about the Nagas ran deep.

'My Lady,' said Athithigva carefully. 'How can we allow this?'

Kali was staring at Athithigva, livid at the humiliation being meted out to her, a Queen in her own right. She touched Sati's arm. '*Didi*, forget this...'

Sati just shook her head. 'Lord Athithigva, Kashi is a shining light of tolerance within India. It accepts all Indians, no matter what their faith or way of life. Isn't rejecting some noble and valiant people, just because they are Nagas, going against the very reasons that make your city a beacon for the downtrodden and marginalised?'

Athithigva looked down. 'But, My Lady, my people...'

'Your Highness, should you give in to your people's biases? Or instead, lead them onto a better path?'

The Kashi king remained silent, wavering.

'Please do not forget, Your Highness, that if the Kashi platoon has returned and the villagers of Icchawar are alive today, it is due to the bravery of Kali, Ganesh and their men. We would all have been killed by the lions. They have saved us. Do they not deserve honour in return?'

Athithigva nodded hesitantly. He looked out of the window of his private chambers. The Ganga flowed languidly, cradling the reflection of the Eastern palace on the far bank. Where his beloved sisters Maya led a miserable life, practically imprisoned. He would have loved to challenge the fear of the Nagas in his people. But had always lacked the courage. The fact that the Neelkanth's wife stood by her family, gave him hope. For who would dare to challenge the Neelkanth? Everyone knew how Shiva had abolished one set of unjust laws. So why not the same for the Nagas too?

The King turned back towards Sati. 'Your family can stay, My Lady. I'm sure they will be comfortable in the wing of the Kashi palace allocated to the Lord Neelkanth.'

'I'm sure they will,' replied a smiling Sati. 'Thank you so much, Your Highness.'

— ⁂ —

Shiva was standing at the head of the ship, Parvateshwar next to him.

'I've doubled the speed of the lead ship, My Lord,' said Parvateshwar.

Shiva had asked Parvateshwar to ensure a quick arrival of their fleet to Kashi. He had been away from his family for more than two years. It was too long a time and he missed them dearly.

'Thank you, General,' smiled Shiva.

Parvateshwar bowed and turned to look at the Ganga again.

Shiva spoke with a hint of a smile on his face. 'So how is married life, General?'

Parvateshwar looked at Shiva with a broad smile. 'Heaven, My Lord. Absolute heaven. A very intense heaven though.'

Shiva smiled. 'Normal rules don't seem to apply, do they?'

Parvateshwar laughed out loud. 'Well, Anandmayi continues to update the rules as each day comes along and I just follow them!'

Shiva laughed loudly as well and patted his friend. 'Follow those rules, my friend, follow those rules. She loves you. You will be happy with her.'

Parvateshwar nodded heartily.

'Anandmayi told me that she has sent a cutter to Ayodhya to inform Emperor Dilipa of your nuptials,' said Shiva.

'Yes, she has,' said Parvateshwar. 'His Highness will be coming to Kashi to receive us. He has promised to hold another, completely extravagant celebration for us in Kashi within ten days of our arrival.'

'That should be fun!'

'Yes, My Lord?' asked Nandi.

Nandi and Bhagirath were with Shiva in his cabin.

'When we reach Kashi, stay close to Prince Bhagirath.'

'Why, My Lord?' asked Bhagirath.

Shiva raised his hand. 'Just trust me.'

Bhagirath narrowed his eyes. 'My father's coming to Kashi?'

Shiva nodded.

'I will be the Prince's shadow, My Lord,' said Nandi. 'Nothing will happen to him as long as I am alive.'

Shiva looked up. 'I don't want anything happening to you either, Nandi. Both of you keep your eyes open and remain careful.'

— ⁂ —

'My son!' cried Sati as Kartik ran into her arms.

Kartik was only three, but, due to the Somras, he looked like a six–year–old. He screamed, '*Maa*!'

Sati twirled her son around happily. 'I've missed you so much.'

'I missed you too,' said Kartik softly, still unhappy about his mother leaving him behind.

'I'm sorry I had to go away, my child. But I had very important work to do.'

'Next time, take me with you.'

'I will try.'

Kartik smiled, seemingly mollified. He then pulled his wooden sword out of the scabbard. 'Look at this, *Maa*.'

Sati frowned. 'What's this?'

'I started learning how to fight the day you left. If I was a good soldier, you would have taken me with you, no?'

Sati smiled broadly and plonked Kartik on her lap. 'You are a born soldier, my son.'

Kartik smiled and hugged his mother.

'You know how you always ask me for a brother, Kartik?'

Kartik nodded vigorously. 'Yes! Yes!'

'Well, I've found a wonderful brother for you. An elder brother who will always take care of you.'

Kartik frowned and looked towards the door. He saw a giant of a man enter the chambers. He was wearing a simple white *dhoti* and an *angvastram* was draped loosely across his right shoulder, his immense stomach jiggling with every breath. But it was the face that startled Kartik. The head of an elephant on top of a human body.

Ganesh smiled broadly, his heart beating uncertainly, anxious for Kartik's acceptance. 'How are you, Kartik?'

The normally fearless Kartik hid behind his mother.

'Kartik,' smiled Sati, pointing at his *elder brother* Ganesh. 'Why don't you say hello to your *dada?*'

The boy continued to stare at Ganesh. 'Are you human?'

'Yes. I am your brother,' smiled Ganesh.

Kartik didn't say anything. But Sati had taught Ganesh well. The Naga held out his hand, displaying a succulent mango, Kartik's favourite fruit. The boy was at once delighted and surprised at seeing a mango so late in the year. He inched forward.

'Do you want this, Kartik?' asked Ganesh.

Kartik frowned, drawing out his wooden sword. 'You are not going to make me fight for it, are you?'

Ganesh laughed. 'No, I'm not. But I will charge a hug from you.'

Kartik hesitated and looked at Sati.

Sati nodded and smiled. 'You can trust him.'

Kartik moved slowly and grabbed the mango. Ganesh embraced his little brother, who immediately got busy, biting strongly into his favourite fruit. He looked up at

Ganesh and smiled, whispering between loud slurps. 'Wow... Thank you... dada.'

Ganesh smiled again and patted Kartik lightly on his head.

— ⅄ⵔ𐌵ፁ⊛ —

The lead ship docked lightly onto the Dasashwamedh ghat. As the gangway was being drawn, Shiva's eyes desperately sought Sati. He could see Emperor Dilipa and King Athithigva standing at the royal platform, with their families. There was a multitude of Kashi citizens thronging the ghats, but...

'Where is she?'

'I'll find her, My Lord,' said Bhagirath as he disembarked, closely followed by Nandi.

'And, Bhagirath...'

'Yes, My Lord,' said Bhagirath, stopping.

'After all this is over, please take Purvaka to the King's palace. Ensure that he is comfortable in my family's area.'

'Yes, My Lord,' said Bhagirath, as he darted away, ignoring Dilipa, his father and the Emperor of Swadweep. But Nandi was surprised at the changes visible in the Emperor. Dilipa looked at least ten years younger, his face glowing with good health. Nandi frowned, before turning to catch up with Bhagirath.

Shiva stepped off the gangway.

Dilipa directed one long hard stare at the retreating form of his son and shook his head, before turning towards the Neelkanth. He bowed low before Shiva, touching his feet.

'May your dynasty continue to spread prosperity, Your Highness,' said Shiva, himself bowing his head with a namaste to Dilipa.

Veerbhadra, meanwhile, had found Krittika and spun her in his arms. An ecstatic yet embarrassed Krittika tried to free herself, blushing as she asked her husband to restrain his public display of affection.

Athithigva also stepped forward and sought Shiva's blessings. Having completed the formalities, the Neelkanth turned, searching for his family. 'Where is my family, Your Highness?'

'*Baba*!'

Shiva turned with a broad smile. Kartik was running towards him. As he lifted his son into his arms, Shiva said, 'By the holy lake, you have grown really fast, Kartik.'

'I missed you!' whispered Kartik, holding his father tight.

'I missed you too,' said Shiva. His pleasure at seeing his son turned into surprise as he recognised the mouth-watering smell of ripened mangoes. 'Who has been giving you mangoes so late in the season?'

Just then Sati appeared in front of Shiva. A smiling Shiva held Kartik to his right and wrapped his left arm around Sati, holding his world close to him, oblivious to the thousands staring at them. 'I've missed you both so much.'

'And we missed you,' smiled Sati, pulling her head back to glance at her husband.

Shiva pulled her close again, eyes closed, taking pleasure in his family's loving touch, his wife and son resting their heads on his shoulders. 'Let's go home.'

— ⁂ —

The carriage was moving slowly down Kashi's Sacred

Avenue. The Emperor of Ayodhya and the King of Kashi followed in their carriages while the brigade that had travelled with Shiva marched behind. Citizens had lined the streets, to get their first glimpse of their Lord after more than two–and–a–half years. Shiva sat comfortably, Sati next to him and Kartik on his lap, waving to the crowds.

Both Shiva and Sati spoke simultaneously. 'I have something to tell...'

Shiva started laughing. 'You first.'

'No. No. You first,' said Sati.

'I insist. You first.'

Sati swallowed. 'What have you found out about the Nagas, Shiva?'

'Surprising things actually. Maybe I have misjudged them. We need to find out more about them. Maybe they are not all bad. Maybe they just have a few bad apples amongst them, like in all communities.'

Sati sighed deeply, finding some release for the tension coiled inside her like a snake.

'What happened?' asked Shiva, staring hard at his wife.

'Umm, there is something that I have also discovered recently. Something very surprising. Something that was kept hidden from me until now. It is about the Nagas.'

'What?'

'I found... that...'

Shiva was surprised to see Sati so nervous. 'What's the matter, darling?'

'I found out that I'm related to them.'

'What?!'

'Yes.'

'How can that be? Your father hates the Nagas!'

'It could be guilt more than hatred.'

'Guilt?'

'I was not born alone.'

Shiva frowned.

'A twin was born along with me. I have a sister.'

Shiva was shocked. 'Where is she? Who kidnapped her? How did this happen in Meluha?'

'She was not kidnapped,' whispered Sati. 'She was abandoned.'

'Abandoned?' Shiva stared at his wife, at a loss for words.

'Yes, she was born a Naga.'

Shiva held Sati's hand. 'Where did you find her? Is she all right?'

Sati looked up at Shiva, her eyes moist. 'I didn't find her. She found me. She saved my life.'

Shiva smiled, not at all surprised to hear yet another tale of Naga heroism and generosity. 'What's her name?'

'Kali. Queen Kali.'

'Queen?'

'Yes, the Queen of the Nagas.'

Shiva's eyes widened in surprise. Kali may be the one who would help him find Brahaspati's killer. Maybe that's why fate had conspired to bring them together. 'Where is she?'

'Here in Kashi. Outside our palace. Waiting to meet you. Waiting for you to accept her.'

Shiva smiled, shaking his head and pulling Sati close to him. 'She's your family. That makes her my family. Where's the question of my not accepting her?'

Sati smiled slightly, resting her head on Shiva's shoulders. 'But she is not the only Naga waiting for your acceptance.'

Shiva frowned.

'Another, even more tragic secret, was kept from me,' said Sati.

'What?'

'I was told ninety years back that my first child was stillborn. As still as a statue.'

Shiva nodded, as though sensing where this conversation was headed, holding his wife's hand tighter.

'That was a lie,' sobbed Sati. 'He...'

'He was alive?!'

'He is still alive!'

Shiva's jaw dropped in shock. 'You mean... I have another son?'

Sati stared up at Shiva, smiling through her tears.

'By the Holy Lake! I have another son!'

Sati nodded, happy at Shiva's joy.

'Bhadra! Drive quickly. My son waits for me!'

Chapter 19

Rage of the Blue Lord

Shiva's carriage quickly turned into the gates of Athithigva's palace. As it sped along the road around the central garden, an excited Shiva lifted Kartik into his arms and reached for the door. He was off as soon as the vehicle stopped, setting Kartik on the ground, holding his hand and walking quickly ahead. Sati followed.

Shiva stopped in his tracks as he saw Kali, holding a *puja thali,* a *prayer tray,* with a ceremonial lamp and flowers.

'What the...!'

Standing in front of Shiva was a splitting image of Sati. Her eyes, face, build — everything. Except that her skin was a jet black to Sati's bronze. Her hair open, unlike Sati who usually restrained her flowing tresses. The woman was wearing royal clothing and ornaments, a cream and red coloured *angvastram* covered her entire torso. Then he noticed the two extra hands on her shoulders.

A nervous Kali continued to stare at Shiva, unsure. Much to her surprise, Shiva stepped forward and embraced her gently, careful not to disturb the puja thali.

'What a pleasure it is to meet you,' said Shiva, smiling broadly.

Kali smiled tentatively, shocked by Shiva's warm gesture, clearly at a loss for words.

Shiva tapped the puja thali. 'I think you are supposed to move this around my face six or seven times in order to welcome me home.'

Kali laughed. 'I'm sorry. Just that I have been very nervous.'

'Nothing to be nervous about,' grinned Shiva. 'Just circle the thali around, shower flowers on me and be sure not to drop the lamp. Burns are damn painful!'

Kali laughed and completed the ceremony, applying a red *tilak* on Shiva's forehead.

'And now,' said Shiva. 'Where's my other son?'

Kali stepped aside. Shiva saw Ganesh in the distance, atop the stairs leading to Athithigva's main palace.

'That's my dada!' beamed Kartik at his father.

Shiva smiled at Kartik. 'Let's go meet him.'

Holding Kartik's hand, Shiva walked up the flight of stairs, with Sati and Kali in tow. Everyone else waited quietly at the bottom, giving the family its own private moment.

Ganesh, in a red *dhoti* and white *angvastram*, was standing at the entryway of his mother's wing of the palace, almost like a guard. As Shiva reached him, Ganesh bent to touch his father's feet.

Shiva touched Ganesh's head gently, held his shoulders and pulled the Naga up to embrace him, blessing him with a long life. '*Ayushman bhav*, my...'

Shiva suddenly stopped as he stared hard at Ganesh's calm, almond-shaped eyes. His hands were rigid on Ganesh's shoulders, eyes narrowed hard.

Ganesh shut his eyes and cursed his fate silently. He knew he had been recognised.

Shiva's eyes continued to bore into Ganesh.

Sati, looking surprised, whispered, 'What's the matter, Shiva?'

Shiva ignored her. He continued to stare at Ganesh with repressed rage. He reached for his pouch. 'I have something that belongs to you.'

Ganesh kept quiet, continuing to stare at Shiva, his eyes melancholic. He didn't need to look in order to know what Shiva was bringing out of his pouch. The bracelet, whose clasp had been destroyed, belonged to him. He had lost it at Mount Mandar. It was frayed at the edges by flames that had tried to consume it. The embroidered symbol of Aum, in the center, was unblemished. But it wasn't a normal Aum symbol. The representation of the ancient holy word had been constructed from snakes. The serpent Aum!

Ganesh quietly took his bracelet from Shiva's hand.

Sati looked on with disbelieving eyes. 'Shiva! What is going on?'

Furious rage was pouring out of Shiva's eyes.

'Shiva...,' repeated Sati, as she touched her husband's shoulder anxiously.

Shiva flinched at Sati's touch. 'Your son killed my brother,' he growled.

Sati was shocked. Disbelieving.

Shiva spoke again. This time his voice was hard, furious. 'Your son killed Brahaspati!'

Kali sprung forward. 'But it was an...'

The Queen of the Nagas fell silent at a gesture from Ganesh.

The Naga continued to look straight at Shiva. Offering no explanations. Waiting for the Neelkanth's verdict, his punishment.

Shiva stepped close to Ganesh. Uncomfortably close. Till his fuming breath blew hard on Ganesh. 'You are my wife's son. It's the only reason why I'm not going to kill you.'

Ganesh lowered his eyes. Hands held in supplication. Refusing to say anything.

'Get out of my house,' roared Shiva. 'Get out of this land. Never show your face here again. The next time, I may not be so forgiving.'

'But... But Shiva. He's my son!' begged Sati.

'He killed Brahaspati.'

'Shiva...'

'HE KILLED BRAHASPATI!'

Sati stared blankly, tears flowing down her cheeks. 'Shiva, he's my son. I cannot live without him.'

'Then live without me.'

Sati was stunned. 'Shiva, please don't do this. How can you ask me to make this choice?'

Ganesh finally spoke. 'Father, I...'

Shiva interrupted Ganesh angrily. 'I am not your father!'

Ganesh bowed his head, took a deep breath and spoke up once again. 'O Great Mahadev, you are known for your fairness. Your sense of justice. The crime is mine. Don't punish my mother for my sins.' Ganesh pulled his knife out, the same knife that Sati had flung at him in Ayodhya. 'Take my life. But don't curse my mother with a fate worse than death. She cannot live without you.'

'No!' screamed Sati as she darted in front of Ganesh. 'Please, Shiva. He's my son... He's my son...'

Shiva's anger turned ice cold. 'Looks like you've made your choice.'

He picked up Kartik.

'Shiva...' pleaded Sati. 'Please don't go. Please...'

Shiva looked at Sati, his eyes moist, but voice ice cold. 'This is something I cannot accept, Sati. Brahaspati was like my brother.'

Shiva walked down the steps, carrying Kartik with him as a shocked Kashi citizenry kept deathly silent.

'Shiva doesn't know the entire picture. Why didn't you tell him?' asked an agitated Kali.

Kali and Ganesh were sitting in Sati's chambers in Athithigva's palace. Sati, torn between her love for her long-lost son and her devotion to her husband, had gone to the Branga building, where Shiva had set up temporary quarters. She was trying to reason with him.

'I can't. I have given my word, *Mausi*,' answered Ganesh, his calm voice hiding the deep sadness within.

'But...'

'No, *Mausi*. This remains between you and me. There is only one condition under which the secret behind the attack on Mount Mandar can be revealed. I don't see that happening too soon.'

'But tell your mother at least.'

'A word of honour does not stop at a mother's door.'

'*Didi* is suffering. I thought you'd do anything for her.'

'I will. She can live without me but not without the Mahadev. She's not letting me leave because of her guilt at not being there for me earlier.'

'What are you saying? You will leave? '

'Yes. In another ten days. Once the Meluhan General and the Chandravanshi Princess' wedding celebrations are done. Then father can return home.'

'Your mother will not allow this.'

'It doesn't matter. I will leave. I will not be the reason for my parent's separation.'

'Your Highness,' said Kanakhala, the Meluhan Prime Minister. 'It is not advisable for you to leave for Swadweep without a formal invitation. It is against protocol.'

'What nonsense,' said Daksha. 'I am the Emperor of India. I can go wherever I please.'

Kanakhala was a loyal Prime Minister. But she did not want her Emperor to commit any act which would embarrass the Empire. 'But the terms of the Ayodhya treaty are that Swadweep is only our vassal and has direct control over its own territory. Protocol dictates that we seek their permission. They cannot deny permission. You are their Lord. But it's a formality that must be completed.'

'No formalities needed. I'm just a father going to meet his favourite daughter!'

Kanakhala frowned. 'Your Highness, you have only one daughter.'

'Yes. Yes. I know,' said Daksha, waving his hand dismissively. 'Look I am leaving in three weeks. You can send a messenger to Swadweep asking for permission. All right?'

'Your Highness, bird couriers are still not set up in Ayodhya. You know how inefficient those people are. And Ayodhya is further than Kashi. So even if the messenger leaves today, he will reach Ayodhya in a little over three months. You will reach Kashi at the same time.'

Daksha smiled. 'Yes, I will. Go and make the arrangements for my departure.'

— ⚹ —

Kanakhala sighed, bowed and left the chambers.

The Emperor of Swadweep, Dilipa, had planned grand festivities to celebrate the wedding of his daughter Anandmayi with Parvateshwar. But the unexpected bitterness between the Mahadev and his wife had soured the mood. However, the pujas could not be cancelled. It would be an insult to the Gods. While all the parties had been put on hold, the pujas to the elemental Gods Agni, Vayu, Prithvi, Varun, Surya and Som were to proceed as planned.

The puja for the *Sun God* was being conducted at the *Surya* temple on the Sacred Avenue, just a little South of Assi Ghat. A grand platform had been erected on the road, directly overlooking the temple. Shiva and Sati were seated next to each other on specific thrones designed for them. Unlike their earlier public appearances, they were sitting stiff and apart. Shiva was not even looking at Sati, righteous anger still radiating from every pore in his body. He had only come for the puja and would return to the Branga residence as soon as it was over.

Every citizen of Kashi, who had never seen Shiva's

temper, was deeply troubled. But none more than Kartik. He had been pestering both his parents to get back together. Knowing Kartik would get even more insistent if he saw the both of them together, Shiva had told Krittika to take Kartik to the park adjoining the nearby Sankat Mochan temple.

Next to Shiva on the platform built for the thrones, were Kali, Bhagirath, Dilipa, Athithigva and Ayurvati. Parvateshwar and Anandmayi were at the temple platform, where the Surya Pandit helped them consecrate their love with the purifying blessings of the Sun God.

To avoid an embarrassing situation, Ganesh had wisely declined his invitation to the puja.

While all of Kashi was at the puja, Ganesh sat by himself at the Sankat Mochan temple. He had first gone to the adjoining park to meet his little brother for the first time in ten days, carrying a sack full of mangoes. After a lively thirty minutes, Ganesh had retired to the temple, leaving Kartik to play with Krittika and his five bodyguards. He sat there quietly, gazing at Lord Hanuman, the most ardent devotee of Lord Ram.

Lord Hanuman was called *Sankat Mochan* for a reason. People believed he always *helped his devotees in a crisis.* Ganesh thought that even Lord Hanuman would find it impossible to help him get out of this mess. Neither could he imagine a life without his mother nor could he bear it if he became the reason for his parents living separately. He had decided to leave Kashi the next day. But he knew that he would spend the rest of his life pining for his mother, now that he had experienced her love.

He smiled as he heard the loud cacophony of Kartik's boisterous antics in the park.

The carefree laughter of a soul strongly nourished by his mother's love.

Ganesh sighed, knowing such carefree laughter would never be a part of his destiny. He drew out his sword, pulled a smooth stone and started doing what Kshatriyas usually do when they have nothing else to do: Sharpen their blades.

So lost was Ganesh in his thoughts that he paid heed to his gut instinct quite late. Something strange was happening in the park. He held his breath and listened. And then it hit him. The park had gone absolutely quiet. What had happened to the loud laughter of Kartik, Krittika and his companions?

Ganesh got up quickly, put his sword into his scabbard and started walking towards the park. And then he heard it. A low growl, followed by a deafening roar. The kill was nigh.

Lions!

Ganesh drew his sword and started sprinting. A man was stumbling towards him. One of the Kashi soldiers, who was slashed across his arm. The clear markings of sharp claws.

'How many?' Ganesh was loud enough for the soldier to hear even at a distance.

The Kashi soldier did not respond. He just stumbled forward, shell-shocked.

Ganesh reached him in no time, jolted him hard and repeated again. 'How many?'

'Thr...ee,' said the soldier.

'Get the Mahadev!'

The soldier still looked shocked.

Ganesh shook him again. 'Get the Mahadev! Now!'

The soldier started running towards the Sun temple as Ganesh turned towards the park.

The Kashi soldier knew what he was running away from and yet his feet were unsteady. Ganesh knew what he was running towards, but his pace was sure and strong.

He used a side stone as leverage to leap over the park fence without a sound.

He landed on the other side, close to a lioness busy crushing the broken neck of a soldier between her jaws, asphyxiating an already dead man. Ganesh slashed at her as he ran by, cutting through a major vein on her shoulder. Blood poured out of the lioness' wound as Ganesh raced towards Krittika, another Kashi soldier and Kartik, who were at the centre of the garden. Two other soldiers were lying dead in a far corner. Judging from their positions, they were probably the first to be killed.

Ganesh dashed to Krittika's side. They were hemmed in from one side by a lioness and a massive liger.

Bhoomidevi be merciful! They have followed us from Icchawar!

The other side was blocked off by the lioness whose shoulder was bleeding profusely after Ganesh's blow.

Kartik, his wooden sword drawn, was ready for battle. Ganesh knew Kartik was childishly brave enough to charge at the liger with just his wooden sword. He stood in front of his brother, with Krittika on one side and the soldier on the other.

'No way out,' whispered Krittika, sword drawn.

Ganesh knew Krittika was not a trained warrior. Her maternal instincts would drive her to protect Kartik, but she probably wouldn't be able to kill any of the cats. The soldier on the other side was shivering. He was unlikely to be much help.

Ganesh nodded towards the bleeding lioness limping towards them. 'She'll not last too long. I've cut a major vein.'

The liger was circling them while moving towards the front, as the lionesses flanked the humans. Ganesh knew it was only a matter of time. They were preparing for the charge.

'Pull back,' whispered Ganesh. 'Slowly.'

There was a hollow in the main trunk of a banyan tree behind them. Ganesh intended to push Kartik in there and defend it from the lionesses.

'We can't last long,' said Krittika. 'I'll try to distract them. You run with Kartik.'

Ganesh didn't turn towards Krittika, staring hard at the liger. But his admiration for Veerbhadra's wife shot up. She was willing to die for his brother.

'That won't work,' said Ganesh. 'I can't move fast enough with Kartik. The walls are high. Help is on its way. The Mahadev is coming. We just have to hold the lions off for some time.'

Krittika and the soldier followed Ganesh's lead as they edged slowly to the rear, pushing Kartik back. The liger and lionesses crept forward, their blind aggression from just a few moments earlier dissipating at the sight of the giant man holding a blood-stained sword.

A little while later, Kartik had been pushed into the banyan hollow, with the tree's hanging roots tied around it to prevent him from charging out. He was safe. At least for as long as Ganesh stood.

The cats charged. Ganesh was surprised to see the limping lioness bounding forward. Krittika was covering that area.

'Stay low!' shouted Ganesh. He couldn't move to support Krittika since the liger could charge through the opening to attack Kartik. 'Stay low Krittika! She's injured. She can't leap high!'

Krittika had held her sword low, waiting for the wounded lioness to reach her. But to her surprise, the big cat suddenly veered left. As Krittika was about to charge after her, she heard a blood-curdling scream.

The lioness from the other side had used the distraction and crept up to the Kashi soldier. He was screaming in agony as the lioness dragged his body back, slashing at him with her claws. The soldier kept screeching, trying to push the lioness back, hitting her with weak blows from his sword. She kept biting into him, finally getting a choke hold on the convulsing soldier's neck. Moments later he was dead.

The liger remained stationary in front of Ganesh, blocking any escape. The other lioness left the dead Kashi soldier and returned to position.

Ganesh breathed slowly. He marvelled at the intelligent, pack-hunting behaviour these animals were displaying.

'Stay low,' said Ganesh to Krittika. 'I will cover the liger and this lioness. You have to focus on the injured one. I cannot see to all three. These animals hunt as a pack. Whoever gets distracted is dead.'

Krittika nodded as the injured lioness started ambling towards her. The animal was losing too much blood from her shoulder injury. She was slow in her movements. Suddenly, she charged at Krittika.

As the lioness came close, she leapt high. As high as her injured shoulder allowed. It was a weak jump. Krittika bent low, holding her sword up high, brutally stabbing it into the lioness' heart. The beast fell on Krittika and was soon dead.

Ganesh glanced at Krittika out of the corner of his eye. Before being felled, the lioness had managed to dig her claws into Krittika and rip away a part of her shoulder. Krittika was bleeding profusely, practically immobile under the lioness' corpse which was pinning her down. But she was alive. She had Ganesh in her line of sight.

Ganesh flipped his shield onto his back, pulled out his second shorter sword and stood close to the banyan tree. The short sword had a twin blade, which clipped together as the victim's body moved. It was a fearsome weapon if it was stabbed deep into a body as it would cut again and again.

Ganesh waited, biding time, hoping the Mahadev would arrive before it was too late.

The liger moved to Ganesh's right. The lioness to his left. There was enough distance between the beasts to make it difficult for Ganesh to observe both of them at the same time. Having established a good offensive position, the animals moved forward slowly, in sync.

The lioness suddenly charged. Ganesh lashed out with his left hand. But the shorter sword did not have the reach. The movement forced him to look left. The liger, taking advantage, charged into Ganesh and bit hard into his right leg, at the same spot that Ganesh had been injured in, at Icchawar.

Ganesh screamed in agony and swung hard with his right sword arm, slashing the liger across the face. The liger retreated, but not before he had bitten off a chunk of Ganesh's thigh.

Ganesh was losing blood fast. He stepped back, leaning against the banyan tree. His kid brother was screaming behind him. Shouting to be let out so that he could battle the lions too. Ganesh did not move. And the cats charged again.

This time the liger came first. Seeing a pattern in their attack, Ganesh kept his eyes dead centre, able to now see both the liger and lioness. He held his right sword out to stop the liger from coming in too close. The liger slowed down and the lioness came in faster. Ganesh jabbed hard with his short sword, straight into the lioness' shoulder, but not before she had bitten into Ganesh's limb. The lioness retreated with Ganesh's short, twin bladed sword buried in her shoulder after having left another gaping injury in Ganesh's left arm.

Ganesh knew that he couldn't stand on his feet much longer. He was losing too much blood. He did not want to fall sideways because Kartik would then become vulnerable. He fell back and sat against the tree, covering the hollow with his body. The animals would have to go through him to get to his brother.

Due to the severe loss of blood, Ganesh's vision was beginning to blur. But despite that, he could see that the wound on the lioness had been telling. She was still struggling at a distance from him, trying to lick her shoulder, unable to stand straight. As she moved, the twin-blade cut further into her, hacking tissue away from bone. He saw the liger moving in from the right, edging closer. Once close enough, the liger bounded and lashed out with his paw while Ganesh slashed with his sword at the same time. The liger's claws tore through Ganesh's face, causing a deep gash on his long nose. Simultaneously, Ganesh's blow gouged the liger's left eye. The animal retreated, howling in agony.

But Kartik had seen what Ganesh hadn't. He was trying

to reach out with his wooden sword. But he couldn't get far enough. 'Dada! Look out!'

The lioness had used Ganesh's distraction to crawl closer. She lunged forward and bit into Ganesh's chest. Ganesh swung his blade, slashing her face. The lioness retreated, snarling in pain, but not before ripping out a large amount of flesh from Ganesh's torso. The Naga's heart, pumping blood and adrenaline through the body at a furious rate, was now working against him as the numerous wounds leaked blood alarmingly.

Ganesh knew his end was near. He couldn't last much longer. And then he heard a loud war cry.

'HAR HAR MAHADEV!'

A warm, comforting darkness was beckoning Ganesh. He struggled to stay awake.

Nearly fifty furious Suryavanshi soldiers charged into the park. They fell upon the two big cats. The weakened animals did not stand a chance and were soon killed.

Through his rapidly fading vision, Ganesh thought he saw a handsome figure rushing towards him, bloodied sword held to the side. His throat, an iridescent blue. Behind the man, he could barely make out the blurred vision of a bronzed woman racing towards him. A warrior Princess, the blood of the liger splattered all over her.

The Naga smiled, delighted to be the bearer of good news to two of the most important people in his world.

'Don't worry... *baba*,' whispered Ganesh to his *father*. 'Your son is safe... He is hidden... behind me.'

Saying so, Ganesh collapsed. Unconscious.

Chapter 20

Never Alone, My Brother

Ganesh thought he should feel pain. But there was nothing.

He opened his eyes. He could barely distinguish the formidable Ayurvati next to his body.

He shifted his eyes down towards his ravaged body; skin torn asunder, flesh ripped out, blood congealed all over, arm bone sticking out, a gaping hole in his chest, ribs cracked and visible.

Bhoomidevi be merciful. I don't stand a chance.

Ganesh returned to darkness.

— ⁂ —

A sharp sting on his chest. His eyes opened slowly. Barely.

Through the slits, he could see Ayurvati changing his dressing.

He could feel again.

A good thing, right?

He slipped into his dream world once again.

— ⁂ —

A soft caress. Then the hand moved away. A sleeping Ganesh moved his head. He wanted the hand back. It returned to his face, stroking it gently.

Ganesh opened his eyes slightly. Sati was sitting next to him, leaning over, her eyes swollen, red.

Maa.

But Sati didn't respond. Maybe she hadn't heard him.

Ganesh could see outside the window behind Sati. It was raining.

The monsoons? How long have I been unconscious?

Ganesh saw a man leaning next to the window, against the wall. A strong man, whose normally mischievous eyes were expressionless. A man with a blue throat. A man staring intensely at him. Trying to figure him out.

Sleep snatched Ganesh away yet again.

— ⁂ —

A warm touch on his arm. Someone was gently applying the ointment on him.

The Naga opened his eyes slowly. And was surprised to see the hand applying the medicine so tenderly was not soft and feminine, but strong and masculine.

He turned his eyes slowly to see the kindly doctor. The torso was powerful and muscled. But the neck! It was different. It radiated a divine blue light.

Ganesh was stunned. A gasp escaped his mouth.

The hand applying the medicine froze. Ganesh could feel a pair of eyes boring into him. And then the Neelkanth rose and left the room.

Ganesh shut his eyes again.

— ⁂ —

Ganesh finally emerged from his sleepy cocoon after a long, long time without the immediate need to slip back into its safety. He could hear the soft pitter-patter of raindrops.

He loved the monsoon. The heavenly whiff of a rejuvenated earth. The melody of falling rain.

He turned his head slightly to his left. It was enough to wake Sati. She immediately rose from her bed at the far end of the room and walked up to Ganesh. She pulled a chair up close and rested her hand on her son's.

'How are you, my son?'

Ganesh smiled softly. He turned his head a little more.

Sati smiled and ran her fingers across her son's face. She knew he liked that.

'Krittika?'

'She's much better,' said Sati. 'She wasn't as badly injured as you. In fact she was out of the ayuralay very quickly. Just two weeks.'

'How long...?'

'How long have you been here?'

Ganesh nodded in reply.

'Sixty days. In and out of consciousness.'

'Rains...'

'The monsoon is almost over. The moisture led to complications, slowing down your healing process.'

Ganesh took a deep breath. He was tired.

'Go to sleep,' said Sati. 'Ayurvati ji says you are well on the road to recovery. You will be out of here soon.'

Ganesh smiled and went back to sleep.

— ⅄⦾Ʊ⇑⊗ —

Ganesh was woken up abruptly by Ayurvati, who was staring at him pointedly.

'How long have I been sleeping?'

'Since the last time you were awake? A few hours. I sent your mother home. She needs to rest.'

Ganesh nodded.

Ayurvati picked some paste she had kneaded. 'Open your mouth.'

Ganesh winced at the foul smelling paste. 'What is this, Ayurvati ji?'

'It will make the pain go away.'

'But I don't feel any pain.'

'You will when I apply the ointment. So open your mouth and keep it under your tongue.'

Ayurvati waited for the medicine to take effect. Then she opened the dressing on Ganesh's chest. His wound had healed dramatically. Flesh had filled up and some scar tissue had formed.

'The skin will smoothen out,' said an aloof Ayurvati.

'I'm a warrior,' smiled Ganesh. 'Scars are more welcome than smooth skin.'

Ayurvati stared at Ganesh, impassive. Then she picked up a bowl.

Ganesh held his breath as Ayurvati started applying the ointment. Despite the anaesthetic, the ointment still stung. She finished applying the paste quickly and covered the wound again with a bandage of neem leaves.

Ayurvati was quick, efficient and sure, qualities that Ganesh admired deeply.

The Lord of the People took a deep breath, gathering some strength. 'I didn't think I would survive. Your reputation is truly deserved, Ayurvati ji.'

Ayurvati frowned. 'Where did you hear of me?'

'I was injured in Icchawar as well. And *Maa* told me that you could have healed me twice as fast. She said that you are the best doctor in the world.'

Ayurvati raised her eyebrows. 'You have a silver tongue. Capable of making anyone smile. Just like the Lord Neelkanth. It's sad you don't have his untainted heart.'

Ganesh kept quiet.

'I admired Brahaspati. He was not just a good man, but a fount of knowledge. The world suffered when he died before his time.'

Ganesh did not respond, his sad eyes looking deep into the doctor's eyes.

'Now, let me look at that arm,' said Ayurvati.

She yanked his bandage open. Hard enough to make it sting, but soft enough to not cause any serious damage.

Ganesh didn't flinch.

— ⁂ —

The next day, Ganesh woke up to find his mother and aunt in the room, whispering.

'*Maa*, *Mausi*,' whispered Ganesh.

Both the sisters turned to him with a smile.

'Do you want something to eat or drink?' asked Sati.

'Yes, *Maa*. But can I also go for a walk today? I've been sleeping for sixty days. This is terrible.'

Kali smiled. 'I'll speak with Ayurvati. For now, stay put.'

As Kali left to find Ayurvati, Sati pulled her chair closer to Ganesh.

'I've got *parathas* for you,' said Sati, opening a small ivory box that she was carrying.

Ganesh beamed. He absolutely loved the stuffed *flat breads* his mother made. But his smile vanished just as quickly when he remembered that so did his step-father, Shiva.

Sati rose to find the mouth rinse Ayurvati had prescribed for Ganesh before he could eat.

'Has father returned to your quarters, *Maa*?'

Sati looked back from the medicine cabinet. 'Now you don't worry about these things.'

'Has he started speaking to you at least?'

'You needn't worry about this,' said Sati as she walked back to Ganesh.

The Naga was staring at the ceiling, guilt gnawing at his heart. He narrowed his eyes. 'Did he...'

'Yes he did,' replied Sati. 'Shiva came to check on you every day. But I don't think he'll be coming from today.'

Ganesh smiled sadly and bit his lip.

Sati patted him on the head. 'Everything will become all right when it is meant to become all right.'

'I wish I could explain what happened at Mount Mandar. I wish I could explain why it happened. I don't know if he would forgive me. But at least he would understand.'

'Kali has told me a little bit. I understand somewhat. But Brahaspati ji? He was a great man. The world lost something when he died. Even I cannot understand completely. And Shiva loved him like a brother. How can we expect him to understand?'

Ganesh looked at Sati with sad eyes.

'But you saved Kartik's life,' said Sati. 'You saved me. I know that's worth a lot to Shiva. Give him time. He will come around.'

Ganesh remained silent, clearly sceptical.

— ⸻ —

The next day, with Ayurvati's permission, Ganesh left his ayuralay room to take a short walk in the garden next door to Athithigva's grand palace. Ganesh walked slowly, leaning on Kali's shoulder, with a walking stick taking the bulk of his weight. He had wanted to walk alone, but Kali would hear none of it. As they reached the garden, they heard the loud sounds of clashing steel.

Ganesh narrowed his eyes. 'Someone's practicing. Practicing hard!'

Kali smiled. She knew Ganesh liked nothing better than seeing warriors practice. 'Let's go.'

The Naga Queen helped Ganesh to the central area of the garden. Ganesh was, meanwhile, commenting on the quality of the practise, based on the sounds he heard. 'Quick moves. These are steel swords, not meant for practice. Accomplished warriors duel over there.'

Kali simply helped Ganesh through the fence gate.

As they entered, Ganesh recoiled. Kali strengthened her hold on him. 'Relax. He is not in danger.'

At a distance, Kartik was engaged in a furious duel with Parvateshwar. He was moving at a speed that shocked Ganesh. The three-year-old may have been the size of a seven-year-old, but he was still significantly smaller than the gargantuan Parvateshwar. The Meluhan General was swinging hard with his sword. But Kartik was using his size to devastating effect. He bent low, forcing Parvateshwar to sweep lower with his sword, an action that most skilled swordsmen were not good at. Nobody trained to battle midgets. Kartik also had the ability to jab and swing with shattering speed and accuracy, swinging up at Parvateshwar at an angle that any grown man would have found impossible to defend. In just a few minutes,

Kartik had already stopped short of three deathly blows at the Meluhan General, all in the lower torso area.

Ganesh stood gaping.

'He's been practicing every day since you were injured,' said Kali.

Ganesh was even more amazed by something he had seen only a handful of warriors do. 'Kartik uses two swords simultaneously.'

'Yes,' smiled Kali. 'He doesn't use a shield. He strikes with his left hand also. The boy says that offence is better than defence!'

Ganesh heard Sati's voice speak out loudly. 'Stop!'

He turned to see his mother rise from a ledge at the corner.

'Sorry to disturb you, *Pitratulya,*' said Sati to Parvateshwar, the man she respected *like a father*. 'But perhaps Kartik may want to meet his dada.'

Parvateshwar looked up at Ganesh. The Meluhan General did not acknowledge Sati's older son, not even a curt nod. He simply stepped back.

Kartik smiled at seeing Ganesh ambling slowly towards him. Ganesh was shocked at the change in Kartik. His eyes didn't have the innocent look of a little boy anymore. They had steel in them. Pure, unadulterated steel.

'You fight very well, brother,' said Ganesh. 'I didn't know.'

Kartik hugged his brother, holding him tight. The embrace hurt Ganesh's wounds, but he didn't flinch or pull back.

The boy stepped back. 'You will never again fight alone, dada. Never.'

Ganesh smiled and embraced his little brother once again, his eyes moist.

The Naga noticed that Sati and Kali were silent. He

looked up to see Parvateshwar turning towards the gate. Parvateshwar banged his right fist on his chest and bowed low, executing the Meluhan military salute. Ganesh turned in the direction Parvateshwar was facing.

At the gate stood Shiva. Arms crossed across his chest. Expression blank. His hair windswept and clothes fluttering in the breeze. Staring at Ganesh.

Ganesh, with Kartik still in his embrace, bowed low in respect to the Neelkanth. When he straightened up, Shiva was gone.

— ⁂ —

'He may not be such a bad man, Shiva,' said Veerbhadra, exhaling the marijuana fumes softly.

Shiva looked up with a deadpan expression. Nandi looked at Veerbhadra in alarm.

But Veerbhadra was adamant. 'We don't know everything about him, Shiva. I spoke to Parshuram. It was Ganesh who assisted him, the one who helped him fight against the injustices he faced. Apparently, Parshuram had been grievously injured when the Brangas first attacked him. Ganesh found the wounded Brahmin on the banks of the Madhumati and rescued him. On hearing Parshuram's terrible story, he also swore to support him in any way that he could.'

Shiva simply took the chillum from Veerbhadra and took a deep drag, not saying a word.

'You know what Krittika said. Ganesh fought like a man possessed to save Kartik, nearly sacrificing his own life in the process. Krittika is a good judge of character. She says that Ganesh has a heart of gold.'

Shiva kept quiet, exhaling smoke.

'I heard from Queen Kali,' continued Veerbhadra, 'that it was Ganesh who arranged for the Naga medicine which saved Kartik's life during his birth.'

Shiva looked up, surprised. He narrowed his eyes. 'He is a strange man. I don't know what to make of him. He has saved my son's life. Twice, if I am to believe you. He saved my wife's life in Icchawar. For all this I must love him. But when I look at him, I hear Brahaspati's desperate cry for help ring in my ears. And then, I want nothing more than to cut off his head.'

Veerbhadra looked down, unhappy.

The Neelkanth shook his head. 'But I know of a man that I definitely want answers from.'

Veerbhadra looked up at him, suspecting his friend's train of thought. 'His Highness?'

'Yes,' said Shiva. 'Kali and Ganesh could not have been abandoned without his consent.'

Nandi piped up for his Emperor. 'But My Lord, Emperor Daksha had no choice. That is the law. Naga children cannot live in Meluha.'

'Well, isn't it also the law that the Naga's mother has to leave society? That the mother should be told the truth about her child?' asked Shiva. 'Laws cannot be applied selectively.'

Nandi kept quiet.

'I don't doubt the love the Emperor has for Sati,' said Shiva. 'But didn't he realise how much he was going to end up hurting Sati by banishing her son?'

Veerbhadra nodded.

'He hid this fact from her all her life. He even hid her twin sister's existence. I always thought the way he examined Kartik's body at birth was strange. Now it makes sense. He acted as though he was almost expecting another Naga.'

'Hmm,' said Veerbhadra.

'And I have a dirty feeling that this is not where the story ends.'

'What do you mean?'

'I suspect that Chandandhwaj did not die naturally.'

'Her first husband?'

'Yes. It is just too convenient that he drowned the day Ganesh was born.'

'My Lord!' Nandi spoke up in shock. 'But that cannot be true. That is a crime. No Suryavanshi ruler will ever stoop so low.'

'I'm not saying that I know for sure, Nandi,' said Shiva. 'It is just a feeling that I have. Remember nobody is good or bad. They are either strong or weak. Strong people stick to their morals, no matter what the trials and tribulations. Weak people, many a times, do not even realise how low they have sunk.'

Nandi kept quiet.

Veerbhadra looked straight at Shiva. 'I will not be surprised if what you suspect is true. It may have been His Highness' twisted way of thinking that he is doing Sati a favour.'

Chapter 21

The Maika Mystery

It had been nearly three months since Ganesh had saved Kartik's life. Though still limping, he had recovered enough to know that he had to go back to Panchavati. He had been conscious for a month now. Each waking moment reminded him of the torment in his mother's heart. The rift between Shiva and Sati was more than he could bear. As far as he knew, the only way out was for him to leave.

'Let's leave tomorrow, *Mausi*,' said Ganesh.

'Have you told your mother?' asked Kali.

'I intend to leave a note for her.'

Kali narrowed her eyes.

'She will not let me go, even though she must.'

Kali took a deep breath. 'So you are just going to forget her?'

Ganesh smiled sadly. 'I have got enough love from her in the past few months to last me a lifetime. I can live on my memories. But she cannot live without the Neelkanth.'

A puzzled Shiva rose to receive Athithigva. The Kashi king had never stepped into the Branga quarters before. He had always waited for the Neelkanth outside.

'What is the matter, Your Highness?'

'My Lord, I just received word that Emperor Daksha is on his way to Kashi.'

Shiva frowned. 'I don't understand the urgency. If you have received word today, I'm sure the Emperor will not be here for another two to three months.'

'No, My Lord. He's coming today. In a few hours. I just received word from an advance party.'

Shiva raised his eyebrows, surprised beyond words.

'My Lord,' said Athithigva, 'I wanted to request you to come to the throne room to take your rightful place so that we may receive the Emperor.'

'I'll come,' said Shiva. 'But please ensure that only you are there. I do not want to receive him along with your courtiers.'

This was unorthodox. Athithigva frowned, but didn't question Shiva's unusual demand. He simply left to carry out the orders.

'Nandi, word may have been sent to Parvateshwar and Bhagirath as well,' said Shiva. 'Please tell them it is my wish that they do not come to the court right now. We will have a ceremonial welcome for His Highness a little later.'

'Yes, My Lord.' Nandi saluted and left.

Veerbhadra whispered to Shiva. 'You think he knows?'

'No. If I know anything about him, he wouldn't have come had he known that Kali and Ganesh were here. He has come in haste, without regard for protocol. It is the action of a father, not an Emperor. He was probably missing Sati and Kartik.'

'What do you want to do? Let it go or discover the truth?'

'No way will I let it go. I want to know the truth.'

Veerbhadra nodded.

'I hope for the sake of Sati,' said Shiva, 'that my suspicions are wrong. That he knew nothing. That the only thing that happened was that Maika's administrators followed the law.'

'But you fear you are right?' asked Veerbhadra.

'Yes.'

'Any idea how we can find out what actually happened that day?'

'Confront him. Catch him by surprise. This is the perfect time.'

Veerbhadra frowned.

'I intend to spring Kali and Ganesh on him,' said Shiva. 'His face will tell me the rest.'

'What is His Highness doing here?' asked Parvateshwar. 'Nobody told me of his plans. How can Kashi do this? This is a breach of protocol.'

'Nobody knew of this, My Lord,' said Nandi. 'Even King Athithigva got to know of it right now. Meluha sent no intimation earlier.'

Parvateshwar looked flabbergasted. Such slips in Meluhan diplomatic procedures were unheard of.

Bhagirath shrugged his shoulders. 'All kings are alike.'

Parvateshwar ignored the jibe aimed at the ruler of his realm about his lack of etiquette and protocol. He spoke to Nandi. 'Why does the Lord Neelkanth not want us to come to the throne room?'

'I couldn't say, My Lord,' replied Nandi. 'I'm just following orders.'

Parvateshwar nodded. 'All right. We'll stay here till the Lord calls us.'

— ⁂ —

'Shiva can have any number of reasons for wanting to meet Kali. But why Ganesh? What's going on?' asked Sati, frowning.

Veerbhadra was stumped. Not only was Ganesh in Kali's chamber, but so was Sati. Considering that Daksha was already in Kashi, he had to get Kali and Ganesh into the throne room as fast as he could. It was entirely possible that Daksha might find out about the presence of his Naga daughter and grandson. Time was of the essence. If their surprise meeting had to work, it had to happen now. Veerbhadra had no choice but to announce Shiva's summons to Kali and Ganesh.

'I'm just following orders, My Lady.'

'Following orders doesn't entail your not knowing what's going on.'

'He wants them to see something.'

'Bhadra,' said Sati. 'My husband is your best friend. You are married to my best friend. I know you. I know that you know more. I am not letting my son go till you tell me.'

Veerbhadra shook his head at Sati's doggedness. He could see what drew Shiva to Sati, despite their temporary estrangement. 'My Lady, your father is here.'

Sati was surprised. Partly at the unannounced appearance of her father, but more so at Shiva summoning Kali and Ganesh to meet Daksha.

Somewhere in his heart, Shiva actually believes that injustice had been done to my sister and son.

'Do you want to go?' Sati asked Kali.

The Naga Queen narrowed her eyes, hand tightening on her sword hilt. 'Yes! Even wild horses couldn't keep me away.'

Sati turned to her son. He didn't want a confrontation. He didn't want the truth to come out. To hurt his mother even more. He shook his head.

Kali spoke up in surprise. 'Why? What are you afraid of?'

'I don't want this, *Mausi*,' replied Ganesh.

'But I do!' said Sati. 'Your existence was hidden from me for ninety years.'

'But those were the rules, *Maa*,' said Ganesh.

'No, the rules are that a Naga child cannot live in Meluha. Hiding the truth from the mother is not part of the rules. Had I known, I would have left Meluha with you.'

'Even if the rule was broken, it's in the past. Please *Maa*, forget it.'

'I will not. I cannot. I want to know how much he knew. And if he did know, why did he lie? To protect his name? So that no one can accuse him of being the progenitor of Nagas? So that he can continue to rule?'

'*Maa*, nothing will come of this,' said Ganesh.

Kali started laughing. Ganesh turned to her in irritation.

'When you were scouring all of India to confront Sati, I had told you this very thing,' said Kali. 'And what had you said? You wanted answers. That you would not be at peace till you knew the truth about your relationship with your mother. That it would complete you. Then why can't your mother want or expect the same from her father?'

'But this is not completion, *Mausi*,' said Ganesh. 'This is only confrontation and pain.'

'Completion is completion, my child,' said Kali. 'Sometimes completion causes happiness and sometimes pain. Your mother has a right to do this.' Saying so, Kali turned to Sati. 'Are you sure you want to do this, *didi*?'

'I want answers,' said Sati.

Veerbhadra gulped. 'My Lady, Shiva only asked for Queen Kali and Lord Ganesh. Not you.'

'I'm coming, Bhadra,' said Sati. 'And you know very well that I must.'

Veerbhadra looked down. Sati was right. She had the right to be there.

'*Maa*...' whispered Ganesh.

'Ganesh, I am going,' said Sati firmly. 'You can either come along or not. That is your choice. But you cannot stop me.'

The Lord of the People took a deep breath, pulled his *angvastram* on his shoulder and said, 'Lead us on, brave Veerbhadra.'

— ⁂ —

'What a pleasant surprise to see you, Your Highness,' said Athithigva, bowing to the Emperor of India.

Daksha nodded as he entered the antechamber of the court. 'It is my empire, Athithigva. I think I can throw in a surprise or two!'

Athithigva smiled. Daksha had his wife Veerini in tow. She in turn was trailed by the famed Arishtanemi warriors, Mayashrenik and Vidyunmali. With Parvateshwar's absence from Swadweep, Mayashrenik had been appointed provisional General of Meluha's armed forces.

Daksha was surprised when he entered the main throne room, as the usual courtly nobles and officials were absent. Only Shiva and Nandi were present. Nandi immediately brought his fist up to his chest and bowed low to his Emperor. Daksha smiled at Nandi genially.

Shiva remained seated, joining his hands in a namaste. 'Welcome to Kashi, Your Highness.'

Daksha's smile disappeared. He was the Emperor of all of India. He deserved respect. Even if Shiva was the Neelkanth, protocol demanded that he stand up for the Emperor. In the past, Shiva had always done so. This was an insult.

'How are you, my son-in-law?' said Daksha, trying to keep his anger in check.

'I am well, Your Highness. Why don't you sit next to me?'

Daksha sat. So did Veerini and Athithigva.

Turning to Athithigva, Daksha said, 'For such a noisy city, you seem to run a very quiet court, Athithigva.'

Athithigva smiled. 'No My Lord, it's just that...'

'My apologies for interrupting, Your Highness,' said Shiva to Athithigva, before turning to Daksha. 'I thought it would be a good idea for you to meet your children in private.'

Veerini perked up immediately. 'Where are they, Lord Neelkanth?'

Just then Veerbhadra walked in. Followed by Sati.

'My child!' said a smiling Daksha, forgetting the slight from Shiva. 'Why didn't you bring my grandson along?'

'I have,' said Sati.

Ganesh entered the room. Behind him was Kali.

Shiva was staring hard at Daksha's face. The Meluhan

Emperor's eyes sprung wide open in recognition. His jaw dropped in shock.

He knows!

Then Daksha swallowed hard, straightening up.

He's afraid. He's hiding something.

Shiva also noticed Veerini's expression. Profound sadness. Eyebrows joined together, but her lips curled up slightly in a smile struggling to break through. Her eyes moist.

She knows too. And she loves them.

Daksha turned to Athithigva and blustered. 'How dare you consort with terrorists, King of Kashi?'

'They aren't terrorists,' said Sati. 'Terrorists kill innocents. Kali and Ganesh have never done that.'

'Does Sati speak for the King of Kashi now?'

'Don't speak to him, father,' said Sati. 'Speak to me.'

'What for?' asked Daksha, pointing at Ganesh and Kali. 'What do you have to do with them?'

'Everything! Their place is with me. Should have always been with me.'

'What? Vile Nagas have only one place. South of the Narmada! They are not allowed into the Sapt Sindhu!'

'My sister and son are not vile. They are my blood! Your blood!'

Daksha stood, stepping up to Sati. 'Sister! Son! What nonsense? Don't believe the rubbish these scum tell you. Of course, they hate me. They will say anything to malign me. I am their sworn enemy. I am the ruler of Meluha! Under oath to destroy them!'

Kali reached for her sword. 'I am in the mood to challenge you to an Agnipariksha right now, you repulsive goat!'

'Don't you have any shame?' Daksha shouted at Kali. 'Do penance for your past life sins quietly instead of creating bad blood between a loving father and his daughter! What lies have you told her about me?'

'They haven't said a word, father,' said Sati. 'But their existence says a lot about you.'

'It's not me. They exist because of your mother. Her past life sins have led to this. We never had Nagas in our family before her.'

Sati's jaw fell. She was seeing the levels to which her father could stoop to for the first time.

Veerini was staring at Daksha, silent anger smouldering in her eyes.

'This is not about past lives, father,' said Sati. 'It is about this life. You knew. Yet you didn't tell me.'

'I am your father. I have loved you all my life. I have fought the world for you. Will you trust me or some deformed animals?'

'They are not deformed animals! They are my family!'

'You want to make these people your family? People who lie to you? Who turn you against your own father?'

'They never lied to me!' shouted Sati. 'You did.'

'No, I did not!'

'You said my son was still born.'

Daksha took a deep breath, looked up at the ceiling as though struggling to regain control and then glared at Sati. 'Why don't you understand? I lied for your own good! Do you know what your life would have been like if you had been declared a Naga's mother?'

'I would be with my son!'

'What rubbish. What would you have done? Lived in Panchavati?'

'Yes!'

'You are my daughter!' screamed Daksha. 'I have always loved you more than anyone else. I would never have allowed you to suffer in Panchavati.'

'It wasn't your choice to make.'

An exasperated Daksha turned to Shiva. 'Talk some sense into her, Lord Neelkanth!'

Shiva's eyes were narrowed. He wanted to know how wide this web of deception spread. 'Did you get Chandandhwaj killed, Your Highness?'

Daksha blanched. Fear was written all over his face. He looked sharply at Sati and then quickly back at Shiva.

Oh Lord! He did!

Sati was reeling, shocked into absolute silence. Kali and Ganesh did not seem surprised.

Daksha immediately regained control. He pointed a finger at Shiva, his body shaking. 'You did this. You choreographed this!'

Shiva stayed quiet.

'You have turned my daughter against me,' screamed Daksha. 'Maharishi Bhrigu was right. The evil Vasudevs control you.'

Shiva continued to stare at Daksha, as if actually seeing him for the first time.

Daksha was boiling. 'What were you? A stupid tribal from a barbaric land. I made you the Neelkanth. I gave you power. I gave it to you so that you would bring the Chandravanshis under Meluhan control. So that I could establish peace in India. And you dare to use the power I bestowed upon you against me?'

Shiva remained passive, making Daksha spew even more venom.

'I made you. And, I can destroy you!'

Daksha pulled his knife out and lunged forward.

Nandi jumped in front of Shiva, taking the blow on his shield. His Meluhan training didn't allow him to draw his sword at his monarch. Kali and Ganesh, however, had no such compunctions, drawing their blades rapidly on Daksha. Ganesh jumped in front of Shiva even as Vidyunmali drew his sword. Mayashrenik, a loyal Meluhan who would have fought to the death for his King, was stunned into inaction. He was deeply devoted to Shiva. How could he draw his sword against the Neelkanth?

'Calm down,' said Shiva, raising his hand.

Vidyunmali still had his sword drawn. Daksha's knife had fallen to the ground.

Shiva spoke once again. 'Nandi, Ganesh, Kali, stand down. NOW!'

As Shiva's warriors lowered their swords, Vidyunmali also sheathed his blade.

'Your Highness,' Shiva addressed Daksha.

Daksha's eyes were glued on a teary-eyed Sati, who had her sword inches away from her father's throat. His face exhibited the sense of betrayal and loss he felt. Sati was the only person he had ever truly loved.

'Sati...' whispered Shiva. 'Please. Put it down. He's not worth it.'

Sati's sword inched closer.

Shiva stepped forward slowly. 'Sati...'

Her hands were shaking slightly, rage driving her dangerously close to the edge.

Shiva touched her shoulder lightly. 'Sati, put it down.'

Shiva's touch brought Sati back from the precipice.

She lowered her sword a little. Her eyes narrowed, her breathing heavy, her body stiff.

Daksha continued to stare at Sati.

'I am ashamed that your blood runs in my veins,' said Sati.

Tears began to flow down Daksha's face.

'Get out,' whispered Sati through gritted teeth.

Daksha was deathly still.

'GET OUT!'

Veerini got a jolt from Sati's loud voice. Her expression a mix of sadness and anger, she walked up to Daksha. 'Move.'

Daksha stood paralysed, shocked at this turn of events.

'Come on,' Veerini repeated louder, pulling her husband by his arm. 'Mayashrenik, Vidyunmali, let's leave.'

The Empress of India dragged her husband out of the room.

Sati was shattered. She dropped her sword, tears streaming down her face. Ganesh rushed towards her. But Shiva caught her even as she fell.

Sati was sobbing uncontrollably as Shiva picked her up in his arms.

Chapter 22

Two Sides, Same Coin

'So what are you thinking?' asked Kali.

Ganesh and Kali were in the Naga queen's quarters. After the drama that had unfolded earlier in the day, Shiva had carried Sati over to their room in Athithigva's palace. Daksha, Veerini and their entourage had departed immediately for the Meluhan capital, Devagiri.

'This was unexpected,' said a pensive Ganesh with a slight smile.

Kali raised her eyes. 'Sometimes your stoicism can be very irritating!'

Ganesh smiled. A rare broad smile from one floppy ear to the other, his extended teeth stretching further out.

'Now that's the face I want to see more of,' said Kali. 'You actually look cute.'

Ganesh's face turned serious again. He raised a papyrus scroll. A message from Panchavati. 'I would have been laughing, *Mausi*. But for this.'

'What now?' asked Kali, frowning.

'It's a failure.'

'Again?'

'Yes, again.'

'But I thought...'

'We thought wrong, *Mausi*.'

Kali cursed. Ganesh stared at his aunt. He could feel her frustration. A final solution was so close. Its success would have completed their victory. Now, there was every chance that everything they had done would be lost.

'Do we try again?' asked Kali.

'I think we have to finally accept the truth, *Mausi*. This route is a dead end. We have no choice. The time has come to reveal the secret.'

'Yes,' said Kali. 'The Neelkanth should know.'

'The Neelkanth?' asked Ganesh, surprised at how much had changed in such a short span.

Kali frowned.

'You didn't use his name. You said the Neelkanth. You believe the legend now?'

Kali smiled. 'I don't believe in legends. Never have, never will. But I believe in him.'

How different would my life have been if fate had blessed me with a man like Shiva. Maybe like didi, *all the poison could have been sucked out of my life as well. Perhaps, even I would have found happiness and peace.*

'We have to show him the secret,' said Ganesh, intruding into Kali's thoughts.

'Show him?!'

'I don't think it can be done here, right? He must see for himself.'

'You want to take him to Panchavati?'

'Why not?' asked Ganesh. 'Don't you trust him?'

'Of course, I do. I would trust him with my life. But he doesn't come alone. There are others who come with him. If we take them along, they will know how to get to Panchavati. This will weaken our defences.'

'I think people like Parvateshwar and Bhagirath can be trusted, *Mausi.* I don't think they will ever go against the Neelkanth. They would give their lives for him.'

'If there is one thing I have learnt in life,' said Kali, 'it is that one should not spread one's trust too thin. And, never take things for granted.'

Ganesh frowned. 'If you doubt all his followers, then what about Parshuram? He already knows the way. You know his devotion to the Neelkanth.'

'Remember, I had told you not to bring Parshuram to Panchavati. But you didn't listen.'

'So, now what, *Mausi*?'

'We'll take them through Branga. They will know how to get to Panchavati, but only from Chandraketu's realm. They will never be able to reach us directly from their own kingdoms. The forests of Dandak would consume them if they were to even try! We can trust the Brangas to not let anyone pass without our permission. Even Parshuram doesn't know any other way.'

Ganesh nodded. 'That is a good idea.'

— ⁂ —

'Thank the Lord, I didn't do anything rash that I would have regretted later,' said Sati.

Shiva was sitting on a long chair in the balcony of their chambers. Sati was on his lap, her head leaning against his muscular chest, her eyes swollen red. From the heights of the Kashi palace, the Sacred Avenue and the Vishwanath temple were clearly visible. Beyond them flowed the mighty Ganga.

'Your anger was justified, my darling.'

Sati looked up at her husband, breathing slowly. 'Aren't you angry? He actually tried to kill you.'

Shiva stared into his wife's eyes as he ran his hand across her face. 'My anger towards your father is because of what he did to you, not what he tried to do to me.'

'But how dare Vidyunmali draw his sword upon you?' whispered Sati. 'Thank God, Ganesh...'

Sati stopped, afraid that her taking Ganesh's name would ruin this moment.

Shiva gave her a gentle squeeze. 'He's your son.'

Sati kept quiet, body stiff, feeling the intense pain that Shiva felt at Brahaspati's loss.

Shiva held Sati's face and looked straight into her eyes. 'No matter how hard I try, I cannot hate a part of your soul.'

Sati sighed as fresh tears escaped silently from her eyes. She held Shiva tight. Shiva did not want to spoil the moment as he held onto his wife. One thing continued to puzzle him. Who's Bhrigu?

— ⁂ —

'The Emperor had got Chandandhwaj killed?' asked a shocked Parvateshwar.

'Yes, General,' said Veerbhadra.

Parvateshwar, numb with shock, looked at Anandmayi and Bhagirath. Then back at Veerbhadra. 'Where is His Highness now?'

'He's on his way back to Meluha, My Lord,' said Veerbhadra.

Parvateshwar held his head. His Emperor had brought

dishonour to Meluha, his motherland. He couldn't even imagine the pain this revelation must have caused to the woman he had always looked upon as the daughter he had never had. 'Where is Sati?'

'She's with Shiva, My Lord.'

Anandmayi looked at Parvateshwar with a smile. At least some good had come out of this sordid episode.

— ⁂ —

The Meluhan royal ship cruised slowly up the Ganga, four ships sailing around it in the standard Suryavanshi defensive naval protocol. Daksha's entourage was on its way home, a day away from Kashi.

Mayashrenik was in the lead boat, maintaining a steady pace. He was still shaken by the incidents at Kashi. He hoped his Emperor Daksha and the Neelkanth would reconcile their differences. He wished to avoid the terrible fate of having to choose between his loyalty to his country and his devotion to his God.

Vidyunmali was in-charge of security on Daksha's ship. He wanted to safeguard against any assassination attempt upon his Emperor by the followers of the Neelkanth. Even though it seemed unlikely, he wanted to take all the possible precautions.

Veerini sat in the royal chambers of the central ship, next to a window, watching the Ganga lap against the ship. She sensed that she had lost all her children now. She turned in anger towards her husband.

Daksha was lying on the bed, eyes forlorn, a lost look on his face. It wasn't the first time he had faced and been overpowered by such terrible circumstances.

Veerini shook her head and turned to look out again.

If only he had listened to me.

Veerini remembered that incident so clearly it was as if it had happened just yesterday. Almost every day, she wondered how her life would have been if things had turned out differently.

It had happened more than a hundred years ago. Sati had just returned from the Maika gurukul, a headstrong, idealistic girl of sixteen. In keeping with her character, she had jumped in to save an immigrant woman from a vicious pack of wild dogs. Parvateshwar and Daksha had rushed in to her rescue. While they had managed to push back the dogs, Daksha had been seriously injured.

Veerini had accompanied Daksha to the ayuralay where the doctors could examine her husband. The most worrying injury was on his left leg, where a dog had ripped out some flesh, cutting through a major blood vessel. The loss of blood had made Daksha lose consciousness.

When he had opened his eyes after a few hours, Daksha's first thought was of his young daughter. 'Sati?'

'She's with Parvateshwar,' said Veerini, as she came closer to her husband and held his hand. 'Don't worry about her.'

'I screamed at her. I didn't mean to.'

'I know. She was only doing her duty. She did the right thing, trying to protect that woman. I'll tell her that...'

'No. No. I still think she shouldn't have risked her life for that woman. I didn't mean to scream at her, that's all.'

Veerini's eyes narrowed to slits. Her husband couldn't be any less Suryavanshi. She was about to say something when the door opened and Brahmanayak walked in.

Brahmanayak, Daksha's father and ruler of Meluha, was

a tall, imposing figure. Long black hair, a well manicured beard, a practically hairless body, a sober crown and understated white clothes could not camouflage the indomitable spirit of the man. He set impossible standards for all those around him with his own great deeds. He was not just respected, but also feared in all of Meluha. Obsessive about the honour and respect that his empire should garner, his son's lack of courage and character was a source of anger and dismay for him.

Veerini immediately arose and stepped back quietly. Brahmanayak never spoke to her unless to give orders. Behind Brahmanayak was the kindly doctor who had stitched up Daksha's leg after the severe mauling it had received.

Brahmanayak, in a matter of fact manner, lifted the sheet to look at his son's leg. There was a bandage of neem leaves tied around it.

The doctor smiled genially. 'Your Highness, your son will be back on his feet in a week or two. I have been very careful. The scars will be minimal.'

Daksha looked for a brief instant at his father. Then, with his chest puffed up, he whispered, 'No doctor. Scars are the pride of any Kshatriya.'

Brahmanayak snorted. 'What would you know about being a Kshatriya?'

Daksha fell silent. Veerini began seething with anger.

'You let some dogs do this to you?' asked Brahmanayak, contemptuously. 'I am the laughing stock of Meluha. Perhaps even the world. My son cannot even kill a dog all by himself.'

Daksha kept staring at his father.

To prevent a further escalation of hostility and to

safeguard the patient's mental health, the doctor cut in, 'Your Highness, I need to discuss something with you. May we talk outside?'

Brahmanayak nodded. 'I haven't finished,' he said, turning to Daksha, before walking out of the chamber.

A livid Veerini stepped up to her husband, who was crying now. 'How long are you going to tolerate this?'

Daksha suddenly turned ferocious. 'He's my father! Speak of him with respect.'

'He does not care about you, Daksha,' said Veerini. 'All that he cares about is his legacy. You don't even want to be King. So what are we doing here?'

'My duty. I have to stay by his side. I am his son.'

'He doesn't think so. You are only someone who would carry forward his name, his legacy. That's all.'

Daksha fell silent.

'He has forced you to give up one daughter. How much more are you going to sacrifice?'

'She's not my daughter!'

'She is! Kali is as much your flesh and blood as Sati is.'

'I am not discussing this again.'

'You have thought about it so many times. For once, have the courage to follow through.'

'What will we do in Panchavati?'

'Doesn't matter. What matters is what we'll be.'

Daksha shook his head. 'And what do you think we'll be?'

'We'll be happy!'

'But I cannot leave Sati behind.'

'Who's asking you to leave her behind? All I want is to unite my family.'

'What?! Why should Sati live in Panchavati? She's not a

Naga. You and I have past life sins that have to be atoned, sins for which we have been punished. Why should she be punished?'

'The real punishment is the separation from her sister. The real punishment is to see her father being humiliated every day.'

Daksha remained silent, wavering.

'Daksha, trust me,' said Veerini. 'We'll be happy in Panchavati. If there was any other place where we could live with both Kali and Sati, I'd suggest that. But there isn't.'

Daksha breathed deeply. 'But how...'

'You leave that to me. I'll make the arrangements. Just say yes. Your father is leaving tomorrow for Karachapa. You are not so badly injured that you can't travel. We'll be in Panchavati before he knows you're gone.'

Daksha stared at Veerini. 'But...'

'Trust me. Please trust me. It will be for all our good. I know you love me. I know you love your daughters. I know you don't care about anything else. Just trust me.'

Daksha nodded.

Veerini smiled, bent closer and kissed her husband. 'I'll make the arrangements.'

A happy Veerini turned and walked out of the room. She had a lot to do.

As she stepped out, she saw Sati and Parvateshwar sitting outside. She patted Sati on her head. 'Go in, my child. Tell your father how much you love him. He needs you. I'll be back soon.'

As Veerini was hurrying away, she saw Brahmanayak walking back towards her husband's chamber.

The Meluhan Queen was jolted back to the present

by some dolphin calls. The more than a century old memory still drew a tear from her eyes. She turned to look at her husband and shook her head. She had never really understood what happened that day. What had Bramhanayak said? All she knew was that when she had gone back to Daksha's chamber the next day with their escape plans, he had refused to leave. He had decided that he wanted to become Emperor.

Your stupid ego and need for approval from your father destroyed our lives!

'The secret?' asked Shiva, recalling his conversation with Parshuram.

Shiva was sitting with Parshuram, Parvateshwar, Veerbhadra and Nandi. Kali had just entered the chamber. Ganesh, still unsure of his position vis-a-vis Shiva, was standing quietly at the back. Shiva had acknowledged Sati's elder son with a short nod, nothing more.

'Yes, I think you need to know,' said Kali. 'It is India's need that the Neelkanth know the secret the Nagas have been keeping. Thereafter, you can decide whether what we have done is right or wrong. Determine what must be done now.'

'Why can't you tell me here?'

'I need you to trust me. I can't.'

Shiva's eyes bored into Kali's. He could see no malice or deceit in them. He felt he could trust her. 'How many days will it take to reach Panchavati?'

'A little more than a year,' answered Kali.

'A year?!'

'Yes, Lord Neelkanth. We will travel up to Branga by river boats, right down the Madhumati river. Then travel by foot through the *Dandakaranya*. The journey takes time.'

'There is no direct route?'

Kali smiled but refused to be drawn in. She didn't want to reveal the secrets of the *forests of Dandak*. It was the primary defence for her city.

'I'm trusting you. But it appears that you don't trust me.'

'I trust you completely, Lord Neelkanth.'

Shiva smiled, understanding Kali's predicament. She could trust him but not everyone with him. 'All right. Let's go to Panchavati. It is perhaps the route I have to take in order to discharge my duty.'

Shiva turned to Parvateshwar. 'Can you make the arrangements, General?'

'It will be done, My Lord,' said Parvateshwar.

Kali bowed towards Shiva and turned to leave, stretching her hand out to Ganesh.

'And, Kali...' said Shiva.

Kali spun around.

'I prefer Shiva, not Neelkanth. You are my wife's sister. You are family.'

Kali smiled and bowed her head. 'As you wish... Shiva.'

Shiva and Sati were at the Vishwanath temple. They had come to perform a private puja, seeking Lord Rudra's blessings. Having completed their prayers, they sat against one of the pillars of the temple, looking out towards the idol of Lady Mohini, whose statue was at the back of Lord Rudra's idol.

Shiva reached out for his wife's hand and kissed it lightly. She smiled and rested her head on his shoulder.

'A very intriguing lady,' said Shiva.

Sati looked up at her husband. 'Lady Mohini?'

'Yes. Why isn't she universally accepted as a Vishnu? Why has the number of Vishnus stopped at seven?'

'There may be more Vishnus in the future. But not everyone regards her as a Vishnu.'

'Do you?'

'At one point of time, I didn't. But now, I have come to understand her greatness.'

Shiva frowned.

'It's not easy to understand her,' said Sati. 'There were many things that she did which can be considered unjust. It does not matter that she did those things to the Asuras. They were still unfair. To Suryavanshis, who follow the absolutes of Lord Ram, she is difficult to understand.'

'So what's changed now?'

'I've come to know more of her. About why she did what she did. So I still don't appreciate some of the things that she did, but perhaps I have more compassion for her actions.'

'A Vasudev had once told me that they believe Lord Rudra could not have completed his mission without her support.'

Sati looked at Shiva. 'They may be right. Maybe, just maybe, sometimes, a small sin can lead to a greater good.'

Shiva stared at Sati. He could see where she was going with this.

'If a man has been good all his life despite the unkindness he has faced, if he has helped others, we should try to understand why he committed what appears to be a sin.

We may not be able to forgive him. However, we may be able to understand him.'

Shiva knew Sati was talking about Ganesh. 'Do you understand why he did what he did?'

Sati took a deep breath. 'No.'

Shiva turned his gaze towards Lady Mohini's statue.

Sati pulled Shiva's face back towards her. 'Sometimes it's difficult to understand an event without knowing everything that led up to it.'

Shiva turned his face away. He shut his eyes and breathed deeply. 'He saved your life. He saved Kartik's life. For that I must love him. He has done much to make me think that he is a good man.'

Sati remained silent.

'But...' Shiva took a deep breath. 'But it's not easy for me. Sati... I just can't...'

Sati sighed. *Perhaps going to Panchavati may make everything clear.*

— ⁂ —

'My Lord, what are you saying? How can I?' asked a flabbergasted Dilipa.

He was sitting at Maharishi Bhrigu's feet in his private chambers in his palace at Ayodhya. Prime Minister Siamantak had become a past master at keeping Bhrigu's frequent visits to Ayodhya a secret. The Maharishi's medicines were working their magic. Dilipa was looking healthier with every passing day.

'Are you refusing to help, Your Highness?' Bhrigu's voice was menacing, eyes narrowed.

'No, My Lord. Of course not. But this is impossible.'

'I will show you the way.'

'But how can I do it all by myself?'

'You will have allies. I'll guarantee that.'

'But an attack such as this? What if someone finds out? My own people will turn against me.'

'Nobody will find out.'

Dilipa looked disturbed. *What have I got myself into?*

'Why? Why is this needed, Maharishi ji?'

'For the good of India.'

Dilipa remained silent, worry lines on his face.

Bhrigu knew the self-obsessed Dilipa would not particularly care about the larger cause. So he decided to make it very personal. 'You also need to do this, Your Highness, if you want to prevent disease from eating up your body.'

Dilipa stared at Bhrigu. The threat was clear and overt. He bowed his head. 'Tell me how, Maharishi ji.'

Within two months of the Naga Queen's request to Shiva, Parvateshwar had made arrangements for travelling to Panchavati.

Shiva's entourage had grown considerably since the time he had sailed into the city where the supreme light shines. Accompanying Shiva on the voyage was his entire family, as the Mahadev refused to leave Sati and Kartik behind. Kali and Ganesh obviously had to be there. Veerbhadra and Nandi were fixtures of the Neelkanth's retinue. And Veerbhadra had insisted on his wife Krittika accompanying him this time, not just because they missed each other, but also as he knew she would not be able to bear parting company from Kartik for so long. Ayurvati was the obvious choice for the physician on board. Shiva also wanted Bhagirath and Parshuram with him. And Parvateshwar, his General and security head, could not leave without Anandmayi.

Parvateshwar had arranged for two brigades to travel with them. So two thousand soldiers, both Chandravanshi and Suryavanshi, travelled in a fleet of nine ships along with the royal vessel carrying the Neelkanth and his close aides. Vishwadyumna, the loyal Branga follower of Ganesh, and his platoon, were also commissioned into the Chandravanshi Brigade.

They sailed slowly so they could keep all the ships together. Two months had passed since they had left Kashi when they neared Vaishali.

Remembering his conversation with Gopal, the Chief of the Vasudevs, Shiva turned towards Veerbhadra, Nandi and Parshuram. All of them, except Nandi, were smoking pot on the deck, contemplating the river.

'Apparently Lord Manu had said that Good and Evil are two sides of the same coin,' said Shiva, breaking the silence of the moment, taking the chillum from Parshuram.

Parshuram frowned. 'I have heard this too. But I could never make sense of it.'

Shiva took a deep drag of the marijuana, exhaled and passed the chillum to Veerbhadra. 'What do you make of it, Bhadra?'

'Frankly, a lot of what your Vasudev friends say is mumbo-jumbo!'

Shiva burst out laughing. So did his friends.

'I wouldn't quite say that, brave Veerbhadra.'

A surprised Shiva turned around to find Ganesh behind

them. Shiva fell silent, all traces of humour dropping from him. Parshuram immediately bowed his head to Ganesh, but did not say anything out of fear of angering the Neelkanth.

Veerbhadra, who was growing increasingly fond of the Lord of the People and believed him to be a man of integrity, asked, 'So what would you make of it, Ganesh?'

'I would think it's a clue,' said Ganesh, smiling at Veerbhadra.

'Clue?' asked Shiva, intrigued.

'Maybe for the Neelkanth to understand what he should be searching for?'

'Carry on.'

'Good and Evil are two sides of the same coin. So the Neelkanth has to find one side of a coin, right?'

Shiva frowned.

'Is it possible to find one side of a coin?' asked Ganesh.

Shiva slapped his forehead. 'Of course, search for the whole coin instead!'

Ganesh nodded, smiling.

Shiva stared at Ganesh. A germ of an idea was forming in the Neelkanth's mind.

Search for Good. And you shall find Evil as well. The greater the Good, the greater the Evil.

Veerbhadra held out the chillum to Ganesh. 'Would you like to try some?'

Ganesh had never smoked in his life. He looked at his father and couldn't read what was written in those deep, mysterious eyes. 'I would love to.'

He sat down and took the chillum from Veerbhadra.

'Place it in your mouth like so,' said Veerbhadra, demonstrating by cupping his hands, 'and breathe in deeply.'

Ganesh did as he was told, collapsing in a severe bout of coughing.

Everyone burst out laughing. Except Shiva, who continued to stare at Ganesh, straight-faced.

Veerbhadra stretched out to pat Ganesh on his back and took the chillum away from him. 'Ganesh, you have never been touched by this evil.'

'No. But I'm sure I'll grow to like it,' smiled an embarrassed Ganesh, glancing for a moment at Shiva as he reached out for the chillum again.

Veerbhadra drew it out of reach. 'No, Ganesh. You should remain innocent.'

The fleet was at the gates of Branga. Parvateshwar, Anandmayi and Bhagirath had transferred into the lead ship to supervise operations.

'I've seen it before, I know,' said Anandmayi, staring at the gates, 'but I still get amazed at their sheer ingenuity!'

Parvateshwar smiled and put his arm around Anandmayi. And almost immediately, much to Anandmayi's annoyance, he turned back to the task at hand. 'Uttanka, the second ship is not high enough. Tell the Brangas to fill more water into the pool.'

Unnoticed by Parvateshwar, Anandmayi raised her eyebrows and shook her head slightly. Then she turned her husband's face and kissed him lightly. Parvateshwar smiled.

'All right, you lovebirds,' said Bhagirath. 'Keep a lid on it.'

Anandmayi laughed and slapped her brother on his wrist.

Parvateshwar smiled and turned towards the gates, to supervise the crossing.

'This crossing will go well, General,' said Bhagirath. 'Relax. We know what the Brangas are doing. There are no surprises here.'

Parvateshwar turned to Bhagirath with a frown. He was surprised the Ayodhyan Prince had used the term 'General'. He could tell his brother-in-law was trying to say something but was being cautious. 'Out with it, Bhagirath. What are you trying to say?'

'We know the path here,' said Bhagirath. 'We know what the Brangas are doing. There will be no surprises. But we have no idea what route the Nagas will lead us on. Only the Almighty knows what surprises they may have in store. Is it wise to trust them so blindly?'

'We're not trusting the Nagas, Bhagirath,' interrupted Anandmayi. 'We are trusting the Neelkanth.'

Parvateshwar remained silent.

'I'm not saying we shouldn't trust the Mahadev,' said Bhagirath. 'How can I? But how much do we know of the Nagas? We're going through the dreaded Dandak forests with the Nagas as our guides. Am I the only one concerned here?'

'Listen,' said an irritated Anandmayi. 'Lord Neelkanth trusts Queen Kali. That means I will trust her. And so will you.'

Bhagirath shook his head. 'What do you say, Parvateshwar?'

'The Lord is My Lord. I will walk into a wall of flames if he orders me to,' said Parvateshwar as he looked towards the banks, where accumulator machines had just been released, pulling their ship forward with tremendous force.

The Meluhan General turned to Bhagirath. 'But how can I forget that Ganesh killed Brahaspati, the greatest scientist of Meluha? That he destroyed the heart of our empire, Mount Mandar. How can I trust him after all this?'

Anandmayi looked at Parvateshwar and then at her brother uncomfortably.

— ⁂ —

'No, Krittika,' said Ayurvati. 'I am not doing it.'

Krittika and Ayurvati were in the Meluhan doctor's office on the royal ship. The hooks on the sideboards of their ship were being attached onto the machine that would pull it through the gates of Branga. Practically everyone on the vessel was on the deck, to see this marvellous feat of Branga engineering in action. Krittika had used the time to meet Ayurvati without Veerbhadra's knowledge.

'Ayurvatiji, please. You know I need it.'

'No you don't. And I'm sure if your husband knew, he would say no as well.'

'He doesn't need to know.'

'Krittika, I am not doing anything to put your life in danger. Is that clear?'

Ayurvati turned around to prepare a medicine for Kartik. He had cut himself while practicing with Parvateshwar.

Krittika saw her chance. There was a pouch lying on Ayurvati's table. She knew this was the medicine she desperately craved. She slipped it quietly into the folds of her *angvastram*.

'My apologies for disturbing you,' said Krittika.

Ayurvati turned around. 'I'm sorry if I appear rude, Krittika. But it is in your own interests.'

'Please don't tell my husband.'

'Of course not,' said Ayurvati. 'But you should tell Veerbhadra yourself. Right?'

Krittika nodded and was about to leave the room when Ayurvati called out to her. Pointing towards Krittika's *angvastram*, Ayurvati said, 'Please leave it behind.'

Embarrassed, Krittika slowly slipped her hand into her *angvastram*, took the pouch out and left it on the table. She looked up, eyes moist and pleading.

Ayurvati held Krittika's shoulder gently. 'Haven't you learnt anything from the Neelkanth? You are a complete woman exactly the way you are. Your husband loves you for who you are and not for something you can give him.'

Krittika mumbled a soft apology and ran from the room.

Chapter 23

The Secret of All Secrets

The convoy crossed the gates of Branga and sailed into the river's westernmost distributary, the Madhumati. A few weeks later they passed the spot where Shiva had battled with Parshuram.

'This is where we fought Parshuram,' said Shiva, patting the ex-bandit on his back.

Parshuram looked at Shiva and then at Sati. 'Actually, this is where the Lord saved me.'

Sati smiled at Parshuram. She knew what it felt like. Being saved by Shiva. She looked at her husband with love. A man capable of pulling the poison out of the lives of all those around him. And yet, he couldn't pull the poison out of his own memories, still being tortured by his own demons. No matter how hard she tried, she could not get him to forget his past. Perhaps that was his fate.

Sati's musings were interrupted by Parshuram. 'This is where we turn, My Lord.'

Sati looked in the direction the exiled Vasudev pointed. There was nothing there. The river seemed to skirt a large grove of Sundari trees and carry on towards the Eastern Sea.

'Where?' asked Shiva.

'See those *Sundari* trees, My Lord,' said Parshuram, pointing towards a grove with the hook fixed on his amputated left hand. 'They lend their name to this area. The *Sundarban*.'

'*Beautiful forest?*' asked Sati.

'Yes, My lady,' said Parshuram. 'They also hide a beautiful secret.'

On the orders of Kali, the lead ship turned into the grove that Parshuram had pointed towards. From the distance of her own ship, Sati could see the figure of Parvateshwar, also on the deck, looking at Kali and trying to argue with the Naga Queen.

Kali simply ignored him. And the ship continued on a course that appeared to be its doom.

'What are they doing?' asked Sati, panic-stricken. 'They'll run aground.'

To their shock, the lead ship simply pushed the trees aside and sailed through.

'By the holy lake,' whispered an awe-struck Shiva. 'Rootless trees.'

'Not rootless, My Lord,' corrected Parshuram. 'They have roots. But not fixed ones. The roots float in the lagoon.'

'But how can such trees live?' asked Sati.

'That is something I have not understood,' said Parshuram. 'Perhaps it's the magic of the Nagas.'

The other ships, led by the royal ship that carried the Mahadev, glided into the floating grove of Sundari trees and entered a hidden lagoon where the gentle waves of the

Madhumati came to a halt. Shiva looked around in wonder. The area was lush green, alive with raucous bird calls. The vegetation was dense, creating a canopy of leaves over the lagoon which was massive enough to hold ten large ships. It was nearing the end of the second prahar and the sun was at its peak. Within the shaded lagoon however, one could mistakenly think it was evening time.

Parshuram looked at Shiva. 'Very few people know the location of the floating grove. I know of some who have tried to find it and have only run their ships aground.'

The ten ships were quickly anchored into long stakes in the banks after being tied to each other and pulled behind a dense row of floating Sundari trees. The vessels were secure and completely hidden from view.

The path now was on foot. More than two thousand soldiers had to troop through the Dandak forests. They were all asked to assemble on and around the lead ship.

Kali climbed up the main mast, so that all could see her. 'Hear me!'

The crowd quietened down. Kali's voice instantly commanded compliance.

'All of you have heard rumours of the *Dandakaranya*. That the *Dandak forest* is the largest in the world. That it stretches from the Eastern Sea to the Western Sea. That it is so dense that the sun hardly ever cracks through. That it is populated by monstrous animals that will devour those who lose their way. That some trees themselves are poisonous, felling those stupid enough to eat or touch things better left alone.'

The soldiers looked at Kali with concern.

'The rumours are all true, horrifyingly so.'

The soldiers knew the Dandak forests were to the

South of the Narmada, the border mandated by Lord Manu. The border that was never to be crossed. Not only were they violating Lord Manu's orders, but they were also entering the terrifying *Dandakaranya*. None of them wanted to push their luck further by being adventurous in these cursed jungles. Kali's words only sealed their convictions.

'Only Ganesh, Vishwadyumna and I know the path through this death trap. If you want to stay alive, follow our orders and do as we tell you. In turn, I give you my word that you will all reach Panchavati alive.'

The soldiers nodded vigorously.

'For the rest of the day, rest on your ships, eat your fill and get some sleep. We leave tomorrow morning at sunrise. Nobody is to go exploring into the Sundarban by himself tonight. He may discover that these forests are more vicious than beautiful.'

Kali climbed down the mast to find Shiva and Sati below.

'How far is the Dandak forest from here?' asked Sati.

Kali looked around and then back at Sati. 'We are travelling in a large convoy. Normally, the distance should take a month. But I suspect we will take two or three. I don't mind that though. I would rather be slow than dead.'

'You have a way with words, sister.'

Kali smiled with unholy glee.

'Is Panchavati at the centre of the Dandak forest?' asked Shiva.

'No, Shiva. It is more towards the western end.'

'A long way.'

'That's why I said it would take a long time. Once in the *Dandakaranya*, it will take another six months to reach Panchavati.'

'Hmm,' said Shiva. 'We should carry enough food from the ships.'

'No need, Shiva,' said Kali. 'Excess baggage will slow us down. The forests are replete with all the food we need. We just have to be careful that we don't eat something that we shouldn't.'

'But food isn't the only problem. We'll be spending nine months in the forest. There are many other threats.'

Kali eyes lit up. 'Not if you are with me.'

— ⁂ —

Dinner had been served on the deck of the main ship. Shiva had decided to honour the Naga custom of community eating, where many people ate from one humongous plate stitched together from many banana tree leaves.

Shiva, Sati, Kali, Ganesh, Kartik, Parvateshwar, Anandmayi, Bhagirath, Ayurvati, Parshuram, Nandi, Veerbhadra and Krittika sat around the massive plate. Parvateshwar found the custom odd and unhygienic, but as always, followed Shiva's orders.

'What is the reason behind this custom, Your Highness?' asked Bhagirath to Kali.

'We Nagas believe Devi Annapurna, the Goddess of food, is one of our collective mothers. After all, doesn't she keep us all alive? What this custom does is that it makes us all receive her blessings together. We eat all our meals, while travelling, in this manner. We are brothers and sisters now. We share the same fate on the journey.'

'That's true,' said Bhagirath, simultaneously thinking that community eating was a good way to hedge against poisoning.

'Is it really that dangerous in Dandak, Your Highness?' asked Parvateshwar. 'Or are these just rumours that ensure discipline?'

'The forest can be abundant and caring like an indulgent mother if we follow her rules. But stray out of line and she can be like a demon who will strike you down. Yes, the rumours help ensure discipline. Nine months is a long time to stick to a fixed path, to not stray. But trust me, those who stray will find that the rumours are not far from hard facts.'

'All right,' said Shiva. 'Enough of this. Let's eat.'

All this while, Ayurvati had been looking at Krittika and Veerbhadra. Between bites, Veerbhadra was pointing towards Kartik and whispering to his wife. They looked at Kartik with loving eyes, almost like he was their own son.

Ayurvati smiled sadly.

— ⁂ —

'General,' said Veerbhadra.

Parvateshwar was clearly irritated. The two men were on the floating dock next to the lead ship, along with a hundred soldiers. At the lead were Kali and Ganesh. No road was visible. Dense bushes covered the path in every direction.

Seeing Veerbhadra, Parvateshwar calmed down. 'Is the Lord coming?'

'No General, just me.'

Parvateshwar nodded. 'That's all right.' And then, he turned towards Kali. 'Your Highness, I hope you do not expect my men to hack their way through these bushes all the way to Panchavati?'

'Even if I did, I'm sure your Suryavanshi men would be able to do so very easily.'

Parvateshwar's eyes narrowed in irritation. 'My Lady, I am at the end of my tether. You either give me some straight answers or I take my men and sail out of here.'

'I don't know what to do to earn your trust, General. Have I done anything in this journey thus far to hurt your men?' Kali pointed in a westerly direction. 'All I need your men to do now is hack their way through these bushes for a hundred metres in that direction.'

'That's it?'

'That's it.'

Parvateshwar nodded. The soldiers immediately drew their swords and formed a line. Veerbhadra joined them. They moved forward slowly slashing through almost impenetrable bushes. Vishwadyumna and Ganesh were at the two ends of the line, swords drawn, facing outwards. It was obvious from their stance that they were protecting the men from some unknown danger.

A little while later, Veerbhadra and the soldiers were surprised to emerge from the dense undergrowth on to a pathway. It was broad enough for ten horses riding side by side.

'Where, in Lord Ram's name, did this come from?' asked an astonished Parvateshwar.

'The road to heaven,' said Kali. 'But it passes through hell before that.'

Parvateshwar turned back to the Naga Queen.

Kali smiled. 'I told you so. Trust me.'

Veerbhadra walked up and stared in wonder at the road ahead. It ran straight, right into the distance. A stony path, it had been levelled reasonably well. Along the sides, running parallel to the trees, were two continuous hedges of long, thorny creepers.

'Are they poisonous?' asked Parvateshwar, pointing at the twin fences.

'The inside one, on the side of the road, is made of the Nagavalli creeper,' said Kali. 'You can even eat the leaves if you like. But the hedge on the outside, facing the forest, is highly toxic. If you get pricked by its thorns, you will not even have time to say your last prayers.'

Parvateshwar raised his eyebrows. *How did they build all this?*

Veerbhadra turned towards Kali. 'Your Highness, is that it? Is this all we have to do? Uncover this road and keep walking? And we find the city of the Nagas?'

Kali grinned. 'If only life was that simple!'

— ⁂ —

The first prahar was just about ending. The sun glimmered over the horizon. Within a few minutes, it would be shining down in all its glory, spreading light and warmth. In the dense Sundarban however, the sun was a shadow of its fiery self. Only a few rays courageously penetrated the heavy foliage to light the pathway for Shiva's convoy.

A company of men had been stationed at the clearing made by hacking the bushes up to the Naga road, with express instructions. Kill anything and everything emerging from the forest.

The foot soldiers marched through the clearing, entering the Naga road with wonder in their eyes. The last thing they had expected was a comfortable and secure road through the forest. The procession was flanked by mounted riders, bearing torches, lighting the way.

Riding a black horse, Vishwadyumna was at the head accompanied by Parvateshwar, Bhagirath and Anandmayi. The Neelkanth's family travelled in the centre, along with Kali, Ayurvati, Krittika and Nandi. Ganesh was at the clearing with Veerbhadra and Parshuram. He would wait till every soldier had passed through. He had a task to do.

'Do we really need a rear guard, Ganesh?' asked Veerbhadra. 'It is almost impossible to find the floating Sundari grove.'

'We are Nagas. Everyone hates us. We can never be too careful.'

'That is the last of the soldiers. What now?'

'Please guard me,' said Ganesh.

Ganesh walked into the clearing bearing a bag of seeds. Veerbhadra and Parshuram walked alongside, their weapons drawn, protecting his right and left flank.

They had been in the clearing for a few moments when a wild boar sauntered in. It was the largest boar Veerbhadra had ever seen. The animal stopped at a distance, staring at the humans, shuffling its front hoof, snorting softly. Parshuram turned to Ganesh. The animal was obviously gearing up to charge. The Naga continued to perform the task of scattering seeds on the ground as he nodded softly. Parshuram lunged and swung hard with his axe, cutting the boar's head off in one clean sweep.

Veerbhadra was edging forward to help Parshuram, when Ganesh stopped him sharply. 'You keep your eyes focussed on the other side, Veerbhadra. Parshuram is capable of handling this.'

Parshuram, meanwhile, continued to hack the beast's

body. He then pulled the fragmented parts of the boar's corpse onto the road.

As Parshuram walked back, he explained to Veerbhadra. 'That carcass will only attract other carnivores.'

Ganesh, meanwhile, had finished scattering all the seeds. He turned and walked back to the road, followed by Parshuram and Veerbhadra.

As soon as they entered the road, Veerbhadra spoke up. 'That was one massive boar.'

'Actually, that one was pretty small since it was young,' said Ganesh. 'Others in its pack would be much larger. You don't want it to be close by when we are defending the road. A sounder of boars in this region can be vicious.'

Veerbhadra turned and looked at the hundred Branga soldiers waiting for them, holding their horses steady. He turned to Ganesh. 'What now?'

'Now we wait,' said Ganesh, drawing his sword, his voice calm. 'We have to protect this gateway till tomorrow morning. Kill everything that tries to enter.'

'Only till tomorrow? Those bushes will not be full grown by then.'

'Oh yes, they will.'

— ⁂ —

Veerbhadra was woken up by the loud snarls of a tiger. Some animal, perhaps a deer, had fallen victim to the mighty cat. He looked around. The jungle was waking up. The sun had just risen. Fifty soldiers were sleeping in front of him. Beyond them was the Naga road on which Shiva's entourage had left the previous day.

Veerbhadra pulled his *angvastram* close around himself,

breathing hard onto his hands. It was cold. He saw Parshuram next to him, sleeping soundly, snoring, his mouth slightly open.

Veerbhadra raised himself on his elbows and turned around. The other fifty soldiers were standing guard, their swords drawn. They had taken over from their fellow soldiers at midnight.

'Ganesh?'

'Out here, Veerbhadra,' said Ganesh.

Veerbhadra walked forward as the guards parted to reveal the Lord of the People. Veerbhadra was stunned.

'By the holy lake,' said Veerbhadra. 'The bushes have grown back completely. It's almost as if they had never been cut.'

'The road is protected completely now. We can ride out. Half a day's hard riding and we will catch up with the rest.'

'Then what are we waiting for?'

— ⁂ —

'You should ask him,' said Veerbhadra to Krittika.

It had been a month of uneventful marching through the Sundarban. Despite the mammoth size of the convoy, they were making good progress. Krittika had slipped back from the centre of the convoy to ride with her husband at the rear. She was enjoying her conversations with Ganesh and had grown increasingly fond of the elder son of her mistress.

Ganesh, whose horse was keeping pace with Veerbhadra's and Krittika's, turned. 'Ask me what?'

'Well,' said Krittika. 'Veerbhadra tells me that you weren't too surprised to hear that Emperor Daksha may have killed Lord Chandandhwaj.'

Parshuram pulled his horse up to fall in line with the others. Curious.

'Did you know?' asked Krittika.

'Yes.'

Krittika stared hard at Ganesh's face, trying to glean some traces of hate and anger. There were none. 'Do you not feel the need for vengeance? A sense of injustice?'

'I feel no need for vengeance or justice, Krittika,' said Ganesh. 'Justice exists for the good of the universe. To maintain balance. It does not exist to ignite hatred among humans. Furthermore, I do not have the power to administer justice to the Emperor of Meluha. The universe does. It will deliver justice when it is appropriate. In this life or in the next.'

Parshuram interjected. 'But wouldn't vengeance make you feel better?'

'You got your vengeance, didn't you?' asked Ganesh to Parshuram. 'Did you really feel better?'

Parshuram took a deep breath. He didn't.

'So you don't want anything to be done to Daksha?' asked Veerbhadra.

Ganesh narrowed his eyes. 'I simply don't care.'

Veerbhadra smiled. Parshuram frowned at Veerbhadra's reaction.

'What?' asked Parshuram.

'Nothing much,' said Veerbhadra. 'Just that I have finally understood something Shiva had told me once. That the opposite of love is not hate. Hate is just love gone bad. The actual opposite of love is apathy. When you don't care a damn as to what happens to the other person.'

'The food is delicious,' said Shiva, smiling.

It had been two months since Shiva's men had marched out of the floating Sundari grove. They had just entered the dreaded Dandak forests. The road had ended in a giant clearing, capable of accommodating many more than Shiva's band of travelling men. As was the Naga custom, groups of people were eating their dinner together on giant plates.

Kali smiled. 'The forest has everything that we need.'

Sati patted Ganesh on the back. He rode separately from the rest of the family, so Sati enjoyed the common dinners where she got to talk to her elder son. 'Is the food all right?'

'Perfect, *Maa*,' smiled Ganesh.

Ganesh turned to Kartik and slipped a mango to his younger brother. Kartik, who rarely smiled these days, looked at his elder brother with affection. 'Thank you, dada.'

Bhagirath looked up at Kali. He couldn't contain himself any longer. 'Your Highness, why are there five roads leading out of this clearing?'

'I was wondering how you had kept yourself from asking that question up until now!'

Everyone turned to Kali.

'Simple. Four of those paths lead you deeper and deeper into the Dandak. To your doom.'

'Which path is the right one?' asked Bhagirath.

'I will tell you tomorrow morning, when we leave.'

'How many such clearings are there, Kali?' asked Shiva.

Kali's lips drew in a broad smile. 'There are five such clearings on the way to Panchavati, Shiva.'

'Lord Ram be merciful,' said Parvateshwar. 'That means

there is only a one in three thousand chance of marching down the right path to Panchavati!'

'Yes,' smiled Kali.

Anandmayi was grinning. 'Well, we better hope you don't forget the right path, Your Highness!'

Kali smiled. 'Trust me, I won't.'

Kali looked at Shiva, Sati and Nandi riding a little ahead of her. Shiva had just said something which made Sati and Nandi crack up in laughter. Then the Neelkanth turned to Nandi and winked.

Kali turned to Ayurvati. 'He has the gift.'

They were marching at the centre of the convoy to Panchavati. It had been three months since the march from the Madhumati river. Deep in the Dandak now, the march had been surprisingly uneventful and probably a little tedious. Conversations were the only relief from the boredom.

'What gift?' asked Ayurvati.

'Of bringing peace to people, drawing out their unhappiness,' said Kali.

'That he does,' said Ayurvati. 'But it is one of his many gifts. *Om Namah Shivāya*.'

Kali was surprised. The Meluhan doctor had just corrupted an old mantra. The words *Om* and *Namah* were only added to the names of the old Gods, never living men.

The Queen of the Nagas turned to gaze at Shiva, riding ahead. And smiled. Sometimes, simple faith could lead to profound peace.

Kali repeated Ayurvati's line. '*Om Namah Shivāya.*'

The universe bows to Lord Shiva. I bow to Lord Shiva.

Ayurvati turned towards Kartik riding a little behind. The boy, a few months older than four, looked like a nine-year-old. He presented a disturbing sight. Scars were visible on his arms and face. Two long swords tied in a cross across his back, no sign of a shield. His eyes were focussed beyond the fence, searching for threats.

Kartik had become withdrawn after the day his elder brother had saved him single-handedly from the lions, nearly dying in the process. He rarely spoke, except to his parents, Krittika and Ganesh. He almost never smiled. He always accompanied hunting parties into the jungle. Many a times, he had brought down animals single-handedly. Awed soldiers had given Ayurvati graphic details of Kartik moving in for the kill: Quiet, focussed and ruthless.

Ayurvati sighed.

Kali, who had developed a strong bond with Ayurvati over the months since they had left Kashi, whispered, 'I think you should be happy he has taken the right lessons from life.'

'He is a child,' said Ayurvati. 'He has many years to go before he grows up.'

'Who are we to decide when it is time for him to grow up,' said Kali. 'The choice belongs to him. He will make all of us proud one day.'

— ⁂ —

It had been eight months since the march from the banks of the Madhumati. The convoy was only a day away from the Naga capital Panchavati. They were camped near the road, next to a mighty river as big as the Saraswati in its early reaches.

Bhagirath thought that this great river must be the fabled Narmada. The border mandated by Lord Manu that was never to be crossed. They were on the northern side of the river.

'This must be the Narmada,' said Bhagirath to Vishwadyumna. 'I guess we'll cross over tomorrow. Lord Manu have mercy on us.'

Parvateshwar spoke up. 'It must be. Narmada is the only river in the southern regions as enormous as the mighty Saraswati.'

Vishwadyumna smiled. They were already far South of the Narmada. 'My Lords, sometimes the mind makes you believe what you want to believe. Look again. There is no need to cross this river.'

Anandmayi's eyes widened in surprise. 'By the great Lord Rudra! This river flows West to East!'

Vishwadyumna nodded. 'That it does, Your Highness.'

This couldn't be the Narmada. That river was known to flow East to West.

'Lord Ram be merciful!' cried Bhagirath. 'How can the existence of such a wide river be a secret?'

'This entire land is a secret, My Lord,' said Vishwadyumna. 'This is the Godavari. And you should see how much bigger it gets by the time it reaches the Eastern Sea.'

Parvateshwar stared in awe. He put his hands together and bowed to the flowing waters.

'The Godavari is not the only one,' said Vishwadyumna. 'I have heard rumours of other such giant rivers further South.'

Bhagirath looked at Vishwadyumna wondering what further surprises lay ahead the next day.

'Ganesh,' said Nandi.

'Yes, Major Nandi,' said Ganesh.

Nandi had slipped back to the end of the caravan to relay a message from Kali to Ganesh. 'The Naga outposts will follow their standard practice vis-a-vis the convoy, irrespective of the fact that the Queen and the Lord of the People travel with it.'

Queen Kali, ever cautious when it came to the welfare of her people, was indirectly referring to the fact that the progress of the convoy would now be monitored all the way to the Naga capital so that any potential threats could be neutralised.

Ganesh nodded. 'Thank you, Major.'

Nandi looked back at the small Naga outpost that they had just passed. 'What security can a hundred men provide, Ganesh? They are isolated, a day's journey from the city. The outpost is not even fortified properly. Seeing all the elaborate security measures the Nagas have in place, most of them bordering on genius, this one makes no sense.'

Ganesh smiled. He would normally not have trusted any non-Naga with details of their security. But this was Nandi, Shiva's shadow. Doubting him was like doubting the Neelkanth himself. 'They cannot offer much protection on the road. But if there is such an attack, they trigger an early warning. Their key task then is to set booby traps along the way to Panchavati as they fall back towards the city.'

Nandi frowned. *An outpost just to set booby traps?!*

'But that is not their primary task,' continued Ganesh, pointing with his finger. 'Their key function is to protect us from a river attack.'

Nandi looked at the Godavari. Of course! It must meet

the Eastern Sea somewhere. An opening that could be exploited. The Nagas truly thought of everything.

— ⚹⚹⚹⚹⚹ —

The faint light of the full moon, breaking through the dense foliage intermittently, had lulled the creatures of the Dandak into a false sense of security. All was quiet in Shiva's camp, everyone fast asleep. Most had been awake till late into the night, eagerly discussing the end of their long and surprisingly uneventful journey through the dangerous woods of Sundarban and Dandak. Panchavati was only a day away.

Suddenly, the quiet of the night was broken by the shrill call of a loud conch shell. Actually, many shells.

Kali, at the centre of the huge encampment, was up immediately. As were Shiva, Sati and Kartik.

'What the hell is that?' shouted Shiva, over the din.

Kali was looking towards the river, stunned. This had never happened before. She turned back towards Shiva, teeth bared. 'Your men have betrayed us!'

The entire camp was up as the conch shells kept persistently sounding out their warning.

Ganesh, closest to the blaring conches at the camp end nearest to the river, was making a beeline for it, Nandi, Veerbhadra and Parshuram in tow.

'What is going on?' screamed Veerbhadra, to make himself heard over the din.

'Enemy ships are sailing up the Godavari,' shouted Ganesh. 'They have tripped our river warning system.'

'What now?' yelled Nandi.

'To the outpost! We have devil boats!'

Nandi turned around and relayed out the order to the three hundred men who had already rallied around to face the unknown threat. The soldiers had been following close on the heels of the four men. They doubled back to the outpost, where the hundred Naga men were already pushing out their devil boats.

Meanwhile Vishwadyumna, at the end farthermost from the enemy threat, rapidly controlled his disbelief and started carrying out the standard drill set in place for such an eventuality. A red flame was lit, warning Panchavati in the distance.

Meanwhile, Bhagirath ran up to Vishwadyumna. 'What are your river defences?'

Vishwadyumna glared angrily at Bhagirath, refusing to answer. He was sure the Nagas had been betrayed.

Bhagirath shook his head and ran to Parvateshwar, who was already gathering soldiers and deploying them in defensive formations along the river.

'Any news?' asked Parvateshwar.

'He won't talk, Parvateshwar,' screamed Bhagirath. 'My fears have come true. They have betrayed us. We walked straight into a trap!'

Parvateshwar clenched his fists, looking at the five hundred men arrayed behind him in battle formation. 'Kill everything that emerges from the river!'

And then, the sky lit up, ablaze at a thousand points. Bhagirath looked up. 'Lord Ram be merciful.'

A shower of fiery arrows flew high. They had obviously been fired from a distance, from the battleships racing up the Godavari.

'Shields up!' screamed Parvateshwar.

At the centre, Shiva and Kali had issued similar orders.

Soldiers ducked under their shields, waiting for the onslaught of flaming arrows to stop. But scores of arrows had already found their targets. Setting clothes on fire and piercing through many bodies. Injuring large numbers and killing some unfortunate ones.

There was no respite. The curtain of arrows kept raining down in an almost continuous shower.

One arrow hit Ayurvati's leg. She screamed in pain, folding her leg closer to her body, holding her shield nearer.

The sudden attack and its severity had forced most of Shiva's camp to cower behind their shields. But real fighting was on at the river end of the campsite, within the Godavari itself.

'Quickly!' screamed Ganesh. If the downpour of arrows continued for a few more minutes, the entire camp would be destroyed. He had to move fast.

His soldiers, the Suryavanshis, Chandravanshis and the Nagas, were swimming hard, pushing the hundred small boats towards the five large ships rowing rapidly up the Godavari. The small boats, with dried firewood and a small flint inside, had been covered by a thick cloth. Once in range, the devil boats would be lit and rammed into the ships. Fire was the best way to destroy such large, wooden ships.

The ships were sailing up river rapidly, the flaming arrows still being continuously shot from their decks. Due to the manic speed of the vessels coming towards them, Ganesh's soldiers didn't have to swim too far to reach the enemy battle ships. The devil boats were already in place, aligned to ram into them.

'Light them!' screamed Ganesh.

Soldiers rapidly pulled the cloth off each boat and struck the flints. The boats were aflame almost instantaneously, before the assassins on any ship could react. Ganesh's men pushed the boats into the sides of the ships.

'Hold them in place!' screamed Nandi. 'The ships have to catch fire!'

The lookout assassins on the ships turned their bows onto their attackers in the water. A hailstorm of arrows started tearing into the brave soldiers in the river, maiming and killing many. The fire from the devil boats was also lapping Ganesh's men, but they grimly kept swimming, pushing the boats onto the ships.

All five ships were aflame within moments, but the loss of life till they had caught fire made it seem like an eternity.

'Back to the shore!' screamed Ganesh.

He knew he had to form his line on the Godavari's banks now. As fire spread through the ships, the assassins would jump over or into lifeboats and row up to the shores to resume battle.

Ganesh's soldiers had barely made it to the riverbanks when they heard a deafening blast. They turned around in shock. The first ship of the enemy fleet had just blown up. Within a few moments, the other ships went up in gigantic explosions as well.

Ganesh turned to Parshuram, stunned. '*Daivi astras*!'

Parshuram nodded, shocked out of his wits. Only *divine weapons* could have led to such explosions. But how could anyone lay their hands on such weapons? And that too in such alarming quantities?

Ganesh rallied his men, counting the living. He had lost one hundred of the valiant four hundred who had charged behind him, mostly Nagas — the only ones who knew the drill. The Lord of the People gritted his teeth in anger and marched towards the camp to find Kali and Shiva.

— ⅄ⵀⵕⵗⴲ —

'You led us into a trap!' a livid Parvateshwar screamed. He had lost twenty men in the hail of arrows.

The number of dead in the camp centre was significantly higher. Close to fifty soldiers had been killed. The highest casualties were of course at the end closest to the enemy warships. Three hundred soldiers had died there, including the hundred that were killed while attacking the enemy ships. Ayurvati, with a broken shaft buried in her thigh, was rushing around with her medics, trying to save as many as she could.

'Nonsense!' yelled Kali. 'You betrayed us! Nobody has ever attacked us from the Godavari. Ever!'

'Quiet!' shouted Shiva. He turned to Veerbhadra, Parshuram, Nandi and Ganesh, who had just arrived. 'What were those explosions, Parshuram?'

'*Daivi astras*, My Lord,' said Parshuram. 'The five enemy ships were carrying them. The fires triggered the explosions.'

Shiva breathed deeply, staring into the distance.

'My Lord,' said Bhagirath. 'Turn back now. More traps await us on the way and at Panchavati itself. There are only two Nagas here. Think of what a fifty thousand could do!'

Kali exploded. 'This is your doing! Panchavati has never been attacked. You led your cohorts here. It was lucky that Ganesh led a fight back and decimated your troops. Otherwise we would all have been slaughtered.'

Sati touched Kali lightly. She wanted to point out

that even Suryavanshi and Chandravanshi men fighting alongside Ganesh had been killed.

'Enough!' shouted Shiva. 'Don't any of you get what really happened?'

The Neelkanth turned towards Nandi and Kartik. 'Take a hundred men and go down-river. See if there are any survivors from the enemy ships. I want to know who they were.'

Nandi and Kartik left immediately.

Shiva looked at the people around him, seething. 'We were all betrayed. Whosoever was firing those arrows was not picking and choosing targets. They wanted us all dead.'

'But how did they come up the Godavari?' asked Kali.

Shiva glared at her. 'How the hell should I know? Most people here didn't even know this river wasn't the Narmada!'

'It has to be the Nagas, My Lord,' said Bhagirath. 'They cannot be trusted!'

'Sure!' said Shiva, sarcastically. 'The Nagas sprung this trap to kill their own Queen. And then Ganesh led a counterattack on his own people and blew them up with *daivi astras*. If he had *daivi astras* and wanted us dead, why didn't he just use the weapons on us?'

Pin-drop silence.

'I think the astras were meant to destroy Panchavati. They planned to slaughter us easily from their ships and then sail up to the Naga capital and destroy it as well. What they didn't bet on was the Naga wariness and extensive security measures, including the devil boats. That saved us.'

What the Neelkanth was saying made sense. Ganesh thanked Bhoomidevi silently that the Naga Rajya Sabha had agreed to his proposal of arming the banks of the Godavari outpost with devil boats for any such eventuality.

'Someone wants us all dead,' said Shiva. 'Someone powerful enough to get such a large arsenal of *daivi astras*. Someone who knows about the existence of such a huge river in the South and has the ability to identify its sea route. Someone resourceful enough to get a fleet of ships with enough soldiers to attack us. Who is that person? That is the question.'

— ⅄ⓄⓊ⍋⊛ —

The sun was rising slowly over the horizon, spreading light and warmth over the tired camp. A relief party from Panchavati had just arrived with food and medical supplies. Ayurvati had finally relented and was resting in a medical tent, after having been assured that most of the injured were taken care of. The death toll had not risen further as the night had progressed. Even those with nearly fatal injuries had been saved.

Kartik and Nandi trooped into the camp after the night long search along the river and went straight up to Shiva. Kartik spoke first. 'There are no survivors, *baba*.'

'My Lord, we checked both the riverbanks,' Nandi added. 'Went through all the wreckage. Even rowed five kilometres downriver, in case some survivors had been washed off. But we found no one alive.'

Shiva cursed silently. He suspected who the attackers were but wasn't certain. He called Parvateshwar and Bhagirath. 'Both of you recognise the ships in your respective countries. I want you to study the wrecks properly. I want to know if any of those ships were Meluhan or Swadweepan.'

'My Lord,' cried Parvateshwar. 'It cannot be...'

'Parvateshwar, please do this for me,' interrupted Shiva. 'I want an honest answer. Where did those Goddamned ships come from?'

Parvateshwar saluted the Neelkanth. 'As you command, My Lord.'

The Meluhan General left, followed by Bhagirath.

— ⁂ —

'You think it's a coincidence that this attack happened just a day before you were to discover the secret?'

Shiva and Sati were sitting in a semi-secluded area along the river near the camp. It was the last hour of the first prahar. The cremation ceremonies had been completed. Though the injured were in no state to travel, the general consensus was that reaching the safety of Panchavati was imperative. The Naga city offered better protection than an indefensible forest road. The Nagas had arranged carts to carry the injured in the convoy to their capital and were scheduled to leave within the hour.

'I can't say,' said Shiva.

Sati remained quiet, looking into the distance.

'You think... that your father could be...'

Sati sighed. 'After all that I have learned about him recently, I would not put it past him.'

Shiva reached out and held Sati.

'But I don't think he can order an attack of this magnitude all by himself,' continued Sati. 'He doesn't have the capability. Who is the master puppeteer? And why is he doing this?'

Shiva nodded. 'That is the mystery. But first, I need to know this big secret. I have a feeling the answers could be deeply connected with all that is going on in Meluha, Swadweep and Panchavati.'

The sun was high when the entourage, bloodied and tired, marched up the river banks of the Godavari to the Naga capital, *Panchavati*. The *land of the five banyan trees.*

These weren't just any odd five banyans. Their legend had begun more than a thousand years ago. These were the trees under which the seventh Vishnu, Ram, accompanied by his wife Sita and brother Lakshman, had rested during their exile from Ayodhya. They had set up house close to these trees. This was also the unfortunate place from where the demon king Ravan had kidnapped Sita, triggering a war with Ram. That war destroyed Ravan's glittering and obscenely rich kingdom of Lanka.

Panchavati was situated on the north-eastern banks of the Godavari. The river flowed down from the mountains of the Western Ghats towards the Eastern Sea. To the West of Panchavati, the river took a strange ninety degree turn to the South, flowed straight down for a little less than a kilometre and then turned East once again to continue its journey to the sea. This turn of the Godavari allowed the Nagas to build grand canals, and to use this cleared part of the Dandak to meet the agricultural needs of their citizens.

To the surprise of the Suryavanshis, Panchavati was built on a raised platform, much like the cities of Meluha. Strong walls of cut stone rose high, with turrets at regular intervals to defend against invaders. The area around the walls, extending a long distance, was used by Nagas for agricultural purposes. There was also a comfortable colony of guest houses set up for regular Branga visitors. A second wall surrounded these lands. Beyond this second wall, land was again cleared far and wide, to give a clear line of sight of approaching enemies.

Panchavati had been established by Bhoomidevi. The mysterious non-Naga lady had instituted the present way of life of the Nagas. Nobody knew the antecedents of Bhoomidevi. And she had strictly forbidden any image of hers from being recorded. Hence the only memories of the founder of the present Naga civilisation were her laws and statements. The city of Panchavati was the epitome of her way of life, combining the best of the Suryavanshis and the Chandravanshis. It loudly proclaimed her aspiration above the city gates. '*Satyam. Sundaram.*' *Truth. Beauty.*

Shiva's convoy was allowed entry from the outer gates and led straight to the Branga guest quarters. Each member of the convoy was assigned comfortable rooms.

'Why don't you relax, Shiva,' said Kali. 'I will bring the secret out.'

'I want to go into Panchavati now,' said Shiva.

'Are you sure? Aren't you tired?'

'Of course I'm tired. But I need to see the secret right now.'

'All right.'

— ⁂ —

While Shiva's company waited outside in the guesthouse, Kali and Ganesh led Shiva and Sati into the city.

The city was nothing like they had expected. It had been laid out in a neat grid-like pattern, much like Meluhan cities. But the Nagas appeared to have taken the Suryavanshi ideal of justice and equality to its logical extreme. Every single house, including that of the Queen, was of exactly the same design and size. There were no poor or rich amongst the fifty thousand Nagas who lived there.

'Everyone lives the same way in Panchavati?' Sati asked Ganesh.

'Of course not, *Maa*. Everyone has a right to decide what they want to do with their lives. But the state provides housing and basic necessities. And in that, there is complete equality.'

Practically all the inhabitants had lined up outside their houses to see the Neelkanth walk by. They had heard of the mysterious attack on the Neelkanth's convoy. The people were thanking Bhoomidevi that nothing had happened to their Queen or the Lord of the People.

Shiva was shocked to see that many people did not have any deformities. He saw many of them cradling Naga babies in their arms.

'What are these non-Nagas doing in Panchavati?' asked Shiva.

'They are parents of Naga children,' said Kali.

'And they live here?'

'Some parents abandon their Naga children,' said Kali. 'And some feel a strong bond with their progeny. Strong enough to overcome their fear of societal prejudices. We give refuge to such people in Panchavati.'

'Who takes care of Naga babies whose parents abandon them?' asked Sati.

'Childless Nagas,' said Kali. 'Nagas cannot have natural

children. So they readily adopt the abandoned children from Meluha and Swadweep and bring them up as their own. With the love and attention that is the birthright of every child.'

They walked in silence to the city centre. It was here, around the five legendary banyan trees, that all the communal buildings were situated. These edifices, to be used by all the residents of Panchavati, had been built in the grand style of Swadweepan buildings. There was a school, a temple dedicated to Lord Rudra and Lady Mohini, a public bath and a stadium for performances, where the fifty thousand citizens met regularly. Music, dance and drama were coveted lifestyle choices and not paths to knowledge.

'Where is the secret?' asked Shiva, getting impatient.

'In here, Lord Neelkanth,' said Ganesh, pointing to the school.

Shiva frowned. A secret in a school? He expected it to be in the spiritual centre of the city, the temple of Lord Rudra. He walked towards the building. The rest followed.

The school had been built in traditional style around an open courtyard. A colonnaded corridor ran along the courtyard with doors leading into the classrooms. At the far end was a large open room. The library. Along the side of the library was another large corridor leading to the playground beyond the main building. On the other side of the ground were the other facilities such as halls and practice laboratories.

'Please keep quiet,' said Kali. 'The classes are still on. We would like to disturb only one class and not all of them.'

'We will disturb none,' said Shiva, walking towards the

library, where he expected the secret of the Nagas to be. Perhaps a book?

'Lord Neelkanth,' said Ganesh, halting Shiva mid-stride.

Shiva stopped. Ganesh pointed to the curtained entrance of a classroom. Shiva frowned. An oddly familiar voice was expounding philosophies. The voice was crystal clear behind the curtain.

'New philosophies today blame desire for everything. Desire is the root cause of all suffering, all destruction, right?'

'Yes, Guruji,' said a student.

'Please explain,' said the teacher.

'Because desire creates attachment. Attachment to this world. And, when you don't get what you want or get what you don't want, it leads to suffering. This leads to anger. And that to violence and wars. Which finally results in destruction.'

'So if you want to avoid destruction and suffering, you should control your desires, right?' asked the teacher. 'Give up *maya*, the *illusion* of this world?'

Shiva, from the other side of the curtain, answered silently. *Yes.*

'But the Rig Veda, one of our main sources of philosophy,' continued the teacher, 'says that in the beginning of time, there was nothing except darkness and a primordial flood. Then out of this darkness, desire was born. Desire was the primal seed, the germ of creation. And from here, we all know that the *Prajapati*, the *Lord of the Creatures*, created the Universe and everything in it. So in a sense, desire is the root of creation as well.'

Shiva was mesmerised by the voice on the other side of the curtain. *Good point.*

'How can desire be the source of creation as well as destruction?'

The students were quiet, stumped for answers.

'Think about this in another way. Is it possible to destroy anything that has not been created?'

'No, Guruji.'

'On the other hand, is it safe to assume that anything that has been created, has to be destroyed at some point in time?'

'Yes,' answered a student.

'That is the purpose of desire. It is for creation and destruction. It is the beginning and the end of a journey. Without desire, there is nothing.'

Shiva smiled. *There must be a Vasudev Pandit in that room!*

The Neelkanth turned to Kali. 'Let's go to the library. I want to read the secret. I will meet Panditji later.'

Kali held Shiva. 'The secret is not a thing. It is a man.'

Shiva was taken aback. His eyes wide with surprise.

Ganesh pointed at the curtained entrance to the classroom. 'And he waits for you in there.'

Shiva stared at Ganesh, immobilised. The Lord of the People gently drew the curtain aside. 'Guruji, please forgive the interruption. Lord Neelkanth is here.'

Then Ganesh stepped aside.

Shiva entered and was immediately stunned by what he saw.

What the hell!

He turned to Ganesh, bewildered. The Lord of the People smiled softly. The Neelkanth turned back to the teacher.

'I have been waiting for you, my friend,' said the teacher. He was smiling, his eyes moist. 'I'd told you. I would go anywhere for you. Even into *Patallok* if it would help you.'

Shiva had rerun this line in his mind again and again. Never fully understanding the reference to the *land of the demons*. Now it all clicked into place.

The beard had been shaved off, replaced by a pencil-thin moustache. The broad shoulders and barrel chest, earlier hidden beneath a slight layer of fat, had been honed through regular exercise. The *janau, the string signifying Brahmin antecedents*, traced a path over newly-developed, rippling muscles. The head remained shaved, but the tuft of hair at the back of his head appeared longer and better oiled. The deep-set eyes had the same serenity that had drawn Shiva to him earlier. It was his long-lost friend. His comrade in arms. His brother.

'Brahaspati!'

...to be continued.

Glossary

Agni: God of fire

Agnipariksha: A trial by fire

Angaharas: Movement of limbs or steps in a dance

Ankush: Hook-shaped prods used to control elephants

Annapurna: The Hindu Goddess of food, nourishment and plenty; also believed to be a form of Goddess Parvati

Anshan: Hunger. It also denotes voluntary fasting. In this book, Anshan is the capital of the kingdom of Elam

Apsara: Celestial maidens from the court of the Lord of the Heavens – Indra; akin to Zeus/Jupiter

Arya: Sir

Ashwamedh yagna: Literally, the Horse sacrifice. In ancient times, an ambitious ruler, who wished to expand his territories and display his military prowess, would release a sacrificial horse to roam freely through the length and breadth of any kingdom in India. If any king stopped/captured the horse, the ruler's army would declare war against the challenger, defeat the king and annexe that territory. If an opposing king did not stop the horse, the kingdom would become a vassal of the former

Asura: Demon

Ayuralay: Hospital

Ayurvedic: Derived from Ayurved, an ancient Indian form of medicine

Ayushman bhav: May you have a long life

Baba: Father

Bhang: Traditional intoxicant in India; milk mixed with marijuana

Bhiksha: Alms or donations

Bhojan graham: Dining room

Brahmacharya: The vow of celibacy

Brahmastra: Literally, the weapon of Brahma; spoken of in ancient Hindu scriptures. Many experts claim that the description of a Brahmastra and its effects are eerily similar to that of a nuclear weapon. I have assumed this to be true in the context of my book

Branga: The ancient name for modern West Bengal, Assam and Bangladesh. Term coined from the conjoint of the two rivers of this land: *Brahmaputra* and *Ganga*

Brangaridai: Literally, the heart of Branga. The capital of the kingdom of Branga

Chandravanshi: Descendants of the moon

Chaturanga: Ancient Indian game that evolved into the modern game of chess

Chillum: Clay pipe, usually used to smoke marijuana

Choti: Braid

Construction of Devagiri royal court platform: The description in the book of the court platform is a possible explanation for the mysterious multiple-column buildings made of baked brick discovered at Indus Valley sites, usually next to the public baths, which many historians suppose could have been granaries

Dada: Elder brother

Daivi Astra: Daivi = Divine; Astra = Weapon. A term used in ancient Hindu epics to describe weapons of mass destruction

Dandakaranya: Aranya = forest. Dandak is the ancient name for modern Maharashtra and parts of Andhra Pradesh, Karnataka, Chhattisgarh and Madhya Pradesh. So Dandakaranya means the forests of Dandak

Deva: God

Dharma: Dharma literally translates as religion. But in traditional Hindu belief, it means far more than that. The word encompasses holy, right knowledge, right living, tradition, natural order of the universe and duty. Essentially, dharma refers to everything that can be classified as 'good' in the universe. It is the Law of Life

Dharmayudh: The holy war

Dhobi: Washerman

Divyadrishti: Divine sight

Dumru: A small, hand-held, hour-glass shaped percussion instrument

Egyptian women: Historians believe that ancient Egyptians, just like ancient Indians, treated their women with respect. The anti-women attitude attributed to Swuth and the assassins of Aten is fictional. Having said that, like most societies, ancient Egyptians also had some patriarchal segments in their society, which did, regrettably, have an appalling attitude towards women

Fire song: This is a song sung by Guna warriors to agni (fire). They also had songs dedicated to the other elements viz: *bhūmi* (earth), *jal* (water), *pavan* (air or wind), *vyom* or *shunya* or *akash* (ether or void or sky)

Fravashi: Is the guardian spirit mentioned in the *Avesta*, the sacred writings of the Zoroastrian religion. Although, according to most researchers, there is no physical description of Fravashi, the language grammar of *Avesta* clearly shows it to be feminine. Considering the importance given to fire in ancient Hinduism and Zoroastrianism, I've assumed the Fravashi to be represented by fire. This is, of course, a fictional representation

Ganesh-Kartik relationship: In northern India, traditional myths hold Lord Kartik as older than Lord Ganesh; in large parts of southern India, Lord Ganesh is considered elder. In my story, Ganesh is older than Kartik. What is the truth? Only Lord Shiva knows

Guruji: Teacher; ji is a term of respect, added to a name or title

Gurukul: The family of the guru or the family of the teacher. In ancient times, also used to denote a school

Har Har Mahadev: This is the rallying cry of Lord Shiva's devotees. I believe it means 'All of us are Mahadevs'

Hariyupa: This city is currently known as Harappa. A note on the cities of Meluha (or as we call it in modern times, the Indus Valley Civilisation): historians and researchers have consistently marvelled at the fixation that the Indus Valley Civilisation seemed to have for water and hygiene. In fact historian M Jansen used the term 'wasserluxus' (obsession with water) to describe their magnificent obsession with the physical and symbolic aspects

	of water, a term Gregory Possehl builds upon in his brilliant book, *The Indus Civilisation — A Contemporary Perspective.* In the book, *The Immortals of Meluha*, the obsession with water is shown to arise due to its cleansing of the toxic sweat and urine triggered by consuming the Somras. Historians have also marvelled at the level of sophisticated standardisation in the Indus Valley Civilisation. One of the examples of this was the bricks, which across the entire civilisation, had similar proportions and specifications
Holi:	Festival of colours
Howdah:	Carriage placed on top of elephants
Indra:	The God of the sky; believed to be the King of the Gods
Jai Guru Vishwamitra:	Glory to the teacher Vishwamitra
Jai Guru Vashishtha:	Glory to the teacher Vashishtha. Only two Suryavanshis were privileged to have had both Guru Vashishtha and Guru Vishwamitra as their gurus (teachers) viz. Lord Ram and Lord Lakshman
Jai Shri Brahma:	Glory to Lord Brahma
Jai Shri Ram:	Glory to Lord Ram
Janau:	A ceremonial thread tied from the shoulders, across the torso. It was one of the symbols of knowledge in ancient India. Later, it was corrupted to become a caste symbol to denote those born as Brahmins and not those who'd acquired knowledge through their effort and deeds
Ji:	A suffix added to a name or title as a form of respect
Kajal:	Kohl, or eye liner
Karma:	Duty and deeds; also the sum of a person's actions in this and previous births,

considered to limit the options of future action and affect future fate

Karmasaathi: Fellow traveller in karma or duty

Kashi: The ancient name for modern Varanasi. Kashi means the city where the supreme light shines

Kathak: A form of traditional Indian dance

Kriyas: Actions

Kulhads: Mud cups

Maa: Mother

Mandal: Literally, Sanskrit word meaning circle. Mandals are created, as per ancient Hindu and Buddhist tradition, to make a sacred space and help focus the attention of the devotees

Mahadev: Maha = Great and Dev = God. Hence Mahadev means the greatest God or the God of Gods. I believe that there were many 'destroyers of evil' but a few of them were so great that they would be called 'Mahadev'. Amongst the Mahadevs were Lord Rudra and Lord Shiva

Mahasagar: Great Ocean; Hind Mahasagar is the Indian Ocean

Mahendra: Ancient Indian name meaning conqueror of the world

Mahout: Human handler of elephants

Manu's story: Those interested in finding out more about the historical validity of the South India origin theory of Manu should read Graham Hancock's pathbreaking book, *Underworld*

Mausi: Mother's sister, literally translating as maa *si* i.e. like a mother

Maya: Illusion

Mehragarh: Modern archaeologists believe that Mehragarh is the progenitor of the Indus

Valley civilisation. Mehragarh represents a sudden burst of civilised living, without any archaeological evidence of a gradual progression to that level. Hence, those who established Mehragarh were either immigrants or refugees

Meluha: The land of pure life. This is the land ruled by the Suryavanshi kings. It is the area that we in the modern world call the Indus Valley Civilisation

Meluhans: People of Meluha

Mudras: Gestures

Naga: Serpent people

Namaste: An ancient Indian greeting. Spoken along with the hand gesture of open palms of both the hands joined together. Conjoin of three words. 'Namah', 'Astu' and 'Te' – meaning 'I bow to the Godhood in you'. Namaste can be used as both 'hello' and 'goodbye'

Nirvana: Enlightenment; freedom from the cycle of rebirths

Oxygen/ anti-oxidants theory: Modern research backs this theory. Interested readers can read the article 'Radical Proposal' by Kathryn Brown in the *Scientific American*

Panchavati: The land of the five banyan trees

Pandit: Priest

Paradaeza: An ancient Persian word which means 'the walled place of harmony'; the root of the English word, Paradise

Pariha: The land of fairies. Refers to modern Persia/Iran. I believe Lord Rudra came from this land

Parmatma: The ultimate soul or the sum of all souls

Parsee immigration to India: Groups of Zoroastrian refugees immigrated to India perhaps between the 8th and 10th century AD to escape religious persecution. They landed in Gujarat, and the local ruler Jadav Rana gave them refuge

Pashupatiastra: Literally, the weapon of the Lord of the Animals. The descriptions of the effects of the Pashupatiastra in Hindu scriptures are quite similar to that of nuclear weapons. In modern nuclear technology, weapons have been built primarily on the concept of nuclear fission. While fusion-boosted fission weapons have been invented, pure fusion weapons have not been invented as yet. Scientists hold that a pure nuclear fusion weapon has far less radioactive fallout and can theoretically serve as a more targeted weapon. In this trilogy, I have assumed that the Pashupatiastra is one such weapon

Patallok: The underworld

Pawan Dev: God of the winds

Pitratulya: The term for a man who is 'like a father'

Prahar: Four slots of six hours each into which the day was divided by the ancient Hindus; the first prahar began at twelve midnight

Prithvi: Earth

Prakrati: Nature

Puja: Prayer

Puja thali: Prayer tray

Raj dharma: Literally, the royal duties of a king or ruler. In ancient India, this term embodied pious and just administration of the king's royal duties

Raj guru: Royal sage

Rajat: Silver
Rajya Sabha: The royal council
Rakshabandhan: Raksha = Protection; Bandhan = thread/tie. An ancient Indian festival in which a sister ties a sacred thread on her brother's wrist, seeking his protection
Ram Chandra: Ram = Face; Chandra = Moon. Hence Ram Chandra is 'the face of the moon'
Ram Rajya: The rule of Ram
Rangbhoomi: Literally, the ground of colour. Stadia in ancient times where sports, performances and public functions would be staged
Rangoli: Traditional colourful and geometric designs made with coloured powders or flowers as a sign of welcome
Rishi: Man of knowledge
Sankat Mochan: Literally, reliever from troubles. One of the names of Lord Hanuman
Sangam: A confluence of two rivers
Sanyasi: A person who renounces all his worldly possessions and desires to retreat to remote locations and devote his time to the pursuit of God and spirituality. In ancient India, it was common for people to take sanyas at an old age, once they had completed all their life's duties
Sapt Sindhu: Land of the seven rivers – Indus, Saraswati, Yamuna, Ganga, Sarayu, Brahmaputra and Narmada. This was the ancient name of North India
Saptrishi: One of the 'Group of seven Rishis'
Saptrishi Uttradhikari: Successors of the Saptrishis
Shakti Devi: Mother Goddess; also Goddess of power and energy
Shamiana: Canopy
Shloka: Couplet
Shudhikaran: The purification ceremony

Sindhu: The first river
Somras: Drink of the Gods
Sundarban: Sundar = beautiful; ban = forest. Hence, Sundarban means beautiful forest
Svarna: Gold
Swadweep: The Island of the individual. This is the land ruled by the Chandravanshi kings
Swadweepans: People of Swadweep
Swaha: Legend has it that Lord Agni's wife is named Swaha. Hence it pleases Lord Agni, the God of Fire, if a disciple takes his wife's name while worshipping the sacred fire. Another interpretation of Swaha is that it means offering of self
Tamra: Bronze
Thali: Plate
Varjish graha: The exercise hall
Varun: God of the water and the seas
Vijayibhav: May you be victorious
Vikarma: Carrier of bad fate
Vishnu: The protector of the world and propagator of good. I believe that it is an ancient Hindu title for the greatest of leaders who would be remembered as the mightiest of Gods
Vishwanath: Literally, the Lord of the World. Usually refers to Lord Shiva, also known as Lord Rudra in his angry avatar. I believe Lord Rudra was a different individual from Lord Shiva. In this trilogy, I have used the term Vishwanath to refer to Lord Rudra
Yagna: Sacrificial fire ceremony

Other Titles by Amish

The Shiva Trilogy

The fastest-selling book series in the history of Indian publishing

THE IMMORTALS OF MELUHA
(Book 1 of the Trilogy)

1900 BC. What modern Indians mistakenly call the Indus Valley Civilisation, the inhabitants of that period knew as the land of Meluha – a near perfect empire created many centuries earlier by Lord Ram. Now their primary river Saraswati is drying, and they face terrorist attacks from their enemies from the east. Will their prophesied hero, the Neelkanth, emerge to destroy evil?

THE OATH OF THE VAYUPUTRAS
(Book 3 of the Trilogy)

Shiva reaches the Naga capital, Panchavati, and prepares for a holy war against his true enemy. The Neelkanth must not fail, no matter what the cost. In his desperation, he reaches out to the Vayuputras. Will he succeed? And what will be the real cost of battling Evil? Read the concluding part of this bestselling series to find out.

Indic Chronicles

LEGEND OF SUHELDEV

Repeated attacks by Mahmud of Ghazni have weakened India's northern regions. Then the Turks raid and destroy one of the holiest temples in the land: the magnificent Lord Shiva temple at Somnath. At this most desperate of times, a warrior rises to defend the nation. King Suheldev—fierce rebel, charismatic leader, inclusive patriot. Read this epic adventure of courage and heroism that recounts the story of that lionhearted warrior and the magnificent Battle of Bahraich.

www.authoramish.com

The Ram Chandra Series

The second fastest-selling book series in the history of Indian publishing

RAM – SCION OF IKSHVAKU
(Book 1 of the Series)

He loves his country and he stands alone for the law. His band of brothers, his wife, Sita, and the fight against the darkness of chaos. He is Prince Ram. Will he rise above the taint that others heap on him? Will his love for Sita sustain him through his struggle? Will he defeat the demon Raavan who destroyed his childhood? Will he fulfil the destiny of the Vishnu? Begin an epic journey with Amish's latest: the Ram Chandra Series.

SITA – WARRIOR OF MITHILA
(Book 2 of the Series)

An abandoned baby is found in a field. She is adopted by the ruler of Mithila, a powerless kingdom ignored by all. Nobody believes this child will amount to much. But they are wrong. For she is no ordinary girl. She is Sita. Through an innovative multi-linear narrative, Amish takes you deeper into the epic world of the Ram Chandra Series.

RAAVAN – ENEMY OF ARYAVARTA
(Book 3 of the Series)

Raavan is determined to be a giant among men, to conquer, plunder, and seize the greatness that he thinks is his right. He is a man of contrasts, of brutal violence and scholarly knowledge. A man who will love without reward and kill without remorse. In this, the third book in the Ram Chandra Series, Amish sheds light on Raavan, the king of Lanka. Is he the greatest villain in history or just a man in a dark place, all the time?

www.authoramish.com

Non-fiction

IMMORTAL INDIA

Explore India with the country's storyteller, Amish, who helps you understand it like never before, through a series of sharp articles, nuanced speeches and intelligent debates. In *Immortal India*, Amish lays out the vast landscape of an ancient culture with a fascinatingly modern outlook.

DHARMA – DECODING THE EPICS FOR A MEANINGFUL LIFE

In this genre-bending book, the first of a series, Amish and Bhavna dive into the priceless treasure trove of the ancient Indian epics, as well as the vast and complex universe of Amish's Meluha, to explore some of the key concepts of Indian philosophy. Within this book are answers to our many philosophical questions, offered through simple and wise interpretations of our favourite stories.

The Immortals of Meluha

Amish is a 1974-born, IIM (Kolkata)-educated banker-turned-author. The success of his debut book, *The Immortals of Meluha* (Book 1 of the Shiva Trilogy), encouraged him to give up his career in financial services to focus on writing. Besides being an author, he is also an Indian-government diplomat, a host for TV documentaries, and a film producer.

Amish is passionate about history, mythology and philosophy, finding beauty and meaning in all world religions. His books have sold more than 6 million copies and have been translated into over 20 languages. His Shiva Trilogy is the fastest selling and his Ram Chandra Series the second fastest selling book series in Indian publishing history. You can connect with Amish here:

- www.facebook.com/authoramish
- www.instagram.com/authoramish
- www.twitter.com/authoramish

Other Titles by Amish

SHIVA TRILOGY

The fastest-selling book series in the history of Indian publishing

The Secret of the Nagas (Book 2 of the Trilogy)

The Oath of the Vayuputras (Book 3 of the Trilogy)

RAM CHANDRA SERIES

The second fastest-selling book series in the history of Indian publishing

Ram – Scion of Ikshvaku (Book 1 of the Series)

Sita – Warrior of Mithila (Book 2 of the Series)

Raavan – Enemy of Aryavarta (Book 3 of the Series)

War of Lanka (Book 4 in the Series)

INDIC CHRONICLES

Legend of Suheldev

NON-FICTION

Immortal India: Young Country, Timeless Civilisation

Dharma: Decoding the Epics for a Meaningful Life

www.authoramish.com

'{Amish's} writings have generated immense curiosity about India's rich past and culture.'

– Narendra Modi
(Honourable Prime Minister, India)

'{Amish's} writing introduces the youth to ancient value systems while pricking and satisfying their curiosity…'

– Sri Sri Ravi Shankar
(Spiritual Leader & Founder, Art of Living Foundation)

'{Amish's writing is} riveting, absorbing and informative.'

– Amitabh Bachchan
(Actor & Living Legend)

'{Amish's writing is} a fine blend of history and myth...gripping and unputdownable.'

– BBC

'Thoughtful and deep, Amish, more than any author, represents the New India.'

– Vir Sanghvi
(Senior Journalist & Columnist)

'Amish's mythical imagination mines the past and taps into the possibilities of the future. His book series, archetypal and stirring, unfolds the deepest recesses of the soul as well as our collective consciousness.'

– Deepak Chopra
(World-renowned spiritual guru and bestselling author)

'{Amish is} one of the most original thinkers of his generation.'

– *Arnab Goswami*

(Senior Journalist & MD, Republic TV)

'Amish has a fine eye for detail and a compelling narrative style.'

– *Dr. Shashi Tharoor*

(Member of Parliament & Author)

'{Amish has} a deeply thoughtful mind with an unusual, original, and fascinating view of the past.'

– *Shekhar Gupta*

(Senior Journalist & Columnist)

'To understand the New India, you need to read Amish.'

– *Swapan Dasgupta*

(Member of Parliament & Senior Journalist)

'Through all of Amish's books flows a current of liberal progressive ideology: about gender, about caste, about discrimination of any kind… He is the only Indian bestselling writer with true philosophical depth – his books are all backed by tremendous research and deep thought.'

– *Sandipan Deb*

(Senior Journalist & Editorial Director, Swarajya)

'Amish's influence goes beyond his books, his books go beyond literature, his literature is steeped in philosophy, which is anchored in bhakti, which powers his love for India.'

– *Gautam Chikermane*

(Senior Journalist & Author)

'Amish is a literary phenomenon.'

– *Anil Dharker*

(Senior Journalist & Author)

The Immortals of Meluha

Book 1
of the
Shiva Trilogy

Amish

HarperCollins *Publishers* India

www.authoramish.com

First published in 2010

This edition published in India by HarperCollins *Publishers* 2022
4th Floor, Tower A, Building No. 10, Phase II, DLF Cyber City,
Gurugram, Haryana – 122002
www.harpercollins.co.in

2 4 6 8 10 9 7 5 3 1

Copyright © Amish Tripathi 2010, 2022

P-ISBN: 978-93-5629-052-5
E-ISBN: 978-93-5629-059-4

This is a work of fiction and all characters and incidents described in this book are the product of the author's imagination. Any resemblance to actual persons, living or dead, is entirely coincidental.

Amish Tripathi asserts the moral right
to be identified as the author of this work.

All rights reserved. No part of this publication may be reproduced, stored in a retrieval system, or transmitted, in any form or by any means, electronic, mechanical, photocopying, recording or otherwise, without the prior permission of the publishers.

Typeset in Garamond by Ram Das Lal

Printed and bound at
Thomson Press (India) Ltd

This book is produced from independently certified FSC® paper
to ensure responsible forest management.

To Preeti & Neel...
You both are everything to me,
My words & their meaning,
My prayer & my blessing,
My moon & my sun,
My love & my life,
My soul mate & a part of my soul.

www.authoramish.com

Om Namah Shivāya

The universe bows to Lord Shiva. I bow to Lord Shiva.

Contents

Acknowledgements

The acknowledgments written below were composed when the book was published in 2010. I must also acknowledge those that are publishing this edition of **The Immortals of Meluha***. The team at HarperCollins: Swati, Shabnam, Akriti, Gokul, Vikas, Rahul, and Udayan, led by the brilliant Ananth. Looking forward to this new journey with them.*

***

They say that writing is a lonely profession. They lie. An outstanding group of people have come together to make this book possible. And I would like to thank them.

Preeti, my wife, a rare combination of beauty, brains and spirit who assisted and advised me through all aspects of this book.

My family: Usha, Vinay, Bhavna, Himanshu, Meeta, Anish, Donetta, Ashish, Shernaz, Smita, Anuj, Ruta. A cabal of supremely positive individuals who encouraged, pushed and supported me through the long years of this project.

My first publisher and agent, Anuj Bahri, for his absolute confidence in the Shiva Trilogy.

My present publishers Westland Ltd, led by Gautam Padmanabhan, for sharing a dream with me.

Sharvani Pandit and Gauri Dange, my editors, for making my rather pedestrian English vastly better and for improving the story flow.

Rashmi Pusalkar, Sagar Pusalkar and Vikram Bawa for the exceptional cover.

Atul Manjrekar, Abhijeet Powdwal, Rohan Dhuri and Amit Chitnis for the innovative trailer film, which has helped market the book at a whole new level. And Taufiq Qureshi, for the music of the trailer film.

Mohan Vijayan for his great work on press publicity.

Alok Kalra, Hrishikesh Sawant and Mandar Bhure for their effective advice on marketing and promotions.

Donetta Ditton and Mukul Mukherjee for the website.

You, the reader, for the leap of faith in picking up the book of a debut author.

And lastly, I believe that this story is a blessing to me from Lord Shiva. Humbled by this experience, I find myself a different man today, less cynical and more accepting of different world views. Hence, most importantly, I would like to bow to Lord Shiva, for blessing me so abundantly, far beyond what I deserve.

The Shiva Trilogy

Shiva! The Mahadev. The God of Gods. Destroyer of Evil. Passionate lover. Fierce warrior. Consummate dancer. Charismatic leader. All-powerful, yet incorruptible. A quick wit, accompanied by an equally quick and fearsome temper.

Over the centuries, no foreigner who came to our land – conqueror, merchant, scholar, ruler, traveller – believed that such a great man could possibly have existed in reality. They assumed that he must have been a mythical God, whose existence was possible only in the realms of human imagination. Unfortunately, this belief became our received wisdom.

But what if we are wrong? What if Lord Shiva was not a figment of a rich imagination, but a person of flesh and blood? Like you and me. A man who rose to become Godlike because of his karma. That is the premise of the Shiva Trilogy, which interprets the rich mythological heritage of ancient India, blending fiction with historical fact.

This work is therefore a tribute to Lord Shiva and the lesson that his life is to us. A lesson lost in the depths of time and ignorance. A lesson, that all of us can rise to be better people. A lesson, that there exists a potential God in every single human being. All we have to do is listen to ourselves.

The Immortals of Meluha is the first book in the trilogy that chronicles the journey of this extraordinary hero. Two more books are to follow: *The Secret of the Nagas* and *The Oath of the Vayuputras.*

List of Characters

Anandmayi: Ayodhyan princess, daughter of Emperor Dilipa.

Arishtanemi: Meluhan militia, protectors of Mount Mandar and the road to it.

Ayurvati: The chief of medicine at Meluha.

Bhadra, a.k.a Veerbhadra: A childhood friend and a confidant of Shiva. He is named Veerbhadra as he singlehandedly fought a tiger.

Bhagirath: Prince of Ayodhya, son of Emperor Dilipa.

Bharat: An ancient emperor of the Chandravanshi dynasty married to a Suryavanshi princess.

Brahaspati: Chief Meluhan scientist; belonged to the swan-tribe of Brahmins.

Brahma: A great scientist from the very ancient past.

Brahmanayak: Father of Daksha, previous emperor of Meluha.

Chenardhwaj: Governor of Kashmir, based at Srinagar.

Chitraangadh: Orientation executive of the immigrants' camp in Srinagar.

Daksha: Emperor of the Suryavanshi Empire of Meluha, married to Veerini and father of Sati.

Dilipa: Emperor of Swadweep, king of Ayodhya and chief of the Chandravanshis.

Drapaku: A resident of Kotdwaar in Meluha.
Jattaa: An official in Hariyupa.
Jhooleshwar: Governor of Karachapa in Meluha.
Kanakhala: The prime minister of Meluha, she is in charge of administrative, revenue and protocol matters.
Krittika: Close friend of, and attendant to Sati.
Manu: Founder of the Vedic way of life; born many millennia ago in Sangamtamil region.
Nandi: A captain in the Meluhan army.
Panini: Associate scientist of Brahaspati at Mount Mandar.
Parvateshwar: Head of Meluhan armed forces; in charge of army, navy, special forces and police.
Ram: The seventh Vishnu, who lived many centuries ago. He established the empire of Meluha.
Rudra: The earlier Mahadev, the Destroyer of Evil, who lived some millennia ago.
Sati: Daughter of King Daksha and Queen Veerini, the royal princess of Meluha.
Satyadhwaj: Grandfather of Parvateshwar.
Shiva: The chief of the Guna tribe. Hails from Tibet. Later called Neelkanth, the saviour of the land.
Tarak: A Karachapa resident.
The hooded Naga: A mysterious leader of the Nagas.
Veerini: Queen of Meluha, wife of Daksha and mother of Sati.
Vishwadyumna: A close associate of the hooded Naga figure.
Yakhya: Chief of the Pakrati tribe, opponent of the Gunas from Tibet.

www.authoramish.com

CHAPTER 1

He Has Come!

1900 BC, Mansarovar Lake (At the foot of Mount Kailash, Tibet)

Shiva gazed at the orange sky. The clouds hovering above Mansarovar had just parted to reveal the setting sun. The brilliant giver of life was calling it a day once again. Shiva had seen just a few sunrises in his twenty-one years. But the sunset! He tried never to miss the sunset! On any other day, Shiva would have taken in the vista — the sun and the immense lake against the magnificent backdrop of the Himalayas stretching as far back as the eye could see. But not today.

He squatted and perched his lithe, muscular body on the narrow ledge extending over the lake. The numerous battle-scars on his skin gleamed in the shimmering reflected light of the waters. Shiva remembered well his carefree childhood days. He had perfected the art of throwing pebbles that bounced off the surface of the lake. He still held the record in his tribe for the highest number of bounces: seventeen.

On a normal day, Shiva would have smiled at the memory from a cheerful past that had been overwhelmed by the angst of the present. But today, he turned back towards his village without any hint of joy.

Bhadra was alert, guarding the main entrance. Shiva gestured with his eyes. Bhadra turned back to find his two back-up soldiers dozing against the fence. He cursed and kicked them hard.

Shiva turned back towards the lake.

God bless Bhadra! At least he takes some responsibility.

Shiva brought the chillum made of yak-bone to his lips and took in a deep drag. Any other day, the marijuana would have spread its munificence, dulling his troubled mind and letting him find some moments of solace. But not today.

He looked to his left, towards the edge of the lake where the soldiers of the strange foreign visitor were kept under guard. With the lake behind them and twenty of Shiva's own soldiers guarding them, it was impossible for them to mount any surprise attack.

They let themselves be disarmed so easily. They aren't like the blood-thirsty idiots in our land who are looking for any excuse to fight.

The foreigner's words came flooding back to Shiva. 'Come to our land. It lies beyond the great mountains. Others call it Meluha. I call it Heaven. It is the richest and most powerful empire in India. Indeed the richest and most powerful in the whole world. Our government has an offer for immigrants. You will be given fertile land and resources for farming. Today, your tribe, the Gunas, fight for survival in this rough, arid land. Meluha offers you a lifestyle beyond your wildest dreams. We ask for nothing in return. Just live in peace, pay your taxes and follow the laws of the land.'

Shiva mused that he would certainly not be a chief in this new land.

Would I really miss that so much?

His tribe would have to live by the laws of the foreigners. They would have to work every day for a living.

That's better than fighting every day just to stay alive!

Shiva took another puff from his chillum. As the smoke cleared, he turned to stare at the hut in the centre of his village, right next to his own, where the foreigner had been stationed. He had been told that he could sleep there in comfort. In fact, Shiva wanted to keep him hostage. Just in case.

We fight almost every month with the Pakratis just so that our village can exist next to the holy lake. They are getting stronger every year, forming new alliances with new tribes. We can beat the Pakratis, but not all the mountain tribes together! By moving to Meluha, we can escape this pointless violence and may be live a life of comfort. What could possibly be wrong with that? Why shouldn't we take this deal? It sounds so damn good!

Shiva took one last drag from the chillum before banging it on the rock, letting the ash slip out and rising quickly from his perch. Brushing a few specks of ash from his bare chest, he wiped his hands on his tiger skin skirt, rapidly striding towards his village. Bhadra and his back-up stood to attention as Shiva passed the gate. Shiva frowned and gestured for Bhadra to ease up.

Why does he keep forgetting that he has been my closest friend since childhood? My becoming the chief hasn't really changed anything. He doesn't need to be unnecessarily servile in front of others.

The huts in Shiva's village were luxurious compared to others in their land. A grown man could actually stand upright in them. The shelter could withstand the harsh mountain winds for nearly three years before surrendering to the elements. He flung the empty chillum into his hut as he strode to the hut where the visitor lay sleeping soundly.

Either he doesn't realise he is a hostage. Or he genuinely believes that good behaviour begets good behaviour.

Shiva remembered what his uncle, also his Guru, used to say. 'People do what their society rewards them for doing. If the society rewards trust, people will be trusting.'

Meluha must be a trusting society if it teaches even its soldiers to expect the best in strangers.

Shiva scratched his shaggy beard as he stared hard at the visitor.

He had said his name was Nandi.

The Meluhan's massive proportions appeared even more enormous as he sprawled on the floor in his stupor, his immense belly jiggling with every breath. Despite being obese, his skin was taut and toned. His child-like face looked even more innocent as he slept with his mouth half open.

Is this the man who will lead me to my destiny? Do I really have the destiny my uncle spoke of?

'Your destiny is much larger than these massive mountains. But to make it come true, you will have to cross these very same massive mountains.'

Do I deserve a good destiny? My people come first. Will they be happy in Meluha?

Shiva continued to stare at the sleeping Nandi. Then he heard the sound of a conch shell.

Pakratis!

'POSITIONS!' screamed Shiva, as he drew his sword.

Nandi was up in an instant, drawing a hidden sword from his fur coat that was kept to the side. They sprinted to the village gates. Following standard protocol, the women started rushing to the village centre, carrying their children along. The men ran the other way, swords drawn.

'Bhadra! Our soldiers at the lake!' shouted Shiva as he reached the entrance.

Bhadra relayed the orders and the Guna soldiers obeyed instantly. They were surprised to see the Meluhans draw weapons hidden in their coats and rush to the village. The Pakratis were upon them within moments.

It was a well-planned ambush by the Pakratis. Dusk was usually a time when the Guna soldiers took time to thank their Gods for a day without battle. The women did their chores by the lakeside. If there was a time of weakness for the formidable Gunas, a time when they weren't a fearsome martial clan, but just another mountain tribe trying to survive in a tough, hostile land, this was it.

But fate was against the Pakratis yet again. Thanks to the foreign presence, Shiva had ordered the Gunas to remain alert. Thus they were forewarned and the Pakratis lost the element of surprise. The presence of the Meluhans was also decisive, turning the tide of the short, brutal battle in favour of the Gunas. The Pakratis had to retreat.

Bloodied and scarred, Shiva surveyed the damage at the end of the battle. Two Guna soldiers had succumbed to their injuries. They would be honoured as clan heroes. But even worse, the warning had come too late for at least ten Guna women and children. Their mutilated bodies were found next to the lake. The losses were high.

Bastards! They kill women and children when they can't beat us!

A livid Shiva called the entire tribe to the centre of the village. His mind was made.

'This land is fit for barbarians! We have fought pointless battles with no end in sight. You know that my uncle tried to make peace, even offering access to the lake shore to the mountain tribes. But these scum mistook our desire for peace as weakness. We all know what followed!'

The Gunas, despite being used to the brutality of regular battle, were shell-shocked by the viciousness of the attack on the women and children.

'I keep no secrets from you. All of you are aware of the invitation of the foreigners,' continued Shiva, pointing to Nandi and the Meluhans. 'They fought shoulder-to-shoulder with us today. They have earned my trust. I want to go with them to Meluha. But this cannot be my decision alone.'

'You are our chief, Shiva,' said Bhadra. 'Your decision is our decision. That is the tradition.'

'Not this time,' said Shiva holding out his hand. 'This will change our lives completely. I believe the change will be for the better. Anything will be better than the pointlessness of the violence we face daily. I have told you what I want to do. But the choice to go or not is yours. Let the Gunas speak. This time, I follow you.'

The Gunas were clear about their tradition. This respect for the chief was not just based on convention, but also on Shiva's character. He had led the Gunas to their greatest military victories through his genius and sheer personal bravery.

They spoke in one voice. 'Your decision is our decision.'

— —

It had been five days since Shiva had uprooted his tribe.

The caravan had camped in a nook at the base of one of the great valleys dotting the route to Meluha. Shiva had organized the camp in three concentric circles. The yaks had been tied around the outermost circle, to act as an alarm in case of any intrusion. The men formed an intermediate ring of defenders to repulse any attack. And the women and children were in the innermost circle, just around the fire. The expendables first, defenders second and the most vulnerable in the inside.

Shiva was prepared for the worst. He believed that there would be an ambush. It was only a matter of time.

The Pakratis should have been delighted to have access to the prime lands, as well as free occupation of the lake front. But Shiva knew that Yakhya, the Pakrati chief, would not allow them to leave peacefully. Yakhya would like nothing better than to become a legend by claiming that he had defeated Shiva's Gunas and won the land for the Pakratis. It was precisely this weird tribal logic that Shiva detested. In an atmosphere like this, there was never any hope for peace.

Shiva relished the call of battle, revelled in its art. But he also knew that ultimately, the battles in his land were an exercise in futility.

He turned to an alert Nandi sitting some distance away. The twenty-five Meluhan soldiers were seated in an arc around a second camp circle.

Why did he pick the Gunas for his invitation to immigrate? Why not the Pakratis?

Shiva's thoughts were broken as he saw a shadow move in the distance. He stared hard, but everything was still. Sometimes the light played tricks in this part of the world. Shiva relaxed his stance.

And then he saw the shadow again.

'TO ARMS!' screamed Shiva.

The Gunas and Meluhans drew their weapons and took up battle positions as fifty Pakratis charged in. The stupidity of rushing in without any thought struck them hard as they encountered a wall of panicky animals. The yaks bucked and kicked uncontrollably, injuring many Pakratis before they could even begin their skirmish. A few slipped through. And weapons clashed.

A young Pakrati, obviously a novice, charged at Shiva, swinging wildly. Shiva stepped back, avoiding the strike. He brought his sword back up in a smooth arc, inflicting a superficial cut on the Pakrati's chest. The young warrior cursed and swung back, opening his flank. That was all that Shiva needed. He pushed his sword in brutally, cutting through the gut of his enemy. Almost instantly, he pulled the blade out, twisting it as he did, and left the Pakrati to a slow, painful death. Shiva turned around to find a Pakrati ready to strike a Guna. He jumped high and swung from the elevation slicing neatly through the Pakrati's sword arm, severing it.

Meanwhile Bhadra, as adept at the art of battle as Shiva, was fighting two Pakratis simultaneously, with a sword in each hand. His hump did not seem to impede his movements as he transferred his weight easily, striking the Pakrati on his left side at his throat. Leaving him to die slowly, he swung with his right hand, cutting across the face of the other soldier, gouging his eye out. As the soldier fell, Bhadra brought his left sword down brutally, ending the suffering quickly for this hapless enemy.

The battle at the Meluhan end of the camp was very different. They were exceptionally well-trained soldiers.

But they were not vicious. They were following rules, avoiding killing, as far as possible.

Outnumbered and led poorly, it was but a short while before the Pakratis were beaten. Almost half of them lay dead and the rest were on their knees, begging for mercy. One of them was Yakhya, his shoulder cut deep by Nandi, debilitating the movement of his sword arm.

Bhadra stood behind the Pakrati chief, his sword raised high, ready to strike. 'Shiva, quick and easy or slow and painful?'

'Sir!' intervened Nandi, before Shiva could speak.

Shiva turned towards the Meluhan.

'This is wrong! They are begging for mercy! Killing them is against the rules of war.'

'You don't know the Pakratis!' said Shiva. 'They are brutal. They will keep attacking us even if there is nothing to gain. This has to end. Once and for all.'

'It is already ending. You are not going to live here anymore. You will soon be in Meluha.'

Shiva stood silent.

Nandi continued, 'How you want to end this is up to you. More of the same or different?'

Bhadra looked at Shiva. Waiting.

'You can show the Pakratis that you are better,' said Nandi.

Shiva turned towards the horizon, seeing the massive mountains.

Destiny? Chance of a better life?

He turned back to Bhadra. 'Disarm them. Take all their provisions. Release them.'

Even if the Pakratis are mad enough to go back to their village, rearm and come back, we would be long gone.

A shocked Bhadra stared at Shiva. But immediately started implementing the order.

Nandi gazed at Shiva with hope. There was but one thought that reverberated through his mind. '*Shiva has the heart. He has the potential. Please, let it be him. I pray to you Lord Ram, let it be him.*'

Shiva walked back to the young soldier he had stabbed. He lay writhing on the ground, face contorted in pain, even as blood oozed slowly out of his guts. For the first time in his life, Shiva felt pity for a Pakrati. He drew out his sword and ended the young soldier's suffering.

— ⁂ —

After marching continuously for four weeks, the caravan of invited immigrants crested the final mountain to reach the outskirts of Srinagar, the capital of the valley of Kashmir. Nandi had talked excitedly about the glories of his perfect land. Shiva had prepared himself to see some incredible sights, which he could not have imagined in his simple homeland. But nothing could have primed him for the sheer spectacle of what certainly was paradise. *Meluha.* The *land of pure life!*

The mighty Jhelum river, a roaring tigress in the mountains, slowed down to the rhythm of a languorous cow as she entered the valley. She caressed the heavenly land of Kashmir, meandering her way into the immense Dal Lake. Further down, she broke away from the lake, continuing her journey towards the sea.

The vast valley was covered by a lush green canvas of grass. On it was painted the masterpiece that was Kashmir. Rows upon rows of flowers arrayed all of God's colours, their brilliance broken only by the soaring Chinar trees, offering a majestic, yet warm Kashmiri welcome. The melodious singing of the birds calmed the exhausted ears of Shiva's tribe, accustomed only to the rude howling of icy mountain winds.

'If this is the border province, how perfect must the rest of the country be?' whispered Shiva in awe.

The Dal Lake was the site of an ancient army camp of the Meluhans. Upon the western banks of the lake, by the side of the Jhelum lay the frontier town that had grown beyond its simple encampments into the grand *Srinagar*. Literally, the '*respected city*'.

Srinagar had been raised upon a massive platform of almost a hundred hectares in size. The platform built of earth, towered almost five metres high. On top of the platform were the city walls, which were another twenty metres high and four metres thick. The simplicity and brilliance of building an entire city on a platform astounded the Gunas. It was a strong protection against enemies who would have to fight their way up a fort wall which was essentially solid ground. The platform served another vital purpose: it raised the ground level of the city, an extremely effective strategy against the recurrent floods in this land. Inside the fort walls, the city was divided into blocks by roads laid out in a neat grid pattern. It had specially constructed market areas, temples, gardens, meeting halls and everything else that would be required for sophisticated urban living. All the houses looked like simple multiple-storeyed block structures from the outside. The only way to differentiate a rich man's house from that of a poor man's, was that his block would be bigger.

In contrast to the extravagant natural landscape of

Kashmir, the city of Srinagar itself was painted only in restrained greys, blues and whites. The entire city was a picture of cleanliness, order and sobriety. Nearly twenty thousand souls called Srinagar their home. Now an additional two hundred had just arrived from Mount Kailash. And their leader felt a lightness of being he hadn't experienced since that terrible day, many years ago.

I have escaped. I can make a new beginning. I can forget.

— ⁂ —

The caravan travelled to the immigrant camp outside Srinagar. The camp had been built on a separate platform on the southern side of the city. Nandi led Shiva and his tribe to the Foreigners' Office, which was placed just outside the camp. Nandi requested Shiva to wait outside as he went into the office. He soon returned, accompanied by a young official. The official gave a practised smile and folded his hands in a formal Namaste. 'Welcome to Meluha. I am Chitraangadh. I will be your Orientation Executive. Think of me as your single point of contact for all issues whilst you are here. I believe your leader's name is Shiva. Will he step up please?'

Shiva took a step forward. 'I am Shiva.'

'Excellent,' said Chitraangadh. 'Would you be so kind as to follow me to the registration desk please? You will be registered as the caretaker of your tribe. Any communication that concerns them will go through you. Since you are the designated leader, the implementation of all directives within your tribe would be your responsibility.'

Nandi cut into Chitraangadh's officious speech to tell Shiva, 'Sir, if you will just excuse me, I will go to the immigrant camp quarters and arrange the temporary living arrangements for your tribe.'

Shiva noticed that Chitraangadh's ever-beaming face had lost its smile for a fraction of a second as Nandi interrupted his flow. But he recovered quickly and the smile returned to his face once again. Shiva turned and looked at Nandi.

'Of course, you may. You don't need to take my permission, Nandi,' said Shiva. 'But in return, you have to promise me something, my friend.'

'Of course, Sir,' replied Nandi bowing slightly.

'Call me Shiva. Not Sir,' grinned Shiva. 'I am your friend. Not your Chief.'

A surprised Nandi looked up, bowed again and said, 'Yes Sir. I mean, yes, Shiva.'

Shiva turned back to Chitraangadh, whose smile for some reason appeared more genuine now. He said, 'Well Shiva, if you will follow me to the registration desk, we will complete the formalities quickly.'

The newly registered tribe reached the residential quarters in the immigration camp, to see Nandi waiting outside the main gates; he led them in. The roads of the camp were just like those of Srinagar. They were laid out in a neat north-south and east-west grid. The carefully paved footpaths contrasted sharply with the dirt tracks in Shiva's own land. He noticed something strange about the road though.

'Nandi, what are those differently coloured stones running through the centre of the road?' asked Shiva.

'They cover the underground drains, Shiva. The drains take out all the waste water of the camp. It ensures that the camp remains clean and hygienic.'

Shiva marvelled at the almost obsessively meticulous planning of the Meluhans.

The Gunas reached the large building that had been assigned to them. For the umpteenth time, they thanked the wisdom of their leader in deciding to come to Meluha. The three–storeyed building had comfortable, separate living quarters for each family. Each room had luxurious furniture including a highly polished copper plate on the wall in which they could see their reflection. The rooms had clean linen bed sheets, towels and even some clothes. Feeling the cloth, a bewildered Shiva asked, 'What is this material?'

Chitraangadh replied enthusiastically, 'It's cotton, Shiva. The plant is grown in our lands and fashioned into the cloth that you hold.'

There was a broad picture window on each wall to let in the light and the warmth of the sun. Notches on each wall supported a metal rod with a controlled flame on top for lighting. Each room had an attached bathroom with a sloping floor that enabled the water to flow naturally to a hole which drained it out. At the right end of each bathroom was a paved basin on the ground which culminated in a large hole. The purpose of this contraption was a mystery to the tribe. The side walls had some kind of device, which when turned, allowed water to flow through.

'Magic!' whispered Bhadra's mother.

Beside the main door of the building was an attached house. A doctor and her nurses walked out of the house to greet Shiva. The doctor, a petite, wheat-skinned woman was dressed in a simple white cloth tied around her waist and legs in a style the Meluhans called *dhoti*. A smaller white cloth was tied as a blouse around her chest while another cloth called an *angvastram* was draped over her shoulders. The centre of her forehead bore a white dot. Her head had been shaved clean except for a knotted tuft of hair at the back, called a *choti*. A loose string called a *janau* was tied from her left shoulder across her torso down to the right side.

Nandi was genuinely startled at seeing her. With a reverential Namaste, he said, 'Lady Ayurvati! I didn't expect a doctor of your stature here.'

Ayurvati looked at Nandi with a smile and a polite Namaste. 'I strongly believe in the field-work experience programme, Captain. My team follows it strictly. However, I am terribly sorry but I don't recognise you. Have we met before?'

'My name is Captain Nandi, my lady,' answered Nandi. 'We haven't met but who doesn't know you, the greatest doctor in the land?'

'Thank you, Captain Nandi,' said a visibly embarrassed Ayurvati. 'But I think you exaggerate. There are many far superior to me.' Turning quickly towards Shiva, Ayurvati continued, 'Welcome to Meluha. I am Ayurvati, your designated doctor. My nurses and I will be at your assistance for the time that you are in these quarters.'

Hearing no reaction from Shiva, Chitraangadh said in his most earnest voice, 'These are just temporary quarters, Shiva. The actual houses that will be allocated to your tribe will be much more comfortable. You have to stay here only for the period of the quarantine which will not last more than seven days.'

'Oh no, my friend! The quarters are more than comfortable. They are beyond anything that we could have imagined. What say *Mausi*?' grinned Shiva at Bhadra's mother, before turning back to Chitraangadh with a frown. 'But why the quarantine?'

Nandi cut in. 'Shiva, the quarantine is just a precaution. We don't have too many diseases in Meluha. Sometimes, immigrants may come in with new diseases. During this seven–day period, the doctors will observe and cure you of any such ailments.'

'And one of the guidelines that you have to follow in order to control diseases is to maintain strict hygiene standards,' said Ayurvati.

Shiva grimaced at Nandi and whispered, 'Hygiene standards?'

Nandi's forehead crinkled into an apologetic frown while his hands gently advised acquiescence. He mumbled, 'Please go along with it, Shiva. It is just one of those things that we *have* to do in Meluha. Lady Ayurvati is considered the best doctor in the land.'

'If you are free right now, I can give you your instructions,' said Ayurvati.

'I am free right now,' said Shiva with a straight face. 'But I may have to charge you later.'

Bhadra giggled softly, while Ayurvati stared at Shiva with a blank face, clearly not amused at the pun.

'I'm sure I don't understand what you're trying to say,' replied Ayurvati frostily. 'Without further ado let's begin with the ablutionary ritual.'

Ayurvati walked into the guest house, muttering under her breath, 'These uncouth immigrants…'

Shiva raised his eyebrows towards Bhadra, grinning impishly.

— ⅄⊚Ʊ⇡⊗ —

Late in the evening, after a hearty meal, all the Gunas were served a medicinal drink in their rooms.

'Yuck!' grimaced Bhadra, his face contorted. 'This tastes like yak's piss!'

'How do you know what yak's piss tastes like?' laughed Shiva, as he slapped his friend hard on the back. 'Now go to your room. I need to sleep.'

'Have you seen the beds? I think this is going to be the best sleep of my life!'

'I have seen the bed, dammit!' grinned Shiva. 'Now I want to experience it. Get out!'

Bhadra left Shiva's room, laughing loudly. He wasn't the only one excited by the unnaturally soft beds. Their entire tribe had rushed to their rooms for what they anticipated would be the most comfortable sleep of their lives. They were in for a surprise.

— ⅄⊚Ʊ⇡⊗ —

Shiva tossed and turned on his bed constantly. He was wearing an orange coloured dhoti. The tiger skin had been taken away to be washed — for hygiene reasons. His cotton angvastram was lying on a low chair by the wall. A half-lit chillum lay forlorn on the side-table.

This cursed bed is too soft. Impossible to sleep on!

Shiva yanked the bed sheet off the mattress, tossed it on the floor and lay down. This was a little better. Sleep was stealthily creeping in on him. But not as strongly as at home. He missed the rough cold floor of his own hut. He missed the shrill winds of Mount Kailash, which broke through the most determined efforts to ignore them. He missed the comforting stench of his tiger skin. No doubt, his current surroundings were excessively comfortable, but they were unfamiliar and alien.

As usual, it was his instincts which brought up the truth: '*It's not the room. It's you.*'

It was then that Shiva noticed that he was sweating. Despite the cool breeze, he was sweating profusely. The room appeared to be spinning lightly. He felt as if his body was being drawn out of itself. His frostbitten right toe felt as if it was on fire. His battle-scarred left knee seemed to be getting stretched. His tired and aching muscles felt as if a great hand was remoulding them. His shoulder bone, dislocated in days past and never completely healed, appeared to be ripping the muscles aside so as to re-engineer the joint. The muscles in turn seemed to be giving way to the bones to do their job.

Breathing was an effort. He opened his mouth to help his lungs along. But not enough air flowed in. Shiva concentrated with all his might, opened his mouth wide and sucked in as much air as he could. The curtains by the side of the window rustled as a kindly wind rushed in. With the sudden gush of air, Shiva's body relaxed just a bit. And then the battle began again. He focused and willed giant gasps of air into his hungry body.

Knock! Knock!

The light tapping on the door alerted Shiva. He was disoriented for a moment. Still breathing hard! His shoulder was twitching. The familiar pain was missing. He looked down at his knee. It didn't hurt anymore. The scar had vanished. Still gasping for breath! He looked down at his toe. Whole and complete now. He bent to check it. A cracking sound reverberated through the room as his toe made its first movement in years. Still breathing hard! There was also an unfamiliar tingling coldness in his neck. Very cold.

Knock! Knock! A little more insistent now.

A bewildered Shiva staggered to his feet, pulled the angvastram around his neck for warmth and opened the door. The darkness veiled his face, but Shiva could still recognise Bhadra. He whispered in a panic-stricken voice, 'Shiva, I'm sorry to disturb you so late. But my mother has suddenly developed a very high fever. What should I do?'

Shiva instinctively touched Bhadra's forehead. 'You too have a fever Bhadra. Go to your room. I will get the doctor.'

As Shiva raced down the corridor towards the steps he encountered many more doors opening with the now familiar message. 'Sudden fever! Help!'

Shiva sprinted down the steps to the attached building where the doctors were housed. He knocked hard on the door. Ayurvati opened it immediately, as if she was expecting him. Shiva spoke calmly. 'Ayurvati, almost my entire tribe has suddenly fallen ill. Please come fast, they need help.'

Ayurvati touched Shiva's forehead. 'You don't have a fever?'

Shiva shook his head. 'No.'

Ayurvati frowned, clearly surprised. She turned and ordered her nurses, 'Come on. It's begun. Let's go.'

As Ayurvati and her nurses rushed into the building,

Chitraangadh appeared out of nowhere. He asked Shiva, 'What happened?'

'I don't know. Practically everybody in my tribe suddenly fell ill.'

'You too are perspiring heavily.'

'Don't worry. I don't have fever. Look, I'm going back into the building. I want to see how my people are doing.'

Chitraangadh nodded, adding, 'I'll call Nandi.'

As Chitraangadh sped away in search of Nandi, Shiva ran into the building. He was surprised the moment he entered. All the torches in the building had been lit. The nurses were going from room to room, methodically administering medicines and advising the scared patients on what they should do. A scribe walked along with each nurse meticulously noting the details of each patient on a palm-leaf booklet. The Meluhans were clearly prepared for such an eventuality. Ayurvati stood at the end of the corridor, her hands on her hips. Like a general supervising her superbly trained and efficient troops. Shiva rushed up to her and asked, 'What about the second and third floor?'

Ayurvati answered without turning to him. 'Nurses have already reached every room in the building. I will go up to supervise once the situation on this floor has stabilised. We'll cover all the patients in the next half hour.'

'You people are incredibly efficient but I pray that everyone will be okay,' said a worried Shiva.

Ayurvati turned to look at Shiva. Her eyebrows were raised slightly and a hint of a smile hovered on her serious face. 'Don't worry. We're Meluhans. We are capable of handling any situation. Everybody will be fine.'

'Is there anything I can do to help?'

'Yes. Please go and bathe.'

'What?!'

'Please go have a bath. Right now,' said Ayurvati as she turned back to look at her team. 'Everybody, please remember that all children below the age of fifteen *must* be tonsured. Mastrak, please go up and start the secondary medicines. I'll be there in five minutes.'

'Yes, my lady,' said a young man as he hurried up the steps carrying a large cloth bag.

'You're still here?' asked Ayurvati as she noticed that Shiva hadn't left.

Shiva spoke softly, controlling his rising anger, 'What difference will my bathing make? My people are in trouble. I want to help.'

'I don't have the time or the patience to argue with you. You will go and bathe right now!' said Ayurvati, clearly *not* trying to control her rising temper.

Shiva glared at Ayurvati as he made a heroic effort to rein in the curses that wanted to leap out of his mouth. His clenched fists wanted to have an argument of their own with Ayurvati. But she was a woman.

Ayurvati too glared back at Shiva. She was used to being obeyed. She was a doctor. If she told a patient to do something, she expected it to be done without question. But in her long years of experience she had also seen a few patients like Shiva, especially from the nobility. Such patients had to be *reasoned* with. Not *instructed.* Yet, this was a simple immigrant. Not some nobleman!

Controlling herself with great effort, Ayurvati said, 'Shiva, you are perspiring. If you don't wash it off, it will kill you. Please trust me. You cannot be of any help to your tribe if you are dead.'

— ⚹ —

Chitraangadh banged loudly on the door. A bleary-eyed Nandi woke up cursing. He wrenched the door open and growled, 'This better be important!'

'Come quickly. Shiva's tribe has fallen ill.'

'Already? But this is only the first night!' exclaimed Nandi. Picking up his angvastram he said, 'Let's go!'

The bathroom seemed like a strange place for a bath. Shiva was used to splashing about in the chilly Mansarovar Lake for his bi-monthly ablutions. The bathroom felt strangely constricted. He turned the magical device on the wall to increase the flow of water. He used the strange cake-like substance that the Meluhans said was a soap to rub the body clean. Ayurvati had been very clear. The soap *had* to be used. He turned the water off and picked up the towel. As he rubbed himself vigorously, the mystifying development he had ignored in the past few hours came flooding back. His shoulder felt better than new. His surprised gaze fell to his knee. No pain, no scar. He then looked incredulously at his completely healed toe. And then he realised that it wasn't just the injured parts, but his entire body felt new, rejuvenated and stronger than ever. His neck, though, still felt intolerably cold.

What the devil is going on?

He stepped out of the bathroom and quickly wore a new dhoti. Again, Ayurvati's strict instructions were not to wear his old clothes which were infected by his toxic perspiration. As he was wrapping the angvastram around his neck for some warmth, there was a knock on the door.

It was Ayurvati. 'Shiva, can you open the door please? I just want to check whether you are all right.'

Shiva opened the door. Ayurvati stepped in and checked Shiva's temperature; it was normal. Ayurvati nodded slightly and said, 'You seem to be healthy. And your tribe is recovering quickly as well. The trouble has passed.'

Shiva smiled gratefully. 'Thanks to the skills and efficiency of your team. I am truly sorry for arguing with you earlier. It was unnecessary. I know you meant well.'

Ayurvati looked up from her palm-leaf booklet with a slight smile and a raised eyebrow. 'Being polite, are we?'

'I'm not all that rude, you know,' grinned Shiva. 'You people are just too supercilious!'

Ayurvati suddenly stopped listening as she stared at Shiva with a stunned look on her face. How had she not noticed it before? She had never believed in the legend. Was she going to be the first one to see it come true? Pointing weakly with her hands she mumbled, 'Why have you covered your neck?'

'It's very cold for some reason. Is it something to be worried about?' asked Shiva as he pulled the angvastram off.

A cry resounded loudly through the silent room as Ayurvati staggered back. Her hand covered her mouth in shock while the palm leaves scattered on the floor. Her knees were too weak to hold her up. She collapsed with her back against the wall, never once taking her eyes off Shiva. Tears broke through her proud eyes. She kept repeating, 'Om Brahmaye namah. Om Brahmaye namah.'

'What happened? Is it serious?' asked a worried Shiva.

'You have come! My Lord, you have come!'

Before a bewildered Shiva could respond to her strange

reaction, Nandi rushed in and noticed Ayurvati on the ground. Copious tears were flowing down her face.

'What happened, my lady?' asked a startled Nandi.

Ayurvati just pointed at Shiva's neck. Nandi looked up. The neck shone an eerie iridescent blue. With a cry that sounded like that of a long caged animal just released from captivity, Nandi collapsed on his knees. 'My Lord! You have come! The Neelkanth has come!'

The Captain bent low and brought his head down to touch the Neelkanth's feet reverentially. The object of his adoration however, stepped back, befuddled and perturbed.

'What the hell is going on here?' Shiva asked agitatedly.

Holding a hand to his freezing neck, he turned around to the polished copper plate and stared in stunned astonishment at the reflection of his *neel kanth;* his *blue throat.*

Chitraangadh, holding the door frame for support, sobbed like a child. 'We're saved! We're saved! He has come!'

CHAPTER 2

Land of Pure Life

Chenardhwaj, the governor of Kashmir, wanted to broadcast to the entire world that the Neelkanth had appeared in his capital city. Not in the other frontier towns like Takshashila, Karachapa or Lothal. *His* Srinagar! But the bird courier had arrived almost immediately from the Meluhan capital *Devagiri*, the *abode of the Gods*. The orders were crystal clear. The news of the arrival of the Neelkanth had to be kept secret until the emperor himself had seen Shiva. Chenardhwaj was ordered to send Shiva along with an escort to Devagiri. Most importantly, Shiva himself was not to be told about the legend. 'The emperor will advise the supposed Neelkanth in an appropriate manner,' were the exact words in the message.

Chenardhwaj had the privilege of informing Shiva about the journey. Shiva though, was not in the most amenable of moods. He was utterly perplexed by the sudden devotion of every Meluhan around him. Since he had been transferred to the gubernatorial residence where he lived in luxury, only the most important citizens of Srinagar had access to him.

'My Lord, we will be escorting you to Devagiri,

our capital. It is a few weeks' journey from here,' said Chenardhwaj as he struggled to bend his enormous and muscular frame lower than he ever had.

'I'm not going anywhere till somebody tells me what is going on! What the hell is this damned legend of the Neelkanth?' Shiva asked angrily.

'My Lord, please have faith in us. You will know the truth soon. The emperor himself will tell you when you reach Devagiri.'

'And what about my tribe?'

'They will be given lands right here in Kashmir, my Lord. All the resources that they need in order to lead a comfortable life will be provided for.'

'Are they being held hostage?'

'Oh no, my Lord,' said a visibly disturbed Chenardhwaj. 'They are *your* tribe, my Lord. If I had my way, they would live like nobility for the rest of their lives. But the laws cannot be broken, my Lord. Not even for you. We can only give them what had been promised. In the course of time my Lord, you can change the laws you deem necessary. Then we could certainly accommodate them anywhere.'

'Please, my Lord,' pleaded Nandi. 'Have faith in us. You cannot imagine how important you are to Meluha. We have been waiting for a very long time for you. We need your help.'

Please help me! Please!

The memory of another desperate plea from a distraught woman years ago returned to haunt Shiva as he was stunned into silence.

— ⅄◎Ʊ⍋⊗ —

'Your destiny is much larger than these massive mountains.'

Nonsense! I don't deserve any destiny. If these people knew of my guilt, they would stop this bullshit instantly!

'I don't know what to do, Bhadra.'

Shiva was sitting in the royal gardens on the banks of the Dal Lake while his friend sat by his side, carefully filling some marijuana into a chillum. As Bhadra used the lit stick to bring the chillum to life, Shiva said impatiently, 'That's a cue for you to speak, you fool.'

'No. That's actually a cue for me to hand you the chillum, Shiva.'

'Why will you not council me?' asked Shiva in anguish. 'We are still the same friends who never made a move without consulting each other!'

Bhadra smiled. 'No we are not. You are the Chief now. The tribe lives and dies by your decisions. It cannot be corrupted by any other person's influence. We are not like the Pakratis, where the Chief has to listen to whoever is the loudmouth in their counsel. Only the chief's wisdom is supreme amongst the Gunas. That is our tradition.'

Shiva raised his eyes in exasperation. 'Some traditions are meant to be broken!'

Bhadra stayed silent. Stretching his hand, Shiva grabbed the chillum from Bhadra. He took one deep puff, letting the marijuana spread its munificence into his body.

'I've heard just one line about the legend of the Neelkanth,' said Bhadra. 'Apparently Meluha is in deep trouble and only the Neelkanth can save them.'

'But I can't seem to see any trouble out here. Everything seems perfect. If they want to see real trouble we should take them to our land!'

Bhadra laughed slightly. 'But what is it about the blue throat that makes them believe you can save them?'

'Damned if I know! They are so much more advanced than us. And yet they worship me like I am some God. Just because of this blessed blue throat.'

'I think their medicines are magical though. Have you noticed that the hump on my back has reduced a little bit?'

'Yes it has! Their doctors are seriously gifted.'

'You know their doctors are called Brahmins?'

'Like Ayurvati?' asked Shiva, passing the chillum back to Bhadra.

'Yes. But the Brahmins don't just cure people. They are also teachers, lawyers, priests, basically any intellectual profession.'

'Talented people,' sniffed Shiva.

'That's not all,' said Bhadra, in between a long inhalation. 'They have a concept of specialisation. So in addition to the Brahmins, they have a group called Kshatriyas, who are the warriors and rulers. Even the women can be Kshatriyas!'

'Really? They allow women into their army?'

'Well, apparently there aren't too many female Kshatriyas. But yes, they are allowed into the army.'

'No wonder they are in trouble!'

The friends laughed loudly at the strange ways of the Meluhans. Bhadra took another puff from the chillum before continuing his story. 'And then they have Vaishyas, who are craftsmen, traders and business people and finally the Shudras who are the farmers and workers. And one caste cannot do another caste's job.'

'Hang on,' said Shiva. 'That means that since you

are a warrior, you would not be allowed to trade at the marketplace?'

'Yes.'

'Bloody stupid! How would you get me my marijuana? After all that is the only thing you are useful for!'

Shiva leaned back to avoid the playful blow from Bhadra. 'All right, all right. Take it easy!' he laughed. Stretching out, he grabbed the chillum from Bhadra and took another deep drag.

We're talking about everything except what we should be talking about.

Shiva became serious once again. 'But seriously, strange as they are, what should I do?'

'What are you thinking of doing?'

Shiva looked away, as if contemplating the roses in the far corner of the garden. 'I don't want to run away once again.'

'What?' asked Bhadra, not hearing Shiva's tormented whisper clearly.

'I said,' repeated Shiva loudly, 'I can't bear the guilt of running away once again.'

'That wasn't your fault…'

'YES IT WAS!'

Bhadra fell silent. There was nothing that could be said. Covering his eyes, Shiva sighed once again. 'Yes, it was…'

Bhadra put his hand on his friend's shoulder, pressing it gently, letting the terrible moment pass. Shiva turned his face. 'I'm asking for advice, my friend. What should I do? If they need my help, I can't turn away from them. At the same time, how can I leave our tribe all by themselves out here? What should I do?'

Bhadra continued to hold Shiva's shoulder. He breathed

deeply. He could think of an answer. It may have been the correct answer for Shiva, *his friend.* But was it the correct answer for Shiva, *the leader*?

'You have to find that wisdom within yourself, Shiva. That is the tradition.'

'O the hell with you!'

Shiva threw the chillum back at Bhadra and stormed away.

It was only a few days later that a minor caravan consisting of Shiva, Nandi and three soldiers was scheduled to leave Srinagar. The small party would ensure that they moved quickly through the realm and reached Devagiri as soon as possible. Governor Chenardhwaj was anxious for Shiva to be recognised quickly by the empire as the true Neelkanth. He wanted to go down in history as the governor who had found the Lord.

Shiva had been made 'presentable' for the emperor. His hair had been oiled and smoothened. Lines of expensive clothes, attractive ear-rings, necklaces and other jewellery were used to adorn his muscular frame. His fair face had been scrubbed clean with special *Ayurvedic* herbs to remove years of dead skin and decay. A cravat had been fashioned of cotton to cover his glowing blue throat. Beads, cleverly darned onto the fabric, gave it the appearance of the traditional necklace that Meluhan men sported during times of ritual. The cravat felt warm around his still cold throat.

'I will be back soon,' said Shiva as he hugged Bhadra's mother. He was amazed to see that the old lady's limp was a little less noticeable.

Their medicines are truly magical.

As a morose Bhadra looked at him, Shiva whispered, 'Take care of the tribe. You are in charge till I come back.'

Bhadra stepped back, startled. 'Shiva you don't have to do that just because I am your friend.'

'I have to do it, you fool. And the reason why I have to do it is that you are more capable than I am.'

Bhadra stepped up and embraced Shiva, lest his friend notice the tears in his eyes. 'No Shiva, I am not. Not even in my dreams.'

'Shut up! Listen to me carefully,' said Shiva as Bhadra smiled sadly. 'I don't think the Gunas are at any risk here. At least not to the same extent as we were at Mount Kailash. But even so, if you feel you need help, ask Ayurvati. I observed her when the tribe was ill. She showed tremendous commitment towards saving us all. She is trustworthy.'

Bhadra nodded, hugged Shiva once again and left the room.

— ⅄⦶Ʊ⇞⊛ —

Ayurvati knocked politely on the door. 'May I come in, my Lord?'

This was the first time that she had come into his presence since that fateful moment seven days back. It seemed like a lifetime to her. Though she appeared to be her confident self again, there was a slightly different look about her. She had the appearance of someone who had been touched by the divine.

'Come in Ayurvati. And please, none of this "Lord"

business. I am still the same uncouth immigrant you met a few days back.'

'I am sorry about that comment, my Lord. It was wrong of me to say that and I am willing to accept any punishment that you may deem fit.'

'What's wrong with you? Why should I punish you for speaking the truth? Why should this bloody blue throat change anything?'

'You will discover the reason soon enough, my Lord,' whispered Ayurvati with her head bowed. 'We have waited for centuries for you.'

'Centuries?! In the name of the holy lake, why? What can I do that any amongst you smart people can't?'

'The emperor will tell you, my Lord. Suffice it to say that after all that I have heard from your tribe, if there is one person worthy of being the Neelkanth, it is you.'

'Speaking of my tribe, I have told them that if they need any help, they can turn to you. I hope that is all right.'

'It would be my honour to provide any assistance to them, my Lord.'

Saying this, she bent down to touch Shiva's feet in the traditional Indian form of showing respect. Shiva had resigned himself to accepting this gesture from most Meluhans but immediately stepped back as Ayurvati bent down.

'What the hell are you doing, Ayurvati?' asked a horrified Shiva. 'You are a doctor, a giver of life. Don't embarrass me by touching my feet.'

Ayurvati looked up at Shiva, her eyes shining with admiration and devotion. This was certainly a man worthy of being the Neelkanth.

— ⅄ⵙႮ⇡⊗ —

Nandi entered Shiva's room carrying a saffron cloth with the word 'Ram' stamped across every inch of it. He requested Shiva to wrap it around his shoulders. As Shiva complied, Nandi muttered a quick short prayer for a safe journey to Devagiri.

'Our horses wait outside, my Lord. We can leave when you are ready,' said Nandi.

'Nandi,' said an exasperated Shiva. 'How many times must I tell you? My name is Shiva. I am your friend, not your Lord'

'Oh no, my Lord,' gasped Nandi. 'You are the Neelkanth. You *are* the Lord. How can I take your name?'

Shiva rolled his eyes, shook his head slightly and turned towards the door. 'I give up! Can we leave now?'

'Of course, my Lord.'

They stepped outside to see three mounted soldiers waiting patiently, while tethered close to them were three more horses. One each for Shiva and Nandi, while the third was assigned for carrying their provisions. The well-organised Meluhan Empire had rest houses and provision stores spread across all major travel routes. As long as there were enough provisions for one day, a traveller carrying Meluhan coins could comfortably keep buying fresh provisions that would last a journey of months.

Nandi's horse had been tethered next to a small platform. The platform had steps leading up to it from the other side. Clearly, this was convenient infrastructure for obese riders who found it a little cumbersome to climb onto a horse. Shiva looked at Nandi's enormous form, then at his unfortunate horse and then back at Nandi.

'Aren't there any laws in Meluha against cruelty to animals?' asked Shiva with the most sincere of expressions.

'Oh yes, my Lord. Very strict laws. In Meluha ALL life is precious. In fact there are strict guidelines as to when and how animals can be slaughtered and…'

Suddenly Nandi stopped speaking. Shiva's joke had finally breached Nandi's slow wit. They both burst out laughing as Shiva slapped Nandi hard on his back.

Shiva's entourage followed the course of the Jhelum which had resumed its thunderous roar as it crashed down the lower Himalayas. Once on the magnificent flat plains, the turbulent river calmed down again and flowed smoothly on. Smooth enough for the group to board one of the many public transport barges and sail quickly down to the town of Brihateshpuram.

From there on, they went eastwards down a well marked road through Punjab, the heart of the empire's northern reaches. *Punjab* literally meant the *land of the five rivers*. The land of the Indus, Jhelum, Chenab, Ravi and Beas. The four eastern rivers aspired to grasp the grand Indus, which flowed farthest to the west. They succeeded spectacularly, after convoluted journeys through the rich plains of Punjab. The Indus itself found comfort and succour in the enormous, all embracing ocean. The mystery of the ocean's final destination though was yet to be unravelled.

'What is Raṃ?' enquired Shiva as he looked down at the word covering every inch of his saffron cloth.

The three accompanying soldiers rode at a polite distance behind Shiva and Nandi. Far enough not to overhear any conversation but close enough to move in quickly at the first sign of trouble. It was a part of their standard Meluhan service rules.

'Lord Ram was the emperor who established our way of life, my Lord,' replied Nandi. 'He lived around one thousand two hundred years ago. He created our systems, our rules, our ideologies, everything. His reign is known simply as '*Ram Rajya*' or '*the rule of Ram*'. The term 'Ram Rajya' is considered the gold standard in how an empire must be administered, in order to create a perfect life for all its citizens. Meluha is still governed in accordance with his principles. Jai Shri Ram.'

'He must have been quite a man! For he truly created a paradise right here on earth.'

Shiva did not lie when he said this. He truly believed that if there was a paradise somewhere, it couldn't have been very different from Meluha. This was a land of abundance, of almost ethereal perfection! It was an empire ruled by clearly codified and just laws, to which every Meluhan was subordinated, including the emperor. The country supported a population of nearly eight million, which without exception seemed well fed, healthy and wealthy. The average intellect was exceptionally high. They were a slightly serious people, but unfailingly polite and civil. It seemed to be a flawless society where everyone was aware of his role and played it perfectly. They were conscious, nay obsessive, about their duties. The simple truth hit Shiva: if the entire society was conscious of its duties, nobody would need to fight for their individual rights. Since *everybody's rights* would be automatically taken care of through *someone else's duties*. Lord Ram was a genius!

Shiva too repeated Nandi's cry, signifying *Glory to Lord Ram*. '*Jai Shri Ram*.'

— ⋆ —

Having left their horses at the government authorised crossing-house, they crossed the river Ravi, close to *Hariyupa*, or the *City of Hari*. Shiva lingered for sometime as he admired Hariyupa from a slight distance, while his soldiers waited just beyond his shadow, having mounted their freshly allocated horses from the crossing-house on the other side of the Ravi. Hariyupa was a much larger city than Srinagar and seemed grand from the outside. Shiva considered exploring the magnificent city but that would have meant a delay in the trip to Devagiri. Next to Hariyupa, Shiva saw a construction project being executed. A new platform was being erected as Hariyupa had grown too populous to accommodate everyone on its existing platform.

How the hell do they raise these magnificent platforms?

Shiva made a mental note to visit the construction site on his return journey. At a distance, Jattaa, the Captain of the river crossing house, was talking to Nandi as he climbed the platform to mount his fresh horse.

'Avoid the road via Jratakgiri,' advised Jattaa. 'They suffered a terrorist attack last night. All the Brahmins were killed and the village temple was destroyed. The terrorists escaped as usual before any backup soldiers could arrive.'

'When in Lord Agni's name will we fight back? We should attack their country!' snarled a visibly angry Nandi.

'I swear by Lord Indra, if I ever find one of these Chandravanshi terrorists, I will cut his body into minute pieces and feed it to the dogs,' growled Jattaa, clenching his fists tight.

'Jattaa! We are followers of the Suryavanshis. We cannot even think of barbaric warfare such as that!' said Nandi.

'Do the terrorists follow the rules of war when they attack us? Don't they kill unarmed men?'

'That does not mean that we can act in the same way, Captain. We are Meluhans!' said Nandi shaking his head.

Jattaa did not counter Nandi. He was distracted by Shiva who was still waiting at a distance. 'Is he with you?' he asked.

'Yes.'

'He doesn't wear a caste amulet. Is he a new immigrant?'

'Yes.' replied Nandi, growing uncomfortable with the questions about Shiva.

'And you're going to Devagiri?' asked an increasingly suspicious Jattaa, looking harder towards Shiva's throat. 'I've heard some rumours coming from Srinagar…'

Nandi interrupted Jattaa suddenly. 'Thank you for your help, Captain Jattaa.'

Before Jattaa could act on his suspicions, Nandi quickly climbed the platform, mounted his horse and rode towards Shiva. Reaching quickly, he said, 'We should leave, my Lord.'

Shiva wasn't listening. He was perplexed once again as he saw the proud Captain Jattaa on his knees. Jattaa was looking directly at Shiva with his hands folded in a respectful Namaste. He appeared to be mumbling something very quickly. Shiva couldn't be sure from that distance, but it seemed as if the Captain was crying. He shook his head and whispered, 'Why?'

'We should go, my Lord,' repeated Nandi, a little louder.

Shiva turned to him, nodded and kicked his horse into action.

— ⅄⦶Ʊ⍋⊛ —

Shiva looked towards his left as he rode upon the straight road, observing Nandi goading his valiant horse along. He turned around and was not surprised to see his three bodyguard soldiers riding at exactly the same distance as before. Not too close, and yet, not too far. His glance also took in Nandi's jewellery which he suspected were not merely ornamental. He wore two amulets on his thick right arm. The first one had some symbolic lines which Shiva could not fathom. The second one appeared to have an animal etching. Probably a bull. One of his gold chains had a pendant shaped like a perfectly circular sun with rays streaming outwards. The other pendant was a brown, elliptical seed-like object with small serrations all over it.

'Can you tell me the significance of your jewellery or is that also a state secret?' teased Shiva.

'Of course I can, my Lord,' replied Nandi earnestly. He pointed at the first amulet that had been tied around his massive arm with a silky gold thread. 'This is the amulet which represents my caste. The lines drawn on it symbolise the shoulders of the *Parmatma, the almighty*. This means that I am a Kshatriya.'

'I am sure there are clearly codified guidelines for representing the other castes as well.'

'Right you are, my Lord. You are exceptionally intelligent.'

'No, I am not. You people are just exceptionally predictable.'

Nandi smiled as Shiva continued. 'So what are they?'

'What are what, my Lord?'

'The symbols for the Brahmins, Vaishyas and Shudras.'

'Well, if the lines are drawn to represent the head of the Parmatma, it would mean the wearer is a Brahmin. The symbol for a Vaishya would be the lines forming a symbol of the thighs of the Parmatma. And the feet of the Parmatma on the amulet would make the wearer a Shudra.'

'Interesting,' said Shiva with a slight frown. 'I imagine most Shudras are not too pleased about their placement.'

Nandi was quite surprised by Shiva's comments. He couldn't understand why a Shudra would have a problem with this long ordained symbol. But he kept quiet for fear of disagreeing with his Lord.

'And the other amulet?' asked Shiva.

'This second amulet depicts my chosen-tribe. Each chosen-tribe takes on jobs which fit its profile. Every Meluhan, in consultation with his parents, applies for a chosen-tribe when he turns twenty-five years old. Brahmins choose from birds, while Kshatriyas apply for animals. Flowers are allocated to Vaishyas while Shudras must choose from amongst fish. The Allocation Board allocates the chosen-tribe on the basis of a rigorous examination process. You must qualify for a chosen-tribe that represents both your ambitions and skills. Choose a tribe that is too mighty and you will embarrass yourself throughout your life if your achievements don't measure up to the standards of that tribe. Choose a tribe too lowly and you will not be doing justice to your own talents. My chosen-tribe is a bull. That is the animal that this amulet represents.'

'And if I am not being rude, what does a bull mean in your rank of Kshatriya chosen-tribes?'

'Well, it's not as high as a lion, tiger or an elephant. But it's not a rat or a pig either!'

'Well, as far as I am concerned, the bull can beat any lion or elephant,' smiled Shiva. 'And what about the pendants on your chain?'

'The brown seed is a representation of the last Mahadev, Lord Rudra. It symbolises the protection and regeneration of life. Even divine weapons cannot destroy the life it protects.'

'And the Sun?'

'My Lord, the sun represents the fact that I am a follower of the *Suryavanshi* kings — the kings who are *the descendants of the Sun*.'

'What? The Sun came down and some queen…' teased an incredulous Shiva.

'Of course not, my Lord,' laughed Nandi. 'All it means is that we follow the solar calendar. So you could say that we are the followers of the "path of the sun". In practical terms it denotes that we are strong and steadfast. We honour our word and keep our promises even at the cost of our lives. We never break the law. We deal honourably even with those who are dishonourable. Like the Sun, we never take from anyone but always give to others. We sear our duties into our consciousness so that we may never forget them. Being a Suryavanshi means that we must always strive to be honest, brave and above all, loyal to the truth.'

'A tall order! I assume that Lord Ram was a Suryavanshi king?'

'Yes, of course,' replied Nandi, his chest puffed up with pride. 'He was *the* Suryavanshi king. Jai Shri Ram.'

'Jai Shri Ram,' repeated Shiva.

— ⅄Ⓞᑌᐃ⊛ —

Nandi and Shiva crossed the river Beas on a boat. Their soldiers waited for the following craft. The Beas was the last river to be crossed after which the straight road stretched towards Devagiri. Unseasonal rain the previous night had made the crossing-house Captain consider cancelling the day's crossings across the river. However the weather had been relatively calm since the morning, allowing the Captain to keep the service operational. Shiva and Nandi shared the boat with two other passengers as well as the boatman who rowed them across. They had traded in their existing horses at the crossing-house for fresh horses on the other side.

They were a short distance from the opposite bank when a sudden burst of torrential rain came down from the heavens. The winds took on a sudden ferocity. The boatman made a valiant effort to row quickly across, but the boat tossed violently as it surrendered to the elements. Nandi stretched towards Shiva in order to tell him to stay low for safety. But he did not do it gently enough. His considerable weight caused the boat to list dangerously, and he fell overboard.

The boatman tried to steady the boat with his oars so he could save the other passengers. Even as he did so, he had the presence of mind to pull out his conch and blow an emergency call to the crossing-house on the other side. The other two passengers should have jumped overboard to save Nandi but his massive build made them hesitate. They knew that if they tried to save him, they would most likely drown.

Shiva felt no such hesitation as he quickly tossed aside his angvastram, pulled off his shoes and dived into the turbulent river. Shiva swam with powerful strokes and quickly reached a rapidly drowning Nandi. He had to use all of his considerable strength to pull Nandi to the surface. In spite of being buoyed by the water, Nandi weighed significantly more than what any normal man would. It was fortunate that Shiva felt stronger than ever since the first night at the Srinagar immigration camp. Shiva positioned himself behind Nandi and wrapped one arm around his chest. He used his other arm to swim towards the bank. Nandi's weight made it very exhausting work, but Shiva was able to tow the Meluhan Captain to the shore, just as the emergency staff from the crossing-house came rapidly towards them. Shiva helped them drag Nandi's limp body on to the land. He was unconscious.

The emergency staff then began a strange procedure. One of them started pressing Nandi's chest in a quick rhythmic motion to the count of five. Just as he would stop, another emergency staff would cover Nandi's lips with his own and breathe hard into his mouth. After which, they would repeat the procedure all over again. Shiva did not understand what was going on but trusted both the expertise as well as the commitment of the Meluhan medical personnel.

After several anxious moments, Nandi suddenly coughed up a considerable amount of water and woke up with a start. At first he was disoriented but he quickly regained his wits and turned abruptly towards Shiva, screeching, 'My Lord, why did you jump in after me? Your life is too precious. You must never risk it for me!'

A surprised Shiva supported Nandi's back and whispered calmly, 'You need to relax, my friend.'

Agreeing with Shiva, the medical staff quickly placed Nandi on a stretcher and carried him into the rest house abutting the crossing-house. The other boat passengers were observing Shiva with increasing curiosity. They knew that the fat man was a relatively senior Suryavanshi soldier, judging by his amulets. Yet he called this fair, caste-unmarked man 'his Lord'. Strange. However, all that mattered was that the soldier was safe. They dispersed as Shiva followed the medical staff into the rest house.

CHAPTER 3

She Enters His Life

Nandi lay semi-conscious for several hours as the medicines administered by the doctors worked on his body. Shiva sat by his side, repeatedly changing the wet cloth on his burning forehead to control the fever. Nandi kept babbling incoherently as he tossed and turned in his sleep, making Shiva's task that much more difficult.

'I've been searching… long…so long… a hundred years… never thought I…. find Neelkanth… Jai Shri Ram…'

Shiva ignored Nandi's babble as he tried to keep the fever down. But his ears had caught on to something.

He's been searching for a hundred years?!

Shiva frowned.

The fever's affecting his bloody brain! He doesn't look a day older than twenty years!

'I've been searching for a hundred years…,' continued the oblivious Nandi. '…I found… Neelkanth…'

Shiva stopped for a moment and stared hard at Nandi. Then shaking his head dismissively, he continued his ministrations.

— ⋯ —

Shiva had been walking on a paved, signposted road along the River Beas for the better part of an hour. He had left the rest house to explore the area by himself, much against a rapidly recovering Nandi's advice. Nandi was out of danger, but they had been advised to wait for a few days nevertheless, so that the Captain could be strong enough to travel. There was not much for Shiva to do at the rest house and he had begun to feel restless. The three soldiers had tried to shadow Shiva, but he had angrily dismissed them. 'Will you please stop trying to stick to me like leeches?'

The rhythmic hymns sung by the gentle waters of the Beas soothed Shiva. A cool tender breeze teased his thick lock of hair. He rested his hand on the hilt of his scabbard as his mind swirled with persistent questions.

Is Nandi really more than a hundred years old? But that's impossible! And what the hell do these crazy Meluhans need me for anyway? And why in the name of the holy lake is my bloody throat still feeling so cold?

Lost in his thoughts, Shiva did not realise that he had strayed off the road into a clearing, where, staring him in the face was the most beautiful building he had ever seen. It was built entirely of white and pink marble. An imposing flight of stairs led up to the top of a high platform, which had been adorned by pillars around its entire circumference. The ornate roof was topped by a giant triangular spire, like a giant 'Namaste' to the Gods. Elaborate sculptures were carved upon every available space on the structure.

Shiva had been in Meluha for many days now and all the buildings he had seen so far were functional and efficient. However, this particular one was oddly flamboyant. At the entrance, a signpost announced, 'Temple of Lord Brahma'. The Meluhans appeared to reserve their creativity for religious places.

There was a small crowd of hawkers around the courtyard in the clearing. Some were selling flowers, others were selling food. Still others were selling assorted items required for a *puja*. There was a stall where worshippers could leave their footwear as they went up to the temple. Shiva left his shoes there and walked up the steps. As he entered the main temple he found himself staring at the designs and sculptures, mesmerized by the sheer magnificence of the architecture.

'What are you doing here?'

Shiva turned around to find a Pandit staring at him quizzically. His wizened face sported a flowing white beard matched in length by his silvery mane. Wearing a saffron dhoti and angvastram, he had the calm, gentle look of a man who had already attained *nirvana*, but had chosen to remain on earth to fulfil some heavenly duties. Shiva realised that the Pandit was the first truly old person that he had seen in Meluha.

'I am sorry. Am I not allowed in here?' asked Shiva politely.

'Of course you are allowed in here. Everyone is allowed into the house of the Gods.'

Shiva smiled. However, before he could respond the Pandit questioned him once again, 'But you don't believe in these Gods, do you?'

Shiva's smile disappeared as quickly as it had appeared.

How the hell does he know?

The Pandit answered the question posed by Shiva's eyes. 'Everyone who enters this place of worship has eyes only for the idol of Lord Brahma. Almost nobody notices the brilliance of the architects who built this lovely temple. You, however, have eyes only for the work of the architects. You have not yet cast even a glance upon the idol.'

Shiva grinned apologetically. 'You guessed right. I don't believe in symbolic Gods. I believe that God exists all around us. In the flow of the river, in the rustle of the trees, in the whisper of the winds. He speaks to us all the time. All we need to do is listen. However, I apologise if I have caused some offence by not being respectful towards your God.'

'You don't need to apologise, my friend,' smiled the Pandit. 'There is no "your God" or "my God". All Godliness comes from the same source. It's just the manifestations that are different. But I have a feeling that one day you will find a temple worth walking into purely for prayer and not its beauty.'

'Really? Which temple might that be?'

'You will find it when you are ready, my friend.'

Why do these Meluhans always talk in bizarre riddles?

Shiva nodded politely, his expression suggesting an appreciation for the Pandit's words that he did not truly feel. He thought it wise to flee the temple before he outlived his welcome.

'I should be getting back to my rest house now, Pandit*ji*. But I eagerly look forward to finding the temple of my destiny. It was a pleasure meeting you,' said Shiva, as he bent down to touch the Pandit's feet.

Placing his hand on Shiva's head, the Pandit said gently, *'Jai Guru Vishwamitra. Jai Guru Vashishtha.'*

Shiva rose, turned and walked down the steps. Looking at Shiva walking away from him, clearly out of earshot, the Pandit whispered with an admiring smile, for he had recognised his *fellow traveller in karma.* 'The pleasure was all mine, my *karmasaathi*.'

Shiva reached the shoe stall, put on his shoes and offered a coin for the service. The shoe-keeper politely declined. 'Thank you Sir, but this is a service provided by the government of Meluha. There is no charge for it.'

Shiva smiled. 'Of course! You people have a system for everything. Thank you.'

The shoe-keeper smiled back. 'We are only doing our duty, Sir.'

Shiva walked back to the temple steps. As he sat down, he breathed in deeply and let the tranquil atmosphere suffuse him with its serenity. And then it happened. The moment that every unrealised heart craves for. The unforgettable instant that a soul, clinging on to the purest memory of its previous life, longs for. The moment which, in spite of a conspiracy of the Gods, only a few lucky men experience. The moment when *she* enters *his* life.

She rode in on a chariot, guiding the horses expertly into the courtyard, while a lady companion by her side held on to the railings. Although her black hair was tied in an understated bun, a few irreverent strands danced a spellbinding *kathak* in the wind. Her piercingly magnetic, blue eyes and bronzed skin were an invitation for jealousy from the Goddesses. Her body, though covered demurely in a long angvastram, still ignited Shiva's imagination into sensing the lovely curves which lay beneath. Her flawless face was a picture of concentration as she manoeuvred the chariot skilfully into its parking place. She dismounted the chariot with an air of confidence. It was a calm confidence which had not covered the ugly distance towards arrogance.

Her walk was dignified. Stately enough to let a beholder know that she was detached, but not cold. Shiva stared at her like a parched piece of earth mesmerised by a passing rain cloud.

Have mercy on me!

'My lady, I still feel that it's not wise to wander so far from the rest of your entourage,' said her companion.

She answered. 'Krittika, just because others don't know the law, doesn't mean that we can ignore it. Lord Ram clearly stated that once a year, a pious woman has to visit Lord Brahma. I will not break that law, no matter how inconvenient it is to the bodyguards!'

The lady noticed Shiva staring at her as she passed by. Her delicate eyebrows arched into a surprised look and then an annoyed frown. Shiva made a valiant attempt to tear his glance away, but realised that his eyes were no longer in his control. She continued walking up, followed by Krittika.

She turned around at the top of the temple steps, to see the caste unmarked immigrant at a distance, still staring at her unabashedly. Before turning and walking into the main temple, she muttered to Krittika, 'These uncouth immigrants! As if we'll find our saviour from amongst these barbarians!'

It was only when she was out of sight that Shiva could breathe again. As he desperately tried to gather his wits, his overwhelmed and helpless mind took one obvious decision — there was no way he was leaving the temple before getting another look at her. He sat down on the steps once again. As his breathing and heartbeat returned to normal, he finally began to notice the surroundings that had been consecrated by her recent presence. He stared once again at the road on the left from where she had turned in. She had ridden past the cucumber seller standing near the banyan tree.

Incidentally, why is the cucumber seller not trying to hawk his wares? He just seems to be staring at the temple. Anyway, it is not any of my business.

He followed the path that her chariot had taken as it had swerved to its left, around the fountain at the centre of the courtyard. It had then taken a sharp right turn past the shepherd standing at the entrance of the garden.

But where were this shepherd's sheep?

Shiva continued to look down the path that the chariot had taken to the parking lot. Next to the chariot stood another man who had just walked into the temple complex, but had inexplicably not entered the temple itself. He turned to the shepherd and appeared to nod slightly. Before Shiva could piece together the information from his observation, he felt her presence once again. He turned immediately to see her walking down the steps, with Krittika silently behind. On still finding this rude, caste-unmarked, obviously foreign man staring at her, she walked up to him and asked in a firm but polite voice, 'Excuse me, is there a problem?'

'No. No. There's no problem. But I feel that I've seen you somewhere before,' replied a flustered Shiva.

The lady was not sure how to respond to this. It was obviously a lie but the voice was sincere. Before she could react, Krittika cut in rudely. 'Is that the best line you can come up with?'

As Shiva was about to retort, he was alerted by a quick movement from the cucumber seller. Shiva turned to see him pulling out a sword as he tossed his shawl aside. The shepherd and the man next to the chariot also stood poised in traditional fighter positions with their swords drawn. In a flash Shiva drew his sword and stretched out his left hand protectively, to pull the object of his fascination behind him. She however deftly side-stepped his protective hand, reached into the folds of her angvastram and drew out her own sword. Surprised, Shiva flashed her a quick, admiring smile. Her eyes flashed right back, acknowledging the unexpected yet providential partnership.

She whispered under her breath to Krittika, 'Run back into the temple. Stay there till this is over.'

Krittika protested. 'But my lady…'

'NOW!' she ordered.

Krittika turned and ran up the temple steps. Shiva and the lady stood back to back in a standard defensive-partner position, covering all the directions of any possible attack. The three attackers charged in. Two more jumped in from behind the trees. Shiva raised his sword defensively just as the shepherd came up close. Feigning a sideward movement to draw the shepherd into an aggressive attack, Shiva dropped his sword low. He hoped to tempt him to move in for a kill wound and in response, he would have quickly raised his sword and dug it deep into the shepherd's heart.

The shepherd, however, moved unexpectedly. Instead of taking advantage of Shiva's opening, he tried to strike Shiva's shoulder. Shiva quickly raised his right arm and swung viciously, inflicting a deep wound across the shepherd's torso. As the shepherd fell back, another attacker moved in from the right. He swung from a distance. Not too smart a move, as it would merely have inflicted a surface nick. Shiva stepped back to avoid the swing and brought his sword down in a smooth action to dig deep into the attacker's thigh. Screaming in agony, this attacker too fell back. As yet another attacker joined in from the left, Shiva began to realise that this was indeed a very strange assault.

The attackers seemed to know what they were doing. They seemed like accomplished warriors. But they also seemed to be in a bizarre dance of avoidance. They did not appear to want to kill but merely injure. It was due to their circumspection that they were being beaten back easily. Shiva parried another attack from the left and pushed his sword viciously into the man's shoulder. The man screamed in pain as Shiva pushed him off the blade with his left hand. Slowly, but surely, the attackers were being worn out. They were suffering too many injuries to seriously carry on the assault for long.

Suddenly a giant of a man ran in from behind the trees carrying swords in both hands. The man was cloaked in a black hooded robe from head to toe while his face was hidden behind a mask. The only visible parts of his body were his large impassive almond-shaped eyes and strong fleshy hands. He charged upon Shiva and the lady as he barked an order to his men. He was too large to battle with agility. But his slow pace was compensated by his unusually skilled arms. Shiva perceived from the corner of his eye that the other attackers were picking up the injured and withdrawing. The hooded figure was performing a brilliant rearguard action as his men retreated.

Shiva realised that the man's hood would impair his peripheral vision. Here was a weakness that could be exploited. Moving to the left, Shiva swung ferociously, hoping to peg him back so that the lady could finish the job from the other side. But his opponent was up to the challenge. As he stepped slightly back, he deflected Shiva's swing with a deft move of his right hand. Shiva noticed a leather band on the hooded figure's right wrist. It had a sharp symbol on it. Shiva swung his sword back but the hooded figure moved aside effortlessly. He pushed back a brutal flanking attack from the lady with his left hand. He was keeping just enough distance from Shiva and the lady to defend himself while at the same time keeping them engaged in combat.

All of a sudden the hooded figure disengaged from the battle and stepped back. Even as he retreated, his swords continued to point menacingly at Shiva and the lady. His men had disappeared into the trees. On reaching a safe distance, he turned around and ran after his men. Shiva considered chasing him but almost immediately decided against it. He might just rush into an ambush.

Shiva turned to the lady warrior and inquired, 'Are you alright?'

'Yes I am,' she nodded before asking with a sombre expression. 'Are you injured?'

'Nothing serious. I'll survive!' he grinned.

In the meantime, Krittika came running down the temple steps and asked breathlessly, 'My lady. Are you alright?'

'Yes I am,' she answered. 'Thanks to this foreigner here.'

Krittika turned to Shiva and said, 'Thank you very much. You have helped a very important woman.'

Shiva did not seem to be listening though. He continued to stare at Krittika's mistress as if he were possessed. Krittika struggled to conceal a smile.

The noble woman averted her eyes in embarrassment,

but said politely, 'I am sorry, but I am quite sure that we have not met earlier.'

'No it's not that,' said a smiling Shiva. 'It's just that in our society, women don't fight. You don't weild your sword too badly for a woman.'

O hell! That came out all wrong.

'Excuse me?' she said, a slightly belligerent tone creeping into her voice, clearly upset about the *for-a-woman* remark. 'You don't fight too badly either for a barbarian.'

'Not too badly?! I'm an exceptional sword fighter! Do you want to try me?'

O bloody hell! What am I saying? I'm not going to impress her like this!

Her expression resumed its detached, supercilious look once again. 'I have no interest in duelling with you, foreigner.'

'No. No. Don't get me wrong. I don't want to duel with you. I just wanted to tell you that I am quite good at sword-fighting. I am good at other things as well. And it came out all wrong. I rather like the fact that you fought for yourself. You are a very good swordsman. I mean a swordswoman. In fact, you are quite a woman…,' bumbled Shiva, losing the filter of judgement, exactly at the time when he needed it the most.

Krittika, with her head bowed, smiled at the increasingly appealing exchange.

Her mistress, on the other hand, wanted to chastise the foreigner for his highly inappropriate words. But he had saved her life. She was bound by the Meluhan code of conduct. 'Thank you for your help, foreigner. I owe you my life and you will not find me ungrateful. If you ever need my help, do call on me.'

'Can I call on you even if I don't need your help?'

Shit! What am I saying?!

She glared at the caste-unmarked foreigner who clearly did not know his place. With superhuman effort, she controlled herself, nodded politely and said, 'Namaste.'

With that, the aristocratic woman turned around to leave. Krittika continued to stare at Shiva with admiring eyes. However, on seeing her mistress leaving, she too turned around hurriedly and followed.

'At least tell me your name,' said Shiva, walking to keep pace with her.

She turned around, staring even more gravely at Shiva.

'Look, how will I find you if I need your help?' asked Shiva sincerely.

Momentarily disarmed, she remained silent. The request seemed reasonable. She turned towards Krittika and nodded.

'You can find us at Devagiri,' answered Krittika. 'Ask anyone in the city for Lady Sati.'

'Sati…,' said Shiva, letting the ethereal name roll over his tongue. 'My name is Shiva.'

'Namaste, Shiva. And I promise you, I will honour my word if you ever need my help,' said Sati as she turned and climbed into her chariot, followed by Krittika.

Expertly turning the chariot, Sati urged her horses into a smooth trot. Without a backward look she sped away from the temple. Shiva kept staring at the fast disappearing profile of the chariot. Once it was gone, he continued to stare at the dust with intense jealousy. It had been fortunate enough to have touched her.

I think I'm going to like this country.

For the first time in the journey, Shiva actually looked

forward to reaching the capital city of the Meluhans. He smiled and started towards the rest house.

Have to get to Devagiri quickly.

CHAPTER 4

Abode of the Gods

'What! Who attacked you?' cried a concerned Nandi as he rushed towards Shiva and examined his wounds.

'Relax Nandi,' replied Shiva. 'You are in worse shape than I am after your adventure in the water. It's just a few superficial cuts. Nothing serious. The doctors have already dressed the wounds. I am alright.'

'I am sorry, my Lord. It's entirely my fault. I should never have left you alone. It will never happen again. Please forgive me, my Lord.'

Pushing Nandi gently back on to the bed, Shiva said, 'There's nothing to forgive, my friend. How can this be your fault? Please calm down. Getting excited will not do your health any good.'

Once Nandi had calmed down a bit, Shiva continued, 'In any case, I don't think they were trying to kill us. It was very strange.'

'Us?'

'Yes, there were two women involved.'

'But who could these attackers be?' asked Nandi. Then a disturbing thought dawned on Nandi. 'Did the attackers wear a pendant with a crescent moon on it?'

Shiva frowned. 'No. But there was this one strange man. The best swordsman among them. He was covered from head to toe in a hooded robe, his face hidden by a mask, the kind I've seen you people wear at that *colour festival.* What is it called?'

'*Holi*, my Lord?'

'Yes, the *holi* kind of mask. In any case, you could only see his eyes and his hands. His only distinguishing feature was a leather bracelet with a strange symbol on it.'

'What symbol, my Lord?'

Picking up a palm-leaf booklet and the thin charcoal writing-stick from the side table, Shiva drew the symbol.

Nandi frowned. 'That is an ancient symbol that some people used for the word Aum. But who would want to use this symbol now?'

'Aum?' asked Shiva.

'My Lord, Aum is the holiest word in our religion. It is considered the primeval sound of nature. The hymn of the universe. It was so holy that for many millennia, most people would not insult it by putting it down in written form.'

'Then how did this symbol come about?'

'It was devised by Lord Bharat, a great ruler who had

conquered practically all of India many thousands of years ago. A rare *Chandravanshi* who was worth respecting, he had even married a *Suryavanshi* princess with the aim of ending our perpetual war.'

'Who are the *Chandravanshis*?' asked Shiva.

'Think of them as the very antithesis of us, my Lord. They are the followers of the kings who are *the descendants of the moon*.'

'And they follow the lunar calendar?'

'Yes, my Lord. They are a crooked, untrustworthy and lazy people with no rules, morals or honour. They are cowards who never attack like principled Kshatriyas. Even their kings are corrupt and selfish. The Chandravanshis are a blot on humanity!'

'But what does the Aum symbol have to do with this?'

'Well, King Bharat created this symbol of unity between the Suryavanshis and the Chandravanshis. The top half in white represents the Chandravanshis.

The bottom half in red represents the Suryavanshis.

The amalgam of these is the emergent common path represented in orange.

The crescent moon to the right of the symbol was the pre-existing Chandravanshi symbol.

And the sun above it was the pre-existing Suryavanshi symbol.

In order to signify that this was a pact blessed by the Gods, Lord Bharat mandated the representation of this symbol as the holy word Aum.'

'And then what happened?'

'As expected, the pact died along with the good king. Once the influence of Lord Bharat was removed, the Chandravanshis were soon up to their old tricks and the war began once again. The symbol was forgotten. And the word Aum reverted to its original form of pure sound without a written representation.'

'But the symbol on the bracelet of this hooded man was not coloured. It was all black. And the parts of the symbol didn't look like lines to me. They looked like a drawing of three serpents.'

'Naga!' exclaimed a shocked Nandi, before mumbling a soft prayer and touching his Rudra pendant for protection.

'Now who the bloody hell are the Nagas?' asked Shiva.

'They are cursed people, my Lord,' gasped Nandi. 'They are born with hideous deformities because of the sins of their previous births. Deformities like extra hands or horribly misshapen faces. But they have tremendous strength and skills. The Naga name alone strikes terror in any citizen's heart. They are not even allowed to live in the Sapt Sindhu.'

'The Sapt Sindhu?'

'Our land, my Lord, the land of the seven rivers. The land of the Indus, Saraswati, Yamuna, Ganga, Sarayu, Brahmaputra and Narmada. This is where Lord Manu mandated that all of us, Suryavanshis and Chandravanshis, live.'

Shiva nodded as Nandi continued. 'The city of the Nagas exists to the south of the Narmada, beyond the border of our lands. In fact, it is bad luck to even speak of them, my Lord!'

'But why would a Naga attack me? Or any Meluhan for that matter?'

Cursing under his breath, Nandi said, 'Because of the Chandravanshis! What levels have these two-faced people sunk to? Using the demon Nagas in their attacks! In their hatred for us, they don't even realise how many sins they are inviting upon their own souls!'

Shiva frowned. During the attack, it hadn't appeared as if the Naga was being used by the small platoon of soldiers. In fact, it looked like the Naga was the leader.

It took another week for them to reach Devagiri. The capital city of the Meluhans stood on the west bank of the Saraswati, which emerged at the confluence of the Sutlej and Yamuna rivers. Sadly, though, her majestic flow and mighty girth had now ebbed. But even in her reduced state, she was still massive and awe-inspiring. Unlike many of the tempestuous rivers of the Punjab though, the Saraswati was achingly calm. The river seemed to sense that her days were drawing to an end. Yet, she did not fight aggressively to thrust her way through and survive. Instead, she unselfishly gave her all to those who came to seek her treasures.

The soaring Devagiri though, was in complete contrast to the mellow Saraswati. Like all Meluhan cities, Devagiri too was built on giant platforms, an effective protection against floods as well as enemies. However, Devagiri differed from other Meluhan cities in its sheer size. The city sprawled atop three giant platforms, each of them spreading over three hundred and fifty hectares, significantly larger than the other cities. The platforms were nearly eight metres high and were bastioned by giant blocks of cut stone interspaced with baked bricks. Two of the platforms, named *Tamra* and *Rajat*, literally, *bronze* and *silver*, were for the common man, whereas the platform named *Svarna* or *gold* was the royal citadel. The platforms were connected to each other by tall bridges, made of stones and baked bricks, which rose above the flood plains below.

Along the periphery of each enormous platform were towering city walls, with giant spikes facing outwards. There were turrets at regular intervals along the city walls from where approaching enemies could be repelled. This spectacle was beyond anything that Shiva had ever seen. In his mind, the construction of a city like this must truly be man's greatest achievement.

Shiva's entourage rode up towards the drawbridge across the field of spikes to the Tamra platform. The drawbridge had been reinforced with metal bars at the bottom and had roughened baked bricks laid out on top so that horses and chariots would not slip. There was something about the bricks he had seen across the empire that had intrigued Shiva. Turning to Nandi he asked, 'Are these bricks made by some standard process?'

'Yes my Lord,' replied a surprised Nandi. 'All the bricks in Meluha are made in accordance with specifications and guidelines given by the Chief Architect of the empire. But how did you guess?'

'They are all of exactly the same dimension.'

Nandi beamed with pride at both his empire's efficiency as well as his Lord's power of observation. The platform rose at the end of the drawbridge, with a road spiralling up to the summit in one gentle turn, facilitating the passage of horses and chariots. In addition, there was a broad flight of stairs leading straight up the incline for pedestrians. The city walls and the platform extended steeply onto the sides around this slope, making it a valley of death for any enemy foolish enough to attack the platform from this direction.

The city gates were made of a metal that Shiva had never seen before. Nandi clarified that they were made of iron, a new metal that had just been discovered. It was the strongest of all the metals but very expensive. The ore required to make it was not easily available. At the platform entry, on top of the city gates, was etched the symbol of the Suryavanshis — a bright red circular sun with its rays blazing out in all directions. Below it was the motto that they lived by '*Satya. Dharma. Maan*': *Truth. Duty. Honour.*

Even this initial introduction to the city had left Shiva awestruck. However, what he witnessed at the top of the platform, within the city gates, was truly breathtaking both in its efficiency and simplicity. The city was divided into a grid of square blocks by the paved streets. There were footpaths on the side for pedestrians, lanes marked on the street for traffic in different directions, and of course, there were covered drains running through the centre. All the buildings were constructed as standard two storied block structures made of baked bricks. On top were wooden extensions for increasing the height of the building, if required. Nandi clarified to Shiva that the layout of the buildings differed internally depending on their individual requirements. All windows and doors were built into the side walls of buildings, never facing the main road.

The blank walls that faced the main roads bore striking black etchings depicting the different legends of the Suryavanshis, while the walls themselves were painted in the sober colours of grey, light blue, light green or white. The most common background colour though, appeared to be blue. The holiest colour for the Meluhans was blue, denoting the sky. Green, representing nature, happened to be placed just after blue in the colour spectrum. Meluhans liked to divine a grand design in every natural phenomenon and thought it wondrous that blue was placed just before green in the colour spectrum. Just as the sky happened to be above the earth.

The most recurring illustrations on the walls were about the great emperor, Lord Ram. His victories over his enemies, his subjugation of the wicked Chandravanshis, incidents depicting his statesmanship and wisdom, had all been lovingly recreated. Lord Ram was deeply revered, and many Meluhans worshipped him like a God. They referred to him as *Vishnu*, an ancient title for the greatest of the Gods meaning *protector of the world and propagator of good.*

As Shiva learned from Nandi, the city was divided into many districts consisting of four to eight blocks. Each district had its own markets, commercial and residential areas, temples and entertainment centres. Manufacturing or any other polluting activity was conducted in separate quarters away from the districts. The efficiency and smoothness with which Devagiri functioned belied the fact that it was the most populous city in the entire empire. The census conducted two years back had pegged the population of the city at two hundred thousand.

Nandi led Shiva and the three soldiers to one of the city's numerous guest houses, built for the many tourists that frequented Devagiri, for both business and leisure. Having duly handed over their exhausted horses to the care of the stable boy, they strode in to register themselves. Shiva took in the guest house with a familiar eye, similar to so many he had seen throughout their journey. There was a central courtyard with the building built around it. The rooms were comfortably furnished and spacious.

'My Lord, it's almost dinner time,' said Nandi. 'I will speak with the housekeeper and get some food organised. We should eat early and get enough sleep since our appointment with the Emperor has been fixed at the beginning of the second prahar tomorrow.'

'Sounds like a good idea.'

'Also, if it is all right with you, shall I dismiss the soldiers and send them back to Srinagar?'

'That also sounds like a good idea,' said a smiling Shiva. 'Why Nandi, you are almost like a fount of brilliant ideas!'

Nandi laughed along with Shiva, always happy to be the harbinger of a smile on his Lord's face. 'I'll just be back, my Lord.'

Shiva lay down on his bed and was quickly lost in the thoughts that really mattered to him.

I'll finish the meeting with the Emperor as soon as it is humanly possible, give him whatever the bloody hell he wants and then scour the city for Sati.

Shiva had considered asking Nandi about the whereabouts of Sati but had eventually decided against it. He was painfully aware that he had made a less than spectacular impression on her at their first meeting. If she hadn't made it easy for him to find her, it only meant that she wasn't terribly stirred by him. He didn't want to compound his mistake by speaking casually about her with others.

He smiled as the memory of her face came flooding back to him. He replayed the magical moments when he had seen her fighting. Not the most romantic of sights for most men of his tribe. But for Shiva, it was divine. He sighed recalling her soft, delicate body, which had suddenly developed brutal, killer qualities upon being attacked. The curves that had so captivated him swung smoothly as she transferred her weight to swing her sword. The soberly tied hair had swayed sensuously with each movement of the sword arm. He breathed deeply.

What a woman!

— ⅄ⓄƱ⍋⊛ —

Early next morning Shiva and Nandi crossed the bridge between the Tamra and Svarna platforms to reach the royal citadel. The bridge, another marvel of Meluhan engineering, was flanked on the sides by a thick wall. Holes punched into the walls enabled defenders to shoot arrows or pour hot oil on enemies. The bridge was bisected by a massive gate, a final protection in the likelihood of the other platform being lost to an enemy.

Shiva was completely taken by surprise when they crossed over to the Svarna platform, not by the grandeur of the royal area but by the lack of it. He was shocked that there was no opulence. Despite ruling over such a massive and wealthy empire, the nobility lived in a conspicuously simple manner. The structure of the royal citadel was almost exactly like the other platforms. There were no special concessions made for the aristocrats. The same block structures that dominated all of Meluha were to be found in the royal citadel as well. The only magnificent structure was to the far right and sported the sign 'Great Public Bath'. The Bath also had a glorious temple to Lord Indra built on the left-hand side. The temple was built of wood and it stood on a raised foundation of baked bricks, its cupola plated with solid gold! It seemed that special architecture was reserved only for structures built for the Gods or ones that were for the common good.

Probably just like how Lord Ram would have wanted.

The only concession to the emperor, however, was that his standard block structure was larger than the others. Significantly larger.

— ⅄ΦŪ⇡⊗ —

Shiva and Nandi entered the royal private office to find Emperor Daksha sitting on a simple throne at the far end of the modestly furnished room, flanked by a man and a woman.

Daksha greeted Shiva with a formal Namaste and said, 'I hope your journey was comfortable.'

He looked too young to be an emperor of such a large country. Though he was marginally shorter than Shiva, they differed in their musculature. While the strapping Shiva was powerfully built, Daksha's body indicated that it had not been strained by too much exercise. It wasn't that he was obese either, just average. The same could be said about his wheat-complexioned face. Average sized, dark eyes flanked a straight nose. He wore his hair long like most Meluhan men and women. The head bore a majestic crown with the sun symbol of the Suryavanshis manifested in the centre through sparkling gem stones. His clothes consisted of an elegantly draped dhoti and an angvastram placed over his right shoulder. A large amount of functional jewellery, including two amulets on his right arm, complemented Daksha's average appearance. His only distinguishing feature was his smile — which spread its innocent conviction all the way to his eyes. Emperor Daksha looked like a man who wore his royalty lightly.

'Yes it was, your highness,' replied Shiva. 'The infrastructure in your empire is wonderful. You are an extraordinary emperor.'

'Thank you. But I only deserve reflected credit. The work is done by my people,'

'You are too modest, your Highness.'

Smiling politely, Daksha asked, 'May I introduce my most important aides?' Without waiting for an answer, he pointed to the woman on his left, 'This is my prime minister, Kanakhala. She takes care of the administrative, revenue and protocol matters.'

Kanakhala did a formal Namaste to Shiva. Her head was shaved except for a tuft of smooth hair at the back which had been tied into a knot. She had a string called the janau tied across from her left shoulder down to the right side of her torso. Though young-looking like most Meluhans, the flab on her torso between the white blouse and dhoti didn't escape Shiva's keen eye. She had a dark and incredibly smooth complexion and like all her countrymen, wore jewellery that was restrained and conservative. Shiva noticed that the second amulet on Kanakhala's arm showed a pigeon. Not a very high chosen-tribe amongst the Brahmins. Shiva bent low and did a formal Namaste in reply.

Pointing to his right, Daksha said, 'And this is my chief of the armed forces, General Parvateshwar. He looks after the army, navy, special forces, police etc.'

Parvateshwar looked like a man that Shiva would think twice about taking on in a battle. He was taller than Shiva and had an immensely muscular physique that dominated the space around him. His curly long hair had been combed back severely and fell from under his crown in a disciplined array. His smooth, swarthy skin was marked by the proud signs of long years in battle. His body was hairless, in a rare departure from the normally hirsute Kshatriya men who considered body hair a sign of machismo. As if to make up for this deficiency, Parvateshwar maintained a thick and long moustache which curled upwards at the edges. His eyes reflected his uncompromisingly strong and righteous character. The second amulet on his arm showed Parvateshwar as a tiger, a very high chosen-tribe amongst the Kshatriyas. He nodded curtly at Shiva. No Namaste. No elaborate bow of his proud head. Shiva, however, smiled warmly and greeted Parvateshwar with a formal Namaste.

'Please wait outside, Captain,' advised Parvateshwar, looking at Nandi.

Before Nandi could respond, however, Shiva cut in. 'My apologies. But is it alright if Nandi stays here with me? He has been my constant companion since I left my homeland and has become a dear and trusted friend.'

'Of course he may,' replied Daksha.

'Your Highness, it is not appropriate for a Captain to be witness to this discussion,' said Parvateshwar. 'In any case, his service rules clearly state that he can only escort a guest into the emperor's presence and not stay there while a matter of state is discussed.'

'Oh relax Parvateshwar. You take your service rules too seriously sometimes.' Turning to Shiva, Daksha continued, 'If it is alright with you, may we see your neck now?'

Nandi slid behind Shiva to untie the cravat. Seeing the beads darned on the cravat to convey the impression that the throat was covered for religious reasons, Daksha smiled and whispered, 'Good idea.'

Even as the cravat came off, both Daksha and Kanakhala moved in close to inspect Shiva's throat. Parvateshwar did not step forward but strained his neck slightly in order to get a better look. Daksha and Kanakhala were clearly stunned by what they saw.

Daksha reached out and lightly touched Shiva's throat in awe, 'The colour emerges from within. There is no dye. It is real.'

Daksha and Kanakhala glanced at each other, tears glistening in their astounded eyes. Kanakhala folded her hands into a Namaste and began mumbling a chant under her breath. Daksha looked up at Shiva's face, trying desperately to suppress the ecstasy that coursed through his insides. With a controlled smile, the Emperor of Meluha said, 'I hope we have not done anything to cause you any discomfort since your arrival in Meluha.'

Despite Daksha's controlled reaction, Shiva could see that both the emperor as well as his prime minister were taken aback by his blue throat.

Just how important is this bloody blue throat for the Meluhans?

'Umm, none at all your Highness,' replied Shiva as he tied the cravat back around his neck. 'In fact, my tribe and I have been delighted by the hospitality that we have received here.'

'I'm happy about that,' smiled Daksha, bowing his head politely. 'You may want to rest a bit and we could talk in greater detail tomorrow. Would you like to shift your residence to the royal citadel? It is rumoured that the quarters here are a little more comfortable.'

'That is a very kind offer, your Highness.'

Daksha turned to Nandi and asked, 'Captain, what did you say your name was?'

'My name is Nandi, your Highness.'

'You too are welcome to stay here. Make sure that you take good care of our honoured guest. Kanakhala, please make all the arrangements.'

'Yes, your Highness.'

Kanakhala gestured towards one of her aides, who escorted Shiva and Nandi out of the royal office.

As Shiva exited the room, Daksha went down on his haunches with great ceremony and touched his head to the ground on which Shiva had just stood. He mumbled a soft prayer and then stood up to look at Kanakhala with tears in his eyes. Kanakhala's eyes, however, betrayed impatience and a touch of anger.

'I don't understand, your Highness,' glared Kanakhala. 'The blue mark was genuine. Why did you not tell him?'

'What did you expect me to do?' cried a surprised Daksha. 'This is his second day in Devagiri. You want me to just accost him and tell him that he is the Neelkanth, our saviour? That he is destined to solve all our problems?'

'Well, if he has a blue throat, then he is the Neelkanth, isn't he? And if he is the Neelkanth, then he is our saviour. He has to accept his destiny.'

An exasperated Parvateshwar interjected. 'I can't believe that we are talking like this. We are Meluhans! We are the Suryavanshis! We have created the greatest civilisation ever known to man. Are we to believe that an unskilled, uneducated barbarian is to be our saviour? Just because he has a blue throat?'

'That is what the legend says Parvateshwar,' countered Kanakhala.

Daksha interrupted both his ministers. 'Parvateshwar, I believe in the legend. My people believe in the legend. The

Neelkanth has chosen my reign to make his appearance. He will transform all of India in line with the ideals of Meluha — a land of truth, duty and honour. His leadership can help us end the Chandravanshi crisis once and for all. All the agonies they now inflict upon us will be over — from the terrorist attacks to the shortage of Somras to the killing of the Saraswati.'

'Then why delay telling him, your Highness?' asked Kanakhala. 'The more days we waste, the weaker becomes the resolve of our people. You are aware of the terrorist attack just a few days back in a village not far from Hariyupa. As our response becomes weak, our enemies become bolder, your Highness. We must inform the Lord quickly and announce his arrival to our people. It will give us the strength to fight our cruel enemies.'

'I will tell him. But I am trying to be more farsighted than you. So far our empire has only faced the morale-sapping influence of fraudulent Neelkanths. Imagine the consequences if people were to discover that the true Neelkanth has arrived but refuses to stand by us. First we must be sure that he is willing to accept his destiny. Only then will we announce his arrival to our people. And I think that the best way to convince him is to share the whole truth with him. Once he sees the unfairness of the attacks we face, he will fight with us to destroy evil. If that takes time, so be it. We have waited for centuries for the Neelkanth. A few more weeks will not destroy us.'

CHAPTER 5

Tribe of Brahma

Shiva was walking in the verdant gardens of the royal guest house. His belongings were being moved into the royal guest house by Nandi along with an efficient aide of Kanakhala. Shiva sat down on a comfortable bench overlooking a bed of red and white roses. The cool breeze in the open gardens brought a smile to his face. It was early afternoon and the garden was deserted. Shiva's thoughts kept going back to the conversation he had had with the Emperor in the morning. Despite Daksha's controlled reaction, Shiva could understand that his blue throat was of great significance to the Meluhans, even to the Emperor. It meant that the legend of the Neelkanth, whatever it was, was not restricted to some small sect in Kashmir. If the Emperor himself took it so seriously, all of Meluha must need the help of the Neelkanth.

But what the bloody hell do they want help for? They are so much more advanced than we are!

His thoughts were interrupted by the sounds of a *dhol*, a percussion instrument, and some *ghungroos*, which were anklets worn by dancers. Someone seemed to be practising in the garden. A hedge separated the dance pavilion from the rest of the garden. Shiva, himself a passionate dancer, would normally have stepped in to move to the rhythm of the beat, but his mind was preoccupied. Some words floated in from the group that was dancing.

'No my lady, you must let yourself go,' said a distinguished male voice. 'It's not a chore that you have to do. Enjoy the dance. You are trying too hard to remember all the steps rather than letting the emotion of the dance flow through you.'

Then a lady's voice interjected. 'My lady, Guru*ji* is right. You are dancing correctly, but not enjoying it. The concentration shows on your face. You have to relax a bit.'

'Let me get the steps right. Then I can learn to enjoy them.'

The last voice made Shiva's hair stand up on end. It was her. It was Sati. He quickly got up and followed the sound of the voices. Coming up from behind the hedge, he saw Sati dancing on a small platform. She had her hands raised rigidly to her sides as she enacted the various movements of the dance. She danced in keeping with the steps, first to the left and then to the right. She moved her shapely hips to the side and placed her hands precisely on her waist, to convey the mood of the dance. He was mesmerised once again.

However, he did notice that though Sati's steps were right, the Guru*ji* had a point. She was moving in a mechanical manner; the uninhibited surrender that is characteristic of a natural dancer was absent. The varying emotions of bliss and anger in the story being told were missing in her movements. Also, unlike a proficient dancer, Sati wasn't using the entire platform. Her steps were small, which kept her movements restricted to the centre.

The dance teacher sat facing her and playing on a dhol to give Sati her beats. Her companion Krittika sat to the right. It was the dance teacher who noticed Shiva first and immediately stood up. Sati and Krittika turned around as well and were clearly astonished to find Shiva standing in front of them. Unlike Sati, Krittika could not control her surprise and blurted out, 'Shiva?'

Sati, in her characteristic composed and restrained manner, asked sincerely, 'Is everything alright, Shiva? Do you need my help?'

How have you been? I've missed you. Don't you ever smile?

Shiva continued to stare at Sati, the words running through his mind, not on his lips. A smiling Krittika looked at Sati for her reaction. An even more serious Sati repeated, very politely, 'Can I help you with something, Shiva?'

'No, no, I don't need any help,' replied Shiva as reality seemed to enter his consciousness once again. 'I just happened to be in the area and I heard your dancing. I mean your conversation. Your dance steps were not loud enough to be heard. You were dancing very accurately. Actually, technically it was all…'

Krittika interjected. 'You know a bit about dancing, do you?'

'Oh, not much. Just a little,' said Shiva to Krittika with a smile, before turning rapidly back to Sati. 'My apologies Sati, but Guru*ji* is right. You were being far too methodical. As they say in the land that I come from, the *mudras* and the *kriyas* were all technically correct. But the *bhav* or emotion was missing. And a dance without bhav is like a body without a soul. When the emotions of the dancer participate, she would not even need to remember the steps. The steps come to you. The bhav is something that you cannot learn. It comes to you if you can create the space in your heart for it.'

Sati listened patiently to Shiva without saying a word. Her eyebrows were raised slightly as the barbarian spoke. How could he know more than a Suryavanshi about dancing? But she reminded herself that he had saved her life. She was duty bound to honour him.

Krittika, however, took offence at this caste-unmarked foreigner pretending that he knew more about dancing than her mistress. She glowered at Shiva. 'You dare to think that you know more than one of the best dancers in the realm?'

Shiva gathered that he may have caused some offence. He turned to Sati in all seriousness. 'I am terribly sorry. I didn't mean to insult you in any way. Sometimes I just keep talking without realising what I am saying.'

'No, no', replied Sati. 'You did not insult me. Perhaps you are right. I don't feel the essence of the dance as much as I should. But I am sure that with Guru*ji*'s guidance, I will pick it up in due course.'

Seizing his chance to impress Sati, Shiva said, 'If it is alright with you, may I perform the dance? I am sure that I am not as technically correct as you. But perhaps, there may be something in the sentiment that will guide me through the correct steps.'

That was well put! She can't say no!

Sati looked surprised. This was unexpected. 'Umm, okay,' she managed to say.

A delighted Shiva immediately moved to the centre of the stage. He took off the angvastram covering his upper body and tossed it aside. Krittika's anger at the perceived insult to her mistress was quickly forgotten as she beheld Shiva's rippling physique. Sati, though, began to wonder how Shiva would bend such a muscular body into the contortions that were required of this dance. Flexibility was usually sacrificed by a human body at the altar of strength.

Playing lightly on his dhol, the Guru*ji* asked Shiva, 'What beat are you comfortable with, young man?'

Shiva folded his hands into a Namaste, bent low and said, 'Guru*ji*, could you just give me a minute please? I need to prepare for the dance.'

Dancing was something Shiva was as accomplished in as in warfare. Facing east, he closed his eyes and bowed his head slightly. Then he went down on his knees and reverentially touched the ground with his head. Standing up, he turned his right foot outwards. Then he raised his left leg off the floor in a graceful arching movement till the foot was above knee height, as he bent his right knee slightly to balance himself. His left foot bisected the angle between his right foot and his face. A calm breeze provided relief to the silence that enveloped the audience. Enraptured, the Guru*ji*, Sati and Krittika gazed at Shiva with amazement. They did not understand what he was doing but could feel the energy that Shiva's stance was emanating.

Shiva raised both his arms in an elegant circular movement to the sides to bring them in line with his shoulder. His right hand was holding an imaginary *dumru,* a small, handheld percussion instrument. His left hand was open with its palm facing upward, almost like it was receiving some divine energy. He held this pose for some time; his glowing face indicated that Shiva was withdrawing into his inner world. His right hand then moved effortlessly forward, almost as if it had a mind of its own. Its palm was now open and facing the audience. Somehow, the posture seemed to convey a feeling of protectiveness to a very surprised Sati. Almost languidly, his left arm glided at shoulder height and came to rest with the palm facing downwards and pointing at the left foot. Shiva held this pose for some time.

And then began the dance.

Sati stared in wonder at Shiva. He was performing the same steps as her. Yet it looked like a completely different dance. His lyrical hand movements graced the mystical motion of his body.

How could a body this muscular also be so flexible? The Guru*ji* tried helplessly to get his dhol to give Shiva the beats. But clearly that wasn't necessary. As it was Shiva's feet which were leading the beat for the dhol!

The dance conveyed the various emotions of a woman. In the beginning it conveyed her feelings of joy and lust as she cavorted with her husband. The next emotion was anger and pain at the treacherous killing of her mate. Despite his rough masculine body, Shiva managed to convey the tender yet strong emotions of a grieving woman.

Shiva's eyes were open. But the audience realised that he was oblivious to them. Shiva was in his own world. He did not dance for the audience. He did not dance for appreciation. He did not dance for the music. He danced only for himself. In fact, it almost seemed like his dance was guided by a celestial force. Sati realised that Shiva was right. He had opened himself and the dance had come to him.

After what seemed like an eternity the dance came to an end, with Shiva's eyes firmly shut. He held the final pose for a long time as the glow slowly left him. It was almost as if he was returning to this world. Shiva gradually opened his eyes to find Sati, Krittika and the Guru*ji* gaping at him wonder-struck.

The Guru*ji* was the first to find his voice. 'Who are you?'

'I am Shiva.'

'No, no. Not the body. I meant who are *you*?'

Shiva crooked his eyes together in a frown and repeated, 'I am Shiva.'

'Guru*ji*, may I ask a question?' asked Sati.

'Of course you may.'

Turning to Shiva, Sati asked, 'What was that you did before the dance? Was it some kind of preparatory step?'

'Yes. It's called the *Nataraj* pose. The pose of *the Lord of dance*.'

'The Nataraj pose? What does it do?'

'It aligned my energy to the universal energy so that the dance emerges on its own.'

'I don't understand.'

'Well, it's like this: amongst our people, we believe that everything in the world is a carrier of *shakti* or *energy*. The plants, animals, objects, our bodies, everything carries and transmits energy. But the biggest carrier of energy that we are physically in touch with is Mother Earth herself — the ground that we walk on.'

'What does that have to do with your dance?'

'You need energy for everything that you do. You have to source the energy from around you. It comes from people, from objects, from Mother Earth herself. You have to ask for it respectfully.'

'And your Nataraj pose helps you to access any energy that you want?' asked the Guru*ji*.

'It depends on what I want the energy for. The Nataraj pose helps me to ask respectfully for energy for a dance that wants to come to me. If I wanted the energy for a thought to come to me, I would have to sit cross-legged and meditate.'

'It seems that the energy favours you, young man,' said the Guru*ji*. 'You are the *Nataraj, the Lord of dance*.'

'Oh no!' exclaimed Shiva. 'I am just a medium for the boundless Nataraj energy. Anyone can be the medium.'

'Well, then you are a particularly efficient medium, young man,' said the Guru*ji*. Turning to Sati, he said, 'You don't need me if you have a friend like him, my child. If you want to be taught by Shiva, it would be my honour to excuse myself.'

Shiva looked at Sati expectantly. This had gone much better than he expected.

Say yes, dammit!

Sati however seemed to withdraw into herself. Shiva was startled to see the first signs of vulnerability in this woman. She bowed her head, an act which did not suit her proud bearing and whispered softly, 'I mean no disrespect to anyone, but perhaps I do not have the skills to receive training of this level.'

'But you do have the skill,' argued Shiva. 'You have the bearing. You have the heart. You can very easily reach that level.'

Sati looked up at Shiva, her eyes showing just the slightest hint of dampness. The profound sadness they conveyed took Shiva aback.

What the hell is going on?

'I am very far from any level, Shiva,' mumbled Sati.

As she said that, Sati found the strength to control herself again. The politely proud manner returned to her face. The mask was back. 'It is time for my puja. With your permission Guru*ji*, I must leave.' She turned towards Shiva. 'It was a pleasure meeting you again Shiva.'

Before Shiva could respond, Sati turned quickly and left, followed by Krittika.

The Guru*ji* continued to stare at a flummoxed Shiva. At length, he bent low with a formal Namaste towards Shiva and said, 'It has been my life's honour to see you dance.'

Then he too turned and left. Shiva was left wondering about the inscrutable ways of the Meluhans.

Late in the morning the next day Shiva and Nandi entered the private royal office to find Daksha, Parvateshwar and Kanakhala waiting for them. A surprised Shiva said, 'I am sorry your Highness. I thought we were to meet four hours into the second prahar. I hope I haven't kept you waiting.'

Daksha, who had stood up with a formal Namaste, bowed low and said, 'No, my Lord. You don't need to apologise. We came in early so that we wouldn't keep you waiting. It was our honour to wait for you.'

Parvateshwar rolled his eyes at the extreme subservience that his emperor, the ruler of the greatest civilisation ever established, showed towards this barbarian. Shiva, controlling his extreme surprise at being referred to as the 'Lord' by the emperor, bowed low towards Daksha with a Namaste and sat down.

'My Lord, before I start telling you about the legend of

the Neelkanth, do you have any questions that you would like to ask?' enquired Daksha.

The most obvious question came to Shiva's mind.

Why in the holy lake's name is my blessed blue throat so important?

But his instincts told him that though this appeared to be the most obvious question, it could not be answered unless he understood more about the society of Meluha itself.

'It may sound like an unusual question your Highness,' said Shiva. 'But may I ask you what your age is?'

Daksha looked at Kanakhala with surprise. Then turning back towards Shiva with an amazed smile, he said, 'You are exceptionally intelligent my Lord. You have asked the most pertinent question first.' Crinkling his face into a conspiratorial grin, Daksha continued, 'Last month I turned one hundred and eighty four.'

Shiva was stunned. Daksha did not look a day older than thirty years. In fact nobody in Meluha looked old. Except for the Pandit that Shiva had met at the Brahma temple.

So Nandi is more than a hundred years old.

'How can this be, your Highness?' asked a flabbergasted Shiva. 'What sorcery makes this possible?'

'There is no sorcery at all my Lord,' explained Daksha. 'What makes this possible is the brilliance of our scientists who make a potion called the *Somras*, the *drink of the Gods*. Taking the Somras at defined times not only postpones our death considerably, but it also allows us to live our entire lives as if we are in the prime of our youth — mentally and physically.'

'But what is the Somras? Where does it come from? Who invented it?'

'So many questions my Lord,' smiled Daksha. 'But I will try my best to answer them one by one. The Somras was invented many thousands of years ago by one of the greatest Indian scientists that ever lived. His name was Lord Brahma.'

'I think there is a temple dedicated to him that I visited on my way to Devagiri. At a place named Meru?'

'Yes my Lord. That is where he is said to have lived and worked. Lord Brahma was a prolific inventor. But he never kept any of the benefits of his inventions to himself. He was always interested in ensuring that his inventions were used for the good of mankind. He realised early on that a potion as powerful as the Somras could be misused by evil men. So he implemented an elaborate system of controls on its use.'

'What kind of controls?'

'He did not give the Somras freely to everyone,' continued Daksha. 'After conducting a rigorous country-wide survey, he chose a select group of adolescent boys of impeccable character — one from each of the seven regions of ancient India. He chose young boys so that they would live with him at his *gurukul* and he could mould their character into becoming selfless helpers of society. The Somras medicine was administered only to these boys. Since these boys were practically given an additional life due to the Somras, they came to be known as the *dwija* or *twice born*. The power of the Somras combined with the tutelage of Lord Brahma, along with their other inventions, resulted in this select group achieving a reverential status never seen before. They honed their minds to achieve almost superhuman intelligence. The ancient Indian title for men of knowledge was *Rishi*.

Since Lord Brahma's chosen men were seven in number, they came to be known as the *Saptrishi*.'

'And these Saptrishis used their skills for the good of society.'

'Yes my Lord. Lord Brahma instituted strict rules of conduct for the Saptrishis. They were not allowed to rule or to practice any trade — essentially anything that would have accrued personal gain. They had to use their skills to perform the task of priests, teachers, doctors, amongst other intellectual professions where they could use their powers to help society. They were not allowed to charge anything for their services and had to live on alms and donations from others.'

'Tough service rules,' joked Shiva with a slight wink at Parvateshwar.

Parvateshwar did not respond but Daksha, Kanakhala and Nandi guffawed loudly. Shiva took a quick look at the prahar lamp by the window. It was almost the third prahar. The time that Sati would probably come out to dance.

'But they followed their code of conduct strictly my Lord,' continued Daksha. 'Over time, as their responsibilities grew, the Saptrishis selected many more people to join their tribe. Their followers swore by the same code that the Saptrishis lived by and were also administered the Somras. They devoted their lives to the pursuit of knowledge and for the wellbeing of society without asking for any material gain in return. It is for this reason that society accorded these people almost devotional respect. Over the ages the Saptrishis and their followers came to be known as the *Tribe of Brahma* or simply, the *Brahmins*.'

'But as with all good systems over long periods of time, some people stopped following the Brahmin code, right?'

'Absolutely, my Lord,' answered Daksha, regretfully shaking his head at the familiar human frailty. 'As many millennia went by, some of the Brahmins forgot the strict code that Lord Brahma had enforced and the Saptrishis had propagated. They started misusing the awesome powers that the Somras gave them. Some Brahmins started using their influence over a large number of people to conquer kingdoms and start ruling. Some Brahmins misused other inventions of the Saptrishis as well as Lord Brahma and accumulated fabulous wealth for themselves.'

'And some of the Brahmins,' interjected Kanakhala with a particular sense of horror, 'even rebelled against the *Saptrishi Uttradhikaris*.'

'Saptrishi Uttradhikaris?' inquired Shiva.

'They were the *successors to the Saptrishis* my Lord,' clarified Kanakhala. 'When any of the Saptrishis knew that he was coming to the end of his mortal life, he would appoint a man from his gurukul as his successor. This successor was treated for all practical purposes like the Saptrishi himself.'

'So rebelling against the Saptrishi Uttradhikaris was like rebelling against the Saptrishis themselves?'

'Yes, my Lord,' answered Kanakhala. 'And the most worrying part of this corruption was that it was being led by the higher chosen-tribe Brahmins like the eagles, peacocks and the swans. In fact, due to their higher status, these chosen-tribes were actually not even allowed to work under the Kshatriyas and Vaishyas, lest they get enticed by the lure of the material world. Yet they succumbed to the temptations of evil before anyone else.'

'And chosen-tribes like yours, the pigeons, remained loyal to the old code despite working for the Kshatriyas?' asked Shiva.

'Yes, my Lord,' replied Kanakhala, her chest puffed up with pride.

The town bell sounded out the beginning of the third prahar. All the people in the room, including Shiva, said a quick short prayer welcoming the new time chapter. Shiva had learnt some of the ways of the Meluhans. A Shudra came in, reset the prahar lamp precisely and left as quietly as he came. Shiva reminded himself that anytime now Sati would start her dance lessons in the garden.

'So what revolution caused the change your Highness?' asked Shiva turning to Daksha. 'You, Parvateshwar and Nandi are Kshatriyas and yet you clearly have taken the Somras. In fact I have seen people of all four castes in your empire look youthful and healthy. This means that the Somras is now given to everybody. This change must have obviously happened due to a revolution, right?'

'Yes, my Lord. And the revolution was known as Lord Ram. The greatest emperor that ever lived! Jai Shri Ram!'

'Jai Shri Ram!' repeated everyone in the room.

'His ideas and leadership transformed the society of Meluha dramatically,' continued Daksha. 'In fact, the course of history itself was radically altered. But before I continue with Lord Ram's tale, may I make a suggestion?'

'Of course, your Highness.'

'It is into the third prahar now. Should we move to the dining room and have some lunch before continuing with this story?'

'I think it is an excellent idea to have lunch your Highness,' said Shiva. 'But may I be excused for some time? There is another pressing engagement that I have. Could we perhaps continue our conversation tomorrow if that is alright with you?'

Kanakhala's face fell immediately while Parvateshwar's was covered with a contemptuous grin. Daksha, however, kept a smiling face. 'Of course we could meet tomorrow my Lord. Will the beginning of the second hour of the second prahar be all right with you?'

'Absolutely, your Highness. My apologies for this inconvenience.'

'Not at all my Lord,' said an ever smiling Daksha. 'Can one of my chariots take you to your destination?'

'That's very kind of you, your Highness. But I will go there by myself. My apologies once again.'

Bidding a Namaste to everyone in the room, Shiva and Nandi walked out quickly. Kanakhala looked accusingly at Daksha. The emperor just nodded his head, gesturing with his hands for calm. 'It's all right. We are meeting tomorrow, aren't we?'

'My Lord, we are running out of time,' said Kanakhala. 'The Neelkanth needs to accept his responsibilities immediately!'

'Give him time, Kanakhala. We have waited for so long. A few days is not going to cause a collapse!'

Parvateshwar got up suddenly, bowed low towards Daksha and said, 'With your permission your Highness, may I be excused? There are more practical matters that need my attention as compared to educating a barbarian.'

'You will speak of him with respect Parvateshwar,' growled Kanakhala. 'He is the Neelkanth!'

'I will speak of him with respect only when he has earned it through some real achievements,' snarled Parvateshwar. 'I respect only achievements, nothing else. That is the fundamental rule of Lord Ram. Only your karma is important. Not your birth. Not your sex. And certainly not the colour of your throat. Our entire society is based on merit. Or have you forgotten that?'

'Enough!' exclaimed Daksha. 'I respect the Neelkanth. That means everybody will respect him!'

CHAPTER 6

Vikarma, the Carriers of Bad Fate

Nandi waited at a distance in the garden as he had been asked to, while Shiva stepped behind the hedge that separated the dance arena from the garden. The silent dance stage had already convinced Nandi that his Lord would not find anybody there. However, Shiva was filled with hope and waited expectantly for Sati. After having waited for the larger part of an hour, Shiva realised that there would be no dance practice today. Deeply disappointed, he walked silently back to Nandi.

'Is there somebody I can help you find, my Lord?' asked an earnest Nandi.

'No Nandi. Forget it.'

Trying to change the topic, Nandi said, 'My Lord, you must be hungry. Should we go back to the guest house and eat?'

'No, I'd like to see a little more of the city,' said Shiva, hoping that fate would be kind to him and he would run into Sati in the town. 'Shall we go to one of the restaurants on the Rajat platform?'

'That would be wonderful!' smiled Nandi who hated the simple Brahmin-influenced vegetarian food served at the royal guest house. He missed the spicy meats that were served in rough Kshatriya restaurants.

— ⅄ⓄⓊ⍋⊗ —

'Yes, what is it Parvateshwar?' asked Daksha.

'My Lord, I am sorry about the sudden meeting. But I've just received some disturbing news which I must share with you in private.'

'Well, what is it?'

'Shiva is already causing trouble.'

'What have you got against the Neelkanth?' Groaned Daksha, rolling his eyes in disapproval. 'Why can't you believe that the Neelkanth has come to save us?'

'This has nothing to do with my views on Shiva, my Lord. If you will please listen to what I have to say. Chenardhwaj saw Shiva in the gardens yesterday.'

'Chenardhwaj is here already?'

'Yes your Highness. His review with you has been fixed for the day after tomorrow.'

'Anyway, so what did Chenardhwaj see?'

'He is also sickeningly taken in by the Neelkanth. So I think we can safely assume that he doesn't have any prejudice.'

'All right, I believe you. So what did he see the Neelkanth do?'

'He saw Shiva dancing in the gardens,' answered Parvateshwar.

'So? Is there a law banning dance that I am not aware of?'

'Please let me continue, your Highness. He was dancing while Sati watched in rapt attention.'

His interest suddenly aroused, Daksha leaned forward to ask, 'And?'

'Sati behaved correctly and left the moment Shiva tried to get too familiar. But Chenardhwaj heard Shiva whisper something when Sati left.'

'Well, what did he whisper?'

'He whispered — *Holy Lake, help me get her. I will not ask for anything else from you ever again!*'

Daksha appeared delighted. 'You mean the Neelkanth may actually be in love with my daughter?'

'Your Highness, you cannot forget the laws of the land,' exclaimed a horrified Parvateshwar. 'You know that Sati cannot marry.'

'If the Neelkanth decides to marry Sati, no law on earth can stop him.'

'My Lord, forgive me but the rule of law is the very foundation of our civilisation. That's what makes us who we are. Better than the Chandravanshis and the Nagas. Not even Lord Ram was above the law. Then how can this barbarian be considered so important?'

'Don't you want Sati to be happy?' asked Daksha. 'She's also called Parvati for a reason — it's because she is your Goddaughter. Don't you want her to find joy once again?'

'I love Sati like the daughter I never had, your Highness,' said Parvateshwar, with a rare display of emotion in his eyes. 'I would do anything for her. Except break the law.'

'That is the difference between you and me. For Sati's sake, I would not mind breaking any law. She is my daughter. My flesh and blood. She has suffered enough already. If I can find some way to make her happy, I will do it. No matter what the consequences!'

— ⲀⲰⲨⲫ⊗ —

Shiva and Nandi tethered their horses in the parking lot next to the main Rajat platform market. Moving forward, Nandi guided Shiva towards one of his favourite restaurants. The inviting aroma of freshly cooked meat brought forth a nostalgic hunger in Nandi that had not been satisfied in the past two days at the royal guest house. The owner however stopped Shiva at the entry.

'What's the matter, brother?' asked Nandi.

'I am deeply sorry brothers. But I too am undergoing religious vows at this time,' said the restaurant owner politely, pointing to the beads around his throat. 'And you know that one of the vows is that I cannot serve meat to fellow religious vow keepers.'

Nandi blurted out in surprise, 'But who has taken religious…'

He was stopped by Shiva who signalled downwards with his eyes at the bead covered cravat around his throat. Nandi nodded and followed Shiva out of the restaurant.

'This is the time of the year for religious vows, my Lord,' explained Nandi. 'Why don't you wait on the side? There are some good restaurants on the street at the right. I will go and see if I can find a restaurant owner who has not taken his vows.'

Shiva nodded his ascent. As Nandi hurried off, Shiva looked around the street. It was a busy market area with restaurants and shops spread out evenly. But despite the large number of people and the buzz of commerce, the street was not noisy. None of the shopkeepers stepped out to scream and advertise their wares. The customers spoke softly and in an unfailingly polite manner, even if they were bargaining.

These well-mannered idiots would not be able to conduct any business in our boisterous mountain market!

Shiva, lost in his observation of the strange practices of the Meluhans, did not hear the announcement of the town crier till he was almost right behind him.

'Procession of vikarma women. Please move!'

A surprised Shiva turned to find a tall Meluhan Kshatriya looking down at him. 'Would you care to move aside, sir? A procession of vikarma women will soon pass this way for their prayers.'

The crier's tone and demeanour was unquestionably courteous. But Shiva was under no illusions. The crier was not *asking* Shiva to move. He was *telling* him. Shiva stepped back to let the procession pass as Nandi touched him gently on his arm.

'I have found a good restaurant, my Lord,' said an ecstatic Nandi. 'It serves my favourite dishes. And the kitchen is open for yet another hour. A lot of food to stuff ourselves with!'

Shiva laughed out loud. 'It's a wonder that just one restaurant can actually make enough food to satisfy your hunger!'

Nandi laughed along good naturedly as Shiva patted his friend on the back.

As they turned and walked into the lane, Shiva asked, 'Who are vikarma women?'

'Vikarma people, my Lord,' said Nandi sighing deeply,

'are people who have been punished in this birth for the sins of their previous birth. Hence they have to live this life out with dignity and tolerate their present sufferings with grace. This is the only way they can wipe their karma clean of the sins of their previous births. Vikarma men have their own order of penance and women have their own order.'

'There was a procession of vikarma women on the road we just left. Is their puja a part of the order?' asked Shiva.

'Yes, my Lord. There are many rules that the vikarma women have to follow. They have to pray for forgiveness every month to Lord Agni, the purifying Fire God, through a specifically mandated puja. They are not allowed to marry since they may contaminate others with their bad fate. They are not allowed to touch any person who is not related to them or is not part of their daily life. There are many other conditions as well that I am not completely aware of. If you are interested, we could meet up with a Pandit at the Agni temple later and he could tell you all about vikarma people.'

'No, I am not interested in meeting the Pandit right now,' said Shiva with a smile. 'He might just bore me with some very confusing and abstruse philosophies! But tell me one thing. Who decides that the vikarma people had committed sins in their previous birth?'

'Their own karma, my Lord,' said Nandi, his eyes suggesting the obvious. 'For example if a woman gives birth to a still born child, why would she be punished thus unless she had committed some terrible sin in her previous birth? Or if a man suddenly contracts an incurable disease and gets paralysed, why would it happen to him unless the universe was penalising him for the sins of his previous life?'

'That sounds pretty ridiculous to me. A woman could have given birth to a still born child simply because she did not take proper care while she was pregnant. Or it could just be a disease. How can anyone say that she is being punished for the sins of her previous birth?'

Nandi, shocked by Shiva's statements, struggled to find words to respond. He was a Meluhan and deeply believed in the concept of karma being carried over many births. He mumbled softly, 'It's the law, my Lord…'

'Well, to be honest, it sounds like a rather unfair law to me.'

Nandi's crestfallen face showed that he was profoundly disappointed that Shiva did not understand such a fundamental concept of Meluha. But he also kept his own counsel for fear of opposing what Shiva said. After all, Shiva was his Lord.

Seeing a dejected Nandi, Shiva patted him gently on the back. 'Nandi, that was just my opinion. If the law works for your people, I am sure there must be some logic to it. Your society might be a little strange at times, but it has some of the most honest and decent people I have ever met.'

As a smile returned almost instantly to Nandi's face, his whole being was stricken by his immediate problem. His debilitating hunger! He entered the restaurant like a man on a mission, with Shiva chuckling softly behind.

A short distance away on the main road, the procession of vikarma women walked silently on. They were all draped in long angvastrams which were dyed in the holy blue colour. Their heads were bowed low in penitence, their *puja thalis* or *prayer plates* full of offerings to Lord Agni. The normally quiet market street became almost deathly silent as the pitiful women lumbered by. At the centre of the procession, unseen by Shiva, with her head bowed low, draped in a blue angvastram that covered her from head to toe, her face a picture of resigned dignity, trudged the forlorn figure of Sati.

— ⅄⓪Ʊ⇞⊛ —

'So where were we, my Lord?' said Daksha, as Shiva and Nandi settled down in his private office the next morning.

'We were about to discuss the changes that Lord Ram brought about, your Highness. And how he defeated the rebellion of the renegade Brahmins,' answered Shiva.

'That's right,' said Daksha. 'Lord Ram did defeat the renegade Brahmins. But in his view, the core problem ran deeper. It wasn't just a matter of some Brahmins not following the code. There was a conflict between a person's natural karma and what society forced him to do.'

'I don't understand your Highness.'

'Let me explain. Do you know what was the essential problem with the renegade Brahmins? Some of them wanted to be Kshatriyas and rule. Some of them wanted to be Vaishyas, make money and live a life of luxury. However, their birth confined them to being Brahmins.'

'But I thought that Lord Brahma had decreed that people became Brahmins through a competitive examination process,' said Shiva.

'That is true my Lord. But over time this process of selection lost its fairness. Children of Brahmins became Brahmins. Children of Kshatriyas became Kshatriyas and so on. The formal system of selection soon ceased to exist. A father would ensure that his children got all the resources and support needed to grow up and become a member of his own caste. So the caste system became rigid.'

'Did that also mean that there could have been a person talented enough to be a Brahmin but if he was born to Shudra parents, he would not get the opportunity to become a Brahmin?' asked Shiva.

'Yes Shiva,' said Parvateshwar, speaking for the first time to Shiva. He noticed that Parvateshwar did not fawn all over him and call him Lord. 'In Lord Ram's view, any society that conducted itself on any principle besides merit could not be stable. He believed that a person's caste should be determined *only by that person's karma*. Not his birth. Not his sex. No other consideration should interfere.'

'That is nice in theory, Parvateshwar,' argued Shiva. 'But how do you ensure it in practice? If a child is born in a Brahmin family, he would get the upbringing and resources which would be different from that of a child born in a Shudra family. So this child would grow up to be a Brahmin even if he was less talented than the Shudra boy. Isn't this unfair to the child born in the Shudra family? Where is the "merit" in this system?'

'That was the genius of Lord Ram, Shiva,' smiled Parvateshwar. 'He was of course a brave General, a brilliant administrator and a fair judge. But his greatest legacy is the system he created to ensure that a person's karma is determined only by his abilities, nothing else. That system is what has made Meluha what it is — the greatest nation in history.'

'You can't underestimate the role that Somras has played, Parvateshwar,' said Daksha. 'Lord Ram's greatest act was to provide the Somras to everyone. The elixir is what makes Meluhans the smartest people in the universe! The Somras is what has given us the ability to create this remarkable and near perfect society.'

'Begging your pardon, your Highness,' said Shiva before turning back to Parvateshwar. 'But what was the system that Lord Ram set up?'

'The system is simple,' said Parvateshwar. 'As we agreed, the best society is the one where a person's caste is decided purely by his abilities and karma. Not by any other factor. Lord Ram created a practical system that ensured this. All children that are born in Meluha are compulsorily adopted by the empire. In order to ensure that this is done methodically, a great hospital city called Maika was built deep in the south, just north of the Narmada river. All pregnant women have to travel there for their delivery. Only pregnant women are allowed into the city. Nobody else.'

'Nobody else? What about her husband, her parents?' asked Shiva.

'No, there are no exceptions to this rule except for one. This exception was voted in around three hundred years ago. Husbands and parents of women of noble families were allowed to enter,' answered Parvateshwar, his expression clearly showing that he violently disagreed with this corruption of Lord Ram's system.

'Then who takes care of the pregnant woman in Maika?'

'The hospital staff. They are extremely well trained,' continued Parvateshwar. 'Once the child is born, he or she is kept in Maika for a few weeks while the mother travels back to her own city.'

'Without her child?' asked a clearly surprised Shiva.

'Yes,' replied Parvateshwar, with a slight frown as if this

was the most obvious thing in the world. 'The child is then put into the Meluha Gurukul, a massive school created by the empire close to Maika. Every single child receives the benefit of the same education system. They grow up with all the resources of the empire available to them.'

'Do they maintain records of the parents and their children?'

'Of course they do. But the records are kept in utmost secrecy and are available only with the record-keeper of Maika.'

'That would mean that neither in the Gurukul nor in the rest of the empire, would anybody know who the child's birth parents are,' reasoned Shiva, as he worked out the implications of what he was hearing. 'So every child, regardless of whether he is born to a Brahmin or a Shudra, would get exactly the same treatment at the Gurukul?'

'Yes,' smiled Parvateshwar. He was clearly proud of the system. 'As the children enter the age of adolescence, they are all given the Somras. Thus every child has exactly the same opportunity to succeed. At the age of fifteen, when they have reached adulthood, all the children take a comprehensive examination. The results of this examination decide which varna or caste the child will be allocated to — Brahmin, Kshatriya, Vaishya or Shudra.'

Kanakhala cut in. 'And then the children are given one more year's caste-specific training. They wear their varna colour bands — white for Brahmins, red for Kshatriyas, green for Vaishyas and black for Shudras — and retreat to the respective caste schools to complete their education.'

'So that's why your caste system is called the varna system,' said Shiva. '*Varna* means *colour*, right?'

'Yes my Lord,' smiled Kanakhala. 'You are very observant.'

With a withering look at Kanakhala, Parvateshwar added sarcastically, 'Yes, that was a very difficult conclusion to draw.'

Ignoring the barb, Shiva asked, 'So what happens after that?'

'When the children turn sixteen, they are allocated to applicant parents from their caste. For example, if some Brahmin parents have applied to adopt a child, one randomly chosen student from Maika, who has won the Brahmin caste in the examination, is allotted to them. Then the child grows up with these adopted parents as their own child.'

'And society is perfect,' marvelled Shiva, as the simple brilliance of the system enveloped his mind. 'Each person is given a position in society based only on his own abilities. The efficiency and fairness of this system is astounding!'

'Over time my Lord,' interjected Daksha, 'we found the percentage of higher castes actually going up in the population. Which means that everybody in the world has the ability to excel. All it takes is for a child to be given a fair chance to succeed.'

'Then the lower castes must have loved Lord Ram for this?' asked Shiva. 'He gave them an actual chance to succeed.'

'Yes they did love him,' answered Parvateshwar. 'They were his most loyal followers. Jai Shri Ram!'

'But I guess not too many mothers would have been happy with this. I can't imagine a woman willingly giving up her child as soon as he is born with no chance of meeting him ever again.'

'But it's for the larger good,' said Parvateshwar, scowling at the seemingly stupid question. 'And in any case, every mother who wants an offspring can apply for one and be allocated a child who suits her position and dreams. Nothing can be worse for a mother than having a child who does not measure up to her expectations.'

Shiva frowned at Parvateshwar's explanation, but let the argument pass. 'I can also imagine that many of the upper castes like the Brahmins would have been unhappy with Lord Ram. After all, they lost their stranglehold on power.'

'Yes,' added Daksha. 'Many upper castes did oppose Lord Ram's reforms. Not just Brahmins, but even Kshatriyas and Vaishyas. Lord Ram fought a great battle to defeat them. Those from among the vanquished who survived are the Chandravanshis we see today.'

'So your differences go that far back?'

'Yes,' said Daksha. 'The Chandravanshis are corrupt and disgusting people. No morals. No ethics. They are the source of all our problems. Some of us believe that Lord Ram was too kind. He should have completely destroyed them. But he forgave them and let them live. In fact, we have to face the mortification of seeing the Chandravanshis rule over Lord Ram's birthplace — Ayodhya!'

Before Shiva could react to this information, the bell of the new prahar was rung. Everyone said a quick prayer to welcome the subsequent time chapter. Shiva immediately looked towards the window. A look of expectancy appeared on his face.

Daksha smiled as he observed Shiva's expression. 'We could break for lunch now, my Lord. But if you have another engagement you would like to attend, we could continue tomorrow.'

Parvateshwar glared at Daksha disapprovingly. He knew exactly what the emperor was trying to do.

'That would be nice, your Highness,' smiled Shiva. 'Is my face such a giveaway?'

'Yes it is my Lord. But that is a gift you have. Nothing is prized more than honesty in Meluha. Why don't you leave for your engagement and we could convene here again tomorrow morning?'

Thanking Daksha profusely, Shiva left the room with Nandi in tow.

— ⁂ —

Shiva approached the hedge with excitement and trepidation. Scarce had he heard the beat of the dhol emanating from the direction of the garden, he despatched Nandi to the guest house for lunch. He wanted to be alone. He let out a deep sigh of ecstasy as he crept up behind the hedge to find Sati practising under the watchful eye of the Guru*ji* and Krittika.

'So good to see you again, Shiva,' said the Guru*ji* as he stood up with a formal Namaste.

'The pleasure is all mine, Guru*ji*,' said Shiva, as he bent down to touch the Guru*ji*'s feet as a sign of respect.

Sati stood silently at a distance with her gaze on the floor. Krittika said enthusiastically, 'I just couldn't get your dance out of my mind!'

Shiva blushed at the compliment. 'Oh it wasn't all that good.'

'Now you're fishing for compliments,' teased Krittika.

'I was wondering if we could start off where we left the last time,' said Shiva, turning towards Sati. 'I don't think I have to be your teacher or anything like that. I just wanted to see you dance.'

Sati felt her strange discomfort returning once again. What was it about Shiva that made her feel that she was breaking the law when she spoke to him? She was allowed to talk to men as long as she kept a respectable distance. Why should she feel guilty?

'I will try my best,' said Sati formally. 'It would be enriching to hear your views on how I can improve myself. I really do respect you for your dancing skills.'

Respect?! Why respect? Why not love?!

Shiva smiled politely. He knew instinctively that saying anything at this point of time would spoil the moment.

Sati took a deep breath, girded her angvastram around her waist and committed herself to the Nataraj pose. Shiva smiled as he felt Mother Earth project her *shakti,* her *energy,* into Sati.

Energised by the earth she stood upon, Sati began her dance. And she had really improved. The emotions seemed to course through her. She had always been technically good, but the passion elevated her dance to the next level. Shiva felt a dreamy sense of unreality overcome him again. Sati maintained a magnetic hold over him as she moved her lithe body with the dance steps. For some moments, Shiva imagined that he was the man that Sati was longing for in her dance. When she finally came to a stop, the audience spontaneously applauded.

'That was the best I have ever seen you dance,' said the Guru*ji* with pride.

'Thank you Guru*ji*,' said Sati as she bowed. Then she looked expectantly at Shiva.

'It was fantastic,' exclaimed Shiva. 'Absolutely fabulous. Didn't I tell you that you had it in you?'

'I thought that I didn't get it exactly right at the moment of attack,' said Sati critically.

'You're being too hard on yourself,' consoled Shiva. 'That was just a slight error. It happened only because you missed out on holding one angle at your elbow. That made your next move a little odd.' Rising swiftly to his feet, Shiva continued, 'See, I'll show you.'

He walked quickly towards Sati and touched her elbow to move it to the correct angle. Sati immediately recoiled in horror as there was a gasp from the Guru*ji* as well as Krittika. Shiva instantly realised that something terrible had happened.

'I am sorry,' said Shiva, with a look of sincere regret. 'I was just trying to show you where your elbow should be.'

Sati continued to stare at Shiva, stunned into immobility.

The Guru*ji* was the first to recover his wits and realise that Shiva must undergo *the purification ceremony*. 'Go to your Pandit, Shiva. Tell him you need a *shudhikaran*. Go before the day is over.'

'What? What is a shudhikaran? Why would I need it?'

'Please go for a shudhikaran, Shiva,' said Sati, as tears broke through her proud eyes. 'I would never be able to forgive myself if something were to happen to you.'

'Nothing will happen to me! Look, I am really sorry if I have broken some rule by touching you. I will not do it again. Let's not make a big deal of this.'

'IT IS A BIG DEAL!' shouted Sati.

The violence of Sati's reaction threw Shiva off balance.

Why the hell is this simple thing being blown completely out of proportion?

Krittika came up close to Sati while being careful not to touch her, and whispered, 'We should go back home, my lady.'

'No. No. Please stay,' pleaded Shiva. 'I won't touch you. I promise.'

With a look of hopeless despair, Sati turned to leave, followed by Krittika and Guru*ji*. At the edge of the hedge, she turned around and beseeched Shiva once again, 'Please go for your shudhikaran before nightfall. Please.'

At the look of uncomprehending mutiny on Shiva's face, the Guru*ji* advised, 'Listen to her, Shiva. She speaks for your own good.'

— ⚘ —

'What bloody nonsense!' yelled Shiva as his disturbed thoughts finally broke through his desperate efforts at silent acceptance. He was lying in his bedroom at the royal guest house. He had not undergone the shudhikaran. He had not even bothered to find out what the ceremony was.

Why would I need to be purified for touching Sati? I want to spend all my remaining years touching her in every possible way. Am I going to keep on undergoing a shudhikaran every day? Ridiculous!

Just then a troubling thought entered Shiva's mind.

Is it because of me? Am I not allowed to touch her because I am caste-unmarked? An inferior barbarian?

'No. That can't be true,' whispered Shiva to himself. 'Sati doesn't think like that. She is a good woman.'

But what if it's true? Maybe if she knows that I am the Neelkanth…

CHAPTER 7

Lord Ram's Unfinished Task

'You seem to be a little distracted this morning, my Lord. Are you alright?' asked a concerned Daksha.

'Hmm?' said Shiva as he looked up. 'I'm sorry your Highness. I was a little distracted.'

Daksha looked at Kanakhala with a concerned expression. He had seen a similar look of despair on Sati's face at dinner the previous night. But she had refused to say anything.

'Do you want to meet later?' asked Daksha.

'Of course not, your Highness. It's alright. My apologies. Please continue,' said Shiva.

'Well,' continued a concerned Daksha, 'we were talking about the changes that Lord Ram brought about in society.'

'Yes,' said Shiva, shaking his head slightly to get the disturbing image of Sati's last plea out of his mind.

'The Maika system worked fantastically well. Our society boomed. Ours was always one of the wealthiest lands on earth. But in the last one thousand two hundred years we have shot dramatically ahead of everyone else. Meluha has become the richest and most powerful country in the world by far. Our citizens lead ideal lives. There is no crime. People do what they are suited for and not what an unfair social order would compel them to do. We don't force or fight unprovoked wars with any other country. In fact, ours has become a perfect society.'

'Yes, your Highness,' agreed Shiva, slowly getting into the conversation. 'I don't believe that perfection can ever be achieved. It is more of a journey than a destination. But your society is certainly a near perfect society.'

'Why do you think we are not perfect?' argued Parvateshwar aggressively.

'Do you think it is perfect Parvateshwar?' asked Shiva politely. 'Is everything in Meluha exactly the way Lord Ram would have mandated?'

Parvateshwar fell silent. He knew the obvious, even if he didn't like the answer.

'The Lord is right Parvateshwar,' said Daksha. 'There are always things to improve.'

'Having said that, your Highness,' spoke Shiva, 'your society is wonderful. Things do seem very well ordered. What doesn't make sense to me then, is why you and your people are so concerned about the future. What is the problem? Why is a Neelkanth required? I don't see anything that is so obviously wrong that disaster would be just a breath away. This is not like my homeland where there are so many problems that you wouldn't know where to begin!'

'My Lord, a Neelkanth is needed because we are faced with challenges that we cannot confront. We keep to ourselves and let other countries lead their lives. We trade with other societies but we never interfere with them. We don't allow uninvited foreigners into Meluha beyond the frontier towns. So we think it's only fair that other societies leave us alone to lead our lives the way we want to.'

'And presumably they don't, your Highness?'

'No they don't.'

'Why?'

'One simple word, my Lord,' replied Daksha. 'Jealousy. They hate our superior ways. Our efficient family system is an eyesore to them. The fact that we take care of everyone in our country makes them unhappy because they can't take care of themselves. They lead sorry lives. And rather than improving themselves, they want to pull us down to their level.'

'I can understand. My tribe used to face a lot of jealousy in Mount Kailash since we had control over the shore of the Mansarovar Lake and hence the best land in the region. But sometimes I wonder if we could have avoided bloodshed if we had shared our good fortune more willingly.'

'But we do share our good fortune with those who wish to, my Lord. And yet, jealousy blinds our enemies. The Chandravanshis realised that it was the Somras that guaranteed our superiority. Funnily enough, even they have the knowledge of the Somras. But they have not learnt to mass produce it like we do and hence haven't reaped all its benefits.'

'Sorry to interrupt, your Highness, but where is the Somras produced?'

'It is produced at a secret location called Mount Mandar. The Somras powder is manufactured there and then distributed throughout the Meluhan empire. At select temples specially trained Brahmins prepare the solution with water and other ingredients and then administer it to the population.'

'Alright,' said Shiva.

'The Chandravanshis could not become as powerful as us since they did not have enough Somras. Eaten up with jealousy, they devised a devious plan to destroy the Somras and hence us. One of the key ingredients in the Somras is the waters of the Saraswati. Water from any other source does not work.'

'Really? Why?'

'We don't know my Lord. The scientists can't explain it. But only the waters of the Saraswati will do. That is why, the Chandravanshis tried to kill the Saraswati to harm us.'

'Kill the river?' asked Shiva incredulously.

'Yes my Lord!' said Daksha, as his childlike eyes flared with indignation at the Chandravanshi perfidy. 'The Saraswati is formed by the confluence of two mighty rivers up north — the Sutlej and the Yamuna. In an earlier era the course of the Sutlej and the Yamuna was considered neutral territory, from which both the Chandravanshis as well as the Suryavanshis drew water for the Somras.'

'But how did they try to kill the Saraswati your Highness?'

'They diverted the course of the Yamuna so that instead of flowing south, it started flowing east to meet their main river, Ganga.'

'You can do that?' asked Shiva in amazement. 'Change the course of a river?'

'Yes, of course you can,' answered Parvateshwar.

'We were livid,' interjected Daksha. 'But we still gave them an opportunity to make amends for their duplicity.'

'And?'

'What can you expect from the Chandravanshis, my Lord?' said Daksha in disgust. 'They denied any knowledge of this. They claimed that the river made such a dramatic change in its course all by itself, due to some minor earthquake. And even worse, they claimed that since the river had changed course of its own accord, we Meluhans would simply have to accept what was essentially God's will!'

'We of course refused to do that,' said Parvateshwar. 'Under the leadership of King Brahmanayak, his Highness' father, we attacked Swadweep.'

'The land of the Chandravanshis?' asked Shiva.

'Yes Shiva,' said Parvateshwar. 'And it was a resounding victory. The Chandravanshi army was routed. King Brahmanayak magnanimously let them keep their lands and even their system of governance. We didn't even demand any war reparations or a yearly tribute. The only term of the surrender treaty was the return of the Yamuna. We restored the Yamuna to her original course which eventually met with the Saraswati.'

'Did you fight in that war, Parvateshwar?'

'Yes,' said Parvateshwar, his chest swollen with pride. 'I was a mere soldier then. But I did fight in that war.'

Turning to Daksha, Shiva asked, 'Then what is the problem now, your Highness? Your enemy was comprehensively defeated. Then why is the Saraswati still dying?'

'We believe that the Chandravanshis are up to something once again. We don't understand it as yet. After their defeat, the area between our two countries was converted into a no-man's land and the jungle has reclaimed it. This includes the early course of the Yamuna as well. We have stuck to our part of the agreement and have never disturbed that region. It appears that they haven't honoured their end of the bargain.'

'Are you sure about that your Highness? Has the

area been checked? Has this been discussed with the Chandravanshis' representative in your empire?'

'Are you trying to say that we are lying?' countered Parvateshwar. 'True Suryavanshis don't lie!'

'Parvateshwar!' scolded Daksha angrily. 'The Lord was not implying any such thing.'

'Listen to me, Parvateshwar,' said Shiva politely. 'If I have learnt one thing from the pointless battles of my land, it is that wars should be the last resort. If there is an alternative available what is the harm in saving some young soldier's life? Surely, a mother would bless us for it.'

'Let's not fight! Wonderful! What a great saviour we have!' Parvateshwar muttered under his breath.

'You have something to say Parvateshwar?' barked Kanakhala. 'I have told you before. You will not insult the Neelkanth in my presence!'

'I don't take orders from you,' growled Parvateshwar.

'Enough!' ordered Daksha. Turning to Shiva, he continued, 'I am sorry my Lord. You are right. We shouldn't just declare war without being sure. That is why I have avoided a war until now. But just look at the facts. The flow of the Saraswati has been gradually waning for the last half century.'

'And the last few years have been horrible,' said Kanakhala as she controlled her tears at the thought of the slow death of the river most Meluhans regarded as a mother. 'The Saraswati doesn't even reach the sea now and ends in an inland delta just south of Rajasthan.'

'And the Somras cannot be made without water from the Saraswati,' continued Daksha. 'The Chandravanshis are aware of this and that is why they are trying to kill her.'

'What does the Swadweep representative have to say about it? Has he been questioned?'

'We have no diplomatic relations with Swadweep, my Lord,' said Daksha.

'Really? I thought having representatives of other countries was one of your innovative systems. It gives you an opportunity to understand them and maybe avoid jumping into a war. I had heard of a diplomatic mission from Mesopotamia coming in two days ago. Then why not have this with Swadweep as well?'

'You don't know them, my Lord. They are untrustworthy people. No follower of the Suryavanshi way of life will sully his soul by even speaking to a Chandravanshi willingly.'

Shiva frowned but didn't say anything.

'You don't know the levels they have sunk to my Lord. Over the last few years they have even started using the cursed Nagas in their terrorist attacks on us!' said Kanakhala, with a disgusted look.

'Terrorist attacks?'

'Yes, my Lord,' said Daksha. 'Their defeat kept them quiet for many decades. And because of our overwhelming victory in the previous war, they now believe that they cannot overpower us in an open confrontation. So they have resorted to a form of assault that only repulsive people like them can be capable of. Terrorist attacks.'

'I don't understand. What exactly do they do?'

'They send small bands of assassins who launch surprise attacks on non-military but public places. Their idea is to attack non-combatants — the Brahmins, Vaishyas or Shudras. They try to devastate places like temples, public baths — areas that might not have soldiers who can fight back — but whose destruction will wreck the empire's morale and spread terror.'

'That's disgusting! Even the Pakratis in my land, a bunch of complete barbarians, would not do that,' said Shiva.

'Yes,' said Parvateshwar. 'These Chandravanshis don't fight like men. They fight like cowards!'

'Then why don't you attack their country? Finish this once and for all.'

'We would like to my Lord,' said Daksha. 'But I am not sure we can defeat them.'

Shiva observed Parvateshwar seething silently at the insult to his army, before turning towards Daksha. 'Why, your Highness? You have a well trained and efficient force. I am sure your army can defeat them.'

'Two reasons, my Lord. Firstly, we are outnumbered. We were outnumbered even a hundred years back. But not by a very significant margin. Today, we estimate that they have a population of more than eighty million as compared to our eight million. They can put up a much larger army against ours — their sheer numbers will cancel out our technological superiority.'

'But why should your population be less? You have people who live beyond the age of two hundred years! Your population should be higher.'

'Sociological causes, my Lord,' said Daksha. 'Our country is rich. Children are a matter of choice, and not a duty. Parents adopt children from the Maika system in small numbers, may be one or two, so that they can devote more attention to their upbringing. Fewer mothers are giving birth at Maika as well. In Swadweep the children of the poor are often treated as mere bonded labour meant only to supplement the family income. Resultantly, the whole country, though deprived, has a large population.'

'And the second reason for avoiding war?'

'The second reason is something that is under our control. We fight in accordance with "rules of war", with norms and ethics. The Chandravanshis do no such thing. And I fear this is a weakness in us that our ruthless enemies can exploit.'

'Rules of war?' asked Shiva.

'Yes. For example, we will not attack an unarmed man. A better-armed person like a cavalry man will not attack a lesser-armed person like a spear wielding foot-soldier. A swordsman will never attack a person below his waist because that is unethical. The Chandravanshis don't care for such niceties. They will attack whoever and however they find expedient to ensure victory.'

'Begging your pardon, your Highness,' said Parvateshwar. 'But that difference is what makes us who we are. Like Lord Ram had said, a person's character is not tested in good times. It is only in bad times that a person shows how steadfast he is to his dharma.'

'But Parvateshwar,' sighed Daksha. 'We are not under attack by people who are as ethical and decent as we are. Our way of life is under assault. If we don't fight back in any which way we can, we will lose.'

'My apologies once again, your Highness,' said Parvateshwar. 'I have never said that we should not fight back. I am eager to attack. I have been asking repeatedly for permission to declare war on the Chandravanshis. But if we fight without our rules, our codes, our ethics, then "our way of life" is as good as destroyed. And the Chandravanshis would have won without even fighting us!'

The conversation came to a halt with the ringing of the prahar town bell, as everyone said a quick prayer. Shiva turned towards the window, wondering if Sati would be dancing today.

Daksha turned to Shiva expectantly. 'Do you need to leave my Lord?'

'No, your Highness,' said Shiva, hiding the pain and confusion he felt inside. 'I don't believe I am expected anywhere at this point in time.'

Daksha's smile disappeared along with his hopes, on hearing this. Shiva continued, 'If it is alright with you, your Highness, may we continue our conversation? Perhaps we can delay our lunch a little.'

'Of course we may, my Lord,' smiled Daksha, pulling himself together.

'I have got the story so far, your Highness. Whereas I can understand your reasons for not wanting to attack right now, I can also see that you clearly have a plan, in which my blue throat has some strange role to play.'

'Yes, we do have a plan, my Lord. I feel that as an emperor, my giving in unthinkingly to the righteous anger of some of our people will not solve our problem. I believe that the people of Swadweep themselves are not evil. It is their Chandravanshi rulers and their way of life that has made them evil. The only way forward for us is to save the Swadweepans themselves.'

'Save the Swadweepans?' asked Shiva, genuinely surprised.

'Yes, my Lord. Save them from the evil philosophy that infects their soul. Save them from their treacherous rulers. Save them from their sorry, meaningless existence. And we can do this by giving them the benefits of the superior

Suryavanshi way of life. Once they become like us, there will be no reason to fight. We will live like brothers. This is the unfinished task of my father, King Brahmanayak. In fact, it is the unfinished task of Lord Ram.'

'That is a big task to take on, your Highness,' said Shiva. 'It is sweeping in its kindness and reason. But it is a very big task. You will need soldiers to defeat their army and missionaries to bring them to your side. It is not going to be easy.'

'I agree. There are many in my empire who have concerns about even attacking Swadweep, and I am putting forth a much bigger challenge to them, of reforming Swadweep. That is why I did not want to launch this without the Neelkanth, my Lord.'

Shiva remembered his uncle's words, spoken many years ago, in what was almost another life. *Your destiny lies beyond the mountains. Whether you fulfil it or run away once again, is up to you.*

As Daksha resumed speaking, Shiva refocused his attention on him.

'The problems that we are facing were prophesied, my Lord,' continued Daksha. 'Lord Ram had himself said that any philosophy, no matter how perfect, works only for a finite period. That is the law of nature and cannot be avoided. But what the legends also tell us is that when the problems become insurmountable for ordinary men, the Neelkanth will appear. And that he will destroy the evil Chandravanshis and restore the forces of good. My Lord, you are the Neelkanth. You can save us. You can complete the unfinished task of Lord Ram. You must lead us and help us defeat the Chandravanshis. You must rally the Swadweepans to the side of good. Otherwise I fear that this beautiful country that we have, the near perfect society of Meluha, will be destroyed by endless wars. Will you help us my Lord? Will you lead us?'

Shiva was confused. 'But I don't understand, your Highness. What exactly would I do?'

'I don't know, my Lord. We only know our goal and that you will be our leader. The path we take is up to you.'

They want me to destroy the entire way of life of eighty million people all by myself! Are they mad?

Shiva spoke carefully. 'I empathise with your people and their hardships, your Highness. But to be quite honest, I don't really understand how one man can make a difference.'

'If that man is you my Lord,' said Daksha, his moist eyes opened wide in devotion and faith, 'he can change the entire universe.'

'I am not so sure about that, your Highness,' said Shiva with a weak smile. 'What difference will I make? I am no miracle worker. I cannot snap my fingers and cause bolts of lightning to descend upon the Chandravanshis.'

'It is your presence itself that will make the difference, my Lord. I invite you to travel through the empire. See the effect your blue throat has on the people. Once my people believe that they can do it, they will be able to do it!'

'You are the Neelkanth, my Lord,' added Kanakhala. 'The people have faith in the bearer of the blue throat. They will have faith in you. Will you help us, my Lord?'

Will you run away once again?

'But how do you know that my blue throat makes me the genuine Neelkanth?' asked Shiva. 'For all you know, there may be many Meluhans with a blue throat waiting to be discovered!'

'No, my Lord,' said Daksha. 'It cannot be a Meluhan. The legend says that the Neelkanth will be a foreigner. He cannot be from the Sapt-Sindhu. And that his throat will turn blue when he drinks the Somras.'

Shiva did not answer. He looked stunned as truth suddenly dawned upon him.

Srinagar. The first night. Somras. That's how my body got repaired. That's why I'm feeling stronger than ever.

Daksha and Kanakhala looked at Shiva breathlessly, waiting for his decision. Praying for his *right* decision.

But why only me? All the Gunas were given the Somras. Was my uncle right? Do I really have a prophesied destiny?

Parvateshwar stared at Shiva with narrowed eyes.

I don't deserve a prophetic destiny. But maybe this is my chance to redeem myself.

But first…

Shiva asked with controlled politeness, 'Your Highness, before I answer, may I ask you a question?'

'Of course, my Lord.'

'Do you agree that honesty is required to make any friendship work? Even if it means deeply offending your friend with the truth?'

'Yes, of course,' replied Daksha, wondering where Shiva was going with this.

'Complete honesty is not just the bedrock of an individual relationship, but of any stable society,' interjected Parvateshwar.

'I couldn't agree more,' said Shiva. 'And yet, Meluha wasn't honest with me.'

Nobody said anything.

Shiva continued in a courteous, but firm tone. 'When my tribe was invited to Meluha, we were under the impression that you needed immigrants to build a work force. And I was happy to escape my benighted land. But now I realise that you were systematically searching for the Neelkanth.'

Turning to Nandi, Shiva said, 'We weren't told that a medicine called the Somras would be administered to us as soon as we entered. We weren't told that the medicine would have such effects.'

Nandi looked down with guilty eyes. His Lord had the right to be angry with him.

Turning to Daksha, Shiva continued, 'Your Highness, you know that the Somras was probably administered to me on my first night in Kashmir, without my knowledge.'

'I am truly sorry for that act of perfidy My Lord,' replied Daksha with folded hands and downcast eyes. 'It's something that I will always be ashamed of. But the stakes were too high for us. And the Somras has considerable positive effects on one's body. It causes no harm.'

'I know. I am not exactly upset about having to live a long and healthy life,' said Shiva wryly. 'Do you know that my tribe was also probably given the Somras that night? And they fell seriously ill, perhaps because of the Somras.'

'They were under no risk my Lord,' said Kanakhala apologetically. 'Some people are predisposed towards certain diseases. When the Somras enters the body, it triggers the immediate occurrence of these diseases, which when cured, never recur. Hence, the body remains healthy till death. Your tribe is actually much healthier now.'

'No doubt they are,' said Shiva. 'That is not the point. Both my tribe and I are the better for it. Yet I hardly expected such deceit in the land of Lord Ram. You should have told us the complete truth at Mount Kailash. Then you should have let *us* make an informed choice rather than *you* making it for us. We probably would still have come to Meluha anyway but then it would have been *our* choice.'

'Please forgive us the deception, my Lord,' said Daksha, with guilty regret. 'It is not our way to do something like this. We pride ourselves on our honesty. But we had no choice. We are truly sorry, my Lord. Your people are well taken care of. They are healthier than ever. They will live long, productive lives.'

Parvateshwar finally broke his silence, speaking about what had always been in his heart ever since the search had begun many decades ago. 'Shiva, we are truly sorry about what has been done. You have every right to be angry. Lying is not our way. I think what was done is appalling and Lord Ram would never have condoned this. Deception is the instrument of the weak and even extenuating circumstances can provide no excuse. I am deeply sorry.'

Shiva raised his eyebrow a bit.

Parvateshwar is the only one apologising instead of making excuses. He is a true follower of the great king Ram.

Shiva smiled.

Daksha let out an audible sigh of relief.

Shiva turned towards Daksha. 'Let us put this in the past, your Highness. Like I said, there are some things about your nation that could be improved. No doubt about that. But it is amongst the best societies that I have seen. And it *is* worth fighting for. But I have a few conditions.'

'Of course, my Lord,' said Daksha, eager to please.

'At this point of time, I am not saying that I can perform the tasks that you expect of me nor am I saying that I cannot do it. All I am saying is that I will try my best. But to begin with, I want to spend some more time understanding your society before I can be sure of how I can help. I am assuming that from now on nothing will be hidden from me nor will I be misled.'

'Of course, my Lord.'

'Secondly, you still need immigrants to expand your population. But you should not mislead them. I think that you should tell them the entire truth about Meluha and let them make an informed decision on whether they want to come here. Or you don't invite them at all. Is that fair?'

'Of course it is, my Lord,' said Daksha. Nodding briefly towards Kanakhala, he committed, 'We will implement that immediately.'

'Furthermore, it is clear to me that I am not going back to Kashmir. Can my tribe, the Gunas, be brought to Devagiri? I would like them to be with me.'

'Of course, my Lord,' said Daksha with a quick look at Kanakhala. 'Instructions will be sent today itself to bring them to Devagiri.'

'Also, I would like to visit the location where you manufacture the Somras. I would like to understand this drink of the Gods. Something tells me that it is important to do so.'

'Of course you may, my Lord,' said Daksha, his face finally breaking into a nervous smile. 'Kanakhala will take you there tomorrow itself. I too will be there along with my family for a scheduled puja at the temple of Lord Brahma. Perhaps we could meet.'

'That would be nice,' said Shiva smiling. Then taking a deep breath he added, 'And lastly, I guess that you would like to announce the arrival of the Neelkanth to your people.'

Daksha and Kanakhala nodded hesitantly.

'I would like to request that you don't do that for now.'

Daksha and Kanakhala's face fell immediately. Nandi's eyes were glued to the floor. He had stopped listening to the conversation. The enormity of his prevarication was tearing him apart.

'Your Highness, I have a terrible feeling that when people know I am the Neelkanth, every action and word of mine will be over-interpreted and over-analysed,' explained Shiva. 'I am afraid that I don't know enough about your society or my task to be able to handle that at this point of time.'

'I understand my Lord,' said Daksha, willing a half-smile back on his face. 'You have my word. Only my immediate staff, my family and the people you yourself allow will know of the Neelkanth's arrival. Nobody else.'

'Thank you, your Highness. But I will say it again: I am a simple tribal man who just happened to acquire a blue throat because of some exotic medicine. Honestly, I still don't know what one man like me can do in the face of the odds that you face.'

'And I'll say it again my Lord,' said Daksha, with a child-like smile. 'If that man is you, he can change the entire universe!'

CHAPTER 8

Drink of the Gods

Shiva strode towards the royal guest house with a leaden-footed Nandi close behind, head bowed in self-recrimination. 'I wish to dine alone,' said Shiva over his shoulder. All Nandi could muster was, 'I am so sorry, my Lord.'

Shiva turned around to gaze at Nandi.

'You are right, my Lord. We were so lost in our own troubles and the search for the Neelkanth that we didn't realise the unfairness of our actions on immigrants. I misled you my Lord. I lied to you.'

Shiva didn't say anything. He continued to stare intensely into Nandi's eyes.

'I am so sorry my Lord. I have failed you. I will accept whatever punishment you give me.'

Shiva's lips broke into a very faint smile. He patted Nandi lightly on his shoulders, signalling he had forgiven him. But his eyes delivered a clear message. 'Never lie to me again, my friend.'

Nandi nodded and whispered, 'Never, my Lord. I am so sorry.'

'Forget it Nandi,' said Shiva, his smile a little broader now. 'It's in the past.'

They turned and continued walking. Suddenly Shiva shook his head and chuckled slightly. 'Strange people!'

'What is it, my Lord?' asked Nandi.

'Nothing really. I was just wondering at some of the interesting things about your society.'

'Interesting, my Lord?' asked Nandi, feeling a little more confident now that Shiva was speaking to him again.

'Well, some people in your country think that the mere existence of my blue throat can help you achieve impossible tasks. Some people actually think that my name has suddenly become so holy that they can't even speak it.'

Nandi smiled slightly.

'On the other hand,' continued Shiva, 'some people clearly think that I am not required. In fact, they even think that my touching them is so polluting that I need to get a shudhikaran done!'

'Shudhikaran? Why would you need that my Lord?' asked Nandi, a little concerned.

Shiva weighed his words carefully. 'Well, I touched someone. And I was told that I would need to undergo a shudhikaran.'

'What? Who did you touch my Lord? Was it a vikarma person?' asked a troubled Nandi. 'Only the touch of a vikarma person would mean that you would need to get a shudhikaran.'

Shiva's face abruptly changed colour. A veil lifted from his eyes. He suddenly understood the significance of the events of the previous day. Her hasty withdrawal at being touched. The shocked reactions from the Guru*ji* and Krittika.

'Go back to the guest house, Nandi. I will see you there,' said Shiva, as he turned towards the guest house garden.

'My Lord, what happened?' asked Nandi, trying to keep pace with Shiva. 'Did you get the shudhikaran done or not?'

'Go to the guest house Nandi,' said Shiva walking rapidly away. 'I will see you there.'

— ⸻ —

Shiva waited for the larger part of an hour. But it was in vain, for Sati did not make an appearance. He sat on the bench by himself, cursing the moment when that terrible thought had entered his mind.

How could I have even thought that Sati would find my touch polluting? I am such a bloody idiot!

He replayed the moments of that fateful encounter in his mind and analysed every facet of it.

'I would never be able to forgive myself if something were to happen to you.'

What did she mean by that? Does she have feelings for me? Or is she just an honourable woman who can't bear to be the cause of someone else's misfortune? And why should she think of herself as inferior? This entire concept of the vikarma is so damned ridiculous!

Realising that she wasn't going to come, Shiva got up. He kicked the bench hard, getting a painful reminder that his once numb toe had got its sensation back. Cursing out loud, he started walking back to the guest house. As he passed the stage, he noticed that there was something lying on the dance floor. He bent down and picked it up. It was her bead bracelet. He had seen it on her right hand. The string did not seem broken.

Had she purposely dropped it here?

He smelt it. It had the fragrance of the holy lake on a

sun-kissed evening. He brought it delicately to his lips and kissed it gently. Smiling, he dropped the bracelet into the pouch tied around his waist. He would come back from Mount Mandar and meet her. He *had* to meet her. He would pursue her to the end of the world if required. He would fight the entire human race to have her. His journey in this life was incomplete without her. His heart knew it. His soul knew it.

— ⁂ —

'How much farther, Madam Prime Minister?' asked Nandi, behaving like an excited child.

A visit to the mythical Mount Mandar, the hub where the drink of the Gods was manufactured, was a rare honour for any Meluhan. Most Suryavanshis considered Mount Mandar the soul of their empire. As long as it was safe, so was the Somras.

'It's only been an hour since we left Devagiri, Captain,' said Kanakhala smiling. 'It's a day's journey to Mount Mandar.'

'Actually the blinds on the carriage windows prevent me from judging the angle of the sun and hence the passage of time. That's the reason why I was asking.'

'The prahar lamp is right behind you, Captain. The blinds have been drawn for your own protection.'

Shiva smiled at Kanakhala. He could understand that the blinds were not for *their* protection, but for the safety of Mount Mandar. To keep its location secret. Very few people knew of its exact location. An elite team of soldiers called the Arishtanemi protected the road to Mount Mandar and the travellers on it. Apart from the scientists of Mount Mandar, the Arishtanemi soldiers or any other person authorised by the Emperor, nobody else was allowed to go to the mountain or to even know its location. If the Chandravanshi terrorists attacked Mount Mandar, all would be lost for Meluha.

'Who would we be meeting there, Kanakhala?' asked Shiva.

'My Lord, we would be meeting Brahaspati. He is the Chief Scientist of the empire. He leads the team of scientists who manufacture the Somras for the entire country. Of course, they also conduct research in many other fields. A bird courier has already been sent to him informing him of your arrival. We will be meeting him tomorrow morning.'

Shiva nodded slightly, smiled at Kanakhala, and said, 'Thank you.'

As Nandi looked at the prahar lamp again, Shiva went back to his book. It was an interesting manuscript about the terrible war that was fought many thousands of years ago, between the *Devas* — the *Gods*, and the *Asuras* — the *demons*. An eternal struggle between opposites: good and evil. The Devas, with the help of Lord Rudra, the *Mahadev*, the *God of Gods*, had destroyed the Asuras and established righteousness in the world again.

— ⚹ —

'I hope you slept well, my Lord,' said Kanakhala as she welcomed Shiva and Nandi into the chamber outside Brahaspati's office.

It was the beginning of the last hour of the first prahar. Days began early at Mount Mandar.

'Yes, I did,' said Shiva. 'Though I could hear a strange rhythmic sound all through the night.'

Kanakhala smiled but did not offer any explanation. She bowed her head and opened the door to let Shiva into Brahaspati's office. Shiva walked in followed by Kanakhala and Nandi. There were various strange instruments spread throughout Brahaspati's large office, neatly organised on tables of different heights. Palm leaf notes were placed alongside each of the instruments where some experiments had clearly been conducted. The room was in muted blue. A large picture window in the corner afforded a breathtaking view of the dense forest at the foot of the mountain. Many simple, low seats had been arranged together in a square in the centre of the room. It was a frugal room, in line with a culture that celebrated simplicity over ostentation at every turn.

Brahaspati was standing in the middle of the room, his hands folded in a Namaste. Of medium height, much shorter than Shiva, his wheat-coloured skin, deep set eyes and well-manicured beard gave Brahaspati a distinguished appearance. Serene of expression and shaven of head, his choti bespoke of Brahmanical learning. His body was slightly overweight. His broad shoulders and barrel chest would have been markedly pronounced if they had been exercised a bit, but Brahaspati's body was a vehicle for his intellect and not the temple that it is to a warrior or Kshatriya. He wore a typical white cotton dhoti and an angvastram draped loosely over his shoulders. He wore a janau tied from his left shoulder down to the right side of his hips.

'How are you Kanakhala?' asked Brahaspati. 'It has been a long time.'

'Yes it has, Brahaspati,' said Kanakhala, greeting Brahaspati with a Namaste and a low bow.

Shiva noticed that the second amulet on Brahaspati's arm showed him as a swan. A very select chosen-tribe among Brahmins.

'This is Lord Shiva,' said Kanakhala, pointing towards Shiva.

'Just Shiva will do, thank you,' smiled Shiva, with a polite Namaste towards Brahaspati.

'Alright then. Just Shiva it is. And, who might you be?' asked Brahaspati, turning towards Nandi.

'This is Captain Nandi,' answered Kanakhala. 'Lord Shiva's aide.'

'A pleasure to meet you, Captain,' said Brahaspati, before turning back to Shiva. 'I don't mean to sound rude Shiva. But would it be possible for me to see your throat?'

Shiva nodded. As he took off his cravat, Brahaspati came forward to examine the throat. His smile disappeared as he saw Shiva's throat radiating a bright blue hue. Brahaspati was speechless for a few moments. Slowly gathering his wits, he turned towards Kanakhala. 'This is not a fraud. The colour comes from the inside. How is this possible? This means that…'

'Yes,' said Kanakhala softly, with a happiness that seemed to emanate from deep inside. 'It means the Neelkanth has come. Our saviour has come.'

'Well, I don't know about that,' said an embarrassed Shiva, retying the cravat around his throat. 'But I will certainly try my best to help your wonderful country. It is for this reason that I have come to you. Something tells me that it is important for me to know how the Somras works.'

Brahaspati still seemed to be in a daze. He continued to watch Shiva but his attention seemed elsewhere. It appeared as if he was working out the implications of the true Neelkanth's arrival.

'Brahaspati…' said Kanakhala, as she tried to call the chief scientist back into the here and now.

'Huh!'

'Can you tell me how the Somras works, Brahaspati?' asked Shiva again.

'Of course,' said Brahaspati, as his eyes refocused on the people in front of him. Noticing Nandi he asked, 'Is it alright to speak in front of the Captain?'

'Nandi has been my friend through my sojourn in Meluha,' said Shiva. 'I hope it is alright if he stays here.'

Nandi felt touched that his Lord still trusted him so openly. He swore once again, on pain of death, to never lie to his Lord.

'Whatever you say, Shiva,' said Brahaspati, smiling warmly.

Shiva noticed that Brahaspati was not submissive or excessively deferential on discovering that he *was* the Neelkanth. Just like Parvateshwar, Brahaspati called Shiva by his name and not 'My Lord'. However, Shiva felt that while Parvateshwar's attitude was driven by a distrustful surliness, Brahaspati's was driven perhaps by an assured affability.

'Thank you,' smiled Shiva. 'So, how does the Somras work?'

— ⅄ⓄƱ⇞⊛ —

The royal procession moved slowly on the road to

Mount Mandar. A pilot guard of one hundred and sixty cavalrymen rode in front of the five royal carriages in columns of four abreast. A rearguard of another one hundred and sixty rode behind the royal carriages, in a similar formation. A side guard of forty each marched along the left and right flanks. Each carriage also had ten soldiers and five serving maids seated on the side supports. The soldiers were the legendary Arishtanemi, the most feared militia in all of India.

The five carriages were made of solid wood, with no windows or apertures, except for upward pointed slits at the top for ventilation. There was a grill in front, behind the rider, that allowed in light and air. This could be shut instantly in case of an attack. All the carriages were of exactly the same dimension and appearance, making it impossible to know which carriage carried the royal family. If a person had *divyadrishti*, *divine vision*, to look beyond what human eyes could see, he would observe that the first, third and fourth carriages were empty. The second carried the royal family — Daksha, his wife Veerini and his daughter Sati. The last carriage carried Parvateshwar and some of his key brigadiers.

'Father, I still don't understand why you insist on taking me along to pujas. I am not even allowed to attend the main ceremony,' said Sati.

'I have said this to you many times,' smiled Daksha, as he patted Sati's hand fondly. 'No puja of mine is complete unless I have seen your face. I don't care about the damned law.'

'Father!' whispered Sati with an embarrassed smile and a slight, reproachful shake of her head. She knew it was wrong of her father to insult the law.

Sati's mother, Veerini, looked at Daksha with an awkward smile. Then taking a quick look at Sati, she returned to her book.

At a short distance from the royal procession, hidden by the dense forest, a small band of fifty soldiers moved along silently. The soldiers wore light leather armour on their torso and had their dhotis tied in military style to ensure ease of movement. Each of them carried two swords, a long knife and a hardshield made of metal and leather which was tied loosely around the back. Their shoes had grooves that could hold three small knives. Two men walked at the head of the band. One of them, a handsome young man with a battle scar embellishing his face, wore a dark brown turban which signified that he was the Captain. His leather armour had been tied a little loose and a gold chain and pendant had slipped out carelessly. The pendant had a beautiful, white representation of a horizontal crescent moon, the Chandravanshi symbol.

Next to him walked a giant of a man covered in a long robe from head to toe. A hood stitched onto the robe was pulled up over his head while his face was covered with a black mask. Very little of him was visible except for his strong fleshy hands and his expressionless, almond-shaped eyes. A leather bracelet was tied to his right wrist with the serpent Aum symbol embroidered onto it. Without turning to the Captain, the hooded figure said, 'Vishwadyumna, your mark is visible. Put it in and tighten your armour.'

An embarrassed Vishwadyumna immediately pushed the chain inside and pulled the two strings on the side of his shoulder to tighten the breastplate.

'My Lord, begging your pardon,' said Vishwadyumna. 'But perhaps we could move ahead and confirm that this is the route to Mount Mandar. Once we know that, we'll be sure that our informant was correct. I am sure that we can come back to kidnap her later. We are dangerously outnumbered in any case. We can't do anything right now.'

The hooded figure replied calmly, 'Vishwadyumna, have I ordered an attack? Where does the question of us being outnumbered come in? And we are moving in the direction of Mount Mandar. A few hours delay will not bring the heavens down. For now, we follow.'

Vishwadyumna swallowed hard. There was nothing he hated more than opposing his lord's views. After all, it was his lord who had found the rare Suryavanshi sympathetic to their cause. This breakthrough would make it possible for them to rip out and destroy the very heart of Meluha. He spoke softly, 'But my Lord, you know the Queen doesn't like delays. There is unrest brewing amongst the men fueled by a feeling that perhaps the focus is being lost.'

The hooded figure turned sharply. His body seemed to convey anger but his voice was composed. 'I am not losing focus. If you want to leave, please go. You will get your money. I will do this alone if I have to.'

Shocked to see the rare display of emotion in his leader, Vishwadyumna retracted immediately. 'No, my Lord. That is not what I was trying to imply. I am sorry. I will stay with you till you release me. You are right. A few hours will make no difference keeping in mind that we have waited for centuries.'

The platoon continued tracking the royal caravan silently.

'At a conceptual level, how the Somras works is ridiculously simple,' said Brahaspati. 'The almost impossible task was to convert the concept into reality. That was the genius of Lord Brahma. Jai Shri Brahma!'

'Jai Shri Brahma,' repeated Shiva, Kanakhala and Nandi.

'Before understanding how the medicine slows down the ageing process dramatically, we have to understand what keeps us alive,' said Brahaspati. 'There is a fundamental thing that none of us can live without.'

Shiva stared at Brahaspati, waiting for him to expound.

'And that fundamental thing is energy,' explained Brahaspati. 'When we walk, talk, think, in fact when we do anything that can be called being alive, we use energy.'

'We have a similar concept amongst our people,' said Shiva. 'Except, we call it Shakti.'

'Shakti?' asked a surprised Brahaspati. 'Interesting. That word has not been used to describe energy for many centuries. It was a term employed by the Pandyas, the ancestors of all the people of India. Do you know where your tribe has come from? Their lineage?'

'I am not really sure but there is an old woman in my tribe who claims to know everything about our history. Perhaps we should ask her when she comes to Devagiri.'

'Perhaps we should!' smiled Brahaspati. 'In any case, getting back to the subject, we know that nothing can be done by our body without energy. Now where does this energy come from?'

'From the food that we eat?' suggested Nandi, timidly. He was finally developing the confidence to speak in front of such important people.

'Absolutely right. The food that we eat stores energy, which we can then expend. That's also why we feel weak when we don't eat. However, you don't get energy merely by eating. Something inside the body has to draw the energy so that we can put it to good use.'

'Absolutely,' agreed Shiva.

'The conversion of food into energy is performed by the air we breathe,' continued Brahaspati. 'The air has various gases in it. One of these gases is called oxygen, which reacts with our food and releases energy. If we don't get oxygen, our body would be starved of energy and we would die.'

'But this is the process that keeps us alive,' said Shiva. 'What does the medicine have to do with it? The medicine has to work on that which causes us to grow old, become weak and die.'

Brahaspati smiled. 'What I've told you does have something to do with how we age. Because as it appears, nature has a sense of humour. The thing that keeps us alive is also what causes us to age and eventually die. When oxygen reacts with our food in order to release energy, it also releases free radicals called oxidants. These oxidants are toxic. When you leave any fruit out and it becomes rancid, this is because it has been "oxidised" or the oxidants have reacted with it to make it rot. A similar "oxidising process" causes metals to corrode. It happens especially with the new metal we have discovered — iron. The same thing happens to our body when we breathe in oxygen. The oxygen helps convert the food we eat into energy. But it also causes the release of oxidants into our body which start reacting inside us. We rust from the inside and hence age and eventually die.'

'By the holy God Agni!' exclaimed Nandi. 'The thing that gives us life is also what slowly kills us?'

'Yes,' said Brahaspati. 'Think about it. The body tries to store everything that you need from the outside world in order to survive. It stores enough food to survive for a few days without it. It stocks up on water so that a few days of thirst will not kill you. It seems logical, right? If your body needs something, it keeps some of it as backup for possible shortages.'

'Absolutely,' agreed Shiva.

'On the other hand, the body does not store enough oxygen, the most crucial component of staying alive, to last for more than just a few minutes. It doesn't make any sense at all. The only explanation is that the body realises that despite being an elixir, oxygen is also a poison. Hence it is dangerous to store.'

'So, what did Lord Brahma do?' asked Shiva.

'After a lot of research, Lord Brahma invented the Somras, which when consumed, reacts with the oxidants, absorbs them and then expels them from the body as sweat or urine. Because of the Somras, there are no oxidants left in the body.'

'Is that why the perspiration released from the body is poisonous the first time a person drinks the Somras?'

'Yes. Your sweat is particularly dangerous the first time you drink the Somras. Having said that, remember, sweat and urine released from the body even after a person has drunk the Somras for years remains toxic. So you have to eject it from the body and make sure that it does not affect anyone else.'

'So, that's why the Meluhans are so obsessed with hygiene.'

'Yes. That's why all Meluhans are taught about two things from a young age — water and hygiene. Water is the cleanest absorber of the effluents that the Somras generates and excretes as toxins. Meluhans are taught to drink gallons of water. And everything that can be washed, should be washed! The Meluhans bathe at least twice a day. All ablutions are done in specific rooms and underground drains then safely carry the waste out of the city.'

'Strict hygiene standards!' smiled Shiva, as he remembered his first day in Kashmir and Ayurvati's strong words. 'How is the Somras manufactured?'

'Manufacturing the Somras is not without its fair share of difficulties. It requires various ingredients that are not easily available. For example, the Sanjeevani tree. The empire has giant plantations to produce these trees. The manufacturing procedure also generates a lot of heat. So we have to use a lot of water during the processing to keep the mixture stable. Also, the crushed branches of the Sanjeevani tree have to be churned with the waters of the Saraswati river before processing begins. Water from other sources doesn't work.'

'Is that the strange noise I keep hearing: the churners?'

'That's exactly what it is. We have giant churning machines in a massive cavern at the base of this mountain. The Saraswati waters are led in here through a complex system of canals. The water is collected in an enormous pool in the cavern which we affectionately call *Sagar*.'

'*Sagar*? An *ocean*? Is that what you call a pool of water?' asked a surprised Shiva, for he had heard legends about the massive, never-ending expanse of water called Sagar.

'It is a bit of a hyperbole,' admitted Brahaspati with a smile. 'But if you did see the size of the pool, you would realise that we are not that off the mark!'

'Well I would certainly like to see the entire facility. It

was too late by the time we got in last night so I haven't seen much of the mountain as yet.'

'I will take you around after lunch,' said Brahaspati.

Shiva grinned in reply. He was about to say something, but checked himself in time, looking at both Kanakhala and Nandi.

Brahaspati noticed the hesitation. He felt Shiva might want to ask him something, but not in front of Nandi and Kanakhala. Brahaspati turned to them and said, 'I think Shiva wants to ask me something. May I request you to wait outside?'

It was a measure of the respect that Brahaspati commanded, that Kanakhala immediately rose to leave the room after a formal Namaste, followed by Nandi. Brahaspati turned to Shiva with a smile. 'Why don't you ask the question you really came to ask?'

CHAPTER 9

Love and its Consequences

'I didn't want to question you in front of them. Their faith is overwhelming,' explained Shiva with a wry grin. He was beginning to like Brahaspati. He enjoyed being around a man who treated him like an equal.

Brahaspati nodded. 'I understand, my friend. What do you want to ask?'

'Why me?' asked Shiva. 'Why did the Somras have this strange effect on me? I might have a blue throat, but I don't know how I am going to become the saviour of the Suryavanshis. The Emperor tells me that I am supposed to be the one who will complete Lord Ram's unfinished work and destroy the Chandravanshis.'

'He told you that?' asked Brahaspati, his eyes wide with surprise. 'The Emperor can be a little tiresome at times. But suffice it to say that what he told you is not completely correct. The legend doesn't exactly say that the Neelkanth will save the Suryavanshis. The legend says two things. First, that the Neelkanth will *not be* from the Sapt-Sindhu. And second, the Neelkanth will be the "destroyer of evil". The Meluhans believe that this implies that the Neelkanth will destroy the Chandravanshis, since they are obviously evil. But destroying the Chandravanshis doesn't mean that the Suryavanshis will be saved! There are many other problems, besides the Chandravanshis, that we need to solve.'

'What kind of problems? Like the Nagas?'

Brahaspati seemed to hesitate for a moment. He replied carefully. 'There are many problems. We are working hard to solve them. But coming back to your question, why did the Somras have this effect on you?'

'Yes, why did it? Why did my throat turn blue? Leave alone stopping the degeneration of my body, the Somras actually repaired a dislocated shoulder and a frostbitten toe.'

'It repaired an injury?' asked an incredulous Brahaspati. 'That's impossible! It is just supposed to prevent diseases and ageing, not repair injuries.'

'Well, it did in my case.'

Brahaspati thought for a bit. 'We will have to do experiments to come up with a definitive answer. For now though, I can think of only one explanation. I have been told that you come from the high lands beyond the Himalayas, right?'

Shiva nodded.

'The air gets thinner as you go higher up the mountains,' continued Brahaspati. 'There is less oxygen in thinner air. That means your body was used to surviving with less oxygen and resultantly was less harmed by the oxidants. Therefore the anti-oxidants in the Somras may have had a stronger effect on you.'

'That could be one of the reasons,' agreed Shiva. 'But if that was the case, then the necks of all my tribesmen should also have turned cold and blue. Why just me?'

'A good point,' conceded Brahaspati. 'But tell me one thing. Did your tribe also experience an improvement in their pre–existing conditions?'

'Actually, yes they did.'

'So maybe the diluted air you all lived in did have some role to play. But since your entire tribe did not develop blue throats, it is obvious that the "thinner air" theory may be a partial explanation. We can always do some more research. I am sure there is a scientific explanation for the blue throat.'

Shiva's piercing look revealed that he had read the intent behind Brihaspati's last statement. 'You don't believe in the legend of the Neelkanth, do you?'

Brahaspati smiled at Shiva awkwardly. He was beginning to like Shiva and did not want to say anything to insult him. But he wasn't going to lie either. 'I believe in science. It provides a solution and a rationale for everything. And if there is anything that appears like a miracle, the only explanation is that a scientific reason for it has not been discovered as yet.'

'Then why do the people of Meluha not turn to science for solving their problems?'

'I am not sure,' said Brahaspati thoughtfully. 'Perhaps it is because science is a capable but cold-hearted master. Unlike a Neelkanth, it will not solve your problems for you. It will only provide you with the tools that you may need to fight your own battles. Most people find it easier to wait for the arrival of the Messiah rather than act to solve their own problems.'

'So what do you think is the role that the Neelkanth has to play in Meluha?'

Brahaspati looked at Shiva sympathetically. 'I would

like to think that true Suryavanshis should fight their own demons rather than put pressure on someone else and expect him to solve their problems. A true Suryavanshi's *duty* is to push himself to the limit of his abilities and strength. The coming of the Neelkanth should only redouble a Suryavanshi's efforts, since it is obvious that the time for the destruction of evil is near.'

Shiva nodded.

'Are you concerned that it may be too much of a strain for you to take up a responsibility that you don't really want, because of the pressure of faith?' asked Brahaspati.

'No, that is not my concern,' replied Shiva. 'This is a wonderful country and I certainly want to do all I can to help. But what if your people depend on me to protect them and I can't? Right now, I can't say that I can do all that is expected of me. So how can I give my word?'

Brahaspati smiled. According to his rule book, any man who took his own word so seriously was deserving of respect.

'You appear to be a good man, Shiva. You will probably face a lot of pressure in the coming days. Be careful, my friend. Because of the blue throat and the blind faith it generates, your decisions will have ramifications for the entire land. Remember, whether a man is a legend or not is decided by history, not fortune-tellers.'

Shiva smiled, glad to have finally found a man who understood his predicament. And more importantly, was willing to at least *offer* some advice.

— ⁂ —

It was late in the evening. Having spent a thoroughly

enjoyable afternoon on a detailed tour of Mount Mandar with Brahaspati, Shiva lay on his bed, reading a book. A spent chillum lay on the side table.

A few aspects of the story he was reading, 'The Righteous War against the Asuras', troubled him. The Asuras were demons and were expected to behave like demons who had a pathological hatred for the Devas. They routinely attacked Deva cities, trying to force them to accept the Asura way of life. This was not a surprise to Shiva. What he hadn't expected though were the unusually unethical means the Devas sometimes adopted in the pursuit of victory. Lord Rudra, though personally a great man, seemed to ignore the indiscretions of the Devas in the interest of the larger good.

Shiva heard a commotion outside the Guest House. He looked out of his first floor balcony and noticed that the royal caravan had just arrived. The Arishtanemi soldiers quickly lined up for the traditional salute. Some people appeared to be disembarking from the far side of the second carriage. Even though they appeared to be the royal family, Shiva noted the absence of servitude and pageantry on the part of the Arishtanemi. Shiva suspected that this could be due to the usual Meluhan obsession with perceived equality.

However, Shiva's equality theory was challenged when he looked at the fifth carriage from which Parvateshwar alighted. Here, the Arishtanemi seemed to be in a tizzy. The senior Captain rushed in front of Parvateshwar and executed a Meluhan military salute — a quick click of the heels, the body rigid in attention and the right hand, balled into a fist, brought rapidly and violently to his left chest. The salute was followed by a deep bow of respect to the commander of the army. The soldiers at the back repeated their Captain's greeting. Parvateshwar formally saluted in return, accompanied with a slight bow of his head. He started towards his soldiers, inspecting them, while the Captain politely fell two steps behind.

Shiva had a feeling that the admiration reserved for Parvateshwar was not because of the post he held. It was for the man himself. For all his surliness, Parvateshwar had the reputation of a brave warrior, a soldier's General respected as a man who was true to his word. Shiva could see the strength of that repute in the eyes of each Arishtanemi who bent low on receiving the attention of his General.

A little while later, Shiva heard a soft knock on his door. He did not need to guess who waited on the other side. Sighing softly, he opened the door.

Daksha's fixed smile disappeared and he started a little as the unfamiliar odour of marijuana assaulted his senses. Kanakhala, standing to the Emperor's right, appeared equally perplexed.

'What is that stench?' Daksha asked Brahaspati, who stood to the left. 'Perhaps you should change the Lord's room. How can you subject him to this discomfort?'

'I have a feeling that Shiva is comfortable with this aroma, your Highness,' said Brahaspati.

'It is a smell that travels with me, your Highness,' said Shiva. 'I like it.'

Daksha was baffled. His face did nothing to hide his revulsion. But he quickly recovered his composure. After all, the Lord was happy with the malodour. 'I'm sorry to disturb you, my Lord,' said Daksha, his smile back in place. 'I just thought I would inform you that my family and I have reached the guest house.'

'It's very kind of you to inform me, your Highness,' said Shiva with a formal Namaste.

'My family and I were hoping for the honour of having breakfast with you tomorrow morning, my Lord.'

'The honour would be mine, your Highness.'

'Excellent. Excellent,' beamed Daksha as he moved on to the question that dominated his mind. 'What do you think of the Somras, my Lord? Isn't it really the drink of the Gods?'

'Yes your Highness. It does appear to be a miraculous drink.'

'It is the basis of our civilisation,' continued Daksha. 'Once you have taken a tour of our land, you will see the goodness of our way of life. I am sure you will find it in your heart to do something to save it.'

'Your Highness, I already think highly of your country. It truly is great and treats its citizens well. I wouldn't doubt that it is a way of life that is worth protecting. However, what I am not sure about is what I can do. Yours is such an advanced civilisation and I am just a simple tribal man.'

'Faith is a very potent weapon, my Lord,' said Daksha, his hands joined in supplication. 'All that is needed is for you to have as much faith in yourself as we have in you. I am sure that if you spend a few more days in our country and see the effect that your presence has on our people, you will realise what you can do.'

Shiva gave up arguing against Daksha's childlike belief.

Brahaspati winked at Shiva before coming to his rescue. 'Your Highness, Shiva looks tired to me. It has been a long day. Maybe he should retire and we could meet tomorrow?'

Daksha smiled, 'Perhaps you are right, Brahaspati. My

apologies for troubling you, my Lord. We will see you at breakfast. Have a good night.'

'Good night,' wished Shiva in return.

— ⅄ↀ⩌⍋⊗ —

Sati waited quietly at the table as Daksha glanced nervously at the prahar lamp. To the left were Kanakhala, Brahaspati and Parvateshwar. To his right was an empty chair. For the 'Neelkanth', thought Sati. Next to the empty chair sat Sati and to her right was her mother, Veerini. Daksha had agonised deeply over the seating to get it exactly right.

Sati looked over the arrangements. A formal table and chairs for breakfast rather than the preferred low table and floor cushions that Meluhans normally sat upon to eat. The beloved banana leaf had been replaced by gold plates. The taste enhancing *kulhads,* or *mud cups*, had been replaced by refined silver glasses. She thought that her father was really pulling out all stops for this breakfast meeting. She had seen him pin his hopes on too many so-called Neelkanths earlier. Miracle men who had turned out to be frauds. She hoped that her father would not have to face disillusionment once again.

The crier announced Shiva and Nandi. As Daksha rose with a reverential Namaste to receive the Lord, Parvateshwar rolled his eyes at the servile behaviour of his Emperor. At the same instant, Sati bent down to pick up a glass that she had accidentally knocked over.

'My Lord,' said Daksha pointing to the people standing around the table. 'Kanakhala, Brahaspati and Parvateshwar, you already know. At the far right is my wife, Queen Veerini.'

Shiva smiled politely as he returned Veerini's Namaste with a formal Namaste and a low bow.

'And next to her,' said Daksha with a broad smile as Sati came up holding the glass she had retrieved, 'is my daughter, Princess Sati.'

The breath went out of Shiva as he looked at his life staring back at him. His heart beat a frantic rhythm. He could swear that he had got a whiff of his favourite fragrance in the world: the aroma of the holy lake at sunset. As before, he was mesmerized.

There was an uncomfortable silence in the room. Except for the noise made by the unfortunate glass which fell from Sati's hand again. The clang of the rolling glass distracted Sati slightly from her fixed gaze. With superhuman effort, she managed to control the look of shock on her face. She was breathing heavily, as if she had just danced a duet with Shiva. What she did not know was that her soul was doing exactly that.

Daksha gazed at the dumbstruck couple with glee. He had the look of a director who had just seen his play being perfectly executed. Nandi, standing right behind Shiva, could see Sati's expression. Suddenly everything became clear to him. The dance practices, the vikarma touch, the shudhikaran and his Lord's anguish. While some part of him was afraid, another reconciled to it quickly. If his Lord wanted this, he would support it in every way possible. Brahaspati stared blankly at the couple, deep in thought about the implications of this unexpected situation. Parvateshwar looked at the goings on with barely concealed repugnance. What was happening was wrong, immoral and worst of all, illegal.

'My Lord,' said Daksha pointing towards the empty seat at his right. 'Please take your seat and we shall begin.'

Shiva did not react. He had not heard Daksha's words. He was in a world where the only sound was the harmonious melody of Sati's heavy breathing. A tune he could blissfully dance to for his next seven lives.

'My Lord,' repeated Daksha, a little louder.

A distracted Shiva finally looked at Daksha, as if from another world.

'Please take your seat, my Lord,' said Daksha.

'Yes of course, your Highness,' said Shiva averting his eyes in embarrassment.

As Shiva sat down, the food was brought in. It was a simple delicacy that the Meluhans loved for breakfast. Rice and some cereals were fermented and ground into a thick batter. Small portions of this batter were then wrapped in banana leaves and steamed into cylindrical roundels. It was served while still draped in the banana leaf, along with some spicy lentils for taste. The dish was called an idli.

'You're the Neelkanth?' a still shocked Sati whispered softly to Shiva, as she had willed some calmness into her breathing.

'Apparently so,' replied Shiva with a playful grin. 'Impressed?'

Sati answered that question with a raised disdainful brow. The mask was back. 'Why would I be impressed?'

What?!

'My Lord,' said Daksha.

'Yes, your Highness,' said Shiva, turning towards Daksha.

'I was thinking,' said Daksha. 'Our puja should be over by this evening. However, I have to stay here for two more days for some reviews with Brahaspati. There is no point in Veerini and Sati getting thoroughly bored out here in the meantime.'

'Thank you, your Highness,' said Brahaspati with a sly grin. 'Your vote of confidence in the interest that the royal family has in Mount Mandar is most reassuring.'

The entire table burst out laughing. So did Daksha, exhibiting a sporting spirit.

'You know what I mean Brahaspati!' said Daksha, shaking his head. Turning back to Shiva, he continued, 'From what I am led to believe, my Lord, you were planning to leave for Devagiri tomorrow morning. I think it may be a good idea for Veerini and Sati to accompany you. The rest of us can catch up with you two days later.'

Sati looked up in alarm. She wasn't sure why, but something told her that she shouldn't agree to this plan. Another part of her said that she had no reason to be scared. In all the eighty-five years that she had spent as a vikarma, she had never broken the law. She had the self-control to know what was right, and what wasn't.

Shiva though had no such compunctions. With very obvious delight, he said, 'I think that is a very good idea, your Highness. Nandi and I could travel with both her Highnesses back to Devagiri.'

'It's settled then,' said a visibly content Daksha. Turning to Parvateshwar, he said, 'Parvateshwar, please ensure that the Arishtanemi escort are broken up into two groups for the return journey.'

'My Lord, I don't think that is wise,' said Parvateshwar. 'A large part of the Arishtanemi are still in Devagiri preparing for the material transfer. Also, the standing contingent in Mount Mandar cannot be reduced under any circumstances. We may not have enough soldiers for two caravans. Perhaps, we could all travel together day after tomorrow.'

'I am sure there won't be a problem,' said Daksha. 'And don't you always say that each Arishtanemi is equal to fifty enemy soldiers? It's settled. The Lord Neelkanth, Veerini and Sati will leave tomorrow morning. Please make all the arrangements.'

Parvateshwar went unhappily back to his thoughts as Shiva and Sati started whispering to each other again.

'You did go for a shudhikaran, didn't you?' asked Sati seriously.

'Yes,' said Shiva. He wasn't lying. He had gone for a purification ceremony on his last night at Devagiri. He didn't believe he needed it. However, he knew that Sati would ask him the next time they met. And he didn't want to lie to her.

'Though I think the idea of doing a shudhikaran is completely absurd,' whispered Shiva. 'In fact, the entire concept of the vikarma is ridiculous. I think it is one of the few things in Meluha that is not fair and should be changed.'

Sati looked up suddenly at Shiva, her face devoid of any expression. Shiva stared hard into her eyes, trying to gauge some of the thoughts running through her mind. But he hit a blank wall.

— ⁂ —

It was the beginning of the second prahar the next day when Shiva, Veerini, Sati and Nandi departed for Devagiri along with a hundred Arishtanemi. Daksha, Parvateshwar and Kanakhala stood outside the guest house to see them off. Brahaspati had been detained by some scheduled experiments.

The entourage had to sit in the same carriage as there were guidelines that a minimum of four carriages had to be kept aside for any caravan that carried the Emperor. Since the royal procession had come in five carriages, that left only one carriage for this caravan. Parvateshwar was deeply unhappy about the unorthodox way in which members of the royal family were travelling without any dummy carriages, but his objections had been overruled by Daksha.

Sitting on one of the comfortable sofas inside the carriage, Sati noticed that Shiva was wearing his cravat again. 'Why do you cover your throat all the time?'

'I am uncomfortable with all the attention that comes along with anyone seeing the blue throat,' replied Shiva.

'But you will have to get used to it. The blue throat is not going to disappear.'

'True,' answered Shiva with a smile. 'But till I get used to it, the cravat is my shield.'

As the caravan left, Parvateshwar and Kanakhala came up to Daksha.

'Why do you have so much faith in that man, my Lord?' asked Parvateshwar of Daksha. 'He has done nothing to deserve respect. How can he lead us to victory when he has not even been trained for it? The entire concept of the Neelkanth goes against our rules. In Meluha a person is supposed to be given a task only if he is found capable of it and is trained by the system.'

'We are in a state of war, Parvateshwar,' replied Daksha. 'An undeclared one, but a state of war all the same. We face a terrorist attack every other week. These cowardly Chandravanshis don't even attack from the front so that we can fight them. And our army is too small to attack their territory openly. Our "rules" are not working. We need a miracle. And the first rule of serendipity is that miracles come when we forget rational laws and have faith. I have faith in the Neelkanth. And so do my people.'

'But Shiva has no faith in himself. How can you force him to be our saviour when he himself doesn't want to be one?'

'Sati will change that.'

'My Lord, you are going to use your own daughter as bait?' asked a horrified Parvateshwar. 'And do you really want a saviour who decides to help us just because of his lust?!'

'IT IS NOT LUST!'

Parvateshwar and Kanakhala kept quiet, shocked by Daksha's reaction.

'What kind of a father do you think I am?' asked Daksha. 'You think I will use my daughter so? She just may find comfort and happiness with the Lord. She has suffered enough already. I want her to be happy. And if in doing so, I help my country as well, what is the harm?'

Parvateshwar was about to say something, but thought the better of it.

'We need to destroy the Chandravanshi ideology,' continued Daksha. 'And the only way we can do that is if we can give the benefits of our lifestyle to the people of Swadweep. The common Swadweepans will be grateful for this, but their Chandravanshi rulers will try everything within their power to stop us. They may be able to resist us, but try as they might, they cannot stop a people led by the Neelkanth. And if Sati is with the Neelkanth, there is no way he would refuse to lead us against the Chandravanshis.'

'But your Highness, do you really think the Lord would come to our side just because he is in love with your daughter?' asked Kanakhala.

'You have missed the point. The Lord does not need to be convinced to be on our side,' said Daksha. 'He already is. We are a great civilisation. Maybe not perfect, but great all the same. One has to be blind to not see that. What the Neelkanth needs is motivation and the belief in himself to lead us. That belief in himself will emerge when he gets closer to Sati.'

'And how is that going to happen, your Highness?' asked Parvateshwar, frowning slightly.

'Do you know what is the most powerful force in a man's life?' asked Daksha.

Kanakhala and Parvateshwar looked at Daksha nonplussed.

'It is his intense desire to impress the person he loves the most,' expounded Daksha. 'Look at me. I have always loved my father. My desire to impress him is what is driving me even today. Even after his death, I still want to make him proud of me. It is driving me to my destiny as the King who will re-establish the pure Suryavanshi way of life across India. And when the Neelkanth develops a deep desire to make Sati proud of him, he will rise to fulfil his destiny.'

Parvateshwar frowned, not quite agreeing with the logic, but keeping quiet all the same.

'But what if Sati seeks something different?' asked Kanakhala. 'Like a husband who spends all his time with her.'

'I know my daughter,' replied Daksha confidently. 'I know what it takes to impress her.'

'That's an interesting point of view, my Lord,' smiled Kanakhala. 'Just out of curiosity, what do you think is the most powerful force in a woman's life?'

Daksha laughed out loud. 'Why do you ask? Don't you know?'

'Well the most powerful force in my life is the desire to get out of the house before my mother-in-law wakes up!'

Both Daksha and Kanakhala guffawed loudly.

Parvateshwar didn't seem to find it funny. 'I am sorry but that is no way to speak about your mother-in-law.'

'Oh relax, Parvateshwar,' said Kanakhala. 'You take everything too seriously.'

'I think,' said Daksha smiling, 'the most powerful force in a woman's life is the need to be appreciated, loved and cherished for what she is.'

Kanakhala smiled and nodded. Her emperor truly understood human emotions.

CHAPTER 10

The Hooded Figure Returns

As the caravan emerged from the carefully chiselled passage leading out of the depths of Mount Mandar, Veerini requested that the carriage be stopped for a minute. Veerini, Sati, Shiva and Nandi went down on their knees and offered a short prayer to the mountain for its continued benefaction. Watching over them on high alert was the Arishtanemi Bhabravya, a strapping man of sixty years with an intimidating moustache and beard.

After a short while, Bhabravya came up to Veerini and said with barely concealed impatience: 'Your Highness, perhaps it's time to get back into the carriage.'

Veerini looked at the Captain and got up with a quick nod. Sati, Shiva and Nandi followed.

— ⁂ —

'It's her,' said Vishwadyumna putting down the scope and turning towards his Lord.

The platoon was at a safe distance, concealed from the caravan. The dense and impenetrable foliage was an effective shield.

'Yes', said the hooded figure and let his eyes linger on Shiva's muscular body. Even without using the scope he was in no doubt that this was the same man who had fought him at the Brahma temple some weeks ago. 'Who is that man?'

'I don't know my Lord.'

'Keep your eye on him. He was the one who foiled the last attack.'

Vishwadyumna wanted to say that the previous attempt failed because it was unplanned. The presence of the caste-unmarked man had little role to play. Vishwadyumna could not understand the recent irrational decisions of his Lord. It was unlike him. Perhaps it was the closeness of the ultimate objective that was clouding his judgement. Vishwadyumna was, however, wise enough to keep his thoughts to himself. 'Perhaps we could track them for around an hour before we attack, my Lord. It will be a safe distance from the Arishtanemi back-up. We can get this over and done with quickly and report back to the Queen that the informer was correct.'

'No, we'll wait for a few hours more till they are at least a half day's distance away from Mount Mandar. Their new carriages have systems that can send an emergency signal immediately. We need to ensure that our task is over before their back-up arrives.'

'Yes, my Lord,' said Vishwadyumna, happy to see that his Lord's famed tactical brilliance had not diminished.

'And, remember, I want it done quickly,' added the hooded figure. 'The more time we take, the more people get hurt.'

'Yes, my Lord.'

— ⅄ⓞ∪↟⊛ —

It was the beginning of the third prahar when the caravan stopped at the half-way clearing for lunch. The forest had been cut back to a distance that made a surprise attack impossible. The Queen's maids quickly unpacked the food and began heating it in the centre of the clearing. The royal party and Shiva were sitting closer to the head of the caravan, in the same direction as Devagiri. Bhabravya stood on the higher ground in the rear, keeping an eagle eye on the surroundings. Apart from the royal party, half the Arishtanemi soldiers had also sat down to eat while the others kept watch.

Shiva was about to take a second helping of rice when he heard the crack of a twig down the road. Stopping mid-way, he listened intently for another sound. There was none. His instincts told him this was a predator, who on realising that he had made a mistake, was now keeping still. Shiva looked over at Sati to see if she had heard the sound. She too was staring intently down the road. There was a soft crunch as the foot on the broken twig eased its pressure slightly. It would have been missed by most, except for a focussed listener.

Shiva immediately put his plate down, pulled out his sword and fixed his shield on his back. Bhabravya saw Shiva across the caravan and drew his sword as well, giving quick, silent signals to his men to do the same. The Arishtanemi were battle ready in a matter of seconds. Their swords unsheathed, Sati and Nandi too assumed traditional fighter positions.

Sati whispered to Veerini without turning, 'Mother, please sit in the carriage and lock it from within. Take the maids inside with you. But get them to disconnect the horses from the carriage first. We are not retreating and we don't want the enemy kidnapping you either.'

'Come with me Sati,' pleaded Veerini as her maids rushed to pull out the holds on the carriage.

'No, I'm staying here. Please hurry. We may not have much time.'

Veerini rushed into the carriage followed by the maids who quickly locked it from the inside.

At a distance, Bhabravya whispered to his aide. 'I know their tactics. I have seen these cowards on the southern border. They will send an advance suicide party, pretend to retreat and draw us into a stronghold. I don't care about the losses. We will chase those bastards and destroy every single one of them. They have run into the Arishtanemi. They will pay for this mistake.'

Shiva, meanwhile, turned to Sati and whispered carefully, 'I think they must be aiming for a high profile target. Nothing would be more significant than the royal family. Do you think that you too should wait in the carriage?'

Sati's eyes darted up towards Shiva in surprise. A pained look crossed her face before being replaced by a defiant glare. 'I am going to fight…'

What's wrong with her?! What I said is completely logical. Make the main objective of the enemy difficult and they will lose the will to fight.

Shiva pushed these thoughts out of his mind so he could focus on the road. The rest of the caravan strained every nerve to listen intently for any movement from the enemy. They were prepared for the ambush. It was the enemy's turn to make the first move. Just as they were beginning to think that it may have been a false alarm, the sound of a conch shell reverberated from down the road — from the direction of Mount Mandar. Shiva turned around but did not move. Whoever was making the noise was moving rapidly towards them.

Shiva could not recognise the cacophonic sound. However, the Arishtanemi from the southern border knew exactly what it was. It was the sound of a *Nagadhvani* conch. It was blown to announce the launch of a Naga attack!

Though impatient to fight, Bhabravya did not forget the standard operating procedures. He gestured towards an aide, who rushed to the carriage and pulled out a red box fixed at the bottom. Kicking it open, the aide pressed a button on the side. A tubular chimney-like structure extended straight up from the box for nearly twenty-five feet. The chimney ensured that the smoke signal was not lost in the dense forest and could be seen by the scouts at both Devagiri and Mount Mandar. The soldier picked up a branch from the fire and pushed it into the last of the four slots on the right side of the box. Red smoke fumed out of the chimney, signifying the presence of the highest level of danger. Help was six hours away. Four, if the back-up rode hard. Bhabravya did not intend the battle to last that long. He intended to kill each of the Nagas and the Chandravanshis long before that.

The attack began from the side of the road leading to Mount Mandar. A small band of ten Chandravanshi soldiers charged at the Arishtanemi. One soldier was holding the Naga conch shell and blowing hard. Another amongst them had covered his entire face and head with a cloth, except for small slits for his eyes. The Naga himself!

Shiva did not move. He could see the battle raging at the far end of the caravan. There were only ten Chandravanshis. The Arishtanemi did not need any support. He signalled to Sati and Nandi to stay where they were. Sati agreed as she too expected this attack to be a ruse.

The battle was short and fierce. The Chandravanshi soldiers fought viciously but were outnumbered. As Bhabravya expected, they turned in no time and retreated fast.

'After them,' yelled Bhabravya. 'Kill them all.'

The Arishtanemi dashed behind their Captain in pursuit of the retreating Chandravanshis. Most of them did not hear Shiva cry out loud. 'No! Stay here. Don't chase them.'

By the time some of the Arishtanemi heard Shiva's order, a majority had already left, chasing the Chandravanshis. Shiva was left in the clearing with Sati, Nandi and just twenty–five soldiers. Shiva turned back towards the side of the road leading to Devagiri — the direction from which the original sound of the cracking twig had come.

He turned again to look at the remaining Arishtanemi. Pointing towards his back, he spoke with a voice that was both steady and calm, 'This is where the actual attack will come from. Get into a tight formation in fours, facing that direction. Keep the princess in the middle. We will have to hold them back for about five or ten minutes. The other Arishtanemi will return when they realise that there are no Chandravanshis to fight in that direction.'

The Arishtanemi looked at Shiva and nodded. They were battle-hardened men. They liked nothing more than a clear-headed and calm leader who knew exactly what he was doing. They quickly got into the formation ordered by Shiva and waited.

Then the real attack began. Forty Chandravanshi soldiers led by a hooded figure emerged from the trees, walking slowly towards the Suryavanshi caravan. The outnumbered Arishtanemi remained stationary, waiting for their enemy to come to them.

'Surrender the princess to us and we will leave,' said the hooded figure. 'We want no unnecessary bloodshed.'

The same joker from the Brahma temple. He's got a strange costume, but he fights well.

'We don't want any bloodshed either,' said Shiva. 'Leave quietly and we promise not to kill you.'

'*You're* the one who's looking at death in the face, barbarian,' said the hooded figure, conveying anger through his posture rather than his voice, which remained eerily composed.

Shiva noticed the brown-turbaned officer look impatiently at the hooded figure. He clearly wanted to attack and get this over and done with.

Dissension in the ranks?

'The only face I'm looking at is a stupid festival mask. And it's soon going to be shoved down your pathetic little throat! Also tell that brainless lieutenant of yours that he shouldn't give battle plans away.'

The hooded figure remained calm. Not turning to look at Vishwadyumna.

Damn! This man is good.

'This is the last warning, barbarian,' repeated the hooded figure. 'Hand her over right now.'

Sati suddenly turned towards the carriage as she realised something, shouting, 'Mother! The new emergency conch shell close to the front grill. Blow it now!'

A loud plea for help emitted from the carriage. Bhabravya and his men had been summoned. The hooded figure cursed as he realised his advantage had been taken away. He had very little time to complete his operation. The other Suryavanshis would be back soon. 'Charge!'

The Arishtanemi stayed in position.

'Steady,' said Shiva. 'Wait for them. All you have to do is buy time. Keep the princess safe. Our friends will be back soon.'

As the Chandravanshis came closer, Sati suddenly broke through the cordon and attacked the hooded figure. Sati's surprise attack slowed the charge of the Chandravanshis. The Arishtanemi had no choice. They charged at the Chandravanshis like vicious tigers.

Shiva moved quickly to protect the right flank of Sati as an advancing Vishwadyumna got dangerously close to her. Vishwadyumna swung his sword to force Shiva out of his way. However, the speed of Shiva's advance left Vishwadyumna unbalanced. Shiva easily parried the blow and pushed Vishwadyumna back with his shield. Nandi meanwhile moved rapidly to the left of Sati to block the Chandravanshis trying to charge down that side.

In the meantime, Sati was attacking the hooded figure with fierce blows. He, on the other hand, seemed intent upon simply defending himself and was not striking back. He wanted her alive and unharmed.

Shiva cut Vishwadyumna savagely across the shoulder that had been exposed when he was pushed back. Grimacing, Vishwadyumna brought his shield up to fend off another attack from Shiva. In tandem, his sword arm thrust at Shiva's torso. Shiva quickly pulled his shield in to protect himself. But not quickly enough. Vishwadyumna was able to slash Shiva's chest. Stepping back and jumping to his right, Shiva brought his sword swiftly down in a brutal jab. While Vishwadyumna promptly brought his shield up to block the attack, Shiva's unorthodox move unsettled him. He staggered back realising that Shiva was an excellent swordsman. It was going to be a long and hard duel.

Nandi had already brought down one Chandravanshi soldier who had broken a law of combat that prohibited attacking below the waist, and cut Nandi's thigh. Bleeding profusely, Nandi was ferociously battling another soldier who had attacked him from the left. The Chandravanshi brought his shield down hard on Nandi's injured leg, making him stagger and fall. The Chandravanshi thought he had his man. Raising his sword high with both his hands, he was about to bring it down to finish the job but he suddenly arched forward, as if a brutal force had pounded him from the back. As he fell, Nandi saw a knife buried deep in the Chandravanshi's back. Looking up, he saw Shiva's left arm continue down in a smooth arc from the release of the dagger. With his right hand, Shiva brought his sword up to block a vicious cut from Vishwadyumna. As Nandi stumbled back to his feet, Shiva reached behind to pull his shield in front again.

The hooded figure knew that time was running out. The other Arishtanemi would be back soon. He tried to move behind Sati, to club her on the back of the head and knock her unconscious but she was too quick. She moved swiftly to the left to face her enemy again. Taking a knife out of her angvastram folds with her left hand, she slashed outwards to cut deep across the hooded figure's immense stomach. The knife sliced through the robe but its effect was broken by the armour.

And then with a resounding roar, Bhabravya and the other Arishtanemi rushed back to fight alongside their mates. Seeing themselves vastly outnumbered, the hooded figure had no choice. He ordered his soldiers to retreat. Shiva stopped Bhabravya from chasing the Chandravanshis once again.

'Let them go, brave Bhabravya,' said Shiva. 'We will have

other opportunities to get them. Right now the primary objective is to protect the royal family.'

Bhabravya looked at Shiva with admiration for the way this foreigner fought, and not the blue throat of which he was unaware. He nodded politely. 'It makes sense, foreigner.'

Bhabravya quickly formed the Arishtanemi soldiers into a tight perimeter and pulled the wounded within. Dead bodies were not touched. At least three Arishtanemi had lost their lives while nine Chandravanshi bodies lay in the clearing. The last one had taken his own life since he was too wounded to escape. Better to meet one's maker than to fall into enemy hands alive and reveal secrets. Bhabravya ordered his soldiers to stay low and keep their shields in front for protection against any arrows. And thus they waited till the rescue party arrived.

'My God,' cried an anxious Daksha as he hugged Sati tight.

The rescue party of five hundred soldiers had reached by the fourth hour of the second prahar. Daksha, Brahaspati and Kanakhala had accompanied the caravan despite Parvateshwar's warnings of the risks. Releasing Sati from his grip, Daksha whispered as a small tear escaped his eyes, 'You are not injured, are you?'

'I am alright father,' said Sati self-consciously. 'Just a few cuts. Nothing serious.'

'She fought very bravely,' said Veerini, as she beamed with pride.

'I think that is a mother's bias,' said Sati, as her serious expression was restored. Turning towards Shiva, she continued, 'It was Shiva who saved the day, father. He figured out the real plan of the Chandravanshis and rallied everyone at the crucial moment. It was because of him that we beat them back.'

'Oh, I think she's too generous,' said Shiva.

She's impressed. Finally!!

'She isn't being generous at all, my Lord,' said a visibly grateful Daksha. 'You have begun your magic already. We have actually beaten back a terrorist attack. You don't know how significant this is for us!'

'But it wasn't a terrorist attack, your Highness' said Shiva. 'It was an attempt to kidnap the princess.'

'Kidnap?' asked Daksha.

'That hooded man certainly wanted her alive and unharmed.'

'What hooded man?!' cried Daksha, alarmed.

'That was the Naga, your Highness,' said Shiva, surprised at Daksha's hysterical response. 'I have seen that man fight. He is an excellent warrior. A little slow in his movements, but excellent all the same. But while fighting Sati he was trying his best not to hurt her.'

The colour drained completely from Daksha's face. Veerini glared at her husband with a strange mixture of fear and anger. The expressions on their faces made Shiva feel uncomfortable, as if he was intruding on a private family moment.

'Father?' asked a worried Sati. 'Are you alright?'

Hearing no response from Daksha, Shiva turned to Sati and said, 'Perhaps it's best if you speak to your family alone. If you don't mind, I will go check if Nandi and the other soldiers are alright.'

— ⅄ⓄƱ⇞⊛ —

Parvateshwar was walking amongst his men, checking on the injured and ensuring that they received medical help. Bhabravya walked two steps behind. The General came up to the Chandravanshi who had been killed by Shiva while protecting Nandi. He roared in horror, 'This man has been stabbed in the back!'

'Yes, my Lord,' said Bhabravya with his head bowed.

'Who did this? Who broke the sacred rules of combat?'

'I think it was the foreigner, my Lord. But I heard that he was trying to protect Captain Nandi who had been attacked by this Chandravanshi. And the Chandravanshi himself was not following the combat rules having attacked Nandi below the waist.'

Parvateshwar turned with a withering look at Bhabravya, causing him to cower in fear. 'Rules are rules,' he growled. 'They are meant to be followed even if your enemy ignores them.'

'Yes, my Lord.'

'Go make sure that the dead get proper cremations. Including the Chandravanshis.'

'My Lord?' asked a surprised Bhabravya. 'But they are terrorists.'

'*They* may be terrorists,' snarled Parvateshwar. 'But *we* are Suryavanshis. We are the followers of Lord Ram. There are civilities that we maintain even with our enemies. The Chandravanshis will get proper cremations. Is that clear?'

'Yes, my Lord.'

— ⁂ —

'Why do you call the foreigner "Your Lord"?' asked an injured Arishtanemi lying next to Nandi.

Shiva had just departed after spending half an hour with Nandi and the other injured soldiers. If one had a look at the injured at this point, it would be impossible to believe that they had fought a battle just a few hours earlier. They were talking jovially with each other. Some were ribbing their mates about how they had fallen for the red-herring towards the beginning of the battle. In the Kshatriya way, to laugh in the face of death was the ultimate mark of a man.

'Because he *is* my Lord,' answered Nandi simply.

'But he is a foreigner. A caste-unmarked foreigner,' said the Arishtanemi. 'He is a brave warrior, no doubt. But there are so many brave warriors in Meluha. What makes him so special? And why does he spend so much time with the royal family?'

'I can't answer that, my friend. You will know when the time is right.'

The Arishtanemi looked at Nandi quizzically. Then shook his head and smiled. He was a soldier. He concerned himself only with the here and now. Larger questions did not dwell for too long in his mind. 'In any case, I think the time *is* right to tell you that you are a brave man, my friend. I saw you fight despite your injury. You don't know the meaning of the word surrender. I would be proud to have you as my *bhraata*.'

That was a big statement from the Arishtanemi. The bhraata system that was prevalent in the Meluhan army assigned a mate of equal rank to each soldier up to the rank of captain. The two *bhraatas* would be like *brothers* who would always fight together and look out for each other. They would willingly fight the world for each other, would never love the same woman and would always tell each other the truth, no matter how bitter.

The Arishtanemi were elite soldiers of the empire. An Arishtanemi offered to be a bhraata only to his own kind. Nandi knew that he could never really be the Arishtanemi's bhraata. He had to stay with the Lord. But the honour of being offered the brotherhood of an Arishtanemi was enough to bring tears to Nandi's eyes.

'Don't get teary on me now,' chortled the Arishtanemi, wrinkling his nose in amusement.

Nandi burst out in laughter as he slapped the Arishtanemi on his arm.

'What is your name, my friend?' asked Nandi.

'Kaustav,' replied the Arishtanemi. 'Someday we shall battle the main Chandravanshi army together, my friend. And by the grace of Lord Ram, we will kill all those bastards!'

'By Lord Agni, we will!'

— ⁂ —

'It was interesting how you got into the Naga's mind,' said Brahaspati as he watched Shiva getting the gash on his torso cleaned and dressed.

Shiva had insisted that his injuries receive medical attention only after every other soldier's wounds had been tended.

'Well, I can't really explain it,' said Shiva. 'How the Naga would think just seemed so obvious to me.'

'Well, I can explain it!'

'Really? What?'

'The explanation is that you are the omnipotent "N", whose name cannot be spoken!' said Brahaspati, opening his eyes wide and conjuring his hands up like an ancient magician.

They burst out laughing, causing Shiva to bend backwards. The military doctor gave Shiva a stern look, at which he immediately quietened down and let him finish tending to the wound. Having applied the Ayurvedic paste and covered it with the medicinal neem leaf, the doctor bandaged the wound with a cotton cloth.

'You will need to change that every second day, foreigner,' said the doctor pointing at the bandage. 'The royal doctor in Devagiri will be able to do it for you. And don't let this area get wet for a week. Also, avoid the Somras during this period since you will not be able to bathe.'

'Oh he doesn't need the Somras,' joked Brahaspati. 'It's already done all the damage it can on him.'

Shiva and Brahaspati collapsed into helpless laughter again as the doctor walked away, shaking his head in exasperation.

'But seriously,' said Brahaspati calming down. 'Why would they attack you? You have not harmed anybody.'

'I don't think the attack was on me. I think it was for Sati.'

'Sati! Why Sati? That's even more bizarre.'

'It probably wasn't specifically for Sati,' said Shiva. 'I think the target was the royal family. The primary target was probably the Emperor. Since he wasn't there, they went for the secondary target, Sati. I think the aim was to kidnap a royal and use that person as leverage.'

Brahaspati did not respond. He seemed worried. Clasping his hands together and bringing them close to his face, he looked into the distance, deep in thought. Shiva reached into his pouch and pulled out his chillum, before carefully filling it with some dried marijuana. Brahaspati turned to look at his friend, unhappy with what he was doing.

'I've never told you this before Shiva and I probably shouldn't as, well... since you are a free man,' said Brahaspati. 'But I consider you my friend. And it is my duty to tell you the truth. I have seen some Egyptian merchants in Karachapa with this marijuana habit. It's not good for you.'

'You're wrong, my friend,' said Shiva, grinning broadly. 'This is actually the best habit in the world.'

'You probably don't know, Shiva. This has many harmful side effects. And worst of all, it even harms your memory, causing untold damage to your ability to draw on past knowledge.'

Shiva's face suddenly became uncharacteristically serious. He gazed back at Brahaspati with a melancholic smile. 'That is exactly why it is good, my friend. No idiot who smokes this is scared of forgetting.'

Shiva lit up his chillum, took a deep drag and continued, 'They are scared of *not* forgetting.'

Brahaspati stared sharply at Shiva, wondering what terrible past could have prompted his friend to get addicted to the weed.

CHAPTER 11

Neelkanth Unveiled

The next morning the royal caravan resumed its journey to Devagiri after spending the night at a temporary camp in the clearing. It wasn't safe to travel at night under the circumstances. The wounded, including Nandi, were lying in the first three carriages and the fifth one. The royal family and Shiva travelled in the fourth. All the soldiers who had fought in the previous day's battle were given the privilege of riding on horses in relative comfort. Brahaspati and Kanakhala walked along with the rest of the troops, in mourning for the three slain Arishtanemi. Parvateshwar, Bhabravya and two other soldiers bore a make-shift wooden palanquin that carried three urns containing the ashes of the martyrs. The urns would be given to their families for a ceremonial submersion in the Saraswati. Shiva, Sati and Nandi too wanted to walk but the doctor insisted they were in no condition to do so.

Parvateshwar walked with pride at the bravery of his soldiers. *His boys*, as he called them, had shown they were made of a metal forged in Lord Indra's own furnace. He cursed himself for not being there to fight with them. He castigated himself for not being there to protect his Goddaughter, *his* Sati, when she was in danger. He prayed for the day when he would finally get a chance to destroy the cowardly Chandravanshis. He also silently pledged that he would anonymously donate his salary for the next six months to the families of the slain soldiers.

'I didn't think he would fall to these levels!' exclaimed Daksha in disgust.

Shiva and Sati, comfortably asleep in the carriage, were woken up by Daksha's outburst. Veerini looked up from the book that she was reading, narrowing her eyes to concentrate on her husband.

'Who, your Highness?' asked Shiva groggily.

'Dilipa! That blight on humanity!' said Daksha, barely concealing his loathing.

Veerini continued to stare hard at her husband. She slowly reached out, pulled Sati's hand in hers, brought it close to her lips and kissed it gently. Then she put her other hand protectively on top of Sati's hand. Sati looked at her mother warmly with a hint of a smile and rested her tired head on Veerini's shoulders.

'Who is Dilipa, your Highness?' asked Shiva.

'He is the Emperor of Swadweep,' answered Daksha. 'Everyone knows that Sati is the apple of my eye. And they were possibly trying to kidnap her in order to force my hand!'

Shiva gazed at Daksha with sympathy. He could understand the outrage of the Emperor at the latest Chandravanshi treachery.

'And to reduce yourself to a level where you use a Naga for this nefarious plan,' said a furious Daksha. 'This shows what the Chandravanshis are capable of!'

'I don't know if the Naga was being used, your Highness,'

said Shiva softly. 'It appeared as though he was the leader.'

Daksha however was too lost in his righteous anger to even explore Shiva's insinuation. 'The Naga may have been the leader of this particular platoon, my Lord, but he would almost certainly be under the overall command of the Chandravanshis. No Naga can be a leader. They are cursed people born with horrific deformities and diseases in this birth as a punishment for terrible crimes that they have committed in their previous birth. The Nagas are embarrassed to even show their face to anyone. But they have tremendous power and skills. Their presence strikes terror in the heart of all Meluhans, and most Swadweepans as well. The Chandravanshis have sunk low enough to even consort with those deformed demons. They hate us so much that they have become blind to the sins they are bringing upon their own souls by interacting with the Nagas.'

Shiva, Sati and Veerini continued to hear Daksha's ranting in silence.

Turning towards Shiva, Daksha continued, 'Do you see the kind of vermin we are up against, my Lord? They have no code, no honour. And they outnumber us ten to one. We need your help my Lord. It's not just my people, but my family as well. We are in danger.'

'Your Highness, I will do all that I can to help you,' said Shiva. 'But I am not a General. I cannot lead an army against the Chandravanshis. I am just a simple tribal leader. What difference can one man make?'

'At least let me announce your presence to the court and the people, my Lord,' urged Daksha. 'Just spend a few weeks travelling through the empire. Your presence will raise the morale of the people. Look at the difference you made yesterday. We actually foiled a terrorist attack because of you, because of your presence of mind. Please, let me announce your arrival. That is all I ask.'

Shiva looked at Daksha's earnest face with trepidation. He could feel Sati's and Veerini's eyes on him. Especially Sati's.

What am I getting myself into?

'All right,' said Shiva in resignation.

Daksha rose and embraced Shiva in a tight grip of gratitude.

'Thank you, my Lord!' exclaimed Daksha, even as Shiva released himself from the warm hug with a sharp intake of air. 'I will announce your presence at the court tomorrow itself. Then you can leave for a tour of the empire in another three weeks. I will personally make all the arrangements. You will have a full brigade travelling with you for security. Parvateshwar and Sati will accompany you as well.'

'No!' protested Veerini in a harsh tone that Sati had never heard her mother use. 'Sati is not going anywhere. I am not going to allow you to put our daughter's life in danger. She is staying with me in Devagiri.'

'Veerini, don't be silly,' said Daksha calmly. 'You really think that something would happen to Sati if the Lord Neelkanth was around? She is safest when she is with the Lord.'

'She is not going. And that is final!' glared Veerini in a firm voice, clutching Sati's hand tightly.

Daksha turned towards Shiva, ignoring Veerini. 'Don't worry, my Lord. I will have all the arrangements made. Parvateshwar and Sati will also travel with you. You will just have to restrain Sati sometimes.'

Shiva frowned. So did Sati.

Daksha smiled genially. 'My darling daughter has the tendency to be a little too brave at times. Like this one time, when she was just a child, she had jumped in all by herself, with nothing but her short sword, to save an old woman being attacked by a pack of wild dogs. She nearly got herself killed for her pains. It was one of the worst days of my life. I think it is the same impulsiveness which worries Veerini as well.'

Shiva looked at Sati. There was no expression on her face.

'That's why,' continued Daksha, 'I am suggesting that you keep her restrained. Then there should be no problem.'

Shiva glanced again at Sati. He felt a surge of admiration coupled with the boundless love he felt for her.

She did what I couldn't do.

— ⁂ —

The next morning, Shiva found himself seated next to Daksha in the Meluhan royal court. The magnificence of the court left him wonderstruck. Since this was a public building, the usual Meluhan reticence had been bypassed. It was built next to the Great Public Bath. While the platform had been constructed of the standard kiln-bricks, the structure itself, including the floor, was made of teak wood. Brawny wooden pillars had been laid into set grooves on the platform. The pillars had been extravagantly sculpted with celestial figures like *apsaras, devas* and *rishis* — *celestial nymphs, Gods* and *sages* — amongst others. An ornately carved wooden roof that had been inlaid with gold and silver designs crowned the top of the pillars. Pennants of the holy blue colour and royal red colour hung from the ceiling. Each niche on the walls had paintings depicting the life of Lord Ram. But Shiva had little time to admire the glorious architecture of the court. Daksha's expectations would be apparent in his speech and were causing him considerable discomfort.

'As many of you may have heard,' announced Daksha, 'there was another terrorist attack yesterday. The Chandravanshis tried to harm the royal family on the road from Mount Mandar to Devagiri.'

Murmurs of dismay filled the court. The question troubling everyone was how the Chandravanshis had discovered the route to Mount Mandar. Shiva meanwhile kept reminding himself that this wasn't a terrorist attack. It was just a kidnap attempt.

'The Chandravanshis had planned their attack with great deception,' said Daksha, drowning out the murmurs with his booming voice.

The talented architects of the court had designed the structure in such a manner that any voice emanating from the royal platform resonated across the entire hall. 'But we beat them back. For the first time in decades, we beat back a cowardly terrorist attack.'

An exultant roar went up in the court at this announcement. They had beaten back open military assaults from the Chandravanshis before. But until today, the Meluhans had found no answer to the dreaded terrorist strikes. This was because the terrorists usually launched surprise attacks on non-military locations and fled before the Suryavanshi soldiers could get there.

Raising his hand to quieten the crowd, Daksha continued, 'We beat them back because the time for truth to triumph has finally arrived! We beat them back because we were led by Father Manu's messenger! We beat them back because the time for justice has come!'

The murmurs grew louder. Had the Neelkanth finally arrived? Everyone had heard the rumours. But nobody believed them. There had been too many false declarations in the past.

Daksha raised his hand. He waited just enough for the anticipation to build up. And then jubilantly bellowed, 'Yes! The rumours are true. Our saviour has come! The Neelkanth has come!'

Shiva winced at being put up for display on the royal platform with his cravat removed. The Meluhan elite thronged around him, their statements buzzing in Shiva's ears.

'We had heard the rumours, my Lord. But we didn't believe them to be true.'

'We have nothing to fear anymore, my Lord. The days of evil are numbered!'

'Where are you from, my Lord?'

'Mount Kailash? Where is that, my Lord? Do you think I could go on a pilgrimage there?'

Answering these questions repeatedly and being confronted by the blind faith of these people disturbed Shiva. The moment he had a chance, he requested Daksha for permission to leave the court.

— ⁂ —

A few hours later, Shiva sat in the quiet comfort of his chamber, contemplating what had happened at the court. The cravat was back around his neck.

'By the Holy Lake, can I really deliver these people from their troubles?'

'What did you say, my Lord?' asked Nandi, who was sitting patiently at a distance.

'The faith your people place upon me makes me anxious,' said Shiva, loud enough for Nandi to hear. 'If there was a one-on-one battle, I could take on any enemy in order to protect your people. But I am no leader. And I am certainly not a "destroyer of evil".'

'I am sure that you can lead us to victory against anyone, my Lord. You beat them back on the road to Devagiri.'

'That wasn't a genuine victory,' said Shiva dismissively. 'They were a small platoon, aiming to kidnap and not to kill. If we face a well organised and large army, whose aim is to kill, the situation may be very different. To me it appears that Meluha is ranged against formidable and ruthless enemies. The solution cannot lie in reposing faith in an individual. Your people need to adapt to the changing times. Perhaps your innocent ways will find you helpless in the face of such a cold-blooded enemy. A new system is needed. I am hardly a God to perform miracles.'

'You are right, my Lord,' said Nandi, with all the conviction of a simple, lucky man not troubled by too many thoughts. 'A new system is required, and I obviously don't know what this new system should be. But I do understand one thing. More than a thousand years back, we faced a similar situation and Lord Ram came and taught us a better way. I am sure that, similarly, you will lead us to a superior path.'

'I am no Lord Ram, Nandi!'

How can this fool even compare me to Lord Ram, the Maryada Purushottam, the Ideal Follower of Laws?

'You are better than Lord Ram, my Lord,' said Nandi.

'Stop this nonsense, Nandi! What have I done to even

be compared with Lord Ram? Let alone be considered better?'

'But you *will* do deeds that will place you above him, my Lord.'

'Just shut up!'

— ⁂ —

The preparations for Shiva's tour of the empire were in full swing. Shiva, however, still found time for Sati's dance lessons every afternoon. They were developing a quiet friendship. But Shiva agonised over the fact that while she showed respect, there was no softening of emotions in her or expression of feelings.

In the meantime, Shiva's tribe had been brought over to Devagiri, where they were given comfortable accommodation and jobs. Bhadra, however, was not to stay with the Gunas. He had instead been assigned to accompany the Neelkanth on his voyage.

'*Veer*bhadra! When the hell did you get this name?' Shiva asked Bhadra, meeting him for the first time since his departure from Kashmir.

'Stupid reason actually,' smiled Bhadra, whose slight hump had disappeared completely, thanks to the magical Somras. 'On the journey here, I saved the caravan leader from a tiger attack. He gave me the title for a *brave man* before my name.'

'You fought a tiger single-handed?' asked Shiva, clearly impressed.

Bhadra nodded feeling awkward.

'Well, then you really deserve to be called Veerbhadra!'

'Yeah right!' smiled Bhadra, suddenly turning serious.

'The crazy label of "destroyer of evil"... Are you okay with this? You are not giving in to these pleas just because of your past, are you?'

'I am going with the flow right now, my friend. Something tells me that despite all my misgivings, I can actually help these people. These Meluhans are completely mad, no doubt. And I certainly can't do ALL that they expect of me. But I do feel that if I can make a difference, however small, I will be able to reconcile myself with my past.'

'If you are sure, then so am I. I will follow you anywhere.'

'Don't follow. Walk beside me!'

Veerbhadra laughed and embraced his friend. 'I've missed you Shiva.'

'I've missed you too.'

'Let's meet in the garden in the afternoon. I've got a great batch of marijuana.'

'It's a deal!'

Brahaspati too had sought permission to travel with Shiva. He explained that a Mesopotamian ship carrying some rare chemicals, essential for a critical experiment, was to dock at the port city of Karachapa soon. His team had to check and obtain those materials anyway. It would be a good idea to do this while travelling with Shiva. Daksha said that he had no problems with Brahaspati joining the tour if the Lord was okay with it. Shiva agreed enthusiastically with the suggestion.

Three weeks after the court announcement about the Neelkanth, the day finally dawned for the commencement of Shiva's tour of the empire. On the morning of the day itself, Daksha walked into Shiva's chambers.

'You could have summoned me, your Highness,' said Shiva with a Namaste. 'You did not need to come here.'

'It is my pleasure to come to your chambers, my Lord,' smiled Daksha, returning Shiva's greeting with a low bow. 'I thought I would introduce the physician who would be travelling with your entourage. She arrived from Kashmir last night.'

Daksha moved aside to let his escort show the doctor into the room.

'Ayurvati!' exclaimed Shiva, his face lit up in a brilliant smile. 'It's so good to see you again!'

'The pleasure is all mine, my Lord,' beamed Ayurvati, as she bent down to touch Shiva's feet.

Shiva immediately moved back to neatly side-step Ayurvati. 'I have told you before, Ayurvati,' said Shiva. 'You are a giver of life. Please don't embarrass me by touching my feet.'

'And you are the Neelkanth, my Lord. The destroyer of evil,' said Ayurvati with devotion. 'How can you deny me the privilege of being blessed by you?'

Shiva shook his head in despair and let Ayurvati touch his feet. He gently touched her head and blessed her.

A few hours later, Shiva, Sati, Parvateshwar, Brahaspati, Ayurvati, Krittika, Nandi and Veerbhadra set off. Accompanying them was a brigade of fifteen hundred soldiers, twenty-five handmaidens and fifty support staff for their security and comfort. They planned to travel by road till the city of Kotdwaar on the Beas river. From thereon, they would use boats to travel to the port city of Karachapa. Then they would move due east to the city of Lothal. Finally, they would move north by road to the inland delta of the Saraswati and then by boats back to Devagiri.

CHAPTER 12

Journey through Meluha

'Who was Manu?' asked Shiva. 'I have heard of him quite often being referred to as "the Father".'

The caravan had been travelling for a few days on the broad road from Devagiri to Kotdwaar. In the centre it consisted of a row of seven carriages identical to the ones used during the trip to Mandar. Five of them were empty. Shiva, Sati, Brahaspati and Krittika travelled in the second carriage. Parvateshwar was in the fifth, along with Ayurvati and his key brigadiers. The General's presence meant that every rule had to be adhered to strictly. Hence Nandi, whose rank did not allow him to travel in the carriage, was riding a horse with the rest of the cavalry. Veerbhadra had been inducted as a soldier in Nandi's platoon. Led by their respective captains, the brigade were in standard forward, rear and side defence formations around the caravan.

Both Brahaspati and Sati started answering Shiva simultaneously.

'Lord Manu was the…'

They both stopped talking.

'After you please, Brahaspati*ji*,' said Sati.

'No, no,' said Brahaspati with a warm smile. 'Why don't you tell him the story?'

He knew whose voice the Neelkanth would prefer.

'Of course not, Brahaspati*ji*. How can I supersede you? It would be completely improper.'

'Will somebody answer me or are you two going to keep up this elaborate protocol forever?' asked Shiva.

'Alright, alright,' laughed Brahaspati. 'Don't turn blue all over now.'

'That is hilarious Brahaspati,' smiled Shiva. 'Keep this up and you might actually get someone to laugh in a hundred years.'

As Brahaspati and Shiva chortled, Sati was astounded by the inappropriate manner in which the conversation was progressing. But if the revered chief scientist seemed comfortable, then she would desist from commenting. And in any case, how could she reprimand Shiva? Her code of honour forbade it. He had saved her life. Twice.

'Well, you are right about Lord Manu being the Father,' said Brahaspati. 'He is considered the progenitor of our civilisation by all the people of India.'

'Including Swadweepans?' asked Shiva incredulously.

'Yes, we believe so. In any case, Lord Manu lived more than eight and a half thousand years ago. He was apparently a prince from south India. A land way beyond the Narmada river, where the earth ends and the great ocean begins. That land is the Sangamtamil.'

'Sangamtamil?'

'Yes. Sangamtamil was the richest and most powerful country in the world at the time. Lord Manu's family, the Pandyas, had ruled that land for many generations. However, from the records left by Lord Manu, we know that by his time the kings had lost their old code of honour. Having degenerated into corrupt ways, they spent their days indulging in the pleasures of their fabulous wealth rather than being earnest about their duties and their spiritual life. Then a terrible calamity occurred. The seas rose and destroyed their entire civilisation.'

'My God!' exclaimed Shiva.

'Lord Manu had foreseen this day and had in fact prepared for it. He believed that it was the decadence his old country had fallen into that had incurred the wrath of the Gods. In order to escape the inevitable calamity, he led a band of his followers to the northern, higher lands in a fleet of ships. He established his first camp at a place called Mehragarh deep in the western mountains of present day Meluha. Deeply committed to establishing a moral and just society, he gave up his princely robes and became a priest. In fact the term for priests in India, pandit, is derived from Lord Manu's family name — Pandya.'

'Interesting. So how did Lord Manu's little band grow into the formidable India we see today?'

'The years immediately following their arrival at Mehragarh were harsh on them. With each year's monsoon, the flooding and sea tides would become stronger. But after many years and with the force of Lord Manu's prayers, the anger of the Gods abated and the waters stopped advancing. The sea, however, never receded to its original levels.'

'This means that somewhere in the deep south, the sea still covers the ancient Sangamtamil cities?'

'We believe so,' answered Brahaspati. 'Once the sea stopped advancing, Lord Manu and his men came down from the mountains. They were shocked to see that the minor stream that was the Indus had now become a massive river. Many other rivulets across northern India too had swollen and six great rivers had emerged — Indus, Saraswati, Yamuna, Ganga, Sarayu and Brahmaputra. Lord Manu said the rivers started flowing because the temperatures of our land rose with the wrath of the Gods. With the rise in temperatures, huge channels of ice or glaciers frozen high in the Himalayas began to melt, creating the rivers.'

'Hmm...'

'Villages, and later cities, grew on the banks of these rivers. Thus our land of the seven rivers, Sapt-Sindhu, was born out of the destruction of the Sangamtamil.'

'Seven? But you mentioned the creation of six rivers in North India.'

'Yes, that's true. The seventh river already existed. It is the Narmada and it became our southern border. Lord Manu strictly forbade his descendants to go south of the Narmada. And if they did so, they could never return. This is a law that we believe even the Chandravanshis adhere to.'

'So what are Lord Manu's other laws?'

'There are numerous laws actually. They are all listed in an extensive treatise called the Manusmriti. Would you be interested in listening to the entire text?'

'Tempting,' smiled Shiva. 'But I think I'll pass.'

'With your permission, my Lords, perhaps we can further discuss Lord Manu's guidance to our society over lunch,' suggested Krittika.

At a short distance from the road on which the Neelkanth's caravan travelled, a small band of about forty men trudged silently along the Beas. One in two men of the platoon carried a small coracle on his head. It was typical of this region. The locals made small and light boats made of bamboo, cane and rope, portable enough to be carried by a single man on his head. Each boat could ferry two people with relative safety and speed. At the head of the platoon was a young man with a proud battle scar adorning his face, his head crowned with a brown turban. A little ahead of him walked a hooded figure. With his head bowed, his eyes scrunched, he took slow methodical steps, his mind lost in unfathomable thoughts. His breathing was hard. He brought his hand up languidly to rub his masked forehead. There was a leather bracelet on his right wrist with the serpent Aum symbol embroidered on it.

'Vishwadyumna,' said the hooded figure. 'We will enter the river from here. Whenever we come close to populated areas, we will move away from the river to avoid detection. We have to reach Karachapa within two months.'

'Karachapa, my Lord?' asked a surprised Vishwadyumna. 'I was under the impression that we were to have a secret audience with the Queen outside Lothal.'

'No,' answered the hooded figure. 'We will meet her outside Karachapa.'

'Yes, my Lord,' answered Vishwadyumna, as he looked back in the direction of the road to Kotdwaar. He knew that his Lord would have dearly liked to make one more attempt to kidnap the princess. He also knew that it was foolhardy to endeavour to do so given the strength of the force accompanying the caravan. In any case, they were behind schedule for their main mission. They had to meet the Queen urgently.

Turning towards one of his soldiers, Vishwadyumna

ordered, 'Sriktaa, place your coracle in the river and give me your oar. I will row the Lord through this part of the journey.'

Sriktaa immediately did as instructed. Vishwadyumna and the hooded figure were the first of the platoon to enter the river. Vishwadyumna had already started rowing by the time his men started placing their boats into the waters. At a distance further down the river, the hooded figure saw two women lounging carelessly on a boat. One of the women was sloppily splashing water from the side of the boat on to her friend who was making a hopeless attempt at avoiding getting wet. Their childish game caused their boat to sway dangerously from side to side. The hooded figure saw that the women had not detected a crocodile that had entered the river from the opposite bank. Having spied what must have looked like an appetising meal, the crocodile was swimming swiftly towards the women's boat.

'Look behind you!' shouted the hooded figure, as he motioned to Vishwadyumna to row rapidly in their direction.

The women could not hear him from the distance. What they did see, however, was two men rowing towards them. They could see that one of them was almost a giant covered from head to toe in a strange robe, his face hidden behind a mask. This man was making frantic gestures. Behind the duo were a large number of soldiers swiftly pushing their boats on to the river. That was all the warning the women needed. Thinking that the men were coming towards them with evil intent, the women put all their effort into hastily rowing away from the hooded figure's boat. Into the path of the crocodile.

'No!' shouted the hooded figure.

He grabbed the oar from Vishwadyumna, using his powerful arms to row rapidly. He was shortening the distance between them by the minute. But not fast enough. As the crocodile closed in on the women's boat it dived underwater and charged at it, rocking it with its massive body. The tiny vessel tilted and capsized, throwing the women into the Beas.

Screams of terror rent the air as the women fought to stay afloat. The crocodile had moved too far ahead in its dash. Turning around, it swam towards the struggling women. The delay of those crucial seconds proved fateful for the women. The rescue boat moved in between the crocodile and them. Turning towards Vishwadyumna, the hooded figure ordered, 'Save the women.'

Before Vishwadyumna could react, he had flung his robe aside and dived into the river. With his knife held tight between his teeth, he swam towards the advancing crocodile. Vishwadyumna pulled one of the women into the boat. She had already lost consciousness. Turning to the other woman, he reassured, 'I am coming back soon.'

Vishwadyumna turned and paddled vigorously towards the bank. On the way he passed some of his soldiers. 'Row quickly. The Lord's life is in danger.'

The other soldiers paddled towards the area where the hooded figure had dived into the river. The water had turned red with blood from the battle raging under water. The soldiers said a silent prayer to Lord *Varun*, the *God of the water and the seas*, hoping that the blood did not belong to their Lord.

One of the soldiers was about to jump into the water with his sword when the hooded figure emerged onto the surface, soaked in blood. It was that of the crocodile. He swam forcefully towards the other woman who was on the verge of losing consciousness. Reaching her in the nick of time, he pulled her head out of the water. Meanwhile, two of the Chandravanshi soldiers dived off their coracle.

'My Lord, please get into the boat,' said one of them. 'We will swim ashore.'

'Help the woman first,' replied the hooded figure.

The soldiers pulled the unconscious woman on to the coracle. The hooded figure then carefully climbed aboard and rowed towards the shore. By the time he reached the river bank, the other woman had been revived by Vishwadyumna. She was obviously disoriented by the rapid chain of events.

'Are you alright?' Vishwadyumna asked the woman.

In answer, the woman looked beyond Vishwadyumna and screamed. Vishwadyumna turned around. On the river bank, the hooded figure was coming ashore carrying the other woman's limp body. His clothes were glued to his massive body. To the disoriented woman, the crocodile's blood all over his clothes, seemed like that of her friend.

'What have you done, you beast?' shrieked the woman.

The Naga looked up abruptly. His eyes showed mild surprise but he refrained from saying anything. He gently laid the unconscious woman on the ground. As he did so, the mask on his face came undone. The woman next to Vishwadyumna stared at him with horror.

'Naga!' she screeched.

Before Vishwadyumna could react, she leapt to her feet and fled screaming, 'Help! Help! A Naga is eating my friend!'

The Naga looked at the fleeing woman with melancholic eyes. He shut the windows to his tormented soul and shook his head slightly. Vishwadyumna meanwhile turned to see his Lord's face for the first time in years. He immediately lowered his gaze, but not before he had seen the rare emotion of intense pain and sorrow in his Lord's normally expressionless eyes. Seething with anger, Vishwadyumna drew his sword, swearing to slay the ungrateful wench he had just saved.

'No, Vishwadyumna,' ordered the Naga. Pulling his mask back on, he turned to his other soldiers. 'Revive her.'

'My Lord,' argued Vishwadyumna. 'Her friend will bring others here. Let's leave this woman to her fate and go.'

'No.'

'But my Lord, someone may come any time now. We must escape.'

'Not till we've saved her,' said the Naga, in his usual calm voice.

— ⁂ —

The royal party, including Nandi and Veerbhadra, were sitting together enjoying their lunch in the courtyard of the rest-house they had stopped at. Half the brigade had sat down for their meal. They needed all the energy they could muster in order to march in this scorching heat. Parvateshwar had come in to check on the food arrangements. He was especially concerned about Sati's comfort. However, he had refused to join them. He was going to eat later with his soldiers.

A loud commotion from the area of one of the perimeter guards disturbed Shiva. He got up to investigate, motioning to Brahaspati, Nandi and Veerbhadra to remain seated. Parvateshwar too had heard the racket and was moving towards the uproar.

'Please save her!' cried the woman. 'A Naga is eating her alive!'

'I am sorry,' answered the Captain. 'But we have strict orders. We are not to leave the vicinity of this rest-house under any circumstances.'

'What is the matter?' asked Parvateshwar.

The Captain spun around in surprise, saluted and bowed low. 'My Lord, this woman alleges that a Naga has attacked her friend. She's asking for help.'

Parvateshwar looked at the woman intensely. He would have liked nothing more than to chase the Naga party and destroy them. But his orders were crystal clear. He was not to leave the Neelkanth and Sati. Their protection was the only objective of the brigade. But he was a Kshatriya. What kind of Kshatriya would he be if he didn't fight to protect the weak? Seething at the restrictions forced upon him, Parvateshwar was about to say something when Shiva appeared.

'What's the matter?' asked Shiva.

'My Lord,' said the Captain in awe. He scarce believed that he was actually in the presence of the Neelkanth. 'This woman claims that her friend has been attacked by Nagas', he gasped. 'We are concerned that it may be a trap. We have heard about the Chandravanshi duplicity on the Mount Mandar road.'

Shiva heard his inner voice cry. *'Go back! Help her!'*

Drawing his sword in one smooth motion he told the woman, 'Take me to your friend.'

Parvateshwar looked at Shiva with respect. It was mild, but it was respect all the same. He immediately drew his own sword and turned to the Captain, 'Follow us with your platoon. Brigadier Vraka, command your men to be on alert for any surprise attack. The safety of our princess is paramount.'

Shiva and Parvateshwar ran behind the woman who seemed to lead them with ease. She was obviously a local. The Captain trailed them with his platoon of thirty soldiers. After sprinting for the larger part of half an hour, they finally reached the riverside to find a dazed woman sitting on the ground. Breathing heavily, she was staring in shock at an imaginary vision in the distance. There was blood all over her clothes, but strangely, no injury. There were many footsteps that appeared to be coming out of the river and going back in.

The Captain looked at the woman who had led them here with suspicious eyes. Turning to his soldiers, he ordered, 'Form a perimeter around the General and the Neelkanth. It could be a trap.'

'She was being eaten alive, I tell you,' screeched the woman, absolutely stunned to see her friend alive and unharmed.

'No she wasn't,' said Shiva calmly. He pointed at the corpse of the crocodile floating in the river. A large flock of crows had settled on the carcass, fighting viciously over its entrails. 'Somebody just saved her from that crocodile.'

'Whoever it was has rowed across the river, my Lord,' said the Captain, pointing towards the heavy footmarks close to the river.

'Why would a Naga risk his own life to save this woman?' asked Shiva.

Parvateshwar seemed equally surprised. This was completely unlike the usually blood thirsty Nagas they had dealt with until now.

'My Lords,' said the Captain, addressing both Shiva and

Parvateshwar. 'The women appear safe. Perhaps it is not wise for everybody to stay here. With your permission, I will escort these women back to their village and rejoin the caravan at Kotdwaar. You could retire to the rest-house.'

'All right,' said Parvateshwar. 'Take four soldiers along with you just in case.'

Both Shiva and Parvateshwar walked back, baffled by this inexplicable event.

— ⁂ —

It was late in the evening. Shiva, Brahaspati, Nandi and Veerbhadra sat quietly around the camp fire. Shiva turned to see Sati sitting on the rest-house veranda at a distance, along with Ayurvati and Krittika. They were absorbed in a serious conversation. Parvateshwar was moving among his soldiers, as usual, personally supervising the security arrangements of the camp and the comfort of his boys.

'It's ready, Shiva,' said Veerbhadra, handing over the chillum to the Neelkanth.

Shiva brought the pipe up to his lips and pulled hard. He relaxed visibly. Feeling the need for respite, he smoked some more before passing it back to his friend. Veerbhadra offered it to Brahaspati and Nandi, both of whom declined. Brahaspati stared at Shiva who kept stealing glances at Sati. He smiled and shook his head.

'What?' asked Shiva who had noticed Brahaspati's gesture.

'I understand your longing, my friend,' whispered Brahaspati. 'But what you are hoping for is quite difficult. Almost impossible.'

'It can't be easy when it's so valuable, can it?'

Brahaspati smiled and patted Shiva on his hand.

Veerbhadra knew what his friend needed. Dance and music. It always improved his mood. 'Don't people sing and dance in this wretched country?'

'Private Veerbhadra,' said Nandi, his tone different with a subordinate, 'firstly, this country is not wretched. It's the greatest land in the world.'

Veerbhadra playfully put his hands together in a mock apology.

'Secondly,' continued Nandi, 'we dance only when an occasion demands it, like the Holi festival or a public performance.'

'But the greatest joy derived from dancing is when you do it for no reason at all, Captain,' said Veerbhadra.

'I agree,' said Shiva.

Nandi immediately fell silent.

Without any warning, Veerbhadra suddenly burst forth into one of the folk songs of his region. Shiva smiled at his friend, for Veerbhadra was singing one of his favourites. Continuing to sing, Veerbhadra rose slowly and began dancing to the lilting tune, now accompanied by Shiva. The combination of marijuana and dance immediately changed his mood.

Brahaspati stared at Shiva, first in shock and then with pleasure. He noticed a pattern in their dancing, a smooth six-step combination that was repeated rhythmically. Shiva reached out and pulled Brahaspati and Nandi to their feet. They joined in, tentative at first. But it was only a matter of time before a reluctant Brahaspati was dancing with abandon. The group moved together in a circle around the fire, the singing louder and livelier.

Shiva suddenly darted out of the ring towards Sati. 'Dance with me.'

A flabbergasted Sati shook her head.

'Oh come on! If you can dance while your Guru*ji* and I watch, then why not here?'

'That was in pursuit of *knowledge*!' said Sati.

'So? Must all dance be solely towards that end?'

'I didn't say that.'

'Fine. Have it your way,' said Shiva with a frustrated gesture. 'Ayurvati, come!'

A startled Ayurvati didn't know how to react. Before she could decide on a course of action, Shiva held her hand and pulled her into the circle. Veerbhadra lured Krittika in as well. The group danced boisterously and sang loudly, making a racket in an otherwise quiet night. Sati got up agitatedly and glared at Shiva's back before running into the rest-house. Shiva's anger increased even more as he noticed her absence when he turned towards the veranda.

Damn!

He returned to his dance, his heart in a strange mixture of pain and joy. He turned once again towards the veranda. There was nobody.

Who's behind that curtain?

Shiva was dragged into the next move by Veerbhadra. It was some time later that he was in a position to look once again at the veranda. He could see Sati, outlined behind the curtain, staring at him. Only at him.

Wow!

A surprised and delighted Shiva swung back into his dance, moving in his prime form. He had to impress her!

CHAPTER 13

Blessings of the Impure

Kotdwaar was decked up in all its glory to receive the Neelkanth. Torches had been lit across the fort perimeter as if it was Diwali. Red and blue pennants, embellished with the Suryavanshi Sun, had been hung down the fort walls. In a rare breach of protocol, the governor had come outside the city to personally receive the Neelkanth. The following day, a public function had been organised after the Neelkanth had met the Kotdwaar elite at the local court. Sixty-five thousand people, practically the entire population of Kotdwaar, had converged for the event. Keeping in mind the vast number of attendees, the event had been organised outside the city platform to ensure that every person could be accommodated.

A speech delivered by Shiva convinced the Kotdwaarans that Meluha's days of trouble were soon to end. The remarkable effect Shiva seemed to have on the people was a revelation to him. Though he was careful with his words, telling them that he would do all he could to support the people of Meluha, the public made their own interpretations.

'The cursed Chandravanshis will finally be destroyed,' said one man.

'We don't have to worry about anything now. The Neelkanth will take care of everything,' said a woman.

Seated with Brahaspati and Sati on the speaker's platform, Parvateshwar was deeply unhappy with the public's reaction. Turning to the chief scientist, he said, 'Our entire society is based on the rule of law and we are not meant to blindly follow anyone. We are expected to solve our problems ourselves and not hope for miracles from a solitary man. What has this man done to deserve such blind faith?'

'Parvateshwar,' said Brahaspati politely, for he greatly respected him. 'I think Shiva is a good man. I think he cares enough to want to do something. And aren't good intentions the first step towards any good deed?'

Parvateshwar didn't completely agree. Never a believer in the legend of the Neelkanth, the General thought that every man or woman had to earn his station in life with training and preparation, and not just receive it on a silver platter because of a blue throat. 'Yes, that may be true. But intentions aren't enough. They have to be backed by ability as well. Here we are, putting an untrained man on a pedestal and acting as though he is our saviour. For all we know, he might lead us to complete disaster. We are acting on faith. Not reason or laws or even experience.'

'Sometimes one needs a little bit of faith when faced with a difficult situation. Reason doesn't always work. We may also need a miracle.'

'*You're* talking about miracles? A scientist?'

'You can have scientific miracles too, Parvateshwar,' smiled Brahaspati.

Parvateshwar was distracted by the sight of Shiva stepping off the platform. As he came down there was a surge of people wanting to touch his hand. The soldiers, led by Nandi and Veerbhadra, were holding them back. There was a blind man amongst them who looked like he might get injured in the melee.

'Nandi, let that man through,' said Shiva.

Nandi and Veerbhadra lowered the rope to let him in.

Another man shouted, 'I am his son. He needs me to guide him.'

'Let him in as well,' said Shiva.

The son rushed in and held his father's hand. The blind man, who seemed lost without his son's hand, smiled warmly as he recognised the familiar touch. He was led close to Shiva and the son said, 'Father, the Neelkanth is right in front of you. Can you sense his presence?'

Copious tears flowed from the blind man's eyes. Without thinking, he bent down to try and touch Shiva's feet. His son cried out in shock as he pulled the man back sharply.

'Father!' scolded the son.

Shiva was stunned by the harshness in the son's tone which was in sharp contrast with the loving manner in which he had spoken so far. 'What happened?'

'I am sorry, my Lord,' apologised the son. 'He didn't mean to. He just forgot himself in your presence.'

'I am sorry, my Lord,' said the blind man, his tears flowing stronger.

'What about?', asked Shiva.

'He is a vikarma, my Lord,' said his son, 'ever since disease blinded him twenty years ago. He should not have tried to touch you.'

Sati, who was now standing near Shiva, had heard the entire conversation. She felt sympathy for the blind man. She knew the torment of having even your touch considered impure. But what he had tried to do was illegal.

'I am sorry, my Lord,' continued the blind man. 'But please don't let your anger with me stop you from protecting our country. It is the greatest land that *Parmatma* created. Save it from the evil Chandravanshis. Save us, my Lord.'

The blind man continued to cry while folding his hands in a penitent Namaste. Shiva was shaken by the dignity of the blind man.

He still loves a country that treats him so unfairly.

Why? Even worse he doesn't even appear to think he's being treated unfairly.

Tears welled up in Shiva's eyes as he realised that he was looking at a man whom fate had been very unkind to.

I will stop this nonsense.

Shiva stepped forward and bent down. The flabbergasted son trembled in disbelief as he saw the Neelkanth touch the feet of his vikarma father. The blind man was at sea for a moment. When he did understand what the Neelkanth had done, his hand shot up to cover his mouth in shock.

Shiva rose and stood in front of the blind man. 'Bless me, sir, so that I find the strength to fight for a man as patriotic as you.'

The blind man stood dumb-struck. His tears dried up in his bewilderment. He was about to collapse when Shiva took a quick step forward to hold him, lest he fall to the ground. The blind man found the strength to say, '*Vijayibhav*'. *May you be victorious.*

The son caught hold of his father's limp body as Shiva released him. The entire crowd was stunned into silence by what the Neelkanth had done. Forget the gravity of touching a vikarma, the Neelkanth had just asked to be blessed by one. Shiva turned to see Parvateshwar's enraged face. Shiva had broken the law. Broken it brazenly and in public. Next to him stood Sati. Her face, her eyes, her entire demeanour expressionless.

What the hell is she thinking?

Brahaspati and Sati entered Shiva's chambers as soon as he was alone. Shiva's smile at seeing two of his favourite people in the world disappeared on hearing Sati's voice, 'You must get a shudhikaran done.'

He looked at her and answered simply, 'No.'

'No? What do you mean no?'

'I mean No. Nahin. Nako,' said Shiva, adding the words for 'no' in the Kashmiri and the Kotdwaar dialect, for good measure.

'Shiva,' said Brahaspati, keeping his composure. 'This is no laughing matter. I agree with Sati. The governor too was worried about your safety and has arranged for a pandit. He waits outside as we speak. Get the ceremony done now. '

'But I just said I don't want to.'

'Shiva,' said Sati, reverting to her usual tone. 'I respect you immensely. Your valour. Your intelligence. Your talent. But you are not above the law. You have touched a vikarma. You have to get a shudhikaran. That is the law.'

'Well if the law says that my touching that poor blind man is illegal, then the law is wrong!'

Sati was stunned into silence by Shiva's attitude.

'Shiva, listen to me,' argued Brahaspati. 'Not doing a shudhikaran can be harmful to you. You are meant for bigger things. You are important to the future of India. Don't put your own person at risk out of obstinacy.'

'It's not obstinacy. You tell me, honestly, how can it harm me if I happened to touch a wronged man, who I might add, still loves his country despite the way he has been ostracised and ill-treated?'

'He may be a good man Shiva, but the sins of his previous birth will contaminate your fate,' said Brahaspati.

'Then let them! If the weight on that man's shoulders lessens, I will feel blessed.'

'What are you saying Shiva?' asked Sati. 'Why should you carry the punishment of someone else's sins?'

'Firstly, I don't believe in the nonsense that he was punished for the sins of his previous birth. He was just stricken by an illness, plain and simple. Secondly, if I choose to carry the weight of someone else's so called sins, why should it matter to anyone?'

'It matters because we care about you!' cried Brahaspati.

'Come on Sati,' said Shiva. 'Don't tell me you believe in this rubbish.'

'It is not rubbish.'

'Look, don't you want me to fight for you? Stop this unfairness that your society has subjected you to?'

'Is that what this is about? *Me*?' asked Sati, outraged.

'No,' retorted Shiva immediately, then added. 'Actually yes. This is also about you. It is about the vikarma and the unfairness that they have to face. I want to save them from leading the life of an outcast.'

'I DON'T NEED YOUR PROTECTION! I CANNOT BE SAVED!' shouted Sati, before storming out of the room.

Shiva glared at her retreating form with irritation. 'What the hell is it with this woman?!'

'She's right Shiva,' advised Brahaspati. 'Don't go there.'

'You agree with her on this vikarma business? Answer from your heart, Brahaspati. Don't you think it is unfair?'

'I wasn't talking about that. I was talking about Sati.'

Shiva continued to glare at Brahaspati defiantly. Everything in his mind, body and soul told him that he should pursue Sati. That his life would be meaningless without her. That his soul's existence would be incomplete without her.

'Don't go there, my friend,' reiterated Brahaspati.

— ⁂ —

The caravan left the river city of Kotdwaar on a royal barge led and followed by two large boats of equal size and grandeur as the royal vessel. Typical of the Meluhan security system, the additional boats were to confuse any attacker as to which boat the royal family may be on. The entire royal party was in the second boat. Each of the three large boats was manned by a brigade of soldiers. Additionally, five small and quick cutter boats kept pace on both sides of the royal convoy, protecting the sides in case of an ambush.

'The rivers are the best way to travel when the monsoon is not active, my Lord,' said Ayurvati. 'Though we have good roads connecting all major cities, they cannot match the rivers in terms of speed and safety.'

Shiva smiled at Ayurvati politely. He was not in the frame of mind for much conversation. Sati had not spoken to Shiva since that fateful day at Kotdwaar when he had refused to undergo a shudhikaran.

The royal barge stopped at many cities along the river. The routine seemed much the same. Extreme exuberance would manifest itself in each city on the arrival of the Neelkanth.

It was a kind of reaction that was quite unnatural in Meluha. But then, a Neelkanth didn't grace the land every day.

'Why?' asked Shiva of Brahaspati, after many days of keeping quiet about the disquiet in his troubled heart.

'Why what?'

'You know what I am talking about, Brahaspati,' said Shiva, narrowing his eyes in irritation.

'She genuinely believes that she deserves to be a vikarma,' answered Brahaspati with a sad smile.

'Why?'

'Perhaps because of the manner in which she became a vikarma.'

'How did it happen?'

'It happened during her earlier marriage.'

'What! Sati was married?!'

'Yes. That was around ninety years ago. It was a political marriage with one of the noble families of the empire. Her husband's name was Chandandhwaj. She got pregnant and went to Maika to deliver the child. It was the monsoon season. Unfortunately, the child was stillborn.'

'Oh my God!' said Shiva, empathising with the pain Sati must have felt.

'But it was worse. On the same day, her husband, who had gone to the Narmada to pray for the safe birth of their child, accidentally drowned. On that cursed day, her life was destroyed.'

Shiva stared at Brahaspati, too stunned to react.

'She became a widow and was declared a vikarma on the same day.'

'But how can the husband's death be considered her fault?' argued Shiva. 'That's completely ridiculous.'

'She wasn't declared a vikarma because of her husband's death. It was because she gave birth to a stillborn child.'

'But that could be due to any reason. The local doctors could have made a mistake.'

'That doesn't happen in Meluha, Shiva,' said Brahaspati calmly. 'Giving birth to a stillborn child is probably one of the worst ways in which a woman can become a vikarma. Only giving birth to a Naga child would be considered worse. Thank God that didn't happen. Because then she would have been completely ostracised from society.'

'This has to be changed. The concept of vikarma is unfair.'

Brahaspati looked at his friend intensely. 'You might save the vikarma, Shiva. But how do you save a woman who doesn't want to be saved? She genuinely believes that she deserves this punishment.'

'Why? I'm sure she is not the first Meluhan woman to give birth to a stillborn. There must have been others before her. And there will be many more after her.'

'She was the first *royal* woman to give birth to a stillborn. Her fate has been a source of embarrassment to the emperor. It raises questions about his ancestry.'

'How would it raise questions about his lineage? Sati is not his birth daughter. She would also have come from Maika, right?'

'No, my friend. That law was relaxed for families of nobility around two hundred and fifty years back. Apparently in the "national interest", noble families were allowed to keep their birth-children. Some laws can be amended, provided ninety per cent of the Brahmins,

Kshatriyas and Vaishyas above a particular chosen-tribe and job status vote for the change. There have been rare instances of such unanimity. This was one of them. Only one man opposed this change.'

'Who?'

'Lord Satyadhwaj, the grandfather of Parvateshwar. Their family vowed not to have any birth children after this law was passed. Parvateshwar honours that promise to this day.'

'But if the birth law could be changed,' said Shiva working things out, 'why couldn't the law of vikarma?'

'Because there aren't enough noble families affected by that law. That is the harsh truth.'

'But all this goes completely against Lord Ram's teachings!'

'Lord Ram's teachings also say that the concept of the vikarma is correct. Don't you want to question that?'

Shiva glanced at Brahaspati silently, before looking out at the river.

'There is nothing wrong with questioning Lord Ram's laws, my friend,' said Brahaspati. 'There were times when he himself acknowledged a higher rationale. The issue is your motive for wanting to change the law. Is it because you genuinely think that the law itself is unfair? Or is it because you are attracted to Sati and you want to remove an inconvenient law which stands in your path?'

'I genuinely think the vikarma law is unfair. I have felt it from the moment I found out about it. Even before I knew Sati was a vikarma.'

'But Sati doesn't think that the law is unfair.'

'She is a good woman. She doesn't deserve to be treated this way.'

'She is not just a good woman. She is one of the finest I have ever met. She is beautiful, honest, straight-forward, brave and intelligent — everything a man could possibly want in a woman. But you are not just another man. You are the Neelkanth.'

Shiva turned around and rested his hands on the craft's railing. He looked into the distance at the dense forest along the riverbanks as their boat glided over the water. The soothing evening breeze fanned Shiva's long locks.

'I've told you before, my friend,' said Brahaspati. 'Because of that unfortunate blue throat, every decision you take has many ramifications. You have to think many times before you act.'

It was late in the night. The royal fleet had just set sail from the city of Sutgengarh on the Indus. The emotions at Sutgengarh had erupted in the now predictable routine of exuberance at the sight of the Neelkanth. The saviour of their civilisation had finally arrived.

Their saviour, however, was in his own private hell. Sati had maintained her distance from Shiva for the last few weeks. His pain was deep, his loneliness constant.

The fleet's next port of call was the famous *Mohan Jo Daro* or the *Platform of Mohan*. The city, on the mighty Indus, was dedicated to a great philosopher-priest called Lord Mohan, who had lived in this region many thousands of years ago. Once he had met with the people of Mohan Jo Daro, Shiva expressed a desire to visit the temple of Lord Mohan. This temple stood further downstream outside the main city platform. The governor of Mohan

Jo Daro had offered to accompany the Lord Neelkanth there in a grand procession. Shiva however insisted on going alone. He felt drawn to the temple. He felt that it would offer some solutions to his troubled heart.

The temple itself was simple. Much like Lord Mohan himself. A small nondescript structure announced itself as the birthplace of the sage. The only sign of the temple's significance was the massive gates in the four cardinal directions of the compound. As instructed by Shiva, Nandi and Veerbhadra, along with their platoon, waited outside.

Shiva, with his comforting cravat back around his neck, walked up the steps feeling tranquil after a long time. He rang the bell at the entrance and sat down against a pillar with his eyes shut in quiet contemplation. Suddenly, an oddly familiar voice asked: 'How are you, my friend?'

CHAPTER 14

Pandit of Mohan Jo Daro

Shiva opened his eyes only to behold a man who seemed almost a replica of the pandit he had met at the Brahma temple, in what seemed like another life. He sported a similar long flowing white beard and a big white mane. He wore a saffron dhoti and angvastram. The wizened face wore a calm and welcoming smile. If it hadn't been for this pandit's much taller frame, Shiva could have easily mistaken him for the one he had met at the Brahma temple.

'How are you, my friend?' repeated the pandit as he sat down.

'I am alright, Pandit*ji*,' said Shiva, using the Indian term '*ji*' as a form of respect. He couldn't understand why, but the intrusion was welcome to him. It almost seemed as though he was drawn to this temple because he was destined to meet the pandit. 'Do all pandits in Meluha look alike?'

The man smiled warmly. 'Not all the pandits. Just us.'

'And who might *"us"* be, Pandit*ji*?'

'The next time you meet one of us, we will tell you,' said the Pandit cryptically. 'That is a promise.'

'Why not now?'

'At this point of time, our identity is not important,' smiled the Pandit. 'What is important is that you are disturbed about something. Do you want to talk about it?'

Shiva took a deep breath. Gut instinct told him that he could trust this man.

'There is this task that I supposedly have to do for Meluha.'

'I know. Though I wouldn't dismiss the Neelkanth's role as a "task". He does much more than that.' Pointing at Shiva's throat, the Pandit continued, 'A strip of cotton cloth cannot cover divine brilliance.'

Shiva looked up with a wry smile. 'Well, Meluha does seem like a wonderful society. And I want to do all I can to protect it from evil.'

'Then what is the problem?'

'It is that I find some grossly unfair practices in this nearly perfect society. And that this is inconsistent with the ideals that Meluha aspires to.'

'What practices are you referring to?' asked the Pandit.

'For example, the way the vikarma are treated.'

'Why is it unfair?'

'How can anyone be sure that these people committed sins in their previous birth? And that their present sufferings are a result of that? It might be sheer bad luck. Or a random act of nature.'

'You're right. It could be. But do you think that the fate of the vikarma is about them personally?'

'Isn't it?'

'No it isn't,' explained the Pandit. 'It is about the society as a whole. The vikarma acceptance of their fate is integral to the stability of Meluha.'

Shiva frowned.

'What any successful society needs, O Neelkanth, is flexibility with stability. Why would you need flexibility? Because every single person has different dreams and capabilities. The birth son of a warrior could have the talent to be a great businessman. Then society needs to be flexible enough to allow this son to change his vocation from his father's profession. Flexibility in a society allows change, so that all its members have the space to discover their true selves and grow to their potential. And if every person in a society achieves his true potential, society as a whole also achieves its true potential.'

'I agree.'

But what does this have to do with the vikarma?

'I'll come to the obvious question in a bit. Just bear with me,' said the Pandit. 'If we believe that flexibility is key to a successful society, then the Maika system is designed to achieve it in practice. No child knows what the professions of his birth-parents are. He is independent to pursue what his natural talent inspires him to do.'

'I agree. The Maika system is almost breathtakingly fair. A person can credit or blame *only himself* for what he does with his life. Nobody else. But this is about flexibility. What about stability?'

'Stability allows a person the freedom of choice, my friend. People can pursue their dreams only when they are living in a society where survival is not a daily threat. In a society without security and stability, there are no intellectuals or businessmen or artists or geniuses. Man is constantly in fight or flight mode. Nothing better than an animal. Where is the luxury then to allow ideas to be nurtured or dreams to be pursued? That is the way all humans were before we formed societies. Civilisation is very fragile. All it takes is a few decades of chaos for us to forget humanity and turn into animals. Our base natures can take over very fast. We can forget that we are sentient beings, with laws and codes and ethics.'

'I understand. The tribes in my homeland were no better than animals. They didn't even want to live a better life!'

'They didn't know a better life was possible, Neelkanth. That is the curse of constant strife. It makes us forget the most beautiful aspects of being human. That is why society must remain stable so that it is not pushed into a situation of having to fight for survival.'

'All right. But why would allowing people to achieve their potential cause instability? In fact, it should make people happier with their lives and thereby make society increasingly stable.'

'True, but only partially. People are happy when their life changes for the better. But there are two situations in which change can lead to chaos. First, when people face a change imposed by others, in situations that they cannot understand. This scares them almost as much as the fear of death. When change happens too fast, they resist it.'

'Yes, change forced by others is difficult to accept.'

'And too rapid a change causes instability. That is the bedrock of Lord Ram's way of life. There are laws which help a society change slowly and allow it to remain stable. At the same time, it allows its citizens the freedom to follow their dreams. He created an ideal balance between stability and flexibility.'

'You mentioned a second situation...'

'The second is when people *cannot* make the transition they want in order to improve their lives for reasons beyond their control. Say there is an exceptional warrior who loses his hand-eye coordination due to a disease. He is still a fighter, but not extraordinary any more. The odds are that he will be frustrated about what he perceives as injustice meted out to him. He is likely to blame his doctor, or even society at large. Many such discontented people can become a threat to society as a whole.'

Shiva frowned. He didn't like the logic. But he also knew that one of the main reasons why the Pakratis had rejected the peace offer made by his uncle years ago was because their diseased and old chief was desperate to live up to his earlier reputation of being an exceptional warrior who could have defeated the Gunas.

'Their combined rage can lead to unrest, even violence,' said the Pandit. 'Lord Ram sensed that. And that is why the concept of vikarma came into being. If you make a person believe that his misfortune in this birth is due to his sins in his previous birth, he will resign himself to his fate and not vent his fury on society at large.'

'But I disagree that ostracising the vikarma can work. It would only lead to a progressive increase in pent up anger.'

'But they are not ostracised. Their living expenses are subsidised by the government. They can still interact with family members. They are free to achieve personal excellence in their chosen fields, wherever possible. They can also fight to protect themselves. They cannot, however, be in a position to influence others. And this system has worked for one thousand years. Do you know how common rebellion was in India before Lord Ram created this empire? And most of the times, the rebellions were not led by farsighted men who thought they would create a better way of life for the common man. They were led by men discontented with their lot in life. People who were a lot like the vikarma. These rebellions usually caused chaos and decades were lost before order was restored.'

'So what you are saying is that anyone who is frustrated with life should simply resign himself to being a vikarma,' said Shiva. 'Why?'

'For the larger good of society.'

Shiva was aghast. He could not believe what he was hearing. He deeply disliked the arguments being presented to him. 'I am sorry, but I think this system is completely unfair. I have heard that almost one twentieth of the people in Meluha are vikarma. Are you going to keep so many people as outcast forever? This system needs to change.'

'You can change it. You are the Neelkanth. But remember, no system is absolutely perfect. In Lord Ram's time, a lady called Manthara triggered a series of events which led to the loss of millions of lives. She had suffered terribly due to her physical deformities. And then, fate put her in a position of influence over a powerful queen and thus over the entire kingdom. Therefore, the karma of one maladjusted victim of fate led to the mass destruction that followed. Would it not have been better for everybody if this person had been declared a vikarma? There are no easy answers. Having said that, maybe you are right. Maybe there are so many vikarma now that it can lead to a tipping point, tumble society into chaos. Do I have the solution to this problem? No. Maybe you could find it.'

Shiva turned his face away. He believed in his heart that the vikarma system was unfair.

'Are you concerned about *all* the vikarma, O Neelkanth?' asked the Pandit. 'Or just one in particular?'

— ⅄ⓄUΔ⊛ —

'What is the Lord doing in there?' asked Nandi. 'He is taking too long.'

'I don't know,' said Veerbhadra. 'All I know is that if Shiva says he needs to do something, I accept it.'

'Why do you call the Lord by his name?'

'Because that is his name!'

Nandi smiled at the simple answer and turned to look at the temple.

'Tell me Captain,' said Veerbhadra coming close to Nandi. 'Is Krittika spoken for?'

'Spoken for?'

'I mean,' continued Veerbhadra. 'Is she off limits?'

'Off limits?'

'You know what I mean,' said Veerbhadra turning beet red.

'She is a widow,' said Nandi. 'Her husband died fifteen years back.'

'Oh, that's terrible!'

'Yes, it is,' said Nandi, as he smiled at Veerbhadra. 'But to answer your question, she is "not spoken for" right now.'

— ⚹ —

'My Lady, may I say something?' asked Krittika.

Sati turned from the guest-room window to look at Krittika with a surprised frown. 'Have I ever stopped you from speaking your mind? A true Suryavanshi always speaks her mind.'

'Well,' said Krittika. 'Sometimes, it may not be so bad to lose control.'

Sati frowned even more.

Krittika spoke quickly, before her courage deserted her. 'Forget about him being the Neelkanth, my Lady. Just as a man, I think he is the finest I have seen. He is intelligent and brave, funny and kind, and worships the ground you walk on. Is that really so bad?'

Sati glared at Krittika; she didn't know if she was more upset with Krittika for what she was saying or with herself for experiencing feelings which were apparently so evident.

Krittika continued, 'Maybe, just maybe, breaking the rules can lead to happiness.'

'I am a Suryavanshi,' said Sati, her voice dropping. 'Rules are *all* that I live by. What have I got to do with happiness? Don't ever dare to speak to me about this again!'

— ⁂ —

'Yes, there is this particular vikarma,' admitted Shiva. 'But that is not why I think the vikarma law is unfair.'

'I know that,' said the Pandit. 'But I also know that what troubles you right now is your relationship with that one in particular. You don't want her to think that you would change the law, however justified you feel in doing so, just to get her. Because if Sati believes that, she will never come to you.'

'How do you know her name?' asked Shiva, flabbergasted.

'We know many things, my friend.'

'My entire life is meaningless without her.'

'I know,' smiled the Pandit. 'Perhaps I can help you.'

Shiva frowned. This was unexpected.

'You want her to reciprocate your love. But how can she when you don't even understand her?'

'I think I understand her. I love her.'

'Yes, you do love her. But you don't understand her. You don't know what she wants.'

Shiva kept quiet. He knew the Pandit was right. He was thoroughly confused about Sati.

'You can hazard a guess at what she wants,' continued the Pandit, 'with the help of the theory of transactions.'

'What?' asked a flummoxed Shiva.

'It makes up the fabric of society.'

'Excuse me, but what does this have to do with Sati?'

'Indulge me for a while, Neelkanth,' said the Pandit. 'You are aware that the cloth which has been spun into your clothes, is created when cotton threads are woven together, right?'

'Yes,' answered Shiva.

'Similarly, transactions are threads that when woven together make up a society, its culture. Or in the case of a person, they weave together his character.'

Shiva nodded.

'If you want to know the strength of a cloth, you inspect the quality of its weave. If you want to understand a person's character, look closely at his interpersonal behaviour or his transactions.'

'Alright,' said Shiva slowly, absorbing the Pandit's words. 'But transactions are...'

'I'll explain,' interrupted the Pandit. 'Transactions are interactions between two individuals. It could be trading goods, like a Shudra farmer offering grain for money from a Vaishya. But it could also be beyond material concerns, like a Kshatriya offering protection to a society in return for power.'

Shiva nodded in agreement. 'Transactions are about give and take.'

'Exactly. According to this logic, if you want something from someone, you have to give that person something he wants.'

'So what do you think she wants?' asked Shiva.

'Try and understand Sati's transactions. What do you think she wants?'

'I don't know. She is very confusing.'

'No, she isn't. There is a pattern. Think. She is probably the most eminent vikarma in history. She has the power to rebel if she wants to. She certainly has the spirit since she never backs off from a fight. But she does not rebel against the vikarma law. Neither does she fade into the background like most vikarmas and live her life in anonymity. She follows the commandments, and yet, she does not whine and complain. However unfairly life treats her, she conducts herself with dignity. Why?'

'Because she is a righteous person?'

'That she is, no doubt. But that is not the reason. Remember, in a transaction, you give something because you want something in return. She is accepting an unfair law without trying to make anyone feel guilty about it. And most importantly, she continues to use her talents to contribute to the good of society whenever she can. What do you think a person who is giving all this in her transactions with society wants in return?'

'Respect,' answered Shiva.

'Exactly!' beamed the Pandit. 'And what do you think you do when you try to *protect* such a person?'

'Disrespect her.'

'Absolutely! I know it comes naturally to you to want to protect any good person who appears to be in need. But control that feeling where Sati is concerned.

Respect her. And she will feel irresistibly drawn towards you. She gets many things from the people who love her. What she doesn't get is what she craves for the most — respect.'

Shiva looked at the Pandit with a grateful smile. He had found his answer.

Respect.

— 𐀀 —

After two weeks, the Neelkanth's convoy reached the city of Karachapa at the confluence of the Indus and the Western Sea. It was a glittering city which had long grown beyond the one platform that it had been built on. The *Dwitiya* or *second* platform, had been erected fifty years ago on an even grander scale than the first one. The Dwitiya platform was where the Karachapa elite lived. The Governor, a diminutive Vaishya called Jhooleshwar, had heard of and followed the new tradition of receiving the Neelkanth outside the city.

Karachapa, with its hundred thousand citizens, was at its heart a frontier trading city. Therefore it was an act of foresight by Lord Brahmanayak, Emperor Daksha's father, to have appointed a Vaishya as its governor over a hundred years ago. Jhooleshwar had ruled the city extraordinarily well, gilding its fate in gold. He was considered its wisest and most efficient governor ever. Karachapa had long overtaken Lothal in the eastern part of the empire to become Meluha's premier city of commerce. While foreigners such as Mesopotamians and Egyptians were allowed into this liberal city, they couldn't travel further inland without express royal permission.

Jhooleshwar escorted the Neelkanth on an excursion to the Western Sea on his very first day in Karachapa. Shiva had never seen the sea and was fascinated by the near infinite expanse of water. He spent many hours at the port where Jhooleshwar proudly expounded upon the various types of ships and vessels that were manufactured at the shipyard attached to the Karachapa port. Brahaspati accompanied them to the port in order to check on the imports he was expecting from the Mesopotamian merchants.

At the state dinner organised for Shiva, Jhooleshwar proudly announced that a *yagna*, a *ceremonial fire sacrifice*, was being organised the next day in honour of the Neelkanth, under the auspices of Lord Varun and the legendary Ashwini Kumar twins. The Ashwini Kumar twins were celebrated ancient seafarers who had navigated ocean routes from Meluha to Mesopotamia and beyond. Their maps, guidance and stories were a source of inspiration and learning for this city of seamen.

After dinner, Shiva visited the chambers where Sati and Krittika were housed.

'I was wondering,' said Shiva, still careful with Sati since she had gone back to being formal with him, 'will you be coming to the yagna tomorrow?'

'I am very sorry, Lord Neelkanth,' said Sati courteously. 'But it may not be possible for me to attend the ceremony. I am not allowed to attend such yagnas.'

Shiva was about to say that nobody would question her since she would be attending with the Neelkanth. But he thought better of it. 'Perhaps we could practice some dance tomorrow? I cannot remember the last time we had a dance session.'

'That would be nice. I have not had the benefit of your instruction in a long time,' said Sati.

Shiva nodded unhappily at Sati — the freeze in their relationship tormented him. Bidding goodbye, he turned to leave.

Krittika glanced at Sati, shaking her head imperceptibly.

CHAPTER 15

Trial by Fire

The little boy hurried through a dusty goat trail, trying to avoid the sharp stones, bundling into his fur coat. The dense, wet forest encroached upon the path menacingly. It was difficult to see beyond the trees lining the narrow path. The boy was sure that there were terrible monsters lurking in the dense foliage, waiting to pounce on him if he slowed down. His village was but a few hours away. The sun was rapidly setting behind the mountains. Monsters love the darkness — he had heard his mother and grandmother say repeatedly when he was being difficult. He would have liked being accompanied by an elder, as monsters didn't trouble the elders.

His heart skipped a beat as he heard a strange heaving sound. He immediately drew out his short sword, suspecting an attack from behind. His friends had heard many stories about the monsters of the forests. The cowards never attacked from the front.

He stood still straining to determine the direction of the sound. It had a peculiar repetitive rhythm and seemed vaguely familiar. He felt as though he had heard it before. The heaving was now accompanied by a heavy grunting male voice. This was not a monster! The boy felt excitement course through his body. He had heard his friends whisper and giggle about it, but had never seen the act himself. This was his chance!

He crept slowly into the foliage, his sword dangling by his side. He did not have to go too far when he came upon the source of the sound. It came from a small clearing. He hid behind a tree trunk and peeped.

It was a couple. They seemed to be in a hurry. They had not even disrobed completely. The man was extraordinarily hairy — almost like a bear. The boy could only see his back from this angle. He had a frontal view of the woman though. She was astonishingly beautiful! Her wavy hair was long and lustrous. The partly torn blouse revealed a firm breast, with deep red welts upon them owing to the brutal intercourse. Her skirt had been ripped apart and revealed exquisite long legs. The boy was excited beyond imagination. Wait till his best friend Bhadra heard of this!

As he enjoyed the show, his disquiet grew. Something seemed amiss. The man was in the throes of passion while the woman lay passive — almost dead. Her hands lay lifeless by her side. Her mouth was tightly shut. She was not whispering encouragements to her lover. Were those tears of ecstasy rolling down her cheeks? Or was she being forced? But how could that be? The man's knife lay within the woman's reach. She could have picked up the blade and stabbed him if she wanted.

The boy shook his head. He tried to silence his conscience. 'Just shut up. Let me look.'

And then came the moment that would haunt him for the rest of his life. The woman's eyes suddenly fell upon him.

'HELP!' she cried out, 'Please help!'

The startled boy fell back, dropping his sword. The hairy monster turned to see who the woman was calling. The boy quickly picked up his sword and fled, ignoring the searing pain on his frost-bitten foot as he ran. He was terrified by the thought of the man chasing him. He could hear the man's heavy breathing.

The boy leapt onto the goat trail and sped towards his village.

He could still hear the heavy breathing. It was drawing closer every second. The boy suddenly swerved to his left, pivoted and slashed back with his sword.

There was nobody there. No sound of heavy breathing. The only sound was the haunting plea of a distraught woman.

'Help! Please help!'

The little boy looked back. That poor woman.

'Go back! Help her!' cried his inner voice.

He hesitated for a moment. Then turned and fled towards his village.

NO! GO BACK! HELP HER!

Shiva woke up sweating, his heart pounding madly. He instinctively turned around, wanting desperately to go back to that dreadful day. To redeem himself. But there would be no redemption. The woman's terrified face came flooding back. He shut his eyes. But how do you shut your eyes to an image that is branded on your mind?

He pulled his knees up and rested his head upon them. Then he did the only thing that helped. He cried.

The yagna platform had been set up at the central square of the Dwitiya platform. For Karachapa, it was not the usual austere affair that was typical of Meluha. The frontier city had decorated the venue with bright colours that vied for attention. The platform itself had been painted in a bright golden hue. Colourfully decorated poles, festooned with flowers, held aloft a *shamiana*, a *cloth canopy*. Red and blue pennants, with the Suryavanshi symbol painted on them, hung proudly from many poles. The entire atmosphere was that of pomp and show.

Jhooleshwar received Shiva at the head of the platform

and guided him to his ritual seat at the yagna. At the governor's repeated requests, Shiva had removed his cravat for the duration of the ceremony. Parvateshwar and Brahaspati sat to the right of the Neelkanth while Jhooleshwar and Ayurvati sat to his left. Nandi and Veerbhadra had also been invited to sit behind Shiva. Though this was unorthodox, Jhooleshwar had acceded to the Neelkanth's request. Jhooleshwar governed a cosmopolitan border city and believed that many of the strict Meluhan laws could be bent slightly for the sake of expediency. His liberal attitude had made Karachapa a magnet for people from a wide variety of races and a hub for the exchange of goods, services and ideas.

Shiva looked towards Sati's balcony, which overlooked the central square in the distance. Though Sati was not allowed to step onto the platform while the yagna was being conducted, she could look on at the proceedings from the safe distance of her chambers. Shiva noticed her standing behind the balcony curtain, with Krittika by her side, observing the proceedings.

As was the custom before such a yagna, the pandit stood up and asked formally, 'If anybody here has any objection to this yagna, please speak now. Or forever hold your peace.'

This was just a traditional question, which wasn't actually supposed to be answered. Hence there was an audible, collective groan when a voice cried out loudly, 'I object.'

Nobody needed to look to recognise where the voice came from. It was Tarak, an immigrant from the ultra-conservative northwest regions of the empire. Ever since Tarak had come to Karachapa, he had taken it upon himself to be the 'moral police' of this 'decadent city of sin'.

Shiva strained his neck to see who had objections. He saw Tarak standing at the back, at the edge of the puja platform, very close to Sati's balcony. He was a giant of a man with an immense stomach, a miner's bulging muscular arms and a fair face that was cut up brutally due to a lifetime of strife. He cut an awesome figure. It was obvious, without even looking at his amulets, that Tarak was a Kshatriya who had made his living working in the lower rungs of the army.

Jhooleshwar glared at Tarak in exasperation. 'What is it now? This time we have ensured that we have not used the white Chandravanshi colours in our decorations. Or do you think the water being used for the ceremony is not at the correct temperature prescribed by the Vedas?'

The gathering sniggered. Parvateshwar looked at Jhooleshwar sharply. Before he could reprimand the Governor for his cavalier reference to the Vedas, Tarak spoke up. 'The law says no vikarma should be allowed on the yagna platform.'

'Yes,' said Jhooleshwar. 'And unless you have been declared a vikarma, I don't think that law is being broken.'

'Yes it is!'

There were shocked murmurs from the congregation. Jhooleshwar raised his hand.

'Nobody is a vikarma here, Tarak,' said Jhooleshwar. 'Now please sit down.'

'Princess Sati defiles the yagna with her presence.'

Shiva and Parvateshwar looked sharply at Tarak. Jhooleshwar was as stunned as the rest of the assembly by Tarak's statement. 'Tarak!' said Jhooleshwar. 'You go too far. Princess Sati is confined to the guest-house, abiding by the laws of the yagna. She is not present on the yagna platform. Now sit down before I have you whipped.'

'On what charge will you have me whipped, Governor?' yelled Tarak. 'Standing up for the law is not a crime in Meluha.'

'But the law has not been broken!'

'Yes it has. The exact words of the law is that no vikarma can be on the same platform while a yagna is being conducted. The yagna is being conducted on the Dwitiya platform of the city. By being on the same platform, the princess defiles the yagna.'

Tarak was technically correct. Most people interpreted that law to mean that a vikarma could not be on the *prayer ceremony platform.* However, since Karachapa, like most Meluhan cities, was built on a platform, a strict interpretation of the law would mean that Sati should not be anywhere on the *entire Dwitiya platform.* To keep the yagna legal, she would either have to move to the other platform of the city or outside the city walls.

Jhooleshwar was momentarily taken aback as Tarak's objection was accurate in principle. He tried a weak rally. 'Come, come Tarak. You are being too conscientious. I think that is too strict an interpretation. I think…'

'No, Shri Jhooleshwar*ji*,' reverberated a loud voice through the gathering.

Everybody turned to see where the sound came from. Sati, who had come out on her balcony, continued. 'Please accept my apologies for interrupting you, Governor,' said Sati with a formal Namaste. 'But Tarak's interpretation of the law is fair. I am terribly sorry to have disturbed the yagna. My entourage and I shall leave the city immediately. We will return by the beginning of the third prahar, by which time the ceremony should be over.'

Shiva clenched his fist. He frantically wanted to wring Tarak's neck but he controlled himself with superhuman effort. Within minutes Sati was out of the guest-house, along with Krittika and five personal bodyguards. Shiva turned to look at Nandi and Veerbhadra, both of whom rose to join Sati. They understood that Shiva wanted them to ensure her safety outside the city.

'It is disgusting that you did not realise this yourself,' Tarak said scornfully to Sati. 'What kind of a princess are you? Don't you respect the law?'

Sati looked at Tarak. Her face calm. She refused to be drawn into a debate and waited patiently for her guards to prepare the horses.

'I don't understand what a vikarma woman is doing travelling with the convoy of the Neelkanth. She is polluting the entire journey,' raged Tarak.

'Enough!' intervened Shiva. 'Princess Sati is leaving with dignity. Stop your diatribe right now.'

'I will not!' screeched Tarak. 'What kind of a leader are you? You are challenging Lord Ram's laws.'

'Tarak!' yelled Jhooleshwar. 'The Lord Neelkanth has the right to challenge the law. If you value your life, you will not defy his authority.'

'I am a Meluhan,' shrieked Tarak. 'It is my right to challenge anyone breaking the law. A *dhobi,* a mere *washerman,* challenged Lord Ram. It was his greatness that he acceded to the man's objection and renounced his wife. I would urge the Neelkanth to learn from Lord Ram's example and use his brain while making decisions.'

'ENOUGH TARAK!' erupted Sati.

The entire congregation was stunned into silence by Tarak's remark. But not Sati. Something inside her snapped. She had tolerated too many insults for too long. And she had endured them with quiet dignity. But this time, this man had insulted Shiva. *Her* Shiva, she finally acknowledged to herself.

'I invoke the right of *Agnipariksha*,' said Sati, back in control.

The stunned onlookers could not believe their ears. *A trial by fire!*

This was getting worse by the minute. Agnipariksha, a duel unto death, enabled a contestant to challenge an unjust tormentor. It was called Agnipariksha as combat would be conducted within a ring of fire. There was no escape from the ring. The duellists had to keep fighting till one person either surrendered or died. An Agnipariksha was extremely rare these days. And for a woman to invoke the right was almost unheard of.

'There is no reason for this, my lady,' pleaded Jhooleshwar. Just like his subjects, he was terrified that Princess Sati might be killed in his city. The gargantuan Tarak would certainly slay her. The Emperor's wrath would be terrible. Turning to Tarak, Jhooleshwar ordered, 'You will not accept this challenge.'

'And be called a coward?'

'You want to prove your bravery?' spoke Parvateshwar for the first time. 'Then fight me. I will act as Sati's second for the challenge.'

'Only I have the right to appoint a second, *pitratulya*,' said Sati, reverentially referring to Parvateshwar as being '*like a father*'. Turning to Tarak, she said, 'I am appointing no second. You will fight with me.'

'You will do no such thing Tarak,' Brahaspati objected this time.

'Tarak, the only reason you won't fight is if you are afraid of being killed,' said Shiva.

Every person turned towards the Neelkanth, shocked by his words. Turning to Sati, Shiva continued, 'Citizens of Karachapa, I have seen the Princess fight. She can defeat anyone. Even the Gods.'

Sati stared at Shiva, shocked.

'I accept the challenge,' growled Tarak.

Sati nodded at Tarak, climbed on her white steed and turned to leave. At the edge of the square, she pulled up her horse and turned to take one more look at Shiva. She smiled at him, turned and rode away.

It was the beginning of the third prahar when Shiva and Brahaspati stole quietly into the local *varjish graha*, the *exercise hall*, to observe Tarak exercising along with two partners. The day's yagna had been a disaster. With everyone petrified that the princess would die the next day, no one was inclined to participate in the ceremony. However, as the yagna had been called, it had to be conducted or the Gods would be offended. The congregation went through the motions and the yagna was called to a close.

Tarak's famed fearsome blows on his hapless partners filled Brahaspati's soul with dread and he came to an immediate decision. 'I'll assassinate him tonight. She will not die tomorrow.'

Shiva turned in stunned disbelief towards the chief scientist. 'Brahaspati? What are you saying?'

'Sati is too noble to meet a fate such as this. I am willing to sacrifice my life and reputation for her.'

'But you are a Brahmin. You are not supposed to kill.'

'I'll do it for you,' whispered Brahaspati, emotions clouding his judgement. 'You will not lose her, my friend.'

Shiva came close to Brahaspati and hugged him. 'Don't corrupt your soul, my friend. I am not worth such a big sacrifice.'

Brahaspati clung to Shiva.

Stepping back, Shiva whispered, 'In any case, your sacrifice is not required. For as sure as the sun rises in the east, Sati will defeat Tarak tomorrow.'

— ⅄ⓞ⊍⇡⊛ —

A few hours into the third prahar, Sati returned to the guest house. She did not go up to her room, but summoned Nandi and Veerbhadra to the central courtyard, drew her sword and began her practise with them.

A little later Parvateshwar walked in, looking broken. His expression clearly conveyed his fear that this might be the last time he would talk to Sati. She stopped practising, sheathed her sword and folded her hands into a respectful Namaste. 'Pitratulya,' she whispered.

Parvateshwar came close to Sati, his face distraught. She could not be sure but it seemed as though he had been crying. She had never seen even a hint of a tear in his confident eyes. 'My child,' mumbled Parvateshwar.

'I am doing what I think is right,' said Sati. 'I am happy.'

Parvateshwar couldn't find the strength to say anything. For a brief moment, he considered assassinating Tarak at night. But that would be illegal.

Just then, Shiva and Brahaspati walked in. Shiva noticed Parvateshwar's face. This was the first time he had seen any sign of weakness in the General. While he could understand Parvateshwar's predicament, he did not like the effect it was having on Sati.

'I am sorry I am late,' said Shiva cheerily.

Everyone turned to look at him.

'Actually, Brahaspati and I had gone to the Lord Varun temple to pray for Tarak,' said Shiva. 'We prayed that the journey his soul would take to the other world would be comfortable.'

Sati burst out laughing. So did the rest of the party in the courtyard.

'Bhadra, you are not the right opponent for the practise,' said Shiva. 'You move too fast. Nandi you duel with the princess. And control your agility.'

Turning to Sati, Shiva continued, 'I saw Tarak practise. His blows have tremendous power. But the force of the blows slows him down. Turn his strength into his weakness. Use your agility against his movements.'

Sati nodded, absorbing every word. She resumed her practise with Nandi. Moving rapidly compared to Nandi's slower movements, Sati was able to succeed in a strike that could kill.

Suddenly, an idea struck Shiva. Instructing Nandi to stop, he asked Sati, 'Are you allowed to choose the combat weapon?'

'Yes. It's my prerogative as I threw the challenge.'

'Then choose the knife. It will reduce the reach of his strikes while you would be able to move in and out much quicker.'

'That's brilliant!' concurred Parvateshwar, while Brahaspati nodded.

Sati signalled her agreement immediately. Almost at the

same instant, Veerbhadra emerged with two knives. Giving one to Nandi, he gave the other to Sati. 'Practise, my Lady.'

— ⋆ —

Sati and Tarak stood at the centre of a circular stadium. This was not the main Rangbhoomi of Karachapa, which was huge in its proportions. This one had been constructed next to the main stadium, for music concerts that the Mesopotamian immigrants in Karachapa loved. The arena was of the exact dimensions required for an agnipariksha. Not so big that a person could simply steer clear of the other contestant and not too small so that the combat would end too soon. There were stands around the ground and a capacity crowd of over twenty thousand had come to watch the most important duel in Karachapa for the last five hundred years.

A silent prayer sprang to every lip. Work a miracle, O Father Manu, let Princess Sati win. Or at the very least, live. Both Tarak and Sati greeted each other with a Namaste, repeating an ancient pledge to fight with honour. Then, turning towards the statue of Lord Varun at the top of the main stand, they bowed and asked for blessings from the God of the Water and the Seas. Jhooleshwar had vacated his ceremonial seat right below the statue of Lord Varun for Shiva. The governor sat to Shiva's left with Ayurvati and Krittika to his left. Brahaspati and Parvateshwar sat to Shiva's right. Nandi and Veerbhadra were in their now familiar position, behind Shiva. A bird courier had been sent to Daksha the previous day, informing him of the duel. However, there wasn't enough time to expect a reply.

At long last, Jhooleshwar stood up. He was nervous

about the agnipariksha, but appeared composed. In keeping with the custom, he raised a balled fist to his heart and boomed: *'Satya! Dharma! Maan!'* An invocation to *Truth. Duty. Honour.*

The rest of the stadium rang in agreement. 'Satya! Dharma! Maan!'

Tarak and Sati echoed. 'Satya! Dharma! Maan!'

Jhooleshwar nodded to the stadium keeper who lit the ceremonial oil lamp with the holy fire. The lamp spilled its fire on to the oil channel; the periphery of the central ground was aflame. The ring for the pariksha had been set.

Jhooleshwar turned to Shiva. 'My Lord, your instructions to begin the duel.'

Shiva looked at Sati with a confident smile. Then turning to the stadium, he declared loudly, 'Truth will always triumph in the purifying fire of Lord Agni!'

Tarak and Sati immediately drew their knives. Tarak held his knife in front of him, like most traditional fighters. He had chosen a strategy that played to his strengths. Keeping his knife in front of him allowed him to strike the moment Sati came close. He did not stir too much, allowing Sati to make her moves in front of him.

Sati, breaking all known rules of combat, held her knife behind her. She shifted the knife continuously from one hand to the other, while keeping a safe distance from her opponent. The aim was to confuse Tarak about the direction of her attack. Tarak on the other hand was watching Sati's movements like a hawk. He saw her right arm flex. The knife was now in her right hand.

Suddenly Sati leapt to the left. Tarak remained stationary. He knew that with her right hand holding the knife, the leftward movement was a feint. She would have to move to the right to bring her knife into play. Sure enough, moving quickly to the right, Sati swung her stabbing arm in an arc at Tarak's torso. But Tarak was prepared. Shifting his knife quickly to his left hand, he slashed viciously, cutting Sati across her torso. It wasn't a deep cut, but it appeared to hurt. The audience let out a collective gasp.

Sati retreated and rallied. She moved the knife to her back again, transferring it from one hand to the other. Tarak kept a close eye on her arms. The knife was in her left hand. He expected her to move to the right, which she did. He remained immobile, waiting for her to swerve suddenly to her left. She did, swinging her left arm as she moved. Tarak acted before her arm could even come close enough to do any damage. He swung ferociously with his right arm and cut her deep in the left shoulder. Sati retreated rapidly as the congregation moaned in horror. Some shut their eyes. They could not bear to look anymore. Most were praying fervently. If it had to be done, let it be done swiftly and not in a slow painful manner.

'What is she doing?' whispered a panic-stricken Brahaspati to Shiva. 'Why is she charging in so recklessly?'

Shiva turned to look at Brahaspati, also noticing Parvateshwar's face. Parvateshwar had a surprised, yet admiring grin on his face. Unlike Brahaspati, he knew what was going on. Turning back to look at the duel, Shiva whispered, 'She's laying a trap.'

At the centre, Sati was still transferring the knife between her hands behind her back. She feigned a move from her right to the left, but this time did not transfer the knife. She flexed her left arm, keeping the right arm holding the knife loose and relaxed.

Tarak was watching Sati closely, confident that he

was going to slowly bleed her to death. He believed the knife was in her left hand. He waited for her to move to the right, and then to the left, which she did in a swift veer. Expecting her left arm to come in, he sliced with his right hand. Sati neatly pirouetted back. Before a surprised Tarak could react, Sati had leapt to her right and brought her right hand in brutally onto his chest. The knife pierced Tarak's lung. The shock of the blow immobilised him. Blood spurted from his mouth. He dropped his knife and staggered back. Sati ruthlessly maintained the pressure and dug the knife in deeper, right up to the hilt.

Tarak stumbled back and collapsed onto the ground, motionless. The entire stadium was stunned. Sati's face had the expression of the Mother Goddess in fury. Eighty-five years of repressed anger had surfaced in that instant. She pulled the knife out, slowly twisting it to inflict maximum damage. Blood spewed out from Tarak's mouth at an alarming rate. Gripping the knife in both hands she raised her arms, aiming at Tarak's heart for a quick kill. Unexpectedly though, her expression then transformed from rage to serenity. It was almost as if someone had sucked out all the negative energy from within her. She turned around. Shiva, the destroyer of evil, sat on his throne, staring at her with a slight smile.

Then she looked at Tarak, and whispered. 'I forgive you.'

The stadium erupted in joy. Even if Lord Varun himself had scripted the fight, it wouldn't have been so perfect. It had everything that the Suryavanshis held dear. Defiant when under pressure, yet magnanimous in victory.

Sati raised her knife and shouted, 'Jai Shri Ram!'

The entire stadium repeated, 'Jai Shri Ram!'

Sati turned towards Shiva and roared once again, 'Jai Shri Ram!'

'Jai…,' Shiva's words were clogged by the knot in his throat.

The Lord won't mind this time if I don't complete the cry.

Shiva glanced away from Sati, lest he show his tears to the woman he loved. Regaining control of himself, he looked back at her with a radiant smile. Sati continued to stare at Shiva. Emotions that had been dormant in her for too long rippled through her being as she saw Shiva's admiration. When she couldn't bear it any longer, she shut her eyes.

CHAPTER 16

The Sun and Earth

There was an impromptu celebration that night in Karachapa. Their princess was safe. The insufferable Tarak had been defeated. Many people in Karachapa believed that even his own mother must have loathed the surly preacher. He had few supporters in the liberal city. But there were rules for duels. Hence the moment Sati had forgiven Tarak, paramedics had rushed in to take him to the hospital. Surgeons had laboured for six hours to save his life. Much to the dismay of the town folk, they had succeeded.

'Have you heard about the poem of the sun and the earth?' Sati asked Shiva.

They were standing on the balcony of the governor's palace while a boisterous party raged inside.

'No,' said Shiva with a seductive grin, coming a little closer to her. 'But I'd love to hear it.'

'Apparently the earth sometimes thinks of the possibility of coming closer to the sun,' said Sati. 'But she can't do that. She is so base and his brilliance so searing, that she will cause destruction if she draws him closer.'

What now?

'I disagree,' said Shiva. 'I think the sun burns for only as long as the earth is close to him. If the earth wasn't there, there would be no reason for the sun to exist.'

'The sun doesn't exist merely for the earth. It exists for every single planet in the solar system.'

'Isn't it really upto the sun to determine whom he chooses to exist for?'

'No,' said a melancholic Sati, looking at Shiva. 'The moment he becomes the sun, he answers a higher calling. He does not exist for himself. He exists for the greater good. His luminosity is the lifeblood of the solar system. And if the earth has any sense of responsibility, she will not do anything to destroy this balance.'

'So what should the sun do?' asked Shiva, his hurt and anger showing on his face. 'Just waste his entire life burning away? Looking at the earth from a distance?'

'The earth isn't going anywhere. The sun and the earth can still share a warm friendship. But anything more is against the laws. It is against the interests of others.'

Shiva turned away from Sati in anger. He looked northward to seek solace from his holy lake. Feeling nothing, he looked up at the skies, towards the Gods he did not believe in.

Dammit!

His clenched fist struck the balcony railing powerfully, dislodging some bricks before he stormed off.

— ⁂ —

Outside the city walls, in a forested area, a few soldiers lay in wait. At a slight distance, two hooded figures were seated on large rocks. The Captain of the platoon of soldiers stood rigid in attention next to the duo. He scarce believed that he was standing next to the Queen herself. The privilege overwhelmed him.

One of the hooded figures raised his hand to motion for the Captain to step closer. On the hooded figure's wrist was a leather bracelet with the serpent Aum. 'Vishwadyumna, are you sure this is where we are supposed to meet him? He is late by nearly an hour.'

'Yes, my Lord,' replied Vishwadyumna nervously. 'This is exactly where he had said he would come.'

The other hooded figure turned and spoke in a commanding voice — a feminine one. A voice used to being obeyed without question. 'That man makes the Queen of the Nagas wait!' Turning to the other hooded figure, she continued, 'I trust you have worked this out in detail. I hope I haven't entered this vile territory in vain.'

The other hooded figure moved his fleshy hands in a motion asking the Queen for patience. 'Have faith, your Highness. This man is our key to giving the Suryavanshis a blow that they will never recover from.'

'Apparently, there was an Agnipariksha fight between the princess and a man in the city yesterday,' said Vishwadyumna suddenly, trying to impress the Queen with his sharp ear for local knowledge. 'I do not have the exact details. I just hope that our man was not involved in it.'

The Queen turned swiftly to the other hooded figure. Then back to Vishwadyumna. 'Please wait with the other soldiers.'

Vishwadyumna sensed he had said something he shouldn't have and quickly retreated before his Lord's stern gaze could reprimand him. This is why he had been told in training school that a good soldier never speaks unless spoken to.

'*She's* here?' asked the Queen with barely suppressed anger.

The other hooded figure nodded.

'I thought I'd told you to forget about this,' said the Queen sternly. 'There is nothing to be gained by this quest. Do you realise that your stupid attack on Mount Mandar might have led them to suspect that we have a mole in their midst?'

The male figure looked up in apology.

'Did you come here for her?'

'No, your Highness,' said the hooded figure with a deeply respectful tone. 'This was the place where he asked us to meet him.'

The Queen reached her hand out and gently patted the man's shoulder. 'Stay focussed, my child,' said the Queen softly. 'If we pull this off, it will be our biggest victory ever. Like you just said, we will strike a blow that they will find very difficult to recover from.'

The man nodded.

'And yet,' continued the Queen, pulling her hand back into the shelter of her black robes, 'your preoccupation with her provokes you into making uncharacteristic decisions. Are you aware of his clear message that she cannot be touched? Otherwise, the deal is off.'

The hooded figure stared at the Queen in surprise. 'How did you...'

'I am the Queen of the Nagas, my child,' she interrupted. 'I have more than one piece on the chessboard.'

The hooded figure continued to look at the Queen, ashamed about his poor call at Mount Mandar. The

Queen's next words added to his shame. 'You are making surprising mistakes, my child. You have the potential to be the greatest Naga ever. Don't waste it.'

'Yes, your Highness.'

The Queen appeared to relax.

'I think when we are alone now,' said the Queen, 'maybe you can call me *Mausi*. After all I am *your mother's sister*.'

'Of course, you are,' said the hooded figure as a smile reached his eyes. 'Whatever you say, mausi.'

— ⚹ —

It had been two weeks since the Agnipariksha. Sati had recovered sufficiently for the convoy to continue its journey to its next destination. Shiva, Parvateshwar and Brahaspati sat together in Shiva's chambers at the guest-house.

'It's agreed then,' said Parvateshwar. 'I will make the arrangements for us to commence our journey a week from today. By that time, Sati should have recovered completely.'

'Yes, I think that is a suitable plan,' agreed Shiva.

'Parvateshwar, I will not be accompanying you any further,' said Brahaspati.

'Why?' asked Parvateshwar.

'Well, the new chemicals that I had ordered have arrived. I was considering going back with the consignment to Mount Mandar so that the experiments can begin as soon as possible. If we can get this right then the consumption of water for making the Somras will reduce drastically.'

Shiva smiled sadly. 'I am going to miss you my friend.'

'And I you,' said Brahaspati. 'But I am not leaving

the country. When you finish your tour, come to Mount Mandar. I'll take you around the sylvan forests near our facility.'

'Yes,' said Shiva with a grin. 'Perhaps you will reveal some of your scientific skills and discover a plausible explanation for the blue throat!'

Both Shiva and Brahaspati burst out laughing. Parvateshwar, who did not understand the private joke, looked on politely.

'Just one point, Brahaspati,' said Parvateshwar. 'I will not be able to divert any soldiers from the royal entourage. I will speak with Governor Jhooleshwar about sending some soldiers along with you on your return journey.'

'Thank you, Parvateshwar. But I am sure I will be fine. Why should a terrorist be interested in me?'

'There was another terrorist attack yesterday in a village some fifty kilometres from Mohan Jo Daro,' said Parvateshwar. 'The entire temple was destroyed and all the Brahmins killed.'

'Another one,' said Shiva, angered. 'That is the third attack this month!'

'Yes,' said Parvateshwar. 'They are getting bolder. And as usual, they escaped before any back-up could arrive to give them a real fight.'

Shiva clenched his fists. He had no idea how to counter the terror attacks. There was no way in which one could prepare for them since nobody knew where they would strike next. Was attacking Swadweep, the Chandravanshi's own country, the only way to stop this? Brahaspati kept quiet, sensing Shiva's inner turmoil. He knew there were no easy answers.

Looking at Shiva, Parvateshwar continued, 'I will also

get my people to make preparations for our journey. I'll meet you in the evening for dinner. I think Sati can finally join us. I will send instructions for Nandi and Veerbhadra to also join us. I know you like their company.'

Shiva was startled by Parvateshwar's uncharacteristic thoughtfulness. 'Thank you Parvateshwar. This is very kind of you. But I believe Krittika, Nandi and Veerbhadra are going to a flute recital tonight. That crazy Veerbhadra has even bought some jewels so that he won't look like a country bumpkin next to Nandi!'

Parvateshwar smiled politely.

'But it will be a pleasure to dine with you,' said Shiva.

'Thank you,' said Parvateshwar as he got up. After a few steps, he stopped and turned around. Overcoming his hesitation, he mumbled. 'Shiva!'

'Yes?' Shiva got up.

'I don't think we've talked about this,' said Parvateshwar, uncomfortable. 'But I would like to thank you for helping Sati in her agnipariksha. It was your clear thinking which led to victory.'

'No, no,' said Shiva. 'It was her brilliance.'

'Of course it was,' said Parvateshwar. 'But you gave her the confidence and the strategy to show her brilliance. If there is any person in the world that I relate to with a feeling beyond a sense of duty, it is Sati. I thank you for helping her.'

'You are welcome,' smiled Shiva, with enough sense to not embarrass Parvateshwar further by lengthening this conversation.

Parvateshwar smiled and folded his hands into a Namaste. While he had still not fallen prey to the country-wide 'Neelkanth fever', he was beginning to respect Shiva.

Earning Parvateshwar's esteem was a long journey that Shiva had only just begun. The General turned around and walked out of the room.

'He is not a bad sort,' said Brahaspati, looking at Parvateshwar's retreating back. 'He may be a little surly. But he is one of the most honest Suryavanshis I have ever met. A true follower of Lord Ram. I hope you don't get too upset by the ill-tempered things he says to you.'

'I don't,' said Shiva. 'In fact, I think very highly of Parvateshwar. He is one man whose respect I would certainly like to earn.'

Brahaspati smiled seeing yet another instance of Shiva's large heart. He leaned closer and said, 'You are a good man.'

Shiva smiled back.

'I had not answered you the last time you had asked me, Shiva,' continued Brahaspati. 'Honestly, I have never believed in the legend of the Neelkanth. I still don't.'

Shiva's smile became a little broader.

'But I believe in you. If there is one person capable of sucking the negative energy out of this land, I think it will be you. And I will do all I can to help you. In whatever way I can.'

'You are the brother I never had Brahaspati. Your mere presence is all the help I need.'

Saying so Shiva embraced his friend. Brahaspati hugged Shiva back warmly, feeling a sense of renewed energy course through him. He swore once again that he would never back off from his mission. No matter what. It wasn't just for Meluha. It was also for Shiva. His friend.

— ⋏◎Ʊ✦⊛ —

Over three weeks after Sati's agnipariksha the seven-carriage convoy set off from Karachapa. Moving in a column, six of them were dummies as compared to the usual five. In the third carriage Shiva sat with Sati along with Parvateshwar and Ayurvati. It was the first time that Parvateshwar was travelling in the same carriage as Shiva. Krittika had volunteered to ride, claiming that she was missing the scenic beauty of the countryside. Veerbhadra was more than pleased to ride along with her in Nandi's platoon.

They had journeyed just a few days away from Karachapa when the convoy was brought to a halt by a large caravan travelling hurriedly in the opposite direction. Parvateshwar stepped out of the carriage to inquire. Brigadier Vraka came up to Parvateshwar and executed a military salute.

'What is the matter?'

'My Lord, they are refugees from the village of Koonj,' said Vraka. 'They are escaping a terrorist attack.'

'Escaping!' asked a surprised Parvateshwar. 'You mean the attack is still on?'

'I think so, my Lord,' said Vraka, his face filled with rage.

'Goddamit!' swore Parvateshwar. Neither Meluha nor he had ever got an opportunity like this. To be present at the right time and right place with a thousand five hundred soldiers while a terrorist attack was in progress. And yet, Parvateshwar's hands were tied. He was not allowed to take on any mission except to protect the Neelkanth and the Princess.

'What nonsense,' he thought to himself. 'My orders forbid me from following my Kshatriya dharma!'

'What's the matter, Parvateshwar?'

Parvateshwar turned to find Shiva right behind him. Sati and Ayurvati were getting out of the carriage as well. Before Parvateshwar could answer, a horrible noise tore through the quiet forest road. It was a sound Shiva had come to recognise. It declared the evil intentions of the conch-shell bearer, loud and clear. It announced that an attack had begun. A Naga attack had begun!

CHAPTER 17

The Battle of Koonj

'Where are they?' asked Parvateshwar.

'They are in my village, my Lord,' said the scared village headman. 'It's a short distance from here. Some five hundred Chandravanshi soldiers, led by five Nagas. They gave us thirty minutes to leave. But the Brahmins at the temple were detained.'

Parvateshwar clenched his fists to regain his control despite his fury.

'Our Pandit*ji* is a good man, my Lord,' said the village headman. Tears streamed out of his eyes. Vraka put a comforting hand on the headman's shoulder. But the gesture only made the headman even more miserable. Not knowing the fate of the village priest added to his guilt.

'We wanted to stay and fight alongside our Pandit and the other Brahmins,' sobbed the headman. 'They are men of God. They don't even know how to raise a weapon. How can they fight against this horde?'

Vraka let go of the headman as anger got the better of him.

'But Pandit*ji* ordered us to leave. He told us to flee with our women and children. He said he would face whatever

Lord Brahma has written in his fate. But if anyone deserves to be saved, it is them.'

Parvateshwar's nails dug into his skin. He was livid at the cowardly Chandravanshis for yet again attacking defenceless Brahmins and not Kshatriyas who could retaliate. He was incensed with his fate for having put him in a position where he could not take action. A part of him wanted to ignore his orders. But he was bound not to break the law.

'THIS NONSENSE HAS TO STOP!'

Parvateshwar looked up to see which voice had echoed his thoughts. The expression on Shiva's face almost rocked him back on his feet for a moment. The intense fury visible in the Neelkanth would have brought even a Deva to a standstill.

'We are good people,' raged Shiva. 'We are not scared chicken who should turn and flee! Those terrorists should be on the run. They should be the ones feeling the wrath of the Suryavanshis!'

A villager standing behind the headman said, 'But they are terrorists! We cannot defeat them. The Pandit*ji* knew it. That is why he ordered us to run.'

'But we have a thousand five hundred soldiers,' said Shiva, irritated with the display of such cowardice. 'And there are another five hundred of you. We outnumber them four to one. We can crush them. Teach them a lesson they will remember.'

The headman argued. 'But they have Nagas! They are supernatural, blood-thirsty killers! What chance do we have against such evil?'

Shiva had the presence of mind to realise that superstition can only be countered by another stronger belief. He climbed the carriage pedestal to stand tall. The villagers stared at him. He ripped off his cravat and threw it away. He didn't need it anymore.

'I am the Neelkanth!'

All the soldiers looked up mesmerised at the destroyer of evil. They were overjoyed to see him truly accept his destiny. Those ignorant of the Neelkanth's arrival beheld the living legend in a daze.

'I am going to fight these terrorists,' roared Shiva. 'I am going to show them that we are not scared anymore. I am going to make them feel the pain we feel. I am going to let them know that Meluha is not going to roll over and let them do what they want.'

Pure energy coursed through the huddled mass that stood in front of Shiva, straightening their spines and inspiring their souls.

'Who's coming with me?'

'I am,' bellowed Parvateshwar, feeling the suffocating restraints imposed on him fall away by Shiva's pronouncement.

'I am,' echoed Sati, Nandi, Veerbhadra and Vraka.

'I am,' echoed every single soul standing there.

Suddenly the scared villagers and soldiers were transformed into a righteous army. The soldiers drew their swords. The villagers grabbed whatever weapons they could from the travelling armoury.

'To Koonj,' yelled Shiva, mounting a horse and galloping ahead.

Parvateshwar and Sati quickly unharnessed the horses from the cart and raced behind Shiva. The Suryavanshis charged behind them, letting out a cry louder than any Naga conch shell. As they stormed into Koonj, the horror of what had transpired hit them. The Chandravanshis had ignored the rest of the village and concentrated on the area that would distress the Meluhans the most — their venerated temple. Decapitated bodies of the Brahmins lay around the shrine. They had been gathered together and executed. The temple itself was ruthlessly destroyed and set aflame. The gruesome sight enraged the Suryavanshis. They charged like crazed bulls. The Chandravanshis stood no chance. They were completely outnumbered and overwhelmed. They lost ground quickly. Just as the Chandravanshis began to retreat the five Nagas rallied them around. Against crushing odds, the Nagas grimly fought the righteous Suryavanshis with unexpected grit.

Parvateshwar fought like a man possessed. Shiva, who had never seen the General battle, was impressed with his skill and valour. Like Shiva, Parvateshwar knew that the key to victory were the Nagas. As long as they were alive, the Suryavanshis would feel terrified and the Chandravanshis would draw inspiration from them. He attacked one of them with frenzied aggression.

The Naga skilfully parried Parvateshwar's attack with his shield. Bringing his sword down, he tried to strike Parvateshwar's exposed shoulder. What he didn't know was that Parvateshwar had deliberately left his flank exposed. Swinging to the side to avoid the blow, Parvateshwar let his shield clap to his back as he swiftly drew a knife held in a clip behind. He hurled it at the Naga's exposed right shoulder. His cry told Parvateshwar that the knife had penetrated deep.

The injured Naga roared in defiant fury. To Parvateshwar's utter amazement, he swung his sword arm – with the knife still buried in his shoulder - and brought it back into play with an agonising grunt. Parvateshwar brought his shield back up and blocked the slightly weaker strike from the Naga. He brought his sword up in a stab but the Naga was too quick and deflected it. Swerving left, Parvateshwar rammed his shield down hard on the knife still buried in the Naga's shoulder. The knife chipped through the shoulder bone. The Naga snarled in pain and stumbled. That was the opening that Parvateshwar needed. Bringing his sword up in a brutal upward stab, he pushed it ruthlessly through the Naga's heart. The Naga froze as Parvateshwar's sword ripped the life out of him. Parvateshwar pushed his sword in deeper, completing the kill. The Naga fell back motionless.

Parvateshwar was not above the Meluhan fascination with a Naga face. He knelt down and tore the Naga's mask off to reveal a horrifying countenance. The Naga's nose was pure bone and had grown to almost form a bird-like beak. His ears were ridiculously large while his mouth was grotesquely constricted. He looked like a vulture in human form. Parvateshwar quickly whispered what every Suryavanshi said when he brought down a worthy opponent, 'Have a safe journey to the other side, brave warrior.'

One down four to go, thought Parvateshwar rising. Correction, two down, three to go. He saw Shiva bring down a gigantic Naga in the distance. Both Shiva and Parvateshwar looked at each other and nodded. Shiva pointed towards Parvateshwar's back. Parvateshwar turned to see a ferocious Naga fighting five Suryavanshis singlehandedly. He turned back to look at Shiva and nodded. Shiva turned to charge at another Naga as Parvateshwar turned towards the one marked for him.

Shiva dashed through the pitched battle scene towards the Naga who had just killed a Suryavanshi soldier. He leapt high as he ran in close, with his shield in front to prevent a swinging strike. The Naga had brought his own shield up to prevent what he expected from Shiva — the orthodox up to down swinging strike from a good height. Shiva, however, surprised him by thrusting in his sword sideward, neatly circumventing the Naga's shield and gashing his arm. The Naga bellowed in pain and fell back. He straightened and held his shield high again, realising that Shiva was going to be a much more formidable enemy.

As Shiva grimly fought the fearless Naga, he did not notice another one at a distance. This Naga could see that their assault was being progressively pushed back. It was a matter of time before the Nagas and the Chandravanshis would have to retreat. This Naga would have to face the ignominy of having led the first failed attack. And he could see that it was Shiva who had led the counter-offensive. That man had to be destroyed for the future of the mission. The Naga drew his bow forward.

Shiva meanwhile, unaware of the danger, had wedged his sword a little into the Naga's stomach. The Naga grimly fought on, stepping back slowly while ramming Shiva with his shield. He tried in vain to swing his sword down to slice Shiva, who kept his own shield at the ready. Shiva kept fending the Naga's blows while pressing ahead, pushing the sword in deeper and deeper. In a few more seconds, the Naga's soul gave up. It slipped away as his body bled to death and collapsed. Shiva looked down at the fallen Naga in awe.

These people maybe evil, but they are fearless soldiers.

Shiva looked to the left to find that Parvateshwar too

had killed the Naga he had engaged. He continued to turn slowly, trying to find the last Naga. Then he heard a loud shout from the person he had come to love beyond reason.

'S – H – I – V – A.'

Shiva turned to his right to find Sati racing towards him. He looked behind her to see if anyone was chasing her. There was nobody. He frowned. Before he could react, Sati leapt forward. A jump timed to perfection.

The Naga at the distance had released the *agnibaan* or the *fire arrow*, one of the legendary poisoned arrows of their people. The venom on its tip burned its victim's body from the inside, causing a slow, painful death that would scar the soul for many births. The arrow had been aimed at Shiva's neck. It sped unerringly on its deadly mission. However, the Naga had not calculated the possibility of someone obstructing its path.

Sati twisted her body in mid-air as she leapt in front of Shiva. The arrow slammed into her chest with brutal force, propelling her airborne body backward. She fell to Shiva's left, limp and motionless. A stunned Shiva stared at Sati's prone body, his heart shattering.

The destroyer of evil roared in fury. He charged at the Naga like a wild elephant on the brink of insanity, his sword raised. The Naga was momentarily staggered by the fearsome sight of the charging Neelkanth. But to his credit, he rallied. He swiftly drew another arrow from his quiver, loaded it and let it fly. Shiva swung his sword to deflect the arrow, barely missing a step or decreasing his manic speed. The increasingly panic-stricken Naga loaded another arrow and shot again. Shiva swung his sword once more, deflecting the arrow easily, picking up more speed. The Naga reached back to draw another arrow. But it was too late. With a fierce yell, Shiva leapt high as he neared the Naga. He swung his sword viciously, decapitating the Naga with one swing of his sword. The Naga's lifeless body fell in a heap as his severed head flew with the mighty blow, while his still pumping heart spewed blood through the gaping neck.

The Neelkanth's vengeance was not quenched. Screaming, Shiva bent down and kept hacking at the Naga's inert body, ruthlessly slashing it to bits. No assertion of reason, no articulation of sanity could have penetrated Shiva's enraged mind. Except for a soft, muffled, injured voice that was barely audible in the din of battle. But he heard her.

'Shiva…'

He turned back to look at Sati lying in the distance, her head raised slightly.

'Sati!'

He sped towards her, bellowing, 'Parvateshwar! Get Ayurvati! Sati has fallen!'

Ayurvati had already seen Sati's injured body. The Chandravanshis were retreating in haste. Ayurvati ran towards Sati, as did Parvateshwar on hearing Shiva's call. Shiva reached her first. She was motionless, but alive. She was breathing heavily as the arrow had pierced her left lung, flooding her innards with her blood. She couldn't speak as the force of the blow had made the blood gush from her mouth. But she continued to stare at Shiva. Her face had a strange smile, almost serene. She kept opening her mouth as if trying to say something. Shiva desperately wanted to hold her, but he kept his hands locked together as he tried frantically to control his tears.

'O Lord Brahma!' cried Ayurvati as she reached Sati and

recognised the arrow. 'Mastrak! Dhruvini! Get a stretcher. Now!'

Parvateshwar, Ayurvati, Mastrak and Dhruvini carried Sati to one of the village houses with Shiva following closely. Ayurvati's other assistants had already begun cleaning the hut and setting the instruments for the surgery.

'Wait outside, my Lord,' said Ayurvati to Shiva, raising her hand.

Shiva wanted to follow Ayurvati into the hut, but Parvateshwar held him back by touching his shoulder. 'Ayurvati is one of the best doctors in the world, Shiva. Let her do her job.'

Shiva turned to look at Parvateshwar, who was doing an admirable job of controlling his emotions. But it took one look into his eyes for Shiva to know that Parvateshwar was as afraid for Sati as he was. Probably more than he had been before Sati's agnipariksha. Suddenly a thought struck Shiva. He turned and hurried to the closest Naga body. Bending quickly, he checked the right wrist. Finding nothing there, he turned and rushed to the other Naga dead body.

Meanwhile, Parvateshwar had rallied his disturbed mind enough to realise the important tasks that needed to be done. He beckoned Vraka and ordered, 'Place guards over the prisoners of war. Get doctors to attend to all the injured, including the Chandravanshis.'

'The injured Chandravanshis have already taken their poison, my Lord,' said Vraka. 'You know they will never want to be caught alive.'

Parvateshwar looked at Vraka with a withering look, clearly indicating that he wasn't interested in the details and Vraka should get to the task at hand.

'Yes, my Lord,' said Vraka, acknowledging Parvateshwar's silent order.

'Arrange a perimeter for any counter-attack,' continued Parvateshwar, his consciousness already drawn back to Sati's condition in the house behind him. 'And…'

Vraka looked up at Parvateshwar, surprised by his Lord's hesitation. He had never seen his Lord hesitate before. But Vraka had the good sense to not say anything. He waited for his Lord to complete his statement.

'And…' continued Parvateshwar. 'There should be some courier-pigeons still alive in the temple. Send a red coloured letter to Devagiri. To the Emperor. Tell him Princess Sati is seriously injured.'

Vraka looked up in disbelief. He had not heard about Sati. But wisely, he did not say anything.

'Tell the Emperor,' continued Parvateshwar, 'that she has been shot by an agnibaan.'

'O Lord Indra!' blurted Vraka unable to control his shocked dismay.

'Do it now, Brigadier!' snarled Parvateshwar.

'Yes, my Lord,' said Vraka with a weak salute.

Shiva meanwhile had already checked the wrists of four of the Nagas. None of them wore the leather bracelet with the serpent aum that Shiva had come to recognise. He reached the last one. The one who had shot Sati. The wretched one who Shiva had hacked. Shiva kicked the Naga's torso with intense hatred before trying to find his right arm. It took him some time to find the severed limb. Locating it, he raised the remnants of the robe to check the wrist. There was no leather bracelet. It wasn't him.

Shiva came back to the hut to find Parvateshwar seated on a stool outside. Krittika was standing beside the hut entrance, sobbing uncontrollably. Veerbhadra was holding her gently, comforting her. A distraught Nandi stood at Veerbhadra's side, his face stunned into a blank expression. Parvateshwar looked up at Shiva and pointed to the empty stool next to him with a weak smile. He was making brave attempts to appear under control. Shiva sat down slowly and looked into the distance, waiting for Ayurvati to come out.

'We have removed the arrow, my Lord,' said Ayurvati.

Shiva and Parvateshwar were standing in the hut, looking at an unconscious Sati. Nobody else was allowed in. Ayurvati had clearly stated that Sati did not need the risk of increased infection. And nobody dared argue with the formidable Ayurvati on medical matters. Mastrak and Dhruvini had already fanned out to support the other medical officers treating the injured Suryavanshi soldiers.

Shiva turned towards the right side of the bed and saw the bloodied tong that had been used to stretch Sati's innards so that the arrow could be pulled out. That tong would never be used again. It had been infected with the agnibaan poison. No amount of heat or chemicals would make the instrument sterile and safe again. Next to the tong lay the offending arrow, wrapped in neem leaves, where it would stay for one full day, before being buried deep in a dry grave to ensure that it would not cause any more harm.

Shiva looked at Ayurvati, his eyes moist, unable to find the strength to ask the question that raged in his heart.

'I will not lie to you, my Lord,' said Ayurvati, in the

detached manner that doctors will themselves into, to find the strength in traumatic circumstances. 'It doesn't look good. Nobody in history has survived an agnibaan which has penetrated one of the vital organs. The poison will start causing an intense fever in some time, which will result in the failing of one organ after another.'

Helplessly Shiva looked at Sati and then turned pleadingly towards Ayurvati, who fought hard to rein in her tears and retain her composure. She couldn't afford to lose control. She had many lives to save in the next few hours.

'I am sorry, my Lord,' said Ayurvati. 'But there really is no cure. We can only give some medicines to make her end easier.'

Shiva glared angrily at Ayurvati. 'We are not giving up! Is that clear?'

Ayurvati looked at the ground, unable to meet Shiva's eye.

'If the fever is kept under control, then her organs will not be damaged, right?' asked Shiva, as a glimmer of hope entered his being.

Ayurvati looked up and said, 'Yes, my Lord. But that is not a final solution. The fever caused by an agnibaan can only be delayed, not broken. If we try and control the fever, it will come back even stronger once the medicines are stopped.'

'Then we will control the fever forever!' cried Shiva. 'I will sit by her side all my life if needed. The fever will not rise.'

Ayurvati was about to say something to Shiva, but thought better of it and kept silent. She would come back to Shiva in a few hours. She knew that Sati could not be saved. It was impossible. Precious time was being wasted in this futile discussion. Time that could be used to save other lives.

'Alright, my Lord,' said Ayurvati, quickly administering the medicines to Sati that would keep her fever down. 'This should keep her fever down for a few hours.'

She looked up at Parvateshwar standing at the back for an instant. Parvateshwar knew that keeping the fever down would only lengthen Sati's agony. But he shared the glimmer of hope that Shiva felt.

Turning back towards Shiva, Ayurvati said, 'My Lord, you too are injured. Let me dress your wounds and I'll leave.'

'I am alright,' said Shiva, not taking his eyes off Sati for an instant.

'No, you are not, my Lord,' said Ayurvati firmly. 'Your wounds are deep. If they catch an infection, then it could be life threatening.'

Shiva did not answer. He just kept looking at Sati and waved his hand dismissively.

'Shiva!' shouted Ayurvati. Shiva looked up at her. 'You cannot help Sati if you yourself become unwell!'

The harsh tone had the desired effect. While Shiva did not move from his place, he let Ayurvati dress his wounds. Ayurvati then quickly tended to Parvateshwar's wounds and left the hut.

— ⁂ —

Shiva looked at the prahar lamp in the hut. It had been three hours since Ayurvati had removed the arrow. Parvateshwar had left the hut to look after the other injured and make the preparations for setting up camp, since the convoy was going to stay in Koonj for some time. That was Parvateshwar's way. If he was confronted with an ugly situation that he could do nothing about, he did not wallow in his misery. He would drown himself in his work so that he did not have to think about the crisis.

Shiva was different. Many years back, he had sworn that he would never run away from a difficult situation. Even if there was absolutely nothing he could do. He hadn't left Sati's side for a moment. He sat patiently by her bed, waiting for her to recover. Hoping for her to recover. Praying for her to recover.

'Shiva…' a barely audible whisper broke the silence.

Shiva looked at Sati's face. Her eyes were slightly open. Her hand had moved indiscernibly. He pulled his chair closer, careful not to touch her.

'I'm so sorry,' cried Shiva. 'I should never have got us into this fight.'

'No, no,' murmured Sati. 'You did the right thing. You have come to Meluha to lead us and to destroy evil. You did your duty.'

Shiva continued to stare at Sati, overcome by grief. Sati widened her eyes a bit, trying to take in as much of Shiva as she could, in what she knew were her last moments. Death brings to a final end a soul's aspirations. Ironically, however, it is sometimes the hovering imminence of the end itself which gives a soul the courage to challenge every constraint and express even a long-denied dream.

'It is my time to go, Shiva,' whispered Sati. 'But before I go, I want to tell you that the last few months have been the happiest in my life.'

Shiva continued to look at Sati with moist eyes. His hands developed a life of their own and moved towards Sati. He checked himself in time.

'I wish you had come into my life earlier,' said Sati, letting out a secret that she hadn't even acknowledged to herself. 'My life would have been so different.'

Shiva's eyes tried frantically to restrain themselves, struggling against the despair that needed an outlet.

'I wish I had told you earlier,' murmured Sati. 'Because the first time that I am telling you will also probably be the last.'

Shiva continued to look at her, his voice choked.

Sati looked deeply into Shiva's eyes, whispering softly, 'I love you.'

The dam broke and tears poured down Shiva's grief-stricken face.

'You are going to repeat these words for at least another hundred years,' sobbed Shiva. 'You are not going anywhere. I will fight the God of death himself, if I have to. You are not going anywhere.'

Sati smiled sadly and put her hand in Shiva's. Her hand was burning. The fever had begun its assault.

CHAPTER 18

Sati and the Fire Arrow

'Nothing can be done, my Lord,' said a visibly uncomfortable Ayurvati.

She and Shiva were standing in a corner of the hut, at what they thought was a safe distance beyond the range of Sati's ears. Parvateshwar was standing beside them, holding his tears back.

'Come on, Ayurvati,' urged Shiva. 'You are the best doctor in the land. All we have to do is wait for the fever to break.'

'This fever cannot be broken,' reasoned Ayurvati. 'There is no cure for the agnibaan poison. We are only lengthening Sati's agony by keeping the fever low. The moment the medicines are stopped, the fever will recur with a vengeance.'

'Let it go, Shiva,' mumbled a frail voice from the bed. Everyone turned to stare at Sati. Her face wore a smile that comes only with the acceptance of the inevitable. 'I have no regrets. I have told you what I needed to. I am content. My time has come.'

'Don't give up on me, Sati,' cried Shiva. 'You are not gone yet. We will find a way. I will find a way. Just bear with me.'

Sati gave up. She didn't have the strength. She also knew that Shiva had to find his own peace with her death. And he wouldn't find that unless he felt he had done everything possible to save her.

'I can feel my fever rising,' said Sati. 'Please give me the medicines.'

Ayurvati glanced at Sati uncomfortably. All her medical training told her that she shouldn't do this. She knew that she was just increasing Sati's suffering by giving her medicines. Sati stared hard at Ayurvati. She couldn't give up now. Not when Shiva had asked her to hang on.

'Give me the medicines, Ayurvati*ji*,' repeated Sati. 'I know what I am doing.'

Ayurvati gave Sati the medicines. She gazed into Sati's eyes, expecting to find some traces of fear or anguish. There were none. Ayurvati smiled gently and walked back to Shiva and Parvateshwar.

'I know!' exclaimed Shiva. 'Why don't we give her the Somras?'

'What effect will that have, my Lord?' asked a surprised Ayurvati. 'The Somras only works on the oxidants and increases a person's lifespan. It doesn't work on injuries.'

'Look Ayurvati, I don't think anyone truly understands everything about the Somras. I know you know that. What you don't know is that the Somras repaired a frostbitten toe that I had lived with all my life. It also repaired my dislocated shoulder.'

'What!' said a visibly surprised Parvateshwar. 'That's impossible. The Somras does not cure physical disabilities.'

'It did in my case.'

'But that could also be because you are special, my Lord,' said Ayurvati. 'You are the Neelkanth.'

'I didn't drop from the sky, Ayurvati. My body is as human as Sati's. As human as yours. Let's just try it!'

Parvateshwar did not need any more convincing. He dashed out to find Vraka sitting on a stool. Vraka immediately rose and saluted his commander.

'Vraka,' said Parvateshwar. 'The temple may still have some Somras powder. It was the main production centre of the area. I want that powder. Now.'

'You will have it in ten minutes, my Lord,' boomed Vraka as he rushed off with his guards.

— ⁂ —

'There is nothing else to do but wait,' said Ayurvati as Sati fell asleep. The Somras had been administered — a stronger dose than usual. 'Parvateshwar, you are tired. You need to recover from your wounds. Please go and sleep.'

'I don't need sleep,' said Parvateshwar stubbornly. 'I am staying on guard with my soldiers at the perimeter. You can't trust those Chandravanshis. They may launch a counter-attack at night.'

A frustrated Ayurvati glared at Parvateshwar, her belief reinforced that the machismo of the Kshatriyas made them impossible patients.

'Are you going to bed, my Lord?' asked Ayurvati, turning towards Shiva, hoping that at least he would listen. 'There is nothing you can do now. We just have to wait. And you need the rest.'

Shiva just shook his head. Wild horses could not drag him away from Sati.

'We could arrange a bed in this hut,' continued Ayurvati.

'You could sleep here if you wish so that you can also keep an eye on Sati.'

'Thank you, but I am not going to sleep,' said Shiva, briefly looking at Ayurvati before turning towards Sati. 'I am staying here. You go to sleep. I will call you if there is any change.'

Ayurvati glared at Shiva and then whispered, 'As you wish, my Lord.'

A tired Ayurvati walked towards her own hut. She needed to get some rest since the next day would be busy. She would have to check the wounds of all the injured to ensure that recovery was proceeding properly. The first twenty-four hours were crucial. Her medical corps had been divided into groups to keep a staggered, all-night vigil for any emergencies.

'I will be with the soldiers, Shiva,' said Parvateshwar. 'Nandi and Veerbhadra are on duty outside along with some of my personal guards.'

Shiva knew what Parvateshwar actually wanted to say.

'I will call you as soon as there is a change, Parvateshwar,' said Shiva, looking up at the General.

Parvateshwar smiled weakly and nodded to Shiva. He rushed out before his feelings could cause him any embarrassment.

— ⋆ —

Parvateshwar sat alone and silent, while his soldiers maintained a distance, out of respect. They knew when their Lord wanted to be left alone. Parvateshwar was lost in thoughts of Sati. Why should a person like her be put through so much suffering by the Almighty? He remembered her childhood. The day when he decided that here was a girl he would be proud to have as his Goddaughter.

That fateful day, when for the first and only time, he regretted his vow to not have any progeny of his own. Which foolish father would not want a child like Sati?

It was a lazy afternoon more than a hundred years ago. Sati had just returned from the Gurukul at the tender age of sixteen. Full of verve and a passionate belief in Lord Ram's teachings. Lord Brahmanayak still reigned over the land of Meluha. His son, Prince Daksha, was content being a family man, spending his days with his wife and daughter. He showed absolutely no inclination to master the warrior ways of the Kshatriya. Neither did he show the slightest ambition to succeed his father.

On that day, Daksha had settled down for a family picnic on the banks of the river Saraswati, a short distance from Devagiri. Parvateshwar was then a bodyguard to Daksha and was conscientious about his duties. He sat near the Prince, close enough to protect him, but far enough to give some privacy to the prince and his wife. Sati had wandered off into the forest in the distance, while remaining close to the river so that she was visible.

Suddenly Sati's cry ripped through the silence. Daksha, Veerini and Parvateshwar looked up startled. They rushed to the edge of the bank to see Sati at the river bend, ferociously battling a pack of wild dogs. She was blocking them to protect a severely injured woman. It could be seen even from the distance that the caste-unmarked, fair woman was a recent immigrant, who did not know that one never approached the banks without a sword to protect oneself from wild animals. She must have been attacked by the pack, which was large enough to bring down even a charging lion.

'Sati!' shouted Daksha in alarm.

Drawing his sword, he charged down the river to protect his daughter. Parvateshwar followed Daksha, his sword drawn for battle. Within moments, they had jumped into the fray. Parvateshwar charged aggressively into the pack, easily hacking many with quick strikes. Sati, rejuvenated by the sudden support, fought back the four dogs charging towards her all at once. Daksha fought ferociously, despite an obvious lack of martial skills, with the passionately protective spirit that only a parent feels for his offspring. But the animals could sense that Daksha was the weakest amongst their human enemies. Six dogs charged at him at the same time.

Daksha drove his sword forward in a brutal jab at the dog in front of him. A mistake. Even though Daksha felled the dog, his sword was stuck in the dead animal. That was all the opening that the other dogs needed. One charged viciously from the side, seizing Daksha's right forearm in its jaws. He roared in pain, but held on to his sword as he tried to wrestle his arm free. Another dog bit Daksha's left leg, yanking some of his flesh out. Seeing his Lord in trouble, Parvateshwar yelled in fury as he swung his sword at the body of the dog clinging to Daksha's arm, cleanly cutting the beast in half. Parvateshwar pirouetted around in the same smooth motion and slashed another dog charging at Daksha from the front. Sati moved in to protect Daksha's left flank as he angrily stabbed the dog that was clinging to his leg. Seeing their numbers rapidly depleting, the remaining dogs retreated yelping.

'Daksha!' sobbed Veerini, as she rushed to hold up her

collapsing husband. He was losing blood at an alarming rate from his numerous wounds, especially from the thigh. The dog's sharp incisor must surely have pierced a major artery. Parvateshwar quickly blew his distress conch shell. A cry for help reached the scouts at the closest crossing-house. Soldiers and paramedics would be with them in a few minutes. Parvateshwar bound his angvastram tight around Daksha's thigh to stem the bleeding. Then he quickly helped the injured foreign woman move closer to the royal party.

'Father, are you alright?' whispered Sati as she held her father's hand.

'Dammit, Sati!' shouted Daksha. 'What do you think you were doing?'

Sati fell silent at the violent response from her doting father.

'Who asked you to be a hero?' harangued Daksha, fuming at his daughter. 'What if something had happened to you? What would I do? Where would I go? And for whom were you risking your life? What difference does the life of that woman make?'

Sati continued to look down, distraught at the scolding. She had been expecting praise. The crossing-house soldiers and paramedics rushed to the scene. With efficient movements, they quickly stemmed the flow of Daksha's blood. After dressing Parvateshwar's and Sati's minor wounds rapidly, they carried Daksha on a stretcher. His wounds needed attention from the royal physician.

As Sati saw her father being carried away, she stayed rooted, deeply guilty about the harm her actions had caused. She was only trying to save a woman in distress. Wasn't it one of Lord Ram's primary teachings that it is the duty of the strong to protect the weak? She felt a soft touch on her shoulder. She turned to face Captain Parvateshwar, her father's severe bodyguard. Strangely though, his face sported a rare smile.

'I am proud of you, my child,' whispered Parvateshwar. 'You are a true follower of Lord Ram.'

Tears suddenly burst forth in Sati's eyes. She looked away quickly. Taking time to control herself she looked up with a wan smile at the man she would in days to come grow up to call Pitratulya. She nodded softly.

Jolted back into the present by a bird call, Parvateshwar scanned the perimeter, his eyes moist with emotion. He clutched his hands in a prayer and whispered, 'She's your true follower, Lord Ram. Fight for her.'

— ⁂ —

Shiva had lost track of time. Obviously, nobody had been assigned to reset the prahar lamps when so many lives were still in danger. Looking out of the window, he could see early signs of dawn. Shiva's wounds burned, crying for relief. But he wasn't going to give in. He sat quietly on his chair, next to Sati's bed, restraining himself from making any noise that would disturb her. Sati held his hand tightly. Despite the searing heat of her feverish body, Shiva did not move his hands away. His palms were sweaty due to the intense heat.

He looked longingly at Sati and softly whispered, 'Either you stay here or I leave this world with you. The choice is yours.'

He felt a slight twitch. He looked down to see Sati's hand move ever so slightly, beads of perspiration gliding down between their entwined palms. Though whose perspiration it was he could not say.

Is it Sati's or mine?

Shiva immediately reached out with his other hand towards Sati's forehead. It was burning even more strongly. But there were soft beads of perspiration on the temple. A burst of elation shot through Shiva's being.

— ⅄ⓄƱ♆⊛ —

'By the great Lord Brahma,' whispered Ayurvati in awe. 'I have never seen anything like this.'

She was standing besides Sati's bed. The still sleeping Sati was sweating profusely. Her bed and garments were soaked. Parvateshwar stood by her side, his face aglow with hope.

'The agnibaan fever never breaks,' continued a stunned Ayurvati. 'This is a miracle.'

Shiva looked up, his face shimmering with the ecstasy of a soul that had salvaged its reason for existence. 'May the Holy Lake bless the Somras.'

Parvateshwar noticed Sati's hand clutched tightly in Shiva's but he did not comment. The bliss of this moment had finally crowded out his instinctive drive to stop something unacceptable under the laws of the land.

'My Lord,' said Ayurvati softly. 'We must bathe her quickly. The sweat must be removed. However, considering that her wounds cannot get wet, my nurses will have to rub her down.'

Shiva looked up at Ayurvati and nodded, not understanding the implication.

'Umm, my Lord,' said Ayurvati. 'That means you will have to leave the room.'

'Of course,' said Shiva.

As he got up to leave, Ayurvati said, 'My Lord, your hands would need to be washed as well.'

Shiva looked down, noticing Sati's sweat. He looked up at Ayurvati and nodded, 'I will do so immediately.'

— ⁂ —

'This is a miracle, Sati. Nobody has ever recovered from an agnibaan!' said Ayurvati, beaming from ear to ear. 'I'll be honest. I had given up hope. It was the Lord's faith that has kept you alive.'

Sati was lying on her bed wearing a smile and freshly washed clothes. A new bed had been brought in with freshly laundered and sterilised linen. All traces of the toxic sweat triggered by the Somras had been removed.

'Oh no,' said a self-conscious Shiva. 'I did nothing. It was Sati's fighting spirit that saved her.'

'No, Shiva. It was you. Not me,' said Sati, holding Shiva's hand without any hint of tentativeness. 'You have saved me at so many levels. I don't know how I can even begin to repay you.'

'By never saying again that you have to repay me.'

Sati smiled even more broadly and held Shiva's hand tighter. Parvateshwar looked on gloomily at both of them, now unhappy with the open display of their love.

'All right,' said Ayurvati, clapping her hands together as if to signal the end of an episode. 'Much as I would like to sit here and chitchat with all of you, I have work to do.'

'What work?' asked Shiva playfully. 'You are a brilliant doctor. You have an exceptional team. I know that every single injured person has been saved. There is nothing more for you to do.'

'Oh there is, my Lord,' said Ayurvati with a smile. 'I have to put on record how the Somras can cure an agnibaan wound. I will present this at the medical council as soon as I return to Devagiri. This is big news. We must research the curative properties of the Somras. There is a lot of work to do!'

Shiva smiled fondly at Ayurvati.

Sati whispered, 'Thank you Ayurvati*ji*. Like thousands of others, I too owe my life to you.'

'You owe me nothing, Sati. I only did my duty.'

Ayurvati bowed with a formal Namaste and left the room.

'Well, even I…,' mumbled Parvateshwar awkwardly, as he walked out.

Parvateshwar was surprised to find Ayurvati waiting for him outside. She was standing at a safe distance from the guards. Whatever it was that she wanted to talk about, she did not want the others to hear.

'What is it, Ayurvati?' asked Parvateshwar.

'I know what's bothering you Parvateshwar,' said Ayurvati.

'Then how can you just stand by and watch? I don't think it is right. I know that this is not the correct time to say anything. But I will raise the issue when appropriate.'

'No, you shouldn't.'

'How can you say that?' asked a shocked Parvateshwar. 'You come from a rare family which did not have even one renegade Brahmin during the rebellion. Lord Ram insisted that the laws had to be followed strictly. He demonstrated repeatedly that even he wasn't above the law. Shiva is a good man. I won't deny that. But he cannot be above the law. Nobody can be above the law. Otherwise our society will collapse. You above all should know this.'

'I know only one thing,' said Ayurvati, determined. 'If the Neelkanth feels it is right, then it *is* right.'

Parvateshwar looked at Ayurvati as if he didn't recognise her. This could not be the woman he knew and admired, the woman who followed the law without exception. Parvateshwar had begun to respect Shiva. But the respect had not turned into unquestioning faith. He did not believe that Shiva was the one who would complete Lord Ram's work. In Parvateshwar's eyes, only Lord Ram deserved absolute obedience. Nobody else.

'In any case,' said Ayurvati, 'I have to leave. I have a theory to think about.'

— ⁂ —

'Really?' asked Shiva. 'You mean it is not necessary in Meluha that the Emperor's first-born son succeed him?'

'Yes,' replied Sati smiling.

Shiva and Sati had spent many hours over the previous week talking about matters important and mundane. Sati, while recovering quickly, was still bedridden. The convoy had set up camp at Koonj till such time as the injured were ready to travel. The journey to Lothal had been called off. Shiva and Parvateshwar had decided that it was better to return to Devagiri as soon as the wounded were able to.

Sati shifted slightly to relieve a bit of the soreness in her back. But she did not let go of Shiva's hand while doing so. Shiva leaned forward and pushed back a strand of hair that had slipped onto Sati's face. She smiled lovingly at him and continued, 'You see, till around two hundred and fifty years ago, the children of the kings were not his birth-children. They were drawn from the Maika system. So there was no question of knowing who the first-born was. We could only know his first-adopted.'

'Fair point.'

'But in addition, it was not necessary that the first-adopted child would succeed. This was another one of the laws that Lord Ram instituted for stability and peace. You see, in the olden days there were many royal families, each with their own small kingdoms.'

'All right,' said Shiva, paying as much attention to Sati's words as to the hypnotising dimples that formed on her cheeks when she spoke. 'These kings would probably be at war all the time, so that one of them could be overlord for however short a period.'

'Obviously,' smiled Sati, shaking her head at the foolishness of the kings before Lord Ram's time.

'Well, it is the same everywhere,' said Shiva, remembering the constant warfare in his part of the world.

'Battles for supremacy amongst the kings led to many unnecessary and futile wars, where the only ones who suffered were the common people,' continued Sati. 'Lord Ram felt it was ridiculous for the people to suffer so that the egos of their kings were fed. He instituted a system where a *Rajya Sabha*, the *ruling council*, consisting of all Brahmins and Kshatriyas of a specific rank, was created. Whenever the Emperor died or took sanyas, the council would meet and elect a new Emperor from amongst Kshatriyas of the rank of brigadier or above. The decision could not be contested and was inviolate.'

'I have said it before and I'll say it again,' said Shiva with a broad smile. 'Lord Ram was a genius.'

'Yes, he was,' said Sati, enthusiastically. 'Jai Shri Ram.'

'Jai Shri Ram,' repeated Shiva. 'But tell me, how come your father became the Emperor after Lord Brahmanayak? After all, his Highness is the first born of the previous Emperor, correct?'

'He was elected, just like every other Emperor of Meluha. Actually it was the first time in Meluhan history that a ruling emperor's son was elected Emperor,' said Sati proudly.

'Hmm. But your grandfather helped your father get elected?'

'I've never been sure about that. I know my grandfather would have liked it if my father had become Emperor. But I also know that he was a great man who followed the rules of Meluha and would not openly help his son. Lord Bhrigu, a great sage respected across the land, helped my father a great deal in his election.'

Shiva smiled at her as he tenderly ran his hand across the side of her face. Sati closed her eyes, exulting in the sensation. His hand glided along the side of her body to rest on her hand again. He squeezed it softly.

Shiva was about to ask more about the relationship between Daksha and Lord Bhrigu when the door suddenly swung open. Daksha, looking deeply exhausted, stormed in. Following him were Veerini and Kanakhala. Shiva immediately withdrew his hand before Daksha could see where it was. But Daksha had noticed the movement.

'Father!' cried a surprised Sati.

'Sati, my child,' sighed Daksha, kneeling next to Sati's bed. Veerini knelt next to Daksha and ran her hand lovingly over her daughter's face. She was crying. Kanakhala remained at a distance and greeted Shiva with a formal Namaste. Shiva returned Kanakhala's Namaste with a beaming smile. Parvateshwar and Ayurvati waited next to Kanakhala, politely leaving the royal family alone in their private moment. Nandi, Veerbhadra and Krittika stood behind them. A discreet aide silently brought in two chairs for the royal couple, placed them next to the bed and left just as quietly.

Daksha, Veerini and Kanakhala, accompanied by two thousand soldiers, had immediately left Devagiri on hearing the news of Sati's injury. They had sailed down the Saraswati to the inland delta of the river and then had ridden night and day to reach Koonj.

'I am alright, father,' said Sati, holding her mother's hand gently. Turning towards her mother, she continued, 'Seriously, mother. I am feeling better than ever. Give me one more week and I'll dance for you!'

Shiva couldn't suppress a grin even as both Daksha and Veerini smiled indulgently at Sati.

Looking at her father, Sati continued, 'I am sorry to have caused so much trouble. I know there are many more important tasks at hand and you had to unnecessarily rush here.'

'Trouble?' asked Daksha. 'My child, you are my life. You are nothing but a source of joy for me. And at this point of time, you can't imagine how proud I am of you.'

Veerini bent over and kissed Sati's forehead tenderly.

'I am proud of all of you,' continued Daksha looking back at Parvateshwar and Ayurvati. 'Proud that you supported the Lord in what had to be done. We actually fought back a terrorist attack! You can't imagine how much this has electrified the nation!'

Daksha soothingly continued to pat Sati's hand, as he turned to Shiva and said, 'Thank you, my Lord. Thank you for fighting for us. We know now that we have put our faith in the right man.'

Shiva could not find anything to say. He smiled awkwardly and acknowledged Daksha's faith with a slight nod and a courteous Namaste.

Turning to Ayurvati, Daksha asked, 'How is she now? I was told she is on her way to a total recovery.'

'Yes, your Highness,' said Ayurvati. 'She should be able to move in another week. And in three weeks, the only memory of the wound would be a scar.'

'You are not just the best doctor of this generation, Ayurvati,' said Daksha proudly. 'You are in fact the best doctor of all time.'

'Oh no, your Highness,' cried a flabbergasted Ayurvati, gently pinching her ear lobes to ward off any evil spirit that might take umbrage at the undeserved compliment. 'There are many far greater than me. But in this case, the miracle was Lord Neelkanth's and not mine.'

Looking briefly towards a visibly embarrassed Shiva before turning back to Daksha, Ayurvati continued, 'I thought we had lost her. She got the terrible fever after we pulled the agnibaan out. You know that there are no medicines to cure the agnibaan fever, your Highness. But the Lord refused to lose hope. It was his idea to give her the Somras.'

Daksha turned to Shiva with a grateful smile and said, 'I have one more thing to thank you for, my Lord. My daughter is part of my soul. I wouldn't have been able to survive without her.'

'Oh no, I did nothing,' said Shiva, self-conscious. 'It was Ayurvati who treated her.'

'Therein lies your humility, my Lord,' said Daksha. 'You truly are a worthy Neelkanth. In fact, you are a worthy Mahadev!'

An astounded Shiva stared at Daksha, his expression serious. He knew who the previous *Mahadev*, the *God of Gods*, was. He did not believe he deserved to be compared to Lord Rudra. His deeds did not qualify him for that honour.

'No, your Highness. You speak too highly of me. I am no Mahadev.'

'Oh yes you are, my Lord,' said Kanakhala and Ayurvati almost simultaneously. Parvateshwar looked on, silent.

Not wanting to press the issue as Shiva disliked being called Mahadev, Daksha turned towards Sati, 'What I don't understand is why you jumped in front of the Lord to take the arrow. You have never believed in the legend. You have never had faith in the Neelkanth like I have. Why then did you risk your own life for the Lord?'

Sati did not say anything. She looked down with an uncomfortable smile, embarrassed and ill-at-ease. Daksha turned to Shiva to see him wearing the same sheepish expression as Sati's. Veerini looked at her husband intently. She waited for him to rise and speak to Shiva. Suddenly Daksha stood up and walked around the bed towards Shiva, his hands folded in a formal Namaste. A surprised Shiva rose and returned Daksha's Namaste, with a slight bow of his head.

'My Lord, perhaps for the first time in her life, my daughter is tongue-tied in my presence,' said Daksha. 'And I have also come to understand that you will willingly give unto others but never ask for anything for yourself. Hence I must make the first move.'

Shiva continued to stare at Daksha, frowning.

'I will not lie to you, my Lord,' continued Daksha. 'The laws classify my daughter as a vikarma, because she had given birth to a still-born decades back. It is not a very serious crime. It could have been due to the past life karma of the child's father. But the law of the land holds that both the father and the mother be blamed for the tragedy. My darling daughter was put in the category of a vikarma, because of this incident.'

Shiva's expression made it clear that he thought the vikarma law was unfair.

'It is believed that vikarma people are carriers of bad fate,' continued Daksha. 'Hence if she marries again, she will pass on her bad fate to her husband and possibly her future children.'

Veerini looked at her husband with inscrutable eyes.

'I know my daughter, my Lord,' continued Daksha. 'I have never seen her do anything even remotely wrong. She is a good woman. In my opinion, the law that condemns her is unfair. But I am only the Emperor. I cannot change the law.'

Parvateshwar glared angrily at Daksha, upset that he served an Emperor who held the law in such low esteem.

'It breaks my heart that I cannot give my daughter the happy life that she deserves,' sobbed Daksha. 'That I cannot save her from the humiliation that a good soul like her suffers daily. What I can do, though, is ask you for help.'

Sati looked at her father with loving eyes.

'You are the Neelkanth,' continued Daksha. 'In fact you are more than that. I genuinely believe that you are a Mahadev, even though I know you don't like to be called one. You are above the law. You can change the law if you wish. You can override it if you want.'

An aghast Parvateshwar glowered at Daksha. How could the Emperor be so dismissive of the law? Then his eyes fell on Shiva. His heart sank further.

Shiva was staring at Daksha with undisguised delight. He had thought that he would have to convince the Emperor about Sati. But here he was, quite sure that the Emperor was about to offer his daughter's hand to him.

'If you decide to take my daughter's hand, my Lord, no power on earth can stop you,' contended Daksha. 'The question is: do you want to?'

All the emotions in the universe surged through Shiva's being. His face wore an ecstatic smile. He tried to speak but his voice was choked. He bent down, picked up Sati's hand gently, brought it to his lips and kissed it lovingly. He looked up at Daksha and whispered, 'I will never let go of her. Never.'

A stunned Sati stared at Shiva. She had dared to love over the last week, but had not dared to hope. And now her wildest dream was coming true. She was going to be his wife.

An overjoyed Daksha hugged Shiva tightly and said softly, 'My Lord!'

Veerini was sobbing uncontrollably. The spectre of a lifetime's injustice had been lifted off Sati. She looked up at Daksha, almost willing to forgive him. Ayurvati and Kanakhala stepped up and congratulated the Emperor, the Queen, Shiva and Sati. Nandi, Krittika and Veerbhadra, who had heard the entire conversation, expressed their joy. Parvateshwar stood rooted near the door, furious with such disregard for Lord Ram's way.

Shiva, at long last, regained control of himself. Firmly gripping Sati's hand, he looked at Daksha, 'But your Highness, I have a condition.'

'Yes, my Lord.'

'The vikarma law…'

'It doesn't need to be changed, my Lord,' said Daksha. 'If you decide to marry my daughter, then the law cannot stop you.'

'All the same,' said Shiva. 'That law must be changed.'

'Of course, it will be my Lord,' said a beaming Daksha. Turning towards Kanakhala, he continued, 'Make a proclamation to be signed by the Neelkanth, saying that from now on any noble woman who gives birth to a still-born child will not be classified as vikarma.'

'No, your Highness,' interrupted Shiva. 'That is not what I meant. I want the entire vikarma law scrapped. Nobody will be a vikarma from now on. Bad fate can strike anyone. It is ridiculous to blame their past lives for it.'

Parvateshwar looked at Shiva in surprise. Though he did not like even a comma being changed in any of Lord Ram's laws, he appreciated that Shiva was remaining true to a fundamental canon of Lord Ram's principles — the same law applies to everybody, equally and fairly, without exceptions.

Daksha however looked at Shiva in shock. This was unexpected. Like all Meluhans, he too was superstitious about the vikarma. His displeasure was not with the vikarma law itself but with his daughter being classified as one. But he quickly recovered and said, 'Of course, my Lord. The proclamation will state that the entire vikarma law has been scrapped. Once you sign it, it will become law.'

'Thank you, your Highness,' smiled Shiva.

'My daughter's happy days are back,' exulted Daksha, turning to Kanakhala. 'I want a grand ceremony at Devagiri when we return. A wedding the likes of which the world has not seen before. The most magnificent wedding ever. Call in the best organisers in the land. I want no expense spared.'

Daksha turned to look at Shiva for affirmation. Shiva looked at Sati to admire her joyous smile and glorious dimples. Turning towards Daksha, he said, 'All I want, your Highness, is to get married to Sati. I wouldn't mind the simplest ceremony in the world or the most magnificent. So long as all of you, Brahaspati and the Gunas are present, I will be happy.'

'Excellent!' rejoiced Daksha.

CHAPTER 19

Love Realised

There was an air of celebration in Devagiri when the royal caravan arrived three weeks later. Kanakhala, who had arrived in Devagiri earlier, ensured that all the preparations for the most eagerly-awaited wedding in a millennium had been accomplished. Her arrangements, as always, had been impeccable.

The various wedding ceremonies and celebrations had been spread over seven days, each day filled with an exuberant variety of events. By the usually sober Suryavanshi standards, the city had been decorated extravagantly. Colourful banners hung proudly from the city walls, splashing festive beauty on the sober grey exteriors. The roads had been freshly tiled in the sacred blue colour. All the restaurants and shops served their customers free of charge for the seven days of revelry, subsidised at state expense. The buildings had been freshly painted at government cost to make Devagiri appear like a city that had been established the previous day.

A massive channel had been rapidly dug along the far side of the Saraswati where a part of the river had been diverted. The channel was in the open in some parts and went underground in others. Filters injected a red dye into the water as soon as it entered the channel and removed it just as efficiently when the water flowed back into the river. The channel formed a giant *Swastika*, an ancient symbol which literally translates into *'that which is associated with well-being'* or very simply, a lucky charm. From any of the three city platforms, a Meluhan could look in reverence at the enormous impression of the revered Swastika in the royal red Suryavanshi colour formed by the flow of the holy Saraswati. Some of the protective giant spikes around the entry drawbridges of the three platforms had been cleared. In their stead, giant rangolis, visible from miles away, had been drawn to welcome all into the capital. Kanakhala had wanted to clear all the spikes surrounding Devagiri, but Parvateshwar had vetoed it, citing security reasons.

Elite families from across the empire had been invited to attend the festivities. People of distinction ranging from governors to scientists, generals to artists and even sanyasis had trooped into Devagiri to celebrate the momentous occasion. Ambassadors of eminent countries, such as Mesopotamia and Egypt, had been given permits for a rare visit to the capital of Meluha. Jhooleshwar had cannily used the distinctive honour granted to ambassadors to wrangle some additional trade quotas. Brahaspati had come down from Mount Mandar with his retinue. Only a skeletal security staff of Arishtanemi soldiers had been left behind at the mountain. It was the first time in history that seven days would elapse at Mount Mandar without any experiments!

The first day had two pujas organised in the name of Lord Indra and Lord Agni. They were the main Gods of the people of India and their blessings were sought before any significant event. And an event as momentous as the wedding of the millennium could only begin with their sanction. This particular puja, however, celebrated their warrior form. Daksha eloquently explained the reason. The Meluhans were not just celebrating the marriage between the Neelkanth and their princess. They were also celebrating the massive defeat of the despised terrorists at Koonj. According to him, the echoes of Koonj would reverberate deep in the heart of Swadweep. The Suryavanshi vengeance had begun!

This puja was followed by the formal marriage ceremonies of Shiva and Sati. After which, though some of the celebrations were still on, Shiva excused himself and tugged Sati along with him.

'By the Holy Lake!' exclaimed Shiva, shutting the door to their private chamber behind him. 'This is only the first day! Is every day going to be as long?'

'It doesn't seem to make a difference to you! You walked out when you pretty well pleased!' teased Sati.

'I don't care about those damned ceremonies!' growled Shiva, ripping his ceremonial turban off and flinging it aside. He stared at Sati fervently, slowly moving towards her, his breathing heavy.

'Oh yes of course,' mocked Sati, with a playfully theatrical expression. 'The Neelkanth gets to decide what is important and what is not. The Neelkanth can do anything he wants.'

'Oh yes he can!'

Sati laughed mischievously and ran to the other side of the bed. Shiva dashed towards her from the opposite side as he hurled his angvastram off in one smooth motion.

'Oh yes he can…'

— ⅄ⵀUⴷ⊛ —

'Remember what I've told you to say,' whispered Nandi to Veerbhadra. 'Don't worry. The Lord will give his permission.'

'What…' whispered a groggy Shiva as he was woken up gently by Sati.

'Wake up, Shiva,' whispered Sati tenderly, her hair falling over his face, teasing his cheeks. 'Careful now,' murmured Sati softly, as Shiva looked at her longingly. 'Nandi, Krittika and Veerbhadra are waiting at the door. They have something important to say to you.'

'Hmmm?' growled Shiva, as he walked towards the door and glared at the trio. 'What is it Nandi? Isn't there someone beautiful in your life that you would like to bother at this hour instead of troubling me?'

'There's nobody like you, my Lord,' said Nandi, with a low bow and a chaste Namaste.

'Nandi, you better stop this nonsense or you are going to remain a bachelor all your life!' joked Shiva.

As everybody laughed loudly, Krittika remained anxious about the task at hand.

'Well, what did you want to talk about?' asked Shiva.

Nandi nudged Veerbhadra roughly. Shiva turned to Veerbhadra with a quizzical look.

'Bhadra, since when do you need the support of so many people to speak to me?' asked Shiva.

'Shiva…' murmured Veerbhadra nervously.

'Yes?'

'It's like this…'

'It's like what?'

'Well, you see…'

'I am seeing Bhadra.'

'Shiva, please stop making him more nervous than he

already is,' said Sati. Looking towards Veerbhadra, she continued, 'Veerbhadra, speak fearlessly. You haven't done anything wrong.'

'Shiva,' whispered Veerbhadra timidly, his cheeks the colour of beetroot. 'I need your permission.'

'Permission granted,' said Shiva, amused by now. 'Whatever it is that you want it for.'

'Actually, I am considering getting married.'

'A capital idea!' said Shiva. 'Now all you have to do is convince some blind woman to marry you!'

'Shiva!' reprimanded Sati gently.

'Well, I've already found a woman,' said Veerbhadra, before his courage could desert him. 'And she's not blind…'

'Not blind?!' exclaimed Shiva, his eyebrows humorously arched in wide disbelief. 'Then she is stupid enough to tie herself for the next seven births to a man who wants someone else to determine his marriage!'

Veerbhadra gazed at Shiva with an odd mixture of embarrassment, contrition and incomprehension.

'I've said this to you earlier, Bhadra,' said Shiva, 'There are many customs of our tribe that I don't like. And one of the primary ones amongst them is that the leader has to approve the bride of any tribesman. Don't you remember how we made fun of this ridiculous tradition as children?'

Veerbhadra glanced at Shiva and immediately down again, still unsure.

'For God's sake man, if you are happy with her, then I am happy for you,' said an exasperated Shiva. 'You have my permission.'

Veerbhadra looked up in surprised ecstasy as Nandi nudged him again. Krittika looked at Veerbhadra, as a long held breath escaped with massive relief. She turned to Sati and silently mouthed the words, 'Thank you.'

Shiva walked towards Krittika and hugged her warmly. A startled Krittika held back for an instant, before the warmth of the Neelkanth conquered her Suryavanshi reserve. She returned the embrace.

'Welcome to the tribe,' whispered Shiva. 'We are quite mad, but at heart we are good people!'

'But how did you know?' said Veerbhadra. 'I never told you that I loved her.'

'I am not blind, Bhadra,' smiled Shiva.

'Thank you,' said Krittika to Shiva. 'Thank you for accepting me.'

Shiva stepped back and said, 'No. Thank *you*. I was always concerned about Bhadra. He is a good, dependable man, but too simple-minded about women. I was worried about how married life would treat him. But there is no reason to worry anymore.'

'Well, I too want to tell you something,' said Krittika. 'I had never believed in the legend of the Neelkanth. But if you can transform Meluha like you have transformed my lady, then you are worthy of even being called the Mahadev!'

'I don't want to be called the Mahadev, Krittika. You know I love Meluha as much as I love Sati. I will do all that I possibly can.' Turning towards Veerbhadra, Shiva ordered, 'Come here, you stupid oaf!'

Veerbhadra came forward, embraced Shiva affectionately and whispered, 'Thank you.'

'Don't be stupid. There's no need for a "thank you"!' said Shiva with a grin.

Veerbhadra smiled broadly.

'And listen!' snarled Shiva in mock anger. 'You are going to answer to your best friend over the next chillum we share on how you dared to love a woman for so long without even speaking to me about it!'

Everybody laughed out loud.

'Will a good batch of marijuana make up for it?' asked Veerbhadra, smiling.

'Well, I'll think about it!'

— ⅄◎ꓵ⍏⊛ —

'Doesn't she look tired?' asked a concerned Ayurvati, looking at Sati.

Sati had just gotten up from the prayer platform as she and her mother had been excused for this particular ceremony. This was only for the bridegroom and the father of the bride. The pandits were preparing for the puja, which would take a few moments.

'Well, it has been six days of almost continuous celebrations and pujas,' said Kanakhala. 'Though it is the custom that all this be done for a royal wedding, I can understand her being tired.'

'Oh, I wouldn't say it has anything to do with the six *days* of pujas,' said Brahaspati.

'No?' asked Kanakhala.

'No,' answered Brahaspati, mischievously. 'I think it has to do with the five *nights*.'

'What?' exclaimed Ayurvati, then blushed a deep red as the meaning of Brahaspati's words dawned on her.

Parvateshwar, who was sitting next to Kanakhala, glared at Brahaspati for the highly improper remark. Brahaspati guffawed as the ladies giggled quietly. An assistant pandit turned around in irritation. But on seeing the seniority of the Brahmins sitting behind him, he immediately swallowed his annoyance and returned to his preparations.

Parvateshwar however had no such compunctions. 'I can't believe the kind of conversation I am being forced to endure!' He rose to walk to the back of the congregation.

This made even Kanakhala and Ayurvati chortle. One of the senior pandits turned to signal that the ceremony was about to begin, making them fall silent immediately.

The pandits resumed the invocations of the shlokas. Both Shiva and Daksha continued to pour the ceremonial ghee into the sacred fire at regular intervals while saying, 'Swaha'.

In between two successive swahas, there was enough time for Shiva and Daksha to talk softly to each other. They spoke of Sati. And only Sati. To any neutral observer, it would have been difficult to decide who loved the princess more. The pandit took a momentary break in his recitation of the shlokas, the cue for Shiva and Daksha to pour some more ghee into the sacred fire with a 'Swaha.' A little ghee spilled onto Daksha's hands. As Shiva immediately pulled the napkin on his side to wipe it off, he noticed the chosen-tribe amulet on Daksha's arm. He was stunned on seeing the animal there, but had the good sense to not comment. Daksha meanwhile had also turned and noticed Shiva's gaze.

'It wasn't my choice. My father chose it for me,' said Daksha, with a warm smile, while wiping the ghee off his hands. There was not a hint of embarrassment in his voice. If one looked closely though, one could see just a hint of defiance in his eyes.

'Oh no, your Highness,' mumbled Shiva, a little mortified. 'I didn't mean to look. Please accept my apologies.'

'Why should you apologise, my Lord?' asked Daksha. 'It is my chosen-tribe. It is worn on the arm so that everyone can see it and classify me.'

'But you are far beyond your chosen-tribe, your Highness,' said Shiva politely. 'You are a much greater man than what that amulet symbolises.'

'Yes,' smiled Daksha. 'I really showed the old man, didn't I? The Neelkanth did not choose to appear in his reign. He came in mine. The terrorists were not defeated in his reign. They were defeated in mine. And the Chandravanshis were not reformed in his reign. They will be reformed in mine.'

Shiva smiled cautiously. Something about the conversation niggled at him. He stole one more glance at the amulet on Daksha's arm. It represented a humble goat, one of the lowest chosen-tribes amongst the Kshatriyas. In fact, some people considered the goat chosen-tribe to be so low that its wearer could not even be called a full Kshatriya. Shiva turned back towards the sacred fire on receiving the verbal cue from the pandit. Scooping some more ghee, he poured it into the fire with a 'Swaha'.

At nightfall, in the privacy of their chambers, Shiva had considered asking Sati about the relationship between Emperor Brahmanayak and his son, Daksha. But for some reason, his instincts told him that he would have to be careful in how he asks the questions.

'How was the relationship between Lord Brahmanayak and your father?'

Sati stopped playing with Shiva's flowing locks. She took

a deep breath and whispered, 'It was strained at times. They were very different characters. But Lord Bhrigu...'

The conversation was interrupted by a knock on the door.

'What is it?' growled Shiva.

'My Lord,' Taman, the doorkeeper, announced nervously. 'The Chief Scientist Brahaspati*ji* has requested an audience with you. He insists that he must meet with you tonight.'

Shiva was always happy to meet Brahaspati. But before answering the doorkeeper, he looked at Sati with a raised eyebrow. Sati smiled and nodded. She was aware that Shiva placed great value upon his relationship with Brihaspati.

'Let Brahaspati*ji* in, Taman.'

'Yes, my Lord.'

'My friend,' said Brahaspati. 'My apologies for disturbing you so late.'

'You never need to apologise to me, my friend,' answered Shiva.

'Namaste, Brahaspati*ji,*' said Sati, bending to touch the Chief Scientist's feet.

'*Akhand saubhagyavati bhav*,' said Brahaspati, blessing Sati with the traditional invocation that may *her husband always be alive and by her side.*

'Well,' said Shiva to Brahaspati, 'what is so important that you had to pull yourself out of bed so late in the night?'

'Actually, I didn't get the chance to speak to you earlier.'

'I know,' said Shiva, smiling towards Sati. 'Our days have been full with one ceremony after another.'

'I know,' said Brahaspati nodding. 'We Suryavanshis love ceremonies! In any case, I wanted to come and speak with you personally, since I have to leave for Mount Mandar tomorrow morning.'

'What?' asked a surprised Shiva. 'You have survived all this for the last six days. Surely you can survive one more?'

'I know,' said Brahaspati, crinkling his eyes apologetically. 'I would have loved to stay but there is an experiment that had already been scheduled. The preparations have been going on for months. The Mesopotamian material required for it has already been prepared. We are going to test the stability of the Somras with lesser quantities of water. I have to go early and ensure that the experiment begins correctly. My fellow scientists will remain here to keep you company!'

'Right,' said Shiva sarcastically. 'I really do love their constant theorising about everything under the sun.'

Brahaspati laughed. 'I really do have to go, Shiva. I am sorry.'

'No need to apologise, my friend,' said Shiva smiling. 'Life is long. And the road to Mount Mandar short. You are not going to get rid of me that easily.'

Brahaspati smiled, his eyes full of love for a man he had begun to consider his brother. He stepped forward and hugged Shiva tightly. Shiva was a little surprised. It was usually Shiva who would move to embrace Brahaspati first, and Brahaspati would normally respond later, a little tentatively.

'My brother,' whispered Brahaspati.

'Ditto,' mumbled Shiva.

Stepping slightly back but still holding Shiva's arms, Brahaspati said, 'I would go anywhere for you. Even into Patallok if it would help you.'

'I would never take you there, my friend,' answered Shiva with a grin, thinking that he himself wasn't about to venture into *Patallok*, the *land of the demons*.

Brahaspati smiled warmly at Shiva. 'I hope to see you soon, Shiva.'

'You can count on it!'

Turning to Sati, Brahaspati said, 'Take care, my child. It is so good to see you finally get the life you deserve.'

'Thank you, Brahaspati*ji*.'

CHAPTER 20

Attack on Mandar

'How are you, my friend?'

'What the hell am I doing here?' asked a startled Shiva.

He found himself sitting in the Brahma temple in Meru. Sitting in front of him was the Pandit whom he had met during his first visit to Meru, many months back.

'You called me here,' said the Pandit smiling.

'But how and when did I get here?' asked Shiva, astounded.

'As soon as you went to sleep,' replied the Pandit. 'This is a dream.'

'I'll be damned!'

'Why do you swear so much?' asked the Pandit frowning.

'I only swear when the occasion demands,' grinned Shiva. 'And what's wrong with swearing?'

'Well, I think it reflects poor manners. It shows, perhaps, a slight deficiency in character.'

'On the contrary, I think it shows tremendous character. It shows that you have the strength and passion to speak your mind.'

The Pandit guffawed, shaking his head slightly.

'In any case,' continued Shiva. 'Now that you are here,

why don't you tell me what you people are called? I was promised I would be told the next time I met one of you.'

'But you haven't met one of us again. This is a dream. I can only tell you what you already know,' said the Pandit, smiling mysteriously. 'Or something that already exists in your consciousness that you haven't chosen to listen to as yet.'

'So that's what this is all about! You are here to help me discover something I already know!'

'Yes,' said the Pandit, his smile growing more enigmatic.

'Well, what is it that we are supposed to talk about?'

'The colour of that leaf,' beamed the Pandit, pointing towards the many trees that could be seen from the temple, through its ostentatiously carved pillars.

'The colour of that leaf?!'

'Yes.'

Frowning strongly, Shiva sighed, 'Why, in the name of the Holy Lake, is the colour of that leaf important?'

'Many times a good conversational journey to find knowledge makes attaining it that much more satisfying,' said the Pandit. 'And more importantly, it helps you understand the context of the knowledge much more easily.'

'Context of the knowledge?'

'Yes. All knowledge has its context. Unless you know the context, you may not understand the point.'

'And I'll know all that by talking about the colour of that leaf?'

'Yes.'

'By the Holy Lake, man!' groaned Shiva. 'Let's talk about the leaf then.'

'All right,' laughed the Pandit. 'Tell me. What is the colour of that leaf?'

'The colour? It's green.'

'Is it?'

'Isn't it?

'Why do you think it appears green to you?'

'Because,' said Shiva, amused, 'it *is* green.'

'No. That wasn't what I was trying to ask. You had a conversation with one of Brahaspati's scientists about how the eyes see. Didn't you?'

'Oh that, right,' said Shiva slapping his forehead. 'Light falls on an object. And when it reflects back from that object to your eyes, you see that object.'

'Exactly! And you had another conversation with another scientist about what normal white sunlight is made of.'

'Yes, I did. White light is nothing but the confluence of seven different colours. That is why the rainbow is made up of seven colours since it is formed when raindrops disperse sunlight.'

'Correct! Now put these two theories together and answer my question. Why does that leaf appear green to you?

Shiva frowned as his mind worked the problem out. 'White sunlight falls on that leaf. The leaf's physical properties are such that it *absorbs* the colours violet, indigo, blue, yellow, orange and red. It doesn't absorb the colour green, which is then reflected back to my eyes. Hence I see the leaf as green.'

'Exactly!' beamed the Pandit. 'So think about the colour of that leaf from the perspective of the leaf itself. What colour it absorbs and what it rejects. Is its colour green? Or is it every single colour in the world, *except* green?'

Shiva was stunned into silence by the simplicity of the argument being presented to him.

'There are many realities. There are many versions of what may appear obvious,' continued the Pandit. 'Whatever appears as the unshakeable truth, its exact opposite may also be true in another context. After all, one's reality is but perception, viewed through various prisms of context.'

Shiva turned slowly towards the leaf again. Its lustrous green colour shone through in the glorious sunlight.

'Are your eyes capable of seeing another reality?' asked the Pandit.

Shiva continued to stare at the leaf as it gradually altered its appearance. The colour seemed to be dissolving out of the leaf as its bright green hue gradually grew lighter and lighter. It slowly reduced itself to a shade of grey. As a stunned Shiva continued to stare, even the grey seemed to dissolve slowly, till the leaf was almost transparent. Only its outline could be discerned. It appeared as though numerous curved lines of two colours, black and white, were moving in and out of the outline of the leaf. It almost seemed as if the leaf was nothing but a carrier, which the black and white curved lines used as a temporary stop on their eternal journey.

It took some time for Shiva to realise that the surrounding leaves had also been transformed into their outlines. As his eyes panned, he noticed that the entire tree had magically transformed into an outline, with the black and white curved lines flowing in and out, easily and smoothly. He turned his head to soak in the panorama. Every object, from the squirrels on the trees to the pillars of the temple had all been transformed into outlines of their apparent selves. The same black and white curved lines streamed in and out of them.

Turning to the Pandit for an explanation, he was stunned

to see that the priest himself was also transformed into an outline of his former self. White curved lines were flooding out of him with frightening intensity. Strangely though, there were no black lines around him.

'What the…'

Shiva's words were stopped by the outline of the Pandit pointing back at him. 'Look at yourself, my Karmasaathi,' advised the Pandit.

Shiva looked down. 'I'll be damned!'

His body too had been transformed into an outline, completely transparent inside. Torrents of black curved lines were gushing furiously into him. On close examination he could see that they were not lines at all. They were, in fact, tiny waves which were jet black in colour. The waves were so tiny that from even a slight distance, they appeared like lines. There wasn't even a hint of the white waves close to Shiva's outlined body. 'What the hell is going on?'

'The white waves are positive energy and the black are negative,' said the Pandit's outline. 'They are both important. Their balance crucial. It will be cataclysmic if they fall out of sync.'

Shiva looked up at the Pandit, puzzled. 'So why is there no positive energy around me? And no negative energy around you?'

'Because we balance each other. The Vishnu's role is to transmit positive energy,' said the Pandit. The white lines pouring feverishly out of the Pandit seemed to flutter a bit whenever he spoke. 'And the Mahadev's role is to absorb the negative. Search for it. Search for negative energy and you will fulfil your destiny as a Mahadev.'

'But I am no Mahadev. My deeds till now are not deserving of that title.'

'It doesn't work that way, my friend. The title isn't at all the result of one's deeds. Deeds, however noble, will follow the rightful belief in you that you are the Mahadev. It matters little what others think. Believe you are the Mahadev, and you will become one.'

Shiva frowned.

'Believe!' repeated the Pandit.

BOOM! A distant reverberation echoed through the ambience. Shiva turned his eyes towards the horizon.

'It sounds like an explosion,' whispered the Pandit's outline.

The distant, insistent voice of Sati came riding in. 'S-H-I-V-A…'

BOOM! Another explosion.

'S-H-I-V-A…'

'It looks like your wife needs you, my friend.'

Shiva looked with astonishment at the outline of the Pandit, unable to decipher where the sound came from.

'Maybe you should wake up,' advised the Pandit's disembodied voice.

'S-H-I-V-A'

A groggy Shiva woke up to find Sati staring at him with concern. He was still a little bleary from the outlandishly strange dream state that he had just been yanked out of.

'Shiva!'

BOOM!

'What the hell was that?' cried Shiva, alert now.

'Someone is using *daivi astras*!'

'What? What are *daivi astras*?'

A clearly stunned Sati spoke agitatedly, '*Divine weapons!* But Lord Rudra had destroyed all the *daivi astras*! Nobody has access to them anymore!'

Shiva was completely alert by now, his battle instincts primed. 'Sati, get ready. Wear your armour. Bind your weapons.'

Sati responded swiftly. Shiva slipped on his armour, coupled his shield to it and tied his sword to his waist. He slipped on his quiver smoothly and picked up his bow. Noting that Sati was ready, he kicked the door open. Taman and eight other guards had their swords drawn, ready to defend their Neelkanth against any attack.

'My Lord, you should wait inside,' said Taman. 'We will hold the attackers here.'

Shiva stared hard at Taman, frowning at his well-intentioned words. Taman immediately stepped aside. 'I am sorry, my Lord. We will follow you.'

Before Shiva could react, they heard footsteps rushing in towards them in the hallway. Shiva immediately drew his sword. He strained his ears to assess the threat.

Four footsteps. Just two men to attack a royal hallway! This didn't make sense.

One pair of footsteps dragged slightly. The terrorist was clearly a large man using considerable willpower to make his feet move faster than his girth allowed.

'Stand down, soldiers,' ordered Shiva suddenly. 'They are friends.'

Nandi and Veerbhadra emerged around the corner, running hard, with their swords at the ready.

'Are you alright, my Lord?' asked Nandi, admirably not out of breath.

'Yes. We are all safe. Did the two of you face any attacks?'

'No,' answered Veerbhadra, frowning. 'What the hell is going on?'

'I don't know,' said Shiva. 'But we're going to find out.'

'Where's Krittika?' asked Sati.

'Safe in her room,' answered Veerbhadra. 'There are five soldiers with her. The room is barred from the inside.'

Sati nodded, before turning to Shiva. 'What now?'

'I want to check on the Emperor first. Everybody, files of two. Keep your shields up for cover. Sati at my side. Nandi in the middle. Taman, Veerbhadra, at the rear. Don't light any torches. We know the way. Our enemies don't.'

The platoon moved with considerable speed and stealth, mindful of possible surprise attacks from the terrorists. Shiva was troubled by what he had heard. Or rather, what he hadn't. Apart from the repeated explosions, there was absolutely no other sound from the palace. No screams of terror. No sound of panicked footsteps. No clash of steel. Nothing. Either the terrorists had not begun their real attack as yet, or Shiva was late and the attack was already over. Shiva frowned as a third alternative occurred to him. Maybe there were no terrorists in the palace itself. Maybe the attack was being mounted from a distance, with the *daivi astras* that Sati spoke of.

Shiva's platoon reached Daksha's chambers to find his guards at the door tense and ready for battle.

'Where is the Emperor?' asked Shiva.

'He is inside, my Lord,' said the royal guard Captain, recognising the Neelkanth's silhouette immediately. 'Where are they, my Lord? We've been waiting for an attack ever since we heard the first explosion.'

'I don't know, Captain,' replied Shiva. 'Stay here and block the doorway. Taman, support the Captain here with your men. And remain alert.'

Shiva opened the Emperor's door. 'Your Highness?'

'My Lord? Is Sati all right?' asked Daksha.

'Yes, she is, your Highness,' said Shiva, as Sati, Nandi and Veerbhadra followed him into the chamber. 'And the Queen?'

'Shaken. But not too scared.'

'What was that?'

'I don't know,' answered Daksha. 'I would suggest that you and Sati stay here for now till we know what's going on.'

'Perhaps it maybe advisable for you to stay here, your Highness. We cannot risk any harm coming your way. I am going out to help Parvateshwar. If this is a terrorist attack, we need all the strength we have.'

'You don't have to go, my Lord. This is Devagiri. Our soldiers will slay all the terrorists dim-witted enough to attack our capital.'

Before Shiva could respond, there was a loud insistent knocking on the door.

'Your Highness? Request permission to enter.'

'*Parvateshwar!*' thought Daksha. '*Observing protocol even at a time like this!*'

'Come in!' growled Daksha. As Parvateshwar entered, Daksha let fly. 'How in Lord Indra's name can this happen, General? An attack on Devagiri? How dare they?'

'Your Highness,' intercepted Shiva. Sati, Nandi and Veerbhadra were in the chambers. He could not allow Parvateshwar to be insulted in their presence, least of all in Sati's. 'Let us first find out what is going on.'

'The attack is not on Devagiri, your Highness,' glared Parvateshwar, his impatience with his Emperor having put him on edge. 'My scouts saw massive plumes of smoke coming from the direction of Mount Mandar. I believe it is under attack. I have already given orders for my troops and the station Arishtanemi to be ready. We leave in an hour. I need your permission to depart.'

'The explosions were in Mandar, Pitratulya?' asked Sati incredulously. 'How powerful must they have been to be heard in Devagiri!'

Parvateshwar looked gloomily at Sati, his silence conveying his deepest fears. He turned towards Daksha. 'Your Highness?'

Daksha seemed stunned into silence. Or was that a frown on his forehead? Parvateshwar could not be sure in the dim light.

'Guards, light the torches!' ordered Parvateshwar. 'There is no attack on Devagiri!'

As the torches spread their radiance, Parvateshwar repeated, 'Do I have your permission, my Lord?'

Daksha nodded softly.

Parvateshwar turned to see Shiva looking shocked. 'What happened, Shiva?'

'Brahaspati left for Mount Mandar yesterday.'

'What?' asked a startled Parvateshwar, who had not noticed the chief scientist's absence in the celebrations of the previous day. 'O Lord Agni!'

Shiva turned slowly towards Sati, drawing strength from her presence.

'I will find him, Shiva,' consoled Parvateshwar. 'I am sure he is alive. I will find him.'

'I'm coming with you,' said Shiva.

'And so am I,' said Sati.

'What?' asked Daksha, the light making his agonised expression clear. 'You both don't need to go.'

Shiva turned to Daksha, frowning. 'My apologies, your Highness. But I must go. Brahaspati needs me.'

As Parvateshwar and Shiva turned to leave the royal chambers, Sati bent down to touch her father's feet. Daksha seemed too dazed to bless her and Sati did not want to remain too far behind her husband. She quickly turned to touch her mother's feet.

'*Ayushman bhav*,' said Veerini.

Sati frowned at the odd blessing — '*May you live long*'. She was going into a battle. She wanted victory, not a long life! But there was little time to argue. Sati turned and raced behind Shiva as Nandi and Veerbhadra followed closely.

CHAPTER 21

Preparation for War

The noise of the explosions stopped within an hour of the first. It wasn't much later that Shiva, Parvateshwar, Sati, Nandi and Veerbhadra, accompanied by a brigade of one thousand five hundred cavalry, were on their way to Mount Mandar. Brahaspati's scientists rode with the brigade, sick with worry about their leader's fate. They rode hard and hoped to cover the day-long distance to the mountain in fewer than eight hours. It was almost at the end of the second prahar, with the sun directly overhead that the brigade turned the last corner of the road where the forest cover cleared to give them their first glimpse of the mountain.

An angry roar rent the air as the soldiers sighted what admittedly had been the heart of their empire. Mandar had been ruthlessly destroyed. The mountain had a colossal crater at its centre. It was almost as if a giant Asura had struck his massive hands right through the core of the mountain and scooped it out. The enormous buildings of science were in ruins, their remnants scattered across the plains below. The giant churners at the bottom of the mountain were still functioning, their eerie sound making the gruesome picture even more macabre.

'Brahaspati!' roared Shiva, as he rode hard, right into the heart of the mountain, where miraculously the pathway still stood strong.

'Wait Shiva,' called out Parvateshwar. 'It could be a trap.'

Shiva, unmindful of any danger, continued to gallop up the pathway through the devastated heart of the mountain. The brigade, with Parvateshwar and Sati in the lead, rode fast, trying to keep up with their Neelkanth. They reached the top to be horrified by what they saw. Parts of the buildings hung limply on broken foundations, some structures still smouldering. Scorched and unrecognisable body parts, ripped apart by the repeated explosions, were strewn all over. It was impossible to even identify the dead.

Shiva tumbled off his horse, his face devoid of even a ray of hope. Nobody could have survived such a lethal attack. 'Brahaspati...'

— ⚹ —

'How did the terrorists get their hands on the *daivi astras*?' asked an agitated Parvateshwar, the fire of vengeance blazing within him.

The soldiers had been ordered to collect all the body parts and cremate them in separate pyres, to help the departed on their onward journey. A manifest was being drawn up of the names of those believed dead. The first name on the list was that of Brahaspati, Chief Scientist of Meluha, Sarayupaari Brahmin, Swan chosen-tribe. The others were mostly Arishtanemi, assigned to the task of protecting Mandar. It was a small consolation that the casualties were minimal since most of the mountain's residents were in Devagiri for the Neelkanth's marriage. The list was going to be sent to the great sanyasis in Kashmir, whose powers over the spiritual force were considered second to none. If the sanyasis could be cajoled into reciting prayers for these departed souls, then it could be hoped that their grisly death in this birth would not mar their subsequent births.

'It could have also been the Somras, General,' said Panini, one of Brahaspati's assistant chief scientists, offering another plausible explanation.

Shiva looked up suddenly on hearing Panini's words.

'The Somras did this! How?' asked a disbelieving Sati.

'The Somras is very unstable during its manufacturing process,' continued Panini. 'It is kept stable by using copious quantities of the Saraswati waters. One of our main projects was to determine whether we could stabilise the Somras while using less water. Much lesser than at present.'

Shiva remembered Brahaspati talking about this. He leaned over to listen intently to Panini.

'It was one of the dream projects of…' Panini found it hard to complete the statement. The thought that Brahaspati, the greatest scientist of his generation, the father-figure to all the learned men at Mount Mandar, was gone, was too much for Panini to bear. He was choked by the intense pain he felt inside. He stopped talking, shut his eyes and hoped the terrible moment would pass. Regaining a semblance of control over himself, he continued, 'It was one of Brahaspati*ji*'s dream projects. He had come back to organise the experiment that was to begin today. He didn't want us to miss the last day of the celebrations. So he came alone.'

Parvateshwar was numb. 'You mean this could have been an accident?'

'Yes,' replied Panini. 'We were all aware that the experiment was risky. Maybe that is why Brahaspati*ji* decided to begin without us.'

The entire room was stunned into silence by this unexpected information. Panini retreated into his private hell. Parvateshwar continued to gaze into the distance, shocked by the turn of events. Sati stared at Shiva, holding his hand, deeply worried about how her husband was taking the death of his friend. And that it may all have been just a senseless mishap!

— ⸻ —

It was late into the first hour of the fourth prahar. It had been decided that the brigade would set up camp at the base of the ruined mountain. They would leave the following day, after all the ceremonies for the departed had been completed. Two riders had been dispatched to Devagiri with the news about Mandar. Parvateshwar and Sati sat at the edge of the mountain peak, whispering to each other. The drone of Brahmin scientists reciting Sanskrit shlokas at the base of the mountain floated up to create an ethereal atmosphere of pathos. Nandi and Veerbhadra stood at attention, a polite distance from Parvateshwar and Sati, looking at their Lord.

Shiva was walking around the ruins of the Mandar buildings, lost in thought. It was tearing him apart that he hadn't seen any recognisable part of Brahaspati. Everybody in Mandar had been mutilated beyond recognition. He desperately searched for some sign of his friend. Something he could keep with himself. Something he could cling on to, which would soothe his tortured soul in the years of mourning that he would go through. He walked at a snail's pace; his eyes combing the ground. They suddenly fell upon an object he recognised only too well.

He slowly bent down to pick it up. It was a bracelet made of leather, burnt at the edges, its back-hold destroyed. The heat of the fiery explosions had scorched its brown colour to black at most places. The centre however, with an embroidered design, was astonishingly unblemished. Shiva brought it close to his eyes.

The crimson hue of the setting sun caused the Aum symbol to glow. At the amalgam of the top and bottom curve of the Aum were two serpent heads. The third curve, surging out to the east, ended in a sharp serpent head, with its forked tongue striking out threateningly.

It was him! He killed Brahaspati!

Shiva swung around, eyes desperately scanning the limbs scattered about, hoping to find the owner of the bracelet or some part of him. But there was nothing. Shiva screamed silently. A scream audible only to him and Brahaspati's wounded soul. He clutched the bracelet in his fist till its still burning embers burnt into his palms. Clasping it even more firmly, he swore a terrible vengeance. He vowed to bring upon the Naga a death that would scar him for his next seven births. That Naga, and his entire army of vice, would be annihilated. Piece by bloody piece.

'Shiva! Shiva!' The insistent call yanked him back to reality.

Sati was standing in front of him, gently touching his hand. Parvateshwar stood next to her, disturbed. Nandi and Veerbhadra stood to the other side.

'Let it go, Shiva,' said Sati.

Shiva continued to stare at her, blank.

'Let it go, Shiva,' repeated Sati softly. 'It's singeing your hand.'

Shiva opened his palm. Nandi immediately lunged forward to pull the bracelet out. Screaming in surprised agony, Nandi dropped the bracelet as it scalded his hand. How did the Lord hold it for so long?

Shiva immediately bent down and picked up the bracelet. This time carefully. His fingers were holding the less charred edge, the part with the Aum symbol. He turned to Parvateshwar. 'It was not an accident.'

'What?' cried a startled Parvateshwar.

'Are you sure?' asked Sati.

Shiva looked towards Sati and raised the bracelet, the serpent Aum clearly coming into view. Sati let out a gasp of shock. Parvateshwar, Nandi and Veerbhadra immediately closed in to stare intently at the bracelet.

'Naga…,' whispered Nandi.

'The same bastard who attacked Sati in Meru,' growled Shiva. 'The same Naga who attacked us on our return from Mandar. The very, bloody, same, son of a bitch.'

'He will pay for this Shiva,' said Veerbhadra.

Turning towards Parvateshwar, Shiva said, 'We ride to Devagiri tonight. We declare war.'

Parvateshwar nodded.

The Meluhan war council sat quietly, observing five minutes of silence in honour of the martyrs of Mandar. General Parvateshwar and his twenty-five brigadiers sat to the right of Emperor Daksha. To Daksha's left sat the Neelkanth, the administrative Brahmins led by Prime Minister Kanakhala and the governors of the fifteen provinces.

'The decision of the council is a given,' said Daksha, beginning the proceedings. 'The question is when do we attack?'

'It will take us at the most a month to be ready to march, your Highness,' said Parvateshwar. 'You know that there are no roads between Meluha and Swadweep. Our army would have to travel through dense, impenetrable forests. So even if we begin the march in a month, we will not be in Swadweep before three months from today. So time is of the essence.'

'Then let the preparations begin.'

'Your Highness,' said Kanakhala, adding a Brahmin voice of reason to the battle cry of the Kshatriyas. 'May I suggest an alternative?'

'An alternative?' asked a surprised Daksha.

'Please don't misunderstand me,' said Kanakhala. 'I understand the rage of the entire nation about what happened at Mandar. But we want vengeance against the perpetrators of the crime, not all of Swadweep. Could we try and see whether a scalpel might work before we bring out the mighty war sword?'

'The path you suggest is one of cowardice, Kanakhala,' said Parvateshwar.

'No Parvateshwar, my aim is to seek our vengeance at minimum cost to Meluhan lives,' said Kanakhala politely. 'After all, discretion is the better part of valour.'

'My soldiers are resolute and will defend Meluha to the death, Madam Prime Minister.'

'I know they will,' said Kanakhala, maintaining her composure. 'And I know that you too are willing to shed your blood for Meluha. My suggestion is that we send an emissary to Emperor Dilipa and request him to surrender the terrorists who perpetrated this attack. We can threaten that if he doesn't co-operate, we will attack with all the might at our disposal.'

His eyes scowling with impatience, Parvateshwar said, '*Request* him? And why would he listen? For decades, the Swadweepans have got away with their nefarious activities because they think we don't have the stomach for a fight. And if we talk about this "scalpel approach" after an outrage like Mount Mandar, they will be convinced that they can mount any attack at will and we will not respond.'

'I disagree, Parvateshwar,' said Kanakhala. 'They have mounted terrorist attacks because they are scared that they cannot take us on in a direct fight. They are afraid that they cannot withstand our superior technology and war-machines. I am only thinking about what Lord Shiva had said when he had first come here. Can we try talking to them before we fight? This may be an opportunity to get them to admit that there are sections in their society who are terrorists. If they hand them over, we may even find ways of coexisting.'

'I don't think Shiva thinks like that anymore,' said Parvateshwar, pointing towards the Neelkanth. 'He too wants vengeance.'

Shiva sat silently, his face expressionless. Only his eyes glowered with the terrible anger seething within.

'My Lord,' said Kanakhala looking towards Shiva, her hands folded in a Namaste. 'I hope that at least you understand what I am trying to say. Even Brahaspati would have wanted us to avoid violence, if possible.'

The last sentence had an effect on Shiva similar to a torrential downpour on a raging fire. He turned towards Kanakhala and gazed into her eyes, before turning towards Daksha. 'Your Highness, what Kanakhala says is right. Perhaps we can send an emissary to Swadweep to give them an opportunity to atone for their sins. Striving for a peaceful resolution will help in avoiding the deaths of innocents. However, I would still suggest that we begin war preparations. We should be prepared for the possibility that the Chandravanshis may reject our offer.'

'The Mahadev has spoken,' said Daksha. 'I propose that this be the decision of the war council. All in favour, raise your hands.'

Every hand in the room was raised. The die had been cast. There would be an attempt at peace. If that didn't work, the Meluhans would attack.

— ⁂ —

'I have failed again, Bhadra,' cried Shiva. 'I can't protect anyone in need.'

Shiva was sitting next to Veerbhadra, in a private section of his palace courtyard. A deeply worried Sati had invited Veerbhadra to try and pull Shiva out of his mourning. Shiva had retreated into a shell, not speaking, not crying. She hoped her husband's childhood friend would succeed where she had failed.

'How can you blame yourself, Shiva?' asked Veerbhadra,

handing over the chillum to his friend. 'How can this be your fault?'

Shiva picked up the chillum and took a deep drag. The marijuana coursed through his body, but did not help. The pain was too intense. Shiva snorted in disgust and threw the chillum away. As tears flooded his eyes, he looked up at the sky and swore, 'I will avenge you, my brother. Even if it is the last thing I do. Even if I have to spend every moment of the rest of my life doing so. Even if I have to come back to this world again and again. I will avenge you!'

Veerbhadra turned towards Sati sitting in the distance, a worried look on his face. Sati got up and walked towards them. She came up to Shiva and held him tight, resting his tired head against her bosom, hoping to soothe Shiva's tortured soul. To Sati's surprise, Shiva did not raise his arms to wrap them around her. He just sat motionless. Breathing intermittently.

'My Lord,' cried a surprised Vraka, as he stood to attention. Respectfully, so did the twenty-four other brigadiers for the Neelkanth had just been announced into the war room.

Parvateshwar rose slowly. He spoke kindly as he knew the pain Shiva still carried about Brahaspati's grisly death. 'How are you, Shiva?'

'I am alright, thank you.'

'We were discussing battle plans.'

'I know,' said Shiva. 'I was wondering if I could join in.'

'Of course,' said Parvateshwar, as he moved his chair to the side.

'The essential problem for us,' said Parvateshwar, trying to quickly bring Shiva up to speed, 'is the transport links between Meluha and Swadweep.'

'There aren't any, right?'

'Right,' answered Parvateshwar. 'After their last defeat at our hands a hundred years ago, the Chandravanshis destroyed the entire infrastructure that then existed between Meluha and Swadweep. They depopulated their border cities and moved them deeper into their empire. Forests grew where cities and roads once were. There is no river that flows from our territory into theirs. Basically, there is no way our huge, technologically superior war-machines can be transported to the borders of Swadweep.'

'That was their intention, obviously,' said Shiva. 'Your superiority is technology. Their superiority is their numbers. They have negated your strength.'

'Exactly. And if our war-machines are taken out of the equation, our one hundred thousand strong army may get inundated by their million soldiers.'

'They have a million strong army?' asked Shiva, incredulous.

'Yes, my Lord,' said Vraka. 'We can't be absolutely sure, but that is our estimate. However, we also estimate that the regulars in their army would not be more than a hundred thousand. The rest would be part-timers. Essentially, people such as small traders, artisans, farmers and any one without influence. They would be forcibly conscripted and used as cannon fodder.'

'Disgusting,' said Parvateshwar. 'Risking the lives of Shudras and Vaishyas for a job that should be done by Kshatriyas. Their Kshatriyas have no honour.'

Shiva looked towards Parvateshwar and nodded. 'Can't

we dismantle our war-machines, carry them to Swadweep and reassemble them?'

'Yes we can,' said Parvateshwar. 'But that is technically possible only for a few. Our most devastating machines which would give us the edge, like the long-range catapult, cannot be assembled outside a factory.'

'The long-range catapult?'

'Yes,' answered Parvateshwar. 'It can hurl huge boulders and smouldering barrels over distances of more than a kilometre. If used effectively they can soften, even devastate, the enemy lines before our cavalry and infantry begin their charge. Basically, the role that elephants used to play earlier.'

'Then why not use elephants?'

'They are unpredictable. No matter how effectively you train them, an army often loses control over them in the heat of the battle. In fact, in the previous war with the Swadweepans, it was their own elephants who brought about their downfall.'

'Really?' asked Shiva.

'Yes,' answered Parvateshwar. 'Our ploy of firing at the mahouts and generating tremendous noise with our war drums worked. The Chandravanshi elephants panicked and ran into their own army, shattering their lines, especially the ones composed of irregulars. All we had to do then was charge in and finish the job.'

'No elephants then.'

'Absolutely,' said Parvateshwar.

'So we need something that we can carry along with us and which can be used to soften their irregulars in order to negate their numerical superiority.'

Parvateshwar nodded. Shiva looked towards the window,

where a stiff morning breeze was making the leaves flutter. The leaves were green. Shiva stared harder. They remained green.

'I know,' said Shiva, looking at Parvateshwar suddenly, his face luminescent. 'Why don't we use arrows?'

'Arrows?' asked a surprised Parvateshwar.

Archery was the battle art of the most elite Kshatriyas, used for one-on-one duels. However, since one-on-one duels could only be fought between warriors of equal chosen-tribes, this skill was reduced to being a demonstration art for the crème de la crème. Archers earned huge respect for their rare skill, but they were not decisive in battles. There had been a time when bows and arrows were crucial in war strategies as weapons of mass destruction. That was the time of the *daivi astras*. Many of these astras were usually released through arrows. However, with the ban on *daivi astras* many thousands of years ago by Lord Rudra, the effectiveness of archery units in large-scale battles had reduced drastically.

'How can that reduce their numerical superiority, my Lord?' asked Vraka. 'Even the most skilled among the archers will take at least five seconds to aim, fire and execute a kill. He will not be able to kill more than twelve a minute. We have only one hundred Kshatriyas who are of the gold order of archers. The rest can shoot, but their aim cannot be relied upon. So we will not be able to kill more than one thousand two hundred of our enemies per minute. Certainly not enough against the Chandravanshis.'

'I am not talking about using arrows for one-on-one shooting,' said Shiva. 'I am talking about using them for softening the enemy, as weapons of mass destruction.'

Disregarding the confused expressions of his audience,

Shiva continued, 'Let me explain. Suppose we create a corps of archers of the lower Kshatriya chosen-tribes.'

'But their aim wouldn't be good,' said Vraka.

'That doesn't matter. Let us say we have at least five thousand such archers. Suppose we train them to just get the range right. Forget about the aim. Suppose their job is to just keep firing arrows in the general direction of the Chandravanshi army. If they don't have to aim, they can fire a lot more quickly. Maybe one arrow every two or three seconds.'

Parvateshwar narrowed his eyes as the brilliance of the idea struck him. The rest of his brigadiers were still trying to gather their thoughts.

'Think about it,' said Shiva. 'We would have five thousand arrows raining down on the Chandravanshis every two seconds. Suppose we can keep this up for ten minutes. An almost continuous shower of arrows. Their irregulars would break. The arrows would have the same effect as that of the elephants in the last war!'

'Brilliant!' cried Vraka.

'Perhaps,' mused Parvateshwar, 'our archers could be trained to release the arrows lying on their backs while holding up the bow with their feet. No doubt, accuracy would be somewhat compromised. But the effect would be far more deadly.'

'Excellent!' exclaimed Shiva. 'Because then the bows can be bigger. And the range longer.'

'And the arrows bigger and thicker, almost like small spears,' continued Parvateshwar. 'Strong enough to even penetrate leather and thick wooden shields. Only the soldiers with metal shields, like the regulars, would be safe from this.'

'Do we have our answer?' asked Shiva.

'Yes, we do,' answered Parvateshwar with a smile. He turned towards Vraka. 'Create this corps. I want five thousand men ready within two weeks.'

'It will be done, my Lord,' said Vraka.

— ⅄ⓄƱ⍋⊗ —

'What do you want to talk about, Shiva?' asked Parvateshwar, as he entered the metallurgy factory. He was accompanied by Vraka and Prasanjit, just as Shiva had requested. Vraka had reluctantly left the archery corps he had been training over the past week. However, he had been motivated to attend in expectation of another brilliant idea from the Neelkanth. He was not disappointed.

'I was thinking,' said Shiva, 'we would still need an equivalent of your stabbing ram to break their centre. The centre is where I assume their General would place their regulars. As long as they hold, our victory cannot be guaranteed.'

'Right,' said Parvateshwar. 'And we have to assume that these soldiers would be disciplined enough to stay in formation despite the barrage of arrows.'

'Exactly,' said Shiva. 'We can't transport the ram, right?'

'No we can't, my Lord' said Vraka.

'How about if we try to create a human ram?'

'Go ahead,' said Parvateshwar slowly, listening intently.

'Say we align the soldiers into a square of twenty men by twenty men,' said Shiva. 'We can have each one of them use his shield to cover the left half of his own body and the right half of the soldier to the left of him.'

'That will allow them to push their spear through, from in between the shields,' said Parvateshwar.

'Exactly,' said Shiva. 'And the soldiers behind can use their shields as a lid to cover themselves as well as the soldier in front. This formation would be like a tortoise. With the shields holding against any attack, much like a tortoise's shell, the enemy will not be able to break through, but our spears will cut into them.'

'We could have the strongest and most experienced soldiers in the front to make sure that the tortoise is well led,' said Prasanjit.

'No,' said Parvateshwar. 'Position the most experienced at the back and at the sides. To make sure that the square doesn't break in case the younger soldiers panic. This entire formation works only if the team stays together.'

'Right,' said Shiva, smiling at Parvateshwar's quick insight. 'And what if, instead of the usual spears, they carried this?'

Shiva raised a weapon that he had designed and the army metallurgy team had quickly assembled. Parvateshwar marvelled at the simple brilliance of it. It had the body of a spear. But its head had been broadened. On to the broadened head, two more spikes had been added, to the left and right of the main spear spike. Assaulting an enemy with this weapon would be like striking him with three spears at the same time.

'Absolutely brilliant Shiva,' marvelled Parvateshwar. 'What do you call it?'

'I call it a trishul.'

'Prasanjit,' said Parvateshwar. 'You are in charge of creating this corps. I want at least five tortoise formations ready by the time we march. I will assign two thousand men to you for this.'

'It will be done, my Lord,' said Prasanjit with a military salute.

Parvateshwar gazed at Shiva with respect. He knew that Shiva's ideas were brilliant. And the fact that he had come up with these tactics despite his profound personal grief was worthy of admiration. Maybe what the others say about Shiva could be true. Maybe he is the man who will finish Lord Ram's task. Parvateshwar hoped that Shiva would not prove him wrong.

Shiva sat in the royal meeting room, with Daksha and Parvateshwar at his side. Two legendary Arishtanemi brigadiers, Vidyunmali and Mayashrenik, sat at a distance. A muscular and once proud man stood in front of Shiva, pleading with folded hands.

'Give me a chance, my Lord,' said Drapaku. 'If the law has been changed, then why can't we fight?'

Drapaku was the man whose blind father had blessed Shiva in Kotdwaar. He had been a brigadier in the Meluhan army before the disease which blinded his father had also killed his wife and unborn child. He had been declared a vikarma along with his father.

But Shiva refused to be rushed. 'Tell me Drapaku, how is your father?'

'He is well, my Lord. And he will disown me if I don't support you in this dharmayudh.'

Shiva smiled softly. He too believed this was a *dharmayudh*, a *holy war*. 'But Drapaku, who will take care of him if something were to happen to you?'

'Meluha will take care of him, my Lord. But he would die a thousand deaths if I didn't go to battle with you. What kind of a son would I be if I didn't fight for my father's honour? For my country's honour?'

Shiva still seemed a little unsure. He could sense the discomfort of the others in the room. It had not escaped his notice that despite the repeal of the vikarma law, nobody had touched Drapaku when he had entered.

'My Lord, we are outnumbered heavily by the Chandravanshis,' continued Drapaku. 'We need every trained warrior we have. There are at least five thousand soldiers who can't battle since they have been declared vikarma. I can bring them together. We are willing, and eager, to die for our country.'

'I don't want you to die for Meluha, brave Drapaku,' said Shiva.

Drapaku's face fell instantly. He thought he would be returning home to Kotdwaar.

'However,' continued Shiva. 'I would like it if you killed for Meluha.'

Drapaku looked up.

'Raise your brigade, Drapaku,' ordered Shiva. Turning towards Daksha, he continued, 'We will call it the Vikarma Brigade.'

— ⁂ —

'How can we have vikarmas in our army? This is ridiculous!' glared Vidyunmali.

Vidyunmali and Mayashrenik were in their private gym, preparing for their regular sword training.

'Vidyu...,' cajoled Mayashrenik.

'Don't "*Vidyu*" me, Maya. You know this is wrong.'

The usually calm Mayashrenik just nodded and let his impetuous friend vent his frustration.

'How will I face my ancestors if I die in this battle?' asked Vidyunmali. 'What will I answer if they ask me how I let a non-Kshatriya fight a battle that only we Kshatriyas should have fought? It is *our* duty to protect the weak. We are not supposed to use the weak to fight for us.'

'Vidyu, I don't think Drapaku is weak. Have you forgotten his valour in the previous Chandravanshi war?'

'He is a vikarma! That makes him weak!'

'Lord Shiva has decreed that there are no vikarmas anymore.'

'I don't think the Neelkanth truly knows right from wrong!'

'VIDYU!' shouted Mayashrenik.

Vidyunmali was surprised by the outburst.

'If the Neelkanth says it is right,' continued Mayashrenik, 'then it *is* right!'

CHAPTER 22

Empire of Evil

'This is the military formation that I think is ideal for the battle,' said Parvateshwar.

Vraka and Parvateshwar were sitting in the General's private office. The formation was that of a bow. The soldiers would be arranged in a wide semi-circular pattern. The slower corps, like the tortoises, would be placed at the centre. The flanks would comprise quicker units such as the light infantry. The cavalry would be at both ends of the bow, ready to be deployed anywhere on the battlefield or to ride along the sides of the bow for protection. The bow formation was ideal for a smaller army. It provided flexibility without sacrificing strength.

'It is ideal, my Lord,' said Vraka. 'What does the Mahadev have to say?'

'Shiva thinks it suits our requirements perfectly.'

Vraka did not like it when Parvateshwar referred to the Neelkanth by his name. But who was he to correct his General? 'I agree, my Lord.'

'I will lead the left flank,' said Parvateshwar. 'And you lead the right. Which is why I need your opinion on some tactics.'

'Me, my Lord?' asked an astonished Vraka. 'I thought the Mahadev would lead the other flank.'

'Shiva? No, I don't think he would be fighting this war, Vraka.'

Vraka looked up in surprise. But he remained silent.

Parvateshwar probably felt the need to explain, for he continued speaking. 'He is a good and capable man, no doubt. But the uppermost desire in his mind is retribution, not justice for Meluha. We will help him wreak vengeance when we throw the guilty Naga at his feet. He won't be putting his own life at risk in a war only to find one Naga.'

Vraka kept his eyes low, lest they betray the fact that he disagreed with his chief.

'To be fair,' said Parvateshwar. 'We cannot impose on him just because he has a blue throat. I respect him a lot. But I don't expect him to fight. What reason would there be for him to do that?'

Vraka looked up at Parvateshwar for a brief instant. Why was his General refusing to accept what was so obvious to everyone? Was he so attached to Lord Ram that he couldn't believe that another saviour had arrived on earth? Did he actually believe that Lord Ram could be the *only one*? Hadn't Lord Ram himself said that he is replaceable, only Dharma is irreplaceable?

'Furthermore,' continued Parvateshwar, 'he is married now. He is obviously in love. He is not going to risk Sati being bereaved again. Why should he? It's unfair of us to demand this of him.'

Vraka thought to himself, while not daring to voice his opinion. *'The Mahadev will fight for all of us, General. He will battle to protect us. Why? Because that is what Mahadevs do.'*

Vraka was not aware that Parvateshwar was hoping for

something similar in his mind. He too wished that Shiva would rise to be a Mahadev and lead them to victory against the Chandravanshis. However, Parvateshwar had learned through long years of experience that while many men tried to rise up to Lord Ram's stature, none had ever succeeded. Parvateshwar had laid hopes on a few such men in his youth. And he had always been disillusioned at the end. He was simply preparing himself for another such expected disappointment from Shiva. He didn't plan to be left without a backup if Shiva refused to fight the battle against the Chandravanshis.

— ✱ —

The war council sat silently as Daksha read the letter that had come back from Swadweep — from the court of Emperor Dilipa. Daksha's reaction upon reading the letter left no doubt as to the message it contained. He shut his eyes, his face contorted in rage, his fist clenched tight. He handed the letter over to Kanakhala and sneered, 'Read it. Read it out loud so that the whole world may be sickened by the repugnance of the Chandravanshis.'

Kanakhala frowned slightly before taking the letter and reading it out loud. 'Emperor Daksha, Suryavanshi liege, protector of Meluha. Please accept my deep condolences for the dastardly attack on Mount Mandar. Such a senseless assault on peaceful Brahmins cannot but be condemned in the strongest of terms. We are shocked that any denizen of India would stoop to such levels. It is, therefore, with surprise and sadness that I read your letter. I assure you that neither me nor anyone in my command has anything to do with this devious attack. Hence I have to inform you, with regret, that there is nobody I can hand over to you. I hope that you understand the sincerity of this letter and will not make a hasty decision, which may have regrettable consequences for you. I assure you of my empire's full support in the investigation of this outrage. Please do inform us as to how we can be of assistance to you in bringing the criminals to justice.'

Kanakhala took a deep breath to compose herself. The anger over the typically Chandravanshi-like doubletalk was washing all over her, making her regret her earlier stand.

'It's personally signed by the Emperor Dilipa,' said Kanakhala, completing her reading of the letter.

'Not *Emperor* Dilipa,' growled a fuming Daksha. '*Terrorist* Dilipa of the Empire of Evil!'

'War!' arose a cry from the council, unanimous in its rage.

Daksha looked over at a scowling Shiva who nodded imperceptibly.

'War it is!' bellowed Daksha. 'We march in two weeks!'

— —

The bracelet seemed to develop a life of its own. It had swelled to enormous proportions, dwarfing Shiva. Its edges were engulfed in gigantic flames. The three colossal serpents, which formed the Aum, separated from each other and slithered towards Shiva. The one in the centre, while nodding towards the snake on its left, hissed, 'He got your brother. And the other one will soon get your wife.'

The serpents to the left and right scowled eerily.

Shiva pointed his finger menacingly at the serpent in the centre. 'You dare touch even a hair on her and I will rip your soul out of…'

'But I…' continued the serpent, not even acknowledging Shiva's

threat. 'I'm saving myself. I'm saving myself for you.'

Shiva stared at the serpent with impotent rage.

'I will get you,' said the serpent as its mouth opened wide, ready to swallow him whole.

Shiva's eyes suddenly opened wide. He was perspiring profusely. He looked around, but couldn't see a thing. It was extraordinarily dark. He reached out for Sati, to check if she was safe. She wasn't there. He was up in a flash, feeling a chill in his heart, almost expecting that the serpents had escaped his dreams and transformed into reality.

'Shiva,' said Sati, looking at him.

She was sitting at the edge of the bed. The tiny military tent they slept in could not afford the luxury of chairs. This tent had been their travelling home for the last one month as the Meluhan army marched towards Swadweep.

'What is it, Sati?' asked Shiva, his eyes adjusting to the dim light. He slipped the offending bracelet that he was tightly holding, back into his pouch.

When had I taken it out?

'Shiva,' continued Sati. She had tried to talk about this for the last two weeks. Ever since she had been sure of the news, she had not found an opportune moment. She had always managed to convince herself that this was minor news and it would not be right for her to trouble her husband with this, especially when he was going through one of the worst phases of his life. But it was too late now. He had to learn from her and not someone else. News like this did not remain secret in an army camp for long. 'I have something to tell you.'

'Yes,' said Shiva, though his dream still rankled. 'What is it?'

'I don't think I will be able to fight in the war.'

'What? Why?' asked a startled Shiva. He knew that cowardice was a word that did not exist in Sati's dictionary. Then why was she saying this? And why now, when the army had already marched for nearly a month through the dense forests that separated Meluha from Swadweep? They were already in enemy territory. There was no turning back. 'Sati, this is not like you.'

'Umm, Shiva,' said an embarrassed Sati. Such discussions were always difficult for the somewhat prudish Suryavanshis. 'I have my reasons.'

'Reasons?' asked Shiva. 'What…'

Suddenly the reason smacked Shiva like a silent thunderbolt. 'My God! Are you sure?'

'Yes,' said Sati, bashfully.

'By the Holy Lake! Am I going to be a father?'

Seeing the ecstasy on Shiva's face, Sati felt a pang of guilt that she hadn't informed him earlier.

'Wow!' whooped a thrilled Shiva as he swirled around with her in his arms. 'This is the best news I have heard in a long time!'

Sati smiled warmly and rested her head on his tired but strong shoulders.

'We will name our daughter after the one who has been the greatest comfort to you in the last two months, while I have been of no help,' said Shiva. 'We will name her Krittika!'

Sati looked up in surprise. She didn't believe that it was possible to love him even more. But it was. She smiled. 'It could be a son, you know.'

'Nah,' grinned Shiva. 'It will be a daughter. And I'll spoil her to high heavens!'

Sati laughed heartily. Shiva joined in. His first spirited laugh in over two months. He embraced Sati, feeling the negative energy dissipate from his being. 'I love you, Sati.'

'I love you too,' she whispered.

— ⁂ —

Shiva raised the curtain to come out of the tent that Sati was ensconced in. Krittika and Ayurvati were with her. A retinue of nurses attended to her every need. Shiva had been obsessive about the health of his unborn child, questioning Ayurvati incessantly about every aspect of Sati's well-being.

The Suryavanshis had moved valiantly for nearly three months. The path had been more challenging than expected. The forest had reclaimed its original habitat with alarming ferocity. The army was attacked by wild animals and disease at every turn. They had lost two thousand men. And not one to the enemy. After weeks of hacking and marching, the scouts had finally managed to lead the Suryavanshi army to the Chandravanshis.

The Chandravanshis were camped on a sweeping plain called Dharmakhet. Their choice was clever. It was an expansive field that had enough room to allow the Chandravanshis to manoeuvre their million strong army. The full weight of their numerical superiority would come into play. The Suryavanshi army had tried to wait out the Chandravanshis, to test if they would lose patience and attack in a less advantageous area. But the Chandravanshis had held firm. Finally, the Suryavanshis moved camp to an easily defendable valley close to Dharmakhet.

Shiva looked up at the clear sky. A lone eagle flew

overhead, circling the royal camp, while five pigeons flew lower, unafraid of the eagle. A strange sign. His Guna shaman would have probably said that it's a bad time for battle, as the pigeons clearly have a hidden advantage.

Don't think about it. It is all nonsense in any case.

Breathing in the fresh morning air deeply, he turned right, towards Emperor Daksha's tent. Nandi was walking towards him.

'What is it Nandi?'

'I was just coming towards your tent, my Lord. The Emperor requests your presence. There's been a troubling development.'

Shiva and Nandi hurried towards Daksha's tastefully appointed royal tent. They entered to find Daksha and Parvateshwar engrossed in a discussion. Vraka, Mayashrenik and Drapaku sat at a distance. Drapaku was a little further away from the rest.

'This is a disaster,' groaned Daksha.

'Your Highness?' asked Shiva.

'My Lord! I'm glad you're here. We face complete disaster.'

'Let's not use words like that, your Highness,' said Shiva. Turning towards Parvateshwar, he asked, 'So your suspicions were correct?'

'Yes,' said Parvateshwar. 'The scouts just returned a few minutes back. There was a reason why the Chandravanshis were refusing to mobilise. They have despatched a hundred thousand soldiers in a great arc around our position. They will enter our valley by tomorrow morning. We will be sandwiched between their main force ahead of us and another hundred thousand behind us.'

'We can't fight on two fronts, my Lord,' cried Daksha. 'What do we do?'

'Was it Veerbhadra's scouts who returned with the news?' asked Shiva.

Parvateshwar nodded. Shiva turned towards Nandi, who rushed out immediately. Moments later, Veerbhadra stood before them.

'What route is the Chandravanshi detachment taking, Bhadra?' asked Shiva.

'To the east, along the steep mountains on our side. I think they intend to enter our valley some fifty kilometres up north.'

'Did you take a cartographer with you as Parvateshwar had instructed?'

Veerbhadra nodded, moved to the centre table and laid out the map on it. Shiva and Parvateshwar leaned across. Pointing to the route with his fingers, Veerbhadra said, 'This way.'

Shiva suddenly started as he noticed the ideal defensive position on the map, deep north of the Suryavanshi camp. He looked up at Parvateshwar. The same thought had occurred to the General.

'How many men do you think, Parvateshwar?'

'Difficult to say. It will be tough. But the pass looks defendable. It will need a sizeable contingent though. At least thirty thousand.'

'But we can't spare too many men. I am sure the battle with the main Chandravanshi army to the south will also happen tomorrow. It would be the best time for them to take up positions.'

Parvateshwar nodded grimly. The Meluhans might just have to retreat and manoeuvre for a battle from another, more advantageous position, he thought unhappily.

'I think five thousand men ought to do it, my Lords.'

Shiva and Parvateshwar had not noticed Drapaku move to the table. He was examining the pass that Shiva had just pointed out.

'Look here,' continued Drapaku, as Shiva and Parvateshwar peered.

'The mountains ahead constrict rapidly towards this pass, which is not more than fifty metres across. It doesn't matter how big their army is, each charge by the enemy into the pass cannot comprise more than a few hundred men.'

'But Drapaku, with a hundred thousand men, they can launch one charge after another, almost continuously,' said Mayashrenik. 'And with the mountains being so steep on the sides, you can't use any of our missiles. Victory is almost impossible.'

'It's not about victory,' said Drapaku. 'It's about holding them for a day so that our main army can fight.'

'I will do it,' said Parvateshwar.

'No, my Lord,' said Vraka. 'You are required for the main charge.'

Shiva looked up at Parvateshwar.

I need to be here as well.

'I can't do it either,' said Shiva, shaking his head.

Parvateshwar looked up at Shiva, disillusionment writ large on his face. While he had prepared his heart for disappointment, he had hoped that Shiva would prove him wrong. But it appeared clear to Parvateshwar that Shiva too would be simply watching the battle from the viewing platform being constructed for Daksha.

'Give me the honour, my Lord,' said Drapaku.

'Drapaku…,' whispered Mayashrenik, not putting into words what everyone else knew.

With only five thousand soldiers, the battle at the

northern pass against the Chandravanshi detachment was a suicide mission.

'Drapaku,' said Shiva. 'I don't know if…'

'I know, my Lord,' interrupted Drapaku. 'It is my destiny. I will hold them for one day. If Lord Indra supports me, I'll even try for two. Get us victory by then.'

Daksha suddenly interjected. 'Wonderful. Drapaku, make preparations to leave immediately.'

Drapaku saluted smartly and rushed out before any second thoughts were voiced.

— ⅄ⵔⵖⵠ⊛ —

In less than an hour the vikarma brigade was seen marching out of the camp. The sun was high up in the sky and practically the entire camp was awake, watching the soldiers set out on their mission. Everyone knew the terrible odds the vikarmas were going to face. They knew that it was unlikely that any of these soldiers would be seen alive again. The soldiers, though, did not exhibit the slightest hesitation or hint of fear, as they marched on. The camp stood in silent awe. One thought reverberated throughout.

How could the vikarmas be so magnificent? They are supposed to be weak.

Drapaku was at the lead, his handsome face smeared with war paint. On top of his armour, he wore a saffron angvastram. The colour of the Parmatma. The colour worn for the final journey. He didn't expect to return.

He stopped suddenly as Vidyunmali darted in front of him. Drapaku frowned. Before he could react, Vidyunmali had drawn his knife. Drapaku reached for his side arm. But Vidyunmali was quicker. He sliced his own thumb across the blade, and brought it up to Drapaku's forehead. In the tradition of the great brother-warriors of yore, Vidyunmali smeared his blood across Drapaku's brow, signifying that his blood will protect him.

'You're a better man than I am, Drapaku,' whispered Vidyunmali.

Drapaku stood silent, astonished by Vidyunmali's uncharacteristic behaviour.

Raising his balled fist high, Vidyunmali roared, 'Give them hell, vikarma!'

'Give them hell, vikarma!' bellowed the Suryavanshis, repeating it again and again.

Drapaku and his soldiers looked around the camp, absorbing the respect that they had been denied for so long. Way too long.

'Give them hell, vikarma!'

Drapaku nodded, turned and marched on before his emotions spoiled the moment. His soldiers followed.

'Give them hell, vikarma!'

— ⅄ ◎ Ʊ ⇞ ⊛ —

It was an uncharacteristically warm morning for that time of the year.

The Chandravanshi detachment had been surprised to find Meluhan soldiers at the northern pass the previous night. They had immediately attacked. The vikarmas had valiantly held the pass through the night, buying precious time for the main Suryavanshi army. This *had to be* the day of the main battle. Shiva was prepared.

Sati stood resplendent as she looped the aarti thali in small circles around Shiva's face. She stopped after seven turns, took some vermilion on her thumb and smeared it up Shiva's forehead in a long tilak. 'Come back victorious or don't come back at all.'

Shiva raised one eyebrow and grimaced. 'What kind of a send off is that?!'

'What? No, it's just...' stammered Sati.

'I know, I know,' smiled Shiva as he embraced Sati. 'It's the traditional Suryavanshi send off before a war, right?'

Sati looked up with moist eyes. Her love for Shiva was overcoming decades of Suryavanshi training. 'Just come back safe and sound.'

'I will, my love,' whispered Shiva. 'You won't get rid of me so easily.'

Sati smiled weakly. 'I'll be waiting.'

She stood up on her toes and kissed Shiva lightly. Shiva kissed her back and turned quickly, before his heart could fill his head with second thoughts. Lifting the tent curtain, he walked out. His eyes scanned the skies, keenly looking for omens. There were none.

Bloody good!

The distant drone of Sanskrit shlokas, accompanied by the beating of war drums in a smooth rhythmic pulse, wafted in over the dry winter breeze. This particular Suryavanshi custom had appeared odd to Shiva. But maybe there was something to the Brahmin 'Call for Indra and Agni', as this puja was called. The effect of the beats and the incantations were akin to a clarion call rousing a fierce spirit amongst the warriors. The beats would quicken once the battle began. Shiva was eager to throw himself into the battle. He turned and strode towards Daksha's tent.

'Greetings, your Highness,' said Shiva as he raised the curtain to enter the royal tent, where Parvateshwar was explaining the plans to the Emperor. 'Namaste, Parvateshwar.'

Parvateshwar smiled and folded his hands.

'What news of Drapaku, Parvateshwar?' asked Shiva. 'The last despatch I heard is at least three hours old.'

'The vikarma battle is on. Drapaku still leads them. He has bought us invaluable time. May Lord Ram bless him.'

'Yes,' agreed Shiva. 'May Lord Ram bless him. He just has to hold on till the end of this day.'

'My Lord,' said Daksha, hands folded in a formal Namaste, head bowed. 'It is an auspicious beginning. We will have a good day. Wouldn't you agree?'

'Yes it does seem so,' smiled Shiva. 'The news of Drapaku is very welcome. But perhaps this question may be better suited for the fourth prahar, your Highness.'

'I am sure the answer would be the same, my Lord. By the fourth prahar today, Emperor Dilipa will be standing in front of us, in chains, waiting for justice to be delivered.'

'Careful, your Highness,' said Shiva with a smile. 'Let us not tempt fate. We still have to win the war!'

'We will face no problems. We have the Neelkanth with us. We just need to attack. Victory is guaranteed.'

'I think a little more than a blue throat will be required to beat the Chandravanshis, your Highness,' said Shiva, his smile even broader. 'We shouldn't underestimate our enemy.'

'I don't underestimate them, my Lord. But I will not make the mistake of underestimating you either.'

Shiva gave up. He had learned that it was impossible to win a debate when pitched against Daksha's unquestioning conviction.

'Perhaps I should leave, your Highness,' said

Parvateshwar. 'The time has come. With your permission.'

'Of course, Parvateshwar. *Vijayibhav*,' said Daksha. Turning towards Shiva, Daksha continued, 'My Lord, they have built a viewing platform for us on the hill at the back.'

'Viewing platform?' asked Shiva, perplexed.

'Yes. Why don't we watch the battle from there? You would also be in a better position to direct it.'

Shiva narrowed his eyes in surprise. 'Your Highness, my position is with the soldiers. On the battlefield.'

Parvateshwar stopped in his tracks. Startled and delighted with having been proved wrong.

'My Lord, this is a job for butchers, not the Neelkanth,' said a concerned Daksha. 'You don't need to sully your hands with Chandravanshi blood. Parvateshwar will arrest that Naga and throw him at your feet. You can extract such a terrible retribution from him that his entire tribe would dread your justice for aeons.'

'This is not about *my* revenge, your Highness. It is about the vengeance of Meluha. It would be petty of me to think that an entire war is being fought just for me. This is a war between good and evil. A battle in which one has to choose a side. And fight. There are no bystanders in a *dharmayudh* — it is *a holy war*.'

Parvateshwar watched Shiva intently, his eyes blazing with admiration. These were Lord Ram's words. *There are no bystanders in a dharmayudh.*

'My Lord, we can't afford to risk your life,' pleaded Daksha. 'You are too important. I am sure that we can win this war without taking that gamble. Your presence has inspired us. There are many who are willing to shed their blood for you.'

'If they are willing to shed their blood for me, then I

must be willing to shed my blood for them.'

Parvateshwar's heart was swamped by the greatest joy an accomplished Suryavanshi could feel. The joy of finally finding a man worth following. The joy of finding a man worth being inspired by. The joy of finding a man, deserving of being spoken of in the same breath, as Lord Ram himself.

A worried Daksha came close to Shiva. He realised that if he had to stop the Neelkanth from this foolhardiness, he would have to speak his mind. He whispered softly, 'My Lord, you are my daughter's husband. If something were to happen to you, she would be bereaved twice in one life. I can't let that happen to her.'

'Nothing will happen,' whispered Shiva. 'And Sati would die a thousand deaths if her husband stayed away from a *dharmayudh*. She would lose respect for me. If she weren't pregnant, she would have been fighting alongside me, shoulder to shoulder. You know that.'

Daksha stared at Shiva, troubled and apprehensive.

Shiva smiled warmly. 'Nothing will happen, your Highness.'

'And what if it does?'

'Then it should be remembered that it happened for a good cause. Sati would be proud of me.'

Daksha continued to stare at Shiva, his face a portrait of agonised distress.

'Forgive me, your Highness, but I must go,' said Shiva with a formal Namaste, turning to leave.

Parvateshwar followed distracted, as if commanded by a higher force. As Shiva walked briskly out of the tent towards his horse, he heard Parvateshwar's booming voice. 'My Lord!'

Shiva continued walking.

'My Lord,' bellowed Parvateshwar again, more insistent.

Shiva stopped abruptly. He turned, a surprised frown on his face. 'I am sorry Parvateshwar. I thought you were calling out to his Highness.'

'No, my Lord,' said Parvateshwar. 'It was you I called.'

His frown deepened as Shiva asked, 'What is the matter, brave General?'

Parvateshwar came to a halt in rigid military attention. He kept a polite distance from Shiva. He could not stand on the hallowed ground that cradled the Mahadev. As if in a daze, Parvateshwar slowly curled his fist and brought it up to his chest. And then, completing the formal Meluhan salute, he bowed low. Lower than he had ever bowed before a living man. As low as he bowed before Lord Ram's idol during his regular morning pujas. Shiva continued to stare at Parvateshwar, his face an odd mixture of surprise and embarrassment. Shiva's respect for Parvateshwar made him uncomfortable with such idolatry.

Rising, but with his head still bent, Parvateshwar whispered, 'I will be honoured to shed my blood with you, my Lord.' Raising his head, he repeated, 'Honoured.'

Shiva smiled and touched Parvateshwar's arm. 'Well, if our plans are good my friend, hopefully we won't have to shed too much of it!'

CHAPTER 23

Dharmayudh, the Holy War

The Suryavanshis were arranged like a bow. Strong, yet flexible. The recently raised tortoise regiments had been placed at the centre. The light infantry formed the flanks, while the cavalry, in turn, bordered them. The chariots had been abandoned due to the unseasonal rain the previous night. They couldn't risk the wheels getting stuck in the slush. The newly reared archer regiments remained stationed at the back. Skilfully designed back rests had been fabricated for them, which allowed the archers to lie on their backs and guide their feet with an ingenious system of gears. The bows could be stretched across their feet and the strings drawn back up to their chins, releasing powerfully built arrows, almost the size of small spears. As they were behind the Suryavanshi infantry, their presence was hidden from the Chandravanshis.

The superior numerical strength of the Chandravanshis was apparent in the standard offensive formation in which their army was deployed. Their massive infantry was arranged in squads of five thousand. There were fifty such squads, comprising a full legion in a straight line. They stretched as far as the eye could see. There were three additional legions behind the first one, ready to finish off the job. This formation allowed a direct assault onto a numerically inferior enemy, giving the offence tremendous strength and solidity, but also making it rigid. The squads left spaces in between for the cavalry to charge if required. A study of the Suryavanshi formation had made the Chandravanshis move their cavalry from the rear to the flanks. This would enable a quicker charge at the flanks of the Suryavanshi formation and disrupt enemy lines. The Chandravanshi General had clearly read the ancient war manuals and was following them religiously, page by page. It would have been a perfect move against an enemy who also followed standard tactics. Unfortunately, he was up against a Tibetan tribal chief whose innovations had transformed the Suryavanshi attack.

As Shiva rode towards the hillock at the edge of the main battlefield, the Brahmins increased the tempo of their shlokas while the war drums pumped the energy to a higher level. Despite being outnumbered on a vast scale, the Suryavanshis did not exhibit even the slightest hint of nervousness. They had buried their fear deep.

The war cries of the clan-Gods of the various brigades rent the air.

'Indra dev ki jai!'

'Agni dev ki jai!'

'Jai Shakti devi ki!'

'Varun dev ki jai!'

'Jai Pawan dev ki!'

But these cries were forgotten in an instant as the soldiers saw a magnificent white steed canter in over the hillock carrying a handsome, muscular figure. A thunderous roar pierced the sky, loud enough to force the Gods out of their cloud palaces to peer at the events unfolding below. The Neelkanth raised his hand in acknowledgment. Following him was General Parvateshwar, accompanied by Nandi and Veerbhadra.

Vraka was off his horse in a flash as Shiva approached him. Parvateshwar dismounted equally rapidly and was next to Vraka before Shiva could reach him.

'The Lord will lead the right flank, Brigadier,' said Parvateshwar. 'I hope that is alright.'

'It will be my honour to fight under his command, my Lord,' said a beaming Vraka. He immediately pulled out his Field Commander baton from the grip on his side, went down on one knee and raised his hand high, to handover the charge to Shiva.

'You people have to stop doing this,' said Shiva laughing. 'You embarrass me!'

Pulling Vraka up on his feet, Shiva embraced him tightly. 'I am your friend, not your Lord.'

A startled Vraka stepped back, his soul unable to handle the gush of positive energy flowing in. He mumbled, 'Yes, my Lord.'

Shaking his head softly, Shiva smiled. He gently took the baton from Vraka's extended hand and raised it high, for the entire Suryavanshi army to see. An ear-splitting cry ripped through the ranks.

'Mahadev! Mahadev! Mahadev!'

Shiva vaulted onto his horse in one smooth arc. Holding the baton high, he rode up and down the line. The Suryavanshi roar got louder and louder.

'Mahadev!'

'Mahadev!'

'Mahadev!'

'Suryavanshis!' bellowed Shiva, raising his hand. 'Meluhans! Hear me!'

The army quietened down to hear their living God.

'Who is a Mahadev?' roared Shiva.

They listened in rapt attention, hanging on to every word.

'Does he sit on a pitiable height and look on idly while ordinary men do what should be *his* job? No!'

Some soldiers were praying inaudibly.

'Does he lazily bestow his blessings while others fight for the good? Does he stand by nonchalantly and count the dead while the living sacrifice themselves to destroy evil? No!'

There was pin-drop silence as the Suryavanshis absorbed their Neelkanth's message.

'A man *becomes* a Mahadev when he fights for good. A Mahadev is not born as one from his mother's womb. He is forged in the heat of battle, when he wages a war to destroy evil!'

The army stood hushed, feeling a flood of positive energy.

'I am a Mahadev!' bellowed Shiva.

A resounding roar arose from the Suryavanshis. They were led by the *Mahadev*. The *God of Gods*. The Chandravanshis did not stand a chance.

'But I am not the only one!'

A shocked silence descended on the Suryavanshis. What did the Mahadev mean? He is not the only one? Do the Chandravanshis also have a God?

'I am not the only one! For I see a hundred thousand Mahadevs in front of me! I see a hundred thousand men willing to fight on the side of good! I see a hundred thousand men willing to battle evil! I see a hundred thousand men capable of destroying evil!'

The stunned Suryavanshis gaped at their Neelkanth as the import of his words permeated their minds. They dared not ask the question: Are we Gods?

Shiva had the answer: '*Har Ek Hai Mahadev!*'

The Meluhans stood astounded. *Every single one a Mahadev?*

'*Har Har Mahadev!*' bellowed Shiva.

The Meluhans roared. *All of us are Mahadevs!*

Pure primal energy coursed through the veins of each Suryavanshi. They were Gods! It didn't matter that the Chandravanshis outnumbered them ten to one. They were Gods! Even if the evil Chandravanshis outnumbered them a hundred to one, victory was assured. They were Gods!

'Har Har Mahadev!' cried the Suryavanshi army.

'Har Har Mahadev!' yelled Shiva. 'All of us are Gods! Gods on a mission!'

Drawing his sword, he pulled the reins of his horse. Rising on its hind legs with a ferocious neigh, the horse pirouetted smartly to face the Chandravanshis. Shiva pointed his sword at his enemies. 'On a mission to destroy evil!'

The Suryavanshis bellowed after their Lord. Har Har Mahadev!

The cry rent the air. Har Har Mahadev!

Victory would not be denied. Har Har Mahadev!

The long spell of evil would end today. Har Har Mahadev!

As the army roared like the Gods that they were, Shiva rode on towards a beaming Parvateshwar who was flanked by Nandi, Veerbhadra and Vraka.

'Nice speech,' grinned Veerbhadra.

Shiva winked at him. He then turned his horse towards Parvateshwar. 'General, I think it's time we start our own rainfall.'

'Yes, my Lord,' nodded Parvateshwar. Turning his horse around, he gave the orders to his flag bearer. 'The archers.'

The flag bearer raised the coded flag. It was red with a vicious black lightening darned on it. The message was repeated by flag bearers across the lines. The Suryavanshi infantry immediately hunched down on its knees. Shiva, Parvateshwar, Vraka, Nandi and Veerbhadra dismounted rapidly, pulling their horses down to their knees. And the arrows flew in a deadly shower.

The archers had been placed in a semi-circular formation, to cover as wide a range of the Chandravanshi army as possible. Five thousand archers rained death on the Chandravanshis as the sky turned black with a curtain of arrows. The hapless Swadweepans were easy prey in their tight formations. The arrows, nearly as powerful as short spears, easily penetrated the leather and wooden shields of the irregular Chandravanshi soldiers. Only the regulars held metal shields. Within minutes, the first legion of irregulars had begun to break their line and yield precious ground. They were taking too many casualties to hold on to their position. The irregulars started running back, causing chaos. Confusion reigned in the legions behind.

Parvateshwar turned towards Shiva. 'I think we should lengthen the range, my Lord.'

Shiva nodded in reply. Parvateshwar nodded to his flag bearer who relayed the message. The archers stopped shooting for just a few moments. Turning their wheels right, they rapidly raised the height of their foot rests.

With the longer range quickly set, they drew their arrows. And let fly. The arrows hit the second legion of the Chandravanshis now. The pincer attack of the retreating first Chandravanshi legion and the concurrent hail of arrows created bedlam in the second legion.

Shiva noticed the Chandravanshi cavalry moving into position to attack. He turned to Parvateshwar. 'General, their cavalry is moving out. They would aim to flank us and attack the archers. Our cavalry needs to meet them midfield.'

'Yes, my Lord,' said Parvateshwar. 'I'd anticipated this move from the Chandravanshis. That's why I had positioned two cavalries, led by Mayashrenik and Vidyunmali, on the flanks.'

'Perfect! But General, our cavalry must not move too far ahead or our arrows will injure our own men. Nor must they retreat. They have to hold their position. At least for another five minutes.'

'I agree. Our archers need more time to finish their job.'

Parvateshwar turned to his flag bearer with detailed instructions. Two couriers set off rapidly to the left and right. Within moments, the eastern and western Arishtanemi, led by Mayashrenik and Vidyunmali respectively, thundered out to meet the Chandravanshi counter-attack.

Meanwhile, the disarray in the second legion of the Chandravanshi army increased as the unrelentingly ruthless wall of arrows pounded down upon them. The Suryavanshi archers, unmindful of their tiring limbs or bleeding hands, bravely continued their unremitting assault. The second legion line started breaking as the Chandravanshis tried desperately to escape the ruthless carnage.

'Higher range, my Lord?' asked Parvateshwar, preempting Shiva's words. Shiva nodded in reply.

Meanwhile the Suryavanshi and Chandravanshi cavalries were engaged in fierce combat on the eastern and western ends of the battlefield. The Chandravanshis knew that they had to break through. A few more minutes of the Suryavanshi archers' assault and the battle would be all but lost. They fought desperately, like wounded tigers. Swords cut through flesh and bone. Spears pierced body armour. Soldiers, with limbs hanging half-severed, continued to battle away. Horses, with missing riders, attacked as if their own lives depended on it. The Chandravanshis were throwing all their might into breaking through the line that protected the archers. But to their misfortune, they had run into the fiercest brigadiers amongst the Suryavanshis. Mayashrenik and Vidyunmali fought ferociously, holding the mammoth Chandravanshi force at bay.

The archers meanwhile had begun their onslaught on the third legion of the Chandravanshis. Their legions were either bleeding to death or deserting in great numbers. Some of them, however, held on grimly and courageously. When their shields were not strong enough to block the arrows, they used the bodies of their dead comrades. But they held the line.

'Do we stop now and charge, my Lord?' asked Parvateshwar.

'No. I want the third legion devastated as well. Let it go on for a few more minutes.'

'Yes, my Lord. We should get half the archers to raise their range farther, so that we can target the forward sections of the fourth legion as well. Confusion would rein right into the heart of their troops if their lines are also broken.'

'You are right, Parvateshwar. Let's do that.'

Meanwhile, the Chandravanshi cavalry on the western flank, sensing the hopelessness of their charge, began to retreat. Some Arishtanemi riders moved to give chase but Vidyunmali stopped them. As the Chandravanshis retreated, Vidyunmali ordered his troops to hold their positions, lest the Chandravanshis launch a counter-attack. Seeing their enemy ride rapidly back to their lines, Vidyunmali ordered a withdrawal to their initial position on the flank of the bow formation.

The Chandravanshis facing Mayashrenik, however, were made of sterner stuff. Despite suffering severe casualties, they fought grimly, refusing to retreat. Locked in battle, Mayashrenik and his men fiercely held their ground. Suddenly, the hail of arrows stopped. The archers had been ordered to stand down. Now that their mission was accomplished without their intervention, the Chandravanshi brigadier ordered a retreat of his cavalry. Mayashrenik, in turn, withdrew his troops quickly to his earlier position in preparation for the main charge, which he knew was just a few moments away.

'General, shall we?' asked Shiva, nodding towards the left flank.

'Yes, my Lord,' replied Parvateshwar.

As Parvateshwar turned to mount his horse, Shiva called out, 'Parvateshwar?'

'Yes, my Lord.'

'Race you to the last line of the Chandravanshis!'

Parvateshwar raised his eyebrows in surprise, smiling broadly. 'I will win, my Lord.'

'We'll see,' grinned Shiva, his eyes narrowed in a playful challenge.

Parvateshwar rapidly mounted his horse and rode to his command on the left. Shiva, followed by Vraka, Nandi and Veerbhadra rode to the right. Prasanjit geared his tortoise corps in the centre for the attack.

'Meluhans!' roared Shiva, dismounting smoothly. 'They lie in front of you! Waiting to be slaughtered! It ends today! Evil ends today!'

'Har Har Mahadev!' bellowed the soldiers as the Meluhan conch shell, announcing the Suryavanshi attack, was blown.

With an ear-shattering yell, the infantry charged towards the Chandravanshis. The tortoise corps moved in their slow, inexorable pace towards the Chandravanshi centre. The sides of the bow formation moved quicker than the centre. The cavalry cantered along the flanks, protecting the infantry from an enemy charge. Courageous remnants of the third and fourth legions of the Chandravanshis meanwhile were rapidly forming their lines once again to face the Suryavanshi onslaught. But the mass of dead bodies of their fallen comrades did not allow them the space to form their traditional Chaturanga formation, which could have allowed some lateral movement. They were huddled together in a tight but thin line when the Suryavanshis fell upon them.

The Suryavanshi battle plan was being executed immaculately. The tightly curved line of highly trained and vicious soldiers had the tortoise corps at the centre with the flanking line of light infantry slightly behind. The unstoppable tortoise corps tore ruthlessly into the Chandravanshi centre. The shields provided protection for the corps against the best Chandravanshi swordsmen, while their trishuls ripped through the Swadweepans.

The Chandravanshis had but two choices. Either fall to the trishul, or be pushed towards the sides where the Suryavanshis were now bearing down hard on them. Even as the centre of the Chandravanshi army broke under the unrelenting assault, the Suryavanshi flanks tore through their sides.

Shiva was leading his flank ferociously into the Chandravanshis, decimating all in front of him. To his surprise, he found the enemy lines thinning. Letting his fellow soldiers charge ahead of him, he rose to his full height to observe the movements. A part of the Chandravanshi line that had been opposing him had withdrawn only to regroup at the centre of the battlefield. They were attacking the only exposed flank of the tortoise corps, their right side, which could not be protected by shields. Someone in the Chandravanshi army was using his brain. If any of the tortoises broke, the Chandravanshis would swarm through the centre in a tight line, devastating the Suryavanshis.

'Meluhans!' roared Shiva. 'Follow me!'

Shiva's flag bearer raised his pennant. The soldiers followed. The Neelkanth charged into the sides of the Chandravanshi lines that were bearing down on the tortoises. Caught in a pincer attack between the trishuls and the charge from Shiva's flank, the spirit of the Chandravanshis finally broke.

What was once a mighty Chandravanshi army was now reduced to independent stragglers fighting valiantly for a losing cause. Shiva and Parvateshwar steered their men into completing the job. Victory was absolute. The Chandravanshi army had been comprehensively routed.

CHAPTER 24

A Stunning Revelation

Sati rushed out of her tent, followed by Krittika and Ayurvati.

'A little slowly, Sati,' cried Ayurvati, running to keep up. 'In your condition…'

Sati turned and grinned at Ayurvati, but did not reduce her pace. She hastened towards the royal tent where Shiva and Parvateshwar would no doubt be after the declaration of victory. Nandi and Veerbhadra stood guard at the entrance. They moved aside to let Sati in, but barred Ayurvati and Krittika.

'I am sorry, Lady Ayurvati,' said Nandi apologetically, his head bowed. 'I have strict instructions to not let anybody in.'

'Why?' asked a surprised Ayurvati.

'I don't know, my Lady. I am very sorry.'

'That's alright,' said Ayurvati. 'You're only doing your job.'

Veerbhadra looked at Krittika. 'I'm sorry darling.'

'Please don't call me that in public,' whispered Krittika, embarrassed.

Sati pulled the curtain aside and entered the tent.

'I don't know, my Lord,' said Parvateshwar. 'It doesn't make sense.'

Sati was surprised that Parvateshwar had called Shiva 'My Lord'. But her joy at seeing Shiva safe brushed these thoughts aside. 'Shiva!'

'Sati?' mumbled Shiva, turning towards her.

Sati froze. He didn't smile when he saw her. He didn't have the flush of victory on his face. He hadn't even got his wounds dressed.

'What's wrong?' asked Sati.

Shiva stared at her. His expression worried her deeply. She turned towards Parvateshwar. He looked at her for an instant with an obviously forced smile. One that was measured, obviously concealing bad tidings. 'What is it, Pitratulya?'

Parvateshwar looked at Shiva, who spoke at last. 'Something about this war troubles us.'

'What could be troubling you?' asked a surprised Sati. 'You have delivered the greatest victory ever to the Suryavanshis. This defeat of the Chandravanshis is even more comprehensive than what my grandfather had achieved. You should be proud!'

'I didn't see any Nagas with the Chandravanshis,' said Shiva.

'The Nagas weren't there?' asked Sati. 'That doesn't make sense.'

'Yes,' said Shiva, his eyes carrying a hint of foreboding. 'If they were so thick with the Chandravanshis, then they would have been present on the battlefield. If they were being used by the Chandravanshis against us, then their skills would have been even more useful in the battle. But where were they?'

'Maybe they've fallen out with each other,' suggested Sati.

'I don't think so,' said Parvateshwar. 'This war was triggered by their joint attack on Mandar! Why would they not be here?'

'Shiva, I am sure you'll figure it out,' said Sati. 'Don't trouble yourself.'

'Dammit Sati!' yelled Shiva. 'I can't figure it out! That's why I am worried!'

A startled Sati stepped back. His uncharacteristic vehemence stunned her. This was most unlike him. Shiva immediately realised what he had done and reached out his bloodied hand. 'I'm sorry Sati. It's just that I…'

The conversation was interrupted as Daksha, accompanied by an aide, raised the curtain and swaggered into the room.

'My Lord!' cried Daksha as he hugged Shiva tight.

Shiva flinched. His wounds hurt. Daksha immediately stepped back.

'I'm so sorry, my Lord,' said Daksha. Turning to his aide he continued, 'Why is Ayurvati outside? Bring her in. Let her tend to the Lord's wounds.'

'No wait,' said Shiva to the aide. 'I had said that I didn't want to be disturbed. There is always time to address the wounds later.' Shiva turned towards Daksha. 'Your Highness, I need to speak about something…'

'My Lord, if you will allow me first,' said Daksha, as enthusiastic as a little boy who had just been given a long denied sweet. 'I wanted to thank you for what you have done for me. For Meluha. We have done what even my father could not do! This is an absolute victory!'

Shiva and Parvateshwar looked briefly at each other before Daksha garnered their attention again.

'Emperor Dilipa is being brought here even as we speak,' said Daksha.

'What?' Parvateshwar's surprise was evident. 'But we have just dispatched soldiers to their camp. They couldn't possibly have arrested him so soon.'

'No Parvateshwar,' said Daksha. 'I had sent my personal guards much earlier. We could see from the viewing platform that the Chandravanshis had already lost by the time the Lord and you had begun the third charge. That is the benefit of the perspective you get from a distance. I was worried that Dilipa might escape like the coward he is. So I sent off my personal guards to arrest him.'

'But, your Highness,' said Parvateshwar, 'shouldn't we discuss the terms of surrender before we bring him in? What are we going to offer?'

'Offer?' asked Daksha, his eyes twinkling with the euphoria of triumph. 'Frankly, we don't really need to offer anything considering that he was routed. He is being brought here as a common criminal. However, we will show him how kind Meluha can be. We will make him such an offer that his next seven generations will be singing our praises!'

Before a surprised Shiva could ask what exactly Daksha had in mind, the crier of the Royal Guard announced the presence of Dilipa outside the tent. Accompanying him was his son, Crown Prince Bhagirath.

'Just a minute, Kaustav,' said Daksha, as he went into a tizzy, organising the room exactly as he would have liked it to be. He sat down on a chair placed in the centre of the room. Daksha requested Shiva to sit to his right. As Shiva sat, Sati turned to leave the tent. Shiva reached out to hold her hand. She turned, felt his silent plea and walked behind his seat to sit down on a chair. Parvateshwar sat to the Emperor's left.

Daksha then called out loudly, 'Let him in.'

Shiva was anxious to see the face of evil. Despite his misgivings about the absence of the Nagas, he genuinely believed that he had fought a righteous war on the right side. Seeing the defeated face of the evil king of the Chandravanshis would complete the victory.

Dilipa walked in. Shiva straightened up in surprise. Dilipa was nothing like what he had expected. He had the appearance of an old man, a sight that was rare in Meluha due to the Somras. Despite his age, Dilipa had a rakishly handsome bearing. He was of medium height, had dark skin and a slightly muscular build. His clothes were radically different from the sober Meluhan fare. A bright pink dhoti, gleaming violet angvastram and a profusion of gold jewellery adorning most parts of his body, combined to give him the look of a dandy. The laughter lines around his lips spoke of his humourous disposition. A trimmed salt and pepper beard, accompanied by thick white hair under his extravagantly coloured crown, completed the effete look while adding an intellectual air.

'Where's the Crown Prince Bhagirath?' asked Daksha.

'I have asked him to wait outside since he can be a little hotheaded,' said Dilipa. He looked only at Daksha, refusing to acknowledge the presence of the others in the room. 'Don't you Meluhans have any custom of offering a seat to your guests?'

'You are not a guest, Emperor Dilipa,' said Daksha. 'You are a prisoner.'

'Yes. Yes. I know. Can't you get a joke?' asked Dilipa

superciliously. 'So what is it that you people want this time?'

Daksha stared at Dilipa quizzically.

'You have already stolen the Yamuna waters a hundred years back,' continued Dilipa. 'What else do you want?'

Shiva turned in surprise towards Daksha.

'We did not steal the Yamuna waters,' yelled Daksha angrily. 'They were ours and we took them back!'

'Yes whatever,' dismissed Dilipa with a wave of his hand. 'What are your demands this time?'

Shiva was astonished at how the conversation was progressing. They had just defeated this evil man. He should have been penitent. But here he was, being condescending and self-righteous.

Daksha looked at Dilipa with wide eyes and a kindly smile. 'I don't want to take anything. Instead, I want to give you something.'

Dilipa raised his eyebrows warily. '*Give* us something?'

'Yes, I intend to give you the benefit of our way of life.'

Dilipa continued to stare at Daksha with suspicion.

'We are going to bring to you our superior way of life,' continued Daksha, his eyes marvelling at his own generosity. 'We are going to reform you.'

Dilipa said with half a snigger, '*Reform* us?'

'Yes. My General, Parvateshwar, will govern your empire as Viceroy of Swadweep. You will continue to be the titular head. Parvateshwar will ensure that your corrupt people are brought in line with the Meluhan way of life. We will live together as brothers now.'

Parvateshwar turned towards Daksha, stunned. He had not expected to be despatched to Swadweep.

Dilipa appeared to have difficulty in controlling his

laughter. 'You actually think your straight-laced men can run Swadweep? My people are mercurial. They are not going to listen to your moralising!'

'Oh, they will,' sneered Daksha. 'They will listen to everything we say. Because you don't know where the actual voice comes from.'

'Really? Where does it come from? Do enlighten me.'

Daksha motioned towards Shiva and said, 'Look who sits with us.'

Dilipa turned to Daksha's right and asked incredulously, 'Who's he? What in Lord Indra's name is so special about him?'

Shiva squirmed, feeling increasingly uncomfortable.

Daksha spoke a little louder. 'Look at his throat, oh king of the Chandravanshis.'

Dilipa looked again with the same arrogance towards Shiva. Despite the dried smattering of blood and gore, the blue throat blazed. Suddenly, Dilipa's haughty smile disappeared. He looked shocked. He tried to say something, but he was at a loss for words.

'Yes, oh corrupt Chandravanshi,' scoffed Daksha, moving his hands for dramatic effect. 'We have the Neelkanth.'

Dilipa's eyes reflected the surprised agony of a child who'd just been stabbed from behind by his own father. An increasing dread gripped Shiva's heart. This was far from what he had expected.

Daksha continued his hectoring. 'The Neelkanth has sworn to destroy the evil Chandravanshi way of life. You HAVE to listen.'

A bewildered Dilipa stared at Shiva for what seemed like an eternity. At long last, he recovered enough to softly whisper, 'Whatever you say.'

Before Daksha could bluster further, Dilipa turned and staggered towards the tent curtain. At the exit, he turned around to look at Shiva once again. Shiva swore that he could see a few tears in those proud, haughty eyes.

As soon as Dilipa left the tent, Daksha got up and hugged Shiva, lightly, so as to not hurt the Neelkanth. 'My Lord, did you see the look on his face. It was precious!'

Turning towards Parvateshwar, he continued, 'Parvateshwar, Dilipa is broken. You will have no trouble controlling the Swadweepans and bringing them around to our way of life. We will go down in history as the men who found a permanent solution to this problem!'

Shiva wasn't paying attention. His troubled heart desperately searched for answers. How could a struggle that appeared so righteous, just a few hours back, now suddenly appear so wrong? He turned towards Sati, forlorn. She gently touched his shoulder.

'What are you thinking, my Lord?' asked Daksha, intruding into Shiva's troubled thoughts.

Shiva just shook his head.

'I just asked if you would like to travel in Dilipa's carriage to Ayodhya?' asked Daksha. 'You deserve the honour, my Lord. You have led us to this glorious victory.'

This conversation did not appear important to Shiva at this point. He did not have the energy to think of an answer. He just nodded in an absentminded manner.

'Wonderful. I'll make all the arrangements,' said Daksha. Turning towards his aide, he continued, 'Send Ayurvati in to immediately dress the Lord's wounds. We need to leave by tomorrow morning to make sure that we have control over Ayodhya, before chaos reigns in the aftermath of Dilipa's defeat.'

With a Namaste towards Shiva, Daksha turned to leave. 'Parvateshwar, aren't you coming?'

Parvateshwar gazed at Shiva, his face creased with concern.

'Parvateshwar?' repeated Daksha.

Taking a quick look at Sati, Parvateshwar turned to leave. Sati moved forward, holding Shiva's face gently. Shiva's eyes seemed to droop with the heavy weight of tiredness. Ayurvati lifted the curtain carefully. 'How are you, my Lord?'

Shiva looked up, his eyes half shut. He was descending into a strange sleep. He yelled suddenly, 'Nandi!'

Nandi came rushing in.

'Nandi, can you find me a cravat?'

'Cravat, my Lord?' asked Nandi.

'Yes.'

'Umm. But why, my Lord?'

'BECAUSE I NEED IT!' shouted Shiva.

Shocked at the violence of his Lord's reply, Nandi hurriedly left the chamber. Sati and Ayurvati looked at Shiva in surprise. Before they could say anything, however, he suddenly collapsed. Unconscious.

He was running hard, the menacing forest closing in on him. He was desperate to get beyond the reach of the trees before they laid their ravenous claws upon him. Suddenly, a loud insistent cry pierced through the silence.

'Help! Please help!'

He stopped. No. He wouldn't run away this time. He would fight that monster. He was the Mahadev. It was his duty. Shiva turned around slowly, his sword drawn, his shield held high.

'Jai Shri Ram!' he yelled, as he raced back towards the clearing. The bushy thorns slashed his legs. Bleeding and terrified, he ran hard.

I will reach her in time.

I will not fail her again.

My blood will wash away my sin.

He sprang through the thicket, disregarding the thorns that cut deep into his flesh. Landing into the clearing, his shield was held defensively, his sword gripped low to retaliate. But nobody attacked. A strange laughter finally broke through his concentration. He lowered his shield. Slowly.

'Oh Lord!' he shrieked in agony.

The woman lay stricken on the ground, a short sword buried deep into her heart. The little boy stood on her side. Stunned. His hand was bloodied with the struggle of his kill. The hairy monster sat on the rocky ledge, pointing at the little boy. Laughing.

'NO!' screamed Shiva, as he awoke with a start.

'What happened, Shiva?' asked a worried Sati, darting to hold his hand.

Shiva looked around the room, startled. A worried Parvateshwar and Ayurvati got up too. 'My Lord?'

'Shiva, it's alright. It's alright,' whispered Sati, gently running her hand along Shiva's face.

'You were poisoned, my Lord,' said Ayurvati. 'We think that some of the Chandravanshi soldiers may have had poisoned weapons. It has affected many others as well.'

Shiva slowly regained his composure. He got off his bed. Sati tried to help him up, but he insisted on doing it himself. His throat felt excruciatingly parched. He stumbled over to the ewer, followed closely by Sati. He reached over and gulped down some water.

'It seems like I have been asleep for many hours,' said Shiva, finally noticing the lamps and the dark sky beyond.

'Yes,' said a worried Ayurvati. 'Close to thirty-six hours.'

'Thirty-six hours!' cried a surprised Shiva, before collapsing on to a comfortable chair. He noticed a forbidding figure sitting at the back, his right eye covered in a bandage, his amputated left hand in a sling. 'Drapaku?'

'Yes, my Lord,' said Drapaku, as he tried to get up and salute.

'My God, Drapaku! It's so good to see you. Please sit down!'

'It is heavenly to see you, my Lord,'

'How was your end of the battle?'

'I lost too many men, my Lord. Almost half of them. And this arm and eye,' whispered Drapaku. 'But by your grace, we held them till the main battle was won.'

'It wasn't my grace, my friend. It was your bravery,' said Shiva. 'I am proud of you.'

'Thank you, my Lord.'

Sati stood next to her husband, gently caressing his hair. 'Are you sure you want to sit, Shiva? You can lie down for a while.'

'I have slouched around for long enough, Sati,' said Shiva with a weak smile.

Ayurvati smiled. 'Well, the poison certainly didn't affect your sense of humour, my Lord.'

'Really? Is it still that bad?' grinned Shiva.

Parvateshwar, Drapaku and Ayurvati laughed weakly. Sati didn't. She was watching Shiva intently. He was trying too hard. He was trying to forget, trying to get others to focus on something other than himself. Was this dream much worse than the others?

'Where is his Highness?' asked Shiva.

'Father left for Ayodhya this morning,' said Sati.

'My Lord,' said Parvateshwar, 'His Highness felt that it would not be right to keep Swadweep without a sovereign for so long, under the circumstances. He felt it was important that the Suryavanshi army marched across the empire immediately, with Emperor Dilipa as prisoner, so that the Swadweepans know and accept the new dispensation.'

'So we're not going to Ayodhya?'

'We will, my Lord,' said Ayurvati. 'But in a few days when you are strong enough.'

'Some twelve thousand of our soldiers remain with us,' said Parvateshwar. 'We will march to Ayodhya when you are ready. His Highness insisted that Emperor Dilipa leave behind one of his family members with our unit as hostage to ensure that no Swadweepan attacks our much smaller force.'

'So we have one of Emperor Dilipa's family members in our camp?'

'Yes, my Lord,' said Parvateshwar. 'His daughter, Princess Anandmayi.'

Ayurvati smiled, shaking her head slightly.

'What?' asked Shiva.

Ayurvati looked sheepishly at Parvateshwar and then grinned at Sati. Parvateshwar glared back at Ayurvati.

'What happened?' asked Shiva again.

'Nothing important, my Lord,' clarified Parvateshwar, looking strangely embarrassed. 'It's just that she is quite a handful.'

'Well, I'll ensure that I remain out of her way then,' said Shiva, smiling.

— ⁂ —

'So this route seems to be the best,' said Parvateshwar, pointing at the map.

Shiva, along with the other poisoned soldiers, had recovered completely over the last five days. The march to Ayodhya was scheduled for the next day.

'I think you are right,' said Shiva, his mind going back to the meeting with the Emperor of Swadweep.

It's pointless feeling sorrowful for Dilipa. I'm quite sure he was posturing during our meeting. The Chandravanshis are evil. They are capable of any deception. Our war was righteous.

'We plan to leave in the morning, my Lord,' said Parvateshwar. Turning towards Sati, he continued, 'You can finally see the birthplace of Lord Ram, my child.'

'Yes Pitratulya,' smiled Sati. 'But I don't know if these people would have kept his temple unharmed. They may have destroyed it in their hatred.'

Their conversation was interrupted by a loud commotion.

Parvateshwar turned around with a frown. 'What is going on out there, Nandi?'

'My Lord,' said Nandi from the other side of the curtain. 'The Princess Anandmayi is here. She has some demands. But we can't fulfil them. She insists on meeting you.'

'Please tell her Highness to wait in her tent,' growled Parvateshwar. 'I will be over in a few minutes.'

'I cannot wait General!' screamed a strong feminine voice from across the curtain.

Shiva signalled to Parvateshwar to let her in. Parvateshwar

turned towards the curtain. 'Nandi, Veerbhadra, bring her in. But check her person for any weapons.'

In a few moments, Anandmayi, flanked by Nandi and Veerbhadra, entered Shiva's tent. Shiva raised his eyebrow at her appearance. She was taller than her father. And distractingly beautiful. A deep walnut coloured complexion complemented a body that was voluptuous, yet muscular. Her doe-eyes cast a seductive look while her lips were in a perpetual pout, sensual yet intimidating. She was provocatively clothed, with a dhoti that had been tied dangerously low at the waist and ended many inches above her knees, while being agonizingly tight at her curvaceous hips. It was just a little longer than the loincloth that the Meluhan men wore during their ceremonial baths. Her blouse was similar to the cloth piece that Meluhan women tied, except that it had been cut raunchily at the top to the shape of her ample breasts, affording a full view of her generous cleavage. She stood with her hips tilted to the side, exuding raw passion.

'You really think I can hide some weapons in this?' charged Anandmayi, pointing at her clothes.

A startled Nandi and Sati glared at her, while Shiva and Veerbhadra sported a surprised smile. Parvateshwar shook his head slightly.

'How are you doing, Parvateshwar?' asked Anandmayi, flashing a smile while scanning him from top to bottom, her eyebrows raised lasciviously.

Shiva couldn't help smiling as he saw Parvateshwar blush slightly.

'What is it you desire, Princess?' barked Parvateshwar. 'We are in the middle of an important meeting.'

'Will you really give me what I desire, General?' sighed Anandmayi.

Parvateshwar blushed even deeper. 'Princess, we have no time for nonsensical talk!'

'Yes,' groaned Anandmayi. 'Most unfortunate. Then perhaps you can help me get some milk and rose petals in this sorry little camp you are running.'

Parvateshwar turned towards Nandi in surprise. Nandi blabbered, 'My Lord, she doesn't want just a glass, but fifty litres of milk. We can't allow that with our rations.'

'You are going to drink fifty litres of milk?' cried Parvateshwar, his eyes wide in astonishment.

'I need it for my beauty bath, General!' glowered Anandmayi. 'You are going to take us on a long march from tomorrow. I cannot go unprepared.'

'I will try and see what I can do,' said Parvateshwar.

'Don't *try,* General. *Do it,*' admonished Anandmayi.

Shiva couldn't control himself any longer. He burst out laughing.

'What the hell do you think you are laughing at?' glared Anandmayi, turning towards Shiva.

'You will speak to the Lord with respect, Princess,' yelled Parvateshwar.

'The *Lord*?' grinned Anandmayi. 'So he is the one in charge? The one Daksha was allegedly showing off?'

She turned back towards Shiva. 'What did you say to trouble my father so much that he isn't even talking anymore? You don't look all that threatening to me.'

'Be careful about what you say, Princess,' advised Parvateshwar fiercely. 'You don't know whom you are speaking with.'

Shiva raised his hand at Parvateshwar, signalling him to calm down. But Anandmayi was the one who required soothing.

'Whoever you are, you will all be finished when our Lord comes. When he descends to Swadweep and destroys the evil of your kind.'

What?!

'Take her out of here, Nandi,' yelled Parvateshwar.

'No wait,' said Shiva. Turning towards Anandmayi, he asked, 'What did you mean by saying "*when your Lord will descend to Swadweep and destroy the evil of our kind*"?'

'Why should I answer you, *Parvateshwar's Lord?*'

Parvateshwar moved rapidly, drawing his sword and pointing it towards Anandmayi's neck. 'When the Lord asks something, you will answer!'

'Do you always move that fast?' asked Anandmayi, her eyebrows raised saucily. 'Or can you take it slow sometimes?'

Bringing his sword menacingly close, Parvateshwar repeated, 'Answer the Lord, Princess.'

Shaking her head, Anandmayi turned towards Shiva. 'We wait for our Lord who will come to Swadweep and destroy the evil Suryavanshis.'

Strong lines of worry began creasing Shiva's handsome face. 'Who is your Lord?'

'I don't know. He hasn't shown himself as yet.'

An unfathomable foreboding sunk deep into Shiva's heart. He was profoundly afraid of his next question. But he knew that he had to ask it. 'How will you know that he is your Lord?'

'Why are you so interested in this?'

'I need to know!' snarled Shiva.

Anandmayi frowned at Shiva as if he was mad. 'He will not be from the Sapt-Sindhu. Neither a Suryavanshi nor a Chandravanshi. But when he comes, he will come on our side.'

Shiva's inner voice whispered miserably that there was more. Clutching the armrest of his chair, he asked, 'And?'

'And,' continued Anandmayi, 'his throat will turn blue when he drinks the Somras.'

An audible gasp escaped Shiva as his body stiffened. The world seemed to spin. Anandmayi frowned, even more confused about the strange conversation.

Parvateshwar glowered fiercely at Anandmayi. 'You are lying, woman! Admit it! You are lying!'

'Why would I…'

Anandmayi stopped in mid-sentence as she noticed Shiva's cravat covered throat. The arrogance suddenly vanished from her face. She found her knees buckling under her. Pointing weakly with her hands, she asked, 'Why is your throat covered?'

'Take her out, Nandi!' ordered Parvateshwar.

'Who are you?' shouted Anandmayi.

Nandi and Veerbhadra tried to pull Anandmayi out. With surprising strength, she struggled against them. 'Show me your throat!'

They held on to her arms and dragged her backwards. She kicked Veerbhadra in the groin, causing him to double up in pain as she turned towards Shiva once again. 'Who the hell are you?'

Shiva stared down at the table unable to find the strength to even glance at Anandmayi. He held his armrest tightly. It seemed to be the only stable thing in a world spinning desperately out of control.

Tottering towards her, Veerbhadra pinned Anandmayi's hands from behind as Nandi threw an arm around her neck. Anandmayi bit Nandi's arm brutally. As a howling

Nandi pulled his arm back, she screamed again, 'Answer me, dammit! Who are you?'

Shiva looked up for one brief instant into Anandmayi's tormented eyes. The pain they conveyed lashed his soul. The flames of agony burned his conscience.

A shocked Anandmayi suddenly became immobile. The misery in her eyes would have stunned the bravest of Meluhan soldiers. In a broken voice, she whispered, 'You are supposed to be on our side…'

She allowed herself to be hauled out by Nandi and Veerbhadra. Parvateshwar kept his eyes down. He dared not look at Shiva. He was a good Suryavanshi. He would not humiliate his Lord by looking at him when he was at his weakest. Sati, on the other hand, would not leave her husband to suffer alone. She came to his side and touched his face.

Shiva looked up, his eyes devastated and filled with the tears of sorrow. 'What have I done?'

Sati held Shiva tightly, holding his throbbing head against her bosom. There was nothing she could say that would alleviate his pain. All she could do was hold him.

An agonized whisper suffused the tent with its resonant grief. 'What have I done?'

CHAPTER 25

Island of the Individual

It was another three weeks before Shiva's entourage reached Ayodhya, the capital of the Swadweepans. They had travelled along a decrepit, long-winding road to the Ganga, and then sailed eastward to the point where the mighty river welcomed the waters of the Sarayu. Then they had cruised north, up the Sarayu, to the city of Lord Ram's birth. It was a long and circuitous route, but the quickest possible keeping in mind the terrible road conditions in *Swadweep*, the *island of the individual.*

The excitement in the hearts of the Meluhan soldiers was beyond belief. They had heard legends about Lord Ram's city. But not one had ever seen it. *Ayodhya*, literally *the impregnable city*, was the land first blessed by Lord Ram's sacred feet. They expected a gleaming city beyond compare, even if it had been defiled by Chandravanshi presence. They expected the city to be an oasis of order and harmony even if all the surrounding land had been rendered chaotic by the Chandravanshis. They were disappointed.

Ayodhya was nothing like Devagiri. At first glance, it promised much. The outer walls were thick and looked astonishingly powerful. Unlike the sober grey Meluhan walls, the exterior of Ayodhya had been extravagantly painted with every possible colour in God's universe. Each alternate brick, however, was painted in pristine white, the royal colour of the Chandravanshis. Numerous pink and blue banners festooned the city towers. These banners had not been put up for any special occasion, but were permanent fixtures adorning the city.

The road curved suddenly along the fort wall to the main entrance, so as to prevent elephants and battering rams from getting a straight run to the mighty doors. At the top of the main gates, a wonderfully ornate, horizontal crescent moon had been sculpted into the walls. Below it was the Chandravanshi motto. *'Shringar. Saundarya. Swatantrata.' Passion. Beauty. Freedom.*

It was only when they entered the city that a blow was delivered to the precision and order loving Meluhans. Krittika described it as a 'functioning pandemonium'. Unlike all Meluhan cities, Ayodhya was not built on a platform — so it was obvious that if the Sarayu river ever flooded in the manner that the temperamental Indus did, the city would be inundated. The numerous city walls, built in seven concentric circles, were surprisingly thick and strong. However, it didn't need a general's strategic eye to notice that the concentric walls had not been planned by a military mastermind. They were in fact added in a haphazard manner, one after the other, when the city had extended beyond the previous perimeter. This explained why there were many weak points along each wall, which an enemy laying siege could easily exploit. Perhaps that was why the Chandravanshis preferred to battle outside in a far away battleground rather than defend their city.

The infrastructure was a sorry indictment of the Chandravanshi penchant for debate as an excuse for inaction. The roads were nothing better than dirt tracks. There was, however, one notable exception — the neatly paved and strikingly smooth *Rajpath*, the *royal road*, which led straight from the outer walls through to the opulent royal palace. The Swadweepans joked that instead of finding potholes on their road, they actually had to search for some stretch of road amongst the potholes! This was a far cry from the exceptionally well-planned, sign-posted, paved and tediously standard roads of Meluhan cities.

There were, what can only be called 'encroachments', all over the city. Some open grounds had been converted into giant slums as illegal immigrants simply pitched their tents on public areas. The already narrow roads had been made even narrower by the intrusion of the cloth tents of the homeless. There was constant tension between the rich home-owning class and the poor landless who lived in slums. The emperor had legalised all encroachments established before 1910 BC. Which meant that slum dwellers could not be removed unless the government created alternative accommodation for them. The minor problem was that the Chandravanshi government was so hideously inefficient that they hadn't managed to build even one new house for slum dwellers in the last twelve years. Now there was talk of extending the deadline further. The encroachments, the bad roads, the poor construction combined to give an impression of a city in a state of terminal decline.

The Meluhans were outraged. What had these people done to Lord Ram's great city? Or was it always like this?

Is that why Lord Ram had crossed the Sarayu river to establish his capital at far-away Devagiri on the Saraswati?

And yet, as the initial shock at the ugliness and frenzied disorder wore away, the Meluhans began to find strange and unexpected charm in this city of constant chaos. None of the Ayodhyan houses were similar, unlike the Meluhan cities where even the royal palace was built to a standard design. Here each house had its own individual allure. The Swadweepans, unencumbered by strict rules and building codes, created houses that were expressions of passion and elegance. Some structures were so grand that the Meluhans were amazed with the divine engineering talent that must have created it. The Swadweepans had none of the restraint of the Meluhans. Everything was painted bright — from orange buildings to parrot green ceilings to shocking pink windows! Civic-minded rich Swadweepans had created grand public gardens, temples, theatres and libraries, naming them after their family members, since they had received no help from the government. The Meluhans, despite finding it strange that a public building should be named after a private family, were impressed with the grandeur of these structures. It was a vibrant city that had exquisite beauty existing alongside hideous ugliness. Ayodhya both disgusted as well as fascinated the Meluhans.

The people were living embodiments of the Chandravanshi way of life. The women wore skimpy clothes, brazen and confident about their sexuality. The men were equally fashion and beauty conscious — what Meluhans would call dandies. The relationship between the men and women could only be characterised as one teetering on extremes. Extreme love coexisting with extreme hate, expressed with extreme loudness, all built on the foundations of extreme passion. Nothing was done in small measure in Ayodhya. Moderation was a word that did not exist in their dictionary.

Therefore, it was no surprise that the mercurial people of Ayodhya scoffed at Daksha's proclaimed intention to 'reform' them. Daksha entered a sullen city, whose populace lined silently along the sides of the Rajpath, refusing to welcome the conquering force. Daksha, who had expected the Ayodhya residents to welcome him with showers of petals since they had finally been freed from their evil rulers, was surprised with the cold reception he got. His mind attributed it to a dictat by the Chandravanshi royalty.

Shiva, who arrived a week later, was under no such illusions. He had expected far worse than just a quiet greeting. He had expected to be attacked. He had expected to be vilified for not standing up for the Swadweepans, who also believed in the legend of the Neelkanth. He had expected to be hated for choosing the so-called wrong side. But while he had begun to suspect that the Chandravanshis were not quite evil, he was not prepared to classify the Suryavanshis as the 'wrong side' either. He still felt that the Meluhans were almost without exception honest, decent, law-abiding people who could be unhesitatingly trusted. Shiva was deeply confused about his karma and his future course of action. He missed Brahaspati's keen wit and advice.

His thoughts weighing heavily upon him, Shiva quickly disembarked from the curtained cart and turned towards the Chandravanshi palace. For a moment, he was startled by the grandeur of Dilipa's abode. But he quickly pulled himself together, reached out for Sati's hand, and began climbing the hundred steps towards the main palace platform. Parvateshwar trudged slowly behind. Shiva glanced briefly beyond Sati, to find Anandmayi ascending the steps quietly. She had not spoken to Shiva since that terrible encounter when she had realised who he was. She climbed with an impassive face, her eyes set on her father.

'Who the hell is that man?' asked an incredulous Swadweepan carpenter, held back at the edge of the palace courtyard by Chandravanshi soldiers.

'Why are our Emperor and the sincere madman waiting for him on the royal platform, and that too in full imperial regalia?'

'Sincere madman?' asked his friend.

'Oh, haven't you heard? That is the new nickname for that fool Daksha!'

The friends burst out laughing.

'Shush!' hissed an old man, standing next to them. 'Don't you young people have any shame? Ayodhya is being humiliated and you think it's a joke.'

Meanwhile, Shiva had reached the royal platform. Daksha bent low with a Namaste as Shiva smiled weakly and returned the greeting.

Dilipa, with moist eyes, bent low towards Shiva. He cried in a soft whisper, 'I am not evil, my Lord. We are not evil.'

'What was that?' asked Daksha, his ears straining to hear Dilipa's whispered words.

Shiva's choked throat refused to utter a sound. Not hearing anything from Dilipa either, Daksha shook his head and whispered, 'My Lord, perhaps this is an opportune moment to introduce you to the people of Ayodhya. I am sure it will galvanize them into action once they know that the Neelkanth has come to their rescue.'

Before an anguished Shiva could answer, his caring wife spoke, 'Father, Shiva is very tired. It has been a long journey. May he rest for some time?'

'Yes, of course,' mumbled Daksha apologetically. Turning towards Shiva, he said, 'I am sorry, my Lord. Sometimes my enthusiasm gets the better of me. Why don't you rest today? We can always introduce you at the court tomorrow.'

Shiva looked up at Dilipa's angst-ridden eyes. Unable to bear the tormented gaze any longer, Shiva looked beyond the Chandravanshi emperor, towards his courtiers standing at the back. Only one pair of eyes did not have a look of incomprehension. It was at that moment that Shiva realised that except for Anandmayi, nobody else in Dilipa's court knew of his identity. Not even Dilipa's son, Bhagirath. Dilipa had not spoken to a soul. Clearly, neither had Daksha. Possibly in the hope of a grand unveiling of the secret, in the presence of Shiva himself.

'My Lord.'

Shiva turned towards Parvateshwar. 'Yes,' he said in a barely audible whisper.

'I will lead the army out since the ceremonial march is over,' said Parvateshwar. 'They will be stationed outside the city in the camp set up for the earlier contingent. I will be back at your service within two hours.'

Shiva nodded faintly.

— ⅄⦶Ʊ⍋⊗ —

It had been a few hours since their arrival in Ayodhya. Shiva had not spoken a word. He stood quietly at the window of his chamber, staring out as the afternoon sun washed the city in its dazzling glory. Sati sat silently by his side, holding his hand, drawing on all the energy that she possessed and then passing it on to him. He continued to stare out, towards a grand structure right in the heart of the city. It appeared to be built of white marble from this distance. For an unfathomable reason, looking at it seemed to soothe Shiva's soul. It was built upon the highest point in the city, on a gently sloping hill, clearly visible from every part of Ayodhya. Shiva mused as to why that building was so important that it occupied the highest point in the city, instead of the royal palace.

A loud insistent knocking intruded upon his thoughts.

'Who is it?' growled Parvateshwar, rising from his chair at the back of the chamber.

'My Lord,' answered Nandi. 'It is the Princess Anandmayi.'

Parvateshwar groaned softly before turning towards Shiva. The Neelkanth nodded.

'Let her in, Nandi,' ordered Parvateshwar.

Anandmayi entered, her smiling demeanour startling Parvateshwar who frowned in surprise. 'How may I help you, your Highness?'

'I have told you so many times how you can help me, Parvateshwar,' teased Anandmayi. 'Perhaps if you listened to the answer rather than repeating the question again and again, we may actually get somewhere.'

Parvateshwar's reaction was a combination of embarrassment and anger. Shiva smiled weakly, for the first time in three weeks. Somehow the fact that Anandmayi seemed to have returned to her usual self made Shiva happy.

Anandmayi turned towards Shiva with a low bow. 'The truth has just come to me, my Lord. I am sorry about my sullenness earlier. But I was deeply troubled at the time. Your being on the side of the Suryavanshis can have only one of two explanations. Either we are evil. Or you are not who we think you are and the legend is false. Accepting either of these explanations would destroy my soul.'

Shiva looked at Anandmayi attentively.

'But I have finally realised,' continued Anandmayi. 'The legend is not false. And we are obviously not evil. It is just that you are too naive. You have been misled by the evil Suryavanshis. I will set it right. I will show you the goodness of our path.'

'We are not evil,' glowered Parvateshwar.

'Parvateshwar,' sighed Anandmayi. 'I have told you earlier. That lovely mouth of yours can be put to much better uses than mere talking. You shouldn't waste your breath unnecessarily.'

'Stop your impudence, woman!' cried Parvateshwar. 'You think we are evil? Have you seen the way you treat your own people? Hungry eyes have stared at me all through our journey. Children lie abandoned on the side of potholed highways. Old desperate women beg for alms throughout your "impregnable city", while the Swadweepan rich lead lives better than a Meluhan emperor. We have a perfect society in Meluha. I may agree with the Lord and accept that maybe you are not evil. But you certainly don't know how to take care of your people. Come to Meluha to see how citizens should be treated. Your lives will improve with our method of governance.'

'Improve?' argued an agitated Anandmayi. 'We are not perfect, I agree. There are many things that our empire could do better, I agree. But at least we give our people freedom. They are not forced to follow some stupid laws mandated by an out of touch elite.'

'Give them freedom? Freedom to do what? Loot, steal, beg, kill?'

'I don't need to argue with you about our culture. Your puny mind will not be able to understand the advantages of our ways.'

'I don't want to! It disgusts me to see the way this empire has been managed. You have no norms. No control. No laws. It is no wonder that despite not being evil, you have contaminated yourselves by allying with the Nagas. By fighting like cowardly terrorists and not brave Kshatriyas. You may not be evil, but your deeds certainly are!'

'Nagas? What the bloody hell are you talking about? Do you think we are mad that we will ally with the Nagas? You think we don't know how that will pollute our souls for the next seven lives? And terrorism? We have never resorted to terrorism. We have strained against our natural instincts to avoid a war with your cursed people for the last hundred years. Hence we have retreated from the border provinces. We have cut all ties with you. We have even learned to live with the reduced flow of the Ganga ever since you stole the Yamuna from us. My father told you that we had nothing to do with the attack on Mount Mandar! But you did not believe us. And why should you? You needed an excuse to attack us again!'

'Don't lie to me. At least not in front of the Mahadev! Chandravanshi terrorists have been found with the Nagas.'

'My father told you that nobody under our control

had anything to do with the attack on Mandar. We have nothing to do with the Nagas. It's possible that some Chandravanshis, just like some Suryavanshis, could have helped the terrorists. Had you cooperated with us, we may have even found the criminals!'

'What rubbish! No Suryavanshi would ally with those monsters. As for some Chandravanshis assisting the terrorists, you'll have to answer for that. Swadweep is under your control!'

'Had you not snapped diplomatic ties with Swadweep it would not be lost on you that we are a confederacy far removed from your authoritarian structure. Ayodhya is only the overlord. Other kings within Swadweep pay us tribute for protection during war. Otherwise, they have the freedom to administer their kingdoms any which way they choose.'

'How is that possible? Are you saying that the Emperor of Swadweep doesn't administer his own empire?'

'Please,' begged Shiva, stopping the argument which reflected the debate raging in his mind. He did not want to be troubled by questions for which he had no answers. At least not just as yet.

Parvateshwar and Anandmayi immediately fell silent.

Turning slowly towards the window again, he asked, 'What is that building, Anandmayi?'

'That, my Lord,' said Anandmayi, smiling happily at being spoken to first, 'is the *Ramjanmabhoomi* temple, built at the site of *Lord Ram's birthplace*.'

'You have built a temple to Lord Ram?' asked a startled Parvateshwar. 'But he was a Suryavanshi. Your sworn enemy.'

'We did not build the temple,' said Anandmayi, raising

her eyes in exasperation. 'But we have refurbished and maintained it lovingly. And furthermore, what makes you think Lord Ram was our sworn enemy? He may have been misled into following a different path, but he did a lot of good for the Chandravanshis as well. He is revered as a God in Ayodhya.'

Parvateshwar's eyes widened in shock. 'But he had sworn to destroy the Chandravanshis.'

'If he had vowed to destroy us, we wouldn't exist today, would we? He left us unharmed because he believed that we were good. That our way of life deserved to survive.'

Parvateshwar's mind searched for answers, disturbed by the strength of her arguments.

'You know what Lord Ram's full ceremonial name is?' asked Anandmayi, pressing home her advantage.

'Of course I do,' scoffed Parvateshwar. 'Lord Ram, Suryavanshi Kshatriya of the Ikshvaku clan. Son of Dashrath and Kaushalya. Husband of Sita. Honoured and respected with the title of the seventh Vishnu.'

'Perfect,' beamed Anandmayi. 'Except for one minor mistake. You have missed one small word, General. You have missed the word *Chandra*. His full name was Lord *Ram Chandra*.'

Parvateshwar frowned.

'Yes, General,' continued Anandmayi. 'His name meant "*the face of the moon*". He was more Chandravanshi than you seem to imagine.'

'This is typical Chandravanshi double-talk,' argued Parvateshwar, gathering his wits. 'You are lost in words rather than focussing on deeds. Lord Ram had said that only a person's karma determines his identity. The fact that his name had the word moon in it means nothing.

His deeds were worthy of the sun. He was a Suryavanshi to the core.'

'Why couldn't he have been both Suryavanshi and Chandravanshi?'

'What nonsense is that? It's not possible. It's contradictory.'

'It appears impossible to you only because your puny mind cannot understand it. Contradictions are a part of nature.'

'No, they aren't. It is impossible that one thing be true and the opposite not be false. The universe cannot accept that. One scabbard can house just one sword!'

'That is so only if the scabbard is small. Is it your case that Lord Ram was not so sublime as to have two identities?'

'You are just playing with words!' glared Parvateshwar.

Shiva had stopped listening. He turned towards the window and faced the temple. He could feel it in every pore of his body. He could feel it in his soul. He could hear the soft whisper of his inner voice.

Lord Ram will help you. He will guide you. He will soothe you. Go to him.

— ⸙ —

It was the third hour of the third prahar when Shiva stole into the chaotic Ayodhya streets all by himself. He was on his way to meet Lord Ram. Sati had not offered to come along. She understood that he needed to be alone. Wearing a cravat and a loose shawl for protection, with a sword and shield as a measure of abundant precaution, Shiva ambled along, taking in the strange sights and smells of the Chandravanshi capital. Nobody recognised him. He liked it that way.

The Ayodhyans seemed to live their life without even the slightest hint of self-control. Loud emotional voices assaulted Shiva's ears as if a hideous orchestra was trying to overpower the senses. The common people either laughed like they had just gulped an entire bottle of wine or fought as if their lives depended on it. Shiva was pushed and shoved on several occasions by people rushing around, hurling obscenities and calling him blind. There were manic shoppers bargaining with agitated shopkeepers at the bazaar and it almost seemed like they would come to blows over ridiculously small amounts of money. For both the shoppers as well as the shopkeepers, the harried negotiation wasn't about the cash involved. It was about their pride in having struck a good bargain in itself.

Shiva noticed that a large number of couples had crowded into a small garden on the side of the road doing unspeakable things to each other. They seemed to brazenly disregard the presence of voyeuristic eyes on the street or in the park itself. He noticed with surprise that the prying eyes were not judgemental, but excited. Shiva noted the glaring contrast with the Meluhans who would not even embrace each other in public.

Shiva suddenly started in surprise as he felt a feminine hand brush lightly against his backside. He turned sharply to find a young woman grin back at him and wink. Before Shiva could react, he spotted a much older woman walking right behind. Thinking that she was the younger woman's mother, Shiva decided to let the indiscretion pass for fear of causing any embarrassment. As he turned, he felt a hand on his backside once again, this time more insistent and aggressive. He turned around and was shocked to find the mother smiling sensuously at him. A flabbergasted Shiva hurried down the road, escaping the bazaar before any more passes could disturb his composure.

He continued walking in the direction of the towering Ramjanmabhoomi temple. As he approached it, the unassailable jangle of Ayodhya dimmed significantly. This was a quiet residential area of the city. Probably for the rich, judging by the exquisite mansions that lined the avenues. Turning to the right, he came upon the road which led to his destination. It curved gently up the hill, caressing its sides in a smooth arc. This was probably the only road in Ayodhya, besides the Rajpath, which was not pitted with potholes. Magnificent gulmohur trees rose brilliantly along the flanks of the road, their dazzling orange leaves lighting the path for the weary and the lost. The path that led to Lord Ram.

Shiva closed his eyes and took a deep breath as anxiety gnawed at his heart. What would he find? Would he find peace? Would he find answers? Would he, as he hoped, find that he had done some good? Good that wasn't visible to him right now. Or would he be told that he had made a terrible mistake and thousands had died a senseless death? Shiva opened his eyes slowly, steeled himself and began walking, softly repeating the name of the Lord.

Ram. Ram. Ram. Ram.

A little farther up, Shiva's chant was disturbed. At a bend in the road, he saw an old, shrivelled man, who appeared like he hadn't eaten in weeks. He had a wound on his ankle which had festered because of the humidity and neglect. He was dressed in a torn jute sack, which was tied precariously at his waist and hung from his shoulders with a hemp rope. Sitting on the sidewalk, his thin right hand scratched his head vigorously, disturbing the lice going about their job diligently. With his weak left hand, he precariously balanced a banana leaf which held a piece of bread and some gruel. It looked like the kind of food distributed at cheap restaurants on the donations of a few kindly or guilty souls. The kind of food that would not even be fed to animals in Meluha.

Intense anger surged through Shiva. This old man was begging, nay suffering, at the doors of Lord Ram's abode and nobody seemed to care. What kind of government would treat its people like this? In Meluha, the government assiduously nurtured all its citizens. There was enough food for everyone. Nobody was homeless. The government actually worked. The old man would not have had to endure this humiliation had he lived in Devagiri!

The anger in Shiva gave way to a flood of positive energy, as he realised that he had found his answer. He knew now that Parvateshwar was right. Maybe the Chandravanshis were not evil, but they led a wretched existence. The Suryavanshi system would improve their lives dramatically. There would be abundance and prosperity all around when Parvateshwar took charge of the moribund Chandravanshi administration. There *will* be some good that will come out of this war. Maybe he had not made such a terrible mistake after all. He thanked Lord Ram. He thought that he had found his answer.

Fate, however, conspired to deny Shiva this small consolation. The old beggar noticed Shiva's stare and met it equally. The warm empathy in Shiva's eyes and the compassion of his smile prompted the ancient man to smile in return. However, it wasn't the smile of a broken man begging for alms. It was the warm welcoming smile of a man at peace with himself. Shiva was taken aback.

The old man smiled even more warmly while raising his weak hand with great effort. 'Would you like some food, my son?'

Shiva was stunned. He felt humbled by the selfless gesture of the man he had thought was deserving of only pity.

Observing Shiva staring fixedly, the old man repeated, 'Would you like to eat with me, son? There is enough for both of us.'

An overwhelmed Shiva could not find the strength to speak. There wasn't enough food for even one man in fact. Why was this man offering to share what little food he had? It didn't make sense.

Thinking Shiva was hard of hearing, the old man spoke a little louder. 'My son, sit with me. Eat.'

Shiva struggled to find the strength to shake his head slightly. 'No thank you, sir.'

The old man's face fell immediately. 'This is good food,' he said, his eyes reflecting his hurt. 'I would not have offered it to you otherwise.'

Shiva realised that he had insulted the old man's pride. He had just treated him like a beggar. 'No, no, that's not what I meant. I know it's good food. It's just that I…'

The old man softly interrupted Shiva's words. 'Then sit with me, my son.'

Shiva nodded quietly. He sat down on the pavement. The old man turned towards Shiva and placed the banana leaf on the ground, in between the two of them. Shiva looked at the bread and watery gruel, which until a few moments back had appeared unfit for humans. The old man looked up at Shiva, his half blind eyes beaming. 'Eat.'

Shiva picked up a small morsel of the bread, dipped it in the gruel and swallowed. It slipped into his body easily, but weighed heavy upon his soul. He could feel his righteousness being squeezed out of him as the poor, old man beamed generously.

'Come on, my son. If you are going to eat so little, how will you maintain your big muscular body?'

A startled Shiva glanced up at the old man; the circumference of those shrunken arms would have been smaller than Shiva's wrist. The old man was taking ridiculously small bites, moving larger portions of the bread towards Shiva. Shiva could not find the courage to look up any more. As his heart sank deeper and his tears rose, he continued to eat the portion the old man had given him. The food was over in no time.

Freedom. Freedom for the wretched to also have dignity. Something impossible in Meluha's system of governance.

'Are you full now, my son?'

Shiva nodded slowly, still not daring to look into the old man's eyes.

'Good. Go. It's a long walk up to the temple.'

Shiva looked up, bewildered by the astounding generosity being shown to him. The old man's sunken cheeks were spread wide as he smiled affectionately. He was on the verge of starvation, and yet he had given practically all his food to a stranger. Shiva cursed his own heart for the blasphemy he had committed. The blasphemy of believing that he could actually 'save' such a man. Shiva found himself bending forward, as if in the volition of a greater power. He extended his arms and touched the feet of the old man.

The old man raised his hand and touched Shiva's head tenderly, blessing him. 'May you find what you are looking for, my son.'

Leaden with guilt and remorse, Shiva rose heavily, his self-rightousness crushed by the old man's munificence. He had his answer. What he had done was wrong. He had made a terrible mistake. These people were not evil.

CHAPTER 26

The Question of Questions

The road to the Ramjanmabhoomi temple clung to the sides of a gently sloping hill and ended its journey at Lord Ram's abode. It afforded a breathtaking view of the city below. But Shiva did not see it. Neither did he see the magnificent opulence of the gigantic temple nor the gorgeously landscaped gardens around it. The temple was sheer poetry, written in white marble, composed by the architect of the Gods. The architect had designed a grand staircase leading up to the main temple platform, which was awe-inspiring and yet inviting. Colossal ornate marble statues in sober blue and grey had been engraved on the platform. Elaborately carved pillars supported an ostentatious yet tasteful ceiling of blue marble. The architect obviously knew that Lord Ram's favourite time of the day was the morning. On the ceiling, the morning sky, as it would have been seen in the absence of the temple roof, had been lovingly painted. On top of the ceiling, the temple spire shot upwards to a height of almost one hundred metres, like a giant Namaste to the Gods. The Swadweepans, to their credit, had not imposed their garish sensibilities on the temple. Its restrained beauty was in keeping with the way the sober Lord Ram would have liked it.

Shiva did not notice any of this. Nor did he look at the intricately carved statues in the inner sanctum. Lord Ram's idol at the centre was surrounded by his beloveds. To the right was his loving wife, Sita, and to the left was his devoted brother, Lakshman. At their feet, on his knees, was Lord Ram's most fervent and favourite disciple, Hanuman, of the *Vayuputra* tribe, *the sons of the Wind God.*

Shiva could not find the strength to look Lord Ram in the eyes. He feared the verdict he would receive. He crouched behind a pillar, resting against it, grieving. When he couldn't control his intense feelings of guilt anymore, his eyes released the tears they had been holding back. Shiva made desperate attempts to control his tears, but they kept flowing as though a dam had burst. He bit into his balled fist, overcome by remorse. He curled his legs up against his chest and rested his head on his knees.

Drowning in his sorrow, Shiva did not feel the compassionate hand on his shoulder. On getting no reaction, the hand squeezed his shoulder lightly. Shiva recognised the touch but kept his head bowed. He did not want to appear weak, be seen with tears in his eyes. The gentle hand, old and worn with age, withdrew quietly, while its owner waited patiently until Shiva had composed himself. When the time was right, he came forward and sat down in front of him. A sombre Shiva did a formal Namaste to the Pandit, who looked almost exactly like the Pandits that Shiva had met at the Brahma temple at Meru and the Mohan temple at Mohan Jo Daro. He sported the same flowing white beard and a white mane. He wore a saffron dhoti and angvastram, just like the other pandits did. The wizened face had the same calm, welcoming smile. Shiva couldn't help noticing though that this one's girth was far more generous.

'Is it really so bad?' asked the Pandit, his eyes narrowed and head tilted slightly, in the typically Indian empathetic manner.

Shiva shut his eyes and lowered his head again. The Pandit waited patiently for Shiva's reply. 'You don't know what I have done!'

'I do know.'

Shiva looked up at the Pandit, his eyes full of surprise and shame.

'I know what you have done, Oh Neelkanth,' said the Pandit. 'And I ask again, is it really so bad?'

'Don't call me the Neelkanth,' glared Shiva. 'I don't deserve the title. I have the blood of thousands of innocents on my hands.'

'Many more than thousands have died,' said the Pandit. 'Probably hundreds of thousands. But do you really think they wouldn't have died had you not been around? Is their blood really on your hands?'

'Of course it is! It was my stupidity that led to this war. I had no idea what I was doing. A responsibility was thrust upon me and I wasn't worthy of it! Hundreds of thousands have perished as a result!'

Shiva curled up his fist and pounded his forehead, desperately trying to soothe the throbbing heat on his brow. The Pandit stared in mild surprise at the deep red blotch on Shiva's forehead, right between his eyes. It was not the colour of a blood clot. It was a much deeper hue, almost black. The Pandit chose silence though his surprise was barely controlled. The time was not yet ripe. The moment of revelation had not yet come.

'And it's all because of me,' moaned Shiva, his eyes moistening again. 'It's all my fault.'

'Soldiers are Kshatriyas, my friend,' said the Pandit, a picture of calm. 'Nobody forces them to die. They choose their path, knowing full well the risk it entails. *And also* the possible glory that comes with it. The Neelkanth is not the kind of person on whom responsibility can be thrust against his will. You *chose* this. You were *born* for it.'

Shiva looked at the Pandit startled. His eyes seemed to ask, 'Born for it?'

The Pandit ignored the question posed by Shiva's eyes. 'Everything happens for a reason. If you are going through this turmoil, there is a divine plan in it.'

'What bloody divine reason can there be for so many deaths?'

'The destruction of evil? Wouldn't you consider that a very important reason?'

'But I did not destroy evil!' yelled Shiva. 'These people aren't evil. *They're just different.* Being different isn't evil.'

The Pandit's face broke into his typically enigmatic smile. 'Exactly. They are not evil. They are just different. You have realised it very quickly, my friend, a lot earlier than the previous Mahadev.'

Shiva was perplexed by the Pandit's words. 'Lord Rudra?'

'Yes! Lord Rudra.'

'But he did destroy evil. He destroyed the Asuras.'

'And, who said the Asuras were evil?'

'I read it...' Shiva stopped mid-sentence. He finally understood.

'Yes,' smiled the Pandit. 'You have guessed correctly.

Just like the Suryavanshis and the Chandravanshis see each other as evil, so did the Devas and the Asuras. So if you are going to read a book written by the Devas, what do you think the Asuras are going to be portrayed as?'

'You mean they were just like today's Suryavanshis and Chandravanshis?'

'More so than you can imagine. The Devas and the Asuras, just like the Chandravanshis and the Suryavanshis, represent two balancing life forces — a duality.'

'Duality?'

'Yes, a duality that is one of the many perspectives of the universe — the masculine and the feminine. The Asuras and the Suryavanshis represent the masculine. The Devas and the Chandravanshis speak for the feminine. The names change, but the life forces they embody remain the same. They will always exist. Neither can ever be destroyed. Otherwise the universe will implode.'

'And they see their fight with the other as the eternal struggle between good and evil.'

'Exactly,' beamed the Pandit, marvelling at Shiva's keen mind even in his time of distress. 'But they haven't been fighting all the time. Sometimes, there have been long periods of cooperation as well. In times of strife, which usually happens when there is evil, it is easy to blame each other. The difference between two dissimilar ways of life gets portrayed as a fight between good and evil. Just because the Chandravanshis are different from the Suryavanshis doesn't mean that they are evil. Why do you think the Neelkanth had to be an outsider?'

'So that he would not be biased towards any one way of life,' said Shiva, as a veil lifted before his eyes.

'Exactly! The Neelkanth has to be above all this. He has to be devoid of any bias.'

'But I was not free of biases. I was convinced that the Chandravanshis are evil. Maybe what Anandmayi says is right. Maybe I am naive, easily misled.'

'Don't be so hard on yourself, my friend. You cannot drop from the sky knowing everything, can you? You would have to enter the equation from one side or the other. And whichever side you entered from, you would obviously be coloured by their ways, while viewing the other side as evil. You have realized your error early. Lord Rudra did not recognise it till it was almost too late. He had nearly destroyed the Asuras before he grasped the simple fact that they were not evil, just different.'

'*Nearly* destroyed them? You mean some Asuras still exist?'

The Pandit smiled mysteriously. 'That conversation is for another time my friend. What you need to understand is that you are not the first Mahadev who was misled. And you will not be the last. Imagine, if you will, what Lord Rudra's feelings of guilt must have been.'

Shiva kept quiet, his eyes downcast. The knowledge of Lord Rudra's guilt did not reduce the shame that racked his soul. Reading his thoughts, the Pandit continued. 'You made the best decision you could under the circumstances. I know that this will be cold comfort, but being the Neelkanth isn't easy. You will have to bear the burden of this guilt. I know the kind of person you are. It *will* be a heavy burden. Your challenge is not to suppress the guilt or the pain. You have too good a heart to be able to do that. Your challenge is to stay true to your karma, to your duty, *in spite* of the pain. That is the fate and the duty of a Mahadev.'

'But what kind of a Mahadev am I? Why am I required? How am I to destroy evil if I don't know what evil is?'

'Who has said that your job is to destroy evil?'

A startled Shiva stared hard at the Pandit. He disliked the irritating word games that these pandits seemed to love to indulge in.

Glimpsing the anger in Shiva's eyes, the Pandit clarified immediately. 'The strength that evil has is overestimated, my friend. It is not so difficult to annihilate. All it takes is for a few good men to decide that they will fight it. At practically all the times that evil has raised its head, it has met the same fate. It has been destroyed.'

'Then why am I required?'

'You are required for the most crucial task: To answer that most important question.'

'What?'

'*What* is evil?'

'*What is evil?*'

'Yes. Many wars have been fought amongst men,' said the Pandit. 'And many more will be fought in the future. That is the way of the world. But it is only a Mahadev who can convert one of these wars into a battle between good and evil. It is only the Mahadev who can recognise evil and then lead men against it. Before evil raises its ugly head and extinguishes all life.'

'But how do I recognise evil?'

'I can't help you there my friend. I am not the Mahadev. This is a question you must find the answer to. But you have the heart. You have the mind. Keep them open and evil will appear before you.'

'Appear?'

'Yes,' explained the Pandit. 'Evil has a relationship with

you. It will come to you. All you have to do is recognise it when it appears. I have only one suggestion. Don't be hasty in trying to recognise evil. Wait for it. It *will* come to you.'

Shiva frowned. He looked down, trying to absorb the strange conversation. He turned towards Lord Ram's idol, seeking some direction. He did not find the judgement-filled eyes he had expected to see. Instead, he saw a warm, encouraging smile.

'Your journey is not over, my friend. Not by a long shot. It has just begun. You have to go on. Otherwise evil will triumph.'

Shiva's eyes cleared up a bit. His burden didn't feel any lighter, but he felt strong enough to carry it. He had to keep walking to the very end.

Shiva looked up at the Pandit and smiled weakly. 'Who are you?'

The Pandit smiled. 'I know the answer had been promised to you. And a promise made by any of us is binding on all of us. I will not break it.'

Shiva gazed at the Pandit, waiting for the answer.

'We are the Vasudevs.'

'The Vasudevs?'

'Yes. Each Vishnu leaves behind a tribe which is entrusted with two missions.'

Shiva continued to watch the Pandit intently.

'The first mission is to help the next Mahadev, if and when he appears.'

'And the second?'

'The second is that one of us will become the next Vishnu, whenever we are required to do so. The seventh Vishnu, Lord Ram, entrusted this task to his trusted lieutenant, Lord Vasudev. We are his followers. We are the tribe of Vasudev.'

Shiva stared at the Pandit, absorbing the implications of this information. He frowned as one inference suddenly occurred to him. 'Did the Mahadevs also leave some tribes behind? Did Lord Rudra?'

The Pandit smiled, deeply impressed by Shiva's intellect. The Mohan Jo Daro Secretary was correct. *This man is capable of being a Mahadev.*

'Yes. Lord Rudra did leave behind a tribe. The tribe of Vayuputra.'

'Vayuputra?' asked Shiva. The name sounded oddly familiar.

The Pandit placed his hand on Shiva's shoulder. 'Leave this for another time, my friend. I think we have spoken enough for today. Go home. You need your good wife's comforting embrace. Tomorrow is another day. And your mission can wait till then. For now, go home.'

Shiva smiled. An enigmatic smile. Out of character with his simple Tibetan ways. But he had become an Indian now. He leaned forward to touch the Pandit's feet. The Pandit placed his hand on Shiva's head to bless him, speaking gently, 'Vijayibhav. Jai Guru Vishwamitra. Jai Guru Vashishtha.'

Shiva nodded, accepting the blessings with grace. He got up, turned and walked towards the temple steps. At the edge of the platform, he turned around to look at the Pandit once again. The Pandit was sitting on his haunches, touching his head reverentially to the ground that Shiva had just vacated. Shiva smiled and shook his head slightly. Looking beyond the Pandit, he gazed intently at the idol of Lord Ram. He put his hands together in a Namaste and paid his respects to the Lord.

His burden didn't feel any lighter. But he felt strong enough to carry it.

He turned and began descending the steps. To his surprise, Sati was right in the middle of the compound leaning against a statuesque Apsara cast in stone. He smiled. There was nobody in the world whom he would much rather see at this time.

Walking towards her, he teased, 'Are you always going to follow me around?'

'I know when you need to be alone,' smiled Sati. 'And when you need me.'

Shiva froze suddenly. He could see a robe flapping behind the trees, a short distance from Sati. The light evening breeze gave away the position of the skulking man. Sati followed Shiva's gaze and turned around. A robed figure, wearing a Holi mask, emerged from behind the trees.

It is him!

Shiva's heart started beating faster. He was still a considerable distance away from Sati. The Naga was too close for comfort. The three stood rooted to their spots, assessing the situation, evaluating the others next move. It was Sati who moved first. Shifting quickly, she pulled a knife from her side-hold and flung it at the Naga. The Naga barely stirred. The knife missed him narrowly, slamming hard into the tree behind him, burying deep into the wood.

Shiva moved his hand slowly towards his sword.

The Naga reached behind, pulled the knife out of the tree and in a strange act, tied it tightly to his right wrist with a cloth band. Then he moved, quickly.

'Sati!' screamed Shiva, as he drew his sword and started sprinting towards his wife, pulling his shield forward as he ran.

...to be continued

www.authoramish.com

Glossary

Agni: God of fire

Agnipariksha: A trial by fire

Angaharas: Movement of limbs or steps in a dance

Ankush: Hook-shaped prods used to control elephants

Annapurna: The Hindu Goddess of food, nourishment and plenty; also believed to be a form of Goddess Parvati

Anshan: Hunger. It also denotes voluntary fasting. In this book, Anshan is the capital of the kingdom of Elam

Apsara: Celestial maidens from the court of the Lord of the Heavens – Indra; akin to Zeus/Jupiter

Arya: Sir

Ashwamedh yagna: Literally, the Horse sacrifice. In ancient times, an ambitious ruler, who wished to expand his territories and display his military prowess, would release a sacrificial horse to roam freely through the length and breadth of any kingdom in India. If any king stopped/captured the horse, the ruler's army would declare war against the challenger, defeat the king and annexe that territory. If an opposing king did not stop the horse, the kingdom would become a vassal of the former

Asura: Demon

Ayuralay: Hospital

Ayurvedic: Derived from Ayurved, an ancient Indian form of medicine

Ayushman bhav: May you have a long life

Baba: Father

Bhang: Traditional intoxicant in India; milk mixed with marijuana

Bhiksha: Alms or donations

Bhojan graham: Dining room

Brahmacharya: The vow of celibacy

Brahmastra: Literally, the weapon of Brahma; spoken of in ancient Hindu scriptures. Many experts claim that the description of a Brahmastra and its effects are eerily similar to that of a nuclear weapon. I have assumed this to be true in the context of my book

Branga: The ancient name for modern West Bengal, Assam and Bangladesh. Term coined from the conjoint of the two rivers of this land: *Brahmaputra* and *Ganga*

Brangaridai: Literally, the heart of Branga. The capital of the kingdom of Branga

Chandravanshi: Descendants of the moon

Chaturanga: Ancient Indian game that evolved into the modern game of chess

Chillum: Clay pipe, usually used to smoke marijuana

Choti: Braid

Construction of Devagiri royal court platform: The description in the book of the court platform is a possible explanation for the mysterious multiple-column buildings made of baked brick discovered at Indus Valley sites, usually next to the public baths, which many historians suppose could have been granaries

Dada: Elder brother

Daivi Astra: Daivi = Divine; Astra = Weapon. A term used in ancient Hindu epics to describe weapons of mass destruction

Dandakaranya: Aranya = forest. Dandak is the ancient name for modern Maharashtra and parts of Andhra Pradesh, Karnataka, Chhattisgarh and Madhya Pradesh. So Dandakaranya means the forests of Dandak

Deva: God

Dharma: Dharma literally translates as religion. But in traditional Hindu belief, it means far more than that. The word encompasses holy, right knowledge, right living, tradition, natural order of the universe and duty. Essentially, dharma refers to everything that can be classified as 'good' in the universe. It is the Law of Life

Dharmayudh: The holy war

Dhobi: Washerman

Divyadrishti: Divine sight

Dumru: A small, hand-held, hour-glass shaped percussion instrument

Egyptian women: Historians believe that ancient Egyptians, just like ancient Indians, treated their women with respect. The anti-women attitude attributed to Swuth and the assassins of Aten is fictional. Having said that, like most societies, ancient Egyptians also had some patriarchal segments in their society, which did, regrettably, have an appalling attitude towards women

Fire song: This is a song sung by Guna warriors to agni (fire). They also had songs dedicated to the other elements viz: *bhūmi* (earth), jal (water), *pavan* (air or wind), *vyom* or *shunya* or *akash* (ether or void or sky)

Fravashi: Is the guardian spirit mentioned in the *Avesta*, the sacred writings of the Zoroastrian religion. Although, according to most researchers, there is no physical description of Fravashi, the language grammar of *Avesta* clearly shows it to be feminine. Considering the importance given to fire in ancient Hinduism and Zoroastrianism, I've assumed the Fravashi to be represented by fire. This is, of course, a fictional representation

Ganesh-Kartik relationship: In northern India, traditional myths hold Lord Kartik as older than Lord Ganesh; in large parts of southern India, Lord Ganesh is considered elder. In my story, Ganesh is older than Kartik. What is the truth? Only Lord Shiva knows

Guruji: Teacher; ji is a term of respect, added to a name or title

Gurukul: The family of the guru or the family of the teacher. In ancient times, also used to denote a school

Har Har Mahadev: This is the rallying cry of Lord Shiva's devotees. I believe it means 'All of us are Mahadevs'

Hariyupa: This city is currently known as Harappa. A note on the cities of Meluha (or as we call it in modern times, the Indus Valley Civilisation): historians and researchers have consistently marvelled at the fixation that the Indus Valley Civilisation seemed to have for water and hygiene. In fact historian M Jansen used the term 'wasserluxus' (obsession with water) to describe their magnificent obsession with the physical and symbolic aspects

of water, a term Gregory Possehl builds upon in his brilliant book, *The Indus Civilisation — A Contemporary Perspective.* In the book, *The Immortals of Meluha*, the obsession with water is shown to arise due to its cleansing of the toxic sweat and urine triggered by consuming the Somras. Historians have also marvelled at the level of sophisticated standardisation in the Indus Valley Civilisation. One of the examples of this was the bricks, which across the entire civilisation, had similar proportions and specifications

Holi: Festival of colours

Howdah: Carriage placed on top of elephants

Indra: The God of the sky; believed to be the King of the Gods

Jai Guru Vishwamitra: Glory to the teacher Vishwamitra

Jai Guru Vashishtha: Glory to the teacher Vashishtha. Only two Suryavanshis were privileged to have had both Guru Vashishtha and Guru Vishwamitra as their gurus (teachers) viz. Lord Ram and Lord Lakshman

Jai Shri Brahma: Glory to Lord Brahma

Jai Shri Ram: Glory to Lord Ram

Janau: A ceremonial thread tied from the shoulders, across the torso. It was one of the symbols of knowledge in ancient India. Later, it was corrupted to become a caste symbol to denote those born as Brahmins and not those who'd acquired knowledge through their effort and deeds

Ji: A suffix added to a name or title as a form of respect

Kajal: Kohl, or eye liner

Karma: Duty and deeds; also the sum of a person's actions in this and previous births,

considered to limit the options of future action and affect future fate

Karmasaathi: Fellow traveller in karma or duty

Kashi: The ancient name for modern Varanasi. Kashi means the city where the supreme light shines

Kathak: A form of traditional Indian dance

Kriyas: Actions

Kulhads: Mud cups

Maa: Mother

Mandal: Literally, Sanskrit word meaning circle. Mandals are created, as per ancient Hindu and Buddhist tradition, to make a sacred space and help focus the attention of the devotees

Mahadev: Maha = Great and Dev = God. Hence Mahadev means the greatest God or the God of Gods. I believe that there were many 'destroyers of evil' but a few of them were so great that they would be called 'Mahadev'. Amongst the Mahadevs were Lord Rudra and Lord Shiva

Mahasagar: Great Ocean; Hind Mahasagar is the Indian Ocean

Mahendra: Ancient Indian name meaning conqueror of the world

Mahout: Human handler of elephants

Manu's story: Those interested in finding out more about the historical validity of the South India origin theory of Manu should read Graham Hancock's pathbreaking book, *Underworld*

Mausi: Mother's sister, literally translating as *maa si* i.e. like a mother

Maya: Illusion

Mehragarh: Modern archaeologists believe that Mehragarh is the progenitor of the Indus

Valley civilisation. Mehragarh represents a sudden burst of civilised living, without any archaeological evidence of a gradual progression to that level. Hence, those who established Mehragarh were either immigrants or refugees **Meluha:** The land of pure life. This is the land ruled by the Suryavanshi kings. It is the area that we in the modern world call the Indus Valley Civilisation

Meluhans: People of Meluha

Mudras: Gestures

Naga: Serpent people

Namaste: An ancient Indian greeting. Spoken along with the hand gesture of open palms of both the hands joined together. Conjoin of three words. 'Namah', 'Astu' and 'Te' — meaning 'I bow to the Godhood in you'. Namaste can be used as both 'hello' and 'goodbye'

Nirvana: Enlightenment; freedom from the cycle of rebirths

Oxygen/ anti-oxidants theory: Modern research backs this theory. Interested readers can read the article 'Radical Proposal' by Kathryn Brown in the *Scientific American*

Panchavati: The land of the five banyan trees

Pandit: Priest

Paradaeza: An ancient Persian word which means 'the walled place of harmony'; the root of the English word, Paradise

Pariha: The land of fairies. Refers to modern Persia/Iran. I believe Lord Rudra came from this land

Parmatma: The ultimate soul or the sum of all souls

Parsee immigration to India: Groups of Zoroastrian refugees immigrated to India perhaps between the 8th and 10th century AD to escape religious persecution. They landed in Gujarat, and the local ruler Jadav Rana gave them refuge

Pashupatiastra: Literally, the weapon of the Lord of the Animals. The descriptions of the effects of the Pashupatiastra in Hindu scriptures are quite similar to that of nuclear weapons. In modern nuclear technology, weapons have been built primarily on the concept of nuclear fission. While fusion-boosted fission weapons have been invented, pure fusion weapons have not been invented as yet. Scientists hold that a pure nuclear fusion weapon has far less radioactive fallout and can theoretically serve as a more targeted weapon. In this trilogy, I have assumed that the Pashupatiastra is one such weapon

Patallok: The underworld

Pawan Dev: God of the winds

Pitratulya: The term for a man who is 'like a father'

Prahar: Four slots of six hours each into which the day was divided by the ancient Hindus; the first prahar began at twelve midnight

Prithvi: Earth

Prakrati: Nature

Puja: Prayer

Puja thali: Prayer tray

Raj dharma: Literally, the royal duties of a king or ruler. In ancient India, this term embodied pious and just administration of the king's royal duties

Raj guru: Royal sage

Rajat: Silver

Rajya Sabha: The royal council

Rakshabandhan: Raksha = Protection; Bandhan = thread/tie. An ancient Indian festival in which a sister ties a sacred thread on her brother's wrist, seeking his protection

Ram Chandra: Ram = Face; Chandra = Moon. Hence Ram Chandra is 'the face of the moon'

Ram Rajya: The rule of Ram

Rangbhoomi: Literally, the ground of colour. Stadia in ancient times where sports, performances and public functions would be staged

Rangoli: Traditional colourful and geometric designs made with coloured powders or flowers as a sign of welcome

Rishi: Man of knowledge

Sankat Mochan: Literally, reliever from troubles. One of the names of Lord Hanuman

Sangam: A confluence of two rivers

Sanyasi: A person who renounces all his worldly possessions and desires to retreat to remote locations and devote his time to the pursuit of God and spirituality. In ancient India, it was common for people to take sanyas at an old age, once they had completed all their life's duties

Sapt Sindhu: Land of the seven rivers – Indus, Saraswati, Yamuna, Ganga, Sarayu, Brahmaputra and Narmada. This was the ancient name of North India

Saptrishi: One of the 'Group of seven Rishis'

Saptrishi Uttradhikari: Successors of the Saptrishis

Shakti Devi: Mother Goddess; also Goddess of power and energy

Shamiana: Canopy

Shloka: Couplet

Shudhikaran: The purification ceremony

Sindhu: The first river

Somras: Drink of the Gods

Sundarban: Sundar = beautiful; ban = forest. Hence, Sundarban means beautiful forest

Svarna: Gold

Swadweep: The Island of the individual. This is the land ruled by the Chandravanshi kings

Swadweepans: People of Swadweep

Swaha: Legend has it that Lord Agni's wife is named Swaha. Hence it pleases Lord Agni, the God of Fire, if a disciple takes his wife's name while worshipping the sacred fire. Another interpretation of Swaha is that it means offering of self

Tamra: Bronze

Thali: Plate

Varjish graha: The exercise hall

Varun: God of the water and the seas

Vijayibhav: May you be victorious

Vikarma: Carrier of bad fate

Vishnu: The protector of the world and propagator of good. I believe that it is an ancient Hindu title for the greatest of leaders who would be remembered as the mightiest of Gods

Vishwanath: Literally, the Lord of the World. Usually refers to Lord Shiva, also known as Lord Rudra in his angry avatar. I believe Lord Rudra was a different individual from Lord Shiva. In this trilogy, I have used the term Vishwanath to refer to Lord Rudra

Yagna: Sacrificial fire ceremony

Episode from *The Secret of the Nagas*

The Gates of Branga

'Why are you back so soon? You have enough medicines for a year.'

Divodas was shocked at the manner in which Major Uma was speaking. She was always strict, but never rude. He had been delighted that she had been posted at the gates. Though he hadn't met her in years, they had been friends a long time back. He had thought he could use his friendship with her to gain easy passage into Branga.

'What is the matter, Uma?' asked Divodas.

'It is Major Uma. I am on duty.'

'I'm sorry Major. I meant no disrespect.'

'I can't let you go back unless you give me a good reason.'

'Why would I need a reason to enter my own country?'

'This is not your country anymore. You chose to abandon it. Kashi is your land. Go back there.'

'Major Uma, you know I had no choice. You know the risks to the life of my child in Branga.'

'You think those who live in Branga don't? You think we don't love our children? Yet we choose to live in our own land. You suffer the consequences of your choice.'

Divodas realised this was getting nowhere. 'I have to meet the King on a matter of national importance.'

Uma narrowed her eyes. 'Really? I guess the King has some important business dealings with Kashi, right?'

Divodas breathed in deeply. 'Major Uma, it is very important that I meet the King. You must trust me.'

'Unless you are carrying the Queen of the Nagas herself on one of your ships, I can't see anything important enough to let you through!'

'I'm carrying someone far more important than the Queen of the Nagas.'

'Kashi has really improved your sense of humour, Divodas,' sneered Uma. 'I suggest you turn back and shine your supreme light somewhere else.'

The snide pun on Kashi's name convinced Divodas that he was facing a changed Uma. An angry and bitter Uma, incapable of listening to reason. He had no choice. He had to get the Neelkanth. He knew Uma used to believe in the legend.

'I'll come back with the person who is more important than the Queen of the Nagas herself,' said Divodas, turning to leave.

The small cutter had just docked at the Branga office. Divodas alit first. Followed by Shiva, Parvateshwar, Bhagirath, Drapaku and Purvaka.

Uma, standing outside her office, sighed. 'You really don't give up, do you?'

'This is very important, Major Uma,' said Divodas.

Uma recognised Bhagirath. 'Is this the person? You think I should break the rules for the Prince of Ayodhya?'

'He is the Prince of Swadweep, Major Uma. Don't forget that. We send tribute to Ayodhya.'

'So you are more loyal to Ayodhya as well now? How many times will you abandon Branga?'

'Major, in the name of Ayodhya, I respectfully ask you to let us pass,' said Bhagirath, trying hard not to lose his temper. He knew the Neelkanth did not want any bloodshed.

'Our terms of the Ashwamedh treaty were very clear, Prince. We send you a tribute annually. And Ayodhya never enters Branga. We have maintained our part of the agreement. The orders to me are to help you maintain your part of the bargain.'

Shiva stepped forward. 'If I may...'

Uma was at the end of her patience. She stepped forward and pushed Shiva. 'Get out of here.'

'UMA!' Divodas pulled out his sword.

Bhagirath, Parvateshwar, Drapaku and Purvaka too drew out their swords instantly.

'I will kill your entire family for this blasphemy,' swore Drapaku.

'Wait!' said Shiva, his arms spread wide, stopping his men.

Shiva turned towards Uma. She was staring at him, shocked. The angvastram that he had wrapped around his body for warmth had come undone, revealing his *neel kanth,* the prophesied blue throat. The Branga soldiers around Uma immediately went down on their knees, heads bowed in respect, tears flooding their eyes. Uma continued to stare, her mouth half open.

Shiva cleared his throat. 'I really need to pass through, Major Uma. May I request your cooperation?'

Uma's face turned mottled red. 'Where the hell have you been?'

Shiva frowned.

Uma bent forward, tears in her eyes, banging her small fists on Shiva's well-honed chest. 'Where the hell have you been? We have been waiting! We have been suffering! Where the hell have you been?'

Shiva tried to hold Uma, to comfort her. But she sank down holding Shiva's leg, wailing. 'Where the hell have you been?'

A concerned Divodas turned to another Branga friend also posted at the border. His friend whispered, 'Last month, Major Uma lost her only child to the plague. Her husband and she had conceived after years of trying. She was devastated.'

Divodas looked at Uma with empathy, understanding her angst. He couldn't even begin to imagine what would happen to him if he lost his baby.

Shiva, who had heard the entire conversation, squatted. He cradled Uma in the shelter of his arms, as though trying to give her his strength.

'Why didn't you come earlier?' Uma kept crying, inconsolable.

The entire crew on all five ships was crowded on the

port and starboard side, watching the operation in awe and wonder. Shiva's men were totally astounded by the Branga gates. They had seen the platform close in on their ship with frightening force. Then the hooks were secured to the chains. The Brangas, after the go-ahead from respective ship captains, began towing the fleet.

Shiva was standing aft. Looking at the office at the gate entrance.

Every Branga not working on the gate machinery was on his knees, paying obeisance to the Neelkanth. But Shiva was staring at a broken woman curled up against the wall in foetal position. She was still crying.

Shiva had tears in his eyes. He knew Uma believed that fate had cheated her daughter. She believed that if the Neelkanth had arrived a month earlier, her child would still be alive. But the Neelkanth himself was not so sure.

What could I have done?

He continued to stare at Uma.

Holy Lake, give me strength. I will fight this plague.

The ground staff got the signal. They released the accumulator machines and the pulleys began turning, moving the ship rapidly forward.

Seeing the vision of Uma retreating swiftly, Shiva whispered, 'I'm sorry.'

Other Titles by Amish

The Shiva Trilogy

The fastest-selling book series in the history of Indian publishing

THE SECRET OF THE NAGAS
(Book 2 of the Trilogy)

The sinister Naga warrior has killed his friend Brahaspati and now stalks his wife Sati. Shiva, who is the prophesied destroyer of evil, will not rest till he finds his demonic adversary. His thirst for revenge will lead him to the door of the Nagas, the serpent people. Fierce battles will be fought and unbelievable secrets revealed in the second part of the Shiva trilogy.

THE OATH OF THE VAYUPUTRAS
(Book 3 of the Trilogy)

Shiva reaches the Naga capital, Panchavati, and prepares for a holy war against his true enemy. The Neelkanth must not fail, no matter what the cost. In his desperation, he reaches out to the Vayuputras. Will he succeed? And what will be the real cost of battling Evil? Read the concluding part of this bestselling series to find out.

Indic Chronicles

LEGEND OF SUHELDEV

Repeated attacks by Mahmud of Ghazni have weakened India's northern regions. Then the Turks raid and destroy one of the holiest temples in the land: the magnificent Lord Shiva temple at Somnath. At this most desperate of times, a warrior rises to defend the nation. King Suheldev—fierce rebel, charismatic leader, inclusive patriot. Read this epic adventure of courage and heroism that recounts the story of that lionhearted warrior and the magnificent Battle of Bahraich.

www.authoramish.com

The Ram Chandra Series

The second fastest-selling book series in the history of Indian publishing

RAM – SCION OF IKSHVAKU
(Book 1 of the Series)

He loves his country and he stands alone for the law. His band of brothers, his wife, Sita, and the fight against the darkness of chaos. He is Prince Ram. Will he rise above the taint that others heap on him? Will his love for Sita sustain him through his struggle? Will he defeat the demon Raavan who destroyed his childhood? Will he fulfil the destiny of the Vishnu? Begin an epic journey with Amish's latest: the Ram Chandra Series.

SITA – WARRIOR OF MITHILA
(Book 2 of the Series)

An abandoned baby is found in a field. She is adopted by the ruler of Mithila, a powerless kingdom ignored by all. Nobody believes this child will amount to much. But they are wrong. For she is no ordinary girl. She is Sita. Through an innovative multi-linear narrative, Amish takes you deeper into the epic world of the Ram Chandra Series.

RAAVAN – ENEMY OF ARYAVARTA
(Book 3 of the Series)

Raavan is determined to be a giant among men, to conquer, plunder, and seize the greatness that he thinks is his right. He is a man of contrasts, of brutal violence and scholarly knowledge. A man who will love without reward and kill without remorse. In this, the third book in the Ram Chandra Series, Amish sheds light on Raavan, the king of Lanka. Is he the greatest villain in history or just a man in a dark place, all the time?

www.authoramish.com

Non-fiction

IMMORTAL INDIA

Explore India with the country's storyteller, Amish, who helps you understand it like never before, through a series of sharp articles, nuanced speeches and intelligent debates. In *Immortal India*, Amish lays out the vast landscape of an ancient culture with a fascinatingly modern outlook.

DHARMA – DECODING THE EPICS FOR A MEANINGFUL LIFE

In this genre-bending book, the first of a series, Amish and Bhavna dive into the priceless treasure trove of the ancient Indian epics, as well as the vast and complex universe of Amish's Meluha, to explore some of the key concepts of Indian philosophy. Within this book are answers to our many philosophical questions, offered through simple and wise interpretations of our favourite stories.